THE JAMES V TRILOGY

Book One
THE RIVEN REALM

Two hundred years earlier Robert the Bruce had driven out the English and restored his nation's pride. But now the King of Scotland lay dead amongst the bloody slaughter of Flodden.

Now as fate decreed, the new king, James V, was a child, just seventeen months old. And that same fate had in store intriguing roles for two young men.

David Lindsay and David Beaton – neither high-born – became friends at the University of St Andrews, and were later caught up in the very centre of the storm of hatred, fear, treachery and ambition that followed the young king's accession to the throne. Buffeted by events that would involve England, France, the Empire and even the Vatican, each was to win his own very special place in history.

THE JAMES V TRILOGY

Book Two
JAMES, BY THE GRACE OF GOD

In the wake of the Battle of Flodden, Scotland was ruled in name only. The boy king, James V, was at the mercy of ambitious rival factions, and beyond them the ever-watchful, ominous presence of Henry VIII of England. The young king was in desperate need of all the good advice he could get.

Escaping from the clutches of the power-hungry Earl of Angus, his most effective guides were two old friends, David Lindsay and David Beaton. But, impetuous and hot-blooded, James was more interested in wine and women than affairs of state, and his royal advisers faced an awesome task as they helped the king attain his regal status in a land full of treachery and danger.

THE JAMES V TRILOGY

Book Three
ROUGH WOOING

Still grief-stricken at the untimely death of his queen, Madeleine, and without an heir, the young James, King of Scots, is a beleaguered man. Both he and his throne are vulnerable, and there are many who seek to supplant or control him.

Even his own mother, Margaret Tudor, plots against him. But then she is the sister of the English King Henry VIII, who sprawls like a bloated spider south of the border, his greedy eyes ever on the realm of Scotland, hungry to bring it within his grasp.

The young king's advisers, the two Davids, have preserved him so far but the threats to James and his country seem to grow by the year.

Also by Nigel Tranter

The Bruce Trilogy
Black Douglas
Children of the Mist
Columba
Crusader
David the Prince
Druid Sacrifice
Flowers of Chivalry

The House of Stewart Trilogy:
Lords of Misrule
A Folly of Princes
The Captive Crown

Kenneth
Lion Let Loose
Lord of the Isles
MacBeth the King

The MacGregor Trilogy:
MacGregor's Gathering
The Clansman
Gold for Prince Charlie

Mail Royal
Margaret the Queen
Montrose, the Captain General
The Patriot
Price of a Princess
A Stake in the Kingdom
Tapestry of the Boar
Unicorn Rampant
The Wallace
The Wisest Fool
The Young Montrose

The James V Trilogy

THE RIVEN REALM
JAMES, BY THE GRACE OF GOD
ROUGH WOOING

Nigel Tranter

CORONET BOOKS
Hodder and Stoughton

First published as three separate volumes:

The Riven Realm: © 1984 by Nigel Tranter
First published in Great Britain in 1984 by Hodder and Stoughton Ltd
First published as a Coronet paperback in 1987

James, By the Grace of God: © 1985 by Nigel Tranter
First published in Great Britain in 1985 by Hodder and Stoughton Ltd
First published as a Coronet paperback in 1988

Rough Wooing: © 1986 by Nigel Tranter
First published in Great Britain in 1986 by Hodder and Stoughton Ltd
First published as a Coronet paperback in 1989

This edition 1995

A Coronet Paperback

10 9 8 7 6 5 4

ISBN 0 340 63766 8

Printed and bound in Great Britain by
Clays Ltd, St Ives plc

Hodder and Stoughton
A division of Hodder Headline PLC
338 Euston Road
London NW1 3BH

Principal Characters

IN ORDER OF APPEARANCE

DAVID LINDSAY: Usher and Procurator to infant Prince of Scotland. Son of Sir David Lindsay of Garleton.

MASTER JOHN INGLIS: Abbot of Culross. Assistant tutor to the Prince.

MIRREN LIVINGSTONE: A mistress of King James the Fourth of Scots.

MASTER WILLIAM ELPHINSTONE: Bishop of Aberdeen and Lord Privy Seal.

JAMES THE FOURTH: King of Scots.

MARGARET TUDOR: Queen of above. Sister of Henry the Eighth of England.

JAMES STEWART: Prince of Scotland and Duke of Rothesay. Infant son of King.

SIR DAVID LINDSAY OF GARLETON: East Lothian laird and former warrior.

LADY ISABELLA LINDSAY: Wife of Lord Lindsay of the Byres.

KATE LINDSAY: Daughter of above.

ARCHIBALD DOUGLAS, MASTER OF ANGUS: Great noble. Later 6th Earl of Angus.

MASTER JAMES BEATON: Archbishop of Glasgow and Chancellor of the Realm.

ALEXANDER, 3RD LORD HOME: Lord Chamberlain. Great Border noble.

SIR ARCHIBALD DOUGLAS OF KILSPINDIE: Known as Greysteel. Uncle of Angus.

MASTER GAVIN DOUGLAS: Brother of above. Provost of St Giles. Poet.

MASTER GAVIN DUNBAR: Tutor to James the Fifth. Poet.

JAMES HAMILTON, EARL OF ARRAN: Lord High Admiral. Cousin of the King.

ANTOINE DE LA BASTIE: French envoy and noted soldier.
PATRICK, 4TH LORD LINDSAY OF THE BYRES: Kate's father.
DAVID BEATON: Lay Rector of Campsie. Nephew of Archbishop Beaton.
JOHN STEWART, DUKE OF ALBANY: Cousin of the King and French citizen.
WILLIAM KEITH, EARL MARISCHAL: Great noble.
MARION OGILVY: Daughter of 3rd Lord Ogilvy of Airlie.
SIR JAMES HAMILTON OF FINNART: Illegitimate son of Arran. Known as The Bastard of Arran.
ARCHIBALD, 3RD EARL OF ARGYLL: Lord Justice General. Chief of Clan Campbell.
MASTER WILLIAM DOUGLAS: Abbot of Holyrood. Another uncle of Angus.

1

The square-faced young man with the darkly-humorous eyes nudged with his elbow his companion standing beside him, and jerked his head half-right, grinning, towards where Mirren Livingstone, the King's newest young lady, was intently inspecting herself inside her notably low-necked gown and scratching comprehensively at the same time—activity calculated to engender interesting speculation in any male worthy of the name. His friend began to smile, then changed to a head-shaking frown. After all, John Inglis was a cleric, Abbot of Culross no less, despite comparative youth, and they were in church, St Michael's by the Palace, at Linlithgow, no place for levity, especially on this solemn occasion. He lowered his head again, presumably in prayer, while the choir of singing boys continued to render sweet background music suitable for a monarch at his devotions.

His younger companion, David Lindsay, maintained his not-too-obvious vigil on Mirren Livingstone, whom he rather admired—at a distance, naturally—whilst dutifully keeping his eye on his beloved King James. The monarch, fourth of his name, knelt at a reading-desk, the only kneeling figure in the crowded south transept of St Michael's, before the altar of St Katherine, where Bishop Elphinstone of Aberdeen was conducting Vespers, a special service. All others must stand. James was a notably pious prince—in a practical way, of course, which would not restrict his other interests. He was here to pray for the success of his forthcoming great venture against his wretched brother-in-law, Henry Tudor, eighth of that name on the English throne. It was St Christopher's Day, 25th July, 1513.

The Queen was noticeably not present.

David Lindsay was not in a particularly worshipful frame of mind, apart altogether from Mirren Livingstone, mainly because he was being expressly excluded from the King's notable adventure. He had pleaded to be taken, along with all the flower of Scotland's chivalry. But James had been adamant. Davie's place was with the little Prince, he had insisted. He was his appointed Gentleman and Procurator, and his place was at the child's side, the heir to the throne. There would be opportunities in plenty for armed prowess and glory, later, never fear. So attendance at this special service was scarcely relevant for him.

Wondering what Mirren would be up to whilst the King was away—since he could hardly take her with him—movement caught David's roving eye. From an archway of the transept, to the right of St Katherine's altar, a figure emerged, a strange, an extraordinary figure. It was that of a tall old man, upright, dignified, with long white hair, parted at the forehead, falling down below the shoulders, dressed in a blue robe tied with a linen girdle, walking with a long white stick like a shepherd's crook. Ignoring the bishop, priests and acolytes at the altar, this apparition came slowly across the chancel, in majestic fashion, seeming almost to glide, towards the head-bowed King. David stared, and not only David. The choir's singing faltered momentarily.

The eye-catching figure moved directly over to the monarch at his faldstool and there stood. James looked up, eyes widening.

Strongly, sternly, the old man spoke, loudly enough to be heard above the singing and chanting.

"Sire—I am sent to warn you. Not to proceed with your present undertaking. You hear? Not to proceed. For if you do, it shall not fare well with either yourself or those who go with you."

He paused, as the King eyed him, astonished.

"Further," he went on, "it has been enjoined on me to bid you shun the familiar society and counsels of women, lest they occasion your disgrace and destruction. Hear you, I say."

"Save us—who a' God's name are you? What . . . ?" It is safe to say that James Stewart had never before been addressed thus.

The other dismissed the question with a wave of the hand. "Heed!" was all he said, but dramatically, and with another jab of his pointing finger, passed on.

The monarch lifted to his feet in a single movement, for he was a very fit man for his forty years although beginning to thicken at the waist. "Wait! Stop! Stop, you!" he commanded.

The oddity paid no heed.

David Lindsay moved sideways and thrust out a hand to detain the old man, but he eluded his grasp and pressed on into the crowd behind, which swallowed him up.

Gazing after him, the King shook his head. "A madman! Or a spectre—which?" he demanded, of no one in particular.

And no one answered, even though it was a royal demand.

"Davie—fetch him for me."

Young Lindsay turned and pushed his way into the throng which filled the side-chapel—lords, lairds, courtiers, soldiers and their women. But they were so close-packed that his progress was slow and, despite the remarkable impact of the strange figure, no sign of it was now evident in the crush.

Urgently David worked through and out of the transept into the main nave of the great church, much less crowded here, although worship was proceeding in some fashion before some others of the two dozen altars therein. Still there was no stranger to be seen. He went to the tall west doorway, to stare out. Nothing. The curiosity seemed to have disappeared into thin air.

Back at the King's side, David had to confess his failure. James, who had exchanged worship for discussion and debate, was surrounded now by a group of his lords, all very vocal although the service was still proceeding up at the altar. At the young man's announcement that there was no trace of the interloper, Andrew, Lord Gray, Justiciary, declared that it was, as he had said, a spectre, a bogle, sent by the Prince of Darkness himself, others agreeing. How else had he won into the church unchallenged and out again? He was from the Other World, clearly, a messenger, a wraith . . .

James frowned, hitching at his waist, a habitual gesture when in doubt or unease, adjusting the lie of the chain which he had worn next to his skin since the day twenty-five years ago when he had looked down on the dead body of his father, the hapless James the Third, and recognised how he, the fifteen-year-old son, had been used by unscrupulous nobles to bring his sire to this grievous pass, and took the chain, a mere harness chain, as reminder of his vow of remorse. That it was the same Lord Gray, old now, who had finished off his injured father with a dirk, on that occasion after the Battle of Sauchieburn, might have added some significance to this present, possibly fateful, interlude.

"You, Davie Lindsay—you were close to this, this creature," the King charged. "And you, Abbot. How say you? Was he honest man, however insolent? Or spirit, phantom, good or ill?"

David shook his head. "I know not, Sire. How can I tell? I have never seen a phantom. He seemed but man to me, although strange. And yet . . ."

"Yet, what, man—what?"

"I thought to grasp him, Highness, as he passed. As you bade. But . . . touched nothing! And then I went after him. But he disappeared. Gone. I, I do not know . . ."

"And you, Abbot John?"

"I would not venture an opinion, Your Grace. I saw nothing to have me think that he was other than an old man, probably deranged in his wits. But—who knows?"

"Aye. Mirren—how say you? You were nearby, also."

The young woman, red-haired, full-lipped, full-bosomed and lively—James had a weakness for redheads—came forward. "I say that he was wraith, Sire. None other would dare to speak you so. Sent to warn you against this invasion. I pray Your Grace to take heed . . ."

"Aye—we all know *your* wishes in the matter, lass!" the King said, with a half-smile. "Some others wish it, too, if for different reasons! But whether Heaven or Hell are so concerned is less certain."

"But you will pay heed, Sire?"

"We shall see . . ." James turned to face the altar, where the venerable Bishop Elphinstone made belated recognition of the fact that his congregation was scarcely with him in worship any longer by winding up the service quickly and signing for the choristers to do likewise. He came hobbling down to the royal group.

"Your Grace is pleased to dispense with further seeking of God's blessing?" he reproved.

"Scarce pleased, old friend. Say provoked. You saw this, this visitant?"

"I saw another old man pass me, who might be more

lacking his wits than even your servant, Sire! Was that sufficient to interrupt this holy office?"

"He miscalled the King. Spoke against this great endeavour. Threatened ill," the Earl of Atholl asserted. "Would you have such go unheeded, Sir Priest?"

"I think to heed Almighty God the more, in this house of His," Elphinstone said simply. His was a fine face, although lined and worn, with the noble features of a saintly yet practical philosopher, who had held the highest offices in the land, including that of Chancellor or chief minister; James's early mentor, who should have been Archbishop of St Andrews and Primate—only the King's own illegitimate seventeen-year-old son, Alexander Stewart, had been given that position.

"Aye, well—enough of this meantime," the monarch said. "Back to the palace. My belly rumbles, spectre or none! Come, Mirren . . ."

Leaving the Bishop to unrobe, they all moved from the church and crossed the mound above Linlithgow Loch, which it shared with the handsome brownstone palace.

At the meal which followed, in the great first-floor banqueting-hall, the talk, needless to say, was all of the apparition and what it might signify—the story, naturally, growing with the telling. Only a few who had been nearby had actually heard the words spoken, of course, so that there was considerable scope for the imagination. David and Abbot John—who was the young Prince's appointed tutor, although at only seventeen months not much tutoring was yet being attempted—discussed the matter back and forth, and although they came to no definite conclusions, certain indications were established for further debate.

It is to be doubted whether any similar progress was being achieved up at the dais-table, or at least at its centre, where the King and Queen scarcely exchanged a word; the French ambassador, on James's other side, had not been present in church and was besides a military man and unlikely to concern himself with metaphysics.

James Stewart and his wife were hardly the best of friends. Married for ten years now, they both bored and were bored with each other. On his part this was little to be wondered at, for he liked vivacious and attractive women, and Henry the Eighth's sister was neither. Margaret Tudor was plump, dumpy and somewhat moon-faced, without personal grace, and although still only twenty-two years old already looked almost middle-aged. Yet she was notoriously highly sexed and her little pig-like eyes, so like her brother's, were shrewd enough and missed little. She was probably the least popular queen-consort Scotland had ever had, and knew it—no pleasant situation for any woman. Their marriage, when she was only twelve, at Henry's urging, had done little to interrupt James's long succession of mistresses. Her own amorous adventures had to be less explicit.

When the Queen and her ladies retired and the men were getting down to serious drinking, a page came down from the dais-table to inform David and John Inglis that the King would speak with them, and to await him at Queen Joanna's Bower in the park, presently. James was abstemious about liquor, whatever else, and frequently left his hard-drinking lords to get on with it whilst he sought a different kind of solace.

The two younger men wandered out into the fine July evening. Of all the palaces of Scotland, Linlithgow was the most picturesquely sited, embosomed in low green hills, with the long, narrow curving town on the south side and the fine broad loch on the north, palace and church sharing the ridge between. With the last of the sunset staining sky and water crimson, black and palest green to the north-west, and drawing long purple shadows out of every fold and hollow of the hills, it was pleasant there amidst the last of the darting swallows and the dusk-flighting duck as the friends walked down to the summer-house known as Queen Joanna's Bower, after Joan Beaufort, wife of James the First.

They were not there long before they saw the vigorous figure of James Stewart come striding downhill, alone.

"Here comes the finest king Scotland has had since my noble namesake, David the First," Lindsay observed, "the Bruce excepted."

"You still say that?" his companion charged, smiling. "After his refusal to take you on this great venture of his? Wise as I would say he is, in that!"

"Yes. He has his reasons, no doubt—although I wish that he had not."

The King beckoned them out. "Come—we shall walk around the loch. No long ears there! And I can do with stretching my legs. Too much sitting and talk in the rule of a nation!" Ever straightforward, James came at once to the point. "This at Vespers. What do you make of it all? You were both close by me. And you both have sound wits, or I would not have chosen you to watch over my young son. You have had time to consider it. How think you?"

The others glanced at each other. Inglis spoke. "We do not think that it was any spectre, Sire."

"No? Nor do I. But—why?"

"Would a spectre lean upon a stick, Your Grace?" David asked.

"Ha! A fair point. Anything else?"

"Would a spectre have entered the chapel from the main church and crossed the aisle thereafter, to you? Would one not rather have materialised directly before Your Grace?"

"Perhaps. I am not wise in the ways of phantoms."

"Nor are we, Sire," Inglis hastened to declare. "If such there be."

"You think that doubtful?"

"With respect, Sire—yes."

"Yet Holy Church speaks much of the spirits of the departed and the like."

"But not as coming to haunt men on earth, Highness. Only as existing in the hereafter."

"Indeed. I bow to your superior knowledge, Abbot John. So—if this was no spectre, what was it?"

"Possibly a seer, Your Grace. Some eremite or holy man believing that he has the sight and can foretell the future. There are some who so conceive, I understand."

"Possibly, yes. I had so considered. Crazed or otherwise."

"I do not think that he was crazed, Sire," David said.

"No? Why?"

"Because of what he said in the second place. The first, about doom and scaith, could have been the babblings of a crazed man. But the second was different, quite. About, about . . ." David looked embarrassed. ". . . this of women, Sire. I misremember the words. But it was to do with shunning familiar women. Something of that."

"I heard," James said grimly. "What of it?"

"That is not, I think, what a seer or a crazed religious would have said. That was a different matter, no prediction but a rebuke, a challenge. That was . . . different."

"So-o-o! There, now, we have shrewd thinking! I had not perceived the difference. Yes, you are right. That was no message from the Other World, nor yet the dreams of a crazed seer. Those were the words of a man with a purpose. But, why? Who was he?"

"Does it matter *who* he was, Sire? That old man. A mummer, perhaps, a play-actor. Rather, who sent him?"

James nodded. "No doubt you are right again, Davie. Where did you win the head on those young shoulders?"

"It is none so remarkable, Highness. Who mislikes both your venture into England, and your, your interest in other women, sufficiently to have contrived this?" David's slight catch of breath at his emphasis on the word "other" betrayed his fear that he might have gone too far.

The King paused in his walking to eye him searchingly. "You mean the Queen, man?"

"Your pardon, Sire—but who else has such good reason? Leastways such *strong* reasons."

James hitched at that chain of his. "True. But . . . would she do this? So fell a device?"

Neither of his companions ventured to answer that.

"It could be," he went on slowly. "In truth she has done all that she can do to halt this project. No doubt at her brother's behest. This could be a last attempt. And she much dislikes the Queen of France's fair words in sending me her glove, and to venture three steps into England for love of her."

This great expedition was being undertaken at the urgent request of King Louis of France under the mutual-aid provisions of the Auld Alliance, whereby Scotland and France had long sought to contain English aggression against either by agreeing each to stage an invasion, south or north, if the other was menaced. Henry was at present engaged in the attempted conquest of Guienne; and James, who had suffered much at his brother-in-law's hands, was only too pleased to accede.

David had a notion that the Queen's objection to familiar women would be apt to be centred nearer home than Versailles, but he did not say so.

"The English were ever great on play-acting, mummery and masques," he mentioned.

"Aye. This could be West's device." Dr West was the

English ambassador. "Although Her Grace has the wits to have thought it up for herself!"

"Will you heed it, Sire?" Inglis wondered.

"I will not. All is prepared. Arran, the admiral, has already sailed from the Clyde with my fleet. Home, with his Borderers, is probing into Northumberland. It is too late to turn back now—even if I could. I go to Edinburgh in two days. And we march some days later."

There was silence for a while as they walked on.

"You will cherish my son for me, while I am gone," the King went on presently, in a different tone of voice. "There are ever ill-intentioned folk in this kingdom, as in any other, who would grasp the heir to the throne if they could, to use him to advance themselves. And I do not trust Henry's ambassador, West. So keep ever close to the lad. I chose you two carefully. You can call on any of my royal guard left behind, at need."

"The Prince is safe with us, Sire," David assured.

They were almost back at the palace when James added his second injunction—and it was clearly to David that he gave it. "Look after Mirren when I am gone," he said briefly, and waved them away.

It was two weeks later, in fact, when David Lindsay and John Inglis stood on the vantage point of the Borestane Knowe and gazed out over the Burgh-muir of Edinburgh, spellbound by the sight. It is safe to say that never had that lofty and extensive moor above the city, traditional mustering place for Scotland's armies as it was, seen such a sight as this. Near and far, from the town walls right to the very slopes of the Braid Hills two miles away, the concourse stretched, not in any wide-scattered dispersal but in close-marshalled, serried and orderly ranks, as far as eye could see, the sunlight gleaming on steel and blazoning the colours of a thousand banners and standards which fluttered in the breeze, the steam of scores of thousands of horses raising a sort of mist above all, the encampment of baggage-wagons, ox-carts and weapon-sleds itself larger than the city below. Men said that there were one hundred thousand gathered there—and although that was probably an exaggeration, even half that number would be a greater army than ever Scotland had gathered before in her long story of warfare and strife. None other than James the Fourth, the most popular monarch ever the land had had, *could* have assembled this enormous host from every corner of his kingdom, from the distant Hebrides to the Mull of Galloway, from Sutherland and Ross to the Borders, the manpower of a score of earldoms, a hundred baronies, thirteen bishoprics and two score Highland clans, townsfolk of every burgh in the land. Great armies had marched from here a many, down the centuries, but never anything like this.

The knoll where the young men stood with their charges was like a small island in the sea of glitter and colour, and itself a crowded island, tight-packed and even more colourful than the rest under its forest of waving lordly pennons and escutcheons and tossing plumes, for here waited the principal nobility of the realm who were not for the moment heading up their armed strength, the officers of state and the leaders of Holy Church. In this galaxy of earls and bishops and lords, Lindsay and the Abbot would have merited no least place—save that they escorted two charges, or three, the seventeen-months James, Prince of Scotland and Duke of Rothesay and his nurse the Lady Erskine, and Mirren Livingstone. The Queen was not present, having remained at Linlithgow.

Young James was a chubby and cheerful infant, well-made and restless—which, considering his present seat on David's broad shoulder, where he could view all, brought its problems. He chortled and pointed, laughed and dribbled and beat on his Procurator's bare head, to emphasise his satisfaction with all the prospect. Mirren, perhaps unsuitably, clutched an arm each of the young men, also exclaiming at all she saw. Lady Erskine was more discreet.

A curious, creaking, groaning, rumbling noise turned all heads northwards, city-wards, but the crowds and the falling level of the land hid the cause, and speculation was superseded by the return to the Borestane Knowe of the tight little group of horsemen under the great Lion Standard of Scotland, spurring from the other direction. Reining up before them, the King raised his hand high.

"All is well," he cried. "The South Galloway folk have arrived. And the Arran Hamiltons. We now but await the cannon."

"We hear it now, I think, Sire," George Douglas, Master of Angus, called. "Listen!"

"Aye*!* They are slow, cannot be other. We shall see them come, then march." James made a splendid figure, in black gold-inlaid half-armour over scarlet and cloth-of-gold doublet and doeskin breeches, with thigh-length riding boots, a purple fur-trimmed cloak flung back from his shoulder. But, as usual, his head was bare, only a simple gold circlet at his brow restraining the long thick auburn hair which fell to his shoulders.

He dismounted, throwing his reins to an esquire and striding up to take his son from David, to toss the gurgling child into the air and catch him, laughing.

"Hey, Jamie Stewart! Ho, Jamie Stewart!" he shouted. "Here's to you, and here's to your sire and here's to this fine realm of ours! Yours, one day! See you yon Lion ramping there?" And he pointed up to the great red and gold tressured banner, held aloft and flapping above the royal charger by his standard-bearer, Scrymgeour of Dudhope. "True Thomas said: 'When Alba's Lion throats a roar; wise men run to bolt their door!' That Lion is throating a big roar this day—and you are hearing it, Jamie. Pray others will also—but scarce in time to bolt their doors! Eh, my lords?"

There was a roar of approval from the ranked nobles. But not from them all. A harsh, rasping voice spoke.

"*I* say, see that your Lion doesna choke on this meal you seek to give it! Or it will no' roar again for long enough!"

There was a shocked hush at that, and then a storm of protest which drowned out even the rumbling, clanking noise.

James raised one eyebrow towards the old man. "You belled the cat one time, Archie Douglas," he said, mildly enough. "But you'll not bell the Lion so easy!"

A shout of mirth greeted this sally. Archibald Douglas, fifth Earl of Angus, had been known as Bell-the-Cat ever since, thirty years before, he had disposed of the man Cochrane and others of the late James the Third's odd minions, by the simple expedient of hanging them from Lauder Brig.

The Earl, head of the great Red Douglas house, irascible always, scowled and, since even he could scarcely challenge his sovereign-lord, rounded on the others instead. "Laugh, dizzards!" he cried. "Laugh whilst you may! For, by the powers, you may not have much longer for laughing if you proceed with this folly. Have you considered what you do? You challenge England's might, in war. How many of you ken what war is? You are bairns in the business—bairns! But Henry's lords are old in war—his father saw to that, in his French campaigns. How many of you have ever drawn sword in battle? You are but tourney fighters! I tell you, this will be no tourney!"

The laughter changed to growling. Even the speaker's eldest son and heir, George, the Master, joined in the hostility. "Too late for doubts now, my lord," he called, embarrassed. "When has Douglas ever been afraid to hazard a toss? Is not this the greatest might our land has ever mounted? And our cause just?"

"Cause! *Whose* cause, fool? Louis of France's cause, not ours. All this, to save Louis! What has Louis of France ever done for Scotland?"

"The Auld Alliance . . ."

"The Alliance is all one-sided. What do we gain?"

"Honour, at least!" somebody shouted.

"Honour! I would choose to die for more than honour! Are all summoned here, my lord King, to die for honour? Whose honour? Last night there was another summons, I am told. Not to flourish empty honour, but to compear before the Throne of Darkness within forty days! On the commands of the Prince of Darkness himself. If you do not turn back. And he named many by name—you, Atholl! And you, Argyll. And you, Glencairn. And Bothwell. Aye, and you Cassillis. And Lyle . . . !" Angus's pointing finger jabbed at the owner of each proud title, under their heraldic banners.

There was a shocked silence as he continued with his grim roll-call. All there had heard how, at midnight a bare twelve hours before, a disembodied voice had sounded at the Mercat Cross of Edinburgh announcing that Pluto hereby required all the earls, lords, barons, gentlemen and sundry burgesses of the city to appear before his master, King of the Underworld, within forty days, under pain of disobedience, designating many of the foremost names in the land, as a consequence of this present expedition.

James frowned. "I say whoever contrived yonder

mummery at Linlithgow, with its mouthings, contrived last night's play-acting also," he said, shortly. "Speak no more of King Henry's friends' inventions, my lord!"

"Such calling up of the powers of darkness is evil and should be cast from our minds," another old voice asserted, that of Bishop Elphinstone. "But I much urge Your Grace nevertheless to consider well your intentions, in this venture. Already you have despatched your fleet to France's aid and to threaten the English coasts. And sent my lord of Home and his mosstroopers into England. I pray you to be content, Sire, to take this great array only as far as Tweed and there rest, on your own side of the Border. Posing sufficient threat to King Henry, without leaving your own territory. The English will well perceive the danger, never fear, and will be as greatly concerned as if you had crossed into their land. But you will have remained on your own soil, as you have all right to do, and no men's lives endangered. Wait this side of Tweed, my lord King—in the name of Holy Church, I beseech you."

As murmurs arose for and against this course, there was a diversion, from behind the King this time, where a gallant youth leapt down from one of the fine horses beneath the standard and strode over to take the infant prince from his father's arms in familiar fashion.

"Come, rascal—to your gossip, Alex," he exclaimed. "And let us tell these greybeards that Holy Church can speak with other voice than trembling caution when the cause is just! I say, enough of gloomy doubts and fears. Let us be doing and on our way! And Saint Andrew of Scotland himself will loud out-voice all these quavering ancients!" This was Alexander Stewart, James's seventeen-year-old son by Marion Boyd, his first mistress, Archbishop of St Andrews and Primate of the Church—even though the only hint of episcopacy about him today was the mitre painted on his gleaming half armour. He bounced his small half-brother about vigorously, apparently to the satisfaction of both.

The cheers which greeted this spirited intervention indicated general support.

The King waved a hand for quiet. "I have heard all, and shall consider all," he said. "But meantime we have this host to set in motion. Here come the cannon, at last. We shall see them past and then be on our way."

He had to shout that, for the rumbling, squealing and growling noise was now so loud as to drown all else. The cause of it all was becoming evident, a vast ponderous cavalcade of horsemen, oxen, artillery, wagons and marchers, half a mile long, before which all the serried ranks of the assembled host had to draw aside, however difficult this was. First came a splendidly mounted figure in emblazoned full armour and nodding plumes, under the three black cinquefoils on white, the banner of Lord Borthwick, Hereditary Master Gunner of the realm; and behind came his sons, vassals and followers. Then trundled his famous Seven Sisters, Scotland's greatest cannon, normally kept at Edinburgh Castle, massive monsters each drawn by a score of plodding oxen, their protesting wheels and axles setting up most of the screeching din, added to by the shouts of the drivers and the cracking of their long whips. Behind were ten lesser pieces, similarly ox-drawn. Then innumerable wagons, carts and sleds carrying the cannonballs, powder-casks and other necessary stores. Finally came a succession of hay-wains, laden with the thousands of eighteen-foot pikes which King Louis had sent from France as his contribution to the invasion, looked at distinctly askance by most Scots although allegedly good for keeping attacking swordsmen at more than arm's length. Over four hundred oxen were required to draw all this cumbersome weapon train, such as no Scots army previously had fielded.

As Lord Borthwick came level with the King, he signed for his banner to be dipped in salutation and raised a hand high, James acknowledging. He did not pause, for once that lumbering cavalcade ground to a halt it would take a deal of starting again. It had fifty miles to go to Tweed and would be lucky to cover it in five days.

Now the royal party stirred, most there eager to be on their way. Alexander Stewart gave the young Prince back to David Lindsay, and the King came to kiss the child goodbye.

"You will see well to this one, Davie," he charged. "He is fell precious. None other near the throne save my cousin Albany in France. Those in Henry's pay will seek to grasp him if they can. And the Queen . . . less than single-minded! See to it."

"With my life, Sire."

"Aye." James turned to Mirren. "So, lass—it is farewell, for this present." He reached into his breeches pocket and brought out a jewelled pendant on a gold chain, rubies glowing richly red. "Here is a keepsake to mind me by while I am gone. These two will look after you," and he gestured to Lindsay and the Abbot. He gave her a smacking kiss, slapped her round bottom and made for his horse. In front of all that company even the non-hypocritical James Stewart had to be casual about his ladies. But he looked back before he mounted. "You said that you were going to Garleton, Davie? Take them with you, I think—both. It might be best, meantime."

"If you wish, Sire . . ."

With the monarch in the saddle and reining round, his herald-trumpeter blew a resounding flourish, and the leadership group was on its way, the nobles and bishops swinging into jostling place behind, flags waving, plumes tossing, armour clanking, harness jingling, a brave sight. Not all there went, to be sure, some few remaining to gaze after the departing company, Bishop Elphinstone, Lord Privy Seal, amongst them, and a proportion of the royal guard—but it was noteworthy that the old Earl of Angus, despite his strictures, rode with the King. The Bishop shook his white head sorrowfully.

David Lindsay, holding the Prince, looked from his friend to the two women, and shrugged. "It seems that we *all* go to Garleton. Why, think you?"

"*I* do not, that is sure," Lady Erskine said decidedly. "And the Queen will expect the Prince back at Linlithgow, forthwith."

"His Grace's command was clear," the Abbot pointed out.

"Not for me. I take my orders from the Queen, now. And I am the child's nurse and keeper."

David eyed her thoughtfully, learning so soon something of the burden of reponsibility and difficulty his liege-lord had laid on his shoulders. "The King's express command must prevail," he asserted. "I am his appointed Procurator for the Prince. He goes to Garleton, with me. As does Mistress Livingstone. Your ladyship must do as you see fit."

"I return to the Queen, then. To inform Her Grace of this . . . this folly. The child needs a woman's care, and should come with me."

"*I* will see to the Prince's needs," Mirren put in.

"I said a woman's care—not a whore's!" Lady Erskine said, and turned her back.

The young men exchanged glances.

"Come, then—let us be on our way," David announced, hurriedly. "We have fifteen miles and more to ride. Mirren—which is your horse . . . ?" And, lower-voiced, he added. "What my father will say to this, the good Lord knows!"

2

Garleton Castle sat snugly beneath the quite steep escarpment of the green Garleton Hills, at the head of its fair hanging valley between the vales of Tyne and Peffer, in East Lothian. It was a pleasant, peaceful place, no mighty fortalice, but sufficiently strong for protective purposes, with its tower, turrets, parapets and shot-holes, its position strong too, as witnessed by the ancient Pictish fort which occupied the rocky spur immediately above. Garleton had been a Lindsay possession for almost four hundred years, ever since in the twelfth century Sir William de Lindsay had wed the Dunbar heiress of Luffness, the great castle and estate two miles to the north, on the shores of Aberlady Bay, and became baron thereof, with this Garleton, Byres, Athelstaneford and much else. Here David had been born and would one day be laird—although for official occasions he was styled Lindsay of the Mount, from a smaller property he had inherited, in Fife, from his mother.

The little company, eight strong, clattered into the courtyard filled with the long shadows of the sinking sun, the small Prince jouncing about in front of David's saddle but making no complaint, indeed almost asleep despite the motion. With the father he had he was much used to horseback travel. They had adopted the King's suggestion and brought along four members of the royal guard as escort.

As David set the toddler down on the yard flagstones and turned to aid Mirren to dismount, a large, burly man of middle years appeared within the arched doorway of the main keep, beneath the coloured heraldic panel with the carven Lindsay arms, the blue and white chequy-fesse on red.

"What a God's name is this, Davie Lindsay?" this individual demanded, in something of a bellow. "You'll no' tell me you've fathered a bairn this age without me kenning! I'll no' believe it!'

"No, sir—no, no!" David disclaimed protestingly. "This is the Prince. Young James, Prince of Scotland. The heir."

"Sakes—here? The Prince? Why? What's to do?"

"The King's command. I will tell you. He is gone to England . . ."

"All the world kens that, boy! I have sent eight stout lads for him. With the Byres' tail. Patrick's gone himself, with his three sons. Would God I could ha' gone myself, but this leg . . . But—no' yourself, it seems, Davie? *You* havena gone!"

"His Grace decided otherwise." That was short. David turned to the others. "This is my father, Sir David, of Garleton. Here is Master John Inglis, Abbot of Culross, of whom I have spoken. Tutor to the Prince. And . . ."

"Aye—and the lassie? You'll no' tell me that you've brought a woman home, at long last? After all your daffery and dalliance? Boy, at your age, I was wed four years, and you were older than this princeling!"

"No doubt, Father. But this lady is Mistress Mirren, kin to my Lord Livingstone. She is a, a friend of the King. He has placed her in my, in *our* care, meantime . . ."

"Ha—is that the way of it? His Grace had ever a guid eye for a horse, a hound and a woman—whoever he had to wed! You should learn frae him, Davie! Forby, mind, I wonder he trusts you with this one!"

His son cleared his throat—as he frequently had to do in Sir David's company. "Mistress Mirren will be tired. We have ridden straight from the Burghmuir of Edinburgh. And the child needing his bed. And feeding, first . . ."

"Aye, to be sure. Bring them in—and welcome. You'll no'want the lady in your own bedchamber, then—nor yet the Abbot's? We'll have to see what we can do . . ."

Mirren giggled, as servitors came to take the horses, the men-at-arms were led to the kitchen premises in the lean-to buildings of the courtyard, and Sir David limpingly conducted his guests into the main keep and up the twisting turnpike stairway to the hall and private quarters. Perhaps because of his bad leg, he found it necessary to grasp the young woman's quite sturdy person round the waist to aid in the ascent, his son sighing behind, but not in surprise.

Later, with young James fed and put down to sleep, the

others sat at table in the hall and discussed the day's events. Sir David lived alone at Garleton these days, a widower for many years now, and his other son and two daughters married and away.

This son was particularly interested in why the King should have deemed it advisable that he brought the little Prince here to Garleton instead of taking him back to Linlithgow Palace. They had puzzled over this as they rode, and come up with no adequate answer.

"He must believe the bairn in danger," the laird said. "He doesna trust that Queen of his—and I blame him not! She is more Henry Tudor's sister than James Stewart's wife!"

"But the Prince will have to go back to his mother sooner or later. We cannot keep him here. Forby, she'll send for him, for sure. We have no authority to hold him here, or otherwhere. He merely said to guard him well. And later, added to bring him here meantime."

"Aye. Then he must have feared some early attempt on the bairn. If Henry's friends could take and hold the heir to the throne, hide him away somewhere, then they have a notable grip on the King. They could force him to turn back on this invasion, perhaps. Every child-king or prince in this Scotland has been grasped or threatened thus—this King Jamie himself. He weel kens the danger. And what better time to grasp at the bairn than now, when none would look for it? When in the care of but yourselves? Before he's back to the safety of yon Linlithgow."

"Then it might not be the Queen at all that the King fears?"

"He said something of Her Grace being less than single-minded," John Inglis pointed out.

"If he feared something of this sort, then why did he bring the boy to Edinburgh? Why not leave him safely at Linlithgow? Or send him to Stirling Castle, where he would be safer still?"

"Who knows, lad. But he would have much on his mind with this great venture to prepare. And he may indeed mistrust Margaret Tudor. The Queen did not come to Edinburgh with him? No—then that might be it. He might not wish to leave the bairn alone, with her."

"He says that Dean West has the Queen in his pocket," Mirren Livingstone made her first contribution. "He much mistrusts the Dean." Nicholas West, Dean of Windsor, was English resident at the Court of Scotland.

"A slimy toad!" Sir David commented. "I've heard that he has the same pocket full of gold, to bribe any who will enrol in Henry's service. And such are no' that hard to find, I fear, where gold is on offer! Aye—and what better time to grasp the Prince, when most leal men are away with the King?"

They digested that thoughtfully, with their cold venison.

"What are we to do, then?" David demanded, presently. "We cannot keep the lad here, over long. Or we ourselves could be thought to have abducted him! The Queen will send for him."

"The good Bishop Elphinstone would hear the King tell you to bring the Prince to Garleton," the Abbot reminded. "He will let it be known that all is in order."

"True. But that would not prevent the Queen sending here. And with His Grace gone, she will now rule the land, not Bishop Elphinstone. Forby, she does not love *him*, either."

"You can but wait, then, to see what transpires," his father said. "And in a day or two, perhaps, send our Abbot friend here to Bishop Elphinstone for his guidance. He is an honest man, and wiser than most. And Privy Seal, forby. He will best advise."

That seemed fair counsel, and they left it there.

David saw Mirren to her room door, presently, and there she seemed reluctant to say goodnight.

"Davie—what is to become of me?" she asked, clutching his arm.

"Why, lass—you will do well enough," he assured.

"Are you sure? *What* am I to do? Where can I go?"

"Go? You have your quarters in Linlithgow. And when the King comes back, all will be as it was."

"The King may not come back."

"Wheesht, Mirren—what way is that to talk?"

"He may not! It is war he goes to. And I am afraid of the Queen!"

That admittedly was not something which could just be laughed away. Margaret Tudor was not the woman to look kindly on a husband's mistress.

"What of your home? Your father's house?"

"My father is dead. There is only my mother and three sisters at Dechmont. They could not save me from the Queen. Nor, nor I think, would wish to!"

"M'mm. And the Lord Livingstone?"

"My uncle is gone with the King. With all his strength."

David frowned. "You can bide here meantime, lass. Never fear—all will be well." Feeling protective, he put an arm round her—he was his father's son, after all. And she responded, pressing her ripely rounded warmth against him.

Somewhat hastily he disengaged. "I . . . ah . . . fear nothing!" he told her. "Goodnight, Mirren—sleep well . . ."

He left her, to mount the stair higher to his own chamber.

They waited a few days before Abbot John went off to consult Bishop Elphinstone, pleasant enough days, with Sir David and little Jamie Stewart getting on notably well together, the child being friendly and easy-going by nature and little trouble to anyone. Which left David free to conduct his friend round the neighbourhood and show him what was to be seen—for John Inglis came from Ayrshire and did not know Haddingtonshire or East Lothian. And inevitably Mirren was apt to come along too, being a little bit chary of being left alone with the laird—in which the son scarcely blamed her—and as inevitably her red-headed good looks, generous endowments and unmistakably approachable character, drew considerable comment and interest. And since it was neither convenient nor suitable to declare to all and sundry that this was the King's present mistress; and since even with the prevailing state of the clergy, with concubines commonplace, it could not be assumed that she was Abbot John's paramour, it was generally taken for granted that she was David's lady, and congratulations were apt to be the order of the day. Which, embarrassing as it was at first—to David, for Mirren was not readily embarrassed—became in time so normal that the embarrassment wore off and was replaced by a sort of mutual and secret amusement, which engendered its own intimacy.

That it was largely female neighbours and friends who jumped to these conclusions added its own dimension to the situation, for the fact was that the countryside, hereabouts at any rate, was largely denuded of its menfolk, so successful had been the King's call to his standard. Every castle, tower and lairdship in that fair county between the Lammermuir Hills and the sea, appeared to have sent most of its manpower on the great adventure, save for the ancient and decrepit—this, of course, by no means diminishing David's own need for explanation as to his non-inclusion.

He had another subject of challenge to counter, in which the other two could nowise come to his rescue—poetry. For David Lindsay was a poet, of sorts, had been since his student days at St Andrews, and had something of a local reputation to sustain, however inadequate he knew his verse to be—and of course used to it being overshadowed by the offerings of the famous William Dunbar and Gavin Douglas, both of whom, oddly enough, hailed from this same county. But the fact was that he had written not a word since he had been summoned, over a year before, to take up this appointment with the infant Prince, his new life at court quite absorbing all his attentions and interests—this despite having previously started on what, in his folly, he had already informed folk was to be a major work and to which he had even presumed to give a title—*The Dream*. Oddly, it was his father who was mainly responsible for bruiting this abroad. The Lindsays had always been fighters, soldiers, as had Sir David himself—his damaged leg was a relic of warfare in King James's Highland campaign—and he was much tickled that the line had at last produced what he referred to as a man of letters, although of course he would have been the first to object strongly if this literary inclination had tended to lead to any lack of manly vigour and spirit in his son.

David himself had said little about this interest of his, latterly—indeed, Mirren knew nothing of it and even Inglis took it to have been a passing youthful concern not engaged in since student days at St Andrews where they had first met. But any secrecy was forfeited when, on the third day at Garleton, they paid a visit to the Byres.

This strangely named property was the next estate westwards, below the green Garleton Hills; indeed, originally, Garleton Castle and demesne had been part of this larger barony, the full name of which was Byres of Garleton. But locally it was known merely as the Byres; and when that branch of the chiefly house at Luffness, now Earls of Crawford, themselves became sufficiently renowned in war and statecraft to be given a lordship of parliament, they deliberately elected to use the title of Lord Lindsay of the Byres. So that, although there were one thousand and one byres in Scotland, every farm having its cowshed so named, there was only the one Byres with a capital B. The present Patrick, fourth Lord Lindsay of the Byres, with all three of his sons gone adventuring with the King, was a far-out kinsman of David's, the first of Garleton being a younger son of the first of the Byres.

They were well received, for this house—despite its name a larger and finer castle than Garleton, and standing within a handsome, high-walled garden—had been a second home for David ever since his mother had died when he was but a boy. He had always called Lady Lindsay Aunt Isabella.

"I am thankful to see at least two sensible young men who have not gone off in this madness of the King's!" she greeted, kissing David warmly after the introductions, a big, strong woman, still handsome. "It has been long since we saw you, David."

"Two years, yes. I have been away with the King's Grace the length and breadth of the land. And last time I was here, you were from home."

"You enjoy the King's service?" It had been largely through the Lord Lindsay's influence that David had won his position with the Prince.

"Indeed, yes. It is good. Because the Prince is so young, I am much with the King himself. He is kind to me. Even though he did not take me with him to England."

"You wished to go? The more fool you!"

"All are going, why not I? The King needs everyone . . ."

"And none left to see to all he leaves behind? James has a realm to rule. Even he could not be so foolish . . ."

"Davie—oh, Davie!" The cry turned him round. A girl had appeared within the hall doorway, gazing great-eyed. She held out her hands towards him and then came running.

David was staring, too, as well he might. "Kate!" he got out. "It's Kate!"

Then she had hurled herself into his arms in headlong, impetuous joy. "At last, at last!" she cried.

"Kate—behave you! You are not a child now, remember," her mother said, but smiling.

The girl ignored her. "Davie—so long! Why? Why did you never come?"

"I, I have been occupied, Kate. Throng with affairs. Busy. Going hither and yon. I am Prince Jamie's Procurator. I, I . . ."

"I know, I know. But you were only at Linlithgow and Stirling . . ."

"And Falkland and Kincardine, at Dumbarton, even Inverness. The King is never in one place for long, lass. And takes his young son, to show to all—the heir." Gently he put her from him, but only to arm's length, where he held her young loveliness. "Lord, Kate—you have . . . changed!"

"I have *not*!" Impulsively she shook her dark head. "*You* may have done. I think that you were unkind. Never to come."

"Heed her not, Davie," the Lady Lindsay advised. "She is but growing up. A process which can be trying. For all!"

He wagged his head. "No, no—not that." But it was that, of course. Kate Lindsay was indeed growing up, and most dramatically. A gawky, angular thirteen-year-old when last he had seen her, now at fifteen she had changed almost out of recognition, become a young woman and a beauty, features firmed and bloomed, person filled out and developing into promising excellence. Dark-haired, dark-eyed, clear-skinned, vivacious, eager, she was no longer the child he had known and looked on almost as a sister.

"Growing up, I see, yes. And I like what I see!" he said.

"You have waited sufficiently long to see it! But, now that you *have* come, you have brought . . . others!"

"Ah, yes. This is Mistress Mirren Livingstone of Dechmont. And the Abbot John of Culross. Friends."

The girl dipped a curtsy towards them, deep enough to be slightly mocking, towards Mirren at least. "Friends of Davie Lindsay's *must* be friends of mine!" she declared, eyes flashing.

"The Abbot is Prince Jamie's tutor," he explained. "And Mistress Mirren is at the King's court."

"Indeed. Have you finished my poem? *Katie Lindsay's Confession*?"

"Ah, no. No, I fear not. I, ah, have not been writing poetry, Kate. So much to do . . ."

"But it was nearly finished. And you promised!"

"I am sorry. But my life now is not helpful to writing poetry, I fear. All bustle and company and travel. Too many people coming and going . . ."

"Too many people, yes!" she agreed, looking daggers.

"Kate—fetch our guests wine and cake," her mother ordered briskly.

"I did not know that you were a poet, Davie," Mirren said.

"Nor am I," he disclaimed. "I used to scribble the occasional verse. Nothing of any real worth."

"That is not true," Kate threw back, from the doorway. "He wrote much that is fine, splendid. *The Dream* is great poetry." She slammed the door behind her.

"So you kept it up," John Inglis observed. "I said that you should. What is this of a dream? Some major work?"

"No, no. Just a few notions and observations. On a—a theme. Nothing of moment."

"I would wish to see it, nevertheless . . ."

"Davie is too modest," their hostess asserted. "Much of his work is very fine—although I know little about poetry. But—I like it. As do many."

"I always said that he had promise. At college . . ."

When Kate brought them the wine, oatcakes and honey, David had managed to get them off the subject of poetry. But that young creature was not to be balked.

"See," she said, "I have here my copy of the *Confession* you wrote out for me," and she drew out from her burgeoning bosom, now just large enough to contain it, a rather grubby wad of folded paper which she thrust at him. "Now you can complete it, Davie Lindsay."

He took it, warm from her person. "It is scarce worth it, lass."

"If it was worth starting, it is worth finishing. For me, Davie."

"Very well . . ."

"I will hold him to it," the Abbot promised, smiling.

After that, Kate was all sweetness and charm, even to Mirren. When the visitors left, she declared that she would come over to Garleton the following day to make the acquaintance of the young Prince.

That evening, Abbot John took the many pages of *The Dream* to bed with him, with a candle. And a little later, David saw Mirren to her room door again, to say goodnight.

"The lassie Kate is a lively one!" she declared. "She did not love me, I think."

"You must not heed her, Mirren. She is young and grown headstrong, it seems. She was not so before. I have known her all her life."

"And been fond of her, it seems."

"Why, yes. Almost like her older brother—although she has brothers of her own. We are cousins, of a sort, after all."

"She sees you as no brother, that one, Davie! And she is going to be very beautiful."

"She is greatly altered, yes. In looks, as in, er, behaviour. I scarcely knew her. In but two years."

"This poem she covets? About herself?"

"In some fashion, yes . . ." Something between a grunt and a snort came from the next room where the laird slept, door open, and lowered David's voice to a whisper. "A childish thing just, suitable for a bairn. I am no true poet."

Whispering in turn, she drew him into her room—for it would be a pity to wake Sir David, if he was indeed asleep. "Why did you never tell me? Does the King know of it? Abbot John thinks that you are good. This poetry. Will you make a poem about me, Davie?"

"M'mm. Well—I am truly not writing poetry at this present, any more, Mirren . . ."

"But you *can*. Am I not good enough, fair enough? Will you not do it? Just a little one? For me . . . ?" She was close, and came closer, gazing up into his eyes, a most natural-born and unashamed wanton. And he, to be sure, was no monk. As her thrusting breasts brushed against him, he put an arm around her, pulled her closer still, and their lips met. She was wholehearted and generous about that, too.

But quickly his conscience got the better of him. After all, she was the King's woman and he the King's servant. This would not do. She was in his care. Almost roughly he pushed her from him.

"No, we must not," he jerked. "This is folly! Worse!"

"Is it? I do not think that James would mind," she whispered. "He is open-handed. In all things."

"Nevertheless . . ." He shook his head. "I will write you a verse. Goodnight, Mirren." He hurried off.

It took him some time to sleep.

In the morning, John Inglis was loud in his praises over *The Dream*, however unresponsive and preoccupied the author. Mirren was her usual uncomplicated self. Poetry, David thought, and indicated, was an unsuitable subject for the breakfast table.

Kate turned up thereafter, in excellent spirits, and made a great fuss over the little Prince, Jamie loving it. Soon she was announcing that she would come each day to look after the child whilst he remained at Garleton. None ventured to say her nay.

The next day Abbot John set off for Linlithgow and Bishop Elphinstone.

With his friend gone and the Prince being more than well looked after by Sir David and Kate, David and Mirren were more and more alone in each other's company, and inevitably the pressure grew. Mirren probably could not help herself, and seemed to make little attempt to do so. David was both mightily exercised and sorely tried. He took occasional refuge in his upper chamber, which opened on to the parapet-walk of the keep, ostensibly to write poetry, which required much privacy.

This was only a moderately successful device, for although it kept Mirren at a distance it had little such effect on Kate, who of course was almost as much at home at Garleton as was David at the Byres. Moreover, the parapet-walk round the tower's wallhead was a favourite viewpoint for young James, from whence he could survey all the countryside around, croodle at the pigeons and watch the darting swallows. Not infrequently, then, the poet had company after all.

At least this had the effect of getting Kate's *Confession* completed sooner than would otherwise have been the case, to the girl's satisfaction. She, of course, promptly showed it off to Mirren—which produced a different variety of pressure on the versifier.

It was five days before Abbot John got back. He had had to go all the way to Stirling to find the Bishop, although the Queen was still at Linlithgow. Margaret Tudor and William Elphinstone failed to get on; and Stirling, to be sure, was the true seat of government, Linlithgow being merely a royal residence and, moreover, the Queen's own jointure-house, settled on her at her marriage.'

The gist of John's report was this. The Queen was displeased at her son being taken to Garleton; but the Bishop had told her that this was at the King's express command. She had done nothing about it, as yet, but Elphinstone judged that it was only a question of time before she sent for the boy. His advice was that they should not wait for this, but return to Linlithgow fairly soon, for there was no point in causing unnecessary unpleasantness. On the other hand, the King's fears for the Prince's safety probably were not wholly ill-founded and further precautions should be taken. There could well be others than Margaret Tudor who had their eyes on the heir to the throne. The Bishop would advise the Queen, in his capacity as temporary chief minister—Archbishop Beaton, the Chancellor, was with the King—that the Prince should be brought to Stirling Castle, for greater security. He would get the Privy Council, or the rump of it left behind, to make this official policy. Then the Queen could scarcely refuse. Young James would surely be safe in Stirling Castle, the strongest fortress in the land.

This all seemed reasonable and wise. It was decided to take the Bishop's advice and return to Linlithgow shortly, and then on to Stirling. Mirren was less than enthusiastic, preferring to have remained at Garleton until the King came back; and for once Kate was in full agreement. The laird also declared that Garleton would be a duller place without them.

All were reluctant to go, in fact.

3

The appalling, unbelievable news reached Linlithgow just three days after their return. It was utter and complete disaster for Scotland. The King was dead. Slain in battle, most of his lords with him, and untold thousands of his ordinary folk. Even his son, the seventeen-year-old Archbishop.

The scale of the catastrophe was beyond all comprehension—twelve earls, two bishops, fifteen lords, innumerable knights, lairds and chiefs of name died with their sovereign lord, together with most of the greatest and most illustrious army the land had ever fielded, cut down in utter bloody ruin, mountains of dead, and the King fallen eventually himself on top of one of these mountains.

His realm reeled.

It had happened, apparently, not far into England, at a place high above the Till valley called Flodden Edge, a strong position which the Scots had occupied but which James had abandoned, allegedly to meet the English army under Surrey on more equal terms. This sounded the completest folly, but James was chivalrously inclined and the entire expedition was a chivalrous gesture towards France and her Queen. At any rate, the entire Scots host had dismounted, leaving their scores of thousands of horses there on the high ground, and charged down the steep escarpment to the waiting English below. And there those eighteen-foot pikes, sent by King Louis of France, had begun the disaster, causing men to trip and stumble and fall in the downhill rush, shafts snapping, jagging, wounding. And into this headlong chaos the disciplined, ranked English bowmen had rained their arrows in unceasing thousands, so that even before true battle could be joined the Scots had lost large numbers and confusion reigned. Thereafter, typically, the dashing James had led like a captain of foot rather than a general, in the very forefront, sword tireless; and one by one his lords and knights and clerics had died around him, the royal standard falling and rising again above him, held up successively by a score of hands. Just when the King, wounded many times, had finally been struck down, reports did not say; but night had descended on continuing carnage and fight—but in the morning only the slain remained on Flodden's field. The pride of Scotland was laid low.

The effect of these fearful tidings was indescribable, the reaction shattering, people just incapable of accepting the magnitude of the calamity. There was scarcely a home in the land unscathed, whole villages had lost their menfolk, many burghs their provosts and magistrates, including Edinburgh itself. And almost the entire government and leadership of the nation had fallen with its monarch. Never, in a thousand years of history, had anything like this befallen.

Linlithgow, and no doubt Stirling too, was as stunned as the rest—except for the Queen, that is. Margaret Tudor gave no impression of being stunned—on the contrary, she had never seemed so vigorous and decisive. If she grieved for her husband, she showed little outward sign of it, apart from ordering court mourning. She took charge—and admittedly it was necessary that someone should do so.

One of her first acts was to send for David and John, to fetch her son to her, from their wing of the palace. Two days before, she had given them a vehement dressing-down for taking the Prince away without her knowledge or permission—to which they could only say that it was done on the King's command. Her displeasure had been pronounced, but against the monarch's authority it had had to be muted. Now that situation no longer pertained.

They found her in a private anteroom of her bedchamber, with a young man of high colour and hot eyes, whom they knew to be Archibald Douglas, son of the Master of Angus and grandson of old Bell-the-Cat, the Earl. Young James eyed his mother doubtfully. She held out her hand to him.

"Come, James," she said, smiling.

Perhaps he was not used to that smile, for he hesitated, and David gave him a little push.

It was unfortunate that there was a bearskin rug on that anteroom floor, over which the toddler caught his feet and fell his length. He was none the worse, indeed chuckled cheerfully as he picked himself up—but promptly his expression switched to alarm at the outbreak of hot words his small mishap produced.

"How dare you, sirrah—to strike the King's Grace!" the Queen exclaimed.

"Oaf—keep your hands to yourself!" the young Douglas jerked, jumping to his feet. He strode over to the boy. "Sire—all is well. Heed him not. Come to Her Grace."

The boy looked him up and down, made a face, and turned to run back to David.

This unfortunate contretemps produced a rather difficult pause.

"Your Grace sent for us," Abbot John said, diplomatically.

"Yes. I require your heedful attention," the Queen asserted, frowning. She was a plump woman, with a round face, heavy-lidded eyes and a long nose, and displayed a lot of bosom. Those eyes were shrewd, calculating. "All is now changed. I have no reason to consider you suitable persons to be so close to the King's Grace."

This seemed a strange announcement, at this stage, until David's mind adjusted to the fact that it was not her late husband to whom the Queen referred but to her little son who was now, to be sure, King James the Fifth. This would take some getting used to. They waited.

"I have many more pressing matters to deal with and put in order than choosing others to take your places," she went on, in her clipped English voice. "So, for this present, you will continue to minister to my son, but you will do so in a very much more respectful way and in entire obedience to my wishes and commands. He is the King's Grace, and will be treated as such, under *my* authority. Is that understood?"

They bowed to that.

"Meantime, you will prepare His Grace, his person and effects, for travel. The court moves to Stirling tomorrow. Lady Erskine has already gone there to prepare suitable quarters in the castle. You will be ready to ride at sun-up. His Grace will ride with the Master of Angus, here."

"Yes, Madam." So Archie Douglas was now being styled the Master. That could only mean that his father, the Master and heir to the Angus earldom, was another of the battle's casualties.

"That is all. You may retire."

Again they bowed. "And His Grace . . . ?" David asked.

"What of him?"
"Is he to remain?"
"Take him with you."
So much for the King of Scots.
As the two young men backed out, their charge running ahead thankfully, they were halted at the door.
"Lindsay—the woman Livingstone," that imperious voice said. "I understand that she was with you at Garleton? Get rid of her!"
As they returned through the palace corridors, they sought to digest all this.
"It seems that our services are not much longer to be required," David commented. "Young Jamie, I fear, is in for change. And not going to like it, King or none."
"Poor laddie! It is hard on him. Not only to lose his father, whom he loved, but . . . all this! I can go back to my abbey and you to your Garleton and your poetry. But for young James . . . ! He hardly knows his mother. And clearly mislikes that Douglas. Nor do I blame him for it. He is a hard one that, I judge. It seems that he is close to the Queen."
"Yes, I had heard some hint of this."
"He is married, is he not? Although young. Younger than the Queen, I think."
"Married to Patrick Hepburn's daughter, the Earl of Bothwell. Married very young. She is frail, it is said. I have never seen her at court. And he will require no frail woman, that one, I swear!"
"Perhaps. And he will be Earl of Angus, one day, head of the Douglases. If he is not, already."
"No—the Queen called him the Master. So his father must have died. But not the old Earl." They had reached their own very modest accommodation, near the servants' wing. "It is strange to think that this bairn is the King of Scots. And in these humble quarters!"
"No longer after today, since we move to Stirling. Davie—what is to be done about Mirren Livingstone?"
"Lord knows! It was difficult enough before. But now that the King is dead . . . ! Yet, he told me to look after her. And I promised."
"I heard, yes. You must do what you can for her. But, Davie—do not wed her! She is attractive, yes. Generous

and good company. But—do not think to carry out the King's charge by wedding her."

"I had no such intention, I assure you!" David said shortly.

"Perhaps not. But *she* might have!"

David looked at his friend strangely. "What makes you say that? Since when has the Abbot of Culross become so informed in the ways of women?"

"Being in holy orders does not make me blind nor witless, man! Mirren is fond of you, and now needs a protector. Aid her as much as you can—but do not wed her. She would not make the wife for you."

"You are very sure."

"I am, yes."

They left it at that. But that evening David went down to the house that King James had found Mirren in Linlithgow town, near to St Lazarus Well.

She greeted him joyfully. Since the news had come of the King's death, she had remained indoors, shut up for fear of the Queen's spite. David came as a deliverer.

In the circumstances, he found it difficult to deliver his message, at least, with her arms around him and her lips on his own.

"I thought that you would never come, Davie," she declared, between kisses. "I have been cooped like a hen in a yard! Oh, it is so good to see you!"

"And you. But . . ." He got no further.

"I have missed you, Davie. So greatly. After all our time together."

"It is only two days, lass . . ."

"It seems eternity!" In his arms, or he in hers, she was all but imperceptibly leading him towards an open door. He was fairly sure that it was her bedroom.

"The Queen sent for us, the Abbot and myself . . ." he got out.

"Do not speak of that evil woman. I hate her!"

"More to the point, lass—she hates *you*!"

"I know it. But not tonight, Davie. You have come. That is what signifies, for this present. And we are alone."

"We shall have to consider it, sooner or later, Mirren," he said, rather feebly. He was ever loth to offend a friendly lady; and Mirren was something rather special.

Within the bedchamber, she detached herself—but only to stand back and look him up and down. "You want me, Davie?" she demanded—although it was much more a statement than a question. "I think that you have always wanted me? As I have wanted you. And, now that James has gone, we can have each other!" She made it sound entirely simple and suitable. To emphasise the point she began to untie the strings of her bodice. No churl, after a moment or two David moved to help her.

No great assistance was required in fact, for her clothing seemed to be fairly loosely attached and largely fell off of its own accord, so that in almost less time than it takes to tell she was standing in a froth of lace and undress. Naked, she was a gladsome sight, strikingly yet satisfyingly made, full-breasted, with large, dark aureolas, a belly frankly round over a fiery-red triangle, and ample buttocks and thighs. Like many titian-haired women, her skin was startlingly white and fine. She stood, arms akimbo, at ease, proud of her body, obviously waiting to see its effect upon him.

He feared that he must appear all too appreciative in one respect, and found nothing to say in another.

She laughed. "Come, Davie—do not say that I strike you dumb! You have seen women so before, I swear!"

"Not . . . like you!" he got out.

"Ah! That, now, is better! Kind. You . . . improve." She held out her hands. "Come—I shall aid *you*!"

"No need . . ." he declared, beginning to unbutton his doublet; but she moved in nevertheless, thereby complicating the business although engendering a certain hilarity, especially when it came to his lower parts. It was in high spirits, then, rather than in high passion, that they tumbled on to the bed.

Once there, however, there was no giggling fumbling. Mirren was clearly expert and David not without experience—he could scarcely have made his year's tour of Europe, after university, without learning certain skills. They found each other's rhythm with minimum delay.

Although the man was sufficiently masculine, the woman's need seemed to be the greater, and, if anything, she took the lead. Her hands active, stroking, feeling, gripping, the insistence of her body did not fail to inflame him, although even so she retained the initiative. Her person was smoothly hot, save for her breasts which were strangely cool against him, in itself arousing. Tongue as active as the rest of her, she took him with her into physical ecstasy. It occurred to him, fleetingly, at some stage, to perceive why King James, so knowledgeable about women, had found this one so greatly to his taste. Also to wonder if Mirren was right in assuming that her late master would not grudge this so swift consolation after his tragic demise. But present imperatives did not allow such considerations to preoccupy him for long.

When they were both sated and lay back, it still seemed no appropriate time to broach the subject of the Queen's command. Especially as after only a brief interval, Mirren was employing her considerable dexterity to ensure a repetition of the engagement.

When that too was over, rather more prolonged delight, the hour was growing late and David, a little concerned now over a possible interrogation by Abbot John, made his excuses—although Mirren undoubtedly would have liked him to stay the night. She did not help him on with his clothing, but lay back on the bed watching, all spread and open invitation in the candle-light.

"This of the Queen," he jerked, more roughly than he knew. "We must speak of it. She ordered us to—to get rid of you!"

She shrugged white shoulders. "So?"

"She meant it, Mirren. She is a hard woman. And she now has almost complete power in this land."

"So you are to get rid of me! Where, Davie? What is to be done with me?"

He shook his head. "I wish that I knew. You cannot remain here, I fear. Although the court goes to Stirling in the morning, Linlithgow remains the Queen's own property. She would not overlook you, here."

"Then where am I to go?"

"Can you not just go home? To Dechmont."

"No. I *will* not go there. My mother will have none of me. Since I . . . went with the King. She names me strumpet, and worse. I cannot go home."

"You will have other kin that you might go to?"

"None. None that would have me. Where do *you* go, Davie? Can you not take me with you?"

"How can I, lass? We will be at Stirling, with the court. Looking after young James still, now the King. It may not be for long, for the Queen does not love us, either. But meantime . . ." He stared at her. "There must be somewhere that you can go?"

"I have no money. How can I go anywhere? Of myself? I have some trinkets which James gave me, but I would not wish to sell them."

"No. I understand that." He paused. "See you—how would it serve if you were to go to Garleton? Back to my father? He would look after you, to be sure. Meantime. He liked you."

"To Garleton? Why, yes—yes, that would be good. Would he have me? And you? You would come?"

"When I could, yes—when I could."

"Oh, Davie—that would be good . . ."

So it was arranged. David would provide a horse, a pack-horse and a groom to escort her to Garleton the next day—and he prayed that his father would find it in him to co-operate.

It was, in fact, long after sun-up before the royal party was ready to move off westwards from Linlithgow, quite a large cavalcade. After handing over a very reluctant small monarch to the haughty Master of Angus, David and the Abbot retired to a much more humble place in the company, to await the Queen's appearance and a start.

There they came across an East Lothian acquaintance, Robert Seton, one of the Queen's pages and grandson of the third lord of that name. A wounded brother had just won back from the defeat at Flodden Edge, telling of the Lord Seton's death, amongst the others. He was able to provide further details of the disaster. It seemed that considerable blame was being attached by the survivors to the Lord Home, who had had command of the cavalry wing of the Scots left, largely Border mosstroopers who were never to be parted from their horses, and which the King had used as a flanking force when all the rest were charging downhill dismounted. It seemed that Lord Home in fact won his encounter with the English right, but then, instead of swinging round behind the enemy rear as required, had gone chasing off after the fleeing English cavalry, deep into the Cheviot foothills, and was seen no more in the battle. This failure undoubtedly contributed much to the eventual Scots defeat.

Then there was the ineffectiveness of the vaunted Scots artillery, stuck up there on the high ground and unable to depress their great muzzles sufficiently to fire down upon the English ranked below, in dire impotence.

Further news was that there had been an angry scene between the King and the old Earl of Angus before the battle was joined, Bell-the-Cat objecting strongly, vehemently, to the abandonment of the strong position on the ridge, declaring it to be romantic folly, and announcing that he and his would have none of it. His son, the Master, however, had taken a different view, accepting the royal decision, and the Douglas armed host had followed his lead, not the old man's. So the Earl had thereupon left them all and ridden off alone, asserting that his liege-lord and son were fools both. It was said that he had since gone in sorrow to the Priory of Whithorn, in Galloway, to end his days—whereas, of course, the Master had ended *his* there and then by dying beside his monarch.

Robert Seton, in fact, proved to be quite a mine of information, as presently they forded Avon, heading for Falkirk and the Carron, on their twenty-mile journey to Stirling. He had been sent by the Queen the day before to Edinburgh Castle, with orders for the garrison there, and had found the city in a state bordering on panic, its provost, dean-of-guild and many of its magistrates lost, and everyone in expectation of early attack by the triumphant English. The citizenry, even women and children, were already being driven into building a great new extension to the city wall, for better defence, houses being knocked down to provide the necessary stone swiftly; and the castle itself was being stocked up with provisions in preparation for siege, its garrison bewailing the loss of its cannon. All Lothian, in fact, was in dread, for having lost much of its manpower the land lay wide open to invasion by Surrey's victorious army.

David, for one, wondered whether, instead of thus heading westwards for Stirling, he ought not to be hastening in the other direction, for Garleton, and his own home area, to help in its defence? Indeed, he asked himself just what he might have sent Mirren into? And, to tell truth, worried still more about young Kate.

Seton, being a page in the Queen's entourage, was also knowledgeable on the present governmental situation, and young enough to be proud to demonstrate the fact. It seemed that this move to Stirling was primarily at the Privy Council's urging, led by Bishop Elphinstone—although the real Chancellor, Archbishop James Beaton of Glasgow, was now said to be there, having wisely escorted the army only as far as Tweed before turning back. The Queen might well have arranged to go to Stirling anyway, of course. They would be as secure there as anywhere in the southern half of Scotland; and could always disappear into the nearby Highland wilderness if the invaders should indeed get that far—something which had been done times without number in the nation's past. A parliament had been called, for ten days hence, to decide on the measures necessary for the realm's defence and rule in this dire situation—called in the young King's name, of course. Normally parliaments required forty days' notice of calling, to allow commissioners to attend from the farthest corners of the kingdom; but such time just could not be spared on this occasion, with invasion threatened and chaos at home. So this would be a very small gathering inevitably, however important, what with the short notice and so many of the nation's leaders dead or missing. Young Seton feared that it would be largely composed of churchmen, God help Scotland! Belatedly he remembered Abbot John's cloth, and made excuse to ride off in others' company.

Deliberately that royal column made as little fuss and display as possible, in the circumstances, with none of the usual panoply of standards, banners, heralds and musicians. What the Queen's own sentiments might be was not to be known, her situation now being quite extraordinarily transformed from heretofore. With the loss of her husband, suddenly she was focus of all attention, not only in that she held the infant monarch, in whose name all must be done, but in that she was the King of England's sister, with all that implied in present circumstances. Before, she might have been at the centre of intrigues against the King, or at least his policies towards England, at the behest of Dean West, the English ambassador, or of various power factions amongst the nobility; now she was openly in command of the situation—although parliament might modify that; also she might be in a position to temper the harshness of Henry's victorious forces. Probably a parliament was the last thing that she wanted; but its calling, in a national emergency, was a constitutional right which she could not gainsay.

It was afternoon before they sighted Stirling from the high ground above the Bannock Burn, the dramatic citadel on its lofty rock towering above the huddled town amongst the great silver loops and meanders of the River Forth before it reached its estuary, with all the blue ramparts of the Highlands behind, one of the fairest and most significant vistas in the land. It took them more than another hour to reach it, however, encircling the skirts of the great Tor Wood and avoiding the wetlands below St Ninians.

The cavalcade thereafter wound its way up through the steeply climbing narrow streets, where folk came out to stare in silence, to the tourney ground extending before the lowermost castle gate and drawbridge. Here a welcoming party was assembled to greet them, with the keys of Scotland's strongest fortress. Robert, fourth Lord Erskine, who claimed to be rightful Earl of Mar, was the Keeper; but he had gone to England with his sovereign and none knew whether or not he had survived. But his young son, John, Master of Erskine, came to present the keys to the infant monarch, accompanied by his mother, Isabella, Lady Erskine—who, of course, had been the Prince's nurse. James had travelled all the way, not very happily, alternately in front of the Master of Angus's saddle, that of his mother, or that of Gavin Douglas, the Master's uncle who was Provost of the Collegiate Church of St Giles, Edinburgh, and a noted poet. Apparently the child had slept fitfully but frequently demanded to be returned to the company of Da, as he called David Lindsay. He was now ordered by the Queen to touch the keys held out to him, and then handed over to Lady Erskine, briefly shown off to the waiting and bowing notables and then whisked off through the portcullis gateway into the castle outer bailey.

Standing beside old Bishop Elphinstone was another and much more richly dressed cleric, a stoutly built, florid and heavy-jowled man, of a dissipated appearance but shrewd and watchful expression, James Beaton, Archbishop and Chancellor of the realm. As senior in both Church and State he greeted the Queen in the name of all, in flowery language but much as he might have recited a litany, with a minimum of feeling behind his words, even whilst remarking on her loss, and the nation's, in the dread death of the King's Grace that was. Margaret Tudor was known to dislike James Beaton even more than she disliked William Elphinstone. David had been a fellow student at St Andrews of the Chancellor's brilliant nephew, David Beaton, who was now making a name for himself at the French court.

The Queen nodded, almost curtly, and forestalled any further speech-making by announcing flatly that she was wearied with travel, in her present state, and would seek her chamber forthwith.

All hastily changed their stance and attitude, to draw aside, bending the head and knee, so that she might ride on inside, after her son.

The great hilltop citadel made a strong but less than comfortable refuge for the court. The Keeper's House, of course, was reserved for the Queen and those closest to her, and, since it was anyway the Lady Erskine's normal residence, she and young James were permitted to occupy a corner of it. The Chancellor, Bishop Elphinstone, and the other Privy Councillors, were already installed in the best of the remaining accommodation, so that the rest of the new arrivals, however illustrious, had to make do with whatever they could find. David and the Abbot rated very low on this scale, and ended up roosting in a mere cellar attached to a powder magazine near the Overport Battery. They hoped that they would not be therein for long; but at least they had it to themselves, preferable to lying on the floor of the great cold Parliament Hall, the fate of most of the Linlithgow party.

In the days that followed, frustrating as they were for active young men, in cramped quarters, with insufficient to do, at least they learned more of the Flodden tragedy and its immediate aftermath. Foremost was the intriguing story that the King had gone into battle without his famous chain. Apparently, dallying at Ford Castle, some miles north of Flodden, waiting for the English army to put in an appearance, he had found convenient solace with Lady Heron thereof—whose husband, incidentally, was a prisoner in Fast Castle, one of the Lord Home's strongholds, on account of cross-Border raiding. And Lady Heron, it seemed, had found the chain round the King's loins uncomfortable, and persuaded him to take it off—the first reported occasion of such nicety, although David for one wondered what Mirren would say to that? At any rate, whether from forgetfulness or otherwise, James had left his chain at Ford, when called to leave in a hurry—and there was no lack of folk to declare that this was behind the débâcle, the royal vow broken. Others recollected the apparition at St Michael's Church, Linlithgow, warning against meddling with strange women.

There was the information, also, from an escaped captive of the English army, that terrible as the disaster had been, it was not all quite so clear-cut as at first thought. It seemed that at nightfall, the Earl of Surrey, the English commander, had still been sufficiently uncertain of the outcome to gather, when darkness precluded further fighting, forty of his captains, and berate them soundly for their tactical failures, a worried and angry man. But when morning dawned and revealed only the Scots dead, including the King and most of his nobility, left lying on the field, Surrey changed his tune to the extent of actually knighting the said forty captains for their military excellence.

The arrival of Lord Home at Stirling, on the fifth day, created something of a to-do, especially as he came, if not exactly cock-a-hoop, at least well satisfied with himself, as the only commander on the Scots side to have won his own part of the battle, apparently quite unaware that he was being blamed for much of the disaster by failing to turn the main enemy's flank and assail his rear, instead of chasing off after the fleeing cavalry. He was hot in defence of his own course, and scornful against stay-at-home strategists. And since he was Lord Chamberlain, and had brought a tail of two hundred Border mosstroopers with him to Stirling, the criticism became muted. Scotland was going to need all such in its present state.

The details of the casualties were gradually becoming known. The Earls of Argyll, Atholl, Bothwell, Caithness, Cassillis, Crawford, Erroll, Glencairn, Lennox, Montrose, Morton and Rothes were all dead, as were the Archbishop of St Andrews and the Bishops of the Isles and of Caithness and the mitred Abbots of Kilwinning and Inchaffray. So many lords that none could name them all, but including the Lord Erskine, Keeper here; also the chiefs of clans from the Highlands, James having been perhaps the only Scots monarch who could have got these to come and fight for him since Bruce the hero king. As for knights, lairds and gentry, these were beyond all numbering; and the common folk in their thousands. Even the French ambassador, de la Motte, was amongst the slain.

The parliament to follow would not be much larger than a normal meeting of the Privy Council.

That parliament, held on 21st September, two weeks after Flodden field, was unusual in other than its scanty numbers. Taking place in the castle's Parliament Hall, cleared of its lodgers for the occasion, on the motion of the Chancellor it went into temporary recess almost as soon as it was convened.

Those attending, with more spectators than commissioners, even so by no means filling the hall, stood for the flourish of trumpets and the entry of the young monarch, led in between the Queen and the Master of Angus, the little boy being deposited on the high throne—on which he promptly stood rather than sat—whilst his mother occupied a lesser throne at his side and Archibald Douglas stood behind. In the Scottish parliament, it was necessary for the monarch to be present in person; otherwise it was no true parliament, only a convention of the Three Estates of lords, shire representatives and churchmen, and could not pass effective legislation. The Chancellor chaired the deliberations but the King presided, and could intervene, join in the debate and close the sitting at will.

Bowing to the throne, Archbishop Beaton made his announcement that, in accordance with ancient procedures this was a proper assembly of the high court of parliament, in the presence of and by the authority of their undoubted liege-lord, James, fifth of his name, by God's grace High King of Scots. However, in order that the parliament's due authority should be effective beyond the least doubt, it was considered advisable, in the present grievous circumstances in which they forgathered, that the monarch's position should be established beyond all possible doubt. Therefore it had been decided that a coronation ceremony should take place forthwith, in the Chapel Royal, whereafter the parliament would be resumed. It was usual, of course, for the coronation to be held at Scone. But this was not obligatory, and in the circumstances the Chapel Royal here would serve. Was this the will of the parliament here assembled?

No contrary voice was raised.

So a temporary adjournment was proclaimed, and all filed out of the hall, behind the royal party, to a different level of the rock-top fortress where the Chapel Royal was situated, no large edifice, so that it was perhaps as well that numbers were so low, otherwise all would not have won into the church. John Inglis, as Abbot of Culross, could have probably claimed a place up in the chancel, but nobody had asked him and he preferred to squeeze in at the back with David.

There followed probably the briefest coronation ceremony that Scotland had ever known, not only on account of the need for haste but because so many who should have taken part were just not present. There was no Lord Lyon King of Arms to pronounce the monarch's undoubted right and genealogy back into the mists of antiquity; no representative of the MacDuff line to act as Inaugurator and bear the crown; no High Constable to carry the sword of state; no hereditary bearers of sceptre, orb and spurs. Home, as Chamberlain, had to shoulder responsibility for most of this aspect of the proceedings, appointing such deputies as he thought fit. There was no lack of ecclesiastics, at least, for the most significant part of the ceremonial.

In the absence of the Primate the only other archbishop, Beaton, with the Abbot of Scone, conducted the service with a minimum of fuss, as though to get all over as quickly as possible, for he was no ritualist. Young James, on whose behaviour so much depended, was remarkably patient for most of the time, although he yawned a lot, fidgeted and stared around him. But by the time that they got to the actual crowning—which was difficult anyway, with the crown far too large to be actually placed on his small head, having instead to be held over him while the necessary pronouncements were intoned—the boy had had enough, and made it sufficiently plain, to the disruption of the proceedings. The Queen came forward to try to soothe him; and when that failed, adopted a sterner stance, actually shaking the monarchial arm in exasperation. This produced a spirited reaction of tiny fists, and when the Master of

Angus moved in with a strong arm, he was met by a howl of fury. James jumped down from the coronation chair, to glare around him, seemingly preparatory to bolting.

In these alarming circumstances, Margaret Tudor did probably all that remained open to her. Presumably from her lofty position up near the high altar, she had seen David and John take their places at the back. Now she looked searchingly in that direction and extending her arm, jabbed an imperious finger towards them, twice, ending in a beckoning gesture.

Distinctly embarrassed, the two young men pushed their way forward through the crush.

They were just in time, with James, having discerned a vestry doorway nearby, about to make a dash therefor.

"Jamie, lad—Jamie!" David called, on impulse. "Wait, Jamie—it is Da."

The boy turned. "Da!" he exclaimed. "Da!" and rushed to hurl himself at his friend.

Not a few folk sighed with relief.

Taking the child's chubby hand, David led him back to the Archbishop. "Not long now, Jamie," he said, low-voiced. "Just a little longer. Be good. You will do very well. Abbot John and I will stay with you. Just a little more . . ."

Doubtfully, clutching his protectors' hands on either side tightly, the King of Scots allowed himself to be taken to the coronation chair and sat thereon. One on either side of it, the young men stood. Ignored, the Queen and the Master returned to their places.

Thankfully, Beaton resumed his delivery, hastening now to get it over and done with. Abbot John thus had his part in the coronation, after all.

The Archbishop finished, a fanfare of trumpets proclaimed the fact that Scotland again had a crowned king. Then there was a hiatus. The clergy formed up to lead the procession back to Parliament Hall. But none could leave, of course, before the monarch. And James clung to David and John, and scowled at everybody else.

After a few moments the Queen, frowning, had to accept the situation. "Escort His Grace to the Hall," she directed abruptly.

So, at the head of all, the boy and the two young men wound their way back.

In the hall, infant majesty was not to be left without his accustomed guardians again; and to save another scene erupting, the Queen signed for them to remain standing behind the throne. Young James, to be sure, was not normally like this; but he had never had much to do with his mother, being very much his father's boy. Now he stood on his throne, back to the assembly, and grinned and made faces at his chosen companions. The Master of Angus stood behind the Queen's chair, muttering.

Chancellor Beaton, content that it was all no worse, reconvened the session.

He began by fairly briefly summarising the situation in which the kingdom found itself, and emphasising its desperate straits in the loss of its beloved monarch and so many of the nation's best, in lords, church and people. He did not require to stress the heavy duty which lay upon them all in this hall, those left to carry the burden of state, with the land reeling, open to invasion, and so much of its might gone. But this must be no session of lamentation, he emphasised. They had no time nor occasion for that; nor was it the spirit which Scotland required this day. Resolute action the nation demanded of them all, from highest to lowest—let none forget it.

He went on to indicate the proposed agenda. First and foremost there must be the matter of the continuing rule and governance of the realm under His Grace, since he was a minor—the question of regency. Also decision as to the succession to the throne, now urgent, with a child monarch. Then there was the filling of offices of state under the crown, so many of which were now vacant, so that the due responsibility for the direction of the kingdom would be apportioned, especially the defence of the realm and the maintenance of the law and public order. Much else would demand their attention, but these were the principal immediate issues for decision—and would more than suffice for this day. Was it agreed that they dealt first with the vital matter of rule and the care and destination of the crown?

None could deny that this was the first priority, since all authority stemmed from the crown—and the said crown was at the moment playing happily enough with the two carved and rampant lions which decorated the back of the throne, David Lindsay endeavouring to keep the royal oohs and ahs and chuckles at as low a key as possible.

The Archbishop had scarcely got his question out before the Queen spoke—and thus early in the proceedings demonstrated something of the problems before that assembly. For in theory she had no authority to raise her voice. There was no place for a queen-consort or queen-mother in the Scots parliament other than as a mere spectator sitting beside her royal spouse or son.

"My lord Chancellor," she said, in that clipped, assured English voice. "I have a statement to make, relevant to my royal son, the King's Grace, and to the succession. I am three months pregnant by my late husband. I expect to bear his child until the month of April next."

This, needless to say, created no little stir in the company, for it is probable that none had really considered this possibility, James and his wife having gone more and more their own ways for some time now. Margaret had borne him two children before this young Jamie, both of whom had died in months. Having at length produced a healthy male heir, it had not been anticipated that she would have risked more.

The significance of this announcement at least provided an excuse for the Chancellor not having to point out that Her Grace was out of order in addressing the parliament.

However, she went on. "I further must state that in the matter of rule and governance, I cannot consider the appointment of any soever, other than myself, to act in my royal son's name. Let this be understood by all."

If the first announcement intrigued the assembly, this bombshell stunned it. Margaret Tudor was highly unpopular throughout the land. Moreover no woman had ever been regent or held supreme power in Scotland—which traditionally required a very strong hand at the helm. Yet here was this Englishwoman as good as claiming that position.

In the appalled silence, with even the normally authoritative Archbishop at a loss for words, another voice spoke up, jerkily forceful and self-assertive, that of Archibald Douglas, from his position behind the Queen.

"I hereby propose and nominate the Queen's Grace to be Regent of this kingdom during the minority of the King's Grace," he declared.

This time there was no awkward hush. Shouts of dissent arose all over the hall.

The Chancellor could deal with this, at least. "Master of Angus," he said severely. "I must remind you that you have no warrant to speak nor make any motion before this parliament. You are not a lord of parliament as yet, nor the commissioner of any shire, nor yet, so far as I know, a representative of Holy Church!"

"I speak, sir, as the head of the house of Douglas!" the young man cried hotly. "Is Douglas to have no voice in the affairs of this realm? My father is dead. My grandsire, the Earl, is retired to a monastery. Who says that I shall not speak for Douglas?"

At that challenge there was uproar in the hall, so that David had to soothe the young James, alarmed at the noise and passion aroused. The Douglases were the most powerful family in Scotland, and the richest, with wide ramifications, more so than the royal line of Stewart itself. Inevitably they had enemies, many resenting their influence. On the other hand they had friends and hangers-on; and there were not a few present in similar position to the Master, heirs of line, unsure whether their fathers, uncles, brothers lived yet or no, and so of their own situation; or kin of fallen shire commissioners, who felt that they should be filling their places in this meagre parliament. In the confusion and shouting, old Bishop Elphinstone rose to his feet and raised a hand. Seeing it Beaton banged his gavel, no doubt thankfully, and bellowed for silence for the Lord Privy Seal.

William Elphinstone was undoubtedly the most respected man in the land, former Chancellor, founder of Aberdeen University, historian, former tutor, friend and confidant of the late King. He had no difficulty in obtaining a hearing.

"My lord Chancellor," he said, his eighty-two-year-old voice surprisingly strong. "I have here something which much bears on this present situation and which should help us in our decisions." He waved a paper in the air. "It is the testament of our late and much loved liege-lord James, whom God cherish in a better land than this Scotland, and where I look forward to joining him before long! His Grace left it in my keeping, as his confessor and friend." He looked over at the Queen. "Amongst other matters which I shall, to be sure, convey to the proper quarters, His Grace has written that, should aught ill befall him, he leaves his son and heir in the hands of the Queen's Grace for his care and protection, as tutrix and guardian—but only for so long as she does not remarry. Should Her Grace indeed remarry, then the young monarch is to be transformed into the care and keeping of whoever is appointed Regent of the kingdom." The Bishop sat down.

Again the assembly sat silenced—save for the child concerned, who chortled on, now playing with the tassels of Abbot John's girdle. But as men took in the implications of this revelation, a stir arose and eager discussion amongst delegates. And not only delegates and men. The only woman present turned in her chair and spoke urgently to the Master of Angus, upset most evident.

Beaton allowed the gathering its head for a few moments, and then claimed order with his gavel. "We have to thank my lord Bishop for his contribution to this discussion," he said. "No doubt the Privy Council will examine this document fully in due course, with action in view. We all know the Lord Privy Seal sufficiently well to be assured that this testament of our late liege-lord is a true and honest one. And we are, to be sure, bound to heed its directions in our decisions. From what has been told us, it seems clear that our newly crowned monarch is to remain in the care and keeping of the Queen's Grace meantime. But this applies to the King's royal person, not to the kingdom. In this testament King James speaks of a Regent, to whom His present Grace would be entrusted in the event of the remarriage of the Queen-Mother. So clearly these cannot be one and the same person. In other words, a Regent to rule the realm in the King's name is required, other than the Queen-Mother. So that, even if the Master of Angus had warrant to move his motion, such motion must fall."

Cheers were raised throughout the hall.

Margaret Tudor sat forward in her chair. Her eyes were not such as could blaze, but the smouldering anger in them was not to be hidden.

"Sir Chancellor," she exclaimed, "not so fast! This is not to be borne! I should have been informed of this testament, my own husband's will—if it is indeed honest in truth, which remains to be proven. I shall, you may rest assured, keep and guard my son—and let none think to ordain otherwise! But, of this of rule and regency, I deny what you may, sir. Nothing in what was reported could exclude me from the regency. Bishop Elphinstone said 'whoever is appointed Regent of the kingdom'. *Whoever!* There is nothing there to say that such Regent shall not be myself."

Into the murmurings, Beaton spoke. "Madam—your royal son could not be transferred from yourself to yourself! *Transferred* is the word. My lord Bishop—I take it that this is indeed the word used by our late liege-lord? In his testament?"

"It is, yes. Transferred to whoever is appointed."

"And you would agree that this must mean that whoever is appointed could not be Her Grace the Queen-Mother?"

"Clearly so, my lord Chancellor. Such was His Grace's intention."

"I deny that!" Archibald Douglas shouted. "This is but clerkly play with words! *Whoever* is appointed does not rule out the Queen's Grace."

"Master of Angus—you have no voice in this parliament!" the Archbishop thundered.

"But *I* have!" another voice spoke up strongly, that of a namesake indeed, Sir Archibald Douglas of Kilspindie, commonly known as Greysteel, fourth son of Bell-the-Cat and commissioner for the shire of Haddington. "And I agree with my nephew, the Master. Nothing in what has been said can debar Queen Margaret from the regency. I so move. Move that this parliament appoints Her Grace as Regent."

"And I second. Who better than our young King's lady-mother? And sister of His Grace of England—and so more able than any other to protect this realm from English spite." That was said in the mellifluous tones of the brother of the previous speaker, Gavin Douglas the poet who, as Provost of the Collegiate Church of St Giles, the capital's principal church, ranked with the mitred abbots and had a seat in parliament.

The house of Douglas was making its position plain.

For good measure, Margaret Tudor went on. "The good Master Gavin is right. In this pass, this kingdom requires above all else the goodwill of my royal brother, Henry. Can any deny it? And can any deny, likewise, that I, the King of

England's sister, am the most like to obtain goodwill from him? Could any other Regent so claim?"

There was silence at that, for a moment or two, before the Lord Home raised his voice. "My lord Chancellor, the King of England's goodwill towards this realm has scarcely been evident hitherto! He has claimed, before many, and to our late King's especial envoy, that *he* was Lord Paramount of Scotland, that he was the very owner of Scotland indeed, his very words. And that the late James only held it of his, Henry's, homage! All know of this, this insolent and vaunty boasting. Are we to believe that with Henry's royal sister here ruling the land in her son's name, the Leopard of England will then become a cooing dove? Rather, I say, he would roar the fiercer! He would take over the realm!"

The shout of support for Home spoke for itself, and did much to reinstate the Chamberlain in esteem.

But the Queen was not finished yet. She raised that minatory finger of hers, to point. "Has my lord of Home overlooked the fact that all is changed? With regard to England. Now that my husband is dead. Before, my royal brother feared James's enmity and spleen—and with reason, as witness this late wicked invasion of England, resulting in such dolour. But now the King of Scots, my son here, is no threat to Henry, and must remain none. So long as he is not, Henry, who is fully occupied in France, will not trouble him, or his realm. *I* can best ensure that." She paused significantly. "And not only not trouble him, but indeed cherish him and his kingdom. For my son is now heir-presumptive to the throne of England! Have none realised it?"

By the gasps and exclamations it was evident that few, if any, had. But it was true, of course. Henry, although married for four years to Catherine of Aragon, was childless, brotherless, Margaret his only sister, and young Jamie his only nephew. There was no one else. If Henry, battling in France, should fall, like his late brother-in-law, this child now behind his throne with his friends, not on it, was next in line for the crown of England. Belated recognition, and the implications, left the company bemused.

Not all of it, however. Bishop Elphinstone rose and spoke into the chatter. "This situation, which some of us have foreseen, must be considered in our decisions," he said calmly. "But with great respect for the Queen's Grace, I do not think that it indicates that King Henry will look more kindly on Scotland. On the contrary, my lord Chancellor, I would say that he will be the more like to seek to grasp Scotland, and probably its young King with it, since he arrogantly claims this realm as his. And so to have his heir in his own keeping. This I believe will be his attitude, not kindly concern. And if so, a woman, and his sister, ruling Scotland, would be as good as an invitation to him to come and take what he wants. I . . ." Cheers drowned out the rest.

Beaton took over. "I have a motion before this parliament, proposed by Sir Archibald Douglas of Kilspindie and seconded by his brother, the Provost Gavin, that Her Grace the Queen-Mother should be Regent of this realm as well as guardian and tutrix of the child King. Before any vote is taken, however, it is my duty as Chancellor to point out that it has always been the custom and tradition of this kingdom, from earliest times, to appoint a near *male* kinsman of the monarch to be Regent during a minority. I do not say that this is incumbent upon us, but it is the custom, on the understanding that the realm requires a strong man's hand in such situation. Are there any other motions before we come to a conclusion on the matter?"

Half a dozen men were on their feet at once. The Chancellor gave precedence to Lord Home.

"I move as amendment that John, Duke of Albany, full cousin of our late King, be appointed Regent," the Chamberlain said. "As well as the closest male kin, he is powerful, Admiral of France, and in kinship by marriage with the King of France. Albany, I say."

There were cries for and against. John Stewart was the son of Alexander, Duke of Albany, who had been younger brother to James the Third and who, after trying to supplant his weak brother on the throne, had had to flee to France, where he had married one of the greatest heiresses, the daughter of the Comte de Boulogne; and this John was the son, a *grand seigneur* of France and to all intents a Frenchman, unable, it was said, to speak a word of English, much less Scots. Nevertheless, he was undoubtedly the nearest male relation to young James, and was known to be highly regarded in his adoptive country.

"I support that nomination," Andrew Forman, Bishop of Moray declared.

"We have, then, John, Duke of Albany proposed and seconded as Regent, instead of Her Grace," Beaton said. "Is there any other nomination?"

"Yes, my lord—I nominate James Hamilton, Earl of Arran, Lord High Admiral." This was another cleric on his feet, and a notable one, John Hepburn, Prior of St Andrews and brother of the Earl of Bothwell, who was one of the fallen at Flodden. An able, not to say unscrupulous and ambitious churchman, although only a prior, his was a position of great influence, for he had long managed the metropolitan see, first for the late King's younger brother and then for his illegitimate son, neither true clerics and uninterested in the archepiscopate save for its powers and revenues. Many bishops were less important. "My lord of Arran is grandson of King James the Second, Lieutenant-General of this realm and Warden of the Marches. He, at least, can speak our tongue! I propose the Earl of Arran for Regent."

"No!" That was Home again, coldly. "How could we trust James Hamilton? Has he not already cost this kingdom dear? Where is he now? None know, for sure. I say that Arran as Regent would be a disaster. I move that he be not considered."

There was uproar in the hall, some shouting that it was not only Arran who had cost the kingdom dear.

"But I second Prior John's nomination!" the Bishop of Dunkeld cried into the hubbub.

"And I Home's!" the Lord Saltoun barked.

Beaton was in a quandary. He rapped on his desk. "I have two new motions, making four in all. I am uncertain whether the Lord Home's second motion is competent, moving that the Prior John's be not considered—when itself is a competent motion. What is the will of the house in this matter?"

"Chancellor," Home insisted, "how can we consider the appointment of Arran? He may not even be alive! Our late monarch sent him, in command of the realm's fleet, to assail the English west coast and so to aid in His Grace's venture. This, weeks ago. He was to distract the English forces. But he did not do so. He sailed off from the Clyde to attack *Ireland* in some ploy of his own—God knows what! None know where he now is, or our ships. Some say that he has sailed them to France. How could this realm consider such a, a weathercock as its Regent?" The Earl of Arran had divorced Home's sister four years earlier.

"Nor Albany either!" the Queen-Mother put in tartly. "A prancing Frenchman!"

The Douglases cheered, the Hamiltons shook their fists and most of the company appeared to be on their feet.

James, King of Scots, not liking the noise, made a dart for the open dais door behind the throne, and out, Lindsay in pursuit.

It was not like James Beaton to be found at a loss, tough character as he was. He looked about him now, almost helplessly, banging for quiet but uncertain what to do with it when he got it.

Again it was William Elphinstone, former Chancellor, who came to his aid, when he could make himself heard. "I suggest, my lord Archbishop, that you should adjourn this sitting. That tempers may abate. We have all heard sufficient to cause us most seriously to think. Better that all should do so with cool heads. Tomorrow will serve us well enough to nominate a Regent, be it the Duke of Albany, the Earl of Arran, or Her Grace." He paused, before going on with a faint smile. "Forby, our liege-lord appears to have put any further debate out of order by abandoning the session!"

Thankfully Beaton nodded. "I accept that as good advice. Tomorrow, then, my lords. At noon." He turned and bowed to the Queen. "After Your Grace . . ."

Margaret Tudor rose and swept out of the hall without a glance at anyone, Archibald Douglas hurrying after. They passed her son, on all fours in the passage outside, equally without glance or pause.

As thankfully as the Chancellor, his two partisans picked up their charge and hurried him off to their quarters.

4

David Lindsay, for one, was well content to obtain his further information about the doings of that momentous parliament at second hand. For, sensibly, the Chancellor and Privy Council contrived a constitutional device whereby the monarch's necessary presence could be presumed, by the substitution of a high commissioner sitting in the royal name. By general agreement Bishop Elphinstone was appointed such commissioner. This spared all concerned, young James from prolonged boredom, the assembly from being at the mercy of an eighteen-month-old child's whims, and David and John from embarrassing attendance. The Queen-Mother's reaction went undisclosed, since she was not consulted—but she continued to attend the sessions.

Instead of listening to speeches, arguments, accusations and proposals, whilst the future of the nation was decided, the two young men and the little boy then entertained themselves as best they might. They were commanded not to leave the security of the fortress; but this was less cramping than they might have feared. Stirling Castle was a hilltop citadel, and within its perimeter walling much space was enclosed, at varying levels, by no means all, or even most, of the area built up with towers, bartizans, parapet-walks, barracks, storehouses, kitchens and the like. There was room for archery butts, a quoiting pitch, a bowling green, even a menagerie, although this was presently untenanted save by a couple of Muscovy bears, trained for dancing but now fat and sleepy. Not only on the rock summit, but part-way down the precipitous sides, were grassy ledges and terraces, with steps cut for access, utilised for gardens and recreational pursuits. In especial, some way down the north-east flank but still within the walling, was a remarkable feature, more than any shelf this, poised dizzily between the plain and the soaring turrets, an irregularly shaped plot of ground amounting to a few acres, which could actually be tilled, and whereon were pastured two or three tethered cows to provide milk for the garrison. This was humorously known as the croft of Ballengeich, and was a favourite venue, for there was a steep and fairly smooth grass slope down to it, much appreciated for the sport of hurly-hackit, a grass-sledging activity. This was played by sliding down the hill on the skulls of cows or oxen, steering by means of the up-curling horns, the name coming from hurl, the Scots for ride or glide, and haukie, the term for a white-headed cow. Spirited competitions and races could be held at this, with attempts to cannon into and unseat opponents adding to the excitement.

This became one of young James's favourite pastimes, at first seated in the lap of one or other of his escorts, later pick-a-back clinging to the shoulders, and finally alone on his own small calf's skull, quite fearless despite all the bumps and spills. He, and for that matter his two attendants, found this a deal better than attending parliaments—even though Abbot John did not like to be seen engaging in the sport, conceiving it to be inconsistent with his abbatial dignity—but, as David pointed out, he was only a titular Abbot, not a true one, any more than the late Alexander Stewart had been a true Archbishop, installed by influence and receiving most of the revenues, but not concerned with the religious and monastic responsibilities. Culross Abbey and its affairs were professionally managed by a genuine prior, and John's commitments were covered by two or three brief visits there each year. Such were the convenient arrangements of Holy Church in this early sixteenth century.

All the monarch's time, of course, was not spent sliding down hills and toiling up again, feeding already overfed bears, playing quoits and bowls and clambering about that rocky plateau. Quite frequently it rained and they had to be indoors; and at the Queen's command some sort of attempts had to be made at lessons and training, although James was much too young for any real schooling. John did his best, as tutor, but it was really only behaviour and manners which could be inculcated at this stage. David, for his part, being musically inclined, played lute and harp and taught the boy songs and ballads and to love words.

Despite enforced proximity in the restrictions of the castle, they saw little of the Queen-Mother and her party.

Bishop Elphinstone, however, took a great interest in the child, and from him they learned the gist of what went on at the parliamentary sessions, slow to progress as these proved to be. The regency question was in abeyance meantime, a large majority having agreed to send to the Duke of Albany, in France, to seek his acceptance of the position. If refused, the Earl of Arran was to be approached—if he could be found. Meantime, a triumvirate of the Privy Council—the Chancellor, Home as Chamberlain, and himself as Privy Seal—were to exercise the regency authority. It seemed that the Queen-Mother's candidacy never really had a chance, only the Douglas faction supporting it.

An equally vexed question appeared to have been that of the Primacy of Holy Church, the appointment to the archbishopric of St Andrews, left vacant by young Alexander. This was most important, given the influence of the Church, especially in present circumstances with the King a minor and so many of the heads of families and the baronage likewise suddenly under full age. The urgency of this appointment was emphasised by the report that King Henry had petitioned the Pope to demote the archbishopric from metropolitan status and place it, and Scotland, under the ecclesiastical jurisdiction of the Archbishop of York, in his campaign to bring Scotland under English control. An embassage was being sent to Rome to counter this; but it revealed the lengths to which Henry would go.

Elphinstone himself had been the almost unanimous choice, it appeared, for the Primacy; but reluctantly he had declined. He explained to the young men that to have accepted would have been folly, and worse. He was much too old. A man in his eighties should be considering the next world, not embarking on a most testing and demanding new responsibility. It would mean a new appointment in a year or two. A much younger and more vigorous man was required in this situation. Admittedly his refusal would entail much bickering and competition amongst other contenders, which was unfortunate. There were three principal candidates—Provost Gavin, the Douglas nominee; Prior John Hepburn, who had in fact been administrating the archdiocese for Alex Stewart; and Bishop Andrew Forman of Moray, a most able cleric. The Queen, of course, supported Gavin Douglas; but parliament was almost equally divided between the other two.

David, for one, wondered why parliament had anything

to do with the election of an Archbishop? Surely this was the business of the Church itself? To which the old man replied that it should indeed be so. But that for long the crown had usurped the Church's privilege in nominating incumbents for high ecclesiastical offices to the Pope for consecration; and now, with the crown in a child's hands and no Regent yet, parliament considered that it must be involved, with so much depending on the appointment. Personally, Elphinstone believed that Forman would be the best choice, a Bishop already and an experienced cleric, and was so advising the Pope. But both the Douglases and the Hepburns were strong, with the armed might of their earldoms behind them, and might could prevail. Such was the plight of Christ's Church.

For the rest, the parliamentary news was more constructive. Many necessary appointments had been made to positions vital for governance—justiciarships, sheriffdoms, keeperships of royal castles, captains of ports, march-wardenships and the like. Inevitably the great families gobbled up most of these; but to be sure they had the power to enforce their authority, once appointed, which was also necessary. The secret was to maintain a nice balance between the Douglases, Hepburns, Homes, Stewarts, Kennedys and the rest—aye, and the Lindsays also—so that none grew *over*-powerful. That was ever the aim of domestic statecraft.

As for the nation's situation, happily full-scale invasion had not developed, as yet. Henry required more troops in France, so Surrey had turned the main army southwards again, for embarkation into ships at Tyne and Humber. Also, the Welsh had taken the opportunity to rise, as so often, and forces were needed to contain them. But Lord Dacre, the English Chief Warden of the Marches, had been given orders to raid and devastate as far into Scotland as he could; and, of course, the south of the country was wide open to his savagery. Towns, villages, abbeys, churches, lairdships, were going up in flames, and terrible things done to the people. The Lord Home had been appointed Chief Marches Warden and charged with somehow halting Dacre. But it would be no easy task.

The day after the parliament ended and the commissioners and lords temporal and spiritual had in the main left Stirling, came the news that other than parliamentary decisions still counted in Scotland. The Douglases had attacked and taken St Andrews Castle, the seat of the archbishops, by armed force. The poet Provost Gavin and his brother Greysteel were now in firm possession, indicating that there were more ways than one of seeking high office in the Church, and that literary leanings need be no bar to such preferment. The Master of Angus was still at Stirling with the Queen-Mother; no criticism of the action emanated from the royal quarters. Clearly it had been carefully timed, so that parliamentary criticism would not be forthcoming either.

The Chancellor and Privy Council were angry, and William Elphinstone grieved—but none was really surprised. This had been the pattern in Scotland for all too long. The late King's strong hand had restrained such activities by the powerful nobles; but it was almost too much to hope for, that, his hand removed, they would not revert. The need for a Regent, and a strong one, was the more evident.

Then, just over a week later, there were further tidings from Fife. The Hepburns under Prior John and his nephew, the new Earl of Bothwell, had assailed St Andrews, town and castle, in great strength and managed to retake both, driving out the Douglases with considerable losses. There was major upset in the Queen-Mother's quarters at Stirling, and the Master of Angus departed eastwards in haste, trumpeting calls for an immediate muster of all Douglas power. Civil war could be in sight, to add to all Scotland's other troubles. The Privy Council, sending out urgent orders for peace and observance of the law, considered recalling Lord Home from the Borderland, the only experienced military leader left in the Lowlands, to try to deal with this situation; but decided that, on balance, Lord Dacre's English raiders were the greater menace at the moment. What the Master of Angus's neglected wife, back at Tantallon in East Lothian, thought about all this was anybody's guess; she was a Hepburn, sister of the new Earl of Bothwell.

Fortunately, the Douglas might always took some time to marshal, being so widely dispersed over the country, men having to march from as far apart as Galloway in the south-west and the Mearns in the north-east, something that the Hepburns would have reckoned on. Also, they had suffered large losses at Flodden, which was bound to have its effect upon a call-to-arms so soon after. This gave time for the Hepburns likewise to summon their full strength, nothing like so great as that of Douglas but more concentrated, in Lothian; also they could call upon more allies, all who feared and resented Douglas. It also gave time for a courier to arrive from Rome, with the word that Pope Leo the Tenth had appointed Bishop Forman of Moray to be the Archbishop of St Andrews, as advised by Elphinstone; and not only so, but as a notable snub to the King of England, had emphasised the full metropolitan status of the Scots archdiocese and even given the hint that a cardinal's hat might possibly be forthcoming for the new Primate. Not only that, but he appointed him Legate, with power to regulate the benefices of Scotland in the papal name.

This development effectively threw a douche of cold water on the Douglas-Hepburn flare-up, since neither could very well continue to contest it once the Vatican decision was made. But of course such powerful and jealous competitors were not to be called off without some compensation. The new Archbishop Forman was, however, a realist, and, in conjunction with Home, came to an arrangement with the Hepburns whereby Prior John, still in possession at St Andrews, was to retain most of the revenues of the see meantime, and also to get Forman's own newly vacated bishopric of Moray, whilst the Prior's nephew received the rich Home Priory of Coldinghame. This, of course, infuriated the Douglases, but also had the effect of further isolating them. And the ousted Provost Gavin was astutely ambushed by the minions of Home, who hated all Douglases, and thereafter clapped prisoner in the Sea Tower of the very St Andrews Castle in which he had recently been lording it—and where, as it was said, he could write poetry to his heart's content.

The Douglas cause was thus in some disarray, for the Provost Gavin could be used as a hostage. Moreover, at this juncture, the voice of old Bell-the-Cat was belatedly raised, from his sanctuary at Whithorn in Galloway, declaring that no more Douglas blood was to be spilled in unprofitable adventures whilst he remained Earl of Angus. So the Master, his grandson, returned to Stirling in nail-biting rage and disappointment. With Margaret Tudor now in mid-pregnancy, it was doubtful whether he even obtained much consolation from that quarter.

All this much interested but did not greatly affect David and John—although, not being enamoured of Archibald Douglas, they were not greatly grieved at his misfortunes. What did concern them, however, was the arrival on the scene of a new tutor for the infant King—as though, at his present age, Abbot John was not more than adequate. But Queen Margaret had not forgotten her announcement, that day before they all came to Stirling, that she did not consider them suitable persons to attend on the King's Grace and that she would, presently, look for others. Since then, to be sure, she had discovered that young James was not to be parted from his friends without dire consequences in his behaviour, highly embarrassing. So, as attendants, they remained. But to assert her authority, a senior figure was to be put over them. She chose Master Gavin Dunbar, a chaplain, nephew of the Archdeacon of St Andrews, another Gavin Dunbar, who was a supporter of Gavin Douglas now incarcerated in St Andrews Castle. As well as having the same Christian name as the would-be Primate this Gavin was also a poet, although a less successful one. Indeed, his lack of success in his career generally, thus far, had been marked, despite illustrious family connections, for he was kin to the most noted poet of all, William Dunbar, who had written so flatteringly of Margaret Tudor in *The Thistle and the Rose*—which was probably why she chose this kinsman to be her son's tutor, even though, as far as the Church hierarchy went, he was actually junior to Abbot John. For all that, the newcomer did not appear to be very grateful for this appointment, clearly considering himself worthy of very much higher office than any mere tutorship, even to his monarch.

So Gavin Dunbar came to Stirling. He proved to be no very striking personality, a studious, bumbling sort of man, somewhat older than Lindsay and Inglis, and with a very considerable chip on his shoulder. But, after the first day or two, the others came to the conclusion that their new senior, properly handled, ought not to prove any great problem to them. For one thing, he was not very fond of children, and recognising that James was far too young for the sort of erudition he was qualified to impart, left the boy largely to his juniors, whilst he pursued his own affairs and studies.

So James now had three tutorial guides and not sufficient

work for one. David, in especial, of a vigorous and restless nature, found life less than satisfying, despite his fondness for his young charge. His thoughts tended more often than not to drift eastwards towards Garleton.

It was with something like stimulation, then, that he greeted developments on the national scene, which at least had the effect of stirring up life for all at Stirling Castle. Three ships from France arrived at Dumbarton, on the Clyde, Scots ships, even though a very small part of the fine fleet which had left the same port under Arran some months before. They brought the said James Hamilton, Earl of Arran, and a most notable Frenchman, Antoine D'Arcie, Sieur de la Bastie, as envoy for the Duke of Albany; and these two, with a considerable and gallant company, came hotfoot to Stirling in mid-November.

They made a brilliant and colourful pair, although so very different in character, both handsome, dashing, voluble and over-dressed by Scots standards, and both in their mid-forties. But there the resemblance ended. Arran was flamboyant, mercurial, rash, having a large way with him—as perhaps befitted Scotland's Lord High Admiral and third in line for the throne, his grandmother having been a sister of James the Third. De la Bastie, although sufficiently lively, was a much more solid individual, without being in the least stolid, one of the most renowned chivalric figures in Christendom, famed for his knightly prowess, much admired by the late King James as a man after his own heart. He came to announce that John, Duke of Albany was prepared to consider the call to the regency but that it must be understood that he could not come to Scotland immediately. He was a French citizen, High Admiral of France indeed, and his country was at war with England. King Louis could by no means sanction his departure at this present stage. But if it was still desired, he would come when possible.

This created problems and considerable discussion. The nation needed authoritative direction *now*, not in the vague future. On the other hand, Albany remained the most obvious choice as Regent. Now that the second choice, Arran, had arrived, the discussion was the more to the point, not to say heated.

First and foremost, James Hamilton had some explaining

to do—and did not greatly impress by his explanations. He declared that he had decided that the best way to aid the Scots invasion had been not to assail the English coastline but to attack them where they were most vulnerable, in Ireland, with the object of drawing off forces from England itself, which his fleet could then attack whilst making the sea crossing. He had therefore landed his own three thousand troops in Ulster and attacked the main English stronghold there, Carrickfergus, whilst the fleet patrolled the narrow seas. His siege of Carrickfergus had been crowned with success and they had captured a great deal of booty—which he had apparently despatched back to his own town and seat of Hamilton in Lanarkshire, via the port of Ayr. Unfortunately, the mainland English had failed to send any reinforcements to Ulster—at least none that his ships had intercepted—and after waiting for some time, he had re-embarked his troops and sailed on southwards, to menace the English west coasts, as arranged. The enemy had not risen to this challenge however, so he had thought it best not to turn back for Scotland but to sail on to France, there to seek either to bring a French army back to Scotland to aid King James, or to encourage the French themselves to stage an attack on south-west England. King Louis had been slow to make up his mind, and while they waited, news came of the disaster of Flodden Edge. So it was too late for any French intervention, with James dead. Then the invitation to Albany had arrived from Scotland, and he had decided to return, with Albany's envoy, de la Bastie.

This sorry catalogue was received at Stirling with some scepticism. Any number of questions presented themselves—in particular, where was the rest of the fleet of thirteen fine vessels, and the three thousand troops Arran had set out with? They were told, in offhand fashion, that the French were a notably parsimonious people and that three thousand men took a deal of provisioning and quartering, so that funds had to be found to pay for them. The only means of paying was in the ships themselves, so they had been forced to sell some to Louis, including the *Great Michael* itself, for forty thousand francs.

Appalled at this, for the *Great Michael* had been the late James's pride and joy, symbol of Scotland's rise to be a maritime power, his hearers had been only very slightly mollified by Arran's assurance that he had gained considerable benefits for Scotland in his French visit, especially the concession that the Auld Alliance provisions should be renewed and that all Scots resident in France should have equal rights with French citizens, and that trade between the two countries should be free of restrictions.

These crumbs of comfort were scarcely sufficient to raise cheers. The Arran-for-Regent faction wilted noticeably.

Nevertheless the regency problem remained. Something would have to be done, or the Queen-Mother would assume the regency almost by default. The urgency became even more apparent when, presently, news came from Whithorn that old Bell-the-Cat had died, and his grandson, the Master, was now Earl of Angus and undisputed head of the most powerful family in the land. Allied with Queen Margaret and her custody of the infant monarch, this was a situation which the Privy Council viewed with the utmost alarm.

It was decided that Albany should be considered, and proclaimed, Regent-elect; and in his absence a council-of-regency should be established to wield supreme authority—this to consist of the Chancellor, the Primate and Bishop Elphinstone; and to balance the three churchmen, the Lord Home, and for the looks of the thing, Arran. Also, to avoid, if possible, outright warfare, the young Angus was invited to join, in the confidence that he could always be outvoted by five to one.

It was not a satisfactory solution, but probably the best that could be contrived in the circumstances. That Yuletide, at Stirling as elsewhere throughout Scotland, was probably the grimmest since Wallace and Bruce and the Wars of Independence—especially as it was desperately cold and wet, and with so many breadwinners gone the harvest had been grievously poor and famine stalked the land. And at Stirling, Bishop Elphinstone was obviously failing in health.

If none of these problems affected the young King of Scots, the same could not be said for his guardians. David and John, along with others in the know, well recognised that it was only a question of time, and no long time at that, until there was dire trouble in the nation. And once the campaigning season started again, with better weather, the English would be here in strength, for sure . . .

5

It was early March before David's distinctly pent-up feelings obtained any real relief, welcome indeed even though the occasion was to say the least ominous as far as the national scene was concerned. He was sent for one day to Bishop Elphinstone's quarters in the castle, out of which the Lord Privy Seal had seldom stirred throughout that dire winter. Indeed David had not seen him for some weeks, and was shocked at the changed appearance of the old man, so bent and frail was he, in his bed-robe, and parchment-white as to features. Archbishop Beaton was with him.

"Davie," Elphinstone said, voice thinner than heretofore, "my lord Archbishop and I have a task for you. Believing you to be the best, probably, to undertake it. Knowing that you are to be trusted—as, I fear, not all here are now. But first, we must know whether you are free to undertake it. With respect to our young liege-lord's care and service?"

"Can you leave him, safely?" Beaton added, more bluntly.

"The King? Surely, my lords. If you mean, for an interval? Not . . . altogether?"

"No, no—only for a short spell, lad," the older man assured. "A week or two. You are James's usher and keeper. More important, his favourite companion. We must know whether His Grace will be well enough, with you gone? He must not be distressed or difficult. Or else his royal mother may take the opportunity to remove him into her own keeping, and that of . . . others. Which would be unfortunate, as you will appreciate."

"My lord of Angus? Yes—I understand. But—His Grace will be very well so long as Abbot John remains with him, I think, my lords. Also, to be sure, there is Master Dunbar . . ."

"Aye, we know of Dunbar!" the Archbishop said briefly. "And place scant trust in him. But John Inglis will keep the child content? This is important."

"Surely, my lord. His Grace is very fond of the Abbot."

"That is well. See you, Lindsay—you are from the shire

of Haddington, and will know it all well. Know its folk, and be known. And, we believe, be trusted. Your father's name is esteemed. We have an errand for you, in East Lothian and the Merse. One which must remain secret."

"Secret . . . ?"

"Privy, at least, Davie," Elphinstone explained. "We need to know certain informations. Without seeming to be enquiring too openly. You, coming from Garleton, and with your Lindsay lands in those parts, can visit there, travel through that land, talk with folk, and none will think it strange. Most others here could not do so. You could learn for us much that we require to know. For the realm's weal."

David waited, more than interested.

"It is Angus. And Home," Beaton, who never had any use for diplomatic and tactful approaches, declared.

"But . . ."

"We are concerned over my lord of Angus and what he may be plotting," Elphinstone went on patiently, holding his chest as though in pain. "You will know that the Queen-Mother is in constant touch with her brother, King Henry of England, through the Lord Dacre, the English Warden of the Marches . . . ?"

"You mean . . . ? He who is devastating the Borderland? Slaying and burning! Our fiercest enemy . . . ?"

"The same, Davie. We have known of this from the start. Dean West of Windsor, Henry's envoy to this court, has the right to send despatches to his master, and does so through Dacre. Queen Margaret does the same, and although this is not correct, we have not protested. But, recently, one of West's couriers fell into Armstrong hands—as you will know, the Armstrongs are perhaps the most practised thieves on the Border, and are waging hottest war against Dacre, in this pass. They should not have assailed the English envoy's courier—but they did. How they used him they have not disclosed. But they took his letters, and read them. And believing that they concerned the safety of the realm, they sent them to the Chancellor. We have, of course, returned them to Dean West, with apologies. But . . ."

"We read them first," the Archbishop said grimly. "And the Queen-Mother's letter commends Angus to Henry and says that he awaits his further instructions and thanks him for his latest payment."

"Lord!" David gasped. "Angus, in Henry's pay?"

"The Tudor will buy any he may, man. So—we had the next courier intercepted. Discreetly, mind. Got him drunken as he journeyed south, in the hospice of the Red Friars at Soutra. Had the priest in charge there steam open the sealed letters, read them, and reseal them, so that naught was known of it. And the later letter implicated *Home*."

"But . . . but, my lord, Home and Douglas have ever been at enmity. They would never work together. Lord Home aided the Hepburns to oust the Douglases from St Andrews. And he was ever strong against the English. He is our Warden of the Marches . . . !"

"When the Archbishop says that the Lord Home was implicated, he means only that his name was mentioned in Nicholas West's letter as possibly worthy of Henry's approach," Elphinstone said. "He writes that Home resents my lord of Arran, who has slighted him, it seems. Also that he had recently visited Tantallon, Angus's stronghold on your Lothian coast. There may be no ill in it. But we require to know. These three, Angus, Home and Arran are all on the present Commission of Regency. If there is treachery, plotting, we have to learn of it. So we want you to go, secretly, to sound out the land. Douglas controls most of the Lothian coast and Home that of the Merse, right to the Border. *You* can move there without being suspect. For there are Lindsay lands there also . . ."

"Dunbar," Beaton interjected. "We want, in especial, Dunbar and its castle considered. Its state now. It could be useful."

"Dunbar is the only stronghold between Angus's Tantallon and Home's Dunglass," the older prelate pointed out. "Since the Dunbar family was brought low, it has been forfeited to the crown. But the late King did little with it. And since it was largely Douglas who brought the Dunbars down, Douglas may now be holding it. We have to know this. And its state for defence and warfare. Master William Dunbar here would have been the best to send there—but he is the Queen-Mother's man and we dare not trust him."

"We wish to know all concerning Dunbar. How many men are required to garrison it? What is its state? What cannon it has and how many? Who commands there? All," Beaton asserted emphatically. "We may have to use Dunbar.

Not only to check Tantallon and Dunglass but because it commands the mouth of the Forth. If Henry sent up a fleet . . ."

"But, my lords—I am no soldier!" David exclaimed. "I know nothing of cannon and fortress defences and garrisons. Nor of the armed strengths of Douglas and Home in Lothian and the Merse. I am not the man you require . . ."

"We know that," the Archbishop interrupted. "You will have one with you who well understands all such matters. But knows not the country."

"Davie—we are going to send Sir Anthony, the Sieur de la Bastie, with you. He is a great knight, a noted commander and a close friend of the Duke of Albany. He is a most useful man. He will survey the land and advise us on matters military. And he is wholly to be trusted. You and he will do very well together. For he writes poetry, also!"

Embarrassed, David shook his head. "I but scratch and scribble, my lord." He paused. "But—the Queen, in all this? Will she agree that I go? Leave His Grace?"

"We shall see that she does. You are the King's servant, not hers."

"We shall tell her that you have the Regency Council's permission, Davie. That you have private matters to attend to at your home. Her Grace will care nothing, I think—for if I mistake not, she loves you little better than she loves me!" Elphinstone attempted a laugh, but it was beyond him, for obviously he was tiring grievously.

Perceiving it, Beaton waved David away. "Tomorrow, then, Lindsay . . ."

So, early next morning, without risking a scene by taking leave of young James, David, de la Bastie, and two of the Archbishop's men as escort, rode quietly out of the citadel and Stirling, the first time David had left the town in almost six months—so that, despite the secret and possibly even dangerous nature of his mission, he felt almost like singing aloud in his sense of freedom from constriction. He was, admittedly, a little bit in awe of the Sieur de la Bastie, with his Christendom-wide reputation for gallantry and daring, champion of tourneys innumerable, and accomplished envoy to many courts. But Antoine, as he asked to be called, was as unassuming and as easy to get on with as he was handsome and personable, with no least condescension towards the younger man, so that very quickly David was on good terms with him. It helped that he had discarded his magnificent clothing for much more modest garb and rusty half armour, in the interests of anonymity, and might have been any small laird—although an unusually good-looking one.

They chatted companionably as they rode eastwards, for Antoine, having visited Scotland twice previously, spoke fair if accented English, the accent partly Scots. David learned much about the Duke of Albany, how highly he was esteemed in France, how rich and influential, how he kept his own court, almost to rival that of King Louis, and how notable a sacrifice all this would be to leave and come to Scotland. Although far too courteous to say so, the Frenchman might inadvertently have given just a hint that he too perhaps was making some sacrifice in visiting this strange northern and war-torn land, threatened with further strife.

How threatened it was was vividly brought home to them at Edinburgh, which they reached well before dusk of a windy March day to find the city gates already about to be shut and barred for the night and the walls manned by the vastly increased and volunteer town-guard, with beacons ready to be lit at quite close intervals along the perimeter. Indeed, the travellers, small party as they made, had some difficulty in gaining entrance to the city, so suspicious of strangers were the guards. David's assertion that he was a kinsman of the Lord Lindsay of the Byres, who was well-known in Edinburgh, however, got them in. They had not ridden far into the narrow street of the West Port when they heard the gates clang shut behind them. The feeling of being beleaguered was very strong.

That night, in an alehouse of the Grassmarket, the talk around them was all of an English raiding force at Peebles, on the upper Tweed, only a score of miles to the south, and of the stories of rapine, slaughter and savagery being perpetrated there. The difference in attitude and atmosphere from that of Stirling, thirty-five miles to the north-west, was very noticeable.

It was only a further sixteen miles due eastwards, fording the Esk at Musselburgh, to Garleton—and once beyond that ancient town, also in a state of wary preparedness, strangely enough there was much less feeling of tension and threat in the countryside, Antoine remarking on it. He asked if this could be because they were now entering Douglas country; and David had to admit just the possibility that this might have something to do with it.

Their unexpected arrival at Garleton Castle produced joy but just a little embarrassment also, when it became clear that Mirren had now moved into Sir David's bedchamber and was more or less acting mistress of the house. David was scarcely surprised and not really upset, although his father tried, not very successfully, to explain it all away by asserting that he had not been very well of late and Mirren, kindly nursing him, had found it convenient to be near at hand. His son gravely hoped that the laird would soon be restored to his normal robust health.

Despite all this, Mirren was most evidently quite bowled over by the Sieur Antoine, all but drooling over his brilliantly well-favoured and assured person. David found her, presently, removing her things back from his father's bedchamber to that which she had occupied previously, and knew a little sympathy for his lame and elderly sire.

He learned that his brother, Alexander, who had been with the King's army in Lord Lindsay's following, had been wounded at Flodden, like his chief, left for dead by the English, but had survived, again like his chief, managed to get back across the Tweed, and after being succoured for weeks in a shepherd's cothouse near Birgham, had eventually found his way home. That home was at the Barony, a subsidiary Lindsay property high on the East Garleton Hill behind the castle, only a mile or so away but hundreds of feet higher. David, of course, felt duty-bound to go at once to visit his brother.

He had never been very close to Alexander, a strange and moody young man who resented the fact that David, only a year older, was not only the heir but had been left also the smaller estate of The Mount, in Fife, by their mother, whilst he had to be content with this crow's-nest of a place on the top of a hill. It was not only that, for they had never got on well, Alexander being very much a physical character, delighting even as a boy in fisticuffs and fighting, in demonstrating his prowess in outdoor sports and pursuits where muscle rather than wits were called for, and despising David, even before he began to write poetry, for his love of music and balladry. *He* had not gone to St Andrews University, nor on the year-long continental tour thereafter—he would have hated both, but nevertheless found these a further cause for grudge. He had married the daughter of a small local laird whom he had got with child; and although David felt sorry for her and did not dislike her, they had little in common.

So he rode up to the Barony, was well enough received by Jean his sister-in-law, but only surlily welcomed by Alexander, whom he found emaciated and obviously still suffering from the effects of his wound. He did not actually say that David had failed in his duty by not being with the invading Scots army, but that was implied, and no explanation that it was by royal command impressed.

David did not stay long, but learned some further details of the battle at Flodden Edge and the mismanagement thereof. His brother blamed King James for his chivalric folly, of course, but reserved his principal condemnation for Home and Huntly with the cavalry wing, and those damnable French pikes. He also scoffed at the prized artillery as a useless encumbrance and declared that the English bowmen were the real victors of the struggle, standing well back out of danger, slaughtering at their leisure, and never having to be within striking distance of naked steel. The cavalry wing, to be sure, should have swung round after its breakthrough and rolled up those archers from the rear . . .

David left his brother to his resentments, and spurred downhill again towards a more pleasurably anticipated meeting—at the castle of the Byres. It was known that Lord Lindsay, wounded likewise, had won home; and Bishop Elphinstone had given David a message to deliver to him. But much as he approved of his chief and kinsman, and of his Aunt Isabella, he had to admit to himself that it was Kate whom he was mainly looking forward to seeing again, the transformed Kate who had been so much in his thoughts these last months.

He found Patrick, fourth Lord, lacking an arm, which had had to be amputated after the battle, gangrenous, superintending the excavation of a new well in the walled pleasance of the castle, a high-coloured, slender man of middle years, fine features rather unbalanced by a great beak of a nose. When he recognised David, he greeted him with his accustomed sardonic smile, waving his remaining arm.

"See who comes!" he cried. "Our sovereign-lord's stay and support! I wonder that you honour this humble house, Davie lad!" That was not said unkindly.

"Your arm, my lord! I did not know. I—I am sorry."

"So am I, lad—so am I! But I might have been a deal sorrier! I was more fortunate than most. What, God help us, is an arm or two? Where have you come from? Stirling? You are not dismissed? Lost your fine place?"

"No. I am on a—a mission. In these parts."

"A mission? On whose behalf? That woman . . . ?"

"No, no. The Queen would never send *me* on any mission. It is Bishop Elphinstone and the Chancellor. They require information. About the Douglases. And others. They also send a message to yourself. They ask that you come to Stirling. Say that such as yourself are much needed there. In the realm's service."

"They do? And how am I to serve the realm, Davie? Part crippled!"

"They did not say. But it will be your counsel that they seek. They are notably short of honest lords! I expect that they want you on the Privy Council."

"Well, we shall see. So you want to enquire into the Douglases? You must needs be careful on that ploy, Davie! What do you want to know?"

David explained the situation. The Lord Patrick was particularly interested to hear of the Sieur de la Bastie's involvement, of whom he had heard great things. He seemed more intrigued by this than by the object of the mission. On the subject of the Douglases, he quite often saw Greysteel and Douglas of Longniddry, near neighbours both; and had heard they had been visiting Tantallon together more than once recently—which looked as though something was being hatched. As to Home, he had heard nothing; but assumed him to be loyal and no friend of Douglas, now or ever. He blamed him for the Flodden business, of course.

It was at this stage that David, looking up, perceived Kate watching them from the garden gateway. How long she might have been there he did not know. No running to hurl herself upon him on this occasion, just this quiet scrutiny. Typically, he was the more eager to detach himself from her father and hurry to her.

The older man saw the direction of his gaze, and smiled. "There is someone who will offer a young man more pleasure than talking to an *old* man about the Douglases! She speaks of you, often."

"I will go to her, sir . . ."

She still waited for him there—and he told himself that he had never seen anyone more lovely, more so even than last time, more graceful, further developed—developed sufficiently, presumably, to preclude impetuous welcomes.

"Kate!" he exclaimed. "How good you are to see! A joy! I have missed you."

"Have you, Davie?" She sounded interested rather than ecstatic.

"Indeed, yes. It has seemed a long time."

"Not so long as before. But six months."

"So—you counted them!" He grinned. "I came so soon as I could."

"Yes. You are so important a man, now! Keeper of the King's Grace, no less! We are fortunate even to see you at all!"

"Your father said something the same! Do I hear some question in your voice, Kate?"

"Why, no. Who would question the King's keeper? Save perhaps, the King!"

"Keeper is scarcely right, lass. Procurator and Usher—these I am, to our young lord. Am I to have a kiss, Kate?"

"If you wish." She held up her face to him. His arms and lips were perhaps a little more enthusiastic than cousinly, but she did not draw back, indeed responded to some degree, before recollecting her now sixteen years and their burden of responsibility, and detached herself. "Court ways!" she got out, a little breathlessly.

He shook his head, ruefully. "Scarce that, lass. Just affection. And esteem."

She turned away. "Have you written any more poetry? Or are you still too full of busyness?"

"A little—only a little." He hesitated, always embarrassed by his versifying. "I am put off it, somewhat, you see. There are too many poets at Stirling. Gavin Douglas is close to the Queen. And now a youth called John Bellenden has arrived. It is strange. It was the late King who liked poets, not Margaret Tudor who, I think, cares nothing for poetry. Yet they gather at court. And do not love each other! I am something off poetry!"

"That is foolish. And wrong. When you have the gift. You could write a poem about the young King—since few can know him better. Do none of your fine court ladies presently inspire you?"

"They never did. Besides, there are few ladies at Stirling. Queen Margaret does not like other women around her, preferring men. Especially Douglases! Indeed the citadel is starved of women . . ."

"Well, your Mistress Livingstone is not like to go back, I think! She is too snug with Sir David, now! I hope that you are not jealous? Of your own father!"

"Lord, Kate—do not talk that way! Mirren means little to me. Or—she is a friend of course, but only that. The King, the *late* King, charged me to look after her. And the Queen-Mother mislikes her. So I sent her here . . ."

Lady Lindsay called to them from a castle doorway and relieved David of his prickly problem for the moment.

The Sieur Antoine was a much safer and surer subject of conversation, and David made the most of it thereafter—although hoping, at the back of his mind, that he was not overdoing it as far as Kate was concerned; the Frenchman might make all too great an impression on that burgeoning young female. When he left, in the gloaming, he was committed to bringing de la Bastie to see them all at the Byres very soon, whether or not that was wise.

Kate saw him to his horse, and her farewell embrace was sufficiently encouraging to send him homewards in a warm glow despite the chill air off the Norse Sea.

Next day the four men rode eastwards, out of the hanging valley of Garleton and down the fertile Vale of Peffer, past Athelstaneford, where Scotland had acquired Saint Andrew as patron saint, past the Pictish symbol stone at Prora, in which Antoine was much interested, and round the southern base of the conical green height of North Berwick Law, where David pointed to the ramparts of a Pictish fort on the summit. The Frenchman was much intrigued by the Picts and their traces, for he was from Brittany himself and the Bretons were traditionally of the same early Celtic stock as the Cruithne—it was the Romans who had called them

Picts because they used a pictorial rather than a written language. But all this concern for the past did not preoccupy their minds to the exclusion of their present task, and as they approached the Tantallon area they grew more wary.

Tantallon Castle, the principal stronghold of the Red Douglas earldom of Angus, was perched on an immensely strong and striking clifftop site three miles east of North Berwick town, a huge place, practically impregnable, of rose-red stone keep and flanking towers, linked by lofty curtain walls topped by parapet-walks, the whole protected from landward by a series of deep moats and dry ditches designed and placed so as to keep any besieging cannon well beyond range of the castle itself. The plan was highly unusual, the towers and curtain walling being in fact little more than a high defensive screen cutting off a thrusting headland from which the cliffs fell sheerly hundreds of feet to the boiling tides; so that behind this great fortress wall what amounted to a township of subsidiary and lean-to buildings could cluster secure, unassailable from land or water. The mighty rock known as the Craig of Bass soared abruptly from the sea two miles offshore, completing a dramatic scene which had Antoine whistling his admiration as they viewed it all from an inland vantage point.

They dared not approach the castle itself, of course; but it had a quite sizeable castleton nearby of cothouses and cabins, even a hostelry, for retainers, servants, farm folk and the trains of visiting lords. To this David reckoned that they might risk a call—but left behind their two escorts as too obviously men-at-arms. Also their half armour.

Their arrival in what was really a village appeared to occasion no great interest, certainly no disquiet, and they found their way to the alehouse where three or four men were drinking. David accounted for himself as a cattle dealer from Leith and his companion as a Low Countries merchant and importer, interested in the trade of salted herring. They were making for Dunbar town, where they understood that the fisherfolk salted and smoked much of their catch. Was there anywhere else on this coast where they might try for regular supplies of barrelled herring, to be exported from Leith?

This, with drinks bought all round, initiated a lively discussion. North Berwick, apparently, was no use, its harbour drying out at low water and so unable to take the larger fishing craft necessary to catch the deep-water herring. The same applied to almost all this shallow sandy Lothian coast until Dunbar. Further south, the Merse coast was better for the herring, with fishing communities at Dunglass, Bilsdean, Pease Cove, Redheuch, St Abbs Haven and Eyemouth. Whether they salted their herring in these havens their informants could not tell them.

But the Merse was Home country, was it not, David pointed out. And the Homes had the name for being difficult folk, Border reivers and lairdly thieves. Was it safe to take their Netherlands friend into such country, especially in present circumstances, with the English raiding over the border?

This leading question elicited a useful crop of responses. The Homes were rogues and scoundrels truly, and usually in a state of war with Douglas. But matters were different at the moment—although how long this would last, none knew. There was a sort of truce for some reason. Indeed, the Lord Home himself had been here, at the castle, only two weeks before, with his kin of Wedderburn and Blackadder, to meet Greysteel of Kilspindie and other Douglas lairds; and it was said that the Douglases could now ride through the Merse unharmed. Whether this would apply to a Leith cattle dealer and a Low Country merchant was another matter. But they could always say that they rode under Douglas protection.

Much appreciative of this kindly suggestion, David ordered more ale. This excellent idea might save them from the Homes, he agreed. But what of the English? Once past Dunbar it was a mere thirty miles to the border at Berwick, was it not? Too near possible raiding Englishry for comfort?

It was the alehouse keeper himself, drawn into the discussion and drinking with them, who answered that one. The English were not raiding Douglas territory, having too much respect for their new Earl who had the Queen in his pocket, the English King's sister. And he had heard that part of the deal with Home was that the English would also avoid Home lands. So the travellers ought to be safe from them too, meantime, if they claimed Douglas or Home protection. Humble folk like themselves had to make use of the great ones' ploys as best they could, to their own advantage!

Heartily agreeing with these sentiments, the visitors expressed admiration and astonishment that the Earl of Angus, great lord as he was, could be said to have the Queen-Mother in his pocket. Was she not reputed to be a hard and strong woman? Surely their friend was mistaken in this matter?

Not so, the other asserted. All men knew how far ben Angus was with the Englishwoman. Indeed, it was said that he would *marry* her, presently. When his present wife died.

David stared. How could that be, he wondered? The Lady Margaret Hepburn—or now, the Countess of Angus—was quite young, was she not? Little older than the Earl Archibald himself.

The lady ailed, he was told shortly. And one of the others, silent hitherto, barking a laugh, added that she ailed indeed—helped on, it was reckoned, aye, helped on! This dire suggestion produced an uncomfortable pause, and then disclaimers and argument, the alehouse keeper declaring that gossip about poison was but the idle chatter of castle servants and not to be bruited abroad, whilst the individual who had suggested it asserted that it was more than gossip, that he had it from one of the kitchen wenches who saw the lady's food prepared.

This indiscreet loquacity producing disapproval amongst the others, and a noticeable change of atmosphere, the enquirers recognised that it was probably time that they departed. One last point David raised—who was now in charge at Dunbar Castle? If they were to do business there, it might be as well to know. He was told, as though he ought to have known it, that of course Sir William Douglas had been master at Dunbar for long, brother of the late Master and of Greysteel.

Provided with considerable food for thought, the visitors made their way back to the two Archbishop's men-at-arms, left in hiding in woodland, before heading on southwards for the Tyne estuary and Dunbar.

Assessing the information thus gained—if it was to be believed—they reckoned that they had made a fair start. It looked as though there was indeed some rather alarming link-up between the long-time enemy clans of Douglas and Home, and with ominous English associations, the more dire in that Lord Home was chief Scots Warden of the

Marches, and that he and Angus were both on the Regency Council. So Elphinstone's and the Chancellor's fears, however aroused, appeared to have some basis. As to the suggestion that Angus was indeed contemplating actual marriage with the Queen-Mother, this seemed scarcely credible, as did the talk of poison for his unfortunate countess. According to the late King's testament, Margaret would lose all control of her son, and any power in the land with it, if she remarried. Surely, unscrupulous as she was, she would not be so foolish?

Although Dunbar was a mere seven miles from Tantallon as the crow flew, the great tidal bay and estuary of Tynemouth had to be circumnavigated by travellers, so that it was nearer a dozen miles, and sundown, before they reached the town. And again the escort, insisted on by Beaton, proved something of a nuisance, for ordinary traders and merchants did not normally go so protected. However, Dunbar was quite a large community, with a number of inns and hostelries, and they were able to deposit their escort in one such whilst they patronised another down near the harbour.

If Tantallon had been an impressive strength, Dunbar Castle was no less so, and although very dissimilar, likewise unique in Scotland, for which it was known as one of the 'keys of the kingdom'. For it was erected, not on any clifftop, but on a number of stacks of naked rock rising out of the sea, its towers limited in size and shape by these rock platforms but linked together by bridge-like covered corridors of masonry above the tide, in extraordinary fashion, so that it sprawled and clung and soared into the waves, completely controlling the narrow entrance to the quite large harbour. It had been besieged times without number, being on the principal invasion route from the border, the most famous occasion when Black Agnes, Countess of Dunbar, had defied a large English army for months in 1339. It had yielded more than once but never been actually taken by force of arms.

It was too late for Antoine to try to assess its military state and capabilities that evening, one of his main tasks; but they were able to glean a fair amount of information in the inn, from fishermen and others, whilst supposedly enquiring about the herring trade. They learned that although in theory a royal castle since the Dunbars were put down it had been firmly in Douglas hands for some years now, Sir William, brother of Greysteel, having some fifty men garrisoning it, with a number of cannon. They took toll of every fishing boat's catch before allowing the craft into the harbour, to the great resentment of the community, then sold the fish back to the merchants and salters. David pricked up his ears at this, perceiving a possible excuse for making an approach to the castle direct. They had to be careful, of course, not to get too deeply committed to this herring business or they might have difficulty in extricating themselves.

On the morrow, then, after visiting some of the smokehouses and salteries, they approached the castle itself, a cautious approach, as it had to be, over a drawbridge above the swirling water to a gatehouse guarded by lounging retainers who were anything but respectful but who eventually, after suitable inducement, consented to escort them over another inner drawbridge to the first tower where they were left while someone more able to talk business was fetched. Meanwhile, Antoine's eyes were busy indeed, assessing, memorising.

Presently a burly individual appeared, all bushy red beard and hair, announcing that he was under-steward here and what did they want? David explained. He had heard that the castle had at its disposal quite large quantities of fish, and wondered if a deal might be done, for their mutual benefit? If the castle were to sell the fish direct to himself and his Netherlands friend here, instead of to local merchants, cargoes of it could be sailed up-Forth daily to Salt Preston, near Musselburgh, where were the salt-pans, thus saving two journeys—the salt being brought here to Dunbar and the salt-fish taken back for export at Leith. For a regular supply, this would enable them to pay a higher price than the Dunbar merchants could afford. Would they consider it?

The under-steward scratched amongst his beard and said that they had better go and see the steward.

So they threaded some of the vaulted corridor-bridges of that extraordinary stronghold, the Frenchman noting all. The steward, one Robert Douglas, young for the position and therefore probably an illegitimate son of Sir William, listened to it all again, arrogantly unimpressed at first but growing interested—too much so presently, so that David began to worry about extricating himself from this tissue of falsehood. But eventually the other declared that he would have to consult Sir William, who was away at present; and thankfully David agreed that they should come back on another occasion. They made their escape, Antoine reasonably content that he had seen enough to make a useful report on the strength of the place.

After that they were in rather a hurry to get out of Dunbar before people began putting two and two together.

Dunglass was their next objective, only eight miles south of Dunbar but in markedly different country, as though emphasising the contrasts between Douglas and Home, between Lothian and the Merse. Here the sandy beaches and fertile fields gave place to rocks and reefs and ravines, to beetling precipices and secret wooded denes, where the Borderland hills came abruptly down to the sea, wild country which had Antoine shaking his handsome head. There were little fishing communities tucked away in hidden creeks and coves, but all too small for any pretence at commercial fish buying. So the cattle dealing aspect was now to be emphasised, with Antoine interested in hides for export.

Dunglass Castle was much smaller than either Tantallon or Dunbar, less dramatic altogether although strong, sited just above the fiercely rugged shore where the Dunglass Burn reached the rock-torn sea at Bilsdean Creek. With no valid excuse for approaching the castle—for a less likely place for cattle rearing would be hard to imagine—they turned inland up the burnside to climb steeply up the dene and into the foothills of the Oldhamstocks area, where cattle did at least graze and there were farmeries and a village of sorts in a fold of the green hills. Here, in a wretched poverty-stricken hovel, they spent the night, the only available shelter; with David apologetic to be subjecting the renowned Sieur de la Bastie to such conditions. But the Frenchman made no complaints and proved entirely adaptable and philosophical. Unfortunately they learned little or nothing of any value on this occasion, save that no English forces had been operating in this area as yet, that Home of Dunglass, brother of the Lord Home, was away operating with other Home lairds in unspecified activities, and that times were hard, hard, and any buying of cattle would be welcomed.

Disappointed with Oldhamstocks and Dunglass, they moved on in the morning, ever southwards. They had two main quests now: to discover, if they could, whether the Homes had come to any arrangement with the invading English; and to consider the land, militarily, for purposes of defensive warfare in case Home and Douglas were not to be relied upon—this, of course, Antoine's remit.

In the days that followed they were able to accomplish a fairly useful survey for the second objective but nothing really conclusive about the first. The only possible indication gained, as it happened, was also their only brush with the English. This was at Ayton Castle, another Home strength, the vicinity of which they were approaching very cautiously, for it was a mere eight miles from Berwick-on-Tweed, when they were all but run down by a troop of English horse, about two score of rough-looking characters, some with women held before them on their saddle bows, most burdened with gear and booty and with a number of laden led-horses, obviously a raiding party. Fortunately these ignored the four travellers and clattered on up to Ayton Castle, no doubt tired after a long day's foraying.

David and Antoine had intended to spend that night at Ayton village but decided that this would be too risky in the circumstances, and so moved back three miles to Reston in the Eye valley. And there they learned that this group of Northumbrians from Alnwick, Percys, were indeed making Ayton Castle their base, and that Home of Ayton was still in residence there. Also that they were not raiding Home lands locally. Admittedly this did not necessarily mean that this Home was actually co-operating with the English—he could be under duress, and the locality being spared for some other reason—but it could be one more indication.

Too near Berwick and the border for comfort now, they turned inland into the Merse proper, that fair, blood-soaked land of low grassy hills, shallow valleys and far horizons, dotted with peel-towers, huddled farm-touns and small ancient churches. And here certain circumstances did not fail to impress them. There were ample signs of earlier raiding—burned homesteads and kirks, ravaged barns and deserted hamlets—but there was nothing recent in all this, the visitors not having to be very experienced to perceive that this was all the result of *last* year's invasions. Life was going on apparently fairly normally round about, with no new devastation nor smoking ruins. The travellers were eyed warily but no one panicked and they were not challenged. Nearly all this eastern Merse area was Home land or that of their allies, the great lairdships of Wedderburn, Bassendean, Blackadder, Manderston, Polwarth, Marchmont, Paxton, Hutton, Whiteriggs and many another. But as they proceeded westwards the picture began to change, with ever-growing signs of savage oppression and wanton destruction: men, women and children hanging from trees, mutilated—and some not many days there—wells choked with bodies, stock wantonly slaughtered, farmeries burned out, towers roofless and abandoned, most of it clearly recently done. They were running out of Home land, here, into the territories of Kerrs, Turnbulls, Scotts, Elliots, Pringles and the rest, and it was evident that these Border clans at least were not being spared. The conclusion seemed, on the face of it, fairly clear—the Homes *were* being protected, for one reason or another.

When in one forenoon they had to avoid English raiding bands twice, fortunate in one case in perceiving new smoke clouds rising ahead and so effecting a quick departure; and in the other in being able to hide in thick woodland; they decided that they had probably learned sufficient and should now return northwards.

That evening, in the Ersildoune area of Lauderdale, they were cheered by the news that at least the raiders were not having it *all* their own way. Apparently a large English band, from the Priory of Hexham no less, ravaging their way up Teviotdale after wrecking the village of Denholm-on-the-Green and on their way to do likewise by the town of Hawick, had camped for the night in the riverside haugh of Hornshole and, glutted with easy conquest, rape, food and liquor, had slept in drunken stupor, failing to set adequate guards. And the youths and boys of Hawick, their fathers and brothers never returned from Flodden, had sallied out with axes and knives and clubs, in their scores, and fallen upon the raiders in the darkness and slaughtered them as they lay, not an Englishman escaping, and had borne back the Hexham Priory banner, blue and gold, to Hawick in triumph.

It sounded a more inspiriting note on which to ride home.

They had been away from Garleton for almost two weeks, and were glad to be back. That night, in his own bed, David heard the door of Antoine's room, next to his own, open quietly and soft steps descend the turnpike stairway. They did not return until nearly dawn.

Next day, the Byres party came up to meet the Sieur de la Bastie and hear the news, a radiant Mirren acting hostess. David watched to see Kate's reaction to the Frenchman, and found himself much relieved when she appeared to be only moderately affected by his charm, good looks and gallantry. That he was becoming jealous of young Kate's favours struck him as rather ridiculous but hardly to be denied.

Lord Lindsay, like Sir David, was eager to hear their account of their travels, and what conclusions they had arrived at. Their inference that it seemed probable that there was indeed some agreement or alliance between the previously inimical houses of Douglas and Home, and that there was an understanding with the English not to attack their lands, left the two older men very thoughtful, and all asking what it might mean. The devastation in the western Merse and Roxburghshire troubled and alarmed. Was it only a question of time before the raiding reached East Lothian? Or would the Douglas influence here protect them? The very enunciation of that thought caused all to eye each other guiltily, suddenly aware of the dangers of more than ravishment. Antoine's military investigations were not reported on in any detail, naturally. But he did say that Dunbar Castle could still be one of the keys of the kingdom, and that it ought to be taken back into the keeping of the crown, particularly in present circumstances.

Out of some discussion, Lord Lindsay announced that when they returned to Stirling, he would accompany them. That would be in two days, they decided.

Mirren looked dashed, but Sir David otherwise.

David himself escorted their visitors back to the Byres that evening, unnecessary as this might be, and thereafter took an unconscionable time over his leave-taking of Kate. They would call for her father two days hence. Meantime, he would scratch out some small verse for her, in appreciation . . .

6

They arrived back at Stirling to some considerable stir, for the Queen-Mother had had her baby only the day before, another boy, who was to be named Alexander, Duke of Ross. Mother and child were well enough, although the infant was small and less than robust.

This development was important in more than any personal aspect, for of course it changed the succession situation, pushing back Albany to third place and Arran to fourth—which might affect the coming of the Regent-elect, to some extent. Also it strengthened Margaret Tudor's position, and therefore Douglas's—which worried the Chancellor and Privy Seal.

These two were still more worried when, closeted in William Elphinstone's bedchamber presently, they heard the findings of the investigative mission, and knew their fears confirmed. If both Angus and Home were in Henry's pay, as now looked probable, the situation was very serious, with these two comprising one third of the Regency Council and Arran not to be relied on. That left only the three churchmen as trustworthy, and Elphinstone, as he sadly asserted, a broken reed indeed. It also meant that no decisions of the regency, or of the Privy Council either, would long be secret from the English. Something would have to be done, and quickly.

Clearly, Albany's coming from France would have to be expedited, if at all possible. But how? They could send urgent envoys, but they had no means of bringing effective pressure to bear on anyone so well-established and authoritative in the French community, especially with the French king loth to let him go.

Antoine had a suggestion to make. The Chancellor's own nephew and former secretary, David Beaton, now studying at the University of Paris, was a great favourite with both old King Louis and Albany himself. Even more so with

Queen Anne of Brittany. And he was most persuasive as well as able. If anyone could convince the Duke to come and the ageing King to permit it, David Beaton could.

The Chancellor seemed scarcely to have realised that his nephew could be so valuable. But it was decided to send an emissary to France and to enlist Davie Beaton's aid. They would send the new under-tutor, John Bellenden, who like David Lindsay had been a fellow student with Beaton at St Andrews and knew him well.

The suggestion, from Tantallon, that Angus had ambitions actually to marry the Queen-Mother aroused much interest—although the two prelates dismissed the poison story as mere idle gossip. But their interest was not so much concern nor indignation as, in fact, satisfaction. For, as they pointed out, if Margaret was fool enough to agree to such marriage, this would play into their hands and give them complete control of the King. It was almost too much to hope for.

Telling of the Hawick youths' triumph over the English raiders in Teviotdale, led David to suggest that more of such spirit was called for, that too much was being accepted as inevitable. They should learn from these boys. Hit back. Surely they could carry the fight into the enemy's territory on occasion? Raid over the border into Northumberland. They had learned where at least two of the raiding parties had come from, Alnwick and Hexham. Scots raids into these parts would soon bring back those beauties, teach them a lesson. Antoine strongly supported this attitude. He, as a soldier, would gladly lead or take part in such a raid. This one-sided terror should not be allowed to continue, since Home, as chief Warden, did not appear to be checking the evil on Scots soil.

Their hearers agreed that this might well be worth a trial.

The two churchmen were glad of the arrival of Lord Lindsay. There would be plenty for him to do. They were dependent on too many clerics and too few seasoned warriors and trustworthy nobles.

Young Jamie's greeting for his returned friend was heartening, all but overwhelming, so rejoiced was he to have back the companion he appeared to believe he had lost for ever. Abbot John said that the child had been inconsolable, often refusing to eat and crying himself to sleep at night. David found it touching to be so favoured, but recognised how tying this could become for such as himself. He settled into the citadel routine again with mixed feelings, his taste of freedom having unsettled him.

So it was that, a week or two later, he was indignant when, Antoine, having been given permission to organise and lead a major foray into Northumberland, he himself was not permitted to go along. This on the grounds that he was too important for the King's well-being to be away again so soon, and on a dangerous employment. Besides, he was no soldier and probably would be of little value. This was not Antoine's decision but the Chancellor's.

That raid was a notable success—although almost certainly more bloody than David would have appreciated. The Scots had not ventured as far south as Hexham and Alnwick but they had brought devastation and alarm to a wide area around the valleys of Till, Glen and Heiton, paying particular attention to Ford—where the late monarch had reputedly discarded his famous chain—Etal, Crookham and the vicinity of Branxton and Flodden, to drive the message home. They had even approached Berwick-on-Tweed, from the south, as near as two miles; but of course were in insufficient strength to consider attacking that strongly fortified walled town. The Sieur de la Bastie and other leaders came back acknowledged heroes—and David muttered his exasperation. He even made a short poem out of it which he entitled *The Complaint of the Unwanted Warrior*.

Perhaps partly as a result of this expedition, King Henry sent a message to the Scots. He had to send one anyway, to congratulate his sister on her successful birth-giving. But he added to it with an angry denunciation of murderers, thieves and robbers daring to invade his territories, and ended up, in extraordinary fashion, by demanding that the Scots parliament should forthwith proclaim himself Lord Protector of Scotland.

Even Bishop Elphinstone, out of his vast experience of erratic human behaviour, conceded that the man must be slightly mad.

But further and still more alarming news from that direction arrived at Stirling shortly—that Henry and Louis of France had patched up a peace, that Henry was to get certain territorial concessions and in return was actually offering his younger sister, Mary, as wife for Louis when a divorce from Anne of Brittany should be effected. Not only did this mean that Henry would now be free to turn his military strength against Scotland, but an ominous clause of the peace treaty was quoted—that Louis had agreed to stop all Scots inroads over the border into England, on pain of major French displeasure. There was no corresponding mention of *English* inroads into Scotland.

This dire stab in the back delivered by their trusted partner in the Auld Alliance, on whose behalf their late King had invaded England at such cost, left the Scots outraged and fearful, its possible effect on Albany's coming clearly serious. A parliament was hastily convened by the Regency Council, once more ignoring the statutory forty days' notice. Representations and protests fell to be sent to King Louis, an answer given to King Henry over his absurd protectorship claim—now seen in a rather different light—and the nation's loins girded anew, however lacking in potency.

Unfortunately, and not for the first time, that parliament was more notable for internal division than united action. The urgent threat produced two violently opposing factions whose arguments went like this. Scotland, in her present state of weakness could not fight both England and France; therefore since England was the closer and greater threat, they must seek to appease France, however badly Louis had behaved. After all, the French had been fighting the English for centuries, and at heart hated them—and had been traditional friends of the Scots. It ought not to be too difficult to bring them back to their accustomed collaboration. The Earl of Arran led this faction. The other persuasion argued that with their young King James heir to Henry's throne, and the safeguard of Henry's sister here in Scotland, they would be wise to make peace with England and avoid further disaster. After all, it would cost nothing to let Henry use the title of Protector, if so he desired; it carried no constitutional authority. Peace with England, then, and an end to all this of fear and folly. Needless to say, Archibald, Earl of Angus was undisputed leader of this party. David, watching and listening, was highly interested to learn whether Alexander, Lord Home would publicly support this point of view; but he remained notably silent.

The Chancellor clearly disapproved of both these attitudes; but it was his duty to chair the proceedings, not to lead the discussion. The split Regency Council's opinions had to be put by the Primate, Archbishop Forman of St Andrews, for William Elphinstone, present but huddled in a furred bedrobe, was now too frail for his voice to be heard. With the Earls of Lennox, Bothwell and Glencairn siding with Arran, and those of Atholl, Huntly and Crawford taking their cue from Angus, and other lords forming up behind each, it was largely left to the clerics to lead the more spirited course. Fortunately the majority of the shires and burgh commissioners followed the churchmen's line and voted for more independent action. Nevertheless, it was a near thing. By skilfully manipulating the voting system so that the pro-French party had usually to support the clerics' motions against the English faction, the Chancellor could largely ensure that the worst follies were avoided. For instance, they got a reply to King Henry passed, stating that while the parliament appreciated his kind offer of protection, it believed that Scotland had the power and the will to protect *itself*, as it had always done in the past.

Other decisions reached included plans for a swift and major mustering of troops, lords' levies, clan forces, lairds' retainers, town train-bands and the like, chains of beacon fires to be lit on hilltops throughout the land as summons. It was agreed to send envoys to Denmark, with which country Scotland had a loose alliance, to request military aid in the present situation, Lord Lindsay to lead such embassy. And various measures were to be put in hand to ensure, as far as possible, the nation's readiness for full-scale war. It would have been as well, in the circumstances, if the Lord Home could have been replaced as chief Warden of the Marches, but none felt sufficiently strong as yet to challenge him, and no real proof of any treachery was available.

The Queen-Mother did not attend this parliament. And two days after it had ended, the word reached Stirling that the young Countess of Angus had died, at Tantallon.

That anxious summer of 1514 passed without the feared invasion, and by August Scotland was daring to breathe again. Surely if Henry had been going to attack he would have done so by then, with the campaigning season nearly over? He was, it was reported, personally busy at Tournai, in Hainault, consolidating his position in the Low Countries territory he had managed to wring from King Louis, although his main armies were not now involved. So the northern kingdom might be safe from assault for another six months or so. Then, on the sixth, the news broke; the Queen-Mother had married Angus, at a private ceremony conducted by a Douglas priest in her own quarters of the castle. It was only eleven months since the late King's death.

If the Chancellor and those close to him were privately elated, the nation at large was scandalised. That Margaret should have esteemed their beloved monarch so little as to marry again so soon was shame; and to one so doubtful in his allegiance added to the disgrace.

Archibald Douglas had been sufficiently arrogant before; now he became insufferable.

Archbishop Beaton was not long, of course, in informing Margaret officially that, under the terms of her late husband's testimony, endorsed by the Regency and Privy Councils, she could no longer retain the custody of the young King, which now fell to the Regency Council. Since that Council included the Earl of Angus, and likewise the Lord Home, the situation was less than clear-cut however, especially with Bishop Elphinstone so ill. It seemed probable that he would not live much longer—nor wanted to—in which event much would depend on the mercurial and unreliable Arran's vote in the then five-man Council. But any tentative suggestion that a new member might be added was countered by Arran himself, who perceived his strong position, and by Home, if not by Angus who suggested that his uncle, Gavin Douglas, would be the best choice. So there was stalemate.

The new situation did somewhat improve David Lindsay's position, however, for, trusted by the prelates, he was placed more firmly in charge of young James, indeed given the new title of the King's Master Usher. Abbot John, also, was made full tutor, Gavin Dunbar's position being left vague.

All this, to be sure, made little difference to the young men's life in Stirling citadel looking after their royal charge. Undoubtedly David felt the constrictions of it to be more grievous than did the Abbot, being of a more restless temperament and energetic nature. No amount of sliding down hillsides on cows' skulls—which had become Jamie's favourite pastime—acting horse, with the monarch on his shoulders as knight, playing bowls, quoits and the like, sufficiently used up that energy; and much as he approved of his small ward, he was constantly seeking opportunity for missions which would get him away from Stirling for brief spells at least. De la Bastie was his principal hope in this respect, but came up with nothing effectual meantime.

William Elphinstone died in October, praising God that he was on his way to better things at last, but bewailing the state in which he had to leave his native land and bequeathing heartfelt advice—never to trust any of the Tudors, and to try to reform Holy Church before it was too late. This last was the gist of his final bedside interview with David Lindsay, clutching his wrist with a claw-like hand, voice only a whisper but an urgent one. The Church had grown shamefully decadent and was destroying itself—yet it could and should be the strongest influence in the land. He, one of its shepherds, had failed it, God forgive him, too occupied with affairs of state, man's business instead of God's. But Davie—he had been given the gift of words. Use it. Words could change the world more surely than the sword, although they had the same letters. Use them to show Holy Church its follies. Folk would often heed a poet when they would not heed a preacher. Christ's Church must be saved . . .

David, no churchman, was troubled by this charge, not seeing what *he* could do about it. He discussed the matter with John Inglis, who himself was something of a symbol of the church's decadence, appointed Abbot by influence at an early age with no responsibilities other than to pay out of the abbey revenues a sub-prior to manage the monastic affairs for him. John thought that the recent battle for the archbishopric of St Andrews would make a dramatic piece—but might not gain the approval of the winner, Primate Forman. Perhaps something less controversial? What about the sale of pardons? A poem about a pardoner—scope for eloquence there, surely? Or one of multiple benefices? David acknowledged the possibilities but wondered as to both popularity and effectiveness. What would the Chancellor say, for instance? How many benefices did *he* hold?

Scotland mourned a great and good man whom it could ill afford to lose.

Lord Lindsay returned from Denmark, empty-handed.

What with one thing and another, that Yuletide was little more joyful than the last.

Nevertheless, in its aftermath it proved to have its compensations, even death revealing a brighter side. For on the last day of the year, another elderly actor on the scene made a final bow—Louis the Twelfth of France—to be succeeded by his nephew and son-in-law Francis the First, aged only twenty. And this young man made a very different monarch from his uncle, as was quickly proved. He sought to reverse the French policy of war with the Empire and the Vatican, which meant that Henry of England was not so important to him; and he saw the alliance with Scotland as worth maintaining. To this end he was prepared to allow his Lord High Admiral, Albany, to leave France at last.

So, when the winter's storms were past, the Regent-elect would sail.

There was other interesting news, belated in its arrival in Scotland, but perhaps with some significance. King Henry, at Tournai, was displeased over his sister's remarriage—mainly, it seemed, because she had not sought his permission, but also in that her new spouse was non-royal and a pensioner of his own.

It seemed that the tide of events could ebb as well as flow.

7

Tides do more than ebb and flow, however. They can storm and flood and divide. The news that Albany would be there to govern them before long had other effect on some than hope and satisfaction. On James Hamilton, Earl of Arran, in especial. It seemed that, by this time, the Lord Admiral had convinced himself that his rival would in fact never be allowed to leave France, and with the Queen-Mother's marriage folly, the way was all but clear for his own assumption of the regency. The death of Louis, and the new French attitude, altered all; and Arran recognised that he would have to act, and act fast, if he was to forestall Albany and grasp the supreme power in Scotland. And act he did.

In a surprise attack, in conjunction with the Earls of Lennox and Glencairn, he took the great castle fortress of Dumbarton, which dominated Scotland's main west-coast port and the Clyde estuary, ejecting the governor Lord Erskine whom, as a Queen-Mother's man, he claimed was not to be trusted. The remaining ships which Arran had brought back from France were still anchored at Dumbarton; and the great Hamilton territories, of course, lay not far to the south.

On word of this extraordinary development reaching Stirling, Angus took it as a declaration of war on himself—which to some extent it undoubtedly was—and stormed off westwards with such force as he could muster, including much of the castle's garrison, calling for more Douglas support to follow on. Suddenly it was civil war.

Chancellor Beaton and his associates were worried and wrathful, but were scarcely in a position to take any very effective action themselves. They could not put large bodies of armed retainers in the field to bring these warring nobles to heel, as they would have wished; and the fact that the opponents were both on the Regency Council made it all the more difficult. Another question was—what would

Lord Home, the third of the five, do now? If, as they feared, he joined Angus, then there would be only the two prelates left in the Council not involved—or, put another way, three fifths of the Council would be at war with each other. It was a dire situation. Whichever side might win in this struggle for supremacy, the lawful and constitutional authority, or what was left of it, was almost bound to suffer.

The Lords Lindsay, Fleming, young Borthwick, and others considered still loyal, were sent off urgently to raise such numbers of men as they could as a possible counter-balancing force.

It was three days after Angus had left that David, taking his charge, now nearly three years old, on his shoulders to the hurly-hackit, was halted by a considerable clamour, shouting and clatter of hooves from the direction of the castle gatehouse and outer bailey. Interested, he turned his steps towards the parapet-walk of the East Battery which overlooked the gateway, drawbridge and tourney ground.

There was plenty to see. The entire approach area was full of mounted men with banners and pennons, sun gleaming on the steel of armour and weaponry. Horsemen at the front of all this throng were streaming in over the drawbridge and under the portcullis, hooves drumming on the bridge timbers; but as fast as the numbers thinned at this end, they were made up for by new riders coming up out of the narrow streets of the climbing town. There were many hundreds involved, clearly.

Young James clapped his hands at all the colour and stir. David was eyeing the colours too, urgently, noting that there was no sign of the blue chief and red heart of Douglas, but plenty of the red and white of Hamilton on display. But almost more interesting was the scattering of the white lion on green of Home amongst them, along with Cunninghame of Glencairn and Lennox. It rather looked as though Lord Home had made a different choice from that anticipated.

David hurried down the twisting stairways to the inner bailey, now packed with the newcomers and their stamping, steaming horses, mud-spattered and foam-flecked. These beasts had been ridden far and fast. There were larger banners here, those of the lords themselves. David would have lowered the child from his shoulders but Jamie beat on his

Procurator's bare head to emphasise imperiously that he wanted to stay where he was, to see all from a height.

The leaders of this invasion were obviously inside the Chapel Royal, which opened off this inner bailey. David pushed his way through to the doorway, guarded as it was by sentries with drawn swords. He continued to advance, despite the glares and threatening gestures of the guards—after all, who had more right to enter the Chapel Royal than the child on his back?

"The King's Grace!" he said authoritatively, and they let him through, if doubtfully.

Inside, the scene was dramatic. Arran, Home, Lennox, Glencairn and other lords, in full or half armour, stood at the transept confronting two other and smaller groups. One consisted of the Queen-Mother, Gavin Douglas, the Lady Erskine and one or two others of the court; the second of the Chancellor, the Bishops of Galloway and Moray and a couple of secretaries.

Arran was speaking. ". . . and I tell you again, this misrule, indeed lack of rule, cannot go on. I will not permit it to go on. The land is without any true governance. It is time and past time that governance was restored. *I* shall restore it."

"The Duke of Albany should be here within weeks," Beaton said. "*He* is the choice of parliament . . ."

"We have been hearing that for a year and more! The nation cannot wait for Albany. We require governance now, not some day."

"Why wait until now to use force, my lord?" the Chancellor insisted. "Now, when Albany has been given permission to come, and but awaits weather and tide?"

"Because Scotland cannot wait on the whim of the King of France! Because I do not believe that Albany *wishes* to come! Because Angus has wed the King's mother and the realm is about to be grasped by Douglas! And worse—King Henry has ordered him to carry our young liege-lord, and his brother, over the Border into England, with their mother . . ."

"That is a lie, James Hamilton!" the Queen-Mother said.

"It is no lie. We have it on the best authority." Arran's glance flickered over to Home. "Your husband, Countess of Angus, has not attempted it yet only because, he writes, that it is too dangerous, lady."

"Address me as Your Grace, or not at all, my lord!"

"As to your style, lady—you should have considered that before you wed Angus!"

"Where *is* my lord of Angus?" Beaton demanded.

Arran whinnied a laugh. "Fleeing for his life—probably for the Border! We taught him and his precious Douglases a lesson! In the Pass of Aberfoyle, when he thought to approach Dumbarton. Save for this lady's feelings, I would say that he was fortunate to escape with his life, if undeserving!"

There were exclamations at that—in which Jamie Stewart took the opportunity to join in, with chuckling laughter; which, of course, had the effect of turning all heads towards where David stood with the child still on his shoulders.

For a moment or two there was an uncertain pause. Then Arran flourished a half-mocking bow, and the other lords followed suit. "Your Grace!" he said.

Embarrassed, David put the boy down—who immediately clamoured to be taken up again, where he could survey all so much better.

"I do not believe you, James Hamilton!" the Queen-Mother announced coldly, ignoring her son's presence. "Douglas is not so easily vanquished! You lie, in this, as in all! Now—I have suffered sufficient of your company," and she turned, for the vestry door.

"I fear that you must needs suffer more of it, Countess," he told her, smiling thinly. "You are coming with me to Edinburgh Castle. And His Grace and his brother also. His Grace will be more secure there. From . . . ill-wishers. Yourself, likewise. We ride within the hour. I pray you, go prepare yourself."

There was a stunned silence in the church.

It was Beaton who recovered his voice first. "My lord—you cannot mean this! It is not to be thought of!"

"We ride within the hour," Arran repeated. "And they ride with us. See to it."

"Are you crazed, man? You cannot do this. I will not permit it. As Chancellor of this kingdom. And senior on the Regency Council."

"You cannot stop me, clerk! My men control this Stirling. The Regency Council has outlived its authority."

"This is treason, against the King's Grace!"

"Not so. We but take His Grace to safety. Here, where Douglas comes and goes at will, is far from safe. Edinburgh *I* control."

"I will not go with you, fool!" Margaret exclaimed.

"You needs must, Countess. Come—or be taken! For nothing is more sure than that you go to Edinburgh this day."

"You, my lord of Home—*you* cannot consent to this, this outrage?" Beaton demanded.

"It is necessary. For the safety of the King and the realm," Home said shortly, his first contribution to the exchange.

"But you have no right . . ."

"One hour," Arran interrupted. "We have seven hundred men here. I do not wish to have to use them! This lady, His Grace and the infant—these only." The Earl came over to David. "Give me the King," he ordered.

David looked over at the Chancellor, who shrugged helplessly. "His Grace will be better with me, my lord . . .

"He will be very well *without* you, sirrah! Come to me, Sire."

James clung to David, and yelled.

"I assure you, my lord, that you will have a deal less trouble if you leave him in my care." David, surrounded by armed men, could by no means resist; but delay *might* achieve something.

Arran, with no desire to look foolish trying to pacify a screaming, frightened child, nodded. "Very well. Have him at the gatehouse, ready to ride, within the hour. Barncluith—go with him. See that all is in order." And he pointed to the door.

An esquire in full armour, dirk in hand, came over to grasp David's arm and propel him and his charge, back on his shoulder, towards the door, beckoning two men-at-arms to accompany them.

Thus escorted they went back to their own quarters, where an unbelieving Abbot John had to be convinced that it was not all some game. Then they gathered and packed a selection of the boy's clothing and gear. There did not seem to be anything else that they could do.

James scowled at the intruders and would not let go of David.

Presently a servitor came for Gavin Dunbar, as usual closeted in his own chamber, requiring him to attend on the Queen-Mother forthwith. It looked as though he it was who had been selected to accompany the royal family to Edinburgh.

When, in due course, they took James to the outer bailey and gatehouse, they found it as they had guessed; Dunbar was to go with the King, and they were to stay. Archbishop Beaton was there, and agreed that there was nothing that they could do meantime but accept the situation. He would never have thought that Arran was capable of this. He wondered whether Home had put him up to it? In which case, had Home's assumed alliance with Douglas collapsed? And did he remain, possibly, in Henry's pay? It was all complicated and confusing. Had all their suspicions been mistaken? Or was Home playing some very deep game indeed?

David ventured the opinion that Home had infinitely keener wits than either Arran or Angus, and therefore he was more likely to use them than they him.

Whatever the answer was, they certainly did not discover it that day, with Home keeping himself very much in the background and Arran very much in charge—and scarcely to be questioned. When the Queen-Mother delayed her arrival, there was an angry scene, with men sent to fetch her without further procrastination, in whatever state she was. Brought in furious protest, with the Lady Erskine carrying the new baby, also Gavin Dunbar looking more than usually unhappy, there was another trying interlude when his mother took James from David and handed him over to Dunbar, amidst shouts and pummellings. This undignified proceeding was clearly unsuitable; and Arran, already impatient, all but bellowed an order to mount and depart, without any further leave-taking. The King of Scots was carried off, in a flood of tears, before a nervous poet-tutor, his young brother happily sleeping through all. Margaret Tudor rode off, set-faced, between guards.

Those left behind eyed each other, at a loss.

Some sort of action fell to be taken, but what, that would be in any way effective, was less than clear. It could be assumed that Angus would quickly recover from this set-back and gather his fullest Douglas strength to hit back. Whether that strength would be sufficient to capture the great fortress of Edinburgh Castle, repossess his wife and the royal children, was another matter. Anyway large-scale civil war seemed now certain. And Henry Tudor's attitude had to be considered. If Arran had thought it necessary to act thus before Albany could arrive, might not Henry think the same, and decide to invade first?

The Scots realm was in utter disarray, and all too aware of it.

Archbishop Forman, who had not been at Stirling for this encounter, was hurriedly sent for, from St Andrews. Whether the archbishops, as representing the rump of the Regency Council, could command any worthwhile authority in the land remained to be seen—after all, Arran and Home together could make an equal claim, and had vast numbers of armed men to back it. Beaton was Chancellor and Forman Primate of Holy Church; but Arran was fourth in succession to the throne and Home was Chamberlain and Warden of the Marches.

David was summoned to the Chancellor's quarters the day after the Primate arrived. He found there the two archbishops and the Sieur de la Bastie.

"Lindsay—come, sit," Beaton said. "We have work for you. With the Seigneur, here. We have got to act swiftly, where we can. Not a great deal is open to us, as you know. But we could, perhaps, take and hold Dunbar Castle. And it is important, and vitally placed, as you also know."

Antoine gestured. "It is strong. But I believe that it could be taken."

David sat and said nothing.

"It is a royal castle, although Douglas-held meantime," the Chancellor went on. "We have reliable word that Angus is mustering all his power, and his allies' power, to defeat Arran. Mustering in Douglasdale, in Lanarkshire. Presumably to attack Arran's main seat and base of Hamilton, in Clydesdale. No doubt in order to draw Arran's strength away from Edinburgh, so that he, Angus, can make a swift dash eastwards and take Edinburgh Castle and so recapture the Queen-Mother and her children. So we assess the situation. Huntly and his Gordons and the Lord Drummond and his Strathearn hosts have already come out in his favour and are marching south. It will be surprising if Angus neglects fully to use his *own* people, such as those under his uncle at Dunbar Castle."

It was not for David, with de la Bastie present, to stress how strongly sited was Dunbar, even if its garrison should be reduced.

"Dunbar, in our hands, would serve two ends—even three—for it is indeed one of the keys of the kingdom, well-named. It would be a blow to Angus. It would be a threat to Home, on the very edge of his territories. And it could menace any English advance by the coastal route from Berwick—as it has done so often in the past. Dunbar should be ours."

"No doubt, my lord. But because it is so close to Home land, and none are more warlike than the Home moss-troopers, even if we can surprise and take it, many men will be required to *hold* it. Or it will again be surprised and taken from us."

"Think you that we do not know that, young man!" Archbishop Forman said. "Your Lindsay levies should be sufficient for that, surely."

"Yes—that is it," Beaton went on. "The Lord Lindsay is already sent to gather the Lindsay strength in Lothian. His is probably the most strong force that we can raise in those parts. So the Seigneur, here, and yourself, will go to the Byres, and use that force which he has gathered to assail, take and hold Dunbar Castle."

Antoine and David exchanged glances. "We can attempt it, to be sure," the former said.

"It is important. One of the most useful things that we could do, without any large army," Forman emphasised.

"It is perhaps the only move that we can make at this stage to warn and threaten Home," Beaton agreed. "And that is vital."

"Have you learned, or come to any understanding, my lords, as to what the Lord Home is at?" David wondered. "Why he seems to have turned against the alliance with Angus? And appears to be working against King Henry now, when before we thought otherwise?"

"It is hard to tell," the Chancellor admitted. "But we see the change as only happening since two matters have become known—Albany's coming and Henry's disapproval of his sister's new marriage, and therefore his disapproval of Angus. If it was indeed these that changed Home, then it could mean that he was most probably working for Henry."

"But—this of taking the Queen-Mother and the King to Edinburgh? That does not look like aiding England!"

"Think you not? I reckon that it could be a deal easier to win the King and his mother out of Edinburgh Castle than out of Stirling here. Especially for the Homes. And the road mostly in Home country thereafter all the way to the Border!"

"You mean . . . ?"

"I mean that if I was James Hamilton, I would be watching my partner Alexander Home with an eagle's eye! Especially if Arran was to have to dash off to defend Hamilton, and left Home in charge at Edinburgh!"

"Lord . . . !"

"That is one reason why haste is advisable for this of Dunbar Castle. Dunbar is on that quickest and best route from Edinburgh to the Border. So—you will ride tomorrow, my friends. And we shall send urgent word to Albany to hasten his coming, by all means . . ."

Whether in fact all this speculation as to Lord Home's duplicity and intentions had any basis in fact, and urgency of the essence, it was good to get away from Stirling and to come to Garleton and the Byres again, Antoine almost as appreciative as was David—and even more effusively received. Unfortunately they were unable to spend as much time thereat, with their respective female attractions, as they had anticipated and desired, for it turned out that the Lord Lindsay had found it more convenient to muster the Lindsay strength, such as it was after the losses of Flodden, at the much larger castle of Luffness on the shores of Aberlady Bay some three miles to the north. David was a little surprised at this, for the castle of Kilspindie, Greysteel's establishment, sat just on the other side of the great bay from Luffness, too near for comfort in the circumstances. But Kate declared that her father had ascertained that Greysteel himself and practically all his men from Kilspindie had gone to join the Earl of Angus's army in Douglasdale, so that there would be no threat from that quarter—which made a hopeful indication for Dunbar's present situation.

Kate indeed rode with them the next morning down to Luffness, to David's satisfaction. They found the place in a great stir, with some ninety men gathered there, in addition to its own garrison, more of a holiday atmosphere prevailing than anything more warlike since nobody knew quite for what they were assembling and it was all a welcome change from the monotony of the daily grind. Luffness Castle had been the first Lindsay property in Lothian, acquired by marriage with a Dunbar heiress in the late twelfth century, and formed a most impressive stronghold, with tall twenty-foot-high curtain walls, topped by parapet-walks forming a square with four-hundred-yard sides, protected by circular angle towers at each corner, all behind a deep water-filled moat. Great drum towers for the drawbridge and portcullis faced the bay, and a massive central keep rose in the midst. It had two castletons or retainers' hamlets, one to the south known as Luffnaraw and one to the east, on the bay shore, somewhat grandiloquently called the port of Luffness although in reality only a small fishing haven. It also had a Carmelite monastery and church to the south-west; and nearer Aberlady village, suitably separated from the monks' establishment, a nunnery. All in all, a fine place. Its superiority belonged to the Earls of Crawford, chiefs of all the Lindsays; but now these were grown so great, with properties all over Scotland, that they but seldom came to Luffness, which had long been left in the care of hereditary keepers called Bickerton but who themselves had fairly recently been superseded by a branch of the house of Hepburn.

They found Lord Lindsay with the present keeper, Sir Adam Hepburn, superintending the conversion of part of the castle's mill premises and brewhouse at Luffnaraw into extra barracks accommodation for the assembling man-power. The Lord Patrick was in two minds when he heard of the newcomers' mission: glad enough of some definite action to put the men to, who were getting somewhat out-of-hand in their mustered idleness; but at the same time concerned that they should be expected to tackle, all untrained as they were, so ambitious a task as trying to take Dunbar Castle. If such concern likewise preoccupied de la Bastie, as seemed probable, he did not show it but maintained a confident front. And, at least, with Greysteel's departure for Lanarkshire with his Kilspindie men to go by, it looked hopeful that his brother, Sir George Douglas, would have similarly weakened the Dunbar garrison.

Antoine emphasised the need for haste and asked how soon he could march, with the maximum numbers of men? Lord Patrick said that there was a sizeable contingent to come across from Lindsay lands in Fife, by boat, any day; but that, anyway, they could not all be armed and equipped for the march before three or four days more, at least. The Frenchman, a stranger on foreign soil as he was, demonstrated his authority of command, as well as that of the Chancellor's orders, by declaring courteously but firmly that that would not serve, that the situation would not allow them so much time. They must move the following night. Dunbar was only fifteen miles away. They could do it in a night march and be in a position to attack at first-light in the morning, with maximum surprise. Lindsay looked doubtful but did not assert that it was impossible.

In the meantime, Antoine went on, David should make openly, alone, for Dunbar. He could go again as cattle dealer and fish buyer. He was known as such there. Learn all he could, spy out the situation at the castle. Then meet the attackers outside the town just before dawn with his information. This could be of great value.

It at least was refreshing to have someone in charge who so knew his own mind.

So David took Kate home, bade goodbye and was instructed on how to take care of himself. Then he changed his clothing, to fit his new merchantly role, and set out for Dunbar.

He met with no problems en route and arrived at the town in the late afternoon, making his way to the same harbourside hostelry which they had used before. He was accepted there without question, remembered by some of the habitués.

It did not demand a great deal of contrivance to bring the talk round to the purchase of fish and the suggestion that in fact the castle garrison might be in a position to sell quantities more cheaply than the fishermen themselves, on account of their levy on catches. This brought forth the anticipated flood of protests and objections. And when he innocently proposed a visit to the castle to check on present terms, he was more blithely told that there was little point in that, for scarcely anybody was left in the place, and nobody of any authority. All were gone on some Douglas ploy in the west, some muster—no doubt to the sorrow of honest folk. There would be nobody to talk to about fish prices.

David did not indicate how glad he was to have this information. But he did ask if the fish levy was being maintained in these circumstances? To be answered bitterly that it was, that the extortioners were still insisting on the castle's full quantity, otherwise they would not lift the boom to allow the fishing boats into the harbour—although what the handful of men did with all the fish only the Devil knew, who looked after them!

This general animosity towards the garrison sparked off an idea in David's mind. When did the boats tend to come in from their fishing, he wondered? Was there a normal time of day for the coming and going? He was told that, at this time of year, there were two favoured times, some fishermen preferring to go out at dawn and return at midday, others to sail at midday and come back at nightfall. The castle people were not prepared to raise and lower their boom across the harbour mouth just whenever it suited the fishermen.

So that meant that a number of craft could be coming in, with their catches, and others going out, empty, at about the same time, at midday? And where were the main fishing grounds? That depended on the weather and the season, he was informed; but at present the herring, the favoured crop, were most readily caught about three miles out, on a stretch running east of the Craig of Bass where the deep water suddenly shallowed to the coastal shelf.

Mulling over all this with his ale, David perceived opportunity. A change of plan was called for. So presently, making excuse that he could use the evening to visit a nearby farmer on a cattle buying project, he went out into the breezy dark, saddled his horse again and rode out of town—not to any local farmery but back north-westwards as he had come. He aimed to intercept Antoine and the Lindsay strength earlier than arranged.

The darkness posed something of a problem, of course, even though he knew the roads hereabouts very well. The difficulty was that he did not know which route his friends would choose to take from Luffness, for marching men. There were three or four possibles. However, all must converge at one point, where the outflow of the River Tyne could be forded by men on foot, at the head of Belhaven Bay. This was some four miles west of Dunbar. He would wait for them there—and pray that they would not be overlong delayed.

It was strange to sit there alone in the chilly, windy darkness, listening to the steady boom of the breakers on the distant sand-bar of the bay, the splash and tinkle of nearer water, the creak and sigh of the trees, the calling of the night birds and the soft horse noises, hour after hour. He got cold, of course, and every now and again had to exercise himself to regain warmth. The quiet peace of it all was in such notable contrast with what was intended.

Eventually, despite the chill, he fell asleep—to waken with a start, cramped and stiff, to the stir, a vibration on the night air rather than any actual sound. He had never experienced this before but recognised nevertheless that it was the quiet approach of a large body of men deliberately being as silent as they could, under strict control. He rose and waded the ford to meet them.

Antoine and the Lord Patrick marched at the head of a fair-sized column, with a local man to act as guide. They were surprised that he had come thus far to meet them.

"I have come because we should change our plans," he announced. "I believe that we can do better than any surprise assault."

Whilst the men were fording the Tyne, in some disarray, he told the leaders what he had learned. "This of the fishing boats," he elaborated. "If we could put men on three or four boats, and looking like fishermen, when they come to hand over their levy of fish to the castle, they could seek to win inside with the fish. There are not many men left in the place. And most would not be manning this boom, surely . . ."

"But how to get our men into the boats? And the fish?" the Lord Patrick demanded. "Talk sense, Davie!"

"See you—this is Belhaven Bay. There is a small fishing village at Belhaven itself. We go there, take over a few of *their* boats. They will not be setting off to fish until dawn, no doubt. We could sail out to the fishing grounds east of the Craig of Bass. The Dunbar boats will be there, soon after sun-up. The Dunbar men hate the castle and the fish levy.

We can use that hate. Get them to work with us. Sail back with them and their catch."

"*Parbleu*—he has it!" Antoine exclaimed. "This could serve us well. How many men could we use in it?"

"Not many. But then, we would not require many, I think. It will depend on the boats. How many there are at Belhaven. And how many Dunbar craft fishing off the Bass. There are five or six fishers to each boat, I learned. We could perhaps put four of our men into each Dunbar boat, at sea, dressed as fishers . . ."

"So we cannot expect to use more than a score of men?"

"They say that there are no more than a handful in the castle, now. I could not ask for numbers."

"I say that it is too risky," the Lord Patrick said. "If it fails, as it well may, then the garrison is warned."

"Then we are no worse off. It would mean a delay in any land assault, yes, if that was to be essayed at first light. Unless it could be done at the same time? But that would be difficult to ensure, almost impossible . . ."

"No—we shall try this of the boats," de la Bastie decided. "But we have one hundred and twenty men here. What to do with the others meantime?"

"There is much woodland behind Dunbar. At Eweford and Lochend. You know it, my lord? Barely a mile from the town. Sufficient to hide our people during the day. If this of the boats fails, then we can rejoin the others at Eweford and put in the dawn assault next morning."

"My friend—you have used your head well!" Antoine commended. "It is worth the trial. How far to this Belhaven?"

"Three miles—less. An hour's march."

Round the head of the shallow sandy bay they went, to ford the Beil Water at West Barns of Beil and come to the village of Belhaven half a mile further. It still lacked a couple of hours to dawn and the place slept peacefully. It was no part of their intention to create an outcry, and they marched their men, still silently, straight to the little harbour. There they counted seven fishing craft as well as a number of smaller boats.

There were perhaps a score of cothouses lining a single narrow street; but there was also a group of hovels close to the harbour itself, with drying nets draped from poles outside. Whichever the others were, these seemed certain to be fishermen's houses. David, with Antoine and Lord Patrick, went to knock on doors.

The first produced an alarmed-looking, elderly man, naked from his bed. Seeking to sound both soothing and authoritative at once, David announced that this was the Lord Lindsay of the Byres and that they came in the name of the King and the Regency Council. They required his help.

Struck dumb, the man stared.

"You are a fisherman? We require fishing boats. We shall pay well for their use. To take some of our men out to the fishing grounds. You have a boat?"

"Yes, Yes, lord. But . . ."

"Who else have boats? Which houses?"

"Many, lord. But . . ."

"Put on some clothes. Quickly. We have need of haste. Show us these other houses."

"Do not gawp there, man!" Lord Patrick barked. "We have not got all night!"

It took longer than they would have wished, but presently they had the owners of five of the fishing craft assembled, and approximately clad, however bewildered, along with sundry other men, and explained to them what was required. If there was no enthusiasm, there was no actual opposition either. Clearly what was wished of them would pay a deal better than any day's fishing.

It was agreed that five of the Lindsay men should sail in each of five boats, with the owner and one other oarsman. They would borrow fisherman's clothing and be taken out to the Bass area, and hope there to be transhipped to Dunbar boats. If by any chance this last was not possible, then they would themselves sail for Dunbar at midday and hope that the castle garrison would be as eager for their fish as that of the local craft.

The Belhaven folk had no love for the Douglases and were prepared to co-operate, for suitable reward.

By the time that all this was arranged, it was time to sail. Antoine elected to go with the boat party and the Lord Patrick was left in charge of the main body, to proceed to Eweford. In a scarlet and gold sunrise they pulled out of Belhaven harbour, David and Antoine advisedly in the same boat.

They had to go north by west for some five miles to reach the fishing grounds, and with a quite stiff westerly breeze and choppy sea the square brown sail was of little use to them. So it was a question of rowing nearly all the way. The passengers took their turn at the oars, if not all expertly, the five boats keeping fairly close together.

They made slow progress and, save for the rowers, it was very cold out there on the water. Presently other boats appeared. Although they all seemed alike to David, the fishermen knew where each came from, Dunbar, North Berwick, Skateraw, Canty Bay or Peffermouth. They kept close to those from Dunbar, of which there appeared to be seven.

When it came to the fishing the local boats acted as one unit, trawling the nets between them for the herring shoals. Long lines, with hooks baited with mussels, were also put out, the boats kept moving slowly with just a couple of oars.

David was impatient to approach the Dunbar men, but Antoine said to wait for a while. They must have fish caught, that was essential. So they fished and drifted and rowed, as the sun rose higher in the sky. Indeed, the passengers were apt to sleep, after their busy night.

After the first up-drawing of the nets, and quite a fair haul of herring, before continuing they rowed over to the nearest group of Dunbar boats, hailing them. David was a little concerned that he might be recognised as the erstwhile cattle dealer; but he saw none that he knew amongst the Dunbar fishermen.

Within easy shouting distance, he explained that he was speaking for the Lord Lindsay and the Regency Council. They intended to take Dunbar Castle back from the Douglases and into the King's hands, as was right and proper. They sought the fisherfolk's help, as leal subjects. And they could promise that when the castle was in leal hands again, there would be no more levies on the Dunbar fishermen.

As expected, this produced wary but no very positive reaction, although the last part had some effect.

David went on to explain what was required. The interest quickened. And when the matter of generous payment was added, he had their attention.

But what if the assault failed, lord, he was asked? What would happen to *them*, the Dunbar men who had helped in it?

Why should it fail, with so few in the castle? But if by mischance it did, they could always say that they had been forced to it at swordpoint.

That was accepted. David asked these men to pass on the word to the other Dunbar craft, taking their agreement as established.

So, after another hour or so's trawling with the nets, the assault party transferred, not without some near-mishaps, to the seven Dunbar boats, after suitable rewards to their Belhaven friends. Then, with a reasonable catch, and the good wishes of the beneficiaries, they set off for Dunbar.

Now the breeze was astern and they could dispense with the oars—which was welcome, with the boats overloaded. After all the waiting and inaction the party evinced a tension now. David's worry was that the extra men in each boat might arouse suspicions in the garrison.

It took barely an hour to run back to Dunbar. And there, keyed-up as they were, they had to linger, under the very castle walls, until the people therein deigned to notice them and lift the massive boom of timbers and chains which barred the entrance. Fretting, they sat in the swaying craft, waiting.

However, the delay at least revealed, presently, that only three men appeared to be on duty to deal with the fish levy, two to crank the great handle of the pulley device which creakingly raised the heavy boom, the other to lower a couple of rope-ladders from the castle walling down to water level. Three only—never had David hoped for anything so fortunate as this.

They let the first boat pull in without making any untoward move. The system appeared to be for some of the fishermen to climb up one ladder with a sample of their catch, in wickerwork baskets, for the garrison to pick their choice. Then they returned down the second ladder whilst others were climbing the first.

Exchanging glances, David and Antoine signed for their own craft to move in to the ladder as the first boat was edging away. Grabbing one of the baskets, David made a somewhat unhandy job of clambering up the swinging contrivance with it. Antoine waited until he was almost up before following.

On the masonry platform David put down his load, wordless, in front of the three men-at-arms. As these stooped, to select the best fish, he looked around him, scarcely able to believe that he could have gained entry to this almost impregnable stronghold so easily. He took in the layout of this part of the strung-out castle. Nobody else was to be seen save these three on fish duty—until Antoine appeared with his basket.

Almost simultaneously one of their men came up the second ladder, quickly followed by another. Antoine threw his basket down beside David's and, catching the other's eye, gave a quick nod.

Reaching inside their borrowed fishermen's smocks, they gripped their dirk-hilts, to wait until all three of the garrison men were stooped over the catches; then, whipping out their weapons, they leapt, to bend and press cold steel to the backs of two red necks.

Startled, the trio straightened up, gasping. The third man reached for his own dagger, but before he could draw it, one of the Lindsay party from the second ladder hurled himself upon him, pinioning his arms. David and Antoine transferred their dirk-points to the front of their victims' throats, and their fourth man disarmed all three.

They stared at each other, almost laughing. In less time than it takes to tell they had achieved an entry, with only four men and not a drop of blood shed.

Signalling for the others to come up, they had to decide how to proceed from here. From their previous visit they had a fair idea as to the plan of the castle, with its various towers and bartizans based on rock stacks and linked by covered bridges and corridors. But they could not know where the rest of the garrison was likely to be found.

De la Bastie had no scruples about methods of finding out. Sizing up the three captives, he chose the weakest looking and flourished his dirktip under the man's chin, pricking it slightly to draw blood.

"Where are the others of your people?" he demanded. "Tell us, if you value your wretched life!"

The other goggled, spluttering, but said nothing.

A second and deeper prick loosened his tongue. He

pointed and gabbled, but so incoherently that the Frenchman was mystified. David suggested that the man should lead them, instead of directing, and Antoine agreed. The other two were tied up and left in the care of some of the fishermen. Others of the boats' crews elected to come on with the two dozen attackers. Pushing their unhappy guide before them, the quite large party set out, dirks, daggers and a variety of improvised weapons in hand.

They went through two tower basements and along two corridors before the prisoner halted and pointed dumbly to a closed door before them. Clearly he did not want to be first through that doorway. Nodding, Antoine gestured the man back, then he and David moved forward quietly. They could hear the murmur of voices from beyond the door.

Waiting until his party were massed close behind him, Antoine raised his hand, flung wide the door, and led the way in at a bound.

The chamber was a vaulted dining hall and about a dozen men lounged about a long table littered with platters and beakers, in every attitude of relaxation, some head on arms, apparently asleep.

They had no chance, of course, outnumbered, in the face of armed and determined intruders. Some attempted resistance but most were simply overwhelmed where they sat. It was all over in moments.

Obviously this was the main residential garrison; but there would almost certainly be a guard on the main gate and drawbridge. So, taking half their strength, Antoine and David made their way in that direction, this part of the castle being familiar to them. They found three men in the gatehouse, very much at ease, the drawbridge up and no access from the land possible. These were so surprised to be assailed from within that they put up no show of opposition.

Dunbar Castle was in the hands of the realm's lawful representatives again, in a coup which could have had few parallels for speed and lack of fighting. David's praises resounded.

Soon they had the drawbridge lowered and David was on his way, on foot necessarily, to Eweford and Lochend, to inform the main body that they could come out of hiding and ride openly and freely to their objective. Perhaps he crowed a little.

8

They sent couriers post-haste to Stirling to inform of the situation. But after two or three days it was decided that David himself should go there, to find out the Chancellor's plans and to learn what went on on the wider scene. The Lord Patrick would accompany him as far as the Byres.

So they rode westwards, released. To David, for one, any fortress was just as tedious as another to be shut up in.

That evening, David lingered long at the Byres, being made a hero of, his protests weakening as time went on. It was late before he knocked up the gatehouse keeper at Garleton. At least there were no problems with Mirren, who was already in bed with his father.

In a long day's riding he made it to Stirling by next evening—and with the news he brought, was well received, his story having to be repeated again and again and, as happens, losing nothing in the telling. Inevitably it was suggested that he should make a poem out of it all.

He discovered that there had been no reports as yet of any major clash between the Douglases and the Hamiltons; but it was only a question of time. However, there was news from France. A courier had come with a letter for his uncle from David Beaton, to say that Albany was about to sail with a large following which would include Davie Beaton himself. Albany would bring back with him the remainder of the Scots fleet left in French ports by Arran, and ought to be arriving at Dumbarton in perhaps two weeks' time after receipt of this letter.

This development, it was confidently hoped, would change the entire situation. Another two weeks . . .

David was not to be subjected to any lengthy incarceration in the fortress on this occasion, for he was commanded to return whence he had come, to tell de la Bastie to remain at and hold Dunbar Castle with whatever garrison was necessary, but to send all the men that he could spare to the Lord

Lindsay, who was then to bring on his main strength westwards. They were going to assemble as large a force as possible at Dumbarton to welcome Albany, since it was by no means certain that his coming would be unopposed. Lennox was holding Dumbarton Castle for Arran and might make matters difficult; and Angus could conceivably put in an attack likewise, although this was less likely in that area.

The new Regent was certainly not coming to any bed of roses.

Back the sixty-five miles to Dunbar, then, David rode, via the Byres—where he learned that the Lord Patrick was again at Luffness with his levies. So once more, with Kate, he proceeded thither—and lingered rather on the way. His relationship with Kate was progressing satisfactorily in one respect, less so in another. She was obviously fond of him and liked to be in his company; but there were inhibitions, mainly on his part. With any other young woman he would not have hesitated. He would have pressed his suit, made his intentions all too clear. But Kate he had looked on over the years as all but a little sister. She was still only sixteen and although she looked a woman now and sounded like a woman, he could not get over the feeling that she was really still only a child, not to be misused, endangered. So he was pulled this way and that, ever seeking her company, hard put to it to keep his hands off her, but always having to restrain himself, a man torn. Perhaps the tearing process did not leave the girl entirely unscathed either.

At Luffness they found that Lindsay had fully one hundred men gathered, some having come back from Dunbar where they were not required for garrison duty.

David proceeded south-eastwards, alone, for Dunbar. There the atmosphere, in town as in castle, was vastly different from heretofore, de la Bastie having already established good relations with the townsfolk. The drawbridge was down and David rode in to the salutations of the guards.

Antoine, surprised to see him back so soon, agreed that probably his garrison could be further pruned without danger. He seemed to be well settled in already, very much in command as captain of a fortress. He was glad to hear that Albany was on his way, although regretting that he himself was not to be at Dumbarton to greet him. There had been no troubles at Dunbar and no signs of any Douglas nor Home counter-measures.

So next day David marched slowly back westwards, at the head of thirty men-at-arms, the fifteen miles to Luffness. Lord Patrick had now managed to muster a total of one hundred and twenty, so that in fact one hundred and fifty set out on the long march across the waist of Scotland, not far off one hundred miles, to Dumbarton.

Going by Leith, Linlithgow, Falkirk, Denny and so into the Stirlingshire hills of Touch, Gargunnock, Kilsyth and Campsie, they crossed the watershed of the land, deliberately going by these unfrequented ways to avoid possible clashes with either Arran's or Angus's supporters. In five days of steady tramping, and in fortunately good weather conditions, they began to slant down towards the Western Sea, in all that time meeting with no opposition—one hundred and fifty men, of course, are not lightly to be opposed. But they saw no sign of hostilities nor destruction either; indeed it would have been easy to conclude that all talk of internecine strife and civil war was mere hysterical exaggeration. But admittedly this area was meantime not the location for any trial of strength.

Marching down into the Vale of Leven they began to meet with other bodies of armed men, large and small, all heading south to the Clyde. All were somewhat wary of each other—Colquhouns, Buchanans, MacGregors, Grahams, Drummonds—as well they might be, since most would be unsure as to which side in this present complicated conflict their various lords and chiefs would be on. This was the area known as the Lennox, and the Earl of Lennox it was who had assailed and taken over Dumbarton Castle from the Lord Erskine, Queen Margaret's friend. And Lennox was for Arran and the Hamiltons.

So the Lindsays followed the River Leven, flowing out of Loch Lomond, as wary as any, down towards Dumbarton itself.

But at the town and port, which huddled below the great conical castle rock, they found vast crowds and an almost holiday atmosphere. The Chancellor and Primate were already there, with a great concourse of nobles, churchmen and their retinues. Lennox had thought it judicious, in the circumstances, to issue forth from the castle in peace and at least seem to take part in the welcoming proceedings, although how he would behave when Albany arrived remained to be seen.

All in all it was a peculiar situation with, on the surface, everybody in convivial mood, waiting for the long looked for coming of the Regent who was to restore and reunite the young King's realm; whilst underneath all was tension, concern with what was likely to follow, wondering who was for whom, assessing of likely strength, debating as to who could be trusted and for how long. Even speculation as to what the Duke of Albany would be like. It was said that he was richer than any King of Scots, rode abroad with a court of two hundred, and could speak only French. How could such a man cope with Scotland and the Scots, in present circumstances?

For the look of things, the Earl of Lennox could scarcely deny the Chancellor of the realm, not to mention the Primate, quarters in Dumbarton Castle, which was of course a royal fortress, like Stirling, Edinburgh and Dunbar; so David Lindsay and his lordly kinsman found themselves in the odd position of being able to ride up to this powerful, enemy-held stronghold and gain admittance without question. Not their men, however; these were told in no uncertain terms that there was no room for men-at-arms. The town being full to overflowing, they had to quarter their people in nearby villages, as did others.

Fortunately, in view of the crowding and the underlying stresses, they did not have long to wait, for favourable winds and fine weather brought the French flotilla in unusually short time; and only two days after David's arrival, fishing boats brought the news that eight large vessels were beating up the Firth of Clyde past the Cloch Point and should make Dumbarton in a couple of hours. The excitement mounted.

When the white sails at length appeared, the castle cannon boomed out in salute and a host of small craft put out to escort the convoy into port. Folk thronged down to the harbour area.

The main jetty had been cleared for the principal ships, but it was not large enough to take them all. Two only came slowly in, furling sails, the rest lying off and dropping anchors. The crowds waited, expectant. There were no cheers. The Chancellor and the welcoming party stood at the pier head, dressed in their best.

However, their best was hardly good enough, when presently the newcomers disembarked in a riot of colour, finery, even perfume wafted before them on the breeze. The first off the gangway, after the sailors had rigged it, was a brilliant figure, superbly handsome and dressed at the height of French fashion, a young man with a small pointed beard and curled hair.

"That is not Albany," the Chancellor said. "Albany is older."

"A papingo, whoever he is!" Archbishop Forman snorted. "These French—vanity of vanities!"

But when this vision came near to them, he hailed them in a good Scots voice. "Ha, Uncle! How good to see you! It is a long time."

"Lord—Davie!" the Chancellor exclaimed. "It's yourself! Sakes—I'd never ha' known you! By the Mass, you've changed!"

"Not for the worse, I hope? The years take their toll, they say—even of you, my lord!"

"H'r'mmm. You have brought Albany, then . . . ?"

"Why, yes. And a wheen more! For your delectation. My lords—your servant!" David Beaton flourished a bow.

Others were descending from the first ship, a chattering, laughing throng surrounding a stately individual of early middle years with a look of assured but somewhat depressed authority; a tall, elegant man with a slight stoop. He seemed to be eyeing all before him with resignation, if not disfavour.

David Beaton turned to wave this group onwards with a large gesture, smiling widely, clearly a man who got much enjoyment out of life. He sang out a flood of fluent French, *Monsieur le Duc* recurring frequently.

Albany came stalking up at the head of an ever-growing retinue of loquacious and overdressed courtiers, who made so much noise that young Beaton had to shout to effect the introduction to the Chancellor, Primate and sundry lords and bishops. Albany acknowledged their greetings gravely, with nods of the head but no words, David Beaton translating the welcoming phrases. It seemed to be a fact that the new Regent spoke no English, much less Scots, and the Chancellor's nephew was there in the role of interpreter.

David Lindsay marvelled that one whose father had been of pure Scots blood, indeed a son of the King of Scots, and who himself bore a notable Scots title and the surname of Stewart, should never have troubled to learn a little of the language—when, for instance, de la Bastie, pure French, had mastered it almost like a native. Most of the Scots nobility knew a little French fortunately, although generally more able to write it than to speak it, like David himself. But communication was clearly going to be difficult.

That language was not going to be the only difficulty was quickly apparent. The Frenchmen, now being reinforced by still larger numbers from the second ship, were not used to walking, it seemed, nor prepared to make a start otherwise on this occasion; and since the castle lay over half a mile from the harbour, and once reached, offered a steep climb up to the residential quarters, horses were now demanded, and were not immediately available. There were plenty of mounts in and around the town, of course, all the lords and lairds and their escorts having come on them, but these were stabled and tethered far and wide, and finding sufficient for a couple of hundred Frenchmen would take time. So an uneasy hiatus developed there at the pier head, with more and more French coming ashore in boats from the other ships, and conversation at a painful minimum. Davie Beaton appeared to find it all an excellent joke, but few others did. It made hardly an auspicious start.

David Lindsay was one of those sent off to find horses, and was glad to escape.

In the end, sufficient mounts were found to carry Albany and his more immediate entourage to the castle, with the Scots, including the two archbishops, walking alongside. Since there was neither room nor welcome for most of the newcomers in the fortress, the rest fell to be quartered in the town, overcrowded already as it was, so that much reallocation of accommodation was required, to the offence of the dispossessed, and less than appreciated by the visitors, who obviously thought it all much beneath them. David found himself involved in this invidious task also, and did not enjoy it.

Later, in the castle after the banquet for the guests, he was approached by David Beaton.

"Do I not remember you, from St Andrews?" he asked,

pleasantly. "Are you not Davie Lindsay? *You* have not changed so very much."

"No. But you have! Become the great man. Confidant of princes!"

"Scarce that. But one lives and learns, especially in France! You are at court, here?"

"I am, and I am not. I am the King's Procurator and Usher. But since the King is taken out of my care, by the Earl of Arran and the Lord Home, I am at something of a loose end. So my Lord Chancellor employs me on this and that."

"Oh, we will get young James back into your good keeping, never fear," Beaton declared with easy confidence. "This nonsense of Arran must be halted, and quickly. He is a weakling and only needs a firm hand. Home I do not know—but he sounds different."

"He *is* different, yes—a strange man. Devious. But clever, I think."

"Perhaps the wits behind Arran?"

"Perhaps. But I fear there is more to it than that. What he intends we know not. But he is a man to watch."

"There are too many of those in Scotland! We shall do more than watch them!"

At his so assured tone, David shook his head. "It will be none so easy. Dealing with the Earl of Angus, in especial. The Douglases are not so readily put down. We have made a start with Dunbar, but . . ."

"We shall divide the Black Douglases from the Red and so halve their power. De la Bastie—you have seen him?"

"Very much so. We have worked together. A fine man."

"He is. And an able soldier. I urged the Duke to send him. He could be very useful."

"Already he has been so. He now holds Dunbar Castle for the King."

"Dunbar, eh? Taken from the Douglases? Useful against the Homes. Aye, and against Tantallon itself. What of Fast? Fast and Colbrandspath Tower, both. Are they taken also?"

"No-o-o." David recognised that he must adjust his opinion of this confident character who clearly knew what he was talking about, and even after years in France remembered the lie of the land and its strategic importance.

"Tell me more of Home, and what he is at. This man to watch."

David informed the other of all he knew and what was suspected and conjectured about the Lord Home and the involved game he seemed to be playing, Beaton making shrewd comments. This developed into something of an inquisition on others of the players on the national stage. To even things up somewhat, David asked about Albany himself. What sort of man was he? This of speaking only French—did it imply lack of interest in Scotland? How strong a man was he? So much was expected of him; would he be able to achieve?

"He is a man it takes time to know. But able, strong of will but not of himself so strong. And with the hottest temper of any I know!"

"Lord! And this is the man who is to save Scotland?"

"He could do well enough, with the right folk to guide him!"

"Such as yourself?"

"Why, yes. And perhaps you?"

"I am hardly so ambitious."

"Nonsense, man! You, the King's guardian! When we get James back to your care, who more to effect? He who holds the King . . . !" He smiled. "What of James? Is he an interesting child? Sound in his wits and person? I have brought him a gift. A parrot."

"You have? A papingo? Apt!"

"How mean you—apt?"

"It was something that the Primate said. About Frenchmen and papingoes."

"Ah, I see. Popinjays! Perhaps Forman is right. But never forget that even parrots have strong beaks and can bite! So—we must get our young monarch back, and present him with the papingo."

"And how do you propose to do that?"

"By using the wits the good God has given us—how else?"

It did not take long for David to discover how justified young Beaton was in his authoritative assurance. With everything having to be translated between the Scots leadership and Albany, and the Chancellor his own uncle, Beaton was in a position to do a lot more than interpret—to adapt, suggest, advise and make his own contribution. And with wits sufficiently sharp, and obvious drive and ambition, he could not only influence but all but direct events.

One very prompt example of his abilities was in the matter of the Earl of Lennox. In a fashion, Lennox was their host here; but of course the fortress was in his hands unlawfully, his position equivocal to say the least. Using this situation in masterly fashion, David Beaton went about the business of transferring Lennox's allegiance from Arran to Albany, by seeming to assume that this was already the case and manoeuvring Lennox into the situation that it was accepted by all—and so, more or less, by Lennox himself. All said in the name of Albany, of course. He confided to David Lindsay that he thought it important not only to detach Lennox but to use him to bring over Arran himself. His cause had been much weakened by Albany's arrival undoubtedly, and being a weak man, he should be the more easily disheartened by desertion. Encourage a Douglas assault on him and his Hamiltons, therefore, by all means possible, and he would come over to Albany, nothing more sure. Then Home could be isolated, and they could deal with Douglas.

David marvelled, but was impressed. Beaton seemed to have formed a liking for him; and quite clearly his was the hand which was going to guide Albany—so that he was worth staying close to.

There was no point in remaining at Dumbarton. So in a couple of days, largely taken up with scouring the countryside for horses, a vast cavalcade set off eastwards for Edinburgh, to be followed, on foot, by what amounted to an army of marching men. Some small evidence of David Beaton's power was demonstrated here, in that David Lindsay, detailed by his kinsman to stay with and lead the Lindsay contingent, on foot, found this arrangement countermanded by higher authority and himself instructed to ride with Albany's group—which suited him very well. In fact, he found himself trotting beside Beaton most of the time. Not far behind rode a French servitor with a green parrot in a cage.

Before setting out, the Chancellor issued a summons to a parliament at Edinburgh, again the forty days' notice having to be dispensed with.

It took the cavalcade three days to reach Edinburgh, having halted at Kilsyth and Linlithgow, their company being joined, en route, by many lords and lairds from the surrounding areas, so that they made an impressive array indeed as they approached. There was some debate as to whether to halt and wait a few miles off for the marching host behind before making an entry, in case of armed opposition, the Chancellor so advising. But his nephew said otherwise. They had heard that Home, as well as holding the castle there and the royal family, had managed to have himself appointed Provost of the city; so, it being a walled town, its defences much improved since Flodden, if Home wanted to oppose, he could easily have all the gates closed against them. They should go forward confidently then, seeming to assume him loyal and welcoming,. They made a large enough party not to be readily attacked within the walls.

Albany accepted this counsel.

They advanced, amidst some tension, but saw no signs of opposition, although their approach must have been visible from the castle for many miles. At the West Port they found the gates open—and not only that but Home of Wedderburn, high in the Home hierarchy, waiting to receive them in the name of his chief with a number of the city magistrates and the new Dean of Guild. The Lord Home greeted the Duke of Albany, the Chancellor and the Primate, he announced, and wished them well. Wedderburn's words were suitably civil, but his looks and attitude were less so.

Filing in a long procession through the narrow streets, across the Grassmarket below the castle rock, and up the West Bow beyond, it became obvious that they were not being conducted to the fortress itself. Albany and the French not having been here before did not perceive this; but the Chancellor asked where they were going, and Wedderburn curtly informed that they were bound for the Abbey of the Holy Rood, the castle being much too overcrowded already.

Digesting this and its implications, they rode on through the crowded streets, the Edinburgh folk eyeing them warily, wisely reserving judgment until certain important matters were clarified, such as relative strengths and attitudes.

Down the Canongate, at Holyrood, the Abbot necessarily accepted the invasion with as good grace as possible, with two archbishops involved; but of course there was accommodation therein for only a very small proportion of the great company, and David once again found himself detailed, with sundry others, to find billets and stabling for large numbers of disgruntled visitors, nearly all of them offended at the quality of lodging eventually provided in the town.

This thankless task performed, he felt distinctly guilty when he discovered that he himself was to share notably superior quarters, next to Albany's own, with young Beaton, who cheerfully took charge of all; even Lord Lindsay had poorer lodging.

That evening, David had his first close demonstration of Albany's quality. He and Beaton were having a quiet beaker of wine together after a somewhat scratch banquet provided hastily by the Abbot, when the Duke himself came storming in from his adjoining chamber flourishing a piece of paper amidst a flood of French. Beaton listened respectfully, his glance on the letter the while.

David knew enough French to get the gist of Albany's complaint. He had sent a herald up to the castle, a mile away, requesting its governor to deliver up the keys to himself, as Regent, whereafter he would come and pay his due respects to the young King of Scots, as was suitable. And now the herald was back with this damnable letter and a garbled report that the Lord Home said that he, Albany, was not Regent yet until parliament confirmed him in that position, and therefore had no authority to demand the keys of Edinburgh or any other royal castle. He could come and pay his loyal duty to King James, but only as a subject and kinsman, and he should come alone and without armed escort.

Beaton nodded, not apparently appalled, and when he could interrupt the flow read aloud the letter's contents which contained approximately the same message and were signed, 'Home, High Chamberlain'.

The Duke scarcely heard him out. Furiously he snatched back the paper, crumpled it up and flung it at the fireplace. Not content with that, he pulled off the handsome velvet and jewelled cap he wore and hurled it after the letter, sweating comprehensively the while. A small fire burned in the grate and the hat, better aimed than the paper, was almost into the flames. Beaton stepped over and rescued it, returning it to its owner with a bow and a smile. Albany grabbed it, glared, and marched back to his own room without another word.

As David stared, the other grinned. "I have rescued that cap, and others, before!" he observed. "I told you that John Stewart had a hot temper."

"Sakes! Scarcely auspicious in a ruler!"

"Oh, we can put up with that. So long as he listens to reason when the temper cools. But—this of Home is interesting. He appears to be playing for time. Putting off any conclusions until after the parliament. Why, I wonder? What will that gain him?"

"Waiting to see how the cats will jump?"

"Perhaps. But from what you tell me, he is a jumper, not a waiter! No—there is more to it than that. There are only three ways for cats to jump, anyway—Albany, Arran and Angus. Home entered this present enterprise of abducting the King and bringing him here with Arran—although previously, you say, he had been in league with Angus. But Arran is the weakest of the three now that Albany is here. So Home has to choose between Angus, who is tied to England, and Albany and France. He keeps Albany at arm's length meantime—so it must be the Douglas. Home, I think, prepares to desert Arran and rejoin Angus!"

"It could be. He and Arran made strange bedfellows from the first."

"So—we must change his mind for him! Douglas! We must whittle away at Douglas. In the interests of Home's future!"

"I would have thought that Douglas, Angus himself, was the greater menace, the most powerful."

"Powerful, perhaps—but a deal less clever. Home I see as the cleverest noble in Scotland today. And wits can usually improve on power."

Some results of Davie Beaton's deliberations on the theme of Douglas were fairly quickly apparent—even though the action seemed to come from others, principally, at this stage, from his uncle. The old Bishop of Dunkeld had died and Gavin Douglas, Provost of the High Kirk of St Giles in Edinburgh, Angus's uncle, was astonishingly offered the bishopric by the Primate, at the Chancellor's bidding. More than that, to ensure a prompt acceptance, the elder Beaton proposed to instal and consecrate the new Bishop, at his own costs, in the Cathedral of St Mungo in Glasgow—it all having to be done forthwith in view of the Chancellor's other pressing commitments. This was too great a temptation for Master Gavin, who had always pined for the episcopate, and he succumbed with the required speed—the first defection in the Douglas camp.

Then the Chancellor acted again. He contrived the arrest of the Lord Drummond, Angus's maternal grandfather and chief of the Douglas's main supporting clan in the Highland area, and confined him in the royal prison castle of Blackness-on-Forth. The charge was that Drummond had insulted and assaulted the Lord Lyon King of Arms, the chief herald of the realm, who ranked as the King's personal representative and whom to strike could be construed as treason. It had all happened some time ago but nothing had been done about it. The pretext served.

It was hoped that Douglas, and likewise Home, would read the signs aright.

Whilst this was going on and the armed strength of the Albany camp was massing in the area just west of Edinburgh as all awaited the opening date of the parliament, David Lindsay was given his own orders. If they came via young Beaton and sounded like suggestions arising out of mutual discussion he had no doubts as to the authority behind them. He was to go to Dunbar and urge de la Bastie to assail and take the small Home strength of Colbrandspath Tower, near Dunglass—Dunglass itself might be too strong. This would serve further advice on Home. And thereafter David was to bring back de la Bastie to Edinburgh. The Lord Lindsay would go with him to take over the captaincy of Dunbar meantime.

David was well enough pleased to get away, as ever—especially as it meant that he could see Kate, coming and going. She was much in his thoughts these days.

A pleasant evening at the Byres and, with a brief call at Garleton in the by-going, they rode on next morning to Dunbar. Antoine was glad to see them, he tending to weary of castle keeping, eager for news of Albany and especially of Beaton, in whom he seemed to have much interest, and delighted to hear of the orders to assail Colbrandspath, to enliven the monotony of garrison duty.

So he and David rode south-eastwards next morning with a small escort to spy out the land. Their objective lay ten miles away on the main route to Berwick and the south at a hazard thereon known as Pease Dean—indeed this was the reason for the existence of the tower, for the precipitous sides of the Pease Burn here forced travellers into a position where they must pass close under the walls of the hold, to which they must pay toll if they were to proceed. Such robber-barons' keeps were all too common; but though impregnable to ordinary travellers and even men-at-arms, they were not usually proof against artillery. Unfortunately the much stronger Home castle of Dunglass lay not much more than two miles to the west, and any approach with cannon must be observed and no doubt contested.

So they took a roundabout route, inland, by Innerwick and Oldhamstocks, and so down the rapidly falling Pease Burn from the Lammermuir foothills. From a vantage point directly above the gut of the steep ravine, they could look down from scrub woodland on the fortalice, and consider.

It was a simple square tower of four main storeys and a garret, set within a small irregular courtyard, all cut out of the hillside in such a way that it dominated the roadway, leaving no other access. It would be a hard place to take defended, all but unapproachable from below and although overlooked by the higher ground this was only at some distance off and the necessary descent would invalidate any possible advantage.

"Cannon," Antoine said. "Only cannon will take that hold without a lengthy siege and starving them out. Cannon, up here."

David nodded. "So say I. But—could cannons' muzzles be depressed sufficiently to fire down there? For the balls not to go high above the tower? At Flodden, they say, all the fine cannon were useless because they could not fire down the hill at the English."

"Downward-sloping pits dug," the Frenchman said. "I have seen it done It should be possible."

"And the noise? Cannon fire will bring out the Home strength from Dunglass and elsewhere."

Antoine nodded. "Then we must counter that. We need few to fire the cannon. Our main strength must mass to seem to besiege *Dunglass*. Keep them held there."

"But—how to get the cannon up here? Up this steep rough hillside . . . ?"

"Dismount them. The smaller guns, falcons, serpentines and the like from Dunbar. On horses. It can be done."

David was doubtful as they rode back.

But Antoine knew his own mind. He had inherited almost a dozen assorted cannon when he took Dunbar, mostly small pieces and fairly old; by detaching three of these from their wooden carriages and then loading barrels, carriages, and ball and shot and powder on a string of pack-horses, he solved the problem of mobility. But for his demonstration against Dunglass—for it was to be only that—he required many men. He had a garrison of only around fifty and some must be left to guard Dunbar Castle whilst some were needed to assault Colbrandspath. So, to make an impressive-looking force to threaten Dunglass, he sought volunteers amongst the townsfolk and fishermen of Dunbar. He had, of set purpose, made himself popular in the town, with the raising of the fish levy giving him a good start; and by offering to pay a suitable wage, he obtained an excellent response, indeed more than he could equip and seem to arm from the castle stores. But fifty he could use, and with a score of his own garrison that ought to make a sufficiently formidable force, at a distance, to keep the Dunglass folk from issuing forth. There was a danger in this device, of course, in that someone in the town, disaffected or merely loud of mouth, might talk sufficiently for word of it all to get to Dunglass and Colbrandspath. Delay, therefore, was to be avoided.

So, with only one day for preparation, they set off before dawn, a somewhat unruly and untidy company, the Colbrandspath assault party with about a dozen local men leading the pack-horses, and, behind, the strung-out seventy or so for Dunglass under Lord Lindsay.

They parted company at the fishing hamlet of Skateraw just as the sun was rising out over the Norse Sea, the attack party to take the more difficult and hidden inland route, the others to march direct for Dunglass on the coast.

It made a slow and taxing journey, with the heavily laden pack-animals having to be led and coaxed over much rough and trackless country, the last miles the worst, down through steep and broken scrub woodland with many fallen trees and the horses slipping and slithering. But at length they won into a position similar to that they had been in two days previously, directly above Colbrandspath Tower, perhaps one hundred and fifty feet higher and giving a range of not much more than two hundred yards for the cannon.

Prospecting the site, Antoine chose a position where they could find sufficient depth of soil, of a sort, to dig his downwards facing pits for the guns at a sufficient angle for the muzzles to bear on the buildings beneath. This entailed much labour and required the erection of a small barrier of stones immediately below each cannon in order that on the discharge and recoil the carriages would not hurtle forward and down the slope.

There was no indication that their activities had been noticed from the fortalice below.

"We shall now waken these sleepers!" Antoine declared. "They have lain long enough . . ." and he stooped to apply the burning fuse to the touch hole of the first cannon, a falcon. The explosion drowned his words.

They could hardly miss altogether at that range but that first ball struck the keep walling about halfway down, creating a shower of dust but doing little damage to the thick masonry. The next shot hit lower still. This would not do. The higher on the walling the thinner was the masonry, always; and the ideal place to bombard was of course the roof and parapet-walk, thinnest of all.

As they raised the gun muzzles a little men appeared on the said parapet-walk shouting and gesticulating. The third cannon's ball went over their heads but sent them scurrying below.

Reloading, they tried another realignment. And although this time two of the shots went high the third did smash into the stone slates of the roofing, tearing a great hole therein and no doubt wrecking the garret chamber beneath. As the echoes died away they could hear screams.

Thereafter, by trial and error, they pounded that hapless tower and its lean-to courtyard buildings with repeated salvoes. And quite quickly what had to serve as white flags appeared at two of the small windows to flap urgently.

"They have had enough," David said. "Nor do I blame them, unable to hit back . . ."

"Listen!" Antoine said.

Clearly, from the north-westwards, came the booming of cannon.

"Dunglass! That must be the Homes, firing on our people. They must have cannon there."

"No doubt. They will have heard *our* guns. Perhaps they think that it is general war!" De la Bastie shrugged and pointed downwards. "These, at least, make conveniently swift submission. Will you go down, my dear David, and accept their surrender? And if, by chance, they play any tricks or make difficulty blow this horn and I will open fire again immediately."

"But—if *our* cannon can thus easily win us this hold, could not the cannon, brought from Dunglass, just as easily win it back?"

"That is true. Therefore, I fear that we cannot hold it. It will be necessary for us to destroy it. With the remainder of our gunpowder. Better so than wasting our strength trying to hold a useless tower."

That made sense. David moved off downhill with most of their party and approached the fortalice, all ready for trickery. But there was none. Eight shaken men, unarmed, and two women emerged, assisting two other men, blood-covered and evidently wounded in the bombardment, one of whom it transpired was Home of Colbrandspath himself. They assured that there was nobody else in the place—only the barking dogs and stamping horses in the courtyard stabling. David was embarrassed by what he had to do and say—he had never thought that there would be women in the hold—but steeled himself to the task. He told them that they were free to remove anything that they especially valued from the tower, which was to be destroyed in the name of the King and his Regent, and that they could go down meantime to the fishing hamlet at the shore below—or elsewhere as they desired, although he did not recommend Dunglass. He enquired for the wounded but although the laird himself seemed to have a broken shoulder and sundry lacerations there appeared to be nothing dangerous, the other man bleeding from a scalp wound, painful but superficial.

David checked indoors to ensure that there were no undisclosed problems and then sent a man up to Antoine to inform that all was well and that he could bring down the powder for the demolition.

So, presently, with the sad tower party sent off to Pease Bay with their wounded, their horses laden with household goods and their snarling dogs but with no actual apologies—although David for one felt like making them—they prepared to blow up the fortalice. The lower six foot thick walling, of course, would defy any powder they had available so they confined themselves to the upper storeys which, wrecked, should serve to make the place uninhabitable for some time. In the end they achieved a great bang and showered stones and fragments and a vast cloud of dust and smoke. Thereafter they set off north-westwards along the coast road, satisfied that Colbrandspath Tower would be no menace to honest travellers nor to the Regent's causes for a while to come.

They picked up their main force sitting well out of range of Dunglass Castle's guns and all marched back to Dunbar, duty done.

Two days later David and Antoine rode for Edinburgh, via the Byres and Garleton and some welcome feminine company for each, leaving Lord Lindsay in charge of Dunbar and its castle.

They were just in time for the parliament, which opened in the large church of the Abbey of the Holy Rood. There was a surprisingly good turnout, considering the short notice and the unsettled, dangerous times, and undoubtedly most present would be supporters of the new Regent. It had been hoped that the young King might have been there for the opening, even under strong Home guard, to lend significance to the occasion; but no response had been received to the invitation sent up to the castle. As a precaution, a large contingent of the force camped outside the city had been brought in to secure the entire Canongate–Holyrood area in case of interference by whomsoever.

Albany not being officially Regent yet, and no high commissioner having been appointed under the seal of the monarch, the Chancellor had to open the proceedings himself, after a fanfare by the herald-trumpeters and an introduction by the Lord Lyon King of Arms. Albany sat to one side with Davie Beaton standing close-by to interpret. Every corner of the great church was filled with spectators, even up in the clerestory galleries, the French contingent making itself notably conspicuous. David Lindsay and de la Bastie perched in a window embrasure of the crossing.

The Chancellor, after prayer, declared, in welcoming all, that this assembly was necessarily a convention at this stage, not a parliament, since a parliament required the King's summons or that of his Regent, and present circumstances precluded either. But since the previous parliament, in the King's presence, had nominated John, Duke of Albany, to be Regent, it but required this assembly to make formal confirmation of the Duke, here present, in that office, for him to *become* Regent in fact and fullest authority. He could then declare the assembly to be a parliament, competent to take all due measures required for the realm's well-being. Was this understood by all?

There were general cries of assent.

He put it to the gathering, then—did the lords spiritual and temporal and the commissioners of the shires confirm the Duke of Albany in the Regency? It did not require to be put in the form of a motion, with proposer and seconder, since it was already a due decision of another parliament. Only any rejection would require to be proposed and seconded.

There was a great shout of acceptance from all parts of the church and continued cheering. There may have been some voices raised in dissent but if so they were completely lost in the din.

The Chancellor took it as sufficient confirmation and did not ask if there was any counter-motion. Instead he turned, in the hubbub of acclaim, with something between a bow and a flourish, towards Albany.

"My lord Duke," he said strongly, "this convention of the Three Estates has duly confirmed you in the office of Regent of this realm during the minority of James, by God's grace King of Scots, with all the authority of that office. Do you now, as is your undoubted right, authorise me to declare this a due and lawful parliament?"

His nephew murmured a translation in the ducal ear and Albany nodded. "*Oui!*" he said briefly.

"Then I do so declare. And, in the name of this parliament of the realm, I request you, my lord Regent, to move to and take the throne here as is your right."

So, amidst further cheering, Albany rose and stalked over

to the high chair set in the midst of the chancel but facing the nave and company, actually the Abbot's seat, and sat. After a moment or two, young Beaton slipped discreetly over to stand behind. He stooped and handed the Duke a paper.

Still sitting—for when the crown stood everybody must stand—Albany read aloud. It was a short speech in English of acknowledgment and thanks—which he mangled sadly—ending with what was presumably a promise to fulfil his duties and honour the confidence all had placed in him to the best of his abilities. This over, he dropped the paper and launched into a flood of French so fast that few in that church who were not his countrymen could have made anything of it. This went on for some time, and ended with a large gesture.

The French spectators applauded enthusiastically—although their part called only for respectful silence—and Antoine smiled.

"If he is as strong as his words, Scotland is safe!" he murmured.

The Chancellor turned. "My lord Regent—if my nephew may repeat in our tongue for those who did not catch every word . . .?"

Davie Beaton offered his own version—and de la Bastie's raised eyebrows once or twice seemed to indicate some slight emendation. He declared that the Regent was determined to restore the royal authority, to ensure close relations with his master in France and peace in the land, to put down all warring factions with a strong hand. First he would require King James to be delivered into his hands, with his royal brother; all royal castles to be yielded up to his keeping; all minions of the King of England, high and low, to be banished the realm; all pensions, subventions and doles paid by the King of England to be stopped and made unlawful, under pain of treason; all justiciarships and sheriffdoms to be resigned into his hands for reallotment, likewise wardenships of the marches; all heads of houses, families and clans to be held responsible for the good and leal behaviour of their people.

All this took a little digesting and there was a deal of talk, exclamation and muttered comment. But on the whole the reaction was favourable—of course Angus, Arran and Home were noticeable by their absence, although some of their supporters were present, for instances the Homes of Wedderburn and Blackadder, as representing the shire of the Merse.

The Chancellor allowed the gathering its head for a little, then rapped on his table for silence. He asked if any wished to question or remark on the Regent's intentions, any or all?

The Earl Marischal rose. "How does the Regent propose to gain the custody of the King's Grace and his infant brother?" he asked. "Is it likely that the Queen-Mother, Countess of Angus, would yield up her sons when she holds them secure in this city's fortress? And is known to have sworn to deliver them to none. Especially as she named the Duke of Albany!"

The Chancellor elected to answer that key question. "The former Queen's attitude and prejudices are well known," he agreed. "Particularly towards my lord Regent. But she cannot deny the expressed demands of parliament, save by putting herself outwith the law. So it is suggested that this parliament names eight lords, of whom four will be chosen by lot, these to represent the parliament, who will go up to the castle and require the lady to hand over the King and his brother. This to *parliament*, not to the Regent. Thereafter, it is hoped that parliament will decide to entrust the royal children into the Regent's good keeping. Is this procedure agreed?"

There was some debate about this, but most acceded that it was clever and should provide a face-saving device for Margaret Tudor, if she could be persuaded that she had little chance of retaining possession of the King.

The Chancellor nodded. "We believe that such persuasion can be effected," he assured. "We have proof that the King of England is still insisting that King James, as his heir-apparent, be brought into his own keeping in England. And has recently sent monies by the Lord Dacre, chief English Warden of the Marches, to Dr West, the English ambassador here, secretly to effect this end, the Queen-Mother agreeing. It must be clear, therefore, to all, to this parliament and to the nation itself, that the Countess of Angus is no fit person to retain the keeping of the King of Scots."

This revelation had the desired effect and the members promptly expressed their approval of the proposed procedure. Eight lords' names were quickly forthcoming and lots drawn produced the Earls Marischal and of Lennox and the Lords Borthwick and Lindsay. The last not being immediately available, the Lord Fleming's name was substituted. David Lindsay was interested that Lennox allowed his name to go forward, putting him more firmly in the Regent's camp.

Since the possession of the King was the key to all, it was decided to adjourn the sitting meantime for resumption when the royal situation was more clear, the rest of the Regent's declared programme being accepted—if it could be implemented. The four chosen lords would repair to the castle forthwith—and most of the parliament with them, obviously.

David, Antoine and young Beaton walked up the Canongate, High Street and Lawnmarket together amongst the crowd of parliamentarians and others. Albany and the Chancellor did not go, recognising that it would look better without them. Most of the French stayed behind also when they discovered that walking was involved.

Up at the final approach to the fortress, where the Lawnmarket opened on to the tilting ground on a sort of shelf of the castle rock, the Lyon King of Arms, who had led the procession, went ahead with his trumpeters to announce the parliamentary delegation. The remainder all held back meantime.

They heard the trumpets sounding and presently the clash and clang of the drawbridge coming down and the portcullis going up at the gatehouse towers. There was a pause, and then Lyon turned to wave the main party up.

There a notable sight met them. Flanked by armed guards, Margaret Tudor stood just within the gateway, fairly obviously pregnant again. She held by the hand King James on her right, and on her left stood Archibald Douglas, Earl of Angus, whom all thought to be besieging Arran at Hamilton. Looking distinctly awkward about it, he held the infant Duke of Ross in his arms. Young James seemed somewhat wan and distinctly sulky.

At sight of the King, of course, everybody had to doff bonnets and bow low. There was some embarrassment, since it meant that in the sovereign's presence all announcements must seem to be addressed to him.

Lyon, with practised eloquence, declared that parliament in its wisdom had decided that, with His Grace's permission, of eight lords nominated four chosen by lot should come to interview the Queen-Mother, Countess of Angus. William Keith, Earl Marischal, a bull-like man of middle years, was clearly somewhat offput at having to address the lady through the child monarch. He cleared his throat.

"Sire—your parliament has decided that, for your realm's weal, Your Grace should be taken into the keeping of the said parliament. For your safety. It has accordingly chosen four lords, of whom I am one and the others are my lords of Lennox, Borthwick and Fleming, here present, of which Your Grace's lady-mother should select three. To whom to deliver Your Grace and your royal brother, forthwith. This is the will of parliament." He ended that abruptly and coughed again.

Margaret Tudor eyed them all coldly. "Your parliament is no parliament—since the King had not called it," she said briefly.

The Earl Marischal frowned. "Ah, but it is, Madam. Since the Regent has named it so."

"I recognise no Regent for my son, other than myself."

"But the parliament of this realm does! The previous parliament nominated my lord Duke of Albany Regent. This parliament has now confirmed that nomination."

"How can it, my lord? Since it is no parliament, only a convention. A convention cannot make or confirm a Regent for the King's Grace. Only a true parliament might do that—which this was not when it sought to confirm Albany."

"But, Madam . . ."

This argument, which looked as though it might proceed indefinitely, was cut short unexpectedly and by the monarch himself. Eyeing all the new faces before him, James suddenly caught sight of David standing there and let out a whoop of joy.

"Da Linny!" he shouted. "Da! Da Linny!" And snatching his hand out of his mother's, he launched himself forward.

But Margaret Tudor reacted swiftly and grabbed the boy's doublet at the neck to jerk him back sharply, and when he yelled, to shake him in markedly unregal fashion, amidst howls of fury.

There followed some considerable upset, with shouted protests, fists shaken, the castle guard closing up and Angus addressing his wife urgently. David Lindsay, at his young charge's salutation, had involuntarily stepped forward also, arms extended, and now found himself in front of all, uncertain whether to go on to James's side or to move back into suitable anonymity.

The Queen-Mother solved that problem for him at least. Turning, she flicked an imperious finger at the captain of the guard and pointed upwards. That man shouted an order, and promptly, with a rattle of chains, the heavy portcullis of iron bars interlocked in a great grid came crashing down to slam into place at the bridgehead, cutting off one party from the other.

Staring through the iron network, both sides considered, whilst their liege-lord bawled and struggled.

The Queen-Mother retained the initiative. "Go back to your convention and your so-called Regent, my lords," she called, above the noise, "and tell them, and him, that I accept neither the one nor the other. Think you that I would give my children into the keeping of a Frenchman who has only these two infants between him and the throne he covets? I hold this castle by the gift of my late husband, your sovereign-lord, who also entrusted me with the keeping and government of my children. Nor shall I yield them to any person whatsoever." She paused. "In respect of this so-called parliament, I require a respite of six days to consider their mandate. You may now leave the royal presence."

In the circumstances that seemed to be that. However, this peculiar confrontation was not quite over yet, for one of the principals, who had hitherto remained practically silent, now chose to speak up, and to odd effect.

"*I* do not deny this parliament and its rights," Angus said abruptly. "And I urge my wife to accept its requirements, as is lawful."

All stared, scarcely believing their ears. All except Margaret Tudor, that is. If she was shocked, she showed no signs of it. She did not even glance at her husband.

"Go back whence you have come, my lords," she repeated. "Tell the Frenchman what I have said. Come back in six days and you shall have fullest response to your unacceptable claims." She turned, dragging James with her, to stalk back through the gatehouse pend, a determined, graceless figure.

For a few moments Archibald Douglas hesitated, still with the apparently sleeping infant duke in his arms. Then he shouted through the iron bars. "I, Angus, call on all to note that I do not dispute the parliament's will and commands and would have consented to surrender these children." He swung round and hurried after his wife.

Into the astonished silence, Davie Beaton's voice sounded clearly. "Now that is the most interesting word spoken this day!"

None there denied it.

On their way back down through the city streets, David asked Beaton what he made of it all. Had they been too clever? Or had the Queen-Mother been cleverer? And this of Angus—what did it mean?

His namesake seemed not at all put out. "One cannot but admire the woman," he said. "She has courage, spirit and wits—a King's daughter indeed. But she cannot win—and knows it. This of six days' interval—she leaves herself a postern for escape. She cannot for long defy the expressed will of parliament. This convention talk is but a device. Angus knows it and so has sought to cover himself. *He* will not have his wide lands forfeited by the same parliament for treason!"

"You think that was it? A strange thing, as against his wife."

"That first, yes. But there may have been more to it. I have heard whispers that there has been trouble between them, despite her being with child by him. This might be important. If we can detach Douglas . . ."

"I think that you go too fast, Beaton," de la Bastie put in. "Why did Angus come here? And secretly. From Lanarkshire. Not to attend the parliament, it seems. He would guess that Albany would demand the King. He is not a fool. Nor craven."

"Yet he covers himself, with this parliament. And opposes his wife before all. I say that is good news."

"Did you not expect, then, to have James delivered to us?" David asked.

"No," the other said simply.

That gave them pause for a while.

"I was much interested to see the young King. And to observe how greatly he seems to love you, friend,"

Beaton went on. "This could be of the greatest import, hereafter."

"I am fond of the child," David said stiffly. "Liege-lord as he is." He changed the subject. "What I would wish to know is where was the Lord Home this day?"

"*Moi aussi*," Antoine agreed.

"No doubt he prefers to keep out of sight leaving others to make the moves he devises," Beaton suggested.

"Nor is he the only one, at that!" the Frenchman answered, smiling.

The other bowed, and shrugged.

Back at Holyrood David was not present to hear Albany's reaction to all this, but he was a witness of the remarkable scene the following day in the abbey church when, at the resumed sitting of the parliament, a messenger came hotfoot in to hurry to the Chancellor's table, there to stoop and whisper. The Archbishop stared, frowned, and started to his feet. Ignoring the Lord Gray, who was holding forth on the need for an increase in the number of sheriffdoms, he went over to the Regent's throne and spoke urgently, his nephew translating, eyebrows raised.

Albany did more than raise his brows. He jumped up, glaring around him, snatched off his velvet cap and, since there was no available fire to hurl it at, flung it to the floor and stamped upon it again and again. Then, amidst a cataract of French eloquence, he left them all standing to storm to the vestry door and out.

The sitting undoubtedly was suspended.

Out of the uproar, the Chancellor eventually gained a reduction of noise. "My lords and commissioners," he exclaimed. "We have just heard that last night, under cover of darkness, the Queen-Mother, with her husband Angus, secretly left the castle, taking the King and his brother, and rode, it is thought, for the north!"

The din resumed. Young Beaton had to shout. "Where is the Lord Home?" he demanded.

It was the messenger who answered. "He remains, it is believed, in the castle."

"This parliament stands adjourned," the Archbishop declared.

9

It was marching again, the thirty-five miles from Edinburgh to Stirling, three days' tramp, the slower in that they had cannon lumbering along—and not just any cannon, minor pieces, but the huge Mons Meg itself, Scotland's mightiest, which even the late King had not aspired to take to Flodden, but which Albany—or more likely, Davie Beaton—had decided was worth the labour of trundling all the way from Edinburgh Castle behind no less than a score of plodding oxen. The army might have made slightly better time than the oxen, all eight thousand of them; but even so, it was slow progress. In the absence of the Lord Patrick, still at Dunbar, David found himself in command of the Lindsay contingent and chose to march with them as often as he rode his horse, in the interests of morale.

Albany had moved with speed and decision. Word had reached him that although Angus had gone on north-eastwards for the Douglas lands in Angus and the Mearns, presumably to raise more men, Margaret Tudor and her children had been dropped off at Stirling. Admittedly that fortress was the strongest in Scotland and presumably she felt that she would be safest there—hence Mons Meg being brought, for if anything could batter Stirling into submission it would be that monster. The attendant army was to ensure that Angus did not return to effect a rescue. So the force which had welcomed Albany at his arrival at Dumbarton and marched with him eastwards to encamp outside Edinburgh all this time, was to see some active service at last, with additional numbers recruited by various lords.

There was urgency about it all for a courier had been intercepted from the Queen-Mother to Lord Dacre with a letter, obviously an answer to one from King Henry, in which she agreed that a sufficiently large English force should be sent to Scotland to achieve her rescue at Stirling where she was now immured and thereafter the delivery of herself and children into Henry's care in England, where James would formally be declared heir-apparent to the English throne, requiring his future domicile in England. The letter added that if she was besieged by the usurping Albany and the parliamentary rebels, she would cause young James to stand in a prominent place on the castle walling, wearing his crown, so that Albany's supporters would see that they were guilty of highest treason in taking up arms against their liege-lord. This courier had been captured, but another might have got through. So Albany tended to glance behind him as it were, as he marched, back towards the Borderland. Home was now believed to be in his own territories there, and Arran was goodness knew where, his present attitude uncertain to say the least.

They reached Stirling on 4th August. Marshalling the mass of troops wherever they would seem to present the greatest threat to the castle—although of course they represented little or no threat in fact—Albany had Mons Meg dragged up to a position on highish ground where it could be seen, and out of range of the citadel's own cannon but well within its own greater range. Then the Lord Lyon was sent forward to repeat his message of two weeks before at Edinburgh Castle, demanding that the keys of this fortress be handed over to the Regent and the King's royal person delivered into the custody of the lords of parliament appointed.

When there was no least reply from the gatehouse towers, Lyon went on to inform the castle's captain, if he had not already perceived it, that the great cannon known as Mons Meg had been brought from Edinburgh and was in a position to hammer this fortress into compliance—if so he and the Queen-Mother chose. But if this had to be done then he, the captain, supposing that he survived the bombardment, would be held responsible for the damage done to a royal castle and would have to pay the price. When still there was no response, Lyon and his trumpeters returned to the Regent's party around the artillery.

The young Lord Borthwick, as Hereditary Master Gunner in succession to his father who had not survived Flodden, thereupon lined up his Mons Meg to try to hit a small flanking tower of the castle which would be well out of the way of any part where the royal family might be lodged—for of course any possible danger to the King and his brother was unthinkable, and much complicated potential gunnery. They had not forgotten Margaret Tudor's expressed intention of putting James in a prominent position to inhibit any assault. Borthwick had never fired this monster previously, with its enormous charge of powder and huge ball, and was distinctly nervous, fearing a misfire or a flashback such as had killed James the Second fifty-six years before. David and all the rest stood well back, leaving the Master Gunner to his privileges.

Despite all the precautions, none were prepared for the tremendous blast of the explosion which seemed to pulverise the senses for a few moments. Mons or Mollance Meg had been founded in the middle of the previous century by a noted blacksmith named Kim of Mollance in Galloway for his Maclellan chief—just why was insufficiently explained—but it had proved so efficacious at James the Second's siege of the hitherto impregnable Douglas castle of Threave that the King had thereupon appropriated it, and it had become the showpiece of the royal artillery, show rather than effect, for it had scarcely been used in other than salute since.

The first shot was sufficiently effective for the most demanding, even though its aim was less than accurate. Pieces were seen to fly off a building well to the left of the tower target, and a barracks behind seemed totally to disintegrate with further unidentifiable damage beyond, so overwhelming was the force of the projectile. All stared as the smoke cloud blew away on the breeze, daunted despite themselves.

Not Davie Beaton however, who cheered loudly, urging Lord Borthwick to try again, bearing a little to the right; the elevation was fair enough. Albany stroked his pointed beard.

It took some time to recharge and reload—and everybody stood still further back, covering their ears, as the fuse was applied for the second time. This shot missed the flanking tower also, but demolished in a cloud of dust a considerable length of perimeter walling and parapet-walk, as well as taking the roofs off some outbuildings further on, part of the menagerie. Beaton applauded again and turned to David to ask, as one well acquainted with the layout of the fortress, where would be the best place to aim a third shot, to have maximum effect on the defenders? Clearly with this brute of a cannon they could pound the place to pieces almost at will.

David was less happy. "I mislike this," he said, inadequately. "It is . . . too much. James will be terrified. Endangered. We do not know where he may be. We dare not fire into the main parts of the castle . . ." He was thinking also of the Abbot John, still presumably therein.

He was interrupted by the boom of lesser cannon and smoke blossomed out from one of the citadel's batteries. Everybody flung themselves down, except Borthwick, who shouted that they need not fear, that they were well out of range here. Sure enough, a fountain of earth and stones erupted fully three hundred yards short of their position. And another shot from a second cannon did little better.

"Where will the young King certainly *not* be?" Beaton demanded. "They have not learned their lesson yet!"

"Who knows, for sure? But—the Well Tower, probably. It is above the old kitchens and brewhouse. They would never be there, surely. That is it, to the right of the Chapel Royal—you can see the chapel gables with their crosses. But, for God's sake, keep well to the right! They might have taken refuge in the chapel . . ."

"You hear, my lord?"

"Have a care, of a mercy . . .!"

Borthwick relaid his piece with suitable solicitude but increased confidence and called on one of his assistant gunners to check the alignment. This time he achieved success, with a direct hit which blew the Well Tower into fragments and went on to shatter further quarters behind.

There was rather more general cheering now; but even so, David Lindsay did not join in—until de la Bastie gripped his arm and pointed. There, from one of the gatehouse towers, a white sheet was being hung out over the walling. David was now prepared to cheer with the rest.

Lyon went forward again, and presently waved all others to approach. As he did so the drawbridge began to descend and the portcullis to rise. By the time that the Regent's group reached the gateway, a small party was waiting for them at the bridgehead. It was uncannily like a repeat of the scene at Edinburgh Castle two weeks earlier. Standing there was Margaret Tudor, holding by the arm King James; and beside her was a man with the infant Duke of Ross in his arms—only this time it was not Angus but the Lord Erskine. There was one other difference—the boy monarch held a great iron key in his hand. No word was spoken on either side. Only the baby whimpered.

The Queen-Mother gave her son a push forward, as once again all bowed in varying degrees. James, scowling uncertainly, moved a few steps out on to the bridge timbers and stopped, in the face of that phalanx of armoured men. He looked as though he might turn and run back, when Beaton nudged David Lindsay.

"Sire! Jamie!" the latter called. "All is well. It is Da. Da Linny." And he pushed his way to the front.

"Da!" the child cried. "Da—oh, Da!" And came running.

David strode out on to the bridge before all to meet him, and caught the boy up into his arms, key and all, to hug him and be hugged.

A great clamour of exclamation and relief arose. The Regent moved forward.

Not so Margaret Tudor. Frowning coldly she turned, and with a swish of skirts stalked back into the castle, still without speech. Lord Erskine, hereditary keeper of this citadel, was left looking uncertain, with the other child sobbing against his shoulder.

Led by Albany, the newcomers surged forward over the drawbridge and in through the gatehouse pend, the King up on David's shoulder now—although he was getting too big for this, at nearly four—somewhere in the midst, still clutching the symbolic key of the fortress, which nobody appeared to want.

Abbot John, pushing against the tide, hurried to greet them.

Joyful was the reunion for those three, whatever the atmosphere of constraint and hostility in the rest of the castle.

In due course they learned what was to happen, from Davie Beaton. During the two days' interval Beaton spent much time with David and the Abbot, and therefore with James, who was now not to be parted from them; he clearly found Lindsay's company to his taste—and no doubt perceived advantage in becoming known and accepted by the child monarch. He revealed that Albany was going to take the Queen-Mother back to Edinburgh and keep her in the castle there, more or less a prisoner and a hostage for the good behaviour of her husband Angus. The King, however, with his brother, would remain here at Stirling, for security, in the care of David and Abbot John, the Earl Marischal being left in command of the citadel. It was not thought to be in any real danger now, from Angus or other, for there was no other cannon like Mons Meg in the kingdom, and that monster was being taken back to Edinburgh also. Arran's attitude, like his whereabouts, was unknown; but in the circumstances he was not the man to besiege Stirling to grasp at the King. And Home was now isolated in his Border area and scarcely in a position to mount any major thrust meantime. In fact, the Regent's situation was now reasonably well-established, his strategy working out well—and young Beaton, without any unseemly flaunting, did not pretend that the strategy was not his own, the success thanks to himself.

So, after two days, Albany and his entourage departed, taking Margaret Tudor with them, the army and Mons Meg following on. If the Queen-Mother was desolated at leaving her children she revealed no signs of it, coldly self-contained throughout; and James, for his part, was not moved to tears. The baby duke was left in the keeping of Lady Erskine, who would remain at Stirling, although her husband would go with the Queen-Mother to Edinburgh.

David, holding the King's hand, watched them go, from a gatehouse tower parapet, with mixed feelings. He had young James and Abbot John again—but he was going to miss Antoine de la Bastie and, yes, Davie Beaton also. And he was back to confinement in a fortress once more, his period of freedom apparently over.

A week after this departure a small group of the royal guard arrived from Edinburgh with a green parrot in a wickerwork cage, as gift for the King's Grace from a devoted subject.

10

In the months that followed, David Lindsay came to the conclusion that he was something of a misfit. He had been greatly pleased and indeed flattered those four years earlier when the late King had appointed him Procurator and companion for his infant son. And still he esteemed that position and would have been much offended had he been displaced by someone else. He was genuinely fond of young James, and more than appreciative of the fact that the boy so evidently approved of himself. Nevertheless, he found the life he had to live both trying and tying, to a degree. It was mainly this of being cooped up in a fortress, to be sure; but it was more than that. He just did not have enough to do. He was a restless, energetic man, and although interested in music and poetry and the like he required physical as well as mental activity. It might have been different had the times been otherwise and peace in the land. Then he and his charge would not have been so confined, and life had been vastly more free, with visiting, riding abroad, even hunting and hawking available for the young monarch and his attendants. Nothing of the sort was possible under present circumstances. He almost envied John Inglis who seemed to suffer from no such cravings for involvement and activity; he probably would have made a good monk, a real monk, not a sham abbot.

There was also the matter of Kate. Being fifty-odd miles from her was damnable. Who knew what might be happening at the Byres? Attractive as she had now become, men would be swarming round her like flies.

The Earl Marischal, in command at Stirling, was not the sort of man who would see any need to cater for a younger man's moods and fancies.

News of the world outside the fortress was but scanty. It had been different before, when the Chancellor was based there, and couriers and letters were arriving constantly to keep him informed. Now the Archbishop remained with the Regent, at Holyrood, and it seemed to be nobody's business to inform the King's guardians at Stirling. Only once, in mid-September, did any near involvement in current events reach them. A hard-riding troop of the Regent's men came pounding up to the castle from Edinburgh, demanding to know whether the Queen-Mother had arrived? When, astonished, the Earl Marischal told them no, and how could she, their spokesman said that if she did appear, she was to be admitted but then held secure until the Regent sent for her. He went on to declare that the lady had told Albany that Edinburgh Castle and its grim towers and cells was no place for a princess to be delivered of her child, and since she was now nearing her time she demanded that she be taken to her own house of Linlithgow for the birth. In a weak moment the Regent had acceded and under guard she had been allowed to go. But before they reached Linlithgow, Lord Home with a much stronger party had ambushed them and had taken the Queen-Mother. Clearly it was all plotted beforehand. Nobody knew where she had gone—the assumption was that she might have come here to Stirling to try to pick up the royal children . . .

This news at least gave them something to talk about in the fortress with much speculation as to where Margaret Tudor might be now and whether she was likely to appear at Stirling, demanding her sons, backed by the power of Home and possibly Angus also. But it did nothing to lessen David's feelings of constriction; indeed the reverse, for the Earl Marischal insisted on tightened security so that even brief visits down into the town by members of the garrison were stopped.

It was some ten days later that there were developments—the arrival, not of Margaret Tudor but of Davie Beaton. He rode up, with only two of his uncle's men-at-arms as escort, but in his usual assured good spirits, paid civil respects to the Earl Marischal, made a fuss of young James and his papingo—which he rejoiced to hear was proving a great success—but made it entirely clear that it was David Lindsay that he had come for and that they had work to do.

David did not think to take amiss such cool authority from this young man, little older than himself and with less official status, being a mere student at the Sorbonne, although apparently lay Rector of Campsie in his uncle's archdiocese to provide him with an income. Seemingly they were for the road, bound for the north, on the realm's business.

Why David should be involved became clearer later. It seemed that still nobody knew where the Queen-Mother was, but it was suspected that she would probably make for her husband who was believed to be still recruiting in Angus, the Mearns and Aberdeenshire. It was important, needless to say, that no large-scale threat should be allowed to develop in that area, especially as the Earl of Huntly and his Gordons were allies of Douglas and the Queen-Mother. It so happened that the alternative powers up there, insofar as the shires of Angus and the Mearns were concerned, were the Earl of Crawford, chief of all the Lindsays, and his son-in-law, the Lord Ogilvy of Airlie. Crawford, an elderly man, had been lying distinctly low during all the national upheavals—he had succeeded to the earldom when his nephew was killed at Flodden. But he was nevertheless one of the most powerful lords in the land—and that same nephew had been married to the Lord Home's sister. It was advisable, then, that Crawford should be convinced that his interests lay with the Regent, and David could see some point in himself being enrolled in the business of trying to influence his chief. But why Davie Beaton should take on the task, personally, was not so clear.

They rode off next morning north-eastwards, across Forth, by Strathallan and Strathearn to Perth, and then onwards through Gowrie into the vast valley of Strathmore, the mightiest vale in all Scotland, fifty miles long by eight to ten wide, of fertile, tilled land and fair pasture, between the green Sidlaw Hills and the majestic blue ramparts of the Highland Line known as the Braes of Angus. Young men, they rode hard, and there was little opportunity for elaboration or discussion—David not complaining, so gratified was he to be out of Stirling and more or less free again. Perth was the same distance from Stirling, in the other direction, as was Edinburgh: thirty-five miles, and they made it in four hours. Then, after resting their beasts, on for another three hours to Meigle, on the Isla, in Strathmore. And there, with the sun sinking and their mounts weary indeed,

David was somewhat surprised when his companion turned northwards, up Isla-side, not onwards for Forfar and Brechin, between which lay Finavon Castle, the main seat of the Earl of Crawford.

"We shall go see my Lord of Airlie first," Beaton explained briefly.

They had another six miles to go, with the scene changing now notably and rapidly, wooded foothills and green cattle-dotted ridges, the river winding in shadowy valleys and always the great purple mountains rearing ahead. David had never been in Angus, and was not unaffected by the mighty barrier of soaring peaks, of rock and heather and high wilderness, which he understood went on from here into infinity, the dread and storied Highlands, which all his life he had been taught to shun and fear.

With the Isla becoming ever more of a torrent, peat-brown, and its valley course narrowing and steepening in the September evening gloom, they came at length to a thrusting headland, almost a vast wedge of cliff, where another lesser but still savagely foaming stream came in a deep ravine to join Isla—the Melgam Water, Beaton mentioned. And up there, at the clifftop, where there was the glow of the last of the sunset, lights glimmered from windows. He set his faltering horse to a daunting zigzag track which worked its difficult way up the flank of this proud prow of land. Clearly he had been here before.

At the top they came out on to a small apron of grass, above which high walling, topped by a parapet, rose beyond a dry ditch cut deep into the living rock, dizzy towers soaring behind. The dark gap of an arched gateway was there and a narrow drawbridge was down, to span the ditch. A group of kilted men, broadswords drawn, stood at the bridgehead, waiting, silent. David did not like the look of them, Highland caterans. Presumably their approach had been observed, despite the evening shadows.

Beaton rode on easily to the bridge, raising a hand high. "We come to see the Lord James. And the Lady Marion," he called. "Friends."

At first there was no response. Then one of the men said, in a softly sibilant Highland voice so much at odds with his wild appearance, "The Lord Seamus is from home, sir. Yourself, who are you?"

"I am Beaton. David Beaton. From France. Is the Lady Marion here, then?"

"I will be after asking if she will see you, sir." Despite the speaker's civil words, when he turned to disappear into the gateway arch the others looked none the more welcoming, closing up to bar the way threateningly.

The visitors sat in their saddles. Beaton said something affable but the guards made no answer. Possibly they spoke only the Gaelic.

They had quite a wait there, in the gloaming, in silence save for the horses' champing and the owls beginning to hoot. Then the original challenger returned, and with him a woman—or, more accurately, a girl, for she appeared to be little older than Kate—a long-legged, slender creature with a cascade of golden hair loosely looped back from winsome features, but with a proud, not to say haughty carriage nevertheless. She was dressed in practical but attractive fashion, in a dark-green gown of woven stuff, shorter than was the Lowland style, over a white short-sleeved bodice which detracted nothing from a shapely figure. She stared out at them, a strange apparition to come across at that harsh fortalice on top of the beetling cliff.

"Marion! It is David—Davie Beaton. Come, come visiting! It is Davie, my dear."

They heard her quickly indrawn breath. But that was all. David was surprised. He had assumed that the Lady Marion named would be the Lord Ogilvy's wife, daughter of the Earl of Crawford. Although this could be *her* daughter . . .

Beaton jumped down and all but ran forward, hand out, eagerness in every line of him. "Lassie—Marion! It is I—Davie. From France. Had you not heard . . . ?"

This was a different man from the one David knew, urgent, no longer assured, acting no part. Clearly this young woman meant much to him.

She scarcely seemed to reciprocate his urgency. "You!" she got out. "Here? I believed you still gone. In France, Davie Beaton. I . . ." She shook her fair head.

The guard drew aside to let him past, arms still outstretched. She made no move forward to him, however.

He faltered, hands dropping to his sides. "I came with the Regent, with Albany. I . . . had to come to see you, Marion."

They looked at each other, in strange, searching fashion for moments.

Then Beaton remembered David and his manners. "Here is David Lindsay of the Mount, the young King's Procurator and guardian."

"Lindsay? My mother was a Lindsay," the girl said, looking up. She sounded almost relieved at the intermission.

David bowed and dismounted.

"You have travelled far, sir?"

"From Stirling, lady."

"Stirling? That is far indeed. Sixty miles and more. Long riding. You will be weary, hungry." She appeared to be a deal more at ease in addressing David. "Come." She turned to lead the way within. "My father is not here meantime, but you are welcome to his house."

Airlie Castle was irregularly shaped, of necessity to conform to its highly defensive but awkward site, larger than Garleton but smaller than the Byres, and much more stark and strong than either. But internally it proved to be more comfortable than might have seemed likely. The girl conducted them through a vaulted great hall and upstairs to a pleasant lamplit chamber where a birch log fire burned cheerfully and aromatically and deer and wolf skin rugs littered the floor. Here she provided a flagon of wine and beakers for their immediate refreshment, whilst she left them to go down to the kitchens to arrange more substantial fare.

The two young men eyed each other. "So this is why we came to Airlie Castle first!" David observed. He almost added, and the reason why you chose to make this northern journey personally, likewise.

The other shrugged. "I wished to see Marion, yes. We are . . . friendly. I have not been here for two years and more. She is important to me. And her father is important to the realm, in this pass."

"To be sure . . ."

Presently they were sat down to an excellent repast of cold meats, with their hostess attentively presiding. She seemed to be a quietly competent woman, as well as attractive—but her hospitable attentions were rather noticeably devoted more to David Lindsay than to David Beaton, with whom there was an obvious sense of strain. She and Lindsay decided that they were cousins, seven times removed. She revealed that her father was at present visiting her grandfather at Finavon Castle. When Beaton asked her if this was by any chance to do with the affairs of the Earl of Angus, she was non-committal, indicating that the Lord Ogilvy did not find it necessary to discuss all his business with her. It was amusing to see her questioner chastened in a way nobody else appeared to be able to achieve.

Interesting as this encounter might be to watch, fairly soon after the meal was over David excused himself to seek his couch, pleading fatigue after too much of being confined within fortress walls. Beaton confessed to no such weariness and did not offer to accompany them when Marion Ogilvy said that she would show the guest his chamber.

At a high tower room, feeling a certain sympathy for his travelling companion, David paused in the doorway. "David Beaton is working hard and doing much good for the realm's cause," he mentioned. "He is able, and wields much power. It could almost be said that he is the power behind the Regent, who speaks only French and depends heavily on Davie for guidance. He relies on him."

"Indeed. Then Master Davie will be well content. Since power is what he seeks, has long sought."

The way she said that gave David pause. "And you feel differently?" he asked.

"My feelings in this matter are neither here nor there, Master Lindsay. Who am I to concern myself with the affairs of the realm? Or of David Beaton!"

"H'mm. Yet—he came all this way, from Edinburgh, to see *you*, I think. Leaving the Regent. And his uncle, the Chancellor. At a time of stress." That was the best that he could do for one whom he was beginning to think of as his friend.

"Then perhaps his judgment is less reliable than the Duke of Albany believes! A good night to you, sir."

Perhaps he had not improved matters for his companion? Anyway, who was he to think to seek to meddle in matters of the heart—he who was scarcely achieving great things with Kate Lindsay?

In the morning, with Beaton taking a delayed and reluctant farewell of Airlie Castle, David forbore to ask, as they rode off down Isla-side again, how his companion had got on the previous night. But, after a while, the other did volunteer some comment. He said that Marion was a notably fine young woman and that he was devoted to her. But that she was somewhat out of sympathy with what he was doing, with the life that he had chosen to live. She did not understand the need for such as himself, with the gifts the good God had bestowed on him in wits and circumstances and family connections, to use them to best effect in the service of Scotland in its hour of need. She would have preferred him, it seemed, to be a stay-at-home, a rustic, a mere farmer perhaps—in which case what chance would he have to aspire to the hand of a great lord's daughter, he the seventh son of an impoverished Fife laird?

David murmured something about France being a long way from the Braes of Angus and scarcely conducive to successful courtship.

France was necessary for him, Beaton insisted. He had gone there of a set purpose, as the swiftest road to influence. He was proficient at languages and France was the key to the struggle between the Empire and the Vatican, and England too. Much that would affect Scotland was to be decided in France—as indeed he had proved. It had been only for a year or two—and Marion was young. But she had been against it.

David observed sagely that women had their own peculiar viewpoints, and they left it at that.

It was a mere twenty or so miles' ride to Finavon, out of the valley of the Isla and over the moors of Kinnordy and Kirriemuir to that of the South Esk, which seemed to indicate that it was important and prolonged business which occupied the Lord Ogilvy there, since he could have ridden that distance and back in one day easily enough.

Finavon Castle was a big place and very fine, but not particularly strongly sited nor strategically placed to be the principal seat of one of the greatest nobles in the realm. Indeed it was strange that the Earls of Crawford should have chosen to live here in Angus at all, considering the vast estates and properties they owned all over the kingdom, particularly in Clydesdale—from which they took their title—Lothian and Fife. But nearby Glen Esk was one of the best hunting forests in the land and moreover, apt to be comfortably out of the way of most of the upheavals which so frequently disturbed Scotland.

The Earl proved to be a burly individual in his mid-sixties, heavy and slow of speech but amiable enough—although clearly a little disconcerted by this unexpected visit of the two young men on the Regent's behalf. He had assembled at Finavon, as well as Marion's father—a pleasantly genial and handsome man—a number of other Ogilvy and Lindsay barons and lairds from the area, and fairly obviously this was no mere hunting party or social gathering.

David found himself in the odd position of being accorded more respect than was his companion, partly no doubt because he was the King's Procurator but more likely because he was a Lindsay, son of the quite renowned Sir David of Garleton and a kinsman of the Lord Patrick, second in the Lindsay hierarchies. However, Beaton, his assurance most patently fully recovered, quickly came to the point of the visit and proceeded, whilst being suitably courteous to the Earl and the other seniors, to take charge of the situation.

At table in the huge hall Beaton declared that he had come directly from and on behalf of the Duke of Albany, to whom he was acting as secretary and assistant. The Regent was concerned about rumours that the Earl of Angus was drumming up support in this north-east of Scotland for a treasonable attempt on the person of the King, contrary to the expressed will of parliament. The Duke, well aware of the undoubted loyalty of the Earl of Crawford, the Lord Ogilvy and others here, believed that they were the obvious magnates to counter any such shameful preparations and hereby called upon them to take every possible step to maintain the authority of the King, the Regent, and parliament in these parts.

This announcement produced a certain uneasy stir amongst his hearers, and the young man proceeded to make it more uneasy still by asserting that the Regent and Chancellor expected the present reliably trustworthy company to keep them well informed as to the whereabouts, movements and probable intentions of the said Earl of Angus and his Douglas associates and allies in treason. Indeed, they had heard just a hint that Angus himself might conceivably be considering a visit in person to those very parts in the immediate future to try to enlist aid for his wicked cause; and part of his, and David Lindsay's, mission was to warn them of this dire possibility.

David swallowed, this being the first that he had heard of it; but he perceived that Beaton had guessed that this gathering might well in fact have been convened for the very purpose of meeting Angus—as had occurred to himself—and was taking a chance.

No one actually said anything although many glances were exchanged.

With seemingly complete innocence of any disquiet caused, the other went on to declare that the Regent had some eight thousand men assembled and ready to embark on shipping at Leith to sail up to this Angus coast and be here in a couple of days if need be, for the reinforcement and support of the loyal forces in the putting down of treasonable activities and the punishment of all evil-doers. Their lordships had only to call for help . . .

Their lordships duly considered that information, however imaginative in its content, features thoughtful.

By the time that Davie Beaton was finished, nobody there was in any doubt that support for the Earl of Angus would be a highly inadvisable policy, that the Regent was already very well-informed, and that treason, a word which had cropped up half a dozen times, with all its dire implications as to capital punishment, would be the charge levelled against all so involved. Oddly, it was only as it were by chance and at the end that a vital fact slipped out from the other side, when David Ogilvy of Inverquharity observed that if the Queen-Mother already had the young King in her keeping and was conveying him to England, as was reported, how could a charge of high treason against the monarch be sustained against supporters of the Queen-Mother's husband?

Swiftly Beaton rounded on the speaker. Who so reported? The King was secure in the Regent's keeping in the castle of Stirling—they had left him there but the day before. Treason was deliberate action against the King in parliament, the supreme authority in this realm. And what was this talk of England? Was Margaret Tudor not here with her husband, in the north-east?

If this tacit admission on Beaton's part that he was not quite so well-informed as he pretended registered with his hearers, it was not sufficient to affect their greater concern that young James was not in fact in his mother's hands, as clearly they had assumed to be the case and as presumably Angus was putting out. Crawford made one of his few contributions, asserting that their information was that the Queen-Mother was in the Borders with the Lord Home, indeed at Home of Blackadder's house, if she had not already crossed into England—as they believed, with the King's Grace.

Beaton recovered his composure admirably, declaring that all this was but a typical example of Angus's lies and duplicity. The King was safe, and if Margaret Tudor was not with her husband but in England so much the better for Scotland, and so much the weaker Angus's treasonable cause, as all must perceive.

David was surprised thereafter to hear his friend announce that they must be on their way back to Stirling and Edinburgh forthwith, that the Duke of Albany could only spare his own humble services for the four days required to come up here and warn and reassure their lordships and loyal subjects of His Grace. Also Lindsay of the Mount had to get back to His Grace's side, as his Procurator.

If this sudden departure seemed at all strange to the company assembled, relief at so expeditiously getting rid of awkward guests overbore it quite. No impediments were put in their way.

As they rode away from Finavon in mid-afternoon, however, David thought that he was entitled to an explanation. Surprised, the other said that it should be obvious. They did not want to be caught at Finavon if Angus arrived—and it looked, to say the least, probable that he was expected at any time. And also it was vital that he got this information about Margaret Tudor back to Edinburgh just as quickly as possible. It could be very important. If instead of being up here, as had been supposed, the woman was in the Borders with Home and Home was in collusion with Dacre the English Warden, and if it was all carefully planned and timed, as seemed likely, then they might well have an invasion on their hands at any moment, King Henry's strategy working out. In that case there could be thrusts on two fronts, Home and the English from the south and Angus from the north—and possibly even the mercurial Arran from the west. The sooner he was at Holyrood Abbey the better as far as Davie Beaton was concerned.

His companion thought that all this was a lot to build up out of what they had learned but did not labour the point with this so assured character.

Beaton was certainly in earnest about the need for haste, and they reached St John's Town of Perth before halting for the night. And, keeping up the pace next day, David decided to display a little initiative and self-assertion on his own part. With the ramparts of Stirling Castle rearing before them as they cantered down into the Forth valley, he informed his companion that he would accompany him on to Edinburgh and then proceed to Garleton. After all, nobody at Stirling would expect them back so soon, after a journey to the north-east. It was an opportunity to pay a much called for visit to his home. Beaton, with no reason to object, said that he would be glad of the continued company. So they rode on past Stirling, David feeling both guilty and elated.

They spent the second night at Linlithgow and by midday following reached Edinburgh, horses sorely tired. David would have headed on at once for East Lothian, but Beaton urged that it would be sensible to visit Holyrood first for news.

At the abbey they learned that word of the Queen-Mother's whereabouts had already reached Albany, from Border sources, that she had indeed been taken to Blackadder in the Merse by Home, but was now understood to be at Dacre's castle of Harbottle in Northumberland awaiting the birth of her child by Angus. Where Home himself was now, unfortunately, was not clear. That he had taken Margaret Tudor to Dacre's house was highly significant, of course. He perhaps remained there, plotting with Dacre; or he might have returned to Scotland. There was a suggestion that Angus was expected at Harbottle for his wife's lying-in, presumably coming by sea from north-east Scotland, but this might be no more than guesswork and rumour. At any rate, the Regent had taken certain precautions. He had signed an edict removing Home from the office of Chief Warden of the Marches and appointed the Sieur de la Bastie in his place, sending him back to Dunbar Castle and from there ordering him to mount a concerted assault on the Home strengths in the Merse, one after another, in a determined campaign to dispose of this menace once and for all.

De la Bastie could call on most of Albany's forces based in the Edinburgh area if need be.

Neither David nor Beaton was happy about this appointment of Antoine, much as they both admired him—not as Warden of the Marches, that is. A Frenchman as good as governor of the entire Border region would not be popular—even though he was probably the best military commander available. However, it was too late to change it now, although the appointment would have to be confirmed by the next parliament.

The suggestion that Angus might join his wife for her confinement was interesting, in present circumstances. If so it would mean that any trial of strength was likely to be postponed until after the birth—which would provide a welcome breathing space. But would he do it, a man not notable for thoughtfulness? Leave his mustered forces in the north-east to make the sea journey, and for an indefinite period, childbirth being notoriously unpredictable? He might, in order to concert plans personally with Home and Dacre. And, after all, the infant to be produced would be his first-born, and, if a boy, heir to all the Douglases, Master of Angus and third in line to the throne of England.

With these thoughts preoccupying his mind, David resumed his journey to East Lothian. They did not predominate for long however—not with Kate Lindsay ahead.

He rode straight to the Byres. His father and Mirren, at Garleton, could wait. David Beaton's involvement with Marion Ogilvy at Airlie and what seemed to him like the mishandling and non-success of that affair, had had quite a major effect on him, teaching him a lesson—or so he conceived. Clearly the diffident, tentative approach was not the right one for spirited young women—and Kate was sufficiently spirited he had no doubts. The firm and decisive attitude, not exactly masterful but as of a man knowing his own mind—as became, for instance, the King's Procurator—was called for, he felt.

At the Byres he could scarcely complain of his welcome, with the Lady Isabella greeting him warmly, the Lord Patrick, new back from Dunbar where he had been replaced by de la Bastie, genially avuncular, and the heir to the house, John, Master of Lindsay, on one of his infrequent visits from Pitcruivie in Fife, in back-slapping high spirits, his wife Eliza effusive. But it did mean that in front of all this amiably exclamatory company his meeting with Kate had to be much more casual and restrained than he had visualised, a quick embrace and chaste kiss being as much as the situation permitted. That she was looking lovelier than ever, and seemingly serenely self-possessed, did not help.

Thereafter frustration grew as, try as he would, he failed to arrange that they could be alone together. Always somebody was present, usually two or three, with endless talk about King Jamie, the Regent, Angus, the present ominous state of affairs, the situation in the north-east, the folly of de la Bastie's appointment as Warden of the Marches, and so on. Kate, in fact, seemed to be the least interested in all this, and so absented herself frequently from the discussion, to David's distraction. Unfortunately, it was a miserably chill day of early October with a thin drizzle of rain drifting in off the Norse Sea, precluding any suggestion of a companionable walk or ride together.

David found himself wondering, sourly, how Beaton would have coped with this? He decided, however, that Kate was not only more beautiful than Marion Ogilvy but even more satisfactorily rounded in places where it mattered, and with a readier smile.

It was not until early evening, the meal over at last, and David getting desperate, that Lady Isabella, informed by one of the maid-servants that a further supply of fish would be required for the morrow's breakfast was instructing her where to find the icehouse key and what fish to abstract when Kate volunteered to go instead, knowing better what was required. David all but knocked over his chair in his haste to offer escort for her to the icehouse—which he knew was dug into a grassy bank of the outer walled garden—to the grins of the company.

"I thought . . . that we were never . . . going to be able . . . to be alone!" he gasped, as he closed the door behind them.

"Alone?" she echoed innocently. "You want us to be alone for some reason, Davie?"

"Lord—of course I do! I have been trying to get you to myself ever since I came, Kate. For a little. But always others were there . . ."

"Why? Have you something to tell me? Show me? A new poem, perhaps? To recite . . . ?"

"No. Or, well, I *am* writing some verses about the King's papingo—a parrot which David Beaton brought him from France. But . . ."

"A parrot? Have you nothing better to write about than that?"

"No. Yes. That is not what I want to talk about, Kate. It is important. I . . . where are you going now?"

"To get the icehouse key. My mother keeps it with her other keys in this aumbry. We keep the icehouse locked, otherwise much meat and fish might be stolen. Do you not, at Garleton?"

"I daresay. But—we must talk. I have so much to tell you, my dear . . ."

"Good. And so you shall." She detached a quite large iron key from a sort of hoop linked to a chatelaine's leather girdle on which were many other keys, and handed it to David. "You take this. I will get a basket for the fish. And perhaps a platter too, for we could do with some more venison whilst we are there . . ."

So presently he found himself burdened with a wicker basket and a large and heavy earthenware platter as well as the key. "Where are you going now?" he demanded, almost plaintively.

"To get a cloak, stupid! It is raining."

Out into the damp evening they went then, and any idea of a romantic arm in arm or even waist-encircling progress was inhibited by the man's laden state and a flapping cloak. She led the way through the pleasance and the orchard, under dripping trees, to the outer herb, fruit and vegetable garden within its high walls, in a corner of which was a grassy mound, part of the natural lift of the land towards the Garleton Hill, which had been excavated to form an underground icehouse. On top was a rustic bower, or arbour, roofed and seated. It had been that bower which had been at the back of the man's mind all along.

Taking the key, Kate opened the heavy, creaking door. Chilly as the evening already was, the shock of cold air met them immediately. It was dark in there, as well as cold, as the girl moved inside, but she obviously knew just where everything was and called in David with the platter and basket after her.

The place was like a long cavern, quite extensive, lined with stone and vaulted as to roof, stacked waist-high on each side with boxes filled with ice, this renewed each winter from the shallow curling ponds and which, hidden in the earth here from sun and summer warmth, retained the required chill throughout most years. On top of the iceboxes were laid trays of meats and fish, sides of beef and mutton and venison, hams, poultry and wildfowl.

The idea of being holed up there in the dark close to Kate had been alluring—but the breath-catching cold and the smells were sufficient to counteract any such effects. Giving three stiff salmon for his basket and taking a solid haunch of roe-venison for herself, Kate pushed past him and out without any lingering.

When she had locked the door again, clutching his fish, David looked upwards. "We could talk in that bower," he suggested. And at the diffident note he himself could hear all too plainly in that, recollected his decision regarding firmness, and added much more strongly, more so perhaps than he realised, "Come—I have much to say to you."

She looked at him curiously. "It is not very warm for sitting outside," she said.

"Never heed. You will be well enough. Give me that meat."

"You are wonderfully fierce of a sudden, Davie! Is this how you treat your fine court ladies! That Mirren, and her like?"

"A plague on Mirren!" he declared, and began to climb up to the arbour. The wet grass proved slippery and weighed down as he was he all but fell twice, cursing under his breath. Even so he heard what in anybody else he would have described as a giggle, coming up behind.

In the wooden open-fronted arbour he dumped his fish and meat on the bench and turned, arms wide, to enfold the girl vehemently as she entered. The damp and voluminous cloak got rather in the way and, not anticipating this move and panting a little from the climb, she all but choked in his arms. Nevertheless her heaving, curvaceous and somewhat unsteady person was eminently claspable, even though the kiss he planted missed its exact target.

"Mary Mother!" she gasped. "What's to do, Davie Lindsay?"

"I . . . ah, sit down," he commanded.

She had to move the venison and salmon, and he had to do so again to make room beside her.

"I am very fond of you, Kate," he announced, strongly.

"Oh? Yes, I know," she agreed. "We have always been friends, have we not?"

"This is different. Kate—you understand? Different."

She stared at him. "What is different, Davie?"

"You. Myself. That was good enough, before. But now—you are not a child any more. A woman now. And I am a man. Wanting you!"

"Wanting . . . ?" Her voice faltered a little at that. Especially as he put his arm round her, or tried to do so, the heavy cloak no help.

"I mean *needing* you. Not just wanting. *You*. You only. As a woman—*my* woman. You and me, Kate!"

"Mercy!" She drew away somewhat, but not very far, for what with the viands and their containers there was not much spare room on that bench. "What has come over you, Davie?"

"Nothing. Or . . . perhaps everything! Do you not understand, girl? I *love* you! Love you, I tell you!"

"Oh—is that all!" Her relief was evident. In fact, she edged back closer. "That is nice, Davie."

It was his turn to stare, all but confounded. "Nice . . . ?" he got out thickly.

"Yes. Very nice. I have always wanted you to love me. You have taken a long time to say so! Why? Were you not sure, before?"

Quite put off his stride, as it were, he shook his head. "You . . . you mean this? You want it? Me? You love me, too?"

"To be sure. I have always loved you, Davie. Ever since I was little. You know that."

"But . . ." He could not, somehow, accept this as it sounded. "I mean *love*, Kate—real love. Not just affection, fondness. Love, the love of a man for a woman."

"Yes, oh yes. That is my sort of love, also. I am glad that you have come round to it, at last, Davie."

Still he found her attitude beyond him, his fine authority

and initiative eroded. "I am not sure . . . that you understand me, lass," he said, as though choosing his words with care. "This love, it is not just something which has grown out of childhood fondness, see you. It is deep, strong, from the heart, for all time, man and woman choosing each other . . ."

"And talking a great deal?" she interrupted, with a little laugh. "I did not think that there would be so many words about it all!" And she snuggled up closer.

He swallowed. "Kate! Kate!" was all that he could find to reply.

She unfastened her cloak at the neck and threw it back at his side. "See you, it is cold in here, Davie. This cloak is quite large. Room for us both in it. We will be warmer this way." And she tucked part of the velvet-lined cloak about him, her arm remaining thereafter round his waist.

The initiative might not be his, after all, but he was not the man to neglect such opportunity. He drew her to him and found her lips without any trouble, parting them after a moment or two.

They dispensed with words for a while, sighs and little moans serving very well.

When, presently, they paused for breath, he was not to be silenced, however. "My dear, my very dear!" he panted. "This is joy, beyond all belief! You are delicious, adorable, and I want you, need you, ache for you. But, but . . ."

"But what, Davie? Do I fail you in some way? Are your court ladies more, more adept? Or . . . ?"

"Lord, Kate—do not say such a thing! You are worth all of them together, and more. You are all delight, all loveliness. It is but that I am . . . afraid. Afraid that you may mistake. May not see this of love as I do. You are young, you see . . ."

"I am seventeen. You just said, back there, that I was a woman now. And I am, never fear!" And reaching down for his arm, around her, she took his hand and raised it to cover, or almost, her full and rounded breast. "Is it not so?"

He could not speak for a little, so moved was he. And when he did find words, it was not to argue the matter.

"My love! My heart! My precious! Oh Kate!" he got out.

"That is better," she nodded. "As to age, you know, I

think that I am older than you are. Not in years but otherwise. I think that all women are."

"Indeed!" But he was not going to argue that one either, not with his hand where it still was, her nipple prominent between his finger and thumb. "Will . . . will you wed me, Kate?" he asked abruptly.

"To be sure. I wondered when you would bring yourself to ask!"

Again she had him silenced. Anyway, words seemed distinctly superfluous in this encounter. They came together again by mutual consent in vehement and comprehensive embrace—so comprehensive that somehow David's other hand found itself inside the girl's bodice and most happy to be there, as well it might be, and apparently welcome.

So they sat within that cloak, whilst the rain pattered on the roof and dripped around them, cold like time forgotten. Such speech as intervened was inconsequential.

That is, until Kate suddenly sat up. "When, Davie?" she demanded.

"When . . . ?"

"Yes, when? When shall we be wed?"

"Oh. Well—we shall have to think on that. I do not rightly know. I have not considered that . . ."

"Not considered! You say that!"

"My dear—how could I tell? I could not be sure . . . you might not . . ."

"How soon, then?"

He shook his head. "I do not know. Much will have to be considered. The times are difficult. The King's service . . ."

"Davie—you are not going to make excuses?"

"No, no. But placed as I am, I am scarcely my own master. And we may be into war, at any time. Would you wish us to start our married life shut up in Stirling Castle?"

"Why not? So long as we are together. As well there as any."

"Well . . . sakes, lassie—do not think that I would delay a day longer than need be! Lord—I want you, Kate, want you *now*! Not, not just some day . . ." This assertion promptly led to further urgent embracing and the postponement of less immediate considerations meantime.

After some indefinite lapse of time, Kate recollected that her family might have been expecting them back somewhat before this. They started up, almost guiltily on David's part—although guilt was not something with which Kate was much concerned—and were half down the slope before they remembered the salmon and venison and key, and had to go back. The man retained sufficient of his wits to reflect that it was probably seldom that comestibles played so prominent a part in the manifestation of true love.

Back in the castle, Kate forestalled any criticism or sly comment by announcing outright even as they handed over the viands, that she and Davie were now betrothed to wed, and was it not splendid? David, embarrassed anyway, was a little perturbed, believing it customary for the man to have to seek the father's permission before any such declaration was made. However, none of the company appeared to find anything unsuitable or even surprising about the announcement, taking it almost as though it had been inevitable—which set David wondering, as he responded suitably to the congratulations.

Leaving Kate that night was a protracted and grievous business, and it was late indeed before he got up to Garleton Castle, to an uproar of barking dogs, a sleepily protesting gatehouse porter, and his father and Mirren, wakened from the same bed but quite unembarrassed about it now, accusing him of thoughtlessness. It was much later still before he slept, his mind busy with so much. Only very minor amongst the recurring thoughts was the question of how effective had been his firm and decisive stance in the matter of dealing with women? Whether in fact the decisions had been all, or mainly, on his part? How much, indeed, had he improved on Davie Beaton's performance.

More vital considerations had no difficulty in imposing themselves.

11

Although the wedding was seldom far from David's mind in the weeks and months that followed, events succeeded each other so consistently, often impinged on each other, and even if they did not always actually involve himself were so apt to involve those with whom he was connected, that marriage seemed out of the question meantime. Indeed, once he had returned to Stirling, two days after that especial October night, he did not see Kate again for a considerable time.

First, there was the news that after a distressing and prolonged labour Magaret Tudor had had her child, a daughter; and that Angus had indeed been present and was said to be grievously disappointed that it was not a son and heir. This in itself was not very important as far as Scotland was concerned, but its repercussions were. King Henry made a great show of congratulating his sister, sending her gifts by the hand of a special ambassador, and took the opportunity to announce that this child, his niece, born on English soil, was henceforth under his personal royal protection and must not be removed out of his domains. Clearly she was to be used as a hostage, both for her mother's co-operation and for Angus's obedience and support. Angus, however, whether in defiance, pique or just his disappointment, abandoned his wife and child promptly and returned to Scotland. Reliable reports had it that he had not gone back to his assembled forces in the north-east but, of all things, had headed westwards to join Arran at Hamilton.

This greatly alarmed the Regent and the Chancellor for their greatest fear was always of a concerted attack by the hosts of the three former members of the Regency Council, Angus, Arran and Home. Hitherto there had never seemed much likelihood of Angus and Arran collaborating, the Douglases and the Hamiltons ever being at daggers drawn.

But this new move of Angus, if accurate, was ominous, especially as Home was known to be assembling his strength in the Borders.

Albany decided to counter this threat by direct action, and ordered his Warden of the Marches to proceed to the immediate arrest of the Lord Home, as warning to the other two. Since de la Bastie would require considerably greater strength than he had based on Dunbar Castle for this formidable task, part of the force kept permanently assembled at Edinburgh was detached; and since this included the Lindsay contingent, David was sent for from Stirling to take charge of this, no doubt at Davie Beaton's suggestion. Unfortunately, speed and secrecy for the operation being essential and David having to come from Stirling, the Edinburgh force was well on its way to Dunbar by the time that he reached Holyrood, and he had to go riding hard after it, without any opportunity to call in at the Byres.

It was good, at least, to be on active service again, and a pleasure to see Antoine once more. There was little time for companionable association however. Nothing was surer than that Home would hear of this armed force coming to Dunbar, well-informed as he must be in this area. So actual surprise would be well-nigh impossible. It behoved them, therefore, to gain surprise by contriving something which Home would not expect. De la Bastie saw it thus. Such a large force coming to Dunbar would be almost certainly aimed at the Homes, since Tantallon was all but impregnable and anyway the Douglas presence hereabouts was much muted these days. So what would Home anticipate? An attack on himself, at Home Castle, which would demand many men and considerable artillery since it was a strong place and surrounded by lesser Home strengths? This was the last thing that Antoine wanted to tackle. But suppose instead they made a gesture of assaulting Dunglass—as they had done before? It would be logical, the nearest Home stronghold to Dunbar—and they had already put nearby Colbrandspath out of action. What would Home do, known to be mustering his Merse forces? He would have to do something, or lose all credit with his own people. Almost certainly he would come to the relief of Dunglass. The problem was, would he come in person, or send others? They wanted the man himself, not some lieutenant—and if possible, without a battle. Antoine believed that if he, de la Bastie, made himself prominent in the Dunglass attack, and made at the same time loud claims that he, as new Warden of the Marches, was going to demonstrate how feeble and ineffective was the previous Warden, Home would be almost bound to respond personally. So—an ambush on the way! When the man was protected by no castle walls.

David agreed that this was sound reasoning. But how could an ambush be successful if Home came with a large force, as surely he would?

Antoine had an answer for that, too; a two-fold answer. The narrow passes and constrictions of Pease Dean, as they had seen, ensured that any company proceeding towards Dunglass from the south must inevitably be stretched out into little more than double-file for almost a couple of miles—that was why Colbrandspath Tower was sited there. The Homes would send scouts ahead to ensure a clear passage undoubtedly; but if the ambushing force was well hidden in the high woodland above, leaving the track free, with timber felled and ready to roll down on the vital part of the elongated column in front and rear, cutting off the leadership group from the rest, then the thing might be achieved at comparatively little cost. Especially if prior to that another contingent was to work its way secretly down through these Lammermuir hills, to come into the Merse from the north-west and appear to be menacing Home Castle. This ought to have the affect of causing Home, assuming that he was indeed with the Dunglass relief force, to send back some part of his strength to the aid of his main seat, so weakening and confusing his strategy.

David was lost in admiration for this elaborate planning but saw not a few points where it could go wrong—and said so. Antoine admitted that this, of course, was so; but basically it was a sound projection, he thought, and militarily valid—for even if it failed in any or all of its aspects, nothing should prove disastrous for their own forces. And David was not forgetting that de la Bastie was one of the most experienced military figures in Christendom.

Without delay, then, the plans were put into operation. The available manpower, including many of the Dunbar townsfolk and fishermen who had co-operated in the previous Dunglass gesture, was divided into three units: one for the distant Home Castle, in the Merse; one for Dunglass itself; and the vital ambushing party for Pease Dean—the two latter to keep together meantime. The Merse contingent, under Sir Adam Hepburn from Luffness, was sent off as soon as it could be got ready that very night, to proceed as far as they could under cover of darkness on their roundabout, thirty-mile journey through the hills. A proportion of the rest were allowed to go roystering in the town, making no secret of the fact that they were bound for Dunglass in the morning—in the confident hope that Home would be apprised of it all almost by the time that they got there.

Not too early next day, and in no great hurry, with sundry cannon to trundle along behind, the quite large force made its way along the coast road south-eastwards the eight miles to Dunglass. As anticipated, when they arrived at the castle it was to find the Home garrison ready and waiting for them, battlements manned, drawbridge up and cannon mounted—indeed a couple of shots were fired at them as warning to keep their distance. Which was all as planned.

Antoine brought up their own artillery to give an answering salvo. But since the cannon on both sides had approximately the same calibre and range, and casualties were not the objective, all remained sensibly at arm's length, content to sound belligerent. Whilst this was going on and the besieging troops were satisfactorily positioned, Antoine and David rode quietly off alone for Pease Dean with prospecting to do, which it was important should not be obvious.

It all reminded them of the previous occasion. But this time they had a different problem. They sought what might not be easy to find, a place well above one of the narrowest sections of the track through the dean, sufficiently well-wooded to both hide a large number of men and to provide tree-trunks to fell and roll down, yet with the slope below steep and clear enough of trees not to impede the downward course of the rolled logs. In well over a mile of the twisting ravine, with the track traversing both flanks, there ought to be some such place?

It took them a good couple of hours to find, at the far south-eastern end of the pass, which was not ideal; and even here some clearing of the slope would be necessary—and such clearance would have to remain imperceptible. On the other hand there was the benefit that here were quite a number of large boulders and rock fragments scattered about which would serve as additional missiles if dug out.

They returned to Dunglass, from which the occasional boom of cannon had been resounding, to wait until dusk. Darkness would certainly not facilitate their task, but it was vitally important that no hint of their activities in the dene should be disclosed. How much time they had was a matter of guesswork—but then, to some extent, the entire exercise was that anyway. They reckoned that to give time for the news to reach Home Castle for a relieving force to be readied—a muster was already reported—and for this to make its way up this far would take most of two days. That is, from the previous night. The Mersemen, like all Borderers, were great horsemen, mosstroopers, and once mounted would cover the ground quickly.

With campfires being lit and the shadows of evening cloaking the withdrawal of the ambush party, they set out, armed with axes, mattocks and ropes as well as their weapons, all on foot. They could follow the road for a mile or so but after that must take to the higher rough ground, to avoid being observed by cottagers, and this made for very difficult progress in the darkness, amongst trees and broken terrain, with muffled cursing as accompaniment. There was no great hurry, however.

It was even difficult to find their chosen spot at night although they had marked it carefully earlier. But eventually Antoine and David were satisfied, and they could get to work. Tree fellers went to chop and lop and trim, well behind the terrace area selected for the launching of the attack, and teams of men dragged the trunks down to position them on the very lip of the steep, held in place by wedges of small stones. Others dug up and rolled rocks and boulders and poised these similarly—this activity at two points about one hundred yards apart, leaving a gap. At least there was plenty of manpower for the labour.

The two leaders were particularly careful about the next phase of the work, superintending all of it personally. The steep bank below their terrace had to be cleared of anything large enough to obstruct the hurtling logs and missiles; but such clearance must not be visible from the track in daylight. There were two or three major trees which could not be disposed of without leaving an obvious scar, and these would have to be left, hopefully; but it was mostly small scrub hawthorn and bushes which could be cut away and the branches and leafage then arranged, to look natural. Fortunately, being October, the foliage was sear and brown anyway.

This all took a deal longer, in the darkness, than might have been expected, and there was more noise than desirable—although nobody was likely to be lurking about Pease Dean during the night. It was almost dawn before de la Bastie was satisfied and the men could take some rest, sleep if they could.

With daylight there was more to be done, chilled as they were, and it all had to be effected most discreetly and silently in case of there being anybody abroad to observe. Assault positions had to be allocated, mostly high above the track but some below it, well out of sight, should there be any breakaway in that direction. Also some men down on the road itself but westwards a little way, towards Dunglass. Then there were lookouts to post, up on the high flank of Eweside Hill, where they could see for miles down the Eye Water valley, the almost certain approach route for any fast-moving company from the Merse.

All this done, they settled down to wait, with strictest orders to all groups to remain hidden from the road and make no noise. Now was the time to catch up on the night's missing sleep. Antoine and David remained with the main high-placed party, about one hundred and fifty strong.

All day they waited, and as the hours passed began to fret. By the time that the autumnal sun was sinking behind the Lammermuir heights to their west, they were worried. Had they miscalculated? Had the required information not reached Home Castle? Or was Lord Home away? Or could he possibly be taking a different route to Dunglass? Through the hills, as they had sent Hepburn, much slower as this would be? Or was he not coming at all, leaving Dunglass to its fate?

By late afternoon Antoine was sufficiently concerned to send a runner up to the lookout position on Eweside Hill, to ensure that the men there had not all fallen asleep or otherwise failed in their duty; but he came back presently to declare that there was no failure up there and that despite the far-flung and all-round prospect, the watchers had seen nothing to report all day.

They were reconciling themselves to the spending of another uncomfortable, hungry and probably wasted night in their hiding places when, with dusk falling fast, a panting, breathless man came bounding and slithering down through the woodland from Eweside. They were coming, he gasped, nearly there indeed. Not coming up the Eye Water as expected, but from the higher ground of Coldingham Muir, due eastwards. A large mounted company, perhaps three hundred or more. Only come into sight of Eweside as they topped the rise by Auldcambus, not much more than a mile away.

Antoine did not wait to hear more, leaping up to shout orders, alerting all and sending messengers racing to warn the outlying units. If the Homes were only a mile away when this man left Eweside Hill, they were less than half that now.

The runners were hardly away and the others hurrying to their action position when David held up a hand. Clearly to be heard was the drumming of distant hooves.

"On us already!" he exclaimed.

Antoine shook his head. "Not many," he jerked. "No large number of horses, there. And going fast. Scouts."

"Aye—that will be it. Home will well know the dangers of this pass, and will be sending scouts through first, to ensure that all is clear. Sakes—I hope . . . !"

The Frenchman nodded grimly. "That none of our people down there attack such scouts! Then all would be lost. They have their orders, but . . ."

There was no time to do anything more about it. Round a bend in the track below came a tight group of about a dozen horsemen, two-abreast, cantering. It was fairly deep shadow down there now, but it was possible to see that they were in half armour, with typical Borderers' helmets and lances.

"No—pray that none challenge them!" David muttered.

But quickly the riders were past the area directly below where the lowermost ambush party were hidden, ensconced behind the trees and cover that was not only to protect them from view but from any boulders and logs which might overshoot their target. Pounding round the next bend in the track, they were no longer visible.

"We shall soon hear if the far party halt them!" Antoine said.

They heard only the hoof beats drumming on, the sound gradually fading. The listeners heaved sighs of relief.

"Home is no fool," David declared. "He came by a roundabout route we did not think on. And he prospects this Pease Dean before entering. But—coming at this hour? You think that he did this of a purpose? To arrive at Dunglass with the dark? To surprise us? Assault by night?"

"It looks so. Some hundreds of cavalry riding down a resting camp in the darkness could make much havoc, cause panic. It could be. Clearly we must not underestimate my lord of Home!"

In a few minutes they heard hoofbeats again, but this time in still lesser volume. Then two horsemen appeared from the west, below, at the gallop now, obviously the scouting party's messengers sent back to advise Home that the pass was clear.

Now—an end to this long waiting.

They stood poised. They heard hooves once more, but different now, many, many, but not drumming, pounding, the jingling of harness and the clank of mail, even the murmur of voices. Antoine had his horn at the ready.

The problem now was the lack of light; the track was deeper than ever in shadow. And it was vital to identify the leadership group as the company filed through—or all their effort could be for naught.

In the event, there was no real difficulty for, after a short column of perhaps a score of mosstroopers had trotted past, a smaller party rounded that bend—and these rode under banners, one large and three less so. None in that cohort was likely to display a great banner save the Lord Home himself. Admittedly the devices on the flags could not be distinguished; but the chances of them being anything but the white ramping lion on green of Home were remote indeed.

"Ha! Pride of birth can prove a weakness," de la Bastie commented. "Now—another few lengths, and then . . . !" With the banner group directly below Antoine blew a single long blast on his horn.

Immediately all was changed, dramatically, violently. Men leapt up to knock away the wedges holding the piled tree-trunks and boulders and to push them over the lip of the slope, to go hurtling down the steep and to keep up the process from the stacks collected—this at the two ends of the hundred-yard gap. Down and down the great logs and rocks plunged and bounded, and on the track alarmed horsemen, staring upwards, reacted urgently, wildly and differently, some rearing their mounts to a curveting halt, some spurring ahead, some reining round and back and even down the farther slope, in utter chaos.

On and on the bombardment of deadly missiles continued, to crash down on the road and beyond, carrying away horses and riders in flailing, yelling disaster at both ends of the gap, but mainly at the southern end where by far the largest concentration of logs had been stacked, stretching towards that bend round which new files of horsemen were appearing to tangle with their fellows who had turned back in dire disorder. And in the middle, isolated in the gap, the banner party circled and huddled and struggled with their terrified horses, cut off front and rear by the smashing cataracts of wood and stone and soil.

Judging his moment, Antoine blew another two quick blasts—this for a few selected trees and boulders to be sent down, spaced in the hundred-yard gap itself, since he did not want the leaders there to reckon themselves to be safe and so have time to recover initiative and seek control of the situation. Nor, however, did he want them, Home himself in especial, to be killed or maimed, so these missiles went off singly and intermittently, allowing time for some avoiding action on the track below.

The Home banner party broke up necessarily and satisfactorily, some hastily dismounting to take refuge down the farther bank and behind trees.

Again assessing the timing heedfully, the Frenchman blew his third signal, three long blasts. And all his people, save for small groups at the two extreme ends who still continued with the bombardment, flung themselves down the slope, swords and dirks drawn, in a tide of yelling humanity, leaping and sliding, David and Antoine with them. At the same time the men from below the road showed themselves and came clambering up to play their part.

It was, at this stage, almost inevitable success, there being no escape for the leaders who were outnumbered ten to one. Most were now on foot amongst the milling horses, and although some put up a token resistance, it was only that. The Lord Home, stocky, grizzled, impassive-seeming, stood, arms folded, in a dignified silence.

Whilst all but a few of the attackers swung left and right to man the barriers of wood and debris which had piled up on and about the shelf which carried the road, to prevent any rallying of the mosstroopers to their lord's aid, Antoine came and bowed courteously, if somewhat breathlessly, to Home.

"I trust that you suffered no hurt, my lord, in this unseemly ambuscade?" he enquired. "It has been lacking in finesse, shall we say? But it is the fortunes of war—since war you appear to have chosen!"

"I would not call this war, Frenchman!" the older man said. "What now?"

"If you will remount, my lord, we shall seek quiet and our evening meal. At Dunglass. No doubt you have ridden far and will be anhungered?" As an afterthought, he added, "My lord Duke, the Regent, would like a word with you."

They found that they had captured the lairds of Wedderburn, Blackadder and Paxton also, these taking their fate less calmly than did their lord.

They collected sufficient horses to mount these four prisoners, David Lindsay and a small escort, and these would make their way downhill through the woodland to a small lower and winding path which led to a narrow ford beneath a waterfall of the Pease Burn and thence up to the main track again, further west by almost a mile. Thereafter it should be a clear ride to Dunglass. Antoine, like any good commander, would remain, to fight off any counter-attack by the mosstroopers which might develop—although such would be difficult to mount successfully in the circumstances—and then to extricate his force, up again through the higher woodlands as they had come, terrain where they ought to be safe from mounted harassment in the almost dark.

So David found himself acting captor to the former Lord High Chamberlain, chief Warden of the Marches and member of the Regency Council, and was less than comfortable in the role. But having gone to so much trouble to take their prisoners he was not going to risk losing them now, and maintained strictest control, with each of the four Homes' horses tied to one of their escort's. In fact, he experienced no trouble, and rode into the campfire-lit siege camp presently, at Dunglass, in some triumph, with the great banner of Home held upside-down.

It was almost two hours before de la Bastie arrived with his force, all in high spirits over their all but bloodless victory, having had little difficulty in persuading the leaderless and bemused mosstroopers that there was nothing to be gained by seeking to attack so potent a force of unknown numbers in the darkness and sloping woodland. These might come on in daylight, although this seemed not very likely.

At any rate, Antoine gave orders to pack up, to harness the cannon, break camp and march, there being nothing for them at Dunglass now. Leaving the fires blazing there, amidst a certain amount of confusion but in cheerful mood, the reunited host turned for its night march back along the coast road for Dunbar.

Next day, at the head of his Lindsay contingent again, David escorted his illustrious prisoners to Edinburgh, passing no nearer to Garleton and the Byres than the town of Haddington, to his much regret.

At Holyrood, handing over the Homes to Albany, he drew considerable praise from both the Regent and the Chancellor—and grins from Davie Beaton—despite his disclaimers that all the credit must go to de la Bastie. The older men appeared to imagine that he was proving to be some sort of military expert—of which, to be sure, Scotland was in all too great need—and would no doubt be useful again hereafter. A little worried about such false pretences, he rode on to Stirling the next day, escape to action over again for the meantime.

Eager as he was for movement, action, enlargement from the confines of Stirling Castle, David could hardly have been more surprised to receive a bare two weeks later a summons back to Edinburgh—or, at least, if not a summons a special courier from Davie Beaton requesting him to come forthwith on the realm's business, which in the circumstances amounted to the same thing. His surprise was the greater when, no details being vouchsafed, all he could elicit from the courier was that he imagined that it would be concerned with the matter of the disappearance of the Lord Home.

Leaving a tearful King James once more in the care of Abbot John, and to the Earl Marischal's disapproval, he set off, wondering.

Edinburgh he found more like an armed camp than ever, more men-at-arms everywhere. At Holyrood he was the recipient of an extraordinary story. Beaton, not in the least chagrined as might have been expected, indeed seeming almost amused at the sequence of events, mischances and apparent misjudgments, recounted it all. The Regent, thankful to have Home safely accounted for and advised that clemency would probably serve better than the mailed fist, at this stage, at least as far as the unpredictable and weak Arran was concerned, decided to try to detach the Hamilton from his new-found ally Angus and so isolate the latter and at least neutralise the second of the troublesome triumvirate. To this end he had prevailed on the Edinburgh city magistrates to dismiss the captive Home as their Lord Provost, an office he had held amongst so many others—the capital found it convenient to have great Lords as their chief magistrates in troubled times—and in his place to appoint the said Earl of Arran, Lord High Admiral. Sending Arran word of this, at Hamilton, with a gracious letter, Albany said that this was an excellent opportunity to settle their differences in a chivalrous fashion and let bygones be bygones, assuring him of safe conduct to Edinburgh and all good treatment thereafter. In token of which, and to demonstrate his good faith, he would then hand over to Arran the erring Lord Home, as a sort of hostage, to his safe keeping. And Arran had come, forthwith, had been installed as Lord Provost, and after an amicable meeting with the Regent had taken Home into his custody. And the very next day they both had left the city, secretly, and ridden post-haste for Hamilton, there to rejoin Angus. The Earls of Lennox and Glencairn had adhered to them there, and all five great lords had signed a band, or contract, to unite all their power to bring down the Regent. So now Albany was assembling the greatest army seen in Scotland since Flodden, to march on Hamilton.

David, needless to say, was appalled at this catalogue of folly and seeming incompetence, with all the good work at Pease Dean undone, wasted, the situation worse than before indeed, the three traitorous lords united and joined by two more. Was the Regent mad? For the first time, David questioned, although not in words, Beaton's shrewdness, since surely Albany would not have done all this contrary to his interpreter's and adviser's counsel?

But the other seemed nowise upset. The situation was now excellent, he asserted—all for the best. Albany was essentially a lazy man, he pointed out, despite his hot temper, much too prone to put off, to leave comparatively well alone. He had to be spurred into drastic action against these lords, military action on a major scale. It had to come to that in the end—to demonstrate who was strongest. Having Home taken prisoner was a useful move, a moral victory which must much decrease that proud noble's reputation in the Borders and amongst his own people. And by exercising clemency towards Arran, the Regent would gain a valuable card to play with parliament and the nation. But hitherto Arran had committed no real offence, nothing with which he could be charged or proceeded against lawfully. Now he had. He had set at large a prisoner of the crown and thus had laid himself open to an accusation of treason. He could, and must, be proceeded against. Moreover, all three highly placed rogues were now conveniently shepherded into a corner together, at Hamilton, and two others of doubtful loyalty now confirmed as traitors. The situation was simplified, the decks cleared.

David had his doubts about all this, but kept them to himself.

The army being assembled again on the Burgh Muir of Edinburgh—to march against the city's Lord Provost—was certainly large enough, Davie Beaton calculating that it would number between thirty and forty thousand all told. But how reliable it might be was another question and, to be sure, it was completely inexperienced as to warfare and less than unified, with constant bickering already breaking out and even bloodshed between the units of the various lords. David was interested to discover that the Lindsay force had been reinforced by almost three hundred and fifty from the Earl of Crawford, and two hundred others had come from the Lord Ogilvy of Airlie; so the visit to the north-east had not been fruitless.

The Lord Patrick arrived from the Byres to take charge of this contingent, with David as second-in-command—which in effect meant that whilst Kate's father rode comfortably with the Regent and other lords, her betrothed had to march on foot with the men. Not that David complained; it was all better than the constrictions of Stirling.

The foot set out on 25th October in crisp autumn weather, good for marching, with almost forty miles to go and three days to do it, to Hamilton in Clydesdale, a straggling, untidy column itself three miles long, this not counting the artillery which came along behind—and which, by the very nature of things was bound to be well known about at Hamilton long before it could get there; but this could not be helped. After a disorganised and delayed start they got only as far as Calder Muir, a mere dozen miles, the first day, all those men scarcely commending themselves to the countryside which they traversed, nor the areas in which they camped, a plague of scorpions sent to scourge them as the Prior of St Cuthbert of Calder picturesquely complained, involuntary host to many. The second day they did better, reaching Allanton on the South Calder Water, this on account of the thin drizzle of chill rain which discouraged delay and foraging; and there, at darkening, they were joined by the Regent and his entourage of nobles and knights, including of course Davie Beaton. Hamilton was only nine miles further, in the wide vale where the Clyde and Avon joined.

A somewhat noisy council of war was held, with too many advisers with scant experience of warfare taking part. David, to his embarrassment, found himself being appealed to for opinions, with his new-minted reputation as a military man, but contributed little other than to declare that while a show of strength with all this host encircling Hamilton town and Cadzow Castle was necessary and valuable, it would be folly to launch any sort of assault as was being suggested until the artillery came up. This was coming along at its usual oxen-paced trundle far behind, the mighty Mons Meg included; and although Cadzow might not be a great fortress to compare with Stirling, Dumbarton and Edinburgh, it could cost dear to take without cannon. This sensible advice did not commend itself to the firebrands loud in favour of martial flourish and knightly derring-do. Some there were unkind enough to suggest that the King's Procurator should stick to tutoring bairns, or even poetry.

However, Davie Beaton, always careful not to seem publicly to overstep his role as interpreter and secretary to the Regent, winked over at his friend in token that he at least got the point.

In the event his counsel turned out to be unnecessary and indeed the entire proceedings a distinct anticlimax for the vast majority, although Albany was probably pleased enough when in early afternoon the forerunners of the great host arrived at the Netherton of Hamilton and began to semi-encircle the town and its adjacent large castle of Cadzow—the presence of the River Clyde, broad and deep, immediately to the north making unnecessary any massing on that flank. While this was proceeding a large white flag was seen to be hoisted from the castle battlements, the drawbridge rattled down and a party rode out under a lesser white flag and a banner bearing gules, three cinquefoils ermine, for Hamilton. As this group neared the Regent's company, it could be seen to include a horse litter under a handsome heraldic canopy, the heraldry impaling the royal arms of Scotland with those of Hamilton.

All stared at this in some doubt.

Surprise was increased when, on closer view, the litter could be seen to contain the tiny figure of a very old woman, shrunken within a voluminous fur cloak yet sitting up straight with confidence and dignity. As this strange equipage came up, one of the attendant riders actually raised a trumpet and blew a resounding flourish, as though calling all to suitable and respectful attention.

The summons over, a voice, remarkably strong and authoritative to issue from such an ancient and withered female, said, "Which of you is John Stewart? Or Johan, as I understand he calls himself! Ah, you is it? So we meet, Nephew, at last."

Albany had understood enough of this to urge his horse forward to near the litter, and after a slight hesitation, to remove his velvet cap and to bow over the claw-like hand outstretched to him. "*Madame ma tante!*" he said. "*Je vous salue . . .*"

"Eh? Speak up, man! And speak so that I can understand you. Or, guidsakes—is it true that you can only speak the French? Alec's son!"

Discreetly Davie Beaton moved up and translated that.

"Who are you, young man?"

"The Chancellor's nephew, Countess. David Beaton, secretary."

"Ha! One of that penniless brood, frae Fife! At least you look as though you might hae mair wits than that turkey-cock of an uncle of yours. Or this Frenchified nephew of mine! And call me Highness, boy!"

"Certainly, Highness."

And Highness she undoubtedly was, as well as sounding it, the Princess Mary, daughter of James the Second, mother of Arran, through whom indeed James Hamilton had gained that title and earldom held by Thomas Boyd her first husband. Now in her eighties, she had been the sister of both James the Third and Alexander, Albany's father—and clearly none were to forget it.

The Regent was at something of a loss as to how to deal with his autocratic ancient relative, but the lady suffered no such problems.

"You, Davie Beaton—come nearer. I refuse to shout to you! Tell this silly son of my pig-headed brother that he must cease all this stupid bickering and marching about the country forthwith. He and my equally stupid son, both! There's been ower much of it and it's to stop! I have told James and now I tell this John. They are cousins and they will behave like cousins, for the realm's weal. Tell him so."

Beaton, bowing, conveyed an edited version of that to the Regent, who looked blank.

"Aye. Now, boy, tell him that I have a paper for him, back there. He will get it when he comes to eat his food. I got my fool James to sign it before I sent him off out of harm's way—no' that far, mind. He can be back in an hour or two—ooh, aye. He has signed that he'll be done with this nonsense, that he'll acknowledge this cousin of his as Regent, that he'll send a' those men of his back where they belong and keep the peace hereafter—a' that, so long as John Stewart does the same, takes a' this unseemly host out of my sight and signs a decent bond o' cousinly love and affection. Tell him."

Even Beaton swallowed at that, and was perhaps less diplomatic about his translation than usual. But Albany got the gist, blinked rapidly, and licked thin lips. He murmured something incoherent in French.

"What does he say, you Davie? Has he no' got even a decent *French* tongue in his heid?"

Actually the Regent had said nothing to the point but Beaton said it for him. "My lord Duke is . . . gratified, Highness. At your wisdom and good offices. But he would wish to know what may be the situation with regard to the Earl of Angus and the Lord Home? With whom, we understand, my lord of Arran has contracted a band against the Regent. And the Earls of Lennox and Glencairn, likewise?"

A pair of washed out blue but still keen old eyes considered him shrewdly. "Those limmers!" she said. "Och, I sent them off three days back. That Douglas is a trouble-maker, if ever I saw one! But then the Douglases aye were that, mind. Alecky Home is different—a fox! You'll have to watch that one—or this Johan will! But Archie Douglas will never come to much."

"Yes, Highness—no doubt." David Lindsay, listening nearby, noted that Beaton did not even trouble to translate all that. "But—where are they? Are they with my lord of Arran? Nearby?"

"Na, na—what do you take me for? I tell you, I sent them off. I'll have nae Douglases in *my* house! Nor Border thieves like the Homes, either. Angus has gone to Douglasdale. Whether Home is still with him, guid kens—but I jalouse he will be gone back to work on his ain Merse reivers, who will not have sae high an opinion of him, I'm thinking. After yon stramash when he was taken like a bairn on a chamber-pot in some dene or other! Lennox has returned to his Heilants—and guid riddance! And Glencairn to wherever he comes frae—Cunninghame, belike."

"So-o-o!" Belatedly, the younger man gave a summary of this to Albany, who clearly could scarcely believe his ears. He launched into a flood of dramatic-sounding verbiage, in which waving hands at least were eloquent.

"My lord Duke says that he appreciates your good efforts, Highness," Beaton told her, carefully selective. "He rejoices in your tidings. But can scarcely believe that this threat to the realm's peace could be so readily disposed of."

"Is that so? But then, he doesna ken his aunt! Mind—it isna right disposed of yet. He has to do *his* share, tell him. To sign a paper for James, *my* James, assuring him of all amity and guidwill. And James is to remain Admiral, see you—that is part of it. They will need to shake hands on it, the two o' them, before all is in order."

"And you, Madame, can ensure that my lord of Arran, the Lord High Admiral, can be here presently for this shaking of hands?"

"Och yes, laddie. I ken where he's at. He'll come—if I tell him. Now—tell my owerdressed nephew that there is meat and wine for him and his, ready in my hall. No' for ower many, mind—two hundred, at the maist." And without further ado, with a gesture to her trumpter who blew a single sustained note, she ordered her litter and escort to be turned round and to head back for Cadzow Castle, without so much as looking to see who followed.

In some little confusion the Regent and his entourage conferred and, since there seemed to be nothing else for it, to do as they were told. They rode on after the old lady, leaving orders for the vast host, with contingents still arriving and the artillery of course still far behind, just to camp where it was, as best it could. Beaton went to the trouble of urging David Lindsay, once he had seen to his men, to join him in the castle—and adding that, by what they had just heard and seen, it looked as though Scotland's troubles might be over and done with if only this old woman had been the Regent!

Cadzow was a fine and extensive castle, although no fortress citadel, and later, David sat down in a comparatively modest place in its huge hall, to an excellent repast, in cheerful, almost boisterous company, much tickled that where they had expected battle they found feasting instead. Nobody appeared to be worrying about the possibility of a surprise attack by Douglas forces.

The meal was almost over and the company getting ever noisier as the drink had its effect, when there was a diversion up at the dais end of the hall. The Earl of Arran himself came clanking in, dressed in spectacular black and gold inlaid half armour, an esquire carrying a crested and plumed helmet, attended by a group of Hamilton knights in heraldic surcoats over steel—all highly impressive. The noise in the hall died away.

Arran bowed to his mother and looked doubtfully at Albany sitting beside her. He said nothing.

The Regent was less than voluble, likewise. He rose to his

feet, but that was as far as his reaction went. Since he represented the crown, most others felt that they ought to rise also. An uneasy pause ensued.

Their hostess, remaining seated, suffered no such restraints. "So there you are, James," she said. "Well—speak up, man. He has seen your paper—this cousin of yours. And is prepared to sign the like, for you. But—you had best speak the French if you want an answer! How any man seeks to rule this unruly realm and yet canna speak the language, guid kens!"

Her son cleared his throat. He had, of course, spent a considerable time in France and had a fair command of French. "I greet you, Cousin," he said, in that tongue, but lacking conviction. "I . . . wish you well. I accept you as Regent for our liege-lord James. I desire peace. I renounce my band with the lords of Angus and Home. I request full acknowledgment of my position as Lord Admiral of this realm. And of fourth person in this kingdom." That all came out like a lesson well learned, levelly but without emphasis.

After a pause, Albany shrugged expressive shoulders. "I accept and agree," he said briefly. "I shall so sign."

Again silence, this time broken by a bark of a laugh from one of the earl's little group of supporters, a markedly handsome young man in a strongly virile, almost animal way, powerfully built and with a glittering eye.

"Lord God—here's a bonny sight!" this individual exclaimed. "A nation's fate decided so. By two such . . . paladins!"

There were gasped breaths throughout the hall—for although these words themselves were innocuous enough, there was no hiding the scorn with which they were enunciated.

"Hold your tongue, sirrah!" the old lady observed, but almost equably. "Or I will have it held for you!"

"Madame!" the speaker said, making a flourish of a bow, difficult in armour.

"The Bastard," the man next to Lindsay murmured. "Sir James Hamilton of Finnart, the Bastard of Arran."

David was as interested as anyone there. Few had not heard of the Bastard of Arran, young as he was, the style by which he was generally known. Arran, although twice married, was a widower, with no lawful son, his daughter married to the Lord Drummond. But he had at least two illegitimate sons, this, and the other Sir John Hamilton of Clydesdale, a man of similar moral fibre to his father. But this Bastard was different, a roystering, quarrelsome, unscrupulous character, but a fighter, brave as a lion and one of the best jousters, sworders and tournament knights in Christendom, in this last respect on a par with Antoine de la Bastie. Most had believed him to be still in France, left behind when his father returned to Scotland.

The Regent was looking at this character, and clearly not liking what he saw. David wondered whether they were going to be treated to a display of the famous Albany temper and cap-hurling—and Davie Beaton, in this instance, not in a position to do anything about it. But the Princess Mary, very much mistress in her son's house, took firm control.

"Shake hands, James," she commanded imperiously. "Do not just stand there. Where is that laddie Beaton, with the paper?"

Thus summoned, Beaton was able to come forward to the Duke's side, producing a document from his doublet and the ink-horn and pen which always hung at his side.

The Regent accepted Arran's reluctantly outstretched hand in no very amiable fashion, quickly dropped it and took the pen and paper from Davie, to lean over the table and dash off a spluttering signature. Then he promptly resumed his seat, duty done. It was left to Arran to pick up the signed agreement, and Davie his pen.

The Bastard hooted another laugh. "God save the King's Grace!" he shouted. Nobody quite knew what to make of that in the circumstances, whether to cheer in the traditional fashion, to ignore it, or just to look embarrassed, sensing that it was perhaps not complimentary to these two close supporters of the crown. Their hostess, however, retained her grip on the proceedings and, rapping on the table, ordered the troupe of musicians waiting in a deep window embrasure to strike up. To the scraping of fiddles and the clang of cymbals, then, Arran stood clutching his paper, looking distinctly at a loss despite all his armoured finery. It was the Bastard who led the way over to a side table, across the dais, where they sat down to eat.

Crisis was over, in the short term—and possibly in the longer term also.

In the chamber which Lindsay shared with Davie Beaton that night, the latter was in cheerful mood—not that that was unusual. Who could have prophesied, he demanded, that it all would go so well, so easily? The dangerous triumvirate was broken. Arran would be no more trouble, he swore, so long as that old woman lived. Home's credit was diminished for the second time, with this contract or band rejected. And Angus was now out on his own. They would march for Douglasdale in the morning, a mere score of miles or so—but he very much doubted if Angus would wait for them there. He wondered whether Albany realised how fortunate he was?

David did not know, but doubted whether the prospects were quite so rosy as all that. Arran was a weathercock and his mother could not, in the nature of things, hold him for long.

Perhaps not, the other acceded. But more pressure could be brought to bear. And there was now a new jouster in the lists—the Bastard. Properly used, that one might serve them very well—and not only with Arran. He had known him in France and had recognised his quality.

A quality for ill, for strife and havoc, David suggested, but Beaton waved that aside. Strife and havoc had their value in troubled times, if suitably harnessed and controlled—and he thought that he could control the Bastard of Arran sufficiently to be of use.

As ever, David wondered at the extraordinary self-confidence of this peculiar friend of his.

They sent word next day for the artillery, wherever it might be, to turn around and go back whence it had come. Then, ordering three-quarters of their vast army to start on its own return journey, and judging that even the remaining ten thousand was over-many to march through the Lanarkshire hills to Douglasdale, the Regent and the mounted portion of his host, to the number of about fifteen hundred, set off south-eastwards up Clyde, leaving the rest to come along at a marching pace. David had little difficulty in contriving that he rode now, rather than marched, with Albany's party. Arran, less than enthusiastic, came along too, and the Bastard with him, much more willingly—and it was to be noted on their journey that Davie Beaton found his way not infrequently to the latter's side.

At Dalserf they turned southwards out of the Clyde and into the Avon valley, but soon left this again to follow up a tributary, the Nethan, to Lesmahagow, all territory belonging to Arran. Thereafter they began to climb through bleak lifting moorland, with the hills drawing ever closer, until they reached the watershed of Broken Cross and the land began to drop again towards the vale of the Douglas Water. Then, in late afternoon, with Douglas Castle itself only four miles away, a scouting party was detailed to ride ahead to discover if possible what was the situation there. Surprisingly the Bastard volunteered to lead this, as a seasoned campaigner, and pointing out that this was his own stamping ground and that he knew every yard of the way, Craignethan on this river being his seat. No one liked to display the suspicion which most felt about this offer, but Davie Beaton typically solved the problem by suggesting that David Lindsay, their own expert on such affairs, should go along too, the Regent relieved to agree and Hamilton showing no resentment.

So Lindsay and the Bastard of Arran set off at the head of a score of horsemen to make a discreet and roundabout approach to Douglas Castle, the den amongst the upper Clydesdale hills which had given birth and name to the great and warlike house which had grown to cut so wide a swathe in Scotland. David found the other a cheerful if daunting companion, full of stories and accounts of exploits which in another would have sounded like idle boasting but in this man somehow rang true. He also commended himself by his evident admiration for Antoine de la Bastie.

Amidst lengthening shadows they reined up on a shoulder of Poneil Hill and looked down the vale to its castle, set strongly between two lochans and marshy areas representing a widening of the Douglas Water, difficult to approach save by the one easily defended causeway, but no very large or impressive place to have been the cradle of so powerful a line, indeed not a great deal larger than Garleton. But it was not so much the size that concerned the observers as the fact that it seemed so entirely peaceful in the fading light, no armed camp around it, no campfires, no bustle of men, indeed little sign of any activity at all.

"I think that our hawk has flown, as I judged he might," Hamilton commented. "But I will ride down openly, to find out. I am known here. They will speak with me at the castle."

"And I will come with you. Look like your esquire," David said firmly. "None would expect to see such as yourself alone, anyway."

The Bastard grinned, unoffended by his companion's obvious doubts, and with a single man-at-arms they spurred down into the valley.

They met with no challenge approaching along the causeway. At the castle they found the drawbridge up and the portcullis down and men watching them from the gatehouse parapet.

The Bastard hailed them. He had a strong and carrying voice. "I am Hamilton of Finnart," he called, in case they did not recognise his heraldic surcoat. "Come seeking my lord Earl of Angus."

"He is not here. He is gone," came back to them. "All are gone."

"Gone where, man? Where?"

"Gone to Cavers in Teviotdale, sir."

"Cavers? Teviotdale? Why there? Has he gone there with the Lord Home? On the way to the Merse?"

"No, sir. The Lord Home did not come here. He went off to the Merse earlier. I believe that my lord of Angus goes to Cavers on his way to England. To Morpeth, in Northumberland, to see Her Highness, his lady wife."

"Ha! England again?" Hamilton glanced at David. "Are you sure of this?"

"So he intended, sir. Do you wish to come inside, Sir James? There is none here but myself, as captain. But you are welcome . . ."

"No—it was the Earl I looked for. But, I thank you. I must return . . ." Waving a dismissive hand, the Bastard reined his horse round.

"That did not take long!" David said.

"It would have taken you a deal longer to learn it, without me!" the other pointed out.

"I recognise that. Was it here at Douglas that you were, with my lord of Arran, when his lady mother sent for him? No, no—it could not be. Too far. You could not have come in the time . . ."

"We were only at Barncluith, a few miles from Cadzow. We watched your host arriving, indeed, from there."

"Yet Angus and Home must have learned of what was done. Swiftly. This breaking of the band. How?"

"That was all done three days past. At Cadzow. When we heard that Albany's great army was on its way. My most formidable grandmother did it all. With a little help from your humble servant! Convinced my poor sire that he was riding the wrong horse. Told Angus that he was a fool and could not win in this struggle. And commanded Home to get out of her house. All done, the band torn up, and Albany's paper signed, three days ago. A pretty scene, I tell you!"

David stared. "Then . . . then we need never have marched at all! Forty thousand men!"

"No harm in a little marching! And it brought about this pleasing association, did it not?" Hamilton laughed mockingly.

They picked up their men on the ridge to return to Broken Cross Muir with their information.

The satisfaction at the Regent's camp could scarcely have been greater at hearing the news. The situation as it had developed had not looked so bright since Albany's arrival in Scotland. Arran had changed sides and ought to be kept so without too much difficulty; Home was isolated and discredited; and Angus sufficiently discouraged to be returning to England and his abandoned wife. Scotland should have a breathing space at least, if not something rather better than that.

Orders were issued for all the various units of the army to head for their home territories and the main body for Edinburgh.

David Lindsay thought that he might at last be able to contemplate matrimony. He might, indeed, be able to arrange a visit to the Byres before his return to Stirling, to discuss times and seasons and other relevant matters.

Alas for such hopes. The Regent's party had only reached the Calder area, in Lothian, when it was met by an urgent courier from the Earl Marischal at Stirling Castle with the tidings that the infant Duke of Ross, the King's brother, had died. The child had never been robust, but there had been no indication that his life was endangered. He had, apparently, suddenly sickened and collapsed, with little warning.

This intelligence had a much greater impact on Albany and his entourage than the natural regret at the cutting off of a young royal life. Inevitably it meant trouble. There would be bound to be accusations of neglect from Margaret Tudor, if not worse. And since the child duke had been second heir to Henry of England's throne also, that awkward monarch would be certain to have something to say about it—and it would put the new daughter of Angus and Margaret into a still more significant situation as far as the English crown was concerned. Still more important, perhaps, it made Albany himself heir-presumptive to the *Scottish* throne, something which could markedly affect events and attitudes.

It affected David Lindsay, at any rate, and right away. For it was decided that he should return forthwith to Stirling Castle, Davie Beaton with him, to discover the full details of the prince's death, for official announcement, and to ensure that all was well with King James. So there would be no visit to Kate Lindsay yet awhile. Disappointing as this was, David was by no means mollified by Beaton's announcement, as the two young men rode away northwards, that after he had investigated matters at Stirling, he thought that he would take the opportunity to go a little further, to Strathmore, and visit Airlie Castle—all, of course, in the interest of ensuring that Angus's potential threat in the north-east could now be discounted, at least for the time-being.

12

It was mid-January before David saw Kate Lindsay again, for after the upheavals of November it was unthinkable that he should leave the young monarch's side during the festivities of Yuletide, which that year were especially prolonged, at Stirling Castle, to try to make James forget the loss of his brother. In January, however, a parliament was called in Edinburgh, despite the bad time of year for travel, for good and sufficient reasons, and it was decided that David Lindsay should be in attendance for possible consultation, along with the Sieur de la Bastie. So the day before, he was able to pay his long-delayed visit to the Byres.

Whilst reproachful that he had not contrived a return before this, and accusing him of lack of enthusiasm, Kate presently displayed sufficient of that quality herself to make the visit memorable. Despite the occasional flurry of snow, she insisted that they go riding and led him down to the coast two miles distant, where on the hard sands of Aberlady Bay, the tide being out, they could gallop wild and free. Kate was an excellent horsewoman and on the two miles long sand-bar to the bay she had ample opportunity to challenge David, putting up groups of wild geese in honking protest in the process. The challenge, and sheer physical excitement of it all, in streaming wind, drumming hooves and splattering surface water, also had the effect of arousing their appetite for each other's persons—if such arousal was necessary—so that, coming off the bay with the fading light, without actually having to discuss the matter, they found themselves conveniently in the vicinity of the monks' hay barn of the Luffness Monastery, just to the west of the castle, near the monastic fish ponds, a most suitable and sequestered place to allow their steaming mounts to cool off and eat some hay. The hay was apt for more than feeding horses, to be sure, and at this time of day the barn the last place the good Carmelites would be likely to frequent, outlying as it was. From tethering their beasts outside, to each other's arms inside, was but a logical step, and to sitting down on the hay a natural sequence. Thereafter nature almost but not quite prevailed, the forthcoming marriage not so much discussed as all but anticipated. They had, after all, already put in overmuch waiting. Perhaps it was the monastic ambience which helped them impose the final restraint.

The return to the Byres was at the comfortably sedate pace necessary for holding hands when on horseback.

Before he left next morning with the Lord Patrick for the parliament, David agreed that the wedding should be, God and the Regent—or Davie Beaton—willing, on St Katherine's Day, 30th April, a propitious date surely, as Kate's saint's-day; and at the monastic chapel of Luffness, not only a mere couple of hundred yards from their hay barn but in which featured the fine recumbent effigy of the illustrious ancestor of them both, Sir David de Lindsay, Baron of Luffness, Regent of Scotland for Alexander the Third, who had died on the St Louis Crusade around 1268 and his body been brought back here by one of the dispossessed Scots monks from Mount Carmel—the reason for the monastery being there in the first place. All most auspicious.

The parliament was again held in the great chapel of Holyrood Abbey, and this time, because of snow-bound hill passes and short notice, there was to be no very large attendance. David found Antoine de la Bastie with Davie Beaton, and the latter explained the urgency for this meeting. Henry the Eighth, no doubt in collusion with his sister, was accusing the Duke of Albany of poisoning his nephew in order to become second person in Scotland, and declaring that clearly the life of the young King James was now at risk. In the circumstances he claimed that it was now vitally necessary to get rid of Albany before he did more and irreversible damage. As Lord Protector of Scotland therefore, he called directly upon the Scots parliament to unseat and banish the Regent and to appoint the Queen-Mother, his royal sister, in his place.

This arrogant formal demand had been delivered by the English ambassador, along with a private warning to Chancellor Beaton that King Henry had now some four hundred prominent Scots in receipt of his pensions, many of them lords, bishops and commissioners to parliament, and these could be relied upon to vote against the Regent. This, Davie Beaton averred, was undoubtedly a gross exaggeration; but even if it was only one-quarter true it could be a serious threat. So it had been felt advisable to call the parliament, necessary to return a suitable reply to Henry, as swiftly as possible to prevent any rallying of pro-English support, which in the nature of things might be expected to be strongest in the distant parts of the realm where the central and loyalist influences would be weakest.

There was another reason for an early parliament. There had been a great battle at Marignano, near Milan in Northern Italy, between the French and the armies of the Emperor Maximilian and the Pope, at which the French had gained a notable victory. This enabled King Francis to grab the major prize of Milan, aim at Venice, and so upset the entire balance of power in Europe, a situation which could affect Scotland. Those in the know—including, it appeared, Davie Beaton—believed that this would make France much too strong for Henry Tudor's liking, and that he would break his truce with Francis, and indeed was being urged to do so by the Pope and Emperor, and being offered Milan itself as reward if France could be defeated, Cardinal Wolsey, Henry's Chancellor and adviser, supporting this course. And if France again became involved in a war on two or more fronts, under the terms of the Auld Alliance Scotland would almost certainly be requested to join in. Also, it must not be forgotten that Albany was still Lord High Admiral of France.

Lastly, the Lord Home had fled to England again and sought the protection of Henry against the Regent. Something drastic would have to be done about Home.

As parliaments went, the one of 1516 was brief to the point of being little more than a formality, all over in an hour or two and with sundry outstanding issues remitted to the Privy Council. The main business, answering King Henry's insolent demands, was swiftly dealt with. If there were any of his bought men or pensioners present, they did not reveal the fact, prudently no doubt in view of the outburst of fury on the part of the great majority when they heard the details. It was indeed some time before the

Chancellor could regain order. There was no dubiety about the reply to Henry, only the ability to make it sufficiently civil in tone for an official document. It was in the end left to the Chancellor to draft a letter, to express the undeniable and unshakeable independent sovereignty of the King of Scots in parliament, that parliament's complete satisfaction with the present Regent which itself had lawfully appointed, its rejection of any theme of protectorship or any need therefor, and its reminder that any claim by the former Queen-Mother for supervision of the young monarch, much less to be Head of State as her brother had suggested, had been invalidated by the said lady's remarriage to the Earl of Angus.

To cool down tempers, the Chancellor brought this item to a somewhat abrupt close, and introduced that of the European situation and the sudden advancement in power of France, with its probable effect on England and therefore on Scotland. This being all less comprehensible to most of those present, and on the face of it less immediately urgent, it would probably have been remitted to the Privy Council to keep an eye on. But at this point in the proceedings the Regent made one of his infrequent interventions. A sudden flood of French and some arm-waving left the majority none the wiser but the Chancellor looking uneasy and even his nephew less sure of himself than usual. Davie's translation, whatever gloss he might seek to put on the matter, could not disguise the core of it—namely that the Duke of Albany desired parliament to grant him leave of absence to return to France.

There was consternation in the chapel, shared most evidently by the Chancellor—which indicated no prior consultation. A score of voices were upraised in protest. The Regent looked surprised but scarcely perturbed.

As the din continued, the Archbishop had a quick word with his nephew, who went back to the Regent and spoke urgently and most evidently persuasively. After some exchange, Davie returned to the Chancellor, who rapped for quiet.

"My lord Regent desires it to be known," the young man declared, "that the absence which he seeks is only for a short period, a matter of a few months. It is vitally necessary for his private affairs that he should return to France for such time. He has not seen his Duchess for long. Properties and estates require his attention. And he reminds all that he is Admiral of France and a French citizen. In the present situation, with warfare in the Middle Sea area, he must be available for consultation by the King of France. His duty."

There were cries about prior duty to the kingdom of which he was the Regent and as to the perilous state of Scotland, particularly with this threat of Henry's spleen—which Davie translated.

"My lord Duke says that there need be no fears. That with my lord Earl of Arran, here present, adhering firmly to the King's cause, the Earl of Angus outwith the country and presently in some disarray, and the Lord Home, of whom more hereafter, no longer a danger, the immediate situation is better than at any time for long. Forby, my lord Regent will be able to concert plans with the King of France, should it come to war, to circumvent any threat to Scotland by the King of England and to arrange for mutual support."

Shouts filled the church to the effect that all knew what had happened when last France had required Scotland's support against Henry. Also that Angus could be back at any time and his manpower still undefeated. And that Home would be a menace so long as he lived.

The Chancellor, and no doubt his nephew likewise, saw that on this issue the parliament was not going to be prevailed upon. He declared that the matter would require further information and debate and, bowing towards the Regent on his throne, proposed that they move on to the next item, the subject of the Lord Home, former Lord High Chamberlain.

This was much more to the assembly's taste, for Home was less than popular, both too arrogant and too clever for most. So the Archbishop had no problem. He declared that Home was now in England, in the care of King Henry, of whom it was believed that he had long been a substantial pensioner, and had appealed to the English monarch against his own liege-lord's Regent and government. This was highest treason. If there were any doubts, it could now be revealed that he had been receiving more than a pension from King Henry. Some time ago, the Sieur de la Bastie, now chief Warden of the Marches, had been commissioned to proceed through the Merse and eastern Borders to enquire into the situation prevailing there and the depredations of

English raiding parties after the disaster of Flodden field. And there he discovered that although the raiding was indeed savage and destructive of life and property far and wide, none of the Home lands were being ravaged. Most evidently there was an arrangement between the Homes and the Lord Dacre, the English Warden—and this at a time when the Lord Home was himself chief Scots Warden. The Sieur de la Bastie was here present this day and would substantiate this.

Antoine called down from the clerestory gallery where, with David Lindsay, he was watching the proceedings. "I so substantiate and declare, my lord Chancellor."

"And David Lindsay of the Mount, His Grace's Procurator and Chief Usher, acting with the Sieur de la Bastie, will so confirm."

"I so confirm," David agreed briefly.

"Does anyone wish to question these most reliable and distinguished witnesses?" the Archibishop asked, as though this was indeed a trial in a court of law.

One man there at least found all this unsatisfactory, the young Earl of Moray. "What need is there for all this?" he cried, jumping up. "This is but beating the air! We all know that Alexander Home had committed the highest treason of all, the murder of his sovereign-lord—my own father! Let him pay the price, I say. Indeed I, Moray, demand it."

There was a tense silence, part embarrassment. Few present had not heard something of the story which this young man had assiduously spread abroad ever since Flodden—and no doubt believed—that in the late stages of that disastrous conflict, the Lord Home had returned to the scene of carnage after chasing the English right wing cavalry deep into the Cheviots, and when the battling and wounded monarch saw him, and upbraided him for riding off and leaving the Scots left flank unprotected, Home in a fury had raised his sword and slain King James. Where the young man had got this story was not clear, for he had not himself been at Flodden; but he propagated it assiduously. This was the first time, however, that it had been raised as it were officially. No one, even Home's most bitter enemies, would have paid much attention had not the Earl James been the late King's illegitimate son by Flaming Janet Kennedy and so a half-brother of their present sovereign-lord.

The Chancellor coughed. "We, ah, note your claim and accusation my lord Earl. But such charge would require strong substantiation. Sound witnesses. If you can produce such witnesses, or other corroboration, an indictment of regicide could be added to the other citations for high treason. But lacking this, I fear, no."

"How can I produce witnesses to that fell deed?" the other cried. "All others around the King my father died with him. Only this, this abject dastard, rode free from that field, to continue with his villainies!"

"Yes. Or, no doubt. Perhaps you will seek or continue to seek, for due corroboration, my lord, so that such possible charge can be made? As, indeed, shall we all. Now—my lord Regent, we pass to a related matter. It is inconceivable that the high office of Lord Chamberlain of this realm should remain in the keeping of so undoubted a traitor as the present Lord Home. Accordingly, it is proposed that the chamberlainship should be removed herewith from the said Alexander Home and bestowed upon the Lord Fleming of Cumbernauld. Is such removal and new appointment approved by this parliament? Or is other nomination to be put forward?"

Acclaim for Fleming, a sound man, was forthcoming and no alternative was put forward. On this convenient note the session closed, leaving the Regent's return to France as it were in the air.

David returned to Stirling with Albany's authority, via Davie Beaton, to inform the Earl Marischal that he should have leave of absence from King Jamie's service for two weeks flanking St Katherine's Day next, 30th April—a mere thirteen weeks to wait.

Well before that time, David was surprised to have a visit from young Beaton, who called in at Stirling Castle on his way back from another assault on Marion Ogilvy at Airlie in the Braes of Angus, using as his excuse his desire to pay his loyal duty to his liege-lord and to see how the papingo was thriving—Beaton, of course, recognising the value of maintaining close links with even an infant monarch, at this stage, to ensure advantage in years to come. He was in especially good spirits on this occasion, for it transpired that he had achieved success with the fair Marion in a sufficient degree to obtain a promise of marriage from her at some unspecified date. They would be wed, he asserted, when he got back from France.

David congratulated him, interested that his peculiar friend should be so obviously set on marriage when he seemed the sort of young man to whom conjugal bliss would be less than a priority. Clearly he was deeply in love—and this side of his vivid character the more commended itself to Lindsay. But what was this of France, he wondered? Was the Regent indeed going, and he with him?

Beaton shook his head, promptly reverting to his more usual image of intrigue and manipulation. No, Albany was sending *him* back to France, to seek to facilitate the ducal return, as a personal ambassador to King Francis. The project was that he should try to convince Francis actually to recall the Duke officially for consultation and advice—which as Admiral and a French citizen the Regent could not refuse; but to sweeten this call, for the Scots parliament, by offering certain advantages to Scotland, a firm treaty, improved trade terms and arms and men. Beaton grinned over this—for, he explained confidentially, he was also going to France as an ambassador for his uncle, the Chancellor, with exactly the opposite secret objective. He was to seek to delay the Regent's departure for as long as possible!

All but incredulous, David shook his head. How was this possible? And to what end? Such deceit and ill-faith. What did it, what could it, mean?

The other objected strongly, if amusedly, to these terms. It was not deceit nor ill-faith but statecraft, diplomacy, for the best advantage of all, he claimed. How did Lindsay think dealings between princes and realms were conducted? By straightforward exchange and handshakes, like buying and selling cattle? Seldom that, but by more devious means. Power had its own requirements and niceties, and could not be manipulated as by a bull charging at a gate! As witness the latest move to bridle Angus. It was expensive and difficult to maintain in arms and idle a great host, as at present, just in case Angus decided to set in motion his undoubtedly massive Douglas might. And it was important that he and Home should not ever again act in concert. They were both presently in England. So a messenger had been sent to Angus indicating that the Regent desired only amity and goodwill between them, unlike Home whom parliament had branded traitor and forfeited from all rights and privileges. The Regent urged Angus therefore to return to Scotland, to aid in the governance of the realm, the more so as he himself was intending a visit to France and would expect Angus to take his due place on the Council of Regency during the French interlude. Albany had further assured that there would be no reprisals or other moves against Angus if he so returned.

David reacted predictably. What was the point in this? Undoing all that had been gained at Hamilton. Asking for further trouble. Putting Angus back into a position to have his way with Scotland.

The other was only too happy to explain—for fairly evidently the strategy was his own. Who were the enemies of the Regent and therefore of the Scots realm, in order of menace? Henry of England, the Queen-Mother, Angus, Home and Arran—others did not matter. Angus and Home, in England, were available to be used by Henry against Scotland, as was his sister. In that five, Angus was the weak spot, for he might be enticed home by offers of clemency and a seat on the forthcoming Regency Council, thus getting him out of Henry's grasp. Margaret his wife was unlikely to return with him, with their baby daughter. And Home dared not return, to face parliament and trial for treason. Angus and his wife were scarcely a happy couple and this would further come between them. Margaret without Angus would have little influence in Scotland. So Henry would be left with Home, whose teeth were largely drawn. It but remained to ensure that the remaining opponent, Arran, now largely tamed, did not come together again with Angus. This could probably be assured through envy and jealousy, for they had never loved each other. They would both be on any Regency Council inevitably, but the other members could be carefully selected to support Arran rather than Angus. And there would be one in particular—the Bastard of Arran! He was twice the man that his father was, ambitious and able however unscrupulous, and he, Beaton, was cultivating him. Given this sudden promotion to a position of power, and recognising whence it came, the Bastard could be relied upon to sway his father and others and keep Angus very much isolated. So, if Albany must eventually return to France for a time, all would be held nicely in balance until his return—God willing!

Left more or less speechless by this intricate web of manoeuvre and interaction, David did not essay argument or even further question. But he did marvel at the character and attitudes of this man, the same who was so sure of his abilities to move great folk and their affairs of state like chessmen on a board, and at the same time to be wholly and humbly devoted to an Angus lord's daughter and grateful that she had consented at last to marry him.

David said goodbye to his friend and wished him God-speed on his visit to France—although wondering how much God would be involved in it all. He himself reverted to more vital contemplations, his own forthcoming marriage.

13

David and Antoine de la Bastie rode downhill towards the sparkling expanse of Aberlady Bay flanked by its twin headlands of Kilspindie and Gullane Points, with the burgeoning young green of the Luffness woodlands filling the foreground, and far beyond the blue sweep of the Firth of Forth, all the long varied coastline of Fife rising to the shapely twin breasts of the Lomond Hills—as fair a prospect under the sailing cloud galleons as any man could look for in all southern Scotland, that breezy, bright last day of April 1516. The two horsemen were scarcely concerned with the view, however, even though probably all the far-flung loveliness of sun and shadow and glitter was not without its subconscious effect on the younger man at least on this long-awaited day. Scotland's fickle weather could have been so much less co-operative, and a repetition of the driving rain of yesterday would have presented a depressing problem and handicap—and even more so for the bride, in the circumstances.

There had been strong objections to having the nuptial ceremony at the little monastic chapel of Luffness, especially from the Lady Lindsay and other females of the two families, even from Mirren Livingstone who now was more or less accepted as a sort of proxy-wife for David's father and who took an almost proprietorial interest in the entire affair as self-appointed adviser and consultant. The obvious place to hold a notable wedding, they all said, was the great church of St Mary, Haddington, a splendid building, all but a cathedral, where there was room for hundreds—not a poky little monastery chapel, however pretty its setting, which would hold no more than a score or two. Even the local parish churches of Athelstaneford or Aberlady would have been better, they averred, with more accommodation, suitable for showing off the ladies' finery—and the bride's also, to be sure. But Kate had been decided—it would be at Luffness Chapel and nowhere else. She did not, of course, detail reasons for this odd choice; that hay barn, visible from the chapel door, certainly never would have occurred to anyone as having any relevance. David himself was entirely happy with the venue. The fewer the folk present the better, as far as he was concerned, his priority to get the business over and done with as quickly as possible with the minimum of fuss.

"What do you intend, David, hereafter?" Antoine wondered. "Where will your Kate live? At her old home, here? At Garleton, with your father and our generous Mirren? Your own property of The Mount, in Fife? That is far away—although not quite so far from Stirling, perhaps. You will not leave the King's service, I think, so you must remain for most of the time at Stirling Castle. But a close-guarded fortress is no place in which to immure a young bride."

"Yet she says that she wishes to stay with me at Stirling. That she does not mind about being enclosed—as long as she is with me." David coughed a little at the sound of that.

"She may think otherwise, after a little."

"I recognise that. But I would not wish her to continue to bide at the Byres—my wife." Again the little cough. "Nor in my father's house at Garleton, with Mirren. And The Mount has been empty and shut up for long. I could not put her there, alone . . ."

"You have a problem. Perhaps if she becomes *désenchantée* with Stirling Castle in time, you could find lodgings for her in the town below. Where she would feel less shut-in—as you yourself do, I know."

"That is possible. But I do not think that the Earl Marischal would permit me to leave the King's side, of a night, to be with her in the town. I sleep in an anteroom of his bedchamber . . ."

"You can scarcely instal Kate there!"

"No. But we can find a room somewhere nearby. Happily Kate is fond of James. When I brought him to Garleton they got on very well. He still talks of her. That should help."

"I wish you well in it, David." That was accompanied by a typically Gallic shrug.

"It should not be so very difficult? You would not have me to give up my position as Procurator and Usher to the King? I would not wish to do that . . ."

Leaving their horses at the castle stables, they walked the few hundred yards to the monastery, where they had a word with the Prior, John Bickerton, who would officiate, assisted by the Athelstaneford parish priest. David would have liked Abbot John Inglis to have at least taken some part in the ceremony—although somehow he would scarcely have felt properly married if John had actually been the celebrant—but the Earl Marischal would not hear of both of them leaving the young King at the same time. Antoine was going to act groomsman, a great honour David acknowledged, and had come from Dunbar for the occasion.

They made their way to the chapel, which stood some distance apart from the other monastic buildings in woodland perched on the lip of a sort of winding water-filled ravine, which was in fact the flooded original quarry out of which the sandstone for the building of both the castle and the monastery had been hewn, over two centuries before. It was no large edifice, normally only required for the worship of about a score of monks; but it had three parts, the raised chancel to the east, the monks' nave in the centre, with its own door, and a slightly larger westerly portion not normally in use—for the castle had its own inbuilt chapel—save as a storage space. This had been cleared for today, and would hold some thirty extra persons standing, although some might not be able to see through the screens all that went on up before the altar in the chancel. Already a number of guests had installed themselves there, in the most advantageous positions, and clearly were not going to allow themselves to be pushed to the sides or otherwise displaced by late arrivals. The monks' nave was reserved for the two families and principal guests. Quite a crowd had assembled outside, monks, men-at-arms from the castle, fishers from Luffness Haven and villagers from Aberlady.

David and his groomsman, having arrived in good time, were uncertain whether to wait inside the chapel or out. They decided that it would be less embarrassing outside. There, a little apart from the rest, they stood, David distinctly ill at ease. Normally he was on the best of terms with the local folk, but today he felt separated from all and uncomfortable—after all, he had never before been one of the principals at a wedding. De la Bastie, however, seemed entirely his urbane self, smiling to all.

They waited.

The hour of three after noon struck on the monastery bell, which thereafter continued to toll, presumably in nuptial joy although it sounded the same as for a funeral. Promptly, through the clangour, the sound of chanting could be heard, getting louder, as down the path from the monastic complex paced a choir of singing boys leading Prior Bickerton, in full canonicals, with two monkish acolytes and the Athelstaneford priest following. Some more monks came along behind in the ordinary off-white habits of the Carmelites.

The Prior sketched a casual blessing over the assembled crowd, the choir continuing to sing and the bell to toll. Bickerton bowed formally to David and gestured for him to follow into the chapel.

Therein, at the chancel step, they were signed to wait whilst the Prior and his assistants went up to their places before the altar. The choristers came in behind, chanting still. David muttered to his friend that there was not going to be much room for the bride and her party with all this lot. And where was she? All was supposed to start at three.

Antoine made soothing noises.

The choir kept up their somewhat monotonous chanting, the Prior seemed lost in contemplation of eternity, the parish priest fretted and the congregation now packing the western extension shuffled and pushed and tried to shoo away new arrivals, their hitherto muted chatter soon all but drowning the singing.

Presently the bell stopped ringing and soon thereafter the choir too fell silent, presumably having exhausted its repertoire or perhaps its lung power. An uneasy hush descended upon those at the back of the chapel, with only whispers and stirrings, although the crowd outside seemed unaffected.

David all but groaned aloud. Who had invented this torture for bridegrooms? It was to have been a quiet, simple wedding. Antoine, spreading French hands, observed philosophically that women were ever thus.

How did *he* know, since he had never been married, the sufferer demanded?

After a further seemingly endless hiatus, it occurred to David, staring at the recumbent effigy of his great ancestor and namesake, carved in full knightly Crusader armour there under his canopy at the left of the chancel, that Sir David de Lindsay, Regent of Scotland two and a half centuries ago, would never have stood for this. And why should *he*? After all, he was the King's Procurator and the principle mover in this distressing affair—at least, if he was not, who was? Moreover his groomsman was Scotland's Chief Warden of the Marches, Governor of Dunbar Castle, and one of the foremost knights of Christendom. Well, then.

Abruptly he turned, glared at the choristers and raised a hand to point. "Sing!" he commanded. Anything would be better than this uneasy hush. Up at the altar the Prior came out of his trance to wave a confirmatory hand. David strode to the arched doorway, to stare out.

The crowd outside gave him a welcoming cheer and the choir inside started up their chant again, if somewhat raggedly. David came back to his friend's side, who smiled, and patted the gold-slashed sleeve of his fine wine-coloured velvet doublet. There were some giggles from behind.

Waiting resumed, and somewhere an argument broke out about positioning.

How much longer the bridegroom could have stood it was uncertain, when a second outburst of cheering outside seemed to indicate developments at least. Even so there was no improvement in the situation for an unconscionable time, until David's brother Alexander came stalking in, dressed more splendidly than the bridegroom, and proceeded to take charge, officiously pushing back people here and there, ordering the choir into a tighter huddle, gesturing towards the Prior and otherwise making himself objectionable. David scowled at him.

Then a new sort of silence fell upon all save the singing boys, and even they distinctly faltered. Kate, on her father's good arm, appeared in the doorway. David's scowl dissolved, to be replaced by an aspect of sheerest wonder and bliss.

Radiant, flushed, eyes shining, dressed all in white satin and silver, he had never seen her more lovely, a vision of lively, challenging beauty and delight.

The singers, recovering, changed their somewhat mournful chant into something more rousing, and to this father and daughter moved forward into the chapel, to be followed by Lady Lindsay and Sir David and the other family and principal guests, two by two. With the place already all but full, very quickly something of a pile-up developed, with Alexander Lindsay unsuccessfully seeking to marshal all and making confusion worse. Protests developed, too.

David found Kate at his side, at last. He took her arm. "Where have you been?" he demanded—but a deal less reproachfully than would have seemed possible a minute or two before.

"Where . . .?" Innocently she gazed at him. "Why, just coming."

Gulping, he nodded, as though entirely satisfied with that explanation.

"Oh, David—at last!" she breathed.

"At last!" he echoed, heartfelt.

It was almost as though Prior Bickerton said Amen to that as he turned to take charge, in sanctimonious but authoritative tones. All was now in hand, even though it was not every day that a monastic leader was called upon to marry anyone, save perhaps to Holy Church. He advanced upon the happy couple, totally ignoring the parish priest, and launched in Latin into what was presumably the marriage rite. David recognised a word or two here and there, but did not greatly exercise himself to construe and try to follow, quite content to eye Kate and let this business get itself over as quickly as possible. It was necessary, he recognised—but as far as he was concerned, their real coming together as man and wife had taken place in that hay barn some time ago.

Surprisingly soon, the ring exchange was indicated, and rather fumbled through, responses muttered, and Antoine and Lord Lindsay stood back to allow the bridal pair to be pronounced duly wed in the sight of God and all present—the only occasion when the Prior reduced his rate of outflow from what had been almost a gabble. Then peremptorily he signed for them to kneel, enunciated a sonorous blessing, and stood back.

Apparently it was all over, and, taken a little by surprise, David was about to raise Kate to her feet when the Athelstaneford incumbent, entirely disregarded hitherto, evidently decided that if he was going to have any part in the proceedings it must be now, and came forward hurriedly to pronounce his own and much more detailed benediction.

The Prior countered by signing to the choir to start up again.

So bride and groom rose and embraced—and promptly were all but submerged in a tide of other embracings, in that very confined space. Chaos prevailed. Outside, presently, David looked longingly beyond the thronging well-wishers to that red-tiled hay barn across the pasture.

Congratulations, salutations and humoursome advice over, they rode in large company back to the Byres, David insisting that his new wife sat before him on his own horse, somewhat uncomfortable for both of them as this was, so that at least he could have his arms around her under the cloak which she donned over her satin and silver. Jogging up and down at a trot, this certainly engendered a distinct emphasis on her femininity, much appreciated by the man. That cloak was a blessing, too.

The feasting and jollifications thereafter seemed interminable, at least to David Lindsay, who was clearly not good at weddings. Speeches and toasts by the Lord Patrick, Sir David and Antoine were all very well, being reasonably brief; but others joined in and were less so, the parish priest for instance who, on the strength of having baptised them both—only yesterday, it seemed to him—and now was a little tiddly, decided to make up for his virtual exclusion from the nuptial ceremony by going on at great length now. When Alexander, David's younger brother, rose to add his witticisms about the married state, conjugal rights and the problems of first nights, the bridegroom had had enough and sought to make it plain by his glowering. He leant over to whisper in Kate's ear—who had hitherto been accepting all this a deal more patiently than had her new spouse.

"Make excuse to your father to leave, for a space," he directed. "Slip away."

"Why?" she asked, surprised.

"Best that way. Do it now, while Alex still havers on."

"How can I? What excuse . . . ?"

"Anything. Say that nature demands it! Go, lass—and wait for me out there. I will join you after a minute or so."

And when she still displayed reluctance, he added, "My first husbandly command, Kate!"

Shrugging, she murmured to Lord Patrick on her other side and rising, made for the dais door behind their top table, all eyes upon her.

Alexander in full flood, did not pause. And after a little more of it, David got to his feet, observed to his host and hostess that he would go see that Kate was all right, and headed for the door also.

He found his wife just outside and looking somewhat bewildered. "Come," he said, taking her arm.

"Where? Why? What has come over you, Davie?" she demanded.

"We go to Garleton. Forthwith."

"No? But why . . . ?"

"Lest worse befall us than listening to endless speeches! A bedding is planned."

"Oh! Oh, no!"

"Yes. Antoine overheard my precious brother discussing it with another. We can do without that, I say!"

"Yes. Yes . . ." She was no longer reluctant or doubtful.

He led her to the courtyard door and the stables.

The age-old custom of bedding the bride was still carried out, on occasion, however unpopular with newly-weds. The tradition was that the happy couple could be escorted to their bridal chamber, the bride by the male guests, the groom by the female, and there ceremonially undressed, to be deposited naked on the marriage bed, the interested and considerate escorts not departing until they were satisfied that the marriage was being consummated in due and effective fashion—frequently, to the consequent *in*effectiveness of the new husband, and the then obvious need for instruction and aid. It could all provide a unique opportunity for those involved, of course—except perhaps for the newly-weds themselves.

Not even delaying to collect Kate's cloak, they unhitched David's horse and rode uphill for Garleton, having instructed the stableboy to inform Lord Lindsay in due course where they had gone.

It was an early hour to seek their couch, but neither found this in any way regrettable. Even the fact that the couch itself was on the small side, being in fact David's own agamist bed, in his topmost tower room, that wherein poetry once had been composed. Now a new idyll and rhapsody was to be essayed—and the door locked.

Kate suddenly was shy, unwontedly silent. David could have done with something of the atmosphere and tempo of that day in the hay barn. But he recognised that his own eagerness was likely to be best served by patience and understanding at this stage. He declared that a beaker of wine was called for on this occasion, and, unlocking the door, left her, to go fetch it.

When, after suitable delay, he returned, it was to find Kate in bed, back turned to the door. He went to her, and sat, to stroke her hair.

"My dear, my dear!" he said.

She kept her head down, face covered.

"It will be . . . very good. You are very lovely. A delight," he went on, stroking, soothing. "So very fair, so darling a creature."

Muffled amongst the bedclothes her voice came. "Oh, Davie—why? Why? When before, I, I . . . !"

"It is but this day's doing, my sweet. All the bustle and the waiting and the many folk, to talk to, all the staring. That time, we were alone, just you and I. But now—now we are alone again. Ourselves. It will be as before. But . . . better."

"Yes. Yes, that is it. I know. I am sorry, Davie . . ."

"Hush you. Fret nothing. Just wait, lass." He slid a hand under the blankets to her bare shoulder, gently to caress it. Gradually that hand moved down, to the swell of her breasts, strangely cooler than the rest, to cup the fullness of one. He felt her quiver and kept his hand still for a while, nor knew any complaint in that. Then slowly he began to stroke the nipple and quite quickly felt it rise and stiffen to his touch. And as it stiffened, so the stiffness and tension began to go out of the rest of her, and her breathing slowed but deepened.

Presently he moved his hand over to the other breast and she stirred a little to receive it, sighing. This nipple required little attention, but got it nevertheless. Her breathing changed again, still deep but faster.

Suddenly she exclaimed and sat up, turning to him, eager now. "Davie! Davie! Davie!" she whispered, and her arms went round his neck, her lips seeking his. "Oh, thank you! Thank you!"

Words superfluous, they clung together. Then, even whilst her breasts pressed and rubbed against him, "Quick!" she breathed. "These clothes . . . !"

"Then let me go for a moment, foolish one!" he chided, smiling. "Loose me—or how may I? A moment—but one moment . . ."

"I will help you . . ."

"Faster without you, lass! See . . ."

Swiftly he flung off shirt and breeches, kicking off shoes, leaving his hose meantime. Impatient, unashamed now, she threw back the bedclothes, waiting in all her urgent loveliness to receive him, a vision of the Creator's most demanding, attractive and essential creation, nubile and vital young womanhood. Groaning his pent-up, hoarded need of her, he stumbled to take what she so unstintingly offered. Their coming together was the most natural and fulfilling thing in the world.

Some unspecified time later there was a knock on the bedchamber door and David's father wondered, mildly for that man, if they were there and in good order? He was lucky to get even a grunt in reply.

Next morning, however sleepy, they were off with de la Bastie eastwards. Oddly, it was the Frenchman who had conceived the notion that they should spend their first days and nights of wedded bliss at Fast Castle on the Merse coast, the most remote of the Home strongholds which Antoine had captured. He asserted that it was the most extraordinary place he had ever seen, away from all the haunts of men, and he could think of nowhere more desirable for a pair of newly-weds requiring only each other's company. David had had no better idea and Kate was happy so long as they should be on their own. Their parents and friends had suggested all sorts of alternatives, indeed scoffed at the thought of going to some barbarous thieves' hold in the Borderland—but then, as Antoine pointed out, none of them had ever been at Fast Castle.

So they rode companionably with de la Bastie and his escort, by Athelstaneford and Markle and Preston-on-Tyne to Dunbar, where Antoine dispensed with all but two of his men-at-arms and picked up instead a middle-aged couple who would act as servitor and housekeeper at Fast, along with a pair of pannier ponies laden with provisions. Thus equipped, they proceeded on in the afternoon, south by east, past Dunglass and Colbrandspath Tower, both now garrisoned by the Warden's men, and up on to the windy heights of Coldingham Muir, with the Norse Sea stretching to infinity on their left and the heathland merging with the Lammermuir Hills on the right, a suddenly all but unpopulated land under great skies, with only a few small farmeries and shepherds' cothouses, where the curlews and the peewits called endlessly and the wild geese flighted.

Across this strange plateau land, odd to be so close to the sea, they rode for a full hour at the sedate pace of the pannier ponies until, with the sun beginning to sink behind them, they came to the most isolated farmery of them all, a place of baaing lambs and lowing calves, called it seemed Dowlaw, the demesne farm of Fast Castle. Beyond it a little way, the moorland appeared to stop abruptly for the sea to take over, although on a very different level.

After a word or two with the farmer, on towards this lip of the world foreground they trotted—to the visitors' mystification, for as far as eye could see there was nothing thrusting higher than a whin-bush or an outcropping rock. Then suddenly they were at the edge, and smiling, the Frenchman drew rein. He did not have to say anything.

Kate gripped David's arm, lips parted but speechless. Sheerly the land dropped away to nothingness, dizzily, a steep apron of heather and cranberries and deer-hair grass for perhaps fifty feet and then vertical, precipitous cliff dropping many hundreds of feet to the wrinkled surging waves of that fierce white-fanged seaboard. In a savage but majestic sweep the land reached away north and south to the extent of vision, the entire vista breathtaking in its immensity.

Antoine pointed, half-right and downwards. There, quarter of a mile away and halfway down the beetling cliff, a tall, slender stack of bare rock thrust up out of the boiling tide close against the main headland. And perched on top of this tapering pinnacle of stone was a similarly slender castle, reddish-brown towers and turrets around which the seabirds wheeled and screamed in white clouds.

"Fast!" de la Bastie said, relishing their reactions. "Or Faux, I understand it was in origin, from our French for treachery!"

"Lord!" David exclaimed. "So *that* is Fast Castle! I . . . I can believe that treachery was hatched there!"

"And you brought us here for our, our . . . ?" Kate left the rest unsaid.

Antoine beamed. "Were *I* new-wed, I could esteem few places more to my taste! No?"

The honeymooners eyed each other and David grinned. "I see what you mean!" he conceded.

The girl made a face, glanced flushing at the Frenchman and then laughed, reining her horse's head round, southwards.

They rode along a dizzy clifftop track for a little way until abruptly they had to urge their reluctant mounts down an ever steepening slope, part heather, part naked stone and scree, with the foaming white breakers smashing far below. Round the lip of a sheer rock chimney they circled gingerly, the horses ever more uneasy. Reining up, where the track was just a little wider, Kate dismounted, preferring to lead her beast and trust her own feet. The others pretended to humour her by following suit, the servitor and wife heaving sighs of relief. Soon the horses were all but squatting on their haunches so steep became the descent, the pannier ponies in fact proving the most sure-footed. In the dark, or in wet weather, that descent would be barely possible.

Perhaps halfway down that towering headland their precarious approach reached a yawning gap between the cliff-face and the insular stack. And across this narrow chasm a slender filament spanned, a meagre gangway, evidently a drawbridge of sorts. The motherly soul who was to act housekeeper, already in a state bordering on terror, let out a wail at the sight.

There appeared to be no place for horses across that alarming access, but a ledge of the main cliff-face had obviously been further excavated and enlarged nearby, with iron rings set in the rock, clearly for tethering beasts. Tying their reins, the visitors stared from this sea-eagle's eyrie of a place to Antoine de la Bastie and back again.

"Will you not do very well here, my friends?" the Frenchman asked. "Sufficiently private, is it not?"

Four figures had come to man the battlements above the gatehouse opposite, waving, grinning. Antoine stepped carefully down to the drawbridge head—for even this approach was no more than naked rock—reaching out a hand to assist Kate. The servitor required David's assistance to get his gasping, protesting spouse even that far.

There was a rope stretched above the gangway on one side, to act as handrail—a help in windy weather, the Frenchman explained unnecessarily, striding across—and gripping this tightly, the newcomers edged after him, forbearing to look downwards.

The stronghold was little less unusual within than without, all floors being on different levels, thanks to the contours of the rock top, vaulted ceilings sloping and often angled and rooms oddly shaped and generally small. But there was a fair-sized hall, strewn with sheep and deer skins, where two great fires of driftwood blazed and sparked and hissed, and a vaulted kitchen down a steep stair cut in the naked rock below, from which arose an appetising aroma of cooking meats.

Whilst the housekeeping pair and the escort were taken down there by one of the four-man garrison, Antoine led the bridal couple up a tightly winding turnpike stair to a little gannet's-nest of a bedchamber skied in the very topmost tower of the place, its windows, when unshuttered, opening on to the most stupendous vistas of ocean and cliff and circling seabirds. But even here a fire burned brightly in a tiny fireplace, and while Kate exclaimed at the view, David asked how on earth they got the fuel for these fires in such a situation—for they had seen no woodland within miles, on Coldingham and Lumsdaine Muirs.

"There is a shaft cut in the rock, part natural crevasse, crevice, is it? This opens to a great cavern in the foot of this pinnacle. There is much driftwood washed up on these so savage shores, and it can be hoisted through the cavern roof and up this shaft. Also stores, fish, gear, for there is a little landing stage for boats down there—but only to be reached in calm weather. Fresh water likewise, led from a well to a rock cistern. Oh, the Home who built this hold knew what he was at!"

"I swear that he must have been a man with an uneasy mind, nevertheless!"

"Perhaps. I doubt whether he built it to bring a bride to, certainly!"

"But you saw it as meet for such purpose!" Kate said. "Why, I wonder?"

"Say that had I been in David's place there is nowhere in this land where I would have preferred to bring you, my dear," de la Bastie told her, deep-voiced. "I thought about it, you see. Yes. I envy this friend of mine—I confess it, frankly!"

Meeting his gaze, the girl flushed and looked away towards the far horizons.

Downstairs, they all partook of a hearty if rough and ready repast prepared by the garrison, the main ingredients being roast lamb, bread, honey and ale. Then Antoine, leaving the two escorts as guardians, took the other four men-at-arms and his departure, kissing Kate and clasping David around the shoulders, his message unspoken but clear.

The new incumbents were left to make what they would, and could, of Fast Castle.

That night, in the lofty roost, to the recurrent thunder of the breakers and the weird chorus of the night birds, they made love with a new passion and abandon, to a repeated satisfaction hitherto undreamed of. Kate proved to be a natural lover, and what was not instinctive, she learned fast.

They wakened early but lay late, encouraged thereto by the elements. For overnight an easterly gale had sprung up, and that precarious steeple-top hold shook and trembled alarmingly to the batter of it, the pounding of the wind, the crash of the waves and what they thought was driving rain against their window until they realised that it was spray from the mighty seas which were exploding in crazy violence on the jagged rocks far below. In the circumstances, bed and mutual comfort were the obvious antidotes.

Later, fed and every corner of that breakneck castle explored—which did not take long for it could not be large by the nature of its position—and the weather contraindicating any outdoors activity, they decided to investigate the rock shaft, which Antoine had mentioned, to the cavern beneath. This proved to be reached from a trapdoor in the floor of a storeroom off the kitchen premises which, when raised, revealed a distinctly frightening black hole in the naked rock, clearly an enlarged natural fissure, down which a rope-ladder disappeared and up which came both a hollow booming sound and a strong smell of decaying seaweed. Despite this daunting approach however, Kate asserted that she wished to discover more, quite prepared to face the swaying ladder—provided that David went first.

So, provided each also with flickering lanterns, they took deep breaths, and the husband, with every appearance of nonchalance, put foot on the first rungs and commenced the formidable descent, his lantern less than helpful. A score or so of rungs down, he called up that it was none so bad so long as care was taken, a fondly foolish injunction. He felt her weight affecting the hang of the ladder thereafter and heard an occasional exclamation.

Such exclamation was as nothing to the one he himself emitted when, presently, with the noise of surging waters suddenly louder, he felt the ladder swing much more freely and, as he realised that he was now entering the cavern proper, he was engulfed in a sort of black snowstorm, all but smothered in a softly buffeting cloud which enveloped him and his lamp. In the consequent darkness it took moments for him to understand that this was in fact a great host of bats, in fluttering panic; and his own sudden panic subsided even as they beat musky-smelling tiny wings about his face. He called up a warning to Kate, assuring, out of swift masculine recovery, that there was nothing to be afraid of.

Swaying to and fro like any pendulum now, he descended further and as the bat cloud thinned his light reasserted itself—but insufficiently to reveal any bounds to this cavern, around or below—although the boom and swish of the waves sounded now very close. Evidently it was a very high and extensive place. Increased outcry from above indicated that Kate had entered the bat-level.

Then, amidst the rush and surge of the tide in that dark, hollow enormity another strange noise became apparent—a whining and groaning, less than reassuring, punctuated by a kind of barked grunting. It took some while, with a subsequent plopping and slapping noise, for him to realise that this must be seals protesting and taking to the water—which presupposed ledges around the cave base. Unfortunately his lantern shed little light downwards. He shouted up this latest information.

When he became aware that the ladder was swaying progressively less wildly, he recognised that it must be anchored somewhere and therefore he must be nearing the bottom. Soon his feet touched solid if weed-hung rock, and lowering the lantern he saw that he stood on quite a wide ledge a few feet above the black swirling water; also that the round eyes of numerous grey seals were regarding him glassily, some in the water, some still on ledges, like old moustachioed men, peering.

Kate arrived breathless beside him, as wide-eyed as the seals, and together they gazed around. The lamps were unfortunately insufficient to do much more than reveal that the cave was huge, only the wet walling immediately nearby being visible. Also to be seen beside them was a rough timber jetty or landing stage, with a quite large coble-type boat tied thereto, high prowed of vaguely Viking ship build, which rose and fell regularly on the tidal surge. What the lanterns did not reveal was any opening for the cavern; and no hint of daylight glimmered anywhere.

What *was* fairly clear was from which direction the booming noise was coming. But since no light showed thereabouts, there must be a major bend in the cave or more than one, before the entrance, making it a secret place indeed.

There were oars in the boat, but they reckoned that with a storm blowing outside, any exploration afloat could wait. They did move around gingerly on foot, the seaweed slippery, where the ledges allowed, disturbing more seals, also birds of some sort which made off unseen but with a great squawking. They established the fact that there were at least one or two branches to the cavern, the floor of one sloping upwards to well above high-watermark, and here they found quite a large store of driftwood stacked; likewise fishing nets and lobster pots.

When they could go no further, in this state of the tide, they returned to the ladder foot, to climb back whence they had come. Going up seemed much less alarming than coming down into the unknown. David, counting steps, came to the conclusion that the cave roof must be over one hundred feet in height, and the fissure shaft at least another hundred feet above.

Safely back within the castle walls, they agreed that their

awareness of what lay beneath them much added to their conception and understanding of the entire Fast establishment, as well as increasing their wonder over the designs and concerns of its builders.

The gale raged for two days and nights of blustering fury, a continuous assault which the castle almost seemed to defy with more than assurance, with sheer malevolence. As Kate imaginatively put it, Fast appeared to cling to its rocky perch with one fist whilst shaking the other in the face of the storm. The honeymooners made no complaint, with other preoccupations to the fore. Indeed the elemental battle outside seemed to enhance the fairly elementary proceedings within.

The third morning, however, dawned calm and bright, with only mild zephyrs of air caressing the cliffs, the sky blue and the sea a gleaming dazzling infinity, innocent of all malice, with only a slow, majestic heavy swell to hint of past confrontation. In these circumstances active young people felt called upon to stretch their legs, and ventured out of their eyrie to make their careful way up the precipitous track to the farmery of Dowlaw, where Antoine had taken their horses to be stabled. Thereafter they went riding far and wide over the folded green and brown plateau land of Lumsdaine and Coldingham Muirs, where the scattered small black cattle grazed amongst gold-blazing whins and wind-twisted hawthorns, arousing waterfowl from the many pools and lochans and setting the blue hares loping off in all directions. Every now and again, in their lively cantering hither and thither, they came back to the clifftop track, with its breath-catching, plunging vistas and the glittering plain of the sea. And each time their eyes were apt to be drawn further south-eastwards still, towards where, a few miles on, a mighty headland reared itself high above the rest of that lofty seaboard, imperious, tremendous.

"That can only be St Ebba's Head," David decided. "The highest ness, they say, in all east Scotland south of the Orkneys. Shall we go?"

Her answer was to spur ahead.

Following, heedfully now, that dizzy track, up and down, round plunging chasms and gaping chimneys, passing many ancient earthworks and Pictish fortlets, after almost three miles they began to climb consistently towards that thrusting promontory of soaring rock which, as they drew near, could be seen to have a permanent halo of thousands of circling seabirds.

The headland surmounted, they were more than rewarded for their trouble, for the place was almost beyond description in its awesome grandeur, character and dimensions. It comprised, in effect, three abrupt hills strung together by green saddles, their seaward faces cut sheer and undercut by the ocean into a succession of fierce crags, stupendous and dropping straight into the seething deeps of the tide from cornice edges, the escarpment honeycombed with utterly inaccessible caves and clefts and guarded by innumerable sentinel stacks and pillars. But breathtaking as all this was, it was the birds which made the greatest impact, tens of thousands, myriads, of fowl not only circling and diving but festooning every ledge and shelf and cranny of cliffs and stacks, clinging crazily almost atop each other, from sea-level to cape-top—gulls of every description, fulmars, kittiwakes, puffins, cormorants, shags, guillemots, divers and a host of others, in their screeching, quarrelling, mating multitudes. Seals dived and bobbed below.

Long the couple stood, dismounted, and stared, Kate clinging to David's arm, not too close to the edge despite his bravado for, calm as the day was, this place appeared to generate its own winds, up and down draughts of sudden vigour which could send them staggering. The horses did not like it at all, and kept pressing backwards, ears flattened.

At length they dragged themselves away, and were re-mounting when they perceived an elderly man coming along the track towards them, leading a stocky garron laden with timber—the first human being they had seen since leaving Dowlaw. Surprised at such meeting up here, they paused to greet him.

"For why do you bring wood to such a place as this?" David enquired. "Do not say that anyone would build up here?"

"Och, it is for the beacon, just." The man pointed to the very topmost pinnacle of the highest hill. "Yonder, Maister. I have to keep the beacon fed. Keep plenties o' wood up there, so it can be lit of a stormy night. Aye, and these last nights it burned a deal, I tell you, wi' yon gale. I'll need twa-three mair loads than this, aye."

"A beacon? Up here? For why?"

"For the shipping, Maister—the shipping, what else? To warn ship-maisters o' this right wanchancy coast, in hard weather. To keep their distance."

"So! Then it is a noble task you perform, friend. Of your own goodwill?"

"Na, na—the nuns o' Coldingham Priory pay me. No' that much, mind—but, och, they're just weemen and dinna ken what it's like here o' a wild night, feeding the fire. Saving your presence, lady!"

"And are there many ships lost on this terrible coast?" Kate asked.

"Ooh, aye—plenties. Plenties. A wheen mair than there need be, forby."

"Why? What do you mean?"

"The wreckers, just, Satan burn them!"

"Wreckers . . . ?"

"Aye, wreckers. Och, they're aye at it."

"What do you mean, at it? At what?" David demanded.

"D'you no' ken, sir? It's a right trade, here—and an ill trade, guid kens! Mind, no' sae much o' it since yon Home o' Fast and his rogues were outed."

"Home? Of Fast?"

"Aye, him. The laird. He was aye the worst—him and them that went before him. Right devils they were."

"You mean that Home deliberately sought to wreck ships? But how?"

"Easy. Douse my beacon and march a tight party o' his men carrying blazing torches along this bit path, northwards, towards Fast. The shipmen reckon it's St Ebba's Head light and ken where they are. In the dark o' a gale, mind, they'll no' ken the light's moving. So it lures them on. The ships may keep their distance off shore, or so they jalouse—but this side o' Fast, and the other side too, there's reefs stretching oot, the Branders, the Souters and the Rooks, and wi' the bend o' the coast the chances are the ships will strike one or the other. Hech, man—that's why Fast was built where it is!"

"In God's good name—can this be true?"

"True, aye—why should I lie? A'body kens it, hereaboots. It's aye been the way, at Fast. Many's the time I've had to run for my life, frae yon beacon, because o' Home's men.

Others too, mind. Ooh, aye—fine pickings they've had frae the wrecked ships, ower the years. And drooned men tell nae tales!"

David and Kate eyed each other, appalled. "So that was it!" he breathed.

"Oh, Davie . . . !"

Taking their leave of the old man, they rode back to Fast, in a very different mood from previously.

Somehow, after that, Fast Castle's remote and extraordinary situation did not appeal so much, especially to Kate. Even of a night the seabirds' wailings were apt to change into the cries of drowning men and women. The castle might, in fact, have been built there for completely other reasons—although they were at a loss to think of any. But the beacon-man's tale rang horribly true.

In a couple of more days they decided that they had had sufficient of Fast, and packed up, to head for home. Their attendants could not have been more thankful. They stayed three further days with Antoine at Dunbar, who proved entirely understanding over their feelings—he had not heard about the wrecking links with Fast—before they returned to Garleton, honeymoon over.

14

David brought his bride to Stirling at the beginning of May, to warm greetings from Abbot John and great rejoicing on the part of King James, both at seeing his friend back at last and at the presence of Kate, with whom he had always got on well. Now five years old, he was a pleasant child, somewhat precocious with being solely in the company of adults, normally good-tempered and fun-loving although capable of tantrums. The Earl Marischal and the Lord Erskine, the castle's hereditary keeper, were glad enough to welcome the Lord Lindsay's daughter also, even though they both clearly considered that her husband had always required keeping in his place. Lady Erskine was less enchanted. Hitherto the only woman of quality resident in the fortress, autocratic and of middle years, the arrival of a young, lively and attractive creature like Kate, higher born than herself—she was a daughter of Sir George Campbell of Loudoun—scarcely appealed.

The accommodation problem was satisfactorily solved by John Inglis vacating the room he had shared with David, an anteroom of the royal bedchamber, for a smaller apartment nearby, leaving the other to the newly-weds—for James would not hear of his beloved Davie sleeping anywhere else but in the next and intercommunicating apartment to his own, but was quite prepared to accept Kate there too. This did mean that the Lindsays' privacy was liable to be invaded frequently by the young monarch; but fortunately he tended to sleep long and soundly of a night—although there were occasions when, after some childish upset or frightening dream, he rushed in to share their bed with them.

The other problem, of Kate possibly feeling that she was too much immured in a fortress, proved to be less trying than David had feared. She did not seem to be so oppressed as was he by the stern enclosing walls and battlements.

Moreover, the land being as nearly at peace at the moment as ever it was, the Earl Marischal—who took his duties seriously—was prepared to let the young couple ride abroad frequently, and even to take the monarch with them on occasion, with suitable escort of course, hunting in the Stirling mosses of the meandering Forth, hawking and visiting. It turned out to be a good summer, and Stirling, on the verge of the Highlands, had some wonderful country on its doorstep, and all new to Kate.

All was not quite peace and harmony in Scotland that summer, of course—it never was—even though David was not personally involved and Stirling only remotely concerned. After some months of welcome quiet for Regent and country, there was an outbreak of trouble in the Borderland, the usual raiding and rapine, at first sporadic then gradually showing a pattern. Lord Dacre's name was much bandied about but the identity cropping up most frequently was Sir Andrew Kerr of Ferniehirst, chief of one of the two branches of that unruly clan; and the raiding and bloodshed was confined to the West Merse, Teviotdale and lower Tweeddale, carefully avoiding the Home country; indeed the Homes of Wedderburn, Polwarth and Cowdenknowes were reliably reported to be taking part. The victims tended to be Turnbulls, Elliots, Pringles, Scotts—and these were all Home foes and rivals rather than Kerr's. It looked somehow significant.

It was de la Bastie's duty, as Warden of the Marches, to deal with all this, but he had insufficient forces at his disposal to tackle the combined strength of the Kerr and Home clans, plus Dacre's Northumbrians. So, whilst appealing to Albany for more men, he sought to demonstrate the crown's authority in the area by making sundry minor but strategic gestures of his own, where he believed that the impact might best tell. And in one of these, a call in force one evening at Home Castle itself, he made infinitely more impact than he could have hoped—for he found the Lord Home himself therein, with his brother Sir William and the wanted Kerr of Ferniehirst, in secret conclave, with only a moderate number of mosstroopers to protect them. After a brief but bloody affray, the Warden's men triumphed, and he took all three notables prisoner, to bear them to Edinburgh next day.

This wholly unexpected development created a great stir. It had not been realised that Home himself had returned to Scotland, from King Henry's care, nor that he had been involved in the present Border turmoils at any more than the longest range. Why he had been rash enough to venture back at this stage was not to be known—although no doubt he had some nefarious end in view. His capture, at any rate, changed the entire situation, with Arran more or less tamed and Angus meantime marking time and watching his step heedfully as he did so. Scotland's major trio of dissidents, for once, were all under control.

This time there was to be no undue clemency or delayed action. Home was promptly immured in Edinburgh's Tolbooth, like any common felon, to be brought to trial for high treason at the earliest possible moment, and his brother and Kerr with him. It was already September and the hearing was set for the beginning of October.

It was at this stage that David Lindsay became involved, if in a minor way. De la Bastie was to be one of the principal witnesses, of course, and he asked for David to substantiate his testimony in respect of some of the earlier charges of treasonable activity. So David went to Edinburgh for the trial, and took Kate home for a visit to the Byres at the same time.

The trial, under the Lord Justice General, the Earl of Argyll, was of course a foregone conclusion, little more than a formality—at least as far as Lord Home was concerned. It was inconceivable otherwise, for his guilt had been so blatant and long-continued that there could be no real defence. Indeed he did not deign to put any forward, treating judges, prosecutor and witnesses with a lofty disdain. His brother and Kerr did however fight their cases, but to no advantage. David's testimony was less than necessary. All three were found guilty of highest treason and condemned to death—although Albany, never a harsh man despite his hot temper, and with a view to Border pacification, remitted Kerr's sentence so long as he kept the peace. But for the Homes there could be no such mercy.

Alexander, third Lord Home, met his end, with dignity, on the scaffold outside the Tolbooth the very next day, 8th October, and Sir William the day following. Their heads were thereafter exhibited on spikes above the said Tolbooth, as warning to others. Neither left any male issue.

Much of Scotland breathed a sigh of relief.

Albany and the Warden thereafter lost no time in leading an expedition in major force—the army which had been assembled in answer to de la Bastie's appeal—to parade through the Borderland, with Sir Andrew Kerr in chains, making an especial demonstration at Jedburgh, the Kerrs' main town, before freeing Ferniehirst to return to his own castle. Dacre and his Northumbrians kept discreetly to their own side of the borderline.

It looked as though the realm might have a reasonably trouble-free winter.

Perhaps that was too much to hope for. The very next month two new and unexpected challenges arose for the Regent and government, both with a personal flavour. The first was odd indeed. The previous Duke, Albany's father, second son of James the Second, had had two wives, the first a daughter of the Earl of Orkney, by whom he had produced a son, Alexander. But this marriage had been set aside by Holy Church as within the prohibited relationship, and thereafter it was pronounced by the Scots parliament of the day invalid. The Duke then married his French countess, and the present Albany was born, and accepted by all as heir. The earlier half-brother had grown up quietly, no trouble to anyone, in his native Orkney. Now this Alexander Stewart, in middle years, unaccountably elected to make formal claim that he was in fact legitimately born, the elder son, the former marriage having ended in divorce, not annulment, and that therefore he should himself be Duke of Albany, second person in the kingdom and Regent, the papal injunction false and the subsequent parliamentary veto nullified. Why, at this late stage, he should have brought forward this extraordinary plea was a mystery—although most assumed Henry Tudor to be behind it, for no one else would seem likely to gain anything by it, and Henry was a born fisher in troubled waters. Albany was flabbergasted. He had never so much as met this curious half-brother, and few in the realm had even heard of him—although he was, to be sure, a grandson of James the Second and a cousin of the late monarch.

The second blow fell within days—the arrival of a new

ambassador from France, one Francis de Bordeaux, with a request, indeed a command from the King of France for the prompt return of his Admiral, the Duke of Albany, and a threat, however diplomatically put, not to renew the Franco-Scottish alliance. The same ship brought a private letter to his uncle from Davie Beaton, informing that King Francis was in fact in process of realigning his policies, and was getting no help from the Emperor and Spain in his efforts to retain his prize of Milan and his other North Italy conquests and so was using possible alliance with Henry of England as threat—hence this gesture towards cancelling the Auld Alliance with Scotland. He, Davie, was doing his best in a difficult situation, but bigger guns than himself were called for. He urged Albany's speedy appearance in France.

In some perturbation, the Regent called an urgent special meeting of parliament.

David Lindsay heard about this from Antoine de la Bastie, who attended the parliament as Chief Warden, and thereafter paid a visit to Stirling to see his friends before returning to his duties at Dunbar. According to him the Alexander Stewart business had been more or less laughed out of court, the assembly refusing to take the Orkney claim seriously; but on Albany's urging, eventually passing a formal renewal of the parliamentary ban on any assertion of lawful status by Stewart, with warning of stern crown action if such claims were persisted in. All saw King Henry's busy hand behind this bizarre incident, but hoped that this reaction would see an end to it.

The French problem was not so readily disposed of. Antoine himself, who knew King Francis personally as something of a weathercock, thought that probably masterly inaction was the wisest course, that Francis and Henry would never be other than essential foes, and that all this would blow over of itself sooner or later. But Albany was worried, declaring that the Franco-Scottish alliance was absolutely essential for the realm's well-being and must be rescued at all costs, and quickly. He reiterated his urgent demand for leave of absence, as Regent, to return to France. Parliament had been loth to agree again, at this juncture, considering possible Orkney developments; and the fact that the Queen-Mother, now back at her brother's court, was demanding the right to return to Scotland to visit her son—and with Henry ever declaring that she ought to be Regent for his nephew, Albany's absence would be as good as an invitation. A compromise had been reached, that the Duke should have parliament's agreement to travel to France on a brief visit, but only when the realm's affairs made this reasonably convenient—an equivocal decision on which both sides put their own interpretation. As postscript to all, the assembly emphasised its acceptance of Albany as second person of the kingdom.

As parliaments went, it was scarcely memorable or decisive. But at least it had produced no rumblings from either Arran nor Angus nor their factions. The former, of course, was upset by the Orkney claim, which if it could be successfully pursued, would reduce him to fourth person instead of third. He had not actually taken part in any of the debates, but his son, Sir James Hamilton of Finnart, the Bastard of Arran, had been very prominent, forceful and effective—a man to watch, clearly. As for Angus, he had in fact spoken against his wife being allowed to return to Scotland, his personal relationship with that awkward princess seeming to preoccupy him more than somewhat.

The parliament over, Yuletide was soon upon them, its preparations and the twelve days of Christmas and New Year celebrations a welcome period of relief for all from problems of rule and governance amongst the nations of Christendom—holy days indeed, however less than holy some of the ongoings. At Stirling, Kate and David enjoyed their first Yule as man and wife, with young James almost like their own son, entering into it all with marked enthusiasm. David wrote a poem to celebrate the occasion, short enough for the King to memorise and declaim it, word-perfect—and to go on declaiming it until they could bear it no longer.

It was in fact June before Albany finally got away to France, with even then the Scots very reluctant to let him go. And before that, much had transpired. The new Regency Council had to be set up, for one thing; and proved difficult indeed, with much rivalry, faction-fighting, lobbying, offence given and taken. Eventually it was composed of the Archbishops of St Andrews and Glasgow and the Earls of Arran, Angus,

Argyll and Huntly—much too large, but each required as check and counter-balance against others. Beaton, as Chancellor, would preside. A majority of this group decided that the young monarch, in the interim, would be safer in Edinburgh Castle than in Stirling, as more effectively under their eyes; and although others doubted, the royal entourage was brought to the capital in May—to David's and Kate's satisfaction at least, so much nearer home and at the centre of things.

Then, as it were, to prepare the way for, it was hoped, successful negotiations with King Francis, Albany sent the French ambassador on ahead with the suggestion that Scotland was prepared to have its young King betrothed to Francis's daughter Louise or her sister Madeleine, a shrewd move advised by Davie Beaton, which would give France pause.

Finally, just before he left, the Duke created a further upset of his own, by announcing, without consultation with others, that he was leaving the Sieur de la Bastie as Lieutenant-Governor of the kingdom during his absence—just like that.

There was, of course, a general outcry and protest, Antoine himself pleading to be excused. He was popular enough, admittedly, but the appointment of a foreigner to such a position was hardly acceptable and the position itself of questionable validity and scope—for where did it place its incumbent in relation to the Regency Council? Which was the supreme authority? No one knew, least of all de la Bastie himself. But Albany was adamant. He wanted someone he could trust absolutely at the helm, he informed privately. And a soldier, not a cleric, he insisted. There might well be the need for swift, drastic and military action, and he certainly could not depend on the squabbling ragbag of councillors to provide it effectively. When Antoine pointed out that any such armed action would be apt to be in the Borders area anyway where he was already Warden of the Marches and had full authority to act, the Duke countered by reminding that, as Warden, he had no power to order a mobilisation of the nation's manpower, nor even any major army, and this certainly might be necessary at shortest notice—and God help the realm if it depended on the Council, all pulling against each other!

This, then, was the Regent's last official act before setting sail for his native land.

So David Lindsay found himself in a rather extraordinary situation for a young man of no especially lofty birth and position, close and most favoured companion of the monarch and intimate friend of the new Lieutenant-Governor. Moreover, being now resident at Edinburgh, he saw much of de la Bastie, who inevitably had to spend a greater proportion of his time in the capital than at Dunbar.

It was not long before there was occasion for Antoine to act. As Warden of the Marches he employed spies along the Northumbrian borderlands to give him prior warning of invading bands; and only a week or two after Albany's departure, one of these sent reliable information that Margaret Tudor was on her way northwards with a large train, clearly heading for Scotland. Obviously she—or Henry—had only waited for the Regent to be out of the country before making her move.

Antoine had to think fast—but he was good at that. The Borders were still in an unsettled state. The Homes had lost their chief and his brother and a third brother, Sir George, was now fourth Lord Home, but a man of retiring disposition. Despite this the clan were seething with resentment and on the look out for vengeance. The Kerrs were certainly not to be relied upon, and the other Border clans were scarcely more so, for in the nature of things these, or their leaders, were the most open to King Henry's briberies and blandishments. Moreover, if Margaret had only been waiting for this opportunity, what of her husband Angus? Although lying low meantime, and seeming not to desire his wife's company, he might also have been waiting—and the Douglases were notably strong on the Middle and West Marches. The Tudor approach *could* be the signal for a major uprising in these parts; and if that happened, what might it spark off elsewhere?

In this first test of his position and authority, the Lieutenant-Governor had to act with decision and tact as well as speed. He had to inform the Regency Council, of course; but fortunately or otherwise its members were apt to be scattered about the face of the land unless specifically called together—and there was no time for that. Getting the Chancellor's agreement without difficulty, Antoine mustered as many men as he could in the Edinburgh area, at short notice, and considered how, as it were, to carry the councillors with him in this matter. Beaton himself was getting too old and corpulent for this sort of foray; Arran was away at Hamilton, and Argyll in the West Highlands. But Angus was only at his castle of Tantallon, and it would be wise to have him under supervision anyhow. So he should be asked to ride to meet his wife, as representative of the Regency but at the Lieutenant-Governor's side. And, as counter-balance, in case of Douglas trouble developing, the young Earl of Morton, head of the Black Douglases, who lived at Dalkeith only six miles south of Edinburgh, should come along too—for the Black Douglases were ever suspicious of the Red, or Angus, line, who had been instrumental in pulling them down in James the Second's reign and rising to power in their stead. The Teviotdale Douglases were Black. In addition, Antoine took David Lindsay along, ostensibly to give the Queen-Mother first-hand information about her son—for nothing was more certain than that she could not be allowed any direct contact with the King.

So, some fifteen hundred strong, they marched eastwards, picking up Lord Lindsay and some of his people at the Byres. At Tantallon, Angus had been sent warning of their arrival but with insufficient time for him to assemble any sizeable force. He came along, distinctly doubtful, with a mere hundred or so of a following.

On southwards through the Home country they headed, their numbers precluding any possible attack by that troublesome lot. Halfway down the Eye Water's valley, one of Antoine's scouts brought him word that the English company, some three hundred in number, had crossed Tweed at Berwick and were apparently coming on. De la Bastie promptly sent Lord Lindsay and David spurring ahead to inform Margaret Tudor that she and her party must not enter Scots territory until given due authority to do so.

With a small escort the two Lindsays rode on at speed, wondering what their reception might be from the autocratic Queen-Mother. Down past Ayton and Burnmouth they cantered, and on beyond, between Lamberton Muir and the cliff-girt coast, with Berwick Bounds now only three miles ahead. But, well before they could reach that so-debatable borderline, itself three miles north of the town, they spied the large company in front of them, near Lamberton Kirk, already a good two miles into Scotland. And, to add to the offence, at the cavalcade's head flew the large red and gold standard of the royal Lion-Rampant of Scotland.

The Lord Patrick swore comprehensively.

He swore again presently even more fluently when, near enough to perceive features, he recognised, riding in front beside Margaret Tudor, none other than the Lord Dacre himself, the English Warden, handsome and arrogant. And on the lady's other side, the grim-visaged Home of Wedderburn.

At the approach of the Lindsays, the oncoming column drew rein. The Lord Patrick was not going to doff his bonnet, in the circumstances, but compromised by raising a hand high in some sort of salute to the King's mother. Before he could say a word she spoke, haughtily, in her clipped southern voice.

"The Lord Lindsay, I see. You are something late to greet me, my lord, are you not?"

Lord Patrick gasped and swallowed. "I . . . I .... Madam, that is not my concern, nor my function. I am here at the command of the Lieutenant-Governor of this realm, and the Regency Council, to remind you that you, and this company, should not have crossed into Scottish territory lacking permission and safe-conduct. You must turn back . . ."

"God's death—how dare you, sirrah! How dare you speak me so? *Me*, lately Queen of this realm and mother of the King of Scots! Have you lost your wits, man?"

"No, Madam, I have not. I but obey the express commands of the Governor and Regency. None from another realm may lawfully set foot on Scots soil without the prior permission of the King's representatives, duly appointed. This has not been obtained . . ."

"Who are you, or any, to speak to me of the King's representatives? The King is my son and I journey to see him. I warn you to watch your words, Lindsay, or you will rue the day!"

The Lord Patrick jutted his chin. "The words are not mine but those who sent me. And you, lady, know well their truth and worth. As does the man who has the effrontery to ride here at your side!"

Dacre grinned but said nothing.

"Who may these be who have sent you? This so-called Governor and Regency," Margaret demanded.

"The Sieur de la Bastie, First Knight of Christendom, whom my lord Duke of Albany appointed Lieutenant-Governor during his absence. And the Earl of Angus, your present husband, representing the Regency Council."

That gave even Margaret Tudor pause. She frowned.

Following up his advantage, Lindsay went on. "The Governor, my lord of Angus, and their host, are on their way to meet you. No great distance off. I require that you return to Berwick Bounds and there await them."

The hoot of laughter from Dacre was eloquent.

"Now we *know* that you are out of your mind, sirrah! You expect me, the Queen, to turn back?"

"You are no longer Queen, Madam, but Countess of Angus. And the Earl of Angus will meet you at Berwick Bounds."

"Is he, then, as besotted as yourself? I shall do no such thing, Lindsay."

They glared at each other, clearly impasse reached.

David coughed. So far he had not spoken, but some moderating intervention appeared to be called for. "My lord—Lamberton Kirk, here?" He gestured towards the small isolated parish church which stood a few hundred yards back from the roadway. "Perhaps the princess could wait there? In the shelter of Holy Church! Medial ground? Since she will not go back."

"M'mm." His father-in-law looked uncertain.

"Not that I would think that even such sanctuary would ensure the Lord Dacre's safety from the Governor's wrath, were he to find *him* there!" That significant addition might serve two ends, he hoped.

Lord Patrick shrugged. "That could serve, perhaps. Madam—you may wait in the kirk, here. For myself, I would hope that this Englishman at your side will wait there with you—that he may receive his desserts so richly earned by his savageries against this realm! I would think that he would hang, here and forthwith!" That enabled him to end on a suitably strong note.

It was Margaret Tudor's turn to look a little uncertain. She turned to confer with Dacre and Wedderburn, who both looked preoccupied. Presently she nodded. "Very well," she said briefly, and reined round her horse's head in the direction of the church.

Dacre spoke. "Then, having seen Your Grace safely to your welcome, in the name of your most royal brother, I shall return to my own place." That was dignity itself.

"And I shall escort my Lord Dacre back to Berwick Bounds and English soil," Wedderburn added, as carefully.

Lord Lindsay smiled broadly.

There was some confusion and toing and froing amongst the company as to whom went where. Presently it became evident that, in fact, the majority behind the Queen-Mother were either Dacre's or Wedderburn's men, and would return with their leaders, leaving only a comparatively small group to go to the church. The Lord Patrick sent David back to inform de la Bastie as to the situation.

He did not have to ride more than four or five miles to encounter the main body. Antoine smiled at his report; Angus frowned.

When they reached Lamberton Kirk it was to find Margaret Tudor within and Lindsay pacing outside on guard, whilst the escorting parties glared at each other like chained dogs. The fifteen hundred marshalled themselves around the place, as though for a siege.

De la Bastie led the way in, Angus with no evident anxiety to greet his wife. That lady was sitting alone up in the little chancel, beside the altar, looking grim. With the newcomers, the church was crowded.

Antoine bowed with Gallic flourish. "Madam, I greet you. I am de la Bastie, the Regent's Lieutenant. You have come further north than we had anticipated."

She ignored him entirely, looking beyond to her husband. "You, Anguish, are in bad company, I see." She had always called him Anguish, but what had started as something of an endearment had for a year or two now held a different significance.

"Lady!" he jerked, and apparently found nothing else to say.

"I have been insulted by this man, Lindsay," she went on.

"Most unkindly handled—I, the King's mother. I look for apologies and better treatment. See to it."

Angus shrugged.

Antoine tried again. "Princess—the Lord Lindsay, I am sure, only carried out his orders. Had you sought safe-conduct and awaited it at Berwick, there would have been no . . . *contretemps*! I should have greeted you there in person."

"Frenchman—*I* do not require the permission of any foreigner, or any other, to enter my son's kingdom. I shall visit James when and how I please. Remember it, in future."

"Madam—it grieves me ever to contradict a lady, in especial a royal one. But you mistake, I fear. When you remarried, according to your late royal husband's express command, you forfeited all rights of guardianship and authority over the young King's Grace, such authority to be vested instead in the regency and parliament of the realm. These, since you left this realm for that of your royal brother, have adjudged you to be, shall we say, an unsettling influence with King James. This you know well, for it is no new development. Therefore you cannot be allowed to visit His Grace. I am sorry, but that is the position."

"How dare you! You would part a mother and her child?"

"*You* did that, Princess. You chose to remarry, knowing well the terms of the late King's edict."

"A dead man's grudging hand!" She turned. "You, Anguish, my husband—you stand there and listen to this, this upjumped Frenchman, miscall and assail me! Are you a man or a louse?"

"Watch your words, lady!" the Red Douglas snapped, stung. "You should not be here. You should not have come, lacking *my* agreement. It is as the Frenchman says. The regency declares that you cannot see the King. You should return whence you came."

"Lord God—this from *you*! You, whom I wed, at such cost! This is not to be borne!"

"You should not have come," the Earl repeated flatly.

"I *have* come. And *will* see my son. None can debar me from entering Scotland—its former Queen."

"Your husband can, Madam," Antoine said.

"He would not dare! I warn him, and you sir, that my royal brother Henry has a long arm and an iron fist! He thinks little enough of you, Anguish, as it is. Turn me back now and I swear that he will make you rue it!"

Angus coughed—for of all Scots he did not have to be told the weight and virulence of Henry Tudor's wrath. "For myself, lady, I do not forbid that you enter this realm. I but repeat that the regency refuses that you see the King." And he looked at de la Bastie.

"It is as my lord says," Antoine nodded. "We do not forbid your visit to Scotland. But you may not see His Grace, Princess."

"We shall see about that!" She rose. "Enough of this talk. I will be on my way."

"And we shall escort you, Madam. Your royal son's Procurator and Usher, David Lindsay of the Mount here, will inform you as to His Grace's well-being and progress. For a mother's comfort." De la Bastie bowed again, and turned to lead the way out.

So, to his alarm, David found himself having to ride at Margaret Tudor's side. Stiffly, jerkily, he forced himself to recount something of James's state and condition, with long silences—the longer in that she showed little sign of interest. However, when after a while she unbent enough to ask a question or two, he warmed a little to his task, unable to keep his affection for the boy wholly hidden. It was scarcely a successful conversation, but by the time that they reached Dunbar, to spend that night before proceeding to Edinburgh, he felt that as well as having done his duty he perhaps had discovered just a little more humanity and feeling in this strange woman than he had believed was there.

He was thankful, nevertheless, when he could leave her, at Dunbar.

15

Margaret Tudor, back in Scotland, was an embarrassment for most who had anything to do with government and the monarchy. And being the woman she was, she did not seek to temper the wind towards any. On her marriage to James the Fourth, Linlithgow Palace had formed part of the marriage settlement, and presumably it was still hers, since no steps had so far been taken to deprive her of it legally. At any rate, it was standing empty, and Margaret promptly headed therefor and took up residence.

Quickly she made her presence felt, with orders to the Regency Council that her son should be brought there to lodge with her. When this was as promptly refused, she demanded that she should be admitted to Edinburgh Castle to visit him, and arrived in the capital in some style, to press her claim. This proving equally unsuccessful, she remained in the city, pursuing an alternative project—none other than seeking to reclaim, at law, the sum of four thousand merks, being rents of her dowry properties in the Forest of Ettrick, uplifted and appropriated by her husband in her absence—embarrassing in a more personal way for that member of the Regency Council, Angus had to defend himself in court, with the plea that a wife's property became legally her husband's on marriage—which the judges chose to uphold. In cold fury the lady then declared that the dastardly Douglas would not find himself in a position to steal any more of her revenues hereafter, since she would be no longer his wife. She would sue for divorce, on the grounds that he was living in sin with Janet Stewart, daughter of the Laird of Traquair. This public washing of soiled linen—which was no news to most in Edinburgh and the Borderland—improved neither her nor her husband's position, especially when it transpired that Home of Wedderburn had married Angus's sister, an injudicious liaison, to say the least. The Red Douglas star was scarcely in the ascendant.

There was worse to come, much worse—and the impact of it was to grieve David and Kate Lindsay sorely. Edinburgh had hastily emptied itself of almost all who could afford to move out temporarily, on account of a visitation of the plague; and the young King and his entourage, for safety, were installed in the castle of Craigmillar, on higher ground some three miles to the south-east of the city, a strong place of the Preston family but pleasantly situated and much less daunting to live in than the grim fortress citadel. It was there that the dire news reached them. Antoine de la Bastie was dead, murdered.

The details were sufficiently clear, indeed flauntingly so, for the Homes were boasting of it. They had hated de la Bastie from the day he had opposed the Lord Home and moved against Dunglass, Colbrandspath Tower and Fast Castle. His appointment as Warden of the Marches had further infuriated them, for they looked on that position as more or less hereditary in their family. Execution of their chief and his brother they blamed largely on the testimony of the Frenchman at the trial. And the confrontation at Lamberton Kirk, in their own Merse, appeared to have been the last straw. They, and Home of Wedderburn in particular, had decided to settle scores.

They had gone about it with some cunning. No large-scale battle was sought, in which the Warden's forces would likely win. The Frenchman had the reputation of seeking to settle problems in his bailiwick in person, where possible. So the Homes had staged a small mock outbreak of lawlessness at Langton, in the Merse, not far from Wedderburn itself, where they had one of the Wedderburn brothers make a minor assault on Langton Tower, a Cockburn place, and create something of a botch of it. No doubt Cockburn was in the plot, for he was married to a Home. Anyway there was much sound and fury, if little else, the word was duly brought to Dunbar Castle, and as expected, the Warden set out, with only a small company, to investigate.

Reaching Langton, some twenty-five miles from Dunbar, without interference, he had apparently found the trouble over and peace returned. But whilst making his enquiries he and his people had perceived that they, and Langton Tower, were surrounded. Large numbers of mosstroopers had hidden themselves in the surrounding scrub-woodland—for like so much of the Merse, the area was boggy and undrained, more or less impassable wilderness, a source of much of the Homes' immunity from the processes of law. Recognising that the encirclers meant business and that he was hopelessly outnumbered, with what looked like the entire strength of the Homes mustered, de la Bastie had sought to form up his modest party into the classical cavalry wedge-formation, to try to drive their way through the encircling host at any weak spot, and then head for home and reinforcements. But his followers, unfortunately, saw this as a forlorn hope, and scattered in panic.

Left with only two or three close companions, Antoine had dashed off, more or less on his own, heading eastwards, as he had come, following roughly the line of the Langton Water by the Nisbet area and Mungo's Walls. On a splendid mount, he forged ahead. But this was the very heart of the Home country and his enemies knew it like the backs of their hands, whereas the Warden did not. Shrewdly, deliberately, they used their knowledge and superior strength to drive and manoeuvre their quarry into ever more swampy ground. Worse and worse became the going and presently the Warden's fine horse was floundering up to its hocks in mire. Alone now, Antoine turned to face his assailants. He had no least chance, of course. Attacked, on foot, by a score of Home sworders, he fought to the last, the death-strokes actually being administered by Wedderburn's two younger brothers, John and Patrick Home. Wedderburn's own part in the proceedings was to come up then, dagger drawn, and raising the Frenchman's handsome head by its long, carefully braided hair, to hack and saw at the neck above the half armour gorget until he had bloodily decapitated the fallen body. Then, swinging the head by its tresses, he ploutered his way back to his horse, mounted and with the grisly trophy at his saddle bow, led his triumphant following back westwards, not to Wedderburn but all the way to Duns town, almost the Home capital. There, he hung the head on the market cross, announcing to all and sundry that this was suitable reward for any who thought to interfere with the Homes in their own Merse. Let all take note. He rode off, leaving his trophy there.

Appalled, the Lindsays mourned a friend, and feared for a land where such a deed could be perpetrated.

There were repercussions, of course, public condemnations and outrage, assertions as to condign punishment and so on; but a marked slowness to take any appropriate action. To be sure, the death of the nation's Lieutenant-Governor and Warden left a power vacuum, and there was much dubiety about who was to fill it. This was for the Regency Council to decide, lacking Albany's instructions, and there was no unanimity there. It was no situation for elderly clerics, and there was no obvious strong man of note outside the said council to bring in. So the choice fell between the four earls thereon, really between Arran and Angus, although Argyll and Huntly were each suggested as possible compromise candidates in place of the two real rivals. But both were, as it happened, Highland clan chiefs, of the Campbells and the Gordons, and the predominant Lowland interests would take ill out of such seeming to hold sway over them. So it came down to the Hamilton and the Douglas, as from the first had seemed almost inevitable.

Arran, of course, as third person in the realm, could claim superiority; and Angus's standing at the moment was not at its highest. But Arran was notoriously weak, a weathercock, and middle aged now; whereas Angus was younger, a fighter if not always a successful one, and head of the most powerful house in the kingdom. The scales were fairly evenly balanced. Meanwhile, nothing effective was done about the Homes.

Then Arran played a strong card—or, at least, his son, the Bastard did. He claimed that Angus had been privy to the entire de la Bastie incident—after all, Wedderburn was his brother-in law—and it was asserted that his brother, Sir George Douglas of Pittendreich, had been visiting Wedderburn the day before. What truth there might be in all this was anybody's guess, but it was sufficient, in the climate prevailing, to swing the vote in Arran's favour.

That ineffectual individual was duly sworn in as not only Lieutenant-Governor of the realm but as Chief Warden of the Marches also. David Lindsay was not alone in fearing the worst.

In this, however, David was mistaken, reckoning without Sir James Hamilton of Finnart, the Bastard. For that young man was the reverse of ineffectual, and suddenly he was powerful indeed. By a strange turn of the wheel of fortune, in fact, from being almost unknown by most he quickly proved to be the real ruler of the realm, *pro tempore*, his father only nominally so. Strong, decisive, ruthless and unscrupulous, he was the sort of character that Scotland was apt to throw up in an emergency—and possibly the sort that awkward nation needed from time to time.

His first move, in Arran's name, was to order the arrest of Sir George Douglas and Kerr of Ferniehirst, as allegedly part and art in the murder of de la Bastie—as warning to Angus. Then he commanded Wedderburn and the other Homes to present themselves for trial. Needless to say they did not do so—nor were expected to. But the trial was held, nevertheless, the Homes *in absentia*, Douglas and Kerr protesting their innocence, Angus lying notably low. The two captives were awarded what amounted to a not proven verdict and dismissed with a warning that any further association with the Homes would seal their fate. Wedderburn and his brothers were found guilty and condemned to death, and the entire clan of Home given notice of dire retribution if there should be any further defiance of the lawful authority.

Then a large force was assembled to march south to the Merse.

David Lindsay found himself sent for, by the Bastard, to accompany this expedition, as a former colleague of de la Bastie and as one who knew the Merse and the Homes passing well, also now with some small reputation on tactics, little earned as this might be. Hamilton had not forgotten their association on the ride to Douglas Castle, it seemed. Always well pleased to escape from the constrictions of fortress life, he went gladly. Since presumably they would be picking up the usual Lindsay contingent en route, he took Kate along, to deposit at the Byres once more, the only woman with the host.

Arran himself was present on this occasion, but very evidently his son was in charge of all, the Earl a mere figurehead. The Bastard welcomed David, not warmly for he was not a warm man, but cheerfully, and was gallant, in a fleering, heavy-handed way, towards Kate. He made no attempt to hide the fact that this was *his* expedition and that all would be done his way. A dashing figure in black, gold-inlaid half armour and plumed helmet, he outlined the projected programme as they rode side by side—without, of course, actually seeking David's advice. The object was not any major confrontation, despite their numbers, he informed—the Borderers were difficult enough folk to conduct without unnecessarily arousing their hostility at the start to the new Warden of their Marches. It must always be remembered that the real menace was Angus and the Douglases, these Homes and Kerrs and the like mere pin-prickers. These must be kept in their place, of course, and shown who wielded the King's authority; but full-scale hostilities were to be avoided. This demonstration in force was more to give warning to the Douglases than to savage the Homes. They would make no uncertain gesture towards the Homes and let the Merse see the power of the Governor and Warden; but thereafter they would proceed through the Douglas lands of Teviotdale and Tweeddale, to leave Angus in no doubt as to the realities of the situation. This was explained as they marched from Edinburgh down the Lothian coast, by Musselburgh and Salt Preston, in order to, as it were, show the flag to the Red Douglas lairdships of Longniddry, Kilspindie, Stoneypath and Whittinghame, and of course, Tantallon itself.

David was less than enthusiastic over all this. To him it sounded more like a development of the Hamilton–Douglas feud than a punitive measure against the murderers of Antoine de la Bastie. He said as much.

Hamilton pooh-poohed that but pointed out that it was essential to recognise that the Douglases and the Homes must not be allowed to become allies, as might well happen; and of course the Douglases were much the more powerful and dangerous, nationwide, not only in the Borders. It was necessary that judgment on the Homes over the murder should be seen to be carried out; but the security of the realm itself was vastly more important, and this expedition was concerned with that also.

So the host of some four thousand men moved in almost leisurely fashion down the coast, impressive as to size and appearance, all banners and armour and even some of the late King's cannon, although not the heavier pieces which would have slowed down progress even further, something like a holiday atmosphere prevailing. No great mileage per day was possible in these circumstances, and not much more than a dozen miles was achieved before the first evening—but that conveniently brought them to the area of Longniddry, Aberlady and Kilspindie, all Douglas territory, where the army could satisfactorily encamp and demand food, forage and shelter—a most suitable method of demonstrating the facts of life to the Douglas lairds, including Angus's own uncle at Kilspindie, without actually having to take overt hostile action. Leaving Arran and the Bastard at Luffness Castle, David was able to take Kate three miles inland to the Byres and Garleton.

Next day the army also came that way, leaving the coast where there were no more Douglas properties meantime, to pick up the Lindsay contingent and proceed south-eastwards over the Garleton Hills and across the Vale of Tyne, skirting Haddington, heading for the Lammermuir foothill lands of Whittinghame and Stoneypath, Douglas places also, where a similar procedure was enacted. The descent of over four thousand men on a property for even one night, requiring their keep and accommodation, was a salutary experience and expense for any laird, and all done in apparent good will and in the name of loyal duty.

They had heard that Angus had left Tantallon and was thought to be at his lesser property of Tyninghame, nearer Dunbar, and this being a mere six miles or so from Whittinghame, the host marched that way the following morning, as it were in the by-going. If Angus was indeed at Tyninghame he did not reveal himself, and the Governor's leadership party made no attempt to call, deeming their close passage sufficiently significant. On past Dunbar they went, where Arran, as new Warden, made a brief token appearance for the benefit of the garrison, and appointed a new keeper. Then on to Dunglass for the night, forfeited Home property, still in crown hands.

Now in almost wholly Home territory, they made their leisurely way next day, by Colbrandspath and through the hills southwards for Duns, the Merse capital. As far as David Lindsay was concerned, there was an air of unreality about the entire proceedings, no least haste, little sign of military aggressiveness nor even preparedness for attack. Nothing was more certain than that their unhurried progress would be well-known to all the Home country. Yet the Bastard was clearly unapprehensive—and David knew him to be a realist. He began to suspect that all had been, somehow, arranged beforehand.

At Duns, after the longest day's march, the army happily quartered itself on the burgh, to the lesser delight of the townsfolk, its respectable women in particular. In the morning, after a late start, they moved on a few miles to Wedderburn and Langton.

Here, nothing could have been more agreeable, and generally welcoming. Both strongholds were thrown open to the visitors. The Homes of Cowdenknowes, Ayton and Polwarth were there to greet the Warden and Governor in most civil fashion, all hospitality offered. Unfortunately Wedderburn himself and his brothers were from home meantime, actually visiting friends over on the English side of the borderline; but they would undoubtedly wish all goodwill to be shown to the new Warden. Their houses were at the Warden's disposal.

Since all the condemned Homes' property was already specifically forfeited to the crown, this might seem an unnecessary gesture.

Nevertheless, Arran accepted all graciously, his son for the most part keeping in the background for the moment. A certain merest token harrying of the properties took place, more or less ignored by the leaders on both sides. And after something like a banquet, Cowdenknowes announced that the new Lord Home himself was awaiting them at the burgh of Lauder, to hand over the keys of Home Castle to the Governor. Lauder was not in the Merse at all, but some twenty miles to the west, in Lauderdale, and almost equally far from Home Castle.

David was more than ever surprised when he heard Arran declare his satisfaction with this change of programme, but to wonder about suitable accommodation en route across the high moorland of Polwarth, Wedderlie and Spottiswoode Mosses? The Bastard put a word in here, to inform that the Douglas tower of Evelaw stood approximately halfway, in the Wedderlie area, and would provide a suitable halting place for the night. Cowdenknowes added that it would be his pleasure to escort them in person.

So this very unusual disciplinary expedition set off due westwards next morning, receiving hospitality in passing at Redbraes Castle, the seat of Home of Polwarth, and proceeded on across the high, barren moors, not really part of the Merse so much as the southern foothills of the Lammermuir range. They came to the remote Douglas hold of Evelaw in the evening—and it was noticeable how much less agreeable was both their reception and their attitude here. Douglas of Evelaw had few cattle or sheep left to him when the host moved on in the morning.

It was only some ten miles, through low green hills and mosses, by Westruther and Spottiswoode, to Lauder town, where they duly found the inoffensive George, fourth Lord Home awaiting them with the keys of Home Castle. This last had been forfeited at the time of his brothers' executions and indeed garrisoned by crown representatives since, so this key presentation was something of an empty gesture. But Arran seemed well enough pleased, and his son was only in a hurry now to get on. When it transpired that the getting on involved, not going back eastwards to the Merse to deal with more Homes, but due southwards to Tweeddale and Teviotdale to further demonstrate against the great Douglas lands therein, the Lord Lindsay, for one, called a halt. He had come, and brought his men, he pointed out, to seek out and punish Homes, not to harry and threaten Black Douglases, with whom he was on friendly terms. Anyway, most clearly his contingent was not required, with hostilities apparently the last thing contemplated. He would return to the Byres.

Arran did not seek to detain him, and the Bastard only smiled. David elected to accompany his father-in-law, having had enough of this odd perambulation. At the head of their Lindsays, therefore, they left and rode off northwards for Lothian again, chewing over the problems of a kingdom with a child as monarch, the struggles for power, and how poor a second justice was apt to come to personal and family ambition. They agreed that Hamilton of Finnart was a man to watch, in more ways than one; and that there was a real danger of civil war again breaking out on a major scale between Hamilton and Douglas, with the nation's weal foundering between them. The sooner Albany came back the better, for Arran obviously was useless, a mere cipher.

Their opinion of the new Governor was by no means revised when, a couple of weeks later, after returning from showing the Hamilton flag rather than the Lion-Rampant through the Borderland, Arran announced that in the interests of peace and the realm's well-being, he was graciously pleased, in the name of the King's Grace, to pardon Home of Wedderburn, his brothers and accomplices, and to remit the forfeiture of their properties, on the understanding that hereafter they remained staunch supporters of the said King and his peace.

Antoine de la Bastie was to remain unavenged.

Chancellor Beaton sent an urgent message to the Duke of Albany, to cut short his visit to France and to return to Scotland before the Regency Council fell apart and the realm with it.

16

It was not Albany who arrived, a couple of months later, in answer to the Chancellor's appeal, but Davie Beaton his own nephew. And very soon after his landing, that authoritative young man arrived at the gates of Edinburgh Castle—to which the young King returned, the plague in the city having died away with the colder weather of autumn. Ostensibly Beaton came without delay, officially to convey the greetings of the King of France, and likewise of the Regent Albany, to the child monarch; but in reality he came to see David Lindsay. He was delighted to find him wed, and declared that, God and a certain young woman willing, he intended to follow him into the estate of matrimony at the earliest possible opportunity.

But much as he made of Kate, and the benefits of marriage, that was not what he had come so promptly to discuss. He proclaimed himself much concerned over conditions prevailing in Scotland since he left, and recognised the need for urgent improvement of the situation. But that would not be so easy now, he pointed out.

"Was such ever easy, in this awkward realm?" David asked. "We are, of all peoples, the most difficult to lead and to manage, I do believe! All pull in different directions, preferring to fight each other rather than the common foe . . ."

"Yes, yes—we all know that," Beaton interrupted impatiently—which was not like him. "But this is different. The present situation. The kingdom is now on a steep slope, with little or nothing to prevent it plunging on downwards to disaster, civil war the least of it. Henry of England, we know, is just awaiting his chance. He intends to take over this realm. And what has happened and is now happening, is just what he requires. He intends invasion—when Douglas and Hamilton are fully at each other's throats and most of the kingdom backing one or the other. Then, fullest invasion, with all his might—and the ground, to be sure, well prepared before him. He intends, this time, to be ruler of Scotland."

"But—has he not always sought that? This is not new . . ."

"It is new—his present opportunity, and new moves. Do you not see it? Never before has all been so greatly in his favour. And he is already moving. Already he has set afoot his first endeavours. He will start the trouble at our back door—the Highlands. He is in touch with Alexander, Lord of the Isles, and other great chiefs, Maclean of Duart, Macleod of Dunvegan and others, to lead a great Highland revolt and assault on the Lowlands, with promises to aid them establish an independent sovereignty—this whenever the Hamiltons and Douglases come to actual warfare. This news the French king has, on best authority—and approves, since it all will keep Henry busy and the *French* back door safe. So that Francis can turn his whole strength against North Italy, without looking over his shoulder across the Channel!" Beaton shook his head, unusually perturbed, exasperated, for that normally so confident young man. "The fools here, Angus and Arran, and this Finnart all speak of—they cannot see it! Or will not. And I, *I* can do little about it, as matters are . . ."

David swallowed at what was implied in that, the assumption that his visitor took it for granted that he *ought* to be able to affect and guide the affairs of nations in some degree, the sublime arrogance of it.

"What can any of us do?" he mumbled, embarrassed for his friend.

"I could have done much. With Albany here. He needs me, as interpreter. And heeds me. So I can effect much. But with him in France, here I have not that power. I am but a Fife laird's youngest son!"

"And the Chancellor's nephew," David reminded.

"That, yes. But you will not have failed to note that my uncle is not the man that he was. He grows old and heavy, heavy in mind as well as in person. He is now something of a broken reed, I fear, as Chancellor—tired. Yet he is all that I have, to help steer this yawing ship of state! So I must needs use him."

Again the other marvelled at the attitude behind that.

"See you," Beaton went on, "Forman, Archbishop of St Andrews and Primate of the Church in Scotland, is worse than my uncle, older, frailer, useless. So the Church, which should be the greatest power in the land next to the throne, is feeble, all but leaderless, its bishops and abbots and priors divided, corrupt and largely ignorant, respected by none. Holy Church therefore counts for little or nothing. This could, and should, be changed."

With that, at least, Lindsay could be in full agreement. "The Church is in sorry state, yes. A shame on the nation. Sunk in sloth. But—what can be done about it? Save perhaps by the Pope in Rome? Who, I fear, cares little."

"Aye—and Henry, who is shrewd, mind you, is using this likewise. His Chancellor, Wolsey the Cardinal, is feeding the Vatican with carefully chosen tidings about the Church in Scotland. We hear much, in France, of both the Papal and English courts. Francis is well served with spies. Wolsey would have the Pope to declare the Scottish Church decadent and in default—and it has not paid its dues to Rome for long! So, its hierarchy could be declared incompetent and removed from office, for the time-being. And, to be sure, the nearest metropolitan set in charge over it, to put matters to rights—the Archbishop of York! That age-old story of the English kings—spiritual hegemony over Scotland, as a first step towards complete dominance, via the archdiocese of York. Believe me, Henry Tudor will stop at nothing."

"But—but surely this is impossible? To put the Scots Church under the English! It is centuries since that folly was brought low, that pretence."

"Not so long. Our Church has always claimed independence, but it was only in the reign of James the Third that we attained metropolitan status and our own archbishops. A mere fifty years—and what is that in the life of Holy Church? Right up till then, the ridiculous claims of York maintained. And what one Pope could ordain, another could cancel. It is a real danger. And how Henry would chuckle! The Pope needs help to save all North Italy from the French, with the Emperor so weak. He might well strike a bargain with Henry."

"This is beyond all. Can your uncle do nothing?"

"He might do much—if he would. If only old Elphinstone had been alive! So I must play on my Uncle James. Play strongly."

"You mean . . . ?"

"My eminent relative has other weaknesses besides corpulence, a fondness for young women and consequent sloth in matters religious! He has ambitions also. He would dearly like to be Archbishop of St Andrews, Primate of Scotland, and a cardinal if possible. For these baubles he would do much, exert himself somewhat, I believe."

"So? And how would the realm benefit, in its present straits?"

"So long as he is still Chancellor, and presides over the Regency Council, in name at least, he could use the revived power of Holy Church to large effect. If he would. Monies, my dear David. The Church is rich indeed—if the siller can be wrung out of it. Bribes—Henry Tudor is not the only one who could bribe adherence. We Scots have a sad weakness for siller! And excommunication—a notable power and threat, feared by most men, even the highest, and fiercest. The Primate can excommunicate!"

David blinked. "You, you think to use this, these powers of the Church, in matters of state? Use Holy Church as a weapon to gain your way?"

"To gain the *realm's* way. The realm's safety. Why not? Other kingdoms do, as I know well—France, Spain, the Empire, Henry himself. Why not Scotland?"

"You will never convince the archbishops and bishops to this, Davie. Even you!"

"Not the others, perhaps. But I think that I need only persuade my uncle, see you. With me behind him, as Chancellor *and* Primate, the others will not matter much. Not *that* much!" And he snapped his fingers.

Helplessly, Lindsay wagged his head. "Even you . . ." he repeated. And then, "But would all this be necessary, anyway? It would take time, after all—much time, surely? And the Regent will be back long before that. Albany—with your help, no doubt!—Albany will come and take charge soon."

"That is where you are wrong, my friend. Albany will not come soon. Albany stays in France."

"But—he was given only four months' leave of absence—and that is now past . . ."

"Think you he takes that seriously? He loves France, his home, a deal more than he loves Scotland, I assure you—and I scarce blame him! He has an excellent life there, all to his every taste—here nothing but troubles. Besides, the King of France will not let him go. Especially now, after de la Bastie. Nothing more sure. Not for a long time, I swear."

"You say so? This is . . . bad. Grievous news. If others knew . . .!"

"Others must not know. Keep it to yourself, David."

"I will, I will. But—your uncle? How will he see all this? Can you bring him to it? If he is so weary?"

"I think that I can. That possible cardinal's hat I shall wave, will beckon him! To be Primate as well as Chancellor—that is something few could hope for. If I can give him that hope, I believe I have him. Ambition he does not lack, only vigour. And that, surely, *I* can supply!"

"But how? I think that you have a sufficiency of ambition yourself, yes. But you are only a nephew . . ."

"I aim to be rather more, my friend. See you, if I was constantly at his shoulder, pushing him, making decisions for him, his left hand if not his right—then it all might be achieved. It would take time, to be sure. The French archbishops have secretaries. I propose to make myself my good uncle's secretary. To his marked advantage—and pray God, the realm's!"

David stared. "You could do this? Have yourself accepted, appointed, to such position? Sufficient to precede others? The Chancellor must have many secretaries and assistants already . . ."

"To be sure but none so close as I shall be. I shall be his *personal* secretary, something he has not got, either as Chancellor or as Archbishop of Glasgow. Oh, it will be a Church appointment, never fear. The archdiocese of Glasgow has lay benefices and offices amany, some with most adequate siller attached! I shall draw one of these out of him, and become lay rector of this or lay capitular of that—and so provide myself with suitable wherewithal to support my new state at the same time! I, after all, require the necessary means to keep a wife hereafter!"

"So-o-o! You have it all thought through."

"Most of it, man—most of it. There are one or two details to decide, still! But none beyond me, or the situation, I think. David—with you ever close to the King, and myself guiding the Chancellor and effective ruler of Holy Church, what may we not achieve?"

"I have no say in matters of rule and policy . . ."

"You are *there*, with much influence over our young monarch. You have more power than you think, David Lindsay of the Mount! You could rise high."

"I have no wish to rise high. I see what happened to one who rose all too high, Antoine de la Bastie! I suggest that *you* should take warning from that—for such could happen to you also, in this sad realm!"

"That would be in God's good hands. I am a great believer in God, David—although not always in His earthly servants, self-appointed as most are! But—this of de la Bastie, yes. A shameful affair, shameful for Scotland—and grievously harmful, forby."

"More grievous for Antoine! He was my friend."

"Mine, likewise. You do not forget that it was I who brought him to Scotland? But, more important for this realm, he was the friend of the King of France and of Albany also. Both are affected, in their different ways. Francis is furious—one of his most favoured subjects savagely murdered, and his assassins pardoned. He sees it all as a blow at France, an insult to himself—and Scotland will be the loser. Partly why he approves this of the Lord of the Isles' revolt. Albany will have to work the harder to win the renewal of any treaty and the proposed betrothal of young James to a French princess. As for Albany himself, he will be the more loth to return to Scotland, I fear."

"Yet he is the more needed!"

"True—but we will have to survive lacking him, nevertheless—of that I am sure. Hence my plans to stir up Holy Church. Who knows—we may yet bring those Homes to justice, and avenge our Antoine."

"I pray so. Indeed, I do."

"Yes. Now, this of Hamilton of Finnart, who appears to be cutting so wide a swathe here today—tell me of him. I knew him in France awhile, but never closely . . ."

Oddly enough, David Lindsay was the means of bringing together, in some measure, these two so very different yet able and effective young men who each thought to play a major role on the Scottish stage. Beaton, learning that

David was not exactly friendly but on fairly familiar terms with the Bastard, sought an arranged private meeting, clearly purposing to make use of Hamilton's qualities of drive and energy, if possible, rather than to see him as a prospective foe. Possibly the other thought along similar lines—although David had little doubt in his own mind as to which would be likely to triumph in any duel of wits. Anyway, he saw no harm in bringing them together, in his own quarters in Edinburgh Castle—for both had occasion to visit the fortress frequently on the business of the Governor or the Chancellor. They made an interesting and dangerous pair, and Lindsay was duly wary of both, but recognised that each had qualities which Scotland required, and might counter-balance the one the other.

They appeared to get on reasonably well together, although David had no doubts but that there would be no hesitation on either's part of promptly discarding the other should they discover any influence to be in the way of their own intentions. On one matter, they were in entire agreement, meantime at any rate—that Angus must be kept very much in his place; likewise his wife.

They were aided in this by that ill-matched pair themselves. Margaret, from Linlithgow, announced that, since her husband now had Janet Stewart of Traquair living in open sin with him at Douglas Castle in Douglasdale, divorce was inevitable and urgent. She therefore made application, through Archbishop Forman, for Papal decree. Angus, for his part, at first made no response to this, no doubt concerned about Henry Tudor's reaction. However, if so. he need not have worried, for that autocrat, well informed by his spies, promptly made declaration that his sister must withdraw her suit forthwith, that divorce was morally wrong and repugnant in the sight of God, especially in a member of his own family. She must be reconciled to her husband. Presumably Henry assessed the Douglas power as too potentially useful to be lost over a mere female whim. Emboldened by this, Angus proclaimed to all and sundry that *he* was in fact the injured party in that his wife was flagrantly consorting at Linlithgow with a very young man, oddly enough a Stewart also, Henry Stewart, son of Lord Avondale. King Henry then made it known that he was sending another Henry, one Chadworth, an Observantine friar, to Scotland to effect a reconciliation between the erring couple, in accordance with the Almighty's holy will and precepts.

This comedy was still not yet fully developed, for of all things, Margaret now appealed to Albany in France, writing in most friendly terms, urging him to use his new influence with the Pope—for his wife's sister had recently married the Pope's nephew, Lorenzo de Medici, Duke of Urbino—and assuring him of her support and goodwill in all matters.

Whilst Scotland buzzed with all this, at least it helped to keep more active hostilities from breaking out that winter and spring, both between the Douglases and the Hamiltons and over the Border from England—and scandal was infinitely to be preferred to civil or national war.

In this pleasing lull, Davie Beaton—source of much of the information—came one day in late April to Edinburgh Castle, to announce to David Lindsay two items. One that he was now official personal secretary to the Archbishop of Glasgow, and lay Rector of Killearn, in the sheriffdom of Stirling; and two, that he was to be married to Marion Ogilvy shortly and desired his friend's company and support on that occasion, and Kate's too if she would come.

So two weeks later it was back to the Braes of Angus, at Airlie, to that frowning castle in the jaws of its glen where, if Marion Ogilvy welcomed them with a quiet warmth, her father did less. Lord Ogilvy clearly considered that his youngest daughter was marrying beneath her, and Marion had no doubt had a hard task in getting him to permit her union with the penniless seventh son of a Fife laird, however notable his uncle. Undoubtedly this indicated some lack of perception in her father; but the Angus glens were far from the hub of power, and Ogilvy was presumably unversed in the realities of the situation.

Marion and Kate got on well from the start, very different personalities as they were: the one calm, restrained, assured; the other lively, demonstrative, eager. Apart from the Lindsays, none others on Beaton's side were present, none of his family—which probably added to Lord Ogilvy's doubts about the match.

The night before the nuptials, David again saw a very different side of his friend's character. The castle was full to overflowing, with much of the nobility of Angus, the

Mearns and Aberdeenshire, and the bridegroom was allotted no very splendid accommodation. In his small tower room, David found him pacing the floor in some agitation, in the May twilight.

"David," he said, "this of marriage. It is . . . difficult. A man requires . . . guidance. So much to put to the test, lacking experience in the matter. Marion is so fine, so gentle. I love her dearly, dote on her—but in some ways I scarcely know her! We have been but little together, see you. I fear to disappoint her, hurt her, offend. *You* are married now, and happy, I swear. Can you help me . . . ?"

David swallowed a grin. "This is not like you, friend! Do not tell me that you are so inexperienced? French women, they say, are none so backward . . . !"

"No, no—but that is different, quite. Not to be considered where Marion is concerned. Handling such women demands but little nicety. But this, the marriage bed, with one gently reared and so delicate of her nature . . ."

"I think that she is probably less delicate than you deem her! What I have learned of women is that they are made of stouter stuff than we are apt to think. In some ways, stouter than are we! I counsel you not to fear for her . . ."

"But—tomorrow. Tomorrow night! The bedding—the marriage bed. That first night together. How do you advise? Leave her, leave her . . . not alone, but, but unassailed? At first? Give her time? Did you . . . ?"

"I did not. Lord, Davie—she is wedding a man, not a eunuch! Even if you are now Rector of Killearn or whatever it is! She will expect a man's attentions, I swear! I say be gentle at first, yes—but not over-gentle! Play the eager husband, or she may doubt your need. Or your . . . capabilities!"

"You think so? Your Kate . . . ?"

"My Kate is all woman—and so is your Marion, or I am much mistaken." David felt that it was time to lead to a change of subject. "I would not have thought you the man to doubt yourself—you, who seek to move men and realms to your devisings! Even your own uncle. Is he falling in with your wishes? Now that he has you as secretary?"

Beaton changed back to normal almost in a breath. "He commences to do so, yes. He makes the first moves to unseat Andrew Forman—although God may do that for him, for the man is sick and failing. I have told him that Angus seeks to gain the Primacy for his own poet-uncle, Gavin Douglas, now Bishop of Dunkeld, perceiving much advantage for his cause in that. This has much spurred on my good relative! It is true, forby—although less urgently so than I have suggested. He, my uncle, has already appointed a new Bishop for Caithness, which was vacant—a brother to the Earl of Atholl, and so it will aid in bringing that useful earldom to our side. And I am seeking to have him translate Abbot David Arnot of Cambuskenneth to the bishopric of Galloway—on condition that Arnot then allots the revenues of the Abbey of Tongland therein directly to the Archbishop at Glasgow! It is a surprisingly rich foundation, I discovered. Other moves I have in mind for the reform of Holy Church!"

"Reform? Scarcely the word, I think?"

"Reform, yes—in a manner of speaking. Making the Church a more effective force in the realm. And I have written to Albany seeking his good offices with the Pope, like Margaret Tudor, to have my uncle's promotion to St Andrews expedited, with the possible cardinal's hat, and to forestall any move by Henry of England and Angus to put Gavin Douglas therein. I have not been wholly idle, you see."

David wagged his head. "I wonder if Marion Ogilvy knows what she is marrying!" he exclaimed. "Have you told her what you are? What you seek to do? The life she is like to lead?"

The other looked away. "I have not troubled her with such matters. Should I have done? That is not a woman's part."

"Nevertheless, if she is going to live with *you*, she will have to live with all that, your life. After Glen Isla and the Braes of Angus, it will be no little change! And, Davie—where are you going to put her? To dwell? Living as you do, ever on the move. At this Killearn?"

"No, no—that would never serve. There is a rectory there, yes—but no place for my wife. I will take a lodging in Edinburgh, near to the Abbey of the Holy Rood, where now I dwell in my uncle's quarters, when in the capital. So she will be near you and your Kate in the castle, also. When I am away she will have your company . . ."

Next day the wedding was celebrated in the castle chapel by the parish priest, reminiscent of David's and Kate's own in that the place was too small for all of the company to crowd in, it all making for a simple ceremony, with the emphasis on the feasting afterwards. The bridal pair gladly took David's advice to avoid any possible bedding spectacle by contriving to slip away before the banquet ended. They arranged to meet the following afternoon at St Mary's Abbey of Coupar-Angus.

David Lindsay's parting with the Lord Ogilvy was little less frosty than his welcome had been although he did bring himself to say that he felt sure that Marion would prove to have wed one of the most important men in the kingdom—a prophecy which was received with blank incomprehension. Kate, as Lord Lindsay's daughter, and attractive, obtained a slightly more genial leave-taking.

They found the bridal couple awaiting them at Coupar-Angus, not in the travellers' hospice but at the abbey itself, where the Archbishop's and Chancellor's secretary had prevailed upon the Abbot to provide them with suitable accommodation for the night, unusual for a monastic establishment as this might be, in principle if not in practice. David forebore to ask the new husband how he had fared, but Beaton was in high spirits and Marion gently glowing, so presumably all was well.

They rode on westwards together, the best of company, heading for Perth, to cross Tay, where they were allotted fine quarters in the famous Blackfriars Monastery—and where Beaton regaled them with the story of the murder of James the First within these same walls less than a century before. The day following they reached Cambuskenneth Abbey, near the Forth crossing at Stirling, and again were received with respect and given excellent hospitality—and free. The others were learning some of the advantages of travelling in the company of one influential in Holy Church.

It was when passing through Stirling in the morning that they found the town buzzing with news. A great Highland revolt had broken out. Donald Galda MacDonald, Lord of the Isles, with Maclean of Duart and Macleod of Dunvegan and many other chiefs, had risen in arms and were marching southwards. Already they were said to have overrun much of Lochaber and were heading towards Atholl, declaring that the Highlands and Isles were about to become an independent realm.

It appeared that Scotland's peaceful lull was over and the Beaton marriage celebrated just in time, the Lord of the Isles presumably having proved too impatient to await Henry Tudor's co-ordinated assault—unless this was already under way. Beaton now was suddenly all the man of action, bridegroomship temporarily forgotten, or at least in abeyance. He must get back to his uncle's side at the earliest possible moment. David Lindsay should bring on the young women to Edinburgh without delay, but he himself would dash on ahead, killing horseflesh if need be. In vain the girls, both excellent horsewomen, protested that they could keep up with him. Davie Beaton left them there on the outskirts of Stirling, spurs digging cruelly. Marion Ogilvy was thus quickly to learn the kind of man she had married.

17

Thanks to the two young men, Beaton and Hamilton, rather than to their elders, the Chancellor and Governor nominally in command, prompt action allowed the kingdom a breathing space. On the recognition that the two important men most immediately threatened by the Lord of the Isles' advance were the Earls of Argyll and Atholl, whose territories lay in the way of the Highland horde and who would therefore be apt to fight most strenuously anyway, these two were given fullest powers and commissioned to go and halt the Islesmen at all costs, with the Gordon chief, the Earl of Huntly, to co-operate on the eastern flank, and the bishops of all the contiguous sees instructed to assist with men and arms, but above all, money, to hire more fighting men, Atholl's brother thus swiftly having to earn his new elevation to the diocese of Caithness. Argyll, the Campbell chief, as Lord Justice General and with most to lose, was put in overall command, appointed Lieutenant-Governor of the Isles, and promised vast grants of MacDonald and other lands if he prevailed.

There was no sign of any increased activity from the English side of the Border, so it appeared that Donald Galda had indeed miscalculated and acted before Henry was ready.

In the event, it was almost wholly a clan battle which took place, with great ferocity, in Ardnamurchan, actually over into Argyll—to the satisfaction of most Lowlanders, who much approved of Highlanders destroying each other, whatever the cause. The conflict was indecisive in that there was no obvious victor; but since the Isles host withdrew back into Lochaber and Morar thereafter, with Donald Galda himself wounded, the winner could be claimed to be Argyll. The Bastard of Arran, who went along in an advisory capacity, as representing his father, certainly so claimed. And when, shortly afterwards the Lord of the Isles died, presumably from his wounds, leaving no near heir, the rising petered out and the island clans returned to their own fastnesses, the thing was accepted as full victory. Whether Argyll could gain possession of the promised territories was another question.

The Hamiltons were cock-a-hoop and somehow appeared to claim most of the credit—to Douglas fury. Davie Beaton made no such boasts, but was quietly satisfied.

However, although the Highland trouble had gone off, as it were, at half-cock and was now disposed of, it had its side-effects in seeming to start off a series of minor outbreaks between Hamilton and Douglas supporters in the Lowlands, as a climate of mounting violence prevailed. None of these could be likened to civil war, for Angus himself lay remarkably low, whether at Henry's behest, who was not yet ready, or in order to provide his wife with no further ammunition in her campaign against him, or even perhaps in preoccupation with his new mistress, was not to be known. The violence, although widespread and worrying, remained small-scale, in the Borders, Ayrshire, Lanarkshire, Dumfriesshire and Galloway—until the April of 1520, when the dreaded major hostilities erupted at last, and in the streets of the capital itself, of all places.

It was sparked off by a conjunction of two official events, called for consecutive days, a session of the parliament to consider what was to be done in view of the Regent's continued absence, and a meeting of the town council and guilds of Edinburgh to elect a new Provost for the city, the day before. The Earl of Arran had been Provost, amongst his other appointments, for a succession of terms—it was a point of pride for the capital city to have one of the leading men of the kingdom as a civic head, even though most of the duties were performed by deputies inevitably, not always a satisfactory arrangement. On this occasion a move was afoot amongst the magistrates and guild brethren to appoint a more practical if less decorative head, and one Robert Logan, of the Restalrig family, a prosperous merchant, was being put forward. This was considered to be an insult, not only by Arran who was seeking re-election but by the nobility and aristocracy generally, and the usual pressures were being brought to bear—and with the town filling up with lords and lairds and their trains for the parliament next day, the said pressures could be powerful, the more so when the Earl of Angus arrived from his western fastnesses, for the parliament, with a tail of no fewer than five hundred fighting men.

Arran and his entourage happened to be at Dalkeith, six miles to the south favouring the Earl of Morton there with his company—it was part of his policy to keep the Black and Red Douglases at loggerheads by all means possible—when he heard, not only that Angus had arrived in Edinburgh after lying low for so long, but that he was making a bid for the provostship, not for himself but for his nominee, his own uncle, Sir Archibald Douglas of Kilspindie, the grim Greysteel. In high dudgeon the Hamiltons set out for the city to put a stop to this.

But on arrival at the Greyfriars Port, the southern gate in the tall Flodden Walls, he and his party found the gates shut and barred against them—an unheard of situation. It was midday, and Arran as well as being Lieutenant-Governor of the kingdom was still Provost of the city until either re-elected or replaced. Outraged, he and his shouted their fury and threats. But demands for the gates to be opened immediately were met with assertions that the closure was on the orders of the magistracy, so that no further lords and their armed men should be allowed in to threaten the town council until the election of the new Provost was duly and satisfactorily effected. No amount of protest and hectoring had any effect—and those massive gates and high walls, so hastily erected and strengthened after the Flodden disaster, were stout and strong. Although the Bastard and others set their men to attempting to break in, without battering rams, cannon and scaling ladders they could do little. So the Governor and Provost had to wait outside in impotent rage until the magistrates eventually gave the order to reopen. And then it was to learn that Sir Archibald Douglas of Kilspindie was indeed effectively, if not perhaps duly, elected Provost of the capital.

Arran, on entry, making his way through the crowded streets seemingly largely filled with hooting and jeering Red Douglas men-at-arms, decided that probably the castle would provide safer lodging, in the circumstances than his usual quarters in Holyrood Abbey, and rode thither in major wrath—and it was only then that David and Kate heard of it all from the Bastard, so isolated was the royal citadel from much that went on in the city below. The Chancellor was sent for from Blackfriars—and needless to say Davie Beaton came with him.

A council of war followed—or better, a council of non-war, for obviously it would take very little now to set off a dire confrontation and slaughter in the streets. Although nominally the conference was between the Governor, the Chancellor and Huntly, as members of the Regency Council—Archbishop Forman was now too frail to leave St Andrews and Argyll was still in the Hebrides trying to subdue the island clans—the Earl Marischal was brought in as responsible for the monarch's security and Lord Erskine as Keeper of the fortress. But probably most were well aware that the real decisions were apt to be made by the two young men there only as advisers, Davie Beaton and Sir James Hamilton of Finnart, and that in the circumstances prevailing these two might well clash since the Hamilton interests were not necessarily best for the realm. The Lord Lindsay was sent for, but until he arrived, Beaton suggested that David Lindsay should sit in, in his place.

After an angry and somewhat incoherent harangue from Arran, embarrassing to all, the Earl Marischal, with sufficient seniority to interrupt, announced that he was much concerned for the safety and position of the King's Grace in this situation—which should be the concern of them all. With the Hamilton faction now more or less occupying the castle—for all Arran's entourage had followed him up into the citadel—the Douglases might well come storming up demanding their ejection. And if this was refused, they could possibly mount an armed attack—which would have to be repulsed. This would have the effect of seeming to put the young King entirely on the Hamilton side, which would be injurious to the royal position and the realm's well-being. The crown must be seen and known to be above all faction fighting. Lord Erskine backed this stance, declaring that if the Douglases did attack the castle, the only effective way of keeping them out was the use of cannon fire. And that would indeed set the city and nation ablaze, initiating civil war, the very thing that they were seeking to avoid.

Arran all but choked in his offence and reproach over this suggestion. Was he not Lieutenant-Governor of the realm? And second person after its monarch whilst Albany was absent? Who had more right to seek the shelter of the capital's castle from the shameful assaults of the blackguardly Douglases?

Huntly supported Arran.

Davie Beaton murmured in his uncle's ear.

It was at this early stage in the proceedings that the captain of the guard came in, to whisper to the Keeper. Frowning, Erskine announced that a large party of Homes had ridden up to the Greyfriars Port from the south, and had been refused admittance by the town guard there, on the orders of Sir John Hamilton of Clydesdale, the other of Arran's illegitimate sons. But they might well get in at other gates.

Arran half rose from his chair in his agitation. "Those scoundrels! Border thieves and murderers! They must not enter. To join with the Douglases! All the gates to be shut and barred. Immediately." He pointed a trembling finger at the guard captain. "You—see to it. Forthwith. All city gates barred."

Davie Beaton spoke up, not having time on this occasion to use his uncle's lips. "But, my lord—is this wise? The Homes, little as we may love them, have every right to be here, to attend tomorrow's parliament. After all, your lordship yourself granted them free and full pardon for de la Bastie's murder! Lord Home is a lord of parliament. And Wedderburn and Cowdenknowes are commissioners for the Merse and Lauderdale." He said that reasonably and respectfully.

The Governor glared at him. "You, sirrah—keep your tongue between your teeth! The gates will be closed. When I require your advice I will ask for it!"

"And I shall be honoured, my lord." That was silky. "But may I remind your lordship that by closing all the ports you will be cooping all the Douglases and their friends within the city streets. An explosive situation! All but seeking for worse troubles. There could be fighting with the town guard."

The Bastard nodded briefly towards Beaton and gripped his sire's arm—but the Earl shook him off.

"All gates will be closed," Arran repeated. "That is my command. As Governor. And I am still Provost of this city, since the appointment of this rascally Douglas is clearly by force, and unlawful."

The captain of the guard departed and there was an uncomfortable silence around that conference table.

The Chancellor broke it, less than confidently. "My

lords—this of the provostship. It could be dangerous, very. Cause an uprising of the citizens. I agree that Douglas of Kilspindie's appointment is wrongous and should not stand. But the magistrates and guilds do seek a change, as is their right. If you, my lord Governor, were to insist on being Provost again, there could be serious disturbances. You could force the citizenry to side with the Douglases. That must be avoided at all costs. It would, I say, be wise to declare that neither a Douglas nor a Hamilton should be Provost, at this juncture. But one of their own choosing. This man Logan was to be their choice as chief magistrate. Let him be installed, then, and the Douglas ousted. Then the citizenry would be your better support, my lord."

Arran began to splutter but his son spoke first. "My lord Governor does not require the provostship of this, or any other town, to support his dignity," the Bastard said strongly. "He has a sufficiency of duties, lacking this! He but recognises that this city, containing as it does this great castle and the King's Grace, must remain in leal hands. As Provost, he can seek to ensure that. But if this Logan, or other, can fill the Provost's chair effectively, and keep the Douglases out, then I am sure that my lord would not object."

This time it was Davie Beaton's turn to nod in the other's direction.

Arran looked at his son doubtfully, cleared his throat but did not speak.

"How can this be achieved, and Kilspindie unseated?" Huntly demanded. "The Douglases will resist it."

"If the Regency Council issued a decree that neither a Hamilton *nor* a Douglas should be Provost in this pass, parliament tomorrow would endorse it and it would have the force of law," the Chancellor declared. "I so propose."

It was not a meeting of the Regency Council as such, but three of its members were present, and the absent Argyll could be relied upon to support the Governor. A nodding of heads seemed to clinch the matter, and Arran did not raise his voice.

Then the Earl Marischal returned to his earlier contention. "I still am concerned for the King's Grace," he said doggedly. "Erskine, and you Lindsay, agree? This royal citadel must not appear to be a refuge of the Hamiltons in this pass. The Governor himself may have good right to be here, but not his people. My duty is to our Prince, in this matter."

"I say the same," Erskine added.

"This is not to be borne!" That was Sir Patrick Hamilton, not entitled actually to take part in the conference but sitting behind his brother, Arran. "Are we to be thrust out, to our deaths? For the sake of some notion of these lords! I am kin to the King's Grace—as are others here. We are entitled to the shelter of this castle until such time as this Douglas menace and riot is lifted."

"To be sure," the Governor agreed. "My people stay."

"My lord Governor—surely you see the danger?" the Marischal insisted. "You give the Douglases a rod to beat you with! They could claim that the Hamilton faction is using the King to shelter behind. That you drag the crown into your feuding. I am the *King*'s governor, appointed by the Regent Albany."

"And I am the Keeper of this fortress—as of that of Stirling," Erskine said. "Also appointed by the Regent. I say that you must leave."

"You will seek to put us out then, my lords?" the Bastard demanded, grinning. "I think that you will have . . . difficulty! We have over five score men with us. How many have you?"

There was a momentary silence as men eyed each other, masks dropped. Into it David Lindsay spoke, scarcely confidently but earnestly. He looked at the Bastard, not at Arran or his brother.

"Have you, Sir James, perhaps overlooked a small matter? This citadel can protect you meantime, yes. But it can also imprison you. You could all be held here . . ."

"*That* none would dare, I vow! Not even the Marischal or Erskine!" the Bastard broke in. "Have you lost your wits, man?"

"Not so—that is not my meaning. It is the Douglases who could imprison you herein. Coop you up like poultry. Merely by encamping on the tourney ground beyond the gatehouse and drawbridge. There is but the one door to this hold. If they sat there, in strength, you could not win out into the city. They could keep you, my lord, from attending the parliament tomorrow!"

He had made his point. The Hamiltons looked at each other.

"The parliament—I *must* be there!" Arran exclaimed. "Forby, it would be no parliament without me, the Governor."

"I think that you mistake, my lord," the Earl Marischal said grimly. "If the King's Grace is there, and the Chancellor, it is a due and proper parliament."

"The child? James . . . !"

"Aye. He is now eight years old and a fine lad, and wise enough for his years. It is time that he is more shown to his people, their sovereign-lord. We say that he should now attend the parliaments, at least the openings. And it would serve to improve it, the proceedings, the royal presence."

The Chancellor nodded. "That is true. The King there, bickering and railing should be less, the Douglases be something restrained. Others likewise."

All saw that, even Arran.

"But this of the castle," he went on. "If we are not to bide here—where? Holyrood is wide open to assault. No defences and a score of entrances, to abbey and church. No safety there. And if we leave the city, go to Craigmillar or Dalkeith, we might not gain entry again, without bloodshed. Angus will stop at nothing . . . !"

Davie Beaton spoke briefly to his uncle and then raised his voice. "My lord Governor—the Archbishop's lodging. The Blackfriars' Monastery—it is the most secure house in Edinburgh. Why my lord Chancellor chooses to bide there perhaps!" And he smiled. "It has high walls and gates easily guarded but opening on to the Cowgate as well as the Blackfriars and Niddrie's Wynds. A large courtyard and sufficient space for your people. And it is Holy Church premises. You would be safe at the Blackfriars, my lord."

The Earl looked at his son, who inclined his dark head. "And getting there?" he asked. "Without attack."

"It is evening now and near dark. Soon the streets will be empty, the Douglas men-at-arms all in the dens and stews and alehouses."

So it was agreed, just as the Lord Lindsay arrived, with a substantial following and the word that they had come in by the East Port and found it broken down and smashed, with bodies lying around, apparently having been attacked and stormed by a party of Homes under Wedderburn, who had been denied entry. While the Governor was exclaiming at this, Lindsay interrupted to say that there was worse news than that. Before leaving the Byres, he had learned that Wedderburn and the Homes had assaulted the Priory of Coldinghame, slain the Hepburn Prior and six of his family and installed as Prior none other than William Douglas, brother of Angus.

It was in a state bordering on consternation that the meeting broke up, therefore, and the Hamilton leaders were escorted by the Lindsays down to the Blackfriars' Monastery, fortunately without incident, their own retainers instructed to find their way discreetly in small groups thither—for it was vital that, if possible, there should be no further and large-scale battling and riot before the parliament, which might make its sitting impossible, in the disorder.

Next forenoon, with the city tense but no rioting having taken place, David and Abbot John prepared their royal charge for his important appearance. James, at eight, had grown into a lively, well-built and good-looking boy; but although normally cheerful and biddable was liable to moods and sulks and flashes of violent temper. On such occasions Gavin Dunbar, now awarded the archdeaconry of St Andrews and the deanery of Moray, but still nominally the royal tutor, could do nothing with him, and even John Inglis had difficulty in coping; only David Lindsay had the boy's unfailing devotion and usually could soothe his tantrums and even prescribe punishments and achieve contrition.

But this April day there were no problems, with James looking forward to his outing although a little nervous—probably less nervous than his elders, at that.

Dressed in his best—and that was less than grand—the monarch, mounted on a quiet horse, rode in procession from the castle down the Lawnmarket, the High Street and the Canongate to Holyrood, through watching but mainly silent crowds. There were a few wavering cheers when some perceived, by the royal standard, that the little boy was their liege-lord, but these came to little in the prevailing perturbation. The citizens feared the worst. James, who seldom indeed emerged from the castle, chatted happily to

David and the Abbot and scowled at the Earl Marischal whom he had never liked, honest and reliable as that man was.

Outside the abbey there was already trouble, clashes between the retinues of lords allied to one side or the other, and the Chancellor and his nephew were thankful for the early arrival of the King, whose presence it was hoped would restrain the trouble-makers.

Within the great church the atmosphere was little less tense, although neither Arran nor Angus had so far put in an appearance. In the chapter-house, James was installed to await his official entry.

From there, presently, a great commotion developed outside, of shouting and clatter, and in a minute or two the Lord Lyon King of Arms, in charge of ceremonial, came hurrying in to urge that the monarch should make his formal entrance immediately, as a calming influence. Angus and the Governor had now both arrived, with their companies, and were facing each other like angry dogs, hurling insults and threats, church or no church.

So the trumpeters and heralds were lined up, a stirring fanfare blown and, led by Lyon, young James made his entry behind the Earl Marischal bearing the sword of state and the youthful Earl of Erroll, the High Constable, carrying the crown on a cushion, David and John Inglis in close attendance, the Chancellor and his secretary and clerks bringing up the rear. The boy was led to the Abbot's chair in the chancel, acting as throne, where he sat, the officers of state flanking him and the two young men directly behind. The Chancellor, at his table near the chancel steps, bowed, sought permission to commence the proceedings, and taking it as granted, called on the Abbot of the Holy Rood to commend their affairs in prayer to the All Highest. It so happened that the said Abbot was none other than Master William Douglas, brother of Angus, who had so recently had himself invested as Prior of the wealthy priory of Coldinghame, in the Merse, also, over the murdered body of the previous Prior. Presumably he had come north therefrom with the Homes. His prayer was sonorous but brief.

Quickly Archbishop Beaton went ahead with the agenda, before any disturbance could develop. "The principal reason for calling this assembly, Your Grace," he read out, "is the difficulties caused by the continued absence of Your Grace's Regent, the Duke of Albany, and what steps can be taken both to expedite his return from France and to ensure good government and Your Grace's peace meantime. To that end, it must be recognised by all, the establishment of a just and peaceful solution to the problems besetting this capital city of Edinburgh is vital. Therefore, with Your Grace's permission, I propose to deal with this matter first. The Regency Council recommends that, in the interests of amity and the realm's weal, the provostship of this city meantime should not be held by either a Hamilton or a Douglas. Robert Logan of Restalrig has been nominated by the magistrates and guild-brethren. It is proposed therefore that the said Robert Logan should be confirmed as Provost of the city by this parliament, all other contenders to stand down."

"Seconded!" the Marischal jerked, almost before the other stopped speaking.

"I protest!" That was Angus, loudly, from the front row of the nave where he was surrounded by his Douglas lords and lairds, prominent amongst whom was his uncle Sir Archibald Douglas of Kilspindie wearing the Provost's chain of office. "I am a member of the Regency Council—and this is the first that I have heard of such proposal. I do protest."

"My lord of Angus, although sought for, was not found," the Chancellor declared speciously. "But of the five other members of the said Council, a majority were in favour of the proposal. Therefore your protest fails, my lord."

"Then I move here and now that this preposterous proposal be rejected."

"And I second!" That was a chorus, from a sufficiency of Douglases.

"Then there must be a vote, since the motion is proposed and seconded, as is the counter-motion. But I would remind all that this decision could seriously affect the peace of this realm. Either a Douglas or a Hamilton as Provost of Edinburgh, in this pass, could well lead to grievous hostilities. As already has been shown. So, think well! I will take the negative first. Those in favour of rejection of the motion, show."

David had been counting heads, as far as he was able in the crowded nave, and concluded that it would be a close thing. The Douglases could rely on the Homes and the votes of most of the representatives of the East and Middle Marches of the Borderland, as well as support from Angus itself, the Mearns and much of Fife. Arran could count on the West March, Galloway, Ayrshire, Lanark, the Chancellor's Glasgow area, and Stirlingshire. And there were the Edinburgh city representatives. Much, he decided, would hang on the attitude of the *Black* Douglases.

A score of Douglas hands were raised immediately, but elsewhere there was distinct hesitation, as men looked around them, calculating, debating, or fearful of the Red Douglas glares. Gradually a few more arms rose. The Earl of Morton, head of the Black Douglases, who had been Arran's host at Dalkeith, ostentatiously stood with arms folded across his chest—which chest was noticeably well-protected by handsome inlaid half armour. David heaved a sigh of relief at the sight.

"Thirty-three!" Davie Beaton sang out. "Thirty-three against the proposal."

"Those in favour, show," his uncle directed, his voice uneven.

Fewer hands went up than David had anticipated—until he noticed that Morton still had his arms folded. He was abstaining; and no other Black Douglases voted either, nor some others who were their friends.

"Thirty-six, thirty-seven, thirty-eight!" Beaton counted, throatily. "No—thirty-nine for the motion, my lord Chancellor."

"Then I declare the motion duly carried," his uncle got out. "Neither Douglas nor Hamilton shall be Provost of Edinburgh meantime, this parliament has declared. Sir Archibald Douglas of Kilspindie will therefore vacate in favour of Robert Logan of Restalrig."

There was pandemonium in the church, voices upraised, fists shaken, hands on dirk-hilts—swords being forbidden at a parliament. Quickly the noise increased. King James, who had sat quietly until this, began to looked alarmed, and turned round to David. The Chancellor beat and beat on his table with his gavel for order, and was ignored.

Not only was no heed paid, but here and there in that nave men actually came to blows, the Homes not backward. As the din grew louder and an ornate lectern crashed over,

James jumped down from his throne and ran behind to clutch David's hand.

David spoke urgently to the Earl Marischal, who nodded and turned to the Lord Lyon, gesturing. That perturbed individual was only too glad to oblige, and ordered his trumpeters to sound. A distinctly uneven flourish followed, and to its ragged blare the royal party marched out, in less than perfect order, to the chapter-house, the session thus abruptly adjourned, leaving chaos behind.

With the noise from the church ever heightening, the Marischal decided that the sooner King James was back in the castle's safety the better, David and all agreeing. Concerned about the Chancellor and Davie, however, the latter suggested that half of the royal guard should wait behind to provide security for the Beatons, and the Earl acceded. So, a reduced company, guard close about them, they emerged into the abbey precinct, clove their way under the unfurled Lion-Rampant banner through the milling crowd of men-at-arms there, mainly Douglases by their colours, to the horses and mounting, set off up the Canongate at a much more spanking pace than they had come down, young James frequently looking apprehensively behind him. The crowds had disappeared from the streets now, doubtless not expecting the parliament to be over so soon, and they clattered the mile of cobblestones up to the castle in short time, thankful when their beasts were drumming hooves on the drawbridge timbers.

David Lindsay, however, felt unhappy thereafter about his role in the situation, recognising that he might seem to have left the Archbishop and Davie rather in the lurch, to scuttle for safety. But his first duty undoubtedly was to the King, whose safety and well-being was paramount—and the position had been threatening, to say the least. What had been developing within the church was bad enough, in all conscience; but what might have happened outside amongst all those unruly retainers, mosstroopers and men-at-arms when word of trouble inside reached them, had been much more dangerous. And the boy had been frightened. He could only hope that the section of the royal guard left behind and his father-in-law's Lindsays would provide sufficient escort for the Beatons. Arran and his Hamiltons and allies could look after themselves.

How the Hamiltons sought to do just that became all too evident presently. The first news of it was brought by Davie Beaton himself arriving up at the castle with the detachment of the guard a couple of hours later. For that so positive character he was in some agitation. He told David that only his uncle's holding up of a crucifix and threat of excommunication had prevented a violent assault on the persons of Arran and other Hamiltons by the Homes and some Douglases at Holyrood—although Angus himself had sought to restrain his followers and had in fact succeeded in keeping most of them in the church, giving opportunity for the Governor and his people to get out and force their way through the thronging, struggling retainers outside to their horses, and so had managed to dash up to the Blackfriars' Monastery's security without major conflict. The Chancellor and Davie had followed with the royal guard. And there they had found the Hamiltons in furious conclave, the Bastard now very much in command. Quickly it became apparent that it was to be open war. The Governor's life had been threatened and the full weight of his authority must be mobilised to punish the offenders. But that would take time. Meantime the Douglases and their savage friends must be shown that they should not meddle with the Hamiltons. Every available man in the city capable of bearing arms was to be mustered forthwith, in the King's name; also the levies of every friendly baron, for the protection of the Governor. Angus was to be summoned to attend an urgent meeting of the Regency Council, there at the Blackfriars. If he came, he was to be held prisoner; and if not, as was likely, a specially selected party of the toughest men-at-arms, under the Bastard himself, would go out and snatch him. With Angus held hostage for their better behaviour, the Douglases would be brought to heel.

Davie said that he and his uncle had protested that this was madness and would only lead to worse violence, outright war in the city, and that the King's name should on no account be brought into it. But they were shouted down, the Bastard refusing to listen to reason. So he, Beaton, had come up to the castle with the borrowed guard seeking aid to try to put a stop to this folly. If the Marischal, the Constable and the King of Arms were to come down to Blackfriars and in the King's name forbid any such use of the royal authority, and seek to dissuade Arran from permitting such madness, then the worst might yet be averted.

David was doubtful, but took the other to see the Earl Marischal.

That sober individual would have none of it. His duty, he declared, was to the King, not to Arran, whom he despised. Let him and Angus fight it out between them—and if they slew each other in the process, so much the better for the realm! The royal guard was certainly not to be involved in such feuding. At Beaton's urging, however, he agreed that he could not stop the High Constable and the Lord Lyon from going to Blackfriars if so they wished—but no royal guard.

Young Erroll and Sir Thomas Pettigrew of Magdalensyde, the Lyon, were more receptive, and agreed to do what they could. David Lindsay, still feeling guilty about abandoning the others at Holyrood, said that he would also accompany them; and with Lyon's trumpeters as escort, the tight little company rode down through the town to Blackfriars. The streets were full of men-at-arms looking for trouble.

Admitted to the heavily guarded monastery, they found the Hamiltons preparing for war, and Archbishop Beaton depressed and more or less resigned to whatever transpired. But he went with the newcomers to reason again with Arran and his son.

The Constable and Lyon made no more impression on the Bastard than did David Lindsay and the Beatons; and his father appeared to be wholly under his influence. Arran's brother, Sir Patrick Hamilton, seemed prepared to listen, but the others ignored him. Speaking for the Earl Marischal, Lyon, supported by David, made it very clear that the King's name must not be used in any mobilisation of manpower. This was feuding between Hamilton and Douglas, that only. It was difficult to demand that the Governor should keep the King's peace, since he it was, in the absence of the Regent, who had the authority to enforce it.

In the midst of this argument it was announced that two representatives of the Earl of Angus were at the gate, requesting interview with the Governor. They were alone, so no trickery seemed probable; and one was clad in a Bishop's habit. Arran was for refusing them a hearing but the Chancellor persuaded him that there could be no harm in learning what they had to say, the Bastard shrugging acquiescence.

The visitors proved to be the brothers, Gavin Douglas, Bishop of Dunkeld, and Greysteel, Sir Archibald of Kilspindie, uncles of Angus. The latter was outspoken, grim and did not beat about the bush. Angus had heard, he said, on reliable authority, that Arran was seeking to raise the city in outright attack on Douglas and was even purposing to capture the Earl himself, by deceit. Any such dastardly attempts would be brought to naught, needless to say, and avenged. But his nephew, desiring the minimum of bloodshed and loss in this personal controversy, proposed that instead of full-scale battle in the city streets, with many innocent lives endangered, they should settle their differences in more knightly fashion by making something of a tourney of it—as had been done a century before at the North Inch of Perth. He, Angus, was prepared to meet the Earl of Arran in single combat at, say, the Netherbow Port. But since Arran was nearly thirty years the elder and might consider the contest unfair, he would be willing to fight any suitable representative—but no bastards or low-born ruffians! If this appeared to hazard too much on a single individual, then they might field perhaps a score on each side, as champions for the rest, the losers to abide by the result. Was this not better than outright war?

While the astonished and uncertain Hamiltons went into conclave over what to do about this, Bishop Gavin drew aside to where the Chancellor, his nephew and David Lindsay stood listening.

"My lord Archbishop," he said, low-voiced but earnest, "as men of peace, surely we can do something to prevent this armed strife and bloodshed? I appeal to you, who consecrated me Bishop, to use your high authority in Holy Church to halt this evil before men die. In the name of God!"

The Chancellor shrugged heavy shoulders. "What can I do? What heed will they pay to me? You, my lord—is it not *you* who should be addressing yourself to your nephew Angus? He it is who is issuing this challenge to arms, is it not? *He* is the aggressor in this sorry conflict."

"He seeks now to limit it, at the least! It is Arran and this Bastard who seek to ensnare and it may be slay Angus. This plot we are told of, to trap him, by calling him to a false Regency Council—you, on that Council, and Chancellor, my lord, cannot surely be party to such shameful villainy?"

"No, no. This is wild talk. Not to be credited. Who, who told you this, man?"

"It matters not—but one sufficiently knowledgeable. You as Chancellor it is who calls the Council meetings, no? You cannot but know of these hostile intentions, I think! When you, as priest, should rather mediate for peace, surely?"

Unhappily the Archbishop wagged his grey head. "Not so, not so!" he exclaimed. "I tell you, I swear that I have no hostile intentions towards Angus. And if others have, I am not party to it. I swear it on my conscience!" In his discomfort and confusion, Beaton smote beringed hand on chest to emphasise his innocence—and unfortunately, the blow clanged hollowly. Presumably he had taken the opportunity, while his nephew was up at the castle, to go and don a shirt of mail below his linen rochet for safety's sake, with trouble looming.

"Alas, my lord, methinks your conscience clatters, and tells another tale," Bishop Gavin said drily, as Davie Beaton grinned widely and nudged Lindsay in the ribs.

Distinctly put out, the Archbishop sought refuge in belated dignity and the claims of seniority. "My lord Bishop—I would remind you to whom you speak! Of your position in my archdiocese! I . . . I . . ."

He was saved further embarrassment by Sir Patrick Hamilton coming over to them from the other group to announce that they had indeed agreed to fall in with Angus's suggestion and meet the Douglases in combat, a score to each side. They would insist, however, on having umpires appointed to ensure fair play and had told Greysteel so.

David Lindsay, for one, did not wonder that the Hamiltons had so decided, since, of their own people, they were probably outnumbered by the Douglases three to one at least. To raise and arm the townsfolk, or some of them, would take time, and probably would arouse but little enthusiasm in the circumstances anyway. The offer seemed much to their advantage.

To restore his credit, if possible, the Chancellor raised his voice to declare that if the Earls of Arran and Angus could agree on such substitute for all-out conflict, why could they not meet together privately and come to some understanding, man to man, as honest Christians should, without the sacrifice of other men's blood? Surely this would be to the credit of both?

The Bastard snorted his reaction to that, and the support of Davie Beaton and Lyon, as well as Bishop Gavin, for the Chancellor only made him the more harshly adamant. With Arran himself leaving all to his son, and Sir Archibald Douglas declaring strongly against any such feeble parleying as the Archbishop proposed, the thing was decided. The Hamiltons would meet the Douglases, a score a side, at the Nether Bow in an hour's time. There was still time to settle this business before the light failed.

So the Douglas envoys departed, and the Bastard at once got down to the task of selecting the twenty toughest warriors to uphold their cause, mainly Hamiltons of course but including some notable champions amongst their available allies. The Master of Eglinton, heir to the Earl thereof and a famous tourney fighter, came into this category, with one or two others. There was no lack of volunteers, and a great sharpening of swords, dirks and spear heads followed. The Lyon and the Constable took their leave, desiring no part in it all.

When all was ready, the Governor's contingent formed up to make a move from Blackfriars, first Arran and his lords and lairds, then the chosen score of stalwarts, then the mass of the Hamilton retainers and their friends, and finally the Beatons, David Lindsay and others, in the part of somewhat apprehensive onlookers. It was Davie Beaton's highly appropriate suggestion to have the entire procession preceded by the monastery choir chanting sacred songs.

Thus they left their secure haven, on foot, for the steeply climbing Blackfriars Wynd and the crowded High Street, the choir a help in gaining them passage. Well before they reached the Netherbow Port, they could see the Canongate beyond wholly blocked by masses of ranked men—the Douglases, most evidently. They noted something else also; all the openings off the High Street, the wynds, alleys and side streets, had been blocked by up-ended carts, barrels and other barriers, an ominous sign.

The Hamilton leadership halted about one hundred yards from the solid front festooned with the red heart under blue of the Douglas banners, the choir stopped singing and discreetly retired, and the chosen twenty moved forward in tight formation. The two sides glared at each other, and there was considerable shouting, jeers and challenges. The citizenry gave all a notably wide berth but folk hung out of the windows of the tall tenements on either side, to watch.

Angus, Sir Archibald and some others came forward a little way, beckoning, but Arran and his people stayed where they were. Laughing, the Douglases came on, to comfortable speaking distance.

"Greetings, Hamiltons!" Angus called, mockingly. "You have come, at last, for our sport! I feared that you had no heart for it. Have you managed to find a score of heroes to face Douglas? Or perhaps do you need *two* score, to our one?"

When he got no answer to that but snarls, he went on. "My lord of Arran, I hope that you will honour us by your presence in the forefront? But if, as I fear, your advancing years and well-kent delicacy restrain you, I trust that your paladins will be led by one worthy of our Douglas steel and no bastard felons! We have our own delicacies, see you!"

The Hamilton growls grew the louder, and sundry insults were thrown back. Arran maintained a dignified silence.

Seeing that he was going to get no satisfaction in this exchange, Angus changed his tone. "This of umpires or arbiters, which you require. They must be men of birth and respect. I suggest two from each side. I have my kind uncles here, Greysteel and the good Abbot William of the Holy Rood. They will serve very well. And you?"

"I will so act," Sir Patrick Hamilton shouted.

"And I," Sir Robert Hamilton of Preston volunteered.

There was some confusion over this, as the Douglases returned to their own stance, for it had been assumed that Sir Patrick would in fact be one of the leaders of the Hamilton twenty, he being a noted tournament performer and having, many years before, defeated the supreme Continental champion, the Netherlands Chevalier Cokbewis, in a renowned fight before James the Fourth. In this misunderstanding, the Master of Eglinton was the obvious substitute but of course he was not a Hamilton and most there felt that one of their own should lead. The Bastard, to be sure, would have led, but Angus's remarks had cut him to the quick, and clearly ruled him out.

In his resentment that fierce young man turned on his uncle, with whom he had never been on good terms. "You—why *you* as umpire?" he demanded hotly. "Is it more to your taste than fighting? You, the celebrated jouster! In your old age, have you grown soft? Fear to put your steel to the test?"

"Damn you—watch your words, sirrah!" the other cried. "I will accept such talk from none, in especial from such as you!"

"Go then, Uncle, and watch bolder men than yourself fight and die!"

"God's curse on you, bastard smaik! I *shall* fight this day where you dare not!" Sir Patrick yelled, raising his fist. But instead of striking his nephew, he snatched out his sword and held it high. "Through them! Through!" he cried, the Hamilton slogan. "At them—the Douglas dogs!" And without waiting to see who followed, or any more formal start to the contest, ran forward towards the Douglas front, half armour clanking.

Friend and foe alike were taken by surprise. Montgomerie of Eglinton recovered first and went racing after the older man; and in something of a straggle the rest of the chosen twenty came on behind, lacking all formation.

The Douglases had little more time to react. Angus drew his sword and waved it right and left, to bring his twenty into the favoured wedge formation with himself at the apex. They were barely in position when with Sir Patrick almost upon them, the Earl leapt to meet him, shouting, "A Douglas! A Douglas!"

The two leaders met in a clash of steel and flurry of strokes. But from the first it was an utterly unequal contest. Hamilton was twice Angus's age, and more experienced or not, had run the intervening distance in heavy armour, was breathless and his sword-work unco-ordinated, his outburst of anger still affecting him. Unsteady on his feet, he stumbled in avoiding only the third major thrust, and in seeking to recover his stance, jerked his head to one side, baring his throat above the steel gorget. Angus saw his opportunity and did not hesitate to take it. He slashed sideways, and his sword half severed the other's neck, the blood gushing forth in a scarlet fountain. Sir Patrick fell to the cobblestones before ever even Montgomerie came up with him.

After that unnerving start it was in fact a massacre rather than any true contest-of-arms. The Douglases were in formation, protecting each other and sure of themselves, whereas the Hamiltons arrived in a straggle, panting, disorganised and already disheartened by the falling of their leaders—for the Master of Eglinton, assailed by two others as well as Angus, went down under a hail of blows. In yelling, screaming, bloody horror the twenty fought and reeled and died, in almost less time than it takes to tell.

Well before the last of them fell, the Bastard's fury and hate triumphed over his judgment, and he launched himself forward from his father's side, sword waving, shouting for all Hamiltons to come and avenge their fellows on the dastardly Douglases. Most followed him, however unwisely.

If it had been a massacre before, it was little better than wholesale carnage now, for with the entire mass of the Douglases and Homes engaged, the attackers were outnumbered at least three to one, and with almost every aspect of the encounter against them, arriving piecemeal against a solid phalanx, lacking any coherent strategy, desperate from the start. The Hamiltons fell in their swathes and few Douglases and Homes fell with them.

The Bastard himself seemed to bear a charmed life. He was an excellent sworder admittedly, and undoubtedly benefited from the fact that neither Angus nor most of his kind deigned to cross steel with one born out of wedlock, even though a knight. He fought on savagely, but presently, standing on a mound of slain, he found himself almost alone, with such Hamiltons as had survived tending to disengage and hurry off up the High Street, even he saw that the cause was lost meantime. Hotly he swung round and hurled his dripping sword at Angus, who stood grinning, and cursing brokenly, turned his back on the shambles, slipping and slithering on the causeway that ran with blood. But he himself refused to run, limping with a kind of dignity, wounded but unbowed, back to where his father, no warrior despite being Governor, Warden of the Marches and Lord High Admiral, waited in misery, wringing gauntleted hands.

"Run, Bastard—run!" Angus called after him, but restrained any from attacking that proud back. "To your sorry sire! Begone, so that Douglas can cleanse this causeway of you and your like! Run, Bastard!"

He still did not run, but reaching his father, who seemed rooted to the spot in his consternation, grasped his arm and all but dragged him off up the street, pursued only by the hoots and jeers of the triumphant Douglases.

The two Davids, Lindsay and Beaton, still watched from a pend mouth, appalled at the slaughter—the Archbishop had already fled. Recognising that in their slaughter-lust euphoria the Douglas men-at-arms might well make little distinction between Hamiltons and mere bystanders in this blood-soaked street, they too made a hurried departure. The last they saw of the Lieutenant-Governor of the realm and his son was the Bastard, perceiving a townsman with a mean horse standing beside one of the up-ended carts, going up and taking over the nag and when the man objected, knocking him down with a mailed fist and then clambering on to the beast's back to pull up the Earl behind him and clatter off up the High Street, a strange sight to see.

When the two Davids reached Blackfriars Wynd, they found it choked full of excited folk and could by no means make their way down to the monastery. Fairly obviously the Bastard and his father could not have got down there either. So they turned back and slipped down Niddrie's Wynd, parallel, and so into the Cowgate, thus managing to reach the monastery from the other side. They found the gate wide and unguarded and sundry drunken characters in possession. A hand-wringing monk told them that all was lost, God had deserted them and the legions of Satan had taken over. It seemed that the Archbishop had come fleeing back, pursued by a mob of Homes and Douglases, and the gate porters had not been able to get the doors closed again in time to keep these out. Alarmed, Davie Beaton hurried in search of his uncle, Lindsay following.

There was no sign of the Chancellor in his own quarters, but another distracted monk directed them to the chapel. And there, amidst much shouting and turmoil, they found James Beaton in dire state, collapsed at the altar, the furnishings of which were part dragged on top of him, being beaten and threatened with swords and staves by at least a dozen mosstroopers, his crimson cape and linen rochet ripped off him and savage hands tugging at the protective breastplate beneath, the better to belabour him.

Drawing their dirks, the two young men ran forward,

shouting to one or two affrighted servants to come and help. Their intervention, if it aided the fallen prelate, had the effect of drawing the fury of the attackers on themselves, and quickly they found themselves back to back, fighting off a rain of blows and thrusts. Fortunately most of their assailants were at least part-drunk and not at their most effective; also they were able to wedge themselves into a corner between the end of the altar and a pillar, which protected them on two sides. Nevertheless, undoubtedly it would have gone ill with them, had it not been for the arrival of more Douglases—but this time of a different status. Bishop Gavin of Dunkeld and another of his brothers, Sir George Douglas of Pittendreich, with their own small escort. The Bishop, taking in the situation, angrily made his presence felt, and succeeded in pulling off the belligerents. Ignoring the two young men, he drew his all but fainting and battered superior-in-God to his unsteady feet, expressing due concern and sympathy—after all, without the Archbishop he would not have had the see of Dunkeld. He solicitously escorted him back to his own quarters, with the others, where Marion, one of the Chancellor's mistresses, and sundry other women had barricaded themselves into the strong vaulted basement kitchen premises—and here they were accorded a reception of emotional relief and touching feminine care.

Clearly however the Blackfriars Monastery was no longer a safe haven for opponents of the Douglas faction, so it was thereupon decided that the Chancellor's party should remove at once up to the security of the castle, Bishop Gavin and company escorting them thither through streets now teeming with riotous men-at-arms. On the way thither they learned from the bishop-poet that Arran and the Bastard had last been seen departing the city in haste and fording the shallow end of the Nor' Loch which lay far below the precipitous castle rock, seemingly heading westwards, both on a single broken-down mount.

Leaving his fellow poet at the drawbridge end, David for one was thankful indeed to hear the heavy portcullis clang down behind them and the rattle of the chains as the bridge rose. Fortresses, however cramping and confining, had their uses.

Marion and Kate fell into each other's arms.

18

So Angus was master of Edinburgh and much of Lowland Scotland—although not of Edinburgh's castle. Also, not of the Homes, who as ever were a law unto themselves and demonstrated it by instituting their own brief reign of terror in the capital for a couple of days and nights when Angus led his Douglases from the city westwards as far as Linlithgow, to ensure that Arran did not muster a force against him in that Hamilton-dominated area, nor possibly come to some sort of terms with Margaret Tudor. In the interim the Homes, led by Wedderburn, rampaged through the town, and made something of a ceremony of taking down the grinning heads of the late Lord Home and his brother from their spikes above the Tolbooth where they had been for over three years, before returning in triumph to their own Merse.

Word of all this reached the castle, in its isolation, gradually. They learned that almost eighty Hamiltons had been slain in that dire street encounter—to which Angus had now given the title of Cleanse the Causeway—fully half the total Arran had had with him. What the Douglas casualties were was not revealed, but were probably not a quarter of that.

News of the Governor, if that term now meant anything, came about a week later, when Angus had returned to his mistress in Douglasdale leaving Greysteel, Bishop Gavin and the Abbot William in command at Edinburgh. A courier arrived secretly by night at the castle, having some difficulty in gaining admittance, with a message from Arran, really from the Bastard. They were at Stirling Castle, secure, and summoning loyal forces. The Earl Marischal was urged to bring the King there just as soon as it was possible, taking of course all necessary measures to ensure the royal safety en route. The visitor added that the Governor had sent a messenger to France informing Albany of the situation and urging his immediate return to Scotland.

It was not so easy, of course, to effect a removal of James and his establishment from one fortress to the other, for the Douglases almost certainly would never permit it. So it would have to be done secretly, by stealth. Fortunately, in Davie Beaton, they had available a past master in the use of stealth and subterfuge; and he it was who concocted the scheme. It now being May and the weather clement, they should send word to the Bishop Gavin, the most reasonable of the Douglases, that the young monarch could do with some country air and space to stretch his growing legs after such long constriction in the citadel. A week or two at Craigmillar Castle would meet the case, where there was excellent hunting and hawking in the royal forest of Duddingston. A safe-conduct would be sought—which even the Douglases could scarcely refuse to their liege-lord—and, to make all seem more innocuous, the Bishop, Greysteel and other Douglas notables could be invited to attend a great royal hunt there one day. This might well appear a wonderful opportunity to snatch the King into Douglas hands, the sort of thing which had happened before to youthful monarchs. Whether or not the Douglases would so attempt was neither here nor there. James in fact would not attend the hunt, on the excellent excuse that his guardians had heard that such a plot was indeed envisaged. The hunt would go on—but, concerned for his royal charge's safety, the Marischal had taken the opportunity to send the King off to Stirling the night previously, under cover of darkness!

This ingenious conception found pretty general favour in the fortress, and seemed reasonably likely to succeed. There were a few doubts, mainly concerned with possible reprisals by the Douglases against any of those left behind, but it was agreed that the arrival of a sizeable force of Lindsays from East Lothian, at the start of the hunt, ought to counter any such development.

All went without any major hitch. A safe-conduct duly arrived from Bishop Gavin, with a reproachful note added indicating surprise that it should have been thought necessary for the sovereign's weal. No time was then lost in moving the royal entourage the few miles to Craigmillar, which Sir Simon Preston held of the crown on condition that he made it available when required. James himself was delighted over the excursion. The womenfolk went along also, meantime.

No incidents took place en route. The hunt was fixed for three days hence, a Monday, with invitations sent out, all to meet at Duddingston village an hour before noon.

On the Saturday David Lindsay escorted Kate and Marion to the Byres, where it was felt that they would face fewer hazards than on a night-time dash to Stirling, although the young women were both loth to leave their husbands. At the Byres, Lord Lindsay promised to bring them on to Stirling when all was signalled as safe; and meantime he would attend the hunt on Monday, with the requisite following, to ensure if necessary that there should be no unpleasantness displayed towards the Earl Marischal and the Lord Lyon.

So, late on Sunday night, a well-mounted party consisting of the Chancellor, the Lord Erskine, the two Davids and Abbot John, with a part of the royal guard, and of course the King, all muffled in cloaks, slipped out of the southern postern of Craigmillar Castle into the half-dark, and turned their beasts' heads west-by-south.

They would have gone more swiftly without the Archbishop who, gross and heavy, was not much of a horseman. But secrecy rather than speed was what was important—and the Chancellor, left behind, could have been used as a hostage, with more effect than could the Marischal or the Lyon.

The route chosen, therefore, was less than direct, in the interests of concealment, keeping well clear of the outskirts of the city, and indeed the villages to the south of it, making for the Pentland foothills where their passage would be unlikely to attract any notice. In May it is never really dark in Scotland, and once their eyes were accustomed to the dusk the horsemen had no difficulty in seeing their way. As far as possible they avoided rough ground and bog, of course. In time they struck the well-defined drove road from Lanark, by Colinton, Currie, Balerno and the Dalmahoy hills. Their liege-lord found it all a most exciting adventure.

By sun-up, and striking ever north-westwards now, they reached the Priory of Torphichen which, besides being a famous sanctuary was the seat or Preceptory of the Order of St John of Jerusalem in Scotland, of which Order the Chancellor was a senior chaplain and the Lord Erskine a knight. So here they could safely wait a while, eat and rest.

Linlithgow, on the main Stirling road, was only four miles away to the north, but with empty hills between. James Beaton was exhausted—as no doubt was the horse which had been carrying his weight.

At midday they were off again, keeping to the high ground of Muiravonside and Redding Muir to the area where Wallace fought the fatal battle of Falkirk. Skirting that town well to the west, they were able to heave sighs of relief when presently they entered the glades of the great Tor Wood, the largest forest in Lowland Scotland after that of Ettrick, which extended almost all the way to Stirling, and where they could feel secure from all eyes. David and Abbot John knew much of its fastnesses reasonably well, having often hunted there, from Stirling.

They came to that town and its fortress as the sun was sinking behind the Highland hills. Never before, so far as he could remember, had David Lindsay taken so long to ride a thirty-five mile journey. But all was well and the Archbishop would recover. James was delighted to be reunited with his papingo, which had been left at Stirling.

After it all, they were surprised to find Arran and the Bastard gone from the castle. They were off to the Hamilton country apparently, raising men.

The Earl Marischal arrived a few days later, having suffered no interference. Not surprisingly, the hunt had not been a great success, with the Douglases much upset and angry, but the Lindsay presence in force sufficient to temper their reactions—Angus himself still being absent, apparently.

So, all seeming to be reasonably settled at Stirling, and a quiet spell likely to develop, David sought leave of absence to go and fetch the young wives, Beaton deciding to accompany him.

At the Byres and Garleton they found all well, and lingered pleasantly for a few days, all glad to be released from duties, as it were, for a while, the Lindsays introducing the Beatons to their area of Lothian, from the bays and sands and cliffs of the fine seaboard to the hills and cleuchs and secret valleys of the Lammermuirs, a carefree interlude made the most of by all four. Davie Beaton, in especial, reverted to perfectly natural and high-spirited good company, the model husband and friend, intrigue and statecraft for the moment forgotten.

Or perhaps not entirely forgotten, for on their fourth day at the Byres another visitor arrived and one of some consequence, the Lord Fleming, a distant kinsman of Lord Lindsay. He it was, it turned out, whom Arran had sent from Stirling to France with the message for Albany. Now he had returned, having taken the opportunity of a passage in a French trading vessel from Dunkirk coming to Dunbar for Lammermuir wool. On his way back to Stirling he called in at the Byres for the night.

Fleming was full of news. Evidently, while the quiet spell had descended on Scotland, there had been major developments elsewhere. The Emperor Maximilian had died and was succeeded, to Francis of France's fury, by his rival Charles the Fifth of Spain. This had precipitated strong reaction from the impulsive French monarch and he had promptly made an extraordinary gesture towards Henry of England, calling for an armed alliance against the Empire, Spain and the Pope and inviting Henry actually to meet him on French soil—or at least on soil which he considered to be French but which Henry claimed was English, in the Pas de Calais. Wolsey, Henry's ambitious Chancellor, pro-French, had favoured this, and the English monarch had gone in great state across the Channel, where he had met Francis between Guisnes and Ardres, to discuss a firm alliance. This had been the situation when Fleming arrived from Scotland; and since Albany had gone with Francis to the meeting, as Lord High Admiral of France, thither Fleming had proceeded also.

Obviously he had been vastly impressed by his experiences there, at seeing this vast assemblage of the pride and nobility of two great kingdoms, each vying with the other in an extravagant display of splendour. For instance, there had been no fewer than two thousand eight hundred great pavilions and tents erected on the plain, many of them covered with gold stuff, and all bedecked with banners and pennons—so that the assembly was being called the Field of the Cloth of Gold. The two monarchs, who had never met previously, had come to terms on mutual support and a treaty of alliance agreed on, with Francis agreeing to Henry keeping Calais but getting Tournai back. In the treaty terms Henry had not failed to involve Scotland, his *bête noire*, claiming it to be under his high protection as Lord

Paramount. Albany, there present, had more or less agreed to these terms—no doubt he had little choice—and ambassadors were being sent, indeed might already have arrived, to convey the details to the Scots Council of Regency. In the circumstances, Fleming's mission to urge Albany's immediate return was scarcely well-timed and to little effect. Clearly, whether Francis would allow the Regent's return, whatever Albany's own wishes in the matter, would depend on the Scots reception of these treaty terms—which were, of course, favourable to Henry Tudor, not to Scotland. It was all highly involved, and boded but ill for the northern kingdom.

All this had the hearers much perturbed, and Davie Beaton particularly so. Ignoring the differences in rank and status, he cross-questioned the Lord Fleming at length and in detail. Then he announced that he must get back to his uncle at Stirling at the earliest. He would leave at first light, whether Fleming came with him or not.

So their brief holiday was at an end, it being agreed that they all might as well go together. What Davie could do in the present situation was not evident, but he could be relied upon to attempt something.

They rode next morning in fine style, for Lord Lindsay himself decided to come with them, for consultation with the Chancellor, and took his usual tail of retainers as escort. With no wish to become involved with the Douglases, who were now in complete control of Edinburgh, they were avoiding the city, skirting to the north of it by the port of Leith. And it was while passing through Leith that they learned that this very morning a French ship was docked, putting ashore a party of French and English magnificoes, ambassadors apparently, who had proceeded with much ceremony up to Edinburgh.

Both Davie Beaton and the Lords Lindsay and Fleming were much interested and eager to learn what would happen now in these peculiar circumstances. They would follow the envoys up to the city—as lords of parliament and the Chancellor's secretary, they were perfectly entitled to do so. But there was always the possibilities of trouble with the Douglases, and it was felt that the women should not be exposed to this. It was decided therefore that David and part of the escort should proceed slowly on their way westwards, with Kate and Marion, and wait at the Priory of St Mary at Queen Margaret's Ferry, till the others came up with them.

In the event, they had some considerable time to wait, indeed were becoming anxious about the safety of their friends, before they perceived the Lindsay colours approaching along the little royal burgh's winding shoreside street. Even so they were doubtful, for this seemed a much larger party than before and there were more colours than the Lindsays' red and blue.

To their great surprise, when the others rode up it was to present to them none other than the aforementioned French and English ambassadors, the Messieurs Lafayette and Cordelle, and Henry's Clarenceux Herald, and their attendants, now it seemed also on their way to Stirling. They did not appear to be in the happiest of spirits.

Davie explained. The envoys had been received with fair ceremony at Edinburgh by Angus himself, who it seemed was back in the capital; but to their bewilderment, despite the Douglas being supported by the Earl of Crawford, the Earl of Rothes and the Lords Glamis, Ogilvy, Kennedy and others, they discovered that these lofty-sounding nobles were not in fact who they had come to see, that Angus was the only member of the Regency Council there, the rest being elsewhere, at this Stirling, and having no dealings with these people. So, although they had explained their business to Angus, the terms of the Franco-English treaty as they affected Scotland and so on, and apparently found him non-committal, they had realised that they would have to travel on to Stirling to see the Governor and the Chancellor and others of the Council. It was at this stage that the Lords Lindsay and Fleming had turned up at Holyrood, where all this was proceeding, and learning that the newcomers were indeed on their way to Stirling had sought their escort thither, Angus scarcely approving but hardly in a position to restrain them. He did, however, curtly refuse to accompany the envoys, to their further astonishment. Clearly they found Scotland a strange country.

The journey was resumed. If the foreigners expected to be presented to King Henry's sister at Linlithgow they were disappointed.

On the way, Lord Fleming, riding beside the Lindsay and

Beaton couples, opened their eyes somewhat to an alternative variety of diplomacy to that practised by Davie—the Bastard of Arran's. For he it was who, in his father's name, had briefed Fleming on his errand to Albany. He had said that the Regent was to be told in no uncertain tones that if he was not back in Scotland by midsummer then the Estates of parliament would declare him not only no longer Regent of the kingdom but unsuitable to succeed to the throne, as second person, and heir-presumptive, in the event of the demise of young James. He would also be declared officially infamous and debarred from any further association with Scotland.

Amazed, the others could scarcely believe their ears, that anyone should so threaten the Regent. Davie Beaton was greatly perturbed, for of course he it was who had all but brought Albany to Scotland in the first place, cherished him as Regent and acted his mouthpiece. He declared that Hamilton must be mad, that such threats were the very last thing to bring that proud man back to Scotland, indeed could almost be warranted to keep him away. Then, as an afterthought, he wondered whether that, in fact, might not be the Bastard's intention? After all, if Albany did not come, and was indeed debarred, then who was heir-presumptive to the throne but Arran himself? Was that it? Arran for king—and the Bastard ruling Scotland for him? In which case, how safe was young James Stewart's life?

Appalled at such possible implications, the others fell silent, until David asked how much of this diatribe Fleming had in fact passed on to Albany, and what his reactions had been? The other admitted that he had indeed toned it down considerably, and the necessary translation from English to French had further modified the message. Even so, the Regent had been less than pleased.

Approaching Stirling, they realised that Arran must be back, for the area to the south and west of the castle rock, around the King's Knot, was like an armed camp with hundreds, perhaps even thousands of men, cooking fires sending up their blue smokes into the evening air, the streets of the town thronged with Hamilton retainers.

They had a mixed reception at the castle, Arran apparently flattered by the arrival of the ambassadors to see him, but less happy to see Davie Beaton back, of whom he was gravely suspicious, probably with reason. Neither did he love the Lord Lindsay. The Chancellor, on the other hand, was greatly relieved to see his nephew, on whom he was being led to rely more and more; but he did not welcome the envoys, recognising that they were not come for the benefit of Scotland. The Marischal, for his part, was thankful to see David Lindsay, as was Abbot John, for the King had apparently been at his most difficult during the interim, refusing to obey anyone and demanding the presence of his beloved Davie-Lin, as he now called him. There was a touching reunion of these two, at least. The Bastard was not present, being away raising more troops in the West.

In theory, the ambassadors had come to see the Regency Council; but this was scarcely practical. Of its six members, Archbishop Forman was now all but house-bound at St Andrews; Huntly was up in his Strathbogie fastnesses and would take at least a week to recall; and Argyll was still conducting what had become almost a private war of Campbell aggrandisement in the Western Isles. The visitors had already seen Angus—which left only the Governor and the Chancellor. At Davie Beaton's suggestion, therefore, a sitting of the old Privy Council, which had more or less fallen into abeyance during Albany's absence, was declared for the next day, which enabled the Earl Marischal and the Lords Lindsay, Erskine and Fleming, all councillors, to attend; and to make it look more authentic still, the monarch should be present for as long as he might stand it. Other members of the Privy Council could be conveniently forgotten.

So something of a round-table conference developed the following noontide, in the castle's magnificent great hall with all ceremoniously rising to bow as young James was led in by David Lindsay and the Abbot. The Chancellor presided, but Davie Beaton was very much at his uncle's back.

From the first, however, the ambassadors made the running, in an odd mixture of French and English, losing no time in stating their terms—since that is what it came to. The most puissant and illustrious Kings of France and of England, they asserted, had come to agreement on many matters of mutual concern for the general weal of both kingdoms, and also that of Scotland happily, for which realm they had much regard. Most of the treaty admittedly little concerned the northern kingdom; but certain aspects most assuredly did.

First and foremost, peace must be maintained between all three kingdoms, in place of the grievous onsets which for so long had bedevilled them. There must be no more armed incursions into each other's territories, either across the Channel or over the Tweed–Esk borderline. The truce presently obtaining between England and Scotland therefore was to be replaced by a permanent state of peace, and any warlike compacts and alliances between any two of the realms were to be done away with.

Secondly, Scotland must make new arrangements for her governance during the remaining years of the minority of her well-beloved but youthful monarch, King James, since by no means could King Francis spare his Lord High Admiral to return to this realm as Regent. However, since His Grace of England's royal sister was King James's mother what could be more suitable than her replacing of the Duke of Albany as Regent, to the satisfaction of all. Especially as this folly of estrangement from her husband, the Earl of Angus, and talk of divorce was to be ended and man and wife brought together again. Thus the so-called English and French parties in Scotland would lose all relevance, including the Douglas and Hamilton factions, and a peaceful and excellent unity would prevail.

Thirdly, the King of France had recently been blessed by God with another daughter, the Princess Madeleine, and she was to be promised as bride for King James, in due course, to the further felicity and well-being of Scotland and the desirable drawing together of all three realms.

Such were the wise and expedient requirements of their Majesties of France and England.

The Scots around the table, whatever their entrenched attitudes and concerns, stared with one accord at the propounders of this astonishing series of statements to the representatives of an independent state—all except its liege-lord, that is who, understanding none of it, was playing with the quill pens he had found on the table before him. All were temporarily reduced to silence—save for Davie Beaton, who quickly leaned forward to whisper in his uncle's ear. Arran looked bewildered and turned helplessly to the Chancellor.

That man cleared his throat. Were they to believe, he wondered, that their excellencies had travelled all the way from France to deliver themselves of this extraordinary pronouncement, this prescription? They made it to sound like an ultimatum—but that was possibly owing to the difficulties of language. Had they come to negotiate on these basic headings? If so, they had not made it sufficiently clear . . .

He was interrupted by Clarenceux, who grimly declared that it was all entirely clear. They had not come to negotiate anything but to inform. These were the parts of the treaty concluded, referring to Scotland. They had been signed and sealed between the two monarchs. Their visit was but a courtesy, to convey these terms.

"Terms!" the Earl Marischal burst out. "Terms, sirrah? Whose terms? Not ours! Who is your Welshman, the Tudor, to make terms for Scotland? Or the Frenchman either? To send you here, with your arrogant decrees!" There were growls of approval for that around the table. Lord Lindsay spoke.

"Englishman—these so-called terms? They were reached by Henry and Francis, them only. They have no references to us, the Scots. None."

"Not so, my lord. They were assented to by your Regent, the Duke of Albany."

"That I do not believe!" the Marischal declared. "Albany is neither so foolish nor so false!'

Arran found his voice. "Besides, the Duke has not been in Scotland for three years. *I* have had the rule of Scotland. If the King of France will not permit him to return here, as you say, how can he assent to anything for this kingdom?"

"He is still your Regent, my lord. While so, he speaks for this young King. Can any of you deny it?"

As shouts arose, the Chancellor sought to control the meeting to something of dignity. "*Messieurs*," he said, careful to address the Frenchmen rather than Clarenceux. "You have brought these informations, which we shall note. As to what you call terms, what if we in Scotland cannot accept them?"

"That is scarcely conceivable, my lord Archbishop," Lafayette said. "The terms are passed, signed, completed. You cannot alter them . . ."

"But we can, and must, reject them!" Marischal interrupted. "And so do, by God!"

"Then you must accept, instead, the consequences, *Monsieur le maréchal!*"

"Which are . . . ?" Lord Patrick demanded.

Clarenceux answered. "Pain of the utmost displeasure of both monarchs and realms, my lord. All measures to be taken to bring about compliance, of the sternest. Trade to be cut off. Hostages taken. No further association with France. And the Princess Madeleine's hand withdrawn."

"All of which we could thole, if necessary!"

Davie was whispering again to his uncle, who nodded. "France and Scotland have been friends for many centuries," he pointed out, reasonably. "The Auld Alliance, we call it. Serving both realms, well, to restrain the aggressions of England. Is all to be thrown over out of one day's talking? Is France so sure that never again will the English invade her soil? That she will not require Scotland's aid, as in the past? Does she trust Henry Tudor sufficiently to throw away Scots friendship? Are the English not still in Calais?" That was perhaps hardly diplomacy as normally practised at Chancellor's level, especially in the presence of a monarch; but as an exercise in driving a wedge between partners it was shrewd and telling, however blatant.

And evidently not wholly unsuccessful, by the expressions of the two Frenchmen and their glances at Clarenceux. They coughed but made no other response.

At this stage, King James yawned loudly, and the Chancellor seized the opportunity to bring the meeting to a close on that note, observing that His Grace had been very patient, and thanking all for their attendance. Even the ambassadors were probably thankful to be done with it.

Next day they departed for Leith again, with an escort of Hamiltons to see them safely past Linlithgow and no interviews with Margaret Tudor—but not to go so far as Leith, in case they ran into Douglases. Lowland Scotland was, in fact, now two armed camps, based on the two great rock top fortresses, with the Queen-Mother sitting exactly in the middle, a peculiar situation which, though she had done nothing to achieve, she might well see her opportunity for profit.

Whether that difficult and unpredictable woman did recognise that her position was now strengthened, and in much more than mere geography, Davie Beaton most certainly did, his acute wits swiftly perceiving the possibilities. He came to David Lindsay within hours of the envoys' departure, where he was playing at the hurly-hackit with his sovereign on the slope above Ballengeich, and whilst joining in the sport on another cow's skull, used his friend as a sounding-board to try out his theories. In between slides down and clamberings up, and with constant interruptions from young James and other distractions, he talked it through, almost as much to himself as to Lindsay, undoubtedly.

In the present dire circumstances, the first priority was to get Albany back to Scotland, somehow. To do that would be difficult, obviously, but surely not impossible. The key seemed to lie with Henry Tudor, of course. His Uncle James had sought to drive a wedge between French and English envoys the day previously— a much greater wedge, between Henry and Francis, was required, for Scotland's sake and for more than Scotland's. That was a large project—but there were various items which might be used in the process. Or, better, personalities. He could think of three—Margaret Tudor herself, Albany and Wolsey. It ought to be possible to use these to play on the weaknesses of the two monarchs—who could not truly love nor trust each other anyway. A fourth, it might be—Pope Leo, who was now said to be dying. Henry sought to use his sister—so could *Scotland* not use her against him?

David, panting his way uphill, dragging his cow's skull, waited.

Margaret was tired of Angus and he with her. She did not want to go back to him; she wanted a divorce. But Henry did not. For his own purposes he required them together again so that he had a further hold on Angus. He wanted the Douglas power in Scotland—it was as simple as that. Now, Albany was seeking to obtain Margaret's divorce, from the Vatican. Why? They had never been friends. But she had written to Albany asking his help, since he now had links with the Medici family to which the Pope belonged. She promised her goodwill if he did this. Henry would know well of that letter, for he had spies everywhere. Suppose that another letter from her to Albany was to fall into his hands—as could be arranged—urging greater efforts while this Pope was still alive, and indicating more than a mere goodwill towards the Duke, actual affection perhaps, or at least the possibility of her favours? Margaret was ever indiscreet and would do almost anything to gain her wishes. What would Henry think of that?

The other wagged his head, lost.

Henry would be furious, that is what. Furious at them both, but especially at Albany. And when Henry was furious, he never failed to act, however rashly. He would attack the Duke in any way that he could. And King Francis was fond of Albany, his friend. That was part of the trouble over the regency, not merely that he was Admiral of France but that Francis wanted him near him. Any attack on Albany by Henry would be an attack on Francis. The first tap on the wedge!

David was perhaps less impressed than he should have been.

The second tap, Beaton went on, in his element, would concern Wolsey. All knew that Henry's ambitious Chancellor was ambitious to be more than just a cardinal—he wanted to be Pope. Equally it was known that Henry was strongly against this, not desirous of losing his clever Chancellor. So, if it could seem that the King of France was working to have Wolsey made the new Pope, with Albany's help—what then?

"But how could this possibly be contrived?" David demanded.

"The same letter, do you not see? If the letter from Margaret was to say that, since Albany and his friend Francis were already seeking Vatican support for Wolsey's bid, surely they could further the much less difficult matter of her divorce? Thus the seed would be planted. It would but require some further watering and nurturing!"

Young James's impatience with all this talk demanded an interval of more active endeavour. On the next climb up, David's doubts erupted.

"These are all but speculations, man!" he objected. "Hopes, not probabilities. And why should Margaret Tudor write such a letter? She is no catspaw, that one."

"I think that I could persuade her. I will go to see her. Assert that this would help her cause. Would bear on Albany. Tell her that I, myself, would be going to France soon and could further pursue her interests, if she thus prepared the ground."

"And would you? Go to France?"

"To be sure. It is necessary, in this pass. I must see Albany. And Francis also. I flatter myself that I have some small pull with that headstrong monarch, for some reason. This letter will, I think, sow the seed, as I said. I needs must go and cherish the growth! I can be of more use to Scotland in France, meantime, than here. Fortunately my uncle's affairs can do without his secretary for a while, I judge. Old Forman will not live another year, and I have been at work amongst sufficient bishops to ensure that he is succeeded as Primate by my good relative. The only real rival is Gavin Douglas of Dunkeld, who covets the position—but I believe that I have his measure. Forby, his fortunes must rise or fall with Angus's, and what I seek to do in France will be to Angus's disadvantage. So I think to serve my uncle's cause, and the realm's likewise, furth of Scotland for a while."

"And you esteem yourself able to effect all this? One man, young and but a secretary at that, no great noble, seeking to change the destinies of mighty realms such as France and England! You have ready wits and a nimble tongue, Davie—but is not this beyond you?"

"It may be, yes—for it is a large matter, a challenge. But not impossible, I think. I will strengthen my hand by having myself sent as ambassador, Scotland's resident ambassador to the French court. Old Bishop Leslie has been there overlong and is of little use. I will replace him, meantime. The appointment is one that my uncle can make, as Chancellor, in the name of the Council. That will aid me, give me greater access to Francis."

David, seating himself on his uncomfortable sled, eyed his friend with a kind of wonder mixed with exasperation. "You have all in your hand, I see! Scots ambassador to France, now. Secretary to the Chancellor and Rector of Killearn. What next, I wonder—for the seventh son of a Fife lairdie?"

The other smiled, shrugging.

"And what of Marion? What says your wife? Does she go to France with you?"

"I fear not. That would be scarcely possible." Beaton's tone had changed. "To my sorrow. I . . . she is with child. It would not serve her, or my mission, to take her to France at this time. Marion will go back to her father's house at Airlie, meantime. It, it is the price I have to pay!"

"And *she* pays! You will leave her, to have her child alone? Is that the honest husband's part?"

"What use is a man, at such time? Better without me, perhaps!" But he did not meet the other's eyes, gazing away towards the Highland Line. "The realm's need is urgent, David. And I believe that only I can meet that need, God willing!"

"God . . . ?" Lindsay acceded to the realm's master's urgency and impatience, and launched himself and the King off downhill, leaving behind a man at war with himself, his heart and his head and his fate.

19

That major hostilities did not break out in Scotland that winter was a near miracle, considering that the land was like tinder only awaiting a spark. There were, of course, minor incidents and clashes innumerable, between Hamiltons and Douglases and their various partisans; but that none of these erupted into outright war was a mercy, and more than interesting to all who considered the matter with any knowledge. David Lindsay, for one, came to the conclusion that it was largely thanks to Angus himself, acting as a restraining influence, out of character as this might seem. It certainly was not thanks to Arran—or, more accurately, tó the Bastard, who now so dominated his father, and who seemed to be almost spoiling for a fight with his humiliation over the Cleanse the Causeway incident to wipe out. Time and again Angus could well have reacted violently, and did not. Why, was unclear. Possibly he was lying deliberately low, wary over Henry's efforts to bring about his reconciliation with his wife, which most evidently he did not want. Or it could be merely that as he reached his thirties he was gaining in responsibility. Or just that he was so enamoured and taken up with his Traquair mistress that he did not want to be distracted. Whatever it was, the kingdom had cause to be thankful—although it did have the effect of encouraging the Bastard towards ever more challenging behaviour.

Another aspect of the situation was that the Homes now had more or less a free hand in the East and Middle Marches, for Arran, as Warden and Governor, could not get at them from Stirling and the West without first passing through Douglas-held territory and the Edinburgh vicinity. The said Homes made the most of their opportunities.

Davie Beaton had departed for France in September. Whatever influence he had been able to exert on the French-English situation, if any, was not apparent from Scotland, keenly as David, for one, awaited indications. It was not until May 1521 that news arrived which might imply some activity, or at least some unexpected change on the diplomatic front. It came in a highly dramatic not to say farcical announcement from King Henry—first that Scotland should be informed that the boy taken from Edinburgh to Stirling the previous May was not in fact his nephew King James but a mere low-born substitute, James himself having been spirited secretly to France, there to be reared as a Frenchman, like Albany, with Scotland to become no more than a sub-kingdom of France; and secondly that the said Duke of Albany was seeking to gain a divorce from the Pope for the Queen-Mother, Countess of Angus, in order that he might marry her himself and thus gain complete control of the Scottish succession.

This extraordinary development, however ridiculous on all counts, held profound significance. For whatever else it meant, it indicated a notable split in relations between Henry and Francis, so soon after the Field of the Cloth of Gold. And although the story about the changeling at Stirling seemed too far-fetched to have emanated from David Beaton, the divorce reference and general attack on Albany sounded very much as though he had been at work.

David pondered long over the English monarch's reasons for putting out this absurd accusation about James having been secretly removed to France and a dummy installed at Stirling—which nobody in Scotland was going to credit and which could be so easily disproved there. Assuming that Henry was not actually deranged, then, it must mean that the tale was not designed for Scots ears so much as for others. Whose, then? And why? Who could it impress and what advantage could it possibly serve? It certainly could not advantage France, and would be laughed at in Scotland. So it must be aimed elsewhere, to some quarter little acquainted with Scotland. It might well be believed in England itself, but Henry did not require to foster anti-Scots sentiment in his own kingdom—it was sufficiently strong without such nurturing. Who else, then? The Vatican? Could it be that? The treaty with France had been anti-Vatican and Empire. Why should Henry seek to delude the Pope, or the cardinals concerned with his successor, over the King of Scots? Rome was usually well-enough informed. None of it appeared to make sense.

It was well into summer before David, and others who had puzzled over this problem, obtained a possible explanation, when the sensational news reached Scotland that Henry had in fact made one more of his notorious about-turns, had had a meeting with the Emperor Charles at Gravelines, near Calais, and come to terms with him.

This totally unexpected development of course completely changed the entire international situation, shattering the so-called French alliance and linking the unpredictable Tudor with Spain, the Empire and the Vatican. Could the King James story have been some sort of preparation for this move? To be used as an excuse towards Charles and Pope Leo? A preliminary stab in the back for France and an indication that Henry was prepared to switch horses? If this seemed scarcely credible, it was no more so than the actual volte-face less than a year after all the elaborate charade of the Field of the Cloth of Gold.

Whether the new Scots ambassador to France had had anything to do with it all, it now meant that what Davie had wished for had come about, that Henry and Francis were once again on opposite sides, that Scotland would once more become valuable to France as an ally, and that the Regent Albany might well be able to serve his friend Francis best in the northern kingdom.

The news had a profound effect in Scotland, encouraging the Hamilton and pro-French faction of course, but also most moderate and peace-loving folk; while no doubt depressing the Douglases. There was other news coming from the Continent also to encourage David Lindsay and sundry others, if not the Chancellor and most churchmen—word of ever-growing disillusionment with the corruption and state of Holy Church and the need for reform therein, the German Augustinian monk Martin Luther leading the way with notable courage and effectiveness, with the backing of his Elector of Saxony. Pope Leo had excommunicated him at the beginning of the year, but Luther was not to be silenced. The Church must reform itself, he insisted, or Christ's cause would go down, and Christendom sink into the new paganism; and large numbers of God-fearing people agreed with him—as well they might, when Pope Leo himself, a cardinal at the age of thirteen, had hanged another of his own cardinals on ascending the papal throne, and had made the notorious statement that "truly the myth of Christ had brought much gain!" That gain the Pontiff now was capitalising, by sending the Dominican, Tetzel, on a tour of Christendom, with a long train of pack-mules laden with indulgences and pardons for sale to cover any and every offence whatsoever—save criticism of the Vatican—even assuring release from purgatory, all on an elaborate scale of charges. David and Abbot John had long debates about all this and particularly the shameful condition of the Church in Scotland—which, to be sure, the latter was not in the best position to defend, with himself holding a wholly empty abbacy—empty, that is, save for the receipt of the revenues thereof. David argued strongly for reform, as he had done with Davie Beaton also; indeed he had written a poem on the subject—which, however, he was not foolish enough to let Archbishop Beaton read.

The word they had all been awaiting at Stirling arrived in a letter to the Chancellor from his nephew in September, that King Francis was going to send Albany back to Scotland, probably within the next six weeks, and he would not be coming alone either, but bringing French military advisers with him, along with a consignment of arms and money.

Relief at the first part of this message tended to be a little dampened, for some, by contemplation of the second part, which seemed to strike a warlike note, although hitherto Albany had been little of a warmonger.

About the same time a letter came to Kate, from the Braes of Angus, to say that Marion Ogilvy had been delivered of a fine son and both were well.

It was, in a way, strange that Albany's second arrival in Scotland should be looked forward to with so much satisfaction and hope, for he was scarcely a beloved figure, nor had ever sought to be, no paladin nor brilliant statesman, and still could not speak the language. Nevertheless, compared with the anarchy which had prevailed before his first coming and which had revived since his return to France, he seemed to represent lawful authority and stable government in place of chaos, and by and large the land ached for peace and an end to feuding and bloodshed. And he *was* the second person in the realm, heir-presumptive to the throne, however much Arran and his people might deplore it.

This time, with Dumbarton Castle presently in Douglas hands, it was considered advisable to bring the Regent's three ships to an alternative landfall, although this had to be on the west coast, for similar reasons. So a small craft was despatched to meet the French vessels in the Firth of Clyde and conduct them up through the maze of sea-lochs and isles which penetrated Cowal, the southernmost part of Argyll, and into the Gareloch, near the head of which the welcoming party would wait. If this might seem an odd place to bring ashore the realm's ruler, to his French associates, or even to Albany himself, it was in fact illustrative of the state of affairs prevailing in Scotland, a locality which ought by its remoteness to ensure a safe and uncontested landing and one to which Arran, the Chancellor and the reception party from Stirling, ought to be able to reach without fear of interception by the Douglases or their friends, as this landfall was only a few miles from Finnart on Loch Long, the Hamilton lands which gave the Bastard his title.

So the welcoming group made its way, by quite difficult routes, up the Carse of Stirling, through the hilly MacGregor lands around Aberfoyle and the head of Loch Lomond, and by fierce mountain passes and wild glens to the head of Loch Long and so down to Finnart, a major journey in November weather. David prevailed on the Earl Marischal to let him go along, restlessness strong upon him again. His was not really a suitable temperament for the kind of life he was being forced to live.

It took them nearly three days, halting at the distinctly inadequate monastic hospices of Portanellen and Arrocher. They found Finnart to be a modest square tower-house within a barmkin or high defensive courtyard wall, but surrounded by quite a community of Highlanders' cabins and hovels and a population of herdsmen and fisherfolk. This was no longer the Bastard's home, of course; he was building himself a fine castle at Cambusnethan in Clydesdale, more in keeping with his present status. Here, in less than comfort, they waited for two more days.

On the nineteenth of November they received the information that the three French ships were in sight, and the party crossed the neck of land between the two lochs to Garelochhead and then down the lochside to Faslane where there was sufficient depth of water for sea-going ships to anchor.

Although Albany had been given only four months' leave of absence by parliament, he had been away for over four years—and by his expression when he came ashore was none too happy to be back, even so. His Frenchmen looked still less appreciative, staring about them at the wild and barren mountainous surroundings in something not far from alarm. The Duke's demands as to why they had had to be brought in here—in French, necessarily—rather spoiled the welcoming ceremony, the explanations taking a little time. David had expected to see Davie Beaton there, but was disappointed, and the interpreting had to be done by a little bumbling fat man, who turned out to be Bishop Leslie, lately Scots resident at the court of King Francis and now replaced by Davie—who, it seemed, had decided to remain on in France meantime for reasons of state, despite having a wife and new-born son to bring him home.

The reception party, learning from the last time, had led a long string of spare horses for the newcomers; but these proved to be not nearly sufficient for the numbers Albany had brought and all the baggage they had with them, and some time thereafter had to be spent scouring the neighbourhood for the rough and shaggy but sturdy garrons which were all that were available in these parts. Fortunately there were plenty of these; but it did mean that most of the Scots there, including David, had to ride all the way back to Stirling on these short-legged, broad-backed and saddleless Highland mounts, the proud Frenchmen far too superior to do anything of the sort, requiring their good horseflesh.

On the journey, Albany made entirely clear what he had come for. The establishment of his due authority and rule could be taken for granted, of course; but his primary purpose and duty was the full-scale invasion of England with a large army at the earliest possible moment. Henry Tudor was preparing to attack France, in conjunction with the Emperor Charles, Spain and the Papal forces, and must be forced to look back over his treacherous shoulder to his northern borders and so to divert at least some of his strength. In other words, that Auld Alliance was to be reactivated and put into practice, now that France needed it;

and Albany was here more as Francis's lieutenant than as Scotland's Regent.

There were some long Scots faces arriving at Stirling, David's amongst them. It was, after all, only eight years since the disaster of Flodden, when this French requirement had last been met.

There was news awaiting them at the castle. Archbishop Andrew Forman, the Primate, had at last died at St Andrews, and the way was open for Davie's scheming regarding Church and State to come to fruition—with crown permission, which meant the Regent's acceptance. Albany saw his opportunity and seized it. He would support Archbishop Beaton's translation to St Andrews and the Primacy, and most certainly block the ambitions of Gavin Douglas—in return for a major subvention from Church revenues to help pay for the hire of armed men by the thousand and the adherence of the not inconsiderable numbers of men-at-arms retained by individual bishops, abbots and priors. James Beaton, pained, reluctantly acquiesced.

Neither the Regent nor the Chancellor lost any time in pursuing their two projects. Beaton was off to St Andrews in Fife promptly, to take over the rule and wealth of Holy Church, taking his election by a majority of his thirteen fellow bishops for granted after Davie's careful arranging. And Albany, equally taking for granted that the assembly of Hamilton manpower, now more or less permanently encamped at Stirling, should form the nucleus of his invasion army, went ahead without delay in sending out summonses to all nobles, lairds, chiefs, churchmen and burgh magistrates to muster there also, with their fullest strength, and at the soonest.

But more than armed men gravitated to Stirling, to the surprise of all concerned. The Regent had not been back one week when a small but brilliant cavalcade came riding up to the castle, under, of all things, the joint royal standards of Scotland and England. This proved to be Margaret Tudor, from Linlithgow, demanding to see and welcome the Duke of Albany. Astonished and uncertain, the captain of the guard kept the lady waiting beyond the drawbridge whilst he went to inform the equally unprepared Regent.

The news went round the castle like wildfire, and practically everyone therein hurried down to the gatehouse battlements to witness the scene—although David was careful not to take young James, who had no fondness for his mother.

He arrived in time to see something he could never have anticipated, Albany walking distinctly doubtfully out over the drawbridge planking in wary greeting to the newcomers, and Margaret sliding down from her saddle in ungainly fashion—for she was a heavily built woman—and actually running forward, skirts hitched up, to meet the other, and then flinging herself bodily upon him, not actually into his arms since he kept them to his sides, and in fact recoiled somewhat at the unexpected embrace. But any seeming reluctance on the man's part the woman more than made up for, clasping him to her bosom and planting kisses on both cheeks, in a demonstration never before witnessed by any present. At the Regent's complete lack of response she drew back, but only a little way, running her hands down his arms to grip his wrists, and so to stand gazing up into his eyes as though in near adoration.

The many watchers gasped their astonishment.

That Albany was equally surprised, not to say alarmed and embarrassed, was evident. He could scarcely shake her off, but he did repossess his wrists and arms, and half turned away, a move which Margaret quite cleverly converted into a civil gesture to draw her round and lead her back across the bridge towards the gatehouse pend, she at his side chattering with every appearance of fondness, eyes still on his rather stiff though handsome Stewart features, and one arm still linked in his.

Few there would ever have believed it had they not seen it with their own eyes, nor conceived the arrogant Queen-Mother capable of such play-acting—if such it was—in public, however she was reputed to behave, on occasion, in private. David, pondering, wondered whether Davie Beaton's persuasions, that day, had been even more effective than he had intended?

Everyone was agog, of course, and speculation ran riot. Was there truth, after all, in King Henry's allegations that Albany had only been working for Margaret's divorce in order to wed her himself? If so, he would require a divorce of his own, for his duchess was alive and well in France. But, by appearances, the Regent was taken by surprise in all this affection—which seemed as foreign to his character as it was to the lady's. If so, what did it mean? Was Margaret setting her cap at him, for policy or other reason? Was this a move to try to get back into a position of rule in Scotland? Or merely a means of showing her spite at Angus? Or even part of a device for getting her son under her influence again? There was no lack of theories.

The expected summons to the Regent's quarters came for David that evening; he was to bring the King to greet his mother—despite it being the nine-year-old's bedtime.

They found Albany and Margaret alone in a small sitting room of the palace building, in candlelight, standing before a blazing log-fire, with a table laden with wines and sweetmeats nearby, a cosy domestic scene into which neither the man nor the woman seemed by their natures to fit. The Regent made a more elaborate bow than his usual to the reluctant James, who clutched David's hand and scowled at his mother. Margaret exclaimed in a painfully sweet voice at how he had grown and how good-looking he was. She had not seen him, to be sure, for long. She held out a hand. David gave his charge a nudge forward, but the boy held back. There was an uncomfortable pause.

Albany made some encouraging remark, in French of course; and although James had been taught that language, he did not respond. Margaret frowned, and drummed impatient fingertips on the table top.

"Come, boy—I am your mother!" she said, her tone less dulcet now.

When James actually drew back, half behind David, that man felt that something had to be done. But what? This was the monarch of them all, after all, and himself a comparatively lowly subject. He well remembered being castigated by the Queen-Mother once before for allegedly improper behaviour towards the royal child when James had tripped and stumbled on being propelled towards her at Linlithgow. Yet the other two were clearly not going to make much impression on the boy, who looked as though he might turn and bolt through the doorway by which they had entered. He decided on a device.

"See, Sire—comfits, sweetmeats!" and he pointed. He did not normally address the boy as Sire in conversation, but this was a special occasion. "Come—I am sure that my lord Duke will let us have some." James had a notably sweet tooth.

The boy looked doubtfully from the table to the pair by the fire, and back again, but allowed himself to be led forward. Only he transferred himself to David's other side, to be as far away from his mother as possible.

"You, Lindsay—you have poisoned my son's mind against me!" Margaret rapped out.

"Not so, Madam," David asserted. But he did not elaborate on that, for it was a difficult charge to deny with any conviction; certainly he had never sought to *commend* the mother to the boy.

Albany coughed and looked disapprovingly at all concerned.

Margaret quickly perceived his attitude and changed her own, moving close to him and taking his hand. "Forgive a woman's chagrin over her child's failings, Monsieur le Duc," she said, in French. "I see him so seldom. Perhaps that situation can now be bettered, no?"

The Regent did not comment on that. Instead he nodded towards James. "His Grace may eat, Lindsay," he said. "A little wine, if so he desires."

The King's French was adequate for that, at least, and he reached out to select a confection, but kept a watchful eye on the others as he ate.

"At what studies are you most proficient, James?" the Queen-Mother asked, with a sort of steely patience. "You understand the French tongue?"

Her son, chewing, nodded briefly.

"His Grace is a willing and able scholar, Madam," Davie declared, a little hurriedly. "At French and Latin he is well versed. And at . . ."

"When I require your comments, Lindsay, I shall ask for them!" Margaret interrupted. "James—greet Monsieur le Duc in French."

The boy scowled again, looking at his least attractive, but at a nudge from David, swallowed and muttered, "*Bonne nuit, Monsieur.*"

Albany nodded. "*Merci. Et Madame la Comtesse?*"

Another nudge. "*Et vous, Madame la Comtesse.*"

"I would prefer that you call me Your Grace," the lady said starchily.

That produced another cough from the Duke and an uncomfortable silence thereafter. James helped himself to another cake.

Belatedly recognising, apparently, that her remark might have sounded as much a rebuke to the man as to her son, Margaret Tudor raised a smile of sorts and moved closer still to the Duke, all but rubbing herself against him. "We wish to forget the Earl of Anguish, do we not, Jean? But James is too young to understand such matters. Pray, select me a comfit before this boy eats them all!" That was coy.

Albany did as he was bidden, although glancing ruefully at David.

Thereafter the woman launched into a lengthy discussion with the Regent on the twin subjects of the wickedness of Angus and the progress of her divorce proceedings, interspersed with endearments and touchings, ignoring her son and his Procurator entirely, all embarrassing for David at least even if not for his charge, who made the most of his opportunities with the sweetmeats. It was this, rather than his own desire to be elsewhere, concern that the boy would suffer for overindulgence thus late in the evening, which caused him to catch the Duke's eye, to indicate the need for retiral. At length he succeeded in this, jerking his head from the King towards the door, and Albany perceived, inclined his own head and waved a lordly hand.

Thankfully David bowed towards the pair, tapped his monarch on the shoulder and pointed. Grabbing a last cake, James went with alacrity, in his turn ignoring the others and the whispered instruction to bow to his mother. That princess equally disregarded her offspring's departure, eyes only for Albany.

Heaving a sigh of relief, David got out and closed the door behind them.

Next day the castle buzzed with talk. It had been late indeed before Margaret Tudor had left the Duke's quarters for those allotted to her, so they had been closeted alone for hours. Needless to say, the worst interpretations were put on this circumstance. The lady was the reverse of popular, and although it all seemed strange behaviour for Albany, men being men . . .

To add to the assumed scandal it became evident that the Queen-Mother was not at the castle to pay any brief visit but appeared to be settling in to stay. This was appreciated by few, for her autocratic ways did not help to endear her and quite quickly she was behaving as though she was indeed châtelaine there again. This affected the Lindsays particularly, for although Margaret sought little further contact with her son she had come with only two or three female attendants and Kate was drafted in as a kind of extra lady-in-waiting, to her displeasure. So David heard quite a lot of what went on in the loftier circles of the establishment, as well as the gossip of the groundlings, and wondered the more. He learned for one thing that Albany was intending to make a move to Edinburgh just as soon as he had sufficient men assembled to make it unlikely that the Douglases would contest it. He considered it unsuitable that the country's ruler should not be based on the capital city. And clearly Margaret assumed that she would be going also. Whether they would take the King remained to be seen.

Midwinter was not the best time for the mustering of armed men in tented encampments but the Regent was insistent on at least a token contingent from each magnate and burgh being sent to Stirling forthwith so that a sizeable force would be gathered, over and above the Hamilton array, available for immediate use, even if the main strength would not be able to be marshalled until the spring. This activity was afoot so that Henry's busy spies would report the presence of a major army mobilising; also the projected move to Edinburgh, that much nearer to the borderline, in the hopes that this might deter that aggressive monarch from making his anticipated attack on France in conjunction with the Emperor when the campaigning season started again. All was assuredly for France's benefit, but at least Albany was going to cover himself by calling a parliament at Edinburgh, just as soon after the twelfth day of Christmas as was possible, to approve his plans. Also he was especially summoning Angus to be present thereat to account for his behaviour, and the Homes to answer for the murder of de la Bastie. Kate said that Margaret Tudor was openly asserting that these summonses would in fact ensure that the Douglases and the Homes would *not* attend the parliament but would in all probability flee into England, into her brother's tender care—and Scotland satisfactorily rid of them.

So that Yuletide at Stirling Castle, even though major

war portended, was quite a gay one—not that either Albany nor Margaret was much inclined for gaiety, but the French visitors had to be entertained and the lords who came with their armed contingents kept happy. Whether the Frenchmen were wholly delighted with what they experienced was another matter.

In mid-January the move to Edinburgh was made, with King James and his attendants included, for it appeared that the Regent desired the young monarch to be present at the parliament. To the regret of most others, Margaret Tudor came along also, and was not dropped off at Linlithgow as some hoped. Just before they left Stirling, news came which seemed to support the lady's judgment in one respect at least; Bishop Gavin Douglas, for one, would not be attending the parliament for he had departed for England, allegedly for Henry's court.

This information encouraged the royal party in the belief that there would be no real Douglas attempt to hold Edinburgh and its fortress against them; as they made their slow progress eastwards—and slow it had to be, with a force of almost five thousand men as escort—reports reached them that in fact the Douglases were steadily deserting the capital, and no Homes had been seen there for some time.

So, although the eventual approach to the city on its ridge above the Nor' Loch was made behind an impressive array of armed men, cavalry, foot and even light cannon, no opposition materialised. Admittedly no relieved welcome from loyal citizenry developed either, but that was scarcely vital. The necessary cautious threading of the narrow streets up to the castle tourney ground was uncontested likewise, and at the fortress itself the Regent and his sovereign-lord found the drawbridge down, the portcullis up and a small deputation waiting to hand over the keys to the King or his representative. It was all as easy as that. The said deputation was not very illustrious perhaps, since all such appeared to have fled the city; but the honours were done, after a fashion, by the worthy Robert Logan of Restalrig, the rightful Provost, in the absence of Greysteel of Kilspindie his supplanter in the civil chair, and the provisional deputy keeper of the castle, who turned out to be Sir Simon Preston of Craigmillar. The changeover of command, therefore, was effected entirely without dramatics, almost in anticlimax, with no one in a position to say where Angus was. Albany saw James deposited in his old quarters in the castle, left Margaret Tudor there also with almost visible relief, sent his troops to camp on the Burgh Muir and in the royal forest parkland around Arthur's Seat, and himself resorted to more comfortable premises in Holyrood Abbey. Arran and the Bastard, who had been notably subdued since the Regent's arrival, went off to their former lodgings in Blackfriars Monastery of distressing memory.

That afternoon the castle's artillery, Mons Meg included, fired off a prolonged cannonade of blank shots to inform the realm that order and due royal authority was re-established in the land—to the delight of the royalest individual to hear it, at least, he being of an age when the louder the noise the greater the attraction.

The parliament was held, at Holyrood, ten days later, by which time it was apparent that there would be no immediate Douglas counter-action; indeed, the previous day, word assessed to be reliable was received that Angus himself had now crossed the Border and was residing with the Lord Dacre, the English Warden, at Morpeth Castle, Northumberland, but not apparently accompanied by any large number of his people. Albany could congratulate himself on a successful and bloodless resumption of power.

Despite all this, however, he had less cause for congratulation over the parliament itself, even though much laudatory speech-making was indulged in, much condemnation of the Douglases and Homes, and no actual reminders that the Regent had outstayed his leave of absence by over a dozen times the allotted span. But Albany had made no secret of the fact that the main reason for this parliament was to homologate his plans for the invasion of England on France's behalf, and this the assembly quite definitely refused to agree to. Standing behind the King's throne in his usual position, David Lindsay heard speaker after speaker condemn the venture as inadvisable, unacceptable, dangerous, folly even, the Flodden disaster quoted again and again. There was not indeed a single supporter to speak up for the project after the Chancellor had so obviously disapprovingly read out the Regent's desires. The Archbishop, now Primate of Holy Church and very grand, might be committed to financing Albany's adventure with Church money, but of his reluctance there could be no doubt. With Bishop Leslie translating all for the Duke, that man's handsome features grew darker by the minute. Presently his famous temper took over and, not having a fire available to hurl his hat into, he smashed a fist down on the arm of his chair, jumped to his feet and strode without a word for the nearest doorway to the chancel and out—quite forgetting that he was in the presence of their sovereign-lord and that none must leave before him or without his permission.

Young James did not himself recognise this, presumably, but everyone else did, and was in a quandary. What now? If the King had not been there, then the sitting was over with the Regent departed, and the Chancellor would declare adjournment; but with James present, and superior to Albany, it could still theoretically be in session. There was much muttering and glancing around, until Beaton, concluding that the Duke was not going to return, turned and signed to David, who nodded and whispered to his royal charge. Gladly the boy vacated his throne and preceded David out, grinning, whilst all there bowed.

It was the briefest parliament on record; and nothing had been decided about Angus or the Homes.

Albany's wrath was not readily assuaged on this occasion, with no Davie Beaton there to cajole him, for this of the invasion was what he had come to Scotland to achieve. Too proud to reconvene the assembly and risk another rebuff, he summoned the most important lords and chiefs to his presence and sought to change their minds; but without success. Scotland seemed to have learned its lesson about sacrificing itself for France. Troops would assemble to defend the realm, to maintain the King's peace and to keep such as the Douglases in their places; but they would not cross the Border unprovoked.

For weeks thereafter the Regent was like a bear with a sore head, a problem for all who had to deal with him. And he was not the only one, for news reached Scotland that Pope Leo had died, and without authorising Margaret's divorce. That princess was furious, and all who had any connection with her were made aware of it. Suddenly her extraordinary interest in Albany was over. He was no longer of use to her in that connection, for he had no pull with the new Pontiff, Adrian the Sixth, a Dutchman firmly in the

Emperor's camp, indeed who had been tutor to the young Charles and later became his Regent in Spain. Moreover the Duke had been almost pointedly keeping his distance from Edinburgh Castle and the lady, to her offence. So that odd interlude was over, and Margaret emphasised the fact by promptly removing herself back to her palace of Linlithgow—to the great relief of almost everybody in Edinburgh's citadel, not least her son.

She had barely gone when more news from the Continent informed them that her brother had in fact invaded France in major strength, from the Calais bridgehead. Also it was learned, from nearer at hand, that he had sent the veteran Earl of Shrewsbury up to put the northern counties of England on a war-footing and threat to Scotland, to reinforce Lord Dacre's forces—his reaction to his spies' reports.

This intelligence stirred Albany into action, parliament's views notwithstanding. He exercised his authority as Regent, and commander of the forces of the crown, to order fullest mobilisation forthwith and a march on the Borderland.

David Lindsay would have liked to accompany this expedition, as a change from fortress-life, but the Earl Marischal, much against the entire project, refused him leave, and there was now no Davie Beaton to pull strings on his behalf. All he was permitted was to take King James up to the Burgh Muir to see the vast concentration of men and to watch the Scots host march off southwards, a situation which David found ominously reminiscent of that occasion nine years before when the King's father led a similar vast army from the same mustering place on a similar venture, never to return. Even the numbers were approximately the same, over eighty-thousand, and although this time they were not burdened with those eighteen-foot French pikes, the French presence was very evident, especially in the abundance of light artillery and bombards shipped north. There was a great blowing of trumpets, waving of banners and dashing hither and thither of colourful heralds, and ten-year-old James Stewart much enjoyed it all, and being conducted round the various contingents to inspect all and wish God-speed to his lords. Nevertheless, despite all this flourish, there was an atmosphere of reluctance and foreboding prevalent which certainly had not been in evidence on the previous occasion. David, if not his charge, was very much aware of it.

There was another difference. When Albany came to salute James finally and then rode, under the Lion-Rampant standard, with his French advisers, to place himself at the head of all and lead off, the host marched away from the Burgh Muir of Edinburgh, to the sound of martial music, in a south-westerly not a south-easterly direction, to skirt the flanks of the Pentland not the Lammermuir Hills. Albany at least was showing some discretion in avoiding the Merse and East March approach for his attempt; for Dacre's forces were based on Morpeth, and Shrewsbury was said to have his headquarters in Newcastle, both on the east side of the country, and, of course, in any action, the Homes might possibly create trouble in the Scots rear in this area. So it was to be the West March and Carlisle, in the hope that this would force the English to make a hurried switch across country and so cause them confusion and disorganisation.

Waving goodbye, the little party with the King rode pensively back to the city.

They had almost three weeks to wait for news. When it came, it was both a relief and a cause of shame. The entire affair had been, not a disaster but a fiasco. At Carlisle, the Scots lords had refused to go a step further. They had crossed on to English soil, and, safely behind Carlisle's massive walls, dug in their spurred and armoured heels. This was as far as they would go, for France. Fuming, Albany had been unable to budge them, the Bastard of Arran leading the revolt. Dacre and Shrewsbury had arrived presently with a force not half the size, but still the Scots would not attack unless they were assailed first. This Shrewsbury would not attempt, well content to neutralise the enemy in inaction—which would serve Henry's cause as well as any costly battle. It transpired later that Dacre had been warned by a courier from Margaret at Linlithgow acting with typical Tudor side-switching, that the Scots had in fact no real intention of invading England and were merely putting on a show. So the two sides sat a mile apart and eyed each other, until the English leadership eventually sent heralds to offer a truce, a non-aggression pact—again to Henry's immediate benefit since he could now concentrate on France with an easy mind—and which Albany was forced to accept, if with ill grace, faced by his obdurate Scots lords now anxious to get their levies home for the hay harvest.

So the ridiculous affair trickled to its undignified closure and the Regent's proud eighty thousand turned and marched home intact but inglorious. It was said that the Duke would not speak to a Scot, even in French, all the way back to Edinburgh, confining his few remarks only to Frenchmen.

At least Angus was not in a position to mock and crow, whatever his wife might do, for it appeared that he himself had fled to France, for reasons unknown.

Henry and the Emperor made major progress, and Francis, fighting on two fronts, sustained a serious defeat at Bicocco. Almost immediately thereafter the Regent announced that he had been recalled to France for consultations. Resentful but disenchanted, the Scots could not stop him from going, but there was murmuring that his tenure of the regency was useless and should be taken from him—as undoubtedly would have been attempted had the alternative been anyone other than the spineless Arran. Albany, however, declared that he would be back shortly, and appointed the same Regency Council as before to deputise for him, with the addition of a Frenchman named de Gresolles, in place of the late Archbishop Forman. He also ordained that King James would be safer back at Stirling in the interim, in case of any Douglas attempt against the capital.

So that October of 1522, Edinburgh saw the departure of its monarch westwards once again, and that of the Regent for France, and knew not whether to be relieved or apprehensive.

20

Scotland was blessed with a comparatively uneventful winter that year, with both Angus and Albany out of the country and the Home leaders still in England. Arran was in theory ruling, which meant the Bastard, but with Albany expected to return in a matter of months, that character was restricted in scope; he also found the Regent's watch-dog, de Gresolles, a thorn in the flesh, since being a member of the Council, which Hamilton was not, he ranked as his superior. In fact, Stirling saw little of either him or his father, and since the Chancellor now spent much of his time at St Andrews dealing with the neglected affairs of Holy Church—largely financial, by all accounts—the royal entourage was afforded an unusually quiet interval. This, to be sure, was much appreciated. Yet, human nature being what it is, some began to find life dullish and time to hang heavily. Certainly this applied to David Lindsay, and to a certain extent to Kate also, still not really adjusted to the cramping life of a fortress. When burgeoning spring, therefore, accentuated young people's restlessness, they sought the Marischal's dispensation for a week or two, and escaped. This time they did not head east, to Lothian and home, but north to the Braes of Angus. They would go and see Marion and her child.

They were joyfully received at Airlie Castle, by the grass-widow at least; and even Lord Ogilvy was prepared to tolerate Lord Lindsay's daughter and the King's Usher. Marion was looking blooming, motherhood evidently agreeing with her, and her husband's continuing absence seemingly bearable. The child, called James after his great-uncle, and now eighteen months old, a grave unsmiling infant, all great watching eyes, seemed to ponder life and reserve judgment, a strange offspring it might seem for the lively and mercurial Davie Beaton.

Marion was eager for tidings of the world at large, for up here in the jaws of the mountains even Stirling and

Edinburgh seemed remote, and news therefrom scarcely frequent. Such as did arrive was apt to come by itinerant chapmen and wandering friars, from the former less than reliable, the latter more knowledgeable about Church affairs than other. So the young woman, in fact, knew quite a lot about what went on in St Andrews and other ecclesiastical centres and the new Primate's relations with various bishops, abbots and priors, even that Gavin Douglas was dead—something which the others had not heard of at Stirling—having apparently succumbed to the plague in London, like thousands of others.

Although the visitors were able to tell their hostess considerably more, as it were in bulk, than she could give them, she did surprise them with information affecting the King's future, which they might have expected to have heard first. It seemed that she got occasional private letters from her husband, sent by the couriers who brought Albany's despatches, and the latest of these had mentioned that he, Davie, had at last prevailed on King Francis to make a formal promise, instead of a mere suggestion, of his infant daughter Madeleine, now aged two, to be betrothed to King James, a considerable step in putting the relationship of Scotland and France on an improved footing, one more in keeping with the northern kingdom's dignity and pride. But whenever Henry Tudor heard of this, apparently, he had immediately declared that his nephew should have *his* daughter Mary for bride, now six years, as much more suitable—only he insisted on the condition that Albany's regency should be terminated and in fact the Duke never allowed to set foot in Scotland again.

David asked the obvious question—did Davie's letters give any indication as to when he would be returning to Scotland? Marion sadly admitted that although he wrote that he was longing to see her and hoped that it would not be overlong before he was back, he gave no hint as to when that might be.

Kate confided to her own husband later that she, for one, would not be married to a man who could behave like that and treat his wife as of less importance than any and every other aspect of his life. David protested on his friend's behalf, but with only moderate conviction.

They remained at Airlie for a full week, rejoicing in their

freedom and exploring the exciting glens of Isla, Clova, Prosen, Lethnot and Esk, a world totally different from any they had experienced hitherto, with a people who spoke only the difficult Gaelic and lived not in villages or hamlets but in wide-scattered groupings of turf-roofed cabins which Marion called townships but which bore no resemblance to what that term conjured up in Lowland minds, a cattle-herding folk, with only scratchings of tilth here and there, in marked contrast to the fertile East Lothian farmlands they knew so well. Although snow still mantled the high ground, the valleys were green, quite well-wooded with scrub-oak, rowan and hawthorn, golden gorse glowing its promise everywhere, the rivers peat-brown, rushing and noisy with melt-water, the haughs alive with quacking duck, flitting dippers and grave-stalking herons, as May brought its benison to the mountain land. Thoughts of war and statecraft and intrigue seemed scarcely relevant up here. They saw no sign of the dreaded caterans, the bogey of Lowlanders.

The travellers were loth to return to Stirling sooner than they must, and made a number of brief visits on the way, notably to the abbeys of Coupar-Angus and Abbot John's Culross in Fife, where St Kentigern or Mungo, conceived in their own area of East Lothian and destined to become the patron saint of Glasgow, had been reared by the good Celtic St Serf. Holy Church had become sadly corrupt since those far-off days, but it still did good service by providing shelter and provision for travellers, and work and wealth by the tilling of the ground, the milling of corn, the weaving of cloth and tanning of hides, even the mining of coals at Culross, all of which might just conceivably be deemed a form of practical worship towards the Creator of it all.

Back at Stirling, they learned that the rival offers of a bride for James, from France and England, had been received officially. Needless to say, there was no question as to choice, Henry's conditional overture being not so much as considered, while the French commitment was received with satisfaction. This could be the most useful match for Scotland available, as well as the most prestigious. Davie Beaton's credit was enhanced. Fortunately the prospective bridegroom did not have to be consulted.

Henry's reaction to this rejection, even though he might have been thought fully occupied in France, was not long in being made evident. The Earl of Shrewsbury was withdrawn, as being insufficiently aggressive, and in his place Thomas Howard, Earl of Surrey, was sent north with explicit instructions to burn and slay. This sounded an ominous note in Scotland for this Surrey was the son of that 'auld crooked carle Surrey', now Duke of Norfolk, who had commanded the English army at Flodden where he himself had played no insignificant part.

Nor were the Scots fears unjustified. In great strength, in late June, Surrey and Dacre crossed Tweed and laid waste the land up to and beyond Kelso, which they burned, slaughtering indiscriminately men, women and children, as directed by their master, not sparing the ancient abbey and its inmates, where many of the populace had fled for sanctuary. The Regency Council hastily gathered together a scratch force and sent it to the Borders under the Bastard; but by this time the English had withdrawn, leaving behind the message that this was just a small sample of what could be expected if the Scots persisted in rejecting the wishes and authority of their Lord Paramount, King Henry. Any retaliation and they would be back, and in less clement mood.

In the circumstances the Bastard hesitated, for he had instructions not to invade England, remained in the stricken area for some time and then returned to Edinburgh a frustrated man. There was one small but significant outcome of his effort, however, in that an English messenger fell into the hands of a Scots scouting party, a courier looking for Dacre and not realising that he had retired to Wark Castle. This individual was bearing a letter from Cardinal Wolsey to the Warden, urging still harsher measures against the Scots, and counselling him "favourably to entertain the Homes and other rebels after the accustomed manner, so that they may continue the divisions and sedition in Scotland whereby the Duke of Albany may, at his coming thither, be put in danger; and though some moneys be employed for this entertainment of the said Homes and rebels, it will quit the cost at length". This letter would at least serve to put a halter round the necks of Wedderburn and his colleagues if they should be caught.

The Scots Chancellor thereafter sent an urgent message, in turn, to France, for Albany's immediate return. And a reply was received rather sooner than previous experience had led them to expect. It came from Davie Beaton. The Regent would be in Scotland in the near future, by October, and he would be coming in major strength, at King Francis's command.

The Scots did not know whether to rejoice or to dread.

Presumably Henry's spy-system worked equally efficiently in France as in Scotland, for a new invasion by Surrey and Dacre was promptly mounted, to demonstrate the price the Scots must pay for Albany's return and any French aid. This time, the lower Tweed area being already devastated, the English marched up Teviot and gave Jedburgh, the Middle March 'capital' to the flames, again with its great abbey, together with all the surrounding villages, communities, peel-towers, churches and farm-touns, leaving behind a vast, smoking wilderness and graveyard of what had been one of the fairest regions of the Borderland.

Whether France got word of this projected attack, in turn, or Albany merely was more speedy than anticipated, even as the terror was being enacted over the border the Regent arrived back in the Firth of Clyde. And this time it was not just three vessels but a fleet which came sailing into the Gareloch, to land no fewer than four thousand French troops, with all supporting artillery, arms and munitions, a sign to all of the importance King Francis was now placing on Scots intervention in his battle for supremacy in Christendom. Not even de Gresolles was there to meet his countrymen in their unexpectedly early arrival. Never had Cowal and the Gareloch seen anything like this, such a concentration of shipping and armed men, since the days of Somerled the Mighty, first Lord of the Isles.

The subsequent march of the newcomers through the Highland mountains had to be something of an epic for a Continental army used to campaigning on the level plains of Northern Europe. It took them longer than the journey from France.

Well before they reached the Forth valley, the Marischal got word of it, and in the absence of the Chancellor at St Andrews, and Arran at Hamilton, and the Bastard and de Gresolles off again to the Borderland to see what could be done there, himself led a welcoming party westwards to meet the Regent, the company including David Lindsay.

They encountered Albany at Aberfoyle, emerging from the mountains, and in no genial frame of mind. Straggling behind for miles was the strung-out host of weary, unhappy and travel-stained Frenchmen.

The Earl Marischal was no French-speaker, which was one of the reasons why he had brought David, who was reasonably proficient in the language. So the latter found himself acting interpreter. Not that he was overworked in this capacity, for Albany was even less informative than usual and the Marischal had never been a man of eloquence. The journey eastwards was largely a silent one.

The Regent made up for this unpromising start by issuing a flurry of orders at Stirling. Fullest mobilisation was commanded forthwith, no excuses to be considered. All harvesting was over by now and the autumn cattle sales could wait. Horses by the thousand must be gathered; all cannon collected from the fortresses; the Church must produce more monies and provender and forage for the largest army Scotland had fielded for centuries—and quickly, for he intended to march just as soon as his French troops were rested and trained for this new sort of warfare. There was to be no delay, and no nonsense this time about calling an unco-operative parliament.

In a mere two weeks, in fact, so great was the Regent's determination to strike before the winter weather made large-scale campaigning impossible, the march southwards began, belated contingents from the Highlands and Isles to follow on. David went too, on Albany's express orders, since he was supposed to know something about warfare in the East March, as a lieutenant of de la Bastie—for this time there was to be no discreet back-door approach through the West March and Carlisle, but a full-scale assault and retaliation where the English would like it least, and where they had themselves been so recently operating. David would again act interpreter, since old Bishop Leslie was now returned to his native Aberdeenshire and was not suitable for this sort of thing anyway. And though the Bastard spoke better French, having lived in France for some time, Albany did not trust him.

Kate was unhappy, not so much at her husband going off to war as that she could not go with him. But at least she made the parting from young James less difficult for she was now almost as popular with the boy as was David, and so long as one remained, the King was less trying.

Margaret Tudor made no sallies from Linlithgow.

By the time that the vast slow-moving host had passed Edinburgh and picked up the Lothian contingents at the Burgh Muir, it was reckoned that the army, with the French force, totalled no less than eighty-eight thousand men. And a more reluctant legion, despite all its pomp and display, would have been hard to assemble.

Lord Lindsay was feeling his age, it seemed, as well as reluctance, and had delegated the leadership of his retainers to his eldest son John, Master of Lindsay, who was normally based on their Fife estates and not on the best of terms with his father. From this brother-in-law, himself less than eager for the fray, David learned much of the attitudes and feelings of the Scots nobles—by no means all of which he passed on to the Regent. Whilst they were eager enough for vengeance on the English, they were very well aware that this entire venture was being mounted on behalf of France, not Scotland, their strength, resources, even their blood perhaps, to be expended to further the ambitions of King Francis. They resented Albany's closeness to his French commanders, whom he appointed to the most senior positions, and his cold distance from themselves—especially the Bastard of Arran, not used to this relegation. Moreover, they were worried about the Douglases who so very obviously had not responded to this national call-to-arms and who, in the event of a Scots defeat or even a victory costly in casualties, would be in a position to rise behind them and take the initiative thereafter, to impose their will on the land. None knew where Angus was now, whether still in France, in Henry's England, or secretly back home. If he was to join Dacre and this Surrey, and called out the Douglases and Homes in their rear . . .

They marched through the Lammermuirs by Soutra Aisle and down Lauderdale to the Tweed between Melrose and Dryburgh Abbeys, both so far unburned, and turned eastwards towards the Merse. Deliberately Albany led his multitude through the devastated Kelso area, in order to rouse the wrath and urge for revenge of his nobles and lairds. But as they came at length, by Eccles, to the Coldstream fords, and stared across Tweed to the English bank, David for one knew that it would not serve. The lords, the Bastard the most vocal, would challenge the English might here on their own soil and fight if need be, but they would not cross into England for the King of France. That lesson had been too dearly learned.

In vain the Regent argued and pleaded, threatened and raged, language barrier or none. In furious French he named the Scots craven, cowards, spineless dogs, traitors even, to no avail but to their fierce offence. The vast army sat down around Coldstream and would go no further. Albany himself went back to Eccles Priory's comfort for the night. And comfort was called for, in body as in mind, for the weather was grim, driving chill rain and sleet. The disgruntled army had to do the best it could with Coldstream's facilities—to its townsfolk's misery.

The following day Albany, in the hope of shaming the Scots into action, made a great play of parading his French forces and leading them into and across Tweed. He declared that since Dacre's nearest stronghold of Wark Castle was only some three miles away, he and his brave Frenchmen would go reduce it. When the Scots had recovered their courage, they could come on after.

It was not quite so easy as that, however, for the river was already running high with the rains, and it was quickly apparent that only the very lightest artillery could be got across, the heavier pieces merely sinking into the river-bed, indeed the oxen drawing them refusing to take to the water however much they were coaxed and lashed. Such pieces as were got across, like the commissariat, had to be manhandled—and that was a sorry business for all concerned, in those weather conditions with everyone soaked and chilled.

David Lindsay was in a quandary. The Lindsays, under the Master, were staying put on the Scots bank along with the rest. But he himself had come on this expedition on Albany's direct orders and therefore had to consider himself in the nature of a personal aide to the Regent. He did not desire to seem to side with the French against the Scots—yet he could not but feel ashamed of his countrymen's so non-heroic stance, their decision to stand by and let the visitors do the fighting. He went, but unhappily.

They marched, shivering in wet gear, upstream the three

miles on the English side to Wark. They found it to be a strong old Norman-type castle, on a mound, consisting of a massive square keep surrounded by an inner and an outer bailey, each defended by high parapeted walling and the whole surrounded by a moat. The outer bailey was notably extensive. That it would be no easy nut to crack was apparent—emphasised when cannon-fire greeted their approach, and fairly evidently heavier cannon than they themselves had been able to get across Tweed. The situation did not look good.

But four thousand men cannot just turn tail when faced with a few cannonballs, and the Scots left behind had to be shamed into co-operating, if possible. So Albany advanced, despite casualties, bringing up his small artillery, to mass them against one restricted section of the perimeter walling to batter solely at that. They suffered losses in men and guns, but the strategy worked in that the masonry gave way, leaving a sizeable gap through which the infantry charged strongly, the defenders being hampered by the presence of large numbers of the local country folk and their beasts and belongings who had been allowed to take refuge in this outer bailey on the approach of the enemy.

There followed bloody chaos in that confined space, crowded with combatants and non-combatants. The French were not backward in cutting down all in their way, but the cramped conditions made effective fighting difficult and prevented any large proportion of the attacking force from getting within the walling. Admittedly the English artillery-men could not depress their cannon sufficiently to shoot down into this bailey, nor indeed could they use their hand-guns and archery to good effect without endangering their own folk. But the attackers were also largely hamstrung, faced with the high walling of the inner bailey, without cannon to batter a hole in it, and the gates barred against both them and the unfortunate English left outside. Scaling ladders and ropes were called for, and for a while it was stalemate, although the slaughter went on.

David Lindsay, forward with Albany, was sickened at the sight of women and children dead and dying.

Then the defenders in the inner bailey and keep brought in a new weapon—fire-arrows, shooting down shafts with blazing tow attached into the crowded outer bailey. This, as well as the still-struggling combatants and the dead and dying, was full of hay, straw and provisions for man and beast, the beasts themselves, the permanent lean-to outbuildings of the castle's byres and stabling, makeshift shelters for the refugees, carts laden with domestic gear and so on. It was at all this that the arrows were aimed and, despite the sleet, with marked effect. The hay and straw in especial caught fire quickly and the outbuildings were soon ablaze. Choking clouds of smoke filled the constricted area, and cattle and horses went mad with the fire and the smell of blood and rampaged around. That outer bailey of Wark Castle became a foretaste of hell itself.

The French infantry therein were scarcely to be blamed if they now struggled as hard to get out as they had done to get in. Blinded by the dense dark-brown smoke, unable to distinguish friend from foe, charged by crazed animals, tripping over bodies and with no means of getting further into the castle, they fought their way out through that narrow gap—or some of them did, for many would never emerge on their feet.

Furious, Albany and his French commanders racked their wits unavailingly for an answer to the problems. Without heavier artillery which could outrange that of the castle all they could do was to sit down at a distance and besiege the place, seek to starve it out. But in the prevailing weather conditions that was hardly practical, especially for Frenchmen used to a kinder clime than this.

It was at this stage that some of the cavalry scouts, prudently sent out to scour the countryside, came back to announce that Dacre himself was assembling a large body of English troops at Barmoor, barely fifteen miles to the east, and that their outriders were considerably nearer. Albany, faced with a hopeless situation, took the inevitable decision and ordered a retiral to the Coldstream fords—spurred on by the Wark artillery, which had opened up again.

They left an estimated three hundred French dead behind, along with the local casualties.

Even now their immediate problems were by no means over, for the river had risen noticeably in the interim with the continuing rain and sleet, which was no doubt of storm proportions in the surrounding hills. Getting the men back across, especially the wounded, was a dire business and much of the artillery, light as it was, plus stores and munitions, had to be abandoned. Angry, wet and disheartened, they then discovered that many of the Scots contingents had already anticipated withdrawal and had set off northwards for home.

The Regent was a man all but bereft of speech. David Lindsay's one attempt at consolation, to the effect that conditions would be just as bad for Dacre and that the English would not find crossing Tweed any easier than they had done so they need not worry about pursuit, met with only a flood of French cursing.

But the order for a return to Edinburgh was given. It was only 4th November and extraordinarily early for such hard weather as this. They moved off northwards actually in a snowstorm, banners furled and heads down.

21

That was the start of a hard winter, in more ways than one. Men could not remember such consistently bad weather, so much snow and continual gales. And everywhere in Scotland dissatisfaction was rife. Possibly shame had something to do with it, a sort of self-disesteem at the inglorious state into which the realm had sunk, allied to fear for the future. The Regent, by all accounts, made unbearable company, and David was thankful that he did not have to see anything much of him, for he made his base at Edinburgh and seldom came near Stirling. The capital, however, could have wished him elsewhere for, apart from his ill-temper and demands, he quartered his French troops on the city, and since they could not be expected to survive in encampments in the appalling weather conditions, they had to be billeted in houses and premises, even churches, in the town, to the great offence of their reluctant hosts. The Regent was not to be moved by any representations over this compulsory quartering, however lofty the objectors—indeed many of the lords complained that he was requisitioning their town-houses deliberately as reprisal for their refusal to invade English soil.

It all made a sorry Yuletide, for the bad weather disorganised transport by land and sea and shortages were general.

Immediately after that less than festive season was over Albany called a parliament, at Holyrood. On this occasion the young monarch apparently was not required and David Lindsay had no call to attend, but he heard all about it afterwards, for the Earl Marischal and the Lord Erskine, from Stirling, sat therein as lords of parliament. It had been an acrimonious affair from the start, with the Regent at loggerheads with everybody else, even including the Chancellor who was, it seemed, refusing to find any more Church monies for Albany. And that man needed money in a large way—indeed that, it transpired, was the main reason for calling this parliament—for the four thousand French troops had to be kept and paid, unlike the levies of the Scots lords, who had to provide military service as part of their feudal dues. The demand for forty thousand crowns set the tone of the entire proceedings, for it was flatly refused by every speaker there, amidst accusations that the Regent had already bled the Treasury white, and that the two abortive expeditions to the Borderland had grievously impoverished the lords, Church and burghs. There had been a violent scene with Albany promptly losing his temper and marching out.

However, he had been persuaded to return by de Gresolles, who was a fair English-speaker and was on this occasion acting interpreter. But a second session was no more satisfactory than the first, for the resentful nobles, supported by the Edinburgh and other burgh representatives, banded together to demand the immediate repatriation to France of the four thousand visitors who were costing the land so dear, consuming the nation's substance, behaving with arrogant insolence and keeping them out of their own houses. Even the Chancellor, financially concerned as he was, felt that this was going too far, and pointed out that this dire winter weather was no time to embark thousands of men on ships for France or anywhere else. But he was shouted down and a vote demanded. Parliament then decided, and by a substantial majority, that the Frenchmen should go, and forthwith. When the Regent, enraged, jumped up to declare that in that case he would go also, the second session broke up with no more dignity than the first.

Albany flatly refused to attend another sitting and the parliament was dissolved. But later, the Regent called together the members of the Regency Council and some senior nobles and officers of state and told them that he was sick unto death of Scotland and the Scots, that he was indeed going to go back to France to consult with King Francis, and whether he would come back depended on much better behaviour, suitable obedience and firm commitment to solid support by all concerned. When he was asked when this departure would be, and they were told just as soon as the weather was suitable for sea-travel, the councillors, mindful of previous long-delayed absences, wanted a specific date for the Regent's return. This he had haughtily refused to give, and there were protests that this was no way to rule a realm. When this predictably brought this meeting also to an abrupt close, the Earl Marischal managed to get in a quick proposal that if the Duke was not back by, say, the end of August at the latest, then it would be assumed that his regency was at an end, and suitable alternative arrangements for the kingdom's governance made. Although this reasonable suggestion was agreed to by all present except de Gresolles, Albany himself made no response, and left them there.

All this David heard in due course, and feared the worst.

But worse indeed there was to come. News reached Stirling some weeks later that, in accordance with parliament's decision, the French troops had in fact marched, not through the mountain passes, which were blocked with snow, but to Dumbarton on the Clyde estuary, where their vessels, which had been lying the while in the Gareloch, were brought round to pick them up. And bad weather or none, they had all set sail for France. Shockingly, off the Mull of Kintyre a fierce south-westerly storm had struck the fleet, scattering it and driving the ships far off course northwards, where some had been wrecked on the savage Hebridean seaboard and isles, with great loss of life.

So much for the Auld Alliance.

The Duke of Albany came to Stirling in early April, to take his leave of the monarch whom he represented. The worst of the weather was over and a voyage could be contemplated now without major apprehension. It made a strange visit, for although the Regent was still that, and in theory only going on another three-months leave of absence, nobody there expected him ever to come back to Scotland. So the occasion seemed to hold something of the nature of a charade, for he went through the motions which implied a return in a short period, appointing a permanent member to replace the late Archbishop Forman on the Regency Council, none other than Gavin Dunbar, the tutor, now titular Bishop of Aberdeen. He also confirmed various incumbents in offices of state, and so on. Two items did, however, ring a rather different note. These were Albany's surprising nomination of de Gresolles as Lord Treasurer—and when that drew astonished protests, the cold intimation that the Frenchman in that position would ensure that the monies owing to him for the payment of the French force's expenses, much of which he had had to meet out of his private fortune, would be remitted to him in France, notably those from Holy Church; the other that, when the Earl Marischal took the opportunity to declare that he wished to be relieved of his duty of guardianship for the young King, which he had sustained for overlong as it was to the detriment of his other interests, the Regent, accepting, nominated *four* others in his place. One, Lord Erskine, was more or less only a promotion for, as hereditary keeper of Stirling Castle, he had been acting as assistant guardian all along; but three others, the Lords Fleming, Borthwick and Cassillis, seemed excessive, and the explanation that this was necessary so that one was always to be in residence at Stirling along with Erskine for the monarch's security, again gave the impression of a long-term policy.

It was with mixed feelings, then, that the Stirling company said farewell and watched the Duke ride away. There were no tears, nor any real sorrow, for this John Stewart was scarcely a character to attract affection; but there were considerable ponderings.

David Lindsay's earlier ponderings had caused him to write a letter to Davie Beaton, which he besought the Regent to deliver when he got to France. In it, he urged his friend to relinquish his ambassadorship and return to Scotland, especially if the Duke decided not to do so. The country, he declared, grievously needed a firm hand to guide its destinies, and while the Chancellor and Primate should be supplying that, in fact his uncle was becoming progressively less capable or even almost interested, it seemed. As he aged, he was growing ever more heavy in person and lethargic in behaviour. He seemed less and less concerned with affairs of state and more and more so in Church matters, in especial its revenues, and was spending most of his time at St Andrews. Perhaps the endeavour to have him succeed to the Primacy had been mistaken? Anyway, his secretary's and nephew's guiding hand was sorely needed, and he, Davie, would surely serve Scotland a deal more effectively at home than in France, in this pass, however able an envoy he might be. He ended by informing Beaton that he and Kate had been to see Marion and their fine son, and although they were both well, they needed the presence of husband and father.

So the Regent left Scotland once more, and an uneasy period of waiting ensued.

Waiting, during that summer, but no inaction. For one thing, the English kept up their raiding over the Border, not in major fashion, for Surrey had gone south again and Dacre had to probe ever deeper into Scotland to find suitable undevastated areas—although he noticeably avoided the Home territories. This kept the Bastard busy, for he appeared to have become more or less commander of the Scots armed forces, and of course his father was still, in theory, Warden of the Marches. David saw little of him that summer, for he seldom came to Stirling. Indeed the castle there seemed to have become something of a backwater, with Arran at Hamilton most of the time, the Chancellor at St Andrews and de Gresolles remaining in Edinburgh. The Marischal departed too, and David missed him, for he was a strong and reliable character, if lacking in social graces.

There were rumours that Angus was now with King Henry in the Calais area, which sounded ominous. No direct word came from France.

It was a poor summer weather-wise, not what was required for the land after so grim a winter. The crops were late and scanty. People worried about food stocks and forage.

August came, and the Regent's three months were more than up since he had left in April. But that Holyrood meeting had given him till the end of August before the regency would be assumed to be over. Those last weeks, all who had any interest in the rule and direction of the nation held their breaths, for if Albany did not come, nothing was more sure than that a dire struggle for power would follow.

On the Feast of St Augustine, 29th August, a single horseman, dressed in the height of French fashion but ill-mounted on a tired beast, came riding up Stirling's narrow, climbing streets to the castle, demanding admittance in the name of the Regent. He was allowed in—but that would be the last exercise of Albany's authority in Scotland ever, it seemed; for it was Davie Beaton, who had resigned his position at the French court and taken passage on a wine-ship trading to Dumbarton. The Duke, he informed, was not coming. Indeed, he was at present acting Lord Admiral of France and fighting the armies of the Emperor. He had had enough of Scotland, and in Davie's opinion, would never return. But he had sent no message, no formal resignation.

His hearers eyed each other in doubt and perplexity. But not David Lindsay. He preferred that it was Davie Beaton who had returned to Scotland, rather than Albany, any day.

22

Kate Lindsay exclaimed with a kind of delight at what she saw, reining in her horse. The land fell away gently before them, eastwards from this Balrymonth Hill, in great sweeps and folds, cattle-dotted on the higher ground, ribbed with the long rigs of strip cultivation on the lower, now yellow with stubble, until it met the limitless ocean, glittering in the golden October sunshine, a fair and fertile prospect. And in the middle distance, under a faint blue haze of wood-smoke, something of a blunt peninsula jutted into that Norse Sea, a most eye-catching feature, a tight-packed walled city of warm brownstone masonry and red pan-tiled roofs, from out of which rose a host, a multitude of towers and spires and pinnacles, so many in so comparatively small a space as to be scarcely credible, but all as it were supporting and building up to a greater soaring square tower, slender but strong as it was graceful, high above all but not dominant—for the dominance was provided by another edifice, a redstone castle which thrust out into the sparkling waters on a mound at the very tip of the promontory, proud, challenging, yet for all that not contrasting with the mellow serenity of that entire fairytale city by the sea.

"It is lovely," she said. "So fair and—and sure. So . . . what is it? Withdrawn from all else. There. I had no notion that St Andrews would be like that."

"Strange that it should seem so," David told her. "Fair, yes, after its fashion. But sure? I would not say so. And withdrawn only in that it turns its back on all else but itself, the Church and its university. St Andrews cares only for itself."

"Yet all Holy Church is ruled from here, in all Scotland? The realm's seat of learning."

He shrugged. "In name, yes. But its rule is concerned with its own pride and glory, the Primacy's Church, I would say, rather than Christ's! St Andrews looks inward, not outwards. And its learning is like the rest, limited, inward-looking, going only a little way towards knowledge and truth, I think. Here those who would pursue real learning and higher things seldom remain, but go on to Paris, the Sorbonne, Leyden, Padua and the rest."

"*You* came here. And Davie Beaton."

"When I was fifteen, yes. Davie and I were classmates. I stayed for four years and then my father gained me the appointment at court. I am no true scholar—but I learned enough to know why the good Bishop Elphinstone founded his own university at Aberdeen. He said that St Andrews had exchanged both piety and probity for pride! I believe that was why he refused the Primacy."

"I never knew him. He refused it . . . ?"

"Oh, yes. He was the obvious choice. He was Chancellor too. But he would not come here. Abbot John said that even Elphinstone was afraid that St Andrews might seduce him! As it seems to have seduced all the others. Once they become Archbishops of St Andrews they change, gradually turn their backs on the rest, the realm, the needs of the people, and become only lords of this city by the sea, and its treasure-chests. It is happening to James Beaton, as it did to Andrew Forman, William Shevas, Patrick Graham, even James Kennedy. Perhaps it is like the Vatican, the Papacy, spiritual power corrupting even worse than earthly power. Although there is little that is spiritual here, I fear!"

Kate eyed him questioningly. "This is strange talk, Davie! Is this what St Andrews does to you? Were your four years here so grievous?"

"No. Not that. But . . . if I was no great scholar, say that I learned more than my tutors sought to teach me!"

They rode on down past Feddinch towards the metropolitan see and ecclesiastical capital of Scotland.

They had been visiting the Mount, David's inherited property in what was known as the rigging or roof of Fife, the high central area of that ancient land. The King's new guardians were much less strict about attendance on the monarch than had been the Earl Marischal, and when David's old maternal uncle died, who had been stewarding the estate all these years, he had had little difficulty in gaining leave to go and inspect it and to make new arrangements. Situated some three miles north-west of Cupar, the county town, and comprising perhaps one thousand acres around the twin hills of Lindifferon and the Mount itself, it was a pleasant place, with a sturdy tower-house within a court, and a south-facing walled-garden and orchard, plus a hamlet, Lindifferon. Kate had quite fallen in love with it and its surroundings. They had thereafter called in at Pitscottie, the home of David's garrulous far-out cousin, Robert Lindsay, another poet of a sort. Now they were on their way to visit Davie Beaton and Marion, at his uncle's archiepiscopal castle of St Andrews.

It was just five weeks since the end of Albany's regency.

The approach to the city was through levelling land, all carefully farmed, productive and well-tended, the ground notably drained, the barns full, the cattle sleek. If the rest of Scotland was going to go short after a poor harvest, St Andrews seemingly would not.

They entered by the twin-towered West Port, ignored by the guards in the livery of the archbishopric, and rode eastwards along the fine and broad central thoroughfare which led straight for over half a mile to the great cathedral, the magnificent tall and slender tower of which, steeple-crowned so notably overtopped all the other spires and domes and pinnacles of that soaring city. Kate was surprised to see that long broad street, finer than any she had seen in Edinburgh or Stirling, and so unexpected in the seemingly close-packed huddle of the walled town. Remarking on it, she had it explained to her that this was in fact a processional street, and that processions meant a great deal in St Andrews—prideful religious processions, of course, which her husband suggested the good Lord was apt to be offered frequently in lieu of more humble worship. David's disillusionment with Holy Church, always fairly pronounced, appeared to be aggravated by St Andrews.

Certainly there was no escaping the ecclesiastical ostentations of the place. The streets were crowded, and every second person was dressed in a religious habit of some sort, many of them rich, ornate, gorgeous even. And of the rest, a notably large proportion were liveried attendants, retainers and servants, all wearing the cross in various shapes and colours or the sacred monogram, or else men-at-arms with mitres painted on their steel breastplates. Ordinary citizens, as well as being in a minority, were apt to dodge and cringe and scuttle, with due humility, amongst all the imperious churchmen and arrogant servitors. Of students, surprisingly, there were few to be seen—no doubt they were presently at their classes.

As they went, David pointed out the innumerable splendid establishments, chapels, oratories, priories, friaries, monasteries, nunneries, chantries, shrines and the like, jostling for space in that crowded metropolis. Every see was represented, every order in Christendom, every division of the Church—Augustinians, Benedictines, Carmelites, Cistercians, Dominicans, Franciscans, Observantines, Trinitarians and others.

The size and splendour of the cathedral silenced even David for a little, until he was able to point out its more modest but admirable predecessor, hidden at first by the greater edifice, but sited immediately behind it, to seaward, the Celtic Church chapel of St Regulus or Rule, also with its graceful tall tower, but all on an infinitely more humble scale, dating from the times before Holy Church lost its integrity, according to that man.

Their wide street ending here, they turned off northwards along another only a little less imposing. And now they could see, half-right, the castle looming before them and, oddly, behind it, the tops of the masts of shipping in the harbour immediately below its mound.

At the gatehouse in more high perimeter walling, they were challenged by men in handsome mitre-decorated armour, and told curtly to wait, even when David named Master Beaton the Archbishop's secretary as authority. But presently Davie himself came to deliver them from the unhelpful underlings, all smiles, genial welcome and compliments as to Kate's good looks. He ordered men to see to their horses, and led them across the large paved courtyard to the finest of the many towers of that palace stronghold, a square, redstone keep of four storeys below a parapet and attic floor above, over all of which flew a huge flag quartering the archiepiscopal arms with those of Beaton of Balfour. Therein, apologising for the climb, Davie took them up the wide turnpike stair all the way to the very top attic storey, within the parapet-walk, which proved to contain a pleasant suite of four chambers, high above all else and with the most magnificent views. This Davie had taken over for his own, to instal his little family. Here they found Marion and the little boy, in a scene of warm domesticity before a blazing log-fire, with three deer-hounds and two cats, all as though settled here for years.

Given a bedchamber with its own access to the parapet-walk, the visitors were made to feel at home, an ambience they had never before really associated with Davie Beaton. Here he seemed entirely the family-man, playing with his son and the dogs unselfconsciously, affectionate towards his wife and a thoughtful host.

But after an excellent meal, with the young women putting the child to bed and tongues busy, over a beaker of wine with David, Beaton reverted to his more accustomed self. He was full of information, and concerned at what he had learned. His uncle might be retiring into his archi-episcopal shell and losing his preoccupation with affairs of state, but most evidently Davie was not. And if, as Stirling Castle had tended to become, St Andrews might seem something of an ecclesiastical backwater at the tip of its Fife peninsula, its spy-system appeared to be in a healthy condition.

When David remarked, far from critically, on the strange situation in which he found his friend, thus all but banished to a comparatively remote corner of the land for a man used to being at the centre of national affairs and so recently Scotland's ambassador to France, the other assured him that, in the circumstances, St Andrews Castle was an excellent place to be in. He and his uncle were tolerably secure thus. And if by any chance King Henry sought to move more directly against them here, a ship was always waiting in the harbour below, ready to sail and spirit them away to some other retreat, France itself if need be.

"Henry . . . ? France . . . ?" David sounded incredulous.

"Aye, man—it may come to that. Although I hope not. The tide is running Henry Tudor's way now. It will take time before we can reverse it."

"But—you cannot believe that there is any danger *here*, surely? From the English? To keep a ship waiting . . . !"

"You think not? Would that *I* could. Had we not good—or shall we say, well-paid—informants in sundry useful places, even now Henry and Wolsey might well have their unfriendly hands on us. I do not know if you heard, but whenever it was clear that Albany was not to return to

Scotland, Henry called for a conference to be held on the Border, to settle amicably, as he put it, the situation between the two realms, that there be an end to bloodshed and raiding. Wolsey would come north in person, Henry being still in France, Angus with him, the Queen-Mother and Arran to be there also. The invitation came to my uncle, as Chancellor, and he would have been hard put to it to make refusal in the circumstances. That is, had we not received information from our spies in Northumberland to the effect that they had intercepted a courier from Wolsey in London to Dacre at Morpeth Castle, carrying a letter which revealed that the conference was no more than a plot to capture my uncle. Arran also. Angus was to effect a forcible reunion with his wife, and they were to take possession of King James and rule Scotland together as a dependency of England. It was to have been happening now, in October. And all Henry's pensioners in Scotland would rise to support it."

"Lord! The dastards! What did you do?"

"We sent warning to Margaret Tudor—who has no wish to be reunited with Angus, whatever her brother says. And to Arran. So—no conference. When the Cardinal-Chancellor of England plans to capture and dispose of the Archbishop-Chancellor of Scotland, at King Henry's behest, it is perhaps time to take modest precautions!"

David wagged his head. "This is beyond all. We heard nothing of it, at Stirling. We hear little there, now. You think that they will try some other villainy?"

"Strange if they do not. And it is not only Henry and Wolsey that we have to watch, but others nearer home. Now that Albany has finally left the scene, there is much activity amongst those left in positions of power. New moves by the old contenders. Margaret Tudor and Arran, for instance. They are in secret correspondence. Both see their ambitions threatened by Henry's. So they are moving together."

"But this is unlikely, surely? They have ever been enemies."

"No doubt. I daresay that they still do not love each other. But they perceive that their causes may be served better, meantime, by working together than by fighting each other. In especial, over the King. We have learned that they are planning to have the Regency Council dissolved, all regency over, and the King declared sufficiently old to rule, themselves of course manipulating him, the power behind the throne."

"James—at twelve years! This is crazy-mad! The boy is no more fit to rule a realm than he has ever been. At twelve, how could he be?"

"To be sure. It is folly, and worse. But he is tall and well-made for his years. Good to look at, likewise. He will serve to *look* the part. And to serve his mother's and Arran's purposes. *They* will rule, through James. They will have little trouble with the Regency Council—for de Gresolles is to be declared incompetent, as a French citizen; Huntly is grievously ill up in his faraway Strathbogie; and Argyll is too busy making himself a king in the Highland West to counter them. That leaves only my uncle and your strange friend, Dunbar, now Bishop of Aberdeen. Arran can get written assent from Huntly and Argyll, and the thing is done, whatever my uncle and Dunbar say."

"And James, in Stirling Castle?"

"His new governors, Cassillis, Fleming, Borthwick, were appointed on Arran's—or his son's—recommendation. And the Bastard is behind much of all this, I reckon. They will not hold out. Arran has got many of the lords behind him, especially those afraid of the Douglases and Angus—such as Lennox, Glencairn, Atholl, Maxwell. He is now, after all, second person in the kingdom. And that is important since—have you heard?—the Duchess of Albany has died suddenly, leaving the Duke with no heir. I judge that he is unlikely to marry again, that one. So, if young James was to die, it would be Arran for the throne!"

"Dear Lord! Fortunately James is healthy, strong."

"Aye—may he remain so! I would say, keep you a sharp eye on our liege, my friend. Only, myself, I would be surprised if you are in a position to do so for much longer!"

"What do you mean?"

"You have always said that the Queen-Mother scarcely loves you. If she gets her son back into her own keeping, will she want *you* along, think you? And is Arran, or the Bastard, so fond of you that they would fight strongly on your behalf?"

"You think that I will be dismissed? Thrown over? James would not like that."

"And do *you* think that the wishes of the sovereign-lord of us all have any relevance or say in all this?"

David stared at him. "I have been with James all his life. Twelve years. It has been *my* life. And . . . I am fond of him."

The other shrugged. "I am sorry. I may be wrong, to be sure. But . . . if I were in your shoes, I would be preparing for a change."

"If the Earl Marischal had not been gone . . ."

"My uncle will do what he can, of course. He likes and admires you. And what influence I have, needless to say, will be exerted on your behalf. But, I fear, the tide I spoke of is against us meantime. We have this little fortress of St Andrews, and Fife, where the Church is strong—strong in power and wealth, if nothing else. And here we must ride out the storm as best we may." That was not like Davie Beaton.

They were eyeing each other a trifle grimly when their wives came back, and although they turned on smiles and suitable banter the young women were not deceived.

"What have you two been saying, that you look so sour?" Kate demanded. "Your faces would have turned the milk! What's amiss?"

"Nothing to worry your bonny heads over, my dears," Beaton said; but his friend was less careful.

"Davie thinks that I may well be in danger of losing my place with the King," he said. "He believes that the Queen-Mother and Arran will take James into their own keeping, and they will not want me there."

"You mean . . . we would have to leave court? Leave Stirling?"

"If they succeed, yes. There would be nothing to keep me at Stirling if James was gone. And if he remained there, but I was not wanted . . ."

"Oh, Kate!" Marion exclaimed. "How sore a trial for you! But—must it be so? It may not. Davie—is this like to happen? How much of it all is but your own overbusy wits at work?"

"Possibly it is but that, my love," her husband conceded handsomely. "Too soon for Kate to be distressing herself, at any rate. All may yet be well . . ."

"I am not distressing myself," Kate denied. "Indeed, in

some way, I would not be sorry. I would win my husband more to myself! I like James very well, but I am a little weary of always playing second to him! And I have had more than enough of being penned in fortresses, always with high walls and drawbridges, like prisons! You, David, cannot deny that, for yourself. No—I would not be heart-broken to leave the royal service for a time. To live in our own house on our own land." She waved a hand to encompass that pleasant room and its domestic atmosphere. "To live like this."

David eyed her thoughtfully.

"Where would you go?" Marion asked. "Back to Garleton or the Byres?"

"A week past I would have said so. But these last days we have been at The Mount of Lindifferon, David's property near to Cupar. It is a fine place. It has been stewarded by his uncle these many years. But he has died, and we thought to find a new steward." She turned to her husband. "We could live there, steward the Mount ourselves. I like it well. No?"

David looked doubtful.

"We would be on our own. No problems with fathers and families. Live as husband and wife should. Work the land—it looked a very fair ground, as good as the Byres. I think that I would prefer that to playing watchdog for a child king."

"Perhaps . . ."

"It might be the best choice," Beaton put in. "You would be near here—safe, in Fife, from much of the troubles which will, I fear, beset the realm. Holy Church can have its uses! And we would be able to see much of each other."

"Yes, yes," Marion exclaimed. "That would be good, Kate. To be near."

David, faced with what looked like a united front, did not commit himself. "We shall see," he said. "It may not come to that, forby."

They left it at that.

The visitors saw little of the Archbishop during their stay at his palace. According to his nephew, who was clearly concerned about him, he was not the man he had been, was drawing in on himself, even talking of resigning the chancellorship—although Davie believed that he had persuaded him not to do that, at least meantime. Certainly he was overweight, seemed preoccupied, and ate and drank too much. In the circumstances, David told Kate, for all Davie's persuasions, poor Scotland needed a stronger Chancellor than this.

After three days, the Lindsays returned to Stirling.

23

If David Lindsay had been inclined to judge his friend's forebodings and warnings as perhaps just a trifle alarmist, he was rudely disillusioned almost on their very arrival at Stirling Castle. For they found Margaret Tudor in residence there, indeed behaving as though she was its châtelaine, and Arran in attendance, apparently almost as much in that lady's favour as Albany had been a year or so before. Young James was the more thankful to see his Procurator and Chief Usher back.

Abbot John was worried. He told David that all the establishment now knew that great changes were on the way. There was to be a council, a Privy Council meeting, held at Edinburgh shortly, not a parliament, and at this Arran and the Queen-Mother were going to propose that the King be declared of age to rule, any regency no longer required, and the court moved from Stirling to the capital. This meant, in effect, that Arran and Margaret would rule, or rather Margaret and the Bastard, for his father was a man of straw. The Bastard it was who was behind it all, or most of it, undoubtedly, and he was cock-a-hoop and scarcely bearable to have around. Inglis feared greatly for the future, particularly their own future.

David, emphasising the folly of pretending that a twelve-year-old could be declared fit to rule a kingdom, said that surely the Privy Council would never agree to this project; but the other told him that the Bastard had been preparing the ground thoroughly and that there had been a stream of callers at the castle these last days, Privy Councillors, no doubt being convinced, bought or threatened—significant figures such as the Earls of Lennox, Glencairn, Atholl, Crawford and others of that order. What they *thought* he knew not, but he was afraid that they would vote as required—for the Bastard seemed entirely confident. And, of course, Cassillis, Fleming and Borthwick, the King's present guardians, were in Arran's faction.

Within hours they had confirmation of all this—and from the highest level. The Queen-Mother herself appeared at the King's quarters that evening, with Arran, unannounced. James, about to go to bed, backed away, scowling, to near the door to his own bedchamber, and so stood as though ready to bolt. Kate, Margaret Tudor dismissed with a flick of a beringed finger.

"So you are returned, Lindsay, from wherever you have been hiding yourself!" she said curtly.

"I obtained leave of absence to attend to my private affairs, lady. After the death of an uncle."

"You will call me Your Grace, sirrah. And you will have sufficient opportunity to attend to your private affairs hereafter, I promise you! You will prepare my royal son to ride to Edinburgh in three days' time, taking all his clothing and personal belongings. We leave Stirling. His Grace will be elevated to the supreme rule in this land thereafter, and his association with yourself and the others here ended. You will bring him to me at the Abbey of the Holy Rood at Edinburgh in three days' time, with all his possessions. You understand? And thereafter you will consider your employment in the royal service at an end. Is that entirely clear?"

David moistened his lips. "Madam—I am devoted to His Grace. All his life we have been close. For his sake, if not my own, I . . ."

"Yes! All his life you have been an ill influence with him! Look at him, there. All but hiding from his mother! *Your* doing, Lindsay. You should never have had the training of the boy. My late royal husband sorely misjudged. But now, that is overpast. The King will be his own governor and will rule. You are no longer required."

"I say that he is! He is!" That was James the Fifth, King of Scots.

He was ignored. "You will inform the others. The man Inglis. And his present tutor, Bellenden, he who followed Dunbar, who is now a bishop. None is any longer in the King's service . . ."

"No! No! Davie is my friend," James shouted. "Abbot John, too. But—Davie Lindsay is mine! Mine! You shall not take him from me—you shall not! If I am King and to rule, I will not let you do this. Davie stays with *me*."

"You do not rule *yet*, James. Mind it! Lindsay goes. You will gain new and better friends . . ."

"No! It is not true!" The boy actually stamped his foot and raised a hand to point at his mother. "You—I *hate* you! I hate you. I stay here, with Davie Lindsay and his Kate." He swung on Arran. "You my lord—tell her. I am the King. She cannot do this. Tell her so."

The Earl spread his hands helplessly and looked unhappy. He said nothing.

"Lindsay—take His Grace and put him to bed," Margaret snapped. "If anything was required to prove the evil influence you have on the boy, this outburst provides it. Take him away. And bring him to Edinburgh in three days." And turning, she swept out.

Arran hesitated, sighed, and sheepishly followed her.

James Stewart flung himself upon David, beating on his chest with clenched fists, babbling incoherently.

It was a long time before either of them slept that night.

For all James's protests and tantrums, and David's reluctance, the one had to deliver the other to Holyrood three days later, with a train of laden baggage-animals. They made a miserable journey of it. Kate came along too, for they were going to the Byres afterwards.

They found that it was Sir James Hamilton of Finnart to whom they were to hand over their charge, with no sign of Arran or the Queen-Mother. The Bastard was amiable and at least superficially sympathetic, conceding that David was the loser by this change but indicating confidentially, if a trifle condescendingly, that he would endeavour to see that some small annual pension should be forthcoming by way of compensation—a suggestion for which the beneficiary appeared perhaps less grateful than he might have been.

The parting from James was grievous for all concerned, and difficult too, for the boy clung to David's person, and since it was *lèse-majesté* to lay hands on the monarch's body, even the Bastard was inhibited from seeking physically to detach him. David himself, much moved, could not bring himself to push the boy away and no urgings from the others present had any effect. It was Kate who eventually solved the problem by taking the King's arm in something nearer an embrace than a grip, and gently easing him away from her husband's and on to her own person, kissing his brow and then holding him at arm's length, whilst soothingly assuring him that they were his friends for always and that they would make shift to come and see him whenever they could—and Sir James Hamilton, she was sure, would facilitate this and look after His Grace well meantime. To which the Bastard hurriedly agreed, asserted entire goodwill as well as his loyal duty and promised that the Lindsays should always be permitted access to the presence, tentatively taking a royal arm as Kate backed away.

He was promptly shaken off, and James stood alone. Hamilton hastily signed to some of the attendants to line up between the King and his friends, at the same time urgently waving the Lindsays away.

Hating to leave the boy thus but recognising that nothing was to be gained by prolonging the misery they raised hands in farewell, David bowed deeply and Kate curtsied, and hurriedly they turned and made their exit, their last sight of their liege-lord standing stricken-featured, desolate, gulping back his tears. Their own vision was not a little blurred thereafter.

They made a silent journey of it to the Byres of Garleton.

The fourth evening of their stay at the Byres, the Lord Lindsay returned—for he had been attending the vital Privy Council meeting in Edinburgh. He came in grim mood and surprisingly, he brought Davie Beaton with him.

It was the latter who did most of the explaining. Much as he loved his good friends David and Kate, he asserted, he was not come on any friendly visitation but practically as a fugitive. Because Lord Lindsay had had his usual tail of armed retainers with him in the city, he had sought his protection and come with him here instead of setting out alone on the long road to St Andrews, unguarded. For the archiepiscopal escort his uncle had brought with him was now disarmed and itself under tight guard in Edinburgh Castle, and the Chancellor himself taken prisoner and confined in Blackness Castle, the state prison near Linlithgow. That Davie was not with him there was only thanks to good fortune and swift preventive action. No least doubt but that he was being searched for in the capital at this moment.

As his friends stared in astonishment at all this, they learned more. The Council at Holyrood had been a disaster. Sundry moderate lords and bishops had been variously prevented from attending, and the Queen-Mother's and Arran's party had had everything their own way. In vain the Archbishop had protested against this device of elevating the twelve-year-old monarch to nominal rule, pointing out that this was a nonsense save in that it gave complete power, without a regency, to those who controlled the child. And who would that be but his mother, not present, but sufficiently well represented? His uncle had been shouted down, but had persisted. Was it sufficiently realised, he demanded, what having King Henry of England's sister controlling the nominal ruler of Scotland would mean, with no Regent? It would mean *Henry's* rule of Scotland, what that monarch had been seeking to achieve all his reign. Already they had sure information from spies in London that Henry was sending up two hundred specially chosen soldiers of his own royal guard to form a close bodyguard for King James, and to this his mother had acceded. Also he was sending a large consignment of gold—no doubt to pay for the bribes offered for a favourable vote in this council! And if that vote should go against him they all knew of his latest threat—that all the property of Scots in England would be confiscated forthwith, and all Scots resident in that realm not only to be banished but to be driven on foot from English soil with no belongings allowed but a white cross affixed to their upper garments, as indication that they were as good as lepers, outcasts of God and man. That was the monarch into whose blood-stained hands they would commit their young liege-lord and his realm if they permitted this folly to be established.

Since the Chancellor presided over this Privy Council meeting, none had been able to silence him. But when Gavin Dunbar, Bishop of Aberdeen, and the Lord Lindsay, sought to support the Archbishop, *they* had been silenced by Arran, at the Bastard's prompting, moving a vote of no-confidence in the present chairmanship, and had it overwhelmingly granted. He then had had himself voted into the chair, as second person in the kingdom, and promptly had put the motion for the elevation of the King to the vote, without further debate. Only three had voted against, the

Chancellor, Dunbar and Lindsay, although there had been two or three abstentions.

The thing was done, the meeting broke up—and the first move of the new regime was to order the apprehension and imprisonment in Blackness Castle of the Chancellor and Primate, and of the Bishop of Aberdeen. Lindsay, learning what was afoot, had wisely left the abbey secretly for the security of his own retinue. Unfortunately, the Archbishop's escort had been rounded up and disarmed whilst the meeting had been going on. So Davie had had to desert his uncle and join the Lindsays, unobserved, and here they were.

Appalled, David and the others listened, comment superfluous.

That night something of a council of war developed. Clearly Margaret and Arran—or his son—had the bit between their teeth now and would stop at little to gain their way, if they could arrest even the head of Holy Church and the realm's chief minister of state, the Chancellor. Undoubtedly those who opposed them were in danger of the same treatment, or worse. All knew that Davie was largely the wits and will behind his uncle and therefore was at real risk. He wanted to get back to the safety of St Andrews Castle just as quickly but unobtrusively as possible, there to do all in his power, and the power of the Church, to gain the Archbishop's freedom. Lord Lindsay was probably safe enough here in his own country, amongst his own folk, with his armed retainers, so long as he did not actively oppose the regime. But David was in a different position, the King's affection for him, in present circumstances, a positive danger. Margaret Tudor hated him, obviously, and although the Bastard was on the face of it on fair terms with him and sought to buy him off with a pension, the Queen-Mother was unlikely to see it that way. He was probably not so much at risk as was Davie Beaton, but danger there was of arrest or other threat. Garleton was too close to the capital for his good, all agreed, and Kate's recommendation of the Mount of Lindifferon as excellent refuge, near to Davie's St Andrews, strongly backed by Beaton, began to look ever more attractive. His father was growing old, but his brother Alexander, at the Barony, was more and more taking over the managing of the property for him, and would not look kindly on David, the older son, coming to supplant him, whilst the Mount required a resident laird.

In the end it was decided that the three of them should indeed make their way secretly to Fife, travelling by night at least for the first part of the journey. It might seem an inglorious business for men who were used to thinking of themselves of some small consequence in the realm, but it was probably good for their souls. They would pay fishermen from Luffness Haven to sail them across the open firth to Pittenweem in East Fife where there was a priory belonging to St Andrews and where they would be able to gain shelter and then horses to carry them on northwards—that way, they ought to run no risk of interception or recognition by enemies.

All at the Byres and Garleton agreed that this was the wisest course both as to the journey and the dwelling in Fife thereafter. Indeed David was a little piqued by the fact that his father and even Mirren seemed less than distressed that he was going off to live far from Garleton and would in the nature of things be unlikely to see much of home and themselves for some time thereafter. Mirren had long settled in at the castle as its mistress, was becoming plump and matronly, and the laird in his old age appeared to rely on her and to be content to be more or less ruled by her. David's presence, not to mention Kate's, probably would have been an embarrassment. And at the Byres itself, although they were very welcome to stay a while, there was no real place for them now, no employment suitable for David.

So, two evenings later, on the Eve of Martinmas, taking advantage of an early frost and therefore calm seas, the travellers made their farewells and rode off down to Luffness, to board a pitch-painted, fishy-smelling coble, just as the November dark was settling on the Forth estuary. It was going to be a cold voyage.

There was little wind, which kept the seas down but which meant that the square lug-sail did not greatly aid them, even though what breeze there was came from the prevailing south-west, the desired quarter since their course was north-east. So the six-man crew had to pull on their long sweeps for the entire fourteen-mile slantwise crossing—although the two Davids were glad enough to take turns at the oars in the interests of keeping warm, being in the circumstances too masculine to take advantage of Kate's offer to huddle with her within the fur wraps she had wisely brought along, even though they would have been delighted to accept.

It took almost three hours to make the crossing, a strange even weird experience for the trio who had never before sailed in a small open boat by night. Their course was never in doubt, at least, for ahead of them all the time, once they had cleared Aberlady Bay's Gullane Point, was the gleam of the blazing beacon on the Isle of May maintained each night by the monks of the same Pittenweem Priory to which they were headed, which isle lay off the Fife coast some five miles—one of the many little-lauded but useful services which Holy Church provided, as Beaton pointed out.

A few miles short of the May, the boatmen changed course to due north, apparently quite sure of their position, and now, calm as the night might be, the swell running in from the ocean began to take them broadside-on, to their increased discomfort. Fortunately there was no lengthy period of this before the loom of the land and the noise of slow rollers breaking on a rock-bound coast, greeted them, and after a little skirting of the shore eastwards, the harbour of what they were assured was Pittenweem opened ahead. All was dark beyond, even though now their eyes were accustomed to the night vision.

Set ashore at a stone jetty amongst moored, bobbing fishing craft, they said goodbye to their boatmen and, stiff with cold, set off uphill in what Davie assured was the direction of St Ethernan's or Adrian's Priory. He knew the area well, of course, and indeed had been here recently, for this was one of the most valuable of the metropolitan see's many daughter-houses. It was nearly midnight, and the little fishing burgh was lightless and asleep. A single lamp did burn, however, at what turned out to be the Priory gatehouse; and when Davie set the great doorbell jangling loudly, it did not take long for a hooded monk to come peering through a grating and demanding to know who dared come disturbing godly men at such ungodly hour? Promptly left in no doubt as to the authority of at least one of his callers, in the name of Archbishop Beaton, he made no delay in opening the postern and admitting them, Davie thereafter demanding the presence of the Prior himself, in bed as he might be. And well aware that the Prior's own house would be the most warm and comfortable in the establishment, he led the way thereto.

An alarmed cleric was presently produced, and a probably deliberate demonstration of the power of the Primate's secretary to achieve results was staged. Soon they were being warmed and restored by a hurriedly prepared meal and excellent wine before a resuscitated fire in the Prior's library, beds were being made up and instructions given as to horses and even an escort to be provided for the morning. This was a masterful Davie Beaton, indicating that the affairs of Holy Church would not be allowed to languish whilst its nominal head himself languished in durance vile.

Kate was interested to hear a female voice plaintively wanting to know what was to do, from the Prior's bed-chamber, as she and David made for their allotted apartment nearby.

Next morning they rode openly northwards, with four of the Prior's armed servitors, through the East Neuk of Fife, by Kellie Law and the high ground of Lathones and Kinninmonth to Pitscottie. Here they had a meal with David's rather odd kinsman, and thereafter parted from Davie, who was turning eastwards for St Andrews, seven miles, while the Lindsays proceeded north-eastwards for Cupar. They promised to forgather soon and to keep in touch always. Davie insisted that they take two of the Prior's men whilst he took the other pair.

They came to Lindifferon as the November day was quietly dying. The twin breasts of its hills swelled gracefully against a pale lemon-yellow sunset, with the tower of the Mount's little castle silhouetted darkly on the flank of the eastern one, surveying all the shadowy, fertile vale of Stratheden. At the sight of it all, they drew rein involuntarily, to pause and gaze, entranced.

"A fair inheritance," Kate said, at length. "A world unto itself. Safe. Secure. Our own. Why did we not come here sooner? Better than palaces and fortresses, courts and intrigues. We shall be happy here, at the Mount, I believe—all three of us!"

"I hope so. I . . . *three*, you say? How three?"

"Three, yes. I have waited to tell you, David, of a purpose. Till . . . now. I am going to have a child, I think. I have wanted it. To be born here, at the Mount of Lindifferon. Oh, Davie . . . !"

"Kate! My dear—you . . . you . . . ! At last—a child! You are sure?" He reined his horse over to hers, hand out—then remembered the escort behind, and moderated his voice and actions, but only a little. "This is . . . joy! Joy! A homecoming, indeed. We have waited so long. Eight years."

"Yes, I am sure enough. So, you see, we start afresh, David Lindsay of the Mount! Come—let us up there and make a beginning."

"With all my heart, my love . . . !"

Book Two

JAMES, BY THE GRACE OF GOD

Principal Characters

IN ORDER OF APPEARANCE

DAVID BEATON: Rector of Campsie and secretary to the Primate.
DAVID LINDSAY OF THE MOUNT AND GARLETON: Usher to the King of Scots.
PATRICK, 4TH LORD LINDSAY OF THE BYRES: Father-in-law of David Lindsay.
ARCHIBALD, EARL OF ANGUS: Chief of the Red Douglases.
SIR ARCHIBALD DOUGLAS OF KILSPINDIE: Uncle of above, known as Graysteel.
MASTER WILLIAM DOUGLAS: Abbot of Holyrood. Another uncle of Angus.
JAMES BEATON, ARCHBISHOP OF ST. ANDREWS: Primate of the Church in Scotland.
JAMES HAMILTON, EARL OF ARRAN: Lord High Admiral.
JAMES THE FIFTH, KING OF SCOTS: Aged thirteen.
MARGARET TUDOR: Queen of the late James the Fourth and sister of Henry the Eighth.
SIR JAMES HAMILTON OF FINNART: Known as the Bastard of Arran. Illegitimate son of that Earl.
JOHN STEWART, EARL OF LENNOX: Chiefest of the non-royal Stewarts.
SIR WALTER SCOTT OF BUCCLEUCH: Warden of the Middle March and chief of the Borderland Scotts.
JOHN STEWART, EARL OF ATHOLL: Great Highland noble.
JANET DOUGLAS: Tirewoman and Wardrobe Mistress to the King, daughter of the Laird of Stonypath.
GAVIN DUNBAR, ARCHBISHOP OF GLASGOW: Chancellor.
ROBERT, 5TH LORD MAXWELL: Warden of the West March.

JOHNNIE ARMSTRONG OF GILNOCKIE: Known as King of the Border. Leader of that notorious clan.
MARGARET VON HAPSBURG, QUEEN OF HUNGARY: Aunt of the Emperor Charles and Governor of the Netherlands.
CHARLES VON HAPSBURG, EMPEROR.
MARION OGILVY: Former wife of Davie Beaton. Daughter of the 3RD LORD OGILVY OF AIRLIE.
BISHOP ANTONIO CAMPEGGIO: Papal Nuncio.
GEORGE, 4TH LORD HOME: Great Borders noble.
HENRY, 6TH EARL OF NORTHUMBERLAND: English Warden of the Marches.
MARIE DE BOURBON: Daughter of the Duc de Vendôme.
FRANCIS DE VALOIS, KING OF FRANCE.
MARIE DE GUISE, DUCHESS DE LONGUEVILLE: Sister of the Duc de Guise and Cardinal of Lorraine.
MADELEINE DE VALOIS, PRINCESS OF FRANCE: Daughter of King Francis.

Part One

1

Half-a-dozen men were working at the hay on the slantwise, south-facing field on the lower slopes of Lindifferon Hill that June afternoon, the horseman noted; but whilst five were toiling near to each other towards the bottom end, one was by himself towards the top. And while the group worked with a slow but steady rhythm of practice and custom, swinging their sickles in smooth, even sweeps, the lone individual seemed to be labouring much harder, stooping and rising more often with more frequent strokes, head down, even at that distance a picture of tense concentration, strange in a sunny hayfield. Without much hesitation, the visitor turned his mount's head in that direction and trotted across and up.

As he drew near, the toiling man seemed loth to stop cutting, even to glance up, although he could not have failed to hear the clip-clop of hooves and jingle of harness. The newcomer's handsome features took on a thoughtful, assessing look.

He reined in his splendid grey stallion only a few yards from the other, who at last looked up. "So, David—you are busy, I see. God bless the work! A fair hay crop, this year, all tell me. It is good to see you, friend."

The toiler straightened an obviously aching back, and nodded, stiff-faced. "Yes," he said, "and you." He did not sound overjoyed, voice level.

"They told me at your castle that you would be here," the horseman added. "Working, always working, they said. You are well enough, David? I have seen you looking better, and with more flesh to your bones."

"Well?" the man with the sickle repeated. "What is well? Or ill? I am not sick, if that is what you ask. Not sick of body."

"Mmm. I am sorry, David—sorry."

There was a pause as they eyed each other.

They made an extraordinary contrast in appearance, those two men, both in their early thirties, the one brilliantly good-looking in a strangely delicate, fine-featured way which could have been almost effeminate save for the strong jawline, firm mouth and keen, lively eyes, the other more rugged both of face and build, muscular but gaunt-looking, clad in old breeches which had been well-cut once and were now stained and worn, with a sweat-darkened shirt of linen, open to the waist, while the horseman was dressed in the height of French fashion, all but dandified, crimson velvet slashed with gold, lace at throat and wrists, the curling feather of his flat jewelled cap held in place by a great ruby brooch.

When the standing man made no further comment, indeed turned to look away down over the lovely prospect of the part of the fertile Howe of Fife known as Stratheden—gentle green swelling hills enclosing the wide farm-dotted vale, with its winding river, scattered woodlands and red-roofed villages, over a thousand acres of which, closest at hand, were his own—then the horseman dismounted and came to stand beside his friend, for these two *were* friends, despite all appearances. He laid a hand on the other's arm.

"They say that time heals all, David," he murmured. "True or not, who knows? But activity makes time pass the faster—which may help. But hay-making, now? I doubt if that is the best time-passer for such as you! Too much time to think. Not so?"

"Perhaps," the other admitted. "But no time, however passed, will find me what I have lost."

"No. Agreed. But you have to go on living, man."

"Aye. All the years."

"To be sure, all the years. You have forty perhaps ahead of you. I say that you will need more than hay-making, or harvesting, or working the land, or yourself too weary to think, to remember. You will need more than that."

"Need? My needs are the least of it, Davie. And what I need I cannot have."

"But . . . there are other needs than just yours, friend. *My* needs. Others'. The realm's needs—this Scotland of ours. There are great and pressing needs thronging the land beyond all this." And he waved his gloved hand to encompass that fair vista. "Beyond the Mount of Lindifferon evil stalks through this kingdom. While you make hay, David Lindsay of the Mount!"

"No doubt. It usually does, God knows! If there is a God. But I cannot help that."

"You can, I think. You have done in the past and can do again."

"Davie Beaton—spare me your scheming and plots and ploys! I am in no state for such, I promise you. I know you. Moving men like chessmen—as you have moved me, in the past. That is over—like so much else."

"Is friendship over, then? Affection? Regard for others, man?"

Lindsay frowned down at his sickle. "No-o-o. Not that. You know that is not true. You know it."

"I know that I, your friend, need you. And, more important than I am, James Stewart needs you. Your liege-lord and mine."

That was shrewd thrusting, and Lindsay started to protest, but restrained himself with an effort. Twelve-year-old King James the Fifth was indeed his friend, as well as his monarch. "James is beyond any help of mine," he said.

"Perhaps not. Help he must have. If he is taken to England, to his Uncle Henry of accursed name, I doubt if we should ever see him again!"

"England? What do you mean, England? How could this be?"

"We have word at St. Andrews that his mother contemplates taking him there, secretly. To prevent him from falling into Angus's hands, she says. You have heard that Angus is back, and he and his Douglases have taken over Edinburgh town again?"

"No. No—I had not heard that. I hear but little here . . ."

"Perhaps you should hear more, listen more, David. For knowing nothing will not save any of us from trouble! Yes, the Earl of Angus and his Douglases descended upon the capital in strength some weeks ago, and took over the city. As he did once before. Arran and his son were at Hamilton, so they had an easy conquest. The Queen-Mother and young James contrived to get up to the castle from Holyrood, with the help of the English guard Henry has provided, and they are secure there, meantime at any rate. Without cannon, Angus cannot take the castle—but it is not beyond him to obtain artillery in time and bombard it. Although whether he would dare that, with the King therein, I doubt. But Margaret Tudor, it seems, thinks that he might—and she ought to know him, having wed him!—and so she is planning secretly to leave the fortress by night and flee with James to England. She has written to this effect to the Lord Dacre, the English Warden of the Marches, at Morpeth—our spies intercepted and read the letter. She asks him to be ready to receive them, and to muster all available forces to invade Scotland thereafter, with King James at the head of his army so that the Scots will be loth to take arms against their own monarch. And so to drive the Douglases out of Edinburgh and restore Margaret to power."

Lindsay shook his head. "So—we are back to that! The same old folly and treachery. Will it never end?"

"Not so long as James is a child, I fear, and his mother holds him. And good men fail to act! It is all part of her brother, Henry Tudor's game to win Scotland for himself."

"Aye. Then I am well out of it all!"

"Spoken like a true friend of Jamie Stewart!" Beaton said, sourly for that honey-tongued individual.

The other drew a quick breath and the knuckles gripping the sickle gleamed white. "I was *put* out of it, I'd remind you!" he jerked. "Dismissed from being the King's procurator and usher—by the Queen-Mother, seven months ago. Besides, what could I do now? The boy himself may like me well enough but his mother hates me. She certainly would not listen to me, even admit me to her presence. I am but a simple Fife laird now. I have nothing to offer in this sorry situation—even if I would."

"I think that you mistake, David. It is not to Margaret Tudor I would have you go. But to someone who will listen to you. To Kate's father. Your own good-father at The Byres of Garleton—Patrick, Lord Lindsay."

His friend stiffened perceptibly at those names and turned to stare at Beaton, eyes narrowed.

Hurriedly the other went on. "The Lord Patrick is an honest man, one of the few on the present Privy Council. The Queen-Mother will have none of him, any more than of you. And that weak fool the Earl of Arran takes his line from her. So Lord Lindsay is squeezed out—like other honest men. And we have heard that Angus has twice been to The Byres to see him."

"What of it?"

"Angus, for that hot-tempered man, has been behaving with some care since he took Edinburgh. He is biding his time, keeping his Douglases under control. He has even moved out of the city himself, to lodge with the Black Douglas chief, the Earl of Morton, at Dalkeith, even though until now they were unfriends. We, my uncle and I, have hopes for the Earl of Angus. Faint perhaps, but hopes!"

"Then I misdoubt your judgement!"

"Ah, but the judgement is not of character but of circumstances! He remains a hot-head, ambitious, untrustworthy, but . . ."

"And in King Henry's pocket! Always he has been. If he has lately come back to Scotland, it is straight from Henry's court."

"Aye—but the conditions are changed, see you. Have you not heard this either? The divorce has been granted. Our friend the Duke of Albany in France has prevailed upon the new Pope to grant it. Paid all out of his own pocket, they say—Lord knows why, save that he hates Angus! So Margaret Tudor is no longer Countess of Angus, and he no longer Henry's good-brother. Thus, you see, he is no longer of the same use to England. Henry cannot command him as he did, or use him, the most powerful noble in Scotland. He has not the same hold over him."

Lindsay shrugged, waiting.

"So, as I say, we have hopes for Angus. In this coil. There are three great factions in this Scotland—the Queen-Mother's, the Earl of Arran's and Angus's. Four, if you count Holy Church! And the young King is the prize. Whoever hold James, rules in his name, now Albany is gone and there is no regent. Arran and his Hamiltons have taken sides with Margaret Tudor, and so presently rule—or *she* does, since he is a weakling. Thus, Holy Church must look elsewhere."

"You mean *you* must look elsewhere! Since you control your uncle, the Archbishop."

"Crudely put, David! As the Archbishop's and Primate's and Chancellor's secretary, I may have some small influence. But to control him, and through him Holy Church, is an . . . exaggeration! Incidentally, my friend, you should speak more respectfully to your old class-mate. For I am now not just Rector of Campsie and Cambuslang but Lord Abbot of Arbroath, no less!"

"You? You—Abbot? Arbroath! How can this be? You are not a priest. Not in holy orders . . ."

"Admittedly. But I am Abbot *in commendam*. A lay prelate, shall we say? A convenient arrangement, is it not? Since Arbroath is the second richest abbey in the land!"

"Convenient! It is shameful, rather. Disgraceful. That the Church should prostitute itself, to give such as you its high office, its wealth and power . . ."

"Sakes—you are in an ill mood this day, David, I must say! Why not me? I will use the revenues of Arbroath to better effect than any of its ordained and priestly abbots for long enough, I promise you—in *Scotland's* cause. Or half of them, for my uncle would only grant it if he retained half! If I am going to do what I seek to do for our realm, I need moneys. So I have prevailed on my good kinsman—unwilling as he was, mind you—to arrange this. And what is so shameful? If the late King, of beloved memory, could make his fifteen-year-old bastard son Archbishop of St. Andrews *in commendam*, why not your humble servant, who has a degree in theology from the Sorbonne? I warrant no other abbot in all Scotland has that! And I *was* Scots ambassador to France. But, you see, it is not only the moneys and status that is important to me, but the fact that the mitred abbacy carries a seat in parliament. *That* is what I require. Hitherto, at parliaments, I have had to sit dumb, like yourself, listen only, and nudge my august uncle, as Chancellor, when advisable! Now, friend, I can speak and urge and vote. Which is partly why I am here."

Lindsay nodded, almost wearily. "You will come to why, Davie, no doubt. In this flood of words. Always you could out-talk anyone I ever knew."

"Exactly! Hence the value of a seat in parliament! Well now, simple Fife laird—here is my mission, and, I hope, yours. If Margaret's wings are to be clipped and James saved, her own and Arran's factions have to be reduced, out-fought. And only by the other two factions working together can this be achieved—that is, Angus's and the Church. That is the simple fact of it. But less simple to achieve, for they have never had aught in common. My uncle and Angus have always been enemies. So—we need a mediator. Lord Lindsay should serve. Will you go to bespeak his good offices for us, David?"

"So that the Church can aid Angus to supreme power? Think you that any betterment for Scotland?"

"That is not the objective—although even Angus, suitably hobbled, might be better than Margaret Tudor, now that he is cut adrift from Henry of England."

"Have we not had enough of faction-fighting, feud and civil war, all these last years, since Flodden?"

"It is not fighting, war, we seek, but the rule of law, the rightful authority of the realm . . ."

"From Angus and his Douglases! Have you lost your famed wits, man?"

"It is a parliament we aim for—do you not understand? Votes in a parliament. My uncle, as Chancellor, can call a parliament in the King's name. The Church and the Douglases together could swing sufficient votes amongst the shire and burgh commissioners, I believe, to gain a majority. One reason why I wanted my abbacy—to speak in parliament. That way we could unite the nation, or enough of it to thwart Margaret and Arran. And to get the King out of her hands."

"And into Angus's?"

"Into the Privy Council's, with honest additions. Will you do it, friend? Go over to East Lothian, to The Byres of Garleton. Tell your good-father what is intended. Seek his good offices. Ask that he will go to Angus and tell him what is proposed. Ask the Earl to come to St. Andrews for a conference. We cannot go to him—my uncle is past skulking travel, so gross has he become. You come from East Lothian, know your way. We would put you across the firth by night, in a boat from Pittenweem, secretly. Go to The Byres. See your own father, whilst there. Back the next night. No difficulty for *you*. Will you do it, David?"

"I . . . I must consider . . ."

"Aye. Do that. And whilst you consider, man, will you not prove yourself more of a host towards an old friend and offer me some small refreshment better than the smell of cut hay? After all, I have ridden fifteen miles from St. Andrews to see you."

"Yes. To be sure. You will forgive me. I am remiss. Come—we will go back to The Mount . . ."

They walked side-by-side, leading the horse, across the field and down through open woodland where cuckoos were calling hauntingly, towards the dip between the twin hills, Beaton holding forth on the possibilities of his plans, the chances of Angus's co-operation and the methods which he would use to seek to ensure that Holy Church gained most from the association, rather than the Douglases—whose menace he by no means underestimated. A tinkling burn ran down the green cleft in the bosom of the hills, and as the well-defined track they were on neared this, to cross it by a plank-bridge, David Lindsay turned off the track right-handed to head through the trees to a lower crossing-place some way down. His companion, who had used the track and bridge on the way out, interrupted his talk to ask why the detour?

"That bridge is where Kate fell," he was told shortly.

Beaton asked no more. At the funeral two months earlier he had heard that Kate Lindsay, seven months pregnant, riding back from some visit, had been thrown from her shying horse at some hazard, to be eventually found dead and her part-born child with her, in some water. Her husband had been a stricken man since.

A narrower and new path leading lower indicated that David Lindsay could not bear to use that bridge any more.

In silence now they strode on round the base of the eastern hill, back on the track again.

Soon they came to the Castle of The Mount, rising before them on a sort of terrace of the hillside, a typical square stone keep of four storeys beneath a parapet and wall-walk, with a garret storey above, all surrounded by a barmekin or high defensive wall with a gatehouse, enclosing a courtyard containing lower lean-to domestic outbuildings. It had been David's inheritance from his mother, so that he had been nominal laird of the Mount of Lindifferon from childhood, although one day, when his father died, he would be Lindsay of Garleton, in East Lothian, a larger property where he had been born. He and Kate had only come to The Mount, hitherto stewarded for him by an older brother of his mother, in the previous November on being dismissed from the position of procurator and usher to King James, which he had held for all twelve years of the boy-monarch's life. Here he was to become the simple Fife laird he had spoken of so bitterly, and here their first child was to be born. Now he saw life bleak and grey, a changed man.

That was David Lindsay.

In the first-floor hall of his little castle, a housekeeping woman provided a cold meal, adequate but unambitious, to which Beaton did justice but at which his host merely picked. The conversation was almost all on one side, and fairly heavy going even for that most eloquent individual. It was not long before the visitor declared that he must be on his way back to St. Andrews Castle, a two-hour ride—and was not pressed to stay.

At the gatehouse farewell, Davie Beaton rode off sad and concerned for his friend. But at least he had his promise that he would go on this mission to East Lothian for him, and with minimum delay, for time was of the essence.

* * *

Three nights later they made another farewell, this time some twenty-two miles to the south-east, at the fishing haven of Pittenweem below the walls of St. Ethernan's Priory. It was not dark—it is seldom really dark of a Scots June night—but after midnight, a strange time to be putting to sea in a small boat.

Both men had very much in mind the last time that they had been here, in similar if darker circumstances, in the previous November, but coming in the other direction—only that time there had been three of them, Kate agog at the adventure of thus clandestinely commencing a new life.

"It is a calm enough night," Beaton said. "You should be over in little more than two hours. Then a bare three-mile walk up to The Byres. There well before breakfast."

The other nodded.

"You have it all? What is proposed. What to tell the Lord Lindsay. What we wish him to put to the Earl of Angus. And the need for haste. A parliament takes time to mount. And Margaret Tudor might make her move any day."

Again Lindsay nodded. "It is all clear enough. Although whether it will come to anything is another matter."

"We must hope so, pray so. For the sake of young James and his realm, for all our sakes. Much will hang on this, I believe."

"*You* do the praying, my lord Abbot!" he was told, almost mockingly. "Which will be a change, I think!"

It was on the tip of Beaton's tongue to say that such words and attitude represented a still greater change in the David Lindsay he had known since they were youths at college, but instead he held out his hand.

"Good fortune and God speed," he said.

"Yes. I will come to you at St. Andrews two days hence. Or three—who knows?"

"Aye. The boat will wait for you at Luffness. And the Prior here will have your horse ready whenever you arrive, and an escort."

Lindsay stepped down into the broad-beamed coble, and the four fishermen, employed by the Priory, dipped in their long sweeps to manoeuvre the craft out from the cluster of other boats at the pier-side, to pull for the harbour-mouth. Their passenger sat hunched in the stern and did not look back.

Out in the open Firth of Forth the sea was less calm than it had seemed from the land, and the fourteen-mile crossing took longer than Beaton had estimated, largely because the oarsmen had to pull all the way, the square lug-sail being of no use to them, for the prevailing south-westerly breeze, although not strong, was in their faces going this way. The glimmer of the beacon on the Isle of May, to their left in the firth-mouth, was much paler in this half-light than it had been in the dark of November, and soon faded from sight altogether. It was chill out there on the water for the passenger who huddled in his riding-cloak. Occasionally a shower of spray came inboard. Only the creak of the rowlocks and the slap-slap and hiss of the seas broke the silence.

After a couple of hours of it, the loom of the land grew vaguely before them, but there was no certainty as to feature or distance, as the oarsmen pulled steadily, rhythmically on. It was sound rather than sight, in almost another hour, which offered any evidence of location, the continuous booming roar from half-right ahead, low but powerful, dominant. David knew what that was; strange if he did not, after all the flighting for wild-geese he had done to its accompaniment. It was the noise of breaking seas on the bar of Aberlady Bay, the three-mile-long, half-mile-wide sand-bar which all but closed the mouth of that great estuarine bight, something which was not to be mistaken in all the scores of miles of either side of the Firth of Forth.

Parallel with that daunting sound, but well back from its origin, the fishermen steered their craft for the bar's entire length, for the navigable entrance to the bay, at whatever state of the tide, was at the extreme west end of it, where the Water of Peffer found its way to the sea from behind the bar. Twin stone pinnacles marked the opening, only some two hundred yards apart, the gateway to the channel—for Aberlady was the port of Haddington—and these stood out clearly enough in the June half-light; but of a winter's night in a gale of wind and spume, it was not difficult to miss them, and many were the ships which had done so, to leave their timbers on that grievous submerged sand-bar.

Once within the calm waters of the bay itself, all was changed and it was like rowing over an inland loch. They turned the boat's blunt prow eastwards again now, well away from the long jetty at Kilspindie where the port shipping tied up, to head towards the very apex of the triangular-shaped bight, the water of which covered a full fifteen hundred acres. The tide was two-thirds in, fortunately, which meant that they would not be troubled by shallows in this fairly flat-bottomed coble.

Near the very tip of the bay, where the Peffer came in from its wide, level vale, they made their landfall at a boat-strand under quite a steep bank, above which reared the lofty curtain-walls and angle-towers of the great castle of Luffness, another Lindsay stronghold owned, but seldom visited, by the chief of all that renowned house, the Earl of Crawford. Below the castle, huddling between its frowning walls and the shore, was a row of cothouses, hovels, tarred shacks for smoking fish and drying nets hung on poles, the fishing hamlet of Luffness Haven. All was dark and asleep here still, although a dog barked at scent of the visitors.

David jumped out on to the shingle, leaving his boatmen there in their craft. They would do well enough with the local fisherfolk when these awakened. He hoped to be back the following night, for the return passage, but if not they should wait another day. If still he had not appeared, and no word sent, they were to go back to Pittenweem on their own—although he did not anticipate that.

Avoiding the castle, for he was uncertain as to its keeper's allegiances, he set off to the west of it, deliberately to pass a certain red-tiled cart-shed in a field belonging to the Carmelite monastery, sited that side of the castle, a place of bitter-sweet memories, where he and Kate had pledged their troth nine years before. Moving inland he came to the monastery chapel where they had been married. He did not go in but stood at the door amongst the ancient trees for a little, his mind a battle-ground for emotions, before sighing, and resuming his walking.

The light was growing now and he reckoned that the sun would be rising in another hour, by which time he ought to have reached his destination. Strangely enough, familiar as it all was to him, he could not remember ever having *walked* this way before, always having come on horseback, even as a boy.

Skirting the monastery grounds between it and its sister nunnery on the outskirts of Aberlady village, he crossed the water-logged Luffness Muir by a track which was almost a causeway, setting up quacking duck by the score and lazy-flapping herons and disturbing roe-deer and hares; a great place for hawking. Over a mile of this and he came to the hamlet of Ballencrieff, where the cocks were beginning to crow and more dogs remarked on his passage. Then the land began to rise, gently, towards the green ridge of the Garleton Hills, another mile or so. And up there, fairly close under the now abruptly soaring heights of the ridge itself, he came to the castle and castleton of The Byres of Garleton, just as the sun was rising in golden splendour above the rim of the Norse Sea, glimpsed from this altitude miles to the east, between North Berwick and Dunbar.

This place, the seat of the Lords Lindsay of The Byres, the second-most-senior line of that powerful family, and Kate's former home, was a fine establishment, not so large as Luffness but a noble house nevertheless, within its walled gardens and pleasances and orchards, a many-towered fortalice of reddish stone lording it over its slantwise fertile lands and cattle-dotted hummocks, with its own chapel, dovecotes, granaries, mill, ice-houses, even a brewery, its castleton greater than many a village. The first blue smokes of morning fires were lifting into the new slanting sunlight as David approached.

Crossing the moat by the drawbridge, which was not raised, as the portcullis was not lowered, he nevertheless had to beat on the massive timbers of the gatehouse double-doors with the hilt of his dirk, with some repetition, before a peep-hole at eye-level was opened and he was inspected.

"Lindsay of the Mount," he jerked, and there was an exclamation of recognition from within.

With a great creaking the gates were thrown open wide and the porter greeted him with warm respect, all incoherent half-sentences about him being a stranger, his sad loss, the earliness of the hour and where had he come from, to all of which he got little response save for a shake of the head and an enquiry as to whether his lordship was at home? He was, yes, he was told, but not likely to be out of his bed yet. No matter, David said, not to disturb him. He would go to the kitchen for some refreshment, and wait there. No need to escort him; he knew his way.

Presently, with a breakfast of porridge and cream, cold venison, oatcakes and honey washed down with ale, and not anxious to be put through an inquisition, however friendly, by the kitchen staff, he allowed his head to droop at the great kitchen table, and promptly fell asleep.

He started awake with a hand on his shoulder and looked up to find a tall woman, still handsome although elderly, and with kind features, considering him.

"David—here's a surprise!" she said. "It is good, good to see you. But—how come you thus? Afoot, I am told. Why by night? Is it trouble, lad? More trouble?"

"Aunt Isabella!" He rose, to kiss and be kissed. Lady Lindsay was not his aunt but he had always called her that, although her husband he never named uncle. "No, no trouble. At least, not for us. Any more than for all. I come on a mission to my lord. From the Chancellor. And best that I be not seen. By unfriends."

"Ah—so that's the way of it! If it is the Chancellor, then it is young Beaton his nephew! And that one can mean trouble enough, I vow! But—at least it has brought you here, David. You are well enough? You look thin, lad."

"I am well enough, yes. I came in a boat, by night. Did not sleep . . ."

Patrick, fourth Lord Lindsay of The Byres appeared, a thin, high-coloured, grizzled man in his late fifties, with hawklike face and minus an arm lost at Flodden-field. An individual of few words, he greeted his son-in-law briefly. His wife informed him of the circumstances.

David, in no mood for small talk anyway, came straight to the point. "Chancellor Beaton has it that the Queen-Mother intends to take King James secretly to England, believing that her former husband, the Earl of Angus, seeks to lay hands on him and use him for his own ends. This would deliver the boy, and the kingdom, into King Henry's hands. It must be stopped. He believes that a parliament called could stop it. He can call a parliament, as Chancellor. But to win a vote against the Queen-Mother's and Arran's parties, he would require Angus's support. Also his assurance that he would not grab the King. So he seeks a conference with Angus, and quickly. You, my lord, he has word have been seeing Angus. The Archbishop asks that you go to Angus, as mediator. He has always been unfriends with the Earl, so he needs a go-between, in this."

The older man eyed him levelly. "I am no friend of Angus, either," he said.

"Yet Beaton says that he has been here to see you more than once, of late, my lord."

"Your churchman is devilishly well-informed! How that?"

"I know not. I think that it is not so much the Chancellor as his nephew. He seems to have spies everywhere . . ."

"Aye—your friend Davie Beaton! This is all *his* device, then, I warrant. Rather than the old man's. Is it not so?"

"It may be. But does that alter the need for this parliament? To save the King. Something must be done."

"Perhaps, but Angus is an ill man to deal with."

"Yet you have been dealing with him?"

"Not me with him, boy. *Him* seeking to use me! He wants my manpower, against Arran and the Hamiltons. He has Crawford on his side, so he wants the rest of the Lindsays."

"Then you have something with which to bargain."

"I am not giving my Lindsays to die for Angus! Or any of them. I have had enough of war and swordery!"

"So say I. And Davie Beaton! Better a parliament to decide matters, the vote not the sword. It's why I agreed to come here."

"Maybe so. But by the same token I have nothing to bargain with, with Angus. I told him that I am not lending him one man."

"Nevertheless, my lord, you still can reach him, have access to him. And Davie Beaton has not. Will you do this? For the young King's sake."

"Angus is one for the sword rather than talk, conferences, voting in parliament. He would laugh at me, belike. He is a devil, that one."

"It is not much to do, Pate," the Lady Isabella said. "Need Lindsay fear Douglas laughter?"

"My lord—at least ask him to come to St. Andrews, to confer with the Archbishop. Angus has an uncle, a churchman, Prior William Douglas. And many other Douglas clerics. *They* would not wish him to reject the Primate's call out-of-hand. He may prefer the sword, but would be a fool needlessly to antagonise the Church, I think."

"You are strong on this, David. Why? If you are so keen, go to Angus yourself."

"He would never see me, only a small laird now, of no consequence. He is proud, arrogant. Besides, I cannot travel the breadth of Scotland to seek him . . ."

"No need. He is not at Galloway or Douglasdale, meantime. He is only at Tantallon—a dozen miles away. Has been these ten days. I will take you to him—but you can do the talking!"

The younger man bit his lip, uncertain now.

"Why not, David?" Lady Isabella asked. "Both go. Better two than one. He will not *eat* you!"

"I was to sail back tonight . . ."

"And still can, if you must. You could be at Tantallon before noon. Back in two hours . . ."

He shrugged.

So, presently, with a tail of a dozen well-mounted armed retainers, without which such as the Lord Lindsay never rode abroad, the two men trotted eastwards down into the Vale of Peffer, by Drem and Prora and Congalton, skirting to the north of the wide boglands where that most curious of rivers arose. For the Peffer was probably the only river in all Scotland to flow in two directions out of its swampy womb of waters, one branch westwards nine miles, eventually to enter Aberlady Bay; the other eastwards only four miles to reach the Norse Sea at Peffermouth; both called Peffer from the Celtic *pefr*, meaning fair, and forming one continuous waterway through one of the most fertile vales in the land.

By the village of Hamer, with its fine and ancient red-stone church, they came in sight of Tantallon, on its cliff-girt promontory, that seemed to shake a fist at sky and sea and the mighty mass of the Craig of Bass which reared out of the tide two miles offshore. It made a striking picture, a vast thrusting pile as red as Hamer Kirk, the Lothian seat of the Red Douglases—indeed some suggested that was how this branch of the family got its name, for its people were in truth no redder in hair or feature than the Black Douglases. No other fortalice in the land was quite like it, for it was really an enormous thirty-foot-high curtain-wall, topped by a wall-walk, cutting off its lofty triangular peninsula of cliff, with a massive gatehouse-keep in the centre and a tall tower at each end, the whole being defended from landward by water-filled moats and deep dry ditches, in series, which prevented even the most powerful cannon from being sited within range to do any damage. It required no defences on the seaward sides, so sheer were the precipices. From the end towers the great red-heart banners of Douglas flapped, while above the central keep flew the Earl's standard, quartering the arms of Angus and Douglas.

Impressed despite themselves, the Lindsays frowned at it all. They had been challenged by Douglas outposts long before they reached thus far, at Hamer and Scoughall and Auldhame, but Lord Lindsay's authoritative reaction had gained them passage without trouble. But at the final drawbridge before the arched pend through the basement of the massive central keep, they were held up for some time while, after demanding their business, the porter sent to discover whether they were to be admitted, scowling men-at-arms presenting a frieze of lances at them as though they were about to try to take the place by storm.

At length they were allowed in, although their escorts were curtly told to wait outside with the horses. They were led through the quite long vaulted passage beneath the great five-storeyed tower by a character dressed in the finery of a herald's tabard, with feathered bonnet, all emblazoned with the Douglas device, to an open space hardly to be described as a courtyard, for it was much larger than that. It was the flat cliff-top area enclosed by the tremendous barrier of masonry through which they had passed, part paved and part laid out in cropped grass as sports-ground for bowls, quoits and even archery, as well as a lady's pleasance with arbours, sundials, paths, shrubs and flowers, a strange place to find behind that frowning exterior. Most of it was surrounded by subsidiary outbuildings, chapel, domestic offices and accommodation, stabling and the like; but directly in front a gap had been left at the cliff's edge, providing an open view over the sea to the Bass and the distant Isle of May—although hoists and crane-like structures with ropes and pulleys and cranks indicated that it was not so much for the vista that the gap was there but for a raising and lowering device for men and goods, so that this all-but-impregnable establishment could be supplied and re-inforced by sea, a notable advantage. Their herald took them to a large well-shaft, with its own hoist, in the centre of the paved area, and there told them to wait.

The Lord Patrick snorted something about over-grown and blown puppies aping royal status, with their heralds and arrogant pretensions; but David was busy taking in his surroundings in detail and perceiving why Tantallon had never been successfully besieged, to date.

They were kept waiting for another considerable period, to the older man's wrath, before the herald returned to announce that the lord Earl would now see them. He conducted them up a straight stair in the thickness of the main curtain-walling—which provided some indication as to the width of the said masonry, since the stair itself was nearly four feet wide—and into an anteroom on the first floor of the central keep, to leave them once more and disappear beyond into a further chamber from which voices sounded. Again they had to wait, with two armed guards in the Douglas colours eyeing them at the connecting doorway. Lord Lindsay, something of an autocrat himself, inevitably stamped back and forth on the stone-flagged floor in unconcealed offence, spurs jingling.

At length the busy pursuivant reappeared, to usher them in, proclaiming in sonorous tones the Lord Lindsay of The Byres to see the most noble and puissant Earl of Angus, Lord of Douglas, Galloway, Nithsdale and Jed Forest, etcetera, whom God succour and assist. He did not mention David.

Lord Patrick stamped in, glaring. Four men lounged at ease around a table laden with flagons and beakers, drinking, and certainly giving no impression of being in council or doing serious business. Three were of later middle years, one much younger, in his late twenties.

"Ha—Lindsay!" the young man said. "So it is yourself. Have you come to see sense, then? Perceived that your refusal was unwise? Belatedly!"

"At Tantallon, so far, Angus, I have only perceived mummery and play-acting! If I had been looking for sense I would have gone elsewhere! To be kept waiting at your doors like packmen . . . !" Which was not how David would have wished to start the interview.

The Earl clenched his fists on that table-top. He was a handsome, fair-haired, hot-eyed man, well-built, richly if carelessly dressed. Undoubtedly he was a man to look twice at—but it was those eyes which made the greatest impression, of palest blue, staring, unblinking.

"Watch how you speak in Tantallon, sirrah!" he jerked. "You come un-announced. Like packmen! If you are not seeking sense, and you have not changed your mind over supporting me, what *do* you want of me, man?"

"Civility is all *I* seek—perhaps too much to expect from

Douglas! It is my friend here who has matters to put to you. Myself, I would have counselled him otherwise!"

"You would . . . ?" For the first time, as it seemed, Angus allowed himself to notice David, and then only briefly. He gave no sign of recognition, although he must have known him, having seen him often enough with the young King. "And what does *he* want?"

"My lord—I come from the Chancellor," David said. "The Archbishop. From St. Andrews. He sends greetings and seeks . . ."

"I addressed the Lord Lindsay—not you!" he was interrupted. "Speak only when you are spoken to, in this house. Well, Lindsay?"

The Lord Patrick stared. "Are you out of your mind, Angus?" he demanded. "Has association with Henry Tudor addled your wits to make-believe Tudor grandeur?"

The Earl half-rose from his seat, in a posture of menace. "If you wish to leave Tantallon a whole man, Lindsay, you will guard your ill tongue! While you still have *one* arm!"

"I lost the other, Angus, on Flodden-field, amongst better men than you! And where the previous Angus rode off the field before the battle started!" That was shrewd thrusting, but hardly fair, for although the fifth Earl, the notorious Bell-the-Cat, this man's grandfather, had indeed left the Scots army before the fighting began, out of disagreement over strategy with James the Fourth, not in fear, his eldest son, the Earl's father, had died there with his monarch.

David, exasperated beyond bearing by all this folly, turned to the other three who sat watching, listening. He knew them all, all Douglases, all uncles of Angus—Sir George Douglas of Pittendreich; Sir Archibald Douglas of Kilspindie, known as Graysteel, neighbour of The Byres and Garleton; and Master William Douglas, Prior of Coldinghame. It was to the last that he addressed himself.

"You, Master Prior—you are a churchman. I come from the Primate of Holy Church with a message. Is it not to be heard? Shall I return to the Archbishop and Chancellor and tell him . . ."

"Silence, fool! I told you—speak only when spoken to in my presence!" the Earl exclaimed. "Think you that coming from that fat slug Beaton commends you to me? If there is any worth in what he has to say to me, then let your good-father reveal it. I do not deal with underlings."

David drew a deep breath. At least the man had revealed that he knew who he was.

The Lord Patrick snorted. "The message is his, not mine. I scarce know the matter. I but brought him here. Would God I had not!"

"Aye—the first fair word you have spoken here, Lindsay!"

There was a cough from the eldest uncle, Pittendreich, who glanced at the Prior. That plumply smooth individual, presumably taking this as a sign to intervene, spoke up.

"Do you not think, Archie, that we should hear at least what the Archbishop has to say?" he suggested. "And since my lord of Lindsay appears not to know the details, it looks as though we must have it from this Lindsay of the Mount. Briefly, to be sure."

His two brothers grunted agreement.

Angus eyed them all from under down-bent brows for a little, silent.

"Better from *this* Chancellor, perhaps, than from the other!" the Prior added, significantly.

That dart found its mark. For the Queen-Mother, Angus's late and hated wife, had recently declared the Archbishop, in the King's name, to be no longer Chancellor, and appointed to the office her present lover, Henry Stewart of Methven—although she had no true authority to do either, the chancellorship being an appointment of the King-in-Parliament. The Earl, who could not be expected to love his successor in Margaret Tudor's bed, shrugged.

"Very well," he acceded. "Out with it."

David felt himself to be at his least eloquent and persuasive, his most terse, in these circumstances. Which was perhaps unfair towards Davie Beaton's mission.

"My lord Archbishop proposes a conference at St. Andrews," he announced jerkily. "He would call a parliament thereafter and wishes to ensure a favourable vote. He has learned that the Queen-Mother intends to smuggle King James out of the country, into England. This must be stopped. He believes that only a parliament can do it, take the necessary steps. And the Douglases, my lord, could much aid the vote in parliament."

"So-o-o! That is the way of it. Henry is to get James into his hands—is that it?"

David nodded.

"When?"

"That is not known. But the Chancellor calls for haste. He believes that the Queen-Mother is but waiting for a message from the Lord Dacre, the English Warden, to whom she wrote."

Angus looked at his uncles. "She fears us, then!"

"Or else she fears that Arran may turn against her! Or that Bastard of his." That was Graysteel, Sir Archibald of Kilspindie.

"Aye, perhaps. You have heard naught of such talk?"

"No."

"It is said that Arran resents Margaret making so much of Henry Stewart," Sir George of Pittendreich said.

"Dacre has been in the south, at London," the Prior pointed out. Having Coldinghameshire property on the borders of Northumberland, and being in league with the Homes, he was in a position to know such things. "He may still be."

"So Margaret waits," Angus said. "And Beaton looks to Douglas to do his work for him!"

"Say, my lord, that he recognises that together Douglas and the Church can sway parliament, and so save the King. Whereas alone, neither could, possibly."

"You think so? Perhaps Douglas should take the King out of Margaret's hands without troubling a parliament! And save him the more surely, that way."

"Since she has His Grace safe in Edinburgh Castle, my lord, it is scarcely likely. It would require a siege, bombardment by cannon. Against the King's royal person . . ."

The Earl glared at David angrily.

"What does the Archbishop suggest . . . in return for this Douglas service?" the Prior asked suavely.

"I know not. But that, perhaps, is what the conference is for!"

"Ah."

There was a silence around that table. It had not been proposed that the Lindsays should sit down, or partake of the wines.

"When?" Angus demanded abruptly.

"So soon as is possible. Since the Queen-Mother may act at any time."

"Why can Beaton not come here? Why should we go to St. Andrews?"

"The Archbishop is not young, and less than well. Also there is less danger for Douglas in travelling the country than for him, is there not?"

"By sea, Archie, we could be at St. Andrews in three hours," Pittendreich said.

David recognised that he had gained his objective.

"Tell Beaton that he had better have sufficient inducements for me, if I come!" Angus said grimly.

"Yes. When shall I tell him to look for you, my lord?"

"That remains to be seen. I do not discuss times and seasons with such as you, nor wait on the convenience of clerks in orders! Tell him so, likewise."

The Lord Patrick grinned. "When the clerk controls more riches than the rest of the realm put together, Angus, I think, will discover his convenience not so difficult!"

It was his turn to be ignored. "You have my permission to retire, Lindsay," the Earl said, but to David now.

"When do we start to name you Your Grace?" the older man mocked. "Come, David—we have had a sufficiency of play-acting for one day!" And without so much as an inclination of his grizzled head towards the Douglases, he turned for the door.

David hesitated, half-shrugged, bowed briefly, and followed him.

Surprisingly for so plump and comfortable a person, they found Prior William reaching the door before them. "I will see them out, Archie," he said, and waved them on.

The herald was waiting in the anteroom beyond, but the Prior gestured him aside. At the stair-foot, he paused.

"Give my lord Archbishop my duty and greetings," he said. "Tell him that I will do what I can, in my humble way. Give me three days, or four, and I think that I may promise that we will be at St. Andrews. A good day to you, Lindsay. And to you, my lord."

As the herald came to take them on to the porter's lodge and drawbridge, the Lord Patrick shook his head.

"An oily scoundrel that," he judged. "A snake, where Angus is but a boar! And greedy, I swear. Seeking a bishopric, no doubt!"

"Perhaps. But greed my be easier to deal with than arrogant pride, I think."

"Easier, man? That one will never be easy. Watch him! Remember how he won Coldinghame Priory—by having the

Homes slay the previous Prior and his monks in cold blood, he watching. The snake is more deadly than the boar—for one gives warning when he strikes and the other does not!"

They rode back westwards, thoughtful.

David called in at Garleton Castle to see his aging father and Mirren Livingstone his mistress, but did not stay long. He was back at Luffness Haven, to the waiting boat, by sundown.

2

David Lindsay certainly had not expected to be travelling back to the south shore of the Firth of Forth again so soon, even though in very different fashion. Again it was the persuasive Davie Beaton who had been responsible, convincing him that he ought to attend the session of parliament, purely as a spectator of course, partly because his advice might be useful, and partly as an opportunity to see his late charge and young friend, King James, impossible these days otherwise. Lindsay had once more been reluctant, but the other pressing—Beaton seemed to have taken it upon himself to try to rouse his namesake and former fellow-student out of his depths of depression.

So now, dressed in what passed for his best, he rode near the head of a glittering cavalcade westwards through the central Howe of Fife—for Archbishop Beaton hated the sea and refused to make the journey to Edinburgh by boat. In fact the Primate travelled very much at ease, lying in a handsome canopied litter, heraldically decorated, slung between two white horses, a gross, overweight, heavy-jowled man in his early sixties, almost purple of feature, with drooping eyelids above small, shrewd pig-like eyes, most splendidly garbed in ecclesiastical finery and decked with jewellery, even for the journey, Holy Church indicating temporal power to match the spiritual. Before and after rode at least one hundred of the archiepiscopal guard in mitred breastplates and liveries embroidered with the arms of the metropolitan see, and behind this personal escort, a colourful cavalcade of clerics, chaplains, confessors and officials; then a train of laden pack-horses burdened with gear, extra vestments, provisions, wines and candles, led by uniformed servitors, and finally another detachment of the guard. David, riding with his friend near the Primate's litter, considered it all a vulgar and unsuitable display, but the Lord Abbot of Arbroath—*in commendam*—declared otherwise, that it was a useful and salutary demonstration to all concerned of the fact that the Church was a potent and effective influence in the affairs of the realm, much needed in the present struggle for rule and government.

The conference at St. Andrews had duly taken place—if such it could be called, when it had been really only a bargaining session between Angus and the Archbishop, or more accurately between the latter's nephew and the former's uncle, Prior William Douglas, who between them had done most of the trading. Lindsay of course had not been present; but when young Beaton had come again to the Mount of Lindifferon, to persuade him to attend the parliament, he had given him some account of the proceedings, with typically humorous and scurrilous comments. Angus had hectored and threatened and insulted, but the fact that he was there at all indicated that he had judged the occasion worth while and therefore could be dealt with. There had been some hard bargaining nevertheless, and Prior William had proved himself an acute and wily opponent—whom Davie Beaton appeared to admire. He did not give details of the terms come to, but no doubt these would become evident in due course. Meantime, the parliament had been agreed to and, because of the necessity for haste, the normal forty days notice had been dispensed with. This would inevitably mean a low attendance, with lords and commissioners from the remoter areas of the country probably unable to make it in time; but it was calculated that the Douglas and Church representation would be apt to gain from that.

So, ten days later, here they were on the road.

With that horse-litter, and the clerical horsemen apt to be no pace-setters, progress was stately rather than speedy; but as Davie Beaton pointed out, the Queen-Mother was unlikely to try to smuggle her son off to England now, with a parliament arranged at which the young King was to be present, and hopefully a rallying-call for her supporters; and, moreover, with the Douglases alerted to the danger, keeping a night-and-day watch on any possible exits from Edinburgh's castle-rock. The Archbishop was prepared to face the mere mile-wide crossing of Forth at Queen Margaret's Ferry, where the great flat-bottomed barges could carry their many horses; but that demanded a journey, through Fife and Fothrif, of some thirty-five miles, and ten miles to Edinburgh on the other side. At their rate of progress, this would require an overnight halt, and the Primate was not the man to put up with scratch lodging in some small monkish hospice or ale-house. So it meant reaching his own princely Abbey of Dunfermline, the richest jewel in the metropolitan mitre—with Arbroath only in second place—even though it was those thirty-five miles from St. Andrews, a long journey for one day for the present travellers, even though the two Davids could have done twice that. If Davie Beaton, who could ride as hard as any, chafed at their unhurried pace, as did David Lindsay, he did not allow it to show.

Since the Archbishop slept for most of the way, his nephew was free to discuss with his friend—or more truly use him as a sounding-board in his calculations—how the parliament was likely to go. Even with Douglas support, they could by no means be sure of success. For the Douglases were hated as well as feared, and Arran's party was strong in the west. Much would depend on lesser factions, in especial the Stewarts. These were a somewhat divided lot, although all of them supported their Stewart monarch. But some, such as the Earl of Lennox, loathed Margaret Tudor, and others, like the Galloway branch, were apt to side with their Douglas neighbours. On the other hand, the main Lanarkshire and Renfrewshire stem, which included the Lords Avondale and Innermeath, were likely to support the Queen-Mother, since Henry Stewart of Methven, her present lover, was Avondale's son. All Davie Beaton's renowned artifice and eloquence was going to be required to win the day, Douglas or none.

It was evening before they reached Dunfermline and the comforts of its great abbey, in the splendid church of which so many of the King's ancestors were interred, including the hero-king Bruce himself. Because it had succeeded Iona as the place of royal sepulture, it had become so well-endowed with lands and riches over the centuries that it was now the wealthiest foundation in the land, and, coming as it did under the metropolitan see of St. Andrews, represented one of the Primate's greatest assets. It was understood that whoever was appointed its abbot passed on half of its vast revenues to the Archbishop; nevertheless there was never any difficulty in filling the position. If the present Abbot considered the invasion of nearly two hundred mouths to feed, with their beasts, an imposition, he was careful not to say so. He would come with them in the morning, for his was another mitred abbacy with a vote in parliament.

They made no early start next day, and, reinforced by the contingents of the Abbots of Lindores and Balmerino, both in Fife, made their way down to the narrows of the Firth of Forth at the Queen's Ferry. This was in fact one of the money-spinners of Dunfermline Abbey, run by that establishment ever since the days of St. Margaret, who had founded it over four centuries earlier. Now all other travellers were pushed aside—to the annoyance of certain lords, also heading for Edinburgh—while the major task of transporting the archiepiscopal following to the Lothian shore proceeded, a protracted business. Perceiving this, Davie Beaton urged his uncle to invite the Earl of Rothes and the Lord Glamis to accompany him across in the abbatical barge and to take wine with them in the hospice at the other side, as they waited—since it would be a pity to lose two votes out of mere injured pride.

It was a major company, therefore, which reached Edinburgh in the afternoon. The hilly city was already packed, seething with incomers, too large a proportion of whom appeared to be wearing the colours of Douglas, and behaving as though the capital belonged to them. Pushing slowly through the thronged narrow streets from the West Port, by the Grassmarket below the soaring castle-rock, to the Cowgate, they came to the Blackfriars Monastery, which was the Archbishop's Edinburgh headquarters—and which he had not dared to visit for long. Commodious as these quarters were, they were filled to overflowing by the new arrivals. The Prior thereof warned all that it would be unwise to venture out into the city streets after dusk, as the town was infested with roaming bands of Douglas and Hamilton supporters, based on Holyrood and the castle respectively, looking for trouble and not only with each other.

It made scarcely ideal conditions for a productive assembly to arrange the nation's affairs.

Of recent times parliaments had been apt to be held in the great church of the Holy Rood—largely because all too often the castle, with its Parliament Hall, was in the hands of one faction or another and barred against the rest. But on this occasion, with the Queen-Mother and her son therein, and she refusing to let King James be taken out, it had been agreed to hold the session there, however reluctantly, as giving advantage to Margaret's and Arran's parties, since it was essential for a true parliament, as distinct from a convention of the Estates, that the monarch should be present in person. It was not really anticipated that, at the last moment, the Queen-Mother would hold the citadel against them and refuse admittance, since that would be to proclaim to the nation that she feared that she had only minority support; but the possibility was always there, Davie Beaton admitted. What would happen if she did was hard to predict. Almost certainly outright civil war would follow.

* * *

Next noontide, David Lindsay sat in a corner, carefully chosen, of the great hammer-beam-roofed Parliament Hall of the capital's fortress, watching and waiting. So far, so good. There had been no attempt by the garrison to prevent ingress, although ranked men-at-arms, mainly wearing the Hamilton colours, lined the climbing route up from the gatehouse and drawbridge to this hall, glaring at all comers belligerently. But they had not done more than that—indeed the Douglases, thronging the tourney-ground approach to the castle, had been much more aggressive in challenging all who sought admittance, indicating that all who entered the citadel did so only with their permission, all unauthorised turned away out-of-hand. Lindsay undoubtedly would not have gained access had he not come with the Chancellor's party. Davie had found him this place to sit, on a stool in an alcove not far from the Chancellor's table and, in fact, directly across the dais from the throne. It was, Beaton said, where he would have sat himself, to be effectively near his uncle, had he not had to take his new place on the ecclesiastical benches, as Abbot of Arbroath.

The hall was by no means full, for it would hold hundreds—and there would be no hundreds attending this parliament. Indeed Davie calculated that there would be no more than sixty present entitled to vote—although of course there were many others: burgh representatives who were permitted to come to ensure that their chosen commissioners voted as their burgh councils had instructed, the eldest sons or heirs of lords of parliament, senior churchmen not in the mitred class, and other privileged spectators. But even of these there were a deal fewer than usual.

With the city bells below the castle-rock striking the hour of noon, a fanfare of trumpets from outside the hall stilled the chatter. All stood, eyes turned to the double doors which opened on to this dais area and which were now thrown wide.

The Lord Lyon King-of-Arms and his heralds entered, all splendid in their colourful tabards, to announce the royal summons and authority for this parliament. Then, preceded by pikemen in the royal livery, he ushered in the procession of state, consisting of those high officers of the realm who were not otherwise involved, or indeed not banished, imprisoned or afraid to appear—the Clerk-Register, the Dempster, the Lord Privy Seal, the Lord High Treasurer—none other than Margaret's paramour and would-be Chancellor, Henry Stewart—the Earl Marischal and the High Constable, the last with the sword of state. These were followed by the justiciars, two-by-two.

There was a pause and then another trumpeting, and two men appeared side-by-side but walking as far apart as the access would permit, each managing to turn a shoulder away from the other in mutual disesteem, but each bearing a purple cushion. That was the only point of resemblance, for one, the Earl of Angus, was young, handsome, upstanding and, oddly for the occasion and a summer's day, clad in half-armour and thigh-length riding-boots, as though garbed for the fray; and the other, the Earl of Arran, chief of the Hamiltons, Lord High Admiral and second person to the King, his cousin, elderly, stooping and over-dressed in velvets and cloth-of-gold. On Arran's cushion lay the sceptre and on Angus's the crown. Clearly hating each other, they marched into the hall and up to the Chancellor's table, where the Clerk-Register had already taken up his position, to deposit their symbols of sovereignty beside the sword of state. They then moved down to the foremost benches of the assembly, there to sit together, but still contriving not to see each other.

Another pause and trumpet-blast and James Beaton came in,

the President of the High Court of Parliament, Chancellor of the Realm, a figure to catch and hold all eyes, his grossness hidden under the most magnificent and costly robes that even an archbishop might aspire to, alb, cope, pallium and stole, all so encrusted with jewels and gold as to make his every movement a blazing scintillation, Holy Church intent on preaching one of its more telling lessons. Archiepiscopal staff in one hand and Chancellor's gavel in the other, he paced his ponderous way to the table, there to remain, standing.

Sir Thomas Clephane, the Lord Lyon, bowing, retraced his steps to the door and out. All waited, on their feet.

The trumpeters this time excelled themselves in a flourish of brassy sound which seemed to shake the ancient stonework. There was a clanking of armour and grounding of pikes outside, but a distinct interval elapsed before Lyon reappeared, his baton upraised, pacing slowly now. Just within the hall he halted, and gazing about him, exclaimed with practised grandiloquence:

"James, fifth of his name, by God's grace, High King of Scots, Duke of Rothesay and Lord of the Isles, our most high and mighty prince and gracious sovereign-lord!"

It is to be feared that the sequel to this stirring announcement was something of an anticlimax, for neither the boy nor the woman who now appeared were such as to especially engage the attention in other circumstances. James, now thirteen, was good-looking enough, well-built for his years, and with a fine head of red hair; but he entered with that head down, and scowling, reluctance in every line of him; and he was dressed in nondescript, not to say outworn, clothing, probably the least fine in all that hall. And his mother, close behind, was neither beautiful nor elegant. Now aged thirty-four, Margaret Tudor looked older, heavily made, hair greying prematurely, her features puffy, pasty—although those close enough to perceive it would recognise spirit in her dull-glowing dark eyes, indicating that here was a woman who could have fierce emotions, who could hate with a smouldering intensity and whose rages were as notorious as her lasciviousness. David Lindsay, as she came near, from his alcove wondered anew that one so, to him, physically unsavoury, could be so concerned with her own body and its functions. Her brother, Henry the Eighth, was similarly gross—but at least he was said to have a certain animal attractiveness. Margaret, who had come to Scotland at the age of thirteen as bride for the dashing and gallant James the Fourth, was undoubtedly one of the Auld Enemy England's most effective disservices to the northern kingdom.

Behind the pair, unlooked-for, unsuitable and causing gasps of offence from the deep-bowing assembly, clanked in a file of perhaps a score of armed men in red livery, their steel breastplates painted with the five-lobed flower device of the Tudor Rose, part of the bodyguard of two hundred sent north by the King of England a month or two before, allegedly for his nephew's protection, a gesture much resented by the Scots.

James, reluctant as he obviously had been, once he was into the hall made for his place, the throne at the rear of the daïs, at more speed than dignity, his mother's barked command to slow down ignored. As a consequence she also had to hurry, to keep up, and the men-at-arms behind likewise, making an unusual royal entry. At the handsome gold-painted chair of state, with its rampant lions as finials, set on its own plinth, the boy sat down without ceremony. Panting a little, and frowning as darkly as her son, the Queen-Mother came up, to pause before seating herself on a chair placed beside and a little below the throne. The clanking escort shuffled to range themselves in a long line behind, facing the assembly.

After a moment or two of silence, all sat who had seats.

The Chancellor rose again, bowed to the throne and raising a beringed hand, uttered a prayer for the proceedings, remarkable in its brevity. He then declared the King-in-Parliament to be duly in session and called upon the Clerk-Register to read out the names of the Lords of the Articles appointed by the last parliament, a sort of executive committee charged with carrying out the broad decisions of each assembly, and whose responsibilities were now ended. It was noticeable that of the ten names given, five were not present today.

Hardly had the Clerk-Register finished before the Queen-Mother was on her feet. "My lord Chancellor, my lords and barons," she said in her clipped English voice which twenty-one years of residence in Scotland had not altered, ignoring the burgesses, "I declare that this parliament is untimely and unnecessary. I do regret, as does His Grace, the inconvenience and cost to which you have all been put, to attend it. The Lords Articular, with my guidance, were well able to conduct the affairs of His Grace's realm in the meantime, there having been no disaster or great event to warrant another parliament. I therefore move that the Lords Articular, those who have done their duty, be reappointed forthwith, and so save much unnecessary talk and labour here."

She sat down amidst a great outcry and stir of excitement. Never had the gauntlet been thrown down so swiftly and unexpectedly, in a trial of strength which could end the proceedings before they were begun.

The Chancellor banged his gavel on the table, jowls wobbling in indignation and outrage, but ignoring him, the Earl of Arran rose.

"I support the Queen's Grace," he exclaimed. "I call a vote."

Before he was finished, Angus, at his side, was on his feet. "My lord Chancellor," he cried, "with all respect for my late consort, I move the contrary. Douglas has not come here for such device. We have come to right the realm's business." No swords other than the sword of state were permitted within the Parliament Hall, but the Earl managed to beat his sheathed dagger metallically against his plate-armour as he sat down.

The Archbishop continued to bang his gavel, almost as though he did not know what else to do, his quandary most evident to all who knew the rules. As President of the session, procedure was difficult, to say the least. The fact was, Margaret Tudor had no authority to speak in that parliament at all. She was not the monarch, nor a lord of parliament, nor a commissioner of shire or burgh and certainly not a representative of the Church. So her speech and motion were *ultra vires*. But Arran, an earl, had seconded it and Angus, another, had made a contrary motion, both within their right. The situation was as complicated as it was embarrassing.

Strangely, relief came for the Chancellor from an unlikely source. It was at this difficult moment that King James, glowering around sulkily, suddenly caught sight of David Lindsay sitting in his corner. His expression transformed, he promptly leapt to his feet.

"Davie! Davie Lindsay!" he shouted gladly, and ignoring his mother's restraining hand, ran across the dais to the alcove and his former procurator and usher.

There was consternation in Parliament Hall.

David's mind became a battlefield of emotions, alarm, uncertainty and gladness that his one-time charge should so clearly delight in his presence. But—how to cope with the situation?

The boy hurled himself bodily upon his friend in a gabble of incoherent greetings and affection, and involuntarily the man's arms encircled his monarch's eager young person, however improper and unsuitable that might be. It was the best part of a year since they had been rudely parted, at Stirling Castle, and David sent packing by the Queen-Mother, James in tears. Nothing could have been more eloquent of the boy-king's misery and hatred for those months than his attitude shown hitherto this day compared with the joy displayed now before all.

But as the youngster clung and laughed and shook his friend in an excess of feeling, David sought desperately for ability to deal with the situation. And not only David; all present with any authority for the parliament were in a like quandary. Never had the like been seen, or any precedent established for dealing with it. James Stewart might be a newly-thirteen-year-old boy behaving in outrageous fashion on a great state occasion, but he was the sovereign-lord of all there, in theory the supreme authority in the parliament as in the realm. No-one was in a position to order him back to his place so that proceedings might be resumed, for although the Chancellor chaired the assembly, the monarch in effect presided over all.

There was an agitated interlude, with the hall loud in exclamation and talk. Margaret Tudor was on her feet, glaring. Archbishop Beaton was twisting his gavel round and round in his uncertainty. The Earl of Arran even turned to stare at his neighbour, who was grinning at it all. One man, however, did more than gaze. The Abbot of Arbroath left his place amongst the clerics to step up on to the dais-platform, to his uncle's side, there to whisper urgently.

The Queen-Mother it was who acted first. Striding out, she came for her son, hand out imperiously.

James, feeling his friend stiffen, turned. Seeing his mother there, he too held out a hand, but palm towards her, in the most eloquent thrusting-away gesture.

"No!" he shouted. "No! Go away. Davie—do not let her . . . !"

That made the situation worse than ever. The previous year Margaret and Arran had, on the Duke of Albany's return to France in resignation, managed to have the regency declared at an end and the King old enough to rule personally as well as reign—they in fact ruling in his name. Nevertheless, James was nominally supreme ruler of his kingdom from that day, and his royal command unchallengeable—even if he would scarcely realise it. Whether the Queen-Mother accepted this momentarily, or was merely shaken by this public exhibition of her son's hatred for her, she faltered.

No-one else was in a position to intervene. Henry the Eighth's English guards looked on helplessly.

Margaret Tudor could not just stand there, in mid-dais. She had to either go forward or back to her seat. "James," she said loudly, "come back to your throne. I, I beg of you." For that woman, that last must have taken a deal of saying.

"No!" her son answered. "Go away."

In the ensuing silence, with all at a loss what to do now, Davie Beaton made a gesture of his hand towards Lindsay and the latter gave a single nod of the head. It had come to him that he alone in all that gathering might solve this problem, and must try to, for everyone's sake, not least that of the boy who still clutched his arm. He drew a deep breath.

"Sire," he said, low-voiced, "I think that you should go back to your place. I will come with you, if you wish. Until you do, this parliament cannot go on. And it should, for your kingdom's sake. The sooner it resumes, the sooner it will be over. Go back to your throne, Sire."

"*You* will come, Davie? You will stay with me?"

"Yes. I will stand behind you. As I have done before."

"Very well. But you must not leave me. Where have you been, Davie, all this time?"

"At my house in Fife, Highness. Come . . ."

Hand-in-hand they crossed the dais, James deliberately looking away from his mother as he passed her. He sat on the throne again, and David stood beside it, close but a little behind on the left, where the boy could, and did, pat his arm. So much for his discreet attendance as a spectator in a corner.

The Queen-Mother returned to her seat, set-faced. Sighs of relief prevailed around. Davie Beaton moved back to his own place, in his splendid prelatical robes for the first time.

Whatever else might result from this incident, it had had more than one effect on the Chancellor who, possibly with his nephew's advice, appeared to have gathered his wits about him in the interim. Bowing elaborately to the throne, he banged his gavel.

"With His Grace's royal permission, we will resume," he announced. "A motion was before the parliament regarding the Lords of the Articles. But I have to rule this out-of-order, as the proposal was not made by a commissioner. I also rule that the appointment of Lords Articular is always made at the *end* of a session, not the beginning, when the decisions which they have to implement are known. It is within my authority to decide. The order of business is the Chancellor's responsibility. Therefore I so rule. We shall now proceed with the agenda. The first matter I have down for consideration is the necessary extension of the panning of salt. The trade to Muscovy and other parts in salted fish demands not only an increase in salt-making but a spreading of manufacture over a wider area of the kingdom. Certain burghs, which have coals nearby, must be encouraged to build salt-pans and take up such manufacture. Holy Church has long taken the lead in this matter, but the realm's trade demands more general development. I understand that the royal burgh of Inverkeithing has proposals?"

If the Chancellor believed that Margaret Tudor had been quelled, and that the introduction of a safe and non-controversial subject such as this would get the session established in orderly and businesslike fashion after a deplorable start, he was to be disappointed. The Queen-Mother was not so easily put down. Before the Archbishop had finished speaking she was on her feet again.

"My lords," she said strongly, "it may suit churchmen and traders to discuss this matter of salt and fish before the vital affairs of the kingdom, but I swear that this is not why most of your lordships have come here today! First things first, I say! And since the conducting of the business of this parliament, since it *has* been called, however unnecessarily, is important, as is the managing of the realm's affairs thereafter, from day to day, I say that the assembly should appoint, as is its right, a new Chancellor, one in better health and fitness of mind, the present cleric being of sere age and having over-long borne the burden of office. He deserves relief! I propose for the chancellorship the present Lord High Treasurer."

At first that bombshell was greeted with an astonished hush. Then uproar broke out, exclamation and shouting. Nor was it all indignation. There was debate, glee—for the Archbishop was not everyone's favourite—even admiration for the sheer effrontery of the Englishwoman in thus making such telling recovery from her humiliation at the hands of her son.

The Chancellor gobbled and blinked, as though scarcely able to believe his ears. He had indeed held the great office of chief minister of the realm for long years, since Flodden indeed, so that he had come to look on it as his own, almost as by divine right, as indeed did others. When he recovered his voice sufficiently to enunciate, however chokingly, he could only fall back on his previous contention.

"Madame," he got out, "I, I must remind you that you have no authority here to propose anything such. Nor indeed even to speak in this parliament, save by my permission. Only members of the Three Estates, lords of parliament, spiritual and temporal, and commissioners of shires and burghs may propose a motion. I must again rule you out-of-order, therefore."

"Then I, my lord Chancellor, move the same instead!" That was the Lord Avondale, Henry Stewart's father, from the lords' benches.

"And I second," came from the Lord Innermeath, his kinsman.

There was pandemonium in the hall, as everywhere men objected, disputed or acclaimed. This cut across all faction-siding and alignments, a totally unexpected issue, irrelevant to most there. Even Angus and Arran for once need not be on opposite sides, Angus because he was against anything his former wife might propose, Arran because he resented her infatuation with and promotion of the upstart Stewart, nine years her junior. Yet the Stewart faction could be strong, if it could be united, which it seldom was; and James Beaton had his enemies.

That man glowered around the assembly heavily. He could not reject the motion, duly moved and seconded by lords entitled to vote. "Any contrary motion?" he demanded.

"I move the contrary," Angus declared briefly.

Arran was half-way to his feet to second, and then just could not bring himself to seem to support his hated rival.

In the pause, Master William Douglas, no longer just Prior of Coldinghame but mitred Abbot of Holyrood with a vote in parliament, part of the price the Archbishop had had to pay at the St. Andrews conference, was first of half-a-dozen Douglases to second his nephew.

Shrugging massive shoulders, the Chancellor nodded to the Clerk-Register, whose duty it was to supervise the counting of votes.

It made an unlikely subject for the first vote of the day, one which would give no true indication as to the way major decisions would go thereafter. Admittedly no Douglases or their close supporters were likely to vote against Angus's counter-motion; but otherwise the result was unpredictable, all depending on how many found Henry Stewart intolerable and how many disliked the Archbishop sufficiently, who had never sought popularity.

On this first vote, the procedure was formal and lengthy, each voter being named and answering individually, a system normally helpful for the humbler and undecided, since the more important came first and so gave an indication as to relative strengths and wise alignments—which was why this first vote was important. The Estate of Holy Church came first, and since the Chancellor himself had to vote last of all, the question was put to the second most important prelate, Gavin Dunbar, Archbishop of Glasgow, the former tutor to the King, who had in fact succeeded Beaton on his promotion to St. Andrews.

"I abstain," that man said levelly, "since I conceive it unsuitable that one archbishop should seem to uphold another in secular office."

There were gasps at this, and immediate conjecture as to whether this lead would be followed by other clerics, the Chancellor and Primate shooting venomous glances at his colleague, with whom he had never got on.

Perhaps fortunately for his cause, the next name to be read out was the previous voter's uncle, of the same name, Gavin Dunbar, Bishop of Aberdeen. He was sound in his Primate's support, and voted accordingly.

Thereafter, although certain of the churchmen abstained, most voted for the amendment, only one against, the Abbot of Paisley, who was a brother of Arran. The lords temporal divided in no recognisable pattern on this curious issue, save that the Stewarts were solid in favour of the motion except, oddly, for their most senior representative, the Earl of Lennox, who abstained. The commissioners of shires and burghs, who unless themselves involved, usually tended to follow the lead of their local magnates, now did just that. The motion was defeated by twenty-three to fifteen, with almost a score abstaining.

The Chancellor looked relieved, but, glancing over to his nephew, David Lindsay saw that Davie seemed less so. This had been no true test of strengths. The real challenge was yet to come.

Clearly Angus also recognised this, and, hardly waiting for the Clerk-Register to finish, was on his feet.

"Before the Chancellor gets back to his salted fish," he announced grimly, "I too say first things first! We are here for one main purpose, on which all hangs—the weal and safety of the King's Grace and therefore the realm's also. Both have been much endangered. There has even been word of His Grace being taken to England." And he stared balefully at his late wife. "The present situation of the King is unsuitable and should be changed—forthwith. Douglas will take better care of the King!" Abruptly he sat down.

All around, men stared at each other, unsure, alarmed. There was no doubt as to what this meant—the Douglases were for taking over the rule of the land if they could, grabbing the monarch. But how? That had sounded like a naked threat. No motion had been proposed. What now?

The Chancellor looked as uncertain as most others as to how to proceed after this flinging down of the gauntlet.

Two people there were in no doubts, the Queen-Mother and Davie Beaton. As the former, white with fury, stabbed a finger towards the Earl of Arran in clearest command for him to rise and rend her late spouse, the Abbot of Arbroath was on his feet, to seek to repair and regularise the situation well before the not-very-effective Lord High Admiral could move into any sort of action.

"My lord Chancellor," he said in clear but modest, almost diffident tones, as though in awe of the company he kept, "I rise reluctantly to speak, well aware of my inexperience and lack of standing in this my first parliament in which I have had a vote. But I beg all to bear with me, for I yield to none in my love for our liege-lord James, whom God defend, and my concern for this my native land—I, who have sought to serve it, and His Grace, these last years, to my best if humble abilities, as the realm's ambassador to France."

The company stirred uncomfortably. It was not used to this sort of embarrassing talk about love and inexperience and humble abilities, from a whey-faced young man almost beautiful enough to be a woman. It might be how they did things in France, but in Scotland its legislators were apt to speak more through clenched teeth and with clenched fists.

As though aware of this reaction, Davie Beaton changed all, with a remark in the same mild and deferential voice, almost as an aside, as though it had just occurred to him.

"And speaking of France, Your Grace, my lords and friends all, I think that you may not have heard—since I only received the news this morning from France—that the King of France has been defeated at Pavia in Italy, and is now captured and in the Emperor's hands. Which, as you will perceive, may well alter much on the stage of our Christendom! I therefore . . ."

His voice was drowned in the clamour of less nicely modulated tongues, as everywhere men exclaimed, agog. For this news did change the entire international prospect, with Scotland bound to feel the effects in a major way, much more closely than the misfortunes of a foreign monarch might seem to imply. Because of the Auld Alliance, the mutual defence treaty, centuries old, between Scotland and France, whereby England could be threatened on its northern and southern flanks if she attacked one or the other, the French dimension was vital for the northern kingdom. Moreover, the balance of power in Europe was maintained largely through the relative positions of the Empire, Spain, the Vatican, France and England, with ever-changing affiliations, to keep any from becoming too powerful. So a weakened France, and her King a prisoner, was bound to change Henry of England's present stance. He had recently been pro-Empire and pro-Vatican, to help keep France in her place; but now, with an imperial victory, and Spain linked dynastically to the Emperor, France would be no danger—whereas the others would. And if Henry came to terms with France, however temporarily, he would have no fears for his southern flank and could turn his aggressive attentions against Scotland with impunity. It had all happened before and all knew the possible consequences.

Having thus exploded, however moderately, his own bombshell and thereby changed the atmosphere in the hall, not least towards himself and his position, Davie Beaton went on as the hubbub died down.

"So, my lord Chancellor, I say that it behoves this realm to take all necessary steps for the defence of its borders and the protection of its sovereign-lord King James. With all respect towards the King of England's royal sister," and he bowed towards that lady, "I submit that King James requires more strong hands for his safety than any woman's can be, however kindly and gentle." If the speaker's references to a gracious kindly, gentle woman were in profoundest mockery towards Margaret Tudor, neither by intonation nor expression did he give the slightest sign of it. "Accordingly, I say that parliament itself, the supreme authority of this realm, under the King himself, should take His Grace's royal person into its own good keeping, for his security. Since, to be sure, a parliament cannot, by its nature, remain permanently in session, nor itself cherish the King from day to day, I propose that it chooses four of its number, of high repute, to be the royal protectors, in turn. Perhaps for three months each, sharing the burden and privilege each year, in the name of the Three Estates of the Realm. My lord Chancellor, with your permission, I so move." He sat down.

There was no doubt as to the impression he had made now, how he had altered the entire temper of the meeting by his news, his skill and eloquence, and his pointing to a seemingly decent way out of the dilemma facing them all. The unctuous voice of William, Abbot of Holyrood, emphasised acceptability by Douglas at least.

"I have pleasure in seconding the motion of my young friend, *in commendam*, of Arbroath."

Arran rose, belatedly. "My lord Chancellor, I move rejection of this motion, this quite unnecessary motion," he declared. "His Grace is well cared for and protected as it is, here in this strong fortress. It is not only his royal mother who tends and cherishes him. *I* do, his Admiral and cousin, second person in this realm. And I have no lack of men to aid me in it! King James requires no change in his care. From Douglas, not long come from England, or other!"

There was something like a cheer for that—and it was not often that lack-lustre individual drew cheers.

"I second rejection," Sir James Hamilton of Finnart, known generally as the Bastard of Arran, the Earl's illegitimate son, called strongly. "When the King requires Douglas protection, things have reached a pretty pass in Scotland!"

As growls and hoots, cheers and counter-cheers filled the hall, Davie Beaton was on his feet again.

"My lord Chancellor, Your Grace, I crave your indulgence, and that of all here," he said earnestly. "Perhaps I did not make myself clear? In which case I tender my apologies. You must put the fault down to my lack of experience in parliamentary speaking. My motion was not that His Grace should be put into the keeping of any one house or party, but that parliament itself should accept the responsibility for his royal care, and appoint its own four guardians."

If that were an urgent attempt to avoid the house having to vote baldly for or against Douglas, it was not to be the last word, for Angus claimed that. Not bothering to rise, but clashing dirk-hilt against his gold-engraved steel breastplate, to draw adequate attention, he barked:

"Douglas has power to protect the King. Greater power, I'd mind all, than any other in this land! And how well does Hamilton presently cherish His Grace?" He jabbed out that dirk towards the rank of impassive English guards standing behind the throne. "Are *those* Hamiltons? Has Hamilton adopted the Tudor Rose as his emblem now? There are two hundred of these in this castle—Henry's men. *They* hold the King! Who votes for that? Vote, I say! And no more talk."

The Chancellor, glancing towards his nephew, shrugged. "Vote, then," he called, flat-voiced. "The amendment first." And he nodded to the Clerk-Register.

This time it was by show of hands. Angus promptly rose to his feet, and turning his back on monarch and Chancellor, stood staring at the company, clearly to note well who dared to vote against Douglas. After a moment or two, Arran did likewise, although he bowed to the throne before turning.

Most hands were slow to go up. The Bastard of Arran's was the first, Archbishop Dunbar's the second, the Abbot of Paisley's the third. Then the Stewart lords, again excepting Lennox. Encouraged by these, the hands of others rose, notably the Earls of Glencairn and Cassillis, west country neighbours of Hamilton, the Earl of Moray and the Lords Maxwell and Ruthven. Lesser men then began to risk a decision. Presently, David Lindsay, at the King's side, was able to count twenty-six hands upraised, three more than the winning total of the previous vote.

There was a tense silence now in that hall, as all perceived how close a thing this was going to be.

"All finished?" the Clerk-Register intoned. "I declare twenty-six against the motion."

"*For* the motion, vote," the Chancellor said.

There was little delay this time, as hands shot up. Assessing, Lindsay knew a thick sensation in his throat. One or two, he noted, had still not voted, the Earl of Lennox and his own father-in-law the Lord Lindsay amongst them. Counting and counting again, he made it exactly twenty-six again, the same as the counter-motion.

As everyone else reached the same conclusion there was uproar, men on their feet, voices raised, fists shaken.

When he could gain approximate silence, the Clerk-Register turned to the Chancellor. "My lord Archbishop of St. Andrews?" he asked, clearing his throat. "Do you vote?"

"I do. I vote for the motion."

If the noise had been vehement before, it was redoubled now.

David Lindsay let his own breath out as he perceived Beaton's brief expression of triumph, quickly replaced by one of more moderate satisfaction. He had won, thanks to his uncle.

"I declare the motion carried." The Clerk-Register had to shout, but probably few heard him. Not that it mattered. Scotland's course had been changed, for good or ill, by that one vote.

Half-a-dozen Douglases rose to speak, but when they saw Angus himself rise, they sat down. Their chief was brief, and definite as always.

"As well this parliament has chosen rightly," he said, nodding significantly. "As well, I say! If I mind aright, the motion said that four guardians should be appointed. These must be of the highest rank and fit for the task. Four earls, then. I nominate, besides myself, my lord of Erroll, the High Constable; my lord of Lennox, and . . ." he turned to his nearest neighbour and bowed, mockingly, "my lord of Arran, the Admiral!"

Swift seizing of the initiative as this was, none could deny that it was shrewd also, indicating that Angus was not all mailed fist and bluster. For these names, on the face of it, were suitable, fair, such as most present could vote for, covering the main factions, Stewart as well as Douglas and Hamilton. The hereditary High Constable, Erroll, chief of the Hays, was in a different category, but senior of the high officers of state, a young man who had recently married the daughter of Lennox. If four were to be the number chosen, it would be difficult to fault these, even though men wondered at Angus's unprejudiced choice.

There was a chorus of seconding.

The Chancellor, recognising the general acceptance, announced that, assuming these lords were willing to accept the duty and responsibility, he saw no reason to seek alternative names and to vote therefor. With parliament's agreement, then, he would nominate the Earls of Angus, Arran, Lennox and Erroll as responsible for His Grace's royal security. In sequence.

There was no contrary reaction, only Angus himself commenting.

"Since the motion was mine, I will accept the first such responsibility!" he observed, again significantly.

For moments there was a sort of general hush, as the assembly considered something about the way that was said.

King James turned to look up at David Lindsay. "I do not like that man!" he said—and in the quiet, most must have heard him.

The Chancellor coughed. "On the matter of the salt . . ." he began, and was interrupted.

"A plague on your salted fish!" Angus cried, now firmly in command. "The Council can deal with siclike merchandise! Douglas did not come here to bicker about salt!" Clearly the Earl's diplomatic interlude was over. "We have settled our day's business. Let us have done."

"My lord Chancellor—the Lords of the Articles . . ." someone called.

"None are required!" That was Angus again.

"My lord!" the Archbishop protested. "This parliament is presided over by His Grace and myself. I . . ."

But it was too late. The Douglas now had the bit between his teeth, and was already on his feet. Ignoring the Chancellor and all others, he strode forward, up on to the dais and straight to the throne. With the sketchiest of bows, he held out his hand.

"Come, Sire," he said, commanded.

The gathering watched, dumbfounded.

James rose from his gilded chair, but not to take that outstretched hand. He shrank back, shaking his red head. He turned to clutch David Lindsay.

The Queen-Mother, too, was on her feet now. "How dare you!" she got out.

"I dare much, anything, in the service of . . . our liege-lord!" Angus answered, with a derisive bow so elaborate as to be almost a genuflection. He looked past her, to the row of Tudor guards. "Out!" he snapped, with a flick of his hand, still holding that dirk, to reinforce his scornful order.

"Fool!" his ex-wife exclaimed. "There are ten score more waiting outside this hall! Have you lost such few wits as you ever had?"

The Earl grinned. "Lady—while this parliament has been sitting, my Douglases have been entering the castle by ten times your ten score! For His Grace's better security! There is some value in talk, perhaps—it gives time for the more active to act!" He raised his voice. "All here will now do as I say—parliament having kindly granted me that authority! *You* may go. Go to your Linlithgow—or to your royal brother in England, if you wish. But send *these* back to him, forthwith, for King James has no further use for them." He turned. "You, boy—come with me. We go to Holyrood. Away from this ill prison on its cold rock, so bad for Your Grace's good health, with its foul airs rising from the Nor' Loch! You, Lindsay, had better come with him, since he seems to esteem you. You will see that he behaves suitably—as you value your skin! Come, both of you." And without so much as a glance at any other, he strode for the dais doorway, and out.

Lindsay looked from James to his mother, to the Chancellor, and got no help from them, or any other. Was there any point in refusing? Would anything such not merely cause more distress for the King? It was utterly deplorable, shameful—but Angus appeared to hold all the cards and everybody there saw it, even the English guards, who were now milling around looking unhappy. Then, with his young charge demanding of him, "What now?" he found the scarlet-robed figure of Davie Beaton at his side.

"Your Grace," that man said, hurriedly for him. "David—better go. No choice. Angus will have it this way, meantime. But—there may be advantage in it, too. If he keeps you with His Grace at Holyrood, you could learn much of use, be of great help hereafter, within Angus's household. I will find a way to reach you. Go now—before there is trouble. Your Grace." Bowing, he hastened over to his uncle.

Lindsay, expressionless, put an arm around the boy's shoulders. "Come, Sire," he said. "I will stay with you."

Without a glance at his mother, James Stewart went with his friend.

3

The man and boy climbed steadily, deep-breathing both, close together, picking their way with practised eyes up the steep grassy slope, avoiding the outcropping rocks, the slippery wet patches and the prickly gorse-bushes, while Holyrood and the burgh of the Canongate and all Edinburgh, hilly as itself was, dwindled and sank below them. But as well as watching where they put their feet their glances were apt to range somewhat further afield too, if not so far as the spread of the city, planning not only the line of their further ascent but picking out hollows, bluffs, dead ground, features of the hill which could hide them in their upwards progress and so confuse the half-dozen horsemen who dotted the slopes below and on their flanks. It was a sort of game that these two played most days, temporarily to lose and alarm the Douglas guards who so assiduously dogged their steps, ordered never to let them out of their sight. These, being mounted men and no hill-climbers, had to take different routes up Arthur's Seat, Edinburgh's main mountain which reared over eight hundred feet above the Abbey, and which, with its surroundings, constituted a royal hunting-park. It gave the climbing pair a certain satisfaction the more they could agitate and upset their inevitable escort, even though they could never elude them entirely. The ascent of a bare, conical-shaped hill precluded any ultimate escape from horsemen.

Most days that summer David and James climbed Arthur's

Seat, from the Abbey at its foot. It was something to do, a kind of challenge, both the mountain and the confounding of the guards, something they could pit their wits and energies against, confined prisoners in all but name as they were. Lindsay had always been a man for action, physical activity, fretting at the constrictions of fortress life when he had been the young monarch's procurator in Edinburgh and Stirling Castles; and latterly at the Mount of Lindifferon, seeking to hammer down the ever-rearing sense of loss of his Kate by sheer, unremitting toil. And James, a growing boy, strongly-built and burgeoning now into youth, as good as a captive all his days, ever sought bodily freedom, any kind of freedom. He was permitted to go riding, even hawking occasionally, and hunting in this his own great royal park, but always with that armed escort of Douglas guards—which ruined all. Only in climbing this mighty hill could he escape their close proximity for a little and gain a momentary illusion of freedom.

It was six weeks since the parliament, six weeks of constraint and surveillance and ordering for both of them. David was kept with the King all the time, slept in the same room and, with his master's degree from St. Andrews University, acted as tutor as well as attendant and companion. They were not ill-treated, so long as they did what they were told, but any resistance or display of independence was dealt with forcefully, the young monarch purely a hostage, an asset to be exploited for its nominal authority, Lindsay a useful servant whose duty was to ensure maximum co-operation. Angus himself was apt to hector them when he deigned to acknowledge their existence; but fortunately Angus was seldom at Holyrood, ever ranging the land he now ruled, putting down any signs of opposition, wielding that mailed fist. His uncle, the Abbot William, was their real captor, a much cleverer man than the Earl and a deal less abrasive to cope with—although by no means to be underestimated as a menace on that account, for he was quite as unscrupulous as his nephew, only more subtle and superficially amiable about it. He was a man unhesitatingly prepared to commit any act—indeed multiple murder, as he had already demonstrated at Coldinghame—to further his ambitions and gain his ends.

In these weeks the Douglases had ruthlessly transformed the governance of Scotland to their own liking—all in the name of James, High King of Scots. Practically every major office of state was now held by one of them, or their nominees. Henry Stewart was dismissed as Lord High Treasurer, and Graysteel, Douglas of Kilspindie appointed in his place, which gave Angus control of the Exchequer, depleted as it was by Margaret's extravagances. Abbot William himself was Lord Privy Seal. Their brother, Pittendreich, was Master of the Household. Douglas of Parkhead was Captain of the Guard, and Master of the Wine-Cellar, Douglas of Drumlanrig was Master of the Larder—positions of more power than their titles suggested. The judiciary, the sheriffdoms, the keeperships of the royal castles, the controllerships of customs and taxation, and naturally the armed forces, were all in the hands of their people. Angus appointed himself, amongst other things, Chief Warden of the Marches, which ensured him personal command of the vital Borders area. The Privy Council had been purged and reconstructed, so that men who could scarcely be got rid of without major armed challenge, such as Arran, the Earl of Argyll, the Campbell chief, Erroll the Constable and the Lord Lindsay, David's father-in-law, could always be voted down with ease. The Chancellor, or chief minister of the realm, was still James Beaton, but he was little heard of and Angus took all the decisions. Scotland was in fact governed from Tantallon Castle now.

The climbers had surmounted the major northern shoulder of the hill and had to circle the corrie at the head of the central probing valley, known as the Hunter's Bog, when James, keen-eyed, scanning the positions of the scattered horsemen now coming into view, noted something else, three riders coming cantering up the slantwise floor of the valley itself, from the lower ground of St. Margaret's Loch. These three looked different from the others, riding purposefully and close together, the central one even at half-a-mile's range seen to be clad in vivid red.

"See, Davie—strangers," the boy said.

Lindsay paused, staring. "Aye. So-o-o! And who do we know who wears scarlet? And only the one, James?" When they were alone, titles of Sire, Grace and Highness were dispensed with.

"Davie Beaton—who brought me my papingo." On a visit from France, years before, Beaton had given the child-king a present of a parrot, which the boy still cherished.

"The same. Now what, say you? We will wait, I think."

"He comes to us?"

"Who else? Up here?"

Their waiting there at the head of the corrie allowed their guards to reach them before the newcomers, suspicious at this change from their usual eluding tactics. The Douglas men sat their beasts a little way off, and were ignored.

The three others, superbly mounted, came pounding up, Davie Beaton sure enough, with two armed attendants wearing the mitred emblems of the archdiocese of St. Andrews on their chests. A splendid figure in his scarlet travelling-clothes, the Abbot of Arbroath jumped down from the saddle, to bow low before the King.

"Your Grace's most devoted subject!" he greeted. And to Lindsay, "Lord, David—you are a hard man to reach! To have to chase you to the top of Arthur's Seat!"

"It gets us out of that Holyrood Abbey, where we are little better than prisoners." The other gestured towards the watching Douglas guards.

"Aye—no doubt. At least you look well on it! A deal better than when last we forgathered."

That was true. Despite the frustrations and constrictions of his present existence, David Lindsay had lost much of the embittered and drawn attitude which had settled on him after his Kate's death.

"And *you* look . . . extraordinary? Less than suitably clad for hill-climbing, I fear!"

"Ha! You would not condemn the Lord Abbot of Arbroath to looking ordinary, man? Especially when he has to make his presence felt. But I daresay that I can climb your hill as well as the next. If I must, to have privy speech with you?"

Grimly Lindsay considered the other's magnificent scarlet-dyed thigh-length riding-boots of softest doe-leather, with their high and spurred heels. "Can you mount yonder steeps in those?" he demanded, and pointed to the roughest and rockiest route up towards the summit. "Where we may get away from those horses."

"Ah—is that the ploy! To be sure, I can." Beaton turned to his two escorts. "Lead my beast and keep us in sight," he directed. "These others will no doubt be doing the same. Now, Sire—lead on!"

Laughing—and it was not often that James Stewart laughed

these days—the King started off upwards, deliberately choosing the most difficult and abruptly-rising route, amongst the outcrops, scree, stunted gorse and wet green aprons of surface-water. The horsemen were left behind to find an alternative way up. But if this might have been a successful device for gaining them private speech, it proved less so in that Davie Beaton was so busy picking his way in those awkward boots, and panting for breath as he did so, that he had little ability to talk. Perceiving this, after letting James have his fun for a little, Lindsay pointed half-right to a sort of narrow terrace on the hill-face, where they could pause, and where no horses could get within three hundred yards at least. Thankfully Beaton made his way thither.

They stood for a minute or two on that eyrie-like ledge, surveying all the land spread like a variegated carpet beneath, down to the blue waters of the Firth of Forth and beyond to the gentle green hills of Fife, before Davie was in a state to talk. He sat down, on a sun-warmed outcrop.

"God save us—I prefer Lindifferon Hill to Arthur's Crag!" he got out. "Why can you not stay on level ground, like other folk, Master Pursuivant Lindsay of The Mount?" David had been appointed an Extra Pursuivant, or herald, to the King, by the Douglases, not out of any desire to accord him status but so that his board and keep could be charged to the crown revenues as part of the Lord Lyon King-of-Arms' establishment.

"Save your breath for more useful talk!" his friend advised. "What brings you here that could not have waited until we were returned to Holyrood?"

"I do not trust that sleek William Douglas. I trust none of them, to be sure, but him least of all. He would be unlikely to let us be alone together—and if he did, might well have listeners behind doors or arras! And what I have to say is for your ears alone. And yours, Sire, to be sure."

"I hope that you are going to contrive some way of getting us out of Douglas clutches?"

"That, too. But seven weeks more, and Arran takes over as guardian of His Grace. It may be better, easier then—if all goes as it should! Meantime we must be as patient as is in us."

"Patient . . . !" Lindsay snorted.

"Aye, just that, David. Patience, using our wits, gathering

support, seeking out Angus's weaknesses. Which is where you are well-placed to learn much. We need to know how united are the Douglases themselves. Angus is not a kindly man—they cannot all love him! How sure is he of his allies—the Homes, the Kers, the Hepburns and the rest? What does he plan for the future—if he has to yield His Grace to Arran? Are all the royal fortresses firm in his support? You, biding within Holyrood, with his Uncle William, who has the wits of the family—however great a scoundrel—must hear much. The other uncles are there frequently, we know. And the rest of Angus's kin. What have you learned?"

"Sakes—have you come only to pick my brains? I had hoped for better than that!"

"All in good time, friend. Do not tell me that you have learned nothing in these six weeks?"

"I have learned to hate the Douglases! And to grieve the more for King James, here." He shrugged. "For the rest—I agree that the Abbot William is the cleverest of them. That he is not to be trusted. That Kilspindie is probably the least ill of them, and disapproves of much that Angus does. He does not like his brother William. Nor does Pittendreich—but he is as big a rogue, only less clever. Angus himself is little here, ever riding about the land, sword in hand. But—all this you must know, and can be of little use to you. What do you want of me?"

"Better than that, yes. Although it is of use to know that Kilspindie, Graysteel, does not always agree with Angus and does not love his brother William, since he is now Treasurer. Perhaps we can use that. What of the Earl of Morton, chief of the *Black* Douglases? How close is he? Angus and he used to be unfriends."

"Nor are they friends now, I think. Morton is seldom at Holyrood. But William and his brothers speak little good of him."

"That is well, then. But Drumlanrig, now Master of the Larder, is one of that line."

"He *is* a friend of Angus, yes. The only one of the Black sort, I think. But—why do you concern yourself with all this? What good can such knowledge do? Angus controls Scotland. Who loves him signifies little—so long they all fear him!"

"Now, perhaps. Because Angus now holds His Grace, here.

But that situation is due to change in October. Then we may see."

"You believe that? From the way the Douglases talk, they see no sudden ending of their power, in October or other. They plan to remain in power."

"Have you heard any word of *what* they intend to do in October, man?"

"No. Nothing plainly, just their general attitude. That they will still be holding Scotland firmly in the future."

"Aye. David—do you think that Angus will refuse to deliver up His Grace to Arran, in October? Despite parliament's instructions—his own proposal?"

"I do not know. But I would not put it past him. That one will care nothing for parliaments, or even for his own given word. Power is what he wants—and he has that power now. I would expect him to try to hold on to it. Would not you?"

"If he believes that he can, that way, any way, yes. If he defies parliament and refuses to yield up His Grace, he unites many against him, since parliament, however muted, is still the voice of the nation. Not only Arran and his Hamiltons, their friends and the Stewarts, but Lennox and Erroll and their people, the other two guardians. And others who voted for that motion—including Holy Church! Argyll, the Campbell chief, resents not being included as a guardian—he was always one of the old Privy Council. Your good-father, Lord Lindsay. The Earl Marischal. Angus could weld most of the realm against him if he did that."

"So long as he holds King James, does that matter?"

"See you—he could avoid that uniting against him if he came to terms with Arran."

"Arran? The Douglases and the Hamiltons in harness! They have ever been foes."

"To be sure. I do not say that they would start to love each other. But if they were to *work* together . . . ! If *I* was in Angus's saddle, that is what I would do. Arran is weak and Angus would dominate, inevitably."

David shook his head, wordless, but obviously disbelieving.

James Stewart it was who spoke now. "The Earl of Arran would like to be King," he said. "He might kill me."

That silenced even Davie Beaton for a moment or two. Lindsay reached out to grip the boy's arm.

"Never that, James—do not fear. Arran is no killer. Never think that."

"But his son, the Bastard is!"

Beaton stared at his young monarch, clearly astonished at the boy's perception rather than his fear, for that was shrewd judging. Sir James Hamilton of Finnart, the Bastard of Arran, *would* kill, to advance himself. His father, second person in the kingdom, was the nearest heir to the throne, with the Duke of Albany gone, a French citizen and obviously no longer interested in Scotland. Arran's mother was the Princess Mary, a daughter of James the Second. The Bastard, being illegitimate, could never aspire to the throne himself, but could hope to rule the kingdom through his weak father.

"Sire—you must not fear anything such," Beaton said urgently. "There is no danger, I swear to you! Sir James Hamilton would never seek to lay hands on the Lord's Anointed. Nor would any . . ."

"Others *have*! Why not him? I would rather be held by my lord of Angus, who would not seek to be King!"

The two men eyed each other, in mutual agreement that the subject should be changed.

"Angus will undoubtedly protect Your Grace—since you are the source of his present authority," Beaton said. "As for Arran, he has become weaker, not stronger, of late. Since Your Grace's royal mother married Henry Stewart . . ."

"Married!" That was Lindsay. "They are *wed*?"

"Yes. Had you not heard? A week past, at Linlithgow."

"But—this is folly! Worse than folly! A man of no account, eight or nine years younger than she is. A young coxcomb! For the former Queen, the King's mother, to wed such . . . !" Glancing at James, David coughed. "I crave your pardon, Sire."

The boy shrugged that aside, clearly not interested in his mother or her antics. "You will always stay with me, Davie?" he demanded. "Even if my lord of Arran gets me?"

"To be sure—if I may, Sire. I shall not leave you willingly. Fear nothing . . ."

"This marriage has driven a wedge between Arran and the Queen-Mother," Beaton went on. "He was wroth when she made Stewart Lord Treasurer without consulting him, or any. For old Avondale, Stewart's father, is a long-time foe of Arran's. But this marriage is too much for him. He has left her side and returned to his castle of Cadzow. So her cause also is the weaker. As is his. If Angus were to approach him now, who knows . . . ?"

"You are not *hoping* for this, man?"

"No. Far from it. But we must consider it, the possibility. So I ask that you listen well to the talk at Holyrood. If you hear any word that Angus is in touch with Arran and the Hamiltons, contrive to let me know. It is vital that we should learn of it at St. Andrews at the earliest."

"Why?"

"Because such alliance would be the worst that could happen for Scotland, and we would have to move heaven and earth to stop it! Douglas and Hamilton together would make a league almost impossible to beat. We would have to try to halt it before it was established."

"How could you? How could any?"

"It would not be easy. But there *are* forces in this land which have not been harnessed as yet in the King's cause, powerful forces seldom considered. In the north, the Highlands, the clans. They are part of the realm, are they not? Always over-busy fighting each other, and so overlooked. Yet they represent a mighty power—if they could be brought into it."

"Aye—but how? Since Harlaw, a hundred years ago, they have shown little interest in Lowland Scotland. Why should they now?"

"Two reasons. Or three. Two men have been ignored by Angus and Arran both—and resent it. Both from the north: Argyll, the Campbell chief, and Huntly, the Gordon; both on the old Regency Council, and now overlooked. Each could put three thousand broadswords in the field—more, if they brought in their friends and neighbours. And the third—Lennox. Also on the fringes of the Highlands. See you, if Arran joined Angus, it would leave the Stewarts stranded. They are not strong enough of themselves to stand alone. They would have either to join Angus likewise, or retire from all but local influence in the land. But there are Highland Stewarts too—Appin, Ardvoirlich, Garth, and of course, Atholl."

"These will not love the Campbells, I think!"

"No. But if it were that or nothing, bowing to Angus, I say that they might well be persuaded. And Lennox, the senior of the non-royal Stewarts, is the key. He is a sound man and of influence, one of the chosen guardians, and holder of one of the most ancient Celtic earldoms. He might bring in Erroll and the Hays."

"I like my lord of Lennox," James put in.

"Might! Could! May be! It is all so much supposition, hope, Davie. Hope, that is all. A Highland host, to beat Douglas! I do not see it."

"It would not be easy, no. But do not forget two other influences, both linked—the Church and siller! Money, friend—money! My uncle controls the deepest purse in this kingdom—and the Highlanders are ever hungry for siller."

"You would seek to buy them? Buy the clans? To fight against Lowlanders."

"If necessary. We must use whatever tools come to hand. Mind—it may never come to this. Angus may yield His Grace to Arran. And even if he does not, he may not think of coming to terms with the Hamiltons. And Arran might reject it. But—we have to be prepared. So you understand how important it is that we have prior knowledge of any movement, any link, between Douglas and Hamilton? *You* are the best situated to learn this, David."

"Mmm. I think you over-estimate the length of my ears! But, if I did hear aught, how would I get word to you? I am never permitted to be outside Holyrood Abbey without guards. As now."

"I know it. But the Sub-Chantor at the Abbey here is one of my people, from St. Andrews. He will convey your messages to me. John Balfour his name—of distant kin."

"I will do what I can . . ."

They moved on, but, taking pity on Beaton in those boots, did not climb all the way to the top of the hill. He was probably glad to reach his horse again.

Before parting company, he retailed one other item of news which might interest them. His minions, notably proficient at intercepting and suborning couriers crossing the border, by means unspecified, but almost certainly at the monkish hospices for travellers at the Tweed crossings, had read a letter from the Queen-Mother to her brother Henry, via Lord Dacre, requesting the despatch of ten thousand English troops to Scotland under the Duke of Norfolk, to enable her to recover possession of her son and so to restore her rule. Later, word from a spy in

Cardinal Wolsey's London establishment informed that this request was refused on the grounds that the King of England believed that it was not necessary, as the Earl of Angus would do his work for him.

On that note they parted, Lindsay thoughtful indeed— not least as to the uses its Abbot made of the rich revenues of Arbroath in maintaining his information network, presumably something else he had learned in France.

As it happened, soon after their return to Holyrood, David learned something from the talk therein, namely that Angus, having heard about the marriage, had gone to Linlithgow and arrested Henry Stewart of Methven on a charge of treason for having wed the King's mother without the King's sanction or knowledge. He was now confined in nearby Blackness Castle, a prisoner. Margaret herself had been conveyed to Stirling Castle and placed in the strict keeping of the Lord Erskine.

Lindsay did not seek to forward this news to Beaton, assuming that he would learn of it speedily enough from his normal sources. It certainly made clear who was in command in Scotland.

4

It was All Hallows Eve, the last day of October—and no change so far had become evident in the dull routine at the Abbey, no arrangements for handing over the King to Arran, or anybody else, nor any suggestions of such a thing. So it seemed that the fears expressed on Arthur's Seat all those weeks before were well-founded; Angus did not intend to yield up his royal hostage to other guardians, parliament or none. There was, however, no air of tension at Holyrood; the reverse, in fact, for the Abbot William, in an excess of amiability, announced that a diet of study and lessons was not natural or proper for young folk, even the Lord's Anointed, and that His Grace deserved a little entertainment. So, it being All Hallows, the traditional time for mummery, guizards and such-like frivolities, he had arranged some small diversion for that evening. There would be a modest banquet in the refectory, with music, dancing, play-acting and the like. His Grace's spirits must be maintained.

David was a little suspicious at this sudden concern for the royal feelings, even whilst welcoming any lightening of the boy's distinctly trying circumstances.

That night the monks' eating-hall was transformed, ablaze with candles, lamps and lanterns (many contrived to look like grinning faces), yew, fir and holly branches decking the walls. The abbatical dais was provided with laden tables flanking a central one which was accorded five chairs instead of the benches elsewhere, leaving the main floor clear for the entertainment.

Led in by the abbey choir chanting a more spirited refrain than usual, James made a formal entry, flanked by the Abbot and his brother, Sir Archibald of Kilspindie—who, as Treasurer, was no doubt paying for all this. David Lindsay and the Prior came behind—and the former was interested to note that there were women present on this occasion amongst the brethren, and not nuns either, something he had not seen before. All bowed to the monarch, the first time anything of the sort had been staged. David wondered the more.

James was seated in the middle, between William and Archibald Douglas, while David sat on the left and the Prior on the right. The latter rose to say a brief grace-before-meat in Latin, and then the lay-brother servitors brought in the steaming dishes. Flagons of wine were already on the tables.

It proved to be quite the finest repast Lindsay for one had tasted for years—soups, salmon, wild duck, venison, pork, sweetmeats, fruits and a variety of liquors. He noted how assiduously the Douglases urged James to partake of all, particularly the wines, and he grew a little apprehensive. Presently he mentioned to his neighbour, Kilspindie, that the boy was not used to so much, especially the liquor—but was pooh-poohed as though a spoilsport.

Whilst the meal proceeded there was entertainment in the form of juggling, singing, fiddling and dancing, taking place on the main refectory floor, not perhaps of the highest standards—save for the last, which was performed by a gipsy group of four. The two men and two women were exceedingly active and talented, the women in especial, who might have been sisters, both darkly striking in appearance, one, seemingly the younger, almost beautiful in a coarse-grained way. They were well-formed creatures and, disporting themselves to the fiddle-music with rhythmic abandon, their notably low-cut bodices and brief skirts hid little of their persons, their breasts bouncing about with eye-catching freedom, indeed those of the younger woman tending to escape their cover altogether on occasion—and not to be put back with any embarrassment or even haste. David noted how young James's eyes were concentrated in that direction, to the neglect of his viands.

When the performance ended, unusual perhaps for an abbey, the King was loudly enthusiastic in his applause, and Abbot William, patting his shoulder, assured him that they would have more of this, if he enjoyed it, when the dancers had recovered their breaths. Beckoning a servitor, he murmered something to him, accompanied by an odd gesture indicating the upper body.

Thereafter there was an interlude with a distinctly moth-eaten performing bear, and some more singing, before the gipsies reappeared, but this time only the two women. And now their offering was frankly and provocatively sexual where before it had appeared to be so only, as it were, by accident. Moreover, both bodices were now so low-slung that quickly the jouncing, twisting movement caused them to slip down to the waist, and after only a token pull or two upwards, so they remained throughout the dance. The older woman was rather less well-endowed but just as active, and the entire display challenging indeed.

When it too finished, to prolonged acclaim, Sir Archibald beckoned both females up to the dais, where he offered the elder his own beaker of wine to drink from, in congratulation, indicating to the King that he should do the same for the younger. James was nothing loth, although clearly suffering from acute embarrassment and fascination mixed—for the tucking-in process as the women advanced had been only partially successful and one of the younger woman's breasts was still fully exposed, and at close range, with the large dark aureola and thrusting nipple, having an almost mesmeric effect on the boy.

While still the dancers, panting effectively from their exertions and exuding a heavy female scent, were sipping the wine, bold-eyed, Abbot William rose to announce that the entertainment would now be general, and that all who cared to dance should do so—adding, with a smile, that for this evening he gave leave for such holy brethren as knew how to join in. He called on the fiddlers to strike up, and then moved round the top table to take the hand of the older gipsy woman and lead her down on to the main floor, beckoning to James to do the like with the younger. It now became apparent that the other women guests were there to provide dancing-partners for at least some of the monks and lay-brothers.

David Lindsay sat still. He had not danced since Kate died, and certainly did not feel like restarting now. He was unsure what to do, if anything. It seemed very clear that all this had been arranged at some expense and for some purpose—and for young James's benefit, if that was the word. Equally clear, that these tough Douglases were not suddenly smitten with concern over their hostage's dull existence and lack of amusement. So what was the object of this peculiar All Hallows celebration, particularly this deliberate exposure of the women to the boy?

Lindsay was no prude, but as well as being fond of James he felt himself to have a duty to guide and protect him in more than tutoring and personal attendance. But was there anything that ought to be done, or could be done, here? Was there any harm in it all, for the King? He was thirteen and although, having been as good as a prisoner all his life, he had inevitably been sheltered from fleshly matters—whatever he thought of his mother's behaviour—he was bound in the nature of things, to learn about women and sex in the near future. Was this way so objectionable? And even if it was, would *his* objections be paid any attention to by those who had gone to the trouble to stage the evening?

At first the general dancing was notably different from what had gone before, formal, graceful, in set patterns, lines and circlings with pacings and much bowing and curtsying. James had done little of this previously, but his present partner was assiduous in his instruction, and no doubt the wine imbibed helped to counter his inhibitions. He was scarcely graceful about it, coltish rather, but picked up the rhythm quickly enough. About a dozen couples took part, Abbot William leading.

Presently the fiddle-music changed tempo and style to a less dignified and more jigging pace, and the formal grouping split up into little clusters and pairs, steps growing lively, the two gipsy women emphasising the change. Abbot William, panting, soon had enough of this and retired, his partner being joined instead by one of the gipsy men, and these two now set a pace which grew ever more vehement. James, out of his depth, was nevertheless guided and led and put up with by the younger woman, in much laughter, suiting herself to his gangling cavortings—which of course soon shook her bosom quite free again. Her partner's concentration on the dancing-steps was no doubt thereby distracted. Presently, either by his own initiative or her guidance, one royal hand was holding at least one of those mobile breasts approximately steady, leaving the other to its jigging.

It was at this stage that David's frowning attention also became distracted. For the Abbot, back at the top table and puffing noticeably, his plump features pink and beaded with sweat, addressed himself to the younger man.

"You do not dance, Lindsay? Because you cannot, or will not?"

"To dance worthily, my lord Abbot, one must feel so disposed. I do not."

"Ah. Do I detect some . . . criticism?"

"Wonder, rather. I wonder what you are at?"

"What but to celebrate All Hallows Eve in a fashion to amuse our young liege-lord. You would not grudge him? He, at least, appears to find it all to his taste."

"As you have gone to some trouble to ensure!"

"We do what we can, although little enough." The other glanced along the table, and gestured. "My brother is no dancer, either! And seems to have had a sufficiency of entertainment for one night! He will be the better of his bed. Will you conduct him to his chamber, Lindsay?"

Surprised, David looked at his neighbour, Sir Archibald, who now lay slumped over the table, head on arms amongst the flagons and beakers, apparently asleep or drunken or both.

"He seems well content!"

"Nevertheless, he would do better elsewhere. He sleeps in the chamber in the foot of the bell-tower."

Shrugging, David rose. He could scarcely refuse this strange request, or command, although one of the monks or lay-brothers would have seemed a more suitable escort if such was indeed required.

The Abbot shook his brother's shoulder. "Rouse yourself, Archie," he exclaimed. "Lindsay here, who appears to think as little of our entertainment as do you, will aid you to your couch. You could do with it. Come, man—on your feet."

Graysteel looked up, blinked, and obediently rose, if unsteadily. But he was sufficiently rational to grab David's arm rather than his brother's. He said nothing, but leaning heavily on the younger man, promptly began to weave his way across the dais towards the door.

Leaving the refectory building, which was separate from the main residential conventual range, they crossed the wide courtyard to the cloisters which skirted the chapter-house and church itself, the bell-tower being at the far south end of the range. The chill night air appeared to do Sir Archibald good, for he began to walk fairly normally, although he clung to the younger man's arm nevertheless—otherwise David would have sought to excuse himself and return to the refectory. They exchanged no conversation.

Even within the main building's candle-lit corridors he was not released. The place seemed to be deserted, all the inmates being at the entertainment, no doubt. Reaching the Treasurer's bedchamber, David's services were still required whilst more candles were to be found and lit, Graysteel suddenly becoming talkative and detaining his escort further with enquiries about the King's progress in his studies, his general abilities and the like, all notably unlike the Douglases.

Wondering the more, David made his escape and headed back for the refectory.

There the dancing was still in progress, amidst much noise. It did not take him long to discern that James was no longer present, nor indeed was the Abbot William. It took only a little longer to recognise that the King's dancing-partner was missing also, although her gipsy colleagues were still there. The Prior was likewise gone from the dais-table.

David sat for a little, sipping his wine, not exactly perturbed, since it all might be explained perfectly naturally no doubt, but just slightly uneasy. That unease grew as time passed and James made no reappearance. At length, he beckoned to a lay-brother servitor and asked him where His Grace had gone. The man expressed ignorance. He moved down amongst the dancers, seeking out the older gipsy woman. Panting, at his enquiry, she too appeared to have no knowledge—but smilingly offered to dance with him. He approached another servitor, and when he gained the same response, asked where the Abbot had gone, frowning now. He was little more successful in that, save for the suggestion that he might well have retired to his own quarters, as indeed might His Grace.

David had to admit that this was a sensible enough supposition, especially if James had noticed that he himself had disappeared from the dais. Perhaps William Douglas had escorted the boy back to his bedchamber, if he had had enough dancing.

So, leaving the refectory again, he returned to the main building and up to the room he shared with his charge. James was not there.

He waited, growing ever more uneasy, as the minutes went by. At length, never a notably patient man, he could stand it no longer. He knew where the Abbot William's rooms were. He would go and enquire there, however unlikely to be well received.

But downstairs, in the most handsome suite of apartments in the great establishment, although candles blazed, and a fine fire crackled on the hearth, there was no sign of the incumbent.

At a loss, David considered. The certainty grew on him that this entire night's proceedings were altogether too out-of-character to be explained away naturally.

It had all been thought out. Why? The Douglases did not usually do things by stealth and subterfuge; they were far too sure of themselves for that. If they had intended to remove James from his own charge and care, they could have done it openly, without all this elaborate play-acting. He could not have prevented it. So, what?

He decided that he at least knew where one of the play-actors was; and Archibald Douglas was easier to deal with and less subtle than his brother. He would go to the bell-tower and try to get to the bottom of this business, even if the Treasurer was now asleep in his bed.

He went out into the chill night air again.

At the door of Graysteel's room he paused, hearing voices

within. After only a moment's hesitation he knocked, and without waiting for permission opened and entered.

The two Douglas brothers sat therein at a table, wine-beakers in hand. They stared at him.

"What's to do? What do you want, Lindsay?" the Abbot jerked, less smoothly than usual.

"I am looking for His Grace," David said flatly.

"Indeed? And why look for him here, sirrah?"

"I left him in your care, my lord Abbot. When you required me to escort Sir Archibald hither." David made a brief mock bow. "I rejoice to see your brother so well recovered!"

The Treasurer cleared his throat. "Is the King not still dancing?" he asked.

"No, sir. Nor is he in the refectory, nor in his own chamber. The hour is late. Where is he?"

"Sakes, Lindsay—what's this? What a pother!" William Douglas had changed his tone. "It is All Hallows Eve, a time for merry-making—not for auld hens' cluckings! His Grace is but a lad—let him have his bit fling."

"As you have most carefully devised!"

"Tut, man—we but contrived a little entertainment for the lad. He has had little enough of such, I jalouse. Let him be, for once."

"He is in my care, my lord. I could let him be more readily if I knew where he was and what was being done with him."

"*Done* with him? Nothing is being done with him, man! Or . . . how could it be? Here in this my Abbey? What he is at, wherever he is, he cannot come to any harm. It is none so large a place, and he'll no' get out. Probably, like Sir Archibald here, he found the wine, the provender and the noise and dancing overcame him somewhat. He will be sleeping it off, belike, somewhere."

"But not where he should be—in his own bed. I must find him."

"You speak like any auld wife, Lindsay! Spare us more of it. Go seek His young Grace, if you must, but leave us in peace, of a mercy!"

"That I will, sir," David said, and turned on his heel. He slammed that door behind him.

Out in the cloisters, he tried to clear his mind of anger and to think constructively. It did not look as though the Douglases were for spiriting James out of the Abbey or planning any major change—not this night, at least. It *could* be all as the Abbot pretended. Yet all this *had* been planned, of that he was convinced, for some purpose. That purpose he must discover. First he must find James in this rambling establishment. Where to look? He could not go prying into every room, dormitory, corner. Between eighty and one hundred souls lived in the Abbey of the Holy Rood. He would have to return to the refectory, to start there, question folk again, try to gain some hint.

On the way, he looked in once more at their own quarters—which were still empty. Back at the eating-hall, he found conditions changed, the dancing superseded by general revelry, drunken singing, horse-play and the like, shameful in such a place consecrated to worship, nobody apparently in charge any more. But James had not returned nor could David see the younger gipsy woman either, although her companions were still present.

So—the chances were that the pair of them were still together, with all that implied. Was that it, then? An assault on the boy's pudency, modesty, virtue? And if so, why? What would that gain the Douglases? These people did nothing without a reason . . .

Putting the whys and wherefores to the back of his mind meantime, David concentrated on the task of finding James. Where to look? If the woman was indeed involved and had taken the lead, then the probability was that, a gipsy and an outsider, she would not know the abbey-precincts throughly and would therefore tend to take the King somewhere near-at-hand and available, easily reached—unless some more elaborate place had been specially prepared for them. So, try this same refectory building, for a start. He had never been through it before. None of the company looking sober, unoccupied or helpful, he went exploring.

Behind the main eating-hall he found the kitchens, larders, storerooms and wine-cellars, in vaulted basements. He unearthed two couples in the warm kitchens, one copulating, the other sprawled in each other's arms asleep—but neither known to him. There was another pair comfortable in an adjoining room full of blankets. Half-way along the connecting vaulted corridor there was a circular stair-tower containing a turnpike.

Two more revellers had reached thus far, one a monk, but presumably had been either in too great a hurry for their satisfaction or found themselves unable to climb the stair, for there on the lowermost treads they lay, clothing markedly disarranged, dead to the world. Deciding to try the upper floor, David stepped carefully over them and mounted the winding stair.

There was a dormitory above, presumably for the domestic and kitchen staff, and from it snores emanated. The door open, David looked in, but although some of the beds were occupied none appeared to contain women or King James. At the far end of this, however, was a shut door with light gleaming above and below. To this the searcher proceeded, and in no mood now for polite knocking, opened and entered without pause.

His quest was over. It was a much smaller apartment, probably the bedchamber of the chief cook, and on the bed two naked figures lay, one on top of the other, the woman uppermost. She at least was not asleep, for she raised her dark head to look towards the doorway. Clothing lay in a pile on the floor. As she lifted her well-made upper half, languorously, James Stewart's red head came into view beneath.

David moved into the room and closed the door behind him, to stand tight-lipped, contemplating the scene.

"Davie!" the King got out, chokingly. He heaved convulsively beneath his partner, managed to wriggle free and rolled over the far edge of the bed and down, out of sight.

The woman, quite unabashed, turned lithely, lowered her feet to the floor and stood up, facing the intruder. She was certainly magnificently formed, a sight to stir any man—or boy.

She smiled invitingly. "You now, sir? Your turn?" she wondered, with an eloquent flourish of the hand.

"Thank you, no!" David said shortly. "This, this is . . . shameful! How dare you! The King's Grace!"

"Och, I dared very well, sir. Nae trouble! And so did this one! For a first time, he did well enough. A quick learner! But, och—you, now, will be mair practised?"

"Be quiet, woman!" he commanded. "Have you no shame? No decency? Our sovereign-lord . . ." As she laughed, he moved round the foot of the bed to where James crouched on his knees, hands over his private parts, peering up, flushed, in an agony of guilt and apprehension.

"Dress yourself," he was told, in no humble tones. "Quickly. We shall talk later." David turned back to the woman. "You were brought here to do this? Paid?"

She shrugged shapely shoulders, her breasts quivering effectively.

"Who by?"

She said nothing, but went to sit on the bed, making no move to pick up and don her clothing.

"Was it Sir Archibald Douglas? The Abbot?" he demanded. "Tell me. Who contrived this, this wickedness?"

"Nothing wicked in it, sir," she assured, easily. "The laddie enjoyed it fine—I saw to that! So did I. So might your ain sel', if you'd tak the glower off your face!"

David realised that he was going to get nothing out of this gipsy. James was struggling into his clothes, not entirely effectively. He turned to give the boy a hand, less than gently. The woman sat watching, amused evidently, and unconcerned with her nakedness.

When he was approximately dressed, the man took the King's shoulder and pushed him towards the door.

"Guid night to you, laddie," came from behind them amiably. "You'll no' forget Jeannie!" That was a statement, and no plea nor question.

James did not look round.

On the way to their quarters across the courtyard, man and boy exchanged scarcely a word. James kept his head down, and David decided that this was not the time for serious talking. Even up in their own bedchamber little was said, the youngster obviously anxious only to get his head down under the blankets in oblivion. The man knew a certain sympathy with him, for it was scarcely James's fault. When he said good night before getting into his own bed, he tried to make his voice sound as normal as possible, not unfriendly. He got only a muffled grunt in reply.

Lying awake thereafter, David went over it all in his mind time and again, trying to discern what was behind the night's events, the reasons for this deliberate seduction of the young monarch. It must have been important, for the Douglases to have gone to so much trouble. It could scarcely be sheer depraved evil-mindedness, in the corruption of a youth. Nor hatred, for they had no reason to hate James. Policy, then? But to what end? To gain some power over the boy? To strike at his now-hated mother through him? To loosen his own, David Lindsay's, hold over the King's affections, for their own purposes? None of these seemed adequate—but he could not think of anything more significant before he slept.

In the morning he saw things more clearly. James was silent, reserved, eyes never meeting his own, so unlike his normal affectionate reliance. Was that it, then—a means of driving a wedge between them? But could that have any importance for the Douglases?

Their silent breakfast over, the inevitable inquest on the affair, which the boy so clearly dreaded, had to be got out of the way before the day's studies began. David sought to be fair, moderate, reasonable, recognising all too well his own difficulties in the matter. After all, this was the King of Scots he was to talk to, his liege-lord; and he had no moral authority over him either now, no longer even his official procurator and usher, but only the ties of friendship and loyalty.

"James," he said, at last, "what happened last night was wrong, very wrong—as I think that you know very well. Wrong in more ways than one. We have to speak of it."

The boy did not answer, looking away.

"What that woman did with you was . . . unsuitable, shameful. Not the act itself only, see you—but how it was done, and with *you*. Men and women do have this, this congress, can fit their bodies together, to enjoy each other, to much satisfaction. But it should be done in love and affection, not coupling in haste like farmyard animals! And you are not a man, not yet fourteen years. Much too young for such."

"I, I was not too young to, to . . ." His voice faded away.

"No, perhaps not. Your body might be able for it—but not *you*, yourself, your inner self. And forby, you are the King. And that woman was a, a gipsy whore, a paid trull, hired to ensnare you."

No response.

"James—we have to speak of this. Why the Douglases did this, I do not know. But they did it out of no love for you, that is sure. They are your enemies, holding you captive for their own purposes. Last night's doings were for their own advantage likewise—no question of that. They hired this woman and her friends to attract you with their dancing, their bodies. They made you to drink more wine than was good for you. Then they got you dancing with her and she making you very free of her person. They pretended that Sir Archibald was drunk, and had me to convey him to his chamber—and while I was away the woman took you off. And you know what followed. Why, think you?"

James shook his head but found words at last. "She was . . . kind," he said.

David sighed. "Kind is not how I would name it. She would be well paid to do what she did. That was no kindness, James."

"How do you know? You were not there!" That was almost defiance.

"For a woman to seduce a half-drunken boy of thirteen years, and her liege-lord, for money, is scarcely kindness. But—she is not the greatest sinner, I admit. Those who paid her to do it are worse. Would that I knew why they did it. But they went to much expense to achieve it. I suspect, to gain some power over you. So—apart from all else, we must not play the Douglases' game for them. Enough that we have to suffer this captivity. Do you understand? Can you not see it?"

The boy certainly gave little indication of understanding, staring down at his hands, set-faced.

"We shall speak no more of this, meantime, lad. I just ask that you consider who are your friends—the Douglases, who devised it all? Or myself, Davie Lindsay, who loves you well? So—enough of that. Now for the Latin . . ."

Throughout that day David debated with himself whether to go and challenge William and Archibald Douglas with his accusations and condemnation, but came to the conclusion that it would achieve nothing. He would leave them in no doubt as to his reaction, but recognised that this was unlikely to distress them unduly.

So his relationship with their captors deteriorated markedly, although the All Hallows Eve incident was not actually discussed. This in itself did not distress David; but what did was that his relationship with James had also suffered some change. They were still close, but the affair with the woman had introduced a shadow between them, something which was not spoken of but which was there, and on which the boy held a view very different from the man's. This was sad, but what made it worse was the fact that the Douglases began to adopt a different attitude towards the King, seeking not exactly to ingratiate themselves with the boy but to show him more respect, to talk to him, even to defer to him on occasion. Especially Sir Archibald who, with sons of his own, was more used to dealing with youngsters than was the Abbot. He presented James with a handsome dirk, which much pleased the recipient, and took him hawking in the adjacent royal park, the first time accompanied by David, the second time not. As Treasurer, he had to be much in the capital, and so was more or less in residence at the Abbey.

Then, one day in late November, Angus himself made one of his infrequent visits, and that night James was invited to dine with the Earl and his uncles—and David was not. When he was brought back, late, the King was distinctly the worse for liquor, and inclined to boast of his success with these Douglases, who were none so ill when one got to know them. His friend was the more anxious. Clearly a new policy was being established—and it was clear that Angus had no intention of yielding up his hostage to Arran or any other. And his own, Lindsay's, influence with the monarch was to be reduced. Presumably, then, the Douglases considered him to be in their way. He guessed that it might be only a matter of time before he was dismissed. Which implied for James—what?

When, just before Yule, another caller at Holyrood was the Bastard of Arran, and his call all but secret, David decided that Beaton should be informed, both of this last and of the new treatment for James. Going in search of the monk Balfour, the sub-chantor whom Davie had named as go-between, he found himself in a part of the establishment hitherto unvisited, and passing the laundry was surprised to see a woman working there—the gipsy Jeannie. She hastily turned her back on him, and disappeared further within, but there was no doubt as to who it was. Considerably concerned, he judged this to be an added threat.

His message to Beaton was the more emphatic.

David's fears were soon substantiated. With the wintry weather limiting his ranging the country, Angus spent most of the Christmas and Yuletide period at Holyrood—and although he was not the man to go in for festivities in any large way, he and his uncles did celebrate to some extent, with feastings and gatherings. In some of these James was included, but David never. On two such occasions the boy was again brought back to his quarters very late and drink-taken, guilt and defiance writ large in his attitude, to be followed in the mornings by sulks and heaviness. When, on a third such night, Hogmanay, he did not return to their room at all, nor reappearing until the forenoon of New Year's Day of 1526, David's anxiety and distress was not to be damped down any longer.

"James—you have been with that woman again!" he charged. "I know it. Every line of you proclaims it. After all I said, all my warnings. Do not seek to deny it. The Douglases have set you to drinking and whoring—and you are playing their game. She is still about this abbey—I have seen her."

The King nibbled his lip, wagging his red head. He looked slack and dull-eyed.

"They are working your ruin, boy—can you not see it? To get you into their pockets, dependent upon them. And you their willing dupe!"

"There is no harm in it," James burst out, thickly. "We hurt none. I . . . I like it. I am old enough, not a child any more. Others do it. Jeannie is kind. She likes me well, says that I am good at it! You, you are hard, would deny me all pleasure."

"Och, James, laddie—I am your friend. Your only friend in this place. That woman is no friend, however warm she seems towards you. She does what she does not out of love for a thirteen-year-old boy but because the Douglases pay her. Like it you may, but it is evil . . ."

"You say that. Others do not. Bedding is natural for any lusty person . . ."

"Who said that to you? Was it Angus? The Abbot? The Treasurer? I swear that you did not make that up for yourself!"

The other looked away. "My mother—she beds whom she will! And my father, they tell me, had many mistresses. When he was young, too . . ."

David looked grim. "Aye—they teach you skilfully! Can you not see what they do? You are not a fool. They make you to *need* them. And they separate *us*, drive a wedge between you and me. Is that what *you* want?"

"No-o-o. But I am no longer to be treated like a child. I am the King!"

"Ha—so that is it, *Sire*! Yes, you are King of Scots, and I am but your humble subject, no more than that. But we have been friends all your days. Your royal father put you in my care. But, if that time is past and Your Grace wishes to be free of me and my guidance and caring, then so be it. You have but to say the word."

Doubtfully now James eyed him.

"See you, Sire—I mislike it here, held as good as prisoner. The Douglases hate me and would be quit of me. I need not be a captive in this abbey. I have my lands in Fife to tend, my own life to live. Only *your* service, and my love of Your Grace keeps me here. If you have no longer need of me, and find my lord of Angus more to your taste, the Douglases' care kinder—then, Highness, say so. I vow none here now would seek to keep me!"

"Davie—no! Oh, Davie!" Abruptly the boy's entire attitude changed. Wide-eyed now he flung himself forward into David's arms. "Do not say it. You must not leave me, Davie. Never! You *must* not. I need you, need you. I will not see her again—Jeannie. I promise! Do not go away."

Much moved, the man nodded. "Very well. I will stay, lad—if they will let me. They may not, mind. Since they wish to separate us, clearly, surely the easiest way to do it would be to send me away . . ."

"I will not let them! If you go, I go. I am the King—my royal command! You stay with me."

"If it was as simple as that, James, neither of us would be here! But—I will stay whilst they allow me . . ."

In the aftermath of that scene there was a marked improvement in their relations and no further talk about women and bodily needs. And when, a few days later, another invitation to dine with Angus came, James curtly refused. This presently brought the Abbot William to the royal quarters, ostensibly to enquire after the King's health, the assumption being that he must be feeling unwell. The boy's jerked assertion that he was not sick but had no wish to dine again with the Earl and his friends, caused the Douglas to look very thoughtful, eyeing David equally with James. He did not cross-question nor seek further details, however, and left them ominously silent.

"I fear that we shall not be long in hearing more of this!" David commented.

They did. The next day it was the man's turn to be

summoned to Angus's presence—and not for dinner. As ever, the Earl did not beat about the bush.

"Lindsay," he said, "we have supported you here sufficiently long. The King, I judge, no longer requires your attendance. We shall provide other and more suitable companionship for him. You will make your arrangements to leave, forthwith."

David took his time to answer that. "I am in the King's employ, my lord—not yours. If His Grace asks that I leave him, I shall leave."

The other's hot eyes flared. "You will leave whether he asks you or no! From all I hear, your influence with him is not good. You are stubborn and unhelpful, and would make him so. He deserves and requires better company."

"Female, I take it? A gipsy laundry-wench. For the King's Grace!"

"Fool! You will address me civilly, or suffer for it. I speak of a tutor and more worthy attendant. Now—be off."

"Gladly. Only, I tell you—if the King stays, I stay. That is his royal wish . . ."

"We shall see . . ."

David waited for three days. But when the summons came it was for James. Angus had gone to Tantallon in the interim but had now returned. At the order, brought by a servitor, the King was for refusing to attend—it was not for a monarch to be summoned by one of his earls. David agreed but, since they were in the Douglas's power, it would serve for James to announce that he would see Angus somewhere of his own choosing, not the Earl's. Say in the abbey-church—a suitable venue to emphasise dignity; for it would be a hard and brow-beating interview concerned with his, David's dismissal. He did not see that James could win.

The boy went, with a mixture of apprehension and determination.

When he returned, it was still with mixed feelings, but now the mixture was different—there was triumph in it. They had won, he declared excitedly. Davie was not to be sent away—he could stay. He had told Angus so, and forced him to agree. They were not to be parted.

That David was surprised went without saying, so improbable did this outcome seem. But behind the boy's satisfaction the man sensed something else, some hint of reservation.

"You won, then. I am glad," he said. "But—at a price, I think? What did you have to pay, James? Angus is not the man to yield to mere pleading, even from his sovereign-lord."

The King looked down. "I have to write a letter—that is all."

"A letter? To whom?"

"To my mother. To tell her that all is well with me. Just a letter."

"James—what is this? Why such a letter? Now? There is something strange here. This was Angus's demand?"

"Yes. That was why he sent for me—that, and to say that you must go. I was to write to my mother, to say that I was well content here, that I was treated kindly. And that I was well pleased to continue to bide with the Earl of Angus."

"So-o-o! That is it! And—you agreed?"

"I said that I would only do it if you were allowed to stay with me, Davie."

"Och, laddie, laddie . . . !"

"It is none so much to do. They *are* being kinder to me now. And my mother cares nothing for me—only to use me, as King, for her own purposes. It is not much to do to keep you, Davie. Is it?"

"More than you think, James. Do you not see? That letter is not really for your mother, at all. Oh, she will get it, no doubt. But others will read it, or learn of it, as well—all the realm will. Scotland will learn that its King is well content with the Earl of Angus and the Douglases, happy in his keeping. This is not for *her* comfort! No—it is for others. In especial, I think, for Arran, Lennox and Erroll, the lords to whom Angus should have delivered you after his three months—and has not. Which means, to be sure, that he is going to keep you still. And more than that, I think. For most will have come to that belief already. He must have some further plan for you, which requires that he seems to have your agreement. What, who knows? But—there is a deal more in this than just a son's letter to his mother. Some subtle scheme—more like the Abbot William's work than Angus's, I'd say. Was *he* there?"

"Yes, he came to the church with the Earl, but said little."

"Aye—that one is a devil . . . !"

"But, Davie—what of it? The Douglases will do what they

will, anyway. We cannot stop them. But *you* stay with me. That is what is important. I'd do more than write any letter, to hold you. You stay!"

"At what cost, I wonder . . . ?"

5

Although superficially the months that followed at the Abbey of the Holy Rood were little different from those which had gone before, there was in fact a notable change. The roles of David and James had altered. The man was there now only on sufferance, dependent wholly on the boy's continuing demand and active bargaining. Their captors demonstrated that all too clearly, showing with scorn and insult that they had no further use for him. And, perhaps inevitably, something of the shift in emphasis began to show in the relationship between the two. James was more and more the King and David the subject, even if the boy did not consciously so intend. It was partly, no doubt, that he was growing up fast now, spurred on almost certainly by his sexual awakening; also the fact that the Douglases were treating him ever more respectfully, on the face of it at least. The pair remained good friends but the balance was changing, especially in authority.

The dinners with Angus or his uncles resumed, David excluded; and after one such, when the boy returned very late, David suspected that he had been with that woman again. A stroll round to the laundry next day revealed that she was still working there. Then, a week later, he was sure of it—James actually smelt of woman when he came back.

In bed thereafter, David debated long with himself what he should do. Was there any point in challenging the boy with breaking his promise and yielding to what was undoubtedly strong temptation deliberately put in his way? Would it do any good? On the contrary, would it not merely worsen the situation between them? Better probably to make no comment, whilst letting James realise that he *knew* what was happening. If they were going to continue to live thus close, for both their sakes he must strive to keep relations as harmonious as possible.

So nothing was said about drinking and womanising, although the King could have little doubt as to his friend's attitude and knowledge.

Then, on the 10th of April, the boy's fourteenth birthday, they learned what was partly behind that letter written to the Queen-Mother. Angus was at Holyrood again, and invited James to attend a ceremony in the abbey-church in celebration, at noon. Wondering, the boy could hardly refuse to attend—but he took David along with him. They were escorted into the chapter-house, to discover Lyon King-of-Arms there, with his heralds and trumpeters. Presently Angus himself came in, bowed low to the monarch, glared at David, and announced that proceedings would commence and the royal birthday be suitably honoured. The trumpets would sound, Lyon would lead the way, and they would enter the church by the chancel doorway. He himself would guide His Grace as to what to do.

James looked doubtfully at David, but the Earl forestalled any questions by signing to the trumpeters to sound. In the confined space of the chapter-house the noise of their fanfare was deafening. The inner doorway was thrown open by a herald, and Lyon formed up his colourful court of pursuivants—at the last moment beckoning for David to join them, since he was, officially at least, one of them—and in great dignity marched in, Angus and the King coming behind together, followed by the instrumentalists, still blowing lustily.

They found the church full, surprisingly, Arran and his son the Bastard with a clutch of Douglas lairds, waiting there in the chancel, with Abbot William and the robed clergy. The abbot's chair had been brought forward to a central position, and to this Angus led the King and, with a flourish, indicated that he should sit. The heraldic group formed up nearby. Angus remained standing beside James.

When the fanfare ended at last, the Earl stepped forward and held up his hand for silence.

"My lords and fellow subjects," he said loudly, "we are here for a purpose. To celebrate the birthday of our gracious sovereign-lord King James. He has now reached the age of fourteen years and enters into manhood. I say that we all wish him well." That was jerked out with more force than eloquence, for Angus was no speech-maker. He turned and bowed towards the throne-like chair.

"His Grace has been well prepared for his high calling," he resumed. "And having now reached years of discretion and judgement, his Council have decided that he is fit and able to govern as well as to reign. Accordingly, as from this birthday, King James the Fifth assumes the rule of his realm. God save the King!"

How much surprise there might be in the crowded church at this announcement, David had no means of knowing—for it might have been bruited abroad beforehand. But for himself, he was astonished. Angus did nothing without hope of advantage for himself and his house—and what advantage was there for Douglas in this? If it meant little or nothing, a mere empty ceremony, as had been the case when the Queen-Mother had made a similar statement almost a couple of years before, then why go to all this trouble? And if it was indeed a significant act—why? Fourteen was still far too young an age for any true rule. And nothing was more improbable than that Angus was voluntarily yielding up effective power and influence.

David's wonderings were interrupted by a further development. Abbot William moved from behind the altar to the King's side, carrying now a handsome cloak of purple velvet trimmed with fur. He placed this ceremoniously about the wary boy's shoulders, and then bowed deeply before him.

"God save the King's Grace! Long may he reign and his rule be glorious!" he intoned, with a practised eloquence in marked contrast to his nephew. "We all acclaim the King's Highness."

Led by the ranked Douglas lairds, the congregation took up the traditional refrain. "God save the King! God save the King! God save the King!" all chanted loudly.

At a sign from Lyon, the trumpeters raised their instruments and blew another stirring flourish.

When this died away, Angus spoke again. "A new beginning. All, I say, wish His Grace well in it. At this fresh start in the realm's governance, all appointments of the crown fall back into the monarch's hands, to be renewed . . . or otherwise." There was a significant pause there. "I myself yield up my position of Chief Warden of the Marches. Others likewise. The King now rules. God save him!"

A little less fervently now the congregation repeated the phrase, but only once.

So that was it! The reason behind all this play-acting—for David was sure that it was little more than that. All offices of state were forfeit at a new rule—to be reallocated to men of Angus's choosing without a doubt. All direction of the realm put lawfully into the hands of a boy who was controlled by Douglas. This was the rest of the plan foreshadowed by that letter to the Queen-Mother—Angus the effective master of Scotland, and for years to come.

As though to emphasise the accuracy of that assessment, Angus now turned and strode back to James's chair, held out a hand to raise the King from it, and taking his arm through that fine cloak, led him off across the chancel to the door by which they had entered, and out, without pause or further ceremony.

Reality had returned, play-acting over.

Apparently taken by surprise, Lyon looked around him uncertainly, decided on a final fanfare, and gestured to his trumpeters. As, somewhat raggedly, this rang out, he looked over at Abbot William, evidently wondering who should go first, and then more or less shooed his heralds out rather like barn-door fowls. The entire proceedings had lasted only a few minutes.

In the chapter-house, David found Angus already gone and James waiting alone, uncertain as to what would happen next, in a notable atmosphere of anticlimax. David nodded to the boy, took his velvet cloak and handed it to the Lord Lyon, for it was fairly evident that in fact nothing happened next, and together man and boy went out into the cloisters and across the courtyard to their own quarters.

The new dispensation and fresh start seemed markedly similar to the old.

And so it remained, in the summer weeks that followed, all as it had been, except for one development—signings. Now, almost daily, large numbers of papers, documents and charters were brought to the King for signature. No explanations and elucidations came with them, just the requirement to sign. This, it seemed, was the monarch ruling in person. It was no part of David Lindsay's remit or duty to advise James not to sign, since refusal would result only in pressure and unpleasantness. But he did suggest a policy of reading first, where possible, so that at least they might be made aware of what the Douglases were up to. Most which they read were appointments to office under the crown and transfers of lands, mainly to Douglases and their friends—although, significantly, some to Arran and his Hamiltons, clearly in token of a bargain struck. But most significant of all was a document addressed to the Archbishop of St. Andrews informing him that his position of Chancellor of the realm and chief minister now, like others, reverted to the crown; and that he, James, had appointed the Earl of Angus thereto, and ordered the return of the Great Seal of Scotland to the said Earl, forthwith.

What the Beatons would do about that remained to be seen.

In early July there were two developments. James was informed that Angus intended to hold justice-ayres in the Borderland—one of the first papers he had had to sign had been the reappointment of Angus as Chief Warden of the Marches—and the Earl deemed it right that the monarch should accompany him on this occasion and learn at first-hand of the administration of justice in his realm; this in a week's time. The second, a day later, was the arrival at Holyrood of the Earl of Lennox, to see Angus—who had gone off to Tantallon only that morning. Before following on thither, Lennox came to pay his respects to the King—and was sufficiently senior to be able to dismiss the functionary who brought him there, so as to have some private converse with the monarch. He was a personable, youngish man, fine-featured but slightly-built, descendant of the ancient Celtic mormaors through the female line, although himself a Stewart.

Alone with James, who kept David by him, he knelt down on one knee to take the royal hand within both of his own, in the traditional gesture of fealty, declaring urgently that he was His Grace's man until his life's end. Rising, he spoke low-voiced and hurriedly. He said that they might well not be left long alone, and so he must say what he had to tell him quickly. First, he had brought a letter from the Archbishop of St. Andrews and the Abbot of Arbroath. This he handed over, recommending that it be hidden meantime—James passing it to David, who pocketed it within his doublet. Secondly, Lennox told them that the King's predicament and shameful captivity was not forgotten or accepted by many of his loyal subjects. Angus seemed to have all his own way for the time being, but forces were being mustered against him and it would not be long before a move would be made to right the wrong. He himself was actively gathering support, especially in the Highlands. Once the harvest was in up there they would march south. The clans would never rise before harvest, since the cattle, their life's-blood, depended on the winter-feed the hay and oats represented. In September then, God willing, they should be in a position to challenge Angus. Not only the Highlanders, of course; many others would rise. From his own Lennox, from the Stewart lands of Renfrew and Bute, from Gowrie, Menteith, Fife and Galloway, even in the Borders many hated Angus who bore hardly on them, using the Homes to do his ill work for him . . .

At mention of the Borders, James interrupted to declare that he was going there, with Angus, in a week's time, on justice-ayres. He had never been to the Borderland, never really been anywhere in the realm save Stirling, Linlithgow and Edinburgh. Could they do anything, speak to any who would help, while they were there?

It was at this stage that Lennox's fears about interruption were proved valid, for the door was thrown open and Abbot William and Sir Archibald Douglas came in, with no pretence at by-your-leave even though they bowed briefly to the King. Graysteel announced that they had some papers urgently requiring the royal signature, and his brother produced some documents.

Lennox took the hint and bowed himself out.

The documents proved to be far from pressing, merely an excuse.

The Douglas brothers gone, David produced the letter Lennox had brought.

It was from Davie Beaton. He too announced that the Holyrood captives were not forgotten and that Angus's power was less complete than it probably seemed to them. Moves were afoot to unite the forces against Douglas. No details in this letter, which could fall into wrong hands; but it was to be hoped that their ordeal would soon be over. Needless to say, the Archbishop would not resign the Chancellorship nor return the Great Seal, recognising that King James would have signed the order only under duress. The Earl of Lennox was to be trusted and had large influence, especially in the Highlands; and Argyll was helping, with his Campbells. Once read, this letter should be burned.

Much heartened, the recipients complied with that last. James was cock-a-hoop, and fell to be warned by his friend not to be over-optimistic, for the Douglases were very strong and in a position to bring much pressure to bear on the fearful and the hesitant. Admittedly their power did not extend into the Highlands, where lay James's best hopes—if those strange warrior-clans could be coaxed southwards. James must seek not to reveal by any evident good spirits that they had received encouraging news, which could alert their captors.

That wise advice was more easily given than acted upon. However, the King's obvious satisfaction at the whole idea of the Borderland assize trip and the comparative freedom it represented, was not dangerous and probably the Douglases put his high spirits down to that. David was to go too, the boy declaring that he himself would refuse otherwise.

* * *

The Borderland episode of 1526 had an extraordinary effect on James Stewart—more so than even David anticipated. Just how enclosed a life the fourteen-year-old had led, shut up in fortresses all his days, was apt to be forgotten. He had been allowed to hunt and hawk and ride short distances from his places of captivity, of course, but always under strict guard, never permitted to roam the land, see new scenes and faces, mix with his subjects, meet the common people. All beyond his keepers and their courts was a new world for him—the more intriguing in that he was nominally the lord of it all. The sheer feeling of space, release from confinement, the illusion of liberty, with the changing scenery, towns, villages, houses, rivers and lochs and moors, gripped him with the excitement of what could be round the next bend in the track. He was still under close watch, to be sure, and still not allowed to mix with others than their hosts at abbeys, castles and towers where they rested and put up; but he was seeing new faces all the time, undergoing new experiences, listening to litigants in the various court-sittings of the justice-ayres, witnessing justice being done, even men being hanged or having their hands chopped off or their genitals emasculated—although blessedly these cases were in a minority, for each holder of a barony had his own powers of pit and gallows and did not require the royal justiciar's authority to imprison or hang in other than pleas of the crown. These summary jurisdictions applied to Holy Church also. Treason, rebellion, theft of royal revenues, assault or robbery on the King's highways, high-seas piracy and such-like did not occur every day. So most of the cases before the justiciar, sitting in the King's name, were disputes about lands and boundaries, rights, privileges and servitudes infringed, inheritances withheld, slanderous accusations circulated, mainly concerning the land-owning classes. All of which was of much educative value for the young monarch, as well as providing interest.

And, strangely enough, it all showed up Angus himself in another light. Where his own personal interests and advantage were not involved, nor those of his friends, he made a generally fair and honest judge, never gentle, admittedly, but equitable, listening attentively to both sides and coming to reasonable and often shrewd decisions. And he was no respecter of persons. James did indeed learn much, sitting by his side in judgement seats.

They went down Lauderdale, to the burgh of Lauder itself, where they hanged certain thieves who had been terrorising and robbing the lieges who had to use the desolate road over the Lammermuirs by Soutra and Fala; and settled a dispute between the barons of Thirlestane and Whitslaid. Then on to the Earlstoun of Ersildoune, where James was more interested in the tower which had belonged to the famous poet and seer, Thomas the Rhymer, than in the rather dull litigation over a boundary demarkation between the common lands and the barony of Cowdenknowes—which being a Home property, the case was decided in their favour. Then on to Melrose, where they passed the night in the great Abbey. No justice was dispensed there, for the Cistercians' foundation had it own regality jurisdiction. Here was the burial-place of many of the Douglases, including the second Earl of Douglas, the hero of Otterburn, and Sir William, the Knight of Liddesdale, alleged Flower of Chivalry. Also, of course, of the heart of Robert the Bruce.

Making their way up Tweed thereafter, they entered the great Forest of Ettrick, for what proved to be a major hanging session at Selkirk, for the Forest, royal lands and covering an enormous area of the Middle March, was the notorious haunt of robbers and broken men; and every now and again batches of these, caught in the interim, fell to be tried and executed by the score, more or less a routine exercise for the justiciar. David Lindsay had expected young James to recoil in horror from all these hangings, but the boy seemed fascinated, observing and commenting on the different attitudes of the victims and how long each took to die.

At Selkirk, Angus's party was joined by a quite large contingent of armed men from the Douglas lands of Yarrow and Megget and around St. Mary's Loch. With these they moved southwards over the hills, by Ashkirk and Synton to the Teviot valley where, at Hawick, a further assize was held and their strength further added to by considerable numbers of the retainers of the Douglases of Drumlanrig and Cavers, the latter hereditary Sheriff of Teviotdale. When they moved on, south-westwards now, climbing towards the high central spine of Lowland Scotland, they had almost a small army with them—which seemed a strange development. Soon it transpired that this was in fact one of the main objectives of the entire expedition—a drive against the Armstrongs.

The Armstrongs were a large and warlike clan of mosstroopers and freebooters inhabiting what was known as the Debateable Lands, of the Middle and West Marches, on both sides of the Borderline—indeed, the term border hardly applied in their area, as the word debateable implied, for the Armstrongs just did not recognise it, and held sway on each side, a law unto themselves. They were a fierce and powerful lot, able to muster thousands on occasion, and normally the Scots and English Wardens left them very much to themselves, as too hot to handle conveniently. But every now and again they tended to overstep the mark and raid properties lying around the perimeter of their area—which, on the Scots side, were apt to be Douglas lands. And when this became serious, punitive measures were called for, and had to be prosecuted in major force, as now.

When James learned of all this, he was much excited, seeing it all as a great adventure, the sort of thing that he had often dreamed of, shut up within fortress walls, stirring battle between knightly hosts and outlaws and rebels. Sadly, however, the King was disappointed, for it seemed that the Armstrongs possessed an excellent information system and were well warned of this Douglas approach. Whether it was the fact that the King was present with Angus inhibiting them, or merely that this July was not a convenient time for them to muster in strength, was not to be known; but they proved entirely elusive, not only not to be brought to battle but not even to be seen. As the Douglas force moved up past Teviothead and over the great watershed at Mosspaul and so down into Ewesdale, heading for the Esk at Langholm, they had scouts well ahead, but these encountered no opposition. Langholm-town itself huddled fearful as they rode through; and beyond was Armstrong country. But it was a deserted land they entered—although only recently deserted. These green hills and dales were never densely populated, but there were not a few farms and upland properties surrounding small stone peel-towers, and all those readily reached from the passes and roads were empty, cattle and even poultry gone with their owners, even though in some peat-fires still smouldered on hearths. That Angus's men left more than peat smouldering at most of these was scant consolation for lack of either slaughter or booty—and anyway, bare stone towers do not burn readily. Where the Armstrongs and their beasts had gone was not clear, but the hills and the hidden valleys stretched away to infinity on every hand, and could swallow up hundreds.

Angus was making specifically for Gilnockie Tower, the seat of the most prominent and notorious of the Armstrong leaders, not the chief himself but his brother, Johnnie Armstrong of Gilnockie, who was renowned far beyond the Borderland for his daring, his disrespect for all authority other than his own, the style he kept—he was reputed seldom to ride abroad without a tail of up to thirty Armstrong lairds—and the fact that he boasted he could raise one thousand mounted men in three days and two thousand in a week. Angus had every intention of hanging this insolent individual out-of-hand if he could catch him; but when they reached Gilnockie, on Eskside some five miles south of Langholm, it was to find the place deserted like the rest. Not only this, but the tower itself was a disappointment for it was no more than a square stone keep within a courtyard, four storeys and a garret in height, with a parapet and wall-walk, sturdy and strong but little larger or more impressive than the other Armstrong fortalices they had already so unsuccessfully tried to burn. It certainly gave no aspect of being able to house and support so puissant a character as the famous Johnnie, much less his reputed entourage, almost the only distinction of Gilnockie Tower being the stone beacon surmounting its topmost gable—this presumably the means by which he summoned his supporting hordes from near and far, with a blazing signal which would touch off other beacons in prominent positions on the surrounding hills, a sort of static fiery-cross.

Angus went to great exertions to ravage if not demolish this small empty stronghold; but with walls six feet thick and precious little woodwork, and no cannon nor gunpowder available, little could be done save to burn the notably simple furnishings left behind, the hay and straw in the stables and byres, and such other perishables as could be found. Presumably more gear was hidden not too far away, but search-parties failed to locate any.

The justiciar's force reluctantly turned northwards again, recognising the hopelessness of probing further into this Debateable Land, and leaving a great column of smoke rising above Gilnockie—mainly burning hay and the thatches of the surrounding shacks and cot-houses—which Angus hopefully described as an alternative beacon to let the Armstrongs know who ruled in Scotland. But it all made a very hollow triumph, and the Earl made irritable company for the next day or two.

A surprise greeted them back at Hawick, where they found the Earl of Lennox and a small company awaiting them. He said that he had come to pay a visit to his kinsman, Sir Walter Scott of Buccleuch, at nearby Branxholm, but had found him from home; and hearing that His Grace and Angus were in the area, he thought it only civil to wait and pay his respects. Angus demonstrated no joy at this encounter, but could hardly banish his fellow-earl from the King's company when he indicated that he would ride on with them.

That evening at Jedburgh, Lennox contrived a brief private word with David Lindsay, having been unable to find James alone. He said that when they had told him at Holyrood of this borders expedition, he had decided to try to make some attempt to rescue the King. He had in fact seen Scott of Buccleuch, who was the Warden of the Middle March, and put the attempt into his hands—for the Borderers were always loth to fight under any but their own leaders. Buccleuch was away now drumming up support amongst his own Scotts, the Elliots and Turnbulls and Pringles of these parts. But they had not expected Angus back from the Armstrong country so soon, and any attack would have to be hastened on or it would be too late to effect it in the Borderland. So he himself was remaining with the royal party, to try to send messengers secretly to Buccleuch as to details of positions and numbers. It was unfortunate that Angus had so large a force with him on a justice-ayres. They had not reckoned on so many.

David, whilst grateful that efforts should be made to free them, was distinctly doubtful over this situation. He understood that Angus was making for Roxburgh, where Teviot and Tweed met, then to move north up Tweed again to Melrose on their way back to Edinburgh. So there would not be much time for Scott to gather an adequate force. It was probable that the Douglases of Cavers and Drumlanrig would leave Angus when he moved out of Teviotdale, so his numbers might be considerably lessened; but even so, there might not be time to assemble . . .

In fact, next day, although the Teviotdale Douglases did turn back, reducing Angus's company by some four hundred, this sadly was more than made up for by the appearance in the afternoon, in the St. Boswells area, of a mixed band of Homes and Kerrs to the number of almost six hundred. And worse, these came because there was a rumour circulating in the East March that Scott of Buccleuch was planning some sort of attack on the King and his guardians.

So Angus was not only reinforced but warned. He ordered more support from the nearby Kerr and Home lands and put his people on the alert, riding in tight formation now. And he turned on Lennox with some suspicion, since he had recently been in touch with Buccleuch. For his part Lennox denied all knowledge of where Scott was or what he was about, and suggested that the tale was a nonsense, for he would swear that none was a more loyal subject than Sir Walter.

Thus, wary and keyed up, they came to Melrose again. Angus decided to remain at the Abbey there for another full day, to give opportunity for further Homes and Kerrs to arrive. These did appear, over the next thirty-six hours, in batches small and quite large, so that the Douglas was able to count a force of little less than two thousand—with Melrose groaning under the impact. No signs of Buccleuch's muster was reported. Whether Lennox had been able to reach them with messengers was not to be known.

They left Melrose on the morning of the 25th of July, to head northwards by a different route, up the Allen Water valley, parallel with the Leader, as being less likely to be watched by potential enemies, and so headed westwards at first, to cross

Tweed by the Darnlee ford. They had gone, in fact, not much more than a mile from the Abbey and were nearing Darnick Tower and hamlet, before the approach to the ford, when all at the head of the long and necessarily strung-out column were surprised by the sounding of horns blown from ahead and to the flank. There was a low wooded hill, scarcely high enough to be so-called in the Borderland, between the road and the river, and rounding the shoulder of this, Angus and his leadership group were astonished to find the track ahead of them barred by a solid phalanx of mounted men, armoured and with banners, more and more riders emerging from the cover of the woodland, more horns blowing. The Douglases drew rein abruptly, with consequent considerable bunching and confusion behind. Angus had no scouts out thus early after leaving the Abbey, and scarcely out of the town.

The barrier of men and horses was perhaps two hundred yards ahead, and at its centre was a group of knightly figures in fine armour and plumed helmets under the blue-and-gold standard of Scott. One of these reined forward a little way and held up a steel-gauntleted hand.

"Hail the King's Highness!" he shouted. "I, Buccleuch, Warden of the Middle March, greet the King's Grace, and request the honour of his escort whilst he is in this March—as is my undoubted right. Will you so honour me, Sire, and receive my homage?"

For moments all around the King were struck dumb by this unexpected development, so different from any assault or ambush such as had been anticipated. Then Angus found his voice.

"Buccleuch—what are you at?" he demanded, having necessarily to shout also, at that range. "This is Angus. King James is in *my* keeping. His Grace requires no further escort."

"In the Middle March he should be in *mine*, my lord. You know it."

"Not so. I am Chief Warden of all the Marches, His Grace remains with me."

It was a highly dramatic and extraordinary situation, the two Wardens facing each other some one hundred and fifty yards apart, each backed by a cohort of armed men—and not only Wardens but cousins, for Buccleuch's grandfather had married the sister of Bell-the-Cat, fourth Earl of Angus, the present

Earl's grandfather. David Lindsay sat tense beside James's horse. Lennox watched, still-faced, nearby.

"Angus—my words are for the King's Grace, not for you," Scott cried. "In the presence of his royal person you have no authority over me or any. Sire—will you come to my good care . . . ?"

Angus precluded any answer from James. "Buccleuch—if you wish to pay your humble duty to His Grace, come you here and do so," he called. "But come alone."

"Is the King of Scots not to be allowed to speak his own mind in the presence of Douglas!"

"Fool! In your insolence you deny His Grace passage. Clear your ruffians from this road. Before I clear it for him! And a new Warden for the Middle March will be required, I swear!"

Lennox raised his voice. "My lords," he began reasonably. "This is folly! King James should surely go forward to receive the homage of these his illustrious subjects. *I* will escort him, Angus, if you fear aught . . ."

"No!" the Douglas barked. "Enough! Begone, Scott—while you still have a head on your shoulders!"

"Not so, Angus. You have held His Grace captive sufficiently long, to your shame and his royal hurt. Now he will go free. Sire—come forward, I pray you . . ."

Angus reined his mount round, almost unsaddling his Uncle Archibald in the process, to lean over and grab James's bridle—eloquent enough answer.

It was sufficiently so for Buccleuch, at any rate. Turning, he raised a curling bull's-horn to his lips and blew a long quivering blast, then lifted his steel-clad arm again and thrust it forward, pointing. And with a roar the ranked horsemen blocking the way lowered lances and whipped out swords and spurred into action. "A Bellendaine! A Bellendaine!" they yelled, the Scott slogan.

There was inevitable confusion in the royal cavalcade at this sudden charge. Most of the column was still out-of-sight around the shoulder of the hill. The leaders wheeled their beasts to get out of the way of the Scott onslaught, some spurring off into the flanking trees, some heading directly back, some seeking to prepare those behind to stand their ground. Angus himself, rearing his mount on its hind legs, yelled to Graysteel to bring the King, and then dashed headlong through the press behind him, cannoning men and horses aside, clearly not in any panic to escape but to gain control of his host further back and to dispose it to face this challenge.

James, David and Lennox found themselves surrounded by a group of Douglas lairds under Sir Archibald, and rudely forced round and driven towards the rear. It crossed David's mind to try to resist, but unarmed and alone he reckoned it would be pointless and might result in danger to the King; besides, the mass of shouting men hurtling towards them in a thunder of hooves was sufficiently daunting to vanquish every other urge than to get out of their way. Back they went amongst the jostling throng.

That bend in the road round the shoulder of hill was the key to the entire encounter. It meant that neither side, at the start, had any clear idea of the other's strength. Also no broad front was possible for the attacking charge, which inevitably had the effect of slowing it down and diluting its force, whilst at the same time preventing those behind the leadership from perceiving what went on, or even being able to receive signals and commands. A better place for a hidden and waiting ambush, and a worse for an onrushing assault, would have been difficult to envisage.

After the first undignified scurry rearwards, the reverse applied to Angus's force. Once back round the bend, there was plenty of space for his people to form up and manoeuvre; likewise to see and follow their lord's orders. The Earl was quick to recognise all this, and acted decisively. Spurring furiously towards his own bewildered and milling main body, he waved his arm urgently right and left, right and left, yelling to divide, divide, divide. How many perceived the implications of his tactics was doubtful; but the way he drove down on his own column, with the waving and shouting, was unmistakable. Men reined aside hurriedly to get out of his way and to give him passage. But once in their midst, he wheeled his spirited but long-suffering charger right round again, it pawing the air, and went on yelling and gesturing to divide into two, that command at least now entirely clear. Jostling and sidling, in something not far from chaos, his following, or the front half of it, did somehow split into two uneven sections, with himself and some of his lieutenants, including David, the King and Lennox, left in the centre.

This was the situation which confronted Buccleuch as he and

his foremost ranks came pounding round the bend. And Angus had guessed aright—not very difficult to do perhaps, for the attackers' obvious strategy on so narrow a front was to constitute themselves into the traditional wedge or spearhead formation and to drive headlong at the enemy front and leadership, bore through it and break it up in confusion, then to wheel round on its rear, a well-proved cavalry device. Buccleuch attempted just that—but found the enemy already divided into two and awaiting him, and only the little group left in the centre as target, leaders though they were. And so close were they that there was no time to change tactics in a thundering charge. Buccleuch, at the head of the wedge, could try to switch his attack somewhat to one side or the other, but that would leave the unassailed section free to assault his wedge in flank, where it was most vulnerable.

Decision had to be taken almost instantly, and Scott, probably advisedly in the circumstances, elected to continue for the centre, where at least he might bring down Angus himself and his leaders and just possibly capture the prize of the King. But this too the Earl had foreseen, using himself as bait. As Buccleuch bore down on him, sword swinging, he yelled to Graysteel, pointing, to take James into the press of his people on the left or south side, while he flung himself, with some others, into the temporary anonymity of the throng on the right—and with only brief seconds to spare. The attackers, quite unable to change course at that range, came crashing down into the now empty gap, still shouting, "A Bellendaine! A Bellendaine!"

What happened thereafter was all but indescribable. Horses at full charge cannot be pulled up in short space, so Buccleuch's formation went plunging down the corridor between the two sections of Angus's force, and these promptly turned in on them on both sides in smiting fury. In moments the scene was utter turmoil, a wild mêlée of flailing, hacking, shouting men and rearing, stumbling, neighing horses. Adding to the pandemonium was the pressure from behind, as more and more of Buccleuch's people came piling in at the gallop, and the rearmost hundreds of Angus's column did the same. It became complete, savage tumult and disorder, with no sort of planning nor direction possible on either side, the leaders themselves lost in the general shambles. Angus was a born fighter and Buccleuch a veteran Border warrior, but as the encounter had so swiftly developed, they were both all but helpless to control their followings. What ensued was not so much a battle as a medley of countless individual combats, in closest proximity and constriction, hopelessly entangled in bloody riot.

In these circumstances, inevitably numbers told, and when everything became evident it was that there was a lot more with Angus than with Buccleuch.

Whenever the clash commenced, David Lindsay saw the safety of the King as his one duty. So, whilst all around him were pressing inwards to the attack, grabbing James's bridle, he sought to push in the other direction, outwards away from the battling. It was anything but easy, forcing their alarmed mounts against the tide of struggling, plunging horseflesh and bawling, sword-wielding men, and more then once they were all but unseated, their knees were bruised, their bodies buffeted. But at length, more perhaps by the tide leaving them than themselves gaining on it, they found themselves free of the press and on a slight grassy rise, from which they could turn and view all.

James was trembling, not with fear but with excitement, gasping incoherent exclamations, questions. Scanning the terrible scene of passion and hatred and bloodshed, David pointed and pointed again.

"Outnumbered!" he cried, above the din. "Aye, outnumbered. Two to one, I'd say. Hard to see . . . who is who. But, see you—Buccleuch can have no more than a thousand there, if that. And Angus twice as many. I fear, I greatly fear . . ."

"Perhaps they will . . . I cannot tell . . . where is Buccleuch? All the banners are down. Davie—what can we do? Surely we can aid them . . ."

"No—we cannot. Nothing that we can do, unarmed. You, the King, must stand safe. That is our only part. *Your* part. You are the King . . ."

For how long that dire struggle lasted there was no knowing, for time was irrelevant, went unnoticed. But gradually some pattern in the disarray did begin to evolve, some recognisable drift—and that drift was westward almost imperceptible at first, then becoming more evident, westwards and north-westwards, the direction from which the attack had come, round that bend in the road and into the woodland. More and more of Buccleuch's people were breaking away, perceiving their fight as hopeless and making their escape whilst they could.

Whether Angus was content with this gradual exodus of his enemies, or was in no position to halt it anyway, the watchers, joined now by Lennox, could not tell. They could not even pick out Angus's person in the mêlée. But presently the trickle became a flow, a flood, and the battle, if such it could be called, more or less ground to a halt.

The Douglases and their allies were left in possession of the field. And that field was a grievous sight, littered with the dead and wounded, riderless horses everywhere, the dark-red stains of blood seemingly splashed over all.

Angus, himself bleeding from a grazed forehead and cheek—for, like most of his lieutenants, he had been caught helmetless by the attack—materialised from the milling throng and came spurring up to the King, hot eyes hotter than ever.

"So much for your friends!" he jerked. "How Buccleuch pays his homage! You are going to require a new Warden of the Middle March!" He swung on Lennox. "And you, my lord—what part did *you* play in that onset? Little that was honest, I swear!"

His fellow earl shrugged. "What part should I have played, Angus?" he asked. "Save to take concern for His Grace's safety. Do you require me to aid you put down but half your numbers of Buccleuch's people?"

"So you stood by and lifted no hand! God's wounds—if I thought that you had helped to bring down those dastards upon us, Lennox, I would, would . . . !" The mailed fist rose, quivering.

Lennox reined back, involuntarily.

"Is, is Buccleuch . . . ? Is he . . . fallen?" That was James, thick-voiced.

"I know not—nor care!" Angus reined his mount round, to ride back to the scene of carnage, where wounded were being picked out from dead, friend from foe. Over his shoulder, he threw back the command. "Lindsay—take His Grace back to the Abbey. Kilspindie will accompany you. We shall wait until the morrow to ride north."

Lennox, when the other was gone, shook his head. "A bungled business!" he said. "A sorry outcome, ill-managed. Myself, I will be off. Nothing for me here. But, Sire—do not lose heart. We shall do better than this, for Your Grace. At the least, it has shown that the Lowlands are not waiting for the Highlands to save the King. The clans will now heed me, I think. This is only the first blow struck in Your Grace's cause." He reached out to take the King's hand, and kissed it, before riding off.

Doubtfully the other two looked after him, as Archibald Douglas came up to escort them back to Melrose Abbey.

They learned, later, that Buccleuch was not amongst the eighty dead and many more left wounded on the field of what Angus called the Scott Skirmish of Darnick.

Next day, still heavily escorted by Homes and Kerrs, they rode by the shortest route, up Lauderdale, for Edinburgh. The Earl was in a black mood, not triumphant over his victory but angry that such a revolt against his authority should have taken place, especially in his own Borderland. Also that he had been caught in a position where he had been unable properly to control and direct his forces, so that they had fought like any rabble. He exemplified his ill-humour, on arrival at Holyrood, by swinging on David Lindsay and telling him, without warning, that he was dismissed from the King's service, and to be gone. He declared that he had seen his head close to Lennox's on more than one occasion—and he believed Lennox to be behind the affair at Darnick. He must leave forthwith.

In vain James pleaded, threatened that he would do nothing that he was told, would sign no more papers, wept even. Angus was scornfully adamant.

David was not allowed even to see the King alone thereafter. With a strained and almost tearful farewell, he rode away from the Abbey of the Holy Rood that same evening.

6

It was almost a repetition of the previous occasion fifteen months before, when Davie Beaton came riding back to The Mount of Lindifferon—save that this time it was the oat harvest, not the hay, which was being gathered, in early September, and a different field in which Lindsay was wielding his sickle, in line with his men. Beaton perceived another difference too, as he came up—his friend no longer bore the former dour, grim expression and bearing but, without being especially lively or demonstrative on this warm afternoon of hard labour, was much more his normal self.

"Is it the scourging of your body for the weal of your soul? Or do you *like* to labour and toil with your hands?" Beaton greeted him, dismounting. "I never knew the like."

"Some honest toil would do *you* no harm!" he was told. "Sweat some of the intrigue and plotting out of you."

"I think not, friend. The talents the good Lord has given my unworthy self to use reside in my head rather than my muscles, I judge! For every man of wits there are a thousand with mere thews. You, it seems, have both, in some degree."

"I thank you! After the months shut up in Holyrood, I find this labour in the fields to my taste. But—what brings you here, Davie? When you come visiting, I fear the worst!"

"Ingrate! You must agree that I bring diversity and interest into your life? Yes, I have word for you of something more lively than reaping oats." Beaton took his friend's arm, to lead him out of earshot of the other workers. "Affairs are on the move, David—at last. Lennox has achieved it—with some help from St. Andrews! He has mustered an army and is ready to march, from beyond the Highland Line. To sweep Angus from power and win James his freedom."

The other made no comment.

"Come, man—this is what we have been waiting for, what I have been working for. In God's name, show some heed!"

"I heed you, yes. But—I was at Darnick!"

"Darnick! That was but a gesture, a shaken fist—and a palsied one! This is otherwise—a stabbing sword! Not a few mosstroopers, ill led, but a great army on the march, the clans moving south. And more than the clans—Gowrie, The Stormounth, Strathearn, Menteith, The Lennox, and others south of the Line. This is the challenge to Angus. Argyll, Atholl, Erroll, Huntly, the Marischal—all these earls are in it, lords and chiefs by the score. And Holy Church paying the siller! This time Angus has war on his hands, not gestures! Do not tell me that you, of all men do not rejoice?"

The other shrugged. "As to rejoicing, I reserve mine, meantime. If James can be won out of Angus's grip, then none will be more glad than I. So long as he is not to fall into other hands little less harsh. But—major war? Scots slaying Scots by the hundred, the thousand—is that the price? Aye—and is that not what Henry Tudor seeks? To weaken the realm so that he can take it over?"

"Angus put down, and the realm united round the young King, would set Henry back, man. That is sure. This is the only way to get rid of Angus. I have been scheming and planning—aye, and paying—for this these many months. While you were shut up in Holyrood, I have been sowing the seed—now, pray God, is the harvest! And a deal more vital for Scotland than your wretched oats, David Lindsay! I lead a party of my uncle's retainers, and some of my own from Arbroath, to join the host at Stirling in four days time. I want you with me. You have had experience of warfare, under the late de la Bastie. I have had none. Nor have most of the Lowland lords who will be there—the legacy of Flodden where all our warriors fell. Do not say that you will not come? You, the King's friend."

Lindsay kicked almost savagely at a sheaf of oats lying there. "Damn you, man—you never let me be!" he cried. "Always you are at me to do this, to do that!"

"You can always refuse, can you not?"

"That is the curse of it! I *cannot* refuse. I never can, the way you charge me with it. Well you know it . . ."

Beaton smiled, and gripped his friend's shoulder. "That is well, then—you cannot refuse! Curse me as you will, so long as you come!"

"You are a devil, abbot as you may be . . . !"

So, three days later, Lindsay rode westwards again, en route for Stirling, with his so-demanding friend, at the head of some four score armed retainers in the fine livery of the archdiocese of St. Andrews, with more to be picked up at the great Abbey of Dunfermline and at the lesser one of Culross. Beaton was in high spirits, eager to see the consummation of all his planning.

By the time they left Culross they had almost two hundred—and had also collected Abbot John Inglis thereof, Lindsay's old former colleague and assistant tutor to James, now back less than enthusiastically to the life religious.

Fife and Fothrif left behind, fifteen miles further west, at Cambuskenneth Abbey under the soaring castle-rock of Stirling, despite almost doubling their strength again, from this place as well as the Abbeys of Lindores and Balmerino, they received news to perturb them. Lennox and Atholl with their army were no longer at Stirling, having left at first light that morning for the east, without waiting not only for the Church contingent but for the Earl of Argyll and his Campbells and the Earl of Moray and a further large company from the far north-east. It seemed that Lennox had learned that Angus had recently taken King James to Linlithgow, because Edinburgh was undergoing one of its periodic visitations of the plague—Linlithgow only eighteen miles east of Stirling. And only last night word had come from there that Angus himself had had to return to the capital temporarily for some reason, so that for the moment James was left in the care of George Douglas of Pittendreich, another of the Earl's uncles. Lennox saw it as a God-sent opportunity to strike swiftly, grab the King whilst Angus was still absent—and do the main fighting later, with James safely in their hands as figurehead. Linlithgow was a palace, no great castle or fortress, and should not be difficult to take.

If Davie Beaton was concerned over this sudden change of plan, he was not nearly so much so as David Lindsay. Lennox was no seasoned warrior, and even though his force, allegedly about five thousand, might well greatly outnumber the Douglases at Linlithgow, Angus would not be such a fool as to leave James less than adequately guarded. It was almost certain that he had heard that a host was gathering against him behind the Highland Line—indeed it was quite likely that he had gone to Edinburgh again to drum up and co-ordinate reinforcements. Besides, Linlithgow area was Hamilton territory and now that Arran was in league with Angus, the country round about would be against them. Not to have waited for Argyll and Moray, in especial, was folly.

That night the two Davids debated as to what they should do—whether to hurry on after Lennox, with their near four hundred, or to wait for the Campbells and Moray men. Lindsay was in favour of the latter, for the Campbells were seasoned fighters and Argyll could put a couple of thousand men in the field, at least; thus they would have a strong and well-led force to go to Lennox's aid, if he needed it. Beaton argued that immediacy was more important. Lennox would take only a few hours to reach Linlithgow. If he needed help, he needed it now rather than vaguely in the future. If Argyll or Moray were not reported nearby first thing in the morning, they should hurry on eastwards after Lennox, with all speed.

Beaton won, of course; the men were his, even though Lindsay was there as the experienced campaigner. And at sun-up, with no word of new arrivals from north or west, Holy Church's contingent set off along the south side of Forth for Linlithgow, with some trepidation.

They went by St. Ninians and the mustering-place for the Bruce's mighty victory at Bannockburn, passing the mill thereof where James's grandfather had died ingloriously, and on through the great Tor Wood which stretched for many miles to above Falkirk, where Wallace had suffered defeat—for this was the cockpit area of Scotland. Thereafter, keeping to the high ground of Muiravonside, they crossed the Redding and Polmont moors until presently they could see the green low hills around Linlithgow some miles ahead, and began to drop down to the lower levels. From here all looked entirely peaceful.

It was as they neared the valley of the Lothian Avon that they caught up with Lennox, relieved to find that so far there had been no hostilities. But that situation appeared to be about to end. Lennox, Atholl and the other lords and chiefs were clustered on the summit of a wooded knoll overlooking the quite deep river-valley, their troops resting all around, part Highland, part Lowland, each category keeping well apart from the other.

The two Davids rode up to the knoll—and Lindsay was surprised to find his father-in-law there, along with the Kennedy chief, the Earl of Cassillis, and a batch of Stewarts, the Lords Avondale and Innermeath, the Bishop of Caithness, and the Highland Stewarts of Appin, Ardvoirlich, Garth, Fasnacloich and Invernahyle. They were loud in argument, amidst much pointing and gesticulation.

The bridge over the Avon could not actually be seen from here—the only one upstream or down for many miles, and carrying the main Edinburgh-Stirling road. It seemed that their scouts reported that the bridge was held against them, by Hamiltons under Arran himself, with some Douglas support. The main enemy force was massed on the up-sloping far side of the river, but a strong party had been thrown forward to this side to hold a bridgehead. The dispute on the knoll was as to tactics. Atholl was a huge, golden man, shoulder-long hair and silky beard gleaming, black armour so chased and engraved with gold that little of the steel was noticeable, known as The Magnificent, on account of his princely extravagance. He was advocating, demanding indeed, direct assault on the bridge, asserting that they could easily over-run the defenders there with a Highland charge and their superior numbers. Cassillis and most of the Highland Stewarts agreed with this. Lords Lindsay, Avondale and Innermeath however, declared that it would be too costly, that even though they won the bridge itself, they could be bottled up at the other side unable to get sufficient men across its narrow passage to break out. They must seek a crossing elsewhere. Lennox himself appeared undecided.

The arrival of the two newcomers went all but unnoticed, save by Lennox—who possibly saw in them the means to help him make up his mind.

"Beaton—Lindsay!" he greeted. "How say you? Linlithgow Bridge is held against us, and Arran masses his Hamiltons beyond. But less than our numbers. Shall we attack?"

Beaton gestured to his friend to speak first.

David shook his head. "It would be folly to assail a held bridge, with a large force waiting behind it. You might capture the bridge itself, but you could get only a few men across at a time. They would be wiped out as they reached the other side."

"What, then?"

"You have little choice. Either you wait here for the enemy—let *them* make the crossing. Or you cross the river elsewhere."

"Another craven!" Atholl exclaimed. "What are we? Bairns, to be given lessons? We have here a Highland host, man—they will take that bridge and swarm beyond it, like bees out of a bike!"

"Ringed in beyond by steel-clad men on horses, my lord, your bees will never win out of their bike to swarm!"

"Where else could we cross?" Lennox asked. "It is a steep valley, although the river itself is not very deep. We cannot just sit here, waiting. *They* will not cross to us, I swear!"

Beaton spoke. "There is a small nunnery something over a mile upstream, the Priory of Emmanuel. Under the protection of the Order of St. John of Jerusalem, whose Preceptory of Torphichen is but two miles further—but at the other side of this Avon. I know it well. There is much coming and going between the two houses. There is no bridge—but there is a ford—the Nuns' Ford. It is narrow for such a host as this, but . . ."

"A ford! Only a mile up . . . ?"

"Here's better talking," Lord Lindsay said.

"Narrow you say?" Lennox asked. "How narrow?"

"I cannot say. I did not measure it. Scarcely made for an army to cross. But . . ."

"Three abreast? Four . . . ?"

"Oh, yes—that, surely."

"Then let us be on our way. We had wasted overlong here . . ."

"Wait, my lord—wait a little," David Lindsay broke in. "This is Hamilton country. The Hamiltons may well know this Nuns' Ford. If Arran is waiting, and watching the bridge, he may be watching the ford also. And if it is narrow, it could be almost as easily defended as the bridge . . ."

"God save us from the fearful!" Atholl cried. "Are we men or, or nuns! I say, let us down to this bridge and see what steel can do, Highland steel! Enough of this talk."

"Wait, John," Lennox said. "Much depends on this." These two, chiefs of independent Stewart septs, were married to sisters. "Lindsay of the Mount learned war with de la Bastie, the First Knight of Christendom."

"Let my lord of Atholl lead his Highlandmen down to the bridge," David nodded. "This I was about to suggest, but to wait, in full view, not to attack. The rest, the horsed host, to make for the ford, unseen. See you, Arran and the Hamiltons will know that we are here—but they cannot see us yet. Nor we them. They cannot know our full numbers. If part of your force shows itself this side of the bridge and seems to prepare to attack, Arran will assume belike that this is the *entire* host. Especially if it displays all the banners, and not a few armoured knights as well as the clansmen. The rest of us, horsed, hasten up to the ford, to cross, out of sight, to win *behind* the Hamiltons. Then we have them front and rear. Even if the ford is watched and word sent to Arran, he will not dare to leave the bridge. He will have to split his force . . ."

"Good! There speaks good sense," Lennox cried. "John—you hear? Take you the clansmen and go show yourselves at the bridge. Make as though to assail it. I will take the horsed people and try to get behind Arran. Give me a little time . . ."

Atholl snorted, but swung his mount round.

With much blowing of horns thereafter the two distinct portions of the army divided, not difficult since they kept well apart anyway, the Lowland cavalry to mount their beasts and the Highlanders to cluster in their clans and sept groupings. There were far more of the latter than the former; nevertheless, the mounted force, including the new Church contingent, which presently set off at speed southwards, numbered above one thousand. Some lords and knights remained with Atholl, to make a show, with all the colourful flags and banners. Whether Atholl, on his own, would wait and be content merely to demonstrate rather than promptly hurl into the attack, was an open question.

Davie Beaton led the way up through the rolling grassy braes and open woodland which flanked this west bank of the Avon, safely hidden from the east or Linlithgow side. It proved to be somewhat more than a mile to the Priory of Emmanuel, but they were soon there. Leaving the cohorts of cavalry to be eyed askance by the alarmed nuns, with Abbot John Inglis to reassure them, the leaders rode down to the riverside, to inspect the ford.

It was as David had feared. A little group of Hamilton horsemen were hanging about on the far side of the river, watching. At sight of the newcomers, these bunched together and came down to the head of the ford, obviously prepared to contest passage.

"No more than a score," Lord Lindsay commented. "These cannot hold us up for long."

"But they can send to warn Arran," his son-in-law pointed out. "Only a mile away, if Arran is but behind the bridge. A mile back—and he could have a force here in only a short time. We will have to get our people across fast, these guards or none."

Davie Beaton was forward, peering into the river. "Twelve feet wide, the causeway, not much more," he reported. "Four abreast at the most. And slippery."

"No delay, then," Lennox decided. "Bring the men, with all haste." His sword drawn, he was the first to urge his horse down into the water.

"Wait, my lord," David advised. "Why fight against odds? Let *them* do that. Now they see only a few men here. But when our host appears, these Hamiltons will perceive that they have no chance of holding us up, and will bolt." He did not add that a field commander's task was to guide and control his force, not to act as outrider, however gallant.

Quickly the first files of the cavalry appeared, and were directed down into the water. Great blocks of stone had been set there, some two feet below the present surface, much shallowing the river. In this early September, after the summer, the water was running low; but this advantage was to some extent offset by the quantities of green slime on the stones, which would be swept clean by winter's floods. Davie Beaton was urgent in advising the horsemen to go slowly, carefully across, as their mounts could so easily slip and fall, to create havoc behind.

Fortunately, as more and more men appeared from the direction of the Priory, the waiting Hamiltons recognised that they could not possibly do more than hold up the first files for a brief interval, and evidently decided that this effort would be pointless. They wheeled around, then, and spurred away up the opposite bank and disappeared.

Lennox was not to be deterred from being one of the first to cross. And once over he still would not wait for all this force to make the passage, but himself pressed on, up the bank and then downstream again, with a mere hundred or so at his back. David Lindsay cursed, shouted to Beaton at the other side that he was going to try to restrain the Earl, and raced off in pursuit.

Up on the higher ground there was still no extended view, owing to the rolling nature of the land hereabouts, certainly no sign of the enemy. David pounded after Lennox, with others coming piecemeal behind him.

He came up with the Earl and his group at the lip of a steep ravine, where a tributory stream came in from the east, Lennox prospecting the best way across. David urged a general halt here meantime, to assemble their host in some sort of battle order before moving on. And if a detachment of Arran's force appeared in the interim, this was a good defensive position to withstand it.

But Lennox would not hear of it. He was not looking for any defensive position, he cried. He was here to rescue the King, at Linlithgow; and that was not to be done by sitting inactive and waiting to be attacked.

He set off zigzagging down into the ravine and up the other side, David following on unhappily.

After a little more riding, this advance-guard began to hear the din of strife ahead of them. Atholl was evidently making no mere demonstration at the bridge but was in action. Lennox grew the more eager.

Breasting one of the gentle green ridges of that terrain, suddenly they obtained something of the looked-for vista. Ahead of them the land sank to a wide area of grassy pastureland, still undulating but open now, dotted with wheeling agitated groups of cattle. Beyond, they could see a confused mass of men and banners, but owing to a further drop in the land-level towards the road and bridge, they could not distinguish details of what went on.

Although more of their mounted men had now caught up with them, including some of the lords and knights, Lennox still would not wait for any marshalling of his force. No point in that, he claimed, until they could see the whole field before them, how the enemy was placed, and decide how they were to attack. Clearly Atholl's people were engaged and would require assistance swiftly. He plunged on.

David found Beaton cantering alongside, and panted out his opinions of Lennox's odd generalship. But there seemed to be nothing that they could do meantime, save to keep up and try to control the situation somewhat once it was clarified.

It was as the Stewart host was thundering in great style but no order at all across the grassland, spread out over a great area, both in length and depth, that David became aware that some, many, of those milling cattle-beasts were behaving oddly, not just charging about in confusion as before but heading in a solid mass—and heading towards them, in a stampede, heads down and tails high, and covering quite a wide front. It took only a little longer to perceive the reason—the banners and pennons and lance-tips showing behind the steaming mass of bullocks. The Hamiltons had seen the Stewart advance and were using the old device of driving a herd of frightened cattle before them, to confuse and break up an enemy formation. The fact that there was no formation ahead of them would not lessen the confusion.

In fact what happened thereafter was even worse than that, absolute chaos, a wild clash of charging bullocks and rearing, toppling horses, riders flung from saddles and trampled on by bellowing cattle-beasts, weapons useless. Lennox, in the forefront, was one of the first to go down, disappearing in the steaming, stinking, neighing press, other leaders likewise. David Lindsay, a little behind, recognising what the impact would produce, had just time to take some avoiding action, pulling his mount cruelly back on its haunches and dragging it right round in the same movement, to spur it in the other direction, backwards, however craven-seeming, and yelling to Beaton to do the same. They did not escape all contact with the hurtling cattle, being cannoned into and jostled. But at least they were now proceeding approximately in the same direction as the crazed animals, and they kept their seats. It was a mad situation altogether, to find themselves actually smashing back amongst their own Church followers.

But, however unheroic in appearance, it served some purpose. For seeing their leaders thus in headlong retreat, the Churchmen sought to slow their onwards rush and slew round after them. This also resulted in dire disorder, but at least most of their people escaped the cattle stampede.

Probably the general wide scattered nature of the Stewart advance had its advantages in some degree, for it meant that quite a large proportion did not become involved in the shambles at the front, even though they were still unco-ordinated and more or less leaderless.

Lindsay and Beaton, once out of danger of being over-run, sought to produce at least some order out of the turmoil. Reining round again, David shouted:

"A wedge! A wedge! Here—to us. A Lindsay! A Beaton! Form a wedge. Quickly! A wedge . . ."

Probably few of those who heard him had any real understanding of what he meant, being only the personal guards of prelates and the like, not trained battle-fighters; but at least they rallied round, thankful for some leadership and command. Urgently David sought to marshal them into something of the traditional arrowhead formation, whilst Beaton, for his part, waved in latecomers of their own or of other groups. How many they mustered thus, they had no opportunity to assess, but there would be well over one hundred.

There was no time to wait for more or to try to form these up in better shape. The priorities were vital and immediate—to present some sort of organised opposition to the Hamiltons, for the rest to rally to; and if possible to rescue Lennox—for any force which discovers its commander fallen is in danger of losing its morale as well as its focal point.

Placing himself and Beaton together at the apex of the distinctly ragged wedge, David shouted for their men to keep tight formation, to protect each other, and if the outer riders tired or were wounded, the inner ones to replace them. That was as much as he could do in the circumstances. He flung his sword-point forward in the advance gesture, and dug in his spurs, Davie at his side.

Ahead, the situation was still in disarray but less densely so, for a fair proportion of the cattle-beasts had made off, singly and in groups, the surviving horsemen were recovering and some of those unhorsed regaining their mounts. But as a fighting force it was a travesty and many bullocks remained in milling frenzy. A tight group of Stewart lairds, dismounted, stood around the fallen Lennox, swords and dirks at the ready. And beyond, a couple of hundred yards or so perhaps, the horsed Hamilton force had drawn up in line, on a minor grassy crest, clearly waiting for the right moment, with the cattle out of the way, to charge down and finish off their utterly disorganised enemy. A number of banners flew above them, but in the centre was one larger than the others, the undifferenced arms, red-on-white, of the Hamilton chief, Arran himself.

As David Lindsay took all this in, he had only moments to make up his mind. If he and his merely went to join the Stewart lairds round Lennox, they would lose all the advantage and impetus of their driving wedge, and just be there to be ridden down also when the Hamiltons charged. On the other hand, a direct assault on the waiting enemy line, whilst risky indeed, possibly disastrous, could have great impact, even change the entire situation by, in turn, disorganising Arran's front and giving more time for the scattered Stewarts elsewhere to rally. Arran was notoriously no warrior and might well not react swiftly. If it had been his son the Bastard's banner there in the middle, it would have been very different.

These thoughts flashing through his mind, another was no less evident. To assail Arran with any element of surprise, it would be necessary to plough his wedge first right through that entanglement of their own fellows, horses and bullocks, a grievous thought. But to seek to ride round it all would lose them impetus and also give the Hamiltons all the warning and time they would require to prepare to meet an attack. Lindsay made his decision and drove on the harder.

Yelling their slogans, mainly "A Beaton! A Beaton!" the wedge-formation crashed headlong into the mêlée of men and animals, hurling aside and knocking over right and left with the speed and weight of their impact. At the tip of it all, the two Davids were all but jerked out of their saddles, but were held approximately in position more by the impetus from behind and the pressure at the sides than by their own efforts. It was grievous to see the Stewarts going down around them, some trampled under hooves.

They drove on relentlessly, to thunder past within a score of yards of the ring around Lennox. Lindsay waved in that direction, but that was all, his attention concentrated on maintaining his position and cutting a way through the crush as nearly directly as possible towards that great banner of Arran's.

Pounding and shouting, at last they were through, leaving a trail of ruin behind, with only that couple of hundred yards between them and the long, stationary Hamilton line. Presumably it only then dawned upon Arran and his people that precipitate assault upon them was intended by this comparatively small company, and that something would have to be done immediately. But these were no more trained cavalry than were their opponents, and the instinctive reaction was to get out of the way of that menacing arrowhead—and Arran himself, although hereditary Lord High Admiral of Scotland, was no veteran general, despite his years. He was indeed almost the first to rein round and urgently seek a less exposed position, cannoning into his banner-bearer and those behind in the process. Others took prompt example from their chief, and the centre of the line broke in disorder.

It does not take many moments for even cantering horses to cover two hundred yards, and in the press and confusion little of escape, and certainly no defensive strategy, was achieved before the wedge struck. Although this clash was against sword- and lance-bearing riders, not cattle-beasts and unhorsed men, the difference was not so noticeable as might have been expected, for the Hamiltons were more concerned with getting out of the path of the attackers than the bullocks had been, jostling and impeding each other in their haste, and so close-packed in consequence that their lances were useless and even swords were difficult to wield. The long line, which had been formed thus mainly to act as a barrier to prevent the mounted Stewarts from reaching and rescuing Atholl's Highlanders at the bridge, although perhaps three hundred yards long was only three or four men deep, and this presented no great obstacle to the charging spearhead, which ploughed through in less time than it takes to tell. Admittedly its members had little opportunity to use their swords either, although they knocked over a few of the Hamiltons mainly by collision; but the principal objective was to break up the lines and to upset the leadership. This certainly was achieved.

Lindsay now was faced with his most difficult task, to swing round his wedge to drive in the reverse direction without losing all formation, a large enough problem even with trained cavalry and almost hopeless with these churchmen's retainers. Nevertheless, yelling repeated instructions and waving his sword in pointing gestures, he attempted just that manoeuvre, pulling round left-about, the direction in which he had seen Arran go, and seeking to make as tight an arc of it as was possible.

It was not very successful, in fact, and the resultant wedge was scarcely recognisable as such. Also speed and impetus inevitably dropped. But, determined to retain as much of their advantage as possible, he shouted his orders to reform, and without waiting for any real improvement, led the way back, still with Beaton at his side, spurring to regain speed.

At least his target was not difficult to identify, for Arran's banner-bearer was faithful and kept close to the Earl, round whom numbers of the Hamiltons were rallying. Directly for the great flag Lindsay headed his now oddly-shaped company.

It was scarcely an acceptable military manoeuvre, but at least it had purpose and drive, which elsewhere was notably lacking on that field. Arran's group were in the main leaders, not the led, but that did not make a unified force of them, especially as they got little lead from their chief. Some were for dispersing, some for forming a wedge of their own, some indeterminate. In these circumstances, the dispersers inevitably won, and the group disintegrated in various directions. David headed, as far as he was able, after Arran and his bannerman and a few others foremost in dispersing.

The situation developed almost farcically, with over one hundred churchmen chasing the Lord High Admiral and about a dozen others—the dozen darting hither and thither making for nowhere in particular. But in the nature of things, one hundred are less easy to twist and turn than are a dozen, also slower, and little was achieved. David was deciding to abandon this profitless exercise when Beaton reached over to grasp his arm, and point. Up on the ridge, almost half-a-mile to the east, a new situation was developing. A long line of horsemen were silhouetted, and being added to, many hundreds with banners innumerable, two in the centre large and unmistakable—the red-on-gold Lion Rampant of Scotland and the Red Heart of Douglas.

"See—Angus! With the King!" Beaton shouted. "Worse trouble, now!"

That Lindsay recognised all too well. The farce was in dire danger of becoming a disaster. He yelled and gesticulated to his following to break off and swing round. He would head for Lennox and his dismounted group, rescue them at least, and then race back to the ford before the Douglases came up with them.

Abandoning pursuit of Arran, this they attempted, and achieved in some measure, quickly driving off the comparatively small numbers attacking the Stewart lairds. Lennox they found to be wounded, but able to stand. Hastily recapturing a few of the riderless horses, they mounted some of the Stewarts and took up the rest behind their own saddles, all the time eyeing that ominous advancing array beneath the flapping standards. It was going to take them all their time to reach the Nuns' Ford unassailed.

They did not quite manage it. A company of the Douglas host detached itself from the left flank of that lengthy front and came driving hard, at a tangent, to cut them off. Spur as they would, David's party could not outride these, who were racing downhill and had not the intervening ravine to contend with. It became obvious that these Douglases knew of the ford and were determined to prevent their crossing.

"We must stand. And fight!" David jerked.

"To what end?" Beaton demanded. "They outnumber us already. The longer we stand the more will come. We will not reach that ford. We are held."

"What, then? Yield?"

"What else? No service to die! For nothing. Yield. Young

James—perhaps he will be the saving of us? If they have him under yonder standard. They will not execute the King's friend out-of-hand! Nor the Abbot of Arbroath, I think!"

It was a hard decision to take, tamely to surrender. But there seemed to be nothing else, in reason, for it. This battle was already lost—if it could be called a battle. Lindsay nodded, and reined over towards a little mound in the levellish area just beyond the ravine, to pull up, waving and shouting to his following fairly eloquently. None of his churchmen looked outraged at this development, whatever the Stewarts' attitude. Some of these spurred off on their own.

They had only moments to wait before the Douglases arrived, pounding up, shouting their slogan, swords drawn, lances lowered. Swiftly, expertly enough—trained mosstroopers these—they surrounded their stationary quarry.

From behind the two Davids one voice was upraised—Lennox's, weak, weary. "All is lost, then? Lost!"

"Only the day is lost, my lord," Beaton answered him. "There will be other days. You are something recovered?"

A burly, stocky, red-bearded man of middle years rode forward out of the milling circle of newcomers, well-armoured. He waved his sword at them, on their mound.

"You—like conies on a warren! Do you yield to me?" That was harshly demanded. "I am Mains. Douglas of Mains."

"We have heard of your name, Aye, we yield—to avoid unnecessary bloodshed," Beaton declared, now taking charge. "I am David, Abbot of Arbroath. And this is David Lindsay of the Mount, King's Procurator and Extra Pursuivant."

The other seemed unimpressed—looking past them, indeed. "Is that not Lennox, I see? The Earl?" Mains demanded, pointing. "Hiding there!"

"Yes. He is wounded, not hiding."

"You say so? My lord—your sword!" The Douglas was undoubtedly concerned for the ransom-value of his prisoners, and assessed one of the most ancient Earls of Scotland a notable prize—although a shrewder captor might have considered the Abbot of Arbroath, the second richest Abbacy in the land, and nephew of the Primate and Chancellor, as still more profitable.

Lennox, in evident pain and half-dazed, had lost his sword in the affray earlier and did not appear to understand what the Douglas wanted. Some of his Stewart lairds were protesting angrily and there was much shouting and altercation, Mains clearly considered to be of insufficient status to yield to for such as themselves. It would have been almost amusing had it not been, in fact, grimly serious.

The real gravity of the situation, however, was demonstrated all too speedily. One of Mains' lieutenants reined close to Beaton, knocking the proffered sword out of his hand but reaching out to wrench the gold chain with the small crucifix from about his neck—the only symbol of his office other than the abbot's ring which he wore—when another company of horsemen came cantering up. This was still more numerous than the Douglas's and under a much larger banner—the white-on-red of Hamilton but differenced by a black diagonal band across from top-left to bottom-right, the bend-sinister or heraldic symbol for illegitimacy. More than one individual was entitled to blazon that device undoubtedly—but one only was likely to flaunt it thus in action—Sir James Hamilton of Finnart, the notorious Bastard of Arran, eldest of the Lord High Admiral's illegitimate brood. The two Davids knew him well, as an unscrupulous but able and ambitious man of about their own age. He was tall and darkly handsome, with fine features and a noble brow but notably thin cruel lips. He carried one shoulder slightly higher than the other. He ignored both Beaton and Lindsay meantime.

"Ho, Douglas," he called authoritatively. "Who commands here? You, Mains? I see that you have netted a pretty parcel of fish! But you have taken one of mine, man." He pointed. "Lennox. The traitor himself!"

"Lennox is mine—*my* prisoner," the Douglas growled. "What do you want with him?"

"Not yours—mine. My people unhorsed him, in fair fight. Before you saw fit to take the field! I want him."

"And shall not have him!" Mains roared. "To me he, and they all, surrendered. You are too late, Hamilton."

"Fool! Do you not know who I am? I am Finnart. Son to Arran, the Admiral, I demand . . ."

"Son o' a sort! I care na whether you were Arran himsel'! Or young Jamie Stewart on his bit throne! Yon's my prisoner—they all are. And bide mine." The older man grinned mockingly and waved a hand. "You can have one o' his esquires, if it suits you . . ."

But the Bastard, paying no least heed, kicked his magnificent mount through the press, to Lennox's side. Cold-eyed, he stared at the Earl.

"So, traitor—it comes to this, does it!" he jeered. "You thought to outmatch Hamilton and grasp the King. We shall teach you better, I swear, than to assail honester men."

Lennox clearly had to exert much effort to speak at all, even to remain upright in the saddle. "It ill . . . becomes you . . . such as you . . . to talk of honester men!" he declared thickly. "Seek you . . . honest parentage first! And to say traitor—you who aid Angus . . . to hold the King's Grace . . .!"

Hamilton's hand shot out, furiously to slap the Earl across the face.

Both Lindsay and Beaton started their beasts forward to intervene, in protest, but it was Mains who got there first.

"Hands off my prisoner, Finnart!" he cried. "Hear you? They all are mine. Douglas's."

"God's curse on you, scum! I told you . . ." The dark man gestured with the hand that had struck the Earl. "A pox—you may have some of these. And this milkmaster of a false priest!" And he flung a scornful glance at Beaton. "But Lennox is my property. Do not meddle with matters too high for you, man. I take him. After all, he is my cousin!"

That was true, at least. Lennox was son to Arran's sister.

"For the last time—no!" Mains raised his mailed arm towards the ranks of waiting Douglases. "Take him—if you dare! There are more Douglases nearby than these, I warn you!"

"Fiends of hell—dare? Finnart!" Handsome features contorted, the Bastard reined the yard or two closer to Lennox. His hand fell to his waist, to his dirk's hilt—he had not deigned to draw his sword. Like lightning he whipped out the gleaming dagger. "By the Christ—if *I* may not have him, none other shall!" he exclaimed.

Ferociously he lunged over, to plunge the steel into the Earl's throat, just above the armour's gorget. Twice, thrice, he stabbed expertly, then wrenched the reddened weapon clear and contemptously wiped it clean on his victim's sagging person, as with a bubbling groan Lennox sank, slewed and toppled from the saddle to crash to the ground, spouting blood.

A short bark of a laugh and the Bastard of Arran spat, reined his horse round and spurred away, without a glance at anyone else, his men falling in behind him. Stupified, appalled, all others stared, at first too shocked to move.

David Lindsay was the first to jump down, to run and sink to his knees beside the prostrate Earl, whilst Douglas of Mains lifted his great voice in furious profanity.

John Stewart of Lennox's last breath choked in a bloody froth.

In the confusion, indignation and recriminations which followed, the other captives, at least, all but forgot their own dangers and problems.

Developments followed fast, however. Arran himself, no longer being chased, rode up, now in the company of none other than Angus. Presumably they had already been told of Lennox's death, for the former, a thin, lantern-jawed ageing man of fine but weak features, went straight to where the body lay, dismounted and bent down, gazing at his nephew, head ashake, slack lips moving.

All around men paused, to turn and watch.

It was Davie Beaton who broke the sudden silence. "Your son did this, my lord," he said evenly, levelly. "Finnart. Slew an unarmed and wounded man. Unprovoked, in wanton spleen. Your son . . ."

The other did not answer, did not so much as look up, but sank on his knees beside the corpse. His hand, trembling a little, went out to touch Lennox's face. Then rising, he took off the handsome cloak he wore over his armour, scarlet with the ermine cinquefoils of Hamilton, and spread it over his nephew. Perplexed, embarrassed, men looked on at the extraordinary scene.

Douglas of Mains found his rough voice. "My lord—Lennox was *my* prisoner. To me he yielded. Then that, that skellum, your Bastard, came up. I told him. But he slew him. *Mine* . . .!" It was to his chief, Angus that he now turned.

"Aye, that is Finnart! Never heed, Sandy—you will not suffer. But these others. *I* want Beaton, nephew to the former Chancellor. Do as you will with Lindsay and the rest. But keep Beaton for me—or, by God's eyes I'll have your head for him! Now—where is the King? Where is young James? I said that he was to be here, to Pittendreich. By the Rood—where is he?"

"Yonder, lord," one of his people said, pointing. "There he comes. Leastways, the royal standard . . ."

Coming now from the general direction of the bridge, the

party with the Lion Rampant flag approached. James was riding beside Douglas of Pittendreich, and Parkhead, the Captain of his Guard, and with a dark scowl on his attractive young face. At sight of Lindsay, however, this vanished, replaced by a wide grin, as he spurred his mount forward.

"Davie! Davie Lindsay!" he cried. "You, here! Good, good—here's joy! It has been long . . ." His voice tailed away as he caught sight of the body part-covered by the rich Hamilton cloak, but not sufficiently to hide the gold-and-blue Stewart surcoat Lennox had worn over his half-armour, and Arran still standing there. The boy stared. "That . . . that is . . . ?"

"Lennox, Your Grace. The Earl—foully slain." That was Beaton.

"Lennox! My lord, fallen? Dead?" It was at Lindsay that he looked, biting his lip. He reined closer to where Lindsay stood, and reached down to touch, to grasp his shoulder, gulping. "Is all lost, then? You—*you* are not hurt? You are well? And, and Abbot Beaton?"

"Unhurt, Sire—but prisoners, it seems. Meantime."

"All not lost, Your Grace—only this joust!" Beaton added, with an assumption of cheerfulness.

Angus, watching and listening with a sort of grim interest, snorted a laugh. "This joust—and the last! And the next, clerk!" he jerked. "Fear not, James—Your Grace is safe from all such feckless plotters and traitors."

"They are not traitors! They are not. They are my friends, my good friends, my lord," the King asserted. "You it is who, who . . ." He restrained himself, changing the direction of his accusation. "If there be any traitor here, I say that it is this man." And he pointed to Pittendreich. "He, he mistreated me. He threatened me, coming here. Is it not treason to threaten the person of the King? He said, he said that rather than his enemies should take me from him, he would lay hold on my body. And, and if it be rent in pieces, he would be sure to take one part of it! Pittendreich said that, in front of these others. Is that not treason?"

As men gasped, Angus glanced at his uncle, and shrugged. "I am sure that Sir George but jested, Sire. He meant no ill."

"He did! He did! All heard him, and laughed. At me, the King! He said he would lay hold on me, rend me in pieces! Davie—is that not treason most foul?"

"I would say that it was, Sire, assuredly."

Angus reined round, indifferent, to watch Arran remount and ride away, alone, seemingly stricken. "Enough of this," he said. "We have more to do here than bicker over words. I want Atholl now. Have these prisoners secured . . ."

"They are mine, lord," Mains repeated. "All mine. Lennox was, forby . . ."

"Yes, yes. Have done, man. You will get your ransoms. But—guard them well. This Beaton in especial. He is a fox! I'll require him at your hands. Your Grace—come."

"Davie—you come with me," James exclaimed.

Lindsay looked from the King to Angus and over to Mains. "Gladly, Sire. But—I am captive. Of Douglas, here . . ."

"No. I want you with me. You *must* come."

"Your Grace—Lindsay must bide with Mains. He has yielded to him. He has the disposal of him," Angus declared, frowning.

But James, having found his friend again, was not going to be parted from him without a fight. "I want Davie Lindsay. He is mine. And I am the King. It is, it is my royal command!" That was defiant.

Angus was put in an awkward position now. However much he might ignore and over-rule the boy in private and behind closed doors, in front of many others, as here, he could scarcely disobey an express royal command. Angrily he waved a mailed hand.

"Very well. Let him come along with us. But only Lindsay. Mains—you will not lose by this. Now—come."

So David made for his horse, receiving a surprisingly mirthful grin from Beaton in the by-going, mounted, and spurred over to the King's side. James patted his friend's arm, and they rode on together after Angus and the royal standard, smiling to each other.

Angus led them back to the bridge area, where, although there seemed to be much confused fighting still going on, it was obvious that the tide of warfare was now in reverse, with Atholl's people retreated but holding the narrow bridge itself against all attacks. This in itself could probably be kept up more or less indefinitely; but the Nuns' Ford was just as much of a back-door for one side as the other, and it would not be long before Angus's men used it to get behind the Stewart defence. No doubt even the brash Atholl perceived this, and had retired from the forefront of his fighters to organise the rear, probably with a view to withdrawal from the scene. Or so Lindsay assessed it. The day was now clearly lost. He wondered what had happened to his father-in-law. He could not see the red-and-blue banners of Lindsay anywhere. The Lord Patrick was an old campaigner and no doubt had seen the way things were being mismanaged and had reacted prudently.

Angus halted well above the bridge conflict to consult with some of his lieutenants. James was chattering incoherently, excitedly to David when the latter suddenly pointed. Coming fast along the far, western side of the river-bank was a large mounted company and at its head, distinguishable even at that distance, was the diagonal black bend across the large banner in the Hamilton colours.

"Finnart—the Bastard!" David exclaimed. "He who slew Lennox. He who slew Lennox. He has crossed the ford. This will finish Atholl, I fear."

The Highland Stewarts saw and recognised the threat, and however martially aggressive, accepted that they had now no chance, no choice. Everywhere the breaking-off process commenced.

Angus, shrugging, turned his horse's head round once more, shouted commands to sundry of his lairds and beckoned for Pittendreich to bring on James, back towards Linlithgow town and palace. This day was done.

David Lindsay rode with them. From here he could not see what had happened to his friend Beaton. He felt somehow guilty of desertion.

7

David Lindsay found himself to be in a most peculiar position, part prisoner yet the King's favourite, treated with hostility by most yet the closest of all to the monarch's person. James, in his determination to hold on to him, threw tantrums if there was any move towards separating them. The boy, if he had not actually matured in the interim, appeared to have become considerably more assertive, not to say hot-tempered. Indeed however warm he was towards David personally, that man grew a little troubled at James's general behaviour and attitude to life. His natural sunny disposition seemed to be somewhat clouded over, his converse abrupt, his manner suspicious. He drank too much wine, he played cards with some of the young Douglas blades, well supplied with money apparently, and his—and their—talk was much of women, in detail unsuitable for a youth of fifteen. It looked as though Angus's campaign to corrupt the lad was being all too successful, like his military efforts.

In his influence with the King, David did find that he had one ally, and a female one at that. James, it transpired, had acquired a tirewoman and seamstress, odd as this might seem. Angus, it appeared, was pursuing a new policy with the boy, whether as part of the corruption efforts or in an attempt to gain his co-operation, giving him splendid clothing, even some jewellery, keeping him supplied with money—most of which he lost at cards back to the Douglases—and similar pamperings. To attend to this new wardrobe, Janet Douglas, daughter of the Laird of Stonypath, had been appointed, a still-faced, quiet young woman, comely without being beautiful. At first, David assumed her to be another like the gipsy wench at Holyrood, but he soon realised that this was not so, that here was a modest, rather shy, not to say reserved creature, no whore nor bought woman. And that she was concerned for more than the King's clothes was soon equally apparent. She was watchful, protective without being assertive, occasionally gently chiding. James had obviously told her much about Davie Lindsay, and her interest in him, although veiled, was evident.

Angus was meantime occupying the Queen-Mother's palace of Linlithgow, a handsome and commodious establishment above its own broad loch, no stern fortress. The King had been given much better quarters than at Holyrood, so conditions were comfortable enough, physically at least.

Part of Lindsay's mental discomfort stemmed from the fact that Davie Beaton was here at Linlithgow too, removed from Mains' keeping and locked in a bare, semi-underground cell three floors below. James had asked that he be accorded better treatment, but Pittendreich, who was in charge while Angus himself was much away, ignored the plea. He was a hard man, the most sour and morose of that family.

However, on the fourth day at Linlithgow, Beaton achieved his own release from durance vile. He actually turned up in the royal quarters to say goodbye, much to Lindsay's surprise.

"How of a mercy did you effect this?" the latter demanded. "Lord—I'd have thought this beyond even *your* clever tongue!"

"I but struck a bargain with Angus," the other assured easily, "when he returned last night from Hamilton—where I gather he is now having trouble with Arran. I had to get out of here somehow."

"A bargain? With Angus? What could you give that man which he would value more than holding your person?"

"One thing only—the Great Seal of Scotland!"

Lindsay stared. "The Great Seal! You mean—man, you have not bartered the Seal for your freedom? Your uncle's office . . . ?"

"I have indeed. It is the one thing that Angus wants, needs. The Chancellor's symbol of office. He has been calling himself Chancellor, and seeking to act it, these many months. But he needs to hold the Great Seal to *make* him Chancellor. And that I can give him. It is at St. Andrews. What use is it to my uncle, in present circumstances? *He* cannot act the part, as matters are. As good as in hiding, cooped up there in his hold on the edge of the Norse Sea. And after that sorry battle at the bridge of Avon, possibly fled to France, when he heard that I was taken. The Seal is but a bauble to him, now . . ."

"Even so, next to the crown, it is the nation's symbol . . ."

"What advantage to the nation that is in chains to Angus? I must be free—to aid the nation. Do you not see? I am of no use to Scotland locked in a vaulted cell. Free, I can act, use my wits—and the power of Holy Church! Work for Angus's fall. Can you not see it, man?"

Lindsay shook his head. By this time, he ought to have been no longer surprised by the other's self-confidence, his utter faith in his own abilities and destiny—which, it had to be admitted, seldom was proved to be seriously misplaced.

"The Archbishop?" Lindsay asked. "Will he agree to yield up the Seal, entrusted to him by the realm?"

"I have no fears as to that. My one fear is that he may have already departed in our waiting ship, for France. And taken the Great Seal with him. But I did not tell Angus that!"

"And what will you do if he has? What will you do, anyway?"

"I go now to St. Andrews. And if Uncle James has gone, I will go after him and bring the Seal back. I have given my word—and even Angus accepts that. But—I think that he will probably be at St. Andrews still, and the Seal with him. I will bring it to Angus. That I have promised. And then—then I will work day and night to bring him down! Angus. I may no longer be secretary to the Chancellor—but I am still Abbot of Arbroath and secretary to the Primate of Scotland's Church. And the Church is rich, see you, rich beyond all telling! Gold, Davie. Gold and wits together may move mountains. With a little faith!"

"So-o-o! And once you start that, will St. Andrews remain a secure haven? Will not Angus come to prise you out of it? Then what of your uncle? And what of your wife and the child?"

"It may well come to that. I will move them to Arbroath Abbey. Then somewhere even more remote, secure, if need be. All Scotland lies before us, the Church everywhere. Angus will learn that!"

"And is this what Christ's Church is for? Fighting your battles?"

"Fighting the nation's battles. It is the nation's Church. It must fight to free the Lord's Anointed—James. If his anointing and kingship mean anything. Somebody must continue the fight—and fight more effectively than did Lennox and Buccleuch and the others."

"That I do agree. And shall do what little *I* can. But I too am as good as a captive here. And with nothing to exchange . . . !"

"You can do much—more than most. For you have the King's ear, and his love. You can influence James more than any, to resist and confound Angus in all ways possible. He needs the royal authority and signature to make his deeds lawful. He will take James with him where he can. If you can go also, you can do much, see you."

"I can try . . ."

They parted, then, Beaton to ride off a free man.

* * *

It was not so easy to deny the King's authority to Angus, however willing James was to co-operate. The Douglases made harsh and determined taskmasters and the boy was entirely in their power. They could make conditions very unpleasant for him, and David saw it as no part of his duty to involve his liege-lord in more trouble and discomfort than was absolutely necessary. James did make himself more difficult to his captors, and suffered for it; but it only really came to delaying tactics. Indeed, one of their most galling failures related to none other than David's own father-in-law. Lord Lindsay, amongst others who had escaped from the disaster of Linlithgow Bridge, was declared to be in rebellion against the King, outwith the King's peace, and required to submit himself to the King's justice forthwith—and when he failed to do so, his lands and property were declared forfeit to the crown and handed over, in theory, to Graysteel of Kilspindie—if the latter could effectively take them. A royal warrant to this effect was amongst the many put before young James to sign—and one that he sought longest to delay, David naturally encouraging him. But the latter came to recognise that the Douglases might well be watching this warrant carefully, making a test-case of it, and could possibly make use of any opposition to give them grounds for parting him from the King's side. In the end, he actually urged James to sign the forfeiture, and in the presence of Abbot William Douglas, esteeming this the lesser evil. He imagined that the Lord Patrick was capable of fighting his own battles.

So that winter of 1527 passed uneasily, with Angus everywhere in command in Lowland Scotland, if not in the Highlands. Or, in command more in name that in fact, perhaps, for a fair proportion of the lords and chiefs were hostile, if meantime quiescent, merely biding their time. The situation could be exemplified by the fact that Graysteel did not indeed take over the Lindsay lands of The Byres of Garleton and elsewhere, contenting himself with a mere token occupation of some small properties in the Ballencrieff and Coates area adjoining his own lairdship of Kilspindie, which the Lord Patrick apparently was prepared to concede for the sake of a precarious peace; no doubt the Earl of Crawford, the Lindsay chief, a lukewarm ally of Angus, was not uninvolved in this, resenting any Douglas encroachment closer to his own superiority of Luffness. Such represented the checks and balances of the feudal realm.

At least Angus gained his official chancellorship, when Davie Beaton, in a couple of weeks, arrived again at Linlithgow with the Great Seal of Scotland. Under the excuse of paying his due homage to the King, he contrived a brief meeting with Lindsay—in which he revealed, in strictest confidence, an astonishing situation. When he had reached St. Andrews, it was to find his uncle fled. On word of the disaster at Linlithgow Bridge and the capture of Davie, the Primate had promptly lifted his archiepiscopal skirts and betaken himself off, anticipating attack by Angus. But he had not departed for France, as feared, but for pastures, sheep pastures, much nearer home. Instead of making for Arbroath Abbey or any other of the Church's major havens to hide in, he had surprisingly elected to go to one of the granges of Cambuskenneth Abbey, a sheep-run in the Ochil Hills called Bogrian Knowe, where he was ostensibly acting as an extra shepherd—although what sort of a hill shepherd the gross and over-weight prelate might make beggared the imagination. Presumably the ex-Chancellor felt safer thus, where he would be unlikely to be traced by the Douglases, the Church's chief shepherd of men become a pastor of sheep. His nephew seemed to find all this amusing in the extreme, but was quite prepared to leave his relative where he was meantime, out of the way, whilst he himself, in the Primate's name, got on with his efforts to deal with Angus.

To Lindsay's questions as to how the other proposed to set about this, Beaton was less specific than usual. In very general terms he indicated that Fife, being notably under Church influence, with its abbeys of Dunfermline, Culross, Inchcolm, Lindores and Balmerino, and its priories of Inverkeithing, Dysart, Cupar, Crail, Pittenweem, Aberdour and others, as well as the great metropolitan complex of St. Andrews itself, might suitably initiate a kind of non-military revolt against the Douglas regime which Angus would find difficulty in countering and which, he hoped, might encourage lords and great ones elsewhere, with Church urging and gold, to do likewise, nationwide, until the Douglases were so stretched and preoccupied, over the country, that a successful military venture could be mounted. If all this seemed distinctly vague, not to say improbable, to his friend, Lindsay did not say so in so many words, acknowledging that the other had a remarkable ability to effect the most unexpected developments.

Before leaving, Beaton divulged that he had removed his wife Marion and their son from St. Andrews to the remote castle of

Ethie, on the Angus coast south of Montrose, which he had purchased and put in Marion's own name, as her property, to give her security and a safe base in the possible event of disaster befalling himself. It was the first time that Lindsay could recollect his so-confident friend ever conceding that such failure was even remotely possible. It took Marion Ogilvy to get beneath his armour.

That difficult and unhappy winter the Lindsay family received three blows in quick succession. First, David's father died, at Garleton. Sir David, in his sixties, had been ailing for some time, nursed by Mirren Livingstone, so this was no great shock, however sad. It made David laird of Garleton as well as of the Mount of Lindifferon; but he was well content to leave the management of the estate in the hands of his brother. What did shock was the news, when he was barely back at Linlithgow from attending the funeral under Douglas guard in Athelstaneford kirkyard, that the Master of Lindsay, Kate's brother, had been killed in a hunting accident in Fife. And this was followed, only a few weeks later, by the sudden death of the Lord Patrick himself, at The Byres, seemingly from natural causes, however unexpected, leaving the Master's young son John to become fifth Lord Lindsay.

David grieved for the old lord, with whom he had always got on well in an undemonstrative way; and more so for the Lady Isabella, his surrogate aunt, who had now lost husband, eldest son and daughter. And of course it left the Lindsay strength in the land direly reduced, with only a child as lord, and the chief of the name, the Earl of Crawford, a feeble and bumbling character.

It was in a belated spring of chill east winds and rain-storms that word of troubles in Fife began to reach Linlithgow. At first it took pinprick form, prayers and preaching against Angus in churches, refusals by parish priests to baptise, marry and give Christian burials to Douglases; threats of excommunication. This might not greatly have worried Angus, but soon what had obviously become a campaign grew, with access to monastic mills being denied to Douglases and their tenants and friends—and two-thirds of all Fife grain was ground at Church mills. Fairs and trysts were barred to them also, grazings of the vast Church lands cancelled, increased tithes and payments demanded, and so on. All this tended to make a laughing-stock of the name of Douglas, and quickly the Fife and Fothrif Douglases and their allies were up in arms, demanding redress and vengeance on the insolent churchmen. Eventually Angus could not ignore this. And when the news was whispered that the Queen-Mother and her new husband, Henry Stewart, now living in Methven Castle in Strathearn, were in some measure behind it all, with Atholl and the Beatons, he had to make a move, despite other pressing problems connected with King Henry, Lord Dacre, the Homes and the Border Armstrongs again. But for policy reasons he was not going to make too much of it, with no desire to give the impression that this was any serious threat. So, in May, he announced that he would escort the King for a visit to the royal hunting palace of Falkland in Fife.

They set off in mid-month, a notably large company for a hunting-party, sending the main body round Forth by Stirling and Kinross whilst Angus himself, with James and his close entourage, proceeded down to the Forth shore nearby to take Queen Margaret's Ferry across by the short cut. Thereafter, carefully avoiding Dunfermline meantime, they rode by Inverkeithing's royal burgh, noting particularly its Dominican priory, and on by Lochgelly and Kinglassie and Leslie, making for the shapely breasts of the twin Lomond Hills, so prominent a sight from the East Lothian coast. They reached Falkland, nestling under the East Lomond, by early evening, although it would take their main company all of another day to get there by the Stirling bridge-crossing.

James had never seen his palace of Falkland, and David had only on occasion passed through its surrounding castleton. It was a pleasant, sleepy sort of place, comparatively small, the palace not in the best state of repair—for the late King had never used it much and it had been neglected since his death. It was famous, of course, the seat of the Stewartry of Fife, having been founded by the MacDuffs, ancient Mormaors of Fife, and taken over by the line of the Celtic kings. Here David, Duke of Rothesay, heir to the throne of Robert the Third, had been starved to death by his uncle, a previous Regent Albany. The palace itself was restricted as to accommodation, having grown out of a simple stone keep, so the township adjoining, raised to the status of a royal burgh despite its modest size, was always used for housing courtiers, and thus possessed some better houses. The royal forest, which included the Lomond Hills, came almost up to the doors.

It became obvious, even the very next day and before the rest of the Douglas contingent arrived, that Angus had not come here to hunt. He and his lieutenants did not even stay in the little palace but lodged outside. Douglas of Parkhead, the Captain of the King's Guard, was in charge of the monarch and remained in close attendance, with his minions; but the others disappeared in the morning and were not seen again for two days.

The Earl was, in fact, showing the Douglas flag in no uncertain fashion and making clear how he felt about Holy Church's campaign against him. He had few doubts, of course, as to who was principally behind it all; but he did not assail St. Andrews at first, electing to take his reprisals against Dunfermline, the richest abbey in the land and not protected by any strong castle, as was St. Andrews, so no siege would be involved. He did not destroy the abbey itself, but much of the town went up in flames, the granaries, mills, brewhouses and warehouses pillaged and destroyed and sundry folk hanged—not clergy, which might have caused repercussions elsewhere. Thereafter, he turned his attention to the Inverkeithing Dominican priory. Presumably he intended to work his way eastwards, ever nearer to St. Andrews itself.

In the meantime, James was taken hunting by Parkhead and Balfour of Fernie, Keeper of Falkland Forest, David Lindsay in attendance. For three days they hunted stags and roe on the Lomonds, revelling in the comparative freedom of the chase even though their guards were ever with them. On the third evening, with Angus said to have gone over to Edinburgh on some urgent business, but with Kilspindie and Pittendreich and others returned to Falkland, there was a diversion. Beaton of Creich, a far-out kinsman of Davie's, who was hereditary Keeper of Falkland Palace but had not so far been in evidence, arrived from St. Andrews bringing a message from the Abbot of Arbroath in the name of the Primate. This was to invite Graysteel and Pittendreich to St. Andrews next day or the day after, to discuss a solution of the present differences between Holy Church and the house of Douglas, which all must agree were to be deplored. Safe conduct for the Douglases was assured and every courtesy proffered. The distressing events at

Dunfermline and Inverkeithing must not be repeated, it was emphasised. It was understood that the Earl of Angus was not presently available, but no doubt his uncles would be able to negotiate in his stead. The said uncles were grimly amused, but apparently prepared to go to see Davie Beaton—and no doubt spy out the land in case of any later assault on St. Andrews.

Beaton of Creich himself did not approach King James. But, for all that, he had a communication, and a significant one, for the monarch and David Lindsay. This was surreptitiously delivered to Lindsay by one of the Falkland grooms, Jockie Hart by name, one of Creich's men, who attended to the horses of the royal party and who had acted as something of a guide and extra huntsman in the chases. Hart, contriving to get David alone, informed him that the proposed St. Andrews meeting was a ruse, in order to get the senior Douglases away from Falkland with most of their following, while Angus was absent. This for the purpose of facilitating the King's escape.

The plan was for James to request and devise a special hunt at some distance from Falkland itself, say in the Balharvie Loch and Moss area, where boars and wolves were reputed still to lurk, and which would require an early start two mornings hence, assuming that the Douglas lords would be away. Parkhead could scarcely refuse this. They would make much preparation for the expedition, and claim to require early bedding the night before. But once the palace was bedded down, Lindsay and the King should slip out quietly, disguised in servants' clothing, and make for the North Park, where the horses were grazed. There he, Jockie Hart, would be waiting for them, with three beasts saddled, and they would make their secret departure and ride for Stirling. The Abbot of Arbroath would have a party waiting to meet them at Strathmiglo, and they would then ride on westwards through the night. Lord Erskine and the Earl of Atholl would be ready to welcome them into Stirling Castle.

Needless to say, David was much exercised by this plot, perceiving more than one point where it could go hopelessly wrong. On the other hand it would be a pity not to try it, an opportunity, carefully contrived, which might not occur again for long enough. When he told James, the boy was agog, eager and in no doubts. They would do it—of course they would do it.

So, all the next day, with Graysteel and his brother departed for St. Andrews, the King made almost too much fuss about his desire to go hunt boar at Balharvie Moss and the preparations which would be necessary, special long spears to be collected for the occasion, extra local men to be engaged as beaters who knew the area and the ways of boar, and so on. James Douglas of Parkhead could scarcely refuse co-operation, and agreed that an early start would be necessary, for Balharvie was on the other side of the Lomonds, on the hillskirts between the two peaks, and a roundabout approach would be advisable to ensure that the hunt took place on ground firm enough for the horses, for much of the Moss was impassable swamp. Sunrise would be around five o'clock, when they would make a start. So the insistence was on early bedding for all concerned.

Jockie Hart managed to smuggle in some rough outer wear, suitable for concealing identity, into the royal apartments that evening, and James and David made the pretence of retiring almost immediately after the evening meal. From then until midnight, the King was in a state of excitement and impatience to be gone, restrained by David. They had to be as certain as possible that no late-bedders remained up and about, to observe the departure.

In the event, there were no problems as the pair tip-toed down the turnpike stair along the vaulted basement corridor to a rear door. This was barred, but the massive draw-bar was well-greased with goose-fat and slid into its wall-socket noiselessly. The door open, they carefully pulled the bar back into place behind them, before closing the door again, so that no early riser would be alerted in the morning to anything unusual. Then they slipped across the courtyard, making for the postern-gate in the surrounding curtain-walling.

This also had a draw-bar but again it was kept greased and presented no difficulty. However, the door itself gave them their only breath-catching moments, for it creaked loudly as they opened it and this set off a dog barking somewhere in the adjoining stables. In their haste to be away from there, they omitted to pull back this draw-bar into the closed position.

Outside the walling they all but ran. It was not really dark—it seldom is in late May in Scotland. They knew the North Park well enough, only some three hundred yards from the palace, where the horses, too many for the available stabling, were enclosed to graze overnight. Here they found Hart anxiously awaiting them, worried at having heard the dog barking. He had the three mounts saddled and ready, and explained that he had deliberately not taken the King's and David's fine beasts, just in case their absence would be noted and cause an alarm any earlier than need be. James suggested leaving the park gate open, so that the other horses might stray out and cause delay in any pursuit; but both David and Hart advised against this, as again capable of drawing early attention to an abnormal situation.

Mounting, they circled the park at a quiet walk and headed northwards into the woodland, before spurring into a trot.

There was a fair road through the forest the three miles to the little burgh of Strathmiglo in the upper Eden vale, but they did not risk a canter, for the trees increased the darkness and they must go carefully however impatient the sixteen-year-old monarch.

At Strathmiglo there was a hitch, for there was no sign of Beaton's promised party as they rode through the sleeping town. There developed, however, a great barking of dogs here also, alarming David and Hart and causing them to decide that they dared not hang about in the town waiting for the missing escort. But as they hastened on, swinging westwards now up the Eden, just beyond the outskirts they were met by a single horseman who greeted them relievedly and explained that his party was hiding in some birch-scrub just a little further on, by the riverside, they also having been scared out of the burgh by the barking dogs.

Their guide led them to a group of about a score waiting in the cover of the young trees, under Beaton of Balfour, Davie's eldest brother, whom Lindsay had not come across hitherto. He had the family's good looks but was much more heavily-built. It was a surprise to find in the company Balfour of Fernie, the keeper of this royal forest, who was to have been one of the leaders of the boar-hunt—and who now proved to have been in the plot from the start; indeed had been supplying St. Andrews with up-to-the-minute information throughout. He would return to Falkland now, and turn up for the hunt at sunrise, his implication unsuspected, he hoped. There were only the briefest and almost casual respects paid to the monarch.

There was no delay thereafter, none anxious to linger in the vicinity. They bade farewell to Fernie and set off up the riverside road, west by south.

It was calculated that they had some thirty miles to go to reach Stirling, following the River Eden almost to Milnathort, then avoiding that town and nearby Kinross by keeping to the higher ground of the Ochil foothills, to join the hillfoots drove-road again in the Carnbo area, with thereafter a straight ride by Yetts of Muckhart, Dollar, Tillicoultry, Alva and Menstrie to the causewayhead of Stirling. They would not be able to ride really fast until Carnbo and daylight, but from then on it should be a clear run of some seventeen or eighteen miles.

At first David and James at least tended to keep glancing behind them, fearing pursuit; but as the light strengthened and they left the riverside flats for the foothill slopes, beginning to be able to see for considerable distances, with no sign of trouble, they were able to relax. Jockie Hart, the only local man, acted as guide.

A pale pink-and-gold sunrise behind them began to fill the Ochil valleys and hollows with purple shadow when they were midway between Carnbo and Yetts of Muckhart. Save for the cattle and sheep which they disturbed, they still seemed to have the morning to themselves. They settled down to steady hard riding. James was an excellent horseman and no hold-up.

They were following down the ever-widening vale of the River Devon now, as breakfast fires began to send up their blue plumes of wood-smoke into the still air; and even David Lindsay, anxious for his charge, was able to accept that they had almost succeeded in their efforts, and the King's long spell of captivity in Douglas hands was over, meantime at least. When, in the distance, the thrusting skyline of Stirling Castle could be distinguished above the morning mists of the vale, to the west, the thing was assured. A new chapter was beginning for Scotland.

Tired and mud-spattered but elated, they clattered through the climbing streets of Stirling town, drawing but little attention from the populace intent on some cattle-fair, and up to the tourney-ground fronting the castle gatehouse. The portcullis was up and the drawbridge down, although the gates were shut. But the newcomers' shouts that here was the King of Scots requiring entry to his royal fortress had scarcely begun when they were thrown wide and the Earl Marischal and the Lord Erskine came, almost at the run, out on to the bridge-timbers, to sink to their knees thereon, before their sovereign-lord, too moved even to speak.

James dismounted and went to raise them up, himself suddenly overcome with emotion. For moments they gazed at each other, words an incoherent jumble when they came. Then urgently the King pushed past them, under the portcullis and into the gatehouse pend, to turn and wave his party in after him.

"Come!" he cried. "In with you, all of you. Down with the portcullis. Up with that bridge. Bar the gates. I am free—free! Back in my own Stirling—the King! Let Archibald Douglas come for me now, and see, and see . . . !" His young voice broke. "Oh, Davie, Davie Lindsay—we're free!"

"Yes, Sire," that man said, riding in. "God save the King!"

8

James Stewart had been a king for fifteen years, but only in name. Suddenly all that was changed. Always he had had someone controlling him, usually more or less sternly, if not harshly; now, that no longer applied. There was no regent; his mother was utterly discredited and living privately in Strathearn; Angus had lost him; Arran held no authority meantime save his nominal position of Lord Admiral. James was in his seventeenth year, a youth rather than a boy, and in many ways, precocious for his age. It dawned on him, as on those around him in Stirling Castle, that he was now the King indeed, nobody in a position to do more than advise him, ruler as well as reigner—so long as Angus could be thwarted.

And, to be sure, now the very means by which Angus had sustained his usurped authority, in the possession of the monarch's person, the royal signature and seal, the final sanctions in the kingdom, were abruptly James's own, to use against Douglas. It took only a little while for this to sink in, although David Lindsay had been thinking along these lines since their escape. James now, as it were, reached out to grasp his sceptre.

But all depended on Angus's effective suppression, and with it, the breaking up of the Douglas power. Nothing was more sure than that Angus would not be long in asserting himself. He probably would not be able to winkle James out of Scotland's strongest fortress, although he might well try; but what use was a monarch permanently shut up in a fortress? To escape was not enough—James had to act.

That very first evening, after he and David had had a sleep, on the latter's advice he called a Privy Council meeting. Nominally this was possible, Atholl, the Marischal and Erskine all being privy councillors, as was the Lord Maxwell who happened to be visiting the castle; and in theory James could swear in anyone else he chose. He wanted to make Lindsay a council member there and then, but David dissuaded him, asserting that this would be unsuitable and could cause resentment amongst the others. If he could attend, as acting-secretary say, that would serve.

So the four lords sat down with the monarch in a corner of the parliament hall, almost like conspirators in that great apartment, with Lindsay sitting in, a little back from the table to emphasise his lower status. But James was not long in demonstrating that council member or none, David was expected to take full part in the proceedings, by addressing direct remarks and questions to him—which, of course, he could by no means fail to answer. James was perhaps slightly over-assertive on this his first council meeting with himself in charge, and of course no Lord Privy Seal present to act chairman. Without preamble he plunged straight into the main urgent business—what were they to do about Angus? He would be wroth and would certainly seek to recapture the King. And he was still as powerful as ever. How was he to be countered?

Atholl, ever brash, declared that *he* would raise the Highlands, the clans again, and come to the aid of their High King. This time there would be no folly of splitting forces, as at Linlithgow Bridge. He would send for Argyll to bring his Campbell hordes, and together they would stamp the Douglas and his Lowland ruffians into their Lowland earth!

This, needless to say, raised Lowland eyebrows round that table, the Earl Marischal snorting, Erskine starting to speak and then thinking better of it, although Maxwell agreed that they should certainly send for the Earl of Argyll, who for too long had been so busy making himself a little king in the Highland west that he had quite neglected his duties to his sovereign-lord and the realm. He was after all, Lord Justice General and hereditary Master of the Household . . .

Erskine frowned. He was married to Argyll's sister.

James interrupted impatiently. "That is as may be, my lords. But anything such will take long, mustering the clans. Angus will be here any day. He will come for me. He will besiege us here, in this castle."

"He will not have cannon, Sire," the Marischal said. "It would take him time to fetch cannon from Edinburgh or Dumbarton. And he cannot take this fortress without cannon. That will give time to muster forces against him."

"And even Angus would scarce bombard a castle, I think, containing his own liege-lord," Erskine asserted.

"But he would shut us up, in siege," James exclaimed. "I would be as good as a prisoner again—only in Stirling instead of Linlithgow or Holyrood. Davie—how say you?"

"We need time, Sire, yes. To summon the leal lords and chiefs and their people, Lowland as well as Highland. But I think that Your Grace has powers which you could use, meantime—against Angus. You can declare him outwith your royal peace. Announce that he must submit himself for trial before either parliament or this Privy Council, on charge of having constrained Your Grace's royal person. Then, if he refused so to submit himself, you can order his apprehension. And meantime, he must not approach your person save to submit, and alone. He must keep a distance of so many miles. If he does bring armed men within such distance, he is openly guilty of highest treason, and when taken must be executed."

They all stared at him.

"Angus would laugh at anything such," Atholl scorned.

"With respect, my lord—will he? Even he will not wish to have a sentence for high treason hanging over his head. Anyone who aids a man under that sentence is himself guilty of treason, I'd mind you. Which means that all his people, his friends and allies, would have this hanging over them also, if they lifted a hand in his service. All such cannot go about guarded all the time. It would become the duty of all leal men to apprehend them in the King's name. Angus would become outlaw, and all who supported him actively likewise. How many would choose to put themselves in that position? All this is in the King's power to proclaim. I have thought much on it, as to what could be done when the King was free."

"My God—he is right!" Maxwell cried. "It could give Angus pause, trouble his people, leave them reluctant."

"I could *do* this?" James asked. "Make such pronouncement?"

"You are the King. It is within your royal prerogative, Sire, to condemn for high treason to yourself."

"How could it be proclaimed?" Erskine demanded. "To be effective, all must know it, hear it."

"This Council can announce it, my lord, in the first instance. Then a parliament should be called, to endorse it. A parliament is now needed, anyway . . ."

"That would take more time. Angus could be here tomorrow," James said.

"If he comes so quickly, then he must be told in person. An envoy from Your Grace must warn him as he approaches."

"He might but spurn it as an empty threat and mistreat the envoy."

"Send someone with authority . . ."

"Send Lyon," Maxwell suggested. "The King-of-Arms. It is in itself treason to mistreat the Lord Lyon on the King's business."

"Yes . . ."

"If there is to be a parliament, you will require a Chancellor," the Marischal put in. "Angus himself is at present Chancellor. Or claims to be . . ."

"Then he must be replaced at once. Who?"

They eyed each other. The chancellorship held great power and authority; but not everyone would want the position or could sustain it. It demanded eloquence, secretarial and clerkly skills, nimble wits, the ability to compromise and deal. Many of the greatest lords could not do much more than pen their own names. Traditionally, too, the office went to a senior churchman.

"Beaton grows old and slow. He held the Seal perhaps over long," Atholl asserted. "He has enough to do as Primate. Forby, none knows where he is! I say appoint my brother Andrew,

Bishop of Caithness. He is to be trusted, leal, and has sound wits."

The Earl Marischal demurred. "He is not so long a bishop. Others are a deal more senior. Holy Church might not like it, when there is the Archbishop of Glasgow, Dunbar, who was Your Grace's preceptor, here."

James made a face. He had scarcely loved Dunbar.

"Aye—if not Beaton, Dunbar. He is sound enough—even if he does write poetry!" Erskine cast a glance at Lindsay.

James also looked at that man, doubtfully. "How say you, Davie?"

The other hesitated. He felt that he owed it to Davie Beaton to support his uncle. Yet he was well aware that the Primate had been neglecting his duties as Chancellor for some time—Davie himself admitted it. But being the Chancellor's secretary gave the nephew much influence.

"The Abbot of Arbroath, Sire—would he not make an excellent Chancellor himself? Few more able in your kingdom. Your true friend. And he did contrive your escape here."

But there were murmurs from the others, mutterings that Beaton was too young, too clever by half, sufficiently up-jumped already, and the like. James darted uncertain glances around.

Lindsay realised that he had probably done his friend no service. "If not Chancellor, Sire, then perhaps some other office, close to your royal self. He has great influence with the Church, the Primate's right hand."

"Yes. Some other place. I would not be here but for him. Archbishop Dunbar, then, for Chancellor meantime? Tell him to call a parliament. Here?"

"I think not, Sire." That was Maxwell again. "It must not look as though you were beleagured in this fortress. Edinburgh is your capital. It should be there for your first parliament as ruling monarch . . ."

So it was agreed. In Edinburgh, as soon as it could be made effective—for this parliament must be well-attended and successful, a demonstration of the nation's support and regard for the young sovereign. Always, of course, assuming that Angus could be contained, if not disposed of.

They did not have long to wait for some indication as to the answer to that question. The very next day, around noon, John Inglis, the Abbot of Culross, sent a mounted messenger hot-foot to Stirling to inform the King that a large company of Douglases under Kilspindie and Pittendreich had halted briefly at his Forth-side abbey on their way to Stirling, declaring openly that they were going to collect the King there, and that the Earl of Angus himself, coming from Edinburgh, would join them at Stirling Bridge. This dire news sent James and many of his people up to the topmost towers of the castle to gaze eastwards by north. And, sure enough, just above the windings of the Forth, spread like a map before them from this lofty vantage-point, some three miles away and plain enough to be seen in the levels of the Powis area, was the dark mass of a sizeable body of mounted men.

The King gripped David Lindsay's arm. "They come! They come!" he exclaimed, thick-voiced. "Davie—what can we do? So soon! Angus coming . . . !"

"Fear nothing—you are safe here, Sire. At the worst, they cannot reach you in this hold. But we must do as we decided. At once. Send to inform Angus, warn him about his being outwith your peace and liable to a charge of high treason. An envoy . . ."

"But it is too late to send Lyon. He is not here. Who else could we send? The Marischal? He is the one of the great officers of state."

"Yes. But . . . better a herald. Not the Marischal himself. Or one of the others. Angus could lay hands on any such without it being treason, claim that he, or other, was but one of the lords against him. But a herald is different, protected. A royal herald . . ."

"But none are here! Save, save *yourself*, Davie. You are a pursuivant, now. They made you a pursuivant . . . You could go."

Lindsay frowned. "Willingly, Your Grace. But I would scarce carry sufficient authority. They know me too well and do not love me! Besides, I was only made Extra Pursuivant by Angus himself at Holyrood to have me paid for by your Treasury. He did it in your name, of course—but he is not going to be impressed by *my* position!"

"But—you say in my name? The King makes the heralds, then? So—I can make you greater than an Extra Pursuivant. Could I not make you Lord Lyon? Now, instead of the man—Clephane, is it?"

"Not Lyon, Sire, that would not do. The Lord Lyon

King-of-Arms cannot be replaced like some servitor. Sir Thomas Clephane is one of the most important officers of your realm. You cannot start by supplanting him out-of-hand."

"Then another, a new important herald, next to Lyon. What are they? Albany? Rothesay? Carrick—no, that is but a pursuivant." James swung on Erskine who had come up. "My lord, what herald could I make Davie Lindsay here so that he can go to Angus in my name and tell him, tell him what we decided last night about high treason? Rothesay and Albany and . . . is there not Marchmont? Marchmont Herald?"

"Marchmont is held, Your Grace. All these are held, already filled. You cannot use them. Likewise Unicorn and Carrick Pursuivants. Aye, and Kintyre also . . ."

"I must! It must be a herald who goes to Angus. So that if he seeks to misuse him it is high treason. There must be something . . ."

"Wait, Sire—there *is* something. There used to be a Snowdoun Herald. Here. This castle of Stirling used to be called Snowdoun, in early days, and there was a Snowdoun Herald. I have heard of it, many times. It has not been used for long, I think, but, yes, it was a senior herald, called after the strongest royal fortress."

"Snowdoun! Aye—Snowdoun! That is it. The old name for Stirling. Davie, I name you Snowdoun Herald, next to Lyon. You go to Angus, to Stirling Bridge, if that is where they meet. Tell him my royal command, he is not to come nearer. Indeed, he is to go away. Not nearer than, than . . ."

"Six miles, Sire, was the old limit," Erskine prompted. "Within six miles of the monarch, when he was in residence, was the royal bourne, precinct . . ."

"Yes. Then six miles. Not to come nearer me than six miles. Indeed, further . . ." In his excitement James all but pushed his friend. "Go, Davie, go quickly, or Angus will be here."

"I will go, Sire, yes. But I have no herald's clothing, no tabard. Nothing to show that I am what I say. They may well disbelieve me."

"A royal standard? Surely there is a royal standard flag in this royal castle? Ride under that. Jockie Hart will carry it for you . . ."

Although it was all the result of his own suggestions, David Lindsay thereafter found himself in a very doubtful frame of mind as he and Hart rode down through the town under an enormous Lion Rampant standard meant for flying from a flag-pole—which seemed quite ridiculous for only two men—heading the half-mile for Stirling Bridge. Just what he had let himself in for he did not know, save that it would almost certainly be unpleasant. Nevertheless he still reckoned it to be their best move in present circumstances, however disagreeable the process.

As they neared the north end of the town they became aware of two aspects of the situation; first, an almost complete lack of citizenry in the narrow streets, an ominous sign; and second, nearing the bridge-head across the now narrowed Forth and the start of the mile-long causeway over the marshland beyond, where Wallace had won his famous victory, the sight of a great concourse of men and horses gathered at this end of the arched bridge, blocking all—the Douglases arrived. The fact that this crowd appeared to be stationary however, waiting, appeared to indicate that Angus himself had not come yet from Edinburgh.

David would have been inclined to hang back and wait, for it was Angus himself to whom his message applied and who would make the decisions, and a preliminary encounter with his uncles was of no benefit. But if he could see the Douglases, they could also see him, especially under this huge and colourful banner; and for the royal standard to hang about in the close-mouth of a Stirling street just would not do.

They rode on.

Their reception at the bridge end was all that David had feared, in laughter, jeers, catcalls. When Lindsay's identity was evident, the mockery became tinged with anger, at least on the part of the leadership, and there were distinctly threatening gestures.

Setting his jaw, David moved forward to well within hailing distance before reining up. "I come in the name of the King," he called. "To speak with the Earl of Angus. Is he there?"

An incoherent volley of shouts answered him. But out of it presently one voice prevailed, authoritative, harsh, Pittendreich's.

"You, Lindsay, you treacherous dog! You dare to show your insolent face before Douglas!"

"I am sent only to speak with the Earl of Angus, Sir George. Where is he?" David tried to keep his voice level.

"Fool! Think you that Angus, or any of us, will pay *you* any heed?"

"I do—since I speak in the name of our sovereign-lord and of his Privy Council. But not to you, sir. Only to Angus."

"We await the Earl of Angus, Lindsay." That was Graysteel, less aggressively. "I cannot think that he will greet you kindly!"

"I do not come for kindly greetings, Sir Archibald. I come only to state the King's and the Council's decisions."

"Such so-called Council can make no decision to effect—since Douglas was not at the making!" Pittendreich threw back. "Angus is Chancellor. Kilspindie is Treasurer. Abbot William is Privy Seal. I am Master of the Household . . ."

"Were, Sir George—*were*! Are no longer. You are replaced, all."

"Dizzard! Have you lost any wits the good God allowed you? Douglas places or displaces—none other!"

"You err. The King makes and unmakes. Have you forgot, sir? The King only, whoever may advise him. Only because you held the King and gained his seal and signature could Douglas hold any places, or bestow them. You no longer hold the King—and he makes other arrangements."

"We shall see about that, numbskull . . . !"

David drew a deep breath. This would not do, it was what he had determined to avoid, a profitless exchange with the uncles. Yet what could he do, until Angus arrived? He could not just sit his horse there, silent. He made up his mind, half-turning in the saddle, and pointing. There was a small mound a couple of hundred yards to the east.

"I shall await Angus there," he called, and reined around, Hart with the standard following.

To the accompaniment of more shouting and jeers they took up their stance on the mound, feeling somewhat foolish and embarrassed but thankful that the Douglases at least did not seem to be going to attack them.

For how long they could maintain this odd situation David dared not assess. But, to his relief, at least for the meantime, after only a minute or two a different quality of shouting rose from the Douglas ranks, with pointing and cheers. Looking behind him, he saw a hard-riding party emerging from St. Mary's Wynd and the North Port, under the great undifferenced banner of the Red Heart. Now for the real test.

Angus and his escort clattered up to the bridge-end company, and if he noted the pair under the royal standard in passing, the Earl gave no sign of it. There followed an interval of evident consultation and discussion amongst the leaders, with occasional glances towards the mound. Then, David staying where he was, Angus and his kinsmen appeared to reach a decision and came spurring over to him.

"Lindsay—what is this?" the Earl demanded hotly. "You have shamefully abused our trust, treacherously removed the King from our good keeping, and now come seeking my presence like some nuncio, some ambassador! It is scarcely to be credited!"

"I come thus because that is what I am, my lord. Not ambassador, since that would imply too high a status for you! But envoy, yes, representing King James. I come as Snowdoun Herald, duly appointed to the Lyon Court, in the name of the King and his Privy Council, to inform you of decisions taken concerning yourself."

"You . . . you do? *You*, an impudent upstart, come to me, Angus, with your empty talk of things too high for you!"

"I do. Since I am come in the King's name and by his express commission. And if anyone knows the worth and power of the King's expressed authority, it is you, my lord of Angus, since you have been using it, or misusing it, for long. But for no longer. I am here to inform you that you are now proclaimed to be outwith the King's peace; that you are now deprived of all office and position under the crown, no longer Chancellor, and will yield up the Great Seal to Archbishop Dunbar of Glasgow who is appointed in your place. All your kin and friends' appointments likewise are revoked, as from last night. Moreover, as outwith the King's peace you will not approach within six miles of the royal person, under pain of treason, save alone, unarmed, to make submission. Finally, you and your kind are required to appear before a session of parliament, day to be decided upon, to answer for your offences against the King's person and freedom. Failure so to appear, unarmed, will be adjudged as highest treason and be visited with the most extreme penalty provided by the law—public execution." If all that tended to come out in somewhat breathless fashion, it was scarcely to be wondered at.

For moments the Douglases seemed to be bereft of speech,

staring, unbelieving. Then a gabble broke out, in furious protest and hot challenge, all talking at once, Pittendreich actually urging his horse forward in menace.

But Angus's voice prevailed. "Have you gone crazed, Lindsay? Forgotten to whom you speak—*Angus*? You threaten Douglas thus? The Douglas power?"

"Not I, my lord—the King! And Council. Nor threaten—proclaim, condemn. Here is not threat. The thing is done. You are proscribed, *now*. Outwith the King's peace. Already you are guilty of treason. Since you are here within the bourne, the six miles distance of the royal presence. That may be overlooked this once if you withdraw immediately, now that you are informed. I have so informed you. I have fulfilled my duty, as Snowdoun Herald. I return to His Grace."

"Think you that I will accept this, this insane folly, man?" Angus was visibly quivering with ill-suppressed rage and resentment. "Douglas will soon show who holds the power in this land."

"I care not, my lord, whether you accept it or no. You are informed, that is all my duty. Indeed, for myself, I would prefer it that you did not accept it, I think—since then you are openly guilty of treason most assuredly, disobeying the King's express command, and so liable to the penalty, you and yours, outlawry, apprehension in due course, and execution when apprehended without need for trial. You, my lord, know well enough this process and what it means. You have used it, in the King's name and recollect the late Lord Home and his kin! I advise you to think well. Now I return to His Grace whom in your prideful disloyalty you can by no means reach in Stirling Castle! You are warned." And with only a curt bow from the saddle, David Lindsay wheeled his horse round and set off for the North Port. He felt like cantering, galloping even, his back as naked as a babe's. But somehow he managed to keep his mount to only a steady walk, under the flapping standard, and did not look back.

Ears stretched for beat of hooves behind them, he all but held his breath—and doubtless Jockie Hart did the same. But, halfway to the town-gate, with no evident developments at their backs, David risked a quick glance over his shoulder. Angus and his lieutenants remained where he had left them, heads together in seemingly earnest debate. With an enormous sigh of relief, he kicked heels to his beast's flanks and headed, at a quick trot now, for the town's streets.

A little later, from the heights of the tourney-ground before the castle, he drew rein, to gaze back and down and his heart lifted. The Douglas host was on the move—but northwards. Banners at the front, it was streaming in a long snaking column back over the narrow causeway, away from Stirling. Whether out of decided policy, prudence, a recognition of facts, frustration, or something of all these, Angus was distancing himself from the King's presence, six miles or otherwise. The first hurdle seemed to be surmounted.

* * *

The days that followed were busy ones at Stirling Castle, with messengers being sent out near and far and, as the news spread, visitors arrived in numbers, important visitors. The leal lords found their courage at last—and others who were perhaps less leal but adept at reading the signs. Soon the Earls of Moray, Eglinton, Cassillis, Glencairn, Rothes, Huntly, and even Arran himself, and Morton of the Black Douglases had come. It was fairly clear that the tide had indeed turned, at least for the time being. The lords of parliament were too numerous to list, but significantly included the new Lord Home, and Glamis, who was married to Angus's sister. And the prelates, headed by Archbishop Dunbar, came in force; also the nearer Highland chiefs, the Stewarts notable despite the memory of Linlithgow Bridge. Even the Queen-Mother's third husband, Henry Stewart of Methven, turned up, to offer his duty and congratulations to the monarch—and James's obvious embarrassment was somewhat dissipated by his councillors' wise advice to make a gesture towards his mother, if possible to prevent more intrigues and complications from that quarter, by creating Stewart Lord Methven there and then.

But in all this influx of well-wishers and place-seekers, it was not until Davie Beaton arrived, with a handsome train, from St. Andrews, that they learned any detailed news as to what Angus was doing. Beaton, always well-informed, announced that the Douglas had retired to his all-but-impregnable stronghold of Tantallon, on the East Lothian coast, presumably to sit out the storm there and await possibly more favourable conditions for regaining power. Although there was no hint of submission or coming to terms, at least there was no present indication of major mustering or armed attack, and it looked as though the treason proclamation was having its effect. Davie Beaton also explained that he would have been to Stirling earlier, but once he learned of Angus's retiral he felt it his personal duty to rescue his uncle from his shepherd's hut in the Ochils and restore him to his archiepiscopal castle of St. Andrews.

James, who seemed to have added years to his stature and carriage in a few days, if at the expense of his temper and patience, welcomed Beaton warmly, suitably grateful for arranging the escape from Falkland, as for all else. He somewhat apologetically explained the appointment of Archbishop Dunbar as Chancellor, pleading the Primate's age and state of health; but sought to compensate by offering Davie a seat on the Privy Council and the grant of any office he chose to ask. Beaton, never backward, there and then suggested the Lord Privy Seal's position so recently held by Abbot William Douglas—which, of course, involved the keeping of the monarch's own personal seal, provided the closest links with the crown, constant access to the royal ear and consequent major influence. James agreed without hesitation, although some of his advisers were less sure. The Abbot of Arbroath quickly showed that he had in fact come there with such appointment very much in mind, and prepared to stay.

When David Lindsay later asked whether his friend was now relinquishing his position as secretary to the Primate, he was informed that it was not so. He believed that he could fulfil both functions. After all, previously he had been secretary not only to the Primate but to the Chancellor. He looked upon this Lord Privy Seal's task as more or less similar to the latter, as senior secretary to the monarch—and he, having some knowledge as to the man Dunbar, rather anticipated that the new Chancellor would have considerably less impact on the realm than had his predecessors. Davie Beaton, in fact, was moving in, with unerring instinct, to assume administrative authority in the new dispensation.

At a second and much enlarged Privy Council meeting, with Lindsay merely sitting back as an observer this time, the Lord Privy Seal, however tactful about it, made it abundantly clear that he, rather than the Chancellor, was going to make most of the running in the developing situation. Dunbar, a quiet and studious man, unlike not a few poets, was watchful and adequate but neither forceful nor initiatory, and Beaton was careful not to seem to be in the ascendant, to him nor indeed to other senior councillors. Nevertheless, most of the decisions taken either started with him or were steered into final form by him, and none which he found occasion to oppose were in the end adopted. James most evidently paid more heed to him than to any other.

Measures against Angus were still the prime consideration, and it was agreed that considerable forces should be mustered for an assault on Tantallon Castle, and before King Henry might seek to take advantage of the situation. Tantallon, as well as being so strongly sited, could be supplied by sea, which would offer Henry opportunity; so the project would have to be very carefully planned. The Earl of Argyll had by now arrived from his West Highland fastnesses, and with so much campaigning experience—as well as his huge numbers of Campbell clansmen—was the obvious choice as military leader; although Arran, as Lord Admiral had to have nominal authority and Atholl be kept sweet by being given a secondary command. To achieve this difficult leadership acceptance, without major clashes of interests, the Lord Privy Seal blandly suggested that His Grace should personally accompany the military expedition, as commander-in-chief—which should ensure Argyll's supremacy. James agreed enthusiastically. The other measures against the Red Douglases, bannings, forfeitures, treason-sanctions, were all approved and added to.

It was decided that a parliament should be held in Edinburgh at the beginning of September when the harvest should be in and this bar to a good attendance removed. In preparation for this, and also better to arrange the assault on Tantallon, the court should remove to the capital city just as soon as sufficient troops were assembled to ensure the monarch's safety from any surprise Douglas attempt.

Many new appointments fell to be made to offices of state. And at Beaton's suggestion, certain prominent lords and barons, not present, who had hitherto supported Angus, were specifically absolved from any punishment and offered acceptance of the King's peace, as a gesture towards unity. Arran and his son, the Bastard, who of course came into that category themselves, made no comment, the father eyeing his fingernails, the son grinning cynically.

Although David Lindsay now reverted to a comparatively modest station, as merely Snowdoun Herald and chief usher to the King, he nevertheless occupied a position of considerable influence, for he remained James's closest companion, as well as being in the confidence of the Lord Privy Seal, and in that of the Chancellor, who had associated with David for years as tutor to the young monarch. Another figure from James's childhood, Abbot John Inglis, was brought back from Culross to be royal chaplain.

In all these appointments there was one in which James himself had a particular interest and which seemed to concern no-one else. That was the Mistress of the Wardrobe. Before being taken to Falkland, the King had been growing ever more interested in fine clothing, a taste which Angus had seen fit to encourage, to strengthen his hold over the youth. James had grown fond of the quiet Janet Douglas, whom Angus had installed as wardrobe mistress and seamstress, and now was worried, both that she could have been whisked away from Linlithgow with the other Douglases, and that his clothes might have gone with her. He ordered David Lindsay, therefore, to go to Linlithgow to discover the situation, and if Janet was still there to bring her back to Stirling, and all his splendid apparel with her. He had been dressed in nothing but his hunting clothes since his release.

David, never loth to escape from fortress walls, found himself quite looking forward to seeing Janet again—if indeed she was still at the palace. He had not realised that he had missed her gentle, unassuming but far from negligible presence; now he had recognised that in fact he had done so, that she had been good and satisfactory company, undemanding but sympathetic, as well as his ally in the task of influencing James for the better.

So it was with a small surge of pleasure that, on arriving at the handsome brown-stone establishment above the loch, he learned from the gatehouse-porter that Mistress Douglas was indeed still there, in fact the only Douglas remaining in the place.

He found her down in the high pleasance near the lochside, amongst the fruit-trees, picking gooseberries.

"David!" she exclaimed. "How good!" That was all, but she

smiled warmly. She was a slightly-built creature but sufficiently womanly, with sensitive features and fine darkly expressive eyes. She was simply dressed, as a country-woman rather than any court lady.

Almost involuntarily he moved forward, hands out—then thought better of it. "Yes," he agreed, making his voice sober, factual. "It is. You . . . look well, Janet. A flower amongst other flowers!" He blinked at himself; he had certainly not intended to say anything like that.

"Thank you, sir." She dipped the hint of a curtsy. "Here is a most pleasant surprise. Is His Grace come back to Linlithgow?"

"No. He is at Stirling. He sent me for you."

"He did? I would have thought that he would have had enough of Douglases to last him for a lifetime! Unless, to be sure, I am to be . . . punished?"

"No, no—far from it, Janet. You are his friend. Mistress of the Wardrobe. He wishes you to be at court. He is his own master now, and chooses his own folk to be about him." He coughed, and being an honest man, added, "And wants his fine gear, the said wardrobe, to be sure!"

She smiled again. "That is more like it. I have been concerned about all the clothing, the jewels and the like, that he would be requiring them. When I heard, I thought to send all to Stirling, but had scarcely the authority. No-one instructed me. So I waited here, caring for it. And, and—oh, I am glad to see you, David!"

That was not her usual, either. They gazed at each other for a little, strangely moved.

"It will be difficult for you, here. Since, since Angus's fall," he said. He had hardly thought of that before, but recognised it now. "Alone, I mean, as a Douglas. All the rest gone and you left. Without word, wondering. We should have thought of you, before." That sounded lame, he realised. "There has been so much to see to."

"To be sure. I rejoiced when I heard of your escape from Falkland. Although it meant, meant problems for me. Is King James happier now, free? And can he remain free?"

"I believe so, yes. We must see that he does. The signs now are good. Angus is isolated. I think that we have his measure. The threat of treason, held over the Douglases." He paused. "I am sorry. You, a Douglas . . ."

"I have not been proud to bear that name, of late," she said. She stooped, to resume her berry-picking. "Even though I have to thank them for bringing me here, to serve His Grace, in however lowly degree as seamstress . . ."

"Mistress of his royal Wardrobe, he calls you now. See—give me your basket . . ."

They moved along the bushes together, the man picking also, and their talking drifted into more casual and companionable vein. Until presently she looked up.

"This is unnecessary now—this of the gooseberries," she said. "If I am to go with you to Stirling, no need for grossarts."

David hesitated, but not for long. "We can eat them when we dine, can we not? Stewed in honey they are very good." It was only early afternoon and, it being but eighteen miles to Stirling, they could be there within three hours. But the man knew an inclination to linger. "No doubt it will take you some time to gather together the King's gear and pack it for the taking. Tomorrow will serve very well."

"It is all but ready. I have kept it so. But—yes, I will cook you grossarts in honey, gladly."

They left it at that, and resumed their picking.

Later, in the royal quarters of the now largely empty palace, after their meal, they sat before a small fire of birch-logs, for the July evening had grown chilly. David told her the details of the Falkland escape and what had transpired since, emphasising Davie Beaton's prominence in all. Janet was a good listener, saying little herself. But she did comment that, grateful as they all must be to the Abbot of Arbroath, she judged him to be a man worth watching.

"You mean that by way of warning?" he asked, interested.

"Partly, yes. He is very able, to be sure, and of great spirit. Charm, also. But he could be quite ruthless, I think. And so, dangerous."

"Possibly. Fortunately, he is the King's friend, and my own. Perhaps James has need of some ruthless friends—since he has ruthless enemies!"

"Perhaps. But if he turned against you . . ." She stopped. "Forgive me speaking so, David, if he is your friend. It is presumptuous of me. I bide here alone, and think too much!"

"So long as you think of such as myself!" he told her, and surprised himself again.

She did not answer that, but changed the subject to James's behaviour. Now that he was his own master, as it were, was he still as concerned with the cards, wine, wagery and, and women?

The way that she said that last gave the man pause. "Did he, did he ever trouble you, Janet, in that fashion?"

"No, no. To me he was always . . . correct. But I knew of his failings, his weakness. I have heard him talking lewdly. So ill to hear in one of his years. And he so pleasing and kind, otherwise."

"Yes. That was Angus's doing. Of set purpose to get James further into his power. And finding women for him—an evil thing. At first, when you came, I, I . . ." He coughed. "I soon perceived that it was not so, that you were . . . different, very different."

She bit her lip. "You thought that? You thought . . . ? And others, perhaps? James himself?"

"Not when we saw you and recognised your, your worth." Hurriedly he changed to another aspect of the subject. "He has been better since Falkland and Stirling. Has been too busy, first with hunting then with taking over the reins of kingship. But I fear that he will always be so inclined. His mother, after all, is a woman of appetites, considerable appetites, as we all know! And his father was ever a lady's man. No doubt Angus reckoned on that when he ordered these temptations to corrupt the boy."

"You believe the Earl so wicked?"

"I do. I was there, saw it all. But James has strengths as well as weaknesses. These must be cherished, nurtured. That is one of the reasons why I am so glad that he wants you at court again. You can have so much effect on him, for good, as a woman whom he likes and admires. But is, is . . ."

She smiled slightly at his hesitation. "But is not attracting him towards her bed?" she finished for him.

"No, no. I mean, yes. Or not in that way. I did not mean . . ." Confused he started again. "Forgive me—you are indeed attractive as a woman to men. But you do not flaunt it, as do some. You will be good for James."

"I thank you. The other reasons you spoke of? You are glad I will be looking after his wardrobe, his clothing, yes?"

"That, of course. But I meant otherwise. I meant that *I* would be glad to have you there. Near to me also. I find your company to my taste, Janet."

"You are kind." She sounded as formal as he did. "I thank you again. I do not find it hard to seek to please such as yourself." As though she were thankful to get that little speech off her mind, she leant slightly forward. "I know how distressed you have been over your wife's sad death. My heart has gone out in sympathy to you. I know something of what you have suffered. For I too lost a dear one. We were not wed—but were going to be. He was slain at the Melrose battle."

"I am sorry. I did not know. I saw that battle. You must have felt very badly towards Douglas's enemies. Of which you must count me one."

"No. Only towards war and the folly of men's ambitions which result in war and battle."

They sat silent for a little after that, thinking their own thoughts. Presently the young woman rose.

"I will go now and prepare all for the morrow, pack the King's clothing for the road," she said.

"And I will aid you."

So together they gathered and parcelled up the contents of the royal wardrobe, the scanty jewels and other personal belongings, no great endowment for a monarch but quite a lot for a sixteen-year-old youth, stowing all in bags and baskets for carriage by pack-horse. It made a companionable task and they became the more at ease with each other. When they had finished, she filled a warming-pan with glowing ashes from the fire, to air his bed in the chamber he had used before, adjoining James's. Then she said that she would seek her couch.

He escorted her to her chamber-door, and reached out to take her arm. "Janet—I have been happier tonight, more, more complete, than I have been for long. Thanks to you," he told her.

"Then I am glad," she said simply.

"You are good for me, I think." The hand which held her slid round to encircle her waist. "I fear that I have been only half a man for too long."

She let him hold her close for a moment or two, and then gently pushed him away.

"Never that, David. Always a full man. Tonight has been good, yes. We both were perhaps . . . lonely. Perhaps *only* that. Perhaps more. We shall see. There is time ahead of us to discover. Good night, my dear." Turning, she left him there, and closed her door firmly behind her.

He went back to his own room, his feelings in something of a turmoil. He could admit to himself that, with the least encouragement, he would have gone in with her and taken her to her bed. Undoubtedly he was attracted, as he had not been since Kate died. Was it just because he needed a woman? A man's need? Or was it more than that? He admired her, as well as being attracted, and admired more than just her person. Was that being disloyal to Kate's memory? Or was he just lonely, as she had said? He did not know—he just did not know. All he knew for certain was that some part of him, the bodily part undoubtedly, felt disappointed, balked. But somewhere, he was relieved also. If she had let him in, so soon, would he have continued to admire her?

He went to bed without the answers to all that, but with the underlying conviction that it had been a good and somehow important evening.

In the morning, enjoying each other's company, with the laden pack-horses, they rode the eighteen miles to Stirling.

9

On the Privy Council's almost unanimous advice, the court moved to Edinburgh in later July; and with the lords and chiefs already mustering their forces in strength around the capital, it was deemed safe enough for James to take up residence in Holyrood Abbey rather than in the forbidding confines of the rock-top castle. And there, although the arrangements for the important parliament went ahead, the preparations for the expedition against Tantallon were the more urgent and enthusiastic, for most. This time, the Douglases were to be taught who ruled as well as reigned in Scotland.

The Abbey was full to overflowing, with nobles, lairds and prelates, and the city teeming with their retainers and clansmen, with consequent disharmony, riot and confusion. James entered into it all with energy and eagerness, the military side of it in especial. But not all his energies were so chanelled, for whether it was the ambience of Holyrood again or the mere availability of the city population, he began to renew his association with young women—and some not so young—despite David's and Janet's influence.

In this matter he found a new purveyor. Arran was amongst the residents at the Abbey, his large Hamilton manpower now judiciously at the disposal of the monarch; and the Bastard came with him. And from the first that determined character perceived priorities and set about making himself useful to the King. No doubt he had similar tastes himself and sensed James's needs. At first James was cold, prejudiced against the man who had murdered his friend Lennox. But Hamilton could be attractive and excellent company when he chose, and quite quickly the King came to accept his company. He played cards, and sometimes let James win. He raced horses, he sang and danced and told hair-curling stories, especially about French women and France—where he had lived for some years. And he appeared to have an inexhaustible supply of girls to make available for the young monarch, outdoing Angus himself in this respect, also a train of young gallants to cater to James's gaming, wagering and other weaknesses.

This situation had the effect of drawing David and Janet still closer together in a sort of frustrated partnership. They plotted and planned to circumvent the Bastard's efforts, not with much success. At the young woman's suggestion David actually composed a poem in aid of their cause, since James was interested in his friend's poetic efforts, indeed tried his own hand at the business on occasion. David left this effusion lying around so that the King was bound to see it. Its lines went thus:

Each man after his quality
  They did solicit His Majesty,
Some gart him revel at the racket,
  Some haled him to the hurly-hackit,
And some to show their courtly courses
  Would ride to Leith and race their horses
And wightily wallop o'er the sands
  They neither sparing spur nor wands,
Casting gambols with bends and becks
  So wantonly might break their necks;

There was no play but cards and dice
  Aye aye Sir Flattery bore the price;
Methinks it was a piteous thing
  To see that fair young tender King
To whom these gallants stood none awe,
  To play with him, pluckt at the craw;
They became rich, I you assure,
  But aye the Prince remainit poor;
There was few of that garrison
  That learned him any good lesson.

It was not one of Lindsay's most profound efforts but they hoped that it might have some effect. The Sir Flattery was, of course, the Bastard.

But it was not left to poetry to insert a spoke in Finnart's wheel. One night, at Holyrood, when he was returning to his own quarters after a roystering evening with the King, he was set upon by a hidden assailant armed with a dagger, in one of the abbey corridors, stabbed in several places and left lying for dead. When he was discovered there was a great hue and cry, the entire establishment aroused. They found the culprit, who had failed to clean his blood-stained dirk, and he proved to be a servant of the late Earl of Lennox, come in the tail of one of the other Stewart lords. The Bastard recovered slowly, and his imprisoned attacker was made to pay the penalty with a vengeance, Hamilton vengeance, for he was tortured to death, paraded through the streets of the city while every part of his body was being nipped with red-hot pincers, a brazier accompanying his cart. His right hand was chopped off before he expired. The man's last words were that it deserved worse than that in having failed to slay his late master's murderer, a remarkable demonstration of Highland loyalty to a chief.

This incident set off a great alarm about the security of the Abbey; if a Stewart clansman could do this, what might not the Douglases attempt? So a twenty-four-hour guard was instituted, and even James insisted on taking his turn as guard-commander of a night—although David Lindsay at least suspected that this was very largely an excuse for secret chambering, the guard being on the lax side about women intruders.

Meantime Davie Beaton was working hard to ensure that

the parliament was a major success, to consolidate the King's new-found power. He coaxed, lobbied, bought with Church money, bribed with promises of position, threatened subtly. He was in a strong position and used it to the full.

The military preparations were more straightforward, assembling troops, arms, horses, stores and searching for suitable artillery. Short-range cannon would be of no use, for the Tantallon approaches were defended by a series of deep ditches to landward, keeping artillery at a distance. Mons Meg was the only really powerful piece available and unfortunately it was said to be not functioning at its best. Argyll was in charge of all this, and although an able and practised campaigner, David wondered how his experiences in West Highland warfare amongst the island clans would fit him to lead an assault on such as Angus and a major fortress like Tantallon.

By the beginning of September, with no sign of any of the Douglases yielding themselves up into ward in response to the Privy Council command—not that anyone expected them to do so—the parliament assembled at the castle, to promulgate the necessary measures and establish to all, not least to Henry of England, King James's new and due mastery. As these affairs went, it was a major success, thanks to Davie Beaton's efforts; but also thanks to James's own contribution, for he played his part well, showing authority tempered with modesty, no cipher now, but courteous with it. He was tall, well-built for his age, and good-looking in his red-haired way, indeed seeming older than his sixteen years, appearing quite the man. The two Davids had schooled him well for this occasion. If the Chancellor, in the chair, was somewhat hesitant, the monarch on the throne was not—any more than was the Lord Privy Seal. David Lindsay for the first time had an official role to play; for Clephane, the Lyon King-of-Arms, had been ill and was now unfit to carry out his duties. James had wanted to replace him and make Lindsay Lyon there and then, but was advised that such quick promotion for a new herald would offend others longer established—and Clephane might recover; so he had put the office into commission, in the names of the five senior heralds, Albany, Ross, Islay, Marchmont and Snowdoun. He had insisted, however, that David took this first important parliamentary duty. So, dressed in Lyon's gorgeous emblazoned tabard and regalia, Lindsay did the ushering, proclaiming and stage-managing for the occasion and thereafter stood close behind the throne—as indeed he had been wont to do in the past in unofficial capacity.

The principal business, the declaring of Angus and the other senior Douglases as guilty of treason, of holding of the sovereign's person against his will by the space of two years, of exposing of his person to battle, and the refusal to yield themselves up to his justice as at present commanded, resulting in their forfeiture and sentence of death, was passed almost without opposition, the nominal disposal of their lives, titles, lands and properties following automatically. Then there was the authorisation for all means necessary to enforce parliament's will, including of course armed assault on Douglas strongholds. This out of the way, the remainder of the programme, the appointment to offices of state, the keeperships of royal palaces, provisions for taxation and revenue-raising to rehabilitate the plundered Treasury, the purging of the judiciary and sheriffdoms, appointment of new ambassadors, and so on, took considerably longer and involved a deal of horse-trading and special-pleading. But it was done at last, and most there were reasonably well satisfied, even Davie Beaton.

Now for Angus.

It was quite a major host which set out four days later for Tantallon, no fewer than twelve thousand men, although David Lindsay, for one, saw little point in taking so many, with all the provisioning and tentage necessary; he knew Tantallon and recognised that it was artillery alone which could encompass its downfall, numbers of men being all but immaterial, and mere siege unlikely to be effective since the place could be supplied by sea. But Argyll was in charge, and he and Atholl—and indeed James also—seemed to have great faith in numbers. At least this host would serve to impress the countryside and commonality with the King's new power.

The artillery-train looked impressive but in fact, apart from Mons Meg itself, there was nothing there which, in Lindsay's estimation, Tantallon would take seriously, falcons, half-falcons, quarter-falcons, sakers, culverins and the like, mainly from Edinburgh Castle, with an effective range of little more than two or three hundred yards. The cannon, drawn by teams of slow-plodding oxen, creaked along behind the infantry, while the cavalry, moss-troopers and mounted lairds and lords rode far ahead.

They went by Musselburgh and Cockenzie, and at Longniddry and Kilspindie gestures were made at 'spoiling' these two Douglas houses. But at neither was there any resistance, and it was tame work, their owners being absent; indeed at Kilspindie it was merely a token harrying, burning a few barns and cowsheds—for James looked at Graysteel with less animosity than on the rest of the Douglases and sought to be lenient, although, to be sure, parliament had passed sentence of death on him also. The King also sent a party to assail Whittinghame Tower, but expressly forbade any attack on nearby Stonypath, this being Janet's home.

Although the advance guard had reached there earlier, the King and his leadership group came to Tantallon that same evening, to set up camp near the Castleton, about half-a-mile inland from the fortress. The place looked serene from a distance, assured, invincible, its towers and battlements rose-red in the glow of the setting sun. But it was not at the soaring walls and pinnacles that the knowledgeable gazed there and then but at those parallel lines, five of them, now filling with the purple shadows of evening, which barred off the entire headland, deep, water-filled ditches, perhaps one hundred yards apart and each with its own earthen rampart in front, to keep cannon out of range. These might be bridged, of course, but only at a price, for all most certainly would be defended, and under the muzzles of the castle's own artillery. Angus had often boasted that he could sit behind his defences from any force in Christendom.

Just before darkening, James sent David and the other heralds, with trumpeters, forward under the royal standard to the first rampart and ditch where, after a brassy flourish, they shouted formal announcement that the King's Grace in person hereby called upon Archibald, Earl of Angus to yield himself, his company and this stronghold, into the King's hands forthwith, or suffer from direst consequences.

There was no least reply from fortress or ramparts; the place might have been empty, abandoned. But later, beacon-fires began to blaze at strategic points along the walling and ditches, revealing that these were manned and that darkness was not to be allowed to provide cover for attack.

In the morning a council of war was held, after scouts had been sent out to investigate all possible aspects and approaches and had come back to report. They said that there was no other access to the castle than the ditched area before them. Right and left were only sheer cliffs and precipices dropping to the sea, and these ditches went right to the cliff-edges. They were well-manned behind their system of ramparts, trenches and saps; and some of the scouts had been shot at by archers hidden there.

The conference thereafter was noisy, incoherent and less than decisive. The up-and-at-them school, led by Atholl of course advocated a headlong assault and capture of the ditches, overcoming by sheer weight of numbers; but wiser counsels prevailed against this as much too costly in men and far from assured of success at that. Some believed that a night attack, despite the fires, would be the best hope, but most agreed that they should wait for the artillery. David Falconer, a noted sea-captain and expert on naval gunnery, whom Arran as Lord Admiral had brought along, advocated an attack by sea, from fishing-craft, using scaling-ladders to mount the cliffs; but that was received with scant enthusiasm.

The ox-drawn cannon still did not arrive, and David Lindsay, who had experience of using fishing-boats and their crews along this coast, volunteered to make an investigatory reconnoitre, taking the man Falconer with him. They rode eastwards by south, to Beilhaven, the nearest fishing village, where they hired a boat and crew to row them up the coast again, the five miles or so.

Two items they learned on that brief reconnaissance. Firstly, that three large vessels were in sight, lying well out to sea, almost hull-down and seemingly stationary, near the Isle of May—and Falconer had little hesitation in declaring them English, even at that range, warships of which the Scots had none on this coast, so it looked as though Angus had not been sitting idle in Tantallon all these weeks but had been in touch with Henry Tudor, soliciting aid, so that no assault on the castle by sea would be practicable. And secondly, close under the Tantallon cliffs themselves, they perceived that any attempted attack by scaling the said cliffs by ladder or otherwise was out of the question. So tall, beetling and over-hung were they, the only access from sea-level was a single, narrow stairway cut in the living rock, a dizzy ascent which could be guarded easily by only two or three men, from fortified ledges, a hoist alongside for the drawing up of supplies from boats. Recognising defeat on this front, they turned and rowed back to Beilhaven, to mocking waving from the soaring battlements above.

There was one less option open to the royal forces.

Next day, with the cannon arrived, hopes rose—but were quickly dashed. The artillery made a heartening banging, when ranged in an impressive row, sending up the seabirds from the cliff-edges in screaming thousands—but making no least impact on the castle, none of the cannon-balls, even from Mons Meg, reaching anywhere near the masonry. Try as he would, by raising muzzle-elevations and using dangerously enlarged charges of powder, the Lord Borthwick, Master of the Ordnance, could not bring those walls within range. Admittedly the shots fell amongst the ditches and ramparts, and may possibly have worked some havoc amongst unseen Douglas men-at-arms, but this was not very likely, for the cannon could not really fire dropping-shots and the earthen banks protected the men behind. So, however satisfying the noise and seeming dramatic activity, it was all fairly profitless.

Argyll accepted that there was nothing for it but to attempt a bridging operation. So parties were sent off to find and fell suitable trees with which to construct the bridges and ramps. There were none near at hand on this open coastline, and all had to be trimmed and dragged for substantial distances. This took much time, and those not so menially engaged perforce had to employ and amuse themselves as best they might. So races were run, knightly joustings held, deeds of physical prowess performed, with wrestling, javelin-throwing and other sports, and altogether an atmosphere of holiday and relaxation began to prevail—less than suitable in a serious military endeavour. Aggressive hostility and daring were hard to maintain.

It took another day to assemble and fabricate the bridges, which had to be light enough to drag and position but strong enough to bear the weight of the cannon. There was some suggestion of making the attempt by night, but with such unwieldy material to transport and position in darkness over uneven ground, this would be more likely to work against themselves than the defenders, even if they manhandled it instead of using oxen.

In the morning, then, in thin rain and a chill wind off the sea, a start was made, a screen of infantry in half-armour behind shields pushing forward to the first of the ramparts, surprisingly without being fired on. More surprising still, when brave men, cautiously clambering up, peered over the earthworks, it was to find the ditch beyond unmanned. Much relieved, they signalled back for the bridging parties to come on.

Dragging the heavy timbers behind long files of men was slow work, and to save time some of the cannon were also manhandled forward immediately behind. Still there was no reaction from the enemy.

The bridging process was fairly straightforward, the only problem being that the ditch was both deeper and wider than they had calculated, so that the timbering had to be laid lower than bargained for, with a consequent longer and steeper descent for the cannon. But the work went reasonably well and presently they had three bridges spanning this first hazard. The builders beckoned on the cannon-teams.

Getting those pieces, heavy in themselves even though light artillery, so-called, up over the rampart and then down the steep slope behind to the bridges, was hard work indeed—and one of the sakers actually rolled off out-of-control, to plunge down into the slimy water of the ditch, whence no amount of heaving would pull it out. But so encouraged were the handlers by being left in peace to do it that there was little grumbling. The pieces had to be pushed across the three bridges and then hauled up the bank on the other side, for further advance almost to the next line of ditch, where it was hoped that the castle walls might be within range. It was just as the first cannon were being positioned there, amidst much shouting and directing, that there came a series of popping noises from the castle, scarcely loud enough to do more than draw a few glances and comments. But swiftly all that was changed, as without further warning, stone and iron balls began to descend upon the would-be attackers, the very dropping shots which they themselves were unable to fire. Bombards. Tantallon must be equipped with bombards, a mortar-type of cannon which fired its missiles high into the air, for the balls to drop on the targets instead of being aimed directly at them. Such fire was less accurate, to be sure, but had the great advantage of being able to hit behind defensive barriers. With carefully calculated charges of powder, and elevations of the short barrels, it was possible to gauge the fall of shot in any given area with a fair exactitude, given practice—and clearly Angus's gunners had had ample practice and knew the precise procedure for dropping their shots on this particular area between the fourth and fifth ditches.

Somehow, missiles falling from the sky seemed direly more alarming than those fired in normal fashion, no cover being possible, no point in crouching or hiding, no way of taking avoiding action. As the balls, the size of a man's head, plummeted down, there was panic amongst the royalist advance parties, those with the cannon, those working at the bridging and those bringing up ammunition. When, added to this, archery opened up from behind the next line of rampart, at short range and with deadly accuracy, the position was seen to be all but untenable. Men went streaming back to the safety of the encampment, abandoning all.

The bombardment continued, however. Clearly the intent was to destroy those cannon and bridges.

It was some considerable time after the cannonade eventually ceased, that a couple of scouts crept cautiously forward to inspect damage. They found two of the three bridges shattered, the third shaky and two of five cannon damaged. These scouts were permitted to return, with their report, unassailed.

Gloom prevailed in the King's entourage.

The demand now was for bombards of their own, so that at least they could hit back behind the nearer ramparts, even if they might achieve little against the castle itself. These pieces were of French origin, called bocards and moyons, founded in brass, mainly used on ships-of-war, where they were useful for reaching behind the defensive bulwarks which protected the vessels' decking. They had been little used in Scotland, where naval warfare had been neglected until James the Fourth had sought to remedy this; and although Falconer had had them on ships of his, none were nearer than the Clyde ports. But David Lindsay seemed to recollect that Antoine de la Bastie had installed one or two at Dunbar Castle, when he was using that place as Warden of the Marches. He offered to go and see whether they were still there, to borrow them, if so.

Dunbar was only a mile or two beyond Beilhaven, its strange castle, so very different from but as unique as Tantallon, projecting into the sea at the mouth of the town's harbour, built on rock-stacks above the waves, these individual towers linked by covered and vaulted bridge-corridors, an odd-looking but very strong establishment. It had been a royal fortress for almost exactly one hundred years, since the downfall of the Earls of Dunbar and March; but parliament had ceded it to the late Regent, the present Duke of Albany, now back in France, who had left his deputy, de Gonzolles, in charge. This Frenchman was notoriously jealous for his master's interests, and on David's enquiry, whilst admitting that there were two bocards and sundry other brass cannon at the castle, refused to yield them up without the firmest surety as to their safe return. When Lindsay, at a loss, asked what sureties de Gonzolles would consider adequate, the Frenchman came up with the extraordinary requirement that three Scots lords or their heirs should be delivered to him as hostages for the return of the undamaged bocards, a demand from which he would not budge. So David had to go back to Tantallon with this odd proposal; and so concerned was the royal leadership over the stalemate in their siege that the terms were agreed. As it transpired, too, they had little difficulty in finding volunteers for the part, some of the less warlike and enthusiastic campaigners being quite content to exchange the discomforts and dangers of this so-far unsuccessful operation against the Douglases for the shelter and ease of a stay in Dunbar Castle. David therefore returned with his three willing hostages, plus an escort, and duly brought back the two bocards and some other pieces, with a supply of ammunition.

However, despite all this trouble gone to, no major breakthrough was achieved with the bombards. Clearly much practice was necessary to obtain accuracy with these weapons, and the royal gunners did not have the ammunition for such practice. Shooting beyond the ditches, they were unable to recover the spent cannon-balls—as the Douglases were able to do of a night. They blazed off their supply of powder and shot, but with only disappointing results as far as their observation could establish. Certainly the effect on the castle was minimal.

There appeared to be nothing for it but to settle down to a prolonged siege, or else pack up and depart in humiliation. Nor was there any real conviction that a siege, however long, would be any more successful, especially with those English ships-of-war standing off to supply the beleaguered garrison and even take off the senior Douglases, if required. And with harvest-time already upon them and most lords wanting their people back on their lands for that most essential activity.

All this much depressed the royal party, with James himself

crestfallen that his first major military venture should be proving so fruitless. He would not hear of giving up, however. Frustration prevailed.

There was a kind of relief from an unexpected source. Home of Aytoun, although nominally an ally of the Douglases, like the other Homes, had a bone to pick with that house. For it had been a kinsman of his who was the Prior of Coldinghame whom Abbot William Douglas had had murdered in order to gain the extensive Priory lands and wealth, Aytoun adjoining Coldinghame. Now he arrived at the King's camp with the surprising information that Angus himself had slipped out of Tantallon, presumably by boat and by night, and was now in fact at Coldinghame conferring secretly with his Uncle William—it was thought with a view to organising a Home and other Border clans uprising in the King's rear. This news coincided with reports coming in that bands of Douglases elsewhere had raided and sacked the two Midlothian villages and estates of Cousland and Cranstoun, likewise two further places near to Stirling, crown properties, clearly as distraction and counter-threat. The King, much excited, insisted there and then on personally leading a hard-riding detachment down into the Merse to catch and apprehend Angus at Coldinghame.

Leading a company of some five hundred of the best-mounted lairds, their retainers and mosstroopers, Lindsay in attendance, James headed southwards that same day, at speed, all glad enough for the activity, something positive to attempt after all the heel-kicking idleness and discomfiture of the past days. They had some thirty miles to go, by Beilhaven again, Dunbar, the Home castle of Dunglass, Colbrandspath Tower—where David had vivid recollections of de la Bastie—and on over the high wilderness of Coldinghame Muir where he sighed for Kate and their honeymoon at Fast Castle there. It was dusk when they arrived in the vicinity of the Priory, set in a deep, hidden valley, on a defensive site at the confluence of two steep-sided burns, not far from St. Abb's Head. The monastic buildings were more like another castle than any sacred edifice, even the church four-square, tough-looking and battlemented—no doubt with reason, in that blood-stained Merse area. Whether warned of the royal approach or not, the place was all shut up for the night behind its high walls, and no amount of trumpeted summonsing produced any acknowledgement or other reaction.

James ordered his force to encircle the establishment, to prevent any escape by Angus, assuming that he was still there, and settled down for a chilly night in the open.

In the morning, although the occasional bell sounded from within the Priory, there was still no response to royal demands for the appearance of the Earl of Angus, Abbot William, the Sub-Prior or anyone else in authority, an infuriating situation which again left James and his people at something of a loss. They had no artillery and no means of storming the high walling. They might contrive scaling-ladders but defenders could fairly easily cast such down and overcome the climbers. In the end it was decided to cut down some trees and try to use the trimmed trunks as battering-rams against the massive wooden gates in the walling. If that failed, they might attempt to burn the gates down by heaping blazing brushwood against them; but that would require the construction of some sort of strong canopy to act as shield over the fire-tenders to protect them from possible missiles, javelins or arrows from above, and such would take time to fashion.

The tree-felling was proceeding, with some local help enforced when, around noon, an alarm was sounded. A large mounted force was approaching down the valley of one of the streams, from the west. They bore no banners to indicate identity.

This disturbed David Lindsay more than it did the King or his other officers, who saw no reason to assume that any hostility was intended to the monarch of them all, that indeed it might well represent support and reinforcement from loyal Border clans, Turnbulls, Elliots, Pringles, Scotts, perhaps Buccleuch himself. David, who had had all too much experience of Border attitudes, under de la Bastie, feared otherwise. This was Home country, after all, and that warlike and unruly house were seldom loyal to any save their friends, usually pro-English, and traditional allies of Douglas, Aytoun being something of an exception. Indeed, at that moment, it suddenly occurred to Lindsay that there might be typical Home double-dealing here. Aytoun, after bringing the tidings of Angus's Coldinghame visit to the King, had not himself come back with them here, although his castle was only a few miles away, pleading weariness of men and horses after his dash north to Tantallon—on consideration a strange admission from a mosstrooping Border laird. Suppose in fact that this was all a plot to get the King detached from his army and into Home and Douglas hands? Suppose, after their departure from Tantallon yesterday, Aytoun had quickly recovered his energies and hurried southwards again on a different route, to inform his Home and other allies that James was now at Coldinghame with a comparatively small company and could be readily captured? Angus indeed might not be here at all! Voicing something of this to the King, he made little impression, the general reaction being that Lindsay was letting his poetic imagination run away with him. But when another scout posted on high ground came down to report that a second sizable cavalry contingent was heading hitherwards down the other burn's valley, from the north this time, there was no more mockery and some serious faces.

David, considerably perturbed now, urged James to order an immediate concentration of their people around his person. They were, at present, hopelessly dispersed, still forming a wide circle around the Priory, to prevent any possible break-out by Angus. If this was indeed an attack developing, then they could hardly be worse placed to withstand it.

James hesitated. If these were friendly folk approaching, as surely was most likely, he would look a fool to summon back all his own men, and offer Angus just the chance he might well be looking for to make a dash for it, and all their effort wasted. Others agreed.

So they waited, David fretting. But when, presently, the first-reported force came into general view topping a gentle rise to the west, a mere quarter-mile away, and there drew up and massed, without signal nor friendly indication, even the most optimistic of the King's companions fell silent. At David's agitated plea, James at last ordered his trumpeters to sound the recall for his scattered company.

And as though those trumpets had been their own command, the serried ranks of the newcomers raised a shout, drew swords, couched lances and surged forward. "A Douglas! A Douglas!" they cried, and "A Home! A Home!"

David took charge, since someone must. He reached out to grasp the King's arm, and pointed due eastwards. There was little choice of direction, with enemy approaching from west and north and the river to the south, but that way also would best enable most of their dispersed people to rejoin them; and the valley narrowing again after the open space around the Priory and its homestead, would help to limit any large-scale fighting.

The royal party that rode behind James and his companion were added to all the time by others from the encirclement obeying the trumpet-call. David, having taken the lead, felt responsible for their further moves and always he felt responsible for the King. He racked his brains. He had been here before more than once and could remember something of the layout of the valley, but little detail. Should they seek a place to stand and fight? Or, with the monarch's safety paramount, was that precluded? What were their chances if they did? Numbers were vital. He had no means of knowing the enemy strength but, at a glance, he would have put the company they had seen on the rise as at least as large as their own. And there was another, of unknown size, bearing down on their left. So they could be outnumbered two to one, or more. And these Homes and Douglases were tough Border reivers, fighting on their own ground, while their own party, hastily culled from the royal army, were untried as fighters. Dare they risk the King's safety, then, possibly his life, in such circumstances? It did not take him long to decide that they dared not.

But flight, however humiliating and feeble-seeming was not likely to be easy or straightforward. Their pursuers were probably just as well mounted and would know the country better. In a long chase, they might well win—and it was thirty miles back to Tantallon. So some sort of diversion, some hold-up of the enemy was called for. An ambush? That would take time to set up and would require suitable ground conditions, unlikely to be readily available. A split-up of their people, to confuse the chase? A rearguard action by the majority, to allow the King to win clear? But would James agree to such a move?

It was while all this was racing through his mind as they galloped, that David suddenly perceived something ahead which he had not recollected, if ever he had noticed it. The St. Abb's road they were pounding along crossed still another stream from the north, by a narrow bridge. It was in no deep or steep valley, this one, to serve as a difficult barrier for horsemen, but a broad and shallow and open declivity. However, by that very token, this burn here had spread itself in marshy meadowland and wet grazing, where cattle stood knee-deep amongst reeds and rushes. Through this the water meandered, the recent rains adding to the boglike aspect, with small pools showing. In consequence, the bridge had to be no high-arched stone structure but long and low and timber-built. Even as they began to thud across this, its planking shaking to the beat of hooves, David decided that here was a chance, possibly their only chance. Taking James's agreement for granted, turning in his saddle, he yelled and gestured right and left.

"Hold the bridge! Hold this bridge!" he shouted back. "Line the bog. Both sides. Hold them here. Here, I say!"

Chaos ensued. It was not possible to halt some hundreds of fleeing horsemen abruptly, especially crossing a long and narrow bridge, to deploy them in a defensive posture at the bridge-end and along an uneven marshy front on both sides, without considerable confusion, misunderstanding and dispute. But the King's presence helped, and he excitedly supported Lindsay.

They were fortunate in that the pursuers had evidently decided on a tactic which allowed their quarry a breathing-space. For although they had sent a group racing on behind the stragglers of the royal party, to keep them in view, the bulk of them had halted near the Priory, no doubt to link up with the second contingent. Which probably indicated confidence that their prey could not escape them. So now this detachment of the enemy, no more than fifty, drew rein near the southern end of the bridge, after the last of the stragglers were over, prudently to await the main body. How many of the royal force had failed to rejoin the King there was no means of telling meantime.

David had a little time, therefore, to seek to organise a defensive stance. There was perhaps four hundred yards of the marshland on the west side of the bridge and a bare two hundred on the east, which offered fair scope for a stand—this being emphasised when the hooves of the flanking parties' horses began to sink into the moss and mire, some up to the hocks. No enemy assault across the stream itself, and then through this, would be easy. But of course a mere six-hundred-yard front could be turned fairly quickly, and David had little idea as to what lay beyond, out of sight, right and left.

So, having made as effective a disposal of their manpower as was possible in these conditions, with about one hundred still congregated at the bridge-end itself, he turned to the King.

"Sire—we can hold them up here, I think, for a little. Not for long, for almost certainly they can outflank us, one side or both.

You must go now. Head back over Coldinghame Muir, with a small escort, for Tantallon. Once there, you can send ample troops to our aid."

"Leave you here, Davie? Whilst I flee? No—never!"

"But, Sire—the only point in making a stand, here or elsewhere, is to effect your escape. It is *you* they want, the King. You escape, and they are defeated."

"I will not go. Like some craven!"

"James, heed me, of a mercy! You are the *King*, the whole realm's sovereign-lord. All the kingdom needs you—not just a few men here. You can do nothing here to advantage the issue, one sword in five hundred. If you are captured, or struck down, or slain, you have failed your realm! Throw away all that we have been struggling for since Flodden-field. Think, James—think! Think what your own father cost the realm there, by fighting like a man-at-arms instead of a monarch, and dying, to leave his kingdom in ruin. Do you not the same!"

"He is right, Your Grace," Lord Maxwell, the most lofty member of this party agreed. "If you were captured here, Scotland would be struck a dire blow. In Douglas hands again, all could be lost."

"Can we not outfight them?"

"Not if they are double our numbers," David said. "And there could be more coming. This is a carefully-laid plot." He tried another tack. "We are near the border here. If you are taken, Sire, the Douglases and Homes could well convey you over into England and hand you to Dacre and King Henry, then Henry could make Angus his governor of Scotland, in your name and his!"

That served. James looked shaken. "No—not that!" he exclaimed. "Not Henry!"

"Then, Sire, go! My lord, will you escort His Grace with a small party? A mile this side of St. Abb's there is a farmery and hamlet, I mind. From it a road of sorts strikes northwards across the muir to Fast. Take that. We will follow—when we can!" David paused. "But wait. Not yet. If those yonder see you go now, leaving most here, they may guess what is done and send a company to cut you off. They will know this country better than we do. Wait, then, until there is the stir of attack—then go. Not openly, two or three at a time . . ."

They did not have long to wait. For even as Lindsay spoke the main mass of the enemy appeared around a bend in the valley, and it was very quickly obvious that they far outnumbered the King's force—perhaps twelve hundred of them, at a guess. They came on at speed to the bridge-end and there halted with the others, a bare two hundred yards away. It was something of an alarming experience just to sit inactive, watching them come so near.

Whoever was leading them was a man of decision for, after only a brief pause, he deployed his people left and right, while keeping about one-third of the total clustered at the bridge-head. Clearly there was to be a concerted attack without delay.

David asked himself what his late friend de la Bastie would have done, the most experienced and able commander he had known. Surprise. Surprise had always been Antoine's tactic—but what surprise was open to them here? The smaller force, and very much on the defensive, the only real surprise would be to attack. But how could that possibly be contrived?

The bridge itself was the only feature to offer the least scope. Its width was no more than eight feet, only just sufficient to allow a cart to cross. So it would take no more than two horses abreast at a time. But it could accommodate four to five dismounted men, shoulder to shoulder. If he were to put forward a screen of say fifty of the best-armoured of his people on foot, they could hold the bridge for some time in hand-to-hand fighting, lancemen in front. The enemy, then, would also have to attack on foot. And while this was going on, others of his folk behind them could be working on the bridge-planking, tearing and prising it up, so that thereafter it would be impassable for horses. So any mounted attack must then be pushed through the river itself and the soft marshy gound on either side, much better for defence than attack.

There was no time for trying to think up alternative strategies. Hurriedly explaining this to the bridge-end grouping, he called for volunteers to dismount and go forward at once. There was no great rush to respond; these were cavalrymen and like all such despised foot-fighters. That is until horns blowing from the opposite end of the bridge indicated that the enemy attack was about to develop, and battle would be joined anyway at one side of the stream or the other, and some choice was still theirs. Not fifty but perhaps thirty stout characters thereupon flung themselves down from their mounts, retaining their lances, and hurried out on to the bridge timbers before the enemy could advance.

So far the device worked. David's men were able to get most of the way across the lengthy bridge before the surprised opposition reacted by spurring forward in a mounted mass. But at the beginning of the timbering they pulled up in very evident doubt as to how to tackle this situation. A few daredevils were either ordered, or elected themselves, to ride on, as though to charge the men on the bridge; and not only the men but the frieze of lances, the front rank kneeling. No doubt the intention was to ride the defenders down by sheer weight of charging horseflesh; but two men side-by-side hardly make a successful charge, even though backed up by other pairs. Also horses have their own perceptions, and that tight wall of men and lances was a daunting barrier for any animal, with the sun glinting on spear-heads and armour. The first two beasts began to rear and shy.

Their riders drove them on, their own lances lowered—indeed, they were pushed on from behind willy-nilly. But it was ten lances against two, for the second rank of dismounted men, standing close behind their kneeling comrades, could thrust their weapons out over the others' shoulders, almost as far. Admittedly the horsemen had the height, but that very elevation took almost three feet off the length of the nine-foot pikes; and they had armoured breastplates and helmets to strike at while the others had unprotected horses' legs—for it was on the horses that the defenders concentrated.

The result was all but inevitable. In whinnying, screaming panic and hurt the front beasts reared up on hind-quarters and sidled. One, tottering, fell over the edge of the railless bridge, throwing its rider before it into the water; the other, hooves lashing, swung back and was cannoned into by the animal behind, and both went down in kicking ruin, totally blocking the bridge. On top of this the following horsemen piled, unable to draw up in time, in indescribable chaos, their long lances adding to the havoc. Two more beasts fell off into the stream, and men were thrown right and left. That assault was over.

David had not waited, however enthralling it might be to watch, but had forthwith sent forward his demolition people to break up the bridge-planking. This was not so easy, lacking tools, on solid, massive timbering; and sundry swords were snapped when used as levers. But enough of the planking came up to make the bridge useless for horses, which was what mattered.

David also had to observe the mounted attacks on the flanks, with hundreds of horsemen seeking to pick their way across wet ground, the muddy-bedded stream and more marshy ground beyond, and the defenders ready to stop any routes which seemed relatively easy. Clearly, whatever the eventual outcome, this was going to be a slow process and no major break-through was likely for some time.

He turned, to find Maxwell urging James to be off, the latter still reluctant. "Now!" David cried. "All are engaged. Slip away now, of a mercy! Go, James—go!" That was as near a command as any subject could give to his monarch.

Maxwell took the King's arm.

David returned to the management of his peculiar battle, the first that he had ever sought to command on his own. He sent a runner forward to tell the people holding the bridge to move back behind the gap made by the demolishers, but to do it in stages behind a protective screen, in case the enemy rushed them again. It would be an awkward process for there was only the supporting framework of the bridge to edge over for about a dozen yards. Belatedly he thought of sending mounted scouts up and down stream to spy out and report back on what lay beyond present vision, and whether their flanks could be easily turned. Then he sent a party to reinforce a point where it seemed as though the enemy might achieve a minor break-through.

Looking behind, he was thankful to see now no sign of the King or of Maxwell.

The enemy leadership appeared to be at something of a loss. It looked as though they were waiting to see how their flanking attacks went before making any new initiative, which suited David.

It was only a question of time before sheer numbers told. Timing, therefore, for himself also. If he could grant James a sufficient start, and then begin to withdraw his force gradually, leaving only a hard-riding rearguard . . . ? So much would depend on what the ground was like, left and right, out of sight.

He ordered more men off to plug another gap in the marsh-line to the west.

His scouts returned. Downstream, it seemed, there was more wet ground, even wider than here, indeed a mere of sorts. But the other's report was less encouraging. Round the upstream bend this side-valley narrowed in, with firm ground, and although the banks were quite steep and the burn itself deeper, there was nothing to seriously hold up determined cavalry for long. Sooner or later the enemy was going to turn that flank.

It was difficult for David to calculate timing in all this stress. How long had James had now? Sufficient to let him get clear away? Probably. So it would be wise to try to begin extricating his force almost at once. Where could he pull out first?

His consideration was interrupted by a new move, an enemy assault on foot on the bridge. This had to be unimpeded until the gap was reached, after which it would pose a problem indeed. Men creeping across the supporting framework could easily be picked off one by one. The enemy answer was to hurl missiles, javelins, stones, even pikes and dirks, across the dozen-yard break, to keep the defenders hiding behind their shields, and at the same time to send a proportion of their dismounted men to jump down and wade the river, which was not sufficiently deep to drown in.

David had anticipated something of the sort from the first, and relied on the muddy bottom of the stream to bog waders down, and the fact that there was at least thirty yards of very soft margin thereafter to cross before firm ground was reached. He sent reinforcements to contest this.

In fact, these were not required. The attackers, being cavalrymen, were almost all wearing spurred leather thigh-boots, and few thought to discard these before jumping. They were the last thing in which to wade a waist-deep stream, for they promptly filled with water, becoming little better than anchors, and the spurs apt to catch on weeds and other obstacles in the mud. So the river-front was no success. Nor was the bridge assault. The missiles, at that range, did little damage, and the few hardy souls who ventured over the bridge-skeleton were quickly disposed of. The entire attack petered out, with minimal effect.

David decided to try to disguise the first withdrawals by seeming to send a mounted group of about seventy dashing upstream and out of sight, as though they had just thought of the outflanking danger, but with the instruction to swing off northwards thereafter, for Coldinghame Muir. When there was no evident reaction to this departure by the enemy, he risked sending a still larger party in the other direction, downstream. This left his defensive force very much depleted, of course, reduced now to about three hundred, but he could not have it both ways.

And now he saw what he had been expecting all along, the opposition deciding on the outflanking attempt and despatching almost half their number upstream—whether in belated reaction to the defenders' recent move or not, who could tell?

Now, then, there could be no more delay nor diversionary tactics. In mere minutes they could be cut off by overwhelming numbers. David ordered their remaining trumpeter to sound the recall, and hoped that the foe would not immediately recognise it for what it was.

His people, needless to say, had been waiting for this and lost no time in obeying the summons. They came streaming back to their horses from marsh and riverside and bridge, and as they came, not waiting for any assembling or formation, David sent them off at speed along the St. Abb's road. Their opponents certainly could perceive what was happening, but there was little that they could do to interfere at this stage, with the barriers still between. All depended on the speed of the flanking-force.

David, fretting with impatience as he was, felt bound to be almost the last to leave. There was still no view of the upstream enemy.

A mere rearguard, they pounded along the road eastwards, David wondering how much of a start they had. At least he had ensured that most of the King's force would escape. That was a satisfaction. Also it was good that his first battle as leader, self-appointed as he might be, had been fairly successful and comparatively bloodless. Moreover, he had a sneaking idea that the enemy pursuit might be less energetically pressed now. After all, this entire plot almost certainly had been arranged to capture the King; and it must be fairly obvious to all now that there was little chance of that happening.

At the farmery a mile short of St. Abb's they swung off due northwards, by the track he had first explored with Kate on their honeymoon, passing behind the mighty headland. They began to climb almost at once, and now, on bare, treeless upland, could see many of their own folk streaming ahead of them. David kept glancing back and presently indeed spied pursuit, almost a mile behind, strung-out and no very large numbers as yet. Encouraged, he spurred on.

They were well up on the moor, half-way to Fast Castle, when they recognised that the chase was being given up. Their pursuers could be seen on a grassy ridge far behind, and it took only moments to perceive that they were stationary there. Even as they looked, they saw these horsemen rein round and turn back.

Some of his people cheered, but David was content to sigh his relief.

About two hours later, near Dunglass, they were met by a large company sent by the King to their aid.

* * *

David Lindsay might have been reasonably satisfied with the outcome of that day's doings but James Stewart certainly was not. Indeed Lindsay had never seen him so dejected and ill-tempered. The youth appeared to see himself as a failure, both in his first military venture, the siege of Tantallon, and in the Coldinghame expedition—and in the latter, moreover, he had been compelled to seem the craven, to flee, leaving his people to their fate. No amount of contrary representation by David had any effect—indeed, David rather bore the brunt of the King's ill-humour, as the one who had insisted on his flight and thereafter won praise where he had failed.

James's disappointment and resentment took practical form. The siege was to be abandoned and a return made to Edinburgh the very next day. Actually this decision was more or less inevitable, for there had been considerable desertion even in the short time he had been away, the entire situation at Tantallon being most evidently unprofitable and the harvest calling men away urgently—for in the long run most Scots lairds depended on cattle for their basic sustenance, and if the harvest was not successfully gathered in, the cattle would not survive the long winter; the economics were as simple as that.

So next morning the packing-up began, a gloomy business but few protesting. They did not know whether Angus was back in Tantallon—whether in fact he had ever left it—but if he was, he would be chuckling, and the thought was galling in the extreme. In his present mood, desirous of putting the entire wretched business behind him as quickly as possible, James was certainly not inclined to wait for the cumbersome artillery, ammunition, tentage and waggon-train; and after sending back the Dunbar cannon to the man de Gonzolles for the relief of his hostages, he rode off westwards with his main force, with scarcely a backward glance, leaving Lord Borthwick, Master of the Ordnance, and the seaman David Falconer, to command the rearguard and bring on the artillery and baggage.

The King rode ahead, silent, desiring no company.

They were at Athelstaneford and David Lindsay was about to seek permission to pay calls at Garleton and The Byres, since his presence did not appear to be particularly welcome to the monarch meantime, when couriers caught up with them from the east. These brought dire tidings. Scarcely had the royal army departed than Angus himself had sallied out of his castle in force to attack the rearguard busy packing up the baggage. He had made an easy conquest, capturing the cannon and burning all the gear and supplies. The man Falconer and many others were slain and the Lord Borthwick a prisoner.

This news was not calculated to raise the royal spirits, but there was nothing that could usefully be done about it all now. James, in a passion, raised clenched fists high and swore on oath that so long as he lived Angus and his Douglases should never have their banishment revoked, nor find resting-place in Scotland.

Lindsay thought it an injudicious moment to seek leave of absence.

10

At Holyrood, in the weeks that followed, James was hard indeed to live with. His pride humbled, his self-esteem shattered, the worst side of his character came to the fore. He was bad-tempered, cross-grained, drank too much, demanded a succession of women, gambled recklessly and generally misbehaved. This was distressing for those fond of him and for those who were concerned with the quality of his rule; but it did have the effect of drawing David Lindsay and Janet Douglas ever closer together, in their joint efforts to save their young monarch from his weaknesses. The less successful they were the more they tried, and the better they came to know each other and appreciate the efforts made. David came to the conclusion that his earlier assessment of Janet's worth and virtues had been well founded, indeed an under-estimate, and that something should be done about it. He did not pretend to himself, or to her, that here was any headlong romance, nothing such as he had had with Kate; but he much liked, admired and even desired this young woman. He had no real urge to remarry, but respecting her, he concluded that it had to be a proposal of marriage.

A suitable occasion arose in mid-November after a distinctly shamefaced Lord Borthwick had presented himself at the Abbey, new-come from Tantallon. He reported that he had had a message for the King from Angus, who had casually released him without ransom, saying that James was welcome to have back him and the royal cannon, which were poor things, he having much better himself. He advised that if His Grace thought of a further call at Tantallon or other Douglas house, he should provide himself with more effective pieces than these, capable at least of knocking holes in a dovecote. So furious was James at this sarcastic and insulting gesture that he there and then commanded Arran, Argyll, Bothwell, Maxwell and everyone else about him out his presence, berating them for failing to rid him and his realm of this vile and arrogant traitor, and declaring on his royal word that they were none of them to dare to return to his court until they had disposed of Angus once and for all. On Argyll, as commander of his land forces, he laid the charge in especial, telling him that he should go forthwith and use any and every means and device known to God or man to cleanse the kingdom of this plague. Thereafter, dismissing them all, he deliberately drank himself into a stupor, and in that state David, with Janet's help, more or less carried him to bed.

Together they stood, side by side at the royal couch, looking from the handsome features of their young lord, flushed and open-lipped in drink, to each other; and suddenly, on impulse, David reached out to grasp the young woman's hand.

"This is . . . this is . . ." he began. "This is our lot, lass—our strange lot. Yours and mine. To cherish and defend and try to succour this, this foolish yet lovable lad. Janet—will you wed me?"

She eyed him, searching his face. She did not seek to release her hand. "Wed, David?" she wondered. "Wed, you say? You would marry me?" She might have been playing for time.

"Aye, wed. You and me. Become man and wife."

"Why?" That was not curt but probing, questioning.

"Why? Need you ask, lass?" He sounded almost impatient. "Is it not clear that we should? Here we stand. Just you and I. Close, together, a man and a woman. Sharing so much. Needed, aye, and needing! Just ourselves—and him. James—in name he has a whole kingdom, multitudes, but in fact he has only us two."

"And does that mean that we should wed, David?"

"Why not? We know each other, now. Trust each other, rely on each other. As he relies on us."

"Yes. But is that sufficient reason?"

"Janet, I greatly admire you. I have come to, to require you, I think."

"You do? How do you require me, David?"

"Why, in all ways, woman!"

"All ways? My company you have, and can have, any time. My friendship and trust and regard is yours already. Fortune I have none. Is it my body, then?"

He wagged his head. "No. Or, yes—that also. But—see you, lass, must we put words to it? Can we not *know* what is best, right, good for us?" He all but shook the hand which he still clutched.

"I think that if we know, we shall find words," she said slowly. "You, a man of words, a poet, should perceive that, surely?"

He stared, biting his lip. "*I* know, if you do not," he asserted. "I know that I want you for my wife."

"And will you think hardly of me, David, if I say that that is not enough? For . . . marriage. *My* marriage."

"What am I to say?"

"If you do not know, my dear, then who am I to tell you!"

"So—you will not wed me, Janet Douglas?"

"I think not. Not . . . at this present. But, I thank you for the asking. And hope that this will not spoil our good friendship, David? Do not let it do that."

He looked down at the slightly snoring youth and shook his head dumbly.

She gently released her hand and left them both there.

Profoundly disturbed, dissatisfied, perplexed, David sought his own chamber. It was his turn for failure. Yet he could not see why, where he had gone wrong. She seemed fond enough of him. All this talk of words, of his being a poet, seemed pointless, lacking in significance—and it was a significant-enough occasion surely, a proposal of marriage? It all appeared contrary to his estimation of Janet's character, as though she were insufficiently serious. And yet . . . ?

In the morning the young woman seemed no different from usual, although the man realised that he himself might well be sounding stiff and abrupt. But there was in fact little scope for any private association anyway, for James awoke in a foul mood, contrary and demanding; and Davie Beaton arrived from St. Andrews, on a matter of urgency, seeking the King's co-operation and not getting it. With all Edinburgh in a stir—for Argyll appeared to be taking his new commission against Angus seriously and was commandeering money and materials as well as men in the city—personal preoccupations were precluded.

After a difficult interview with the monarch, Beaton came seeking Lindsay's help. "What is wrong with James?" he demanded. "He is as cross-grained as a Muscovy bear! I can get nowhere with him."

"He is not at his best, no. He has a sore head, from drinking too much, and otherwise working off his disappointments. You have heard of this latest affair of Angus?"

"The sending of Borthwick back with the cannon? Yes, the city buzzes with it. And Argyll's intentions with the Homes . . ."

"The Homes? What is this?"

"It seems that he intends to detach the Homes from Angus somehow. The word is that the King has given him a free hand, all the royal power, to get rid of Angus; and he sees the Homes as the Douglas's weak spot. Many of them are under sentence of banishment and forfeiture for their crimes on the border, as well as for supporting Angus. They say that Argyll will offer to remit these, and even give them moneys, in exchange for Angus's betrayal. Who knows—it might serve some purpose."

"It will not prise Angus out of Tantallon Castle."

Beaton shrugged. "The Campbells are cunning cairds. Argyll will have some scheme. But that is not my concern. I require the

King's assent to a matter of some importance to the Church—and he will scarce listen to me."

"The Church? Do *you* require the royal authority in Church matters?"

"It is not quite that. It is the matter of Patrick Hamilton, Abbot of Fearn. You will have heard of him?"

"I have heard the name, that is all. Is he not some kin of Arran's?"

"That is the trouble, or part of it—the lesser part. The greater is that he is therefore also some kin to James. His father is Sir Patrick Hamilton of Kincavil, Arran's brother. Which puts him in cousinship to the King."

"And that is . . . awkward?"

"Very. For the Abbot is a thorn in the flesh of Holy Church, which requires to be plucked out!"

"I see. So James's permission is advisable? What has this Hamilton done? Fearn is far away, is it not? In Ross?"

"Aye. But our Patrick unfortunately does not confine his activities to Ross. Indeed, I would say that he has not visited Fearn for years. He was given the abbacy as a mere youth, to provide him with funds and a seat in parliament. No—he elects to make a nuisance of himself much nearer home. In St. Andrews itself, in fact!"

"Ah—too close to the bone! What is his offence?"

"He is one of the so-called reformers, and determined with it. And voluble. At St. Andrews he studied under John Major, the historian—not noted for his orthodoxy! There he appears to have imbibed even more dangerous doctrines than we did! Then he went to the Continent, to Wittenberg, where he sat under the man Martin Luther, the schismatic, and then went to this new dissenting university of Marburg. Now he has come home, full of these heresies, and insists in trumpeting them abroad. Even in my uncle's own city. He must be stopped."

"Why? The Church stands in great need of reform, surely? You have said so yourself. The very fact that you are Abbot of Arbroath, yet not in holy orders, and he is Abbot of Fearn from youth, speaks for itself."

"To be sure. But such reform must be orderly, come from the Church itself, from the top, not from beneath. Hamilton preaches otherwise, to the masses, fomenting strife. It is revolt that he advocates rather than reform. He objects to churchmen having any power in the state—as did Major—a dangerous doctrine."

Lindsay grinned.

"You may smile, my friend—but if the Church did not play her part in the state, it would be in a sorrier case than it is! Lord—half of the lords secular can scarcely sign their names! But this Patrick Hamilton preaches other follies—that man has no free will, that children, after baptism, are sinners, that no man is justified by works, only faith, that faith, hope and charity are so knit together that lacking one, a man lacks all. And so on. Many are heeding him and he must be silenced."

"You admit the need for reform, man. But say that it must come from the top. But all know that Rome is the last place to look for betterment. The very worst shameful abuses come from the Vatican itself, the corrupt papacy, the sale of bishoprics and other benefices, even cardinalates, child prelates, the trade in indulgences and the like. Who can look to Rome?"

"Watch your words, Snowdoun Herald, when speaking to the Primate's secretary!" The other smiled as he said that. "You could find yourself excommunicated! But, no—I do not mean that the papacy itself will initiate reform. Not as present minded. By the top, I meant the Church hierarchy in other lands, where is vision and vigour. As here in Scotland! And in those Germanic states and the Netherlands. Even in England, where Wolsey seeks the papal throne for himself. There are stirrings. But the movement must come from above, from the appointed leadership, or Rome will never accept it."

"But *will* it? Can it? It is the very hierarchies which are most at fault. Here not least, man."

"Oh, it can, yes. Many times Holy Church has reformed itself, from within. Nearly all the great orders represent a reformation of sorts—the most recent, the Cistercians. But others, the Benedictines, the Dominicans, the Franciscans, the Observantines and the like, they all started as reformist movements. That is the way it must be done, not by fanatics and mobs."

"And *you*? You who now all but control the Primate and so much of the Scots Church—do you intend reform?"

"I do. Reform in many ways. But not Patrick Hamilton's way. Challenging all established authority, advocating *dis*order and violent change. He must be silenced, or he will do untold harm."

"And you need James's agreement?"

"Not need it perhaps, but prefer it. James himself has little interest in the Church, I think, in religion itself. Nor, probably, have Arran and his Hamiltons, in the main. But they are interested in power, wealth and kinship. Another of Arran's brothers is Abbot of Paisley, and a difficult man. Then there is the Bastard, who could well be awkward. This Patrick is his cousin. They could all bear on the King. So I must needs act, and quickly."

"You? Or your uncle?"

"Let us say both!"

"And what do you want of me?"

"Only your good offices with James. I cannot wait long. Hamilton is apprehended and in a cell at St. Andrews Castle, to appear before a court of the Church in a matter of days."

"I see. I fear that I cannot help you, Davie—even if I would. At present James scarcely loves me. He blames me for making him seem to act the craven at Coldinghame when I persuaded him to flee to avoid capture by the Douglases and Homes. No advocacy of mine would help your cause."

"And, do I take it, you would be loth to give that advocacy anyway?"

"Yes. I am sorry. But I would not be a party to persecution of reformers however . . . inconvenient! I believe that the Church *needs* reform, and is unlikely to get it from your hierarchies."

Beaton eyed him thoughtfully. They had disagreed on minor points and procedures before on many an occasion, but this was the first time that Lindsay had taken an opposing stance on a matter of principle.

"Then I too am sorry," he said simply.

The Lord Privy Seal remained only two days at Holyrood, and on the second came to take his leave of Lindsay in the royal ante-room. On this occasion Janet Douglas was present.

"I have made a little progress with James," he reported. "But only a little. He accepts that authority must be maintained, in Church as in state. But does not commit himself as to Patrick Hamilton. So—now I go to see the Bastard of Arran, who so largely sways his father, and who is all but recovered of his wounds, they say."

"And what do you hope for, from that one? He will have little love for Holy Church, I think."

"No—but he will have much love for James Hamilton of Finnart, unless I much mistake! So I must seek to provide for that."

"Provide? Then you will be wagering with the Devil!"

"No doubt. But I have had some practice at that!"

"My lord Abbot—that man is wicked, a murderer," Janet said. "Surely the Church can have no truck with such."

"It is a wicked world, my dear. If the Church has no truck with wicked men, how shall it make any headway?"

"Headway towards what?" Lindsay demanded. "Can it deliberately use evil to bring forth good?"

"If there is no other road open, and we have a fair destination, we must take the one there is, friend."

"Are you so sure? That way could lead to damnation!"

"Not if one watches where one treads! Use the wits God has given. Though I walk through the valley of the shadow of death, I will fear no evil!"

That silenced Lindsay, but not Janet Douglas.

"I think that David is right," she said. "Is there not a road to hell, to destruction, broad and fair? How is it paved?"

"Ha—wisdom crieth without, she uttereth her voice! Even Solomon had to accept it. I swear I have no chance with the pair of you!"

"But you *will* go to chaffer and deal with James Hamilton of Finnart?"

"I will, yes. And seek to prove you both wrong."

"We shall see. If I cannot wish you well, I can at least wish the Church well."

"Then with that I must rest content. Mistress Janet—of your charity, do not think too hardly of me. I have much on my shoulders, and must carry the burden as best I may."

"Did you not *choose* your burden, my lord? Elect to carry it your own way? David is right, surely. For myself, a mere woman, my notions matter little. But you should heed David Lindsay. Now I will leave you . . ."

"A notable and attractive young woman, with a mind of her own," Beaton observed, when she had gone. "Interesting. And not uninterested in yourself, I would say?"

"That *I* have not noticed."

"No? But perhaps you are hardly a noticing man, where women are concerned?"

"On the contrary. I . . . I much appreciate women."

"But not this one?"

"Why, yes—since you ask. I find her to my taste. But . . ."

"But not sufficiently to seek her favours?"

The other frowned. "If by favours you mean seeking to bed her—no! She is not that sort of woman."

"Ah, do I detect more interest than I had thought? A more serious concern? You could do with a wife, you know, my friend."

"Whether I could or no is of little matter. Since she will not have me."

"You say that? Sakes—that I can scarce credit! The way she looks at you. Have you asked her?"

"I have. And she refused me."

"Then I must indeed be losing my judgement! I would have said . . ." He paused. "You really asked her to wed? Not merely hinted, gave her to understand?"

"I asked her to be my wife, and she said no. As you say, she has a mind of her own."

"I esteemed that I knew women better than this! You must have trodden wrongly, somewhere."

"I asked her plainly, honestly. I could do no more."

"So! Plainly? Honestly? Perhaps now we have it? How plainly, Davie? Women may not always esteem mere plainness in a proposal of marriage."

"You are become very knowledgeable, of a sudden about women! I do not remember you being so sure of yourself when you were courting Marion Ogilvy! I told Janet that I admired her, trusted her, even needed her—at least, I think that I did. That we could rely on each other . . ."

"Admire? Trust? Rely? Aye, but did you tell her that you loved her? Love—that is what women want to hear. Did you tell her that?"

"Why, perhaps not. Love is, is a word which can mean much or little, anything or all but nothing . . ."

"Nevertheless, it is the word that women want. If you denied it her, it may be that she likewise denied you her hand. Until you should . . . learn!"

"But that would be madness! To refuse marriage for lack of one foolish word!"

"Madness or none, it could be your trouble. Try her again,

man. And tell her that you love her. Tell her again and again. I think that it might serve."

"That would be folly . . ."

"Folly? You do love the woman, do you not? After your fashion?"

"What mean you—after my fashion? Of course I love her. Would I ask her to wed me if I did not?"

Beaton threw up his hands in defeat. "I go. I go. Have it as you will. But I have given you good advice—better than you have given me! Now for the Bastard of Arran!"

David Lindsay, of course, was not going to take seriously his peculiar friend's theories on the approaches to matrimony—who was Davie Beaton, after all, to pontificate, a man who had taken years to put his own case to the test and who, once wed, could leave wife and bairns for months at a time? This talk of love was ridiculous as a kind of key to open the gate to marriage, surely. Marriage, the sharing of a man's whole life and future and fortune with another person, was much too important a step to contemplate to depend on any mere form of words, this one or other. Yet, to be sure, Janet had said that about words, claimed that as a poet he should be something of a master of words. So he might be; he seldom had any difficulty in finding apt words for his verses. But matrimony was not poetry, it was reality if anything was. He had *been* married, after all, even if Janet had not, and he knew. This of love—he did love her, to be sure, not as he had loved Kate, of course, but sufficiently to want her to share his life as well as his bed. He supposed that there might be no harm in saying so . . .

He did not see Janet alone again that day; but next evening, with James entertaining a wild party—with, it was interesting to note, the Bastard of Arran attending, and providing some of the women—David sought alternative accommodation and, it being cold outside, after a brief walk, thought of the warmth of the abbey kitchens. And there he found Janet, likewise escaping the riot in the royal quarters, and being entertained by the monkish cooks. He was glad to join that quietly cheerful company and to participate in their provision.

When, presently, the young woman declared that she would seek her bed, David pointed out that, with the noise generated by the King's group, sleep would be impossible for hours yet, and suggested that they might go walking for a little while, a couple of monkish cloaks borrowed against the cold . . .

If she thought this an odd suggestion for a winter's night, she did not say so, and they sallied out of the warmth into the starlit dark, making for the slopes of Arthur's Seat.

When Janet stumbled over an unseen stone, David took her arm and, this being awkward through the heavy cloth of the cloak, she drew aside that flap of it so that he might hold her more comfortably. It was pleasant, companionable, walking together thus, and leaving the lights of the Abbey behind them. They did not talk much. But at length the man spoke up.

"Davie Beaton thinks that I should marry again," he declared, rather abruptly, "that I need a wife."

"Oh," she said. And, after a pause, "Perhaps, in that, he is right."

"Yes. It may be so. But, it is not so simple. Since, since I cannot marry anyone whom I do not love." He had got it out.

He felt rather than heard the intake of her breathing, the lift of her bosom against his arm. But she made no other comment.

"So, my choice is much restricted," he went on—and felt very self-conscious, something of a fool even, as he did so. "Since *you* will not have me."

Still she was silent.

"Perhaps I seek too much?" If that sounded ponderous, she certainly was not making it easy for him. "Love, as well as trust? And, and admiration, was it?"

She halted now. "David!" she got out, distinctly breathless. "What are you saying? Is it . . . ? Are you . . . ? Oh, Davie!" She was clutching him now, hard.

"Why, lass, I am but trying to say what I said before. Only . . . better! I am not good at this, I fear. Saying that I love you and need you and want you. Want you for always, to be my wife. And if you will not wed me, I must needs go wifeless all my days. For I can love no other. It is as simple as that . . ."

And astonishingly, she burst into tears and threw herself against him, small fists beating at his chest—which was difficult in all the monkish cloaking.

Somehow he got his arms around her and rocked her to and fro, his lips in her hair. His sudden spate of eloquence was gone now, so that it was only incoherencies which he mumbled against her head.

But Janet found her tongue instead, however muffled it was. "Oh, Davie, Davie! You fool! You fool! Why could you not say so before? My dear, my very foolish dear! Or is it myself the fool? To have been so lack-witted, childish? So difficult? But I, I needed to know, to be sure. Forgive me, a wilful, silly woman!"

Through all that he picked his way. "Are you saying that . . . perhaps you will? That you might wed me, after all? Or, or . . . no?"

She raised her head, to peer up at him in the darkness. "Davie, my beloved—can you not understand? I love you, have loved you for long. But dared not hope that you might love *me*. I feared . . . and because I feared, I had to be sure. Do you not see? To be sure that you *loved* me also. Not only liked, wanted. You did not say so. Although I tried, I tried, to make you say it! Nothing else would do. Oh, I have been so wilful, stupid."

"Then it is true, Janet? You will wed me? Dear God—you *will*!"

"Of course I will! It is my heart's desire. I tell you, I . . ."

But she had told him enough, at last, words no longer necessary. He picked her up, bodily, seeking her mouth with his. "A plague on these cloaks!" he gasped.

Her peal of laughter was breathless still, but joyous. He stopped all that with his lips.

It was hours before they won back to Holyrood Abbey, by which time even the royal cantrips had died down and peace of a sort reigned, however drunken. They had been quite unaware of the cold, as of the passage of time.

* * *

Neither of them desired a large or spectacular wedding, nor did either want delay. So they decided just to ask the Sub-Prior at the Abbey to marry them, there in its church, or in one of its side-chapels, in ten days' time.

Those were an eventful ten days, as it happened. For they saw, after so long, the removal of the Angus threat, meantime at any rate. Considering all that had gone before, it all seemed somehow ridiculously simple and undramatic. Argyll's strategy worked where that of more straightforward, chivalrous or merely warlike characters did not. The Home bribery move was successful, the Earl decoyed back to Coldinghame—if he had ever been there in the first place—and there he was cornered in a secret raid by Argyll. Cornered, but not captured, for Angus was holed up in his uncle's well-defended priory, and, it being traditional Home property, those curious folk would not hear of it being bombarded by artillery or otherwise damaged, even threatening to use their full force against Argyll if he attempted it. However, Angus himself presumably did not know of this and, unable to break out against the Campbells' vastly superior force, agreed, in exchange for his personal liberty, to yield, go under escort to St. Abb's and there take boat to exile in England, his uncle and other Douglases with him. So now he was gone, and Scotland could heave a sigh of relief. Admittedly he could come back—although he had promised not to until the King recalled him and cancelled the sentence of treason—for Tantallon was still unsubdued and he could reach it from the sea at any time. But it was all a notably improved situation, and Argyll came back to general plaudits and royal favour.

This success had the effect of much restoring James's good humour, so much so that he expressed himself delighted with David's and Janet's betrothal and indeed assumed that he would attend their wedding celebration.

So, the King present, others of the court came too, and the affair became much more ambitious than the principals had planned, being held in the great church itself, not in any side-chapel, even the Bastard of Arran being there. Davie Beaton came specially from St. Andrews—of all attending probably the best entitled. But none of all this, if undesired, in any way invalidated the essential joining together of the pair in one and at least they were spared the embarrassment of any attempt at a bedding ceremony, thanks to James who, strangely, considering his own behaviour and tastes, was much offended at any suggestion of it for these two. Probably he esteemed them in something like a parental role.

They made their own bedding ceremony later, and bliss it was—with promise of still better thereafter. And next day they left, on leave-of-absence, for The Mount of Lindifferon in Fife, Beaton and his archiepiscopal bodyguard as escort for most of the way. James would summon them back when he so desired.

Part Two

11

At Janet's urging, David sought to develop further his undoubted poetic gifts. In the first happy carefree weeks of their marriage he did turn out two or three small things, mainly on the themes of feminine beauty and wedded bliss, even love, suitable for the occasion. But for some time he had been contemplating a much more ambitious project, something which indeed he had started in a modest way long before but had laid aside—a major poem dealing with the manners and conceits, the moral and political follies of the day and the state of the realm, which he had tentatively entitled *The Dream*. Kate had encouraged him in this, but after her death he had not had the heart to continue with it. Now he returned to it, or rather, largely rewrote what he had previously penned, in the light of his own greater experience and maturity—and the impact of ongoing events. He was now thirty-eight and recognised some of his earlier views and judgements as all but juvenile, however finely poetic. So, as the weeks passed into months, and still the King did not send for them, did not even communicate in any way, and he grew just a little hurt, not to say resentful, the role of the monarchy and James himself tended to be alluded to more frequently in the composition, something not contemplated before. Janet backed him in this aspect, indeed they discussed the matter and its relevance and suitability. They assured each other that it was not just injured pride and pique, but for James's own good and guidance—for undoubtedly the poem would eventually go to the King when completed. After all, David had been James's closest companion and trusted friend all his life, his keeper as an infant, his boyhood guide and guard, his youthful instructor, his fellow-captive and now his personal herald. To be seemingly forgotten after all that was galling, for affection was involved as well as service and duty; but it was not so much that as with the King's own moral well-being that they were concerned—or so they told each other—for the monarch, of all people, must learn who to trust, who to turn to in need, how to reward faithful service, and so on. Presumably this present neglect or disfavour still stemmed from the business at Coldinghame, although Janet thought that it was more likely to be because of their united and undoubted disapproval of the King's present excesses in the matter of women, drink and gaming. At any rate, this poetry was a good way of working off disgruntlement and feelings, as well as making comment on, as it were from afar, the way they thought that Church and state were being mismanaged.

All this did not imply that these weeks and months were less than happy ones, or that they were much concerned with matters other than personal. On the contrary, they were prolonged satisfaction in living together, working together, learning to know each other to the full. And there was always plenty to be done at The Mount of Lindifferon, which had been neglected of late. But that was a long winter and late spring, and evenings by the fire lent themselves to such talk and composition.

If there was no news from James at Stirling (whence he had apparently removed again) there was plenty from nearer at hand, enough to resound throughout the kingdom and further afield—to Rome, undoubtedly. For the reformist Abbot of Fearn, Patrick Hamilton, was haled before a consistory court, found guilty of major, prolonged and unrepentant heresy and condemned to be burnt at the stake. At his trial, Sir James Hamilton of Finnart, the Bastard, had been one of the principal witnesses against his cousin.

These unpleasant tidings much concerned David, mainly in the new light it threw on his friend's character. For undoubtedly much of the responsibility for the entire affair must lie with Davie Beaton, even though the fate of the unfortunate Abbot was promulgated by a court of Holy Church. Without Beaton almost certainly little of it would have taken place, the final burning in especial, with the details of that horrific in the extreme, the gunpowder charges which were intended to expedite the burning of the wood twice failing to do so but each time blowing pieces off the wretched victim before he succumbed to the flames. That Davie could have approved of anything such, as well as contriving the situation whereby the Bastard (and therefore his father Arran) far from being a danger became an accomplice, revealed a side of him profoundly disturbing to Lindsay. And that the Church in Scotland could descend to such methods, whatever went on elsewhere, was a dire thought, and indicative both of the malaise which afflicted it and the threat it considered these reformist clergy posed, reforms which Lindsay for one largely agreed with.

As if that were not enough, a further and almost unbelievable aspect of Beaton's attitude towards the Church, and indeed towards life in general, was revealed shortly afterwards. He appeared to have been keeping his distance from the Mount—understandably enough, in Lindsay's opinion—but one day in May he turned up there, unannounced and without his usual impressive escort. He was greeted rather less warmly than usual.

Nevertheless he seemed his normal, cheerful if slightly cynical self, behaving as though nothing had transpired to in any way alter their long-standing friendly association. But even he could not ignore indefinitely his host's stiff reaction and Janet's cool correctness.

"Do I detect some hint of reserve, possibly even some soupçon of criticism?" he wondered presently, smiling unabashed. "Or do you deem me a carrier of the plague, perhaps?"

"Can you expect us, or any decent folk, to approve of what you did to that Patrick Hamilton?" Lindsay demanded. "You sickened not only ourselves but most of the land, I would say."

"Then you, and most of the land, lack judgement and a due responsibility, my friends. Your responsibility, as well as others', see you. For you are all members of Holy Church, baptised into its fellowship, are you not? Bound by solemn vows to its support and maintenance. Yet when the Church is under dire threat and attack from those who would destroy its very foundations, you turn the other way, do nothing and condemn those who do act!"

"Is the burning of a man, a priest, any way to serve God's cause, the God of love?"

"If that priest is destroying the faith of others, the faith of thousands, he must be stopped, punished . . ."

"But burned to death! How could you authorise that?"

"Burning is the Church's long-standing penalty for persistent and unrepented heresy, not mine. Cleansing by fire. Hamilton knew the price he would have to pay, was warned, pleaded with, time and again, but was obdurate. He had to be silenced, and others given warning."

"Surely you could have banished him, spared him, a young man, so cruel a death?" Janet said.

"And sent him back to Luther and Melancthon and the rest,

to learn worse heresies? The Church is world-wide, Janet. Despatching a heretic merely to another part of it is no answer."

"Was the answer to make a martyr of this Hamilton?" Lindsay asked. "You talk of warning others. A martyr could do the reverse, *encourage* others."

"Perhaps. But scarcely so many. There will be a deal fewer candidates for martyrdom than for mere attack on the Church! We must choose the lesser evil."

"God's Church surely should not choose *any* evil? We said that you were playing with evil when you chose to trade with the Bastard of Arran. We were right, it seems. Anything that man touches is tainted. For immunity from the other Hamiltons you bought him in. Now *you* are stained with his evil."

"I doubt your judgement, friend. But if I am, and it is to the benefit of Holy Church, then I must just thole it. As I and my Marion are tholing a more personal burden."

"Marion . . . ? What has Marion to do with your Church's burdens?"

"A deal, to my sorrow. I fear that I must take holy orders."

"What . . . ? You! How can that be? It is impossible."

"Not so. It is . . . inconvenient, but not impossible."

"But—you are married, with a family. How can such be a priest?"

"It is difficult. But steps can be taken to alter that situation, in cases of great need. And such need is now. Seldom greater."

"What do you mean? Steps—and great need?"

Even Davie Beaton took a breath before answering that. "It is necessary," he said slowly. "My uncle, as you know, has long been failing, less than himself. Now not only his body but his wits are going. He is becoming senile, and it will grow worse. Yet, he is the head of Holy Church in this land, and seldom has that Church more needed a strong, able and vigorous leader."

"I am sorry for your uncle. But, there is always Dunbar. Archbishop Dunbar of Glasgow, the Chancellor."

"He will not serve, in this pass. He is essentially a weak man, talented but weak. You have seen how he acts at a parliament. He holds back, hesitates, thinks perhaps, but does not act. *He* will not save the Church."

"*Save* the Church?"

"Aye, save. It is as serious as that. See you—why do you think I was so strong against Patrick Hamilton? I, who believe that the

Church needs reform. Because he represented a much greater threat, he only the froth on the top of the ale. There are much more powerful figures behind him, who required to be warned. Henry is behind this . . ."

"Henry? King Henry Tudor?"

"The same. You heard that he has, they say, four hundred Scots in his pocket, pensioners? I do not know about four hundred—but I do know he has many. And some of these are bishops, as well as abbots and priors. All accepting Henry's accursed gold."

"Bishops? Save us—for what?"

"The old story. Henry wants Scotland, at any cost. All the English kings have done so, but he in especial. He sees Scotland as a threat in his rear to his continental ambitions. And Wolsey, his Chancellor, aims for the papal throne and would have the Scots Church behind his claim as well as the English. Moreover, he is Archbishop of York, and York has always sought ecclesiastical hegemony over the Scots Church. These two see us with a failing Primate and a weak Chancellor-Archbishop, and the reformist agitation growing. Likewise a young, inexperienced and headstrong king. And the Douglas power still, in fact, unbroken. So, the Church, instead of being the nation's strength and stay, as in the past, could be its weakness. And the bishops—many are ignorant, unlettered and corrupt anyway, the bastards of lords and other bishops! That is Holy Church today! Now do you see what I am fighting against?"

"Save us, is it so bad as that?"

"Worse. I do not know one prelate strong enough to be trusted to succeed my uncle as Primate, to keep the Church together and hold off Henry and Wolsey. Not one. So, I must take holy orders, it seems."

"*You* must? I do not understand?"

"Yet it is simple enough. As Abbot of Arbroath, *lay* Abbot, I am well enough, fit to be the Primate's secretary and aide, but not to be the Primate himself. That requires priesthood, holy orders. Although, mind you, our late liege-lord's bastard son Alexander was made Archbishop of St. Andrews and Primate at fifteen years, lacking holy orders. But that was, shall we say, a special case. I am no king's son . . ."

"But, but . . . ? You mean that *you* . . . ?"

"To be sure. I plan to take over from my uncle. When finally he becomes too addle-pated and feeble to provide even a figure-head, as now. Or dies first. None other can I be sure of."

They stared at him, wide-eyed, trying to take in all that was implied in this extraordinary announcement.

"You, you think to be Archbishop of St. Andrews, Davie? You?" Lindsay demanded. "Head of the Church and all the bishops. You cannot mean it? How? Who would ever allow that? Who agree to it?"

"Why, the Pope in Rome would—which is what signifies, is it not? If I have put down heresy in Scotland, and maintained the Church, where others have not."

"Ha—so that is it! Hence Patrick Hamilton! This is scarcely to be credited!"

"And what of your wife?" Janet wondered. "What of Marion? And the children?"

"Marion understands. She has . . . agreed."

"Agreed to what?" Lindsay demanded. "How can this be? A married man may not be a priest. Whatever steps you claim to take, you are still a married man. In the old Celtic Church it would have been different, but Rome is stern on this."

The other was less than his usual assured self. "It will be necessary to alter Marion's status," he said carefully. "Unfortunate, but necessary. She, she will no longer be called my wife. We shall, to be sure, remain together as before. It will be but a matter of name."

"Name! You are saying that you will actually put Marion away, as wife? Your Marion!"

"No, no—not put away. All will be the same, I tell you. Save that in Church matters I will not call her wife."

"But this is . . . damnable! She *is* your wife, mother of your bairns. To shame her thus, before all. What of *your* vows? To keep, honour and cherish her all your days, till death do you part?"

"And so I shall, man. I tell you, nothing will be changed. Save that so far as Church affairs go, she will no longer be called wife . . ."

"What, then? Concubine? Marion!"

Even Davie Beaton flushed, the first time Lindsay had ever seen such a thing. "That is an ill name. Can you not see it? To all save the officials at the Vatican she will still be my wife. There I will have dispensation, setting the marriage aside, so that I may take holy orders. It is a device, no more. But a device which could save Scotland!"

"You say so! I say that you rate yourself altogether too high—and Marion Ogilvy altogether too low!"

"Then you are wholly wrong. I love and respect Marion more than I can say. This grieves me more than anything that I have ever had to do, believe me, but I see no other way. Somehow I have got to take over my uncle's position, to save Holy Church. Then to displace Dunbar as Chancellor, to save the realm, and your James's throne. Otherwise, this time, Henry Tudor will win. And Scotland will become but a poor and despised province of England, with Angus Henry's viceroy."

There was silence for a while.

"So your mind is made up?" Lindsay said at length. "When does this . . . demotion take place?"

"I have already made the first moves. Letters to Rome." Beaton hesitated. "David—I wish with all my heart that you could see this as I do, or more nearly. If Marion can, why not you? So much hangs on it. Your fate, as well as mine, and so many others. Try to understand. You are my friend . . ."

"I cannot believe it to be right, whatever the cause. I am sorry, but I cannot."

They perforce left it at that. Beaton took his departure shortly afterwards, the atmosphere at the Mount of Lindifferon less than happy.

Afterwards, for long, David and Janet discussed it all, trying to see light in the darkness. Since they had to respect Beaton's wits and abilities and believed him when he said that he loved and respected Marion, there had to be something to be said for his extraordinary point of view, however hard for them to perceive. That he was personally ambitious went without saying; but surely not to the extent of deliberately wrecking the lives of his wife and children? Could he really be so devoted to the Church that he would sacrifice all else? David had known him since college days, and did not believe that; indeed he had never thought him as even a very religiously-minded man. It was merely that he used the Church to advance himself and his causes. What, then? It could only be Scotland itself, the realm and nation. Was Davie Beaton a patriot before all else? Did his love for his native land so consume him that he was prepared to give up all for it? Others without number had given their lives for their country, admittedly, down the ages. Was Beaton's patriotism of a still more determined kind? Whereby he planned and schemed and sacrificed all for the sake of his country? He was no modest man, and had infinite faith in his own abilities—and had proved that assessment right, time and again. He appeared to believe that he could save Scotland from disaster and that only he could do so. Could he be right? Was the danger indeed so great? It seemed less so, on the face of it, than for some years. But clearly he believed otherwise.

That he apparently planned to replace Dunbar as Chancellor, however arrogant the sound of it, could all be part of the same assessment and conviction, the belief that he would make a more effective chief minister than the Archbishop, or anyone else. Whether, of course, all the necessary personal advancement could be achieved, was another matter; but obviously he conceived it as possible.

David, debating all this, wondered whether there was something here, more than merely dramatic, for him to put into his poem, *The Dream*? Or was that unsuitable, as well as unkind?

12

Curiously enough, despite the disagreements and lack of harmony on that last meeting, it was Davie Beaton who, having as Lord Privy Seal frequent audiences with the King, arranged Lindsay's eventual return to court. Or, more properly, to James's service, for it was for military duties that he was recalled, fairly early in 1529.

A parliament had been called the previous December, to deal with developments on the English and Border fronts. King Henry had sent a peremptory demand for the reinstatement of his friend Angus, with sundry other requirements, to James's fury and that of most of the parliament. But Davie Beaton had managed to convince them that, in view of their own military unpreparedness and the disaffection of the Douglases and their allies, most of the Border clans, any outright challenge to the English might at this stage would be major folly. So, a diplomatic and comparatively soft answer had been sent to Henry, rejecting any outright pardon for Angus but remitting the sentence of death, so long as he remained in England, and on condition that Tantallon and the other Douglas strongholds were yielded up. James also added, at Beaton's suggestion, that he was grateful to Henry for all the many favours shown to him during his long minority; but now that he had attained man's estate, he would endeavour to stand on his own feet and hoped no longer to be any concern to his uncle or to require further guidance. This piece of semi-hypocrisy took a deal of swallowing by James, but was acceded to in the end as a wise precaution against the difficult, vain and unpredictable Tudor. It was also an indication of Beaton's influence with the King, and to the possibilities of obtaining his desired advancement.

In addition to this measure it was decided that something must be done to demonstrate both to Henry and to the rest of Scotland that James was no weakling nor puppet any more and that the Douglases and their Border allies must be warned as to the consequences of rebellion or any moves in favour of Angus. That individual, as chief Warden of the Marches, had set up an elaborate system of bonds of manrent, as they were termed, whereby each chief and leader of a borderland clan was bound to him and to each other in mutual armed support against all others, even the monarchy. This had to be countered and shown to be worthless. So an expedition through the Borderland was organised and David Lindsay, considered rightly or wrongly to be experienced in Border warfare, was sent for.

As a preliminary gesture of warning, again on Beaton's advice, a number of the most prominent Border lords, many of them more or less attendant on the King, were placed under token arrest at Stirling, with varying degrees of willingness. These even included the Hepburn Earl of Bothwell who had succeeded Angus as Warden of the Marches. Also the new Lord Home, the Lord Maxwell, Scott of Buccleuch himself, Home of Polwarth, the Kers of Ferniehurst and Cessford and the chief of the Johnstones of Annandale. These, allegedly as prisoners and hostages for their clans' good behaviour, were to accompany the royal army of some eight thousand.

James greeted David Lindsay in casual friendliness, as though there had been no rift and no prolonged parting. He was now entering his eighteenth year and had grown and filled-out considerably, looking older than his years, quite the man in his handsome, red-headed way. He had gained much in bearing and confidence of manner in the interim, but there were clear signs of his addiction to liquor and other excesses and his eye was apt to have a cynical glint. This expedition was accompanied by three ladies for his entertainment.

Argyll, under the monarch, was in overall command, with Lindsay somewhat unsure as to his own role. Beaton did not go along; he did not see military affairs as his responsibility.

They marched southwards by Falkirk and across the bleak moorlands of Central Scotland, making for Clydesdale, where they were to pick up Hamilton of Finnart at his castle of Craignethan—for the Bastard was now a firm favourite of James—and an accession of strength. David, for one, did not greet Hamilton with any enthusiasm, although admittedly he was an able soldier and useful man in any battle. Increased in numbers, they proceeded on into Douglasdale, to show the royal standard in that birthplace of the troublesome house. They found the area all but deserted—that is, by the lairdly occupants, the common folk being less able to up and depart when it seemed wise to do so. They did some token burning and despoiling, the Bastard foremost in this, and pressed on. More and more it was Armstrong which was the name on the men's lips now.

With vivid memories of the last time that they had sought to settle differences with that unruly and far-flung clan, under Angus himself three years before, David was very doubtful as to success whatever their armed strength and military expertise. But James was determined to show who ruled here—for Armstrong of Gilnockie was known as the uncrowned King of the Border, capable of raising all the Debateable Land in arms in a day or two, threatening both the Scots and English Wardens of the Marches with dire reprisals should they interfere with him, and acknowledging no man as his master. James also was anxious to prove that he could succeed where Angus had failed. Moreover, the Bastard appeared to have some private quarrel with Johnnie of Gilnockie and was vociferous for his fall.

However, they did not proceed directly to Annandale and Eskdale, electing to march by upper Tweed and down Ettrick and Yarrow, through the great Forest of Ettrick, haunt of thieves and outlaws from time immemorial. Apparently they had lesser fish to fry before seeking to arrive at conclusions with the formidable Johnnie Armstrong.

The Ettrick Forest, generally known merely as The Forest in Scotland, was vast, indeterminate of boundary but covering an area of perhaps some one-hundred-and-fifty square miles, from mid-Tweeddale and mid-Teviotdale westwards and southwards and including much of the high watershed of Southern Scotland where rose the great rivers of Clyde, Tweed, Annan, Nith, Esk and Teviot and a host of lesser streams, refuge for broken men, outcasts and patriots too on occasion, where Wallace and Bruce had been able to elude and defy their hugely-outnumbering foes. In this inaccessible sanctuary certain robbers and reivers were inevitably more successful and powerful than others, especially those with the deepest roots in the Forest, and Adam Scott of Tushielaw actually rejoiced in the self-styled title of King of Thieves—not quite bold enough to risk offending the much more powerful Armstrong of Gilnockie further south by calling himself monarch of more than reivers. James Stewart proposed to show them both what the royal style and title really meant.

Leaving Tweed near Selkirk they went up Ettrick past its junction with Yarrow, where they entered the more constricted dale. Now the great cavalcade grew elongated indeed, winding through the narrow valley mile after mile, with David urgent on sending out scouting parties in front, rear and flanks, recollecting all too clearly how de la Bastie had ambushed even the experienced Lord Home in such country, dividing up a large strung-out company into gobbets to be devoured piecemeal, starting with the main leadership group. Little attention was paid to his representations however, the King, Argyll, the Bastard and the other nobles being quite satisfied that their daunting strength in armoured knights, horsed men-at-arms and running, bare-shanked Highland swordsmen would inhibit even the most aggressive Border thieves and mosstroopers from provoking attack.

Whether or not this was an accurate assessment, they were not challenged as they proceeded up Ettrick Water. In the upper reaches of the twisting valley, with the trees thinning to scrub birch and hawthorn, James was persuaded to send out fairly strong flanking parties to seal off the various side-glens of Hindhope and Gilmanscleuch, Deloraine and Rankle, by which Scott of Tushielaw might seek to make his escape from any direct approach to his peel-tower.

It was as well that this was done for, a bare three miles short of Tushielaw, one of the said parties came back in triumph with Adam Scott himself, captured when departing discreetly over the high pass of Rankle, southwards towards Buccleuch, with a score of his mosstroopers. These had put up a spirited resistance but had been overcome, with heavy loss, and those remaining alive brought back, all wounded.

Their leader and laird proved to be a brash character in his late thirties, with a ruddy countenance, a fleering eye and a distinctly twisted neck—which the Bastard promptly declared to be in need of straightening with a rope. James agreed, but ordained that all must be done lawfully and in due order. So the wounded captives, tied to their own shaggy horses, were carried on to that hub of waters where four major streams joined Ettrick and Tushielaw Tower sat on its hillside high above all.

There was no resistance. The tower, a typical plain Border keep, square, gaunt and tall within a high-walled courtyard, appeared to have been hastily abandoned, although smoke still rose from one of its chimneys, poultry clucked around and women's clothing lay drying over a garden-wall.

James wasted no time. Calling on Argyll, who amongst other offices held that of Lord Justice General, to try the prisoners there and then, the Earl, without so much as getting off his horse, asked the near-swooning Scott if he could deny giving himself the style of King of Thieves. The other found strength to correct that to King of Reivers. Argyll pointed out that that was the same thing, even though it implied that it was cattle only which were stolen. Therefore they had an admission of stealing cattle, siller on the hoof, which was all that was required in law for judgement and sentence. The said judgement therefore was guilty and the said sentence was hanging. Turning in the saddle, the Earl pointed grimly to a nearby isolated tree, ancient and gnarled, from a limb of which three desiccated, shrivelled corpses already dangled, the laird's gallows-tree—for, as holder of the old barony of Tushielaw, he had the power of pit and gallows. Hamilton of Finnart, laughing, volunteered to carry out the sentence, and, finding halter-rope in the tower stabling, went to work with zest. Scott and the seven of his following who had survived thus far—and who could be assumed not to require any separate trial—were strung up, as it were at his own door and with his own facilities, all in the most businesslike fashion. Thereafter the King ordered Tushielaw's head to be cut off, to be sent back to Edinburgh for due and proper exposure on a spike above the Tolbooth.

Most of the royal army, far from being able to enjoy this spectacle, did not even glimpse it, for they were still winding their way up the long, narrow Ettrick valley.

James did not wait for them. The afternoon was well advanced and he had further justice to dispense before they camped for the night. With Scott of Buccleuch as guide—not mourning his fellow-clansman, who had been a thorn in his flesh for long—they turned due northwards, up the Tushielaw Burn, to commence a long climb through bare wild hills, by a well-trodden drove-road, all but paved with the dried droppings of cattle innumerable, no doubt the highway by which the late freebooter had brought home his reived beasts from near and far, over the years. Near the lofty pass at the head of this, they turned off left-handed, westwards again, downhill now by a much-less-well-defined track, from which presently they could gaze down over a wide-opening vista of upper Yarrow, where two lochs gleamed in the sinking sunlight, one large and one small, separated only by a tiny neck of land, St. Mary's Loch and the Loch of the Lowes, where the Meggat Water joined Yarrow. Down to this narrow isthmus their track led them, to cross it to the far side at Oxcleuch. Buccleuch explained. This way, their approach would remain hidden by intervening ridges from Henderland Tower, their next target, up its side-glen at Cappercleuch, whereas had they continued on the main drove-road over the pass, they could have been visible for miles, and Piers Cockburn warned.

As it was, turning right again along St. Mary's Loch, after less than two miles they reached and forded the inflowing Meggat Water, proceeding up it for another half-mile, and there, sitting in the mouth of its steep little glen, not much more than a corrie, was Henderland Tower, almost a replica of Tushielaw but slightly smaller.

Here, with no warning and no chance of escape for the Cockburns, all went rather differently. Piers Cockburn, younger than might have been expected from his freebooterly reputation, came out from his gatehouse in his shirt-sleeves to greet the newcomers, surprised but not apparently alarmed; and was promptly informed that he was in the presence of the monarch and that his sins had caught up with him, that he would be tried forthwith and the penalty paid. He made no least protest at this abrupt intimation of doom, no comment even, but requested that he might be permitted to take leave of his wife and bairns. This was granted by James, but Argyll advised that any farewells should take place in their sight, lest Cockburn tried any tricks. Many castles and towers had secret underground passages, after all, and escape into the hills might be attempted. So the wife, Marjory, and two children, a boy and a girl aged six or seven, were brought out from the tower, fearful and bewildered, the woman attractive, dark where her husband was fair. They ran to the man's side where he stood, held by half-naked Highlanders, and presently a wail went up as the woman learned his fate—to Cockburn's very obvious embarrassment. As the distressful noise went on, fearing hysteria and an unsuitable scene the Bastard hustled mother and children away, pointing her guards down into a deep ravine nearby, with its rushing stream where, as he thoughtfully pointed out, they would not hear her caterwauling any more than she would hear what went on up here.

All this satisfactorily arranged, James decided that the most telling place to hang Piers Cockburn, since he did not appear to possess a gallows-tree, Henderland not being a barony, was from his own gatehouse. So, that individual's quiet acceptance of his doom, plus his farewell to his wife, being taken as acknowledgement of guilt and no trial necessary, without more ado the miscreant was conducted up to the little gatehouse above the pend into his courtyard, and there dropped out of its only window on the end of a length of harness-chain, to be brought up sharp, to dangle and twitch over the archway. It was all over in seconds, for almost certainly the sudden jerk on the chain broke the young man's neck, despite the subsequent convulsive movements of the body.

James had thought to pass the night at Henderland but its situation within the jaws of this little side-glen was quite inadequate for a large encampment—not to mention the disturbance which might well be caused by a hysterical female. Buccleuch however, whose clan territory this was in the main, pointed out that there was an intrusive Douglas property nearby, down Yarrow, only some four miles away, where they had insolently actually given their name to a glen and burn. Almost certainly these Douglases would be aware by now of this force's presence, and would probably have abandoned their Blackhouse Tower there. But it would be salutary to spoil their glen and farmeries, and there would be plenty of room for the army to camp around their hamlet of Craig Douglas at the mouth of the glen.

This was agreed and a move made down the main dale to Glen Douglas, where that township perforce provided cattle and poultry and meal to feed the host; and while the slaughtering and cooking went on, a sizeable company was sent up the valley, under the ever-enthusiastic Bastard of Arran to deal with Blackhouse Tower and its associated homesteads and crofts, some two miles up. These were late in getting back, and returned hungry but otherwise well-satisfied. Most of the area they had found deserted, as anticipated, but they had discovered some women in hiding, which had evidently been a considerable compensation; and the sky lit up redly behind them indicated that more justice had been effected.

Duty done, all settled down for a well-deserved night's sleep—even though David Lindsay, for one, had his doubts about much of the day's doings. But then he was an awkward character, and a poet into the bargain.

In the morning, leaving Craig Douglas township ablaze behind them, they set off for the Armstrong country, back over the pass to Tushielaw and then on eastwards over the Rankle Pass and the empty hills of the great watershed, past Buccleuch itself, where they halted for the night, a small and remote place to give its name to the Scott chiefs, but one which they had long outgrown, their main seat at Branxholme being many miles on, in Teviotdale. Thence, still eastwards, by Bellendean—from which came the Scott war-cry—and the rushing Ale Water, they hastened past Alemuir Loch, haunted as all men knew by a bloodthirsty water-kelpie and not to be ventured near between dusk and dawn. On down Borthwick Water, past Roberton and Highchesters, they reached the Teviot and Branxholme the second night.

Here was a major castle, one of the greatest in the Borderland, in a key position. James was so well entertained here that he decided to stay and rest his people for a couple of days after their gruelling cross-country march. Also they were now nearing the edge of the Armstrong territories and there was the question of strategy to be resolved. Johnnie of Gilnockie would not allow himself to be crept up on, undoubtedly, and would know well of their approach. James was anxious not to repeat Angus's fiasco in this respect and wondered how to get at the elusive King of the Border without having to pursue him deep into the trackless wastes and morasses of the Debateable Land—where of course the Armstrongs would have all the advantages. There were a number of suggestions put forward, none very convincing, David Lindsay's advice being merely to make a sort of royal progress through the Armstrong country, a demonstration of strength rather than taking any punitive measures, in the hope that Gilnockie would recognise realities and come to some suitable understanding with his liege-lord. The Bastard, needless to say, saw this as spineless weakness to be rejected out of hand. But Buccleuch largely supported Lindsay, knowing the problems and asserting that they would only waste their time and strength in trying to come to grips with Johnnie Armstrong in his own country. If the King was not content to do some token burning and harrying, as before, then his suggestion was that James adopted very different tactics in place of the mailed fist, that in fact he sent a messenger ahead to Gilnockie seeking a meeting with Johnnie. The man was proud, pretentious and might well respond to such invitation from the monarch. Better than the ineffectual chasing around the Debateable Land.

Despite Hamilton's jeers, with Argyll tending to agree with Buccleuch, James acceded. He would summon the Armstrong to his presence. If he did not come, time enough then to go hunting him down.

To make the summons sound suitably enticing to this arrogant freebooter no ordinary courier should be sent, it was agreed. What better than to send one of the royal heralds—and David Lindsay, Snowdoun Herald, was the only one present. He should go on, then, with a small escort, and if possible bring the Armstrong to the King.

David, although far from eager for the encounter, reckoned that it was probably all a deal better than any more pointless burning and slaying. So, provided with a royal Lion Rampant banner and a dozen Scott men-at-arms, he set off from Branxholme up Teviot.

Gilnockie lay southwards some twenty-three miles, in the valley of the Esk, and to reach it they had to ride up past Teviothead, over the major pass of Mosspaul and down Ewesdale beyond to its junction with Esk. The Scotts knew the way, but warned that they were unlikely to get far beyond Mosspaul without being approached by the Armstrongs.

In the event, approached was hardly the word. They had only turned the second of the many bends in the twisting drove-road below the pass itself when they were suddenly confronted by a solid phalanx of mounted mosstroopers, fully a score and bristling with arms, sitting their horses silent and completely barring the way. Even as they stared, a clatter behind turned their heads, to see a similar group emerge from a ravine just passed, to block off any retreat. No words were spoken.

David, shrugging, told his standard-bearer to unfurl the royal banner. He raised his voice. "Who are you who dare to block the way of the King's lieges?" he demanded. "I am David Lindsay of The Mount, Snowdoun Herald, on business of His Grace King James with Armstrong of Gilnockie."

That produced some discussion amongst those in front. A man held up his hand, announced that he was Armstrong of Eweslees, and pointed out that it was customary for travellers seeking to traverse Armstrong country to gain permission before they did so.

David retorted that be this as it might, they scarcely could expect the representatives of the King's Grace to seek any subject's permission to ride through His Grace's realm? This elicited no response other than the announcement that the Armstrongs would conduct the visitor to Gilnockie.

In convoy, then, they proceeded down Ewesdale in dashing style and at a spanking pace. David noted how well-equipped and well-horsed were these people, Eweslees himself being finely dressed and turned-out, however rough his manner. There was little converse on that fifteen-mile ride.

They joined Eskdale at Langholm, a sizeable town and something of an Armstrong capital obviously. But they did not pause there, pounding on down the now broad Esk in a richly-wooded valley remarkably narrow for so major a river.

They came to Gilnockie in five more miles, one more typical

Border peel-tower, square and strong, five storeys high with parapet and wall-walk, but unusual in being provided with a stone beacon or fire-basket at its gable-top, no doubt for summoning the clan in haste. The tower itself was little larger than most of its kind, but its courtyard and outbuildings were much more extensive than usual, and the castleton nearby constituted a major township.

Their arrival appeared to be anticipated—which might indicate an excellent communication-system—and they were met at the gatehouse by an imposing individual wearing a heraldic cloak of the Armstrong colours of red-and-white bearing the mailed-arm device and carrying a white-tasselled staff of office. He was flanked by half-a-dozen acolytes wearing a sort of uniform in the same colours. This character bowed elaborately and intoning, sing-song fashion, requested to know who might honour the puissant, honourable and high-born Armstrong of Gilnockie, Holehouse, Enthorn and Thorniewhats with their presence this day?

Unprepared for such reception, David repeated what he had told Eweslees earlier. Bowing again gravely at this information, the unlikely functionary turned and paced back within the gatehouse-arch and out of sight, leaving his assistants impassively to face the visitor, who was still flanked by his large escort of mixed Scotts and Armstrongs.

David waited, and presently was astonished to hear music sounding from within the courtyard, the sweet music of lutes and fiddles, extraordinary for such a place at such a time. The impressive usher or seneschal, or whatever he might be, reappeared then with four instrumentalists playing as they walked. He announced, against the background melody, that Gilnockie would see King James's herald and representative, and to follow him within.

Dismounting, David was led off between the musicians in front and the silent six behind, an odd procession, while his Scott supporters were hustled off elsewhere.

Across the paved courtyard with the wall at its centre they came to the tower itself. And within its heraldic-lintelled doorway a man stood to welcome him, deerhounds at his knees.

David all but halted in his measured pacing which the music rather imposed, so unexpected a sight was this. Presumably in that stance it would be none other than Johnnie Armstrong himself. Yet anyone less like a notorious Border reiver and freebooter would have been hard to imagine. He saw a dashingly handsome dark man in his mid-thirties, slender, graceful even, and dressed in the height of French fashion, from long curled and ribboned hair, jewels at his ear-lobes, to gleaming gold dirk-belt and silver-buckled shoes. Standing smiling there, assured, at ease, he would have outshone anyone at court, even Davie Beaton.

"Greetings, sir," this elegant called out. "Do I understand that you are a Lindsay? I am John of Gilnockie."

"Then it is you that I have come to see. The King's Grace has sent me, the Snowdoun Herald, with a message for yourself."

"Ah, yes," the other nodded, as though messages from the monarch were everyday occurrences at Gilnockie Tower. "Then welcome to my humble house, Master Herald, for some small refreshment. You will be weary after your ride from Branxholme."

"You are well informed, sir," David observed, as he was ushered in through the six-foot-thick walling.

"I require to be, friend. I would not wish to have to counter what happened at Tushielaw, Henderland and Glen Douglas unprepared!"

That caused the visitor to swallow.

He was led past the basement vaults and up the turnpike stair to the roomy first-floor hall, where a cheerful fire burned under another great heraldic lintel and the long dais-table was already set with an assortment of flagons, beakers and goblets, dishes of cold meats and fish and sweetmeats sufficient for a score. The walls of this chamber were hung with costly tapestries, the floor strewn with handsome rugs of skin and weave, and the window-seats cushioned in silk. David sought not to appear over-impressed.

The usher, who had followed them up, now began to ply the visitor with food and drink, snapping his fingers to have his aides bring different varieties of wine, French, Italian and Rhenish. The laird accepted a beaker to drink with his guest whilst standing easily by the fire. The sound of the music still drifted up softly from the courtyard.

Twice David began to deliver his message but each time he was waved to silence and courteously urged to finish his refreshment in peace. Only when the visitor expressed himself as more than satisfied did Armstrong dismiss the attendants and indicate that they could now talk in private.

"My errand is simple," David informed. "His Grace sends his greetings and requests your company. No more than that."

"Requests or summons?" That was mildly put.

"Requests. It is not a royal command."

"As well, sir—that is as well! When and where is this meeting desired? His Grace would be most welcome at this my house."

"Yes, no doubt. But my orders were to bring you to the King, and so soon as . . . convenient."

"Bring . . . ?"

"Escort, shall we say? As I was escorted here!"

"Ah. Convenient, you say? Now that is most . . . civil."

"Yes. Save that, to be sure, His Grace would not wish to have to wait overlong."

"At Branxholme?"

"That was where I left him, yes."

"Very well. We will ride tomorrow."

Was it to be as simple as that? David scarcely believed it.

Yet Gilnockie appeared to assume that all was settled. After some casual conversation he declared that, unfortunately, he had sundry matters to attend to, and that Wat—presumably the usher—would show his guest to his chamber. His men, Scotts though they were, would be well cared for. A woman would be available to ensure that he had a satisfactory night, if so desired. They would ride at sun-up.

Somewhat bemused, and dispensing with the proffered feminine company, David sought his couch. He heard much to-ing and fro-ing and clatter of hooves outside Gilnockie before he slept that night.

He was in no danger of oversleeping in the morning on account of similar and continuing coming and going beyond the courtyard. He was brought breakfast in his room, and when thereafter he was led down and out, it was to discover an extraordinary situation. A great concourse of men and horses was assembled outside; but these were not mosstroopers nor ordinary men-at-arms. All were dressed in fine clothing, not half-armour and helmets but doeskin, broadcloth, velvets, silk shirts and feather caps. Their mounts were as notable as themselves, as handsome a collection of horseflesh as David had ever seen at one time, all splendidly caparisoned. About them milled a host of attendants; but there was no mistaking the one for the other.

Johnnie Armstrong appeared, a sight to draw all eyes, dressed for riding but outdoing all in richness of apparel yet managing to avoid vulgar ostentation. He wore a fur-trimmed velvet cloak embroidered colourfully with the Armstrong arms over a cloth-of-gold doublet and breeches, and long doeskin thigh-boots which were gold-fringed and golden-spurred; his gold sword-belt was a hand-span in width and studded with rubies, and his flat velvet cap, hung with no fewer than nine gold or silver tassels, sat jauntily on his curled dark hair.

"Ah, Lindsay—a good morning to you," he greeted. "I trust that you had a fair night and are adequately rested and refreshed? We are all but ready to ride to meet King James. Here is my brother, Thomas of Mangerton, chief of all the Armstrongs."

Surprised, David looked from his host to the quietly-dressed, diffident-seeming man at his side, tall but apparently slightly lame. "I thought . . ." he began.

"I am but a second son," he was told. "Thomas is head of our house, and worthily so. He must represent Armstrong before King James. And these are our escort, suitable for the occasion. Here is Dod Armstrong of Kershopefoot. And this is Armstrong of Dinwoodie. And Armstrong of Whithaugh. Armstrong of Sorbietrees. Armstrong of Bruntshiels. Armstrong of Sikehead. Armstrong of Woolhope . . ."

The list went on and on. It dawned on David what was here being demonstrated. These were all *landed* men, lairds in their own right, all these well-dressed characters, not retainers nor tenants even. This was a *court* being used as escort, how many he was uncertain but not far off two score. Here was pride and display indeed, on a scale hardly to be rivalled in the land—but pride backed by might. If Johnnie Armstrong, or his brother, could produce all these lairdly supporters at a night's notice, what could he not raise amongst their mosstroopers and retainers? That he should have chosen to take these, apparently, before the King, rather than any host of armed men, was significant surely?

Introductions over, Gilnockie gave the signal to mount. Clearly, whatever their relationship, *he* was in command. David's own Scott escort was then brought forward, to fall in behind the gallant company of lairds, seemingly in good shape. And not only these, the musicians reappeared, in double the number, and horsed now, fiddles and lutes exchanged for flutes and horns. With these preceding them and playing more stirring tunes now, a start was made.

As far as Langholm they processed thus, in no great hurry, cheered and waved to by the country folk, a holiday parade. But thereafter, with the land beginning to rise up Ewesdale, the musicians put away their instruments and harder riding was called for. They settled down to covering ground expeditiously.

As they rested their horses at Mosspaul summit, Gilnockie asked what sort of man young King James was? He had heard that Angus sought to lead him into ill ways, and that he had a temper to go with red hair? David cautiously agreed with that, but declared that James had many virtues and would make a good monarch once he became a more experienced judge of character.

Riding on down towards Teviothead, they were not long in coming into view of a vast concourse of men and horses, the entire valley seeming to be filled as far as eye could see, all gleam and glitter in the sunlight.

"Ha—your King travels in some company, I see!" Johnnie Armstrong observed. "Does he intend an invasion of England, with all these?"

David was about to point out that James was as much Armstrong's King as his own, but thought better of it. "The Borderland is unsettled country and less than law-abiding," he contented himself with saying. "It behoves His Grace to show who rules, even here!"

That drew only a smile from the other.

As the two companies, so contrasting in numbers, neared each other, in the vicinity of Caerlanrig, it could be seen that the royal entourage heading the host drew up at a wide, grassy hollow, clearly to await the arrival of the Armstrongs. For his part, Gilnockie ordered the pace to be slowed, the instrumentalists to start up again and his impressive escort to form up as many abreast as the drove-road would allow—which proved to be nine at a time. They made four spectacular rows—so there were in fact thirty-six of the lairds. Thus, to the sound of music, they proceeded now at a walking pace.

James's company was, of course, illustrious, including many of the greatest names in Scotland. But all had been on the march for a week, were anyway dressed for campaigning not display, and were in no particular order. In consequence they presented a much less eye-catching picture despite the vast numbers behind, than did the Armstrongs.

Gilnockie, slightly in front, with his brother on one side and David Lindsay on the other, reined up about fifty paces from where James sat his horse under the royal standard, and so waited whilst the musicians finished the few more bars of their refrain. Then he whipped off his tasselled bonnet and made an elaborate bow from the saddle—as did all behind him in fair unison.

"Armstrong to greet Your Grace!" he called cheerfully. "Welcome to our country."

James was staring, as indeed were all his company. No response was immediately forthcoming.

David stepped into the breach. "Sire, here is John Armstrong of Gilnockie, his brother Thomas of Mangerton, and, and other Armstrong lairds. Come at your royal behest."

The King looked round at Argyll, Bothwell, Maxwell, Buccleuch, the Bastard and others flanking him. "Yes," he said, uncertainly. "All, all Armstrongs? These? Reivers? Outlaws?"

"Scarcely that, King," Johnnie corrected. "We have our own laws on the Border—and abide by them."

"Insolent!" That was the Bastard.

The change in Gilnockie was immediate and dramatic. "Who speaks so in Armstrong country?" he demanded, suddenly all the debonnaire flourish replaced by a narrow-eyed, menacing stare.

"I am Finnart, Hamilton of Finnart, miscreant! Watch your tongue!"

"I might have known it! Bastards are ever loud-mouthed! Does the King of Scots depend on such to speak for him?"

That spurred James. "You, sirrah—are you he who calls himself King of the Border?"

"No, Sire. Others may, but not I!"

There was a growl from all around the monarch.

"That is little better," James asserted, scowling. "I think that Sir James is right, sir—you are insolent!"

"Then you misjudge," the other said simply. "I assure you that I did not come here, and bring all these, to appear insolent. I came to greet you, in friendship."

"Friendship. *You*—to the King's Grace!" Argyll barked. "Here's a bold rogue, by God!"

David felt somehow responsible, having brought the Armstrongs here. "Sire," he interposed, "Gilnockie and his people, or his brother's people, have ridden far to welcome you to their lands. They hope that Your Grace will visit their houses. I have been kindly treated."

James still looked doubtful, in youthful indecision, but about him voices were all raised in offence and condemnation, the Bastard the loudest.

"I mislike his manner," he said.

"And I mislike the manners of your King's friends!" Armstrong declared, to Lindsay, but loud enough for most to hear.

"Of a mercy, watch how you speak!" David muttered, in an aside. "Inform him of your Armstrong lairds."

Gilnockie nodded. "King James—here is my brother, Mangerton, head of our house. And these are all gentlemen of the name—Kershopefoot, Dinwoodie, Sorbietrees, Whithaugh, Sikehead, Eweslees, Bruntshiels, Woolhope, Birkenbower, Patelaw . . ."

"Lord, enough! Enough! What is this? A, a retinue, a suite? All these!"

"The King of the Border's court of thieves, Sire!" the Bastard asserted.

"Aye—what lacks this knave that a king should have! See how he is dressed! Hear him! His prideful bearing, his, his train! This is an arrogant rascal!"

"And more in need of a hanging than even Tushielaw or Henderland!" the Bastard persisted.

"Aye, the rope for him! For them all. Murdering robbers! Where did they win all that finery? The gold? Those horses? Slain men's gear!" That was Ker of Ferniehurst, who was scarcely in a position to talk.

Gilnockie laughed. "Do I hear mice squeak, coneys roar? Save us from such terrors!"

"Have a care!" David warned.

"What are Your Grace's commands?" Argyll asked, clearly impatient with all the talk.

James drew a quick breath. "Take them," he said.

Argyll urged his mount forward to Gilnockie's side. "I arrest you in the King's name," he said.

"Arrest me? Why? Are you crazed, man?"

"I am Argyll, Lord Justice General of this realm. You are now in the King's custody."

"You must have taken leave of your wits, then, Campbell! We are not in your barbarous Hielands, here, see you. This is the West March of the Border, and *I* say who is in custody and who is not!"

"No more, thief! Your day is done."

"You say so? Myself, or all these?"

"You, and them all."

Gilnockie hooted an eloquent laugh.

It was his hitherto silent and retiring brother who spoke now. "My lord, you cannot mean this? You, a justiciar! What have we done to deserve custody?"

"You have robbed and slain and made terror on the Border these many years."

"We have hurt, and slain no Scots. Only the English, the King's enemies."

"Not as we have heard it. You lie, man!"

Gilnockie reined close. "No man says that to Armstrong!" he rasped. "You will take back that word, Campbell!"

"Fool! Hold your insolent tongue or I will have it torn out! Before you hang!"

"Hang . . . !" That word seemed suddenly to convince Johnnie Armstrong that this was all serious, no mere gesturing and play-acting. He gazed from Argyll to the King—and saw nothing in their faces to reassure. He saw something else, however. Hamilton, a man for action always, had utilised the period of this exchange with Argyll to summon and lead forward a troop of horsed men-at-arms, and with them was now riding to get round behind the Armstrongs with the obvious intention of cutting off any line of retreat.

For a moment or two it looked as though Gilnockie would choose to do just that and lead his people in fast retiral. But pride triumphed over such caution and he spurred forward almost justling Argyll's horse aside right over to the King himself.

"We are here at your invitation. Under safe conduct," he said to the monarch.

"I said nothing of safe conduct," James declared, almost defiantly.

"Your herald invited and brought us, at your behest."

"That does not imply safe conduct for a traitor!"

"Traitor . . . ?"

"Aye, traitor. Think you we do not know of your dealings with the English? You claim to assail only them. But say naught of your traffic with them, of payments you accept from them."

"Mail paid, that I leave them their cattle! Such as will pay, the wise ones!"

"Dacre himself pays you, they say."

"Dacre has many cattle, and owns lands near the borderline!"

"False—all false! You have boasted, man, that you acknowledge the authority of neither the King of England nor the King of Scots. Can you deny it?"

"Only in the Debateable Land. Where, as all men know, the writ of neither runs, only that of the sharpest sword."

"Well, we shall see who wields the sharpest sword here! You will hang, Armstrong—hang!"

"You cannot mean that, James Stewart! Would you hang one who can give you what I can give?"

"What you can give, I can *take*!"

"Not so. Can you take the rents of every fair property between here and Newcastle town? *I* can give you them!"

"I do not believe it. Nor would I accept them, if I could."

"Could *you* take any English noble, be he duke, earl or baron, that you named, out of all that land. I could bring you any, by a certain day, either quick or dead."

There were guffaws from the King's companions who had now gathered round to listen.

"I desire none such," James said, frowning.

"I can give you four-and-twenty fine horses, milk-white and matching beasts. And as much yellow gold, English gold, as four of them can carry. Could *you* take that?"

"You rave, man—rave! And I do not need your horses nor your gold."

"You and yours may need bread, King, if this harvest fails, as it is like to do. I can give you four-and-twenty good-going mills, and the grain to keep them grinding round the year."

"The harvest is not like to fail. Have done, boaster!"

"With such as Your Grace has around you here, scoundrels all I judge, you could do with an honest guard for your royal person, I vow! I can give you more trusty and leal gentlemen than even you see here, Armstrong gentlemen, as your guard.

Say forty, who would lay down their lives for you at my behest. How say you?"

"*I* say that with forty thieves around you, Your Grace would never pass another peaceful night!" The Bastard had returned. That produced grins.

James drew himself up in his saddle. "I believe none of all that you offer," he said. "And your forty thieves will hang with you, for company! My Lord Argyll, do your duty." He pointed. "Up there. There are sufficient trees on yonder ridge to accommodate them all, I swear!"

There was a shout of laughter at this royal sally, which James self-consciously acknowledged.

Johnnie Armstrong made a gesture partly resignation, partly defiance. "I was a fool to look for warm water beneath cold ice!" he said. "A fool to seek grace at Your Grace's graceless face! A fool to come at all, trusting your messenger. Had I known that you would take my life this day, I should have stayed away and kept the Border in despite of King Henry and you, both. For I know that Henry Tudor a blithe man would be this day, and would downweigh my best horse with his English gold to know that John Armstrong was condemned to die. Which proves who lacks in judgement, does it not? I tell you . . ."

"Enough!" Argyll interrupted. "Come, or we shall be here all day. We shall still this insolent tongue once and for all." And he signed for his men to grasp Gilnockie.

"A moment," James said. "What are these targets you wear on your cap?" And he pointed to the gold and silver tassels. "Eight, nine of them."

"I won them in the field, fighting the English—as your royal father dared but I think *you* would not! Each from a different knight's helm."

"Off with him!" the King jerked, turning away.

Armstrong shook off the hands which would have grasped him. "I need none to drag me to my death!" he said. He looked over towards his brother. "God be with you, Tom. We will be together again one day, in a better kingdom! Tell Kirsty . . ."

"He will tell none!" Argyll assured. "You are not parting from him. He hangs with you, as do they all. We shall see an end to the Armstrongs on the Border."

Surrounded now by overwhelming force, there was nothing that any of them could do. The Armstrong lairds, taking their lead as ever from Gilnockie, did not struggle nor plead nor rail, but accepted their fate with quiet dignity. A general move was made up towards a slight grassy ridge whereon grew a group of twisted, wind-blown Scots pines.

David Lindsay hastened to the King's side. "Sire—this is madness! Wrong, wrong! And a sin. You cannot mean to go on with this? To hang him, them all?"

James turned his face away, unspeaking.

"Sire—hear me. This is shame. It will stain your royal name, for ever. The Armstrongs came here at your invitation. Safe conduct *is* understood and accepted in such case. Otherwise he would not have come. To slay him now is, is unthinkable!"

"He is a robber and a murderer. A traitor, and arrogant. He deserves to die."

"So is the Bastard of Arran! But you do not hang *him*!"

By the look the King gave him, David recognised that that was a mistake. He changed his approach. "Your Grace, I am your friend. Always have been, and I pray always will be. Yet you grievously injure *me*, in this. You sent me as herald to bring him to you. My name and repute is concerned. If you hang these men, *I* am diminished. Made accomplice, a deceiver."

"It was the only way to lay hands on him, Davie. He would have escaped justice for ever, at large in the Debateable Land."

"And you name this justice, Sire?"

"I do. Now, if you have no fairer words for me than this, leave me!"

Sorrowfully David reined away.

They hanged the Armstrongs on the trees of Caerlanrig, two or three to a tree, still in their saddles from which they had ruled the West Border, by the simple expedient of putting ropes around their necks and over a bough above then driving their horses from under them. The musicians went with the rest, the Bastard master-of-ceremonies. It was inevitably a haphazard business and not always expeditious, but they all died in the end. It was the Bastard's inspired suggestion that Gilnockie himself should be left to the end, so that he would have the benefit of watching his brother and all his presumptuous crew die first.

Thereafter a return was made to Branxholme, most in high good-humour but James himself silent and withdrawn. They left the forty-odd corpses swinging in the breeze.

Next day, with any further Border campaigning bound to seem

in the nature of an anticlimax, the return march to Edinburgh and Stirling was commenced. At Stirling, Lindsay made a stiff leave-taking of his monarch, who was still morose and difficult and who made no suggestion that David should stay at court. That man would be glad to be back with Janet at Lindifferon.

13

Davie Beaton looked from his host to Janet, and back. "The question is, do you, with all your gifts, abilities and experience, wish to use them, to do something of worth with them, of value to this our realm? Or do you seek to be only a simple Fife laird?"

"Can I not be both?"

"I fear not. I think that you must choose. Here you have no influence on men nor events. Even your poems reach little further—St. Andrews perhaps, no more. You should be at court, where events happen and are made to happen, where men are to be reached, where a little faith can move mountains!"

"I mislike the court as it now is."

"You mean that you mislike some of those who frequent the court? The Bastard and his ilk? You could help to counter their influence with James."

"I have tried that, and failed. I find James himself less and less to my taste, spoiled by the company he keeps."

"The more reason that you should seek to save him from them, and himself. Is it no less than your duty, man? You are his oldest true friend, cherishing him from infancy. James *needs* you, David."

"I think that he is scarce aware of it, then, since he never looks in my direction now."

"Perhaps he does, more than you think. I speak to him of you, and he sounds sufficiently interested. I gave him your *Dream*. He read it and praised it greatly. He even said that since King Henry had a Poet Laureate—he gives the man a yearly grant of wine!—*you* should be the Laureate of the Scots court."

"But does not want me at court to be so?"

"Do not be so thin of skin, friend! Think you all at court are there by express royal summons?"

"If James *needs* me, he can send for me. After all, I am still his Snowdoun Herald. And Janet is Mistress of his Wardrobe—leastways we have heard of no replacements."

"I think that I detect here injured pride?"

"Not so. But after Caerlanrig and the Armstrongs, I hold my distance from that young man unless, as my liege-lord, he summons me."

"Do you agree with this, Janet?"

"David knows best," she said simply.

"Ah, but we are all the better of occasional good advice, especially from our wives."

"*You* to say that!" Lindsay all but snorted.

"Indeed yes. My Marion advises me not a little. More than ever, indeed. Janet must have her views?"

"I have told David on occasion that he might find more, more fulfilment than just in farming The Mount of Lindifferon," she said, carefully.

"And you are right. I say that he has a part to play on a wider stage than some few hundred Fife acres." Beaton paused. "See you, David, I have a proposal for you, a tentative proposal. As ever, I am seeking to contain Henry Tudor, so far as Scotland is concerned. James himself is seemingly little interested. With England and France once again hand-in-glove since Wolsey's fall, the Emperor Charles is bound to be perturbed. Now, Scotland has an ancient treaty with the Netherlands, a treaty of mutual assistance, made a century ago when that land had not been occupied by the Empire and the Spanish. Few know of it, now. I did not my own self, but as Lord Privy Seal I learned of it. One of its clauses is that its term is of one hundred years, and could be renewed thereafter. Those hundred years are all but up. It occurs to me that a renewal might well suit the Emperor Charles, at this juncture, as warning to the ever-aggressive Henry—as it certainly would suit Scotland. A treaty in fact, if not in name, with the Empire, whilst France fails us. But, to be sure, Charles is unlikely to know of its existence. So I propose that James sends an embassage to Brussels to seek renewal of this treaty. How think you?"

"I think that it all sounds entirely like Davie Beaton!"

"That is scarcely the point. What would you say to going on such an embassage?"

"Me? Why me? I have no knowledge of statecraft, no honeyed tongue to persuade rulers—as I have proved!"

"Perhaps not. But you are to be trusted, as are not all. And you do not lack wits—in most matters. In some, mind you, I find you remarkably obtuse! But, see you, this embassage might serve *you* well, equally with the realm. It would bring you back into the royal service in worthy style, allow James to show you his kinder side again. For perhaps he has his pride also, David!"

"This talk of pride is foolishness. I think that you came here today to talk me into this of Brussels for your own ends! Admit it!"

"Scarcely for my own ends. But, yes, I would wish you to do this. I think that I have convinced James that the mission is important, and he suggests sending his latest drinking-companion, Campbell of Lundie. You may not know him, the late Argyll's cousin. You heard that Argyll had died suddenly? This Campbell I do not trust—but can scarcely say so to the King, who esteems him. David Paniter, the new royal secretary, I do trust—since I gained him the appointment!—and he may go also. But he is young yet and lacks experience. You would make the admirable third."

"I do not know . . ."

"I think that you should do it, David," Janet said. "You have been restless of late. There is insufficient here to content you for long, after the life that you have lived. Such a mission would be good for you."

"I shall think on it."

"Do that," Beaton nodded. "But do not think for too long. It is now June and the embassage should depart within a month or so, to gain good sailing weather there and back. Three men are always sent as such envoys—in the hope that one at least will be honest! Choosing three, who may counter each others' weaknesses, can be difficult. I shall endeavour to hold a place for you so long as I may."

"You are kind." That was Janet, not her husband.

"I am very kind, yes," the other agreed, wryly. "In especial, after all the ill things said by this character about Holy Church and its servants, such as my poor self, in *The Dream*! I could have had him excommunicated for less!"

"It all required to be said," Lindsay averred.

"That is debateable, shall we say. I told you, I see betterment, improvement, coming from within the Church rather than without."

Janet smiled. "Be that as it may, I fear that there is even worse to come, my lord Abbot. David has written two more poems in the months since the Borders expedition. And they are . . . stronger! They are named *An Answer to the King's Flyting* and *The Complaint of Our Sovereign Lord's Papingo*."

"Sakes! The papingo? That old bird still squawks?" Davie Beaton it was who had brought the boy-King the parrot or papingo, from France many years before. "And *The King's Flyting*, you say? So, do I take it that James is the target this time, rather than the Church?"

"Not target. A, a reminder, merely, on some of the follies of the royal court." Lindsay shrugged. "Short things they are, of no real merit."

"But sufficient to destroy your repute at that court, man, I've little doubt! I would keep these from James and his friends for a time, if I were you."

"For whom they were written!"

"No doubt. But you self-appointed reformers sometimes require to be protected from yourselves. Does Janet not agree?"

She did not commit herself, but smiled quietly. She had a talent for quiet smiling, that woman.

When Beaton left The Mount, although his friend had not committed himself to Brussels and the embassy, it was understood that he would seriously consider the matter.

* * *

David Lindsay had to admit that his reception by his liege-lord, when two weeks later he did present himself at Stirling Castle, was friendly, even handsome. For, although James was guarded at first, less than at ease, very quickly he relaxed and became almost embarrassingly amiable—which tended to have something of the opposite effect on his visitor. However, when presently the King raised his voice to address a wider audience—they were outdoors on the grassy lip of the castle-rock above the terrace known as the Croft of Ballengeich, preparatory to indulging in James's favourite sport of hurly-hackit—Lindsay's embarrassment gave way to astonishment.

"Bring me a sword," James called out—for none, by custom, wore swords in the presence of the monarch, and they would have been no aid to the sport of hurly-hackit anyway. "My old gossip Davie Lindsay is come visiting, on his way to Brussels on our behalf. We have not seen him for long, and must mark the occasion. If Davie is going to chaffer with the Emperor Charles, it has been represented to me that he must needs go as better than but Snowdoun Herald. Our old Lyon King, Sir Thomas Clephane, long a sick man, has died, and a new Lord Lyon King-of-Arms is required. I therefore so now name and appoint Davie Lindsay of The Mount, our Laureate, to that office, as chiefest herald of this realm. Now—that sword."

One of the royal guard on duty produced a weapon, and taking it, James turned back to David. "Kneel," he ordered.

Scarcely able to grasp what was happening, that bewildered man sank on one knee, while his liege-lord tapped him on each bent shoulder with the long blade.

"I hereby dub you knight, Davie Lindsay, raising you to that most honourable estate, in the name of God the Father, the Son and the Holy Spirit. I charge you ever to serve me well and my realm likewise. And to remain a good and true knight until your life's end." That was said parrot-fashion and sing-song. "Arise, Sir David Lindsay of The Mount, Lord Lyon King-of-Arms."

To a certain amount of applause from some of those around, Davie Beaton leading, the new knight rose to his feet, bereft of words. It was not so much the knighthood which affected him, surprise as it was—after all, his father and grandfather had been knights before him; it was the appointment as Lyon. For this was no ordinary or merely decorative office, sufficiently decorative as it certainly was; for one thing, it was an appointment for life; it carried the rank and status of an ambassador; it ensured a unique relationship with the monarch, for whom Lyon could stand as personal representative, to the extent that to strike Lyon was the equivalent of striking the King himself, and as such high treason; moreover he ranked as one of the realm's justiciars, with his own court, supreme arbiter in more than heraldry, coats-of-arms, baronial status and feudal jurisdiction; also as master-of-ceremonies at the royal establishment, the position could be influential indeed.

James was clearly enjoying the sensation he had produced in Lindsay and in others, slapping his former usher and procurator on the back and proclaiming that *he* was now the only man who could thus strike Da-Lin, his childhood name for his friend and guardian.

Beaton came up. "May I be first to congratulate my Lord Lyon, Sire?" he asked. "Sir David—my felicitations! May this Lyon roar to good effect in His Grace's Scotland, and furth of it!"

Shaking the proffered hand, Lindsay had little doubt as to where the initiative for this development had originated.

James announced that, in suitable celebration, his new Lord Lyon—who after all had first taught him the diversion of hurly-hackit, here on this very slope of Ballengeich—should now engage his erstwhile pupil in a race. Just the two of them. And let the best man win!

David, who had not taken part in this basic, indeed fairly childish sport for years, could scarcely refuse, although he had no desire to participate. For one thing, he knew his sovereign well enough to realise that he would want to win—indeed he was already wagering with his courtiers on the result; and that might be a little difficult to arrange without it being obvious—which would, in its turn, offend. Also, there was always a certain amount of danger to life and limb—not that that would greatly worry him but the man who might cause the *monarch* to become a casualty would be less than popular.

They went to choose their skulls. The sport was of the simplest and consisted merely of sliding downhill on a cow's skull, using the horns as handlebars as it were to steer with—hackit or hawkie being but the Scots word for an old cow, and hurly referring to the hurtling motion. In theory this was straightforward enough, but in practice it was less so. For one thing, skulls, of cattle or other, are not the easiest objects to steer when sitting upon. For another, although the start of the steep slope was grassy, half-way down it became complicated with a series of outcropping rocks, little terraces and drops, some of them of a few feet, jaggy whin-bushes and other obstacles. All of which, approached at major speed, even on a wooden toboggan, would demand a deal of negotiating; on a cow's skull the hazards were not lessened. Yet this was James's favourite pastime, outdoors that is.

There is not a lot of room for a grown man on a skull, although those of typical shaggy Highland cattle tend to be broad, flattish and wide-horned. Selecting the flattest, the contestants dragged them to near the lip of the slope and there drew lots for the left or right course. The least hazardous was the right, and David gained it and wished that he had not.

James, who at eighteen now probably considered his opponent as an old man of not far off forty, was supremely confident.

The new Earl of Arran, the Bastard's half-brother—the old Earl and Admiral had died—gave the signal for off. To start well was important, for it was a test of agility, seated, to propel the skull forward the few feet to the edge, using the heels, and might in fact determine the outcome of the race there and then.

But these two were experts, and David's muscles kept in good state by his outdoor life at Lindifferon. They reached the lip exactly level, and plunged over, to the yells of the onlookers, almost all, naturally, shouting for the King.

The descent started fairly moderately, with heels still urging the sleds on. But quickly gravity took over and the speed of the glissade increased. The grass slope was about two hundred yards long, and before they were half-way down this they were bounding and bouncing at an exhilarating rate, rather extraordinary for so clumsy-seeming mounts, the men perched awkwardly, with their feet up now, knees bent, soles of boots pushed against the horns between their hand-grips. Balancing in this position and at speed was an art in itself.

They could scarcely be described as running neck-and-neck, for the two courses diverged considerably, to take advantage of the best routes through the assorted obstacles further down, so far as this was possible with the rough-and-ready steering. But there was little for the wagerers to choose between them.

David himself was so concerned with watching James's progress that he all but came to grief at the second little ledge-and-drop, taking it a foot or two from the right spot and so careering over a fall of nearly four feet, to land with a jar. Only the speed of his descent and the consequent angle at which he hit the ground saved him from overturning and parting company with his hackit, not to speak of injury. Sobered, he reminded himself of priorities.

Going more heedfully if no less swiftly, and using the occasional heel to pivot slight changes of direction, he threaded his way through the hazards in fair style, considering the interval since last he had done this—too fair indeed, for traversing a brief levellish terrace of grass he had opportunity for just a glance leftwards, to see that he was slightly ahead of James. And for the remainder of the run, his course was, if anything, more free of obstacles than was the King's.

His thinking had to be as swift as his progress. No obvious slowing-up would serve, nor would any deliberate collision or upset. A diversion in the route, then? Only if it could be achieved as seemingly advisable.

There was a patch of wet ground ahead, drainage-water off the great rock, which normally, on this course, was avoided left-about. If he could approach this further to the right, so that to take the left side at the last moment would seem difficult, then right-about would look natural enough. And just a little too far to the right and he would be into an apron of scree and rubble thereafter, which ought to slow him up without actually capsizing him.

Even as he visualised this possibility he was acting on it, the bright green of the damp sump directly in front. Slewing right, he swept round it—and perceived that the scree was further over than he had recollected. Another jerk to the right was necessary, whether it looked natural or not to those watchers above, or he was going to win this race in only a few seconds time. He slewed again, leaning over.

Too late, he realised that he had overdone it, no doubt the effect of the speed, the incline and his heel combined. He was swinging much too far over—and that way lay trouble, actually a sort of quarry where stone had been excavated in years past.

David tried to pull round, back on course, but it was too late. He was heading straight for the rim of the crescent-shaped gouge in the hillside, and no amount of slewing was going to avoid it. He must either throw himself off his hackit, or go over the edge. He could not remember just how deep a drop there was—anything from a dozen to a score of feet probably. And one of the basic understandings of hurly-hackit was that only novices and weaklings deliberately ejected from their sleds, come what might.

It was all over in less time than it takes to tell. The new Lord Lyon King-of-Arms shot over the lip, out into space, still clinging to his cow's horns.

Because of the speed of his take-off, he and his skull did not drop with anything like verticality, hurtling through the air in a sort of sagging arc, to crash to earth, eventually near the mouth of the little quarry, into a pile of rubble, stones and nettles.

It was as well perhaps that those nettles were there in such profusion, for they helped to cushion the stones and debris. Even so, every bone in David's body was jarred and jolted, and the wind knocked out of him.

Too shaken to do more than lie there, gasping for breath, he was also afraid to try to move lest he discovered bones to be broken. He was quite unaware of comprehensive nettle-stings.

Presently, gingerly he stretched one arm, then the other, then his legs. Soreness but nothing worse, he assessed, thankfully. Slowly, painfully, he raised himself on all fours, gulping as he straightened one knee—something damaged there. The other one seemed to be all right. Cautiously he achieved the upright, actually using a clutch of nettle-stems to pull himself up. There and thus he stood, swaying, nerving himself to risk a step or two out from that uneven stance. Surely, seldom can the accolade of knighthood have been so oddly celebrated.

James himself was the first on the scene, part concerned, part amused, "Davie—here's a stramash! What happened? Are you hurt? How did you do it, man?"

"I . . . misjudged," David said briefly.

"You did so! Sakes—did you forget about this quarry? The times you have warned me of it!"

The other was in no mood nor state for any inquest. "I misjudged, I say." Scowling unsuitably at his sovereign, he held out a hand for aid to get him out of that rubbish-heap. James obliged with an arm, and stiffly, awkwardly, David clambered over to level grass, wincing with the pain of that knee.

"You *are* hurt," the King declared. "Your leg. And you have torn your breeches. I'd scarce have believed it of you, Davie."

"Nor I!" That was grimly said.

Leaning on the royal arm, and limping, David had to listen to an exposition on the finer points of hurly-hackit as regards this Ballengeich course, and where his one-time mentor must have gone wrong, the inference being that age would account for much and a failing memory was all but inevitable. This was mercifully cut short by the arrival of the rest of the company, come hurrying down the steep, in slithering disorder, to congratulate royalty on its splendid win and mockingly commiserate with the sorry loser.

Davie Beaton took over from James as support. "That was not

like you," he observed. "Were your new honours too much for you? Or do I sense something here more than met the eye?"

"I misjudged." That repetition was distinctly sour. "It was advisable that James should win."

"Ah! I begin to perceive light. Yes, I see. So it was policy, going a little astray? It happens to the best of us."

"Thank you!" Lindsay changed the subject. "I expect that it was you who were behind this of the Lyon's office? And knighthood?"

"Not altogether. James desired to show you some mark of favour. I think that his conscience might have been troubling him. I was concerned that you should be sufficiently senior, on this Brussels embassage, not to be outranked by the other two. Campbell, of course, is a knight and kin to Argyll. And Paniter is Abbot of Cambuskenneth and Bishop-Elect of Ross. So something of some standing was required for you. And Lyon is always knighted."

"I do not like being beholden . . ."

"Do not be so prickly, man! You were a senior herald anyway, and best man for the position. You will make a better Lyon than we have had for long. And Janet deserves to be Lady Lindsay."

Getting back up that hill with a damaged knee was no pleasant experience, and further converse was limited, to say the least, until Lindsay was safely installed on a settle in the Lord Privy Seal's comfortable quarters on the south side of the Upper Square.

There they discussed the forthcoming mission to the Low Countries, to which Lindsay now seemed committed. It was considered advisable that they should travel in a French ship, as less likely to be attacked by English vessels. One such would sail from Dumbarton in ten days' time, the west-coast route being infinitely safer from the said English than the east. This would entail landing at a French west-coast port, Brest or possibly St. Malo, not risking the narrows of the Channel, and travelling across France to the Netherlands, but this should produce few difficulties—even though it suited Francis to be friends with England meantime and therefore he was anti-Scotland, he had no animosity against the Scots themselves, indeed his personal guard was composed of Scots.

At Brussels they would probably have to deal with Margaret, Queen of Hungary, the Emperor's aunt, who was at present governing the Low Countries for her nephew. Beaton had never met her but she was reputed to be as plain as she was autocratic and nobody's fool. But, in his experience, plain women were more profitable to deal with than beauties, heedfully handled, being more appreciative of flattering references where looks were concerned, and of recognition of their strengths in other respects. Paniter would be little use at this, he guessed, and Campbell was an arrogant soldier who treated women like chattels.

Lindsay was extremely doubtful about all this, especially when he heard that Scotland had really nothing to offer in this treaty-renewal negotiation other than her geographical position as an ever-present threat in England's rear—that and her traditional trading links with the Netherlands, especially with the Flemings for whom she was the main source of wool for their great weaving and cloth trade. If this seemed to Lindsay precious little to offer, the other appeared to believe that, properly handled, it would be sufficient for present circumstances.

David's knee-cap was badly swollen but nothing appeared to be broken, and in a day or two the contusion went down and he was able to walk reasonably well again although the leg tired quickly. For the rest, his body was a mass of bruises, but these would fade, and there was nothing to prevent him sailing on the due date. But before that, he was eager to go back to Lindifferon to take farewell of Janet. Neither James nor Beaton had any objection, so long as he reached Dumbarton in time; but the King suggested that he should bring Janet back to court, on the way, to resume her duties as Wardrobe Mistress. David did not commit her to this, as it was not put as a royal command.

So, with riding no difficulty, he returned to The Mount, having a look at Luthrie in the by-going, this modest barony in North Fife being always allotted to the Lord Lyon as a kind of fee for his services and expenses. He was reasonably well pleased with what he saw there, although the property had been sadly neglected under the ageing and ailing Clephane. Only some six miles from The Mount, it would be comparatively easy to manage it more effectively from Lindifferon.

Janet was delighted to hear of her husband's new status and what was, she declared, his long overdue promotion—she was not informed deeply on the hurly-hackit incident. But now that their parting was imminent, she was a little anxious about thc dangers implicit in his mission overseas, storms, attacks by the

English, foreign travel generally and other unspecified hazards, all of which David of course pooh-poohed, even hinting that the sport of hurly-hackit was in fact more dangerous. She declared that she did not want to go back to Stirling on her own meantime, preferring to remain at The Mount until David returned, when they could resume court life together.

So, after a couple of days, farewells were said and the traveller set off for Dumbarton, knee almost recovered. He still could not really think of himself as Lord Lyon King-of-Arms nor even as Sir David.

14

It took him two days to ride across Scotland to the Clyde estuary, some of the time through the skirts of the Highland Line, MacGregor, Macfarlane and Colquhoun country, where timorous folk said that he should not venture without a well-armed escort, advice which he likewise pooh-poohed, and experienced no problems. He arrived at Dumbarton to find the quite large trading vessel, *La Couronne*, waiting and already laden with a cargo of Lammermuir wool brought by pack-horse from Lothian for the weavers of Rennes in Brittany. Abbot Paniter was therein installed, with two servants. Campbell had not yet appeared.

Paniter proved to be a serious man of about thirty, scion of a Montrose family, young to be a bishop-elect—but then, Montrose was within the Abbot of Arbroath's sphere of influence and friends and neighbours of Davie Beaton were well placed for promotion. David anticipated few problems with him but did not see him as exciting company.

The problems proved to arrive with Sir John Campbell of Lundie, last to appear, probably because he had least distance to travel. Indeed he came two days late, by which time their French shipmaster was in a state of much and voluble agitation. This did not worry the Campbell in the slightest; what did concern him was that there did not seem to be accommodation on board for the dozen Highland clansmen, with less than which apparently he never travelled. It did not matter, evidently, where and how these kilted characters were bestowed, but sail they must. The shipmaster capitulated with ill grace, the Highlandmen bristling with arms, but he demanded more money. David foresaw continuing complications.

Campbell, a man of about Lindsay's own age, was cheerful enough in a loud way, big, florid and dominant, who over-ate, over-drank and over-reacted with a sort of jovial ferocity, hardly the conventional choice as an ambassador. David perceived why Beaton had felt that a counter-balancing presence, other than the reserved Paniter, would be advisable, and why such presence should be invested with some authority.

They sailed on the first tide.

Despite the greatly increased distance involved, they avoided the inner passage of the Irish Sea and voyaged instead around Rathlin Isle and Malin Head, to sail down the west coast of Ireland, where they could expect to escape the attentions of the English pirates, who could not be relied upon to know, or care, that King Henry was at present on friendly terms with King Francis, possible Atlantic gales being considered infinitely the lesser hazard. In fact, there were no storms, the breezes were consistently favourable and without incident they made excellent time—which was probably as well considering the state of the Campbell clansmen roosting in the hold amongst the smelly wool-bales.

Six days, and with hardly another sail sighted until they were into French coastal waters, they entered the Rance estuary and reached the Breton port of St. Malo on its rocky isle and defensive causeway to the mainland, David for one thankful indeed to step back on dry land. It was not that he was a bad sailor but he had had enough of being cooped up in constricted space with John Campbell, his loud voice and peculiar brand of humour. Admittedly they were going to be together for a long time yet, but on horseback, and on overnight stops in inns and hospices and the like, he could surely keep his distance better than in a cramped and low-ceiled cabin.

St. Malo was *La Couronne*'s home port, it transpired, and the travellers asked their skipper's advice as to where they might hire the necessary horses. It was then that they discovered this to be no problem, for the wool cargo would all be going by pack-horse-train to Rennes, fifty-odd miles on their way, and they could get mounts from the same source and indeed journey that far in convoy. This arrangement seemed convenient and would help to initiate them into French travel conditions. Beaton had obtained for them a safe conduct from his friend King Francis, so that no difficulties with the authorities were to be looked for.

There was considerable astonishment at the stableyard-compound across the causeway which linked St. Malo island with the mainland when it appeared that the seventeen Scots required only five horses, and three pannier-ponies, the Campbell henchmen being running-gillies who scorned horseflesh. When even David and Paniter objected that these footmen would be bound to hold up their rate of progress, Lundie hooted his scorn. They would be no such thing, he asserted, able to outrun any pack-horses, keep going longer and eat less fodder; used to traversing mountain country, this flat France would be bairns'-play for them.

And so indeed it proved. As the long cavalcade proceeded southwards through the Breton countryside, the Highlandmen, trotting at either side of their chieftain, had positively to slow their accustomed pace to avoid outdistancing the rest, with Campbell complaining that they would be better off on their own and make much better time. But David and Paniter declared that, as there was no desperate hurry and the sea voyage had been so expeditious, it was sensible to remain with the pack-train meantime, to be thus painlessly introduced to French ways and customs. Paniter spoke French of a sort, David less so and Campbell not at all, so some such assisted initiation was valuable.

They covered the distance to Rennes in two days, halting for the first night at Combourg in the Dol area, where the Stewarts had originated, where indeed they had been Stewards of Dol for the Norman Counts of Dol and Dinan. At the end of this twenty-five miles, the running-gillies appeared to be almost as fresh and unconcerned as they had been at the beginning, cheerful, undemanding individuals despite their fierce aspect, who spoke only the Gaelic and appeared to find foreign travel to their taste. The Breton horse-leaders, after eyeing them askance at first, seemed to get on well with them and in fact were able to communicate with them better than with the gentry, their own dialect sounding not unlike Gaelic, to David at least; the Bretons were themselves in origin a Celtic people, of course.

They found Rennes, Brittany's capital, to be quite a large, bustling town standing where the River Vilaine joined the Ille, the riversides lined with warehouses—to two of which their wool was consigned—mills manufacturing cloths and linen, breweries and the like. As became a commercial centre, there were plenty of inns for travellers, but here again the Campbell gillies proved something of a problem, not in themselves but in the local reaction to them and their peculiar ways—for these did not require nor desire normal inn accommodation but were happy to forage for their own food and to bed down anywhere that took their fancy, on the hay or straw of stables, on sail-cloth stocks, or just in the open air, wrapped in their stained tartan plaids. All of which somewhat disconcerted the innkeepers and town-guards. However, Sir John was liberal with moneys, and this smoothed the way for them fairly effectively. One unforeseen development, first seen at Rennes, was the attraction of these brawny and underclad clansmen for the street-women with which the place seemed to abound, and who obviously found their so evident magnificent physique and good-humoured attitudes much to their taste, a state of affairs which tended still further to complicate the bedding-down arrangements. Not that Lundie himself was in any way concerned; he found his own women and left his henchmen to it. The two other ambassadors were content to behave more conventionally, as became a bishop-elect and Scotland's Lord Lyon King-of-Arms.

The following day, on their own now, they did make much better time, reaching Laval, a good fifty miles, the clansmen, as promised, not holding up the horsemen in the least, whatever their nocturnal activities. Thereafter they crossed some higher ground to Le Mans, the capital of Maine, another fifty miles. David and Paniter were much impressed with this city on the Sarthe, the birthplace of England's Henry the Second and burial-place of Richard Lion-Heart's queen, Berengaria. The Campbells however found it less hospitable.

To avoid the Paris area, advisedly, they now turned almost due northwards by Alençon, Verneuil and Bernay, consistent fifty-mile days, making for Rouen, extraordinary progress David had to admit. At the Normandy capital, with its no fewer than three cathedrals, one archiepiscopal, its rampart-walls and its palaces, scene of the burning of Joan of Arc and tomb of Berengaria's Richard, David was greatly taken, even if his companions were less so, it bringing to mind so much that he had learned and all but forgotten, and stirring his poetic urge. He began to bless Davie Beaton.

Now in order to avoid the English-held Pas de Calais, they headed for Amiens and then St. Quentin, in both of which the great concentrations of woollen-mills and weaving-sheds along the many-channelled Somme gave David the notion of increased Scottish trade being possible. They were nearing the edge of France here, and indeed the day after leaving St. Quentin they came to the border fortress-town of Valenciennes on the Scheldt, with the Netherlands before them and only the county of Hainault between them and their Brussels destination.

After crossing Scheldt they were immediately into war-torn territory, with blackened ruins, abandoned farmsteads and wasted countryside on every hand, for this land had been fought over for generations between the Empire, France and the Dukes of Burgundy; indeed peace of a sort had only come as lately as the year previously, with the Treaty of Cambrai, the 'Ladies' Peace' as it was called, contrived by the two redoubtable queens, Louise of France, mother of King Francis, and Margaret of Hungary, aunt of the Emperor Charles. The travellers, proceeding across-country by Mons, the Hainault capital and Waterloo, became in consequence the more conscious of the problems and responsibility ahead—or two of them did. Suddenly their mission seemed altogether more real, more demanding.

In Brussels, as elsewhere, their escort of running-gillies drew much attention and comment, the like undoubtedly never before seen. It was a great and strange city, built on two distinct levels, the Lower Town and the Upper, with a hillside between them sufficiently steep to be mounted largely by means of steps and stairs, so contrived as to be used by horses. The Lower Town, built along the ditch-like River Senne, and carved up by canals, was the commercial quarter, extensive, thronged with folk, smelly, humid and foggy in this summer weather, with warehouses, granaries, mills, wharves, drinking-dens and the like packed together in the narrow streets and wynds in stirring, teeming confusion, with Flemish spoken, unintelligible to the visitors. The Upper Town was altogether different, airy, spacious, gardened and tree-girt, where was the royal palace and the houses of the nobility, with many fine religious buildings—even though most prominent of all was the renowned Hotel de Ville, below, with its seven storeys of arcading and its extraordinary spire no less than three hundred and sixty-four feet high. French was the language of the Upper Town. Here the visitors found a hospice attached to a Blackfriars monastery, not far from the royal palace, to take them in, although, as ever, the Highlanders were accepted by the friars with considerable doubts.

Paniter's French was good enough to gather from the monks that Queen Margaret was in residence but not the Emperor himself—although he was expected shortly from Italy. However, they also learned that, since it was for negotiations that they had come, the aunt was probably of more use to them than would be the nephew, for reasons unspecified.

Next morning David made his way to the palace, alone. It was felt that he, as a herald, ought to go, to announce their arrival and try to arrange an audience. Getting past the guards at the magnificent gates was not easy, what with his feeble French, his unspectacular Scots broadcloth and his lack of attendants—he had had no hesitation in refusing an escort of the Campbell clansmen on this occasion; but when it occurred to him to produce the safe conduct provided for them with the King of France's signature, that gained him entry.

Oddly enough thereafter there were no more difficulties, indeed it was all almost laughably simple. None of the handsomely-clad throng of nobles, prelates, courtiers and flunkeys who paraded and hurried or idled through the vast and ornate establishment did more than glance at him, his very modest attire probably suggesting that he was some sort of senior servant or messenger. He wandered about the seemingly endless succession of halls, salons, arcades and corridors more or less at will. Once or twice he asked obvious servitors where he would find the Chamberlain, Master of the Household or even a secretary, but received either blank looks, off-putting or incomprehensible directions.

At a loss, he was following a sauntering pair of exquisites along a mirror-walled corridor graced with highly-indelicate marble statuary when the couple in front suddenly drew aside into an alcove and bowed deeply. A thick-set, dumpy woman of middle years, almost as plainly dressed as was David himself, was coming in the other direction, with two much more richly-clad younger females behind and a scarlet-robed cleric following on.

There being no convenient alcove available for him, David merely stood back, wondering whether this could be the Queen-Governor herself, undistinguished as she looked. He bowed, in case, but not deeply.

The lady looked at him and seemed about to stump past. Then she paused, eyeing him up and down frankly. "A stranger, I think?" she said, in French. She had a deepish voice.

David understood that, at least. "Yes, madam," he agreed. "Very much so. From Scotland." At least, that is what he meant.

"Ah—one of the Scots." That was in English very much better than his French. "More fully clad than the others, from what I hear!"

He blinked. News evidently travelled fast in Brussels. "Those are Highland gillies, running-gillies, clansmen, madam. In the train of one of my colleagues. I am no Highlandman."

"Indeed. We have differences in race and style in the Netherlands, also—but scarcely in states of nakedness, monsieur!"

"Men who run all day, even outrun horses, are best with little clothing," he asserted, a little stiffly.

"These run? All day? Outrun horses, you say? Surely not?"

"Not in speed, madam, but in distance. These gillies will run fifty miles and more, with scarce a pause. And little to eat in the running."

"You astonish me, monsieur. I must hear more of this. Come." That was somewhat peremptory.

"I am seeking the Chamberlain here, or other officer of this household, who may gain us an audience with the Queen of Hungary. So far I have not found one . . ."

"*I* am Margaret. You are one of the Scots come to sign a renewal of the treaty, I presume? So you will have to wait until the Emperor comes, for *his* signature must be appended, not mine. I am but his governor here. So, come. This of the runners? Is the like much done in Scotland? I have never heard of it."

"Only in the Highlands, Highness." David produced another little bow at that, and fell into step beside the lady as they moved along down the corridor. He tried to explain the clan system, the patriarchal relationship between chiefs and clansmen, the difference between Highlands and Lowlands, but found it hard to keep his mind on what he was saying, so affected was he by what *she* had said. She had sounded as though this treaty-renewal was almost a foregone conclusion, only formal signing to be required. Perhaps he had misheard, or mistaken? But it had sounded that way. What, then . . . ?

They turned off into a smallish apartment, lined with books like a library but equipped with paper-littered tables and desks, as in some office. Here this businesslike Queen paused, to pick out one paper amongst many, was handed a quill and inkhorn by one of her ladies, and signed the document promptly, without any of the flourish and curliques beloved of most lofty signatories; and handing the paper to the cleric, dismissed him with a wave.

"A pity that we cannot dispose of *your* concordat thus easily, but my nephew Charles insists on signing and sealing all treaties and the like in person. However, he should be here in a matter of days—and it will give me opportunity to see more of you and learn more of your country. Your name, monsieur?"

"Lindsay, Highness—David Lindsay."

"And you, Monsieur Lindsay, represent the chief of your mission to sign this treaty-renewal? Who is he?"

David coughed. "I suppose, Highness, that *I* am." That sounded apologetic almost. "At least, I represent King James. Since I am his Lord Lyon King-of-Arms, Sir David Lindsay of The Mount."

"You say so! All that! Then I am more pleased to welcome you here, Sir David. Modest men in high places are as rare as modest women in courts!" And she glanced over at her two ladies.

He smiled, feeling strangely at ease now with this Queen.

"I was only made Lord Lyon a few weeks past, to come on this embassage," he confessed. "I am scarce used to the position yet."

She gave a deep throaty chuckle and tapped his forearm. "Honest as well as modest!" she said. "I think that your King James chose well. Yet I understand that he is a somewhat loose young man, even for a king! And not always wise? Although perhaps it was Abbot David of, of Aberroath, is it?—the Abbot who chose you?"

"You are well informed, Highness!"

"I would not long remain Governor of the Netherlands if I was not, my friend!"

He accepted that. "Abbot Beaton is a power behind the throne, yes—and behind the Church. But King James, my liege-lord, is no cipher. And he has his virtues, many of them. His failings stem from his early debasement by the Earl of Angus, who long had him in his power, deliberately done to gain better control of him and therefore of his kingdom."

"Ah, yes, I have heard of Angus. Friend to Henry of England, is he not?"

"A friend of sorts! I would not wish that man as *my* friend!"

"Nor Henry himself, I think? Hence your treaty?"

He nodded. "Yes—England must ever be . . . contained." He hesitated. "This treaty, Highness, to be renewed. You anticipate . . . no difficulty?"

"Why should I? It is very ancient, and should serve both our causes. Does anything concern you over it?" That was quick.

"No." He took a chance. "It is but that it appears to be somewhat one-sided. You—or the Empire—gain an ever-present ally in England's rear. But we—what does Scotland gain? I do not look to see the Emperor ever invading England on Scotland's behalf! The Netherlands might have done so, once—or threatened it. But the Empire . . . ?"

"You think not? There are other ways to trouble Henry than by armed invasion, Sir David. But—you seek something more?"

"Only trade, Highness. Scotland is not a rich country, save in sheep and cattle, fish and salt and the like. On our way here, and in Brussels itself, we have seen much of woollen-spinning and cloth-making, tanneries for hides and the like. Clearly much wool is required, also skins. Perhaps salt, or salted fish likewise. We could supply it, to our profit—and probably yours."

"Then why do you not, friend, already?"

"In part, that we have not known sufficiently of the possibilitie. But mainly in that our ships to carry the trade would be attacked and captured by the English pirates or by Henry's ships-of-war. They swarm everywhere in the Norse Sea and the Channel, as you will well know. Even this mission had to sail west-about round Ireland to escape them. Now, the Netherlands are namely for their shipping, as are the Empire's Hansa ports. If Netherlands vessels could come to Scottish eastern ports or, better still, have Scottish vessels sail protected by Empire ships-of-war, then much trade could result and wealth be created."

"I see. You are a man of some vision, I perceive, Sir David. Are you concerned in trade, as well as this of heraldic jurisdiction and the Laws of Arms?"

"No. But I do produce much cattle and sheep on my lands in Fife and Lothian."

"Ah. So you would have something to gain in the matter?"

"I, and a great many others, Highness."

"That is honest, likewise. I shall speak to the Emperor on this. And he may well approve—for he ever requires money and more money! *I* see the importance of trade, if he does not! Perhaps not a clause to the treaty, but a separate agreement?"

"I thank Your Highness."

"Now—you have gone to lodge with the good friars at the Dominican monastery, I am told. That will not do. You will bring your people here, to this palace. All, including your runners. I must see these. We shall have a demonstration, no? In the hunting-park. You, and the other envoys will dine with me tonight. Meantime, I have others awaiting me . . ."

David, bowing, was given a hand to kiss and, much heartened, took his leave.

So commenced what was, on the whole, a very pleasant interlude—even though it became rather more extended than anticipated, first by the delayed arrival of the Emperor and then by his imperial command. But meantime the Scots found themselves, as it were, in clover, most hospitably and flatteringly entertained and in great demand—indeed most embarrassingly so. This partly on account of David's obvious favour with the Queen and partly with the popularity of the running-gillies, who found themselves an unfailing attraction for not only the court but the Brussels establishment generally, all taking their cue from Margaret Hapsburg. After the first arranged demonstration of their normal abilities, they were constantly involved in races, short-distance against local champions and long-distance against each other and horsemen, with much wagering and excitement; also other feats of endurance, wrestling, cannon-ball throwing—at which they excelled, not unlike their own Highland stone-putting—Highland dancing to their own mouth-music, tossing tree-trunks, something never before witnessed here, and general display of muscular prowess. And surprisingly—at least to David and Paniter, who had looked on such clansmen as little better than heathen barbarians, in typical Lowland prejudice—they behaved throughout almost without exception in exemplary fashion, modest, well-mannered and amicable, rather astonishing considering how completely novel an experience this was for men who had never before left their upland glens, and especially the way women, court ladies included, all but threw themselves at them. Sir John Campbell himself, although he gained a sort of reflected glory from his virile henchmen, became all but jealous, an extraordinary state of affairs. Although, of course, the gillies never actually dined in the royal presence, and Margaret was sufficiently tactful not to have them brought on like paid entertainers at the banquets, they certainly suffered no lack of evening and night activities and fed better than they ever could have believed possible.

In all this, significantly, there was no talk of treaty terms, although trade was discussed once or twice, particularly with the burgomaster and other city representatives introduced by the Queen.

So one August week was extended into two and three, and still the Emperor Charles did not appear. Nobody seemed very surprised, although his aunt was not exactly apologetic but understanding over her guests' delay. Not all of them were anxious to be off, admittedly, even though David was, being somewhat impatient by nature and concerned about harvest at The Mount and Luthrie, his new fief. He was also missing Janet. But the waiting was made pleasant indeed, with Paniter spending much time at the many religious institutions of the city and Campbell adequately catered for in all respects.

Then on the 2nd of September, the Emperor arrived with his vast entourage and conditions at Brussels underwent major change. It was not that Charles Hapsburg was unpleasant, domineering nor intentionally arrogant, merely that he was difficult to deal with, almost diffident in fact, with a nervous jerky manner which was apt to put everyone around him ill-at-ease. A man of thirty, he had been King of Spain since sixteen and Emperor since nineteen, and like many another youthful successor to a great man—his grandfather, the famous Emperor Maximilian—had not had an easy time of it. His natural reticence was no help. Peculiar looks likewise did not assist, a sharply-receding forehead and notably high hairline being countered by a thrusting pointed jawline, the famous Hapsburg chin, so that his features seemed to slant downwards at a distinct angle, an impression accentuated rather than aided by a bushy black beard. Emperors and monarchs admittedly did not have to depend on their looks for effectiveness, but Charles did almost appear to be embarrassed by his appearance, and in consequence embarrassed others. Perhaps to compensate he dressed dramatically all in black, with a white ruff and silver facings, his thin, bony legs in trunks and hose seeming notably long.

David and his colleagues were presented to this, arguably the most powerful man in Christendom, by Queen Margaret, and gained the impression that they were quite unimportant and indeed rather a nuisance. It took a little while for them to realise that this was the normal reaction. Charles did not look at any of them as he talked in a hurried, clipped voice, and seemed only anxious to be elsewhere. Yet, when he did move away, abruptly, it was only to go and behave the same way to other groups and individuals, and presently to pace over to one of the great windows of the ornate salon, to stare out, alone. David noted that the imperial fingers, hands behind back, fidgeted and twisted.

Queen Margaret appeared not in the least put out by this behaviour, and almost casually mentioned that her nephew would sign the treaty on the morrow. Astonished that no gestures at negotiation appeared to be envisaged, they were led off.

It was Abbot Paniter who, after discreet enquiries amongst his clerical acquaintances, came up with the likeliest explanation for this attitude towards treaty terms. The Emperor, it seemed, was much preoccupied with two main dangers to his power, now that he had more or less put France in its place—the threats from the Turks and from the followers of Martin Luther. The former was more than a threat, for the Turkish Sultan, Sulieman the Magnificent, had invaded the Empire territories, had captured Belgrade, driven the Knights of St. John out of Rhodes and was now preparing to attack Hungary. This challenge had to be met, and swiftly; but the second problem, that of the new doctrine of the so-called Protestants led by the monk Luther, seriously hampered Charles's military efforts, for his most useful and effective forces were led by the Germanic princes and *landknechts* and these were the very people most affected by Luther's demands for reform. Charles himself had at first been somewhat sympathetic towards Church reform, but the demands of the power-struggle with France and King Francis—who actually had proposed that *he* should be Emperor—required the Empire and Rome to be close allies. So Luther had to be denied. The Diet of Augsburg the previous year had been an attempt to find a middle course, but had not really satisfied the reformers. Now Sulieman was taking full advantage. It was against this background that a more positive alliance with Scotland was being envisaged. For Scotland, especially with Beaton believed to be firmly in the ascendancy, was solidly in the Papal camp—as evidenced by the burning of Patrick Hamilton—and Henry of England, since his demotion of Cardinal Wolsey from the chancellorship, was known to be toying with this reformist heresy for his own purposes. Briefly, then, the Emperor required allies, even as modest as Scotland.

All this set David Lindsay thinking. He recollected how Davie Beaton had indicated at Stirling that this ancient treaty would not be difficult to renew, despite changes in the Netherlands, without going into details. So this was behind it all. Beaton was as ever notably well informed.

The next day, nothing was said about treaty signing, but Queen Margaret was informed that Charles was anxious to see the Scots running-gillies in action and so there was another demonstration in the palace hunting-park. This apparently greatly impressed the Emperor—although he did not say so to the envoys—so much so that the Scots were to be included in a great tournament and display to be held the following week in Antwerp, in honour of Margaret herself. This was the first that the visitors had heard of such an event. It seemed that in appreciation of his aunt's effective rule of the hitherto troublesome Netherlands and to consolidate his position there, Charles was about to promote Margaret from Governor to Regent, and this entertainment was to celebrate the occasion. For political reasons it was to be held at Antwerp rather than Brussels. Antwerp was in fact the commercial capital of the world and full of foreigners apparently, with the representatives of almost every kingdom, principality and duchy in Christendom based there, for financial rather than political reasons, and so was the place *par excellence* to make any significant announcement. Seemingly this tournament and display was more important than merely a celebration of Margaret Hapsburg's promotion. When

David indicated that he was duly impressed—but when was the treaty to be signed, the Queen told him not to be impatient. Did he not desire trading concessions? Well, then—Antwerp was the place for that.

So their sojourn in the Netherlands was further prolonged.

The move to Antwerp was effected in great style, in an enormous and glittering procession of armoured knights, churchmen, carriages, horse-litters, banner-parties, mounted choirs and instrumentalists, with retainers by the hundred and caravans of elaborate refreshment and cheer, which, considering that the distance between the two cities was only twenty-seven miles, meant that the vanguard was almost at the one before the rearguard left the other. The Scots were positioned up at the front, with the Campbell gillies, running on either side of the Emperor and Queen, much admired.

They went down Senne, picking up additional numbers with the Cardinal-Primate, at Mechlin, where the lace was manufactured, and on to the Scheldt again, now a notably wide slow-flowing river dotted with vessels large and small. There was little sign of war damage here.

The visitors were all but overwhelmed by Antwerp itself, much the largest city they had ever seen, and seemingly the richest, making Edinburgh and Stirling appear like huddled villages below their rock-citadels. Although still fifty miles from the sea, the Scheldt was here navigable for the largest ships, and the city was a major port, berthing craft from every corner of the world. David was informed that Antwerp's trade amounted to forty million ducats each year, a sum quite outwith his conception. It made his notions about Scots exports seem all but pointless.

Oddly enough, although the city, within its great walls, seemed to be full of palatial buildings and splendid edifices, with a new Bourse or Exchange being erected, seemingly as much glass as wall, the largest building the Scots had ever set eyes upon, yet there was no royal palace here, only the old cramped castle down amongst the riverside wharves, many-towered but less than commodious. So the Emperor's huge entourage had to be disposed elsewhere, in scores of different premises. However, presumably through Margaret's influence, the Scots were amongst those lodged in the castle itself—although sundry courtiers observed that they might be more comfortable otherwhere.

Their stay in Antwerp started inauspiciously, for when their identity was known they were met on all sides by long faces, head-shakings and condolences, since it was rumoured most persistently that their liege-lord James, King of Scots, was dead. Appalled, the envoys demanded authentification, details, but received neither. Queen Margaret was only moderately sympathetic, expressing doubts and advising caution, for it was strange that her own sources of information had sent no word of this. There appeared to be three differing versions of the story—that the young King had been poisoned, that he had been thrown whilst hunting and that he had been drowned whilst crossing a river. All could not be true—so the possibility was that none was.

It occurred to David that, if all nations maintained agents in this commercial capital, Scotland probably did so. He went seeking any such, and found one, Andrew Nisbet, a merchant from Dysart in Fife, with a dockside warehouse not far from the castle. Dysart was no great distance from Cupar and Lindifferon, and this grizzled veteran of foreign trade knew of The Mount and its lairds and greeted Lindsay warmly. On the subject of the tales of King James's death, he declared that he personally believed none of them. *He* had had no such word and in his position it was essential that he knew what went on. He had traced the rumours all to the English community here, which was quite large and very active in more than money matters. It was perhaps significant that the stories only began to circulate when it became known that a Scottish embassage had arrived at Brussels. David asked whether any of the versions indicated a date for this alleged disaster, and was told that one circumstantial story said that the drowning in the River Forth had happened on the Nativity of St. John the Baptist, Midsummer's Day. Since David himself had taken leave of James two weeks after that, he reckoned that he could dismiss the entire affair as one of Henry Tudor's extraordinary devices, presumably concocted with the aim of spoiling any Scots-Empire treaty negotiations. He reported to that effect to Queen Margaret.

The tournament was held two days later, on Holy Cross Day, on the extensive fair-ground of this staple-city in front of a vast crowd. Before the open-air proceedings commenced, the Emperor addressed the assembled princes, nobles and notables in a huge gilded pavilion erected for the occasion, jerkily announcing the elevation of his esteemed aunt, lately Queen of

Hungary, to be his Regent of the Netherlands, this in order that she should have fullest powers in all matters of policy and rule, on his imperial behalf, whereas hitherto, as merely Governor, her powers had been limited. This was of vital importance for next year he, Charles, intended to lead in person one of the largest armies ever assembled, against the insolent Infidel Sulieman, who was at present actually threatening Vienna. This great Christian crusade would require vast amounts of money; and the Netherlands, Antwerp in particular, was where moneys could best be raised.

The cheers which had greeted the announcement of the crusade against the Infidel notably died away at this emphasis on money.

Staring up at the coloured tented ceiling, so that his strange chin jutted almost horizontally, the Emperor went on. Measures would have to be taken to raise that money; and let none doubt that the Queen-Regent would have the power and ability to do so. All knew her vigour and resolution. A significant pause here. In especial there was this matter of the two million crowns ransom for the two captured sons of King Francis of France, agreed on at the Treaty of Cambrai last year. This had still not been paid and the money was urgently needed. He was reliably informed that the money-dealers and exchangers here in Antwerp could arrange a transfer of this amount from France's trade credits to his own with entire ease, indeed all but overnight. This should be done forthwith, or the Queen-Regent would have to take the necessary steps to enforce it.

Abruptly the Emperor was finished, and indicated a move out to the tourney-ground. Listening, David had conceived a new image of Charles Hapsburg. The tournament started with a lot of long faces amongst the rich and powerful.

As a sporting event, however, it all was a major success, with some dramatic jousting both of individuals and teams of knights, sword-fighting, javelin-throwing, feats of horsemanship, racing, wrestling, archery and other contests, with huge sums won and lost in wagering. Once again the Campbell gillies distinguished themselves, to general applause, even David himself winning a white rose from a lady's lips as prize for javelin-throwing at which he was proficient.

At the feasting afterwards, in the open for the multitudes and in the pavilion for the privileged, the Emperor withdrew early, to the relief of all, leaving his useful aunt to preside over the subsequent entertainment, which she did admirably. Later, back at the castle, she sent for David as he was about to retire for the night and, in her chamber, smilingly handed him the two copies of the Scots treaty, both already duly signed by the Emperor and counter-signed by herself as Queen-Regent of the Netherlands, these now only requiring his own and his colleagues' signatures. When he did not hide his surprise at this peculiar way of concluding a treaty between nations, he was informed that Charles always had his own way of doing things; but that in fact this was *her* way of ensuring that the terms would be well kept, by appending her signature for the Netherlands as well as his for the Empire. This was why she had waited until now, with her regency established. It also meant that she could add a rider to the effect that increased Scots trade with the said Netherlands was to be encouraged by all means, including the protection of Scots shipping by Netherlands warships, where possible.

So all was gained, all in the end successful, and this strange dumpy woman proved not only clever and effective but a good friend.

David took the treaty copies back to his room. He was inclined to wake his fellow envoys with the news; but recognised that Sir John at least would be too drunk to sign anything that night. Tomorrow would do. And then, home.

As a final gesture, Margaret Hapsburg arranged that the Scots party should sail back directly from Antwerp in a Netherlands vessel bound for Sweden but directed to call in at a Scots east-coast port first.

They did not see the Emperor privately again but parted from his aunt in warmest fashion.

15

The ambassadors' return to Scotland, mission successfully accomplished, indeed improved upon by the valuable trade concession, gained them perhaps less appreciation than they deserved. For they came back to something of a crisis, with the minds of those concerned with rule preoccupied with other than long-range foreign policy and trade. James, who proved to be very much alive and well, had, during the months they were abroad to some extent kicked over the traces. Allegedly under the influence of the Bastard of Arran, who now that his sire was dead and his half-brother the new Arran not very effective, was very much wielding the full power of Hamilton, the King had suddenly initiated a campaign against many of his over-powerful nobles—and incidentally those who rivalled Hamilton—as being a danger to his throne and kingdom. He had started with the Campbells. The late Earl had been not only too influential but too strong for James to overturn, Lord Justice General, commander of the army and Lieutenant of the Isles, known indeed as King of the Highlands. But his son, Colin, fourth Earl, was less experienced and potent, and when this young man had requested that the said Lieutenantship of the Isles be vested in himself, so that he could take due order with unruly clans, James had instead appointed his principal rival, Alexander MacDonald of Islay, one of the claimants of the Lordship of the Isles put down by the King's late father. When Argyll had protested, James took the opportunity to throw him into prison. So poor Sir John, returning home in something like triumph, found the Campbells in eclipse and his chief a captive—and retired to Lundie in some haste.

Argyll was not the only one in prison, it appeared. James had decided on a clean sweep. He would clip the wings of others whom he—or perhaps the Bastard—felt were waxed too mighty for his comfort. These included the Earls of Bothwell, Crawford, the Lindsay chief, Moray, the King's own illegitimate half-brother, Cassillis, and the Lords Maxwell and Glamis. And not only these, for James Beaton, Archbishop and Primate, was also in Blackness Castle. It seemed that his nephew Davie had protested against this new policy, as unwise, and against the Bastard's evil influence, and James in consequence had been going to imprison even him. However, the Lord Privy Seal's efficient warning system informed him in time to make good his escape; but his old uncle at St. Andrews, less agile, had been taken into custody instead, more or less as hostage for Davie's good behaviour. All this in the seven or eight weeks of the envoys' absence. If word of it had reached the Netherlands it would not have helped the embassage.

David Lindsay was welcomed back kindly enough by the monarch, who seemed however more concerned to hear about his reported death than about the details of the mission. But with the ominous atmosphere prevailing at court, plus his dislike of the Bastard, now so evidently in the ascendant, David sought almost immediate leave-of-absence—and had no difficulty in gaining it. Almost it seemed as though the Lord Lyon King-of-Arms was a less essential prop of the crown than the title implied.

So it was back to The Mount of Lindifferon, where he had a gently rapturous reception from Janet. He found all in order, the harvest in, and the upsets at court little regarded—save for the imprisonment of Archbishop Beaton which did worry Janet. This was no way to treat an old man, head of the Church, and who had been chief minister of the realm for so many years. He was failing in health and this might be the death of him. Davie Beaton should not allow it. He should yield himself up to let his uncle go free. Where *was* Davie?

Her husband did not know, but guessed that he would be somewhere sufficiently secure—and probably not very far from Marion Ogilvy at Ethie Castle in Angus, on whom he seemed to home when in difficulties. He did not think, however, that the Archbishop would be in any great danger nor discomfort. Blackness Castle, the state prison for the lofty, in West Lothian, was commonly asserted to be more comfortable than the houses of many of its inmates.

Janet declared that there were problems at Luthrie. The steward there and his people had been used to going their own way and in their own time with absentee lairds and little supervision; they resented a woman like herself coming and telling them what to do. But that harvest was much behind that of The Mount, both in yield and ingathering; and many of the much-neglected buildings, which David had ordered to be repaired, were still untouched. So it was decided that Luthrie must be visited, and promptly.

There was also considerable work piled up for David, sent by the Lyon Clerk and the other heralds, requests for grants of arms, complaints of infringements, genealogical descents to be proved, documents to be scanned. So he was kept busy, even though the King himself did not seem to need him.

After a few days, one evening at dusk a visitor arrived, almost stealthily, well mounted but plainly clad and without distinguishing marks heraldic or otherwise. He asked for a private interview with Sir David Lindsay.

He came, he revealed, from the Lord Abbot of Arbroath. His lordship would be grateful for some converse with Sir David. Unfortunately he could not come to Lindifferon in present circumstances, nor anywhere near St. Andrews, which the Hamiltons were watching like hawks, but he urged Sir David, for the realm's sake, to come to him in Angus. If Sir David would journey to Ethie Castle, south of Montrose, to visit the Lady Marion, the Lord Abbot would endeavour to arrange a meeting. It would be best if Sir David could bring the Lady Lindsay with him, and possibly call at the Paniter house, Newmanswalls, near Montrose first, so that the visit would not arouse the suspicions of Hamilton spies. They could make use of all the facilities of Holy Church on the journey.

David was intrigued by this rather extraordinary *cri de coeur* coming from the normally so assured and authoritative Davie Beaton. He could scarcely refuse.

The unnamed messenger left as discreetly as he had come.

Janet proved to be entirely willing to accompany her husband on an excursion to Angus in a golden autumn before winter closed in. She was fond of Marion Ogilvy, considered that she had been shamefully treated, and had not seen her for long. So, early in October, they set off northwards, modestly escorted by two armed attendants.

Janet was a less eager horsewoman than Kate had been, but there was no need to travel other than leisurely. Lindifferon was only some sixteen miles from Ferry-Port-on-Craig, where there was an established ferry across Tay, to Broughty on the Angus shore. In the interests of discretion, if not secrecy, after the crossing, they did not risk an overnight stop at the ferry-inn, so near to Dundee, but rode on a further few miles to the Grange of Monifeith, one of the many farms of Arbroath Abbey, where there was a travellers' hospice, where they put up under names of Davidson of Balgarvie and wife—this being a small subsidiary property of The Mount.

The next day, in a chilly grey haar off the Norse Sea which, however suitable-seeming for secrecy, offered no inducements for lingering, they covered a fair distance. They avoided Arbroath itself, with its great Abbey which might be watched in case of a visit from its Abbot, turning inland up the Elliot Water at Abirlot to make for St. Vigeans, where there was a renowned ancient church and another grange of Arbroath, famed for its apiary. Candles made from beeswax were despatched all over the land, one of the many sources of abbey wealth; also renowned was the echo here, of no fewer than four syllables, from a nearby rock. Janet found the ancient church, its Pictish symbol-stones, the echo and the bee-management, of much interest. David, for his part, enjoyed these days in the saddle with his wife, her company considerably to be preferred to that of his recent travelling companions. She was observant, appreciative of what she saw, uncomplaining over difficulties and knew when to talk and when to keep silence. And at their halts she conformed suitably to the style of Mistress Davidson.

They learned at St. Vigeans that it was only some fourteen miles on to Montrose and that the Paniters' house of Newmanswalls was a bare mile north of the burgh. Not that Abbot Paniter himself would be there, only his uncle and aunt.

They proceeded northwards, crossing the Lunan Water at Balmullie and then mounting over the high ground of Rossie Muir and down to Montrose town beside its vast tidal basin. They had no difficulty in finding Newmanswalls, a small property on the north shore of the basin, loud at this season with the wild trumpeting of greylag geese and the quacking of mallard. Here they were well received by the laird and his lady, a quiet and well-doing couple, who were clearly very proud of their nephew, despite his birth, and whom they had brought up. He was, to be sure, the illegitimate son of the laird's brother, the still more famous Patrick Paniter, likewise Abbot of Cambuskenneth and royal secretary in the previous reign, one of the finest Latinists in Christendom. This little lairdship amongst the wildfowl-haunted marshes of North Angus seemed a strange place to have produced these two, although the brother and uncle appeared much more typical. Here, naturally, the Lindsays had to reveal their true identity, their hosts being obviously impressed. But since their nephew owed his swift promotion in Holy Church largely to Davie Beaton, there was surely no danger to the latter here. However, the visitors did not inform that they were going on to Ethie Castle, merely saying that, as Lyon, David had a number of matters to see to in North Angus and the Mearns, and had called, in passing, to tell them in some measure of their nephew's Netherlands venture. They allowed themselves to be persuaded to stay the night.

In the morning they set off southwards, but this time circling the great tidal area to the west, to avoid the town, and back up on to Rossie Muir. Ethie stood on a cliff-top position near the mighty foreland of Red Head, at the southern horn of the lovely Lunan Bay, some nine miles south of Montrose itself and six north of Arbroath, near enough to the latter to be convenient for Davie, but sufficiently remote to be suitably private.

The visitors came to Davie's real home—although it was in fact Marion's house, bought and chartered in her name—on a crisp afternoon of vivid autumn colours, with the sigh and scent of the sea pervading all and the cries of the seabirds which wheeled endlessly in the pale blue of the sky. Sky and sea were very evident at Ethie, set high on bare upland near the cliff-tops.

The little castle which Davie had bought for his wife when his abbatical revenues began to accumulate—half of Arbroath's income, of course, never reached him, being retained by his uncle—was a simple square tower of the previous century, within a walled courtyard, but with more ancient foundations. He had added a wing to it, for more accommodation and comfort, and now it was a pleasant red-stone pile of medium size, with a walled garden and orchard, sheltered by some wind-blown trees. Isolated on its grassy height, with no other house in sight, its vistas were tremendous, lovely this October day but a wild place of a winter's storm, undoubtedly.

Marion Ogilvy and a clutch of children met them at the little gatehouse—for any visitors could be espied a long way off, and three men with a woman were unlikely to represent danger. When she perceived the identity of the callers her fine features lit up and she came hastening, obviously delighted to see them. Four children, two boys and two girls, the eldest perhaps ten years, held back shyly.

Marion, daughter of Lord Ogilvy of Airlie, was a good-looking creature, still trim of figure and attractive despite all the child-bearing, now in her mid-thirties. If she felt in any way embarrassed over her peculiar circumstances, she gave no sign of it.

Out of much talk, presently, they learned that she saw Davie quite frequently, he often slipping into the castle of a night and out again before sun-up, but never risking any longer stay, for occasional parties of armed men arrived without warning, undoubtedly looking for the missing Abbot. These had never maltreated her, for the present Lord Ogilvy, her brother, lived only a score of miles away and was too powerful in these parts to offend; but Davie was determined not only not to be caught but to cause no trouble for herself and the children if possible, and to give no hint that he was dwelling in the vicinity.

And indeed he was hiding nearby, she revealed, no more than three miles away. These cliffs, some of the most lofty and impressive on all the east coast of Scotland, were honeycombed with caves; but the cliffs almost everywhere dropped sheer into the sea, so that most caves were either inaccessible or only to be reached by boat. One of the most notable of these was called the Gaylet or Geary Pot, less than a mile south of the fishing-village of Auchmithie. As well as being one of the largest, this cavern was unique in having a peculiar open shaft reaching up from its head right to the cliff-top level but some two hundred yards inland. This strange feature gave this cave an emergency escape-route for the nimble, valuable indeed. Davie was roosting in this Gaylet Pot—or at least, he was using it as his refuge and base, for much of the time he was roaming the countryside in disguise. She never knew when he would make an appearance.

That night there was no visit from the fugitive, and next day Marion proposed that, rather than waiting indefinitely, they should themselves pay a visit, discreetly, to the Gaylet Pot. Davie might not be there at present, but they could at least leave a message for him. This could be done without too much risk. The castle had its own tiny fishing community, perching on a terrace of the cliff-foot half-a-mile to the north, called Ethiehaven. The fishermen were all to be trusted there, and one of their boats could take them down the coast to the Gaylet Pot without arousing suspicion, for they had lobster-pots all along the shoreline which had to be tended. This was how Davie was provisioned.

So, leaving Janet to look after the children, dressed in the oldest clothing, Marion, wrapped in a shawl, led David to Ethiehaven, down a zigzag path at a break in the sheer cliff-face. The hamlet consisted of just a few low-browed cot-houses crouching under the precipices on a mere shelf a few feet above the tide and turning gable-ends to the sea—as well they might, for undoubtedly in a storm the waves would be battering against the walling. Below was a little harbour, part natural, where three fishing-cobles were moored, bobbing in the swell.

Marion had no difficulty in persuading a couple of the fisherman to take them, for these were their own tenants and devoted to the castle service. They would visit some of their lobster-pots on the way.

They rowed out in the high-prowed coble into Lunan Bay, to turn southwards round the mighty cape of Red Head. Seen from the sea, its soaring stacks and precipices of red sandstone, thronged by thousands of screaming birds, was a fearsome sight, even in this comparatively calm weather its base spouting high columns of white in the Norse Sea swell.

The fishermen had their lobster-creels marked in position by floating blown-up sheep's bladders attached by ropes. Drawn up, three of the wickerwork cages proved to have trapped the pink, clawing creatures, to the boatman's satisfaction, as they worked their way down the coast.

In about three miles they passed under the larger fishing village of Auchmithie, set higher this, on the cliff-edge. They exchanged hails with two boats out from its harbour.

David had noted the yawning mouths of caves great and small, all the way, in the tremendous barrier of rock. Soon now Marion pointed out a fissure rather than a cavity, a sort of wide crack in the precipice face, reaching right down into the tide. Towards this the oarsmen steered.

It proved to be a re-entrant in the towering rock formation, into which the coble nosed its way carefully, rising and falling quite alarmingly now on the surge of the seas against the cliff-tops. They turned into a narrow dog's-leg channel, all but enclosed and too constricted to row in, the men using the oars as both poles and fenders.

Rounding that bend, there was the cave-mouth ahead, hidden hitherto, and large, high, with the sea running right in. They halted just within the entrance, and hallooed. As result the hollow echoing produced a flurry of wildly-flapping rock-doves but no answering call.

There was a distinct shelf, perhaps three feet wide, weed-hung, a few feet above the water-level. The fishermen moored their coble against this and helped the passengers out and up, with cautions to tread warily on the slippery seaweed. They led the way along, deeper into the cavern.

The large mouth of it meant that light was good for a considerable distance. They passed a small side-cave opening off this shelf, in which were some wooden boxes, evidently stores. A little further and there was a larger aperture and into this the two men turned, most clearly knowing their way. There was just enough light to see that this was about a dozen feet deep and fitted up after a fashion, with a rough fireplace, cooking-pots, torch-holders, two mattresses of heather, blankets, spare clothing and so on. It seemed an extraordinary lodging for the mitred Lord Abbot of Arbroath and Scotland's Privy Seal.

They had come prepared for Beaton to be absent, and left a note on one of the beds to say that the Lindsays were at Ethie, as requested. But before leaving, they went deeper into the main cavern, to let David see the place's special feature. The light was fading noticeably thus far in, but rounding a major bend, perhaps seventy yards in, a new source of light was revealed, admittedly pale and faint. To say that it increased as they gingerly progressed would be to give a wrong impression; but it maintained and became more localised and presently developed into a sort of circular pool of luminosity ahead. This, when reached, proved to be water, a tidal pond reflecting the sky far above, down a great funnel or shaft in the solid rock, a wide chimney soaring well over one hundred feet. Down its wet walling, where ferns grew, a long knotted rope hung.

Marion pointed. "Davie's back-door," she said.

"He climbs that! Davie does?"

"If he must. Not otherwise, I think! In a storm, this cave cannot be left or entered from the sea. And he might be trapped by searchers in boats."

"I would not have believed him to be so agile, so strong of thew! To climb that, or to descend it."

"Davie is . . . . Davie! What he sets his mind to, he usually does."

"Even so . . ." David stared up. "This is a strange place indeed. How was it formed? Could the sea do this? Or is it some break in the rock?"

"Davie says that it would have been the sea. In a gale the waves come roaring in here, he says, frightening in their power, and laden with stones and pebbles. Perhaps there was softer rock here, harder beyond. So the force strikes upward into the soft stone, and over the ages this is formed. The folk here say that on a very bad winter's storm spray comes spouting out of the top there, above the cliffs. But I have never seen that."

They returned to the boat, the visitor much impressed.

That very night Davie Beaton turned up at the castle, having apparently missed them at the Gaylet Pot by only an hour or two. He would have been hard to recognise as the handsome courtier and cleric, dressed now in stained and ragged fishermen's clothing, long hair uncombed, pointed beard untrimmed. But there was nothing of the fugitive and furtive about his manner, his cheerful assurance seemingly proof against present difficulties and discomforts. He greeted the Lindsays with a flourish.

"My apologies for not being present to receive you, my friends, either here in Marion's house or in my own present hermitage under the cliffs—suitable for a religious, is it not? I was haunting the port of Montrose, for news, and heard that you were come. So I hastened back."

"You *heard* that we were here? In Montrose?" David wondered. "How could that be? We told none, save the Paniters. And they did not know that we came on to Ethie."

"You would be surprised how word gets around! Not your names, to be sure—but a man and a woman, with two servants, obviously gentry, strangers, picking their careful way. I have my sources of information, see you. I have to have."

"The last who said that to me was Queen Margaret of Hungary, in Brussels," Lindsay remarked.

"Ah, yes, Margaret. An excellent woman, is she not? Your visit to the Netherlands was a success, I hear. The trade matter a useful addition."

"Your hearing is acute, attuned to near and far it seems. I know not how you do it."

"Siller, man, siller. With a sufficiency of moneys, news is . . . available! It is expensive, but it is worth it. And, fortunately, Holy Church, whatever else it may lack, has siller aplenty! Ears to hear can be bought, eyes to see, and tongues to whisper! You would scarce credit who and where and how!"

When Beaton had changed into more seemly clothing and much improved his appearance, he ate hungrily, meanwhile telling his children highly improbable stories of his adventures to hoots of laughter. But when the two women went to put the youngsters to bed, he changed his tune to the sufficiently serious.

"It was good of you to come, Davie—and so promptly. Good of Janet, likewise," he said. "I am grateful. There is need. I would not have called you, otherwise."

Lindsay nodded, waiting.

"The kingdom is in grievous danger. It always is, to be sure. But now more than usual, I fear. Our James is playing the fool, and could even lose his throne."

"That is scarce new."

"The present situation is. James is almost wholly in the grip of the Bastard of Arran. And the Bastard is more dangerous than any yet. More dangerous than Angus or Home or any of them. For he is able, as well as evil, clever as he is without scruple."

"Is that not itself of some advantage to the realm? I much mislike the man, but agree that he is no fool. If he controls the King, it may not be to James's moral well-being, but the kingdom should not be endangered. As well as being able and courageous, shrewd after his fashion too, Hamilton is a soldier. Could that not be something of what the realm needs? *You* have found him useful in the past!"

Beaton ignored that last. "Wait, you. James is unwed—however well-bedded! So there is no son, no close heir to his throne. Who is the nearest lawful heir? Who but the young Arran, since Albany rejects all, and remains a French citizen. Arran—a weakling, like his father, and the Bastard's half-brother. Have you considered that?"

The thought admittedly did jolt the other. The Hamiltons' ancient grandmother, the Dowager Countess of Arran, had been the Princess Mary, James the Third's sister. "You are not suggesting . . . ?"

"Would you put anything past that man? You who saw him murder Lennox, his own cousin. Who saw him at his hangings, in the Borderland? When I urged more than once that James should seek a wife, the Bastard each time said no haste, time enough for James to enjoy himself first. If the King was to die unwed, the Bastard would rule Scotland in the name of his feckless brother."

"You say that he is all but ruling it now."

"Aye, and to its cost. This policy of bringing down the leading nobles is his, rather than James's own. All the rivals of Hamilton are to be brought low. He started with Argyll but now it is Bothwell, Crawford, Cassillis, Eglinton, Argyll's good-brother,

Maxwell, Home, Sinclair, Buccleuch, even Moray. All imprisoned. Bishops too, my aged uncle included. And I was to be in with them! James is to rule without the aid of his nobles—only Hamilton."

"All this happened while I was in the Netherlands. Only Bothwell was in custody before that."

"Bothwell, yes. The Hepburn has escaped, however, and is now over the Border in England. And is like to join Angus."

"One more traitor will make little difference."

"Be not so sure. Bothwell is dangerous. He has renounced his allegiance to King James and calls on other Scots nobles to do the same, not only those presently in custody. He has joined the English Warden, the Earl of Northumberland, and urges actual invasion of Scotland, saying that all followers of the imprisoned lords, and others threatened, will flock to join the invaders. Bothwell is Lord of Teviotdale, so there is menace in this. Northumberland has written to King Henry to the effect that he looked to see more of the great Scots nobles agreeing to crown him, Henry, in the town of Edinburgh as King of Scots and in only short time! Friends of mine intercepted the courier—as they frequently do."

"Lord—the folly of it!"

"Worse than folly—real danger. For Angus has now sworn fealty to Henry. If only one or two others do likewise, then the thing could become a spate, especially in the Borders. If Buccleuch's and Home's clans, in the east, and the Maxwells and others in the west, let their resentment boil over, then think what that would mean. The Armstrongs are already seething. With Bothwell's Hepburns and the Douglases up in arms, the entire Borderland would be wide open to the invaders. Do you not see it?"

Lindsay wagged his head. "I see it, yes—but what can we do? You, a fugitive, and myself little more than a figurehead. Lyon has not real power . . ."

"You are James's oldest and truest friend, as I have told you before. He knows it, however little he may seem to heed you these days. You must *make* him listen to you. Seek to counter the Bastard's influence, somehow. Stay at court—you have every right to be there, duty indeed, as Lyon. Do not hide away at The Mount. Be always at James's elbow. The Bastard cannot always be there—he has all the great Hamilton interests and properties to see to. James knows he is a rogue, even though he lets him sway him."

"You credit me with an influence I have not got!" Lindsay protested. "James may have some fondness for me, from times past. But he heeds me little and needs me less, now . . ."

"Be not so sure. He often mentioned you, when you were away. He acts headstrong, but he is insecure of himself beneath it all—and that is why he is so easily led by the Bastard. *You* could lead him, likewise, for he knows you to be honest, faithful. And there is your poetry, do not overlook that. James much admires it. He has little real interest in ruling his kingdom, but he loves poetry, women—and, to be sure, hurly-hackit! He thinks to write poetry himself. I have seen some of his verses and they are fair enough. Less than profound—but one could scarcely expect that. He would not show them to you, for he looks on you as the master, and would fear your scoffing. But encourage James to write poetry and you have something the Bastard has not got. James made you Laureate as well as Lyon, after all."

"I did not know of this, of his continuing writing. Childish verses, yes, but nothing more."

"He would like to rival his great-great grandsire, James the First, who was no mean poet. You mind *The King's Quair*? His verse—young James's, I mean—tends to be about women, as you might guess! Some of it is sufficiently . . . detailed!"

"I *can* guess! A pity . . ."

"Do not be over-hard on it, man. If it is women who inspire him to it, use that, and them. That way you may reach him."

"You would have me whoremonger, now!"

"Scarce that. But it is a fool who cannot use a man's weaknesses for a good cause! You will not change James over women now. So you might as well make use of them. And be careful how you talk of whores! Some of the loftiest in the land welcome our liege-lord and theirs to their beds. Margaret, daughter of the Lord Erskine is, I think, the favourite. But there is Euphemia, daughter to the Lord Elphinstone, and a pack of Elizabeths—Lord Carmichael's daughter; Elizabeth Shaw of Sauchie; my own kin, Elizabeth Beaton of Creich; Elizabeth Stewart of Atholl . . ."

"Sakes—all these! I thought that it was women of the common sort that he went for? So all the tales tell."

"Yes, yes—these also, to be sure. It is as the Gudeman o'

Ballengeich that he pursues such—not as the King! All but every night he sallies forth from Stirling Castle, alone, seeking his sport. A right potent prince our Scotland has, in some respects! Would that he was as hot on kingcraft! How many bastards has he sired already, only the good Lord knows!"

"And you would have me to encourage him in this, to make poetry out of it all?"

"Why not? Make some degree of good out of the ill. What you cannot alter, make the best of, I say! You might even use his fondness for women to spur him on to marriage! For marry he must, and the sooner the better. Scotland direly needs an heir, other than Arran. Even if he married Margaret Erskine . . ."

"Erskine's daughter, queen? Surely not!"

"No? Other kings have wed their nobles' daughters. Robert Second and Robert Third. James's own father would have wed Margaret Drummond had Henry Tudor not had her poisoned. Would God he had, then we would never have had Margaret Tudor to deal with! A suitable foreign princess, see you, would be better, I agree, to mortar together some useful alliance. Perhaps the Emperor or his aunt could find us one? But wed James should be . . ."

The return of Marion and Janet gave this talk a different slant, the two women being intrigued with the subject, both agreeing that the King should be allowed to marry for love rather than foreign policy, since he so regarded their sex, David surprised that they sounded less critical of James's amours than he, for one, would have expected. But Beaton cheerfully encouraged them, perhaps incautiously for that normally calculating individual. For it emboldened Janet to voice, however gently, what had been on her mind for long.

"I am a little surprised, my lord Abbot, to hear *you* championing marriage for love," she averred, flushing as she dared it. "After, after what you have done to your wife!" That came out in a rush.

If she feared any indication of offence from her host, she was relieved, for he laughed with seemingly genuine amusement, and turned to Marion.

"What have I done to you, my dear?" he asked. "Deserted you for Holy Church? Shamed you in the sight of honest men? Left you bereft? Now is your opportunity to belabour me!"

She smiled. "My complaint is only a small one—that so many

godly abbesses and prioresses now consider that you are fair game for their blandishments! Your abbatical visits to nunneries!" Marion looked at Janet. "My lord and master's embracing of Holy Church has its dangers! Although I must confess that I have seen more of him since he took holy orders and I became a fallen woman than ever I did before!"

That left the visitors with nothing to say, if somewhat embarrassed. Probably perceiving it, Beaton grimaced.

"The sorriest part of it all is the siller!" he declared lugubriously. "The cost to my purse. For now I must needs pay the Vatican, and sweetly, to legitimise our already legitimate children, suddenly become otherwise. As is necessary before they can inherit any of the properties their so loving sire intends to bestow on them in due course! You will admit that it is hard?"

Before they sought their beds that night, Beaton, declaring that he would not see them in the morning, urged his friend to return to court, to try to counter the Bastard's influence in all ways possible, to use his poetry to best advantage, to urge James towards marriage—and, to be sure, to work for the reinstatement of the Lord Privy Seal, for the realm's weal.

16

David Lindsay did not have to make any pride-swallowing gesture over returning to court, for on their return to Lindifferon they found a worried courier from the King awaiting them, with a command that the Lord Lyon King-of-Arms should attend his monarch forthwith on a progress into the Highlands. The messenger, one of the Lyon Clerk's men, had been at The Mount for three days and by this time was in a state of considerable agitation.

Enquiries as to why his presence should be required for a jaunt into the Highlands elicited for David the information that this was more than any jaunt, that it was in fact a large-scale, almost formal, expedition for the edification and entertainment of the papal envoy. Mystified, David asked what papal envoy and why any such should be taken to the Highlands, of all places, for edification?

The courier explained, as far as he was able. The Pope, informed of the imprisonment of the Scottish Primate, Archbishop Beaton, and sundry other clerics, had sent a Legate, one Antonio Campeggio, to discover the situation and make representations, indeed threatening dire reprisals, even excommunication. So the old Archbishop had been hurriedly released from Blackness, assurances given that there was no assault on Holy Church intended, and the Legate having expressed a desire to see something of the Scottish Highlands, which he had heard referred to as the arse-end of the world, the King had diplomatically arranged this progress. The nuncio, apparently, was also anxious to meet the Queen-Mother, in connection with her brother Henry's threats to divorce himself and England from adherence to Rome, because the Pope had refused him a divorce from his queen, Catherine of Aragon, and it was hoped that Margaret Tudor could act as mediator—after all, she should be grateful for her own divorce. So the said lady was to be invited on this Highland expedition also.

It all seemed a scarcely believable development to David Lindsay and he felt that there must be more behind it than the mere wish of the papal visitor to see the Highlands, even though it was necessary to placate him. Possibly it was all part of James's, or the Bastard's, campaign to bring down the power of the Lowland nobles by using the Highlanders to help. At any rate, there was no refusing the royal command to attend. Nor delay—for the messenger was urgent that they should be off at once, saying that the royal cavalcade would almost certainly have left Stirling by now. He had been waiting here for three days . . .

So, changing into finer clothing and donning his splendid Lyon's tabard, David took a hasty farewell of Janet, and set off again, westwards.

The courier, convinced that it was a waste of time to go to Stirling, advised that they make directly for Methven in Strathearn, where the Queen-Mother now lived in retirement with her third husband. No doubt the King would pick her up there and there would be almost certain delay. They might catch up at Methven.

Through North Fife and the south side of Tay, riding hard

now, they came by Lindores and Abernethy to the flat lands at the mouth of the Earn. Following that fine river westwards still, they could see, by the tracks and horse-droppings, that a great company had passed that way, probably only the day before. Darkness fell by the time they reached Tibbermore, but the wide drove-road was clear enough and they carried on. Before long they were heartened by a ruddy glow in the sky ahead, which they guessed would be from the cooking-fires of the royal escort encamped around Methven Castle.

This proved to be an accurate assessment, as presently they rode up the steep grassy slope above a small loch, its dark waters reflecting the glow, to the impressive terrace site where the fairly large castle reared its red masonry the more ruddily for the firelight. The tents and pavilions of scores of men-at-arms and retainers covered the area, and horses were tethered in long lines.

David had never thought to visit the home of Margaret Tudor, a woman he cordially loathed. As Lyon he had no difficulty in gaining entrance at least.

The first person of note he encountered was Hamilton of Finnart himself, who greeted him with a mocking bonhomie.

"Ha—the Laureate in person! Emerged belatedly from wrestling with the Muse, no doubt? We are all the richer, I swear! Welcome to this royal love-arbour, friend!"

"Thank you. Where do I find His Grace, Sir James?"

"Where but in his lady-mother's boudoir—whence I have just escaped!" Evidently the Bastard did not love Margaret Tudor either. "And scarcely happy therein. Come—I will escort you thither, but not within, my Lord Lyon—not within! I have had sufficient for one day!" And he took the newcomer's arm.

David would have liked to shake off that hand. But he restrained himself. He greatly disliked this man, but recognised that nothing was to be gained by deliberately antagonising one so much in favour with the King. Moreover, from their first meeting at Cadzow all those years ago, the Bastard had always shown a cynically amiable face to him, as though they shared some secret amusing view of life and men—although surely nothing could be further from the fact. Lindsay was scarcely an affable man, but found it difficult to be intentionally discourteous.

He was led upstairs to a second-floor chamber, where two

of the royal guard stood on duty at the door. Hamilton knocked and without waiting threw open the door.

"Your Grace," he called, "Sir David Lindsay of The Mount, Lord Lyon King-of-Arms and ornament of your court—when present!" His voice dropping to a whisper, he added, "God help you!" and pushing David within, shut the door behind him.

Four people sat in the overheated room, where too large a fire for the season blazed under a great heraldic overmantel—the King, his mother, her husband the weedy-looking Henry Stewart, Lord Methven, and a darkly smooth individual of indeterminate age, richly dressed in approximately clerical garb. All stared.

"Davie!" James half-rose from his seat before he remembered his royal dignity. "You have come, then!"

"You sent for me, Sire."

"Yes, I did. I require you, Davie. You are . . . overmuch away." Again the need to assert authority. "You have taken your time, man!"

"I was in the north, Sire. Won back to The Mount only today."

"Aye. As well." He turned towards the others. "My royal mother you know, and my Lord Methven. And here is His Holiness the Pope's nuncio, the Bishop Antonio Campeggio."

David made a composite bow.

Margaret Tudor turned a fleshy bare shoulder on him, her husband taking his cue from her. She was now in her early forties and looked older. Never a beautiful woman, she had grown heavy and coarse looking, and the display of her person for the occasion consequently a mistake. But her eyes were still vital, searching.

"This is the poet Your Majesty told me of, is it not?" That was the stranger, in good but heavily-accented English. He raised a beringed hand in something between a salute and a benediction. "I greet you, Sir David."

James coughed, mopping his brow with his doublet-sleeve, obviously feeling the heat. "Yes. Sir David has been my, my mentor, always. Sit you, Davie. Where were you in the north?"

"Angus, Sire. Monifeith, Montrose and elsewhere. As Lyon, I must needs travel the land on occasion."

"Yes, yes. Sir David is my King-of-Arms, my lord Bishop. And has lately been to the Netherlands, to conclude a treaty between myself and the Emperor Charles." That was said with some emphasis.

"Ah, so. Your Majesty mentioned that."

David recognised discomfort in that room, in more than the heat, and on various levels. He saw why the Bastard had been glad to escape. He did his poor best for James.

"You are bound for the Highlands, Your Grace, I am told? Is this a progress, a surveillance, a strategy or a hunting?"

"Something of all. Bishop Campeggio desires to see those parts and their folk. He has heard much of their strangeness and would see for himself. We go to Atholl, where it is not too barbarous and there is excellent hunting. My lord of Atholl has promised me notable sport—boar, wolves, even wildcats, and deer beyond number. It will make a pleasing diversion before the winter sets in."

Atholl, David noted. The Lady Elizabeth Stewart, he recollected, was one of the high-born women whom Davie Beaton had named as welcoming James to their beds—a daughter of the Earl of Atholl.

Again the silence descended.

David tried once more. "What has His Excellency the Bishop heard of our Highlands which so interests him, may I ask?"

"Ah, much, much." Campeggio fluttered those eloquent hands. "The mountains, so strong, so fierce. Less high than our Alps but more terrible, they say. The lakes, the rivers, the torrents—most remarkable. The animals and fowls and fishes, of such abundance. And the people, savages, all but naked, but noble after their fashion, their coats of many colours—when they wear coats! Like Joseph's! Some do say, because of this, and their language, which is reputed to be like to that of the Galatians, that they are one of the ten lost tribes of ancient Israel. I would myself see, and report to the Holy Father."

Blinking a little at this, David looked at the King, who eyed them both askance. "I hope that Your Excellency may not be disappointed," was all that he could think of to say.

Methven whinnied a laugh. "A likely tale, I'd say!"

"Did any ask *you*?" his wife snapped, her first contribution since David's arrival.

"But Israelites? Hielantmen!"

"If His Excellency considers it possible, who are you to question it?"

James cleared his throat. "We ride for Atholl in the morn. By Glen Almond and Strathbraan to Dunkeld. Beyond that I know not. Have you ever been there, Davie?"

"No, Sire. Nor know any who have!"

"Wonderful! The more wonderful!" the envoy declared. "*Terra incognita*!"

"Aye, well," the King said doubtfully. "Atholl says that he will give us fair lodging and this notable sport. So, we must be up betimes. It is a long ride. I will seek my couch." He rose—so must they all. "You, my lord bishop have matters to discuss with my mother. I bid you a good night."

Margaret promptly sat down again. "You, Harry, leave us alone." That was brusque dismissal.

The two men followed James out, none reluctant. As they came to the stairway, the guard behind, the King turned to glower at Methven—who hurriedly bowed, seemed to recollect urgent business elsewhere, and went upstairs instead of down.

"*He* will not last much longer with that woman!" the monarch confided. "Nor any loss, mind!"

Discreetly David made no comment.

"She will have some other bed-fellow in mind, I've no doubt. Think you she has an eye for the Florentine, Davie?"

Lindsay found the subject difficult, unsuitable. "I have no notion, Sire." He could scarcely any longer tell his liege-lord, now a grown man in his nineteenth year, that this was no way to speak about his mother, even such a mother. But it did occur to him that perhaps James was the less to be blamed for all his womanising, with such parentage—for his late father had been as popular with the ladies as with his people generally, and had never failed to take advantage of the fact.

Going down the stair the King lowered his voice confidentially. "See you, Davie—this nuncio has to be sent back to Rome happy. He came breathing threats and ill will. Excommunication, no less. The reduction of Scotland from metropolitan status, in the Church—that old story! Putting us under York . . ."

"*Only* threats, Sire, surely? No Pope today would ever revert to that folly. Especially with King Henry snapping his fingers at the Vatican!"

"Part *because* of that. Do you not see? Wolsey disgraced and now dead. If the Pope could offer *ecclesiastical* dominion over Scotland to England, Henry might change his attitude. Putting the Scots Church under York would much aid Henry's hopes. It is all part of a plan to keep England in allegiance to Rome. This Campeggio said that clearly I did not rate highly the metropolitan status, for I had imprisoned the Metropolitan, that old fool Beaton!"

They had reached a doorway on the first floor, and James drew David into what was apparently his own chamber, untidy as such always was, shutting out the guard. "So I had to release the old man, and other bishops. At least until the Florentine has gone."

"Sire—I believe you to be mistaken in this," David said, taking a chance. "This of the Primate. The Archbishop is *not* plotting against you. Indeed he is past any plotting . . ."

"Perhaps—but his nephew is not! Which comes to the same thing, since Davie Beaton rules the Church through the old man. I would have arrested *him* if I could have found him, I promise you!"

"James—hear me." It was not often that Lindsay called his sovereign by his Christian name, but he did it deliberately now, as reminder of past relationship and his own faithful service and reliability. "I know Davie Beaton—probably better than any other man in your realm. I know that he does not plot *against* you. He is a plotter, yes, a born plotter—but he is entirely loyal to yourself and your interests, Scotland's best interests. He is, I believe, the most able man you have in your kingdom, and should not be a hunted fugitive, just because Hamilton of Finnart does not like him!"

"Tut, Davie—it is more than that. We know that he was working against my policies."

"Only the policies he believed to be harmful to you and your realm, Sire. As many others believe. As do I, indeed. This of pulling down the nobles and the Church both, it cannot succeed. You need them, need them both. The Hamiltons will not replace them . . ."

"Och, man—quiet you! I did not bring you here to hear your views on policy. Nor Davie Beaton's! It is this Florentine—he is the problem, meantime. I want you to work on him. To convince him that I am a better ally to the Pope than is Henry. Send him away well content with Scotland."

"Me? How can *I* do this? I have no skills for this, no experience. Davie Beaton, yes—but not me."

"Man, did you not lead the successful embassage to the Netherlands? You did well there. You convinced the Emperor, and Margaret of Hungary. Speak with this man. The Vatican needs the Emperor's support. Tell Campeggio that Charles esteems an alliance with Scotland. That he has ordered his warships to protect Scots vessels against the English. That the Pope should be aiding me, not threatening me. You are the man to do it, new back from Brussels. He will heed you, who have been close to the Emperor."

"Scarce close, Sire. Charles is not an easy man to win close to . . ."

"To his aunt then, Davie—of whom you spoke so well. He relies on her, all know. Do your best, Davie. I need you in this."

Lindsay could be an opportunist when the occasion warranted. "I will try, James. But—it would help if I could tell him that you were recalling your Lord Privy Seal to your court. This Legate must know that you are presently at odds with Davie. Also that he is the real power in the Church here, behind the Archbishop. While you reject him, Rome cannot but suspect you. Bring him back and you will be much the stronger."

"Well . . ."

"Forby you *need* him, Sire! You need his wits. Your present Chancellor, the Archbishop of Glasgow, is a good man—but he is not experienced or very able at statecraft. Nor is David Paniter, your secretary. Nor, I swear, is Finnart, however able a fighter! Beaton is the man you require. Fetch him back, Sire."

"I do not know where he is."

"I do—or, leastwise, I know how to reach him! But, James, he will not come, I think, unless he is assured of his safety. Assured that Finnart will not prevail on Your Grace against him again. If I have your royal word on that, I will do all I can on this of the Italian. And all else."

James looked at the other from under lowered brows. "You seek to bargain with me, the King, Davie Lindsay?"

"Yes, Sire, for your own good. And your realm's." That was brief.

James nodded, laughing suddenly. "Och, Davie—you are the honestest man I know, I do declare! However prickly! Very well, it shall be as you say. Bring Beaton back—he will be safe enough. And do your best for me with that nuncio. If my mother gets her claws in him, God knows what will be the end of it!"

"I thank Your Grace. You will not regret this, I promise you. Now, with your permission, I will retire. I have ridden far this day and am weary."

"Aye, Davie—off with you. I am relying on you, mind."

Next morning, David found it none so easy to play the part allotted to him, for the papal nuncio elected to ride beside Margaret Tudor, and even the Lord Lyon King-of-Arms could hardly attach himself to that pair unasked. They rode due northwards, over the high ground, out of Strathearn and into Glen Almond, David close enough behind the Queen-Mother to hear Campeggio rhapsodising over the prospect of the heather-clad mountains opening so splendidly directly ahead, his companion sounding supremely uninterested. It was this situation which presently gave David his opportunity, for, entering the quite dramatic jaws of the true Highland Line, at a dog's-leg bend of the upper valley, known locally as Glen Beg or the small glen, he spurred up alongside the envoy, to point.

"Excellency—your first Highlandman in his native heather!" he exclaimed. Up on a shelf of the otherwise steep hillside, amongst the outcropping rocks and boulders, was a single low-browed hovel, seeming to grow out of the broken ground, and beside it a man standing, watching the cavalcade pass below. Scattered around nearby were small shaggy black cattle. Even at that range the watcher could be seen to be wearing some reddish tartan and a flat bonnet. "You would look, inspect?"

"Yes, yes, Sir David. Assuredly."

The Italian followed his guide eagerly as David picked a way for the horses up that harsh incline, uncaring for Margaret's frowning. Cattle careered away, then stopped to stare. None followed the pair up.

The Highland herdsman stood his ground. As they drew near he could be seen to be a middle-aged man, distinctly fierce of appearance, with down-turning moustaches and an untidy forked beard, clad in a stained and ragged short kilt with a tartan plaid above slung across one shoulder, but otherwise bare of torso. On his feet were a pair of rawhide brogans. When they came up, he bowed strangely courteous and despite his villainous looks gave them a smile. He said something in the Gaelic.

"Good day to you," David greeted. "We are travelling

to Atholl. My friend, from Rome, would speak with a Highlandman."

The other spread a hand apologetically and spoke more Gaelic.

"I fear that he speaks only his own language," David said to Campeggio. "I have none of the Gaelic. You, Excellency, have no knowledge of this tongue you spoke of? The Galatians' was it?"

"Alas, no. Is he not a splendid savage?"

"I would scarce call him savage. He has his own manners, I think."

"The coloured clothings, they are different. The skirt, from the above. Different colours. Most manifest."

"Tartans, yes. There are many forms, designs, I am told. Perhaps with some meaning—I know not."

It was a little uncomfortable just to sit staring at the herdsman, without being able to communicate—at least for David, although the man himself did not appear to be in any way put out, nor the bishop indeed. Then the latter pointed.

"See—a woman! The house, let us see the house. So small, so miserable. Come."

Still more uncomfortable, David thought to suggest that this would be unmannerly on their part, but the nuncio dismounted and hurried forward towards the hovel. Two wide-eyed, all-but-naked children now shared the doorway with the woman.

Looking almost apologetically at the Highlander, David got down also. Gravely the other man inclined his head, and they followed the Legate.

The woman also wore a tartan plaid or shawl, evidently over some sort of brief bodice, and a skirt not a kilt, although shorter than the Lowland fashion, of homespun wool dyed a rich red-brown. She looked from the visitors to her man and smiled nervously. Behind her and the children, oddly, a cow stared out.

Exclaiming, Campeggio pointed and waved his hands about, in a flood of presumably Italian eloquence. Incomprehensible as that was, it was evident that he desired to enter the house, which was built of drystone masonry from the hillside up to about shoulder-height and thereafter thatched with turf, in rounded conformation without gables. Blue smoke curled up lazily from what must have been a hole in the roof, for there was no chimney.

The herdsman, still co-operative, signed to the woman and children, who retired inside, and waved the visitors within, as though it had been something of a palace. That left the cow still looking out interestedly—although it now became evident that there was a partition of about shoulder-height again, just within the doorway, dividing the premises into two, with the beast occupying the lower and smaller portion. Much intrigued, the bishop was gesticulating about this when he was rudely interrupted by some squawking poultry which came flapping out of the dark interior past him, to his sudden alarm.

"This will be a milk-cow for the family," David sought to explain. "I have heard of this—it is done in the rest of Scotland also—beasts and folk under the same roof. But always on the lower side, so that the, the glaur drains out. It helps to keep them warm in winter, I suppose."

Pushing past the cow, the Highlander ushered them into the upper three-quarters of the hovel, the visitors catching their breaths, indeed Campeggio starting to cough chokingly. It was partly the smell of cow and peat-reek and other things, but largely the actual smoke which seemed to serve for atmosphere instead of air.

Blinking and gasping, they peered about them. At first they could see little or nothing, for all seemed black within, save for a red glow in the centre of the floor from which came the smoke—for there were no windows in this building and any light came feebly from the hole in the roof and from the doorway, which of course was still partly blocked by the cow and which the visitors' own persons tended to obscure further.

Loud in his astonishment, Campeggio blundered about. It took some time for their eyes to adjust in some measure to the lack of light. When David's did, it was to perceive that the herdsman was holding out to him a wooden two-handled cup of flat design. Surprised, he accepted this, with thanks. The woman proved to have another, for the envoy, who at first did not recognise what it was and in fact spilled some of the contents on the earthen floor.

"Hospitality," David said, sniffing at it. "The drink of the Highlands. Not wine—whisky. Their water-of-life. Have a care, for it is a strong brew."

Their host had now filled a cup for himself from a dark leathern bottle, and raising it towards them said something no doubt complimentary. He thereupon tossed off the shallow cupful in a single gulp. David nodded, but sipped his carefully. However, the Italian, despite the warning, took a good mouthful—and promptly choked again, spluttering and gasping, as the fiery liquid burned his throat, spilling the rest in the process. Panting, he turned and hurried for the doorway, and out.

David, concerned over manners to match those of their host, finished his own drink, smacked his lips appreciatively, and handed the cup back with a bow. He could see better now, and noted the stark simplicity of the furnishings, if such they could be called, the benches and chests, the cooking-pots around the central fireplace, the boxed-in beds against the stone walling, all blackened with the prevailing peat-smoke. Feeling rather foolish, he bowed again and followed the bishop out.

That individual, still holding his wooden cup, met him with a flood of Mediterranean eloquence, much affected by his experiences. When the herdsman emerged, he thrust the cup back at him, and, delving into an inner pocket, produced a silver piece which he held out to the Highlander.

That man actually drew back a little, looking uncomfortable for the first time. But, the prelate insisting on presenting the coin, he took it, turned it over as though examining it interestedly and then, bowing in turn, handed it to David.

Lindsay cleared his throat. "Time that we rejoined His Grace, perhaps," he suggested, and gestured towards the horses.

Their leave-taking of the cottagers was all smiles and incoherence. When they were mounted, David handed the coin back to Campeggio. "Money they do not accept." He thought that was the best way of putting it. "A sort of pride. Forby, they would have little use for it, I think."

As they rode back downhill, the prelate was full of it all, the strangeness, the behaviour, the darkness of the hovel, the fierce liquor, the cow and poultry. Words, in English or Scots, failed him.

Back at the drove-road, they found that the cavalcade had moved on but that James had left a small escort to wait for them. David now had the opportunity he sought.

"You have travelled much in strange lands, Excellency?" he asked, as they rode on northwards.

"Much," the other agreed. "But in none so strange as this."

"Do not all lands have their own strangenesses? I am recently back from the Netherlands and France, and saw much that surprised me."

"Ah, so. France I have visited. The Netherlands, no."

"I went on King James's behalf. To conclude a treaty with the Emperor Charles, and the Regent, Margaret of Hungary. Have you met the Emperor, Excellency? Or the Queen?"

"No. I have heard that he is . . . difficult? A man much troubled in the spirit, no?"

"As to that, I do not know. But he was sufficiently gracious towards us. But then, his aunt, Queen Margaret, assured us that he thought highly of King James and the Scots nation. That may have aided us."

"Ah."

"Yes. He was eager to sign the treaty. Indeed he signed it before we ever discussed all the terms. The Queen did the bargaining, or any there was. It seems that he sees Scotland as necessary, as having its importance in his struggle against the Grand Turk, the Infidel."

"So? How could that be? This far land?"

"The Emperor fears Henry of England. Henry is like any wild bull, cunning, deceitful, unpredictable—but ever ready to take advantage of weakness anywhere, for his own gain. Does the Holy See not recognise that also?"

The other did not commit himself.

"If the Emperor marshals much of the strength of Christendom against Sulieman, as he *is* doing, and marches on Austria, then the northern parts of the Empire will inevitably be weakened for a time—and Henry might well strike. France at present is scarcely friendly towards the Empire, nor towards Rome, you will agree? So King Francis cannot be relied upon to counter any English move across the Channel. But Scotland, now—Scotland can!"

"You say that Scotland will attack England if Henry attacks the Empire?"

"That is King James's policy, yes."

"I understood, Sir David, that so it was the policy towards *France*, not the Empire? As the King's father proved, did he not, at the price of his life? The ancient alliance?"

"Yes, but not only France. The treaty with the Netherlands is a renewal of one ancient also, of mutual help against England. It has stood for one hundred years."

"Henry of England could be . . . bought, perhaps?"

"By offering him *spiritual* overlordship of Scotland? The Pope reducing St. Andrews from a metropolitan see and putting in under York? It would not serve, not in any way."

"You are so sure, yes?"

"Yes. Oh, Henry would accept it and gladly. But it would not change his course by a hand's-breadth. And *Scotland* would not accept it. You might force King James into the very evil from which you would restrain King Henry—breaking spiritual allegiance to Rome."

"That is *your* belief in this, Sir David. Others may believe differently, no?"

"Not mine only, Excellency. The Queen of Hungary so believes—and therefore the Emperor, whom she much advises. Also Abbot Beaton of Arbroath, Scotland's Privy Seal."

"Ah, the good Abbot David! Where is he? I had looked to see him. His Holiness sent him a message. But he is not to be discovered. I am told that he is in disfavour, no? The Archbishop, his uncle, likewise . . ."

"That is past. A misunderstanding, just. All is well again . . ."

"Yet the good Abbot, whom we all so greatly admire, is not here with your King."

"He *will* be here, Excellency. He is at present up in his own abbatical lands. But he is recalled to court. The King told me so, only last night."

"So? And he, Beaton, will again advise your King on his policies? His Holiness has much faith in the Abbot's wisdom."

"To be sure. King James also recognises the value of his advice. And is apt to act upon it."

"That is well. In Rome they will be much pleased to hear this."

They were in sight of the rear of the main party now, strung out in file as they lifted out of the glen to cross the high pass to Amulree at the mouth of Glen Quaich. David felt that he had done as much as he could for his liege-lord, and hoped that he had not perjured himself in the process.

At Amulree, amongst high moors of heather, ringed by mountains, the company swung off east by north down Strathbraan, to reach the Tay at Dunkeld, passing the striking Falls of Braan, where that river fell over three hundred feet in a mile—to the applause of the papal nuncio. Dunkeld, amongst its steep wooded ridges, was the ancient seat of the Celtic mormaordom of Atholl, the holders of which were hereditary Primates of the Columban Church—hence the name, the fort of the Keledei, or Friends of God. It was still a possession of the Earls of Atholl, although now they had their main seat at Blair, some twenty miles to the north. The Earl John Stewart had sent a large party of his clansmen to meet them here; but it was decided that a halt should be made for the night, for the Queen-Mother's and her ladies' sake, if not the nuncio's. There was a Romish abbey and cathedral here, successor of the Celtic one, and in it the travellers could put up in comfort. It was not stressed that, until a few days previously, the absent bishop thereof had been one of Archbishop Beaton's fellow-prisoners in Blackness Castle.

James was glad to hear David's report of his session with Campeggio, and agreed that in the circumstances it would be politic to send for Davie Beaton, if possible to join them forthwith at Blair-in-Atholl, a royal messenger to ride at once. Lindsay felt, however, that Beaton might well be wary of such summons, fearing a trap, and declared that it would be best if he himself were to go, to reassure his friend. He calculated that it would be about fifty miles to Ethie, certainly over some difficult country, and finding Beaton at the other end might take time. For how long did His Grace intend to remain in Atholl? Three days? Four? He hoped that they could return by that time.

So, instead of settling down for the night in the comfort of the Abbey, David, with two of the royal guard as escort, set off eastwards there and then—for it was only late afternoon and he could get in many miles before darkness. They rode hard, now, up out of Strathtay, over more high forested ground and into a long and very strange wooded valley containing a remarkable succession of lochs. Oddly enough, considering that their ultimate destination was the Angus river called Lunan, bringing them to Lunan Bay, this present twisting high-set glen was the valley of another Lunan Water, mile upon mile of it threading the hills of East Atholl and the Stormounth and enfolding the series of lochs into which the river kept widening—Craiglush, Lowes, Butterstone, Clunie, Drumellie, Rae, Fingask and Stormounth, this last in the mouth of the great vale of

Strathmore, into Angus. The horsemen did not get all that way that evening, but reached an upland grange of the Abbey of Coupar-Angus, on the shore of Loch Drumellie, where they passed the night.

Down Strathmore next day they passed Coupar Abbey itself and on to the town of Forfar, capital of Angus, where they swung off eastwards again to follow the second Lunan Water, by Restenneth and Rescobie and Guthrie, towards the sea. By mid-afternoon they had covered another thirty miles, to Ethie.

That Marion Ogilvy was surprised to see Lindsay back so soon went without saying, but she made him entirely welcome, even though she had mixed feelings about this summons for Davie back to court—for however much *he* might desire it, undoubtedly she would see a deal less of him than she had been doing lately. He had indeed been at Ethie Castle the previous night and she expected him back that evening.

Weary with hard riding, David was in fact in his bed when, late that night a knock at his door announced the Lord Privy Seal, clad, as before, like a fisherman. Davie at least had no doubts about the situation, once he had Lindsay's assurance that no trickery would be involved. The Bastard might prove dangerous, admittedly—but then he was always that; so long as James himself remained trustworthy, Davie thought that he could cope with Hamilton. He was grateful to his friend for achieving this recall. He had heard about the Papal Legate's visit and had been wondering how to contrive some secret meeting.

In the morning, then, two of Scotland's great officers of state left that cliff-top hold and a resigned woman and children, Beaton now transformed, in fine clothing, hair and beard trimmed, a glittering figure. They proposed to reach Blair-in-Atholl by nightfall, if their escort could keep up with them.

Tired indeed, and mounts all but foundered, in the event they came to the wide strath of the Garry, in which lay Blair, not by darkening but soon after—and for the last miles the sky was lit up for them adequately enough by such a blaze of fire ahead as to make the illumination at Methven a few nights previously appear as no more than candlelight. As they rode near enough to look down into the valley, it was to see that this was not caused merely by cooking-fires but came from hundreds of flaming pitch-pine torches set in long rows along the level lands where the River Tilt met the Garry. Never had they seen the like, as though a city had sprung up there in a Highland strath.

Down on the low ground the impression was less of a city than of the camp of a great army, but one where feasting, sport and jollity were the order of the day, or night, not warfare. Hundreds, probably thousands, of Highlanders swarmed everywhere, in the light of the torches and fires, singing and dancing to the music of fiddles and pipes, playing games of muscular prowess, dragging vast quantities of timber for the fires, eating and drinking. No tents were here however; presumably the clansmen despised such, sleeping in their plaids whatever the weather.

Further on they did come to a tented encampment, but this was obviously that of the royal company. Yet, riding through it, the newcomers saw no sign of the King nor his close entourage and important companions. They were looking, of course, for Blair Castle itself as destination, and were presently surprised to discover, amongst all the flaring torchlight, two castles, some little way apart, one huge, one only moderate in size, both blazing with lights. The sound of more music emanated from the larger. To this they headed.

Their surprise grew to astonishment when, drawing close, they perceived that the greater building was in fact not a castle at all; or, at least, it was a sham castle constructed wholly of timber, and green timber at that, still with the foliage attached, Scots pine and birch and rowan, in an amazing flourish. Yet it had great round towers at each end and a pair of typical drum-towers in the centre, flanking the doorway, which was guarded by the usual gatehouse and drawbridge, even its portcullis being constructed of new birchwood. The windows were glass-filled, some of colourful stained glass, and above all a row of flags flapped on poles, lit up by their own torches, mainly Stewart banners naturally but topped by a huge Lion Rampant standard.

The two Davids stared at all this in wonder, even Beaton at a loss for words.

Over the drawbridge and inside, they found themselves walking on a floor of clipped grass, the turfs fitted together closely but patterned with designs and strewn with flowers and sweet-smelling bog-myrtle. This vestibule, arched with greenery, led into a vast hall, where Highland dancing was in progress before the feasting company, with a score of kilted fiddlers playing in lively unison, a scene of extraordinary vigour, spirit and colour.

The newcomers made their way towards the dais-table, where sat the Queen-Mother, the papal nuncio, a middle-aged man in full Highland costume, John Stewart, Earl of Atholl, and sundry others. The King was not there, but a quick survey revealed him to be dancing with a dark, bold-eyed and notably low-gowned young woman, both with considerable vivacity. With his red-haired good looks, they made a striking couple. The Bastard of Arran could be seen similarly engaged nearby.

Since they must pay their respects first to the monarch, the visitors waited apart, although Bishop Campeggio waved to them. When that dance ended, James, who had evidently noticed them, came over, still holding the lady close, her prominent and delectable bosom heaving tumultuously with her exertions.

"Ha, Davie Lindsay—you have found our errant Privy Seal, I see, and brought him back to the fold!" he exclaimed. "Welcome, my lord Abbot!"

"Thank you, Sire. I was never far from Your Grace in spirit," Beaton returned, bowing. "Only I fear my so craven spirit shrank from lodgings in Blackness Castle! So . . . draughty!"

"H'rr'mm." James cleared his throat. "You know Libby Stewart?"

"I have the honour, Sire. Lady Elizabeth—your servant."

They moved up to the dais, where Atholl, who knew them both of course, offered them greeting and refreshment after their long riding. Margaret Tudor ignored them but the Legate was all but effusive in his reception of Beaton, making room for him to sit beside him, where they conversed volubly in Italian, in which Davie appeared to be fluent. Lindsay went and found a more lowly seat.

There, presently, the Bastard came to him, in passing. "So you brought our clever friend back from wherever he has been hiding," he commented. "Clever clerks are very well, in their place—but must not be allowed to get above themselves! I am sure that you will agree."

"Where do you consider that place to be, Sir James?" David asked. "After all, a long line of clerks, clever or otherwise, have governed this realm, as chancellors for the King. As at this present."

"Ah, but this Dunbar is not *too* clever, God be praised! Which makes all the difference. Your friend should note it."

"Is this some sort of a warning, Hamilton?"

"Warning? No, no—just my humble advice. Why should I warn Davie Beaton?"

"That I wondered!"

"He and our Italian visitor appear to be mighty close."

"Perhaps we may all have reason to be thankful for that!"

"You think so? I wonder."

"His Grace does not. Hence, surely, all this!" And he gestured at all their extraordinary surroundings.

"Ah, this play-acting and mummery? This is done for various reasons, not all to impress our papal friend. Admittedly, Atholl was stung when he heard that the Italian had described the Highlands as the arse-end of Christendom, and would show him otherwise. But there is more to it than that. James is concerned to use the clan chiefs to reduce the power of the Lowland lords who plague his peace. These despise the Highlanders. This display is to let them see that there is more in the Highlands than mere hordes of savage caterans. Few Lowland earls could contrive this spectacle and flourish. Save, perhaps, my brother Arran!"

"I see. But why should *Atholl* go to such expense? This must be costing him dear, indeed."

Finnart nodded towards where James sat with the young woman. "There is your answer, man. Atholl would have our James *wed* his daughter Libby, as well as bed her! This is all to aid in his project to be the King's good-sire! It will not serve, of course—but he hopes that it may!"

"You sound very sure."

"Why, yes," the other said easily, and moved on.

David sought a bed soon thereafter, finding a room allotted to him in the true Blair Castle nearby. He left Beaton still in deep converse with the nuncio. James had disappeared. So had the Lady Elizabeth Stewart.

Next day was devoted to hunting. Not the horsed chase, as practised in the south, nor yet individual stalking of beasts, but a very different kind of venery known as a deer-drive—although more than deer were apt to be involved. This was more like warfare than sport, with the hunters setting elaborate ambushes and hiding behind elaborate grass-grown ramparts specially designed for the purpose. A complicated pattern of these deer-dykes was established up on the rising ground of the hillsides a mile or two from the castle, laid out geometrically in long lines and re-entrants, so that driven deer were funnelled into strategically-placed gaps, behind which the hunters were hidden with their bows and arrows and javelins. From before sun-up great numbers of men had been out in the surrounding mountains, not exactly rounding up the herds but causing them to drift uneasily in the desired direction. This was an expert business, much more finesse being required of the deer-movers than of the killers themselves, for although the hills were full of vast herds, thousands Atholl assured, they could so easily break away in alarm and disappear into the endless mountain wilderness. To get them to move gently towards the deer-dykes area and then, at the last moment to drive them in through the gaps to the waiting hunters, was an art, the more difficult in that it had to be done in carefully-timed stages so that most of the animals did not go hurtling through in one mad stampede but in spaced-out batches, to allow maximum slaughter. If it was scarcely a sporting proposition, such as stalking or even the chase, it was certainly a most effective way of amassing large amounts of venison.

With many hunters to be accommodated, more than one of the dyke complexes were manned, and David Lindsay was sent to a different one, higher up the hillside than that appointed for the King and his principal guests. Nevertheless he had more than sufficient activity, indeed grew sickened by the killing long before the day was over. The deer came drifting across the mountainsides in their hundreds, but spread out, singly and in groups, urged on by men and dogs who now allowed themselves to be seen. But when the creatures reached the barriers of the dykes, they had to turn up or down them, and so began to bunch. By the time that they reached one of the carefully-sited gaps they were packed in dense racing columns, jostling and stumbling in panic, utterly unlike their usual graceful bounding gait. Thus they streamed past the waiting marksmen, who shot their arrows and threw their javelins into the red-brown mass, and could scarcely fail to hit, so solid a target did they present, the only problem being the restringing of arrows and replacing of javelins sufficiently fast. Needless to say most beasts were not killed outright in this battue, and had to be despatched later.

The heaps of the slain mounted as fresh herds were driven in. Roe, blue hares, even foxes also got caught up in the stampede, providing more difficult marks.

When David had had more than enough, he moved over to join the beaters and, in fact, found their demanding activity more to his taste.

When all was over, the triumphant young monarch declared that they had slain a grand total of six hundred harts and hinds, apart from lesser creatures. Had that ever been surpassed?

That evening Atholl had a new wonder for his guests, fountains contrived in the turf spouting different wines, muscatel, hippocras and alicant—this in addition to the previous provision of claret, malmsey and whisky available to wash down the banquet of moorfowl, capercailzie, blackcock, swan, heron, even peacock, which supplemented the venison, beef, lamb and salmon.

For their final day's entertainment, they were taken hunting in different style, down amongst the flooded water-meadows and marshy scrub and woodlands of the strath floor and lower slopes, this done on horseback, more like Lowland sport. This dissimilarity was in the quarry, for although there were deer here also, heavy woodland beasts with great spreading antlers, there were also wolves, wild boar, badgers, even wildcats. The bag, needless to say, was infinitely smaller but the challenge much greater. The Bastard distinguished himself by notching up the highest score.

The royal party left Blair the following morning—and even then the Earl of Atholl had something spectacular to show them. For as they formed up to mount, taking their farewells, he ordered his gillies to light more torches and go into that great greenwood palace and set all on fire, furnishings, bedding, hangings, unconsumed provisions and wines, everything, the structure itself included. When, all but appalled, the nuncio demanded why, why, Atholl told him that it was so that quarters which had sheltered the King's Grace, his lady mother and the Papal Legate should never be profaned by less illustrious lodgers. Besides, it was an old Highland custom to burn temporary overnight accommodation behind them when the clans moved on. He said this with a grin—and not all his hearers perceived the allusion to that other Highland custom of feuding, and destroying their neighbours' property after a raid.

So the visitors rode away southwards from Blair-in-Atholl, for Methven and Stirling again, leaving behind them a great brown pillar of smoke rising high above the mountains, from their late luxurious lodging. Atholl and his daughter accompanied them, the Earl to turn back at the limits of his own territory beyond Dunkeld, the Lady Elizabeth to remain with the King. On Lindsay's suggestion they were escorted also by a large company of running-gillies, and Antonio Campeggio was just as impressed by these as had been the Emperor Charles and the Netherlanders.

Davie Beaton confided in his friend, as they rode, that Atholl had admitted having spent the almost unbelievable sum of three thousands of pounds on this three-day royal entertainment.

17

The months that followed, the winter of 1531 and the spring of 1532, although superficially an unusually quiet and uneventful period in the troubled reign of the fifth James Stewart, were in fact anything but, just below the surface, at least for those in the know, especially those at court. For an intense struggle, a battle indeed, was going on, for the will and guidance, if not the mind and soul, of the said James, a war none the less sustained, unrelenting, for being undeclared. The protagonists were Sir James Hamilton of Finnart on the one hand and the two Davids, Beaton and Lindsay, on the other. It would be difficult to say who gained most success in this tug-of-war; certainly neither could claim to win, for James, although weak in certain aspects of his character, was anything but in others, and went his own way most of the time. But, on balance, probably the Davids achieved most. Undoubtedly the Bastard lost some ground previously held—and fought the harder and more unscrupulously in consequence. And Hamilton was a fighter, whatever else.

Beaton and Lindsay held certain advantages, to be sure. The former, as Lord Privy Seal, was in a position to influence much in the sphere of government, especially with a lack-lustre although honest Chancellor; and as effective ruler of Holy Church with its great power and revenues, his uncle becoming ever more of a cipher. And Lindsay, for his part, had the effect of years of boyhood guidance on James, a reliance on him as mentor and friend never entirely outgrown. Moreover, strangely, his poetic abilities had quite a major impact on the young monarch. James had always admired David's writings, indeed envied them, for he himself sought to emulate David and compose verse. The court diversion known as flyting gave scope for this. The King's father had been a great flyter, and young James revelled in it. Flytings were exchanges of abuse in rhyme, humorous and usually ribald, often quite provocative, and James's own were the most outspoken and derogatory, as they could afford to be—although he by no means resented quite blatant attacks on himself, unthinkable on any other occasion. Most of these efforts were in fairly crude doggerel, to be sure; but David Lindsay's were apt to be of notable quality and effectiveness, and the King's own frequently far from feeble. In the long winter evenings, as the winds off the Highland mountains howled round Stirling Castle's lofty walls, flyting was a popular entertainment in torch- and firelight and over brimming beakers of wine and ale—when James was not otherwise engaged.

The King did not often single out Lindsay as the target for his wit, but on one occasion he did launch a fleering volley at his Lyon's unlionlike attitudes towards drinking, gaming, tourney-fighting and even hurly-hackit, accusing him of being a dullard in sport and a laggard in love. David did not reply in more than a few words there and then, but took the opportunity to turn the occasion to good use by composing quite a major poem as response, which in due course he read out at another flyting and then presented the written offering to his liege-lord. Simply entitling it *An Answer to the King's Flyting* he was forthright in his criticism of James's immoralities and extravagances. And he stressed the need for settling down, a satisfactory and virtuous marriage, in the interests of the succession to the throne, a vital matter for the realm's peace and weal. The younger man took this very well, all things considered. It probably had more effect on him than other more normal advice and counsel.

David also composed, at this time, another piece, *The Complaint of Bagsche*. Bagsche was the King's old hound and the poem took the form of its discussion with the current favourite dog Bawtie as to the follies of the court, a satire on the behaviour of courtiers, and incidentally the monarch himself. This earned him few friends, although it much tickled the King.

David's attempts to influence his sovereign's life-style were not confined to the poetic. For instance, on an occasion when Janet, as Wardrobe Mistress, informed him that a new master tailor was to be appointed, Lindsay, before all the King's entourage, personally applied for the position. To the monarch's astonished reaction that surely *he* knew nothing about tailoring, and laughingly doubting whether he could shape or sew, David retorted that, as he had served his liege-lord long, he looked to be rewarded as others were. That he could neither shape nor sew was of no matter, for had not His Grace given even bishoprics and benefices to many standing there amongst them who could neither teach nor preach, and other offices to those with no qualifications? Why not to himself as master tailor? James was amused, if others were less so.

The Bastard of Arran sought to counter all this by encouraging the King in ever wilder extravagances of behaviour and expenditure, catering assiduously to James's weaknesses, predilections and indiscretions, and surrounding him with as raffish a crew of courtiers, male and female, as was to be found anywhere in Christendom, Beaton asserted. Davie asserted too that Hamilton did this not only to maintain his influence over the younger man but in the hope that one or other of the many and repeated excesses might result in the death of James, since his own half-brother would then be eligible for the throne. This was no far-fetched improbability, for the King took enormous risks, in the hunting field, in sports and jousting at hurly-hackit, and especially in his night-time exploits as Gudeman of Ballengeich. Night after night he used to ride out, alone, from Stirling or Falkland, Dunfermline, Linlithgow or Edinburgh, seeking his most favoured sport, the company and attentions of strange women, seeking them in the streets of towns, in alehouses and brothels, in lonely farmsteads and cottages equally with castles and towers, insatiable. The dangers were self-evident, to his person, his health and his pocket, from angry husbands and fathers, robbers and disease. The Earl of Angus's early indoctrinations were producing a bountiful harvest. How many bastards the royal adventurer produced likewise was anybody's guess. As excuse for these nocturnal excursions James claimed that he was concerned to discover at first hand and anonymously how his subjects lived and fared, for their better governance.

These risks were well exemplified by the occasion when, riding out alone after a Privy Council meeting at Holyrood Abbey, in Edinburgh, James found his satisfaction at a low alehouse at Cramond Brig, some six miles from the city, near where the River Almond reached the Firth of Forth. Afterwards, starting off on his return to Edinburgh, he was set upon by a band of ruffians, who no doubt thought the young man a pigeon worth plucking, was dragged from his horse and belaboured with cudgels. Although able to give a fairly good account of himself, he was hopelessly outnumbered and might well have ended his reign there and then had not a stalwart countryman named Jock Howieson heard the rumpus and come to his aid. Together they fought the robbers to a standstill, then to flight. Howieson took the battered monarch to his mill-cottage, bathed and bound up his cuts and bruises and provided rough refreshment. The grateful James, ever open-handed to a fault, revealed his identity and promised his rescuer the freehold of the lands on which the assault had taken place, on condition that the new laird and his descendants should always offer the King and his successors a basin of water and a napkin, and some small hospitality, if they passed that way—a custom which was in fact to be kept up for centuries to come.

But some incidents, however romantic-sounding, were a grievous worry to the King's responsible advisers and made them redouble their efforts to bring James to a greater sense of his duties and position. Marriage, in especial, was considered ever more advisable, not only to keep him home of a night and provide an heir to the throne but to help fill the royal coffers, emptied by the years of mismanagement, hungry nobles and general extravagance. So a royal bride with a rich dowry was called for—this effectively ruling out almost all James's acknowledged Scots mistresses, such as the Elizabeths Erskine, Stewart and Beaton.

This was very much Davie Beaton's problem, for the King himself was less than interested. Davie knew all the royal houses of Christendom and approximately their state of wealth and the advantages or otherwise of their alliance with Scotland. There was no lack of possibilities. By the treaty of Rouen, of course, the daughter of King Francis of France had been named as possible bride for James at some future date; but the Princess Madeleine was very delicate and probably not a practical proposition. However, Francis found three alternative names, all rich and notably high-born Frenchwomen—Marie de Bourbon, daughter of the Duc de Vendôme; Marie de Guise, daughter of the Duc de Guise; and Isabeau D'Albret, daughter of the King of Navarre. Not to be outdone, the Emperor Charles put forward his niece Mary of Hungary, like his Aunt Margaret now widowed; but she was considerably older than James, although she had proved her fertility at least. Then the King of Spain suggested Princess Mary of Portugal, while the deposed King Christian of Denmark offered either of his daughters Christina or Dorothea, plus the only firm cash commitment, ten thousand gold crowns—this in return for the promise of Scots aid to recover his crown from the usurping Frederick. There was still another possibility, the wealthiest of all, the Florentine Catherine de Medici, daughter of the Duke of Urbino, ward of Pope Clement and niece of the Duke of Albany, Scotland's recent Regent. All this galaxy of riches and influence, if not necessarily pulchritude, Davie Beaton debated, weighed up and prepared to juggle with. He would have gone prospecting Europe in person, however unenthusiastic his liege-lord, but recognised that it would be dangerous to leave Scotland for any such prolonged tour at this juncture. He prevailed on James to send Sir Thomas Erskine of Haltoun as roving ambassador when David Lindsay declined the task.

Nobody in Scotland, save perhaps Margaret Tudor, so much as considered Henry of England's daughter Mary as bride for the King of Scots, although that objectionable monarch was more or less demanding it as the price of an end to his attacks on the northern kingdom.

All this marital odyssey had unexpected results and odd repercussions. The reformation agitation in Holy Church was boiling up on the Continent and the princes of Christendom becoming involved on one side or the other. Scotland, from being a small and comparatively unimportant realm on the outskirts of Europe became quite suddenly of some moment as an ally, particularly on the pro-Romish side, especially with Henry Tudor ever more at odds with the Vatican, not so much on religious grounds as at the refusal of the Pope to grant him a divorce from his Queen Catherine of Aragon. The Pope, now, instead of excommunicating James, authorised, indeed commanded the Church of Scotland to pay his treasury large sums of money, for so long as he remained faithful to Rome, the sum of ten thousand pounds annually plus one tenth of the revenues of all benefices for three years—a generosity which even Davie Beaton, and certainly his uncle, considered to be excessive. The Emperor sent James the much-prized Order of the Golden Fleece, never before awarded to a King of Scots. And not to be outdone, Francis of France conferred on him the Order of St. Michael.

All this, of course, much gratified James Stewart, especially the financial relief—for he had been reduced actually to borrowing three thousand merks from the Earl of Huntly. But Beaton, rather ruefully in this instance, finding himself or the Church, which he seemed to look upon as more or less the same thing, the victim of his own cleverness, sought to rescue something from the Pope's devious generosity with other folk's money by instituting a much needed reform in the sphere of government, a project which he and a clerical friend, Alexander Mylne, Abbot of Cambuskenneth, had long discussed—this before James might squander all the ecclesiastical windfall in riotous living. The project was the setting up of a permanent court of justice, other than the judgements of parliament, the *ad hoc* courts of the Lord Justice General, the lordly sheriffdoms and the barons' powers of pit-and-gallows, all, as it were, amateur and casual. Abbot Alexander had studied in Pavia and had been greatly impressed by the standards of justice meted out by a court established there with permanent members qualified in law and paid annual salaries to make informed and equitable judgements. None could deny that such was overdue in Scotland and this seemed an ideal opportunity. So the two churchmen devised a scheme and prevailed on James and his Privy Council, in the first flush of enthusiasm over the unexpected largesse, to endorse it. A college of justice would be established, to be called the Court of Session, in that it would sit permanently as distinct from casually, with fifteen members. And to ensure that Holy Church had major control over this, and clerics gained a suitable proportion of the cash involved—since it was Church money that paid for it—it was stipulated that seven of the members should always be churchmen, plus a clerical president—the first president to be Alexander Mylne himself. This excellent development, to become so much part of Scotland's scene, was an unforeseen bonus to come out of the King's tentative marriage enquiries.

Strangely enough, and sadly as far as David Lindsay was concerned, and the King himself to a lesser extent, one of the first cases to come before the new Lords of Session referred to another Abbot, none other than David's old friend and colleague, James's assistant tutor, Abbot John Inglis of Culross. When the monarch outgrew tutoring, Inglis had reverted to his abbatical duties in Fife and Fothriff, but he and David had kept in touch. Unfortunately he had become involved in a dispute over certain lands held by his Abbey in which Sir John Blackadder of Tulliallan claimed interest. The Abbot granted a tack or lease of these lands to the Lord Erskine, and the fiery Blackadder was sufficiently incensed actually to waylay Inglis at the Loanhead of Rosyth in Fothriff, and slay him—not so unusual an event perhaps in baronial circles, but notable in that the victim was an abbot. A warrant for the arrest of the Baron of Tulliallan was duly made out but the matter became complicated by the accused fleeing to take refuge in the sanctuary at Torphichen, in West Lothian. This ancient Girth, or traditional place of sanctuary for fugitives and wrong-doers, was an area around the Preceptory of the Knights Hospitaller of St. John of Jerusalem, marked out by girth-crosses, part of an ages-old privilege of that chivalric order, by this time little used. Nevertheless, John Blackadder claimed sanctuary there, to the embarrassment of the St. John knights and everybody else. A churchman murdered, Holy Church declared that this ancient privilege was outdated and void, and an armed party sent to Torphichen to bring the murderer to Edinburgh and justice. There however, Blackadder and his friends appealed to the King and Privy Council that he had been forcibly removed from an established sanctuary, which had never been reduced from that status. So the matter came before the new Lords of Session for decision. Cautiously at this stage, they compromised, in an awkward situation. They sent Blackadder back to Torphichen meantime under security of five thousand merks put up by his friends that he would not abscond. Then they settled down judiciously to try the double issue, first the inviolacy or otherwise of the sanctuary and secondly the murder itself—which last was more or less admitted. In due course their lordships found that the sanctuary was in fact a provision of Holy Church in the past and therefore could not be used to protect an offender against the said Church; and secondly that Blackadder was guilty of the murder of Abbot John of Culross and should be beheaded in the Grassmarket of Edinburgh in consequence.

It made a strange baptism for the new administration of justice, and a strange postscript to the life of John Inglis, who had always been a quiet and inoffensive individual. King James and his court went to witness the beheading, as indicating royal support. Sir James Hamilton absented himself, however.

An interesting by-product of this case was the unearthing of the fact that certain churchmen appeared to have been in the habit of making personal gain out of such sanctuaries, in providing criminals with protection, for reward. This discovery resulted in an act of parliament putting an end to all such miscarriages of justice.

18

All this domestic advancement and preoccupation could not last, of course, not with Henry of England's marriage offer being spurned and his burning ambition to be overlord of Scotland unabated. When he heard of Sir Thomas Erskine's bride-prospecting mission to France and the Empire, and the competition in offering James orders of chivalry, he made his own typical gesture towards his troublesome nephew—invasion. He sent the Earl of Northumberland across Tweed from Berwick, with a large army, with instructions to lay waste the lands of the Merse and Lothian, and to assist in the matter he sent also the Earl of Angus and Sir George Douglas, with the renegade Earl of Bothwell, to raise their people on the English behalf.

So it was back to normal in Scotland, after the so unaccustomed interlude, with trumpets sounding to arms again.

Unfortunately James's, or rather the Bastard's, policy of

reducing the power of the great Lowland nobles, however seemingly effective in some respects, especially in promoting Hamilton hegemony, told against the realm's needs in such sudden crisis as this. The lords' levies just failed to respond in any numbers to the call-to-arms; and producing any large host of clansmen from the Highlands and Islands took much time. So mustering to repel the invaders was slow indeed on the Burgh Muir of Edinburgh, the traditional rallying-place for warlike endeavour, and it was basically a Hamilton force of only a few thousand which presently was despatched southwards in the first instance to counter Northumberland, Angus and Bothwell, while James himself remained at Edinburgh to try to raise a large host to bring on as soon as might be. But by the same token, as well as the shortage of lords' men-at-arms, Scotland in these circumstances was notably short of commanders of any experience. The Bastard himself was probably the most able soldier available, for, whatever his failings, he was a bold and effective leader of men. Although his half-brother the new Earl of Arran in theory headed the Hamilton advance force, the Bastard was in fact in command. David Lindsay went along too, partly because of his experience of Border warfare with the late de la Bastie, partly at Davie Beaton's urging, to keep an eye on the Bastard himself, whom Beaton felt was not to be trusted in any crisis. Lindsay went with less than martial fervour in the circumstances.

Nevertheless, once they were on their way, through the western Lammermuirs by Soutra and down Lauderdale, his spirits picked up somewhat, for there was always something invigorating, enheartening, about riding at the head of a great column of cavalry. Moreover, the Bastard, in his element, could be good company when he wanted to, and he seemed to prefer David's company to that of his half-brother, whom he obviously despised.

Reaching Tweed at Leaderfoot, near Melrose, they turned eastwards, to start climbing. And almost at once, above the hills which flanked the great plain of the Merse, they saw the vast billowing clouds of smoke which soared like thunderheads to stain all the sky ahead blue-black and murky brown. To account for all that, the whole land must be ablaze. Hamilton spirits sobered. The smoke-pall extended considerably and ominously northwards.

The Bastard, perceiving sundry bands of Home moss-troopers also heading eastwards, from Cowdenknowes and Drygrange and Redpath and Brothersdene, decided to make for Home Castle, where these would be headed, in the first instance. The present Lord Home was a comparatively inoffensive character, unlike his predecessor and so many of his lairds, and had shown himself to be anxious to remain on good terms with his monarch, lest he too ended up with his head on a spike on Edinburgh's Tolbooth. Yet it looked as though he were summoning his supporters. It could be only to try to protect his lands from the invaders, of course; but in the past the Homes had all too often sided *with* the invaders, for their own gain. It would be as well to investigate.

In the early evening, topping the Smailholm ridge before the dip of the Eden valley, with all the Merse of Berwickshire then spreading before them, they drew rein almost in shock, even the tough Hamiltons appalled. It was at a credible representation of Hell that they stared, endless miles of fire and smoke as far as eye could see, the flames shooting high, but far above these the clouds streaked and glowing with scarlet and crimson. Against this terrible backcloth the walls and towers of Home Castle, on its isolated hill five miles ahead, stood out in silhouette black, stark.

Grimly they rode on.

At Home, presently, they found its agitated lord in a state of indecision, torn between his own fears and the advice of his militant supporters. Clearly his inclination was to be elsewhere and to leave his strong castle well-garrisoned enough to withstand any possible attack by the invaders, even though it looked as though these were going to leave Home alone, at least meantime, since the tide of fire and ravishment seemed to have come no nearer than a couple of miles eastwards. But some of his lairds were urging a more active programme than that, assault on the invaders; and the newcomers suspected, even though they were not so informed, others advised *joining* the English as the surest way of protecting their properties. Lord Home, in fact, appeared quite to welcome the arrival of the Hamilton force, both as added protection and as more or less taking the decision out of his hands.

All that night bands and groups of Home and other Merse residents kept arriving at the castle, as reinforcements, as refugees from the violence and as typical fishers on troubled waters prepared to pick up any advantage to themselves in a fluid and chaotic situation. It was a strong party of these last, turning up in the small hours with a considerable haul of booty taken from English raiders who had previously taken it from unspecified victims, who also brought with them a couple of Northumbrian prisoners whom they conceived to be sufficiently prosperous as to be worth ransoming, in true Border fashion. And these prisoners had been prevailed upon to talk, to the effect that this great incursion was in fact a raid rather than any major invasion, specifically ordered by the King Henry, with limited aims, these the spoiling and devastation, not the occupation, of the land, no attempt to be made on this occasion on Edinburgh, Stirling or other centres of population. The destruction of Dunglass Castle, south of Dunbar, was indeed given as the main objective—this because it was being used as the headquarters base of the Scots Chief Warden of the Marches and so had a special significance as well as being stocked with much gear, arms, ammunition, coin, horseflesh and the like, worth abstracting.

This information shed a different light on the situation, both for the Bastard's people and for Home's. For Dunglass was a Home property, their furthest north and second strongest hold, even though presently held by the crown. Although they were little concerned as to what happened to its present garrison, they had no wish to see the place destroyed. It was near Angus's great fortress of Tantallon and they suspected that this might well be another reason for making it the prime target, for the Douglases would rejoice to see it demolished, a rival strength so near. So the Homes felt impelled to do something about Dunglass.

The Bastard, and David also, saw the need to prevent the Scots Warden's base from being brought low. But still more important was the knowledge gained that this was all only a punitive raid, a short-term gesture with limited purposes. It meant that Northumberland and his host would be turning back for home before long, quite possibly before King James and his main army could be brought to bear on the situation. This, in turn, must affect any strategy of their own. Dunglass was fully twenty-five miles north of Home Castle, into Lothian, not in the Merse at all, and probably more or less the limit of the English thrust—since to go much further would be to near Edinburgh and involve major confrontation.

So next morning, with no assault on Home Castle having developed during an all but sleepless night, the Bastard announced his plans. Couriers would be sent to King James to inform him of the position and urge that he should bring on with all speed such troops as he had managed to assemble, by the shortest route to Dunglass area, that is by Haddington and the Vale of Tyne to Dunbar; whilst he and the Homes made simultaneous but separate approaches to the same area, threatening the invaders from the south-west whereas the King would come from the north-west. Between these three forces, even though they might still not equal the enemy strength, it was to be hoped that they might trap and confound Northumberland and his traitorous allies.

This seemed a sound programme in the circumstances, to all concerned, and preparations were made to move. But before the two forces separated, Hamilton informed David Lindsay that he wanted him to remain with the Homes, ostensibly to act as a sort of liaison-officer but more particularly because he did not trust them. With the Lord Lyon King-of-Arms' presence, the notoriously truculent Home lairds would be less apt to controvert the authority of their indecisive lord. David scarcely relished this employment but could hardly refuse.

It was agreed that the Hamiltons should take the more northerly approach by the Whitadder Water, into the southern skirts of the Lammermuirs, there to turn eastwards and descend on the Dunglass area of the coast by Oldhamstocks, this giving them useful hilly cover right up to the last mile or two. The Homes would advance by the twin river, the Blackadder, to cross the high ground of the Drakemire vicinity to the upper Eye Water and so threaten the English from the Colbrandspath and Pease Dean area, from the south. The conformation of the land thereabouts, with the hills coming down close to the sea, meant that inevitably the invaders would be strung out in elongated files and at their most vulnerable. David was grimly amused that it seemed that he was bound for action with the Homes at the very place where he and Antoine de la Bastie had ambushed the previous Lord Home and his people, many of them here present, all those years before.

As he rode with the Home leadership, at the head of almost

one thousand fierce mosstroopers, as wild a force as he had ever accompanied, David was interested to note that they were in fact, all the way north-eastwards, skirting just to the west of the devastated area, still smoking from yesterday's burning. The invaders appeared to have laid waste a swathe of country between five and eight miles wide, from the coast inland, proceeding northwards; but this wholesale destruction clearly had a fairly well-defined limit westwards. And it did not take him long to perceive that this limit more or less coincided with the boundaries of the major Home lands of Polwarth, Edrom, Blackadder, Wedderburn and the rest, all of whose lairds were riding here with him and their unenthusiastic lord. Obviously, then, the Homes were being deliberately spared from assault by Northumberland—and were aware of it. Why? Presumably so that the invaders' left flank would, in turn, be spared from attack. Which made David consider how genuine was this present sally, how much a mere gesture to keep the Bastard content, with no real hostilities intended? That shrewd individual had probably good reasons for his suspicions of these doubtful allies, and for leaving David himself with them as a sort of watchdog. It was all fairly typical of Borders attitudes and policies, he supposed, where national interests were quite normally subordinate to local and clan allegiances. He gathered that something of the same point-of-view was apt to prevail on the English side of the line also.

He began to doubt whether, in fact, he would see any fighting. He did not rate his chances highly of being able to persuade these Homes to war, however warlike they seemed.

They reached the Blackadder in the Kimmerghame vicinity, when a new development in the situation became apparent. This was that a mounted host, presumably enemy since the Bastard's force had ridden many miles to the west, had recently ridden this way, as evidenced by tracks and horse-droppings and hastily-abandoned farmsteads and cottages. Yet the land here was not burned nor ravaged, whereas all to the east the smoke-clouds continued to rise. Evidently therefore the invading army had divided, for some reason, and part taken this Blackadder valley. This evidently much interested the Home leadership, although none of them actually discussed the matter with David Lindsay.

A few miles further on, in the Bonkyl area, they obtained the answer to any questioning. North of Blanerne, a Lumsden place, the ground sank away to a great sump of marshland, where the Fosterland, Lintlaw and Draden Burns emptied themselves. This was the extensive swamp known as the Billiemire, covering four or five square miles. On a sort of island of firm ground in the midst, protected as by an enormous moat, rose the fortalice of Billie Castle, a remote Douglas hold belonging to Angus. David had heard of the place—indeed it was somewhere near here, in similar marshland, that his friend de la Bastie had been slain by the Homes, fifteen years before.

It was not at the Douglas castle that his present companions drew rein, to stare. At the far side of the mire, to the east, a great cavalry host could be seen to be drawn up, stationary, in ordered ranks. Even at that range, the keen-sighted could discern the prevailing colours of the many banners to be the blue-and-gold of Percy of Northumberland and the blue-and-white of Douglas.

The Homes sat their mounts, considering.

David Lindsay's mind was busy, likewise. This, of course, changed all. There could be no surprise in any force seeking to attack the Dunglass invaders from this direction. Clearly Angus, who knew the country hereabouts almost as well as any Home, had foreseen the danger and blocked off this approach, still ten or more miles from Dunglass, Colbrandspath and Pease Dean. To reach there now the Homes would have to fight and vanquish this host. Whether any similar force would be confronting the Bastard, further north, there was no knowing. But here was challenge indeed. For the enemy, first on the scene, had chosen their position with care and were strongly placed, protected in front and on one flank by all but impassable mire. Any assault on them would be difficult and costly. But, by the same token, theirs was a *defensive* position, difficult to attack from. The inference was obvious. The enemy were warning-off rather than seeking a fight. Undoubtedly they knew with whom they were dealing.

David looked at his companions. "What now?" he asked. He looked past the Lord Home to old Wedderburn, the senior of the Home lairds, and the fiercest, he who had cut off de la Bastie's head to hang at his saddle-bow and be carried to Duns Cross. Any decision made here would be apt to be his rather than his chief's.

"We wait," Wedderburn said briefly.

"Wait? For what?"

"For so long as is required, man!"

"That would be wise, yes," the Lord Home agreed relievedly.

"Wise, my lord? Is wisdom the part we are here to play, today? Are we not here rather to teach the English that it is not wise to invade and savage Scotland?"

"And how would you do that, herald?" Wedderburn demanded grimly. He pointed. "These are in a strong position. They could scarcely be stronger placed. To assail them, on this ground, we would be but throwing our lives away."

"If you assailed them from here, yes. But no need for that. Outflank them. Force them to move. You have miles of land to use. Circle to the south and east," David waved his arm right-abouts, "amongst those banks and ridges. Get behind them, between them and the Eye valley. Aye, and between them and Dunglass and their main army. Then they would *have* to move, or be trapped against this mire."

"You are bold, sir, for a pursuivant! Bold with other men's lives!" Home of Broomhouse, Wedderburn's brother said. "Why should good men die when by sitting here we can gain all that is required?"

"That from a Home! On Home ground!"

"See you, Lindsay," Wedderburn jerked. "We know what we are at, if you do not. We are here to support the Bastard Hamilton, and so King Jamie, are we not? By waiting here, we do just that. We keep that large company yonder of no use to their main host just as surely as if we fought them. More surely. For if we fought and lost, they could rejoin Northumberland, if so be he is at Dunglass. With us here, they dare not. We hold them. Hamilton should thank us!"

There were growls of approval, and some grins, from around them.

David shrugged. "This will be a tale to tell!" he observed. "How Home supports his friends and liege and fights his enemies!"

The growls changed from approval to a kind of menace, but not directed towards the foe.

So they waited. And the enemy waited, an extraordinary situation, there around the Billiemire, as the sun crept round the smoke-filled sky, hour after hour. Both sides dismounted but neither moved any distance from their horses. For such fierce-seeming, heavily-armed folk the improbability of it all was striking.

David Lindsay debated with himself whether he should leave the Homes to their inaction and ride northwards alone, seeking the Hamilton force, to acquaint them with the position—if he could find them. But he decided against this. If he did leave them, these Homes, so reluctant to challenge the enemy, might quite possibly just turn round and ride home, leaving the force opposite free to rejoin and reinforce their main body, to add to the Bastard's and the King's difficulties. Besides, by the time he found the Hamiltons it might well be too late to affect the issue. In a state of impatience and disillusion, he whiled away what seemed to be an endless day.

At long last it was the enemy who made the move, as the sun was casting long shadows amongst the Lammermuir dips and hollows. Stir and mounting across the marshland heralded an orderly forming up into troops and cohorts and then, massed banners at the head, in long column-of-route they left that place. And surprisingly, at least to David Lindsay, they set off *south*-eastwards, not north-eastwards, very distinctly so, and continued in that direction for so long as they remained in sight.

This must mean, surely, that their task here was accomplished and that they no longer needed to protect Northumberland's rear and flank. And the direction taken implied that the Dunglass area was no longer of importance. So presumably Northumberland had now turned back and was heading south again, for England. And would likely be moving fairly fast, for the area he must traverse was devastated and not for lingering in. In other words, whatever had happened in the Dunglass vicinity and on the skirts of Lothian, the great raid was probably over.

This conclusion obviously had been reached by the Homes also, for they too began to pack up and mount, to turn their beasts' heads southwards whence they had come, not to follow the others, their task likewise accomplished evidently.

With no desire to remain in their company any longer, and certainly not to return to Home Castle, David announced that he would leave them, to rejoin the Bastard's force—which would no doubt be strongly harrying the English retiral, if such it was. None took him up on that, and their parting could hardly have been in less mutual esteem.

David knew the territory hereabouts only well enough to reckon that if he followed the Whitadder upwards, west by north, he ought to be on the trail of the Hamilton host—and he could see the long depression of the Whitadder valley, in the Edrom and Blanerne area, from this present position. He rode, thither, alone.

Once by the riverside road he had no difficulty, for nearly four thousand horsemen leave a trail easy to find and follow.

Up into the southern skirts of the Lammermuirs he cantered, glad enough for the action after the long hours of waiting. Quickly the character of the land changed, with the green hills drawing in closer, and now he rode in ever-deepening evening shadows. After about a dozen miles, at Nether Monynut, the tracks he was following turned from the side-valley of the Monynut Water eastwards, to commence the quite major climb over the high ridges of the Monynut Edge. It grew somewhat lighter as he mounted out of the valleys, despite the onset of the dusk, partly because there were fewer shadows up here but also in that the sky ahead was again lit up by flame, eastwards; although to the south, where before it had been so, the evil glow had now died down.

When he began dropping again into the east-facing valleys, with the glare before him outlining the remaining Eweside ridge blackly stark, it was to indicate to him that this new fire must be coming from the Dunglass area itself. When he rode into the valley-floor village of Oldhamstocks, it would have been dark but for the ruddy sky. No doors opened to him from silent church and huddled cot-houses.

He could not see the tracks of thousands of horses now, but did not need to. Surmounting the last ridge, he looked down on the narrow coastal plain, ablaze. The fires did not extend far to the north, towards Dunbar, but southwards they made a more or less continuous line of angry red until the thrust of the hill-mass hid them, where Cove, Colbrandspath, Aikieside, Aldcambus and Redheugh had been set alight. But the largest conflagration was directly below, only a mile away, obviously Dunglass Castle itself, with its castleton and fisher-haven. The smell of burning was strong on the night air.

Descending towards it all, David found the lesser fires of the Hamilton force's camp to the north-west of the burning area, which the prevailing wind kept clear of the smoke. He found the

Bastard enjoying a meal of new-slaughtered beef, of which there was no lack, dead beasts lying everywhere—and not only beasts. Hungry, he was glad to eat as he informed of the Home situation and learned in turn what had transpired here.

Finnart showed little surprise at David's account of the day's doings, indicating that he had expected little else of the Homes, especially when his scouts to southwards had reported no signs of the looked-for parallel thrust towards the enemy, from the Eye valley. But it was all another cord to hang those Homes with in due course, he asserted, grinning. For himself, he had waited, up at Oldhamstocks, not only for the Homes but for King James, who had likewise failed to appear. With his force of less than four thousand quite inadequate to attack Northumberland's main host down here sacking Dunglass, all he could do was to show groups of his people to the enemy in various strengths and positions, in the hope of appearing stronger than he was and so making the English uneasy. He believed that he had been successful in this. Northumberland had in fact not lingered long at Dunglass, nor ventured further north, but presently, after setting all afire, turned back whence he had come. The Bastard seemed quite satisfied with this, even though he had not so much as struck a blow. Now they awaited the King.

David Lindsay sought sleep that night, to the crackle of flames and the wailing of women and children, feeling less than glorious.

In the early morning a courier from James arrived, to announce that the King was on his way down the Vale of Tyne with another four thousand men and hoped to be in the Dunglass area before midday. Hamilton appeared to be quite content to wait for him; but when David protested that they ought to be hot-foot after Northumberland and Angus, harassing their rear if they could do no more, the other shrugged and asked what good that would do? Lindsay's answer that it would at least demonstrate *some* spirit amongst the Scots drew a mocking smile but the permission to take a party of Hamiltons, say five hundred, and do that, if he was so keen on profitless gestures.

David took him at his word—although he found that he had Hamilton of Barncluith as co-commander of this detachment and had little doubt as to whose lead would be followed.

So they set off southwards after the retiring invaders. As the

Bastard said, it was more of a gesture than anything else, for there was really little that they could hope to do. It was a grim business from the start, through devastated country all the way. There was scarcely a house unburned, large or small, castle or hovel, churches, barns, mills, cow-byres likewise, anything which would blaze, growing crops trampled, stock and poultry slaughtered, wells stuffed with bodies, animal and human. It was these last which especially sickened, bodies everywhere, in the villages and farmsteads, in the fields and pastures, in ditches and burns, hanging from trees, the women usually stripped naked, children frequently likewise. As for the survivors, only glimpses could be caught, for such would flee and hide from any armed horsemen soever for long to come. David's party could do nothing about all this, even if they had had time, so comprehensive was the scale of it. They could only press on after the perpetrators.

But these were not readily to be caught up with. They had had a long start and, having savaged the land on the way north, there was little for them to do or to detain them on their return. Also they would expect some retaliation and, sated with slaughter and laden with booty no doubt, they would not be apt to linger.

It was not until they reached the lower lands of the Merse, where these began to slope down to the Tweed valley itself, that they made any contact with the enemy. There, in the vicinity of Mordington and Halidon, they came on fresh tracks and many cattle-droppings, which indicated that a fairly large herd had recently been driven this way, branching off a little westwards from the main retiral line—and nobody else was likely to be driving cattle at present but the invaders. So they hurried on, following this more hopeful course, until, surmounting a west-reaching shoulder of Halidon Hill, they saw before them, a bare mile off, a mass of men and beasts moving slowly southwards. How many was hard to assess at that range, but certainly nothing like their own numbers. Thankful for some action at last, the Hamiltons spurred in pursuit.

Their approach was quickly spotted by the cattle-drovers of course, and these no doubt perceiving themselves to be much outnumbered, made no bones about fleeing there and then, abandoning their stolen herd. This was scarcely surprising but what was unanticipated was the direction of their flight, for they rode off almost due westwards, whereas the Scots would have expected them to head either due east for Berwick or south for one of the nearer fords of Tweed, to reach their main army or at least English territory, at the soonest; whereas westwards, hereabouts, would bring them to a difficult U-bend of the lower Whitadder, with steep banks and deep pools, unsuitable for fording. They could well be trapped if they continued in that direction.

Once the group in front drew away from the cattle it could be seen that there would not be more than four score of them. And they rode fast, faster than the pursuers were able to do, indeed, for a smaller company always outpaces a larger; moreover the Hamiltons had been riding at a good pace for over twenty miles by this time, their horses far from fresh. Still, so long as these English continued on that course they would have them, cornered against that difficult stretch of the Whitadder.

This area off the main track of the invading host had been only partially burned. Past the blackened farm-toun of Laigh Cocklaw the two groups pounded in turn, half-a-mile apart. And still the fleeing enemy maintained their lead and their direction. It was no more than a mile now to the Whitadder.

David Lindsay was conjecturing as he spurred. These people looked as though they knew where they were going. Could it be, in fact, that it was *themselves* who were heading for a trap? Being led to what perhaps was a major force of the invaders, in the Whitadder vicinity? It seemed an unlikely spot for such, but there must be some accounting for this odd line of flight. He was about to communicate his apprehensions to Barncluith, at his side, when another thought struck him, occasioned by what his eyes now told him. For into view ahead had just appeared the topmost tower of Edrington Castle, a strong Lauder hold, strategically placed at the very apex of the river's U-bend, on a rocky bluff. Could it be there that their quarry was headed?

He shouted this suggestion to Barncluith, who shrugged.

Soon it was evident that it was indeed towards this castle that the party in front were making—a strange destination, unless it was being held by the English—although so far David had seen no tower or stronghold taken over and occupied, but all burned or made untenable.

Trees and the lie of the land presently hid temporarily both enemy and castle; but when they came into sight again, a mere quarter-of-a-mile off, the situation was resolved. The fleeing party were in fact riding in through the gatehouse arch of the fortalice on its thrusting rock, which was far from burned, indeed with a Douglas banner flying at its tower-head. Even as the Scots approached, the massive doors below the gatehouse clanged shut, the portcullis dropped into position and the drawbridge rose.

Cursing, denied their quarry at the last moment, the Hamiltons reined up.

"Douglas!" Barncluith snarled. "Douglas there! This Edrington is a Lauder hold."

"Or was," David amended. "I know the Lauders. They hold lands near my Garleton. Indeed they own the Craig of Bass. They do not love the Douglas. So—why this?"

None could answer that.

Frustrated, they drew back out of bow-shot after a warning arrow or two came from the castle battlements, along with shouts and fist-shakings. What to do? Clearly they could by no means take this strong fortalice without cannon, and large cannon at that. David and Barncluith made a circuit and survey of the place, as close as they dared go, and saw no weaknesses. The perimeter wall was fully twenty feet high and clearly well-guarded—the garrison would now be reinforced by some eighty men, moreover. The river itself protected the place on three sides, with a wide moat cutting off the rest. And its people were unlikely to be starved out, for down at the riverside, at its only levellish access but within the curtain-walling, were actually two meal-mills, side by side, using a lade from the Whitadder for power, a highly unusual feature; so presumably there would be grain stored there.

Balked, they returned to their people. There seemed to be nothing that they could usefully achieve there. Many of the Hamiltons seemed more interested in taking over the abandoned herd of cattle than in anything else, Barncluith far from reproving them. It was decided in the end that David and a small escort should return to meet the King and the Bastard and inform them of the situation, while the rest of the force moved on discreetly down to Tweed, to discover the position of Northumberland's main army and whether or not they had yet crossed back into England. No doubt the cattle would go with them.

So, in the late afternoon, David rode north-eastwards again, over Halidon Hill and on through the devastation towards Eyemouth and Coldinghame. At Aytoun he found the royal force, now of some seven or eight thousand, settling for the night in an area blessedly saved from the general ravishment—Aytoun, significantly, being a Home lairdship and had interestingly been spared.

James greeted David warmly and seemed less distressed by all the desolation and suffering than might have been expected. He was angered, however, to hear of the Douglas take-over of Edrington Castle—anything relating to Angus could be calculated to upset him—declaring that this must be put right forthwith. They would move on towards Berwick in the morning, and then deal with the Douglases.

No doubt Northumberland and Angus were well warned of the royal approach in force, and presumably had no desire at this stage to engage in battle, for all were safely within the walled burgh of Berwick, or across Tweed into England well before the arrival of the Scots army. This, for its part, was not equipped with cannon and siege-engines to attempt the conquest of that great fortress town. So, after contenting themselves with making a large demonstration outside the massive walls and bastions of Berwick and its castle, and along the north bank of Tweed nearby, James and the royal host turned and headed westwards, upriver, for its junction with the Whitadder and thereafter northwards to Edrington Castle.

Not that there was in fact anything more that they could do here than at Berwick, for although it was not to be compared with that important citadel, nevertheless it was a very strong place, both as to site and defensive features, and not to be taken without heavy artillery, battering-rams and the like, none of which were available. But James shook his fist at the hold and its defenders and vowed that he would be back, to drive the insolent Douglases from Scottish soil, once and for all. David Lindsay was interested in this rather myopic attitude, for of course the mighty Tantallon Castle, Angus's main seat, was still firmly in that Earl's hands as were other Red Douglas strongholds, with no major campaign mounted against them.

Thereafter, less than triumphantly, the army returned to

Edinburgh. Lindsay was no fire-eater, but he felt the entire affair to have been distinctly feeble—even though his liege-lord and Hamilton of Finnart betrayed no such sentiments.

* * *

Back at Stirling, however, the Lord Lyon King-of Arms and the Lord Privy Seal, if not others, decided that some more assertive follow-up gesture and protest was required, to convince Henry and the English that such savage invasion and devastation was not to be tamely accepted and should not be repeated. Beaton's nimble wits came up with a two-part offensive, mainly diplomatic and negotiable but also with a cutting-edge, since Henry Tudor was a man more likely to be brought to the one by means of the other. He argued thus:

Henry was much preoccupied at present with his domestic affairs and policies and his ongoing battle with Rome over the denied divorce. Also he was short of money—not as James was but on a vaster scale altogether, his continual foreign wars being enormously costly and his extravagance proverbial. All knew that he was going to break with Rome, not just quarrel with Pope Clement but actually detach England from Holy Church. The English parliament had been debating this for years without coming to a conclusion. But matters were coming to a head. Henry was seeing a great deal of a certain young woman. He had many mistresses of course but this one, Anne Boleyn, was a grand-daughter of the Duke of Norfolk, Earl Marshal of England, and not to be treated in any casual fashion, even by Henry, without provoking dire trouble with the Howards, the most powerful family in his realm. Moreover, she was, Davie's spies assured him, a woman of character and spirit and was insisting on marriage before conceding her favours. Yet recently she had been considerably more free and open in her behaviour with the King—which implied that divorce was near. And since Holy Church was adamant in denying that Henry should put away his Queen Catherine of Aragon, it followed that the break with Rome must be at hand. Archbishop Cranmer of Canterbury was prepared to declare the Church in England independent, with Henry its head, not the Pope, and thereafter to grant him divorce—but the break would first have to be declared by parliament. Thomas Cromwell, who had succeeded Wolsey as Chancellor, was saying that he could be sure of a favourable majority, and the defeat of the Church party, by the spring. Therefore all would probably come to a head then—the break with the Vatican, the setting up of a new Church of England, Henry grabbing the old Church's wealth and lands, divorce declared and marriage with this Anne Boleyn.

In these circumstances even Henry Tudor was unlikely to desire any large-scale military adventures for the next few months, here or on the continent—which must be Scotland's opportunity. No doubt this raid of Northumberland's had been planned to ensure that Scotland lay low for a while. So Scotland should *not* lie low, but rather strike whilst the iron was hot. Then by the said vital spring, vital for Henry, Scotland should be in a position to wring major concessions and a substantial peace treaty out of the Tudor.

All this David Lindsay accepted, for Beaton was always well informed. But what could they do? Scotland was in no state to mount a major invasion of England. James, in deliberately reducing the power of his nobles, had also offended almost all but the Hamiltons—and they were the source of his armed power. It was not only the Douglases and Homes and Hepburns and the like who were resentful. Few of the great lords would willingly lift a hand to aid James to muster a great army.

Beaton admitted it. They could only use the tools that were to hand, therefore. But skilfully used, these might suffice. Not for any major invasion, which anyway would only unite and rouse the English. It must be to strike against carefully selected targets. They did have two tools to hand, two sources of manpower which James had not offended—the Hamiltons themselves and the Highland chiefs. A retaliatory raid on the North of England forthwith, for revenge and plunder, was just the sort of thing that the Bastard of Arran would love to lead—indeed he was already proposing it. If to that was added something much more telling, on another front, Henry could be worried. Where were the English most vulnerable? Where but in Ireland, where their occupying forces were constantly being harassed by uprisings of the Irish petty kings and native chiefs. The Western Highland clans looked on raids on Ireland as almost part of their yearly calendar. It would not be difficult, surely, to persuade say Alexander of Islay, who should be Lord of the Isles, to take a large-scale Highland host across the Irish Sea the short distance to Ulster, there to assail the English garrisons and encourage the

Irish to further rising. The Irish were strong for Holy Church and Henry's feud with Rome anathema to them. Rebellion there could spread like a heather-fire. Nothing would be more apt to worry Henry at this juncture and bring him to talk peace with the Scots.

Lindsay could not deny the validity of this reasoning—if the Highland chiefs would agree.

They would agree, Beaton asserted confidently—especially if they were promised freedom to claw back lands the Campbells of Argyll had stolen from them!

And James? Would he agree?

The other grinned.

19

David Lindsay had scarcely expected to be back at Berwick-on-Tweed so soon, especially to be admitted at its so jealously-guarded gates and to pass through its narrow streets unmolested down to the riverside and across the lengthy wooden bridge which spanned Tweed, scene of so much clash and bloodshed down the centuries, and on to English soil beyond. He had never set foot in England hitherto, and felt a strange excitement to be doing so, however similar the scenery to that which he had just left north of Tweed. Admittedly no smiles or other welcome greeted them—but then nothing of the sort had been evident as they had passed through the Merse either, that land making only slow recovery from its dire experiences of the previous autumn.

He was heading further south still, for Newcastle-on-Tyne, and under a safe-conduct letter signed by Henry of England himself, riding at the head of a well-turned-out and splendidly mounted company of about five score, under the royal Lion Rampant banner of Scotland with, at his side, Master William Stewart, the new Bishop of Aberdeen, and Sir Adam Otterburn of Reidhall, Provost of Edinburgh, as fellow commissioners.

They were on the second stage of Davie Beaton's two-part programme to tie the bloody hands of Henry Tudor, the diplomatic and negotiatory stage. That the situation had reached thus far was witness to the success of the earlier gestures. The Bastard's raid on Northumberland and Cumberland in the late autumn had been sufficiently savage and punitory to please even that ruthless individual, with Finnart boasting more towns, villages and houses destroyed, more folk hanged and more cattle, horses and sheep herded back over the border than even the thousands claimed by the English on *their* raid—however few of these found their way to the original owners. And the Highland expedition to Ireland had been even more successful—and still was, for Alexander of Islay and his fellow chieftains of the Clan Donald federation were still over there, still causing maximum havoc and stirring up the Irish to rise against the occupying English garrisons. It was, almost certainly, to get this stopped and the MacDonalds out of Ireland, that the present treaty negotiations had been hurriedly set in train at Henry's urging as early in 1533 as this March–April. That monarch was indeed having a busy spring.

Beaton undoubtedly would have enjoyed being on this Newcastle mission in person, to seek to complete the success of his planning; but a still more urgent priority had dictated that he should be elsewhere. He had gone to France to complete with King Francis final arrangements for the marriage of King James. The two monarchs had now agreed in principle that the bride should be a French princess, but there remained doubt as to which.

King Francis was still offering his kinswomen Marie de Bourbon, Marie de Guise or Isabeau d'Albret of Navarre. Sir Thomas Erskine had already been to France on this quest, but had come back bemused and confused, unable to give his liege-lord any firm guidance on so delicate a matter. Not that James, less than enthusiastic for marriage at all, was in any hurry as to choice, indeed would have used the situation to postpone the entire notion of matrimony. But Beaton had been persistent. The succession must be ensured, if possible; the realm's well-being demanded it. A French match was much the best. So these three French ladies must be more carefully surveyed, much more thoroughly than Sir Thomas Erskine had done, and the best choice selected. Beaton was on friendly terms with King

Francis, and also the Duke of Albany, who could be helpful. It would all have to be done with much care and tact; for she who was selected had to be presentable, suitable to be queen in Scotland and above all, fertile, capable of bearing the required heir to the throne. It remained unstated that she must be reasonably attractive, physically, to James. Beaton considered himself to be apt for the task as any.

So, before departing for France, he had advised James to appoint this trio as commissioners for the English treaty bargaining, Lindsay, Bishop Stewart and Provost Otterburn, and schooled them fairly closely as to their role.

William Stewart, who had been Provost of Lincluden Collegiate establishment, and now appointed not only Bishop of Aberdeen but Treasurer of the Realm, was one of Beaton's own protégés, typical of the men he was seeking to manoeuvre into positions of power in Church and state, youngish, hard-headed, cool, shrewd, more politician than pastor. When old Bishop Dunbar of Aberdeen, uncle of the present Chancellor, had died, there had been murmurings at the appointment of this quite junior cleric, of no especially illustrious background, to one of the most senior bishoprics in the land—done in the name of the Primate, Archbishop of St. Andrews, of course—but like so many of Davie's contrivances it had gone through. Lindsay did not particularly like the man but recognised that he might well be a useful ally in any debate or argument. Sir Adam Otterburn was a very different character, bluff, hearty and jovial in manner, but alleged to be cunning, of middle years, and with keen grey eyes. He made good company—although Beaton had warned David not to trust him in all things. Lindsay was a little uncertain as to who, if any, was leader of this trio; but as Lord Lyon, one of the great officers of state and the King's personal representative, he almost certainly ranked first, however powerful the Bishop-Treasurer.

This was their third day on the road and they were due at Alnwick that night. Alnwick Castle was the principal seat of the Earl of Northumberland, now English Chief Warden of the Marches, the same who had led last autumn's invasion of Scotland. It would be as strange as riding unchallenged through Berwick to sleep under the walls of the Percy's castle.

In the event they slept *within* the Percy's walls, for on the outskirts of Alnwick, at dusk, they were met by the Earl himself, who announced stiffly that such distinguished visitors must on no account put up in any mere hospice or hostelry but should accept the hospitality of his poor house—this from the man who had laid waste half of Berwickshire. He was a tall, thin, foxy-faced individual, unimpressive as to appearance.

The same could not be said of his castle, at least, an enormous establishment, almost a town of itself behind its extensive perimeter-walls, nothing like any Scots castle the travellers had ever seen, scarcely a fortalice or stronghold at all, more of a palace, even more palatial than royal Linlithgow. The visitors eyed its proud magnitude rather askance. No doubt this reception was part of a sort of conditioning for the Scots, preparatory to the negotiations, an impression reinforced on them when Northumberland informed that it had been expressly ordered by King Henry himself. Presumably thereafter the Earl felt that he had done as much as could be expected of him, in meeting and quartering these wretched Scots, for after ushering them through his august portals and handing them over to his chamberlain, they saw no more of him. They were all, however, excellently housed and fed.

In the morning they rode on southwards, their company, formerly seeming quite imposing, now looking a mere undistinguished handful, hemmed in front and rear by what amounted almost to an army of Northumbrians, the huge concourse led by the Percy and a glittering entourage of lords, knights, squires and clerics. The Scots, in fact, rather gave the appearance of captives of a conquering host—which was no doubt intended.

By Coquetmouth and Morpeth they came at length to the shallow valley of the Northumbrian Tyne, so very different from the East Lothian river of that name, and the large walled town and port of Newcastle, a place they found comparable with Berwick in situation and size although less strongly defended and further from the sea. Here, in the late afternoon, the visitors underwent another change in conditions, being conducted to distinctly poor and cramped quarters in a monastic establishment of the Grey Friars and then left abruptly by Northumberland and their resplendent escort, without instructions or further guidance, as it were to kick their heels. In bare and basic premises, very different from Alnwick Castle, after eating plain fare, they passed the night.

And therein they spent the next day also, seemingly ignored if not forgotten, expecting all the time to be led and introduced to their opposite numbers, Henry's commissioners. But nothing of the sort transpired and enquiries from the sub-prior in charge of their lodging produced no information as to who these persons were, where they were to be found or even whether they had yet reached Newcastle—although the negotiations were timed to start that day. All they elicited from the sub-prior was that it was inadvisable for the visitors to venture out into the streets in case they were attacked by the citizens, who had no love for the Scots.

Another night passed and a second day and still they were left cooped up like prisoners and uninformed. By late afternoon, impatient and angry, Davie demanded that he should be escorted forthwith to wherever the Earl of Northumberland was lodged, to protest at the delay and the treatment of the King of Scots' representatives and to discover the situation. The sub-prior declared that he had no authority to do this nor to allow any of the Scots to be endangered in the town; but that he would send one of his monks to his lordship of Northumberland to enquire as to their disposal.

This quest, if it were indeed put in hand, produced no evident results.

It was in mid-evening that a clattering and shouting outside the monastic gates heralded some development. An officer, dressed in the English royal livery adorned with Tudor Roses, marched in on them as they sat at their frugal meal and announced in ringing tones that His Excellency Master Thomas Cromwell, Principal Secretary of State to His Majesty, summoned the representatives of Scotland to his presence.

Staring, at the newcomer and at each other, the three Scots found words slow in coming. The Bishop pursed thin lips and Otterburn hooted. David spoke.

"Summons, sirrah? Did I hear you aright? Your Master Cromwell *summons* us to his presence? The ambassadors of the King of Scots!"

The officer nodded. "Those were my instructions, yes."

"Then, sir, I must bid you return whence you come and say that King James's envoys greet Master Cromwell and will be glad to meet him in due course. At a convenient time and on suitable invitation."

The other frowned. "I was to bring you forthwith," he said.
"Then your are now better informed."
"Off with you, laddie," Sir Adam advised, grinning. "While we finish this, this monkish banquet!"
"You, you refuse to accompany me? To His Excellency?"
"We do."
For moments the officer glared. Then abruptly he turned on his heel and stamped out.
The sub-prior wrung his hands.
The trio at the table were almost equally offended by the ill manners of this summons as they were impressed by the fact that it apparently came from Thomas Cromwell himself. That Henry should have sent his redoubtable chief adviser and evil genius to the negotiating table, the most powerful man in England now next to the King, was a thought to consider. That he was starting out in this fashion was likewise thought-provoking.
They debated what their further reaction should be. If a revised and acceptable invitation arrived, should they accept, at this hour? Or should they declare that they would confer next day? Bishop Stewart pointed out that if they further piqued Cromwell, he might well keep them waiting here for long enough. Having made their gesture, it would probably be wiser to go meet him now.
They had not long to wait—which seemed to indicate that the English commissioners were installed somewhere nearby. The officer reappeared, but now he had with him a cleric, who announced that he was Master Felix St. Fort, a secretary to His Excellency the Chief Secretary and Vicar-General—this last a new title for the Scots. His Excellency hoped that the King of Scots' envoys had enjoyed their repast and invited them to take wine with him in the castle, preparatory to their discussions on the morrow—this said in measured, almost fruity tones.
David conceded that, since the night was yet young, they would be pleased to come.
They were less than pleased, however, when outside the monastery they were lined up by the officer within tight files of the guard of torch-bearing men-at-arms, and marched at a brisk pace through the streets—this allegedly to protect them from the fury of the mob, which remained in fact unseen.

It was not far to the strange castle which gave the town its name, new only in that it was not the first on the site, and strange in that its walls rose directly from the town streets, not surmounting any rock or knoll, four-square and very tall, seven storeys of it, and in the darkness looming enormously hostile, like some great prison into which the captives were on their way to be incarcerated.

This impression was enhanced by the clanging iron doors and portcullis, the shouted challenges of the guards and the armed men who lined the steep mural stairway so that there was scarcely room for the visitors to climb up. However, at the third floor, past more scowling sentries, they were ushered into a large and well-lit chamber, where a great fire of coals supplemented the many flickering candles, the walls hung with colourful arras and the stone floor strewn with skins. Here a number of men lounged at ease around a long table littered with flagons, beakers and wine-cups.

"The Scotch envoys, my lords," their cleric guide announced.

Some of the loungers rose to their feet at this introduction, but three most noticeably did not. David knew two of them, the Earl of Northumberland, and Doctor Fox who had been an English envoy to the Scots court, an elderly stooping man with a long nose and rat-trap jaws, never known to smile. The third was otherwise, a thick-set, bullet-headed individual, swarthy, coarse of feature, red of face, plainly dressed compared with the other two but with a grinning air of authority. In the circumstances, this could be none other than Thomas Cromwell.

For a few moments nobody spoke, as both sides eyed each other. Then Fox cleared his throat.

"Lindsay of The Mount I know. And Sir Adam Otterburn. The other, the clerk, I know not," he said. He obviously was addressing the thick-set man, and made his statement sound anything but complimentary.

"He is Master William Stewart, my lord Bishop of Aberdeen. Sir Adam Otterburn is Provost of the city of Edinburgh and lately Lord Advocate; and I am His Grace's Lord Lyon King-of-Arms," David returned, level-voiced. "You Dr. Fox, *I* know. My lord of Northumberland all know. Others are strangers to us." That was the best that he could do at the moment.

"One of you is probably the man Cromwell, who invited us to

wine?" Otterburn added, for his part, looking round the entire company enquiringly.

There was a profound hush. Then the red-faced man slammed a hand on the table-top, but barked a laugh. "I am Cromwell," he jerked. "No lord—but at your Scots lordships' service! You sound dry, as though needing a drink. Does the good friars' hospitality fail? Come—sit." The man's voice was as thick and plebeian as his person.

They moved forward to the table, David for one the more wary over the other's reaction.

Only under such as Henry Tudor perhaps could a man in Thomas Cromwell's position have risen to his present heights. The son of a Putney blacksmith and no cleric, without the Church's educational advantages, from being a mere merchant's clerk he had been sent to the counting-house of an English factory in Amsterdam, and thence to Rome, where he had made sufficiently good use of his time amongst the churchmen to be recommended to Cardinal Wolsey on his return home. That ambitious and able prelate and Chancellor, recognising a like spirit, had in due course made Cromwell his confidential secretary. So the younger man learned statecraft and the like in the toughest school, was privy to secrets which could raise or damn even the great and powerful, and inevitably came to act as go-between with his master and King Henry—who also came to recognise his abilities. He was inserted into parliament, where he was very useful on occasion. And on Wolsey's fall he defended him, in parliament, to great effect. But not sufficiently to save the Cardinal from Henry's wrath and spleen over failure to gain him his divorce. However the King did not want to lose both useful servants at the same time and took Cromwell into his own employ. Now he was not only chief Secretary of State but a sort of lay inspector of all Church institutions, properties and privileges, with the odd style of Vicar-General, assessing the wealth and personages in bishoprics, abbeys, monasteries and lands, a position of enormous influence in present circumstances. None was now more useful and close to his monarch than Thomas Cromwell, the blacksmith's son.

"You have been delayed in reaching Newcastle, sir?" David asked, pouring himself wine. "We had looked for you . . . earlier."

"Scarcely delayed, no. My lord of Northumberland took us

hunting. Dr. Fox is a great huntsman, although you might not think it to look at him! Myself, I find my distractions otherwhere!" That was said with a fleeting glance at the other two English commissioners.

David recognised the challenge implicit in those seemingly casual comments. This man was entirely sure of himself, despised both the aristocratic earl and the academic diplomat and their attitudes, showed who was in command here, and indicated that he had no hesitation in keeping the Scots waiting if so he pleased.

The quiet Bishop Stewart it was who answered. "We were grateful for the opportunity to rest and refresh ourselves, after the long journey." That lie was calmly declared.

Cromwell looked at the speaker assessingly.

"We hope that your hunting was sufficiently successful to outweigh your reluctance, Mr. Secretary?" Otterburn added, not to be outdone. "Putting you in good fettle for our discussions."

"That fettle you will discover in due course!" the other snapped back. Then he shrugged burly shoulders. "Not that great discussion will be required, I think. For the issues are straightforward, are they not? We both desire peace and an end to profitless bickering, no?"

"The peace, yes. It is the price to be paid for that peace which will require the fettle in discussion," David said.

"So-o-o! You Scots have come to haggle? To chaffer? Merchants, eh? Despite your so-lordly styles. I remind you, *I* was bred a merchant's clerk and know the trade—even if others do not!" Again the glance at Northumberland and Fox.

David perceived that there would be tough bargaining ahead of them. But he also thought that he perceived perhaps a chink in the English armour. There was no love lost between King Henry's commissioners, and this might be exploited. Also Cromwell was emphasising his humble origins overmuch, which could represent an aspect of weakness.

"Trade requires buyer and seller both," Otterburn observed. "*We* have much to sell. If you have the wherewithal to pay!"

"We are not here in a marketplace, sirrah!" Fox declared frostily. "*We* are here representing the King's Majesty, to conduct business of state. In, in dignity. However you deal with such matters in Scotland!"

Cromwell smiled broadly. "What have you to sell that England needs to buy?" he asked. "We have heard that Scotland is scarcely rich!"

"Yet you are here to bargain. The Secretary of State himself!" David rejoined.

"We have much that you need," Otterburn went on. "Your king desires peace on his northern borders, while he battles with Rome. He desires peace in Ireland—at which King James might assist. He desires recognition of a divorce from his queen, and his remarriage, from a monarch loyal to the Vatican. He wishes our liege-lord to wed his daughter, the Princess Mary, and an end to talk of a French match. England requires Scots wool, and could buy it instead of stealing it! England is . . ."

Bishop Stewart cleared his throat. "We are here, by invitation, to drink wine, are we not?" he suggested warningly. "Rather than to debate terms at this present. Tomorrow will serve for that."

David agreed with that. The hearty Otterburn might be forcing the pace somewhat. A more methodical approach than this was called for. "No doubt we shall rehearse all such matters with clearer heads in the morning," he declared. "Unless our English friends are going hunting again!"

Cromwell hooted. "Well said! The morrow it is. But, on your couches this night, before sleep, consider this. King Henry *requires* none of these things, however desirable they may be or may not be. Whereas his nephew King James, does require peace. His lords are in revolt—not only Angus and Bothwell and Cassillis, others also. Some are imprisoned—Eglinton, Sinclair, even Moray, we hear. Others sulk in their castles. I note that none such are here with you today! So James cannot raise an army of any size. Nor can he dare war, for fear of who may rise behind him. His treasury is empty, so that he had to get the Pope in Rome to command Beaton to give him the Church's gold, to pay his debts. He *requires* to sell his wool! He needs a wife with a large dowry; any the French can offer could be outdone by King Henry. And Highland barbarians, tasting their power, love not Lowland Scotland, and could slaughter and slay in more than Ireland, if sufficiently . . . induced! Think of these things my friends, ere you sleep."

That was plain talking indeed from a plain man, and all too true. The Scots recognised it, as they sipped their wine, even though Otterburn snorted and waved a dismissive hand.

The lists then were marked out for the morrow.

Fairly soon thereafter the visitors took their leave. The Earl of Northumberland had not said a word throughout.

Next forenoon, back in the same chamber of the castle, in a very different atmosphere and mood, they all sat down to business, formal, stiff, wary—although that last hardly seemed to apply to Thomas Cromwell. From the start he made the running, taking the line that, despite the fact that Henry it was who had called for this conference and possible treaty, England as it were held all the cards. They were here because his English Majesty, at last to be freed from the bonds of an unfruitful and deplorable marriage and to rewed, also about to take over the headship of the Church in England, with all its shamefully-gained power and wealth, desired to mark his felicity and satisfaction by a gesture of goodwill and affection towards his nephew of Scotland, and put an end to disagreements between the greater nation and the lesser.

He, King Henry, therefore proposed not any mere truce but a full and enduring treaty of peace between England and Scotland, to endure indeed for the lifetime of whichever monarch should first die—if not in fact for longer. This treaty of peace, goodwill, mutual trade and general harmony, conditional only on the most generous of terms.

Silent the Scots waited.

Firstly, the savage Highland forces to be withdrawn from Ireland forthwith, and undertaking given that they would not return. Secondly, that the Lady Mary Tudor should be wed to the Scots king at an early date, a substantial dowry to be negotiated. Thirdly, that King James should pronounce his recognition of the divorce from Queen Catherine and the marriage to the Lady Anne, and should inform the other princes of Chistendom of that recognition and acclaim. Fourthly, that King James and his advisers should now consider a like rejection of the insolent shackles of Rome and declare the independence of the Church in Scotland. And lastly, that the thieves and robbers of the Scots Border Marches, especially the West March Armstrongs, should be restrained from raiding into England and due punishment and reparation made for their ravages.

Perhaps it was strange that it was this last, the least significant and far-reaching in fact, which should have the effect of raising the Scots' temperatures almost to boiling point; but after Northumberland's so recent savageries in Scotland, such a stipulation seemed almost beyond belief. Otterburn half-rose out of his chair in angry protest, fists clenched. David drew a long quivering breath, but spoke before Sir Adam could find words.

"We . . . we can only believe that these terms which you have put forward are scarcely to be taken seriously," he said, seeking to keep his voice under control, "judging by that last! The folly of it! This lord," and he pointed to Northumberland, "this lord himself led an invasion into our land only a few months ago, which outdid, by a score of times and more such damage as the Armstrongs and their like may have wrought in their reivings—which, as you know well, have been part of the Borders way of living, on both sides, for centuries. If this is an example of how you seek to bargain, then we may as well leave this table here and now!"

"Aye—I say more!" Otterburn burst out. "It is bad enough to have to sit at a table with that murderer of women and bairns, there smirking! He who has boasted that he left no single tower, farmstead, house or cot unburned, or a tree without its ill fruit of hanging bodies. Without having to listen to claims for damage and punishment for a few cattle-stealing Borderers! I say that we should halt this talking here, and return to Scotland."

The Bishop raised an episcopal-ringed hand. "Unsuitable and reprehensible as that item was, I would point out that there were other references more important and no less obnoxious," he said levelly. "This of seeking Scotland's rejection of the authority of Holy Church, for instance. Not to be so much as considered."

"Ha—there speaks one who *must* so speak!" Cromwell observed, dismissively. "Lest he lose his mitre and wealth! As for the other, my lord of Northumberland's excursion into Scotland was no reiving raid but a duly authorised strategy by the chief Warden of the Marches, in retaliation for numberless Scots assaults on our territories, at the behest of His Majesty's Privy Council—an entirely different matter." He shrugged. "It is partly to end the need for further such gestures that His Majesty has called this conference."

David drew another breath. "This, sir, I would point out, is *not* a conference called by the King of England, but a possible negotiation between the representatives of the King of England and the King of Scots, with a view to proclaiming a treaty of peace. There is a notable difference."

"Call it what you may, Sir David. It comes to the same in the end."

"I think not, sir—since the end is either a treaty, or none. And on the style of your present submissions, it is like to be none!"

"Then we are but wasting our time," Fox declared. "We are not here to split hairs over nice wording and empy phrases."

"You will pay heed to our Doctor!" Cromwell added, but mockingly. "If you do not like our words and phrases, my friends, let us hear yours."

David glanced at Stewart. Was there any point in going further with these people? They seemed as inflexible as they were arrogant. Yet Cromwell was no fool, as his whole career proved. He had presumably been sent to negotiate, as had they themselves. This attitude could be only a preliminary bargaining stance designed to upset them and so impair their judgement.

The Bishop nodded as though he read David's mind. "We have our own terms," he agreed.

David had notes but scarcely required to consult them. In view of the English attitude, he enunciated the Scots headings more baldly than he might have done. All raids on Scotland were to cease, and reparations be made for damage done in the late invasion. Harassment of Scots shipping and traders was to cease forthwith. The Earls of Angus and Bothwell were to be returned to the justice of the King of Scots, as others of the King's enemies who had fled his realm. The long-trumpeted assertions of the Archbishops of York to spiritual hegemony over the Scottish Church were to be disclaimed—not difficult if the Church in England was no longer under Rome. The terms Lord Paramount of Scotland and Lord Protector of Scotland, used by English kings for centuries, were to be discontinued, Scotland having been an entirely independent kingdom always. All pensions paid by King Henry to subjects of King James were to cease, and no further interference in the affairs of the Scottish realm be permitted. The castle of Edrington in the East Merse, presently unlawfully occupied by Douglas and English invaders, along with the premises known as the Caw Mills, were to be returned to the Lauder owners forthwith. These, the requirements of the King of Scots.

For a little there was silence around that table, save for the scraping of the quills of clerks sitting at another table and taking notes. Then, without consulting his colleagues, Cromwell spread his stubby-fingered hands.

"We have heard you with more patience than you heard me!" he said. "Your claims, to be sure, lack all reality and are no basis for any negotiation. But they will be duly considered, as you will consider ours. Who knows, some might be possible to grant." He smiled, as though that was only a pious hope. "Now—as to concessions. We have exchanged demands. What is there that each side might possibly concede, if such concession aided a settlement? I say only possibly. You will agree that some such indication would be useful to our further and private considerations, and save time?"

David nodded.

"Very well. Here are some that King Henry might be prevailed upon to accede to—*might*, I say. Further military incursions to cease, so long as this applied to both realms. Certain payments to be made to the Scots Treasury, as a gesture of goodwill not in any reparations for my lord of Northumberland's expedition—for anything such would be but cancelled by our similar demands from the Armstrongs. The Archbishop of York's claims might be foregone, in present circumstances. Also certain styles and titles modified. Shipping might be protected on the high seas, but only on condition that Scottish pirates such as the man Wood and the brothers Barton were restrained from attacking English ships. These might be considered."

The Scots exchanged glances. These were, on the whole, better than they had anticipated. Which in itself was suspicious, perhaps?

"Come—what have you to say to that? And what may *you* concede?" Cromwell challenged.

The Bishop it was who answered. "We stated our moderate requirements, sir. So we do not reduce these by seeming concessions. We can but assure you that Scotland will not be unhelpful in attaining a settlement by refusing to yield on a minor matter here or there."

"Your are grudging, Sir Priest. As, for instance?"

"His Grace could possibly request the return from Ireland of MacDonald of Islay and his people . . ."

"Request! King Henry does not *request* his lords, he commands! Is this the best that you can offer?"

David added a suggestion, something Stewart could scarcely say, as a prelate loyal to Rome. "King James might agree to recognise King Henry's divorce and remarriage," he said. James had indeed already more or less assumed this, since there was nothing which he could do to change matters—nor did the matter greatly concern him.

"And so inform other princes?" That was quick.

"It may be that could follow." Clearly this issue assumed an importance to the English, or at least to Henry, unlooked for by the Scots.

"Very well. If that is the best that you can say, we shall adjourn and consider. Tomorrow we shall meet again." Abruptly, the man stood, pushed the chair, and strode to the door and out.

Otterburn gobbled in astonishment and offence, and David all but protested, at this extraordinary way of conducting negotiations; but since such protest could only be made to Fox and Northumberland, he forbore. Bowing stiffly to the Englishmen, he led the way out.

Nevertheless, back at the Grey Friars, the Scots, on consideration, were far from depressed, however much they deplored their opposite numbers' behaviour. It seemed, indeed, as though much that they had expected to have to fight for was going to be granted. And the English demands, however arrogantly put, were on the whole less difficult than they might have been. Admittedly nothing had been said or conceded about Angus and Bothwell, nor Edrington Castle, two matters on which James was adamant. And, of course, the suggestion that Scotland should also break with Rome was not to be considered for a moment. But their other requirements, the cessation of raiding and of attacks on shipping, the end of the ridiculous York claims over the Scots Church, the English kings' pretentious titles, and the resumption of trade, appeared to be conceded—with some unspecified financial payment offered into the bargain. That left only the question of the Princess Mary's marriage not touched upon—which to be sure was not to be contemplated, with reports of the lady being plain in the extreme, a matter important to James, and a French match more or less decided on.

The Scots commissioners sought their couches in a better frame of mind.

The next day's session, although no more satisfactory as regards procedure, with Cromwell acting as though he were in command of a class of students, and ignorant ones at that, confirmed the Scots' conclusions of the night before. King Henry must want this peace treaty quite urgently.

It came down then to the four outstanding issues—the marriage; the Angus and Bothwell repatriation; the yielding up of Edrington Castle; and the secession of the Scots Church from Rome. On these Cromwell would not budge, nor would the Scots.

The sitting was fairly brief. This time, before Cromwell could repeat yesterday's tactics, David proposed adjournment for further consideration. Grimly the others could not but accede.

Not that there was really anything for them to consider. On these four items the Scots could by no means give way. James and Davie Beaton, apart from others, would never concede any of them.

The next day they were informed by their sub-prior that the English commissioners would not be available for discussion. Whether it was more hunting, or just teaching the Scots a lesson, was not vouchsafed.

The day after they were still left to their own devices—which, within the confines of that small monastery, were limited to say the least. When in late afternoon, it was apparent that no call was forthcoming, David sent a message to the castle declaring that if a session was not held the next morning, preferably here in the Grey Friars' monastery, he and his colleagues would return to Scotland for conference with King James and his advisers.

That provided the expected summons, but once again to the castle. And there, with no apologies nor explanations for delay, Cromwell, after making it clear that there was no weakening in the English position, announced that he was a very busy man with many responsibilities and must return to London forthwith. Their conference should resume in one month's time—when it was to be hoped that the Scots would have come to their senses. He thereupon made one of his purposeful exits, an expert at having the last word.

His two so-silent colleagues hurried off after him, as the clerks, who had scarcely begun their note-taking, stared, at a loss.

So it was dismissed and back to Stirling for the Scots.

* * *

As it transpired, and as David had recognised, there was really nothing for them to debate with James and his Privy Council, as distinct from their reporting. Although most were gratified at the progress made, there was to be no weakening on their position as to the issues remaining. James was inflexible about Angus. Bothwell's treachery might be overlooked if need be, if not forgotten. But the Red Douglas was different. All James's life he had suffered at the hands of Angus; now he would have his revenge. He saw Edrington Castle's surrender in the same light, for the Douglases were holding it in the English interest. As for the proposal of an English marriage, this was still further negatived by the arrival of a messenger from Davie Beaton in France, informing that King Francis was now urging marriage with his kinswoman, Marie de Bourbon, daughter of the Duke of Vendôme. The Lady Marie was not uncomely, of a good form and a fertile family and should make a suitable match for King James. Beaton had sent a portrait by his courier, the artist painting an attractive picture of a plump-featured, well-built, smiling young woman with prominent breasts. James, although still less than enthusiastic, decided that he might do much worse in the circumstances. He sent the messenger back with a gift of jewellery for the lady and a provisional suggestion to wed. As to any break with Rome, none, even those like David Lindsay most critical of the corruption within Holy Church, considered for a moment taking any parallel action with the English. After all, it was not so much the reform of corruption which was motivating Henry but anger and spleen over the divorce, ambition to rule all himself and greed for the Church's great wealth.

So David and his fellow commissioners received no new instructions for their further negotiations, no major conciliatory gestures, save in some small matters already more or less conceded—not from Scots sources that is. But from England, during this month's interval, came a pointed and fairly typical Tudor gesture of persuasion—a lightning and particularly bloody raid on Teviotdale by a force under Sir Robert Fenwick, one of Northumberland's lieutenants. The fury this aroused at Stirling had a contrary effect from what was presumably intended. That this raid coincided with Henry's marriage ceremony to Anne Boleyn did nothing to commend the latter to the Scots; and James considered countermanding the tentative agreement that he would recognise the divorce and remarriage of his uncle and inform other rulers that he had done so. But since a peace treaty was as needful as ever for Scotland, it was decided that this rejection should not be emphasised but might be kept in reserve as a possible bargaining counter.

As an aid to the commissioners it was proposed that they should take with them, on their return to Newcastle, Monsieur de Bevois, the French ambassador, an able and friendly individual. His presence might exert a beneficial influence on Cromwell, who would be concerned not to offend King Francis, especially over the marriage proposals. A couple of days before they were due to ride, however, news arrived from England which rather made such persuasion redundant. King Henry, presumably as part of his triumph over poor Queen Catherine, or perhaps as some sort of flourish towards his new bride—who was known to be far gone with child by him—made a declaration that his former marriage having been no true marriage, it followed therefore that his daughter by that marriage, Mary, was in fact illegitimate and should on all occasions be recognised as such. This extraordinary statement, which could only confirm the impression that Henry was in some respects mad, could scarcely be expected to make any easier Cromwell's remit to try to marry the unfortunate young woman to the King of Scots.

The month's interval, therefore, far from improved the situation.

The Scots deliberately delayed their return to Newcastle for two days beyond the stipulated date, in retaliation for their own treatment earlier. Even so, their English counterparts did not put in an appearance for still a further couple of days, so the gesture fell notably flat.

There were no apologies from Cromwell and Dr. Fox—the Earl of Northumberland appeared to have been dispensed with, no doubt so that he would not have to answer difficult questions about Fenwick's recent raid. He was no loss to either side, for he had hardly uttered a word previously. Cromwell, who greeted de Bevois a deal more affably than he did the Scots, appeared to be in a brisk and businesslike frame of mind, adopting from the start the attitude that all was more or less settled and that all that was now required was to agree a few outstanding details and sign the treaty. The Scots intimation that this was not quite the situation was made therefore to seem the more querulous and unhelpful.

For his part, David first made strong and vehement protest about the raid on Teviotdale since they had last met—to be countered by the almost casual assertion that this was just one more of the reivings and forays of these Borderers, something which might be expected from the Armstrongs, for instance, almost at any time. Stung, David opted for bluntness thereafter. Without any diplomatic preamble, which obviously would be wasted on this man, he stated that the Scots position was unchanged. What had been tentatively agreed previously was accepted by King James. But the four outstanding items remained, on which they were instructed not to compromise—King James would not marry the Lady Mary, the more definitely in that she was now disgraced and lowered in status from a princess; the Scots Church would not break with Rome; Edrington Castle and the Caw Mills must be evacuated forthwith; and the Earl of Angus must be returned to Scotland to answer for his misdeeds—although an exception might be made of the Earl of Bothwell, a lesser offender, who could return under pardon so long as he promised to refrain from all futher acts inimical to his liege-lord.

Cromwell's reaction was less fierce than might have been expected. He pooh-poohed these assertions, still seeming to treat them as bargaining points rather than final stances, and proceeded to whittle away at them, even when the Scots reiterated their finality. However, when de Bevois sought permission to speak, and announced that the King of France had agreed that his kinswoman Marie de Bourbon should marry the King of Scots, and that their betrothal would be officially announced shortly, it left even Thomas Cromwell without the wherewithal for riposte. And when the Frenchman added that His Most Christian Majesty most strongly advised King James not to consider any possible disloyalty to the Pope and Holy Church, the English position was still further prejudiced. In essence there remained therefore only the two Douglas matter of Angus and Edrington Castle.

It was, on the face of it, strange that the English should

consider these points as of major importance; yet on them Cromwell refused to budge. They were in fact comparatively minor matters in the affairs of both nations, and yet here they were seeming to produce the final stumbling-block. When neither side would yield, Cromwell declared another adjournment. Whether it was the presence of the Frenchman or no, he was less cavalier in his manner than heretofore.

Back in the monastery the Scots debated long. It seemed absurd to hold up this so desirable peace treaty for the sake of Angus and one small castle. Yet they were there in the name of King James, and these were the issues on which James was most determined. He was the monarch, and they just could not go back and tell him that on these they had capitulated. On the other hand, to return without the treaty, after all the rest had been gained, would be folly. In the end, they came to the conclusion that the only gesture they might risk making was to concede that Angus need not be forcibly returned to Scotland, if he elected to remain in England as an English subject—since it was apparently Henry's contention that he would not and could not deliver up one of his subjects, as Angus had become, to a foreign power. This concession made on condition that Edrington was yielded up. And of course, if Angus did return at any time to his native land, he would have to stand trial. This was the best that they could do, and they hoped that not only Cromwell but James would accept it.

It proved, in fact, sufficient, when at the next sitting Cromwell presumably saw it as a face-saver and conceded the surrender of Edrington and the Caw Mills, with the proviso that the Douglas and English occupiers thereof should be granted safe conduct into England.

So, suddenly, after so long and grievous a struggle, the thing was done. Only, lest he seem to have yielded too much, Cromwell insisted that he—and presumably the Scots also—were only competent to sign the peace treaty as it were tentatively. They would therefore commit the two nations to it for one year only, by their own signatures, although they recommended jointly that it should apply for the period of the two monarchs' reigns, to be ended on the demise of whichever died first; although it was hoped that it would then be renegotiated; it was unsuitable to commit a new monarch on either side. The clerks would draw up these terms.

Two days later, then, with minimal ceremony, the commissioners signed the two copies of this momentous treaty of peace between the realms—peace but scarcely love, for they parted thereafter in no more friendly fashion than they had started, their farewells less than cordial.

For his part, as they rode northwards from Newcastle, David Lindsay wondered how worth it all their efforts had been, and whether indeed the treaty would hold. Henry Tudor was namely as a breaker of truces; would a full treaty be sacrosanct? Only, he imagined, whilst it suited Henry's convenience.

Back at Stirling, James was not happy about the Angus concession, but reluctantly agreed to endorse it, along with the other terms. He was cheered by the news which arrived not long afterwards that the new Queen of England had been delivered of the child on which so much depended. But it was a girl, not the son Henry longed for, and he was reported to be beside himself with disappointment and anger, the poor mother almost as unpopular as had been her predecessor. The baby was to be called Elizabeth.

James was elated.

20

The court at Stirling was in a stir. Four arrivals ensured that. Davie Beaton was the first to come, back from France, full of news. Pope Clement the Seventh was dead, and had been succeeded by a very tough character, Alessandro Farnese, to be called Paul the Third, who was taking a much stronger line with the reformers and heretics who were plaguing Holy Church, and demanding vigorous action against English Henry from all the rulers of Christendom. Also he informed that the Duke of Albany had died lacking male offspring—this left the Bastard's half-brother, the Earl of Arran, undoubted heir to the Scots throne until James produced a lawful child, a situation which made the royal marriage even more urgent. On this subject, Beaton rather ruefully confessed very confidentially to David Lindsay that Marie de Bourbon was in fact considerably less good-looking and attractive than implied by the portrait he had sent; but she was a pleasant-enough female and King Francis was very anxious for the marriage to take place, and quickly.

The next arrivals, only a day or two later, were from England, surprisingly from Henry himself, the Lord William Howard, brother of the Duke of Norfolk, and Master William Barlow, Bishop-Elect of St. Asaphs. These revealed that Henry, despite the peace treaty agreements, had not changed. Howard, who was a son of that 'auld crooked carle' Surrey, the victor of Flodden-field, and so scarcely likely to be popular in Scotland, brought James as gift from his uncle the Order of the Garter, to celebrate the said treaty. But at the same time he pressed anew for the marriage of the Lady Mary to James, officially illegitimate or not, promising an almost unlimited dowry. And Barlow came to further urge a break with Rome, bringing with him details of the vast wealth Henry was garnering in taking over the bishoprics, churches, abbeys and monasteries in England, a magnificent windfall which James might duplicate in Scotland. It seemed as though all the bargaining and negotiations at Newcastle could be ignored, as far as Henry Tudor was concerned.

Then the fourth arrival, while the Englishmen were still at Stirling, was none other than the Papal Legate, Bishop Antonio Campeggio, back again, sent by the new Pope Paul, his remit this time to counter the English machinations, to encourage James not only to remain loyal to Holy Church but to make this evident to all by taking stern and vigorous action against the heretics and so-called reformers who were injuring Christendom in Scotland as elsewhere; and as earnest of papal favour and support to confer on the King of Scots the title of Defender of the Faith.

This explosive mixture of visitors set the court by the ears and the situation was not helped by James himself paying the while very public attentions to his currently favourite mistress, Margaret Erskine, daughter of Stirling Castle's hereditary keeper —and so conveniently on the spot—who had just had the felicity of presenting the King with a fine son, over which infant the father positively drooled. Undoubtedly he had already produced numerous bastards, but this was the first one he not only publicly acknowledged but was permitting him to be named James Stewart and promising continuing favours. Indeed the proud mother was indicating, if only privately to her friends, that it was only right that the boy should be so called, since she and his sire had gone through a secret marriage of the handfast variety.

In the circumstances, those whose task it was to steer the ship of state were not a little bemused. Even Davie Beaton was less calmly confident than usual. As well as Lord Privy Seal he was now also a bishop, albeit a French one, for King Francis seemed to have made him Bishop of Mirepoix and the new Pope had confirmed it.

Davie had come back, inevitably, to many problems which had arisen during his absence abroad, in Church as well as state, most of which he could cope with readily enough. But the matter of heresy, or at least active support for the reforming doctrines of Martin Luther, Melancthon and others on the Continent, was serious, especially in view of Campeggio's mission, the new hard line in the Vatican and the English separation from Rome which had its sympathisers in Scotland. Whilst Davie was in France, owing to the feebleness of his uncle and the *laissez-faire* attitude of the Chancellor, Archbishop Dunbar, the lead in Church affairs had been taken over by Bishop Hay of Ross, a vehement individual, who had ordered the arrest of certain determined dissenters. Most of these, deliberately given due warning to save trouble, had discreetly left the country, these including the brother and sister of the Abbot of Fearn, Patrick Hamilton, who had been burned at the stake some years before, the Canon Alexander Aless of St. Andrews, and a university divine there named MacBeth or MacBee, who was known in the city as Maccabeus. But two named 'reformers' had not taken the hint and continued their public denunciations of Church error and corruption, one David Straiton, a brother of the Laird of Laurieston, in the Mearns, the other Master Norman Gourlay, a parish priest. These now languished in prison at St. Andrews, for the Abbot of Arbroath, Bishop of Mirepoix and Lord Privy Seal to deal with.

Beaton, taking the entire situation into consideration, came up with a fairly typical gesture. He decided that Campeggio and the Pope could be satisfied, James committed firmly to the Romish cause, attention diverted from the Erskine folly, Henry

Tudor's representatives shown once and for all that their cause was hopeless, likewise due warning given to other heretics, all by staging an elaborate trial of the two dissenting culprits, with the King himself sitting in judgement along with the appointed ecclesiastics. This high court of the Church should be held not privately at St. Andrews but publicly at Holyrood Abbey in Edinburgh, and this whilst the various awkward visitors were still with them. He convinced James that this would solve many of his current problems.

When David Lindsay was told of the project he was much against it. Not only did he largely sympathise with the reformers but he felt that such trial and its results might well be counter-productive. There had been considerable unrest throughout the kingdom after Patrick Hamilton's burning. This trial would be almost certain to find the prisoners guilty, and in that case the prescribed penalty for heresy, shameful as he for one considered it, was the stake. If this were carried out there would be more trouble, and the movement for reform could well be encouraged by making martyrs of the pair. Also it would be dragging King James into controversy and endangering his popularity with not a few of his subjects.

Beaton countered that by declaring that every effort would be made to induce the prisoners to recant. They were neither of them figures of importance, and could probably be persuaded both to save their lives and gain themselves preferment in due course by taking the sensible line. Even if not, once the visitors were gone, sentence could probably be commuted to banishment.

The two so different friends agreed to differ, as so often.

It took a few days to arrange this piece of stagecraft to Beaton's satisfaction and to move the principal actors therein, along with most of the court and the audience for whom it was to be played, from Stirling to Edinburgh. James himself seemed to see it all in the nature of an entertainment and diversion, although Davie deplored this, since it would give the wrong impression to the visitors. But it was in something like a holiday spirit that the royal cavalcade proceeded by way of Linlithgow to Edinburgh, to take over the Abbey of the Holy Rood for the occasion. The King, with so many boyhood memories of the place, was much exercised. He insisted that David Lindsay and himself should make their quarters in the same chamber which had been theirs all those years before. The Bastard, for one, was incensed that he should be excluded—for he frequently nowadays shared the royal bedchamber.

Beaton had got Lindsay's Janet busy beforehand, for as the King's Wardrobe Mistress she was responsible for the royal tailoring, and it was decided that James should be clad wholly in scarlet, the traditional colour for judgement, for the occasion. So, a striking figure in rich red, to match his long red hair, rubies from Elie in Fife reflecting the sun from bonnet and breast, and wearing all the newly acquired orders of the Garter, the Golden Fleece and St. Michael, the King led the procession to the great abbey-church from the monastic quarters, where he was greeted by the Abbot of Holyrood and conducted to a throne in mid-chancel, all the rest filing in to fill the nave, although David, as Lord Lyon, followed the monarch, to stand behind the throne, as so often he had done in a different capacity. The commissioners of the ecclesiastical court were already there, at the other side of the chancel, bishops, abbots and priors. The Primate should have presided, but old James Beaton was far too heavy and lethargic to travel from St. Andrews, and Bishop Hay of Ross acted Commissary in his stead. Davie Beaton remained discreetly out of evidence. The Abbot of Holyrood, bowing to James, moved over to join the judges.

David Lindsay, however loth he was to be present, still had his official duties to perform. Once all were inside, he rapped three times on a reading-desk with his baton of office, ordered the doors to be closed and declared that they were here in the name and presence of His Grace James, High King of Scots, descendant of a hundred kings, at a consistory of the highest ecclesiastical court in the land, called by the Primate of All Scotland, to see justice done. He called upon the Lord Abbot of Holyrood to open the proceedings with prayer.

After that, Bishop Hay, a short, wiry individual whom Beaton had privately described as a mitred weasel, having requested the King's permission, declared that in the regretted absence of the Primate, the Archbishop of St. Andrews, on account of bodily indisposition, he had been appointed to head up the commissioners of Holy Church to enquire into and decide upon a matter of great concern, with His Grace's concurrence, to the realm as well as the Church. As most present would be aware, there was a grievous tide of heresy flowing in various parts of Christendom, seeking under guise of reform to undermine the doctrines and integrity of Holy Church and overthrow its age-old institutions and God-given authority. This must not be allowed to happen in Scotland, however close the threat might have come. And the Bishop glanced over to where the distinguished guests sat in the south transept, Lord William Howard and William Barlow amongst them.

Under instructions from the Holy Father in Rome, the Church in Scotland had been seeking to set its house in order, in this respect as in others, reform being good and proper so long as it was ordered and undertaken with the due consent of those ordained to oversee the worship of God's people. But instigated by sources outwith this realm, for their own purposes, certain misguided persons had been seeking to persuade others publicly to rebel against divinely appointed authority and openly preaching heresy and division, even denying the very doctrines of the Catholic faith. The leaders of Holy Church had been patient, perhaps too patient, with these subverters of truth and order, and had warned them frequently. Some had taken heed, some had elected to leave the realm altogether, but some had persisted deliberately in their wrong-doing. Reluctantly the Primate and bishops had been forced to act against these determined heretics, and today two of the most inveterate offenders had been brought before this high court of the Church to make answer for their sins. With His Grace's royal permission he would call on the officers to bring them before the court.

At James's nod, the Bishop called the names of David Straiton and Master Norman Gourlay, priest.

From the chapter-house the prisoners were marched in, under guard. Straiton, young, stocky and defiant seeming, the other middle-aged, frail and bent. They were brought to stand at the chancel steps. The company sat forward, even the King.

"Norman Gourlay and David Straiton," Hay intoned, "you are here before the highest authority in Church and realm this day, in His Grace's presence, to answer charges of heresy and incitement to heresy, after due and repeated warnings and in full knowledge of the penalties prescribed for such offence. In the King's name and of his royal mercy, I give you one last opportunity to recant. Do you, either or both, repent you of your heretical statements, and urgings of others to rebel against the authority of Holy Church? If you will recant as publicly as you first proclaimed your error, and promise never again to repeat the offences, you shall go free from this place."

Hardly waiting for the Bishop to finish, Straiton spoke out strongly. "I recant nothing. I deny, in God's name, that I have ever pronounced heresy but only God's holy Word and Christ's own teaching as contained in Holy Writ."

A murmur ran round the church.

"So be it. And you, Norman Gourlay?"

The older man's voice quavered. "My lord Bishop . . . Your Grace . . . I am a sinner and one of God's weakest vessels. I have failed in much, in my ministry as in my daily life. But I cannot confess to heresy. Heresy, as I understand it, is the holding of false doctrines and the propagation of teachings contrary to the Word of God. Of such I am not guilty, nor ever would be. I but bewail, as I must as God's humble servant, the errors and malpractices which men have introduced into the observances of Holy Church. This surely is the duty of all of us, especially those ordained in holy orders. Of this I cannot recant."

David Lindsay, for one, felt like cheering, but remembered in time that he was the realm's Lord Lyon King-of-Arms.

Hay, after a glance at his fellow judges, who all displayed expressions of disapproval, offence, if not shock, gestured towards the King.

"Your Grace, you have heard these two accused, this defiance and refusal to repent, and even determination to persist in their opposition to the authority and teachings of the Church. There is, indeed, no need for any further indictment, since they have already confessed to the offences charged. But that fullest justice should be seen to be done, even to these wilful offenders, it is proposed that some examples of their offences should be put before Your Highness."

"So I would expect," James said.

"Yes, Sire. This David Straiton is brother to the Laird of Laurieston, in the Mearns, and has properties on that coast near the havens of St. Cyrus and Inverbervie. He owns fishing-cobles and smoke-houses and makes considerable moneys from the sale of fish, especially from smoking and salting. For these profits he has the duty to pay tithes to my lord Bishop of Moray, as is right and proper. But he has resolutely refused so to do. And when my lord Bishop sent his officers to collect the said lawful tithe, the man Straiton, before all at the haven, told his fishermen that they should throw every tenth fish that they caught back into the sea, and advised my lord's officers to go seek the Bishop's tithe where it was to be had in abundance! Such infamy . . ."

A titter ran through the company, and the King smiled broadly.

Hay frowned. "My lord King, this is a fell serious matter, not only denying the Church its due tribute on God's providence and on the labours of others, but contrary to and contesting the very right of Holy Church to its tithes and teinds. Moreover, when the Bishop's representatives upbraided him, for impiety and public denial of God's ordinances and bounty, warning him of the penalties therefor, this Straiton blasphemously there, before a large company, sank to his knees and declared in shameful mockery that Scripture said that our Saviour would deny before His Father and the holy angels anyone who denied Him before men; and he swore to God that although he was a great sinner, he would not deny Him or his truth for fear of bodily torments. We could call a score of witnesses to this wickedness and impiety. But no need, for the man has confessed and not denied it, many times since, and indeed glories in his shame."

Amidst considerable mutterings and murmurings, James cleared his throat.

"And is this heresy?" he asked. "It seems to me . . . otherwise. Play-acting and disrespect for the Bishop, perhaps. But scarcely heresy."

"With due respect, Sire, since you ask, heresy, as even the prisoner Gourlay has admitted, is the holding of false doctrines and the proclamation thereof, the propagation of teachings contrary to the Word of God. This the man Straiton has committed." And Hay turned to look at his fellow commissioners, all of whom nodded solemnly.

James shifted uncomfortably on his throne. "I must accept that assertion of Holy Church as to what is heresy and what is not," he conceded. "But since *I* would not have considered this act and behaviour of the prisoner as heresy, however foolish and disrespectful, then perhaps neither did he. So, if heresy was not intended . . ." The King's voice rather tailed away.

Bishop Hay's certainly did not. "Sire—the thing was done deliberately and of forethought, before many. Making a mock of Holy Church and its ordinances. And blasphemously calling Almighty God to aid him in his apostacy. This is heresy most vile!" Again the waspish prelate turned to his colleagues. All expressed their agreement.

James, clearly out of his depth, spread his hands. "I must bow to your decision, my lord spiritual," he said. "But in this case I suggest mercy. Also recommended in Holy Writ, is it not? Since the penalty laid down for heresy is dire, my judgement in the matter would be a warning on this occasion, on condition that the prisoner pays his tithes in future without such play-acting."

There was silence for moments, Church and state at loggerheads.

When the Bishop spoke, he sounded not a little strained. "With all respect, may I remind you, Sire, that in matters of heresy Your Grace does not have the prerogative of mercy?" he said. "Nor indeed have I!"

A single hoot, compounded of astonishment, laughter and scorn, sounded through the church. It came from Hamilton of Finnart.

James turned in his chair, features almost as red as the rest of him, to look at David Lindsay.

Almost hurriedly Hay went on. "David Straiton, you stand condemned. Norman Gourlay—do you recant?"

The whisper was barely audible. "No, my lord. God . . . giving me courage."

"So be it. You also stand condemned. For you have preached heresy from the very altar-steps of your parish church, as you will not deny."

"I have preached God's Word, as proclaimed by Christ Jesus. On that I must stand, weak as I am."

"On that you shall burn, sir! Since you set yourself up to know better than the Church which gave you any authority you have. You but add blasphemy to heresy." The Bishop turned to his coadjutors. "Does any wish to add to what has been said? Or to offer any reason why the penalty decreed by Holy Church for the vile sin of heresy should not be carried out?"

All there shook their mitred heads.

"Then it falls to me, in the name of the Primate, to pronounce sentence on both heretics. They shall be taken forthwith from this holy place to Greenside-under-Calton, outwith the Canongate burgh bounds and near to the refuge of the lepers, and there their bodies shall be burned with fire. And may Almighty God have mercy on their souls thereafter. This sentence to be carried out in the presence of all true servants of Holy Church, in whatever degree. Officers—conduct the prisoners hence."

Abruptly James rose from his throne and, without a word, stamped out.

Lindsay after a moment or two followed him.

* * *

In the royal bedchamber of the monastery, a little later, Davie Beaton joined an angry monarch and Lindsay. James rounded on him at once.

"You, Beaton—*you* are responsible! You talked me into this. You contrived all. I have been made to look a fool, before all. Over-ruled by a clerk—I, the King! Brought to sit in judgement, and then ignored and controverted. In front of Henry's servants. It is not to be borne! You have failed me, man—failed me!"

"Sire—it is none so ill as that!" Davie asserted, soothingly. "Hay overstepped himself, yes, and lacked tact. But there is no great harm done. You . . ."

"I was insulted and made a laughing-stock. As good as told to hold my tongue! By that up-jumped bishop *you* appointed!"

"Scarce that, Your Grace. Hay spoke rashly, unsuitably. I have already had a word with him—and will have more! He saw his opportunity before the papal nuncio to demonstrate his own fervour and strength for Holy Church, so that the message would be carried back to Rome. Possibly he thinks to see the Primacy itself within his grasp one day! But not if *I* have aught to do with it. But you, Sire, have not suffered over it all, I swear. I have already heard men praising you, admiring your plea for mercy. You will have gained much in repute as the merciful monarch. Yet lost nothing with Campeggio and the Pope who, had the prisoners indeed been reprieved, would have been incensed against you. This way, you have the best of it. The nuncio will return to the Vatican satisfied. Henry will see that he had no hope of turning Scotland against Rome. And Your Grace will be advanced in the affection of your people. What could be a more satisfactory outcome?"

James rubbed his chin, considering.

Not so David Lindsay. "Satisfactory?" he demanded. "Not for

those two poor wretches who go to a terrible and shameful death! Have you forgot *them*, in your satisfaction? Sacrificed for your statecraft—a burnt sacrifice! For holding to what they believed . . ."

"They condemned themselves. They have only themselves to blame."

"You say that! You, who spoke to me of mercy, of reprieve, banishment at the most. Was that but lies and deceit?"

"I hoped that we could persuade them to reason. As we have tried. If not to recant, at least either to remain silent or to indicate regret, so that mercy could be shown. But they remained obdurate, knowing the penalty. They *sought* martyrdom . . ."

"Aye, martyrdom! That is what they will achieve. And your cause will suffer. Each such burning and martyrdom but further condemns the Church in the eyes of all but the clerics. I tell you, it is *Henry's* cause which may well benefit from this day!"

"Henry is concerned only with his own power and with grasping the Church's wealth. He would not care for a thousand martyrs . . . !"

James intervened. "Enough of this. The burning—must I go to this Greenside to watch? I have no wish to do so. Let your Church do its own ill work."

"I fear that you must, Sire. Not to go would look as though you disassociated yourself from the findings of the Church court, undo what good there is in it. Campeggio will be there, and the Englishmen. If *you* are not, all will say that you disagree. So all the benefit towards Rome and Henry will be nullified. These two must die, by the laws of the Church. At least let them not die in vain!"

"Lord!" Lindsay exclaimed.

"Be not so squeamish, my lord Lyon King-of-Arms!" Beaton said. "We have a realm to govern for His Grace, and cannot all afford such delicate stomachs!" He paused. "But, Sire, there is something that you could do there to, shall we say, mitigate sentence. Aye, and further demonstrate Your Grace's mercy. The Church says that heretics' bodies must burn, for the saving of their souls. But it does not say that they must be *alive* when they burn! If you were to order a quick death first, by hanging or the axe, then burning thereafter, it would be less dire, would it not?"

"Ha! Yes, that is a notion. I could do that?"

"To be sure. None can stop you, Sire. Certainly not Bishop Hay. And it would not do your cause any harm at Rome."
"Good! Then we will do that. See you to it, Beaton, in my name."
"There are gallows always ready at Greenside, Sire. For the hanging of malefactors outwith the burgh of the Canongate."
"Very well. Let us get the business over and done with."
"Sire, I seek Your Grace's permission not to attend you on this occasion, as Lyon," Lindsay said. "This once."
James looked from one David to the other, and nodded.

21

James Stewart paced up and down the timbers of the quayside at the port of Leith, as the last of the stores and baggage was being loaded aboard *The Fair Maid*, in a mood compounded of almost boyish excitement and impatience, tinged with annoyance that the sovereign-lord of the realm should be kept thus waiting by the laggardly efforts of common porters and shipmen who should have had all loaded and ready long before this—that, and disapprobation directed towards the man he was leaving behind, to rule, in effect, the said realm for him, even though nominally Archbishop Dunbar the Chancellor would be in charge; Davie Beaton, who stood by, expression inscrutable, David Lindsay at his side.

For Beaton was, if not in disgrace, at least in his monarch's deep disesteem. James had not really absolved him from blame over involving him in the burning of Straiton and Gourlay those months before—the resentment including all the Church's leaders, to be sure. And when the new Pope Paul had sorely failed the King of Scots shortly thereafter, the entire exercise appeared to James a sorry episode, ineffective as it was upsetting, and its instigator and moving spirit, Davie Beaton, to blame. Moreover he suspected Davie of a further offence, of secretly contriving the marriage of his favourite, Margaret

Erskine, to Sir William Douglas of Lochleven, one of the Black Douglases—this to ensure that he, the King, did not marry her, as he was every now and again threatening to do, despite the proposed French match. This secret marriage had struck James sorely, in his pride and self esteem, for he had believed that the lady loved him truly, as well as bearing his son, and he conceived that Beaton had arranged it somehow in order that nothing should interfere with the French connection. In reaction, the King had written directly to the Pope, asking him to annul this wretched union, assuming that, as Beaton had averred, the Vatican would now be well disposed towards him, after the heresy trial and such clear support of Holy Church. When the Pope had declined to do any such thing for a third party, even the esteemed King of Scots, James was the more wrathful, suspecting that here again Beaton was involved. And when, as a final blow, a Hamilton new back from France had informed the Bastard, and he the King, that the Lady Marie de Bourbon was a deal less well-favoured than the portrait Beaton had brought, in fact that she and her sister were both sore made awry, as the informant put it, his anger at his clever Lord Privy Seal reached the stage when something had to be done about it.

That something had developed into this extraordinary adventure, starting at Leith haven, the port for Edinburgh. Margaret Erskine out of the running as a wife, and the proposed French bride allegedly highly unattractive, James had decided to trust no more envoys and match-makers but to go himself, secretly, on the quest for the required wife. King Francis was offering an annual pension of no less than twenty thousand livres for the French match, to outdo Henry, so obviously to France he ought to go. But go in disguise, anonymously, to see with his own eyes what this Marie de Bourbon was like, and if, as seemed probable, she displeased, go seek another French lady more to his taste. There were allegedly plenty of highly attractive women in that fair land. This rather juvenile and romantic knight-errantry all the King's advisers, without exception, had been against; but James was not to be dissuaded. He was going, and taking only a very small company with him, in this one ship—since anything larger would reveal him as someone of importance. His Lord Privy Seal would most certainly not be going with him.

David Lindsay would, however, as would the Bastard of Arran and a few others who knew France and the Continent.

Beaton smoothed hand over mouth and neat pointed little beard. "Try to steer him, if you ever get so far, towards Marie de Guise," he advised, low-voiced. "I fear that he will have none of the Bourbon, when he sees her, in his present mood. The de Guise is not beautiful but she has her attractions, very rich, and she is an able young woman who would make a good queen. She might be good for James—and he sorely needs a good strong wife!"

"He will gang his ain gait, in this, that one!" Lindsay said. "I fear that I will be able to do little. The entire ploy is a folly . . ."

"A folly, yes. But like so many follies, we must make the best of it. I need not say to do your best for James. But watch Finnart. I would that *he* was not going. He will cause trouble if he can."

"What could he do, in this? In France . . ." Lindsay got no further with that, for heavy spots of rain began to fall and James decided to leave the quayside for the shelter of the ship. He came up to them.

"Come aboard, Davie. You, Beaton, see to all in my absence—but heedfully, see you. No clever ploys! I warn you, I shall require a close accounting when I return. They are near finished loading now. We shall sail forthwith."

"Sire, the weather is not of the best. Fishermen I spoke with say that they expect it to turn for the worse. I advise that you delay sailing . . ."

"Nonsense, man! Old wives' havers! *I* know you. You are against me sailing, at all. Be off, or you will be soaked. Come, Davie . . ."

Lindsay raised a hand to his friend, and followed his liege-lord up the gangplank on to the vessel.

The shipmaster, a burly Fifer, was also concerned about the weather, but James was already tired of delay and insisted that a start be made. At least there was no lack of wind to assist them in casting off and, sails filling, they moved out into the open water.

Beaton and the others left behind made a bolt for cover.

The steady rain which developed, the cramped and less than comfortable quarters, and the overcrowding of the small ship, made it an inauspicious start; but the King, now that he was actually on his way, was in high spirits even if nobody else was. As they heaved and tossed their way down the Firth of Forth, no wettings from rain or spray damped his enthusiasm, his interest in the handling of the ship, the setting of the sails, the views of the shores and islands of Lothian and Fife. Although the motion of the craft, in increasingly disturbed waters, together with the smells of stale bilge-water, tar and oily wool-bales from the hold, sent most of the passengers hurrying below, pale of face, not so their sovereign; he appeared to be immune to sea-sickness. Fortunately Lindsay was also a good sailor; and although the Bastard was less so, evidently, he resolutely remained on deck with his monarch.

The wind was gusting from the north-east, unusual in July, and this entailed continual tacking, much delaying their progress. Not that this concerned James. He kept urging the shipmaster, in his necessary beatings back and forth across the firth, to go ever closer to either shore, so that he might try to recognise the various locations and landmarks as seen from this unaccustomed viewpoint, exclaiming at the isle of Inchkeith, the headland at Kinghorn where his ancestor Alexander the Third had fallen to his death, the roaring white breakers on the sand-bar of wide Aberlady Bay, and the cliffs and rocks of Elie where the rubies came from. With the mighty towering stack of the Craig of Bass off North Berwick, he was duly impressed, pointing delightedly at the basking seals and the thousands of screaming, diving gannets.

But once past the Bass, they were out of the firth and into the open Norse Sea, and the difference was very quickly apparent, as the seas grew in steepness and the wind stiffened to a steady half-gale. *The Fair Maid* rolled and pitched grievously in the cross seas as they turned due southwards, and the deck lost its attractions even for the King. Anyway, there was nothing more to see now, with night falling and the land only faintly looming on their right. Thankfully his companions led him below for a meal of sorts.

There was no great demand for food that evening, but a drinking session developed amongst those so capable and inclined. David Lindsay retired to his bunk early—but not before they had a visit from the shipmaster, who came to announce gruffly that wind and seas were still rising steadily. If it got much worse they might have to run for shelter in some haven or anchorage. Did His Grace have any views on the matter?

James, distinctly drink-taken now, told the man not to be so craven. They must be off the coast of England by now, and the last place he would wish to reach was his Uncle Henry's domains. He pressed wine on the skipper to improve his courage.

Before falling asleep, David heard the King being assisted to his bed by the Bastard, who had a notably good head for liquor. Despite the strange conditions, the heaving, the creaking of timbers and the thick atmosphere, Lindsay had a fairly good night.

There was no light in that pit of a cabin when he awoke, and he had no idea as to the time. But after lying for a while, listening to the snores of his companions, he was aware of clatter and footsteps on the deck above his head. Also the motion of the ship was much less pronounced. When he smelt what he decided was cooking ham, from the nearby galley, he reckoned that it was probably morning. He rose, stretched, and made his way up the ladder to the deck.

It proved to be broad daylight, even if a dull and grey morning. Hamilton, looking enviably fresh, was standing beside a bleary-eyed shipmaster. He grinned at the newcomer.

Yawning, David looked about him. Land was visible, not much more than a mile off. It took a moment or two for its significance to register. It lay to leeward, to their *left* side, not to the right as was to be expected. Then he realised that, although there was no sun visible as yet, such lightness as the sky held was astern to them. So they were heading westwards, not southwards or eastwards, parallel to the shore. And his glance astern registered something else. Behind them, some miles, a great lump of rock rose out of the sea, and even at that range there was no mistaking its bulk and contours. It was the Craig of Bass. Bewildered, he peered landwards. Yes, there was North Berwick Law and his own Garleton Hills. They were back in the Firth of Forth, sailing for home.

Astonished, he went over to the Bastard. "What is this?" he demanded. "Why are we here? What has happened?"

"You must have slept well, man," Hamilton said. "We had to turn back. The storm grew too great for us. We could no longer hazard the King's safety. It was either this, or running for an English harbour—which James had forbidden."

"But . . . but . . . Sakes—this is beyond all! To turn back altogether. To return home. The seas are less high . . ."

"Here in the firth, yes. Out there it was otherwise. You must be a sound sleeper, my Lord Lyon!"

"But why come all the way back? We are off Aberlady Bay. Why not shelter in the south of the firth and then resume our voyage when the seas go down?"

"Because the storm has loosened some timbers, our shipmaster says. We are taking water. Some spars were broke. We must return for repairs."

"Lord! Does James know?"

"Not yet. Like you, His Grace sleeps sound! We did not think to disturb him."

"He is not going to like this."

"Better than a watery grave, man!"

"*You* may tell him, then. I prefer not!"

It was quite some time before James appeared. They were by then off Musselburgh, and with the crouching-lion outline of Arthur's Seat looming large ahead, there could be no least doubt, even at first glance, as to where they were. The King stared. His arm extended, to point at the great hill. No words came.

The Bastard produced something between a bow and a shrug. "Safe back from the storm, Sire," he greeted. "Preserved from the perils of the deep, God be praised!" he added piously.

James transferred his stare from the view to the speaker. "You . . . turned . . . back!" he got out.

"To be sure. All was at stake. Your Grace's very life. The storm grew ever worse after you retired. We were in danger of sinking, timbers sprung, taking water. We could not run for an English harbour, for you had said not that. We only prayed that we could win to the calmer waters of this Forth again, in safety . . ."

"You turned back, Hamilton, without my permission! Knowing that I would not give it. You did this, against my wishes. You did it . . . because you were against this venture from the start. Would not have me to go to France. Would not have me to marry. So that, so that *Hamilton* might one day gain my throne! You, you Bastard indeed!"

"Sire—no! Hear me. We could not go on, in the storm. The seas were beyond belief. It was an English haven, or return here. You were asleep and in wine. The shipmaster was much in fear. I took the only decision possible . . ."

"You took a decision that you will regret, Hamilton! This I

will not forget." Without another word, the King swung around and went below again.

Back at Leith, James sent for David. He did not wish to see the Bastard again. Have him away and out of his sight. They would require to hire horses, to ride up to Holyrood. Send a messenger ahead to prepare all. He would speak with none. His name and fame had been brought low in the sight of all men. This was the sorriest day of his life.

Lindsay sought to comfort and reassure. A storm was beyond anyone's control, even a king's. None would think the worse of him . . .

James silenced him with a gesture and waved him out of the foul-smelling cabin.

The King would not disembark until he was assured that Finnart had gone, and the others with him. Thereafter he and David alone rode in cloaked anonymity the two miles up to the Abbey of the Holy Rood.

* * *

There followed a strange interlude. James, humiliated and angry, was at his sourest. He would have none of his court around him. Those at Edinburgh were sent packing back to Stirling, and none from there summoned. David Lindsay was almost his only companion, as he had been here all those years before when Angus had ruled. They went daily walks up Arthur's Seat, but these were scarcely pleasant occasions, with the King poor company indeed. He drank steadily.

Then, after five days of it, Davie Beaton turned up, unbidden, from St. Andrews, having heard the news. At first the King would not see him either; but after the two friends had had a conference, Lindsay convinced James that Beaton not only had matters of state which called for the monarch's attention, but had proposals, interesting proposals, as to the present situation and the French visit. This procured an interview.

After sympathetically listening to a diatribe against the Bastard and the shipmaster of *The Fair Maid*, Beaton, agreeing with all the King had said, suggested tactfully that the French visit should not be abandoned but amended and proceeded with forthwith. But not in any secret or clandestine fashion. Let James go openly, as King of Scots, and with a goodly squadron of ships, as befitted a royal suitor, such as would impress the

King of France, whose favour was of course essential, especially if the Lady Marie de Bourbon was to be rejected. And in view of those twenty thousand livres of pension! With a number of larger ships there would be little chance of any repetition of being turned back by storm. Also no risk of attack by English pirates.

James very quickly began to cheer up, but wondered where he could get a sufficiency of ships, and how to pay for them, in the chronically empty state of his Treasury? Davie answered to leave that to him, and to Holy Church. *He* would find and pay for the ships. There were many fine vessels trading out of Fife—from St. Andrews itself, from Dysart and Kirkcaldy, from Inverkeithing and Culross. Give him two or three weeks. And with His Grace's permission, this time he would accompany the expedition himself. And there would be no turning back!

James, much enheartened, could produce no objections.

Beaton did not actually say that he expected something in return for his generosity, but he did indicate that His Grace could usefully fill in some of the time, while the ships were being found and a suitably illustrious company assembled to accompany the King to France, by making a brief pilgrimage, which would benefit the Church and please the Pope in Rome, also further confound King Henry. A new shrine had recently been set up to Our Lady of Loretto, at Musselburgh. There had been no such place of pilgrimage in South-East Scotland since St. Margaret's Black Rood had been stolen by English Edward from Holyrood three centuries before. They had Whithorn in Galloway, St. Duthac's at Tain in Ross, and of course Iona in the Hebrides; but nothing save the small shrine of the White Kirk of Hamer, near Tantallon, where the holy well had rather fallen into desuetude. This new chapel, shrine and image at Musselburgh, founded by the hermit-monk Thomas Duthie three years before, was just what was needed for the faithful of Edinburgh, Lothian and the East Borderland. But so far few knew about it and it was therefore not attracting the desired numbers of pilgrims. If His Grace would go there, preferably on foot—it was a bare five miles from Holyrood, after all—then all the realm would hear of it and take note. Also, since it commemorated the marriage of the Virgin Mary with Joseph, as well as the Annunciation, it was a highly suitable venue for the King to offer prayers for the success of his matrimonial journey—and no more storms!

James, scarcely a religious character as he was, saw no serious reason why he could not co-operate in this, if his Lord Privy Seal thought it important. It would only take one day, after all.

Later, Lindsay taxed his friend with this pilgrimage project. Was it not all something of a nonsense? He had heard something of this hermit Duthie and his claims. Were there not grave doubts about it all?

"Of course there are, man—as there must be about anything with claims towards the miraculous. This Duthie may well be an imposter, the relics of his own devising—although perhaps not, who knows? What is important is that folk, ordinary folk, need the reassurance of such places and persons, such spiritual comfort. Their belief is what matters, not what may or may not be material. Such shrines fulfil a need amongst the faithful." He smiled slightly. "And are very profitable for Holy Church!"

"Aye—there we have it! Profitable. And it matters not that all may be pretence? Not true?"

"What *is* truth, Davie? What a man *believes* can be more potent than what may be proven fact. This of Loretto. The image and relics the man Duthie may truly have brought from Italy, or may not. But then at that Loretto itself—what of that? The tradition is that the very house in which the Virgin Mary lived in Nazareth, miraculously uplifted and brought through the air from Galilee to Ancona in Italy, was set down there three centuries ago. Do *you* believe that?"

"I think not."

"Yet many do. Sufficient, I am told, to bring one hundred thousand pilgrims there each year, giving thirty thousand crowns in offerings! Moneys which can be useful indeed for God's work."

"Or for priests' and prelates' pouches!"

Beaton shrugged. "Some of it, perhaps. But most serves its good purpose. And the Church in Scotland can do with the like." He grinned again. "If James makes a pilgrimage to this Loretto, sufficient will follow to pay for these ships I am to charter for him!"

"Sakes! So that is it!"

"Part of it. I am a practical man, you see."

So four days later a somewhat embarrassed James Stewart led his first, and probably his last, holy pilgrimage. Beaton had organised it with his usual efficiency, and all Edinburgh turned out to watch, not a few to take part. It should have been a barefoot progress, according to Vatican traditional rules, but ever since, almost exactly one hundred years before, Aeneas Piccolomini, later Pope Pius the Second, had made the pilgrimage from Dunbar to the White Kirk of Hamer in frosty weather, and suffered rheumatism in his feet for the rest of his life in consequence, he had accepted that barefoot pilgrimages were scarcely suitable for Scotland and amended the regulations for northern climes accordingly.

But walk they did, starting from Holyrood. A large choir of singing boys and instrumentalists went first, followed by a notable contingent of clergy led by David Beaton himself, for once in episcopal robes and wearing a mitre, not as Bishop of Mirepoix but as Abbot of Arbroath. Then came James, walking alone, dressed soberly, such great officers of state as were available just behind, the Earl of Erroll, High Constable and Lindsay, Lord Lyon. Then the earls, lords, barons, knights, lairds and chiefs, with the new Lords of Session. Finally the Edinburgh magistrates and guild deacons led by Sir Adam Otterburn, as Provost—who, as again Lord Advocate could have walked beside David Lindsay, but chose to lead his own grouping. A flock of citizenry trailed along behind, with children, packmen, beggars, even dogs. The royal guard was dispensed with, for this allegedly religious occasion.

In the pleasant early August sunshine, it made an agreeable enough stroll, through part of the royal hunting-park which surrounded Arthur's Seat, past St. Margaret's Loch, over a shoulder of hill to the Fishwives' Causeway and across the Figgate Whins to the coast. Less than two miles, following the sandy shore, brought them to the haven of Fisherrow, near the mouth of the River Esk. Not having horses to ford the shallows of the little estuary, they had to turn upstream to cross by the hump-backed stone bridge. Here they were met by the Provost and baillies of Musselburgh, who escorted the royal procession through their burgh, which prided itself on its ancient and honourable status as the honest toun, so called by Thomas Randolph, Earl of Moray, Bruce's nephew, regent of the infant David the Second, when it had succoured him in his and the kingdom's need. The house where the sick regent had lodged was proudly pointed out to the present monarch.

Only a little further, beyond the east end of the High Street, was the site of the new shrine, a small chapel of no real distinction, erected beside a feeder of the Pinkie Burn—to provide the necessary holy water. James was not the only one to declare himself unimpressed by the object of their pilgrimage.

They were greeted by Brother Duthie, suitably hairy but otherwise unhermitlike, a powerfully-built youngish man in the Carmelite habit, who claimed to have occupied a cave on Mount Sinai before being taken by the Infidel and held captive for years. He had eventually escaped from the Turks to Italy and gone to Ancona, where he had, he asserted, been in the famous Casa Santa, the house of the Blessed Virgin miraculously transported from Nazareth, now encased in white marble, and had actually seen the window through which the Archangel Gabriel had appeared to Mary—whose sub-angels, no doubt, arranged the said transportation.

The chapel was so small that only a very few of the visitors could get in, and Beaton murmured to Lindsay that they would have to build something better than this once the money began to flow in. Inside, amidst the incense-smoke and many flickering candles, they found an altar on which there were a number of rather gaudily-painted iconlike pictures, surrounding a small wooden statuette of the Virgin and Child, brought from Italy but which appeared to have been freshly and vividly painted for the occasion. They were assured that those privileged to touch it could be cured of sundry diseases and ills, including scrofula, cold griefs, dropsy, and it was singularly helpful in resisting witchcraft. The King duly touched, muttered a Hail Mary, and coughing in the incense-smoke, was for getting out when Beaton restrained him, and launched into a stirring petition to the Almighty for the success of the forthcoming royal journey to France in search of a fair, virtuous and fertile bride and queen, who should, they prayed, be the earthly counterpart of the heavenly one they were here to celebrate, and from whom Scotland would gain great blessing.

Outside, after depositing the all-important offerings in a capacious kist, they found the great concourse, unable to get into the chapel, settled down in holiday fashion to picnic on the banks of the burn—for enterprising hucksters and packmen had appeared, selling viands and drink as well as miniature images, pictures, beads, crosses, charms and the like. Concerned that the available moneys brought could mostly be spent in such competing fripperies instead of on the object of the exercise, the hermit-custodian proclaimed in a stentorian bellow that all should form up to file into the chapel in turn, to gain its undoubted blessings and contribute accordingly; and that meantime most there might elect to wash their feet in the burn's holy waters, duly blessed for the occasion, for which only a small charge would be made but which would banish not only weariness from walking but rheumatics, swellings, varicosity and likewise generally uplift the spirits.

James, however, had had enough, and having had the forethought to arrange for horses to come along behind them, was able to ride back to Holyrood at a brisk pace to better than any *al fresco* meal amongst the multitude.

Davie Beaton was reasonably well satisfied. A worthwhile harvest would almost certainly follow this planting of seed.

By first September, Beaton's efforts had borne fruit, and no fewer than seven fine ships were assembled at the port of Kirkcaldy in Fife—which had a more sheltered anchorage for such a squadron than had St. Andrews—one, the flag-ship, of as much as seven hundred tons. The royal procession which wound its way the forty miles from Stirling, mounted this time, consisted of no fewer than five hundred souls, an illustrious company, all clad in their best. It included four earls, Argyll, Moray, Rothes and Arran—the last taken along to keep him from mischief-making with his half-brother the Bastard, who was being most ostentatiously left behind, also, of course, he was hereditary Lord High Admiral. The Lords Maxwell, Fleming and Erskine were there, and numerous heirs and cadets of noble houses—amongst whom was a very good-looking and dashing young man named Oliver Sinclair, of the line of the St. Clair Earls of Orkney and Caithness, on whom the King's favour was increasingly being bestowed since the fall of Finnart. Davie Beaton superintended all on this occasion. There was only the one woman, Janet, Lady Lindsay of The Mount, who was considered suitable to attend on the hoped-for bride, none of the King's many mistresses being apt for the occasion.

They sailed on the evening tide, an impressive flotilla, not only the flag-ship decked with Lion Rampant standards and banners. And the sky was clear and the breeze only adequate to fill the sails—whether at Our Lady of Loretto's behest or otherwise.

22

They reached Dieppe on the 10th of September, after a pleasant, swift and uneventful voyage, admittedly dogged by English ships, but these had kept their distance, in view of the size and quality of the Scots squadron.

Their arrival at the French port created a great stir. Beaton had, of course, despatched a courier in advance to inform King Francis of their coming, and that monarch had sent what he no doubt considered to be the most suitable and illustrious deputy to welcome his royal visitor, the Duc Charles de Vendôme himself, which, in the circumstances, was something of an embarrassment to James. The Duc proved, however, to be an amiable elderly man of far from daunting character, which was something of a relief. With the Scots five hundred and the Duc's own five score, they made almost an army, to ride in leisurely fashion east by south through the Picardy plain to Aisne and St. Quentin, where it appeared that the Duc and his family were presently residing and like any and every army, they inevitably made themselves less than welcome to the ordinary folk of the countryside in passing. The provision of sufficient horses for the visitors was in itself a major undertaking, and the feeding en route likewise, with overnight accommodation a headache. All was done in the King of France's name, fortunately, and at his charges. It was almost one hundred miles to St. Quentin, and they made the two overnight stops, the first at Bethune, on the River Brette, which Beaton was concerned to show off, for this was where his ancestors had come from to Scotland in the twelfth century, the name Beaton being merely a corruption of Bethune.

The Duc Charles had brought them ill news.

The Dauphin Francis, young as he was, had died, leaving as heir to the French throne his brother Henry, a much more feeble individual with whom his father did not get on well. King Francis was prostrated with grief, at Lyons. It all made an inauspicious start to the Scots visit.

The second night they passed at Amiens, the capital of Picardy, which David Lindsay had visited on his way to Brussels six years earlier. St. Quentin also he had passed through, which they reached the next day, a large town on the Somme, with a magnificent twelfth-century church and a handsome town hall. Here the ducal palace was too small to house the great Scots retinue, presumably larger than expected, and most had to be billeted in the town—with the inevitable attendant problems of precedencies and choosing who should lodge where, a task which fell to David Lindsay, as Lyon, to arrange.

There was no lack of hospitality and entertainment, however, on the part of their host and his son, the Count Antoine; indeed a most ambitious programme of events, sports, a jousting, bear- and bull-baitings, hunting, even a carnival and circus, and of course banqueting, had been organised—which was distinctly awkward, since, within the first half-hour of arrival, the King of Scots' one preoccupation was to get away from that place as quickly as possible. For Marie de Bourbon was indeed far from physically attractive and to a man of James's all-consuming interest in women, scarcely conceivable as a wife. Without being actually deformed, she had stooped shoulders almost constituting a hunched back, short legs and short neck. She was not ugly of feature but her squarish face had a masculine cast to it, very like her father's—and unfortunately an incipient moustache to go with it, which shaving could not wholly hide. Her pleasant smile, which the portrait-painter had been at pains to emphasise, was insufficient to compensate, as far as James Stewart was concerned. And her younger sister, who might have provided an alternative choice, was very similar, but without the smile.

So the problem was how to make a fairly speedy departure without causing major offence. Beaton and Lindsay had all along recognised that some such situation might arise, and they now sought to restrain James's eagerness to be off. Their efforts were hardly aided by Marie herself, who most obviously found the good-looking and romantic prince from afar who had, she assumed, come all this way just to wed her, entirely to her taste, and made no attempt to hide the fact. In these conditions, James could not avoid her company, and not being unkind by nature, was much troubled, insisting that his closest aides should if possible never leave him alone with the lady, and in especial that Janet Lindsay should attach herself to Marie at every opportunity. At the public and outdoor events this was not difficult; but there were numerous occasions indoors, some undoubtedly contrived by Marie herself, when it was all but impossible for others to cling to the King's side. Janet found it all trying in the extreme, the more so in that she esteemed the Frenchwoman so pleasant a character.

Six days, and worse, six evenings, of this, and James was becoming desperate—an extraordinary situation for him with any woman—when unlooked for relief arrived in the shape of Henry, Duc de Guise, from Lyons. A stiffly handsome man of some thirty years, and brother of the second of the ladies suggested as possible bride for James, he came with King Francis's command to conduct the King of Scots, and all others, to him at Lyons forthwith, no explicit reason being given. However, James thankfully all but embraced the haughty de Guise, and set about preparing to depart almost too promptly for good manners. Probably their host was somewhat relieved also, since he could hardly have failed to recognise that his royal guest was hardly overwhelmed with admiration for his daughter; also the transference elsewhere of the cost of entertaining five hundred Scots could scarcely be unwelcome. What Marie herself thought, she did not vouchsafe; but probably she saw no objection to continuing her courtship amidst the splendours of Francis's court.

So a day or two later the move was initiated. From St. Quentin to Lyons involved a major journey, down through the centre of France, of almost four hundred miles, so that the royal entourage became almost an expedition, taking practically two weeks. Although James had to ride for some part of the way at Marie's side, no intimacy was called for; and since they put up en route almost entirely at abbeys and bishops' palaces, with accommodation inevitably and conveniently crowded, embarrassing proximity could be avoided. All the way they went by, and followed, great rivers, by the Oise and the Aisne to Rheims, then by the Marne to Chalon and so to reach the upper Seine at Troyes. They crossed the higher ground of Burgundy to the

Yonne and on thereafter through the Nivernais to the Saône, to the other Chalon. Finally down that river, in the Cote d'Or, to its junction with the Rhone, where stood Lyons, the second city of France. Taken leisurely, it made a pleasant and rewarding journey, although for David Lindsay it was spoiled by the continuing necessity of reconciling individuals to their overnight lodging, the Scots lords and lairds being supremely touchy about inferior accommodation.

They found Lyons to be a great and prosperous walled city, within two rows of fortifications, hilly, teeming with folk, with many great churches and public buildings. Nevertheless the dominating theme was wealth, trade and commerce, with the warehouses which lined the riverside quays seeming to represent the spirit of the place, something the visitors had not encountered hitherto, although Lindsay had seen something of the same at Brussels. King Francis, always extravagant, had recognised how much money was to be made by the manufacture of silk, and was determined to make Lyons the silk capital of the world, and so spent much time here. He had no palace, however, and made that of the Archbishop of Lyons his headquarters. Thither the Duc de Guise escorted the visitors.

Here James had a surprising reception. For they were met by the eighteen-year-old Henry, the new Dauphin, a slight, weedy and pimply young man who, when de Guise announced the King of Scots, came running forward and actually threw his arms around him, gabbling a mixture of welcome, admiration, apologies and explanations. Distinctly taken aback, James if he did not recoil scarcely responded, eyeing de Guise over the youth's head. The Duke had warned him that this Henry was not a strong character, inclined to be emotional, and all but despised by his father; but he was unprepared for such a display nevertheless.

The Dauphin, clutching James's hand and leading him onward, ignoring the Archbishop and other waiting dignitaries, launched into a breathless exposition. His father, who sadly hated him, without cause, and loved his brother, had taken to his bed in dolour and would not be comforted. He, Henry, had had done what he could. He had his brother's Italian body-squire—who undoubtedly had poisoned the Dauphin at the behest of the Emperor Charles—flayed and tortured to death; but nothing would assuage the King's grief. This God-sent arrival of His

Majesty of Scotland would, Heaven willing, serve to arouse his royal father and soften the pain.

They came to a door in a long corridor, flanked by resplendent guards. On this the young prince beat unceremoniously with his fists, for apparently it was locked from within. Repeated banging at length produced a hollow voice demanding to know who was there and daring to disturb a man undergoing the sufferings of the damned? To which the Dauphin shouted that he had the King of Scotland come to see His Majesty and give him comfort.

Unprepared for this role of deliverer and consoler, James was the more astonished when, after a sort of bellow from within, the door was suddenly thrown open and His Most Christian Majesty appeared in his bedgown, hair awry, beard untrimmed, tears streaming down his face, to gaze at his tall and handsome visitor and then to launch himself bodily upon him, even more comprehensively than his son had done a few minutes before, clutching him to his inadequately-clad and paunchy person and loudly thanking his Maker for His beloved goodness and great benefits in sending to him a brother-monarch to share his pain and help take the place of him whom the same Almighty had so cruelly removed.

Overwhelmed physically and otherwise by this extraordinary introduction to the de Valois father and son, James Stewart failed to respond in kind. Unprepared for such presumably Gallic demonstration, especially in one who was renowned as an inveterate fighter of battles, a notable political intriguer and the most extravagant man in Christendom, he tended to stiffen and hold off, even though his own nature was apt to be on the impulsive side. But this exaggerated mummery towards a complete stranger, although perhaps flattering, was over-much for any Scot.

Francis, however, did not appear to notice the lack of response. He drew James into the untidy bedchamber, exclaiming volubly. The Dauphin followed them in, but the others remained in the doorway, uncertain as to procedure. No more uncertain than James himself, admittedly, who glanced behind him as though for help. Fortunately perhaps, the other monarch, turning to glare at his son, perceived Davie Beaton standing amongst the others, and reacted with a further display of fervour, exclaiming his delight to see again his dear Scots David, whom the good Saviour had also sent to his aid in this pass, and beckoning him within—to James's marked relief. De Guise, Vendôme, the Archbishop, David Lindsay and one or two others, also entered now.

Thereafter, apparently recovered from his prostration, the French monarch shouted for his gentlemen-of-the-bedchamber with his clothing, these appearing from an anteroom, there before them all His Majesty was stripped of his bedgown and dressed in the elaborate finery of silken shirt and starched ruff, velvet and cloth-of-gold, padded shoulders and slashed sleeves, chains and jewellery, talking the while incessantly. He was a man of forty-two, formerly well-favoured in a dark and sallow way but now somewhat ravaged and puffy with ill-health and many indulgences, his over-large nose and heavy eyelids seeming scarcely to match his vehemence and lively facial expression. He held forth eloquently on his sorrow-turned-to-joy, his grievous loss but his new-found felicity, how he would demonstrate his welcome and his favour. They would go to Paris and forget this unhappy Lyons—and he looked balefully at his son and their unfortunate archiepiscopal host.

Thoroughly roused and revived now, Francis de Valois showed that he would prove his words. Nothing was good enough for his guests. Not only the Archbishop's palace but Lyons itself was set in a stir to provide them with princely hospitality. This king clearly did what he chose to do in no uncertain fashion, whether it entailed mourning a son or entertaining important visitors.

But not for long, here. There were restrictions even for him in playing this role, at Lyons. Paris was the place for it. Moreover, when James admitted that Marie de Bourbon was hardly his notion of a suitable wife, however admirable in birth and fortune, Francis said that he sympathised and understood, and declared that his friend must lose no time in meeting the other possibility, Marie de Guise—since tragically his own daughter Madeleine, whom with all his heart he would have had James to wed, and thus made him into a son indeed to replace the lost one, was in no state of health to marry, the apple of his eye but sadly stricken with a wasting sickness.

So, within a week, the vast train set out for the north again. This journey involved more river-following, France clearly a notable country for great and noble rivers. This time it was the Loire, which took them up through the Bourbonais and the

Orleanais, by Roanne and Digoin and Nevers, to Montargis, where they branched off due northwards to follow the Loing, as the greater river swung westwards for the distant Bay of Biscay. By Nemours they came to Fontainebleau, and the magnificent new palace which Francis had built, after two hundred and twenty miles and six days of travel. And here, strangely enough, the French king left them, with Paris only a day's journey ahead, saying that he had to ride to Rambouillet, where there was a royal chateau in which dwelt his famous and formidable sister, Marguerite, Queen of Navarre, author of the *Heptameron* and supporter of the reformers, whom James must meet. Why Francis must go for his sister in person was not explained; but de Guise hinted that a favourite mistress lived at Etampes, en route to Rambouillet. When James enquired where was the Queen of France, Eleanor of Portugal, the Emperor Charles's sister, there was a pause before de Guise indicated that the lady was not spoken of and lived in retirement. Before Francis left them, however, he sent instructions ahead for the deputies of the French parliament to be present to receive the Scots monarch at the city limits the next day, and to come dressed for the occasion in scarlet gowns—something apparently only done hitherto for the reception of a new Dauphin; of course the Dauphin Henry would be there, with James, but Francis assured his royal guest that it was in *his* honour.

The following afternoon, then, with no sign of King Francis or his sister, the great cavalcade duly arrived at the French capital, reaching the Seine at Ivry. At the outskirts the red-robed parliamentarians were waiting, with a large crowd of others in finest array, with speeches of welcome and a mounted band to lead them into the city.

Paris was undoubtedly the greatest metropolis that any of the Scots had ever seen, save perhaps Davie Beaton who had been to Rome. It was now spreading far beyond its early walls and outer fortifications, an extraordinary mixture of magnificence and squalor, of unbelievable wealth and grinding poverty, with mean stinking hovels cheek-by-jowl with palatial mansions, splendid public buildings and noble churches and monasteries set amongst crumbling ruins, wide squares and marketplaces crowded by narrow, twisting streets and lanes into which daylight scarcely penetrated.

Through all this the lengthy, brilliantly-clad company wound, de Guise's guards clearing their way with lance-butts and the flats of swords. Davie Beaton, who was very familiar with it all, pointed out the sights to the Lindsays. The mighty and lofty cathedral of Notre Dame drew all eyes with its twin towers and slender spire soaring above all else; but soon thereafter a rival edifice began to dominate the urban scene—although the word edifice might give a totally wrong impression. This was an enormous riverside citadel, of a grandeur scarcely to be taken in at first sight, curtain-walls within curtain-walls, courts within courts, with no fewer than sixteen tall, conical-roofed and parapeted towers, turrets and bastions without numbers, storeyed roofs rising row upon row, all islanded within a series of canal-like moats fed from the Seine which lapped the walls.

This apparently, The Louvre, was their destination—although there was another royal residence in the city, the Palais Royal, more modern but smaller and so less suitable for the numbers now to be entertained. The Dauphin led the company, of nearly one thousand now, in over three different drawbridges and through three outer baileys, into a vast central courtyard, where even these numbers did not appear to crowd the place—for The Louvre was itself a town within a city.

They were greeted here by a tall elegant in his mid-twenties, handsome in a saturnine way and dressed all in crimson velvet, in the height of fashion, whom the Dauphin, now seeking to assert himself apparently, introduced, although sourly, as Charles de Guise, Cardinal of Lorraine. The visitors knew this famous character to be the younger brother of the Duc de Guise, and of Marie de Guise. Next to King Francis he was the most powerful man in France despite his comparative youth, clever as he was good-looking, able as he was subtle and ambitious, effective head of the Church, and the King's all-important link with the Vatican. He and Davie Beaton, obviously well-acquainted, made a pair indeed. No doubt this was the real source of the latter's bishopric of Mirepoix.

If the Cardinal was surprised not to see his master, King Francis, with James, he gave no sign of it but welcomed the King of Scots and his entourage in a speech which could not be faulted for grace and diplomacy. It was by no means overlong, to be tedious, nevertheless James's attention strayed, taken up by a lady who waited at the forefront of the glittering throng behind the Cardinal, a tall, graceful creature, not beautiful but with an arresting appearance, dark, full-figured, with a long, swanlike neck and a glowing eye and very direct glance. Quick to notice the chief guest's interest, Charles de Guise, glancing at his brother, turned to introduce her, before any of the others, as his sister Marie, the widowed Duchess de Longueville. As she curtsied low, James hastened forward to raise her up, thereafter retaining her hand for some few moments.

Davie Beaton nudged David Lindsay, and they both looked towards Marie de Bourbon.

After the other presentations, they moved indoors and through what seemed an endless succession of splendid halls, statue-lined corridors and picture-hung galleries, unexpected in a medieval fortress, James walking between the Cardinal and his sister, the Duc de Guise and the Dauphin immediately behind. It was noteworthy how the Duc Henry, somewhat haughty and proud as he seemed hitherto, now gave place to his younger brother. Presently, leaving the major portion of their followers behind, after a wave of the Cardinal's hand towards a chamberlain, they came to a comparatively small apartment, modest in size if not in its quality and furnishings, circular in shape and obviously occupying one of the many round towers, only James's closest companions being ushered in here. It was a strange room to find there, or anywhere for that matter, giving a great impression of light and glowing brightness, for not only were there many windows but the intervening wall-space was all but filled with tall mirrors from floor to pastel-painted ceiling, reflecting the sunshine outside. Despite the warm autumn weather, large fires blazed on two white marble hearths, so that the heat struck the visitors forcibly. The plenishings and decor were all of white and gold, the floor itself white and scattered with rugs and skins. Two persons occupied this extraordinary chamber, a young woman sitting on an ornate couch, and a turbaned black slave-boy standing behind.

James was not the only one to catch his breath, and not merely on account of the heat. The girl sitting there was quite the loveliest creature that David Lindsay, for one, had ever set eyes upon. Slender, fair, great-eyed, with perfectly chiselled features, pale but with a flush to her cheeks, she was dressed simply in white silk and pearls. She gazed at James, then slowly smiled and rose.

For perhaps the first time in his adult life James Stewart was abashed. He stared, biting his lip and finding no words.

"Her Highness Madeleine, Princess of France, Sire," the Cardinal declared, bowing.

She came forward, small hand out, her whispering silk the only sound in that chamber other than the faint background crackle of the fires. James seemed rooted to the spot, so that she had to come all the way to him. She was beginning to curtsy when he came to himself, and reached out almost abruptly to stop her doing so, roughly grasping her hand, her arm, to bend over and kiss it. In that moment, Marie de Guise was as forgotten as was Marie de Bourbon, behind.

The royal pair, each so striking in appearance, continued to eye each other as though there was no other person in the room.

Cardinal Charles coughed. "I have told His Majesty of Scotland that in the absence of your royal sire that you, Princess, with His Highness the Dauphin of course, will entertain King James," he said smoothly.

"We shall do our best, Your Eminence," she acceded. "Sire, we are at your command. It is my joy to welcome you. I have heard much of you."

"And I of you, Princess. But, but nothing to prepare me for this, for your beauty and fair delight!"

After that there was no separating these two. Suddenly, completely, James Stewart was in love. Attracted as he had been to unnumbered women, he had never before been really in love, even with Margaret Erskine. Now he was so, headlong—and Madeleine appeared to be almost equally so. From that first encounter no-one else seemed to matter—and being who they were, no-one else was in a position to say them nay.

Those concerned did try at least to warn, to damp down this spontaneous combustion, pointing out that the Princess's health was precarious, that she was inevitably restricted in what she might do and the life she must live. Also of course that her father considered that she was unfit to marry. The Cardinal and Beaton were equally worried, from their different points of view, however tactful and respectful they had to be about their advice—the latter even pointing out that Madeleine was unlikely to be able to produce the necessary heir to the throne which was the object of the expedition. David Lindsay also urged caution, the poet in him declaring that the Scottish climate was scarcely one in which this lovely but frail flower would be likely to flourish. No doubt the French advisers made similar representations to the young woman. But the pair brushed all such aside. James of course could and did quote the terms of the original treaty made so long ago when, even as a boy, Madeleine had been promised to him. And the only voice which could pronounce the direct negative was that of the absent King Francis.

With that monarch still not putting in an appearance, the Cardinal did his best at least to provide distractions. He organised daily excursions and diversions, and of the sort which by their outdoor nature the Princess would be unable to attend. He took the visitors on lengthy horseback tours of the environs, visits to great houses and abbeys, even arranged a special auto-da-fé, a mass burning of fifty heretics, men and women, at Gisors, found guilty of reformist activities, himself applying the first brands to the fires. He planned a further and dramatic display of pious devotion to Vatican policy, with a mass drowning in the river for the day following—but cancelled this on indications that James was less than enthusiastic. And he urged his sister to use her very considerable abilities to provide alternative attraction for an impressionable young man. Short of actually throwing herself at James, Marie de Guise did her best, but failed to provoke more than superficial appreciation. Poor Marie de Bourbon might not have existed.

It was five days before King Francis arrived in his capital with his sister of Navarre, with no explanations as to the delay. Marguerite de Valois proved to be a handsome woman of notable strength of character, in her mid-forties. Her *Heptameron*, the book of seventy-two stories, of picturesque and uninhibited forthrightness, had made her famous, but her leanings towards the reforming heresy would have made any other woman endangered.

Whether or not Francis was upset by the association which had developed between his daughter and his royal guest, he did not show it. He may have chosen to follow de Guise's policy of trying to keep James busy, if not tired out, with strenuous activity by day and prolonged feasting and entertainment by night, or that may have been his own notion of suitable hospitality; but that was what followed at almost increased pace and endless succession, with much of which his daughter was quite unable to cope. There was hunting in the Bois de Vincennes and other royal preserves, joustings in lists set up in The Louvre's own great courtyard, full-scale tournaments elsewhere, horse-racing, archery contests, sailing regattas on the Seine, masques, balls, play-actings and nightly feastings, such as to leave even the most vigorous of the visitors all but dizzy and exhausted. But nothing quenched James Stewart's preoccupation with Madeleine de Valois, his utter determination to have her, nor her obvious joy in him; and her father, who clearly found it difficult to deny her anything, more and more came to accept the situation. Whether or not it was being in love which was responsible none could say, but the young woman showed little signs of ill health save in that she tired quickly. She attended some of the outdoor events, which apparently she had not done for long, and altogether seemed to take on a new lease of life, all remarking upon it. Francis could not but be delighted, and whatever his misgivings, gradually it became acknowledged that the royal pair were made for each other and that marriage could scarcely be forbidden. Marguerite of Navarre positively encouraged them.

September passed and October showed no let-up in the entertainment, with no word of the visit ending. Many of the Scots, Beaton and Lindsay amongst them, began to grow concerned over such prolonged absence from home and what might be happening there, with a lethargic Chancellor and ailing Primate in charge in the interim and the Bastard of Arran no doubt in resentful mood. But James showed no anxiety, wholly taken up with what was clearly the most enjoyable interlude of his life. He began to talk about the wedding-day.

By mid-November, Beaton and the others recognised that no suggestions of delay, with final decisions after the return to Scotland, were going to be effective. James was not going home without his beloved. With Francis acceding now, the matter was clinched. The actual marriage contract was signed on 26th November. They would wed here in France on the first day of the New Year.

Now all was changed, life at the court geared for preparation for the great event; and a great event it was going to be. There was so much to be done, the most elaborate arrangements made, Francis being the man he was. All was to be at his expense, his famed extravagance given free rein, his generosity almost beyond belief. Never were the tailors of Paris so busy. Everyone remotely connected with the ceremony, and many who were not, were to be dressed anew in the most splendid attire, all at the King's cost. Paris was to be transfigured for the occasion, with triumphal arches, street decorations and bunting, the thoroughfares cleaned up, beggars herded out of sight. The Louvre itself was to be turned into a palace of love and romance, with hundreds of painters, woodworkers and plasterers brought in to effect the transformation. While this was going on, Francis decreed that the court must move out, to the royal palace of Blois, near Orleans, the Princess making the hundred-mile journey wrapped in white furs in a special silver chariot with six white horses, leading a lengthy train of carriages for the other ladies. Fortunately the weather was remarkably clement for the time of year.

At Blois the tempo was maintained. James was given his wedding presents from his father-in-law to be—twelve magnificent warhorses and their full and rich accoutrements, several suits of gilded tilting armour, much jewellery and twenty thousand livres of dowry money; a thoughtful gesture this, towards one whose pockets were never overflowing and now practically empty. As well, there was the promise of two fine ships-of-war, fully manned and furnished with guns, to join the waiting Scots squadron at Dieppe.

All moved to Chambord, still another royal chateau, for Christmastide—which was by no means to be skimped on account of the wedding to follow. David Lindsay was very much interested to find the French ideas for celebrating the festive season differing in many respects from the Scots, with less emphasis on Yuletide, the new year and the sun's rebirth, and more on St. Stephen's martyrdom and singing angels on the one hand and playing curious games and not a little saturnalia on the other, echo of the pre-Christmas feast of Saturn.

Three days after Christmas they moved northwards to Fontainebleau, to be better placed to make a grand entry, or re-entry, into the transformed Paris. This was effected on the last day of 1536, to thunderous gunfire, fountains spouting wine, choirs singing at every street-junction, addresses of welcome from fir-and holly-decked arches and the scattering of largesse to the crowds.

What with all the festivity, excitement and seeing in the New Year, Scots fashion, many, including the bridegroom, never got to bed that night.

The wedding ceremony was to be at noon, in the great cathedral of Notre Dame, three different processions setting out thereof from different gateways of The Louvre. The first to leave was the clergy, and this was in itself as large as it was splendid—for, to indicate Vatican approval of the occasion, no few than seven cardinals were present, each with his own train of dignitaries; also archbishops, bishops, abbots and priors by the score. Then emerged the bridegroom's cavalcade, or rather retinue, for they did not ride but walked the bare mile to the cathedral, through the garlanded, crowded streets. This was in fact the smallest procession of the three, despite its five hundred Scots. James looked magnificent in white and gold velvet, bare-headed, his high colouring and red hair contrasting vividly, the effect only a little marred by the bruising on brow gained in a tournament at Blois. Happily the weather continued to co-operate, so that all declared that Heaven smiled on the match. The bride's array came last, the largest of all, she and her father sitting in the first of a train of white carriages drawn by white horses with tossing golden plumes and gilt harness, all behind a choir of one hundred singing boys. It was remarked upon that although Marie de Guise was well to the fore, in her own carriage, there was no sign of Marie de Bourbon who had quietly disappeared from court.

The vast church was packed with the flower of France, so that there was some considerable pushing and even altercation before all the Scots contingent could be got in. Even the chancel and transept was crowded, spacious as it was, to accommodate all the clergy, and despite being close on the heels of the bridegroom, Beaton and Lindsay had to squeeze into a corner behind sundry cardinals. Janet, for this occasion, had ridden with Marie de Guise, and did rather better. Henri D'Albret, King of Navarre, was present, with his Queen, so that there were three monarchs there—but no Queen of France. These, the bride and the celebrants, were almost the only ones who were not uncomfortably cramped as to space.

James's entry had been greeted by a great blaring of trumpets and clashing cymbals; but Madeleine's appearance, on her father's arm, was to the accompaniment of sweetest singing. She was looking at her most lovely, with a delicate and ethereal beauty to lift the heart. Dressed all in white as usual, and eschewing all fancy and elaboration, she was probably the most simply-dressed woman in the cathedral, with that very simplicity only enhancing the delight of her person. Admittedly she looked slight and frail, but it was with a willowy and not really a brittle fragility. When she came to stand beside her tall and lissome bridegroom, they made a pair to gladden the eye.

Of all the Princes of the Church present, Francis had chosen Vendôme's younger brother, the Cardinal de Bourbon, to conduct the service, no doubt as some sort of compensating gesture over the rejection of his niece. The ceremony itself was fairly brief, basic, although the musical accompaniment and priestly processional, the to-ing and fro-ing with crosses and candles, seemed to the Scots excessive, almost as though all these cardinals and prelates were more important to the occasion than were the nuptial couple. These two, however, obviously blissfully preoccupied only with each other, betrayed no impatience.

As the final benediction was pronounced, and the bells high above them began their clamorous acclaim—which was to continue for hours and be taken up by every church, monastery and religious house in Paris—James, radiant, turned his bride round proudly to face the great congregation, arm around her. Scotland had a queen again.

* * *

In the days and weeks which followed, as James delayed his departure, it was said that France had not known such jubilation and revelry since the days of Charlemagne. The reasons for this were hard to pin-point. French monarchs had married, their daughters had wed greater kings than James Stewart, resounding triumphs of war and diplomacy had been celebrated, yet not on this scale. It was probably Francis's especially extravagant nature, combined with his great fondness for Madeleine; and perhaps something to do with reaction from his recent prostration and mourning for his dead son. Also this closer alliance with Scotland was a gesture in the directions of both Henry of England and the Emperor Charles, a warning that France was strategically strengthening her position, likewise buttressing the Pope and Holy Church against the reformist influences in England and the Germanic states. Whatever was behind it, the scale of festivities, jubilation and revelry, hectic enough before the wedding, now attained an unprecedented pitch, attained and continued. Every day some great event was organised, every night its counterpart. Nothing appeared to overtax Francis's ingenuity, nor it seemed, his treasury—as indicated by the great chests full of gold and silver coins, kept replenished and unlocked in the corridors of his palaces, for his guests to help themselves whenever their pockets felt empty. There were mock-battles with actual armies taking part, knightly chivalry, armoured foot, squares of pikemen, ranked bowmen, cannoneers, even siege-engines to batter down temporary forts and palisades. There were sea-fights in miniature on the Seine, with fleets of small ships and barges, their gunfire, using blank shot, shaking the entire city. Pageants in every conceivable form took place almost daily, many of them with the most elaborate and ambitious refinements, for instance flying dragons spouting flame and smoke, and a complete troupe of dancing bears. Deer, rounded up from many a park and forest, were driven into the city for hunting and slaughter in the streets and wynds; and bull-baiting, cock-fighting and gladiatorial combats became part of the Paris scene.

Not that all this merry-making was confined to the capital. All France was ordered to celebrate, and the royal company and at least part of the court moved around the country attending, with great nobles and municipalities vying with each other to provide welcomes and spectacles. One of these excursions took them to Vendôme, but although her sister was in evidence, there was no sign of Marie thereof. The rumour went round that she had decided to retire from the world and enter a convent, a suggestion which did distress James Stewart somewhat.

And so the weeks passed, and many of the Scots grew more and more restive, anxious now to be gone. Beaton was kept fairly well informed, by regular couriers from David Paniter and others, as to events in Scotland; and fortunately nothing of dire consequence appeared to be happening there, on the national scene at least, however many private problems might be arising. Nevertheless, few were unconcerned about this prolonged absence from home, and even their royal host's most ingenious diversions tended to pall in time. But Francis appeared loth indeed to let his daughter go; and James was probably one of the least anxious of his company to be off, the business of statecraft and rule never having much appeal to him. Also, of course, there was the excuse of Madeleine's health. On the whole this remained fairly good, although she tired very quickly and took little part in much of the excitements; but it was felt that a long voyage in winter seas would be unwise. So Francis had written to Henry Tudor seeking a safe conduct for his daughter and son-in-law through England, and Henry had made no reply, wait as they would. Despite offended pride at this discourtesy, the doting father made another approach, sending an envoy to London this time; and when this representative eventually returned, it was to announce that the King of England would not give the desired assurance of safety and non-interference for his nephew and new wife if they traversed his land, grossly insulting to all concerned as this was.

So a sea voyage it had to be.

And now it was the weather's turn to delay them. That winter had been quite remarkable for its mild geniality, at least in France; but March and April saw a change to gales and storms; and Francis would not hear of his beloved daughter venturing to sea in such conditions. The most that he would concede was that the court and guests should make the move towards the coast, so as to be ready to take advantage of any sustained improvement in the weather. Dieppe itself was scarcely a suitable place for any royal sojourn, so they would travel down Seine, in boats, to Rouen and wait there, a mere day's journey from the port.

Rouen it was, then, and here there was occasion for further festivities, for the end of April saw James's twenty-fifth birthday, a significant milestone at which, by old Scots tradition, a new dispensation began. One of the more important aspects of this was the almost automatic cancellation of all crown appointments and offices made hitherto. Most holders were re-appointed forthwith, to be sure, but not all. It was a recognised opportunity for a cleansing of the royal stables and a general reassessment. Few changes were actually promulgated there and then at Rouen, of course; but the Bastard of Arran was one of the immediate casualties, losing his positions as Gentleman of the Bedchamber, Master of the Horse and Keeper of Carrick. James, despite present euphoria, had a retentive memory. Amongst others to fall was the Lord Forbes, Justiciar of the North, and his son, the Master, suspected of plotting with the

Douglases. Needless to say, both Beaton and Lindsay retained their offices.

Eventually the winds moderated and the skies cleared, with the weather-prophets foretelling better things. So at long last the move was made to Dieppe, nine months after disembarking there.

A great host of shipping was now waiting at the port, for as well as the Scots squadron and the two wedding-gift vessels, *Salamander* and *Morsewer*, Francis had ordered a French war fleet to accompany them to Scottish waters, to ensure his daughter's safety from English attack. A tearful leave-taking followed, with Francis all but proposing to accompany them all the way to Scotland, so reluctant was he to part from Madeleine. Prolonged were the farewells, Frenchly demonstrative the endearments. Overloaded with gifts, oversated with excitements, overfed and all but overwhelmed in emotion, they sailed on the 10th of May, an impressive convoy.

As well that they were, perhaps, for the English ships picked them up within the first twelve hours and shadowed them thereafter. There were usually only two or three of these, being relieved each day, but undoubtedly, had the Scots been weaker, these could have called out a major force to try to capture James or even slay him. Without any close heir to the Scots throne, Henry would have been well placed to take over, especially with Angus his ally and his sister placed as she was.

Oddly enough, the other side of the Tudor coin was demonstrated on the fifth day out when, somewhat becalmed off Scarborough Head on the Yorkshire coast, a flotilla of small boats put out towards them, flying white flags. Suspicious but intrigued, James waited for these to approach, under the loaded guns of his escorts. They proved to be a group of Yorkshire knights and squires, who presumably had been waiting ready for the Scots convoy, come to seek King James's aid in ousting the tyrant Henry Tudor from the English throne and restoring the authority of Holy Church in England—a surprising development. Coming aboard, they were obsequious to James and loud in their complaints as to misrule and persecution, with assertions of widespread resentment, unrest in the land, faithfulness towards the Pope and Rome and admiration for the King of Scots' stand against the forces of heresy. They declared that much of England, especially the North, and all of Wales, would rise against Henry if James would provide the lead. And if France would join in, of course, victory would be assured.

This extraordinary situation intrigued James and his advisers; but in his present blissful preoccupation with Madeleine he was scarcely in a state to consider it seriously. However, he did agree to meet another and more senior delegation a little further north, off the Tees, for which it seemed this group were only forerunners; and meanwhile to ask the French admiral to chase away the English ships, which, hull-down to the south, still dogged the convoy, so that word of this meeting with the northern lords would not be reported to Henry.

In this delay in the voyage, James decided to send his Lord Lyon ahead, in a light, fast ship, to prepare a suitable reception and welcome at Leith and Holyrood for the new Queen of Scotland. Davie Beaton would have chosen to accompany him, anxious to get back to the direction of affairs in Scotland, but felt that he should remain with James during any interview with English dissenters, to try to ensure that no unwise commitment were entered into—he being very doubtful as to the wisdom of any Scots entanglement in English affairs, however tempting.

So David and Janet transferred to another vessel and set off on their own. At first they took a while to distance themselves from the others, owing to the prevailing calm, but presently the wind freshened from the south-west and, their sails filling, they began to make good speed. The Lindsays were in fact delighted to be on their own together, after nine months of crowded company.

Unfortunately the freshening wind, although timeous and in the right direction, outgrew its usefulness when it developed into an untimely early-summer storm, and the little craft, the smallest in the entire combined fleet, although seaworthy enough, reacted to the stresses in boisterous fashion, tossing and heaving and spiralling crazily in the wild waters. Janet was sick, and although David was spared that misery, he dared not eat anything substantial for two days. However, they made reasonably good progress up the Northumberland and Berwick coasts, and when they turned at last into the mouth of the Firth of Forth the land quickly began to shelter them and they went along on a more even keel.

On the fourth day after leaving the others they sailed into

Leith harbour, thankful to set foot again on their native soil. They had had sufficient foreign travel to serve them for a considerable time.

Although they would have liked to have gone straight home to The Mount of Lindifferon, they had to plunge into urgent activity. Hiring horses, they repaired to Holyrood Abbey, there to instruct the Abbot and his monks to prepare the royal apartments and in especial heat them adequately for a queen used to a warmer clime than Scotland's. David summoned Sir Adam Otterburn, in his capacity of Provost, and with him put in hand arrangements for an official welcome to the capital city. They could not attempt anything on the Paris scale, but triumphal arches, platforms and street decorations were to be erected; greenery and fir-branches hung; bonfires prepared; carriages made ready, and the folk urged to be ready to line the streets. Janet for her part informed the abbey kitcheners as to suitable cooking for the French party, and gathered a group of ladies to attend on the Queen, also filled the royal bedchamber and anterooms with such flowers as mid-May might provide. They did not know, of course, just when the royal company would arrive, which was awkward. So look-outs were sent up Arthur's Seat to keep watch, from the summit of which it was possible to see down the thirty-odd miles to the mouth of the firth. It was calculated that they probably had at least two days, although the convoy might arrive by night, hence the bonfires.

During all this activity the newcomers learned something of what had been going on in Scotland in the past nine months. The Bastard of Arran seemed to have been lying decently low in his own Hamilton country, which was a blessing. There had been some English raiding, but Scott of Buccleuch, the Black Douglases of Cavers and Drumlanrig, and other Middle March clans, had driven them off, and the Armstrongs and Johnstones, on the West March, had retaliated in kind. Margaret Tudor had been creating a new scandal, falling out with and actually leaving her third husband, and declaring that she was going to get another divorce, from the new Pope, and remarry her second spouse, Angus. Home of Wedderburn, the main firebrand of that troublesome lot, had died, and his sons, squabbling over the inheritance, tended to confine their depredations to their own Merse. And so on.

On Whitsun Eve, the 19th of May, the watchers up the hill

reported that a great fleet of ships was in sight beyond the Craig of Bass. All moved into action.

At this stage, David had concentrated on the port of Leith rather than on Edinburgh itself. Hurrying down there, he got all in train, and was ready before the first sails appeared in view from the haven. Only a small proportion of the vessels would be able to tie up at the wharves and jetties, but they had cleared as many of the harboured craft there already, as was possible, to make more room.

The King's ship, with its Lion Rampant standards, came in first, and David had a band of musicians to play it in, and a large company of notables under a gaily-flapping canopy—in case of rain—to give welcome. When the business of berthing was completed, to music, and a gangway was run out, there was a pause. Then King James appeared at its head, Madeleine at his side. And waving to the crowd he suddenly turned and impulsively scooped her up in his arms and thus burdened, strode down the gangplank on to his Scottish soil—a nice touch. Loud and long was the cheering.

For her part, when the new Queen of Scotland was set down, she swayed as though dizzy for a moment or two, then sank down on her knees before all, and in a fair attempt at Scots speech, thanked Almighty God for safely bringing her husband and herself to this their own land. Which said, she scraped at the sandy soil there with her slender fingers, to pick up two handfuls of the earth and kiss it. The crowd shouted its acclaim and James beamed on her, and all, proudly.

But David Lindsay did not, for he was shaken by the changed appearance of the young woman, however warmly she smiled and gestured. It seemed scarcely possible that there could be such alteration in three or four days. She was drawn, wan of feature, large eyes dark-ringed, thinner, slighter altogether. That storm had obviously taken its toll of Madeleine de Valois.

There was no glooming nor haste, no hustling her off to the waiting carriages, however. David would have foregone the presentation of the long line of dignitaries, but clearly both King and Queen expected to go through with this, and did so genially, James at his most amiable. Behind the notables, the ordinary folk of Leith were packed in a cheering, surging mass, and to these Madeleine smiled and waved and mouthed pleasantries. For his part, James waved forward his new favourite, Oliver

Sinclair, with a large bag of coins, into which the King dipped and threw, dipped and threw—all French silver, David noted.

At length it was over and a move was made over to the waiting carriages and horses, for the couple of miles ride up to Holyrood. David sought out Beaton, to ride beside him.

"The Princess? The Queen?" he asked, leaving the rest unsaid.

"Aye, poor lass—she took sore ill out of that storm. Not just the sea-sickness. Much worse—vomiting blood. I fear, I fear . . . She has spirit, but . . ."

"What can be done?"

"We can pray!" Bishop Davie said simply.

At Holyrood, Janet, after one look at Madeleine, to whom she had become much attached, asserted herself, as so seldom she did, and put the Queen to bed, with warming-pans and possets of curdled-milk and wine. The evening's banquet had to make do without the guest-of-honour.

A night of high fever followed, and the next day's ceremonies and celebrations were cancelled. The Queen kept her room.

Two more days of this and James at last began to show signs of worry and agitation. Madeleine herself remained quietly cheerful, but her weakness could not be denied. Physicians were sought, although James professed no faith in such—a view which seemed to be substantiated when these all made differing prognostications and prescribed different treatments.

Then the invalid rallied a little, and a limited programme of introducing her to her new subjects was put in hand, although the state entry into the capital, for which Lindsay, as Lyon, had made all the arrangements, was still postponed. But during the evening's feasting the Queen collapsed at table, amidst general consternation, and had to be carried in her husband's arms back to bed. That night she coughed more blood—which seemed to make a distinct nonsense of the blood-letting advised by the physicians.

There followed a week of prostration and consequent deep gloom, James seldom leaving his beloved's chamber. The weather by no means helped, strong cold winds and driving rain playing a mournful tattoo on the abbey windows. Deputations from all over the land, nobles, clerics, lairds, merchant and trade guilds, provosts and ordinary citizens, came with gifts, addresses of welcome and messages of goodwill. Prayers were said in the churches.

Davie Beaton, who had gone to St. Andrews on urgent business, returned and, much concerned, recommended that the Queen should be moved to the Abbey of Balmerino, in North Fife, not far from Lindifferon, renowned as the most salubrious and healthful place in the land—that is, if she was strong enough for the journey. She could go by boat—but she quailed at the thought of further sea travel. James, ready to clutch at a straw, agreed, and had a canopied horse-litter prepared. But the starting day had to be put off and put off, as Madeleine, despite her brave smiling, grew progressively weaker.

On the night of the 7th of July, six weeks after landing in her new country, Madeleine de Valois choked to death in a red flood of her own blood.

James Stewart was as a man bereft of all sense.

The bells of all Scotland tolled out thereafter, as long and loud as those of France had done so short a time before, but with a very different tempo and note.

The funeral over, and burial in the abbey-church, the distracted King went off to shut himself up in Stirling Castle, all his court dismissed.

The Lindsays rode home to The Mount of Lindifferon at long last, David thankful for only one thing—that he had not been chosen to convey the tidings to Francis de Valois. They went speaking little, he beginning to compose, in his mind, an elegy for a queen.

The Bastard of Arran may not have smiled, but the day was his.

Book Three

ROUGH WOOING

PRINCIPAL CHARACTERS
IN ORDER OF APPEARANCE

JAMES THE FIFTH: King of Scots.
MASTER DAVID BEATON: Abbot of Arbroath, Bishop of Mirepoix, Lord Privy Seal.
SIR DAVID LINDSAY OF THE MOUNT: Lord Lyon King of Arms, Poet Laureate.
MARGARET TUDOR: Mother of James the Fifth, now wife of the Lord Methven, sister of Henry the Eighth of England.
OLIVER SINCLAIR: A Favourite of King James.
MASTER GAVIN DUNBAR: Archbishop of Glasgow.
GEORGE GORDON, EARL OF HUNTLY: Great Scots noble and chief of the Gordons.
JANET DOUGLAS, LADY LINDSAY: Second wife of Sir David, and Wardrobe Mistress.
MARION OGILVY: Former wife of David Beaton, daughter of the Lord Ogilvy of Airlie.
MARIE DE GUISE, DUCHESS DE LONGUEVILLE: Second wife of James the Fifth.
CHARLES DE GUISE: Cardinal of Lorraine, brother of Marie.
MARQUIS D'ELBEOUF: Another brother
DUC DE GUISE: Eldest brother.
ARCHIBALD CAMPBELL, EARL OF ARGYLL: Lord Justice General, great Highland chief.
JAMES HAMILTON, EARL OF ARRAN: Great Scots noble, Lord High Admiral.
RODERICK MACLEOD OF THE LEWES: Highland chief.

SIR JAMES HAMILTON OF FINNART: Illegitimate brother of Arran. Known as the Bastard of Arran.
GEORGE, FOURTH LORD HOME: Great Border noble.
ARCHIBALD DOUGLAS, EARL OF ANGUS: Great noble, second husband of Margaret Tudor.
MATTHEW, EARL OF LENNOX: Great noble.
MARY, QUEEN OF SCOTS: Only legitimate surviving child of King James.
JOHN DE HOPE: Edinburgh merchant burgess and banker, of French extraction.
HENRY THE EIGHTH: King of England
MARGARET OF HUNGARY: Regent of the Netherlands.
POPE PAUL THE THIRD: Allesandro Farnese.
JOHN STEWART, EARL OF ATHOLL: Great noble.
MASTER GEORGE WISHART: Former priest and reformer.
MASTER JOHN KNOX: Former priest and reformer.
MACBETH MACALPINE otherwise MACCABAEUS: Scots doctor of divinity in Denmark.
CHRISTIAN THE THIRD: King of Denmark.
JOHN MAJOR or MAIR: Provost of St. Salvator's College, St. Andrews.

Part One

1

Three men stood looking out of a window of the royal quarters of Stirling Castle, gazing down on the forecourt area where there was considerable stir, dismounting from horses and shouting for grooms. Of the trio, one was in his mid-twenties, and two of an age, in their forties. The young man was tall, red-headed, high-coloured and good-looking, and named James Stewart. But despite the fact that he was King of Scots, fifth of that name, and in the strongest fortress of his kingdom, he looked the least at ease, almost agitated in fact, for one who was normally rather too carefree, not to say irresponsible, as a monarch, for some of his advisers. Of the two said advisers who were with him now, one was notably handsome in a smooth and almost delicate way, splendidly elegant, dressed all in scarlet; the other was much more rugged of feature and person but with a strong, plain face and keen eyes, plainly clad. They were respectively Davie Beaton, Abbot of Arbroath, Bishop of Mirepoix in France, Coadjutor and nephew to the Primate of Holy Church in Scotland, and Lord Privy Seal of the realm; and Sir David Lindsay of the Mount, Lord Lyon King of Arms, chief Usher to the King and Poet Laureate. These two eyed each other and their liege-lord significantly, as much as they considered what went on below.

"See you – you are to bide, both of you. Even though she bids you begone," James said. "I want you to be present. To note. And, and to support me. If necessary. She will be difficult. She, she always is. You understand?"

"Have no fear, Sire," Beaton told him, easily. "The situation is entirely clear, and all in your favour. We shall . . ."

"Who speaks of fear, man? Sakes – I do not *fear* her! It is but . . . awkward."

The other shrugged eloquent, red-velvet shoulders.

Lindsay said nothing. Despite being the poet and playwright, the man of words, he was a deal less prompt of speech than was his friend.

Presently they heard voices from the stairway. Then, without the usual preliminary knocking, the door was thrown violently open so that it banged to the wall, and a woman swept in, followed by an overdressed young man of almost beautiful appearance but looking distinctly unhappy, not to say dishevelled, just then, hand out, seeking to restrain her, members of the royal guard behind.

The lady, notably small eyes blazing, paused after a couple of paces into the chamber, then swinging round on the young man who was in the act of making a hasty bow towards the King, actually pushed at his chest, thrusting him back through the doorway with no little force, into the arms of the guard. Then she grabbed at the door again and slammed it shut in his face, before turning to confront the waiting trio.

"God's mercy – the insolence of that cub!" she exclaimed. "It is not to be borne! I will not be treated like some serving wench – I, Margaret, I tell you! Do you hear? Dragged here by that fopling and his ruffians!"

"*I* sent Oliver Sinclair to bring you, Madam," James said. "I, I desire words with you."

"The more you are to blame, then, James!" she snapped back. She was a stocky, short woman of thick waist and middle years, sallow of complexion and unbeautiful, but with a very distinct presence and an inborn authority which by no means required her over-aggressive speech and manner to be effective. Dowdily dressed, she was nevertheless overloaded with jewellery for horseback-travel.

"Blame! *You* to speak of blame! You, who would betray me to my enemies! Who plot my downfall and scheme against me. You talk of blame to me! I'd have you to know, Madam, that your treasonable doings are revealed, your letters intercepted . . ."

"Ha! Spying, is it? Creeping and peeping and prying? As well as subjecting me, *me*, to indignities! I will not have it, James – do you hear? You go too far!"

"No! I will go further. I am the King . . .!" But James's need to assert the fact implied a certain lack of the authority so evident in the woman. After all, it is difficult, unnatural, for a son openly to controvert his mother.

Her glance slid over towards the two others standing there listening; as indeed did the King's.

It was in answer to the young man's unspoken appeal for help that there was reaction, the churchman seeking to provide it.

"Lady Methven – Madam – His Grace, in this, has the rights of it. The matter is serious, grievous, the safety of the realm involved. This must be dealt with in due and decent fashion. For the sake of all . . ."

"Silence, sirrah! Speak when you are spoken to, not before! And do not name me Methven – never that! Highness, from you, Beaton. Remember it."

He inclined his head, but only slightly. It was not easy to put down Davie Beaton, as many a great one had discovered. "As the Lord Methven's wife, lady, I but address you in that style."

"I have no further part nor concern with Methven. He is a scoundrel and a deceiver. I shall divorce him. He has stolen my rents and taken a mistress. When I am finished with him, he will regret deceiving Margaret Tudor!"

Her son cleared his throat. "This is why I required to see you," he declared. "This of divorce. And . . . remarriage. I will not have it, Madam – I will not!"

"*You* will not? My marriage has naught to do with you, James."

"I say that it has. Since, of all follies, you are proposing to rewed my greatest enemy, Angus. I tell you, we have read your letters. It shall not be."

"You cannot stop me. I shall wed whom I please."

"Angus is your brother Henry's tool, lackey, lickspittle! Has sworn him fealty and become an Englishman – a Scots earl! Henry wants him only to try to unseat me and so gain Scotland. You, Henry's sister, will not aid him, I say, against my realm. You will not remarry Angus."

"And I say again, you cannot stop me."

"You cannot rewed lacking a divorce from Henry Stewart of Methven."

"The Pope will grant me that divorce. With Methven in open adultery."

"Not if I urge him not to. And if Holy Church in Scotland requests Rome otherwise. There will be no divorce."

She glared, first at her son and then at Beaton. "This, then, is *your* doing, you clerkly snake, you viper! I might have known it. You have ever hated me – both of you." And she turned on Lindsay also. "From the first you have wrought me only ill, poisoned my son against me, as a child and as a grown man. You, Lindsay, first; then this upstart priest. Always you have been my enemy."

"Not your enemy, Madam – only the King's friend, however humble."

"Liar! I have watched you . . ."

"Madam – instead of miscalling my friends, answer me this," the King intervened. "John, Master of Forbes, is *your* friend. Married to Angus's sister. Can you deny being close to him? Sending secret messages? We have your courier. And Forbes plotting my death."

"I know naught of such. Scurrilous tales. John Forbes is an honest man."

"Yet he plots to slay me. With gunfire. A culverin, no less. When I go to Aberdeen, on justice-eyres. And you are his friend."

"Lies – all lies."

"And lies also that Angus's other sister, the Lady Glamis, likewise your friend, threatens to poison me? As she poisoned her first husband? And now you plan to marry Angus again!"

"You believe such fables, James? Are you fool enough for that? Tales devised to cozen you against me. No doubt by such as these two here!"

"They have served me long and well . . ."

"They have served *themselves* well! A versifying small laird and an upjumped clerk! Who now dare to insult me, a queen and princess. And would rule you, the King. If we are to have further privy talk together, James, have them out of here."

"No. They stay. This is not privy talk. It is the realm's business. Henry is ever plotting against me. He would reign in Scotland, as well as in England and Wales and Ireland. And you, his sister, would aid him. It may be that you think to be his viceroy, with Angus? It will not be, I tell you! You will not wed Angus again. You will remain wedded to Methven. That is my will, my, my royal command. Seek a divorce, from Rome, and you will be imprisoned. For the remainder of your days."

That silenced even Margaret Tudor for a space. Her mouth worked but no words came. Then she got it out. "You, you would not dare . . .!"

"Dare? I need not to *dare*, Madam. I am the King. My word is sufficient. For too long you have intrigued against me, your brother's accomplice in this my kingdom. You talk of snakes and vipers. What are you but Henry's viper here at my very throat? No more, I say. You will plot no more on Henry's behalf."

"It is not true. You haver, you wander in your mind! I have not worked against you. I know nothing of Henry's plottings."

"Your letters belie you. You should be more careful, Madam, of what you pen on paper. You accept Henry's gold. Why, when I have given you sufficient lands, properties? Aye, and your friends get more, as you know well. Four hundred pensioners Henry keeps, in my Scotland. *Four hundred*! Why? Not out of love for them, or for me, I swear! This Master of Forbes, no doubt amongst them. And Angus's kin and other Douglases. But – no more, I say. It is to stop."

"This is crazy-mad! You have been fed lies, falsehoods, I tell you. By these, these creatures." And her beringed finger jabbed venomously towards the two Davids. "You cannot do this to me, your father's queen, a princess of England. Halt my divorce."

"You think not? I could do more. I could summon you before my courts. Both as prisoner and as witness. John Forbes is arrested and will be tried, in Edinburgh, in a few days. The Lady Glamis likewise. Shall I summon *you*? To compear there? For them. Or against them? There, before all. How say you to that, Madam?"

She actually stepped back, as though she had been struck. "No! No – never that! You would not, could not . . ."

"I could, and would. If need be. So consider well. You will plot no more, with Henry and Angus and the Douglases. You hear? I have been patient overlong. You will go back, under escort, to Methven Castle. And remain there, married to Henry Stewart. Applying for no divorce. Or you will come to court, accused of art and part in treason. That is my royal word."

There was silence in that room, for a space.

James resumed. "Now, Madam – you have my leave to retire. Oliver Sinclair will conduct you to your quarters, and tomorrow, back to Methven. Go."

Tense, without a word spoken, Margaret Tudor went, and closed that door quietly behind her.

"I did it! I did it!" James exclaimed then, his voice quivering a little. "I told you that I would. She, she knows now who is master!"

"Yes, Sire – that was admirable," Beaton said. "You are greatly to be congratulated. The lady will now know her true position, I think. Not before time."

Later, in Lindsay's more modest quarters of the fortress, the two so strangely different and often differing friends, exchanged impressions.

"I am surprised that James was able to be so firm with that dangerous woman," Beaton admitted. "When I first spoke with him, after coming from St. Andrews, I feared that it would be merely myself and you who would have to confront her, on his behalf. As in the past. What has changed him? He has ever been afraid of her – and not without cause. Could it be the death of Madeleine?"

"I think that may have had much to do with it, yes. His wife's death has greatly affected him. He is altered in some ways. It has much sobered him, to be sure. But he is more readily angered. He was always hot-tempered, but now he angers more deeply and frequently. It is as though the loss of his new queen and love is to be worked off in wrath, hitting at what offends. Perhaps his own hurt seeking easement in the hurt of others? Or that may be but a fancy. But this of the Master of Forbes and the Lady Glamis – he is hot against them. With what true cause I am not sure. He has had them both taken into custody. He would have had them both condemned out-of-hand, I believe, but we persuaded him to bring them to open trial, at least. Any with Douglas connection are now endangered. Always he has had reason to fear and resent Angus and the Douglases. But now it is sheerest hate. As though they were in some way responsible for Madeleine's death."

"This trial? In Edinburgh, he said? And threatened to hale his mother before it?"

"Two trials. Separate. One, of Forbes, for conspiring to shoot him. And the other of Lady Glamis, Forbes's good-sister. Since mere talk of threatening to poison the King would be difficult to prove, as treason, she is to be tried for practising witchcraft – which is a deal simpler! I mislike it, for I fear, whatever the justiciars find, that James will have these two guilty and condemned. Because of their connection with Angus. Perhaps, Davie, if *you* could be there, attend the trial, be with James, even if only to plead mercy? He much respects your judgement. And you speak with the voice of Holy Church . . ."

"I do not think that will be possible, my friend. When are these trials, do you know? Two weeks hence? Then, no, I cannot be there. I shall be in France. Or on my way there."

"France? You – again? What is this?"

"It is necessary. That is why I have come here, now. To convince James. And *have* convinced him, I think. This morning I had much talk with him, alone. See you, Queen Madeleine has died, yes. And James is shattered. But the realm's need is not altered. An heir to the throne is necessary, all-important. Or Scotland will be on the road to disaster. You know that. With the creature Arran as next in line, and his brother the Bastard steering him,

James *must* produce a true heir. That he ever wed Madeleine is, in fact, the tragedy, brief joy as it brought them both. I blame myself that I did not seek more strongly to stop it . . ."

"You, man – even you could not have damped down that sudden fire! That flame of love was beyond all quenching."

"Perhaps. But I believe that I could have persuaded King Francis to have forbidden the marriage. He was loth, as it was, recognising his daughter's weakness. And, I flatter myself, he heeds me in not a little. My wits told me that it was all a mistake, as did her father's. I knew that, frail and sickly as she was, she could never bear James the child he needed, his kingdom needed. Even though she had not died thus soon."

"Aye. But it is too late to repine."

"Too late for Madeleine. But not for James. He must marry again. It will not be the same, no hot love-match. But that is not necessary. Most monarchs do not wed for love. For this realm, nothing is altered from one year ago. The succession must be assured. Or Henry will have us, one way or another. He, or the Bastard of Arran – or both, in concert. France is still the key to Henry's postern-door. We need France's aid, and not just in the Auld Alliance, but in her active support. So it must be a French princess again."

"But – so soon! It is but weeks since Madeleine died."

"Aye – but these things take time to arrange. And much time we have not got. Henry is busy, always. And the Douglases readying. James is not wholly mistaken in this hatred of his for that house. And the Hamiltons but bide their time. The Bastard is building a great new castle, a fortress indeed, at Craignethan – have you heard? He is vastly extending the old tower of Draffane, a former Douglas place. And on the very edge of the Douglas territories. Why, think you? Well away from the rest of Hamilton land. I have heard that he intends to make common cause with Angus, he who has always been that earl's enemy – this since James has dispensed with his services. No doubt, he hopes to gain Douglas support, for his half-brother Arran as king. Should James happen to die! And James *could* die so easily, and without heir. This of shooting by Forbes, or poison by Janet of Glamis – they but represent a continuing and wider threat. Then there is this new reforming heresy, in the Church. The reformers are the supporters of Henry, now that he has parted with the Vatican – and Henry supports *them*, for his own purposes. They see James as a stumbling-block to their aims. So James needs France and Rome for *his* active support. I have convinced him of the urgency of it. So, I sail, with his authority, in but a few days."

"Authority to do what?"

"To find him another wife – and quickly."

"But . . . six months after his wedding to Madeleine? This is indecent! Too soon."

"It will be a year before all is arranged. We cannot wait. And, fortunately, I have something to start from. There were *three* French ladies offered, in the first place. Madeleine, Marie de Bourbon of Vendôme, and Marie de Guise, Duchess de Longueville. Poor Marie de Bourbon is not to be considered now – James would not have her, for her looks; and forby she is now wed to Holy Church and become a nun, in her disappointment. But the de Guise – that is different. Until he met Madeleine, James was well pleased with her. She is handsome, lusty, able, and she liked him well, clearly. He should have wed *her*. She is a widow and has proved herself fertile. Unless she has wed someone else in these last months, it is not too late. And she would, I swear, make an excellent Queen of Scotland – better than the fragile, beauteous Madeleine ever could."

"So, that is it! Marie de Guise. And James – he agrees to this?"

"He is scarce fervent, admittedly. But, yes – he accepts the need. And would find her . . . bed-worthy! You know him – that is mighty important with him. And since he is not in love with her, only admired her person and spirit, it need not too much restrict his adventures otherwhere!"

"Lord, Davie – I sometimes think that you are a devil, rather than any churchman!"

"I am but a practical man, my Lord Lyon King of Arms – as I have told you before. And since the Church is in this sorry world, and must deal with it, the Church needs practical men, as well as saints!"

Lindsay shook his head. "And Francis? And the Duchess Marie herself? How will they consider this? So soon after the other marriage? Doting on his daughter as he did, will Francis not hate the very name of Scotland?"

"I think not. He is a king as well as a father. He will be concerned still to have a Frenchwoman as queen here. He must seek ever to contain Henry of England. He would have Scotland an ever-present threat at England's back. As for Marie de Guise, that one made it clear that she did not mislike James Stewart! And she would be a queen, I have no doubt, if she might. Forby, her uncle, the Cardinal of Lorraine, whose word counts for much in France, is my friend."

"So you have it all thought through. As ever! But, would James go to France a second time? Leave his realm again, for weeks, months. That would be dangerous, in these circumstances. We took sufficient risks before."

"No, not that. It will have to be a proxy wedding. In France. James to send someone as representative. Then the full ceremony here, when the bride arrives. That will have to be understood. It might be unacceptable in some case. As it would have been for Madeleine. But the de Guise is different. She is not a king's daughter. And has already been wed. I think that she will be prepared for such arrangement."

"Will you be away for long? You are needed here, more than in France, I think."

"For so short a time as is possible to contrive it all. I shall not linger, I promise you. My uncle is all but senile, and I cannot afford to leave him, and Church affairs, for long. Even though I have good deputies. In the present state of both kingdom and Church I need to be back quickly."

"Must it be *you* that goes, then?"

"I fear so. Both Francis and the Cardinal are friendly

towards me, from previous years. I shall need their aid, probably."

"Your Marion will see but little of you, at Ethie, these days."

"To my sorrow, yes. She has the bairns, of course – three now. I miss her damnably. But . . ."

"But you are David Beaton. And Church and state stand or fall by your efforts! And Marion is only . . . Marion!"

"Damn you . . .!" For a moment that normally so imperturbable individual lost his calm control, eyes flashing quite as hot as Margaret Tudor's had done earlier. But swiftly he recovered himself. "That is scarcely just, my friend. I must seem to neglect her grievously, yes. But it cannot be otherwise, placed as I am. Marion understands. She has known, from the first, that it would be this way. She knows that she has my love and devotion. And I get to Ethie oftener than you may think, even if only for brief visits. I have a small ship constantly ready at St. Andrews haven, which in any passable weather can win me up to Ethiehaven in three hours. It is but a score of miles, by sea. I must needs fail Marion much – but never in my love. *You* are more happily placed. You can have your Janet here at court. I can by no means do the like."

"No. I am sorry, Davie. It is easier for me. But – we often grieve for Marion Ogilvy. We are fond of her."

"I know it. If you could contrive to visit her at Ethie, perhaps, while I am in France, it would be kind."

"We shall try, yes."

"Good. Now – I must back to St. Andrews, if indeed I am to see her before I sail. Wish me well . . ."

The trial of John, Master of Forbes, in the great hall of Edinburgh Castle on 16th July 1537, was a show and demonstration as much as an impeachment – and by the same token, the verdict was scarcely in doubt, from the first. This was to be a counter-stroke against Angus, the Douglases and Henry Tudor, and at the same time some sort of strange salve for James Stewart's hurt and sorrow.

Both kingdoms were to know it, so the hall was full, great numbers of the most influential of the land summoned to attend, almost as though it had been a parliament. Since the charge was high treason, this was not a matter for the new-founded Court of Session, but for the Privy Council itself. James, although very much present, was not to take active part. And the Lord Privy Seal, Beaton, being off to France, the Chancellor of the realm, Gavin Dunbar, Archbishop of Glasgow, deputised for him; the other members of the court, all privy councillors, being the Earls of Atholl and Cassillis, the Lord Maxwell and the Master of Glencairn, carefully chosen. David Lindsay was there, as Lyon, but only formally to open the proceedings in the King's name.

On the stroke of noon, splendidly attired in the vivid red-and-gold Lion Rampant tabard of his office, and flanked by his heralds and trumpeters, he paced into the crowded hall, on to the dais at the west end, and after a fanfare by the instrumentalists, announced the arrival of James, by God's grace High King of Scots.

To another blare of trumpets James came in, carelessly dressed as usual, all men bowed and, as the monarch seated himself on the throne, Lindsay declared that His Grace's Privy Council was hereby commanded to hear the lord Earl of Huntly's charge of high treason against two of His Grace's subjects. In the absence overseas of the Lord Privy Seal, the Lord Archbishop of Glasgow, Chancellor, to proceed, with His Grace's royal permission.

Gavin Dunbar, who had once been James's tutor, looked unhappy in this situation. He was a mild, studious man, no proud prelate despite his lofty position, who had been appointed Chancellor, or chief minister, when his predecessor, Archbishop James Beaton of St. Andrews, had become incapable of continuing as such, in order to maintain Holy Church's power in the state. In fact, of course, Davie Beaton, his uncle's secretary and coadjutor, wielded the true power, with Dunbar more or less a figurehead. His discomfort on this occasion was obvious to all. Without preamble, he called for George Gordon, Earl of Huntly.

Huntly, chief of the great north-east clan of Gordon, who rejoiced in the hereditary appellation of Cock o' the North, a dark, spare, lantern-jawed young man of twenty-four years, stood forward. His mother had been an illegitimate daughter of the King's father, James the Fourth. This being that highly unusual occurrence, a public meeting of the Privy or Secret Council, the normal trial procedure was not used. There was no crown prosecutor, as such, no judge and jury in name, merely this panel of councillors at a hearing. But none doubted their ability to pronounce and impose due judgement.

Huntly, bowing to his uncle by blood, announced that in his country and sheriffdom of Strathdon, Strathdee and Strathbogie, there had long been a general belief that certain highly placed persons were less than leal subjects of the King's Grace, supporters of the renegade Earl of Angus and in frequent communication with the King of England. As Justiciar he, Huntly, had been concerned and perturbed, but had no proofs or certainties on which to take action. And in view of the status and rank of the persons involved, this much distressed him. Then, a month or so past, he was approached by one, a man of some substance in Strathdon, a laird by name Thomas Strachan of Lynturk, a vassal of the Lord Forbes, who informed him, as a leal subject of His Grace, that there was a plot to murder and slay the King's Grace, the instigator of which was none other than John, Master of Forbes, son and heir of the said Lord Forbes, one of those long suspected of treasonable correspondence with Angus and England. The said Lynturk's declarations and assertions were so specific and grievous that he, Huntly, had conceived it to be his bounden duty, as Justiciar, forthwith to apprehend the Master of Forbes and his father, the Lord Forbes, since His Grace's royal person could be endangered, and have the matter enquired into by His Grace's Privy Council, the Lord Forbes himself being of that Council and so entitled to go beyond the justiciary court. Hence this sitting and hearing.

Archbishop Dunbar nodded and murmured something about it being most correct and duteous of the lord Earl.

Were the accuser and the accused here present for the Council to question? Then let them be produced.

Officers thereupon escorted in two men, one elderly and the other in his thirties. Both were tall and good-looking in a florid way, clearly father and son, although they held themselves very differently, the Lord Forbes distressed and apprehensive, the Master defiant and with a sort of inborn arrogance. They bowed towards the throne, low and less low. From another door, a third man was led in, of an age with the Master but short, stocky and ill-at-ease, the Laird of Lynturk.

The Chancellor looked uncertain as to how to proceed, this all being a new experience for those present, the trial of a privy councillor and his son by a committee of that Privy Council at the instance of another privy councillor, the accuser being merely a nobody, but the instigation undoubtedly coming from the monarch himself. Dunbar waved a hand towards Huntly.

The Earl turned to the King. "Sire – is it your royal will that this Strachan of Lynturk should here repeat, before all, what he revealed to me of this matter?"

James shrugged. "Address your questions and remarks, my lord, to the Chancellor. He presides. I but observe."

Looking more uneasy than ever, the Archbishop said, to no one in particular, "Proceed."

Another voice spoke up, and strongly. "Before anything further is said, my lord Archbishop, I would have all present to know that I, and my father, protest, most strongly protest." That was John Forbes, glaring around him. "Protest that we should have been brought here like felons, and held imprisoned. The Lord and Master of Forbes! Of a line more ancient, honourable and illustrious, I dare to say, than any, any soever in this hall today, MacFirbis, a power in this land when it was still Celtic Alba, and when the forebears of most here were still horse-holders and scullions in Normandy-France!" At the growls that produced, he merely raised his voice the higher. "And this treatment at the hands of one who is our house's enemy, our *recent* enemy, since this man's Lowland ancestors, Normans, only came into our north but two centuries ago, there to crow like any cock on its midden, and be sufficient proud to name himself so. Worse, this man's grandsire only changed his name from Seton to Gordon a few years back! And he dares to accuse Forbes! On the trumped-up testimony of a forsworn small tacksman of ours, who holds a grudge against me over a wench!" He did not deign to glance over at Strachan, reserving his ire for Huntly. "This, I say, you should all know, before proceeding further."

There was uproar in the hall, unprecedented at a Privy Council meeting, Lowland lords of Norman pedigree shouting, the Chancellor flapping his hands, and Huntly shaking his fist, bony features contorted, at this attack on the Gordon origins – Gordon in fact being a place in the Berwickshire Merse, and the family only marrying into the Highland polity two centuries before, and another century later a Sir William Seton, another Norman-line Lowlander, wedding the Gordon heiress and taking the name. Even James Stewart sat forward on his throne scowling; for after all, the Stewarts got their name from being Stewards of Dol, in Normandy, before ever they became High Stewards of Scotland.

The Chancellor, unable to obtain silence, looked appealingly at David Lindsay, who nodded and signed to one of his trumpeters. A blast on an instrument achieved quiet.

"Sir," the Archbishop said, "your words, however unsuitable here, have been heard and noted. Hereafter, you will speak only by my permission. This is a council meeting, in the presence of His Grace, not a cattle-market! Now – my lord of Huntly."

The Earl, mastering his wrath, turned to Strachan. "Lynturk – give your evidence," he said tersely. "And make it the truth."

That man, looking even more nervous now, spoke only hesitantly. "My lord . . . my lords . . . Sire . . . I swear it is truth. I but did my leal duty. Could do no less. When I heard of the Master's design to slay the King's Grace, I could not stay silent. I must needs tell it. I went to my lord the Justiciar . . ."

"Yes, yes, man," Huntly intervened. "All accept that. Come to the heart of the matter."

"Yes, my lord. It was in May month. While His Grace was still in France. The Master spoke with some close to him. I was there. He said that the King always came to Aberdeen town to preside at the justice-eyres in the autumn, in September or October months. And to hunt, with you my lord Huntly, in Strathbogie. He said that the next time, His Grace should die, be slain. That he was no good king for Scotland. That he was against the Highlands and the north. That he was destroying the old order. That he was over-fond of France. That my lord Earl of Arran would make a better king. That he, the King, hated my lord of Angus, the Master's good-brother . . ."

"The plot, man – the plot?"

"Yes, my lord. The design was to shoot His Grace as he passed through the streets of Aberdeen, to open the justice-eyres."

"And how was this to be done?"

"It was to be done by cannon-fire, my lord. A culverin. To ensure that there should be no miss, no mere wounding. Cannon-fire at the King's person . . ."

The noise in the hall drowned the rest.

When order was restored, Huntly went on. "This dastardly design – was it agreed?"

"*I* spoke against it, my lord. But the Master was strong for it. Said that it was necessary for the realm. That King James must die – and before there might be a son born to heir the throne . . ."

"You disagreed. But others did not? Who else?"

"Three others. I do not know their names. Forbeses, no doubt."

"No doubt will not serve, sir," the Chancellor said severely. "Was the Lord Forbes present?"

"No, my lord. Just these three. Whom I did not know."

"Have you reason to believe that the Lord Forbes was privy to this evil plot?"

"No-o-o, my lord."

"Then why, my lord Earl of Huntly, when you arrested

the Master, did you also arrest my Lord Forbes, his father?"

"Because, when Lynturk brought me this word, as Justiciar, I considered it to be wise. Forbes has ever been a friend of Angus and the Douglases – as, to be sure, is the Master, married to Angus's sister. I feared that if I left the father free, he might well seek to rescue his son, with his Forbes caterans, of whom none are more unruly in the north. Or with Douglas mosstroopers in the south here. Forby, we do not know that the Lord Forbes was *not* in the plot, or was at the least aware of it. Prudence made his arrest advisable."

"Prudence, aye, my lord. But you have no true charge against the Lord Forbes?" That was a different voice, that of John Stewart, Earl of Atholl. His aunt, after all, had been Forbes's first wife.

"Nothing that I could prove, no."

"Then, my lord Chancellor, I say that the Lord Forbes should be permitted to stand down."

Dunbar cast a quick glance at the King, who gave an almost imperceptible nod. "Very well," he said. "My lord, you may go. Leave this hearing."

"I thank your lordships – but may I first speak?" the older man asked. "I am, after all, a member of this Privy Council." And when the Archbishop inclined his head, went on more strongly. "I swear before God and you all that I am innocent of any plot to slay His Grace – whom may Heaven preserve! I would never, never I say, seek hurt towards the King, to whom I have sworn sacred oath of support. But, my lords, equally with that I say that neither is my son guilty of this charge. It is untrue, I do assure you. This man, Strachan of Lynturk, is not to be trusted. He was dismissed from my son's service. He is a noted troublemaker in Strathdon. Because time and again we have had cause to rebuke him, he has become the enemy of me and my house. You cannot, in all decency and honesty, accept the word of such a man against that of Forbes!"

There was a stir and murmur throughout the hall, not all of it unsympathetic. Not many lords present would be prepared to have one of their vassals' or tacksmen's word accepted in preference to their own.

Recognising it, Huntly spoke up sternly. "My lords, the Lord Forbes accuses this Lynturk of being a troublemaker. As to that, I have no knowledge. But what I do know is that there are few greater and more notour troublemakers in all Scotland than John, Master of Forbes! As Justiciar in the north, I can assure you of that. It is none so long past that he was involved in the murder of Seton of Meldrum, in the Garioch – and did boast of it! He it was who, when the late Regent, the Duke of Albany now dead, led the Scots host to assail the English some years back, headed the refusal of many to cross Tweed and attack Wark Castle, and so caused the failure of that expedition. Always this man has worked in the English interest and supported Angus. Can he deny that he receives frequent payments in siller from King Henry? A pension, indeed!"

Taking this as permission to speak, the Master raised his powerful voice. "I do so deny. Deny all these charges. Brought against me by Huntly out of pure spite and malice. None can be proved. It is all hearsay, based on the lies of this Strachan, an arrant rogue . . ."

"Silence!" Huntly cried, reinforcing the Archbishop's feeble flappings. "Still that evil tongue, sirrah, in the King's presence! Your denials are of no worth, man. For the charges are *not* but hearsay, or merely on Lynturk's testimony. You were unwise, Forbes, to write letters. To the Lady Margaret of Methven, His Grace's mother."

That produced sufficient effect. The company was suddenly stilled, almost breath-held, all eyes turning on the King, who sat expressionless, staring ahead of him. As for John Forbes, he was abruptly changed in his entire stance and attitude, the arrogant confidence wilted. He moistened his lips but did not attempt speech.

Huntly himself seemed less than triumphant over this dramatic stroke, as though uneasy about the revelation and what was implied. No doubt he was unsure as to how James would react to the public introduction of the Queen-Mother's name into the affair, how much the monarch might wish to be known, or hinted at, of her intrigues and behaviour. Certainly the Chancellor appeared to be distinctly agitated; and Atholl, the senior of the councillors, was frowning.

Almost hurriedly, Huntly went on. "So Master of Forbes, your guilt can be substantiated, in measure, your denials worthless. My lord Chancellor – I think that sufficient has been said for the Council to make decision?"

With obvious reluctance, Dunbar nodded. "I thank you, my lord." Almost with a sigh he turned to his fellow-members of the panel. "Do any wish to question the accused? Or the witness? Or my lord of Huntly?"

With varying expressions the four shook their heads.

"Very well. Remove the prisoner, John Forbes. Also the witness Strachan. My lord of Forbes may remain present, if so he wishes."

"I say no, to the last." That was Kennedy, Earl of Cassillis, his first contribution. "It would be more suitable, less difficult, if the Lord Forbes was . . . absent."

"As you will. My Lord Forbes – you will leave us, meantime."

When the Forbeses and their accuser were gone, there was a change of atmosphere in the hall. Everyone eyed the King rather than the Chancellor and his colleagues. But James gave no sign.

Dunbar wagged his grey head, but knew what was expected of him. "My lords – you have heard. We have to decide. John, Master of Forbes, is before us on a charge of high treason. Not of being a troublemaker nor of being concerned in a previous felony. Such is not our concern here. We must say whether or not he is guilty of treason towards his liege-lord and realm. That only. My lord of Atholl – how say you?"

"Guilty," that man jerked briefly.

"My lord of Cassillis?"

"Guilty, my lord Chancellor."

"Aye." That was heavy. "My lord Maxwell?"

"I can only find him guilty, my lord Archbishop."

"And you, Master of Glencairn?"

"I also say guilty, my lord."

Dunbar bowed to the inevitable, inevitable from the first. "Who am I to adjudge *you* mistaken? I must accept your decision. There is, then, only the sentence. What shall it be?"

"There is only one sentence for high treason, as all men know," Atholl said woodenly. "Death. Hanging, drawing and quartering."

The others nodded.

"There is the royal prerogative, my lords – mercy!"

Again all eyes were on James Stewart. And again he stared ahead of him, expressionless.

Seconds passed as the Archbishop waited, until at length he sank his head between hunched shoulders. "So be it," he got out thickly. "Guard – bring in the Master of Forbes."

In tense silence the company watched the prisoner being brought back. He appeared to have recovered his defiant attitude, jaw out-thrust. Undoubtedly he knew the verdict, and his fate.

"Master of Forbes," the Chancellor said tonelessly, "you have been found guilty by the Council of the offence of high treason, in that you have conspired against the life, well-being and rule of your sovereign-lord King James. As a consequence, you will die, and at a time and place to be decided by His Grace. May Almighty God have mercy on your soul!"

Forbes bowed, ironically. "And on yours, my lord Archbishop, for condemning an innocent man!"

As though he had been struck, the prelate shrank back in his chair.

Abruptly, James Stewart rose, and without a word stalked from the hall.

As men scrambled to their feet, David Lindsay signed to his trumpeters to blow, and, with what dignity he could muster, hurried after the monarch.

It was Huntly who shouted after him. "Lindsay – discover when and where? The execution?"

James was at his royal quarters before David caught up with him – and few would have risked speech, in view of the King's expression. But Lindsay had been his childhood companion and only real friend, the first and most enduring influence in the royal life.

"Sire – are you indeed set on that man's death?" he asked. "Would not banishment serve? Send him to join his good-brother Angus?"

"No." That was sufficiently certain. "He dies."

"Then, my lord King, they must know when. And where." The criticism in the other voice was as certain.

"Forthwith. Lest the Douglases attempt a rescue, or other move. Today, here, at this castle. He goes not outside these walls again. Now – leave me."

So, on the Castle-hill of Edinburgh, that same afternoon, John Forbes went to the gallows, bold, challenging to the end, the King watching from a distant window of the rock-crowning fortress. As for mercy, the gruesome drawing and quartering was postponed until life was considered to be extinct.

But James Stewart, in his heartbreak over Madeleine de Valois and his resentment and fear of Angus, the Douglases and Henry his uncle, was not finished. Lindsay had never seen him like this, so dour, sullen, set in his vindictiveness – for normally he was a cheerful, casual young man, verging on the irresponsible, pleasure-loving and easy-going, more concerned with women, hunting, sport and gaiety than affairs of state. He promptly ordered the trial of the Lady Janet Douglas, widow of the Lord Glamis, to be held before his return to Stirling four days later.

It proved to be scarcely a repetition of the Forbes hearing, although it was held in the same hall and before much the same large company, for the actual charge here was not to be treason, although that could be inferred, but witchcraft – and witchcraft was an offence against Holy Church. So it was not a Privy Council matter nor the concern of the justiciary nor the new Court of Session.

Three prelates were the judges, resplendent in magnificent vestments, the Bishops of Dunkeld and Ross, and, just that there should be no mistake, the King's secretary, David Paniter, Prior of St. Mary's Isle.

The monarch was ushered in by Lyon in the usual way.

On this occasion, at least, there was no reluctance nor hesitation on the part of the presiding judge. Bishop George Crichton of Dunkeld was an amiable, chuckling, uncomplicated character, who appeared to extract maximum enjoyment out of life, even witchcraft-trials – very different from his superior the Archbishop of Glasgow, who was not present on this occasion. Beaming around him, once the King was seated, he called for the accused.

Lady Glamis was brought in, a handsome, well-made woman in her late thirties, carrying herself assuredly, with no lack of Douglas pride. She bowed to none.

The Bishop waved to her genially, and ordered a chair to be brought for her; but evidently she preferred to stand, for she ignored it, and him.

"You are Janet Douglas, sister to Archibald Douglas, Earl of Angus, now a subject by choice of the English king, rejecting his own liege-lord?" Crichton observed, as though he found the matter amusing, intriguing. "You were married firstly to John, sixth Lord Glamis, who died of a poisoning. Commonly said to have been administered by your ladyship in a posset of Bordeaux wine!" The Bishop smiled cheerfully at this tit-bit of relevant information. "Since when you have wed a Hielantman, one Campbell of Skipnish. We trust that *he* keeps well, my lady?"

She eyed him coolly. "Well, my lord Bishop. And you, I understand, are a bastard son of a small Lothian laird. Who has boasted that he has read neither the New nor the Old Testament of holy scripture!"

Delightedly the Bishop rubbed plump beringed fingers. "Ha! Spirit, I see. A lady of birth and spirit, indeed! Excellent! And right on both counts, forby. Holy Church looks after the faithful, however humbly-born and unlettered. We are not all witches and warlocks, only simple men. As to scriptures, I have my breviary, and have ever found it sufficient." He turned to his fellow-judges. "Eh, my friends?"

James Hay, Bishop of Ross, made a gesture which could

have meant anything; and David Paniter, a learned man and protégé of Davie Beaton, produced a wan smile.

"Now, to our task, lady," Crichton went on, pleasantly. "You dabble in poisons, it seems. An art, no doubt – even if it is a black one. Little known to such as us here, simple men – even more so than holy writ, heh? Enlighten us, lady. How do you discover these infusions? By much reading of dark books? Through secret conclaves? Or by witchcraft and consultation with Satanicus?" He hooted. "With Auld Hornie – Satanicus. Lord of the Powers of Darkness? He has his auld and new testaments, too, they do say! But you will put us right on that, no doubt?"

The woman looked at him disdainfully. "Do you wander in your mind, my lord Bishop? Or is this some play-acting? I know nothing of the powers of darkness. Any more than I do of poison. Or of witchcraft."

"Och, modest, modest! Suitable in a woman, to be sure. But scarce helpful to our enquiry. Never heed – your friend the barbour and chirurgeon has been more forthcoming, see you – the mannie John Lyon. Lyon, now – that is the Glamis name, is it not? Some kinsman, eh?"

That altered her attitude not a little. "What mean you?" she demanded quickly.

"Why, but that a sawbones and trimmer of beards being so close to a lord's lady and earl's daughter, could be the better understood if he was of your late husband's kin."

"A servant of my lord, that was all. Not close to me. I am not close with servants!"

"Ah – then he is a teller of tales as well as a cutter of hairs and letter of blood! A man of many talents, to be sure. It seems a weaver of spells and brewer of potions also? And the tales he has told us! In yonder Tolbooth." Crichton positively beamed.

Lady Glamis looked wary. "What is this? What tolbooth? Spare me your riddles, my lord Bishop."

"Why, lady, the Tolbooth of this Edinburgh. Down the High Street. Where now lie your friends, this John Lyon, Patrick Charteris of Cathelgurdy, a priest whose name I misremember – and, to be sure, your present husband

and your son, the young Lord Glamis. Forby, these two are now bestowed up here, in this castle. A notable company – and they have been enlightening us with their own riddles! Interestingly, I say – interestingly."

"My son! You have my son? How dare you! What have you been doing to John? In that hell-hole, the Tolbooth? He is but sixteen years . . ."

"And well-advanced for such years, lady. A fine lad. He told us much, after a little while."

"If you have been torturing my son, priest, you, you will . . .!"

"Tut, lady – no need for torture. No, no. A mere sight of the thumbikins and he could not have been more helpful. Told us much. As did they all, indeed – most informative. Och, we are much the wiser, improved in our knowledge." He snickered. "Even Holy Church can learn, we do confess. So now – we seek your own confession, lady, as is right and proper."

"I have nothing to confess – to you, sir, or other. You can bring no true charges against me. For I have committed no offence."

"No? How fortunate you are to be able so to say! Few can be quite so sure, in this sad world! So your son, your present husband, Cathelgurdy, the priest and the barbour – they all lie? Only your ladyship speaks truth?"

"I have not been put to the torment. As yet! What charges do you raise against me?"

Crichton consulted his papers. "We have it here, somewhere. Ah, yes – that you, the Lady Janet Douglas, did conspire and imagine the destruction of the most noble person of our serene lord the King, by poison and witchcraft. Aye, that is the heart of it. To the point, you will agree, lady?"

"I deny it. False as it is foolish."

The Bishop of Ross spoke up. "Let us have done with this. We get nowhere with this woman. We know the worth of her denials. We know her past offences. We know that she has spoken against the King's Grace on many occasions. That she actively supports her brother, the outlawed Earl of Angus. That she visited him in

England, with Charteris of Cathelgurdy, at King Henry's court. That she is in constant communication with Douglas factions and their friends up and down this land . . ."

"Aye, Jamie, aye – but this of poison and witchcraft is our especial concern this day, see you. On all you say, the lady is no doubt to be condemned. Sins against the realm. But witchcraft now, could be accounted the sin against the Holy Ghost! The business of Holy Church. Forby, it is fell interesting, you will admit?" Crichton turned back to the prisoner indulgently. "Lady, you will admit to attending secret meetings by night in the kirkyard of Glamis? Of digging up skulls and bones therein buried? Of uttering curses at the full of the moon? Of fire-raising? Of examining the bellies of hares and the like for omens? Of colloguing with the barbour John Lyon, and a man he named as Mackay, in the concocting of potions and poisons, for administration to the King's Grace . . .?"

"All folly! All lies! How could I administer poison to the King? I have never been in the King's company."

"Ah, but you have friends, good friends, who do frequent His Grace's court. Highly placed friends, who could have the poison administered." He chuckled. "You'll not deny that, a bonny woman like yourself!"

"I do so deny."

"Tut, lass – I have the names somewhere. Aye – what of the Lords Ruthven and Oliphant, eh? And others?"

"Mere neighbours and friends of my former husband."

"Scarcely *his* friends, lady . . .?"

The third member of the panel, David Paniter, the King's secretary, intervened, reading in level tones from a paper. "In the year 1532, the accused Lady Glamis stood trial at Forfar justice-eyres on a charge of fire-raising. And of poisoning her husband, the Lord Glamis, four years earlier. That trial was abandoned for the refusal of witnesses to compear. Also of justices to attend, to the number of twenty-eight, although summoned. For fear of witchcraft and threats to their persons."

That flat statement quite notably changed the character

of the proceedings. The slightly unreal atmosphere engendered by the Bishop of Dunkeld's genial handling of the matter gave place to tension.

"Idle talk," the prisoner said into the silence. "The ignorant clack of groundlings."

"Scarcely groundlings, Lady Glamis," Paniter said. He read again. "Amongst those fined by the justiciary for refusal to attend as justices were the Lords Oliphant and Ruthven and the barons of Moncrieffe, Ardoch and Tullibardine. Over a score of others."

Crichton wagged his head wonderingly. "That was right effective witchery, lady. How did you do it? Hech, hech – over a score of them, afeard. Explain it to us, simple churchmen, if you please."

"It is all lies, I tell you. Talk. Without substance."

"Was it without substance that you were tried and found guilty, the year before, of conspiring with the King's rebels and using unlawful means to persuade others to betray their allegiance?" That was Paniter again. "For which you fled the realm. And your property was forfeited. As in 1528, nine years ago, you were summoned to appear before parliament itself, charged, with Home of Blackadder, Kennedy of Girvanmains and others, of aiding the Earl of Angus to convoke the King's lieges for invasion of His Grace's royal person, at the age of seventeen years."

"I was acquitted on that occasion," she declared, but her voice faltered for the first time.

"But not on *this* occasion, I say," Bishop Hay declared heavily. "What need we of further talk? This woman is long set in her wickedness and sins. She is utterly unrepentant. We but waste the time of His Grace and all here. Her guilt is clear. I say that it is only for us to pronounce sentence."

"I agree," Paniter nodded.

Almost reluctantly Crichton spread his hands. "As you will," he allowed. "Although who knows what we might learn, to add to our poor knowledge of such dark matters? If this lady could be persuaded to inform us." He shrugged. "So, Lady Glamis, you have heard? My godly colleagues find the charges proved against you. Myself, I can do no other. As to sentence, I am thankful that it is not for us to decide. Holy Church in its wisdom has only the one sentence for witchcraft – the stake. But you will know that well, I am sure. Thus may cleansing fire consume and purify the ill in you, and you will go on your way to grace and better things, not only forgiven by a merciful God but purged, refined." That was benevolence itself. "Will the morrow serve for your . . . translation? Here, on the Castle-hill? So be it."

Expressionless the prisoner inclined her handsome head. "May I see my son?" she asked.

"Surely, surely – His Grace permitting." For the first time, the Bishop addressed the throne. "Sire, Holy Church has heard, examined, decided and spoken. We pray God's blessing on Your Grace and your realm."

"I thank you, my lord Bishop." James rose, staring at the Lady Glamis. "There remains but Angus and his brother," he added, but so low that probably only David Lindsay, standing behind him, heard it.

The trumpeters sounded.

2

David Lindsay, straddling two gnarled boughs of an old apple tree in the orchard at the Mount of Lindifferon, picking the last of the fruit in the October sunshine, declared, certainly not for the first time, that he *was* being careful, that he well realised that he was no longer a young man, in fact that he was in his forty-seventh year – but that did not mean necessarily that he was a decrepit cripple nor a witless idiot. He dropped another apple into the apron his wife held out beneath him, to catch the fruit without it bruising.

Janet Douglas smiled gently – she was good at that. "It is merely that I rate your worth higher than a few apples! Even wise and agile men of whatever years can fall if the branch breaks under them – and the one under your left foot looks like to do so. Or should I say sinister foot, for my lord Lyon? Lord Ape would suit you better, I swear, at this present!"

"Quiet, woman! I have had enough of that already, from Sandy Moir."

"Sandy has the rights of it. Kings of Arms and Poets Laureate, to say nothing of privy councillors, should not climb trees. You should leave those top apples to Sandy."

"Sandy is old enough to be my father! And an auld wife, forby! There now," he exclaimed, as an apple missed the apron and fell to the grass. "That one will not keep. If you were to stand in the right place instead of clucking at me like a broody hen, we'd do the better!"

Janet made a face up at him. She was his second wife, she was not beautiful nor yet handsome, but undeniably attractive nevertheless in a calm and comely way, her years sitting but lightly upon her. The royal Wardrobe Mistress, she was the only Douglas the King would have about his court – but then, she was a Black Douglas, not a Red of the Angus line, and despite having the same name as the late Lady Glamis, there was little else to link them.

It was the disapproving Sandy Moir, handyman and as much of a gardener as the Mount boasted, who raised his voice from a little way off. "Maister – see yonder! Doon by. Company." Sandy always had had difficulty in his addressing of Lindsay. A sturdy, independent Fifer, he had known his employer since childhood and had never managed to get his tongue round Sir David, still less my lord Lyon. If he was being particularly critical, he called him Laird.

Looking where the man pointed, southwards, downhill through the autumn leafage, David saw the three horsemen come trotting up the quite steep winding track to the Mount, one most kenspeckle in vivid scarlet. There was only one man he knew who habitually dressed all in red – and he had believed that man to be still in France.

"Davie!" he exclaimed. "Davie Beaton – home again!"

Janet sighed. "Then there is an end to apple-gathering. At least we will get you down from this tree!" She wagged her expressive head. "I am fond of Davie, as you know – but his comings are apt to spell trouble." She went to empty her apronful into one of a row of baskets.

The estate and barony of the Mount of Lindifferon covered the twin hills of that name which rose out of the green vale of Stratheden in the Rigging of Fife, some three miles north-west of the county town of Cupar, a pleasant place of steep fields, hanging woodlands and far-flung vistas, with a square stone tower within its curtain-walled courtyard, its pleasance and orchard and a dovecote. David had inherited this property as a child, from his mother, long before he fell heir to his father's larger lairdship of Garleton, in East Lothian, just across the Forth estuary; and having always been known as Lindsay of the Mount, had not bothered to change his style to Lindsay of Garleton, on his father's death. He looked on this isolated and lofty Fife demesne as his home; and Janet preferred it to Garleton, where he had a younger but not particularly congenial brother as incumbent. Here they came whenever they could get away from their duties at court.

Lindsay was still dusting the green of the tree off his far from elegant homespun clothing when the other David rode up, a picture of fashion and style in red velvet and satin, with nothing particularly clerical about him save for the gold crucifix on the chain against his doublet. His two attendants made up for it, however, heavily armed, in mitre-painted steel breastplates and the embroidered livery of the archiepiscopal see of St. Andrews. They reined up well back from their master.

Doffing his jewelled and plumed bonnet in a sweeping homage to Janet, at the same time as he dismounted lithely, Beaton produced that most winning smile of his.

"The fairest sights and scenes these eyes have been favoured with for many a day!" he announced gallantly. "Bless you both – how good to see you again." There was little of prelatical benediction about that.

"So you are back," Lindsay said. "Sooner than we looked for you."

"A plague on it – what sort of a welcome is that!" the other demanded, laughing. "Janet – can you not do better for me?" He strode forward to embrace her.

"It is good to see you, Davie," she assured him. "You should know this bearlike husband of mine by now, eloquent only on paper, the most unlikely poet even Scotland has produced! We have missed you these months, despite his greeting. When did you return?"

"Only yesterday my ship reached St. Andrews. And here I am on my way to Stirling, to James. I could not pass without calling, to see if you were here."

"You will have the shorter journey, then," Lindsay told him. "James is hunting, at Falkland, here in Fife. He does not require us, for that – so here we are."

"Good. Then I have only another dozen miles to ride. Which means that I can bide with you a while. For James, hunting, will not want to see me, or any, until he has eaten and is rested. How is he? Still mourning Madeleine?"

"Aye. Although managing to console himself, in some fashion!"

"No doubt. Well, I have consolation for him. Marie de Guise will wed him. And King Francis not only agrees but will provide another dowry, of one hundred and fifty thousand livres, no less! So all is well. Mind you, it was not all simple to achieve. For Henry of England is looking for still another new wife, and his eye fell on the de Guise. But I convinced Francis of the folly of permitting that. And the lady of the dangers of being wed to Henry Tudor!"

"But – is he seeking *another* divorce? He is married now to this Jane Seymour . . ."

"Sakes, man – she is dead! Have you not heard? After giving birth to the son he so greatly coveted and needed, this Prince Edward, she sank and dwindled. Bleeding never ceased, they say. She died, and within days he was seeking a fourth wife."

"Lord – that man is beyond all! A monster! This Frenchwoman should thank you, then."

"I hope that she may. And that James will also. As Francis has done. Likewise Pope Paul." That was just a trifle smug.

"So greatly favoured! I wonder that you deign to darken our poor doorway!"

"Which you have not yet invited him to do!" Janet reminded. "Come – favour *us*, favoured as you are, Davie. You will be the better of some refreshment, I warrant."

But Beaton actually caught her arm as she was moving off, holding her back. "You speak truer than you know, both of you," he declared. "I would have you the first to know, to hear it, here in Scotland. I am to become a cardinal, a Prince of the Church!"

"Wha-a-at!" Lindsay stared. "Cardinal? You, you jest!"

"No jest. I am to become the Cardinal of St. Stephen of the Caelian Hill. When James marries the de Guise."

"But . . . why? You, Davie Beaton, a cardinal? You are clever, yes. Able. Have much influence here in Scotland. But, at Rome? Why, man?"

"You scarcely flatter! There is reason enough. Francis urged it on the Pope. Scotland must be strong for Holy Church, this reforming heresy controlled. Henry of

England will have Scotland if he can. Having it throw off allegiance to Rome would greatly aid him. He tries all the time, with intrigues and pensions, as you know well. And the Church here is *not* strong, at this present. My uncle, its head, is little better than a cipher, senile. He will not live much longer. Dunbar of Glasgow is weak. An honest man, yes, but not a fighter, not one to be Primate, and save the Church from Henry and the heretics. And the other bishops – can you see any of them strong enough, with sufficient vigour and resolve? For that task? Old bumbling Dunkeld? Ross already a sick man. Galloway aged. Aberdeen lost in his books. Some already accept Henry's gold, I know. So . . ."

"So? You mean . . .? *You*?"

"Aye, myself. There is nothing else for it, David. Do you not see it? *I* can preserve Holy Church in Scotland – and I know no other who could. So I must succeed my uncle, when he goes. But I am not even a bishop in Scotland, only in France. To become Archbishop of St. Andrews and Primate I must have undoubted episcopal authority, to be accepted. As a cardinal, that is . . . undeniable!"

At a loss for words, Lindsay gazed at his one-time fellow-student.

Janet looked from one to the other. "A cardinal is still but a man," she said. "And a man requires sustenance after a long ride. If Your Eminence-to-be will come this way?" And she led them out of that orchard towards the little castle, directing Sandy Moir to look after the two men-at-arms.

Later, with no more to be said on Beaton's soaring prospects, the talk turned to the present situation in Scotland, with that man wanting to know all of significance that had transpired during his four-months' absence. Lindsay told him about the trials at Edinburgh and his own concern thereat, not only at what he feared might well be the injustice perpetrated – for he was by no means convinced that either of the accused had been guilty – but at the new development in the King's character, a ruthless severity and resentment not hitherto evident. Presumably it was the death of Madeleine which had brought this out. The Tudor blood in him coming to the surface, perhaps . . .

"The more this new match is needed, then," Beaton asserted. "Marie de Guise is a strong-minded woman. She will be good for James. *He* is not a strong character – we have always known that. He needs a guiding hand, closer to him than mine, or even yours. As to the trials, those two, Forbes and the Lady Glamis, they may not have been guilty of all they were accused of, but they deserved to die, I swear. That woman was evil, dangerous, apart altogether from being Angus's sister. And Forbes was a murderer."

"Perhaps. But that was not what they were tried for. It was treason. And witchcraft. I cannot think that the King's justice – and the Church's – nor their repute, profited. *You*, Davie, I vow were thankful to be spared sitting as one of the judges? Indeed, I think that you may even have contrived it all, so that you would *not* be there! And appointed judges who would do it all for you!"

"You esteem me, if that is the word, of greater power and authority than ever I am blessed with!" the other returned lightly. "Give James himself a little of the credit!" And, in a different voice, "You say that he is changed? And for the worse. He is still mourning Madeleine – but consoling himself meantime! With whom? The usual tribe of noble sluts and common whores?" He waved. "With my apologies to Janet!"

"These, yes, in some measure. But that is not what concerns me most – for it has ever been that way." Lindsay hesitated a little. "It is this of Oliver Sinclair. He is . . . doting on that young man."

"Doting? You do not mean . . .?"

"I do not rightly know. It scarcely seems possible, in a man so taken up with women. Yet they are seldom apart now. Sinclair has taken over the place of the Bastard of Arran, only more, more intimately. He shares his bedchamber not infrequently – but the Bastard used to do that also . . ."

"And as did you, over many a year, my friend!"

"To be sure. But that was . . . otherwise. There may be no ill in that. But Sinclair is no good influence on James, I feel sure. He encourages his new harshness. I do not like that young man."

"But he is not displacing the women, you say?"

"No-o-o. But he presumes. Interferes. Gives himself airs. And James appears to see no fault in him. Many complain to me."

"Such familiars and favourites come and go. Most rulers have the like. It is a lonely life, to be a monarch."

"True. Perhaps I make overmuch of it. Janet says that I do. But – I believe that he is worth watching. If King Henry could get at Oliver Sinclair . . .!"

"M'mm. Yes, I see. I will keep an eye on him. He will be at Falkland with James? I scarce know the man."

"He is kin to the Earl of Caithness, of that savage house."

"David will see no good in him," Janet said. "I think there is little harm to Oliver Sinclair, that a few more years will not put right. This new marriage will help the situation, belike? When is the wedding to be?"

"James will have to decide that. Francis suggests May. Which is probably right . . ."

"Not another months-long jaunt to France!" Lindsay protested. "So soon after the last. This kingdom could not be doing with that."

"No, I agree. Nor the French, either. I doubt whether James would wish it, forby. I am going to suggest that he sends one of his lords for a proxy wedding in Paris, Erskine perhaps, or Maxwell. Then the true ceremony when the bride gets here."

"Will the Duchess Marie agree to that?"

"I believe so. She is a sensible woman, pleased to be becoming a queen. And she was much taken with James – as he with her, before he met Madeleine. Forby, she is no girl, and has been wed before."

"Poor Marie de Guise!" Janet murmured. "I wonder whether she has any notion of what she has ahead of her, as Queen of Scotland!"

The men did not venture an opinion on that.

"Did you see Marion while I was away?" Beaton asked, changing the subject.

"Indeed yes. We visited her at Ethie Castle for a day or two in August, after we had the harvest in. She was well, and the children. But missing you. A woman in a thousand, that."

"Do I not know it! I will go there whenever I can get away from James. See you – why not come with me, both of you? Sail from St. Andrews in my vessel. It would be a joy."

"Yes, David – why not?" Janet exclaimed. "That would be so good."

"If the King does not require our services . . ."

"If he is having fair sport at Falkland, he will not, my friend," Beaton assured. "Kings of Arms and Wardrobe Mistresses, even poets, are scarcely essential to stag-chasing! I will seek leave-of-absence for you . . ."

To the Lindsays the speed and ease of the voyage by sea, compared with the journey by land which they had had to make hitherto, was scarcely believable. Whereas it required two long days of riding, even using the ferry across Tay, from Lindifferon to Ethiehaven on the Angus coast, going by ship it was a mere twenty miles or so, on this breezy October day and took them only three hours. Sailing in Beaton's own – or at least Holy Church's – shallop, *Eden Lass*, from St. Andrews quayside, they headed north by east on the steady south-west wind, out of the bay and crossing the mouth of the Tay estuary, to pass between the long, low headland of Buddon Ness and the menacing reef of Inchcape, which was spouting high spray even on this relatively calm sea, the most fatal hazard on all the east coast of Scotland according to Beaton. He explained that it was a long ridge of rock, entirely hidden at high-water, threatening the shipping routes to both the Forth and Tay firths, on which more vessels had struck and foundered than anywhere else on this seaboard. With some satisfaction he pointed out the slender scaffold or timber frame rising from the rock, on which hung the great bell which they could just hear intermittently out of the contrary breeze, and which had been erected there, after great endeavours, by a former Abbot of Arbroath, its constant tolling to warn mariners by day and night – so that the reef was often called the Bell Rock; and which the dastardly pirate, Sir Ralph the Rover, had deliberately cut down in order to lure more ships to their doom – and was himself wrecked and drowned on the same shoal within the year. The Abbey of Arbroath still took pride in maintaining this dangerous belfry in the ocean, he assured them.

Soon thereafter they were level with the town of Arbroath itself, its great red-stone abbey rising proudly above the huddled houses and harbour, its smoke-sheds for curing fish sending up blue clouds, all helping to provide wealth for the Abbot, and this the second-richest religious foundation in all Scotland. From there on they sailed parallel with a wild and cliff-girt coast, the precipices growing ever higher and more savage, their feet smothered in spume, until Red Head itself, one of the loftiest promontories in the land, loomed before them in towering majesty. Just round this daunting foreland, where the seas boiled more whitely than anywhere else they had seen, beyond all seeming reason the *Eden Lass* turned directly in towards the turmoil of waters, heaving on the cross-tides, yet with the calmer waters of Lunan Bay inviting only a little further. And there, tucked in behind the soaring cape, was a cleft in the wall of rock, sheltering the tiny harbour of Ethiehaven, which crouched under the cliffs. A less likely destination for a Prince of the Church would have been hard to imagine.

Their skipper was practised at entering this difficult refuge, and they tied up expertly at a breakwater under a huddle of fishers' cottages which sat on a mere shelf of the promontory. Disembarking, after a greeting for the fisherfolk, with whom Beaton was obviously on excellent terms, they commenced the ascent of the cliffs by a steep zig-zag which was more stone step-ladder than path, the seabirds wheeling and screaming around them.

At the summit, breathless, they gazed around them at the farflung panorama of land and sea, the great crescent of Lunan Bay ringed with golden sands where the cliffs sank away to marram-grass dunes, the green braes inland, cattle-dotted, the wind-blown woodlands all bending away from the sea, and the distant blue ramparts of the Highland Line enclosing all to the west.

Breath recovered, Beaton led them off inland, following first the bank of a small burn which poured in a cloud of spindrift over the precipice, and then a track which climbed through rising grassland, past a lonely chapel, to a green ridge. And just over this ridge and protected by it, within a fringe of its own twisted trees, rose a fine red-stone castle, with courtyard, outbuildings and farmery, with scarcely another building in sight anywhere.

"My hermitage!" Beaton said.

"Or Marion Ogilvy's!" Lindsay amended. Although he spoke ironically, that was in fact correct. For Beaton had put this property in Marion's name while they were still husband and wife.

"To be sure," the other nodded. "Hermitage and sanctuary."

The children were doing what the Lindsays had been at when their father had called at Lindifferon, picking the last of the apples, in the walled orchard, when James, the eldest, now aged twelve, saw the trio approaching and, with shouts, led the others, two girls and a brother, to greet them. They were a lively, bright and attractive-looking lot, and the meeting was excited, not to say riotous, with the father little more restrained than his offspring, an extraordinarily different man from the normally suave and imperturbable courtier. For a moment, the childless David Lindsay was envious. One of the little girls ran to fetch her mother.

Marion Ogilvy met them at the gatehouse-pend of Ethie Castle, a good-looking and gracious woman now in her late thirties, tall, slender and lissome despite all the child-bearing. Surprised as she must have been to see any of them, she showed only quiet delight. But then, that woman had had long practice in restraining her emotions in public.

Courteously but with her own warmth, she welcomed

the Lindsays first, embracing Janet and kissing David, before turning to her husband, or former husband if that were the required description of their curious relationship. They still looked upon each other as husband and wife, although Beaton had in fact had to demote her to the status of mistress, so that he might take holy orders, some years previously – for he was a latecomer to the ministry although, as secretary to his uncle, the Primate, he had been secular Commendator-Abbot of Arbroath. It must have been a dire decision for Marion to accept, this extraordinary reduction in position in the sight of all; but having done so, for the sake of her husband's career, she appeared to have come to terms with her situation with remarkable equanimity. She and Beaton clung to each other, now, for a moment or two, wordless.

Ethie Castle thereafter became a cheerful place indeed.

Nevertheless that evening, before a great log fire in the hall, the children abed, the two Davids came as near to open quarrel as they had ever been in their long friendship, with Janet the unwitting cause. The first notes of their disharmony had been there for years, to be sure, with two such different and differing characters, each having strong views. But hitherto they had managed to keep their disagreements within the bounds of amity, accepting each other's rights to his own opinions. But that evening at Ethie saw the beginning of a new phase.

They were talking of France and court life there, with Beaton enlarging on the poetry of Clement Marot and its effect on Marguerite, Queen of Navarre, Francis's remarkable sister, who was toying with the Lutheran heresy, when Janet informed their hosts that David was working on a great new poem, really a verse-play, which she was sure was going to be the most exciting and important that he had yet attempted. It was, like this Marot's work, a satire based on the follies they saw all around them, at court, in council, in the Church, in the cities and towns and in everyday life, richly comic and colourful. She thought it a wonder, so far as it had progressed.

Her husband pooh-poohed, but the Beatons demanded to hear more.

Janet said that it was to take the form of a sitting of the Estates of Parliament, with the King there in person, and mocking examples of the great and less great, lords, bishops, knights and burgesses, all boasting and making display. Then a poor man coming before them with complaints, he and his like harried by the lords, rents increased by the lairds, abused by the prelates, their wives and daughters stolen, and the like. She particularly relished the verses about the Pardoner, with his relics for sale; and urged David to recite a few lines of that jewel, for their edification.

He asserted that he did not remember any sufficiently.

"What nonsense!" she exclaimed. "You have told me them many a time. That line about Johnnie Armstrong? 'The cord so long, which hanged Johnnie Armstrong; sound hemp and, and . . .'"

"No, no –

> Here is the cord, both great and long,
> Which hangit high Johnnie Armstrong,
> Of good hemp, soft and sound . . ."

"There you are! You remember it perfectly well. You but pretend."

"Yes, let us hear some of this epic, man," Beaton declared. "What is this of Armstrong of Gilnockie? You were at his hanging, were you not?"

"Aye, to my sorrow. That was one of the worst of James's acts. The Bastard of Arran urging him to it. But the verses are not about that. It is a Pardoner's follies . . ."

"Well, out with it. Do not cozen us further."

"It is but a conceit. About the shams and frauds of such folk."

Shrugging, he commenced:

> "My potent pardons you may see,
> Come from the Khan of Tartary,

Well blessed with Easter shells;
  Though you have no discretion
You shall have full remission
  With help of Book and bells."

He had begun hesitantly, embarrassed by his own words; but his voice strengthened as he went on,

"Here is a relic stout and strong,
  From Fionn MacCoull's own true cheek-bone;
Here is the cord both great and long
  Which hangit high Johnnie Armstrong,
Of good hemp, soft and sound.
  Good holy people, I do afford,
Whoever is hangit by this cord
  Needs never to be drowned."

"I told you," Janet said. "And the piece about Saint Bridie's cow, David. Go on."

"The anus of St. Bridie's cow,
  The snout of good St. Anthony's sow,
Which bore his holy bell;
  Whoever hears this bell to clink,
Gives me a ducat for to drink,
  He ne'er shall go to hell.

Who love their wives not with their heart
  I have the power to set apart;
Methinks you deaf and dumb!
  Has none of you cursed shrewish wife?
Who harries you with pains and strife?
  Come, take my dispensation,
Of that beldame I'll make you free,
  Even though you to blame may be.

Good masters, come these pardons buy,
  With meal or malt or good money,

For cock or hen or honey from hive,
Of relics here I have a score;
Why come you not? Your need is sore.
I promise you Holy Church will shrive."

When he finished, the women clapped their acclaim. But Davie Beaton, although he smiled, sounded less than delighted.

"Much wit and jollity!" he conceded. "Shrewd thrusting. But – it might be bettered with some slight amendment, I think."

"To be sure. It is but a first draft. It can be much improved."

"I would say so, yes. Just a word or two, perhaps. For instance, the line about remission, with the help of Book and bells, was it? And the promise that Holy Church would shrive. These are . . . unwise."

"Unwise? Sakes – they are the very heart of it! The shame and cheat and deception of those clerkly impostors – all should know it, recognise it."

"This could be taken as an attack on Holy Church, David."

"If Holy Church sanctions such lies and deceits – as not infrequently it does, as you know well – then it merits attack. The selling of pardons and indulgences for money is surely a notable sin?"

"Perhaps. But that is the Church's affair, not yours. And the Church is under sufficient attack at this present, without David Lindsay's assaults!"

"But, man – are we all to be dumb in face of wrong, blind to blatant error? Just because you see the Church endangered by reform? Is it not such very faults which bring grain to the reformers' mills?"

"I have told you before, the Church will do its own reforming. That is part of *my* task. I am entrusted by Rome with this, and saving Holy Church in Scotland from the heretics. If such as you, the Lord Lyon King of Arms and King's Usher, give aid and comfort to the heretics, then my task is the sorer. You must see that."

"I see the price of your red cardinal's hat, at least!"

"Watch your words, man!"
"Oh, David . . .!"
"I think that enough has been said on this," Marion put in, quietly. "This, my house, at least is not the Three Estates! Nor St. Andrews Castle!"
"No, my dear. I am sorry. But – this matter must be faced. If the Church is direly threatened, so is the realm. Henry Tudor but waits his chance. Indeed, he does not wait, but stirs up the heretics. Pays the reformers. Incites by every means to undermine the Church. For one purpose only – not reform of wrongs and follies, of which there are sufficient, God knows! But to win Scotland as part of *his* realm, like Wales and Ireland. He has tried war and intrigue and treachery – and failed. Now he uses religion – he who has no least religion in him! He must not succeed. If such as David here aid him, by turning the common folk, and even those higher, against the Church, this ancient kingdom could go down. It is as grievous as that."
"And how are *you* going to save the Church?" Lindsay demanded. "It is rotting before our eyes. Not only this of pardons and indulgences and the sale of relics, real or false. But shame and corruption everywhere. Bishoprics sold to the highest bidder. Prelates who cannot read holy writ or even recite Our Lord's Prayer. Abbots and priors keeping mistresses openly in their monasteries. Nunneries little better than whore-houses. Churchmen refusing to baptise or wed or bury without ever-increasing payment – which the poor can by no means find. Is this, and more, all to be accepted without murmur? For fear of Henry and the English? Or for fear of the wrath of Rome!"
"Not so. But betterment should and must come from within, from the top, not from beneath. The common folk cannot reform the Church, only those with the knowledge and power. I see the need, yes – as do others. But it cannot be done overnight. It will take time. And meanwhile Henry plots and rouses and uses."
"You have not answered me. What will *you* do to aid reform?"
"I will see that better men get the bishoprics and

abbacies. I will have visitations of parishes, monasteries and nunneries by inquisitors. I will get rid of the pardoners and relic-mongers . . ."

"And the heretics! The reformers!"

"Those too, since they endanger us all. So, my friend, amend your verses, just a little, of a mercy!"

"I am not wholly convinced . . ."

The women took over then and achieved a change of subject and some lightening of the atmosphere.

But matters were not the same thereafter between the two men, and the Ethie visit was less successful than heretofore. After two or three days, Lindsay said that they must be returning to Fife, and Beaton made no great efforts to change his mind. He put his shallop at their disposal, to take them back, but said that he would delay his own departure for a day or so more.

They parted amicably, but the shadow was there.

3

The two Davids inevitably saw a lot of each other about the court at Stirling and Edinburgh, as Lord Lyon and Lord Privy Seal, and superficially they got on well enough, agreeing to differ. Few would have guessed that a rift had opened between them. Especially when, the following May, they had to work together to a major degree in the King's marriage ceremony and celebrations. James had sent the Lord Maxwell to Paris to act as proxy at a preliminary wedding at the cathedral of Notre Dame – where he had been married to Madeleine only eighteen months before – and Maxwell was due to return to Scotland with the bride towards the end of May. It had been decided that the final nuptials should take place at St. Andrews, the metropolitan see, and it was to be a great occasion, to avoid any anticlimax as an obvious second-choice as queen, and to try to banish any lingering sense of misfortune. To Beaton was allotted the responsibility for the religious ceremonial, and to Lindsay the welcoming pageantry and entertainment. All was to be on a major scale, hardly to rival the nine months' junketings in France over the Madeleine wedding, but showing that Scotland could rejoice in its own fashion.

So co-operation was the order of the day, and Lindsay in fact went to take up temporary residence in St. Andrews Castle well in advance of the due date, to plan and prepare.

The ecclesiastical metropolis at the extreme eastern tip of the great Fife peninsula between the firths of Forth and Tay, was certainly a splendid setting for the dramatic activities envisaged. A moderately sized city, entirely contained within its high encircling walls, it was so crammed with religious institutions and seats of learning as, at first sight, to leave no room for any ordinary housing, most of those in evidence having spires, pinnacles, towers, steeples and belfries, so that from a distance the city looked as though it were reaching for the sky, if not heaven, with a myriad competing arms upraised. Despite this crowding, however, the principal streets, of which there were four, were not only straight and long, but notably wide, designed indeed for processions and parade, unexampled elsewhere. Flanking these broad thoroughfares was such a concentration of fanes, churches, chapels, oratories, shrines, monasteries, nunneries, hospices and preceptories, of every order known to Christendom, such as to defy enumeration, all of course supporting and leading up to the mighty soaring cathedral which dominated even that ambitious scene. The wealth represented here was beyond all computation, the more extraordinary in a nation esteemed poor in money terms, if not in resources and skills, with an almost permanently empty royal treasury. And over it all Davie Beaton, seventh son of a Fife laird, ruled supreme, in fact if not yet in name – for his uncle, the Archbishop, was now seldom seen or thought of, in a state of advanced and gross senility. All of course, was done in his name, as Primate, by his Coadjutor and nephew.

David and Janet – for she, as Wardrobe Mistress, was much involved in the designing and making of costumes and effects – took up quarters in the courtyard of the red-stone castle which jutted on its promontory into the sea, sheltering and protecting the harbour beneath. The old university, at which the two Davids had first met as students, the colleges of St. Salvator and St. Leonard, was nearby, with the later St. Mary's College, founded by James Beaton in his more effective days, a little further off.

Davie had sent his fast shallop to Dieppe, with one of his minions, not to escort the bride's and Maxwell's ship but to come back in advance of it, when both sailed for Scotland, bringing word as to just when the other would be arriving, so that a suitable welcome could be mounted. The *Eden Lass* duly returned, on 8th June, with the news that the larger and slower vessel, with its escort of French warships to ensure its safety from English pirates, was on its way but would probably not arrive until a couple of days later, laden down as it was with treasure and gear as well as the parties of the bride and her three brothers, the Duc de Guise, the Cardinal of Lorraine and the Marquis d'Elbeouf, who were coming to see her settled in her new land. The weather had been kind, and all was in order.

Lindsay sent one of his heralds in haste to Stirling to fetch the King.

Overnight, the weather changed. A north-easterly gale blew up, unseasonable as it was inconvenient – for inevitably it would delay the French convoy, which would now have to battle into headwinds. More inconvenient still, possibly, was the fact that St. Andrews harbour, situated where it was, faced and opened north-eastwards, and stormy seas from that quarter made it dangerous, all but impossible to enter. Many had been the shipwrecks on its flanking reefs. Anxiously, those responsible watched the seas rise. Soon a mist of spray was shrouding even the castle on its cliff.

Beaton, consulting Jock Fernie of the *Eden Lass*, and other shipmasters, did not take long to come to a decision. By no means could they allow the great French vessel bearing the new Queen to try to enter this harbour in the storm. With no sign of the wind abating, the convoy must somehow be diverted. To have it lie off this dangerous coast in a nor'-easter would be almost equally hazardous, as well as most uncomfortable for those on board. The answer seemed to be to bring the visitors ashore at a more sheltered port in the Forth estuary, Crail, the nearest, about a dozen miles to the south. But to get such instructions to the French shipmen would involve sending out a vessel as pilot. And no craft could issue from St. Andrews harbour against the gale and these seas, any more than enter it.

The only thing for it was to try to get a boat out from Crail itself. There would be only fishing-craft there, but these were sturdy vessels, small as they were, and their crews used to negotiating these turbulent waters. But they could scarcely send out some rough fishermen to greet the new Queen of Scotland and order her French skippers to change course for a different landfall.

David Lindsay, as King's Usher rather than Lyon, conceived it to be his duty to go – much to Janet's alarm.

So, uncertain as to when the French ships would arrive, he set off with minimum delay, taking Jock Fernie with him as adviser. They rode southwards by Kingask, Boarhills, Kingsbarns and Wormistone, in the blustering wind and almost horizontal rain-showers.

It was evening before they reached Crail, a little town a mere three miles west of the thrusting headland of Fife Ness, and the first of the long series of Fife ports on the Forth's north shore. Even the sight of Crail harbour gave the newcomers pause indeed, with great rollers smashing in and white spume flying, the huddled fishing boats hiding behind the harbour wall tossing and plunging crazily.

Jock Fernie shook his greying head less than hopefully, not so much at the heaving boats as at the harbour entrance itself, where the cross-seas broke in daunting fury.

"You'll no' get any big craft in yonder," he averred. "A sma' bit boatie, maybe, wi' oars, that can hug the pier-end and tak its chance. But no' a great vessel wi' sails."

"Then, what . . .? One of the other Forth ports?"

"Anster, Pittenweem, Siminnans – they'll be the same, wi' cross-seas. I hadna thocht they'd be running sae bad up the firth. It maun be right rough outby, to dae this."

"Lord – I hope . . .!" The rest was left unsaid. One royal bridal tragedy was more than sufficient.

Fernie led the way down to a quayside alehouse where the fishermen were apt to congregate. There they announced their requirements to a blank-faced audience, which clearly thought them next to crazy. But when they persisted and David offered very substantial payment for services rendered to the King's Grace, and Fernie added his assessment that Crail fishers were not likely to be afraid of a whistle of wind and a bit jabble of sea, they began to get some response. Two youngish men asked for more details.

The situation as to the French ships was explained, and elicited the opinion that any such convoy should stay at sea, riding it out, rather than try to make a port in these conditions. All agreed that large ocean-going ships would not be able to enter Crail harbour so long as this gale lasted, nor would any of the other Fife havens be much better. One of the young fishermen said that he would be willing to try to take them out, and go looking for the Frenchies, in the morning; but unless there was a big and unlikely change in the weather, he could not see any docking for ships.

There was a hospice at Crail, an outpost of Pittenweem Priory, and here the visitors put up for the night of blattering rain squalls and howling winds.

In the morning, conditions were unchanged. David was at his wits' end, when the young fisherman who had doubtfully volunteered his services, turned up with a suggestion. If it were all that important for some of the Frenchies to come ashore, they could probably do so at Balcomie. That was two miles to the east, a mile this side of Fife Ness itself. There was no true harbour there, but there was a little headland with a natural harbour amongst the rocks behind it, this side, where small boats could land. It would be protected by the headland from these seas running in from the east. The large ship itself could not put in there but could lie off under the headland, and the Queen and others board a small craft, his own fishing-boat, then they could be put ashore. The big ships could then sail on up Forth to the nearest sheltered port, probably Dysart.

This solution seemed the best that could be hoped for in the circumstances, however undignified a landing for a queen; and Jock Fernie agreed that it should serve, although the trans-shipping might prove difficult in rough seas. If the fisherman thought that he could get his craft out of this Crail harbour . . .?

Clearly that young man so thought, and without more ado they moved down to the pier.

Their helper, a red-haired and bearded, stocky individual named Dod Cairnie, went off to assemble his crew.

Normally, apparently, he manned his boat with three others but with the amount of oar-work which would be called for today, they would be better with two more. He did not seem to anticipate any difficulty in finding them.

Reaching Cairnie's craft was in itself a hazardous business, for there were fully a dozen fishing-boats in the harbour and this one was one of the farthest out from the pier, one of the largest. They were all tied together, but in the wind and spray there was a real danger of falls and broken bones.

The boat, of the yawl type, proved to be almost a quarter-full of water, which had to be baled out, a wetting process. But all were already fairly wet and would be more so. Fortunately it was not cold, and Lindsay and Fernie were told grimly that, since they would have to keep up the baling while the others rowed, they would not grow chilled. There were six long oars to the boat, although normally it seemed that they used only four, one man to each. There was a mast and square sail, but obviously these would be of little use today.

Cairnie did not put his planned procedure into words, but it appeared to be to propel his craft out as closely under the east harbour wall as possible, to its mouth, and then, choosing his moment, to make an abrupt turn outwards, with the fullest power of the six oars, to direct their bluntish bows into the oncoming seas. Obviously it would be a dangerous few moments, and they would ship water; but so long as they did not allow themselves to swing broadside-on, they ought to get through. If they failed, the probability was that they would either be rolled right over or smashed against one or other of the pier-heads.

In the event, David, busy baling near the stern and gasping for breath anyway, nearly choked as he was all but overwhelmed by water and thrown backwards almost out over the side, amidst the shouts of the rowers. The wave that hit him was not an incoming sea but the water already in the forward part of the boat spilling down on him as the bows shot up almost vertically. He had a moment's vision of the oarsmen seeming poised above him, feet braced against the stays, mouths open, sweeps awry, as though all would topple down on him. Then the yawl smashed down forwards, the bows dipping deep, and more water flooding in as he and the stern rose high. He was flung forward on top of Jock Fernie, and both against one of the rowers, who breathlessly cursed them.

Cairnie yelled at them to bale, bale, and for the oarsmen on the windward side to dig deep, as the craft was swept sideways and the western pier-head loomed close.

The bows started to rise again but more heavily now. Half-filled with water as they were, the weight at least provided some ballast, and the stern this time did not rise so high. But another cross-sea flung them to within inches of the streaming pier-head stonework, so that the leeward oars could not function. Desperately their opposite numbers dug and backed-water, Cairnie panting instructions. The backwash of that wave spun them round and for moments they were broadside-on, with a great white-laced comber soaring above them. It hit them abeam, and much of it came inboard; but, waterlogged as they were, it swept them on past the pier-head almost near enough to touch.

They were out, wallowing but still afloat, outside the harbour mouth.

Cairnie ordered the two sternmost rowers to ship their oars and aid in the baling, while he and the other three sought to keep their bows head-on to the seas, a less complicated task now. There were still cross-seas and backwashes, but each yard they edged from the land the less dangerous these were, although the main rollers by no means lessened. These grew ever the more consistent and predictable, however, and the yawl was built to cope with the like – although possibly not when half-filled with water. Baling therefore was the priority. Fortunately, recognising the probable need, Cairnie had brought extra beakers as balers, and although two were lost overboard, the four men managed to get most of the water out, despite every now and again another wave-tip coming in.

So breathlessly busy was David Lindsay at this slaistering toil that it was some time before he realised that in fact the worst was now over, that they were out in the open firth mouth; and however violent the motion of the boat, it was regular, repetitive and, carefully handled, the craft could master the conditions. It had been the conjunction of sea and land which was the main menace.

They were heading due eastwards now, the Isle of May four miles to the south-east and Fife Ness ahead, no towering headland, however notable a feature. The fact that they could see both, despite the spindrift, was a good sign, for visibility was bound to be important this day. Peer as David would each time they topped a wave-crest, he could see no sign of shipping.

However slow their progress, it did not take long to bring them level with the lesser Balcomie Point, before the main Fife Ness – lesser but higher, rising to quite a cliff-girt summit of perhaps one hundred feet. Dod Cairnie said that they should move in thereto, on this sheltered western side of the headland, to see how a landing would go. They slanted in thereafter at a wide angle, to avoid any broadside-on approach.

Quite suddenly they felt the protection of the headland. The water was by no means calm, of course, but the surface although veined with white above much surge and undertow, grew steadily less turbulent the nearer they approached land. By the time that they drew into a sort of cove amongst the rocks, the motion was only moderate.

Two weed-hung arms of reef thrust out, to offer them protected entry to this inlet which, after a hundred yards or so, ended in a shingle beach. Up and down this the tide surged, but presented them with no major difficulty, and they were able to run their yawl's prow up over the pebbles and jump ashore. After all the trials and hazards, this vital part of the plan seemed ridiculously easy.

David decided that it would be worthwhile to climb to the summit of the headland while they were here, to gain the wider view offered by that height. And this change of exercise proved rewarding, for from up there they were able to spy four ships far to the south-east, fairly scattered but clearly of one group, proceeding under very scanty sail. Fernie reckoned them to be about six miles off.

"Can we reach them? Before they pass Fife Ness?" David demanded. "They will be making for St. Andrews. It is the French, for sure."

Cairnie thought that they probably could, even in the face of these easterly seas. The ships would be coming half-towards them, after all, and having to tack against the north in the wind.

So they hurried back down to the boat and pushed off again, with easy going until they rounded the headland, when once more they were into steep seas. But apart from an awkward moment or two amongst back-surges and undertows rounding the point, it was merely back to straightforward if very uncomfortable and tossing progress, if hard work for the rowers.

Anxiously David now watched for the French convoy, as they topped each roller; but for a considerable time he could see no sign of them at all, from this lower position. At length, however, one of the ships came into view, half-right, Fernie estimating it to be some two miles off still. He reckoned that their present courses should bring them within perhaps half a mile of each other. The fishing-boat would be very limited as to any alteration of course, since they had to keep its bows head-on to the seas out of danger of swamping.

David now gave up baling and, bracing himself against the mast, sought to tie thereto the wet Lion Rampant flag which he had brought for this purpose, wrapped sash-like around his middle – no easy task in that plunging craft. He did not get the banner very far up the mast, but sufficiently to stream out above the rowers' heads. It was to be hoped that their boat and flag would be perceived from the ships, and the significance recognised. Lord Maxwell, at least, and his Scots party, should get the message.

Soon all four ships were in sight, and although not really on a converging course, drawing nearer. The fishing-boat admittedly would look very small from the Frenchmen, but the gold-and-red flag should stand out.

It was the keen-eyed Dod Cairnie who first saw that the

foremost of the vessels was itself flying a large yellow-and-red standard as well as the blue-and-white of France. This, no doubt, was the one carrying Marie de Guise. And presently this flagship could be seen to be changing course – and yes, it was almost directly towards them.

David heaved a sigh of thankfulness.

The great and small craft closed on each other in those tempestuous seas, the lesser often hidden in troughs. David stood, clutching the mast for support, while Cairnie guided his oarsmen to pull in to get under the lee of the galleon without becoming broadside-on to the seas in the process. It was a difficult manoeuvre, for the large ship could not come to any sort of halt in the following wind, and actually passed them before they could draw close enough. After a difficult turn, they had more or less to chase it, in stern-seas now.

At length they were near enough to hail.

"Ho, there," David shouted. "The Lord Maxwell? Is the Lord Maxwell there?"

"I am Maxwell, yes," came back thinly, from a group of huddled figures on the high poop of the galleon. "Who is that? What is to do?"

"I am Lindsay. The Lyon. Can you hear me? You cannot enter St. Andrews harbour. Nor any other hereabouts. In this storm. You hear?"

"Aye, aye. We feared that. What, then?"

"Have your shipmaster make for Balcomie Point. Yonder. Just west of Fife Ness. Round that into sheltered water. No haven, but you could anchor. And put down Her Highness and others into this boat and so land. You have it?"

"Leave this ship? For that! The Queen!" Maxwell sounded highly doubtful, even at that range. "Is this necessary, Lindsay?"

"Aye. With harbours all closed. That, or remaining aboard till seas drop. A welcome is prepared at St. Andrews. The King . . ."

"Aye, well." The two craft were proceeding more or less side by side, now, the oarsmen having to pull hard to keep up.

"Is all well with Her Highness?"

"Been sick. All have. But better now."

Shouting in the wind and noise was tiring. "Make for Balcomie Point. A mile west of Fife Ness. Anchor behind the headland. You have it?"

A waved hand as acknowledgment.

Although the fishing-boat tried to maintain the galleon's speed, even with the latter's sail reduced to a minimum the larger vessel steadily drew ahead. Presently Maxwell's shout reached them again, to say that the French shipmaster was offering to tow them. Was this desired? Cairnie was glad to accept and save his oarsmen's weary arms. A rope was thrown and secured, and thereafter better progress made. The three other French ships followed their flagship dutifully.

It seemed a much briefer journey back to Balcomie in these conditions. Skirting the point warily, the French skipper brought his galleon round into the sheltered water. No doubt he was concerned about shallows, but Cairnie shouted that there was plenty of water. The bay, if so it could be called, was perhaps a quarter-mile deep, and the Frenchman risked only about half that before dropping anchor. Although it was a vast improvement in calmness, it was by no means a good anchorage for large ships, and there were anxious faces above the fishing yawl as they pulled alongside. Clearly the sooner the trans-shipping was over the better. The three warships lay off.

A rope-ladder was lowered from the galleon and David Lindsay caught it and clambered up, less than nimbly owing to the swell and heave. On the well-deck, Maxwell and others awaited him, swathed in cloaks. Soaked, wind-battered and unsteady on his legs, he bowed in some fashion to Marie de Guise, who extracted a hand from her wrappings to hold out to him, achieving a certain dignity about it. Lindsay had got on well with her during their recent French visit.

"Highness!" he jerked, in fair French. "This is no kind welcome to Scotland. I am sorry. But – even kings, queens and cardinals cannot command the winds!"

"Alas no, Sir David. We can but face them with such,

such assurance as we may summon." That was in English, although heavily accented. "We must descend to your little boat?"

"I fear so, Highness. His Grace is eager to see you, I do assure you. He will be awaiting you at St. Andrews where all is prepared for your welcome. No harbour in this East Fife will be open to your ships in this storm. It could be days . . ."

"Very well. I shall trust myself to the good God and your hands, Sir David!" She looked round at two of her ladies. "One of these must needs likewise! We at least will have Holy Church's prayers – however unavailing they have been with this storm!" And she smiled at her brother just behind her, the Cardinal of Lorraine.

That handsome and notably suave individual gestured and shrugged. "We must leave the miracles to the Scots!" he said. "I salute you, Sir David, in venturing out in that frail craft."

"These are sturdy boats, Eminence. And manned by stout fishers who know what they are at. Any credit is theirs. Now – how many to come ashore here? As you can see, the boat will only take a few at a time."

After some brief discussion it was decided that Marie de Guise and her three brothers, one of her ladies and the Lord Maxwell were all that should leave the galleon meantime, for the French shipmaster was afraid of his vessel dragging her anchor in the swell and running aground, and did not want to wait for a second ferrying. David called up Jock Fernie to stay with the skipper and pilot him and the others to the nearest accessible port, probably Dysart. Then he urged a prompt trans-shipping to the yawl.

The Marquis d'Elbeouf, the youngest of the de Guise brothers, volunteered to go first down the rope-ladder. He clearly found it no very difficult feat, although timing the last steps from the swinging ladder to the heaving boat demanded judgement, even with helping hands to receive him. The Duke, the eldest brother, went next, more cautiously. Both called up advice to their sister, who replied that she would manage very well.

David and Maxwell aided her over the side. She showed no fear or hesitation nor made any to do about her skirts and the length of leg she inevitably revealed. The said skirts did get in the way of her descent of the ladder-rungs of course, but taking it slowly, she effected all with a minimum of fuss, her brothers' arms receiving her. Her lady-in-waiting, with this example, could not but emulate her coolness.

The Cardinal and Maxwell followed, their cloaks no help, and David Lindsay, giving final instructions to Fernie, came last down to the overcrowded yawl. Cairnie pushed off, and they rowed the couple of hundred yards to the beach.

Helped ashore on to the slippery, weed-hung rocks, Marie made no dramatic gestures as to kissing the soil of her new country, but briefly expressed her thankfulness to be safely on land. David decided that this was a calm, competent and effective woman and that Scotland was probably very fortunate in her new queen, however odd a way this was to receive her.

They were wet, and in that blustering wind the exposed headland was no place for them to linger. Dod Cairnie said that the Learmonths' Balcomie Castle lay about a mile to the north, where they could shelter meantime and gain refreshment. So, pulling the yawl up out of danger, the entire party set off inland without delay.

Once clear of the mist of blown spume, they could see Balcomie Castle rising tall and grey on a slight ridge amongst wind-blown trees. They battled their way thither, bent against the gale.

It was a bedraggled party which presented itself at the heraldically decorated gatehouse arch, seeking shelter and sustenance in the King's name. An astonished gatehouse-porter, peering out through a narrow arrow-slit, evidently distrusted them despite the resounding summons, and left them standing outside the massive closed gates while he sought higher authority.

Presently a female voice spoke from the arrow-slit, wanting to know who they were and what they wanted at this hour and in this weather? Lindsay's answer that he was the Lord Lyon King of Arms and that he had here the King's bride, the Duchess Marie – he did not call her Queen, for she was not officially that until fully wed to James – elicited gasps from within. But presumably the woman conceived that no one would be likely to invent such an identity, and she ordered the gates to be opened.

In the paved courtyard the lady, in a distinct flutter, proved to be the Lady Learmonth's sister, presumably there in a housekeeperly role. Sir James and his wife, it seemed, had gone to St. Andrews to attend the royal festivities.

This unlooked-for visitation set Balcomie Castle in a stir, indeed. However, food and drink were produced and some dry clothing for the two ladies, the men electing to steam before large log fires. David was concerned to find horses to carry them all to Crail, but unfortunately most of the establishment's riding mounts were gone with the laird's party to St. Andrews and only three nondescript beasts were available – unless some of the party chose to ride on lumbering plough-horses from the farmery. This being declined, after an hour or so for refreshment, the two ladies mounted and the remainder set out on foot for Crail, two miles westward. At least they had the wind behind them.

Even before they reached the little town they could see that something unusual was astir there; and closer approach revealed that the place was full of men and horses. King James himself had come to Crail, from St. Andrews, in haste.

They found James at the same hospice where David had passed the night, preparing indeed to set off westwards, storm or none, having been informed that four great ships, obviously the Frenchmen, had been seen running up Forth. His astonishment at the arrival of his bride and party, wind-battered, poorly mounted, in borrowed and ill-fitting clothing but in fair spirits, was nevertheless almost laughable.

The meeting of the royal pair therefore was scarcely according to plan or suitably regal or dignified, even though duly effected by the authority responsible for such ceremonial, the Lord Lyon King of Arms – but perhaps, in the event, none the worse for that. James, staring, came running to Marie's horse, exclaiming incoherences, to reach up and lift her down and in the process to hug her to him. Words came pouring from him, in no very logical sequence but eloquent enough, of concern, apology, regard and thankfulness, while he clutched her, all but shook her. For her part, Marie did not attempt to compete, but smiled and nodded. She had a natural dignity. The brothers and sundry lords looked on with varying expressions.

After gabbled and garbled explanations and assertions, it belatedly occurred to the King that they would be better indoors out of the gale, and a move was made into the hospice.

Therein, rather more formal greetings over, goodwill messages from the King of France and the Pope delivered, decisions fell to be made. The journey to St. Andrews, where all was in readiness for a formal reception of the royal bride, could be commenced almost forthwith, or delayed, at Marie's choice; and she decided that, despite the inclement riding conditions, and since it was only some ten miles, she would prefer to go right away, to where she could settle in comfort and find suitable clothing. David Lindsay would go on ahead, to announce the royal arrival and see that all was prepared for this different reception. Meanwhile, a party would ride westwards down the coast, to discover which port the French ships would enter, and to bring on the remainder of the visitors.

So this very active day saw David, on his own horse again, hurrying back to St. Andrews, not a little concerned about how much of all the elaborate ceremonial, decorations and tableaux he had arranged would be practical to produce in these weather conditions. Who could have visualised such a storm in June?

In the event, after consultation with Davie Beaton, it was decided that the outdoor reception celebrations would have to be scaled down to a minimum, or postponed – for surely this unseasonable weather could not last, although admittedly easterly gales were very apt to continue for three days. It was really out of the question to try to perform much of the pageantry devised, the set-pieces, the dancing and singing and speech-making, in the streets. Nor would the royal couple enjoy it. So the programme was hastily amended and drastically curtailed, to the relief of almost all.

Anyway, it was in fact late afternoon before watchers posted on the lofty tower of the cathedral reported the distant approach of the royal party. David sent off a herald to request the King to enter the city by the new Abbey Port, which was the most apt for their purposes; and also sent trumpeters and officers through all the town to summon the loyal subjects of His Grace to the vicinity of the said gate, weather or none. At the arched gateway in the city-wall itself, facing south-east, he hurriedly gave his instructions to those concerned there, and made last-minute adjustments and scaling-down of the projects.

When, presently, the King's train came into sight of all, descending Kinkell Braes, David sent out the massed choirs of men and boys drawn from all the many monasteries, churches and colleges, to meet them and escort them in, with song and chant. They went off doubtfully, for inevitably it would make for breathless singing, under grumbling choirmasters, heads bent into the gale, vestments flapping. Fortunately the rain had ceased. Beaton declared that, despite being two hundred strong, they would be happy if any of their singing was to be heard above the incessant roar of the seas smashing on the nearby rockbound shore.

The waiting crowds did in fact hear snatches of chanting as the royal company drew near, ragged admittedly but that could be the effect of the gusting wind. David, dressed now in his heraldic finery, with Lion Rampant tabard and wildly waving bonnet-plume, David Beaton in gorgeous canonicals and a great concourse of lords spiritual and temporal and other notables, stood just outside the imposing open gateway.

When the newcomers came within seventy yards or so, Lindsay raised his baton-of-office as signal, and promptly massed trumpeters launched into a lengthy and stirring fanfare of welcome. This at least prevailed over the noise of the elements, and thankfully the panting choristers desisted.

The blaring trumpeting ending, David turned towards the gateway behind him and raised his baton again. A new sound become evident to those near enough to hear, a mechanical creaking and squealing and rumbling. And down from the parapet and wall-walk above the gateway, hitherto hidden under billowing sail-canvas, was lowered an extraordinary object, not at first easy to identify, seeming to be contrived out of a mixture of painted parchment and fluffed-up fleecy wool. The wind, unfortunately, battering at this, rather blew it all out of shape, and bits of the materials fluttered loose. Halfway to the ground this odd contraption halted, with something of a jerk, and to more creaking, the thing opened, two wings swinging apart to reveal a sort of platform covered in goose-down – which the wind sent swirling off – in front of a painted backcloth of great clouds, sunbeams and cherubs, so that the fleece and curling parchment in front were now identifiable as representing more substantial clouds. And on the downy platform stood a beautiful young woman, fair of hair and person, most diaphanously clad, with a pair of angel's wings sprouting at her back. In one hand she held an illuminated scroll, in the other a large golden key. The wind, plastering her filmy covering against her body, made it entirely clear that she was wearing nothing beneath. Loud cheers greeted this apparition.

When these died away, the angel began to speak. But her voice carried no distance in the prevailing hubbub, and Lindsay halted her with his raised baton, and waved forward the royal couple invitingly. James, nodding, dismounted, and aiding Marie down from her saddle, they walked up close to the heavenly platform, their entourage pressing in behind them.

The angel tried again, reading an elaborate address of welcome in fairish French, declaring that the city of St. Andrews, and indeed all Scotland, was at the new and beauteous queen's disposal; and that this key presented to

Her Highness was not only to open every door in the city to her but the hearts of all therein also.

Marie accepted the key graciously, amidst loud applause, and with a renewal of creaking and groaning the platform and its occupant ascended whence it had come, although in fits and starts.

David Lindsay now took its place in the archway, summoning up his eloquence and lung-power both. Their late celestial visitant, he declared, voice raised to carry, had suitably delivered the greetings of this fair city and metropolis of Holy Church. It fell to himself, as Lyon, now to convey, however inadequately and briefly, the welcome of the realm at large to the new consort of their well-loved and puissant monarch, James, High King of Scots. This he did right joyfully. Large and aspiring plans had been made to demonstrate this welcome in better than these poor words, but the boreal blasts of these northern climes had produced their own over-vehement reception, quite outmatching anything which even the most appreciative of mere men could provide. In the face of these demonstrations of elemental enthusiasm for Her Highness, it behoved lesser forces, such as the nation's officers-of-state and lords spiritual and temporal – for whom today he was the humble mouthpiece – to be content to praise and give thanks in their hearts rather than in gasped and broke-winded words, postponing their other efforts until the aerial display ended.

Panting indeed over this shouted deliverance in competition with superior forces, he gulped to recharge lungs sufficiently to end on the required note. He praised their queen-to-be as a fair, gracious, brave and noble lady, meet wife for their sovereign-lord; and adjured her as spouse and helpmeet, as the good God commanded, ever to cherish and obey her husband, to serve that God and the realm, and to maintain her winsome person in beauty and purity. God save Their Highnesses!

Thankful to have got this over, at this stage of a long and tiring day, David bowed, and gestured in some relief to the trumpeters. He stood aside then, and waved on the royal couple to proceed, behind the instrumentalists, into the city.

Conceiving that Marie and her people would have had quite enough of reception meantime, it had been hastily arranged that the trumpeters should lead the procession directly through the crowded streets to the abbey's recently completed extra hospice accommodation, known as the New Inns, set aside for the occasion to serve as the bridal palace, whilst this night King James would sleep in the archiepiscopal castle. There, after a fairly brief private interval, the royal pair separated, to rejoin in an hour or so at a banquet in the castle, given by Davie Beaton.

After all the climatic punishment, the evening seemed almost blissfully felicitous however exceptional, without any hitches. Beaton, to be sure, made an admirable host, and with all the revenues he had at his disposal, the entertainment and provender were of the highest standard, rivalling anything the French might have produced. The numbers attending were comparatively modest, for even the great hall of the castle would not accommodate a great many in comfort; but that was as far as the modesty went. Their host was determined that the visitors should be disabused of any idea that Scotland was an impoverished and backward country, however comparatively small in population, and nothing was spared to inculcate this message. The banquet itself ran to no fewer than fifteen courses, including such extravagances as roasted peacocks enhanced with the glory of their spread tails, swans seeming to float in claret-flavoured jelly, whole salmon which opened to reveal whole trout within, young wild boar cooked in honey, and confections moulded and sculpted in fantastic shapes and colours supporting a set-piece of the Lion Rampant and the Lilies of France, all to be washed down by a scarcely believable choice of wines and liquors. The accompanying divertisements were on a comparable scale, with dancers, acrobats, jugglers, performing bears and apes, and playlets performed by talented actors, two of which were based on poems by David Lindsay, soft music accompanying all. Wisely, speech-making was avoided, apart from a brief but adroit welcoming address from Beaton himself in the form of grace-before-meat and a suitable thanks-after-meat at the end by the Cardinal of Lorraine. It all made a most agreeable close to a long and eventful day, as bride and groom parted for their pre-nuptial beds. Throughout, there had been no sign of Archbishop James Beaton, nor indeed any mention of him, so accepted now was the situation.

David Lindsay, for one, was thankful to sink into his wife's arms in their own very post-nuptial couch, and to let the gale batter and rage outside.

In the morning, the wind had sunk considerably and, although the seas continued to pound and thunder, the streets of the city were reasonably possible for the processions and crowds, which was just as well. Parties were out early clearing those nearest to the shore and harbour area of seaweed, starfish, mussels and the like, cast up by the storm.

The wedding ceremony, which was not of course exactly that, was scheduled for noon; but it was decided that there must be some postponement to allow the remainder of the bride's and Maxwell's company to get to St. Andrews from whichever port they had eventually reached, such delay arousing no great objections after the experiences of the day before. In the event, the missing guests turned up on hired horses, from Dysart, just before mid day, and the word was sent round the town that the ceremony would commence in two hours' time, all of St. Andrews' innumerable bells to ring out until then.

So the processions started, a plethora of them, demanding all the Lord Lyon's organising ability to ensure that they did not collide and get hopelessly entangled in the city streets, as they all converged on the cathedral; for they came from all quarters, the two colleges of the university, those of the various ecclesiastical dignitaries and great lords, the trades and guild brethren, the fisherfolk and shipmen, and of course the magistrates and town council. The last to move out, when all was clear for them, were three, two from the castle, the King's own and Beaton's, and the bride's from the New Inns.

Nearly all had musical accompaniment as they paraded through the crowded town, singers, fiddlers, trumpeters and cymbalists, so that an extraordinary cacophony resounded under the continuing jangle of the host of bells.

It was, of course, important that neither the monarch nor Marie should have to hang about outside the cathedral for any reason, and it demanded all Lindsay's expertise to ensure that they arrived sumultaneously, James at the door to the north transept, the bride at the great main west entrance to the nave, officers hurrying to and fro between them to contrive this. Beaton's clerical party had come in by the south transept, just previously. So, as the officiating clergy moved into the chancel, to sweet singing from choirs skied in the clerestory galleries, David Lindsay watched, from a vantage-point behind the magnificent chancel-screens, for the signals from his minions. When these came, after only a brief delay, he strode forward, backed by his corps of heralds and pursuivants, to a central position at the transept-crossing, and raised his baton. A single blast of a trumpet stilled the singing, and after a moment's quivering silence – spoiled only by the distant pealing of some errant church-bell – the great organ crashed out in thundering pride which seemed to shake even that mighty building. David pointed his baton north and then west, in a strangely commanding gesture, and to the tremendous beat of the organ-overture the two royal processions moved slowly in towards the chancel-steps, while the vast congregation craned necks and exclaimed.

The King's party had much the shorter distance to cover, so that James was duly in position at the steps and facing the high altar well before his bride arrived. He made a brilliant picture, with his long red hair constrained by the simple but regal circlet of gold, dressed today all in cloth-of-gold trimmed with scarlet, the Orders of the imperial Golden Fleece, St. Michael of France and the Garter of England glittering on his breast.

The bride – whose luggage had only just arrived in time, from Dysart – had chosen silver and blue, her national colours, for her splendid gown rather than any unsuitable virginal white, and with her superb figure and assured carriage, gleaming diamonds and duchess's coronet, looked every inch a queen. She was flanked by her eldest brother, the Duc de Guise, and the Lord Maxwell her proxy-husband, and backed by the colourfully stylish band of her French courtiers, all looking quite remarkably different from their storm-battered appearance of a few hours earlier. As they came up to the steps, James turned, to hold out his hand to take Marie's. He had no groomsman.

Side by side, with the Duke and Maxwell half a pace behind, they moved up into the chancel.

Davie Beaton and the Cardinal of Lorraine awaited them there. Beaton was in fact the more magnificent of the two now, clad today in the full splendour of Archbishop and Primate rather than in his bishop's and abbot's vestments, fine as these had always been; for today he was acting as Coadjutor, his absent uncle's representative and substitute. And he looked the part indeed, fully as did the other two principals. He took charge as though to the manner born.

It made a strange service, safe to say unique to all present except possibly the Cardinal. For it was not really a wedding, that having already taken place by proxy in Paris. But it was the *celebration* of a wedding, and at the same time the effective union of two persons and the creation of a queen. Beaton had planned it all effectively, juggling with the various parts of the marriage service, omitting this and substituting that, confidently weaving his way to a satisfactory and significant climax when James exchanged one ring on Marie's finger for another and finer, and with a smile turned and handed the former to Maxwell as keepsake.

The benedictions thereafter were bestowed on the couple by Beaton, and on the congregation as a whole by the Cardinal, with sonorous solemnity.

David Lindsay watched all with heedful concern – but could not help perceiving at least nine of the King's mistresses prominent amongst the concourse.

After the blessing he, as Lyon, was the first to move.

He paced out from his place at the side of the chancel steps to the centre. Whereupon James swung right round to face the congregation and taking Marie's arm, stepped forward with her. Lindsay sank down on his knees before them, and held out both hands to take the Queen's, not exactly in the gesture of fealty, since that was for the monarch alone, but in a token indication of acceptance as queen-consort.

"Your Grace!" he murmured. "I am your servant. This is a happy day for Scotland. May it prove as greatly so for you. God save Your Grace."

Thereafter the other great officers-of-state, the Chancellor, the High Constable, the Earl Marischal, the Lord Treasurer and so on, came forward to render their especial obeisance. Then, to triumphant music, the King and Queen paced down the central aisle to the west doorway, through the bowing assembly. This Queen looked a deal more likely to survive than the last.

David Lindsay's responsibilities were by no means over for this day, for all the individual, corporate and ecclesiastical welcomes and receptions planned for the French visitors, which had had to be postponed from yesterday, still fell to be staged; and Queen Marie, when it was put to her back at the archiepiscopal castle, expressed herself as entirely willing to go through with this straight away, lest any be disappointed. James, however, was less condescending, declaring that it was scarcely the way to spend a wedding day. When Lindsay ventured to point out that many bodies and groups had gone to much labour and expense to prepare their demonstrations of salutation and loyalty, and would be much upset if their efforts were to be ignored, Marie at once agreed that that would never do, and that she would wish to satisfy all, to her best endeavour. But James jutted his chin and maintained his attitude. The Queen could parade around the town if she so wished, but for himself he had had enough of ceremonial and processions for one day. Smiling but no whit abashed, Marie said that she quite understood. She would go with Sir David, to seek to become better acquainted with her new countrymen – which, to be sure, His Grace had no need to do; and would return to his good company the better consort for the King of Scots.

His Grace had the grace to look a little shamefaced at this, but evidently found it too much that he should change his royal stance. He said merely that he would await his new wife's return with due impatience.

Lindsay was much interested in this exchange, and early indication of attitudes and reactions. That James should show what he considered amounted to irresponsibility was, in his opinion, as significant as it was disappointing, and tended to bear out the feeling which had been growing on him for some time that the King's general behaviour was in some measure deteriorating. Also it might be some indication as to his personal standpoint on this new marriage, that he should so swiftly be prepared to let his bride perform a quite important duty alone. And, of course, it further revealed Marie de Guise to be an independent-minded and reliable woman, prepared to pursue her own courses.

Thereafter, with the weather steadily improving, Lindsay conducted the Queen and her brothers on a tour of St. Andrews, calling necessarily only briefly at the university colleges and many of the churches, monasteries and shrines as well as at the tolbooth, courtrooms and other offices of the city administration and magistracy, with visits to selected viewpoints from which some idea as to the surrounding countryside might be gained. In all of which Marie showed interest and appreciation, with no signs of merely performing a duty. When, after almost three hours of it, they returned to the castle, it was to find James sitting at wine with Oliver Sinclair and other courtiers, including some of his mistresses. To his enquiry, with a hint of sarcasm about it, as to whether she had enjoyed her inspection of the city's delights, the Queen assured that indeed she had never seen, in France or any other land she had visited, so many good faces in so little room and so much of true worth in short time, as this day in St. Andrews. And at her husband's raised eyebrows, she added that in France it was often said that Scotland was but a barbarous country, destitute and devoid of commodities common elsewhere – as perhaps he had gathered; whereas now she most certainly knew differently. That was said with obvious sincerity.

The King, surprised, barked a laugh. "You say so? Forsooth, Madam, if that is how you view this small churchman's town, you shall see better ere you go, God willing!"

Marie de Guise was not alone in fairly evidently wondering just how to take that and just what it might signify, Beaton and Lindsay exchanging glances; but James was clearly somewhat drink-taken, and perhaps it meant little.

The Queen inclined her head and said that she would anticipate such further edification eagerly. Meanwhile, with His Grace's approval, she would seek her chamber and rest awhile.

Belatedly accepting his husbandly role, James offered to conduct her to their nuptial quarters, and to bows all round they went off, her arm in his.

Not a few, undoubtedly, would have been intrigued to witness what went on behind the royal doors thereafter.

If the King was eager to demonstrate to his wife that St. Andrews was indeed only a small and far from representative corner of Scotland, he scarcely showed it, for the court remained based there for no less than forty days, as guests of Davie Beaton and Holy Church, at incalculable cost. Admittedly the royal party ranged far and wide in Fife and even over into Angus in the interim, hunting, hawking, horse-racing, attending jousts and sporting contests, fairs, historic sites, beauty spots and great lords' houses. James was, to be sure, seeking to match in some measure the elaborate and prolonged round of entertainment and festivity which had featured so largely in his French visit of two years before – mainly no doubt for the benefit of the de Guise brothers, so that they would go back and inform King Francis that Scotland was indeed a worth-while ally and no poor relation. Whether the Queen found it all to her taste was not to be known; but certainly she betrayed no signs of weariness nor impatience. She was an excellent horsewoman and proficient at archery, falconry and other outdoor activities, and in the evenings her dancing, singing and lute-playing were much admired.

James and his realm were to be congratulated. Whether Marie was, perhaps remained not so certain.

4

All Stirling was agog. The great ones, with their trains of supporters and men-at-arms, had been arriving for the Privy Council these last two days, and the mighty fortress and the town below itself were full to overflowing, noisy and tense, with the minions of the lords and bishops ever looking for a fight with rivals, packmen, chapmen and street-whores doing a roaring trade, pardoners and sellers of indulgences loud on their business and a holiday atmosphere prevailing. It was after all, Fastern's Eve, with Lent looming ahead. Even up in the rock-bound castle itself, that February noontide, there was an air of expectation, especial anticipation of great developments. Davie Beaton had ensured that.

In the Queen's personal retiring-room of the royal quarters, which had windows offering an excellent view down over the castle forecourt and tourney-ground to the upper approaches of that hilly town, three persons stood watching and waiting, Queen Marie herself, David Lindsay and his wife Janet. David was much in the Queen's company these days, for he got on with her notably well, better indeed than he now did most of the time with his old pupil the King; moreover, Janet had graduated from being the King's Wardrobe Mistress to being the Queen's, a much more rewarding position.

"Our eminent friend delays," Marie commented. She had to raise her voice above normal to make herself heard – they all did these days in Stirling Castle, for the place resounded to the incessant banging of hammers, chipping of masonry and clatter of planking, James having started the ambitious building of a great new palace there on the rock-top, within the towering curtain-walls, fit for a monarch with an increasing conception of his status and authority, if not necessarily his dignity. The man they all awaited was, of course, paying for it.

"Of a purpose, no doubt," Lindsay answered. "He does nothing lacking such."

She looked at him. "You sound . . . wary, Sir David? I understood that Monsignor Beaton, or the Cardinal as we must now name him, was your friend. Your old and close friend?"

"He is, yes, Your Grace. We have been friends since student days at St. Andrews University. But – that does not blind me to perceiving the man he is. And being, as you say, wary. It behoves all to be wary of Davie Beaton."

"Are you perhaps warning me, Sir David?"

"I would scarcely so presume, Madam. But it is as well, perhaps, to recognise that he is the cleverest man in Scotland and is apt to use his cleverness, use all indeed, for his various purposes. With I fear but little scruple."

"He will seek to use *me*, you think?"

"If he can, yes. As he uses all. Myself. His Grace indeed. Mainly with no ill intent, no doubt, and for what he esteems important. Always he has done this. And now, more powerful than ever before, he will endeavour to use all the more."

"David is too hard on him, I think, Your Grace," Janet put in. "Cardinal Davie uses *himself* harder than any. He believes strongly in certain causes and courses – as who shall say is wrong? And uses all his powers and abilities, and these are great, to further them."

"And his own advantage!" her husband added.

"That only in the second place, I think."

"As, I am told, he used his wedded wife and young family, in order to take holy orders?" the Queen observed. "Do you condemn that, Sir David?"

"I do." That was blunt.

Janet did not contest it, but added, "This realm and his Holy Church. For these, I believe, Davie Beaton would sacrifice all."

"Should not we all?" Marie asked simply.

They heard the music, even above the hammering, before they saw the first signs of what they were waiting for, the great bannered procession appearing out of the jaws of the climbing street from the lower town. Brilliant with colour, and the gleam of steel in the thin wintry sunshine, behind a large band of horsed instrumentalists and a troop of splendidly liveried cavalry, came a phalanx of mounted clergy all in gorgeous array and on white horses. After these came an extraordinary scarlet-canopied litter, emblazoned heraldically and slung between six more white horses, in which sat an upright figure, all in red, undoubtedly Beaton himself. Behind rode a further troop of helmeted and armoured guards.

Lindsay barked a laugh at the sight of his friend being borne in a litter like some old, decrepit man, he who had shared so much rough riding and scrambled, dangerous journeyings. He could not but recollect, also, how it was not so long ago that that same red-clad figure had stood with himself and King James, at a similar window to this, indeed in the next chamber, watching the arrival of the King's mother, Margaret Tudor, and what had transpired thereafter.

"He makes a fine entry, if belated," the Queen said. "You believe of a set purpose?"

"Aye. There speaks power. Davie keeps even the King waiting. And the entire Privy Council of Scotland. No other would so dare. Nor even he until now. It is a demonstration. And he will have a reason for it. Not mere vainglory, that is certain."

"To be revealed at the council meeting?"

"It would seem likely. He it is who has called this Council, as Lord Privy Seal, rather than His Grace."

"Then I would wish that I might have attended it. But, alas, I am a mere woman!"

"I shall inform Your Grace, in due course." Bowing, David Lindsay left the ladies to go down to his duties at the council chamber.

He found James playing dice with some cronies, including Oliver Sinclair his now constant companion, in an ante-room of the great hall, wine-flagons much in evidence. David was struck anew by the impairment of the King's appearance of late, the blotchiness of colour, the puffiness and thickening of figure, the heaviness of carriage. Clearly his health was not what it had been. It certainly did not look as though marriage was agreeing with him – although the fault could be scarcely that, for he was known to be far from neglecting his mistresses. Yet he was a young man still, only of twenty-seven years. He was drinking immoderately, of course.

"His Eminence the Cardinal has now come, Sire," Lindsay announced. "All is ready when Your Grace is."

"Let him wait, man," James said thickly. "He has kept *me* waiting."

"Yes, Sire. But it is others, the many others. The greatest lords in this land, who have also waited long."

"If their liege-lord must wait for this clerk, so must they!"

"As you will, Sire . . ."

So there was further delay, with the score or so of Privy Councillors restive indeed. Lindsay went in search of Beaton, who had not appeared at the council chamber. He found him, with some of his entourage of abbots, priors, secretaries, even a chamberlain, inspecting the progress of the builders at the new palace-block.

"Ha – David! There you are," he was greeted. "This is all very splendid, very assertive, is it not? If costly." Beaton waved a beringed hand at the soaring, carved stonework, seen to be richly decorative behind the scaffolding.

"Aye – almost as splendid and assertive as yourself, Eminence! You come late."

The new Cardinal shrugged elegant scarlet shoulders. "So many matters to attend to. I cannot pass *my* time playing dice and drinking, see you!"

Lindsay blinked. That came too pat to be wholly coincidental. Beaton must have efficient spies here in Stirling Castle, as elsewhere, prompt with their information.

"Even so – you were only at Cambuskenneth Abbey." Cambuskenneth, where Beaton had spent the night, was a mere three miles away across Forth. "You called this meeting for noon. The lords do not all play dice!"

"Lord, man – why this fuss? What is an hour or so? With the realm's future in the balance? *Someone* must take heed and see to affairs of state and Church, even though the monarch and his lords do not!"

"So that is what delayed you?" Lindsay sounded sceptical. "At Cambuskenneth? I thought that perhaps you did it to prove something. That all must now wait on the Cardinal!"

"Ever suspicious, David," the other said lightly. "How is Her Grace?"

"Well. And wishing that she might attend this council."

"James could so invite her, if he chose. To sit in. He is lord of all."

"I think that he would be unlikely to do that."

"For some reason?"

"It may be that he conceives her as over-interested in matters of rule and governance. He does not look for that in a wife!"

"Aye, she is an able woman. She would make a better monarch than James. I have little doubt . . ."

He paused as an officer of the royal guard came up. Lindsay turned, expecting that the message would be for himself, to attend the King. But it was to the Cardinal, not the Lord Lyon, that this individual addressed himself, informing him that His Grace was about to leave the ante-room for the council chamber. Beaton nodded and dismissed the man, Lindsay recognising the significance of this incident. It was Beaton who was important rather than himself, who as master-of-ceremonies had to usher in the monarch. And that Davie's information service at Stirling included officers of the royal guard.

Lindsay hurried back to duty, whilst the Cardinal made his dignified way, without haste, to the meeting-place.

David found the King impatient now to proceed. A Privy Council meeting was no occasion for trumpeters, but the monarch could not just walk in unheralded. So, bowing, he declared that all was ready, the Lord Privy Seal present, and led the way to the chamber, there to announce their liege-lord, all to be upstanding.

The room was full, the councillors round the great table, clerks and secretaries disposed around. Davie Beaton was at his place at the foot of the table. James came in, not entirely steady on his feet, to take his seat at the head, without gesture or acknowledgment of all the bowing. Lindsay, who as Lyon was *ex officio* a member of the Council, drew up a chair near the throne.

All seated, Beaton, who as Lord Privy Seal chaired the Privy Council, as the Chancellor chaired parliament, with the monarch in a presidential capacity at both, spoke up.

"Your Grace, my lords and friends, I declare this Secret Council in session. It is called for good and sufficient reasons. His Grace's realm has been endangered times without number. But I venture to assert, seldom more dangerously so than at this present." At murmurs of disbelief from around him, he raised a hand. "You think not, my lords? You think that all is well? Then, hear you. Some may already have heard that Donald Greumach of Sleat has threatened to raise all the Highland West against the King, and to take back the Lordship of the Isles which His Grace's royal father reduced and incorporated in the crown thirty-five years ago. This Donald MacDonald claims to be the lawful heir of the last Lord of the Isles and Earl of Ross. Only this morning I have had sure word that this is indeed no mere threat but dire fact. He has left his isles, with a great army of fifteen thousand broadswords and over one hundred galleys, and has invaded mainland Ross. He has already defeated the loyal clans at Kinlochewe and is marching south, his galley-fleet accompanying him down the coast. He has called on all the Westland clans to rise against the King."

That certainly shook the company. Lindsay, like others no doubt, had heard rumours of unrest in the Highlands and Islands, but this was so normal a state of affairs in those parts as to arouse little heed. But major armed revolt against the crown was something different.

The Earl of Moray, the King's half-brother, illegitimate son of James the Fourth by Flaming Janet Kennedy, pooh-poohed it. "These Highland caterans are ever at each other's throats. They march and slay and shout their threats endlessly. But hate each other more than they hate the King. Mackenzie of Kintail and others will halt this MacDonald of Sleat."

"Mackenzie of Kintail is already defeated, my lord. He it was who lost at Kinlochewe. MacLeod of Dunvegan with him. These were the King's best friends in the north-west."

Into the silence with which this was received, Beaton went on. "If this were the only danger, my lords, I would say, as would others here, let His Grace marshal a host under my lords of Argyll, Huntly, Atholl or others, who know these parts, to deal with Donald the Grim. But there is worse to consider. As you all will know, many English have been flooding in to take refuge in Scotland these last months, victims of King Henry's hatred of the Pope and Holy Church. In his zeal, not for reform of worship but for moneys, power and lands, he has been sorely persecuting those who remain loyal to their faith. Your Grace will recollect how some of the north of England squires and lords came out to your ship, when you were returning from France, seeking your protection? Near ten thousand have died at Henry's hands, in martyrdom. That north of England, Yorkshire in especial, remains largely true to Holy Church, and many there rose against their king's savageries. That rising has been called the Pilgrimage of Grace. But it has been put down, and with great cruelty, more thousands dying. So, many have sought refuge in our realm, which remains faithful to Rome. Henry Tudor will now use this against Scotland. I have it on most reliable authority that he is to send envoys to Your Grace accusing you of harbouring his enemies, demanding the return of all such into his hands, with compensation to be paid for injury done. Not only that, but he is demanding that the two realms must come into a closer relationship – by which he means that the larger will swallow the lesser! And to aid him in this, Scotland must reform her Church, as he has done in England, throwing off the Vatican, that there be no further cause for disharmony. To ensure all this, Your Grace is to be summoned, *summoned*, mark you all, to York to meet King Henry, there to agree to all and sign away your kingdom's independence. So the Tudor will gain all that he has sought for so long, and Scotland will be but an English province!"

Even James, who had seemed almost uninterested hitherto, all but dozing, sat forward at this. "How do you know all this, man?" he demanded. As though recollecting, he changed that last word to Eminence, less than respectfully.

"I have my sources at the English court, Sire. If you doubt the truth of it, remember these names when Henry sends his summons. Sir Ralph Sadler and the Bishop of St. Davids are already appointed as envoys."

This naming of names sounded convincing, and the King shrugged. "I shall not go," he said.

"To be sure, Your Grace. And Henry assumes that you will so decide. So he promises outright invasion, on a mighty scale, full war, if these demands are rejected. And there, too, he has chosen his men. His army will be commanded by the Duke of Norfolk, whom he has named the Scourge of the Scots. With the Lords Dacre and Musgrave, lieutenants. And the assault will be over the West March."

There was no lack of reaction to that, all round the table. Norfolk was the son of that auld crooked carle, Surrey, who had been the victor of Flodden, that disaster which still cast a shiver down Scottish spines, this son having been to the fore in it all. And Dacre's ruthless hatred of the Scots was known to all.

Beaton went on. "My guess is that Henry would have wished his attack to coincide with this rising of Donald Greumach – which he may well have encouraged and partly paid for. But the MacDonald has moved over-quickly, not awaiting the campaigning season. February is early to be on the march in those parts, with the Highland passes still blocked with snow. But that makes his galley-fleet the more significant, important. For the ships, keeping abreast of the clan-army, can take off the men where the choked passes may hold them up. You know that sea-board, with all its great sea-lochs and sounds. The ships can reach far inland."

"What, then, of the English?" the Gordon Earl of

Huntly asked. "Since you say that the MacDonald has already started. Norfolk will not invade, surely, until we reject their terms. So we have time to defeat Donald before we need face the English."

"If we can, my lord – if we can! We can produce the men, perhaps. But where are we to get the ships to challenge that great fleet? My lord of Argyll can no doubt raise galleys and birlinns, and his Campbell chieftains more. But not one hundred, I think?"

MacCailean Mor, Earl of Argyll, shook his head. "Forty perhaps. Fifty at the most." Even that was grudging, for James had maltreated the Campbells in his prolonged efforts to reduce the power of his great nobles.

"We must defeat him on land, then," Huntly asserted. "Somehow we must get through those passes. Or else wait until he reaches the Lowlands, where we have the advantage in cavalry and armoured knights."

"That would mean abandoning Argyll and Cowal to the MacDonald hordes!" the Campbell exclaimed. "That is not to be considered."

David Lindsay spoke. "These Isles galleys are notable vessels, dangerous and faster than any other that sail the seas. But they are light and of ancient design, little more than the Viking longships. So they can carry no cannon. They can outsail any ships that Your Grace can send against them. But they could not fight great ships carrying cannon. Such could sink the galleys at a distance. So, I say we should threaten this Donald's fleet. Assemble such large ships as may be found in our ports. Load them with all the cannon we can muster. Send them up the west coast waters, to challenge the MacDonald galleys. A tight squadron, bristling with cannon. That will give the Islemen pause, I swear. Blast the galleys with cannon-fire, from a distance. Donald the Grim will surely halt his advance southwards, on land, if his fleet is dispersed. For His Grace's ships could then go on to attack Skye and the Isles."

"Aye – excellent!" Beaton said. "My Lord Lyon has the rights of it. That might well serve. At the worst it would delay Donald and give us time to muster an army."

"Can we find sufficient large ships, quickly?" Moray asked. "In the east coast ports, perhaps yes. Leith, Inverkeithing, Dysart, Dundee, Aberdeen and the rest. But to assemble and arm all these, and then sail them right round Scotland to the north-west coast, would take much time. Arran – this is *your* concern. Can you find sufficient large ships in the west? Since time will be all-important."

The Hamilton chief, Earl of Arran, half-brother of the disgraced Bastard, was no heroic figure, a somewhat feeble character. But he was hereditary Lord High Admiral of Scotland; and, of course, his territories were in the south-west. He shrugged narrow shoulders.

"Who knows? But Dumbarton is the greatest port in the land. And Greenock and Cartsdyke, Gourock, Irvine and Ayr, are busy havens."

"A dozen large vessels should be sufficient," Beaton said. "Is Your Grace agreeable that these ships should be sought and mustered? And the cannon?"

James nodded, making his first contribution. "My royal castle of Dumbarton itself has many cannon. Also Renfrew, Dundonald and Turnberry. If there is time, some can be taken from this Stirling. Even Edinburgh."

"Yes, Sire. Then is it agreed by this Council? My lord of Arran to assemble the ships. My lord of Borthwick, Master-Gunner, to find the cannon, powder and ball. All to be contrived forthwith, in all haste. For MacDonald will not wait for us!"

None contraverting, the thing was passed.

"Now – Henry!" Beaton resumed. "Which is more difficult. Sadler may arrive at any time – although I have had no word of him on the way, as yet. But he could come by sea. I think not, however, in February. We must be ready for him."

There was silence around that table as men considered the size and complexity of being ready for Henry Tudor's active aggression.

"As I see it, the English threat comes under three heads," Beaton went on. "There is this of the victims of his spleen who have taken refuge here, and whom he wishes to have returned to him – and to their deaths, undoubtedly. There is this demand that Holy Church here should be reformed, as he names it, in line with his English rejection of Rome. I am informed that he is instructing the Archbishop of York to raise again those ancient claims of spiritual hegemony over Scotland, which date from the days of the Columban Church. Thirdly, his summons to His Grace to attend on him at York – York again, mark you! Sadler will raise all these matters. On how we answer him will depend the issue of war or . . . I do not say peace, but relief from immediate attack. How say you, my lords?"

A new voice spoke up, that of the Cunningham Earl of Glencairn. "Since the first issue, on which the rest hangs, is this of the English fugitives, I do not see why we should endanger our realm's safety for *their* sakes! We owe the English nothing, whether they be churchmen or so-called heretics. Most of these are from the north of England – and it is from the north of England that for centuries the worst raiding and war has come. If Henry wants his subjects back, why should we risk all to keep them here?"

There were one or two murmurs of agreement with that.

"You ask why, my lord," the Cardinal took him up. "I say that there is good reason why. First, in that if we yield to this, we will be expected to yield on the rest. And there will be a succession of further demands, you may be sure. But, more important, this realm is part of something even greater, the one Holy, Catholic and Apostolic Church of Christ, which it is our very Christian duty to support and maintain. These fugitives are faithful to that Church. That is why they are here, suffering for their faith, at the hands of the apostate Henry. You, my lord, may possibly have leanings towards heresies – but I hope and pray not!"

Glencairn spluttered angrily at that, the cold glare and significant pause, while many shifted in their seats uncomfortably. A council meeting was surely not the place for personal accusation. There was greater discomfort to come.

"Secondly, there is this insolent requirement that the Scottish church should be reformed in accord with the

English, and allegiance to His Holiness and Rome cast off. Linked with this threadbare claim of the Archbishops of York to spiritual lordship over Scotland – which means, to be sure, *Henry's* overlordship of Your Grace's kingdom, as Lord Paramount. I say that not only should this wicked presumption be fought to our last breath and drop of blood – but that it *will* be! That I promise you."

Eyes blinked at that, not only at the words themselves and their vehemence but at the sheer authority with which they were uttered. Lindsay for one had never seen Davie Beaton, usually so suavely debonair, thus sternly assertive. To the Privy Council and in the monarch's presence, it seemed scarcely suitable.

Clearly others felt the same, whatever James thought.

"Your Eminence sounds almost as though you held yourself responsible for the realm's weal and direction!" the Earl of Rothes asserted. "We all here are equally concerned for His Grace's support, even though we are not all clerks and churchmen! Does not the High Constable, the Earl Marischal, the Admiral, the Warden of the Marches, even the Chancellor, sit at this table?"

There was a considerable murmur of approval now.

"I rejoice that this is so, my lords," Beaton acknowledged, but far from apologetically. "All have their important parts to play. But since Holy Church's integrity and indeed survival is at stake, as well as the realm's, *I* have an especial charge and duty. From His Holiness himself. In His Grace's polity I am but Lord Privy Seal, yes. But His Holiness the Pope has appointed me to be *Legatus a Latere*. I repeat, *Legatus a Latere*. With the prescribed task of saving the Scots Church, thwarting Henry Tudor and rooting out dangerous heresy!"

There was all but stunned silence, as that announcement sank in. A Lateran Legate was almost an unheard-of appointment, as far as Scotland was concerned. None indeed would have been able to recall a Scot ever before having been so elevated. It far exceeded the authority of a cardinal or archbishop, or even a nuncio, papal ambassador or normal legate. It was in fact the delegation of full papal powers to the individual concerned, authorising him to act in every respect as the Pope himself, without prior reference to Rome. So, suddenly David Beaton *was* the Pope in Scotland, with absolute pontifical authority, to bind or loose, to raise up or demote, to absolve or to condemn. And not only within the Church. For he could excommunicate at will, refuse baptism, wedding or burial, declare any marriage invalid or otherwise, impose ecclesiastical taxation on any subject, pronounce on what was heresy and what was not, suspend the application of laws, and much more. No man, even the King, had ever held such powers in the land – for so long as Beaton remained *Legatus a Latere*.

None present, even James Stewart, was anxious to be first to voice comment, as men eyed each other.

It was David Lindsay who did find speech. "The Pope must indeed be concerned over the Church in Scotland. Is it so grievous that such a step is necessary?"

"It is. If you do not know it, I do, to my sorrow. Aye, and shame. For shameful it is. Heresy is ever growing, evil doctrines rampant, disobedience on all hands. All fostered by English gold. You would scarce believe what Henry is spending in Scotland, to undermine Church and then state. And out of moneys stolen from the Church in England!" He paused significantly, and his glance traversed the company deliberately. "Or perhaps some of you could indeed believe it! Even here!"

That thinly veiled suggestion of complicity drew shocked expressions and resentful glances.

"You are not accusing any on this Council of being in Henry's pay?" Rothes demanded.

"I am not accusing, my lord. I leave that to the consciences of any who may be concerned. But consider this. Two years ago, we learned that four hundred in Scotland were in receipt of Henry's pensions. Today I would say that there are four or five times that number. I cannot even trust all my own bishops!"

"*Your* own bishops . . .!" the Chancellor, Archbishop Dunbar of Glasgow, quavered.

"Aye, my lord – as Legate, mine."

With the company digesting that and its implications,

Beaton went on. "The rot, so sedulously nurtured by our enemies, must be cut out, and swiftly, before it spreads and contaminates all. This I shall do. It must be done ruthlessly, if others are to be deterred. But that, I agree, is not the concern of this Privy Council, save in that you should be informed and prepared. What is your concern is this third matter – the summons for His Grace to go to York, to meet Henry . . ."

"It need concern none here," James interrupted. "I have already said that I shall not go."

Most there nodded approval.

"Right and proper, Sire," Beaton agreed. "But, put thus, wise? We have to hold Henry off, since we can scarcely defeat him by power of arms, for he has ten times our numbers. So we must use our wits to reinforce those arms. Keep him unsure and delayed. I would suggest that Your Grace offers indeed to meet him, not necessarily at York. But only if the King of France is present also. That should hold him! Say that your alliance with France, strengthened by your two French marriages, demands this. That the three monarchs meeting together could well bring all differences to an end. Francis would be unlikely to go, to be sure – but the thing would give Henry pause and give us time."

On this occasion there was only approval and acclaim around the table, for what all recognised was a brilliant suggestion. Neither the King nor any other voiced any objection.

Always one to recognise and seize his moment, Beaton waved an acknowledging hand and declared that since this all seemed to be satisfactory, he thought that the Council had come to the end of its present business. Unless any member had other matter which he might wish to raise?

In the circumstances, all had had enough. It was agreed that those concerned with raising the forces and shipping to counter Donald Greumach should remain behind to decide on details. Then the King rose, and all with him, and without comment or remark, gestured for Lyon to lead him out. That he had nothing to say to Beaton was perhaps significant.

Later, the new Lateran Legate came seeking David Lindsay in his own quarters, alone.

"So, my good David – what is the verdict?" he greeted lightly enough. "I think that you are critical? Not for the first time, to be sure! I was watching your face at that meeting. You have very expressive and readable features, you know! You did not approve of much that I said there?"

"Who am I to approve or disapprove? To disagree with the Lateran Legate? As much as a man's life is worth! Or his eternal soul?"

"There you are. Prickly as ever. You frown on my appointment? You think that I soar over-high?"

"I fear for what you may seek to do with your power."

"There are times when it is necessary to be harsh to be kind. You know it. And this is one such."

"Then be harsh with your own Church, Davie. Start there. Is there not sufficient folly, corruption and shame in the ranks of the clergy to keep even a Lateran Legate busy? Commence a true reform of the ill-living prelates, the grasping, ignorant priests, the pardoners, the relic-mongers and the rest. Then King Henry and his English Church will seem less to be emulated. You said once that reform should come from above, not below. Now *you* are above, the summit. Reform, then."

"In due course, David – in due course. Give me time. I will reform, never fear. But first things first. I *shall* be harsh with the Scots Church. But the more pressing enemy at the gates, the wolves, must be dealt with before the rats and mice which gnaw within. The Pope has so charged me. First root out the heresy and wrecking doctrines. Then cleanse the house."

"I say that you put the cart before the horse. First cleanse your stable. Then the heresies and mistaken doctrines will find less welcome."

"We must differ in our priorities, friend. You are the poet and dreamer. I am the artificer, the carpenter. You pen your plays, I must labour at the playhouse and stage

– and with what tools I have!" He paused. "But, David – be not *too* sweeping with your so-eloquent pen! Lest you raise devils on my stage which you cannot control. Nor I!"

"You are warning me, my lord Cardinal?"

"Not warning, counselling. Some of your verses might even be named heretical!"

"So – we have reached this far, have we! After all the years!"

"Do not be a fool, man! We are friends. And will remain so. I but urge . . . discretion. For all our sakes." He gestured and changed tone of voice. "Now – enough of that. James – he looks less than well."

"That is so."

"What ails him? He is seeming older than his years. Heavier, thicker. He was near drunken, to be sure."

"Perhaps if you had not kept him waiting for an hour, he would have been less in wine! But, yes – he seems to sicken. What is wrong I do not know. But he has been misusing himself for years, as you know. All these women, night after night . . ."

"The Queen? Does she not satisfy him? She would seem bed-worthy, to me!"

"No one woman will ever satisfy James. He leaves the Queen's bedchamber, to go roaming, as he has always done. I am sorry for her. She must wonder indeed what she has wed. I hope, I hope that his sickness is not, not . . ."

"You mean – he might pass it on? Lord – not that!"

"No – it is but a fear I have, on occasion. His ailing is probably otherwise. Insufficient sleep and too much wine, aiding. Angus deliberately corrupted him, as a boy, and now the price is being paid. He is a man driven."

"Are not we all?" That sounded strange, coming from Davie Beaton. "There is no sign of the Queen's pregnancy? Scotland needs that heir. It is eight months since she came. And they are both fertile enough. She had a son by Longueville. And he has bastards innumerable."

"I have heard of nothing such. And Janet would know, I think. They are close."

"Aye. Well, I go seek her now. She has her part to play in our battle to save Church and realm. She is sounder in her faith, I think, than is her husband!"

"*Our* battle?"

"Aye, ours. Your cause as much as mine, David."

"I do not think that we fight the same battle, Eminence!"

"Do not be so stiff, man! And it *is* the same battle. You are concerned for James and his kingdom, I for the Church. But both are essentially linked. And I fight as much for the one as the other. If the Church goes down, Henry will have won and *Scotland* will go down. *You* should have concern for the Church."

"I do. But for its truth and spirit, not its power and vainglory! That is why I have written my poems and plays. Do not think that I have no concern for the Church."

"Believe you that your verses will aid in this great struggle? From what I have heard of them they will but spread greater doubts and confusion. And undermine due authority. My authority now, whether I like it or no."

"Oh, you like it!"

"That latest great play you were working on? Have you finished it? Have you a name for it?"

"Finished, yes – if any play or writing is ever finished, since it can always be improved. I have thought to name it a satire on current follies. In Church, yes – but in the kingdom also. I spare none, not myself, not the clergy nor the lords nor James himself. *A Satire of the Realm*, perhaps? Or *The Satire of All Estates of the Realm*? That is too long. *A Satire of the Three Estates* – lords, Church and people."

"Whatever you name it, think you it will effect anything for good? Verses and mummery? It may well rouse the common folk, make them more discontented. But those that matter, those who endanger the realm? How much heed will they pay to play-acting?"

"Is not much of your Church display mummery of a sort? Your fine vestments and processions and relic-worship? Yet you use it to great effect."

"Perhaps. But it does not sway the great and powerful, I fear. That council meeting today – how many there would be moved over-much by the Church's mummery any more than by yours? It is power, lands, money, position that stirs these. Aye, and threats!"

"That was what you were doing? Threatening? As *Legatus a Latere*? Threatening even Scotland's Privy Council!"

"With good reason. I could have named three, probably five, sitting at that table, in receipt of Henry's pensions! Some in constant communication with Angus in England. Some ready to rise against James, if the English invade. Some, if not themselves prepared to betray, with kin who are. Two of this last, in especial, whom I deliberately singled out to take major part in this of resisting Donald MacDonald's assault. Arran and Borthwick, the Admiral and the Master-of-the-Ordnance. To ensure that they were committed to James's cause, before all. Arran's half-brother, the ineffable Bastard, is lying low, but he is not down. He intrigues and conspires. I let Arran know that I know it, to warn him to keep the Bastard under. Borthwick is a better man, stronger. I have no reason to believe *him* false. But his kinsman, Sir John Borthwick, Provost of Linlithgow, and in a key position, keeper of the Queen's dower-palace, is deep in communication with Angus and the English. We have intercepted some of his letters. He must be dealt with. I would rather that he was warned, and fled the country, than have to engage in a great struggle here, with sides taken. But I will unmask him, if I must. So – I warn the Lord Borthwick. His Grace's Privy and Secret Council, you see my friend, is scarcely unimpeachable however privileged!"

"I can hardly believe all this."

"Yet it is true. Like a lot more I could tell you. And I must deal with it – since none other will, it seems. But first I will deal with the churchmen, to let all see that I am in earnest. I am going to bring some quite senior clergy to open trial for heresy. The Dean of Dollar and Canon of St. Colm's Inch. Two Dominican friars. An ecclesiastical notary. As warning. I have the names and offences of many others – a long list. We shall see if it will be necessary to try them all!"

"Trial, you say? Are they not already condemned, before trial?"

"Say that I would not be bringing them to trial were I not convinced of their guilt."

"And the price these will have to pay? That others may be warned?"

"They none of them are ignorant of the price of heresy."

"So – these men are doomed to death by fire! On *your* decision. I would not be in your shoes then, Cardinal Legate! For all the power the Pope or other can bestow."

"No. That I can believe," David Beaton said levelly. "Nor, my friend, many a night, would I! I pay part of the price myself, you see." And he left, to go in search of the Queen.

5

David Lindsay peered out from the dais-doorway of the great hall of Linlithgow Palace, watching for the signal of one of his heralds stationed down at the far main entrance. All was ready, the hall filled to overflowing, almost all who mattered in Scotland present – although not, he observed, Cardinal Beaton – the minstrels' soft music barely to be heard above the chatter of tongues, a glittering, colourful company. He only awaited the royal entry and all could commence. The Queen would tonight ensure that James would not be late.

Waiting there, his thoughts went back to that other evening, twenty-six years before, when he had awaited James's father in this same hall, after that other grim play-acting, when the strange apparition of an ancient weird man had materialised before the King in the adjoining St. Michael's Kirk, to warn him against invading England at the behest of the Queen of France, and the price he would have to pay if he did. That mummery had been of Queen Margaret Tudor's arranging, almost certainly, on her brother's behalf; and a month later, Flodden-field had been the outcome, disaster, and the death of the King, with young James succeeding to the throne at the age of seventeen months, himself his usher, procurator and guide. Had he failed the child? And the father who had laid that task upon him? None could deny that this James had turned out less admirable a man and monarch than might have been hoped for. How much of the responsibility was perhaps his? Or could he comfortably blame all on the Tudor blood in his veins and the baleful influence of the Earl of Angus? And now, here he was about to demonstrate most overt criticism of monarch, court, Church and kingdom – and incidentally of himself – in front of all the criticised.

Was he a fool to be doing this, a presumptuous fool?

Davie Beaton most certainly would say that he was, if in less forthright words.

How would they take it, here? Much would depend on James himself – and it was one item in the King's favour, his ability to laugh at his own faults and accept criticism, although seldom to act on it. And the Queen would help, for she had had many of the verses read to her privately by Janet, and had shown no offence. The lords and courtiers would not like much of it, but they would be apt to take their tone from the monarch; and they would enjoy the castigation of the clergy which was, after all, the major theme. David counted four bishops present, five mitred abbots and fully a score of priors, deans, canons and other senior churchmen. Beaton undoubtedly was absenting himself deliberately, and lacking his presence these might well follow the lead of the Chancellor, the Archbishop of Glasgow, who was sitting there in the front row.

Well, it was too late now for doubts and second thoughts. The thing was in train. Anyway, he could not draw back, even if he would. It had become something of a war between himself and Davie Beaton. The Cardinal had had his grim demonstration to all, the trial and death by burning, for heresy, of Dean Forret, the Black Friars Keillor and Beveridge, the notary Forrester and a priest, Simpson; and Sir John Borthwick, who had prudently bolted to England, had been tried in his absence and condemned. Now it was *his* turn to make his very different affirmation and challenge, his counterblast.

A hand raised by the herald stationed at the other door ended Lindsay's cogitations. Moving out on to the dais itself, he stepped down to the main floor level and strode to the other end of the hall, along the central aisle left between the crowded benches, a brilliant figure in his emblazoned heraldic tabard, baton in hand. He passed through the inner doorway to the outer, his waiting trumpeters falling in behind him, and was ready on the steps to receive the King and Queen as they came round the inner courtyard from the royal quarters of the palace – for tonight *they* would not be gracing the dais-platform.

"God's eyes, Davie – it is a cold night to be taking us away from our firesides! Your entertainment had better be good, man, to compensate!" James greeted. Blessedly, he seemed to be in a good mood.

"Oh, it is, James," Marie said, smiling. "I have heard a little of it."

"I thank you, Madam. It is well-intended at least, Sire," he answered bowing. "Some will take offence, I do not doubt – but not Your Grace I think, since the king portrayed tonight is not your royal self but one made up of many princes less gracious – more like unto King Henry, perhaps!" God forgive him that hypocrisy, but it was the best that he could do in the circumstances.

"You say so? A pity, then, that the Englishman Sadler has come and gone, with his message and reply. He could have taken back word of this night's doings to my deplorable uncle also!"

David did not comment on that, but signed for his trumpeters to blare their introductory fanfare. Then he led the way inside, as all rose, and the minstrels in the gallery changed their tune to a rousing march.

The royal couple proceeded up the aisle through the bowing and curtsying company, James's hand heedfully on Marie's elbow. He was taking ostentatious care of her these days, for she was five months pregnant with the heir he and all Scotland had long looked for.

Lindsay conducted them up to the front rows of seats below the dais, where the Chancellor and other great officers of state sat, and there left them, to mount the dais again and disappear through its private doorway. In the ante-room behind, where the players crowded, he took off his gorgeous Lyon's tabard and plumed cap and laid aside his baton-of-office. Raising a hand for quiet, he wished the excited actors well and reminded them that, if they forgot any of their lines and verses not to stand dumb but to improvise, use their wits, say anything that seemed apt – and none would know the difference. Then he went back into the hall, in his ordinary and far-from-resplendent clothing, and at the front of the dais waited for approximate silence.

"Your Graces, my lords, excellencies and honoured guests," he declared, "tonight it is my pleasure to present before you an offering, an entertainment, a dramatic diversion. I have named it *A Pleasant Satire of the Three Estates*, and I emphasise that such is what it is – a satire. Such as a device, a parable, an allegory, a contrivance in exaggeration, to convey a message or contention, with humour if possible, not to make charge or indictment. So, while all should heed and note, aye and smile and perchance even weep a tear, let none, I say, take umbrage or point the finger at another." He paused significantly. Then he added, "As to the play itself, if aught seems amiss, blame not the actors, who but seek to do their best with my poor words. If blame there is to be, blame David Lindsay. Your Grace – have I permission to proceed?"

Turning, he gestured at the stage itself, furnished with a great table and many chairs, one a throne, but also with a stocks with jougs or handcuffs, and a gibbet. He waved to the dais-door and a trumpeter stepped out, hooded and cloaked now, to blow a prolonged flourish, while David stepped down and went to take his seat, not amongst the officers-of-state but in a more modest row of benches, beside Janet.

The trumpeter retired and out from the ante-room came a grey-bearded individual of noble and dignified appearance, dressed in a long robe plain but rich. In authoritative tones he announced that his name was Diligence and that all good and honest folk in this renowned audience should heed him well, for his was the duty to usher in, to introduce, to announce and explain, aye and to prove and reprove, to praise and dispraise. Some, to be sure, might like and some mislike what they saw and heard; but let none take it ill to their persons, for what was to follow was of general import, not personal, for pastime and for play. Heed then, great and less great, saints and misdoers alike!

A telling pause there. Then, in a loud voice, he called for their sovereign-lord and king – whom God save and faithful folk cherish and obey, that no man be wronged or woman either, even His Grace's past paramours!

As the company gasped at that, there issued on to the stage a royally clad personage bearing a crown in one hand and a sceptre in the other, his lengthy and handsome velvet-and-fur cloak held up by two capering courtiers, while a third, overdressed and bent almost double, ushered them forward with extravagant bows and flourishes, gabbling obsequious and fulsome nonsense.

With a stern gesture Diligence, the presenter, silenced this character and observed that he was called Solace, or if preferred, Pleasure, and that he had altogether too much to say and overmuch influence in the realm whose liege-lord was this King Humanitas – who also could well do without the other two courtiers, Wantonness and Placebo or Pleaser. If these would be quiet, His Grace would now address all.

Solace thereupon produced no trumpet but a tin-whistle on which he blew a mocking piping note or two, and King Humanitas raised voice to declare that the Lord of lords and King of Kings should be his guide in all things, supporting him in all his business, giving him grace to use his diadem to God's pleasure and his own comfort, defending him from all temptation and disfame . . .

Wantonness here interrupted outrageously to reprove the monarch for making such dreary cheer. After all, so long as he had himself and Placebo in his close company, he would live right merrily and want for no pleasure, Sandie Solace here ensuring that likewise – for had he not the Lady Sensuality happily available for His Grace?

At this cue there entered three females, the first a splendidly built and distinctly underclad young woman, golden-haired and good-looking, with painted lips and darkened eyes, her gown so low-cut as barely to contain her thrusting breasts – not that this made as much impact as it might since her clothing was of such diaphanous stuff as could be seen through at every movement. The audience duly exclaimed at the sight, as well they might, for Lindsay had persuaded Margaret Erskine herself, now wife to Sir William Douglas of Lochleven, here present, James's favourite mistress, to play the part. She was supported by two simpering maidens. As the lady smiled roguishly around on all, Diligence asserted disapprovingly that this was the Lady Sensuality, especially released for the occasion by the Prioress of the nunnery of Balmerino, the monks of the adjacent abbey begrudging.

Sensuality bowed, and in a clearly enticing throaty voice urged all lack-lustre lovers to awake and behold what was on offer for most pleasant pastime and dalliance, her fair face and gay attire, her features flaming warm as fire, her paps of outline quite perfect, her limbs and loins without defect, all her tributes of delight offering pleasure infinite, to all, even the Kings of Christendom in especial to the court of Rome.

King Humanitas was clearly smitten, and asked Wantonness, his secretary, to present the lady. Thereafter, as she all but rubbed herself against him, dismissing her maids, he was obviously going to lead her off on his private interests when Diligence protested, and reminded His Grace that he was here for a serious purpose, not gaping nor copulation but to consider the better rule of his kingdom, with his councillors.

Reluctantly the king returned, but still kept an arm around Sensuality's pulchritude. Scowling, he gave orders for his councillors to assemble. Then he and his court left the stage temporarily, Solace as he went suggesting that while His Majesty Serene awaited a fair and prudent queen, he could well use a concubine of quality since he lacked the gift of chastity.

A choir of the common folk came on to sing an interval, and the audience were able to express their opinions of the performance so far, which they did loud if not clear, for the impact most evidently varied greatly, Lindsay and his wife seeking to measure and compare. There was no obvious disapproval from the royal couple.

The singing died away at the arrival of another venerable and sober individual whom Diligence introduced as Good Counsel, now returned from banishment and come to advise the monarch and his officers. But he was quickly thrust aside by three fashionable lordlings, who called themselves Devotion, Sapience and Discretion – although Diligence declared that their real identities were Flattery,

Falsity and Deceit. Good Counsel sought to assert that without his guidance and wisdom no emperors, kings nor potentates could advance; and whoever held him in delusion would come only to confusion. But the three lords chased him away, with abuse and mockery, before King Humanitas reappeared, still with Sensuality, he now tottering significantly limp after obvious exertions, although she was as bright as ever.

While Flattery, who clearly was to be the clown of the piece, and his colleagues fawned upon king and lady, two more and very different females appeared on the scene, decently-clad and modest of mien, announced as Verity and Chastity, the former holding an open Bible. These were jeered at by Flattery and company, and when Verity commenced a reproof against careless and unjust rulers she was quickly silenced by the trio and hustled over to the stocks and clamped therein. When Chastity protested and declared that she herself had been similarly abused by all three Estates, in especial by the Spiritual Estate, the Church, whose bishops said that they knew her not, whose abbots preferred the Fairy Queen and whose nuns shut their doors in her face, Falsity made to grab her and she ran to throw herself on the mercy of the king, who looked down at her doubtfully. But Lady Sensuality did not, and signed for Falsity to take her and put her in the stocks beside Verity.

At this shameful development, with the watching company reacting loudly and variously, a trumpet-blast of great power heralded the arrival of a dramatically impressive newcomer, wearing a crown and regal robes but also sporting a pair of angel's wings. This imperious apparition, silencing even Diligence, proclaimed that He was King Correction Himself, come down in wrath from the seat and source of all power, in order to censure and judge. He glared around him, pointing at each and all.

The king hung his head, Sensuality rushed off, crying that she would be safe with the clergy, Flattery, Falsity and Deceit cast themselves to the ground, Good Counsel reappeared, and at Correction's command released Verity and Chastity from the stocks, all the while relating the wickedness of the courtiers, the lords' selfishness, the shame of the Church and the greed of the burgesses, together with the utter inaction of the monarch.

Correction, with a flick of his hand, dismissed the rest and turned on King Humanitas. He reminded him how one, King Sardanapall, sported his lust amongst fair ladies for so long that his neglected lieges rebelled and threw him down, as he, Divine Correction, would do likewise unless there was improvement. Remember Sodom and Gomorrah!

The king, contrite, came to throw himself upon Correction's mercy, and was commanded to commence immediate reform of behaviour and of governance. Let this latter be initiated by a session of the Three Estates forthwith.

Hurriedly the monarch shouted the order for the assembly of a parliament. All left the stage save Diligence, who announced the end of the first act, and an interval. In the minstrels' gallery musicians struck up.

Animated discussion filled the hall. Faces turned to eye David Lindsay.

The second and principal act started with a poor man, Pauper, coming from Tranent in Lothian, entering and seeking alms from Diligence, asserting that he had either six or seven bairns to feed, he could not recollect which, and naught to feed them on; for when his father, mother and then wife had died, one after other, the Tranent vicar took his three cows, all he had, as price to pay to bury them. Pauper got scant sympathy from Diligence. Then a Pardoner appeared on the scene, in monkish habit and ringing a bell, with a boy pushing a sort of trolley laden with strange gear; and perambulating round the stage, declared that he was Sir Robert Rome-Raker, public Pardoner personally licensed by the Pope. He was followed in by some ordinary citizens, including a souter or shoemaker and a tailor, with their wives. Diligence ignoring him, the Pardoner turned to these two tradesmen, dismissing Pauper as unprofitable, and launched into an exhibition of his wares and relics from the cart, declaiming the verses which David had read out that evening at Ethie Castle – here was Fionn MacCoull's true jaw-bone with teeth complete; the cord which hanged Johnnie Armstrong; the anus of St. Bridle's cow and the snout of St. Anthony's sow; and other wonders. Whoever bought what he had to sell need never fear to go to hell. Come then, buy.

When no offers were forthcoming, the Pardoner moved to more particular devices, turning to the souter and the tailor, declaring confidentially that he had the power, from the Pope himself, to set apart those who loved their wives without full heart. Was neither of them cursed with a shrewish wife, who harried them with pains and strife? The souter, admitting that his dame was a slut and a scold, and asking how much his divorce would cost, for he had only five shillings and his cobbler's knife, was interrupted by the lady herself, who denounced him as a whoreson, cold and dry and useless in bed. How much would it cost *her* to be rid of him? She could offer only a pair of his shirts, but of cloth excellent once they were washed. The Pardoner agreed to accept both these fees and declared that, to seal the deal, they must there and then each kiss the other's backside for the last time, and part for ever with his blessing. He thereupon raised the woman's skirt the better to facilitate this parting exchange.

The audience erupted in a great outcry of mixed abuse and delight, shocked offence and outrage from some, laughter and advice from others. The clergy of course were especially voluble and angry. But it was at King James that David Lindsay looked anxiously, for that reference to Johnnie Armstrong cut close, he well realised. James had personally ordered the hanging of Armstrong and his troop of forty-eight Border supporters ten years ago, on the urging of the Bastard of Arran but against the pleading of others, including Lindsay himself, one of the blackest marks on his reign. But although his one-time pupil's back-view was all that was visible, James seemed to be taking it well enough, indeed to be one of the laughers – which would influence others undoubtedly.

The Pauper was now approaching the Pardoner to help him get back his cows from the Vicar of Tranent, but had only one groat to offer, and was being scornfully rejected, when Diligence clapped his hands for silence, for the re-entry of the monarch and Sensuality and the arrival of the Three Estates of the realm. King Humanitas paced to his throne and took his seat, Sensuality perching on its arm, and to the piping of the tin-whistle the three groups of parliamentarians entered backwards, the Temporality, the lords and lairds, led in by the lordling Flattery; the Spirituality, bishops and priors, by Falsity; and the burgh representatives, merchants and tradesmen, by Deceit, their tripping, stumbling backwards progress sufficiently significant to all. The king cried out what folly was this? How could his parliament know where it was going if it went backwards? Solace and Wantonness answered that in one way, and Good Counsel the opposite, until Divine Correction silenced all and demanded the reason for this regression, to be answered by the leading bishop, doffing his mitre, to say that they had all gone this backside-way for many a year and most pleasantly. Sternly Correction ordered them all to turn and face the monarch, and thereafter hear and attend to the just complaints of all the lieges who had suffered by their wicked reversal of progress.

King Humanitas then announced that the Estates were in session, and that they all were his members and he their head. Also that he was determined, as instructed by Correction, to reform each Estate, as was sorely required, and to punish all who might oppress the common-weal.

A great panic ensued amongst all three groups at this royal threat, all gabbling protest, with Holy Church, much the loudest, advising His Grace not to be hasty and suggesting postponement until another day, when he would be in a better mood and this uncomfortable Correction out of the way . . .

King Humanitas, with an unusual exhibition of decision, cut the bishop short and signed for all commissioners to take their seats around the great table. Then he called for the first complainant to appear before the assembly.

Diligence selected one of the watching citizens, and announced him as John Common-weal.

Bowing humbly before the throne, this John poured out his troubles and indictments, his voice strengthening as he went on. He had for long been misgoverned, abused and defrauded by all three Estates, and was like to be so still, despite His Grace's belated attention, so long as the said Estates were guided by their respective Vices, Flattery, Falsity and Deceit. He urged that these three be dismissed, that they might better proceed with this session. When, at Sensuality's whisper, the monarch shook his head, John appealed to Divine Correction, who promptly ordered three sergeants to arrest the Vices and put them in the stocks where Verity and Chastity had been shackled. He also commanded Sensuality to leave the scene, which she did tearfully but promising in loud asides to return in due course, the monarch nodding and patting her arm.

Thus chastened, the Three Estates prepared for business.

John Common-weal was joined now by the poor man called Pauper, who reverted to his claim that the vicar of Tranent had taken his cows, all three, as grave-dues before he would bestow Christian burial on his dead father, mother and wife. He craved parliament's condemnation of this theft, for that is what it was, when a single chicken would have been adequate payment for each. And he could name many others equally defrauded by priests. John Common-weal was weighing in with similar charges against grasping clergy when Spirituality, the senior bishop, angrily rose to interrupt, declaring that such impious whoresons as these must not be allowed to insult Holy Church and that they should not only be dismissed but taken out and scourged. Correction had to intervene to silence him and his clerical colleagues, and John, proceeding, charged the churchmen not only with greed for money and gear but with prelatical plurality of benefices, the adulteries of priests, monks and nuns, and the arrogance of bishops, abbots and priors. He demanded that the other two Estates, of lords and burgesses, should herewith censure the Estate Spiritual. Furiously the bishop rose again to assert that if there were any such move he would appeal directly to the Pope in Rome for excommunication of all concerned.

Correction here once more stepped in, declaring this to be of none effect, and urging the Estates to their duty. King Humanitas unwillingly agreed that they would have to consider a motion of censure.

John Common-weal and Pauper retired and were succeeded by the two wronged ladies, Verity and Chastity. These also launched into accusation against the Spiritual Estate, Verity recounting how she had been done violence to and placed in the stocks, and Chastity telling that she had been flung out of her nunnery by its Prioress. They had complained to higher ecclesiastical authority but received only abuse. They asserted the ignorance of the clergy, high and low, saying that some could neither read nor write, few ever preached and many knew neither the Old nor New Testaments.

Once more the bishop thundered condemnation and anathema, until Correction had to halt the proceedings. Sternly he ordered the other Estates to censure the Spiritual, censure now, not merely consider censure.

Sheepishly the lords' and burgesses' spokesmen rose to make mumbling but official reprimand of the Church. Correction, turning to King Humanitas, ordered him there and then to suspend all prelates from the sitting, and to dismiss them from his presence. Hesitantly, uneasily, the monarch obeyed.

Angrily the bishops, mitred abbots and priors rose from their places and, snatching off their magnificent jewelled copes and canonicals, threw them at the scribes and clerks. They then marched out, shouting that they were bound straight for Rome, and all who had been concerned in this shameful event would live to rue it here and hereafter. But as they went, Spirituality himself mentioned in a loud aside that since it was quite a long way to Rome, they would all go sup with Lady Sensuality in the by-going.

Correction ordered the finest of the prelatical robes to be recovered and put upon John Common-weal and Pauper, and these sat down in the clerics' places at the table.

Diligence then announced that this most important sitting of the realm's Estates would suitably end with a proclamation of Acts of Parliament here passed and to be enacted, and called on the chief scribe to proclaim them to all. A trumpeter blew for full attention, and the clerk read out five Acts, commanding, in the name of King and Estates, the improvement of government and justice; the reform of the Spiritual Estate; a decree that priests shall be allowed to marry, in order to maintain matrimonial chastity; a ban on Lords Temporal marrying the bastard bairns of clerics; and a campaign to be mounted against thieves and robbers of all sorts and degrees, starting with the Border reivers.

This over, King Humanitas and the parliamentarians rose; but before departure signed for the sergeants to loose the prisoners from the stocks and to convey them to the gallows, for a final scene – the hanging of Deceit, Falsity and Flattery, in that order. This was effected most realistically, with a deft substitution, behind a screen, of a dummy figure, identically dressed for each of the Vices, being hoisted on a rope while the actors crept away unseen, after each had issued farewell advice to his particular Estate of burgesses, lords and clerics. By a notable device a live crow, hitherto hidden, was released, to flap away from the dummy Falsity, to represent the departure of his black soul – this to the cheers of the entire house, players and audience alike.

Diligence had the last word, in theory – but none heard him in the hubbub.

David Lindsay, heart-in-mouth, moved out from his seat to go apprehensively to the front, below the dais, that there should be no doubt that blame, reproach, anger, must lie with the author not with the actors. As he went he was aware of movement at his back, and there was Janet coming with him, proudly to take his arm. Heart in its right place again, and courage returned, he moved on.

James stood up, and so must all, talk and exclamation dying away. For a moment there was silence. The Queen, with her own woman's gesture, also placed her hand on her husband's arm, smiling.

"Bravo!" she murmured quietly, and inclined her head towards the Lindsays.

James, glancing at her, cleared his throat and then stared David in the eye. There was much in that look, question, assessment, resentment, warning but also something of acknowledgment, respect, even affection. He raised his hand.

"Hear all," he said. "Tonight we have been entertained indeed. Aye, and admonished and instructed – some might say belaboured! Some may find cause for censure indeed, even reprisal and reckoning. But not I, my lords and lieges, not I! My old friend Davie Lindsay has been teaching me lessons all my days, some none so gentle! Tonight he has returned to his tutoring – and he does not spare the rod! Yet, he is a kindly chiel at heart, as I know well. So I bend the back to his rod. As must all here."

He paused and looked all round, in the silence, drawing himself up a little. In a changed tone of voice he went on, turning on the Chancellor and other bishops.

"You, my lords of Holy Church, have heard and seen – and, I swear, seethed within you! Seethe you, then – but to good effect. Take due heed, I say. The scourging the Spiritual Estate has received this day is for the good of Holy Church, of which you are the shepherds and guardians. That you have failed in your shepherding, all can see. I advise that you improve it hereafter."

Archbishop Dunbar wrung his hands, and when that was all he did, James Hay, Bishop of Ross, a less studious but more forthright prelate, raised strong voice.

"Sire – what perforce we have witnessed and listened to this night was shameful, yes. But in its falsity, its ill-speaking, its wicked assault on God's Church. Here was a crying sin, I say, a bad and vicious scandal, to be deplored utterly. By this, this demagogue! To mount such affront, before Your Graces and us all . . .!"

At the nodded agreement of other clerics, James interrupted him. "Silence, my lord! Remember before whom *you* speak! If Lindsay exaggerates, here was sufficient of truth to condemn the rule of you and your like over the Church in this my kingdom. I charge you, and *you*, my lord Archbishop, and all other bishops and prelates, that you reform your fashions and manners of living, you and those who take their monition from such as you. Or by God's bones I will send the six of you here to my uncle of England, to learn how he treats ecclesiastics! And send others after you, if they amend not. You hear me?"

Dunbar found his quavering voice. "Your Grace – fear not. Fear not, I say. We, we have heard and noted. Aye, noted. We shall . . . act. One word from Your Grace's mouth suffices. It is our commandment. I, I promise amendment."

"Let it be so, then. Gladly I bestow any words of my mouth that can amend your Estate. See you to it, my lords Spiritual." And waving a dismissive hand, he took the Queen's arm and turned to head for the hall-door.

Hastily David reverted to being Lord Lyon, abandoning Janet meantime and hurrying down the aisle before the royal couple, while one of his trumpeters, on his own initiative, contributed a valedictory fanfare.

David escorted them across the torchlit courtyard to the entrance to the royal quarters, and there bowed low.

"I thank Your Grace," he said. "And you, Madam."

"Aye, Davie Lindsay – well may you!" James returned, almost grimly. "Some monarchs would have had your head for that, yonder! But – for auld times' sake . . ."

"I know it, Sire. But – I think that I know Your Grace likewise!"

"Then you will know how close a miss it was!"

"*I* think that you did passing well, Sir David," Marie de Guise said, and they moved inside. "A good night to you."

After a step or two, James threw back over his shoulder, "I advise that you watch how you tread, Davie, hereafter. All are not so forbearing as am I. The churchmen will hang you, with Johnnie Armstrong's rope, if they can! And what will the *Legatus a Latere* have to say to this . . .?"

Lindsay wondered that also. He wondered indeed whether he had been wise, or even sensible, to make this night's gesture, at all? Might it not have been better if Donald Greumach MacDonald of Sleat had not had the misfortune to be killed whilst besieging the Mackenzie castle of Eilean Donan in Kintail, and his entire southwards drive thereby suffered abortion, so that now he, David Lindsay, would have been away on a military campaign in the north and Highlands instead of risking his whole future in challenging Church and state in this fashion? What had made him do it?

6

David Lindsay got his campaigning in the north and Highlands, after a fashion, despite Donald Greumach's death and the impact of *The Three Estates*. For in May that year, 1540, Queen Marie was delivered of the son her husband and his subjects, or most of them, had been longing for, a new James Stewart, Duke of Rothesay; and now, two weeks later, another cherished desire of James's, instigated in the first place by Davie Beaton, was coming to fruition likewise. This was to be a great expedition, part military, part political, part royal progress, round the entire Scottish seaboard, with especial attention to the insurgent and troublesome Highland West and the Lordship of the Isles, showing flag and mailed fist but also displaying the monarch in his majesty.

Now all waited, at the port of Leith, eleven large ships – or not quite all, for they awaited one more. And if it might seem unsuitable that the King of Scots, the Lord High Admiral, the commander of land forces, the High Constable, the Earl Marischal and scores of lords and knights, with a couple of thousand men at arms and seamen, should have to wait for the seventh son of a Fife laird, it had to be recognised that the missing entity was in fact the most powerful individual in the land, monarch scarcely excepted, Papal Legate, Cardinal, Archbishop of St. Andrews and Primate – for old James Beaton had at last passed on and been succeeded by his coadjutor and nephew. Moreover Archbishop Dunbar of Glasgow had been persuaded to resign the position of Chancellor of the realm, or chief minister, and Davie Beaton had taken over that office also – which left little else for him to aspire to. As well as all this, he was more or less paying for the entire expedition, out of the enormous revenues of the Church he now controlled. Nine of the ships waiting there, including the King's, had been chartered by him, three of them victuallers laden with provisions, gear and extra arms and ammunition. Only two, those of Arran, the Admiral, and Huntly, the military commander, were not of his providing. Now his own vessel, coming from St. Andrews, was due to join the fleet at any time.

As Lyon, David Lindsay sailed on the King's ship. This had been handsomely, indeed luxuriously, appointed for the voyage, the royal cabins tapestry-hung and carpeted, with even gold plate to eat and drink from and musicians to play accompaniment. Unfortunately the vessel's domestic arrangements were in the hands of Oliver Sinclair, the favourite, a young man whom David misliked, whose arrogance made him few friends but who was always attended by flattering toadies and place-seekers, appealing to his influence with James. David would have preferred to sail on one of the other ships – although not necessarily Beaton's. He had seen nothing of Davie since that evening of the Linlithgow play-acting, and had only heard it reported that the Cardinal had been most displeased over it all – as was only to be expected, of course. But there had been no direct repercussions from St. Andrews, for soon thereafter, on his uncle's death, the Legate had had to make a brief visit to Rome in order to be ordained and consecrated Archbishop and Primate of the Scots Church. He had only been back a week or two. And coming home via France, he had brought back with him a renewal by King Francis of the provisions made by the French parliament in 1513, immediately after the disastrous Battle of Flodden, giving all Scots subjects citizenship of France, with all the privileges and benefits of that status – an extraordinary gesture of support for the smaller nation, which had been rather overlooked but which could have major impact, not only on trade and commerce and international relations, but on the strength of Holy Church, in view of France's strong adherence to the Vatican.

When the Cardinal's ship appeared, it proved to be quite the largest and finest of the fleet – as it required to be, for it turned out to have no fewer than five hundred men aboard, all well-armed and equipped, the Church

Militant indeed. And when Davie Beaton came to pay his respects to the King, it was to make it clear to all, however courteously put, that whatever notions the Admiral and Huntly and others might have about it all, this excursion would be conducted more or less on the terms of the man who was paying for it all, himself. If there were scowls and mutterings, that did not worry Davie, who could take all such in his stride. James acquiesced.

Before heading back to his own vessel, Beaton had a private word with Lindsay. "This expedition could achieve great things," he asserted. "James has never been north of Aberdeen and Argyll. All the north-country, east and west, has been unaware of him, and like a dagger at our backs for long – the same sort of dagger that we and France together threaten Henry with, should he attack one or the other. These Highland folk, near half of the kingdom, scarcely recognise James as their liege-lord. He means little or nothing in the north. And Henry Tudor can use that. Do not think that his English pensions stop at the Highland Line! It was his misfortune that Donald MacDonald caught that arrow at Eilean Donan. But there could be others to use, and *will* be, if we do not set our house in order. This voyage must be the start of that. Showing the north who rules in this land. But also seeking to give the Highlandmen some fellow-feeling that they share the King, laws and rights, aye *rights*, with the rest of us. And share the same Church, forby."

"Aye – and there we have it, I think! The Church in the north is strong. Is little concerned with reform. You could call on that, use it, in your struggle against reform here."

"And why not? If we are all one kingdom. And if we have the most powerful chiefs in our grip – as I intend that we shall have before we return – then we have the means to muster a great new army, thousands of the best fighting men in Christendom. For the Highlanders are that, whatever else. And we are going to need these, once Henry perceives that he is not going to win Scotland save by war."

"So – you have it all thought through, as ever, Davie. I

might have known that you were not spending all this siller just to pleasure James!"

"Someone must try to bind this kingdom into one. And who else is doing so? Not yourself, my friend – not *you.* With your play-actings and assaults on the Church. You are *dividing* the realm, not uniting it, as it needs. Playing into Henry's hands."

"Not so. I seek a Church and a realm purged of corruption. A corrupt Church means a corrupt people. And such can never be strong. We need to cleanse ourselves of inner enemies before we seek successfully to fight our outward ones."

"You think that what you are doing, ridiculing the priesthood, undermining clerical authority, causing doubts and unrest – you think that is cleansing and strengthening Scotland, man?"

"I think that it is a beginning. Which must start somewhere."

"*I* do not. So we differ, my friend – not for the first time! But . . . I have the means to see that my way prevails, I'd remind you!"

"I wondered when it would come to this!"

"Well might you. I have been very patient. Had it been other than yourself, my oldest friend . . . I did not come to your play, recognising that I could probably not have sat through it without halting it, as sacrilege. I took no steps against you, thereafter – as I was urged by many to do. Thankful indeed to be off to Rome and France, so that I need not do aught about you! Which is not my way, as you know! But, David – do not try me too hard. For I have more than friendship to consider."

Lindsay nodded grimly. "I am warned," he said. "We shall see."

"I hope, even pray, that you *do* see. And that I never have to choose too sorely between friendship and duty." Then shrugging, and changing his tone noticeably, Beaton smiled that winning smile, and touched the other's arm. "Enough of that. We set out on something of an adventure which we can both enjoy. Let us do so. It should be a notable ploy. I suppose that you must bide in this, the

King's ship? As Lyon. For I would have wished you to sail with me. Later perhaps . . ."

The fleet weighed anchor an hour later and stood out, twelve sail, into the Forth, while from two miles away the banging of a royal salute came echoing from the cannon of Edinburgh Castle.

With a band of instrumentalists playing on the high stern-castle of the royal flagship, they crossed the firth, to sail in leisurely fashion along the Fife coast, passing sundry of the ports and havens from which in fact most of the ships had come, Kinghorn, Kirkcaldy, Dysart and Anstruther. As they neared Fife Ness itself, David was able to point out to James just where the incident with the de Guise ships had been battled out, and where he had thereafter put the Queen-to-be ashore at Balcomie. But it all looked so calm and fair a scene on this fine June day that the entire business now seemed remote and unlikely.

Rounding the Ness they turned northwards, passing St. Andrews, source of all the funding for this venture, and headed out across the mouth of the Firth of Tay, the smoke of Dundee in the distance. It was evening before they were level with Arbroath, the towers of its great redstone abbey, the start of all Davie Beaton's power, glowing in the sinking sun. But it is never dark of a northern June night, and when the cliffs of Red Head loomed mightily abeam, the two Davids at least picked out the twinkle of light from the Ethie Castle window, where Marion Ogilvy would be keeping her lonely vigil – this before they retired to their bunks.

They had passed Stonehaven and Aberdeen and were approaching Buchan Ness, that great thrusting fist of Scotland shaken in the face of the Norse Sea, the most easterly tip of all the land, when David Lindsay arose and went up on deck. Apparently they were making for the burgh of Banff, where James was to make his first landing and preside over a justice-eyre, Beaton having arranged this in advance with the Bishop of Moray.

Once past another frowning cape, known as Kinnaird's Head, they found themselves sailing due westwards, not north, and as far as eye could see, so odd was the configuration of the land. This, according to the shipmaster, was the Firth of Moray, or at least the mouth of it, although it appeared to be the open sea, with no sighting of an opposite shore, so wide was it. Inland they could see what was obviously a fertile broad coastal plain and then endless ramparts of blue mountains.

Some three hours' sailing along this coast brought them to Banff Bay, where the fleet could anchor in sheltered water whilst the King went ashore. The royal party was greeted by Patrick Hepburn, Bishop of Moray and brother of the Earl of Bothwell, with a local chieftain in tartans, Alexander Fraser of Philorth, with the Provost and magistrates of the town, for this was an ancient royal burgh. Indeed there seemed to be two towns, the sea-town and the low-town, separated by the mouth of a river, the Deveron, neither impressive, with an old tumble-down royal castle in between, once allegedly a seat of the Celtic kings, MacBeth, whose calf-country this was, and Malcolm Canmore who slew him. The folk of Banff showed no great interest in the visitors.

The Bishop led them, not to the castle which was too derelict for use, but to a Carmelite priory, where the justice-eyre was being held. James's half-brother, illegitimate son of James the Fourth by Flaming Janet Kennedy, the Earl of Moray, was Justiciar here of course; but since he had never been in the area in his life and knew little Gaelic anyway, his deputy, this Fraser of Philorth, conducted the proceedings, James and Moray sitting-in, as it were. James himself had a smattering of the Gaelic but not sufficient to follow much of the charges, evidence and pleadings. Most of the cases seemed to be concerned with cattle-stealing, theft and rape, by Highland caterans, which produced evidently automatic sentences of hanging, accepted apparently by all concerned, even the prisoners, as unexceptional. But there was one issue where a group of Ogilvies were charged with murdering no fewer than fourteen Rosses or Roses. This, however, was dismissed by Philorth as no business of the court, it all being undoubtedly part of a traditional feud between the two clans, and by ancient custom permissable – for had not the Roses the previous year burned two Ogilvie villages and all therein?

Getting only the mere drift of all this, James Stewart soon had had enough, and decided that there might probably be more interesting things to do in Banff; so Lindsay had to halt the proceedings to announce the monarch's departure.

Davie Beaton now led the way to a second priory, unexpected perhaps in such a location, and unusual in that it was a house of the Observantine friars, a strict offshoot of the ancient Franciscan Order, who had been settled here for centuries, and were rarely to be found in Lowland Scotland. The monks here, although poor-seeming and humble, nevertheless provided a meal for the King's party, simple but adequate, and with large quantities of most potent local whisky to wash it down – which had its due effect. Since the Prior and brothers were Gaelic-speakers with little English, Beaton provided an after-dinner oration on the customs and disciplines of the Observantines, which in fact related more to the former Columban or Celtic Church of their ancestors than to the Romish one, he drawing a parallel with the Celtic foundations of His Grace's throne, the northern origins of the High Kings of Picts or Cruithne, and why James was styled King of Scots and not King of Scotland. David Lindsay was highly interested in this, not only in the historical significance but in the fact that Davie Beaton should obviously have studied it all, and despite his so strong Vatican connections, spoke sympathetically. It is to be feared, however, that his lecture otherwise fell largely on somewhat deaf ears, for whether it was the effect of the whisky, the flood of earlier Gaelic-speaking or less than sound-sleeping during their first night at sea, most of the company, including the monarch, tended to doze off.

After a rest, the party made a tour of the upper and lower towns – which did not take long, for they were no more extensive than they were imposing, finishing up with a look at the castle, where they heard some history from the Cardinal. Then back to the ships.

And there Lindsay, for one, gained another insight into Beaton's wide-ranging interests and concerns, hitherto unsuspected. For in Banff Bay a young man from St. Andrews University, of his own surname, William Lindsay obviously a protégé of the Cardinal's, was taking soundings from a small boat, measuring, assessing and charting, and apparently had been doing so, in less detailed fashion, all the way up the seaboard. He was, in fact seeking to make the first coastal survey of Scottish waters, in the interests of better navigation and the safety of mariners as well as in the advancement of knowledge. Even James was impressed by this, and agreed that they should all spend the night in Banff Bay, in order to give the young man time to finish this detailed part of his task.

In the morning, grey and threatening rain, they turned their prows due northwards instead of continuing along the Moray shoreline, to cut right across the so-wide mouth of this so-called firth, making for the coast of Ross. This meant missing Cawdor, Nairn and Inverness, which Beaton had proposed to visit as important for the King's itinerary; but Oliver Sinclair, who clearly found all this appearance-making something of a bore, prevailed on James to change the programme and make directly for Caithness, where he had family connections with the Sinclair Earl thereof, promising excellent hunting, splendid feasting and notable women. The Cardinal did not hide his disapproval, for he had arranged a great reception for the King at Inverness, the ancient royal Celtic capital; but he could not prevail on the monarch. So he said that he would carry out this visitation himself, in the King's name, and they would meet up again at Castle Girnigoe, the Sinclair's main seat on the north coast of Caithness in four days' time. Beaton's ship, therefore, sailed westwards alone, and William Lindsay was able to continue with his coastal survey. David Lindsay would have preferred to go with Beaton, but this was not to be considered; Lyon's place was at the King's side, as usher and herald.

It seemed a long time, six hours indeed and over fifty

miles, before they made their next landfall, for they had the mouths of two more firths to cross, those of Cromarty and Dornoch. And then they were beyond Easter Ross and skirting Sutherland, a strange name for the second most northerly earldom and county of Scotland, but so called of course because it had always been dominated by whoever ruled in Orkney, rather than in Scotland proper, and to such it *was* a southern land.

It seemed a wild territory, with the mountains nearer and coming down to high moorland right to the coastal cliffs, with little signs of townships or villages but many fierce-looking small castles perching on the said cliffs. The Lowland lords eyed it all askance, as though at a foreign and barbarous land.

By evening, although the cliffs, castles and moors were still in evidence the mountains had drawn back and the fleet was off Caithness, the ultimate tip of the mainland. Oddly, as it seemed, this was a more populous country – explained by the fact that while it was remote indeed for what was looked upon as the rest of the kingdom, it was close to that other entity, the last addition to the realm, the Isles of Orkney, with their totally different character, people and history.

Presently a deep bay opened before them, at the head of which could be seen the blue haze of smoke of what must be quite a large town. This was Wick, they were told, the Norse word *vic* meaning just that, a bay. From now on all the names would be Norse. The smoke was not only from domestic fires but from the large number of smoke-houses for the curing of fish, which was the principal trade of these parts.

The squadron did not head in for Wick however, but continued northwards, to round a bold headland called Noss Point. And thereupon opened a vastly larger and more open bay, fully six miles across – Sinclair's Bay, James's favourite announced proudly. And crowning a spectacular rock-pinnacle about a mile in, seemingly all but detached from the sheer beetling cliffs which enclosed this great semi-circle, rose the tallest and most slender fortalice any there had ever seen, appearing almost part of the cliff-formation itself, Castle Girnigoe, their immediate destination.

As they approached that extraordinary hold it was obvious that there was no convenient harbour or even anchorage in sight – clearly the cliff-girt place was not intended to be accessible. Oliver Sinclair said that they would have to put off in their small boats, and make for a tiny pebble cove under the frowning precipices, from whence there was a steep zig-zag track, or more of a stone step-ladder, up to the cliff-top a couple of hundred feet above. It would make a strange approach for a monarch. Clearly no large company could land here, and it was decided that only James and his immediate close entourage should disembark, and then the squadron should turn around and go back to shelter in Wick Bay and land at the town – for here was no place for shipping to lie off.

David Lindsay wondered why they should have come here in preference to Inverness, the Highland capital.

He wondered even more as they made their difficult landing on slippery weed-hung rocks in a surge of swell which wet not a few courtly feet, including the royal ones, and then faced the dizzy crawl up the cliff-face, largely on steps cut in the living rock. However, because it was his honest Oliver's idea, James took it all with good grace – and others could not protest too loudly when their liege-lord did not.

At the top they found a ferocious-looking band of armed men awaiting them, with no hint of welcome, not tartan-clad these for they were out of the Celtic area here. These people were all but threatening, totally unimpressed by shouts that this was the King of Scots, until Oliver announced that he was Sinclair of Pitcairns and kin to their earl, whom he had brought King James to visit. This had some effect, and surrounding the party with scant courtesy, the guards marched them off along the winding cliff-top path towards the castle, almost as though they were prisoners.

Seen from the land, Castle Girnigoe was no less dramatic, perched on its independent stack of rock and reachable only by means of a drawbridge over a yawning abyss, which Sinclair called a geo, at the foot of which the tide burst in white spray. Indeed Girnigoe meant apparently the gaping or yawning inlet. There were two main towers to the place, linked by lower building, one six storeys high the other five, and with the curtain-walls, gatehouse and lesser works, all were crammed into such huddled and limited and awkward space as the stack-top provided, on differing levels. As a sea-eagle's eyrie it might be apt enough; but as the principal seat of an earldom, it struck a strange and somehow ominous note.

Still more ominous was what the visitor saw when they had crossed that breath catching, sideless drawbridge – that is, after noting the swaying ranks of no fewer than fifteen corpses in various stages of decomposition, hanging in chains from a sort of scaffolding projecting from the gatehouse; and that was how, at the inner bridge-end, callers had to turn sharply but carefully right-handed on a narrow base of bare rock – or else plunge straight down a very steep and greasy incline to the lip of the cliff, and over. Clearly this was a device for discouraging rushed or unauthorised entry; but in wet or frosty weather it would surely be apt to present an alarming hazard for the castle's own inmates. James and his party negotiated it with extreme caution, despite the urgings-on of the guards.

Once within the castle, with sighs of relief, they discovered that the Earl of Caithness was not in fact at home. His countess was, however, and did not seem to find the royal arrival of great convenience, for she appeared to be sharing a bed-chamber with the Bishop of Caithness in the interim. She was a lean and hungry-looking woman of middle years, with traces of former good looks, the Lady Elizabeth Graham, sister of the Earl of Montrose and mother of six. And the Bishop was the notorious Andrew Stewart, brother of the Earl of Atholl here present, who was much better known for conquests military, feuding and feminine, than spiritual.

That castle was as peculiar to dwell in as it was to behold, since, on account of its necessary slenderness and height, much of the available space seemed to be taken up by staircases, which the occupants had to spend much of their time ascending and descending. Nobody appeared to know just where the Earl was; and it was only just before they left that they discovered that his eldest son and heir, the Master of Caithness, had been on the premises all the time, but confined in one of the many pits or prisons cut in the solid rock below. Why was not explained – but the Sinclairs were like that.

Oliver, of course, was faced with the task of proving to James that Girnigoe was all that he had boasted it to be, difficult in these circumstances. But he did his best. Admittedly there was no lack of food and drink; and the next day's hunting was sufficiently exciting, for it provided sport not hitherto sampled by the King nor almost any of his party, the quarry being wolves – and not just the odd wolf, which might be found elsewhere, but large packs of the brutes, which appeared to terrorise these parts, although probably less direly than did the noble Sinclairs themselves. This chase, with its spice of danger – for the horses ran scared of wolves and a thrown rider could be torn to pieces by a pack in a matter of seconds – was much appreciated by James and the younger lords. And in the evening, they found that their hostess and the Bishop had rounded up a different sort of pack, women, to suit all tastes, from girls in their early teens to mature dames whose experience and ingenuity compensated for any lack of youthful charm. Anyway, James for one had always been catholic in his attitudes. Where these all came from was not disclosed. They decided that this was probably all part of the Scandinavian inheritance, from the Norsemen and Vikings.

So passed four days, in which David Lindsay wished that he had indeed gone with Davie Beaton to Inverness, for there were no duties here for a Lyon King of Arms. Then the Cardinal arrived, and, summing up the situation quite quickly, decided that this was scarcely what he had financed this expensive expedition for, and persuaded the King that a move over to Orkney was indicated and would be rewarding. No King of Scots had visited the islands since MacBeth's time. Oliver Sinclair produced no objection. Beaton knew why. It seemed that Sinclair was pressing James to create him Earl of Orkney, on the grounds that it was only just, his forebears having held that rank under the Norse crown. Beaton was advising strongly against this, however. Caithness was dominating Sutherland; and if Orkney, which included the lordship of the Shetland Isles also, was handed over to Sinclair, this would create a vast semi-independent fief, almost a Sinclair kingdom, Norse-inclined, which could be highly dangerous, especially in its possible alliance with the Hebridean and West Highland chiefs. This was the real reason for taking James to Orkney – to let him see how important strategically, and how valuable a dependency, it was for the Scots crown.

So the rest of the fleet was sent for from Wick, and they sailed next morning, northwards, to cross the stormy and fabled Pentland Firth, no firth at all, of course, but a ten-mile-wide strait between the Atlantic and Norse oceans. The weather fortunately was fairly calm, but even so the seas were impressive and the ships tossed about direly, to the distress of the poorer sailors. They had brought along an experienced skipper from Wick, who knew these waters, for their hazards were legendary and none of the dozen shipmasters of the squadron were conversant with them. This pilot steered the flagship well clear of the dreaded Pentland Skerries, which could be seen to the east ominously spouting high clouds of spray; but also kept their route well to the east of the isolated Isle of Stroma, off which was one of the notorious roosts or whirlpools which bedevilled the Orkney seas, this one known as the Swelkie. These races, caused by the mighty Atlantic tides striking the shallow underwater tableland of the archipelago and swirling round the islands, had sunk ships innumerable.

Twenty miles north of Girnigoe they safely reached Brough Ness, the most southerly tip of Orkney, on the island of South Ronaldshay, to exclaim at its wild coastline of red-brown precipices, stacks, pinnacles, geos and caves, with inland apparently only endless moorland. Some six miles of this and they could see their sea-way narrowing notably before them, as other islands began to crowd in; and presently they entered a narrow passage between islands their pilot called Flotta and Burray, the Sound of Hoxa, where, despite the limited sailing-space, the vessels had to tack this way and that to counter the tide-race, a process which strung out the fleet.

However, once through this strait, they sailed into what was almost an inland sea, some eight or nine miles across, almost totally enclosed by islands, the mountainous Hoy to the west, the others low-lying and green. This was Scapa Flow, and after all the rough seas, its calm waters were like a benison.

But they were not to enjoy much of this, for their guide quite quickly ordered steering to starboard, apparently heading for an impassable barrier of islands reaching north from Burray. But at the last moment a passage opened through these, and they slipped through in line astern, to round another great ness, which was apparently the tip of Pomona, or the main island of the Orkneys – of which they were informed there were over sixty, not counting the innumerable small and uninhabited holms.

Sailing north again and then west, round a bewildering succession of isles, as the sun was sinking they saw ahead of them the smoke of what must be a town at the head of a deep bay. This it seemed was Kirkwall, the Orkney capital. It was obviously a large place, the biggest community they had touched at since leaving Leith. And closer approach showed it to be no mere huddle of hovels or decayed fishing-haven but a substantial burgh of good stone buildings, dominated by a great and handsome red-stone cathedral. The visitors were considerably impressed.

The harbour area was extensive, with many quays, for necessarily most traffic in Orkney would be by water. This was emphasised when they landed, for they found the streets of the town to be mere paved and narrow lanes between the houses, so winding and constricted as to make even Edinburgh's wynds seem like wide thoroughfares by comparison – but clean and uncluttered where the latter were apt to be filthy and obstructed with booths and stalls. Obviously horses and wheeled-vehicles were not to be looked for here. This, of course, had been a Viking town and Vikings were not horsemen nor anything but sailors.

There was no room for crowds in these strange streets either, but faces watched the new arrivals from every window and doorway, guarded, largely expressionless, silent, evoking a strange air of tension to temper the prevailing air, which was redolent of peat-smoke and fish.

None of the royal party ever having been here before, procedure was uncertain. Beaton suggested that the obvious place to make for was the cathedral, where someone ought to be found to direct them to the bishop's residence. Since the removal of the Sinclair earldom to Caithness there was no feudal lord here – indeed the land-holding system was not feudal at all, nor even clan-regulated, but udal, a kind of yeoman-freehold, after the Norse custom, and unfamiliar to the Scots. But the Bishops of Orkney were appointed from St. Andrews, and the present incumbent was in fact Robert Maxwell, kin to the Lord Maxwell, here present, and acted more or less as the crown's representative in the islands as well as the Church's.

At least it was easy enough to find the cathedral, even in that dense pack of buildings, for it occupied a gentle eminence, and anyway soared mightily above all. Emerging into the open space around it, even the most unimpressionable of the visitors could not but be struck by the splendour of this great edifice, by its sheer size, unexpected in such a remote area, but still more by the beauty of line and architecture, the symmetry of design and quiet restraint of ornament – all that in a pleasing warm rose-red stonework. Davie Beaton knew all about it, of course, although he had never before seen it, and explained something of its story. It had been built in 1137 by the Norse jarl Rognvald in fulfilment of a vow taken before a battle with his cousin Hakon, who had foully murdered *his* cousin the saintly Jarl Magnus; and so this great church was named St. Magnus's Cathedral, saintly jarls being distinctly uncommon here as elsewhere. Beaton was proposing that they move inside to inspect the renowned interior, when he was interrupted by a group which came hurrying down the road from westwards, a party of men-at-arms escorting an extraordinary equipage, something like a canopied horse-litter but borne by eight men in episcopal livery, not animals, in the cushioned and tasselled magnificence of which sat a plump and staring cleric. This entourage approached at the trot, to halt in front of the admiring company. The prelate held out a beringed hand, pointing.

"What is this? Who are you? Those ships – what are they?" he demanded. "I am Robert, Bishop of Orkney. Who are you who land here unbidden? Why am I not informed . . .?"

"Wheesht, Rob – wheesht!" Lord Maxwell exclaimed. "Can you no' see? Here is His Grace the King come visiting. Aye, and the Cardinal-Legate, forby."

"Save us – is that yourself, my lord?" The Bishop peered, evidently short-sighted. "The Cardinal, you say? The King? Lord have mercy . . .!" Convulsively he sought to get out of his litter but made an awkward job of it until his gawping bearers set the thing down and he stumbled out, waving agitated hands in incoherent apology.

"Never heed, my lord, never heed," James said. "We could not inform you of our coming. This is a fine kirk you have here. If your palace is of a like quality, we shall fare none so ill!"

"Eh . . .? Ah . . . umm. Yes, Sire – to be sure, Sire. My poor house is at your command, your disposal. If, if so you wish. If . . . it is not far." That sounded less than hearty, as the Bishop appeared to be counting heads.

"Then lead us there, my lord," Beaton commanded crisply. "We can see your cathedral tomorrow."

Hastily agreeing, Bishop Robert asked if the King would travel in his litter, and when James dismissed the suggestion, perforce waved the thing away, since he could hardly ride whilst the monarch walked. They moved off in a straggle.

It was no distance to go to what was now the seat of government of Orkney; indeed it was just across the road, although the courtyard-entrance and gatehouse was round a corner and down a long range of building. An extraordinary building it was too, although scarcely rivalling the noble cathedral, handsome as it was commodious and longer than any to be seen in Scotland. At one end was a great round tower, and a splendid oriel window projected from what must be the hall, supported on elaborate corbels. The courtyard was flanked by further fine subsidiary and domestic quarters. Few of the great nobles present could boast so fine a residence. Nor, to be sure, could any claim that a king had died in their house – for herein had the Norse King Hakon expired after the disastrous Battle of Largs in 1263.

Catering for this unexpected influx of important visitors undoubtedly taxed the Bishop and his staff, but however humdrum the provision it surprised them to find it served on magnificent gold and silver plate, in a hall hung with notable tapestries and floored with rich carpets. James remarked to the Cardinal that he saw now why he had advised this visit to Orkney, and the assertions that it ought to be a brighter jewel in the Scots crown. Beaton nodded and took the opportunity to point out, low-voiced so that Oliver Sinclair at the King's other side would not hear him, that it would be folly indeed to grant away all this, and what it represented in wealth and manpower and trade, as an earldom. Orkney should remain a crown fief, and be better developed as such. Give away some other token, a grant on its customs or rentals, if so desired, but keep the lordship.

In the days that followed, James came to recognise the wisdom of that advice, as he saw more of Kirkwall and the nearer Orkney Isles, discovering with some surprise that it was all far more populous and prosperous than he had had any idea of or thought possible. Like most other Lowlanders he had scarcely considered these far-northerly islands as other than a mere remote and probably barbarous fringe of his kingdom, when he had considered them at all. The Hebrides and the isles of the West Highlands were different, for they kept pushing themselves into the southron consciousness, in revolt, challenge and the warfare of clan rivalries. But Orkney . . .

There was another aspect of the islands, or at least of the islanders, which presently manifested itself all too evidently – their sturdy independence and toughness of character. This, forcibly demonstrated, indeed hastened the royal departure after only three days. It was the Kirkwall folk's reaction to the southern invasion of soldiery and seamen from the fleet, these tending to behave as idle fighting men are apt to do everywhere – to the much offence of the townspeople. There were riots and battles in those narrow, twisting streets, broken heads and limbs. When the locals threatened to bring in reinforcements of fishermen and farmers from the surrounding islands to teach the Lowlanders a lesson, the King recognised that it was time to be gone. His armed force had been brought to teach their own lesson to the Highland West, not to upset the inoffensive Orkneymen. Besides, James soon had had enough of the place's attractions. There was no hunting here worth considering, and though no lack of women, these did not find their way up to the Bishop's palace – and there was overmuch competition, for the monarch, down in the town. He had presided over the one justice-eyre – although they did not call it that here – but since the language used was a form of Norse, and unintelligible to him, as were the udaller customs, he quickly grew bored.

So, on the fourth day, they all re-embarked and set sail, and undoubtedly Orkney was glad to see its liege-lord go, even though in a gesture James created Kirkwall a royal burgh, with the privileges that status implied. Also, to console Sinclair over not getting the earldom, he bestowed on him the collection of the rentals on payment of two thousand pounds to the crown, which would work out very profitably for all concerned, save the udallers.

Now the fleet voyaged south by west, back into the Pentland Firth and along the attractive north Caithness and Sutherland coast, this becoming ever more scenic and Highland as they went west, with golden beaches, offshore islands, sea-lochs and mountains rising higher and more spectacular. In the face of a westerly breeze, with much tacking, it took them all day to reach and round the mighty Cape Wrath or Hvarf, meaning the turning-point, the extreme north-west tip of mainland Scotland, its soaring cliffs in unending battle with the Atlantic rollers. They sailed on westwards into the sunset, making for Lewis and Harris and the Outer Hebrides, forty miles more.

David Lindsay went on deck to a surprise, next morning. It was to what seemed almost like a new world, in the early sunshine, a world of colour and light and beauty such as he had never experienced before, breathtaking. The ships were at anchor in a bay of size and shape none so different from the one they had left at Kirkwall. But the difference was extraordinary nevertheless, and not only in the surroundings, the hills and valleys – no mountains these – the scattered woodland, missing on Orkney, the flaming gorse-bushes and gleaming birch-trunks. It was the colour which seemed to change all, a strange lucency in air and sea as well as in the hues of rock and vegetation. It took him some time to reach some conclusion on what might be responsible for this, before deciding that it was probably the sea itself basically, that the water seemed to be clearer and somehow warmer than that of the Norse Sea, and that the seaweeds which it supported were not the usual dark greens and dull browns but multi-coloured and vivid reds and yellows, emerald and even purple. Not only this but the sand so evident below the clear water was pure white, presumably formed of ground up cockle-shells rather than rock sediment, and this had the effect of enhancing the colours and producing a lightness over the entire scene. The reason for all this he knew not, but the poet in him rejoiced and marvelled at such transformation, overnight, sudden and unexpected as it was.

There was no actual town here, flanking the deep bay they were in, apparently, but a prolonged scatter of low-browed, thatched housing stretching almost as far as eye could see just back from the shoreline and dotting the lower slopes behind, but not reaching far up into the heather moorland and low hills which obviously comprised most of the interior. This was the Isle of Lewis, the shipmaster informed, and this bay, anchorage and community was called Stornoway. They had come here for Roderick MacLeod, one of the chiefs who had supported Donald Greumach's rising. This was allegedly his chief place, but where his castle might be was unclear, for there was no sign of anything such in view.

Later, when the King and his company went ashore, their attitude and that of the entire expedition was as different from what it had been hitherto as was the colour, scene and climate. Now all was stern, military, even threatening. It was not the progress of a cordial monarch through his so-far unvisited domains, but the descent of a punitive war-lord on a rebellious area. Not that there was the least sign of rebellion or even hostility now on the part of the populace which turned out to greet them, and Lewis was evidently populous; only interest, wonder, sometimes even hesitant gestures of welcome. The large guard around James, bristling with arms, and the cannon threatening all from every ship, seemed rather ridiculous in the circumstances.

When the visitors' fluent Gaelic-speakers asked where was the castle of Roderick MacLeod of the Lewes, as he was styled, they were directed to something called Dun MacNicol, the chief's house, north-west along the loch shore, hidden behind a shoulder of hill but not far distant, they were assured.

Whatever the distance, they did not have to go all the way, for presently the royal party met another group coming towards them, at speed, and eyecatching by any standards. This consisted of one enormous man dressed in tartans, mounted on a shaggy Highland garron and flanked by fully a score of running-gillies, bare save for short ragged kilts but each bearing an unsheathed broadsword over one naked shoulder and a gleaming dirk in the other hand. These came on at a fast run and faltered nothing at sight of the approaching company.

They halted in dramatic fashion only a few feet in front

of the visitors – who for their part *had* faltered a little at this headlong encounter, even though five times as many.

"MacLeod," the big man barked briefly; and in a single shout his escort repeated the name, bringing their broadswords from the slope into a forward-pointing position, a highly effective introduction.

Even Davie Beaton was at something of a loss as to how to counter this suitably. Lindsay conceived it to be his duty to try, at least.

"Then, MacLeod, here is your liege-lord James, High King of Scots, come with his court. And the Cardinal-Legate, Archbishop of St. Andrews. And the High Constable of this realm. And the Lord High Admiral. And, and others." That was the best that he could do.

The chief stared, and blurted out something in the Gaelic. It did not sound complimentary.

"I am James," the King said. "Are you Roderick MacLeod? Of the Lewes?"

"I am."

"Then get you down from that horse, man. Do you sit while your king stands?"

"Are you in truth James Stewart? What brings you here? To the Lewes?"

"*You* do! I have come for you, MacLeod. Tell him, Davie."

Lindsay coughed. "I am Lord Lyon King of Arms," he informed. "His Grace has come to these parts to enforce his royal authority. After the wicked and treasonable rising, led by Donald Greumach MacDonald of Sleat. In which rising you, sir, took armed part. His Grace now comes to make a reckoning."

The other, still sitting his garron, looked incredulous. "A reckoning . . .?" he wondered. "Here? With MacLeod?"

"Aye, man – with MacLeod!" the King exclaimed. "And not only with you. With all the treacherous Highlands and Islands rogues who rose against me, a year past, at the behest of Henry of England – MacDonalds, Mackenzies, Macleans and the rest, as well as MacLeods. I will have no more of it. I take you back with me to Stirling, you and the others. Hostages. Do you hear – hostages? For the good behaviour hereafter of these rebellious isles."

"Myself? MacLeod! You think to take *me* prisoner, James Stewart?" The disbelief on the big man's face was almost laughable.

"I do. But I said hostage, not prisoner."

Davie Beaton spoke up. "I am Beaton, the Papal Legate. His Grace makes a notable distinction, MacLeod. A hostage goes as the King's guest, not as a captive. As a gesture of goodwill and promise of betterment. No prisoner but a guest."

"And what if I refuse this king's hospitality, Sir Priest? Preferring my own isles to his Lowland fortress!"

"Then it might be necessary to seek to persuade you more strongly, my friend. But . . . let us hope not!"

"We have sufficient of persuasion here, MacLeod," the Earl of Huntly put in. "Two thousand of broadswords in yonder ships!"

"And cannon enough to blow your castle and every hovel on this island to pieces!" Arran the Admiral added. "Even now they are trained on this Stornoway."

"Choose you," James said.

Roderick MacLeod was clearly a man of decision as well as of presence. With an extraordinary change of stance, in more ways than one, he stepped down from his horse – stepping was almost all that was required, owing to his length of legs and the shortness of those of his mount – and swept off his bonnet, with its three chiefly feathers, in an elaborate bow, smiling broadly.

"At such kind urging, who could refuse, whatever!" he declared. "I, and mine, are at Your Grace's service, I do assure you."

"Ah! I . . . ah . . . umm." James looked around him, at a loss as to how to deal with this sudden change of attitude.

Beaton was more agile. "Excellent! I was sure that MacLeod of the Lewes would respond to royal courtesy," he said pleasantly.

"To be sure. What else, at all? MacLeod can offer his own courtesies. To you all. My poor house is yours, for your refreshment. After shipboard fare, you will favour it, no doubt. You have not far to go. Beyond the trees, there. It will be my pleasure." And abruptly vaulting on to his horse again, the man jerked a single word to his clansmen and, wheeling the beast round, without another glance, set off at the trot whence he had come. The escort turning about as one man and, swords on shoulders again, ran alongside.

Astonished, the royal party stared after them and at each other, exclaiming, some declaring insolence, some that the man was mad, others that it was but a trap to ensnare them. But Beaton held otherwise, pointing out that Highland manners and customs differed from their own and that MacLeod was but making the best of a bad situation. Lindsay agreed, asserting that the chief had clearly been impressed by word of the numbers of swords and cannon against him, and the threat to his people; and that would prevail over any notion of an attack hereafter. If MacLeod were to be taken as a hostage, then they had better follow him to his castle and achieve their aim with the least possible trouble.

James accepted this advice, and they moved on.

Rounding the wooded shoulder, they came upon a small and hitherto hidden inlet of the main bay, above the head of which rose a rocky mound, crowned by a peculiar building, at least to Lowland eyes, not the sort of castle they were used to. This appeared to consist of only curtain-walls, following the shape of the site, but rising considerably higher than usual, fully forty feet, and obviously topped by a parapet and wall-walk on which sentinels could be seen to pace. There was no keep nor angle towers, merely this lofty walled enclosure, no moat nor drawbridge nor portcullis. A great arched gateway therein stood open. Scattered around, landward, were cothouses and barns, with small black cattle grazing.

As they approached, MacLeod reappeared in the gateway, to wave them on. At the same time he waved in the other direction, and out from the interior marched a couple of his clansmen; but these, if they were the same, had exchanged their swords for bagpipes. Playing lustily some stirring air, this pair came on to meet the visitors, and in front of the King wheeled round to lead the way back to that strange castle.

The royal company followed on, not without embarrassment, some stepping out to the brisk music, if that is what it could be called, some deliberately not.

"Welcome to Dun MacNicol," MacLeod boomed out at them, and ushered them in through the walling.

Within was a further surprise. It was as though they had entered a walled town in miniature, more spacious than it appeared from outside, and all open to the sky. Lean-to buildings surrounded what was really a great courtyard, unpaved; but there were other buildings erected therein also, including a long hallhouse, clearly the chief's own quarters. Domestic constructions appeared to include stabling and byres as well as storehouses, brewery and the like, also servitors' housing. Milk-cows were tethered beside bog-hay heaps and poultry clucked around.

The Lowland lords stared in disbelief at this chiefly establishment.

Nevertheless, MacLeod was all the attentive and courteous host now, leading his guests through the clutter to the hallhouse, and ordering a steward to provide the men-at-arms with ale and whisky. Indoors, in a huge raftered hall with a central fireplace, the peat-smoke from which rose to escape through a hole in the roof, blackening the said rafters, women were laying out cold meats, curds, oaten cakes, honey and bread, with a variety of wines unexpected, and, of course, the local whisky in inexhaustible supply.

James was somewhat doubtful about partaking of this hospitality, when he was about to remove the chief from his hearth and home, however odd; but MacLeod seemed to take the situation for granted now, asking how many supporters he might take with him, how long he would be likely to be away, and so on – which was a help. Incidentally, he volunteered details of the late Donald Greumach's end, which had brought the recent rising to an untimely close, how, outside Mackenzie's castle of Eilean Donan, Donald had been struck by a MacRae arrow, and choosing to pluck it out from his leg there and then, he had burst the major artery and bled to death – an impatient man according to MacLeod.

Refreshment partaken of, James declared that they must get back to the ships. Was MacLeod ready? The chief, making no fuss nor plea for delay, said that the King's pleasure was his own. So, the visitors somewhat bemused, by more than the whisky, the move out was made. As a gesture, MacLeod offered the King his garron to ride, and when this was declined, promptly mounted the beast himself, and with his team of running gillies forming up around him again, and the two pipers blowing in front, led the way back to Stornoway haven, in surely as strange a hostage-taking as any there had ever experienced.

They sailed with the evening tide, after declining an escort of MacLeod galleys and birlinns.

Next day they called in at Harris, the southern part of what was known as the Long Island, different in character from the Lewis end, mountainous and highly picturesque. The MacLeods were a double clan, descendants of the two sons of Leod, himself a son of Olaf, King of Man in the twelfth century. These sons, Tormad, or Norman, and Torquil, founded the Siol Torquil of Lewis, and the Siol Tormad of Harris and Dunvegan. Their present hostage's opposite number, of Harris, turned out to be at his other seat of Dunvegan, on Skye, in the Inner Hebrides. They took his bewildered brother as security meantime, however, his Lewis kinsman laughing heartily.

The squadron visited North and South Uist, still in the Outer Hebrides, MacDonald territory, but found no chiefly personages there worthy of taking hostage. Despite its intended punitive character the expedition was developing ever more of a holiday atmosphere, sailing in brilliant weather through perhaps the most lovely scenery in Northern Europe, with no signs of opposition, indeed welcome of a sort wherever they chose to land. James, who even managed some hunting here and there, quite fell in love with the Isles, and declared that he would incorporate its lordship into the Scottish crown in perpetuity, so that he himself would now be the famed Lord of the Isles.

They sailed eastwards from Lochboisdale in South Uist the thirty miles across the Sea of the Hebrides to Skye, its spectacular mountains beckoning them on. The strange flat-topped summits of two, which were apparently called MacLeod's Tables, guided them towards the scenic Loch Dunvegan, where, in another of the strange fort-like West Highland castles they found the chief of Siol Torquil, Alexander MacLeod of Harris, a younger man with a still younger wife and two babies, and less resigned than his kinsman of the Lewes to accompany the royal party. But shown that there was no option, he capitulated with a decent grace, and at Roderick's suggestion offered the King a day or two's hunting and hawking, before the move was made.

Thereafter they went east-about round the northern tip of Skye and down the Sound of Raasay, on their way to Sleat, the late Donald Greumach's own lands. Half-way, at evening – and these were no waters to negotiate even in the half-dark of a Highland summer – James was interested to pay a call at the main Skye anchorage of Portree, under the challenging Cuillin Mountains for here King Hakon of Norway had put in on his way to his great defeat by the Scots under Alexander the Third at Largs, in 1263, a victory which ended the Norse and Viking domination of this whole seaboard. He learned that was how the place got its present name, *port-an-righ* meaning merely the haven of the King, which was formerly called Kiltaraglen. Liking Portree, James remained there for a few days.

Perhaps that was foolish for, when they moved on down the narrow Sound of Raasay and through the still narrower Kyles of Lochalsh and Rhea into the Sound of Sleat, in that network of islands, sea-lochs and channels, it was to discover when they came to Armadale Castle, on the Sleat peninsula, that their main bird had flown. This was Donald Gorm MacDonald, son of the late Donald Greumach, who was now presumably claiming the lordship of the Isles in his father's stead, and who, because of the delay at Portree, had had time to hear of the royal presence and to make his escape. According to locals interrogated at Armadale, he and some of his near kin had sailed forthwith for England and the protection of King Henry. So the holidaying fell to be paid for.

The King was annoyed, but there was compensation. They learned also that before sailing, young Donald Gorm had thoughtfully sent a messenger to warn another of the MacDonald chieftains, John Moidartach, Captain of Clanranald, the one they had failed to find on the Uists but who at present apparently was staying at a secondary house of his at Trotternish in the north of Skye, an area they had already passed. So it was turn around and sail back northwards, right to the tip of that huge island, round which, on the west coast, they came with all speed to the isolated castle of Duntulm only a couple of miles from the topmost cape, Hunish. And whether the messenger had been slow, or chosen a different route, or Clanranald unheeding, they found him at Duntulm, actually out hunting; and not only so, he had with him as guest none other than the third of the MacDonald chiefs, Alexander of Glengarry. So, with the mere minimum of trouble, they were able to collect two-thirds of the MacDonald hierarchy.

At Duntulm James decided on another gesture – this against the advice of both Beaton and Lindsay but at Oliver Sinclair's urging. While he was up here, he would go and take in John of Kintail, chief of the Mackenzies – after all they had passed the mouth of Loch Duich, at Kyle of Lochalsh, where presumably he was to be found. Protesting that this was pointless, for John had been *against* Donald Greumach's rising, the two Davids pointed out that it was while attacking the Mackenzie castle in Kintail that Donald had died. But Sinclair argued that all these Highland chiefs were dangerous, treacherous dogs and should be taught a lesson. He prevailed with the King, and they sailed round Hunish again and down the long east coast of Skye back to the narrow Kyle of Lochalsh, from which opened Loch Duich and Kintail, on the mainland now.

Eilean Donan Castle, built on a tiny island on the mouth of the loch, the Mackenzie seat, was a notably strong place and all but impregnable to ordinary assault; but not to heavy cannon-fire. And even the heroic defiance of the hereditary MacRae defenders thereof, known all over the north-west as 'Mackenzie's Shirt of Mail', could not hold out against the squadron's artillery bombardment – the only opportunity so far to use the cannon. John Mackenzie surrendered, protesting that he was a loyal subject, but was sent to join the other chiefs. They made an interesting, colourful and indeed impressive group, however much most of the Lowland lords shunned them.

There was only the one more hostage-to-be on James's list now – Maclean of Duart. His stronghold was on the large island of Mull, some eighty miles to the south. On the way, they called in at Castle Tioram, on Loch Moidart, Clanranald's main seat, to inform his lady that he would be absent for a season, and to engage in some further hunting and feasting. Then on past the tremendous peninsula and headland of Ardnamurchan, the most westerly point of mainland Britain, before turning eastwards into the long Sound of Mull.

Hector Maclean of Duart was renowned as a notably fiery character of independent if unpredictable views and with a large and powerful clan, and it was feared that here, at the last, the expedition might have a fight on its hands. All were warned to be ready for action. But in the event there was none, for arriving at Duart, a magnificent stronghold towering over bay and Sound, on a rocky bluff, they found a galley-fleet at anchor below, but no sign of the Maclean. On a wet morning, the King and company went ashore unassailed, and were being entertained by Lady Maclean when Hector came sailing into his bay in a small sixteen-oared birlinn, from Morvern, and was promptly apprehended by the royal forces and sent to join the other chiefs, to his much bewilderment.

The fine weather seeming to have broken at last, and James having had almost a sufficiency of cruising, it was decided that enough was enough. They would head directly down to the Firth of Clyde and disembark at Dumbarton, a mere three days' voyage, round the Mull of Kintyre.

This they did in driving rain and freshening winds, with domestic comforts consequently beginning to appeal to all, even the hostages. They arrived at Dumbarton in early August, after six weeks' cruising and not a single real battle, with the principal Isles chiefs safely in custody and the north-west tamed, for the time-being at least. King and court and hostages commandeered horses for the thirty-five-mile ride to Stirling, and the shipmasters were instructed to reprovision their vessels and sail back right round Scotland again to their east coast ports.

Davie Beaton confided to Lindsay that he was satisfied with his investment of moneys.

7

Despite the undoubted success of the sea-borne expedition, his effective marriage and the birth of the long-desired heir to the throne, James Stewart was depressed and more moody than he had ever been – to the concern of many but especially of three, the Queen naturally, David Lindsay and Davie Beaton. Marie de Guise, who was pregnant again, confided in Janet Lindsay that she was sure that the King was not well, in person and mind both, instancing his sudden and unaccountable outbursts of hot temper, followed by periods of extreme lassitude, his complaining of abdominal pains and, significantly, his unusual lack of interest in matters of sex. Others were aware of this last, for James had never sought to hide his roving after women, marriage notwithstanding, and he was still only in his late twenties.

But what was causing almost more concern was in these circumstances the King's turning ever more and more to Oliver Sinclair for company and, unfortunately, guidance and advice. Beaton in particular worried over this, as countering his own influence in affairs of state, since he, and others, had no illusions as to Sinclair's competence or wisdom. James was now more apt to have that young man sharing his bedchamber than the Queen, of a night. Not that that necessarily implied a catamite relationship; but in view of the King's lifelong preoccupation with women, it was a strange development.

One result of this intensified association of the two young men was a course of action which hitherto none of the monarch's other advisers had been sufficiently ruthless to urge or contrive. Sinclair had developed a smouldering hatred and jealousy for the Bastard of Arran – who, after all, had himself shared the royal bedchamber in the past – and now prevailed on James to do more than merely banish him from the court. The Bastard had been lying fairly low of late, as far as national affairs were concerned, although cutting a wide swathe in the Clyde valley and Hamilton area, and devoting his undoubted energies and skills to the building of a magnificent castle at Craignethan, near Lanark, suitable for a man who amongst other offices of profit had been the King's Palace-Master and Surveyor of Buildings. Now Sinclair persuaded James to authorise him to take a troop of horse unannounced to Lanarkshire, arrest the Bastard secretly and hurry back with him to Stirling.

This was done, and the first that David Lindsay and others heard of it was that Sir James Hamilton of Finnart was bestowed in a deep dungeon of Stirling Castle in durance vile, not like the Highland hostages who were ensconced in reasonably comfortable quarters there, as more or less honoured guests.

When Beaton heard of this, he came hot-foot from St. Andrews to see the King. Thereafter he came to the Lindsays, in considerable agitation for that cool customer.

"This is folly," he declared. "And highly dangerous. The Bastard was meantime doing no harm, posing no threat to the realm. Now he is made into a martyr, for no reason. And the whole house of Hamilton angered. Over nothing, save this Sinclair's spleen."

"I know it. I urged James to hold him hostage, if he must, like the Islesmen. Not necessarily here at Stirling. But he would not."

"He is going to bring him to trial. On a charge of high treason! Can you credit it? The danger of that. With all the Hamilton ramifications."

"What treason is this?"

"What but that old story of twelve years ago! The alleged plot to slay the King, by the Earl of Angus and his Douglases. You remember it? Now James is saying that he has evidence that the Bastard was involved also. Finnart, who has always been the enemy of the Douglases! He says that another renegade Hamilton has come forward with the evidence – James Hamilton of Kincavil, Sheriff of Linlithgow, who was brother to the Abbot Patrick Hamilton of Ferne . . ."

"Ha – the one you burned! As heretic. And whom the Bastard helped you to condemn!"

"He *was* a dangerous heretic. The Bastard did only his duty. But – this is crazy-mad! To make enemies of the Hamiltons without cause. And now! They are the second most powerful house in Scotland, after the Douglases – who are already James's enemies. Arran, the Bastard's half-brother, is still next heir to the throne if the new baby-prince should not survive. As well as being Admiral, he is allied to half of the noble houses of the south-west. To alienate the Hamiltons, when Henry is threatening invasion with Douglas aid, is beyond all in folly. But James is adamant, I find."

"He is not well. He is acting very strangely, in more than this. Can you not do anything? As Papal Legate, even?"

"What can a Legate do in this? High treason is one offence outwith my powers. Henry Tudor will rub his blood-stained hands! For whatever else, the Bastard has always been *his* enemy."

James and Oliver Sinclair had their way in this matter. They arranged a quick and almost secret trial before a small group of carefully selected Privy Councillors, officers-of-state rather than great nobles, the result of which was a foregone conclusion, despite the Bastard's fleeringly skilful defence and challenge to put the issue to the test of armed personal combat with his namesake and accuser. He was found guilty and condemned to execution there and then, with no delay permitted.

David Lindsay perforce had to observe the execution, since the King was present to see it done. He watched the beheading with reluctance and distress, but also with mixed feelings about justice. For, of course, James Hamilton of Finnart was a scoundrel who, if any did, well deserved death, having been responsible for innumerable killings in his day, including the cold-blooded murder of the Earl of Lennox, unarmed and wounded after the Battle of Linlithgow Bridge in 1526, this before Lindsay's own eyes. That he himself was now dying on a trumped-up charge, admittedly held a sort of grim irony. He died well, defiant to the end.

The threatened visit of the English envoys, Sir Ralph Sadler and the Bishop of St. David's, materialised soon thereafter, enjoyed by none. James left most of the dealings – they could scarcely be called negotiations – to Beaton as Chancellor; and if the Bishop of St. David's was somewhat overawed by having to cope with a cardinal and *Legatus a Latere*, clearly Sadler was not, even though the situation was otherwise embarrassing; for the main burden of Henry's message was for James to get rid of Beaton and initiate a taking over of the Scots Church after the English model. Sadler was a shrewd and experienced ambassador, but arrogant, and on this occasion made little concession to diplomatic convention or even simple courtesy. He had come to deliver an ultimatum, and that was all. King Henry required an interview with King James, to settle outstanding differences, as well as the matter of the Church; and if this was not forthcoming he would invade. It was as elementary as that. He would make one conciliatory gesture, by coming half-way to meet the Scots, namely to York, where he would look to see his nephew at a date to be arranged, the following year. When Beaton pointed out that York was still in the middle of England, and so an unsuitable venue for any meeting of independent monarchs which, if held at all, should obviously be on the borderline. this was brushed aside as irrelevant, and indications given of the size and quality of the forces King Henry was prepared to allot for the successful conclusion of the problems between the two kingdoms. That was it, that was all – an ultimatum. The Scots, for their part, were perhaps less straightforward if more diplomatic. They said to tell King Henry that these weighty matters must necessarily be discussed by the parliament of the realm, before King James could come to any final decision, this being the Scottish way, if not the English.

The envoys departed, in mutual disesteem.

James himself seemed strangely uninterested in all this, although clearly with no intention of meeting his uncle at York or anywhere else. But a parliament was duly called for just before Yuletide.

As parliaments went it was an unexciting and predictable affair, with no real attempt made to consider the English proposals, which all agreed were quite unacceptable. What was conceded was that the best way to avoid Henry's threatened invasion was to make clear and evident military preparations to resist anything such, so that Henry would recognise, well informed by spies as he was, that the cost of any such attack would be high. So the assembly was concerned mainly with arrangements and promises for the mustering of men – and here James's deliberate policy of lessening the power of his great nobles told against him grievously, notably now the Hamiltons, for it was from the levies of the lords that the main manpower of the nation was to be raised. It was agreed that some of the Highland hostages should be offered their freedom to return home, if they promised to raise their clansmen for the army – although this was recognised as having its dangers if these should choose to change sides at a time of crisis.

For the rest, the parliament was concerned mainly with the annexation of the Hebrides to the crown in perpetuity, and further secular measures against reformers of the Church, on the demand of the Papal Legate.

Yule festivities at Stirling obviously going to be much muted on account of the King's lassitude and the Queen's pregnancy, David and Janet Lindsay were able to obtain leave-of-absence to return to the Mount of Lindifferon for their own quiet celebrations.

The spring of 1541 started well, with the birth of a second son to James and Marie, to be called Arthur, Duke of Albany, so that the succession now appeared to be fairly surely established. Then, soon after, Margaret Tudor died, at Methven – and although this should hardly be hailed as good news, and the court went into nominal mourning, the fact was that the Queen-Mother's departure came as a relief to almost everyone, for she had always been a difficult and aggressive woman and a disruptive influence in the kingdom. Whether Henry, at Windsor, mourned his sister any more than did her son at Stirling, was not to be known; but having just married his fourth wife, Anne, daughter of the German Duke of Cleves, he perhaps was finding consolation. Whether, then, it was these events or merely the effects of spring, James's spirits improved somewhat, to the relief of Queen and court; and he chose to demonstrate this by a return to his enthusiasm for the handsome reconstruction of the palace within Stirling Castle, and also a wider campaign of improvement of various royal castles and houses, particularly the extensions to the Abbey of the Holy Rood at Edinburgh to be a palace independent of the monastic premises – where, of course, he had been held as good as prisoner for so much of his boyhood, this to replace the distinctly cramped and primitive royal quarters in Edinburgh Castle. His advisers were glad enough to encourage him in this preoccupation, even though it might seem an odd activity for a monarch awaiting almost certain invasion.

And then disaster struck. Not the feared English armed assault yet but a more personal tragedy. James and Marie were returning from a visit to Aberdeenshire and Angus, surveying royal castles, when an urgent messenger from the Lord Erskine, Keeper at Stirling, reached them with dire tidings. The baby Arthur Stewart of Albany had died. Not only so, but his brother James, Duke of Rothesay, was ill, vomiting and eating nothing. Appalled, the royal party spurred for home.

They arrived to further horror. The child James was dead also.

The King, with the hand of God so clearly upon him, sank into utter dejection and depression. Marie bore up bravely.

There were, of course, the usual suggestions of poison or even witchcraft. But both Janet and the Lady Erskine had been with the little princes throughout their sicknesses and could assure that there had been no suspicious circumstances, no strangers present, and they vouched for the integrity of the nurses. Such ideas therefore gained no credence.

Gloom lay upon the land, with a sense of foreboding, despite an unusually fine summer.

Davie Beaton, with David Paniter the King's secretary, went off to Rome, to report progress, and to France to seek some sort of threatening gesture against England, to inhibit Henry in his designs on Scotland.

It was in these circumstances that Sir Ralph Sadler paid a second brief visit to James, and in still more arrogant mood than previously. The brevity of both stay and his message was to be emphasised. Henry would be at York in early October for one week. He would look to see his nephew there at that time. Or else . . .

James Stewart, in his present state, more or less shrugged this off. And in Beaton's absence abroad, Sadler was sent whence he came without much attempt at diplomatic nicety. He had announced, incidentally, that Henry had now proclaimed himself to be King of Ireland, and left the significance of that to sink into Scots minds.

With James turned almost recluse and desiring only Oliver Sinclair's company, there was little of official duty for the Lord Lyon, and the Lindsays were able to spend much of the summer and autumn at Lindifferon – which suited them very well, although Janet's increasing closeness to the Queen was a limiting factor. Marie de Guise was proving not only a far better wife than James deserved but an admirable queen-consort, taking on not a few of the duties which the monarch ought to have carried out, deputising for him with quiet and gracious assurance. She was a woman of experience, of course, and had been reared in the courtly and powerful Lorraine family, and as the former Duchess de Longueville, used to exercising authority for an ailing husband.

October came and went, and instead of being interviewed by Henry Tudor at York, his nephew granted interview to a deputation of Irish chiefs and kinglets who came to offer him the throne of All Ireland, as counter to the Tudor's arrogant assumption of that crown. James, with no intention of doing so, said that he would consider the matter with his advisers.

Beaton's return from France and Rome was followed almost immediately by a demonstration that Henry had been making no idle threats over non-compliance with his demands. It was not yet full-scale invasion – possibly the ostentatious massing of French troops and shipping and talk of a pact between the Emperor, the Vatican and France to bring down Henry and restore the establishment of Holy Church in England, all sedulously propagated by Cardinal Beaton, although there was little real truth behind it, had something to do with it; but it was a raid in strength over the Border into Teviotdale, in the Middle March, led by the English Warden and Captain of Norham Castle, Sir Robert Bowes, a veteran commander.

The Scots, to be sure, had been anticipating something of the sort and had plans made. The Warden of their March, Sir Walter Ker of Cessford, sought to contain the thrust from his base at Roxburgh, while he sent for reinforcements from the King. But the attack developed along a wide front – Bowes had three thousand men it was said, and the Warden required many more men to hold it. And when word was forthcoming that the renegade Earl of Angus was with Bowes, with his brother Sir George Douglas, seeking to rally his Douglases to rise on Henry's behalf, then it was recognised that a major reaction was necessary. The Earl of Huntly, who these days was accepted as the kingdom's foremost soldier – which was perhaps not very significant, for Scotland had not been involved in full-scale warfare since Flodden, almost thirty years before – was sent south with a similar number, three thousand, and instructions to involve the Lord Home and his East March clan, who were to be given this opportunity to redeem themselves over past misdeeds, and prove a counter to the Douglases. And David Lindsay found himself conscripted to accompany the force, on the supposition that he was an expert on borderland fighting, thanks to his co-operation with the late Sieur de la Bastie, when that gallant Frenchman was Warden of the Marches. Also he had had ample experience of dealing with the Homes, which might be useful.

Mustering on the Burgh Muir of Edinburgh, they rode southwards by Fala and Soutra and the western Lammermuirs, and down Lauderdale. At Cowdenknowes, just beyond the Earlstoun of Ersildoune, where the fifth Lord

Home tended to reside, Home Castle itself, ten miles to the east, having become too battered during his difficult brother's and predecessor's days to provide comfortable living, they found the Homes sufficiently apprised of the situation, indeed better informed than they were. Lord Home himself had already gone east to raise the bulk of his clan, presumably in the interests of self rather than national defence. David Lindsay was deputed to go after him and bring him and his people on to join Huntly's force in Teviotdale. Home Castle itself was, of course, the traditional clan rallying-place.

That castle, on its isolated ridge in the Merse, the great rolling, fertile plain of the East March so largely composed of Home lairdships, was already thronged with armed and horsed men, hundreds of them, when he reached it, the tough mosstroopers of the Borderland, the best horsemen in the kingdom. Home himself was there, and greeted David warily. He was a very different character from his executed brother, retiring, almost diffident by nature, and a strange leader for his warlike house. But the Home relationship with the crown, indeed with the rest of Scotland, had long been uneasy. However, when he heard that Huntly had three thousand men and that the King looked to him to prove the Home loyalty and help, not only to drive the English back over the Border but to keep the Douglases from rising to aid them, he made no objection, indeed more or less admitting that this last was what they had been mustering to do anyway, the Home-Douglas rivalry being long-standing, traditional.

Home, who had many messengers out to gather in the manpower of the outlying lairdships, said that he had four hundred assembled already, but could double that in a couple of days. His information was that Bowes and Angus were burning their way down Teviotdale, probably to attack Jedburgh. Ker of Cessford was doing his best to delay and divert them, but he was heavily outnumbered.

David declared that in these circumstances time was of the essence. They must save a massacre at Jedburgh if at all possible. Huntly would require immediate aid. Waiting for two days could be fatal. Let them ride at once with the four hundred, the others to follow on later.

Home and his lairds accepted that and a move was ordered.

There was no point in heading back to Lauderdale and the upper Tweed, so they rode almost due southwards for Kelso and Roxburgh, where Tweed and Teviot joined, some six miles. And at that fair town they gained news. The Earl of Huntly and his force had managed to reach Jedburgh first, and were now occupying the town, eleven miles west of Kelso. The invaders had moved on eastwards, just why was not certain, but in the circumstances it looked as though they might well be awaiting reinforcements and possibly cannon, before attacking a walled town now held by a force as large as their own. The Border in this area was only a few miles away, and Norham, Bowes's headquarters as English Warden, comparatively close, some fifteen miles from Kelso. He would have cannon there. So that *could* be the strategy. To wait near the Borderline, for artillery and more men, and then to attack. And not necessarily Jedburgh first. Kelso itself would be nearer and less defensible.

David asked the town's provost what the Scots Warden, Ker of Cessford, was doing? Nobody knew for sure, but it was assumed that he was still harrying the English flanks without risking an outright clash.

What to do, then? Just to ride west and join Huntly in overcrowded Jedburgh seemed pointless and a waste of this so mobile force of horsed fighting men. But four hundred were not such as might usefully attack almost ten times as many, even in conjunction with Ker. Yet this would be the time to assail the English, while they were waiting, idling – if that indeed were the position.

Home sent out three groups of scouts, south-east, south and south-west to try to locate the enemy. Once they knew just where the English were, David proposed that he should himself ride west to Jedburgh and try to persuade Huntly to sally out and attack, the Homes to put in a flanking assault.

This agreed as probably the best tactics, they had not

long to wait before the first of the scout-parties arrived back, that from the south-east. In some excitement they reported that the invaders were, in fact, only about four miles away, encamped on the higher ground between Kelso and the Borderline, in the vicinity of Haddon Rig.

This certainly made sense. Haddon Rig was the traditional meeting-place for the Wardens of the Marches, Scots and English, to hold parleys, discuss infringements of border laws and hang offenders. Bowes, as English Warden, would know it well. There was much open space up there, water, pasture for horses, a likely place to camp.

David Lindsay was just about to leave for Jedburgh with this information when the second scout-party arrived, their news equally significant. Huntly had not waited at Jedburgh. He was pressing on eastwards down Teviot, and was indeed only about the same distance off as was Bowes. Clearly he intended attack.

Some of the Home lairds now asserted themselves. They knew the Haddon Rig area very well, having driven many a prey of cattle, English cattle, home that way, before crossing Tweed. If this Huntly earl made a frontal attack on the enemy there, they themselves might improve on the situation. The Haddon Rig ridge of high ground was over a mile long, and at its east end was a large wood. Although from most of the ridge the views were wide open and clear, with an east-about approach, from the *English* side, it was possible to reach the woodland unobserved from the main ridge, or should be. If they were to do this, the Home force could get into the trees and hide there. It was a large wood. Then out on the enemy when Huntly attacked.

This seemed to all an excellent suggestion. The problem was to know Huntly's intentions and strategy.

Home of Aytoun pointed out that there was a small intervening ridge beyond the Redden Burn valley, at Kerchesters, midway between Kelso and Haddon Rig. From its summit they ought to be able to view the entire western approaches to that upland area. Watchers sent up there, while the rest of them remained hidden in the

Redden valley, would ensure that they knew what was transpiring.

It was now late afternoon, and there were doubts that any effective fighting would be done that day. But a move towards this Redden Burn was made, the anxious Kelso citizenry waving them on.

In the event, they hardly required to send scouts up on to the Kerchesters summit, for even before they reached the quite small Redden valley they could hear the clash of arms, the neighing of frightened horses and the shouting of men, distant but unmistakable as battle and no mere sounds of an armed camp. Presumably Huntly had decided to strike at once, rather than make a night assault or wait until the next day.

The Homes were divided as to procedure now. Some were for dashing straight over the intervening ridge and uphill to the attack, and not wasting time on the proposed hidden approach from the English rear. But senior leaders were for holding to the original plan. Charging from here, as well as being a long pull uphill, slowing them down, would also mean that there could be no real surprise, for they would be in sight of the English position for half a mile, perhaps more. Whereas the wood would give them cover almost to the last. Forby, it would not take long to get there; only a three-mile ride.

So it was hard spurring eastwards and then southwards, round that haunch of upland – it could hardly be called a hill, although the eastern flank proved to be quite steep, almost a bluff. They were actually in England here, so erratic was the unmarked borderline.

A burn-channel took them zig-zagging up the slope, in single file, and brought them out directly into the woodland. There was no noise of battle here. The hot-bloods feared that all could be over, one way or the other, and themselves with no part played; but their elders declared that the trees would muffle the sounds.

There was fully half a mile of that scattered woodland, thorn and birch and scrub-oak, to traverse, difficult riding for four hundred horsemen. Gradually they began to hear the clash again; so the fighting still raged, with the light failing now.

When at length they came to the western limit of the trees, it was to an arresting scene. Far and wide under the sinking sun the upland system of gentle green ridges and shallow hollows spread, the latter now filling with lilac shadows, all ever rising towards the high Cheviot Hills. In the immediate foreground the contrast with that far-flung and peaceful scene was shocking. Armed struggle hit the eye, but not such as might have been visualised as a battle, two forces engaged in regular conflict, two combatant sides facing each other. Instead was merely an incoherent mass of men and horses, in no sorts of formations, facing all ways, men battering and hacking and stabbing, some mounted, some afoot, some standing on mounds of slain, beasts rearing and braying. There were flags and banners here and there admittedly, but not in any line or pattern to indicate a front or leadership group. It was in fact a spectacle of utter and bloody chaos.

Lindsay and the Homes stared. They had thought of it as charging an enemy rear. But here was no rear any more than a front, enemy and friend inextricably mixed. What could they usefully do?

Home of Blackadder had his answer. They could do much to resolve this clutter. Let them form four wedges of a hundred men each, and charge down on the mêlée on a wide front, drive four lanes right through it. Then turn and sweep through again. That would break up the fight and clear the way for a decision.

David protested that that would be riding down friends as well as foes; but the others said what of it? They would be shouting their slogan of "A Home! A Home!" The English would quickly know what that meant and recognise that the game was up. Huntly's people would have the battle won for them, and would not bewail a few men knocked over.

Despite Lindsay's doubts, this commended itself to the other Home lairds; and David could think of no effective alternative. They formed up into four great arrowheads, under Blackadder, Whitsome, Aytoun and Polwarth,

David with Lord Home and one or two of the older lairds grouping in a small rearguard. Then, at a horn-blow signal, they burst out of the trees, in line abreast, lances lowered, swords drawn, using the flats of these to beat their mounts right into a full gallop.

It was slightly downhill at first, which gave them impetus, and the four wedges thundered on, each about seventy yards apart and so forming a front of over three hundred yards. Bellowing "A Home! A Home!" they bore down upon the battling mass. And without the least lessening of pace, they smashed in, all along the line.

The impact was, of course, shattering, terrible, and what had appeared sufficiently chaotic before now became beyond all description. Yet the confusion was strangely one-sided, in that it applied only to the vast struggling multitude of six or seven thousand and not to the four hundred, who, in their tight spear-headed galloping groups, clove on through the all but stationary congestion without disintegration and with purpose clear and undeflected. There was inevitably some diminution in speed caused by the press, the trampled bodies and the heaps of slain already littering the ground; but the wedge-formations were especially designed for such cleaving progress, with sufficient speed and momentum, each horseman supporting and supported by his neighbour and all backing up and thrusting forward the apex of the arrowhead. Although the charging Homes wielded swords right and left, as they rode, they probably did little damage with these, the main impact being caused by the sheer weight of trampling horseflesh and lashing hooves.

So, yelling their challenge, they drove on through, leaving four bloody avenues of broken men and animals behind them, and so splitting the battle area into five sections of mixed friend and foe, all equally shaken and for the time-being at a loss.

But the bewilderment and disarray was not quite equal, however similar might be the casualties suffered on each side. For there could be no doubt as to which side these latest attackers were on, their shouted Home slogans, and their lairds' banners making their identity abundantly clear. And, as the wedges came out into the clearer area beyond the battleground, and wheeled round, still in approximate formation, to resume their onslaught, the English inevitably recognised that their position was now all but hopeless, split up as they were, initiative forfeited and central leadership lost. Moreover, their own border was only a mile away, and comparative safety not much further – a significant factor for desperate men. As the Homes bored in again, everywhere individuals and groups began to break away and stream off eastwards. Quickly this became a general drift and then a flood. The battle of Haddon Rig was suddenly over.

Now, as far as the Home lairds were concerned, it was business, the capture of ransom-worthy prisoners, the urge to kill yielding to the urge for profit. As with one accord, the wedges became hunting-parties, seeking the English leaders; and these, many seeking to rally their disheartened men-at-arms, were the last to bolt.

For his part, David Lindsay, in the rear, found himself, with Lord Home, in the midst of a torrent of fleeing humanity. None sought to assail him, nor he to halt them. He went in search of Huntly, through the ghastly debris of the battlefield.

He discovered the Earl and most of his lieutenants in a group towards the eastern limits of the conflict area, almost as bewildered as were the enemy at this abrupt ending of the engagement. They were relieved, of course and pleased that the victory was evidently theirs – but undoubtedly not a little hipped that it was all so obviously the Homes' doing, distinctly galling for the King's officers. This reaction was scarcely soothed by the arrival, presently, of Home of Blackadder with, as prisoner, no less than Sir Robert Bowes himself, whom he handed over in grinningly patronising style – while retaining ransom rights, to be sure.

As the Scots force sought to sort itself out and count its heavy casualty-list, there were not a few dark looks cast at the arrogant-seeming Homes. Probably only a very small proportion of the Scots fallen and injured could be attributed to their indiscriminate charge, but despite its winning effect there was resentment.

The triumphant Homes did suffer one setback, however, for one of their lesser lairds had actually captured the Earl of Angus; but as he was bringing him in, yielded though he was, and disarmed, that fiery character had suddenly turned on his captor, snatched out the Home's dirk and stabbed him to the heart with it, before running to leap on a stray horse and make his escape. Such behaviour all condemned as unworthy.

There was no concerted attempt to pursue the fleeing enemy into England, where they could soon find protection in Wark, Norham, Twizel and Heaton Castles. It was almost dark now anyway, and the abandoned English camp offered provisions, comforts of a sort, a place where the wounded could receive rough dressing. The dead could be buried next day. Huntly and most of the leaders moved down to spend the night in Kelso; but the Homes, darkness or not, rode off northwards with their prisoners, with only grudging thanks for their intervention.

David remained with Huntly. In the morning, after burying the slain, a move was made up Tweed for Lauderdale and home to Edinburgh, some fifty miles, riding slowly because of the wounded.

By the following afternoon they had climbed out of Lauderdale, over Soutra and could see Edinburgh's castle-rock and Arthur's Craig, when at Fala, they met King James himself, coming to reinforce them with a great army of no less than thirty thousand. There was, needless to say, much satisfaction over the Haddon Rig victory and the consequent lifting of the current invasion threat. Nevertheless that appreciation was somewhat spoiled by the development thereafter of a major disagreement. James, supported by Oliver Sinclair, wanted to press on southwards with this fine army and teach the English a lesson, by crossing the Border and taking fire and sword into Northumberland; but the Scots lords, whose levies formed most of the force, were solidly against this. They asserted that they had mustered to defend Scots territory not to invade England. Their loyal duty to the crown was the defence of the realm, not foreign adventure. The victorious Huntly, who had had sufficient of fighting meantime, agreed with this attitude. James was very disappointed and incensed, but apart from the royal guard and a few others, the thousands assembled would do as their lords told them.

A return was made to Edinburgh, triumph muted.

As it transpired, the King's intention on this occasion was proved to be the right one. For, only days after Haddon Rig, Henry's general, the Duke of Norfolk, Earl Marshal of England and son of the victor of Flodden, led ten thousand men over the Border again, presumably in a gesture designed to wipe out Bowes's sorry defeat; and in a brief few days' raid, created havoc along the Scots East March, burning Kelso, Roxburgh, Coldstream and scores of villages, hamlets and farm-touns, before retiring whence he came. If James, and three times his English numbers, had proceeded southwards, that would not have happened, and Norfolk would either have turned back or been defeated.

The thing rankled.

8

That disagreement at Fala, below Soutra in the Lammermuir Hills, was to prove a deal more significant for Scotland than anyone could have foreseen, both in its effect on James Stewart and on the national situation, immediate and longer-term. The King's resentment at the power of his nobles, always pronounced, grew notably stronger, and was not to be confined to words. Gradually it became evident that James and his nobility were on a collision course. Appointments hitherto almost automatic, were not confirmed by the crown, offices of state were left unfilled, charters of land were denied the royal signature, and, more and more, churchmen were being used to fill vacancies in the administration of government and justice, national and local, almost all of which had in the past gone to the lords and their kin. It was this last aspect of the situation which most perturbed David Lindsay, since it seemed to imply that Davie Beaton was supporting the monarch in this campaign, for it could hardly have been possible otherwise. A parliament was being called, and with anger growing amongst the nobility and landed men, there would be trouble thereat. With Henry of England threatening dire things, this was no time to alienate the sources of Scotland's manpower.

David sought leave-of-absence to attend to pressing matters at Lindifferon – but actually to pay a call upon Beaton at St. Andrews, from which place the land was now so largely governed. It was not difficult to obtain, for these days James was ever more preoccupied with his building programme, in especial the Stirling palace, which was the most ambitious architectural project seen in Scotland since David the First's great abbey-building strategy; and the Lord Lyon's services were not in demand for that. Indeed, Oliver Sinclair, who had gifts in the artistic sphere if in little else, sufficed the King for company and advice.

On a May morning, with the gorse ablaze, the first swallows darting and the cuckoos calling, Lindsay rode through the East Neuk of Fife to St. Andrews Castle.

The Cardinal-Archbishop was away addressing a convocation of new priests in St. Mary's College but was expected back by midday. David went down to the quayside and watched the shipping. St Andrews had become a very busy port, with the Archbishop as effective at encouraging trade as at most else that he turned his hand to, the profits accruing mostly to Holy Church but partly to himself. He was said now to be the wealthiest individual in the kingdom.

Davie Beaton came to the harbour to find his visitor, and greeted him with his accustomed cordiality. "How good to see my oldest and best friend, colleague and mentor!" he exclaimed. "I did not know that you were in Fife, or I would have called at The Mount."

"I came only yesterday, Janet not with me. A hurried visit."

"Ah! Do I detect urgency? And to see *me*?"

"Aye. To see Your Eminence."

"Sakes – when you name me so I fear the worst! You come in disapproval, is it?"

"Say that I come seeking information. If not reassurance. Being . . . perturbed."

"Perturbed? Are we not all? Who have this realm's weal at heart. All the time."

"Perhaps. But this is more immediate. And you, Davie, are involved. Indeed, there is little in the realm in which you are *not* involved, I think!"

"And my involvement perturbs you?"

"Yes. The present situation regarding James. His attitudes and actions. I believe that you are supporting him and them. To the danger of all."

"Is it not our simple duty to support our liege-lord?"

"Do not mock, man! You know of what I speak. James's warfare against his nobles. It is dangerous folly.

Especially now, when we may expect invasion at any time."

"James has reason to distrust his nobility. You know that. *You* were there when they refused to follow him to the border and over, to teach the English their lesson. And not for the first time. And so cost Scotland dear."

"With hindsight we know that now. They did not, then. But – this sustained attack on the lords and lairds and chiefs, curtailing their privileges, revoking their appointments, replacing them with churchmen, this could spell disaster when Henry moves against us, as move he will soon, I believe."

"And you blame me for this?"

"James could not be doing it without your aid. All these clerics gaining high position in the land. You rule the Church completely. These are *your* men. You are moving them into more and more positions where they can control the kingdom. Do not tell me that this is by chance. I know you better than that!"

"And you hold this to be wrong? May not my churchmen be better servants for James than many of these arrogant lords?"

"That may be so. But they cannot produce large numbers of armed men, such as will be required to repel a great English invasion."

"Be not so sure. *They* may not, but Holy Church could."

"What do you mean?"

"I mean siller, David – siller! Gold, indeed. The Church has more money than all these lords and lairds added together. And siller will buy anything, armed men included. If I offer sufficient, the King will not lack hired soldiery. These very lords who deny James their support will be the first to *sell* me their men! Take my word for it."

Lindsay stared. "So that is it! Money!"

"A useful commodity, I have found out. The mammon of unrighteousness, to be sure – but put to good purpose, invaluable!"

"And you are willing to use the Church's wealth, thus?"

"If need be, yes. And my own likewise. The realm must be saved from Henry. And the Church too. For he would bring it down, as he has done the Church in England, nothing surer."

"I see. You play a deep game, Davie – but then you always did. Is it the Church or the crown you seek to save, by encouraging James in this?"

"Both. And this strange entity which we call Scotland. Its ancient Church and still more ancient crown."

"A corrupt Church. And a weak king."

"No doubt. We can only use the tools which come to hand."

"And does that mean prostituting the Church's offices, amongst other things, as well as spending her treasure? Giving great abbacies to mere boys?"

Beaton eyed him assessingly. "You refer to the King's bastards?"

"Aye. I hear that six of them, the eldest only fifteen years – for James himself is only thirty – are appointed Abbots of Holyrood, Kelso, Melrose, Coldingham, St. Andrews here, and Inchcolm. Children!"

"*Commendator* abbots. There is a difference, man. As *I* was Commendator of Arbroath before I took holy orders. I do not like it, mind you, would not choose it. These love-children of the King's women. But it is part of the price I have to pay."

"For what?"

"For James's support in the saving of Holy Church. It is not all one way, see you. I have to trade."

"Need you? With all your siller?"

"I need to force the hands of many. The said lords. *Some* will not take my money for their men. Also, many are for this heresy of so-called Church reform! *You* know that, since in some measure you have encouraged them! So I must prevail on them, both for men for the army and to protect the Church. And for this I require James's agreement. The royal seal and signature, in parliament."

"Ah. So the parliament is at your bidding?"

"Not entirely. It is necessary. For the realm's security."

"What is this of forcing the hands of the lords?"

"I have a list. A long list. Of lords, barons, lairds and chiefs. Over three hundred of them, no less. Many Henry's pensioners, secretly. Many sworn to sever the Church from Rome. Other enemies of James himself. These must be shown who rules in Scotland. They will either agree to provide troops, at this parliament, and cease support of heresy – or that list will be read out, a roll of treason! Infamous! Lands to be forfeited to the crown!"

"Lord – you would go that far?"

"If need be, yes."

"Am *I* on that list?"

"None would accuse the Lord Lyon King of Arms of treason, I think!"

Lindsay considered that oblique answer. Both were silent for a little.

"So you have it all in hand," he said, at length. "I might have known it. I am glad that you are, as you say, my friend and not my enemy, Davie Beaton!"

"Enemy? I have but one enemy – Henry Tudor! And against him I will marshal all I have and am."

"And you think that you can beat him? Henry of England?"

"I can try. But I need time. Time to bring all the pressure required."

"And that he may not give us. It is said that Norfolk has thirty thousand now, mustered at York."

"More. Forty thousand," Beaton amended. "He has been given vice-regal authority over all the north of England, to raise men. And as aides the Earls of Southampton, Shrewsbury, Derby, Rutland and Cumberland. So we must try to *make* time. Another reason for this parliament. It must authorise commissioners to go to York. Quickly. To tell the English that James regrets that he was unable to meet his uncle there in the autumn, owing to his mother's dire illness. That should give Henry pause! To declare that warfare is no way to settle disputes between neighbours, and to ask for a truce and conference, as between equals. It will not be granted, but it may give us the time we need. For Henry will not be at York. He is in Wales, threatening Ireland – so couriers would have to be sent seeking him with our message. It will all delay Norfolk, while he awaits an answer."

That at least Lindsay agreed with.

After a meal, he rode back to Lindifferon, a thoughtful man. This parliament was going to be a vital one. He, as Lyon, could take no part in it, other than ushering in the monarch; but his name had frequently been put forward as a commissioner for the royal burgh of Cupar, three miles from the Mount. A word in the right ears, and he could be nominated to take his seat, after bringing in the King. It might be that his voice could usefully be raised on that occasion.

For so important an event, the parliament of June 1542, at Edinburgh, was singularly quiet on the face of it, non-controversial, formal – although it could nowise be called dull because of the underlying tension, of which none could be unaware. It was particularly well-attended, in all three Estates, the circumstances assuring that.

David Lindsay had had no difficulty in being nominated member for Cupar, in the Third Estate, and in obtaining the royal permission to take his seat, after his formal introduction of James – who told him that he must support the Cardinal's efforts to bring the nobles to heel. In fact, no great support was required, for Beaton had done his preliminary work most thoroughly, and all Scotland knew now of his Black List, as it was being called, and the threat behind it, of publication and forfeiture of lands and offices – his revelation of it to Lindsay at St. Andrews having no doubt been no mere friendly, confidential gesture but part of his strategy.

Beaton indeed dominated the session, in his Chancellor's function as chairman. As *Legatus a Latere*, Cardinal-Archbishop, Primate, Privy Seal, King's principal adviser and paymaster of all, it could hardly be otherwise; and with invasion threatening, all played into his hands. The lords were in the main sullen and unforthcoming, to be sure, but they did not risk confrontation, and the various items on the agenda were passed one after another with very little discussion and practically no opposition.

The twin themes of dealing with the English threat to state and Church were skilfully linked by Beaton, who gave fuller information about the enemy's armed build-up and revealed that King Henry had ordered his Archbishop of York to assemble all necessary documentation to attempt to substantiate the ancient canard that the Scottish Church was in fact a sub-church of that of England and that the Archbishops of York were metropolitans over Scotland, the St. Andrews primacy invalid; so with the English rejection of the Papacy, the Scots Church was likewise divorced from Rome, and all appointments therein now subject to York. And, of course, as now lawful head of the Church of England, Henry's own claim to be Lord Paramount of Scotland was obviously further confirmed.

This, needless to say, served to arouse the parliament to a suitable anger, even those in favour of reform, and aided the acceptance of both the military and diplomatic plans put forward. The Cardinal did not actually mention his Black List, but twice hinted at it, the treasonable danger to the realm by those accepting money payments from Henry – the names of whom were known – and the grievous folly of those who, in the name of reforming Church failings, undermined it from within, thus aiding the enemy. Those so inclined were also known.

It was at this last theme that David Lindsay rose to make his comment. He said that while His Eminence's intimations and revelations were timely and should be heeded by all, the Church's hold on the hearts and minds of the nation would be much strengthened, and its cause protected, by a more evident and vigorous purging of the faults and excesses and abuses of her clergy, by her leaders, from within. A united people facing the English threat was essential; and this could be greatly enhanced by an immediate campaign of cleansing in ecclesiastical affairs, such as the esteemed *Legatus a Latere* had ample powers to carry out, and the removal of the offensive accusation of heresy from those who merely sought Church reform.

This brought forth the first applause of the session,

but black looks from the clerical benches; although the Cardinal-Archbishop himself accepted it all smoothly and even thanked the commissioner for Cupar, Fife, for his observations.

The military strategy was then dealt with, the Cardinal's indication that substantial moneys would be forthcoming for the hire of troops from lordships, baronies and burghs, arousing considerable interest. It was agreed that there should be two forces mustered, to move to protect both East and West Marches, with close liaison between them to ensure, if possible, swift switching of manpower to whichever side proved to be under greatest threat in invasion. Lindsay spoke to this, indicating the lessons learned at Haddon Rig, and the value of utilising to the full the Borderland moss-troopers' light cavalry tactics and their knowledge of the ground.

The matter of sending envoys to York meantime produced the only real controversy of the day, for many there thought it not only unnecessary, undesirable, but almost humiliating. And it was difficult to explain the need to the gathering, that it was merely delaying-tactics; for, of course, Henry Tudor was almost as well served with spies in Scotland as was Davie Beaton in England, and he would very quickly be supplied with information as to this parliament and its decisions, so that the real reason for the embassage had to be played down and the suggestion put forward that King James's royal dignity required this move, and parliament was bound to endorse it. Even James looked doubtful about that. In the end it was agreed that two envoys, Sir James Learmonth, the Treasurer, and the Bishop of Orkney, should leave for England very shortly.

The assembly broke up, with acceptance of large-scale mustering. Ecclesiastical developments were less clear.

After all the planning, mustering and preparations, a distinct lull developed thereafter, during the summer of 1542. Learmonth and the Bishop of Orkney came back from York, rejected – although they had never expected anything else. Whether their embassage had, in fact, gained the required time was hard to say. Certainly no English attack developed, and no move was reported northwards from York meantime; but as the weeks went past, it seemed less likely that the envoys could take credit for this. What was restraining Henry Tudor even Davie Beaton did not claim to know. But something was.

Reaction in Scotland was mixed. Many were relieved of course, but others were impatient; having screwed themselves up for war, the delay irritated. Also large numbers of armed men, mustered but idle, were a problem, for commanders as well as for the local citizenry. But at least it allowed, first the hay harvest and then the corn to be gathered in, always important – perhaps that might have had something to do with the English delay also? Sections of the assembled host were allowed to return home for harvest work, by rotation, prepared for urgent recall.

It all made a most unsettling season.

Then, in October, Henry did act, and in a way that he had never done before – he formally declared war, a strange development. Who this was to impress, none knew. For reasons for the war, he cited James's alleged broken faith in failing to come to meet him at York; Scots support for his 'Irish rebels'; likewise for harbouring the so-called Pilgrimage of Grace Catholic traitors. This seemed quite inadequate for a declaration of war between two realms – and he had never before considered anything such necessary before his armed assaults. But the Tudor was a law unto himself, and scarcely to be judged by other men's standards.

Remustering was the order of the day, the main assembly to be, as usual, at the Burgh Muir of Edinburgh.

It was late in the year for invasion, with the days closing in and the winter weather worsening. But, in early November, the word reached Edinburgh that an English force estimated at about ten thousand had crossed Tweed into the East March. This, of course, faced the Scots command with a problem. Norfolk was known to have at least forty thousand at York, so this was either only an advance-thrust, or the main assault was to be elsewhere, presumably on the *West* March. How to react?

A council-of-war was hastily called – and it was not a happy or encouraging one. There were divided counsels, but that was not the principal source of the trouble. The blame was James's own. When it had been agreed that about one-third of the Scots muster should immediately head south-eastwards, under the Earl of Arran, Lord Admiral, to deal with this initial assault, it was decided that most of the main force should move south-westwards for Dumfries-shire and the West March. A residue of a few thousand would remain at the Burgh Muir, to reinforce whichever army most needed help. And the major south-western host itself would divide at some point, near Langholm perhaps, where one detachment of it would still be able to switch to the East March without too much difficulty, if the call came from there. The residue remaining at Edinburgh would hope to be much added to, as the outlying and Highland levies came in, in a day or two. This was felt by the majority of the lords as the best that could be contrived in difficult circumstances – although some disagreed, declaring that this dividing up of the Scots numbers was highly dangerous.

It was then that the King exploded his bombshell. He declared that the commander of the main force for the West March should be, not Huntly nor Argyll nor even the Earl Marischal or the High Constable, but his good Oliver Sinclair.

This, needless to say, produced consternation, offence, fury, all but mutiny, amongst the senior nobles and officers of state. The like had never been heard of, an unpopular and inexperienced young man in his twenties, with no armed tail of men of his own, given authority in the field over the earls and lords and chiefs and their thousands. Utter demoralisation threatened.

Davie Beaton had gone off eastwards with Arran, to seek to put stiffening into that rather weak individual. David Lindsay sought to do, or undo, what he could of the damage. When James retired in sulky obstinacy he followed him into his pavilion, to urge reconsideration privately. Nothing could be more productive of damage to their hopes and cause than the disaffection of the nobles, already long the target of the King's personal distrust, although in this national crisis they had been prepared to put their united strength at the royal disposal; but not under an untried and junior commander, however trusted by the monarch. When James refused to reconsider, David urged on him that in that case he himself must assume the nominal command, supreme; none could object to that. With Sinclair acting under him, directly.

This was eventually agreed, and a move south-westwards was ordered, along the foothills of the Pentland Hills, by Penicuik and Biggar and Tweedsmuir, to the head of Annandale.

James was in one of his worst moods, sour and difficult – which was strange, considering that the Queen was pregnant again and a child was expected soon in December. He was not well, undoubtedly; indeed he had been ailing, with some unspecified complaint, for long – Beaton was not the only one to suggest that it was some disease contracted through his indiscriminate womanising. Whether that was true, it much affected his spirits and temper – and all suffered, even Sinclair.

Some sixteen thousand of them headed south-westwards, the majority on foot, scouting-parties well ahead. The mounted contingent, of course, soon grew tired of keeping to the pace of the infantry and moved even further in advance.

They settled to camp early that first day, at Biggar, for the King was clearly unwell and found the riding a trial. The Lord Fleming had a seat here, where James could rest, Boghall Castle. An atmosphere of gloom lay upon the expedition.

In the morning, James sick, vomiting, was in no state to proceed. But when it was suggested that he return to Edinburgh, he curtly refused. Although David Lindsay was concerned, he was in a way relieved at that refusal. For, of course, if the King had indeed gone back, the fiction of his being in supreme command of the army could not have been maintained and crisis over Sinclair precipitated.

So next day, with James delaying the pace, the mounted chivalry got only as far as Moffat, at the head of Annandale, after the high crossing of Tweedsmuir. Here they were reached by a messenger from one of the scouting parties. The English, under Norfolk himself, were massing at Carlisle, in major strength. They could not give numbers, but it looked as though the main thrust were indeed to be on this West March. Carlisle was only some forty miles from their present position. The news produced a new tension in the host, but no great increase of confidence.

There was as yet no information from the East March force as to the situation there. It was agreed to go on as far as Morton, between Eskdale and Annandale, and only a few miles from the borderline, and there to decide on tactics while awaiting the foot – who were, of course, now far behind. James had to be supported in his saddle for the last ten miles of the thirty.

Morton was a modest place to have given title to an earldom, a Black Douglas property and parish on the edge of the Debateable Land, with a small but strong old castle which but seldom saw its lord in this remote spot, the Earl – who was with the King now – having many finer lairdships. Fairly obviously, however, he must have a working arrangement with the Armstrongs, who dominated all hereabouts, and who were conspicuously out of evidence on this occasion.

At Morton Castle, James retired to bed, while they awaited the foot and further news from the scouts.

It was 28 November, in chill, rainy weather, when the infantry arrived from the north and couriers from the south. The latter informed that Norfolk, with the main English array, had moved out of Carlisle towards the Border at the Solway shore, but he also had sent lesser forces, under Lord Dacre and Sir Thomas Wharton, inland, north-eastwards, probably with the same strategy in mind as had the Scots.

The council held in the royal bedchamber at Morton

was little more satisfactory than was the previous one, now that it was obvious that James was in no condition to lead, or even to proceed with the force. The lords were sullen, unhelpful. Oliver Sinclair, however, kept notably quiet, which was something. It was the Lord Maxwell who took such lead as there was – this was, of course, his own home territory and he was indeed Warden of the West March. He declared that they were in no strength to meet Norfolk's main force. That must be postponed until their major reinforcements arrived from Edinburgh, and their foot here were rested after their long, hard marching. They should also send to Arran on the East March for some part of his strength, since it was clear that this area was where the principal English thrust was taking place. But meantime, there was something useful that they might do, with the cavalry, to harass and unsettle Norfolk. They were about six miles from the River Esk, which here constituted the Borderline. Leaving the foot at Morton, they could ride down to a little-known ford of that river, cross into England and there strike south-westwards between Dacre's and Wharton's forces, and so get behind Norfolk, between him and Carlisle, which would be his base of supply. This should cause maximum enemy concern and some disruption, without any major fighting, while they awaited their additional strength.

There being no better, or alternative proposals, this was accepted.

The King's position had to be decided upon. This small, cramped fortalice, high on the moorlands, was no suitable resting-place for a sick monarch, and it was much too near the Borderline for safety should there be any hurried retiral. James himself saw that, and suggested going to the old royal castle of Lochmaben, a Bruce stronghold in mid-Annandale; but although strong enough in position, it was in a poor state of repair, neglected and semi-ruinous. Maxwell again took charge, and said that his own great castle of Caerlaverock, near Dumfries, the main West March stronghold, was the place for the King. It was secure from all but the heaviest of artillery, which

Norfolk certainly would not have. And it was roomy, comfortable.

So next morning, a horse-litter was contrived for James, and after farewells, emotional in the case of Oliver Sinclair, he went off, with a strong escort of the royal guard and some Maxwells, for Caerlaverock.

The mounted chivalry thereafter, to the number of some three thousand, made a move down towards the fords of Esk.

They were in constant touch with their scouts, no great distance ahead, and these informed that the two lesser forces under Dacre and Wharton were now proceeding westwards about six miles apart, the former along the Lyne valley, the other further north in the Netherby area. Fairly clearly they knew the Scots present position and were seeking to outflank it, and probably at the same time form a line with Norfolk, who was now reported to have reached Annan on the Solway shore.

Maxwell declared that the Hopesyke ford was the place for them, midway between Dacre and Wharton. Across Esk they could turn either north or south, to threaten the rear of whichever enemy group seemed best. No actual battle, at this stage, would be wise.

Due southwards after only a few miles, they reached the River Sark, which entered the Esk estuary through the marshland of the Solway Moss. But before that boggy ground was entered they swung left-handed, over firmer terrain, and came to the broad river opposite the Hopesyke woods. These provided useful cover from view on the English east and north.

The ford proved to be a narrow one, involving a strung-out and therefore prolonged crossing, but there was no interruption.

Once all were across and Maxwell was sending out more scouts, north and south, to ascertain the actual positions and strengths of the enemy now, Oliver Sinclair asserted himself. He ordered the remainder of the royal guard to contrive a sort of platform for him out of lance-shafts and shields, raised on the shoulders of about a dozen men. He had a trumpet blown – to the alarm of the lords, who scarcely relished this possible drawing of attention to their arrival on English soil – mounted his shaky dais, a paper in hand, and called for silence. He read from the paper. It was a proclamation from the King, naming him supreme commander of the Scots forces in the royal absence, and requiring all loyal subjects to obey his commands and directions.

The hubbub of fury, protest and contumely which thereupon broke out was predictable, earls, lords, lairds and chieftains shouting their offence and resentment, Maxwell, the Warden, notably and understandably angry. Everywhere there were threats of non-co-operation.

Sinclair gained quiet by more trumpeting. This was a royal command, he reiterated, and refusal to accept it was highest treason. He demanded immediate and entire obedience, in the King's name. From now on, this expedition would be fought on his orders.

Again the uproar, followed by further blowing of trumpets.

David Lindsay pushed forward to the side of the curious platform, and spoke up urgently.

"This is folly, Sinclair!" he asserted. "Offending the lords, now, will gain nothing, win no warfare. The men-at-arms are theirs. You *need* their favour, aid, support. Their goodwill rather than mere obedience. The men will obey their chiefs, not you. Maxwell knows what he is doing here, and they will work with him. He is the Warden. Pass the command to him."

"Not so. I but carry out James's royal wishes. *I* command."

"Then appoint Maxwell your lieutenant, man. And let him order the day. With your authority. That might serve."

"Serve you and your grudging like, perhaps! But not me, nor the King's Grace. No – you, and all others, will do as I say."

During this exchange the noise and disturbance had grown again, and another instrumental blast, loud and prolonged, was required to gain approximate hush.

Sinclair raised his voice. "We shall not waste time

assailing either Dacre or this Wharton," he announced. "These do not matter greatly. Norfolk is the true danger. We cannot attack *him* until our foot and new strength reaches us. But we can do better than harry these others. We can ride directly to Carlisle and set it ablaze! It is but six or seven miles. They will expect nothing such. It is Norfolk's base, from which he will be supplied. Nothing will more grievously trouble him, and the others, than Carlisle taken behind them. They must halt, turn back. That will give us more time . . ."

The appalled silence which had greeted this declaration of intent now erupted into yelling opposition, contradiction, dispute. The thing was madness, impossible, bairn's dreaming. If they ever reached Carlisle they would be trapped there. It was a great walled city. Even if they won inside, the gates could be shut behind them. If Norfolk, Dacre and the rest did turn back, again they would be trapped – never get back to Morton. Once their men were dispersed in the city streets, they would be in no position to fight. And so on.

Oliver Sinclair ignored all. They would do as he said, he insisted. All commanders back to their companies, ready to move off, forthwith.

That abrupt directive was just too much. Outright rejection was the effect on most of those present. It could scarcely be called mutiny since few there accepted that Sinclair had any authority anyway. Everywhere there were cries of complete refusal, dissent, abuse. Only a few moved towards their men-at-arms.

Sinclair jumped down from his platform, pushing Lindsay out of the way, and went to mount his own horse, ordering the standard-bearer to unfurl the royal Lion Rampant banner and the trumpeters to sound the Advance. Reluctantly David went after him.

Few others did. The nobles gathered in groups, arguing, gesticulating. Even when Sinclair, with very small support, spurred forward to a second rendering of the Advance, he was followed mainly by jeers and catcalls.

And then, out from the cover of the Hopesyke woodland burst the English cavalry.

Whether they had been there all the time, or whether it was all the trumpeting which had brought them to the area, was not to be known. But out they surged from the trees, charging in line, in half a dozen orderly wedges, yelling, 'A Dacre! A Dacre!', and thundering down upon the completely surprised and disorganised Scots.

It was utter and shameful rout, inevitably. The attackers had only a few hundred yards to cover, somewhat downhill. Most of the Scots were not even beside their horses, much less mounted. There was no time to organise any defence, any counter-measures, no time even for most of the leaders to reach their own units, before the enemy wedges were upon them, slashing, thrusting, slaying.

David Lindsay, seeing a brief mind-picture of Haddon Rig in reverse, found himself, oddly enough, in the only group of Scots which was in any position to do anything effective, the small party behind Sinclair, mounted and already on the move. They were far too few to offer any real resistance, to be sure, but at least they might survive that first charge and thereafter be able to achieve some small rescue, perhaps.

David took charge, since Sinclair merely stared, dumbfounded. Shouting to form a wedge, a wedge behind him, he wheeled his beast round to face the onrush. The people with him were by no means the most valiant and expert fighters of the host, and no coherent group either; they did not dispose themselves into any very tight or effective spearhead-formation therefore, indeed had little time to do so before the English were upon them. But they did present the enemy with a fairly solid and somewhat ordered array, whereas all else was disorder and confusion. As a result, almost inevitably, the charging foe tended to avoid them meantime, to hurtle on past to more easy and profitable targets. The outer left flank was swept aside in the rush, but most of the party found themselves bypassed.

David recognised certain realities. First, that his group was still more or less intact. Second, that no further wave of attackers had materialised behind. Third, that the enemy themselves, in the chaos they had flung themselves into, would be unlikely to be able to maintain any very organised and controlled momentum – and there were no great numbers of them, far fewer than the unprepared and disconcerted Scots. Shades of Haddon Rig again. So there was just the possibility of making some useful contribution.

He reined round again, yelling to the others to do likewise, to reform their wedge and to drive back down on the rear of the English attackers. But it was one thing to visualise and decide on this, and quite another to transmit the notion and determination to others, especially a hotchpotch of others who were not any recognised unit and who owed him no personal allegiance. Some of these obviously saw the situation in a very different light, escape not foolish heroics their priority. Had Oliver Sinclair himself backed Lindsay it might have helped; but that young man was not only completely out of his depth but clearly stricken with fright. He acted, but in no useful fashion, suddenly digging in his spurs and dashing off on his own, northwards, away from the turmoil, towards a great bend in the river. Some streamed after him. Others fled elsewhere.

David was left with the standard-bearer and about a score, mainly of the royal guard. He realised that it was far too small a group to make any real impact on the situation. They would be overwhelmed. But they might effect something limited, rescue a few . . .

The scene ahead of them now beggared description, with confusion reigning, the English wedges absorbed and largely disintegrated in the mass of men and horses, the only recognisable and positive action being the efforts of some of the wedges to retain some sort of formation and controlled mastery, and some small clusters of Scots standing their ground – that and the tide of men seeking to flee to the Esk, to cross back into the Solway Moss, where cavalry would be at a disadvantage compared with foot.

A hasty scanning of that dire scene showed David only one point where he thought that he might possibly achieve something effective, in however small a way. Amidst all the chaotic mêlée there appeared to be only one grouping where any sort of unified resistance was being offered to the attackers, a huddle of men forming a kind of hedgehog, lances and spears thrust out in a defensive roundel by the dismounted majority, horsemen with swinging swords in the centre. Above these last fluttered the black saltire on white of the Maxwell banner. Perhaps not to be wondered at, the Warden of the March was putting up the best performance in this sorry disaster. English cavalry were wheeling round and round this tight formation, held at bay by the thicket of lances but seeking an entry.

Lindsay slashed down his drawn sword to point thereto, and waved his little party on, spurring hard.

It was no very impressive charge but at least it had direction and some impetus. They had to plough through the seething mass of struggling humanity to reach the Maxwells, and shut their minds to the horror of riding down friend as well as foe – and many more of the former than the latter. But it was that or nothing. Shouting, smiting, they clove their way to the circling English.

Their onset had its effect, temporarily at any rate, breaking and scattering the surprised enclosing ring and all but crashing into the dismounted spearmen. The Lord Maxwell and his mounted lairds reacted promptly, surging forward and through their men-at-arms screen, to meet the newcomers. For a few moments all was as chaotic as the rest of the scene.

Maxwell took charge. Yelling to his unhorsed people to mount – by which he meant either to grab riderless horses, of which there were innumerable milling about, or else to clamber up behind those already in the saddle – he pointed north by west, jabbing with his sword. Then, flanked by his banner-bearer and lairds, he spurred onwards, the others following, including Lindsay's group, in no sort of order but with definite solidarity and purpose.

They were in fact only joining in what had become a general movement, however erratic and hindered, towards the Esk. But there was a difference in their flight, from the rest. It was faster, more assured, informed – for Maxwell knew the exact location of the narrow ford, and few others did.

On their headlong way thither they were joined by others, who could detach themselves from the fighting, and who had acquired horses. David Lindsay was in two minds about this very evident flight and desertion of the field; but it was entirely obvious that they could not materially affect the issue by staying, for the day was hopelessly lost. Lords and men were throwing down their arms all around. Better that some should escape than none.

Maxwell led them straight to the ford, and across. They had to string out, and although one or two plunged off the line of it in their haste, and into deep water, most won over. At the far side, they drew up, to turn and look back. Such pursuit as had developed had halted on the English bank, since it was clear that any enemy riding across in file could be picked off with ease, by the defenders. But by the same token, of course, it meant that these English could block the ford at their end and prevent any more escapes.

The situation behind them was becoming stabilised – stabilised in complete defeat and humiliation, such fighting as there had been dying away. Many were still streaming down to the Esk, however few would actually get across; but the majority were evidently surrendering, proud nobles and lairds and humble men-at-arms equally. Also evident was how greatly the vanquished outnumbered the victors.

Maxwell wasted no time on fruitless repinings. Ordering a group of his mosstroopers to remain to guard the ford-head, he told others to go along this northern river bank and collect survivors who were managing to win across – then to bring them on to Caerlaverock or Dumfries by an inland route through the foothills, to avoid Norfolk's host on the coast road.

With a grim last glance at the site of possibly the most shameful débâcle in all Scotland's stormy story, the Warden pointed northwards and nodded.

By the round-about route through the upland areas of Kirkpatrick, Brydekirk and Mouswald, they came down to the Solway again at the Nith estuary, where the mighty, rose-red Caerlaverock Castle sat securely within its loch-like but man-made cordon. They had seen no sign of Norfolk's force, not even his scouts. Possibly, with the news from Solway Moss, he had halted in the Annan area, some dozen miles to the east.

Now they had to break the news to the King. They found him in bed and looking poorly indeed, and David Lindsay's heart ached for his monarch and long-time friend, however misguided. But there was no way that they could spare him this additional pain and burden. He and Maxwell had to recount the disaster and the reasons for it.

James's initial reaction seemed not to be consternation at his army's defeat and shame, but entirely personal.

"Oliver?" he demanded. "Where is Oliver?"

"The last I saw of him, Sire, he was fleeing. Alone. Northwards. Towards Netherby. I know not whether he escaped."

Maxwell muttered something beneath his breath.

"Oliver – fled? My Oliver – fled?" James started up, hand out. "No! No!"

They gazed at their liege-lord, silent.

"I will not believe it. He will come back to me. Oliver will come, I tell you."

"Your Grace has more to concern yourself with than Oliver Sinclair!" Maxwell began, when Lindsay gripped his arm, and shook his head.

"Not now, my lord – not now."

The King sank back and closed his eyes. "Bring Oliver to me when he comes," he said. "Now – leave me. Leave me."

They had, of course, more to worry about than James's aberrations over the ineffable Sinclair. First and foremost, the Duke of Norfolk. Maxwell had scouts out eastwards, and at any time they expected to be informed of the English approach. Probably Norfolk could not take Caerlaverock without heavy artillery; but one of the last things desirable was for the King of Scots and themselves to be cooped up in this Border fortress, besieged, and Scotland leaderless in this crisis. Somehow they must get James away to the north and safety. The awaited reinforcements should be arriving soon, on the Biggar – Tweedsmuir – Moffat line of march. To join these as quickly as possible would be best. But James was in no state for long or hard riding. A horse-litter, slung between two beasts, could not cover many miles a day in comfort.

Survivors kept arriving from Solway Moss. They told a variety of stories, out of which it was possible to piece together some overall picture of the situation there. Probably the numbers slain were not great, and of the dead most had almost certainly drowned in seeking to cross the Esk, to escape. But those captured would be between one and two thousand, including the Earls of Cassillis and Glencairn, the Lords Somerville, Gray, Fleming and Ruthven and hundreds of lesser lairds, knights and chieftains, Oliver Sinclair amongst them, he having been seen by more than one witness being brought back under guard. Others might have escaped who had not found their way to Caerlaverock. But the scale of the catastrophe was overwhelming.

When James heard that Sinclair was captured he wept like any child.

Information from the Annan area was that Norfolk had meantime encamped at that town, no doubt awaiting Dacre's and Wharton's reports.

It was decided that, first thing in the morning, a move should be made, with the King, firstly to Lochmaben Castle in mid-Annandale, some fifteen miles. James would be safer there, while they sought to contact the hoped-for forces from Edinburgh.

Next day then, David escorted the silent James, in his litter, past Dumfries to Lochmaben, while Maxwell went seeking the reinforcements the Earl of Atholl should be bringing to their aid, and to link these up with the Scots infantry still presumably waiting at Morton.

At Lochmaben Castle, islanded in its curious group of lochs, James came to himself after a fashion – at least, he began to assert himself, however curious his decisions. He declared that it was all really Angus's doing – the Earl of Angus was known to have been sent north by Henry with Norfolk, and James had an almost pathological preoccupation and hatred for the man who had all his life been his incubus. Oliver, his friend, would now be in Angus's evil clutches. He must be rescued, at all costs. And the way to achieve that was to go and take Tantallon Castle, Angus's favourite seat, and offer it back to the Earl in exchange for Oliver Sinclair. They must go, at once.

David Lindsay sought to negative this astonishing proposition, but the King was adamant now. Clearly his mind was affected, as well as his body, probably had been for some time, to account for his recent behaviour and indeed his infatuation with Sinclair, so unlike his previous attitudes. But he was still sovereign-lord, and his commands had the force of law. David pleaded with him to wait at least until Maxwell could come to Lochmaben with news of Atholl and the foot; but the King would not hear of it. He was all in a fever now to strike a blow for his beloved Oliver. They must be off forthwith, before Oliver suffered more. With no option but to obey, Lindsay left a message for Maxwell, and started out on the long cross-Scotland journey to the Lothian coast.

It was a slow progress indeed, right over the high watershed of the Lowlands, for however determined and eager James was, his physical weakness was not to be denied, and each day's journey in the litter grew the shorter and the more trying. It took them five grievous days to reach the Merse, the last lap over the Lammermuir Hills a nightmare, the King all but comatose. They saw no sign of Arran's army, nor indeed of any English invaders.

And at Tantallon's frowning walls and multiple moats, of course, no amount of shouting in the royal name to open to the King had the least effect on the Douglas garrison, who sat assured of their complete security in that impregnable stronghold. But by now James was barely aware of what was going on, rambling in his speech when he spoke at all. Lindsay, on his own initiative, decided that enough was enough and that the care of physicians was what the monarch needed most, and ordered a move back to Edinburgh. It is doubtful whether the man in the litter knew what transpired.

At Holyrood they found Arran and Davie Beaton in a considerable state of agitation, unsure what had happened, what to do in consequence, and how and where the King was. Beaton's relief at his friend's arrival with the missing monarch was soon lost in further concern at James's state. He had just come from a hasty visit to Linlithgow Palace, where the Queen was about to give birth, and was much worried about her husband.

At least the English threat appeared to have receded meantime. Presumably Norfolk considered that he had achieved sufficient, with his enormous haul of prisoners and hostages from Solway Moss; or it may have been that he preferred in the circumstances not to challenge Atholl's reinforcing army. At any rate, he had turned back to Carlisle, and was reported to have gone south in person to confer with King Henry.

Two days in the physicians' hands in Edinburgh, with much dosing and blood-letting, and James, although still direly weak, appeared to be a little better, and was again demanding news of Oliver Sinclair. They could tell him nothing, but suggested that he should go to his wife at Linlithgow, in this her time of stress, with an heir to Scotland about to be born, hoping that this would distract and possibly cheer him. He did not react with any enthusiasm, but did not refuse to go. He declared that he would proceed to Falkland Palace and wait for Oliver there, calling in at Linlithgow in the by-going.

So, accompanied by the physicians, Arran and sundry courtiers, they set out westwards, James in his litter again, but a better and more comfortable one than Lindsay had been able to improvise. Even so, it took them all day to cover the eighteen miles. James was exhausted by the time they reached his wife, and instead of cherishing and supporting her, it was the other way round, with Marie seeking to comfort and look after him. She was obviously very near her time but was cheerful and practical as usual.

She wanted James to stay with her, naturally enough; but in his strangely obstinate mood he was set on getting to Falkland, apparently caring little about the child-to-come. He seemed to link Falkland and Sinclair in his bemused mind. He had much improved the old hunting-seat of late, Oliver aiding him.

The two Davids, both of whom admired and esteemed Marie de Guise, were loth to take her husband away from her at such a juncture, but James was insistent. So, after three days, they left for Fife. To shorten the journey for the sick monarch, instead of riding all the way round, by Stirling Bridge, they crossed Forth by the Queen Margaret's Ferry, and thence by Inverkeithing some eight miles to Hallyards, where the new Treasurer, Sir William Kirkcaldy of Grange, had a castle, where they spent the night. By the following evening they reached Falkland Palace, under the East Lomond Hill.

Despite his anxiety to get there, James showed little joy at arriving. Perhaps he was past joy. Dispirited, he sought his bed forthwith.

Davie Beaton had intended to proceed on to St. Andrews, but, the King's condition by no means improving, he decided that Holy Church's affairs must wait another day or two.

On the second day, a messenger arrived from Linlithgow. The Queen had given birth to a fair child. Both were well. It was a girl, and she proposed that they call her Mary, since she had been born on the Feast of the Immaculate Conception of the Virgin.

The effect of the news on James was profound. It was as though he had now received a final judgement upon him. He stared up at the ceiling, from his bed, for long moments, silent. Then his lips moved, soundlessly at first, before he got the words out.

"It came . . . with a lass," he whispered. "And it will go . . . with a lass!"

Slowly, ponderously, without looking at any present in the bedchamber, he worked his body round, to face the wall, and said no more, answering nothing to the empty compliments and well-wishings presented to his back.

Not all there probably would recognise to what the King's curious and rambling-seeming comment referred. But David Lindsay, for one, knew it as no rambling. James, whatever the state of his mind, had given voice to the most significant remark he had uttered for long. He alluded to the fact that the throne had come to the house of Stewart, back in 1370, on the death of Bruce's son David the Second, without heir; and the hero-king's grandson by his daughter Marjorie's marriage with Walter the High Steward, had succeeded as Robert the Second. So now James saw the writing on the wall, his own death and only a female child to carry on the line, or to fail to do so.

For five days thereafter Falkland Palace was in a strange state indeed, of almost suspended animation, as men waited, waited for what they scarcely admitted to themselves but which all in fact knew must happen. Some lords, such as Argyll and Rothes – whose heir, the Master, was one of the captives of Solway Moss – arrived, to join the all-but-silent, apprehensive company. The air of unreality was extraordinary. Yuletide was approaching, but there was no thought of preparing for the usual celebrations. Men almost tip-toed about the place. Since the rulers of Scotland were there, work did go on, but in low key and as it were unobtrusively. The least busy of all were the physicians, for James would have none of them near him, on his royal command. Apart from muttered conversations with the absent Oliver, he spoke to none, not even to David Lindsay – although he was the only one whom the King would bear to remain by his bedside for any length of time. He ate nothing, however much the cooks sought to tempt him. In fact and most evidently, he was willing himself to die.

And on that 14th December of 1542, die James Stewart did, aged only thirty-one years, six days after the birth of his daughter Mary, the end as strange as what had led up to it. For, after calling out, the first time for days, and with a sudden accession of strength, which brought men running, he was found to be sitting up in bed. Eyeing them all with an expression of surprising concern, not to say sweetness, he kissed his hand towards them in an almost childlike gesture. Raising that hand higher, he pointed upwards. Then, without a word spoken, he fell back on to his pillow and stopped breathing. It was as simple, and yet as extraordinary, as that.

David Lindsay, for one, shed tears – but then, as others remarked, that was only to be expected of poets and the like.

Beaton did not. But presently he remarked on it, as they left the royal bedchamber. "Dry your eyes, man," he said, but not unkindly, an arm around his friend's shoulder. "Time for that is past. For too long there has been gloom and inaction. There is now a realm to run. Now we have work to do, you and I – or others will do less well!"

Part Two

9

Work to do there was, that Yuletide and for months thereafter, in Scotland. Seldom indeed could the realm have been in a sorrier state, and consequently in such danger. After the most humiliating defeat in her history and with a large proportion of her leading figures captive in England, plus the months past of neglect in rule, suddenly she was left without a king and figurehead and with a week-old baby as monarch, and a girl-child at that. If indeed the infant Mary *were* to be the monarch, only lawful offspring of the dead king as she was. Scotland had never had a queen-regnant – unless the child Maid of Norway, who had never been crowned and never set foot in Scotland proper, was to be counted. Many held, in principle, that the idea was not only unsuitable but unconstitutional. The kingdom had always required a strong sovereign-lord, the *Ard Righ* or High King. By no stretch of the imagination could a woman fill that role, much less a week-old girl. Needless to say, the Earl of Arran, Lord Admiral, and his Hamilton faction, proclaimed this theory most strongly – since Arran, whose grandmother, the Princess Mary, had been a sister of James the Third, was next heir to the throne. So there was an immediate move to disinherit the child Mary and make Arran king.

But there was a still stronger move against anything such, led by Cardinal Beaton and Holy Church, and supported by most of the remaining great lords and officers of state. Arran was weak, amiable enough but indecisive. Moreover, weakness ran in the family, his eldest son quite mad and locked up. Such a one would make no worthy King of Scots. The child Mary was scarcely the ideal occupant of the throne, but she was the late monarch's only legitimate heir; and there was nothing in the dynastic code to say that a Queen of Scots, instead of a King, was ruled out. Moreover, any supercession of the child would be accounted a grave affront to France and King Francis. Unfortunately, although the first message to Falkland had declared mother and child to be well, when the court and officers of state repaired to Linlithgow, with the royal corpse, they found the child to be sickly and weak, an added worry. Marie de Guise herself was wel' enough – this was, after all, her fourth child-birth – and took the death of her husband with suitable sorrow but no extravagant bewailing; and needless to say she was strong in favour of her daughter's elevation to the throne, indeed astonished that there could be any other view.

This matter for urgent decision had to be dealt with at the same time as her father's funeral and the nation's mourning period, of course. These solemnities were David Lindsay's responsibility, as Lyon, and he ordered it all efficiently and with dignity. The King was buried at Holyrood Abbey, where so much that had been important in his young life had taken place and where sundry of his ancestors were interred, the body carried through the crowded Edinburgh streets with due pomp and ceremony, lighted torches flanking it, mourning trumpets blown and the nobility, gentry and officers of state all clad in black. Probably the citizenry grieved for him more sincerely than did most of the official mourners, for James's curious exploits amongst them as the Gudeman of Ballengeich had somehow endeared him to the common folk.

Thereafter pressing matters of governance fell to be decided, and quickly. The actual succession proved to be not too difficult, for most of the lords who might have supported Arran's claim were at present King Henry's prisoners in the south of England, and Beaton and Marie de Guise, with the useful aid of the Highland Earls of Argyll, Huntly and Atholl, sufficiently swayed a hurriedly called Privy Council to accept the child Mary, to be Queen of Scots. But, in fact, although this might seem all-important, more vital still was who was to *rule* Scotland during the infant monarch's long minority, who was to be Regent?

The Queen-Mother was the obvious choice. But there

was overmuch objection to that. She was too much of a newcomer to the country. There was a prejudice against a woman, especially with a female monarch also. The last Queen-Mother, Margaret Tudor, had been a disaster. And Marie herself was not keen. Arran, of course, was the next possibility; if he could not be king at least he could be Regent, his supporters claimed. But he would make but a feeble ruler and tend to be influenced by stronger and more ruthless men than himself. A powerful faction was against him, led by Davie Beaton. *He* had his own solution, to be sure, and came out with the claim that he had the late King's own support for it, in the form of a will – namely a Regency Council consisting of four of the great earls, Moray, James's illegitimate half-brother, Argyll, Huntly and Arran, with the Cardinal himself as chairman or preses.

This created a major furore, grave doubts being expressed on all hands as to the authenticity of this alleged document. David Lindsay himself was distinctly dubious about it, for he had heard nothing of it hitherto and he had been much closer to James than Beaton ever had; and the late monarch had never given the slightest hint that he was considering anything such or even interested in what would happen when he was gone.

Lindsay challenged his friend on the subject. "This will – it is strange that I never heard anything of it. You never spoke of it. I find that curious."

"It is scarcely a will – save that it *is* the expressed will of the departed James," the other said easily. "The *uninformed* are calling it a will. Our legal friends would name it a notarial instrument! James's wishes written down by another, and witnessed by Kirkcaldy of Grange and Learmonth." Sir William Kirkcaldy was the Treasurer and Sir James Learmonth of Balcomie the Master of the Household.

"When was this . . . acquired?"

"Soon after the birth tidings. James could not write nor sign, but he still could speak."

"Yet he said naught to me. Nor did you!"

"Why should I? It was not so important – not then. But

– be not so carking, man. It is the best answer, is it not? For the realm. A Regency Council. With three of the earls safe men."

"And you controlling all!"

"Scarcely that. But able perhaps to guide here and hinder there, when necessary."

Not wholly convinced, Lindsay left it at that.

It would have been hard to say whether Beaton's notarial instrument was a success or a failure at this stage. It convinced many – or perhaps it was the idea of the Regency Council which was approved; but it also aroused grave suspicions in many, and the Hamiltons were assiduous in spreading their assertions that it was a forgery.

With so many of the former Privy Councillors captive in England, there was a problem in assembling a Council carrying sufficient authority to decide effectively on the regency question. In theory, since it was the monarch's own council, it automatically dissolved on the demise of the sovereign. But since an infant could not choose new councillors and there was no Regent as yet to do it for the child, the general solution was for the former members to remain so until replaced or reappointed. But in present circumstances, finding a sufficiency of councillors was difficult. Both sides were reduced to introducing nominees who were not in fact true councillors – and of course these were contested.

Nevertheless, Beaton's and the Queen-Mother's faction, which perforce included David Lindsay since he could by no means bring himself to support Arran, looked like being able to produce a clear majority of votes, and a date for the necessary council meeting, towards the end of January, was being canvassed, after a busy month indeed. And then the situation was abruptly changed, all dramatically altered. Henry Tudor took a hand.

It was not war again, invasion or the threat of it, this time – indeed almost the reverse. Henry sent his prisoners back, unransomed, indeed laden with gifts.

So Scotland was treated to the extraordinary sight of a large proportion of her lords, lairds and chiefs riding home, on English horses, somewhat sheepishly, admittedly, free men – at least, free on certain conditions. They had a strange story to tell. At first, it seemed, Henry had treated them badly, mockingly, parading them through London streets tied together with ropes, like felons. And then, when the news of the birth of a princess and the death of King James reached them, all was different. Henry suddenly lifted them out of their cells and dungeons, announced that they were all his honoured guests, and showered hospitality upon them. They were to return to Scotland, which clearly needed them. And here they were.

It did not take long for their shrewder compatriots to elicit the reasoning behind the Tudor's unaccustomed clemency. None came home who had not agreed to give an undertaking to support the policy of a marriage of the infant Queen of Scots to Henry's five-year-old son, Edward, Prince of Wales; and to vote for the appointment of the Earl of Arran as Regent.

So, thus unexpectedly, Beaton and Marie de Guise were confounded. Not all the captured Scots nobles had agreed to Henry's terms, but sufficient had to ensure Arran's victory on any Privy Council – many, of course, were of that faction anyway, men James had antagonised.

Despite desperate delaying tactics, the Cardinal could not hold up the vital council meeting indefinitely. The vote was taken, and setting aside the alleged royal will, which speaker after speaker denounced as a blatant forgery – although it was not produced there and then – Arran was declared Regent and Governor, by a clear majority. And thereafter, on the urging of his clamorous supporters, as his first official acts, he pronounced this to be a true and effective meeting of Her Grace's Privy Council, and ordered the immediate arrest and imprisonment of the former Lord Privy Seal, the Archbishop of St. Andrews, on a charge of most treasonably forging the late King's signature for his own purposes. Beaton's assertion that no such signature was involved and that he could produce the notarial instrument, witnessed by the two officers of state, was shouted down and he was hustled away and put in the care of the Lord Seton, to be immured in Blackness Castle – Seton being one of those returned from London.

Thereafter all became a clean sweep for Arran and his supporters. The Council learned that another of King Henry's requirements was the return of the Earl of Angus to Scotland forthwith, for purposes undisclosed.

A very worried Lord Lyon King of Arms had to do the honours for Scotland's new Regent.

There followed a most unsettled and unsettling period for all who had any say in the rule and direction of the kingdom, notably so for David Lindsay, whose duties required that he remained close to both the Regent and the infant Queen, however uncomfortable a situation that might be. Arran made his headquarters in Edinburgh Castle, for security reasons, he being a somewhat timorous man; and Marie and her child remained at Linlithgow Palace, which was traditionally the jointure-house of the queens-dowager. So Lindsay had to wear down a trail between the two places, his horses almost capable of making the eighteen-mile journey on their own. It was no weather for such continual ridings, in what was proving to be one of the hardest winters in living memory, with even the seaside harbours and havens frozen over. The only consolation was that Janet was back at Linlithgow, reinstalled as Marie's lady-in-waiting. It was perhaps ironic that on each journey Lindsay had to pass near the walls of Blackness Castle, just five miles from Linlithgow, where Davie Beaton was held prisoner. Not that the captive's state was very grievous; indeed he was very comfortable, as he cheerfully admitted when his friend, using his authority as Lyon, called one day to interview him, ostensibly on behalf of the Regent. He would soon be out of there, Beaton assured, sitting before a roaring log fire, wine-beaker in hand; after all, he was the Papal Legate, and could excommunicate Arran and all his tribe at a nod of the head. He had not done so only because the business of the realm had to go on, and an excommunicated Regent would be unable to operate in many aspects which affected the Church; moreover, anathema emanating from Rome might possibly drive the feeble Arran further into Henry's arms and just conceivably cause him to turn reformer and seek to bring the Church here into line with that of England. Nevertheless, the Hamilton could not long hold the Legate, Cardinal and Archbishop prisoner – for instance, the child-Queen's coronation could not be held without his authority. Meanwhile, in this hard weather, he was very well at Blackness, with Seton wisely being accommodating. He was busy perfecting plans for the better rule of Scotland hereafter. Arran was a weakling and would find that not only was it unwise to antagonise Davie Beaton, but that he needed him.

Lindsay marvelled but did not totally disbelieve.

The matter of the coronation was, in fact, much troubling Arran and the Council. It was necessary that it should be put in hand without undue delay, but, being very much a religious ceremony, the Church's co-operation was essential – and with the head of the Church imprisoned, that was not forthcoming. Oddly, the most urgent pressure for the thing came from none other than Henry Tudor, who now sent his envoy, the arrogant Sir Ralph Sadler, to insist on an early ceremony, since he, the King, was not going to have his son Edward affianced to any but a crowned queen – presumably he feared that Arran might still himself try to take the throne. The implication that the marriage was more or less being taken for granted in England was not lost on the Scots.

Arran as Regent and Governor was scarcely a success. He was not an evil nor vicious man, but indecisive, vacillating, pulled this way and that by the ambitious and the unscrupulous. Problems demanding major and swift decisions came thick and fast, and he was not the man to make them. Moreover, the problems were much added to by an extraordinary claim put forward at this late stage by Lennox, the son of the earl whom the Bastard of Arran had cold-bloodedly murdered at Linlithgow Bridge sixteen years before. He now asserted, in a letter to the Privy Council from France, where he had been in semi-exile, that Arran himself was illegitimate, in that his late father had never been properly divorced from his second wife when he married his third, and Arran was the fruit of that third lady – who, strangely enough, was a cousin of Davie Beaton's – Janet, daughter of Sir David Beaton of Creich. Therefore, as illegitimate, he could not be a true claimant to the throne; and since his position as Regent was dependent upon being next heir, he now held that office by default. In fact, he himself, Lennox, should be Regent: for the Lennox Stewarts descended legitimately from a daughter of the same Princess Mary, source of the Hamilton claim. Added to this pronouncement was the information that he, and the Duc de Guise, were assembling an expedition, and squadron of ships, to come to Scotland to secure the safety of the Queen-Mother and her child and the relief of Holy Church.

This, of course, much encouraged what was being called the Church faction, as opposed to the English faction – and they required encouragement, for as well as Beaton their leader being imprisoned, the Earl of Angus had now returned and proved to be little improved for his long exile in England. He was his accustomed fiery and overbearing self, and although sent by Henry ostensibly to support Arran as Regent, in fact much offended the Hamilton by his clear assumption that he and his Douglases were the true power in the land again and that Arran held his position more or less thanks to *his* recommendations to King Henry. He demanded Douglas appointments to many offices of state.

The earls whom Beaton had proposed for his Regency Council, minus Arran himself, Huntly, Moray and Argyll, sought to achieve something on their own, and assembled at Perth with a fair number of their people, drawn mainly from beyond the Highland Line. They were joined there by other lords opposed to Arran, including even some of those returned from London captivity, such as the Earl of Bothwell, who now declared that their agreements to Henry's demands had been obtained only under duress and therefore were not binding. Huntly had a letter from the Cardinal, smuggled out of Blackness Castle. Plans were made for an advance south over Forth and on to Linlithgow, there to take the baby Queen and her mother into their protection and to convey them to the security of Stirling Castle, to be held against Arran and Angus both – for it was anticipated that the Douglases would try to get the little monarch into their own hands, as they had done with her father.

Spies alerted the Regent to this project, and alarmed, he called a parliament – which he was fairly sure that his faction could control, with Douglas aid, and which these so-called rebel lords could not attend without leaving their forces and so aborting their attempt. In this emergency he dispensed with the customary forty days' notice for summoning the Three Estates. He ordered David Lindsay to repair to Perth and officially summon these lords to parliament; also to disband their forces on pain of treason.

Lindsay, on this occasion, took a chance and declared that this was not a suitable task for Lyon, the crown's personal representative. The Albany Herald was sent in his stead.

This summons put the Perth earls in a predicament. To accept it was feeble; but to refuse to attend, and have parliament declare them in treason, would not help their cause, putting a dangerous weapon in the hands of Arran. In the end they compromised: Huntly, Moray, Bothwell and the others would attend the parliament; but Argyll, affecting sickness, would retire westwards with the assembled forces towards his own country, there to collect more of his extensive Campbell manpower, to be ready for more positive moves thereafter.

The parliament was held on 12th March in the great hall of Edinburgh Castle, and thanks to the desire of both factions to parade their fullest support, it was the best-attended for many a year. David Lindsay, ushering in the Regent to the throne, was impressed by the numbers present and was not long in weighing up the approximate strengths. At a guess, he made the two sides more or less equal in their known adherents. It was the uncommitted, therefore, who would decide the issues – and there were plenty of them there that day.

The Chancellor now Dunbar, Archbishop of Glasgow again, promptly put the first and essential motion – that the Estates confirmed the appointment of the Earl of Arran, Lord High Admiral, as Regent of the kingdom for her Grace, Mary, Queen of Scots. Thus early was the glove thrown down. The counter-motion for the Regency Council was put by the Earl of Bothwell. However, this was scarcely the most significant issue. Many who would have supported Beaton's proposal in the first instance were now loth to upset all. Even some churchmen, led by the Abbot of Paisley, Arran's illegitimate brother, voted for the motion. It was carried by a clear majority.

Arran, from the throne, thereupon declared that the Estates had many matters of importance to decide upon, but that first and foremost was the vital issue of the defence of the realm from attack and invasion. All recognised the dangers of the situation at present. But, fortunately, the King of England was now proving helpful in this situation. He had not only restrained his forces from further assault but had offered terms of peace. The most important of these was that their new Queen should be promised in marriage to his own son and heir, Edward Prince of Wales. Such union would effectively end the state of war between the two realms – which all would agree had for too long bedevilled them. He therefore commended the proposal to the assembly, and asked for acceptance. Almost as an afterthought, he added that King Henry required an affirmative answer by June month at latest, otherwise war would be declared.

This, needless to say, set the company in an uproar. Probably all there had known of the marriage proposal, but scarcely of the bald threat behind it. A dozen men were on their feet immediately, shouting, waving hands, protesting. A loud banging triumphed over the noise – but it was not the Chancellor's gavel. It was the hilt of the Earl of Angus's dirk, hammered on the back of his bench.

"Silence!" he exclaimed dramatically. "Douglas speaks!"

It was fifteen years since that voice had been upraised in parliament, and it had lost nothing of its authority and threat in the interim. Angus glared, not so much at Arran or the Chancellor but all around him at his fellow-commissioners. "Hear this – for I come from King Henry's self, and speak his further will. King Henry, in view of the unsettled state of this northern realm, requires the young Queen to be sent, for her safety, into his good keeping in England, on being affianced to his son. He requires also that . . ." He got no further, not only on account of the hubbub but because of more loud banging, this time by the Earl of Huntly's dirk-handle on wood, in emulation.

"My lord Chancellor," the Gordon chief cried. "I do protest. The Earl of Angus has no right nor permission to speak here. He was forfeited by the late King and by parliament. That has not been rescinded. Forby, he is now an English subject, swearing fealty to Henry. He cannot address the Scots parliament."

Again general outcry and disturbance, with the Douglases on their feet, and the Archbishop feebly beating his gavel, Arran half-risen from his throne. Never was it more evident that stronger hands were required for the control of Scotland's destinies.

With no lessening of the din, David Lindsay took a hand, ordering one of his trumpeters to sound a long blast. Into the sudden quiet that did achieve, he spoke strongly.

"As Lyon, the crown's usher, I command order and obedience to the Chancellor's ruling of this assembly. Otherwise I shall advise the Regent to adjourn the sitting."

That gained Archbishop Dunbar a hearing. His voice quivering somewhat, he announced that the Earl of Huntly's objection to the Earl of Angus's speech and presence was valid, under a previous parliament's forfeiture. But if parliament had power to forfeit, it also had power to lift forfeiture. If the assembly so desired, it could now do so.

He had barely finished when half a dozen Douglases and supporters were proposing and seconding such motion. Huntly moved the negative, and was seconded by Moray.

Angus, for his part, still standing, turned and eyed the entire gathering, slowly, deliberately, menace in every line of him. "Douglas counts!" he said, raising a hand to jab here and there with that dirk. "Douglas will not forget!"

With the Douglases still undoubtedly the most powerful house in Lowland Scotland, and their chief back with them, the threat could not fail to have its effect on the vulnerable and less courageous spirits. When the Chancellor called the vote, there was a small majority in favour of withdrawing Angus's forfeiture.

"The Earl of Angus may speak," Dunbar said, glancing unhappily at Arran.

The Douglas grinned. "As well," he commented briefly. "As I was saying, King Henry restrains his armies until June. In return, he requires agreement of the betrothal of his son to the infant Queen. The delivery of the said Queen into safe keeping in England meantime. Also the ending of the French alliance, and the handing over of the man Beaton into his custody – he who is most behind the French folly. This done, he will ensure that his English fleets prevent any French expedition under the renegade Earl of Lennox and the Duke of Guise from reaching Scotland. Lastly, he requires all royal castles and fortresses in Scotland to be yielded to officers appointed by him. These terms agreed, and there is peace between England and Scotland."

The comparative hush which followed as Angus sat down, was not acquiescence but appalled reaction to the implications. These were not terms for a peace treaty or even a royal betrothal. They were the announcement of a complete takeover of Scotland by Henry Tudor, his aim for thirty years, and which the Scots had been resisting since before Flodden.

Into the pause, Robert Reid, Bishop of Orkney, spoke up calmly. "My lord Chancellor – does the Earl of Angus appear here as the envoy of the King of England? I understand that was the role of Sir Robert Sadler, rather than any Scots earl!"

There was a sustained murmur of acclaim for that, not only from the clerical benches.

"I but put the facts before you," Angus said, not getting up. "Lest you mistake."

Huntly rose. "Since my lord of Angus is so close to King Henry, let him take back this message to his master. The Queen of Scots will never be delivered up to the English, save over the dead bodies of her people! She is but three months old! Whom she marries there is time and to spare to decide, at a later date. The royal fortresses are hers, not parliament's, to yield to any. And the Cardinal-Archbishop Beaton, far from being sold to Henry, should be released from imprisonment forthwith. He has done no ill to the realm; on the contrary. And as we all know, to the entire kingdom's hurt, no christening, marriage or burial is being permitted by the Church, in the Pope's name, because of this imprisonment. This cannot continue."

There was a mixed reception for that, the factions lining up again.

"That is no motion, my lord," the Chancellor observed. "We all wish to see the Cardinal released and the proper functions of Holy Church being resumed. Do you so move?"

"I do."

"And I second," Moray said. "I would add that, with my lords of Bothwell and Argyll, not present, and I am sure Huntly himself, we would offer our surety that the Cardinal will remain available to answer any charges the Regent or this parliament may prefer against him. That this kingdom may no longer suffer deprivation of its Christian services and solace. Also, the holding up of her Grace's coronation."

That was shrewd bargaining, for many there, whether they loved Davie Beaton or no, were much exercised over the Papal Legate's ban on services – baptisms postponed, weddings delayed, corpses unburied, last rites to the sick denied. And the coronation must be celebrated soon.

"I move contrary," Angus said. "Let us be quit of the Pope's lackeys – as England has done."

This time the vote was almost equal. Arran resolved the issue by promising due consideration of the Cardinal's position, with probably relaxation of his conditions.

Angus conceded, shortly, that so long as Beaton was

kept secure, either in Scotland or England, that would suffice. He must not be allowed to flee to France, to make more trouble. Undoubtedly he it was who had instigated Lennox and de Guise to threaten invasion.

Heartened, Huntly was up again. This of the royal fortresses – he moved rejection of any and all foreign demands for their yielding. That was agreed by a sizeable majority.

Angus, presumably recognising that he had overplayed his hand, did not retract – he was not that sort of man. On the contrary, he rose to challenge further. If Henry invaded, he pointed out, he could *take* any and every royal fortress in the land – as indeed could Douglas, if it were for the realm's good. None was as strong as his own Tantallon. Words and resolutions would not halt Henry – only the sharper sword. And Douglas could wield the sharpest sword in the land. Let none forget it.

Huntly was not to be put down thus. He moved that on no account was any consideration to be given to handing over the child-Queen to the English. Moray, more carefully, seconded, with the amendment that this should apply until Mary was at least ten years old.

That again was accepted by the majority.

But now, at last, came the great decision, which could not be put off any longer and on which war or peace hinged – the marriage proposal itself. Few there desired it, indubitably. But fewer still were prepared to risk Henry's fury by outright rejection. After Solway Moss Scotland was not ready for full-scale war. Even Huntly was cautious.

Arran it was, strangely enough, who took the initiative, a weak man's device – suitable perhaps for a weakened nation in divided condition. Despite his earlier initial request for an affirmative answer, he now proposed, to avoid any outright rejection and war, and to carry the parliament with him, that they should send ambassadors to Henry's court, to discuss the matter further, all the details and conditions – these not to commit the parliament but to report back. This, although Angus and his Douglases snorted and sneered, commended itself to most there as getting them off the hook, meantime at least. Coming from the throne, it was accepted without a vote, amidst muted acclaim.

There were other matters of routine for the Estates to deal with, but that was the principal business covered, both factions having had their successes and failures. What remained included a number of offices of state, sheriffdoms and the like being confirmed to Douglases. One of the last items was a directive that, on a convenient occasion, the Lord Lyon King of Arms should embark on a tour of the capitals of Christendom, in order to return to the rulers thereof the orders and decorations awarded by them to the late King James. This was always done; and was opportunity to forge new links.

David Lindsay wondered when, in fact, the occasion might be convenient, in present conditions, however appealing the notion.

10

It seemed some time since David Lindsay had ridden that well-known road from the Mount of Lindifferon to St. Andrews, by Cupar and Pitscottie and Strathkinness – not indeed for a couple of years, what with one thing and another. And even now it was scarcely convenient, and had been quite difficult to arrange. For his duties as Lyon were onerous and taxing these days, with his presence required at both the Queen-Mother's and the Regent's establishments – and in the circumstances, these were never close. Gone were the days when King James had been content enough to dispense with David's services for quite long periods, and he and Janet could live their own lives at Lindifferon. It had not been easy to gain leave-of-absence, even for a few days, from both courts, in answer to Davie Beaton's urgent plea that he should call at St. Andrews Castle at the soonest.

So this day in early July, with the hay being cut again on all the rich farmlands of the Howe of Fife, he rode unescorted eastwards, and was glad enough to be away even for a brief period from all the pressures and strains of his life, set between the two factions which were pulling Scotland this way and that, under English threat – even though he was well aware that Beaton, summoning him thus, was not likely to add to his peace of mind.

The Cardinal had in fact been back at St. Andrews for almost a month, but in theory still a prisoner therein. This was typical of Arran's reaction to pressures – compromise. Parliament's urging that Beaton should be freed in order that Church services could be resumed, had produced this, a deal. In return for lifting the ban on burials, baptisms and weddings, and the threat of excommunication, the Archbishop and Legate should return to St. Andrews and the direction of ecclesiastical affairs – but not state affairs. And he should still be nominally captive, forbidden to leave the primatial city. But if the Regent believed that this would prevent Beaton from dipping his oar in the realm's business, he did not know his Cardinal.

When presently Lindsay rode in through the West Port gate, he was struck anew by the city's atmosphere of timelessness. Nothing ever seemed to change. Students and clerics thronged the streets in their unhurried strolling, gowns and robes and vestments rivalling the rainbow for colour, bells tolling from monasteries, priories and chapels, chapmen peddling books, tracts and relics, and fishwives singing stridently their wares – all as it had been when he himself had been a student here all those years ago, and Davie Beaton also.

In name, the Lord Seton was still the Cardinal's gaoler and was therefore theoretically in command at the castle; but the fiction of that was manifested by the splendidly uniformed archiepiscopal guard, with their mitred breastplates, who kept the gatehouse-pend and suspiciously and arrogantly scrutinised all callers, even Scotland's King of Arms.

When he was ushered into the Cardinal's presence in the Sea Tower, it was to find him closeted with another and younger man, slightly-built and sharp featured, who eyed the newcomer suspiciously.

"Ah, David!" Beaton exclaimed, rising, both hands out. "So you have effected your release from Arran's clutches! I am grateful. It is good to see you." He turned. "This is Matthew, Earl of Lennox. And here, my lord, is Sir David Lindsay, Lord Lyon."

David was surprised, naturally. "Lennox . . .? My lord, I did not know. I had not heard . . ." He bowed slightly. "I knew your father. Indeed I witnessed his grievous death. I greet your return to Scotland. In sorry circumstances."

Matthew Stewart inclined his head but did not rise nor speak.

"My lord has been here for three days," Beaton said. "Hence my hurried message to you, since he cannot long keep the others waiting, in the said sorry circumstances."

"Others . . .?"

The Cardinal took David's arm and led him over to the

window, to point seaward. Far out, on the horizon indeed, it was just possible to discern perhaps half a dozen specks, which must be ships, and at that range, large ships.

"The Frenchmen? The French squadron?" Lindsay exclaimed. "So – Henry did not turn them back, after all."

"The Tudor is not always so effective as his threats! As we shall further prove, God willing! They sailed east-about, near to Denmark, and so here. But – those ships cannot linger out there overlong. And to land their people just at this present might be . . . unwise."

"They have already waited too long," Lennox jerked. "And the weather may change." He sounded sour.

"Yes – so there is need for haste."

"Haste for what?" Lindsay asked warily.

"For a betterment of this unhappy realm's state, my friend. And a setback to King Henry. You will agree that is necessary?"

The other waited, aware of Lennox's continued suspicions of him.

Beaton went on. "Arran will never stand up to Henry. Nor indeed to the Douglases. He must be replaced." He gave a side-glance at Lennox. "But that may take time. Meantime we must make him *wish* to be replaced, make the regency most difficult for him. He is a weak man, lacking stomach for a struggle . . ."

"*I* should be Regent," Lennox interjected. "The Hamilton is illegitimate, born out of true wedlock. I am next heir to the throne."

The Cardinal nodded. "To be sure. But Arran *is* Regent now, and replacing him will not be achieved by such assertions, however true, my lord. What will most grievously disconcert his regency, short of civil war – of which Henry would take full advantage? What but the abstraction of the infant Queen from his power and grasp. As Regent, he does all in the Queen's name. If she were clearly and most evidently beyond his care, and in the keeping of others, so that he could not approach her, he would be gravely weakened in his authority. In especial since *I* hold the Privy Seal. I have never yielded it up."

"So that is it!" Lindsay exclaimed. "You would take a leaf out of Angus's book? Abduct James's daughter, as Angus abducted James!"

"I do not like the word abduct. Say rescue, or at least take into safe keeping. For there is word that Angus himself is thinking to do the same – only, he will deliver the child to Henry. Another cause for haste."

"So – why send for me?"

"You can greatly help. I am held here in St. Andrews, meantime – at least, I may not go to Linlithgow to see and warn Queen Marie. You can. We would wish her to be ready to move, with the child, to Stirling Castle, when we come for them. We will come in force – my lord here, Huntly, Argyll, Moray, Bothwell and other sure lords. Erskine, at Stirling, will receive us in the castle. It is the most secure fortress in the land, as *you* know well. Therein the young Queen will be safe from Arran and Angus both, and so from Henry. Arran will not be able to see her, save by our permission. So we can guide his feeble hand and, if may be, convince him that he is not the man who should be Regent. If any of the said lords were to appear at Linlithgow before that, they would be suspect and Arran forewarned – Angus also, for we know that he has his spies there. But *you* can come and go freely."

"And you believe that the Queen-Mother will agree to this?"

"I do. She has no love nor respect for Arran. And well recognises the menace of Angus . . ."

"Tell her that I am here, man. With ships and troops from her brothers in France," Lennox put in. "And the King of France's blessing."

"Is the Duc de Guise out there with the ships, my lord?"

"No. He did not sail. My lord Cardinal here advised against it."

"It was too dangerous. If Henry had attacked and captured the Duke, it would have precipitated war – for which we are not ready. France likewise. Better that my lord's force should be seen as a Scots one, with only French stiffening. For the same reason, better that the

French troops do not land here, as yet. Until we have the Queen safely in Stirling. It would give Arran, and Angus too, comfort to say that a *French* army had taken over the child-Queen of Scots – offend many who might support us. As I have explained to my lord here. His ships cannot sail out there endlessly, to be sure. The troops could land somewhere hidden, meantime – at my town of Arbroath, perhaps, to await our summons." Davie Beaton sounded just a little less confident and assured than was usual about that – perhaps why Lennox was sour-seeming.

"When do you intend this descent on Linlithgow, in force?"

"Very soon, it must be. For this treaty of Arran's has been signed at Greenwich. On the first of this month. Agreeing that the child-Queen should be placed in Henry's care, soon, and the marriage agreed. Arran has yielded, as I knew he would do. So, we have not long – for either Angus will seize the child or Henry will send for her. A week, ten days, and we shall come. Argyll and Huntly are assembled west of Perth, others coming also. We shall then march, leave a strong guard at Stirling, and then make for Linlithgow. It is our hope that you will have all ready for us."

"And my duty to the Regent, as Lyon?"

"Your prime duty is to the Queen, surely. To the Regent only as deputy to the Queen. If the Regent fails the Queen, agrees to deliver her up to her enemies, as he has done in this Greenwich treaty, then he has clearly forfeited Lyon's support and duty – as that of all other leal men."

That seemed undeniable.

Presently Lindsay said that he must go, if he were to be back at Linlithgow next day. Beaton personally escorted him downstairs, to see that he obtained refreshment for his journey back to Lindifferon. In the process he confided in his friend that Lennox's arrival at this moment, with his Frenchmen, was in fact something of a nuisance. He had encouraged him and de Guise to assemble a force and shipping, yes, but more as a threat to Henry and Arran than any outright challenge; and certainly not to sail until called for. He did not greatly like this son of a fine father;

and while his claims about Arran's illegitimacy were useful to help in unseating the Regent, Lennox himself was, he felt, unsuitable material to replace the Hamilton, and was not to be encouraged. Somewhat wryly Lindsay sympathised with him on the problems which were apt to beset the intriguer.

On a final note, Beaton divulged that he had it on reliable authority that, to ensure the signing of the marriage-compact and treaty, Henry was offering Arran's mad son his daughter by Anne Boleyn, Elizabeth, as wife – which looked as though the Tudor was less sure of himself and his Scottish plans than he seemed to be.

The Cardinal and his confederate lords – Seton, his alleged gaoler now appeared to have become one – duly arrived at Linlithgow ten days later, with no fewer than seven thousand men, of whom some five hundred were Frenchmen that Lennox had insisted that he brought along. Marie de Guise welcomed them without reserve, Lindsay having had no difficulty in persuading her that the move to Stirling was in the best interests of herself and her daughter. She clearly trusted Davie Beaton's judgement; and the French contingent with her brothers' support helped.

The march of so large a company from Perth to Stirling, and then to Linlithgow, could not have been accomplished unobserved, needless to say, and the Regent must have been informed, for he hastily rode out from Edinburgh with a force mainly of his Hamiltons. But his information must have been updated as to numbers, for he halted discreetly at Kirkliston, midway between the capital and Linlithgow and sent a herald forward to demand who and what and why.

The arrival of one of his own pursuivants was somewhat embarrassing for David Lindsay. He decided that he should go in person to Arran and clarify his own position as well as that of the Queen-Mother, the Cardinal and his lords. If necessary, he would resign as Lyon.

But that was not called for when he had ridden the eight miles to Kirkliston with the pursuivant. Arran proved to be more agitated than incensed, and was almost relieved to see his Lord Lyon. Apparently he was expecting to have to do battle, and was in no position to contemplate its outcome with equanimity – having less than two thousand men with him at present. When he heard that Beaton's intention was only to escort the infant Queen to Stirling, for her safety, he made no great outcry, beyond asserting that he ought to have been consulted first. He declared that David must go back and tell the Cardinal and his associates that he, the Regent, must have access to the monarch at all times. Also that he required the Privy Seal to be available or else delivered up to him. And, a final and very significant point which in part explained his fairly conciliatory attitude, he wanted to know when the Cardinal was prepared to celebrate the Queen's coronation, which must be effected soon. This was, of course, something of a trump card in Beaton's hand, for Henry was demanding a crowned bride for his son; and anyway, tradition required an early ceremony. In theory, it might have been possible for the Archbishop of Glasgow to officiate, instead of the Primate; but the Cardinal could rule that out – and undoubtedly would. So the Regent was held.

The Lord Lyon was able to return to Linlithgow, therefore, as the envoy of the Regent now, and no resignation called for.

Thereafter, although some hot-heads, including Lennox, advocated an advance on the Hamiltons and their supporters there and then, defeating them and possibly capturing Arran himself and then taking Edinburgh, while they had the chance, the more responsible countered that. Beaton always preferred negotiation and diplomacy to battle, and pointed out that such a course would play into *Angus's* hands, give the Douglas his excuse to rise in arms, allegedly to defend the Regent but really to make a bid to take over Scotland himself, calling on English troops to assist.

So, instead, the seven thousand plus the royal household trooped unhurriedly and in almost holiday spirits back to Stirling, almost an anti-climax as it was.

At Stirling, David Lindsay found his position little changed from heretofore – only now he beat his trail between *Stirling* and Edinburgh, between *Beaton* and Arran. It was a curious situation, for he was by no means approving of all the Cardinal's activities and methods, nor yet had any use for Arran as Regent. Yet as Lyon, he had to act the representative of both, sometimes seeming to advocate moves contrary to his own beliefs, yet trusted by both protagonists.

For there was much negotiation between the two, Beaton on the surface appearing to accept the Regent's authority while seeking to establish his own ascendancy and policies, indeed all but imposing them on Arran, who tended to give in on major issues while being placated on minor ones.

The Cardinal made the most of his two great advantages, the Regent's fear and hatred of Angus and the need for the coronation. Beaton postponed the latter deliberately in order to wring the maximum concessions out of the Regent. Until the Queen was crowned that man could not fulfil for Henry the terms of that infamous Treaty of Greenwich. This could not go on indefinitely, of course; September was probably as late as it could be left. But Beaton was adept at finding excuses meantime – and in persuading Marie de Guise to wait also.

Oddly enough, on the other side of the exchange, Lindsay found himself in agreement with at least one of Arran's projects, and indeed urging it on the Cardinal. This was a call to permit the reading of the scriptures in the churches in the vernacular, instead of in Latin, a reform surely in the interests of true religion but which Holy Church was strangely reluctant to grant, apparently on orders from Rome. Preaching and the Lord's Prayer also should be offered in a tongue folk could understand. Beaton was not prepared to authorise this reform, declaring that it would but bring others in its train. He asserted that Arran had been got at by the so-called reformers and would have to be shown his errors of judgement. A breach between two old friends was widened.

Meantime Angus was not idle that summer. He appeared to be making a fairly comprehensive personal tour round Scotland, or at least the Lowlands of Scotland for he did not venture into the Highlands. Davie Beaton made it his business to find out what was the object of this exercise, for although the Earl had been absent from the country for fifteen years, that man was surely not just renewing his acquaintance with the land and former friends. Presently the Cardinal became convinced that he was, in fact, visiting in turn almost all the recipients of King Henry's pensions and subsidies – of which Beaton had a list of over three hundred, some even his own bishops and senior clergy – no doubt with the object of reminding them of their obligations to the donor, and of support for himself in a push for power.

Lindsay, for one, was astonished at Beaton's reaction, which was to send his own envoys in Angus's wake, to offer still larger bribes to cancel out the English ones. It seemed that the de Guises had sent money as well as troops, with Lennox, a treasure-chest to aid their sister's and niece's cause. It all sounded unsavoury in the extreme; but the Cardinal's policy was usually to use all weapons which came to hand.

Scotland balanced uneasily on this seesaw of conflicting powers, threats, inducements and loyalties.

As a further example of Beaton's opportunism, Lindsay was sent to Arran to inform him of this latest activity on the part of Angus and to suggest that it called for a conference between Regent and Primate, since clearly it could affect them both. He proposed that they meet at a midway point, Callander House, near Falkirk, the main seat of Lord Livingstone, one of the Beaton supporters. Lindsay was instructed to intimate to Arran, as a confidential aside, that Holy Church was in fact seeking to outbid Angus and Henry financially in this matter. To his surprise, David found the Regent to be much exercised over this development, worried about a possible rising of Henry's pensioners against himself, and with no large funds at his disposal, other than his private fortune, the more appreciative of the Cardinal's largesse. He agreed to the proposed meeting at Falkirk, but declared that it must be kept secret.

So these two so unequally-endowed competitors for the rule of Scotland duly came together on a day of early August, in Callander House, near where Wallace had lost his Battle of Falkirk, the Regent all but alone, having slipped out of Edinburgh secretly with only his illegitimate half-brother, the Abbot of Paisley – who was having an ever-greater influence, and at the same time ambitious for Church preferment, and coming more and more towards the Cardinal's camp; and Beaton attended by their host, Livingstone, and David Lindsay. The latter felt not a little sorry for the well-meaning but simple and indecisive Hamilton, come to parley with one of the cleverest men in Christendom. The outcome could scarcely be in doubt.

Even so, Lindsay was surprised at the ease and completeness of Beaton's victory on almost every count that mattered. Eventually the two men actually shook hands, on as extraordinary a compact between a ruler and a subject as could have been envisaged. Arran was to remain Regent, to have access to the Queen and Privy Seal when necessary – and his brother to have the next vacant bishopric. Also the coronation would be held in September. On the other hand, Beaton would retain the Queen at Stirling; Arran would refuse to carry out the terms of the Treaty of Greenwich, and the Tudor marriage-compact would be cancelled; and they would unite against Henry and Angus both. Moreover, Arran would reject the offer of the Princess Elizabeth for his son; and, astonishingly, he would agree to give up his reformist tendencies and pressure to have the scriptures read in Scots – and to make this conversion suitably apparent to all, he would go through a ceremony of repentance and reconciliation, say the day before the coronation, indication to troublemakers everywhere that Holy Church was not in a mood to put up with harassment. Beaton shot a half-amused, half-warning glance at David Lindsay as Arran bowed to this requirement.

The Regent rode back to Edinburgh leaving Davie Beaton master of Scotland in all but name.

On 8th September 1543 the extraordinary drama was enacted, rivalling anything that Lindsay could have devised in his *Satire of the Three Estates*, of the Governor, Commander-in-Chief and Lord High Admiral of Scotland doing public penance in the chapel of the Franciscan monastery at Stirling, in the most thorough and unequivocal form. Much of the senior nobility as well as the Church hierarchy was present to see it performed, that there be no doubts. The Earls of Argyll and Bothwell held the required towel over his head as he knelt, while the Regent confessed his apostasy and vowed repentance and no further backsliding, in a gabble of words dictated by the Franciscan prior, before receiving absolution and the sacrament from the Cardinal. Lyon, in attendance, was almost ashamed to be a witness.

The coronation next day of Mary Queen of Scots, delayed as it might be, was a great occasion, as well it might be, unique as it was. Never before had a queen-regnant been crowned in Scotland, the unfortunate Maid of Norway not having got that far. Whether it was an event for national congratulation was another matter which only time would prove; but meantime it ought to be something to celebrate, to sing about perhaps, possibly even to shout about, for a people long depressed, threatened and misgoverned. Davie Beaton at least was determined that it should be so, and in a position to ensure it. David Lindsay, as Lord Lyon, was inevitably intimately involved; but as playwright and poet laureate also, Beaton calling on him to organise something suitably spectacular and memorable – not the religious part so much, which had to be formalised and approximately traditional, but for the ceremonial and subsequent jubilations. In a way, as Lindsay pointed out, it was an inauspicious date, for 9th September was the anniversary of the disaster of Flodden-field; but it was also the Feast of the Nativity of the Blessed Virgin, and so chosen.

The actual crowning ceremony was held in the chapel of Stirling Castle, which being of only modest size, meant that but a limited number could be present. The great coronation chair, or throne, was placed up before the altar, with a lesser one nearby for the Queen-Mother. A choir of boys sang sweet music. Clergy with censers swung their aromatic incense, and the bishops and mitred abbots all but filled the chancel, while the nobility packed the nave. Greenery and flowers were everywhere.

To a flourish of trumpets, Lindsay led in the Earl of Argyll bearing the sword of state, the Earl of Lennox carrying the sceptre and the Earl of Arran with the crown on a cushion. These three were all of royal descent. Thereafter came the Queen-Mother carrying in her arms the all-important infant, followed by seven more earls, Erroll the High Constable, the Marischal, Moray, Atholl, Huntly, Montrose and Bothwell – this to emphasise the continuing tradition that the High King of Scots, and before that, of Alba, was always appointed, from Pictish times, by the seven earls or mormaors. At the same trumpet-call as these entered by the main west door and up the central aisle, the Cardinal-Primate entered alone at the north transept from the chapter house, gorgeously vested, and so was able to be at the altar when the main procession arrived.

Unfortunately the trumpet-blast had alarmed the child-monarch, who was now protesting vigorously, her mother smilingly soothing. The seven earls looked somewhat offput, but not Davie Beaton, who chuckled and waved a reassuring hand.

With no preordained formula for crowning a baby girl, Beaton more or less made it up as he went along, and since the child was being a little fractious, cut it all down to a blessed minimum. Having silenced the choristers with a gesture, he intoned a brief intimation to their Creator that the service had begun and His blessing would be convenient, and moved to receive the infant from Marie de Guise. He cradled her genially, even competently – after all, he had experience of five children by Marion Ogilvy – and then nodded to David Lindsay, who came to take her, a little less confidently. Queen Marie went to her lesser throne and when she was seated Lindsay, feeling rather a fool, moved to the true throne and there stood, not behind it as he had done so often for the child's father, nor at the side, but right in front, close up but with his back to it. He did not actually sit, of course. The child had stopped crying, gazing up and apparently fascinated by the jewelled cross-of-office he wore in the front of his Lyon's tabard.

Mary Stewart had got over her early weaknesses and was now a spirited infant of nine months, still thin but well-made, with her father's red hair and the great Stewart eyes. She was used to David Lindsay's company, of course.

Argyll with the sword and Lennox with the sceptre took up their positions on either side of the coronation chair, while Arran stood facing Lindsay. At the altar again, Beaton consecrated a chrismatory of oil, and with this came to anoint the child on the brow, similarly to baptism. With no hostile reaction, he patted the red head, then turned to take the glittering crown from Arran, handing him the oil-chrism instead, and returning to the altar. There he said a sonorous prayer, held the crown high to invoke a special blessing. Bringing it back, flanked by the Archbishop of Glasgow and the Abbot of Scone – this latter to emphasise the continuity of tradition from the times when the monarchs had been crowned at Scone sitting on the fabled Stone of Destiny – he signed to Lindsay.

That man now had the distinctly awkward task of holding out his royal charge at arms' length, over the throne, in an approximately upright position, praying the while urgently that Mary would not struggle nor wriggle. Well recognising the problem, the Cardinal made no delay but came close to hold the crown above the infant's head. It was far too large actually to place thereon of course, but he allowed it to touch the reddish hair. Mary was beginning to whimper at all these curious attentions, when a beam of the midday sunlight slanting in through a stained-glass window caught and reflected on jewels on the crown, and the whimper changed to a gurgle of pleasure.

Thankfully Beaton announced loudly that in the name of God Almighty, the Father, the Son and the Holy Ghost he crowned Mary, by the grace of the same Almighty

God, anointed Queen of Scots, one hundred and seventh of her line, the most ancient in all Christendom. Let all men see, hear and give thanks and leal duty and service.

As cheers rang through the chapel and were taken up by the great throng outside, Beaton handed back the crown to Arran and took the chrismatory, while David Lindsay dealt with his next problem. This was to seat the little monarch on the throne, if only briefly. This was less simple than it sounds, for there was a lot of coronation chair for a very small person, and although Mary might just be able to sit, her bottom was as yet distinctly egg-shaped, and the seat of the throne, even though cushioned, was wide. It was a matter of propping her up in a corner against one of the arms, but she promptly slid down on to her back. He tried again, with the same result. Then Marie de Guise came to his aid. Rising from her own chair, she took from Arran the cushion on which the crown sat, leaving him to hold the diadem, and went to set her daughter upright, tucking the cushion against her. This sufficed, but she remained standing at the side, holding the child's arm. David took up his position at the other side. Sighs of relief were evident around.

The Cardinal raised his hand high. "God save the Queen!" he cried.

And from all present thundered the refrain, "God save the Queen! God save the Queen! God save the Queen!" Again and again, echoing from beyond the walls, in roared acclaim.

The noise not unnaturally somewhat upset Scotland's monarch, and with her lower lip beginning to tremble, her mother took her up in her arms and so held her. As well that she did, for nearby the group of trumpeters blew a loud and prolonged fanfare, which seemed to shake the very foundations of that comparatively modest building, and caused Mary, wide-eyed and wide-mouthed, to seek her mother's breast in comfort.

This over, Lindsay signed to the Rothesay Herald, who handed to him a rolled parchment scroll. Raising his hand for attention, he began to read or rather recite. "Hear the descent of this, our anointed and crowned Queen of Scots

– the illustrious Mary, daughter of James, son of James, son of James, son of James, son of James, son of Robert, son of Robert, son of Marjorie, sister of David and daughter of Robert . . ."

On and on he read, back past the descendants of Margaret and Canmore, past MacBeth and Duncan, to the Malcolms and Kenneths and all the curiously named Dungals, Aeds, Girics and the rest of the long centuries of the Pictish line, and beyond into the misty realms of myth and legend. He did not read the entire list of one hundred and six, since even imaginative Celtic sennachies had not found names for many in prehistoric times; but sufficient to satisfy the most demanding of genealogists and traditionalists of this most ancient of kingdoms, as was done at every coronation.

Mary fell asleep.

This was really the end of the religious ceremonial. Led by the choristers singing a triumphal anthem, the official party processed out to show the monarch to the waiting crowds, the Queen-Mother still carrying her daughter, Beaton and the clergy following on. Tumultuous scenes ensued.

Thereafter there was feasting, in the great hall for the nobility, clergy and gentry, and outdoors on the tourney-ground for the commonality and the citizenry of Stirling, all paid for by Holy Church, nothing stinted. While this was proceeding, David Lindsay staged his pageantry, each item performed first indoors and then out, with the weather fortunately reasonably kind. These consisted of a series of tableaux depicting suitable incidents in the lives and reigns of Mary's predecessors, enacted by a large team of not only players and mummers but by not a few scions of noble and chiefly houses and their ladies, whom David had enrolled for the occasion. He had chosen his episodes carefully, that they might be both dramatic and significant, indicative of Scotland's enduring *people's* monarchy as distinct from the feudal dominance of other kings, including the English, emphasising that their true and cherished style and title was *Ard Righ*, or High Kings of Scots, high intimating the foremost of others, or of lesser kings, the electing mormaors, now earls; and of the Scots, not of Scotland, underlining the same message, the father of the people not just their lord, in fact the supreme clan-chief, an image all could understand.

To demonstrate this theme, he started with a tableau of Kenneth MacAlpin, general and King of the Scots of little Dalriada, marrying the heiress of Brude, High King of Alba, in 843, and so uniting the Pictish and Scottish polities. Then he showed Malcolm the Third, The Terrible, defying Knud, or Canute, Emperor of the Angles, Saxons and Danes, at this same Stirling, to emphasise the basic and long-continuing struggle of the Scots for independence and freedom against southern efforts at domination. Then MacBeth, grandson of the last, issuing his enlightened code of laws which had so ensured and protected the Scots' essential freedoms. David the First he depicted as signing the charters creating Scotland's splendid galaxy of abbeys, Melrose, Kelso, Jedburgh, Drybourgh, Cambuskenneth and the rest; and the parallel instituting of the parish system of local government, to limit the oppressions of the great lords. Bruce, the hero-king, he presented watching the signing of the famous Declaration of Independence at Arbroath in 1320, and accepting that if he failed the ideal of freedom, even he, or any other monarch, should be dismissed and replaced. James the First he presented as returning from his long imprisonment in England to cleanse his country of its oppressors. James the Fourth assuming the title of Lord of the Isles, after bringing the Highland West under the crown. And finally the new Queen's father instituting the Court of Session, which was to ensure the continued operation of MacBeth's laws of equity for all citizens. It was all somewhat idealised, to be sure, but its message was plain – and was directed towards Davie Beaton as much as to anyone else present.

The Cardinal applauded as loudly as any, too.

So coronation day came to a well-acclaimed close, only Sir Ralph Sadler reporting sourly in a despatch to his master in London that Mary had been crowned with "such solemnitie as they do use in this country, which is not very costlie".

Beaton was now firmly in the saddle, and showed it, which moved his critical friend to wonder when he would take over the regency also, even the throne perhaps, since he now had everything else! To which the other replied, unoffended, that it was much better to keep Arran as Regent, so long as he did what he was told and was there to take any blame for mishaps. And mishaps there were bound to be, for Henry Tudor would not take all this lying down, his imposed treaty torn up, his marriage offer rejected. Angus and his supporters, including the Earls of Glencairn and Cassillis, although summoned to the coronation, had boycotted the ceremony, and could be expected not to be long now in showing their teeth. A strong hand was needed at Scotland's helm – and there was no doubt as to whose the Cardinal believed that hand should be.

11

The King of England's fury knew no bounds, as was only to be expected, verging indeed on madness. But it so happened that other aspects of his madness were pre-occupying him and his realm that autumn, nearer home, and he was hindered from unleashing his fullest wrath on Scotland there and then. After creating the forceful Thomas Cromwell, Earl of Essex, he decided that he was getting altogether too uppish and had him executed. In his place he took as principal adviser the Duke of Norfolk, lately invader of Scotland, his trusted soldier, despite the Duke being an obstinate Catholic, even going so far as to marry, as his fifth wife, Norfolk's niece, Catherine Howard – the fourth, Anne of Cleves having proved unsatisfactory, like all the others. But the Howard woman did not come up to Henry's exacting and peculiar standards either, and so had to tread the well-worn path to the scaffold also – which put the King at odds with his best soldier and the most powerful family in England, and threatened further Catholic revolt. So the commander-in-chief of his military forces was not now to be trusted for an invasion of Scotland, or anything else. And the Tudor was involved in marrying Catherine Parr, which was causing some trouble.

Despite all this, however, Scotland did not escape all the consequences of her defiance, far from it. Henry had his fleet seize a group of Scottish ships in the Norse Sea, alleging an act of war in invading England's sea-space – this although the vessels were in fact unarmed merchanters loaded with salt fish for France, a regular trade. He ordered the new Chief Warden of the Marches to release all Armstrongs whom he had in captivity after one of the less fortunate of that lawless clan's Cumbrian forays, on condition that they returned over the Border to devastate the properties of all the Scots nobles who had so notably failed him over the Solway Moss release, specifically and extraordinarily the Douglases – for he was now blaming Angus for having achieved nothing on his behalf, after all his cherishing. He also promised to burn Edinburgh as well as a host of lesser places, and to provide every Scots tree with its fruit of hanging men, women and children. And, rather more subtly, he offered the Earl of Lennox his niece in marriage. This was the Lady Margaret Douglas, daughter of Margaret Tudor by Angus; and though partly to display the royal spleen against her father, was also to wean Lennox into the English camp, in his place. That young Earl had been very disgruntled in not getting Arran's place as Regent, and had fallen out with Beaton in major fashion, to the extent of purloining ten thousand silver crowns sent by King Francis and the de Guises; the French ships, with fifty pieces of artillery also aboard, to avoid English attack had sailed round Ireland and put into the Clyde at Dumbarton, where as it happened Lennox was holed up in Dumbarton Castle of which he was hereditary keeper; and not knowing of his disaffection, the Sieur de la Brosse had handed over the money in good faith.

All this David Lindsay learned from the Cardinal on the eve of a parliament to be held in December, the first of the new reign. It was at Edinburgh and Beaton himself was to chair it.

And as ever that enterprising individual had the ability to surprise and intrigue his friend – if, as usual, somewhat to alarm him also. He was not the man to cower, of course, under Henry's threats, however demonstrated; but his principal reaction this time was unexpected indeed. He actually was seeking to win over Angus. The Douglas was bound to be furious at these two offences against him by Henry, and with the way things were going in Scotland, ripe for conversion – or so Beaton averred. He had already been in communication with the Earl, who was presently sulking at Douglas Castle in upper Lanarkshire, preparing to protect his Border lands against Armstrong raids, and had not been rebuffed. It would be an enormous gain if the Douglas menace could be removed, even temporarily, and worth considerable effort.

As to the matter of Lennox, something must be done. The Cardinal was arranging for Arran to take a force to Dumbarton to try to recover the ten thousand crowns. But he, Beaton, was anxious not to offend the powerful Stewart clan, which also included Moray, Atholl, Ochiltree, Avondale and the Highland branches, and so drew the line at an outright attack on Lennox in Dumbarton, if he resisted – especially as that fortress was a very strong place. Nor did he want, as it were, to drive him into Henry's arms, to become another Angus. But he must be got out of the country, if possible, for he was now even suggesting that he might wed Marie de Guise herself. So Beaton had a task for the good Lord Lyon King of Arms. He should go to France and persuade King Francis and the de Guise brothers to recall Lennox thither. That Earl owed much to the French, apart from the ten thousand crowns, having been in exile there since his father's murder and made much of at the French court, indeed had only returned to Scotland at French expense.

Lindsay protested. It was no part of his duties as Lyon to go to France on any such intrigue. Let Beaton send one of his own minions, if it were so important. Henry's fleet was attacking all Scots vessels, and probably French also, so it was dangerous as well as unsuitable . . .

Soothingly the Cardinal explained. The last parliament had instructed the Lord Lyon to return to the princes of Christendom the orders and insignia presented by them to the late King – as was always done. This had not yet been accomplished, and no doubt this new parliament would order a prompt compliance. So he would be going to the King of France anyway, with the Order of St. Michael. Not only that, but the Garter would have to be returned to Henry. Even that tyrant could not refuse a safe-conduct for such a courtesy-mission – so David would be able to travel in safety to London and on to France, none knowing of his secret message.

The other shook his head, wordless, as not for the first time.

Beaton went on. "After France, you will go to the Emperor, with the Golden Fleece. Or, if he is not to be found – and Charles is ever on the move, a man of restless spirit – to his aunt, your friend, Margaret of Hungary, at Brussels. She indeed would be better. You gained from her a great increase of trade with the Low Countries, those years ago, and the protection of Netherlands warships for our shipping in that trade. Too many of our vessels have been falling victim to the English pirates and the trade is much fallen off. I know well, for much of it is Church commerce. If a convoy system could be set up again, with the Netherlands guarding it, that trade could be recovered and increased. We might offer special terms, in Lammermuir wool in particular, which the Flemings much seek. Then on to Rome . . ."

There was, of course, no way Lindsay could contest this major assignment. And possibly he would quite enjoy the tour – although scarcely the first part of it, in London. He bowed to the inevitable.

That parliament of December conformed to a predictable pattern, since there was practically no opposition. Angus and his Douglases stayed away. Lennox likewise, and such of the English faction and Henry's former pensioners as were present did not seek to draw attention to themselves. From the throne Arran presided in theory but left all to the Chancellor-Cardinal who ran it like a carriage on well-greased wheels. Everything that he proposed or had engineered was passed, usually with a minimum of debate, in matters domestic as well as diplomatic – and few would assert that they were not in fact mainly good and worthy measures, deserving of support, save for the controversial item on action to be taken by civil courts in matters of heresy, where such affected public as distinct from ecclesiastical jurisdiction – for instance, demonstrations in universities and rabble-rousing in the streets of St. Andrews and Aberdeen by so-called reformers. Apart from this issue which was put forward largely for the benefit of Marco Grimani, Patriarch of Aquileia, sent by the Pope to aid his Legate in purging the Scots Church, who was there for the winter and in which David Lindsay spoke up against the clerics, as commissioner for Cupar rather than as Lyon, but in which the Church won easily, the sitting was one of the most productive and yet expeditious on record. The English match was officially negatived, with the overall decision that no marriage proposals should be entertained until the child Queen was at least ten years old. Guardians were appointed for her security, the Earls Marischal and Montrose and the Lords Erskine, keeper of Stirling, Livingstone, Seton and Lindsay, the last David's brother-in-law. In a significant move by the Chancellor himself, the attainders on the Earl of Angus and other Douglas notables were reversed, many wondering audibly. Scotland's essential independence and liberties were re-emphasised and the principle laid down that she must always have a *native* ruler. The always thorny problem of the succession was got over in the meantime by the acceptance of a declaration that in the event of the death of the Queen, which God forbid, the crown should pass to the nearest lawful heir, provided that he or she was of sound mind. And finally, parliament noted its concern that the late King's orders of knighthood had not yet been returned to their esteemed donors, in the traditional fashion, and instructed that this should be done forthwith.

As the Chancellor was winding matters up, a belated and hurried announcement was made by the Provost of Dunbar that the man Oliver Sinclair was known to have returned from captivity in England and was said to have been seen lurking in the Home country of the East Merse and Lammermuir. No one, however, deemed this of sufficient importance for any steps to be taken.

The entire session might almost have been a play-acting produced by Davie Beaton instead of David Lindsay, had not its findings represented the nation's expressed will, with the force of law.

12

Strangely, despite his many journeys abroad, David Lindsay had never been in England – save a mile or two over the Border, on occasion, on tactical business – a circumstance which applied to many other well-travelled Scots, the Auld Enemy's welcome being problematical, to say the least. Now, equipped with a safe-conduct bearing King Henry's own seal and signature, while welcome might still be too much to expect, attack, assault at least ought to be spared them.

This would have been less assured by sea, where English ships were apt to attack first and enquire afterwards; so they journeyed by land, which was more practical in winter anyway. Horseback travel in February could be less than enjoyable, but storm hazards at least were minimised. It had been decreed that this February start was necessary if David were to be back in time for a very special occasion, in the autumn, the marriage of the Cardinal's eldest son, James Beaton, to David's own niece by marriage, Margaret Lindsay daughter of John, fifth Lord Lindsay of the Byres. Indeed he would have been off earlier had the safe-conduct taken less time to arrive.

So he rode southwards through England, on cold days, mainly of frost with occasional faint snow-flurries, but nothing to halt them and thankfully little rain, which in the saddle can be misery indeed. David did not ride alone, since apart from some sort of escort for security purposes, it would not have been suitable for Scotland's Lord Lyon on a representative mission. On the other hand, he wanted no large entourage which would have profited nothing and probably caused delay and possible complications. Davie Beaton had solved the problem in typical fashion by urging that Lindsay take along one John de Hope, a prosperous Edinburgh merchant and banker, whom he declared could be very useful. For Hope was in fact a

Frenchman who had come to Scotland in the train of the Princess Madeleine, James's first and tragic bride, trusted by the King of France to aid her; and having married a Scotswoman, settled down in Edinburgh to ply his trade there, and quickly made his mark. It transpired that Hope had more than this French connection to recommend him, for he had trading and banking links with many lands, including the Netherlands, the Hanseatic cities of the Empire and the Italian states. Also it so happened that much of his trade was in fine velvets, silks, silver and gold thread and the like, much sought after for the splendid vestments of high churchmen, and becoming exceedingly difficult to import owing to the English blockade; so a safe-conduct passage from Henry Tudor would be a convenience. It also so happened that John de Hope had later brought over from France a son by an earlier marriage, Edouard, or Edward Hope, and this bright young man, as well as taking over much of the banking and money-lending business, had become one of the extra-pursuivants of the Lyon Court, as an expert on Continental heraldry, and there commended himself to the Lord Lyon.

So with the two Hopes and three troopers of the royal guard, David headed down through the English counties, for London.

Although the days were short, it was not weather for lingering and they made good time, even though the Hopes were not the most practised of horsemen. Averaging perhaps thirty-five miles, it took them eleven days. They scarcely saw the English countryside at its best, but were impressed nevertheless with the general richness and fertility and the vast number of fine manors and great houses it supported.

London, however, when eventually they reached it, did not impress David Lindsay at all, although the Hopes seemed rather more appreciative. It was certainly large, although no larger than Paris or Brussels, but it was incredibly dirty, smelly and congested, its streets so narrow and crowded with jostling buildings, tier upon projecting tier, so as to all but hide the sky and to deny all but noonday glimpses of the sun. No wind penetrated therein, unlike Scots cities which were all built on hilly ground and consequently breezy, so that there seemed to be no air as well as no vistas, the stench of humanity, excrement, animals and their dung, tanneries, breweries, smoke-houses and the like all but breath-stopping, even in February. Not that it appeared to affect the breathing of the citizenry, who were in fact excessively vocal, yelling and hooting at the visitors, youths and children throwing insults and offal, dogs snapping and snarling at the horses' hooves. Uncertain how best to deal with this, the travellers were presently instructed when a stylishly-clad individual came clattering up behind them with half a dozen shouting mounted attendants who slashed right and left rhythmically with long whips, ensuring free passage – indeed all but riding down the Scots party in the process. Thereafter the visitors, lacking whips, drew their swords and swung the flats of these as they rode through the capital of Tudor England.

They made a number of attempts at asking directions before they found someone able or prepared to understand their Scots accents and tell them how to get to Whitehall Palace. They found it eventually by the riverside, a great spreading establishment, almost a walled town in itself. Yet within the perimeter walling there was no aspect of a fortress or stronghold, indeed the Scots' first impression was of the great number of large windows, something not to be seen in their own land where security and the weather both tended to decree thick stone walls and small windows. There were splendid formal gardens dotted with statuary, and a curious feature which much intrigued the heraldically-inclined visitors, over thirty tall stone columns bearing heraldic beasts, the significance of which was not clear. Oddly, closer to the palace itself was a large tilt-yard or tourney-ground, with stands for spectators on three sides, the fourth being directly under windows of the house – no doubt so that its royal denizens might watch in privacy. This magnificent place had been built by the late Cardinal Wolsey, at the height of his power, and taken over by his envious master after his execution.

Their reception at Whitehall was cool, indeed they had difficulty in finding anyone to attend to them, the unpopularity of the Scots made entirely evident. Apparently the King was not in residence at present, being at Greenwich Palace, some distance down-river. Enquiries as to how to get there, and how long it would take, were met with scorn for such ignorance; but it transpired that Henry was expected back here the next day. So they decided to wait. No offers of accommodation forthcoming meantime, and too proud to ask for any, they moved out into the town again and found quarters in a nearby inn or hostelry. There was, of course, a Scottish embassy building not far away; but this had been closed up for some time. They were, in fact, glad enough to rest quietly after their long riding, especially the Hopes.

King Henry did arrive the next afternoon. In fact they actually saw him, for he came by river, with a squadron of oared and gaily canopied barges, musicians playing. Thus heralded, citizenry flocked to welcome him for, surprisingly in view of his bloodthirsty habits and unpredictable temper, the Tudor was popular with the people, who called him their Bluff King Hal. The Scots had a good view of him disembarking, amongst a drove of courtiers. There was no doubt as to which of the colourful crowd was the monarch, not only on account of the obsequious attention paid to him but because of the enormous bulk of the man. He was huge, gross, shapeless, almost as broad as he was high, florid of feature as of dress. So heavy indeed was he that he seemed scarcely able to walk and was solicitously aided into a decorative litter borne by a full dozen stalwart bearers in Tudor Rose livery – all of whom were needed to carry that weight, even the short distance to the palace. The musicians forming up, Henry moved off, waving to the cheers of the crowd.

When no summons reached the Scots by evening, David went alone to present himself again at the palace, to announce his mission. But although he waited for almost two hours, there was no reaction. With vivid memories of Thomas Cromwell's similar behaviour at Newcastle those few years earlier, he made repeated reminders as to his presence, eventually demanding to see the Lord Chamberlain. That luminary did not appear but presently sent a minion, who curtly announced that the Scots envoys would be summoned to appear when and if His Majesty decided to grant them an audience. David, never the most patient of men, suggested that since he had no particular desire nor need to speak with King Henry perhaps it would serve if he merely handed over the insignia of the Order of the Garter to some underling, himself possibly, and so waste no more of his own time nor His Majesty's? The other was distinctly taken aback at this, and hurriedly declared that he had no authority to accept anything such, and must go and make further enquiries.

The man was gone for some time, leaving David with two Yeomen of the Guard eyeing each other with mutual lack of appreciation. When he did return, it was to announce that, as a particular favour, His Majesty would grant brief audience now. Would Sir David follow him?

Along corridors and through galleries and ante-rooms, they came to a large chamber filled with a chattering courtier-throng. A silence descended on these as David was marched through. At the far end, near a closed door guarded by two more Yeomen, he was handed over to a still haughtier individual who eyed him superciliously and, without a word, gesturing him to wait, knocked at the closed door, opened and entered, shutting it carefully behind him. He was back quite quickly, to usher David in.

"The Scotch envoy, Your Majesty," he announced.

There were some half-dozen men there, in a smaller, dark-panelled room lit by many candles and a blazing fire. They lounged round a table laden with wine-flagons and platters of broken meats. Henry sprawled largely at the head. Seen thus close he made an extraordinary impression, imposing in his sheer bulk but also in the strange animal vigour he exuded, however physically-inert seeming. Now in his fifty-fourth year, he was unlike any other man David had ever encountered, a monster perhaps and larger than life, but a challenging, vital, even fascinating monster, dominating all not so much by his power and royal authority as by his personal force and magnetism. Despite looking grievously unhealthy, his florid flesh blotchy, discoloured and glistening with sweat, his small pig-like eyes were brilliantly alive. Notably broad of feature, as of body, his mouth was tiny. He appeared to have no hair under the flat jewelled cap he wore. Altogether, Henry Tudor was a shock to meet, in various aspects of the word.

"Ha – Lindsay!" he greeted, grinning. "The poet! Who mislikes the Romish mountebanks! Mocks them to their pious faces. A man after my own heart, heh? Or no?" He had a wheezy voice, to suit the mouth rather than the rest of him, still with something of a Welsh intonation – the Tudors or Theodores were Welsh, of course, and although born at Greenwich Henry had grown up amongst Welsh-speakers.

Uncertain how to respond to that, David bowed. "Your Majesty," he said warily.

"The rogue Cromwell spoke of you. He did not love you, I recollect. So, since he was a rogue, it could be that *you* are honest, heh? A rare quality, I have found – in men, and still less in women, I swear! How honest are you, David Lindsay of the Mount? Are you to be the first honest Scotsman I have met?"

That was difficult to answer, also. "You must have been unfortunate, Sire," he said. "As, so far, *I* have been. In England."

"Ho, ho – a rejoinder! A surrebutter, heh?" Henry looked at his companions. "Hear you that? From this honest rarity from Scotland, the land of crawling turncoats, bootlicking time-servers and begging bowl liars! Remarkable, a peculiar. Like his very style. Lindsay of the Mount. *The* Mount, mark you – when, I am assured, Scotland is a land of naught but mounts. Which mount, man, is yours? The highest? The lowest? Or but the only honest mount?"

David sought to keep his voice level. "I am flattered that Your Majesty should be aware of my humble style.

Also my poor efforts at verse and play-writing. My Mount is that of Lindifferon, in Fife, modest but sufficiently fair. A fairer hill indeed to lift the eyes to, as the scriptures advise, than any I have seen since leaving those of Cheviot! Perhaps Your Highness has been misled about Scotland and the Scots. By rogues such as the late Master Cromwell – whom you ennobled!"

There were indrawn breaths at that, from around the table. Henry's little mouth puckered up meanly.

"Watch how you speak in my presence, sirrah!" he jerked. "Honest you may be – but I find you insolent."

"I regret that, Sire. Since I am sent here to speak, not as David Lindsay but as spokesman for the Scottish Queen and realm, Lord Lyon King of Arms."

"Arrogant also, then! And impatient, I am told. Demanding audience at *your* convenience rather than awaiting mine. Is that how you were instructed to behave? By the man Beaton?"

Lindsay blinked. "I represent the crown and parliament of Scotland, Highness, not the Cardinal. It was scarcely impatience but rather concern for the dignity of my mission and the parliament I represent. Which commanded me to deliver up, with its greetings and respect, the insignia of the Order of the Garter Your Majesty graciously bestowed on our late and well-loved sovereign-lord King James." He delved into the leather satchel hung at his belt and drew out the package, bound and sealed, to hold it out. "This highly-honoured mark of England's esteem I believed that you would not wish to remain lying in the lowly quarters of a London hostelry for any length of time. Was I mistaken, Sire?"

The King chose to ignore that and its implications, but signed to one of his company to take the package.

"You are glib along with the rest, Master Poet," he asserted. "But my nephew James died more than a year past. Another day or so we might have put up with! And he scarcely proved worthy of the Garter, in the first place, I judge!"

David had no answer to that. He had fulfilled his mission. Now he only sought escape.

But Henry was not finished with him. "Since you claim to represent your Scotch parliament, Lindsay, when you return, tell them this. That although they seem to forget it, I, as King of England, am Lord Paramount of Scotland. That I require the terms of my Treaty of Greenwich to be fulfilled forthwith. That the betrothal of my son to the daughter of my nephew must be announced and ratified without further delay. That all royal strongholds and fortresses in Scotland be delivered into my care. And that steps be taken immediately to throw off the shackles of the Romish Church and reform instituted."

David remained silent.

"You hear me, man? You hear me?"

"I hear, Sire. And having nothing that I may say – save that these demands have all already been specifically rejected by the Three Estates, our Scottish parliament."

"So much the worse for them, then! What they insolently have rejected they can and will concede. Or I declare a state of war. I will send my armies and fleets in fullest might to enforce them. And at no light price, Lindsay – no light price. Go back and tell them so. You hear?"

"I do, Sire. And shall do so in due course. But meantime I am on my way to the other princes of Christendom with *their* orders of knighthood also. I would suggest, therefore, that your envoy in Scotland, Sir Ralph Sadler, would be the more appropriate and speedier bearer of such message."

Henry's little eyes narrowed and he leant forward over the table. For a moment or two he emanated a sudden sheer ferocity, intense enough to be almost a physical blow. Then he leaned back, and achieved a humourless gap-toothed grin, flicking a dismissive finger. "You have my permission to retire," he wheezed. "But remember this, Lindsay of the Mountain – an honest tongue requires to be schooled with discretion, else its owner may lose it! And his head with it! Begone!"

David bowed and left, almost too swiftly for the dignity he was concerned about. Outside, the door closed behind him, he was all but shaking, so venomous and alarming had been that last glimpse of the essential Henry Tudor, brief and so swiftly restrained as it was. Thankful to be away, he found his own way out of that palace, the courtiers ignoring him now. The sooner he was away from it the happier he would be.

That feeling remained with him overnight. Sleepless for long, he got the notion that Henry in his spleen might withdraw his safe-conduct, or otherwise prevent him from proceeding on his way, might even arrest him – for the man was capable of much worse than that, even to an accredited envoy. So he was up early next morning and with the Hopes hurried down and across London Bridge to the dock area on the other side of the river, seeking a ship to take them to the Continent, and one which was sailing as soon as possible.

David was not greatly concerned over which monarch he went to next, although in the nature of things he would have been apt to make for Paris and King Francis, with his messages from the Queen-Mother and Beaton and the Hopes' French interests. But at present, Henry, with his bewildering changes in alliances, was associating with the Emperor Charles and therefore in a state of undeclared war with France – indeed, so unpredictable were his political alignments that he was actually aiding the Emperor to put down militarily a group of German Protestant princes and dukes who were supporting the doctrines of Martin Luther. So shipping from London was very much available to the Empire ports, which included the Netherlands, but not to France. Henry's weathercock policies must have made life extremely difficult for English traders and shippers. In the event, the travellers found that they had a choice of vessels, three indeed about to sail for Antwerp, which was the main base for English troops going to the Emperor's campaign. Shipmasters were seldom averse to making a little extra from fare-paying passengers, without enquiring too closely into the business thereof; so they settled on the first craft due to sail, with the noonday tide, a transport named the *Heron*. So preoccupied was David Lindsay with the fear that Henry Tudor might decide on his arrest that, having selected the ship, he remained on board, sending back

Edward Hope and one of the guards to sell the horses for what they would fetch and to bring on their baggage from the inn.

This was achieved without undue delay, there always being a ready market for horseflesh in London; and with sighs of relief they sailed, in the early afternoon, down the broad Thames, thankful indeed to see London fading behind them, with its dangers, smells and smoke – and as the threat of it faded, not a little tickled in fact to be travelling in one of Henry's own transports. It transpired that the troops aboard were almost all German mercenaries, Henry being a major employer of such, and their officers, with whom the Scots had to share somewhat cramped quarters, appeared to have no bias against them.

From the Thames to the Scheldt was no lengthy voyage, a mere hundred miles or so of open sea, although the two estuaries themselves added up to almost as much again. The winds being fresh westerly and their course almost due east, they made good time, and having no need to avoid the English warships which infested these narrow seas, they were into the wider mouth of the Scheldt after only two days' sailing.

Thereafter their progress was less expeditious, for if the Scots had thought that the Thames was a crowded waterway, it was a deal less so than was the Scheldt. Antwerp, which lay fifty miles up its long, winding reaches, was in fact the commercial capital of the world, and here came the merchant shipping of all nations. So navigation had to be strictly controlled, and was indeed in the hands of local pilots who sought to regulate all. It took the *Heron* two more days to reach the city and to find a berth in its vast sprawling dock area.

Antwerp made even London look small, full of magnificent buildings and palatial edifices, its huge cathedral having a spire no less than four hundred feet high and with a carillon of ninety-nine bells. The Exchange was the largest building in the world, allegedly, and the quays extended for over two miles on each side of the river, backed by warehouses, breweries, granaries, mills, roperies and the like. Yet here, in this richest city of Christendom

– its trade reputed to amount to over forty million ducats each year – was not the seat of the Regent of the Netherlands; this was at Brussels, another twenty-seven miles inland, up a tributary river, the Senne. So the Scots did not linger here but hired horses and set off on their own, glad enough to be so and to savour the exercise and feeling of freedom after shipboard.

They had no difficulty in reaching Brussels before dark, and there David went straight to the imperial palace, familiar as it all was to him. Margaret of Hungary was still Regent of the Netherlands for her nephew the Emperor Charles. David had no fears as to his reception here.

It was thirteen years since he had last seen Margaret of Hungary, and she was now an old lady. But although white-haired, thinner, more frail, she gave no impression of having lost any of her authority and decision. She greeted David warmly, told him that she had often thought of him and wondered how he fared. She agreed that she was competent to accept the Golden Fleece insignia on behalf of her nephew – whom it would have been difficult for David to run to earth anyway since he was engaged again in his running war with the Turks under Suleiman the Magnificent at the same time as seeking to put down the rising of his Protestant princes – which was why he needed Henry of England's help – and might be sought for almost anywhere in the east of his Empire.

They passed four days at Brussels, based on the imperial palace, well-spent days in which David achieved the renewing of the convoy system for Scots merchant shipping trading with the Netherlands, and the Hopes made many commercial contacts and deals, bought quantities of velvet, lace and gold thread, and even arranged to establish a new branch of their banking-house at nearby Liège, Amsterdam being their only Netherlands base hitherto. Brussels was a strange city, on two distinct levels, the commercial and manufacturing town on low land alongside the river, and the residential area with its nobleman's palaces, monasteries and rich merchants' houses high above, on abruptly rising ground, well above the fogs and meaner streets. The rise between was surmounted by innumerable steps and stairs, but made accessible for horsed traffic. Below the stairs Flemish was spoken, while above it was French.

Well satisfied with their visit, the Scots bade farewell to the Regent, to make for Paris.

Since the Empire was, in theory, at war with France, although no actual fighting was in progress meantime, Margaret had advised that they did not risk land-travel and crossing guarded frontiers but to go by sea. To some extent, of course, the same problem applied with shipping, since Netherlands vessels, like English, could not sail into French ports; but the ships of Papal states could, and there were always some of these in Antwerp docks, doing a useful trade between the various combatants.

So it was back to that city, where they had little difficulty in finding a Genoese shipmaster prepared to carry them to France on his way back to Italy. Indeed, they persuaded him, for only a modest extra charge, to take them up the Senne estuary as far as Rouen, from whence it was only some ninety miles to Paris.

David was shocked at the change in King Francis, when finally they reached him at the Louvre. It was not, after all, so very long since he had last seen him, barely seven years from James's ill-starred marriage to Madeleine in 1537. Yet, from an admittedly mercurial but active, indeed flamboyant character, he had dwindled to become a shrunken, cadaverous and querulous elderly-seeming man, although aged only fifty, almost a recluse, hiding himself away in that vast fortress. Clearly his health was not good, but there was more to it than that. The death of his daughter, in Scotland, his favourite child, had struck him grievously, especially after losing his eldest son, the Dauphin Francis, two years earlier; and he had never got on with his second son, the present Dauphin Henry, a weakling whom he looked upon as all but imbecile. To all intents Charles de Guise, Marie's brother, Cardinal of Lorraine, was now ruling France – as his friend, Davie Beaton, was ruling Scotland.

David was lodged in the Cardinal's wing of the palace, and was well entertained by that shrewd and able if ruthless cleric. He was eager to hear of his sister, of whom he was very fond – indeed his affection was well-known in Scotland on account of the frequent gifts he sent her, in great variety and sometimes bulk, for he even sent wild boars to improve the Scots strain for hunting, pear and plum trees, equipment to mine gold on Crawford Muir, besides more normal presents for a woman – also to be sure, a succession of architects, artists and artisans, for improving the quality of life in a far northern land.

The interview, arranged by the Cardinal, was of the briefest, despite the momentous decision taken thereat – for David had more to effect here than merely hand back the Order of St. Michael. Beaton was very keen that a project of much significance to Scotland, and to a lesser extent to France also, should be proceeded with. It was not his own idea, indeed it was a thirty-year-old plan, the conception of the young Queen's grandfather James the Fourth. He had devised the ambitious theory of mutual citizenship. He argued that if Scots nationals were automatically citizens of France, and vice versa, this would be of major advantage to both realms, facilitating relations, trade, culture and, of course, helping to contain the aggressive proclivities of the English. Indeed this had been one of the terms proposed when James agreed to 'break a lance' in chivalric fashion, for the French Queen's sake, and to move a yard or two into England, in 1513, to help dissuade Henry from attacking France on that occasion; the result, of course, had been the disaster of Flodden, the death of James and Scotland stricken. In consequence, the mutual citizenship, although agreed to by Louis the Twelfth and the French Estates, had never been officially implemented. Now Davie Beaton saw it as one more weapon to use in his ongoing war against Henry Tudor, and by letter had more or less persuaded his fellow-cardinal to promote it.

For so important and visionary a design it all proved to be ridiculously simple to arrange, so far as David Lindsay was concerned. He had a private discussion on the pros and cons of it with the Cardinal, who, when he took the Scot for his audience with the King, merely mentioned this subject, after the handing back of the Order, observing that it had already been passed by an earlier French parliament and assuming that His Most Christian Majesty approved? Francis's nod was all there was to it, before he looked away and remained so doing, as an indication that the audience was over. Whether he remembered David from previous encounters was not to be known. Nothing more clearly demonstrated whose hand was now on the helm of France than this interview.

It took even David some time really to appreciate that from now on all his fellow-Scots were citizens of France also, with all that might entail.

The Cardinal's help was invaluable also in the matter of the Scots' onward journey. For, of course, he was in constant touch with Rome, and arranged for them to take passage in one of his own ships sailing in a few days from Rouen again, thus saving them a long and possibly trying journey by land. They had only two more honours to deliver, and were making excellent time thus far.

The voyage round the Brittany peninsula, across the great Bay of Biscay and past Portugal and Spain, was somewhat delayed by contrary winds and high seas; but this was compensated for by the comfort, for it seemed that the representatives of Holy Church liked to travel in style, in France as elsewhere. Never had they sailed in such state, in company with a bishop-protonotary and two monsignors, concerned to be affable towards any friends of the great Cardinal of Lorraine.

Once through the Straits of Gibraltar and into the Mediterranean their navigation problems eased notably and they ran expeditiously before a westerly breeze in suddenly balmy temperatures.

A pleasant voyage thereafter of five days, over intensely blue sea and past sundry islands, brought them through the narrow Strait of Bonifacio, between Corsica and Sardinia, to the Italian coast, the mouths of the famed Tiber, and Ostia the port of Rome.

The visitors were grievously disappointed at this first

approach to the fabled Eternal City. Its port was set amidst dismal marshlands and a desolation of ruins, and itself was a dreary and uninspiring place, its river banks yellow mud. Here they disembarked, for the Fiumicino, as this branch of the Tiber was called, was navigable further only by shallow-draught vessels. The road thereafter was good, paved in great stone slabs and clearly very ancient, but the countryside, for some ten miles, was poor and neglected. The churchmen travelled it in horse-litters but the Scots hired mounts to ride alongside.

If the land seemed dull and uncared-for, this impression was certainly heightened by the vast number of ruins with which it was littered; everywhere, as far as eye could see, was crumbling stonework, the remains of ambitious even mighty structures, colonnades, towers, plinths, tombs, statues, bridges, all shattered and creeper-grown, abandoned, in the midst of reedy swamps where poor cattle wallowed. Possibly the Scots had expected too much of the Roman terrain; used to the dramatic shores of their own land, mountains and cliffs, sea-lochs, forests and islands, this was a sorry approach. Rome, they had heard, was built on seven hills; but to their perhaps prejudiced eyes there was not a hill worthy of the name in sight.

The city itself impressed, to be sure, but mainly as a tremendous monument to past magnificence rather than as one of the world's greatest capitals. The best of it, indeed, was ruinous, and not only the ancient parts, for much of the more modern suburbs appeared to be in an abandoned state. The bishop-protonotary explained that this was not the Church's responsibility. Nevertheless the grandeur of the mighty works of the past did not fail to stir and excite the Scots, the tremendous enclosing walls, the Aurelian, twelve miles in circuit they were told, the innumerable aqueducts, the Colosseum, the temples, obelisks, arches, basilicas and forums – although they still looked in vain for the seven hills.

The Leonine or Vatican city, when they reached it, was quite otherwise, all splendour, flourish and extravagance, palaces, churches, shrines, galleries and statues, rather like St. Andrews magnified a score of times, all mounting up to the cathedral of St. John Lateran, which made even that of St. Regulas look puny – although the admittedly prejudiced visitors preferred the latter's simple serenity and soaring purity of line to all the Lateran's pillared and domed magnitude.

At the Vatican, although they were palatially housed and well provided for, thanks to their clerical fellow-travellers, the Scots found greater difficulty in gaining access to the Holy Father than they had to more earthly monarchs, even Henry Tudor. Innumerable papal watch-dogs had to be got past, chamberlains, referendaries, recorders, preceptors and the like, many of whom expected payment for their good offices. It took them a full week to reach the Pontiff, in the castle of St. Angelo – and then it was all over in a matter of moments, much less time even than with the King of France.

Pope Paul the Third, formerly Allesandro Farnese, was a tall, stooping, long-nosed man, now in his seventy-third year but failing nothing in vigour, determination and acquisitiveness, noted for his public works, his political dexterity but also for his nepotism, his promotion of his illegitimate sons and nephews in the hierarchy of the Church, and his amassing of treasure. Now he spoke no English and showed no interest in the proffered Order of the Holy Sepulchre, which he signed to one of his proud-looking young ecclesiastics to take – after all, it had not been granted by himself but by his predecessor – and asked, in French, after Davie Beaton; and without waiting to hear, launched into a denunciation of the rampant heresy in Scotland, intimating the terrible wrath of Holy Church, and as reinforcement, of Almighty God, on all shameful upsetters of the divine order. David Lindsay recognised that this was neither the time nor place to enter into any exposition of a contrary opinion, but was unprepared to accept these strictures totally without demur. However, he had barely commenced a tactful indication that it was not so much heresy as discontent with the corruption of the clergy which was the trouble in Scotland, when he perceived the pontifical hand out-thrust for him to kiss the papal ring, and the interview over. He retired, backwards, making the required number of bows, but only perfunctorily, duty done.

There remained only the Neapolitan Order of the Blessed Annunciation. This presented something of a problem, such as none of the others did. For the Kingdom of Naples had been taken over, first by Spain and then by the Empire, and there was now no King of Naples to return the Order to. Margaret of Hungary had refused to accept it, on behalf of her nephew, and had advised that since it was a dynastic or family honour, even though there was now no actual monarch, his heir still represented the fount of the honour, and should be given it back. Ferdinand the Fourth of Naples' heir, displaced from the succession, was another, suspected to be illegitimate, Ferdinand; and the Emperor allowed him to call himself Duke. But he was not permitted to live in Naples and dwelt in semi-exile in a remote town of the Abruzzi, Pescara, on the Adriatic coast.

Since Pescara proved to be almost exactly one hundred miles east of Rome, David decided it was worth making the journey.

They set out next morning, on more hired horses, indeed with a pack-horse train now, for the Hopes had not wasted their week in Rome, acquiring large quantities of fine vestments, rich fabrics, embroidery, church decorations and the like. They had to cross the spine of the land, and found it all interesting and instructive. For, once clear of the coastal plains, they were into increasingly hilly land, which in fact, the further east they went, became actually mountainous and very attractive. This was the Abruzzi, and in every way in marked contrast to the lowlands, terraced with vineyards and olive gardens and tended by an industrious and cheerful peasantry. At first the hills were small, by Scottish standards, but much more effectively utilised than at home, in the terracing and banking especially. Noting it all, David Lindsay saw features which he might, with profit, try at the Mount of Lindifferon – although the ingenious little irrigation canals would scarcely be necessary in its climate.

They halted for the night, somewhat delayed by the

pack-horse train, at a monastic hospice at Sulmonia, where they were kindly received, and got a much better impression of Italian churchmen.

They did not reach Pescara until the following evening, for they had had to climb into ever more steep and rugged country, around the mountain complex known as the Gran Sasso, the highest altitude in Italy, reaching over nine thousand feet, twice as high as anything in Scotland. Much impressed now, they slanted slowly down steeply to the Adriatic seaboard.

Pescara was a small port on a rock-bound coast, the only one in hundreds of miles apparently, its town of clustering houses and narrow lanes climbing the hillside behind and culminating in a cliff-top castle, all towers, pinnacles and battlements. Here they found Duke Ferdinand, a rumbustious character more like a condottieri captain than a descendant of monarchs, holding court with an entourage mainly of luscious ladies. He welcomed his visitors genially, seemed to assume that they had come to stay, gave them a complete if somewhat broken-down tower to themselves for lodging, and indicated that female company would be available if desired. He spoke neither English nor French but Edward Hope had a fair grasp of most Italian dialects and could translate. The handing back of the Order of the Blessed Annunciation assumed no importance at all, indeed some levity, David getting the impression that if he had desired it for himself he could have had it, with pleasure.

They went hawking the next day with Ferdinand and his ladies, the sport here being the seabirds which nested along the cliffs, varieties of duck, divers and cormorants – in David's opinion, all inedible. The test and problem was, of course, to retrieve the struck fowl, which were all too apt to fall into the sea. The hawks were trained, allegedly, to drive the birds inland and not to strike over water – but this by no means worked out, and much of the bag was lost, and constant wagers lost with them.

Despite the Duke's enthusiastic hospitality, the Scots were not disposed to linger at Pescara. It was not that they were greatly concerned about timing, for the mission had in fact been more expeditious than they had anticipated. But obviously Ferdinand was a great one for gaming, wagering, and clearly for high stakes, and his guests did not aspire to such heights, even though the Hopes were undoubtedly sufficiently wealthy, less so as was David Lindsay. Moreover, there was still a part of their task unfulfilled. They had so far acquired no flints. If this might seem a strange concern for a diplomatic, banking and merchanting mission, it was not entirely so. Flint and steel was the sole means of making fire, required in every home be it cothouse or castle; also needed for firearms and cannon and several other uses. And Scotland did not produce flints. These were a product of limestone and chalk countries, the flints not themselves limestone but quartz-like mineral formed of fossilised shells compressed down the ages between layers of chalk and lime. The Scots had, in the past, got their flints from England, plentiful in some southern parts. But since Henry's wars, this source of supply was cut off and there was a famine in the spark-creating material, causing major inconvenience, and the price consequently soaring. So, since churchmen required flints for lighting candles and censers, as well as trading in them commercially, Beaton had ordered the Hopes to bring back as large quantities as they could. So far they had come across none.

However, at Pescara, they learned that just across the Adriatic, in Dalmatia, was where the Abruzzi folk got their flints, a land almost made of limestone, and only two days' sail distant.

There was another aspect of their situation. It would be much more convenient and speedy to sail home rather than to travel overland, especially with all the merchandise they had collected. This little port of Pescara seldom indeed saw ocean-going ships, only coastal traders and fishing-craft, but over in Dalmatia was the great port of Ragusa, a mercantile city-state where there were always ships of all nations – perhaps not Scots but certainly Dutch and French, the busiest trading centre of the Adriatic next to Venice.

So, since one of the local shipmen would put them and

their baggage across to Ragusa without any difficulty, this course was decided upon. The Duke Ferdinand gave orders accordingly.

They embarked on a small two-masted vessel, with all their accumulated gear, leaving the Duke to dispose of their horses. Their elderly shipmaster, who spoke fair French, eager apparently to demonstrate his linguistic ability, also indeed his general knowledge and wide-ranging experience, was highly loquacious and informative. Presumably he did not often get foreign travellers to entertain. Before long his passengers began to feel that they would have to discourage their enthusiastic skipper, as they sailed across the sparkling Adriatic towards Dalmatia.

That is, until Guiseppi mentioned Henry of England. This occurred when he was telling them that although he had never before encountered Scots, he had known Englishmen, indeed he had worked with them only a few years before, helping them with their trade in altars. At his hearers' expressed mystification over such an odd-sounding commerce, their new friend explained that the English ships laden with King Henry's altars were often too large to enter the smaller harbours, especially on the islands, and so his own vessel was useful to serve as a tender, trans-shipping the heavy altars ashore.

David was still nonplussed. "But ... altars?" he demanded. "What has Henry Tudor to do with altars? They are not something the English make. You Italians, yes, with your marble and alabaster, but not the English. And Henry is the great Protestant!"

"Why, Monsieur, the English did not *make* the altars; most were made here, no doubt. The English king *stole* them. He took over all the abbeys and monasteries and churches of England for himself, putting down Holy Church, God curse him! The abbeys he destroyed – but he took the altars out and loaded them on his ships, to sell to good Catholics all around these seas. You had not heard of this?"

"Save us – no! This is scarce believable! Henry, the Protestant champion! The leader of reform! Selling stolen

Catholic altars back to Catholics! A wonder indeed. You say he sold many?"

"Many, yes. Many shiploads. I myself worked with three English ships. One I unloaded not far from where we sail now – the island of Lopud. We shall pass it tomorrow, seven miles out from Ragusa."

"Could I see one of these altars?"

"If you wish, Monsieur. There were four, I think – yes, four, on Lopud. They will be in chapels there. There are many chapels, for it is a very holy isle."

"Take me there, then. In passing." It did not demand much imagination on David's part to perceive what Davie Beaton could make out of this information.

Next noonday, then, they put in at the crescent-shaped western bay of the island of Lopud, one of the Elaphite group, by no means the first they had sailed past, nor the largest, for this Dalmatian seaboard, like the Hebrides, was alleged to have a thousand islands – indeed the entire scene greatly resembled the Scottish West Highland coast, with its rocks and skerries, straits and sounds, its hilly, pine-clad hills and isles of all sizes. Lopud was perhaps six miles long but not much more than a mile wide, but it apparently supported a quite large population. According to Guiseppi there were at least thirty chapels here – which seemed excessive even for a particularly holy place.

Their shallow-draught craft was able to draw in directly to the stone jetty, under a large church with a campanile, attached to what looked like a monastery, and on the hillside high above, a castle. The island was richly wooded and very hilly, the pine trees coming right down to coastal rock-slabs, this limestone shoreline seemingly everywhere except at the wide western bay, which boasted a rim of golden sand. Houses lined the bay, on one side of the single street, some of them quite ambitious as to architecture, with stone balconies, sculpture and heraldic decoration, evidently the summer houses of prosperous Ragusa citizens.

Disembarked, Guiseppi led the visitors up to the church and its attached range of buildings, which turned out to be a Franciscan monastery and associated convent. The prior in charge, a notably handsome young man, dark of eye and with dashing down-turning moustaches, unusual in a cleric, could speak only his native Serbo-Croat tongue, but was entirely ready to be helpful when Guiseppi addressed him in his own language. Yes, he knew of the English altars. There were four of them on Lopud, one not very far away, at the church of Our Lady of Sunj. If the foreign lords so desired, he would take them there personally. Would they walk, or ride on donkeys?

All hastily agreed that they would walk.

As they set off along the town's single street, the west side open to the sandy beach, the houses set off by palm trees, their prior proved to be voluble and informative, Guiseppi kept busy translating. He named the families who owned most of the larger houses, pointing out their heraldic door lintels. It seemed that the Dubrovnik Republic – for that is what he called Ragusa – was an extraordinarily aristocratic one, with a duke as president, or rector, as he was termed, and counts in charge of attached districts, one here at Lopud, whose castle was sited high above the monastery. Most of these leading families had noble pretensions. These islands even had their own bishop, under the Archbishop of Dubrovnik, his house duly pointed out – although, like most of the others, it seemed, he normally spent only the summer months on the island, when the city grew unbearably hot.

Half-way round the bay, at another monastery, Dominican this time, they turned inland – and quickly they perceived why they had been offered donkeys. There were no real roads on this island, only innumerable steps and stairs up and down the steep wooded hillsides, and traffic tended to be on donkey-back. Up an endless series of these ladder-like flights they climbed, the young prior active as a goat, long grey robes hitched high, the travellers less so after sea-voyaging, court-attendance, riding and no walking. On the lower slopes were terraced gardens, olive groves, orange and apple orchards, but these soon giving way to woodland mainly of ancient pine and juniper. As they rose even higher, with only goats to be seen amongst the trees and outcropping white rock, it seemed a strange route to a chapel deemed worthy of one of Henry Tudor's bartered and no doubt expensive altars.

However, when at length the breathless Scots perceived an end to the steps, they found themselves in a curious hanging valley between the island's two lofty ridges, and the mystery of the missing population was partly solved. This valley was, in fact, one prolonged vineyard and olive grove, running almost the length of Lopud, unseen from below, with houses and farmeries, barns and olive and grape presses, watch-towers and wells, dotted throughout.

They did not remain long in this valley but turned off to the south, to climb again through more woodland, presently coming out in a clearing, which proved to be near the lip of a long, steep slope down to a most lovely hidden sandy bay. In this clearing was an ancient church, surrounded by a graveyard, a charnel house and a watch-tower.

"The Church of Our Lady of Sunj," the prior announced proudly. "Erected by the Crusader Visconti in gratitude for his safe return from the Holy Land in 1098."

And in this sequestered chapel above the attractive Bay of Sunj, they found the altar, a handsome thing of marble, green-blue, with onyx and jacinth intaglio, too ornate by far for this quiet, tree-girt sanctuary, and probably originating in Italy. What English church, abbey or monastery had it come from, the viewers wondered? There was nothing to give a clue. But the prior assured that it had been bought, at considerable cost, from the King of England. He could take them to others, if so they desired.

David expressed himself as satisfied, and they turned back for the harbour.

They left Lopud with some regret, for it was the most delightful place they had come across on their travels; but there were no flints to be had here, nor, of course, sea-going vessels for home.

Once their craft was round the bulk of the island, and past its neighbour, Kolocep, they were able to see Ragusa or Dubrovnik ahead – they were unsure now what to call it, the latter being the native name, Ragusa being that imposed by its Venetian conquerors. Even at six or seven miles' distance it looked dramatic, soaring in mighty walls, bastions and towers above the sea, on a rock-bound coast, with great white limestone mountains rearing abruptly behind. A proud city-state, it looked every inch the part.

Closer approach only emphasised the impressiveness of it all, as the scale of the walling, bartizans, parapets and other prodigious fortifications became evident. That there was a town, a city, within this vast citadel, a cathedral, churches, monasteries, palaces as well as ordinary housing for a large population, markets, warehouses and the rest, was only to be guessed and wondered at, not seen.

Their shallow-draught Pescara vessel was able to tie up in the old town harbour directly under the tremendous walling, to the south; but this was not where they would look for deep-sea shipping for their homeward journey. The deep-water port was apparently at Gruz, on its separate bay to the north a mile away.

David had no official business here, so there was no real need for him to identify himself to the authorities. But he was, after all, one of Scotland's principal officers-of-state, and it might be courteous to pay a call on the Duke-Rector. Also he might learn more about the Tudor's trade in altars. So they entered the huge citadel by the harbour gate, and found themselves almost at once in quite a wide central avenue, the Placa, unexpected in such a crowded concourse of buildings. Here they quickly came on the arcaded and handsome Rector's Palace, at the south end of this Placa, where they were received in a shady, pillared atrium or central courtyard, with marble flooring and balustered stairways. However, the Rector was absent on a visit to Montenegro, to the south, and apparently the Archbishop with him. But they learned from one of the civic dignitaries there that scores, possibly hundreds, of the English altars had been hawked around the Mediterranean and Adriatic seas by Henry's captains, after his break with Rome, many coming to these parts. They were also informed that there was a considerable trade in flints hereabouts. Most foreign ships which called at Gruz took a barrel or two away, at least. They could buy from the merchants at Gruz, or if they wanted large quantities more cheaply, they could visit the great limestone quarries at Brgat, up on the mountainside a few miles inland.

Before proceeding northwards through the crowded narrow alleyways of tall buildings which branched off from the Placa, they paid the required visit to the cathedral, in its own square to the west, a magnificent edifice built, oddly enough, or at least paid for, by an Englishman, King Richard Coeur de Lion who, returning from another Crusade, was shipwrecked in a storm on the nearby island of Lochrun. In gratitude for his rescue and escape from death, he decided to endow a great church on that isle; but the sensible folk of Dubrovnik persuaded him that it would be wiser, and more pleasing to the Almighty, to make it a cathedral in the city itself.

They found other squares, also, as they proceeded northwards, with fountains and statuary, in that extraordinary city, despite the constriction. How many thousands lived in it, nobody could tell them.

They passed out through the mighty north gate, with its moat, drawbridge and portcullis, and over a shoulder of hill to the port of Gruz. This was busy, thronged with shipping, but still a dull place compared with Dubrovnik itself. However, this was their ultimate destination, the turning-point of their long journey. The bay of Gruz was really only the widening of the estuary of a river issuing from the enclosing mountains, and this was lined with fully a mile of docks, havens, shipyards, warehouses and workshops, the source of the walled city's wealth.

Enquiries by Guiseppi as to shipping elicited the information that there were two Netherlands vessels and three French here at present, so there could be a choice. But it turned out that one of the Dutchmen was sailing the very next day for Antwerp, whereas the other had only just arrived and would be at Gruz for another week, at least; and it would be easier, undoubtedly, to get onward passage from Antwerp to Scotland than from one of the French ports, which would probably entail having to sail west-abouts round Ireland to avoid English warships in the narrow seas. So, not desirous of kicking their heels here for many days, they sought passage on the first Dutch ship, although this meant that they would not have time to go to buy flints at the quarries but must get them in lesser quantity from Gruz merchants. However, even so they proved less expensive here than the Hopes had anticipated and they ordered a dozen casksful, to be delivered forthwith to their ship, confident of selling them at a fair profit in Scotland.

Next day, then, all their purchases loaded, they said farewell to Guiseppi and Dalmatia, and set sail on their long voyage for Antwerp, reckoned to take at least a month. Their accommodation was scarcely as fine as on the clerical vessel the Cardinal of Lorraine had found for them, but it was comfortable enough and reasonably roomy by shipboard standards.

It had been an interesting, informative and probably profitable expedition, and this last lap the best of it, David particularly intrigued by the altars and the Hopes pleased to have made new trading contacts. But it would be good to be back in Scotland again, even with all its problems.

13

The problems were not long in asserting themselves to the homecomers, once Scotland's soil was under their feet, that midsummer. A Flemish trader from Antwerp had landed them at Dysart, on the southern Fife coast, one of the main trading ports of the land, and they were at the Mount of Lindifferon that same evening, and David Lindsay thankfully in his Janet's arms. And from her they learned something of the situation which had developed in their absence.

There had been a sufficiency of developments. King Henry had not been inactive, in especial. On the first day of May a vast fleet of English ships had sailed into the Firth of Forth, two hundred vessels no less, flying the flag of the Lord High Admiral of England, the Lord Lisle. No doubt well informed that there were cannon protecting Leith harbour, the port of Edinburgh, these sailed further west a couple of miles, and taking the Scots entirely by surprise were able to disembark, at Granton, a great army under the Earl of Hertford, all but unopposed. This force had then marched back to Leith, while Lisle unloaded the heavy artillery. Soon the port was in flames. For once Beaton's vaunted sources of information had failed him and Scotland, presumably because the fleet had travelled north more swiftly than the tidings. Hastily thereafter, the Cardinal had issued a mustering call to the nation, in the Regent's name, but that, of course, had taken time to achieve results. Meanwhile he and Arran had gathered what they could of armed men, mainly their personal followings, and hurried to meet the invaders. But they were much too late to save Leith and too few to halt Hertford's thousands. Beaton had sent Sir Adam Otterburn, the Edinburgh Provost, and Lord Advocate, under a white flag, to seek terms and delay, but Hertford had scornfully rejected this, declaring that the city would be sacked unless the young Queen was delivered up to him forthwith, along with all the principal fortresses of the kingdom. This being as promptly rejected, the English advance up to the capital continued. Recognising that they could by no means prevent the fall of Edinburgh and anxious not to become cooped up in its castle, Beaton and the Regent retired on Linlithgow, with many of the citizens, others fleeing as best they could. At Linlithgow they awaited Huntly, Argyll and other lords, with their general muster. And, taking a major risk, the Cardinal had sent to Angus at Douglas Castle, seeking his aid, trusting that he was now sufficiently out-of-love with Henry after the last English raiding when Douglas lands had not been spared. Angus had indeed responded after a fashion, but not before Edinburgh was taken and ravished mercilessly. For three days the city blazed, with a terrible slaughter of the common folk who had not been able to escape. Even Holyrood Abbey and Palace had been battered by artillery and set on fire. But the castle, under Hamilton of Stenhouse, had held out, with its heavy cannon able to keep the invaders at bay. Then, when at last the Scots lords had assembled their strength at Linlithgow, the Douglases amongst them for once, and marched eastwards, the English retired, without battle, Hertford south-eastwards overland for the border, burning Seton, Haddington, Dunbar and Reston in the bygoing, Lisle back to his ships at Granton with the artillery and booty. It had been a grim demonstration of Henry's hate and power.

Nor was this the end of the Tudor's spleen, for the meantime. A month later the Earl of Lennox, now at the English court, had led a flotilla of ten ships through the Channel and up the west coast, to attack the isles of Arran and Bute and thereafter to assail the royal castle of Dumbarton, on the Clyde estuary, of which, to be sure, he was hereditary keeper. His own deputy, however, when he learned that the Earl was leading an English force, refused to yield it up, and the invaders then went on to raid and harry Kintyre and other lands of the Campbells. However, the Campbell Earl of Argyll could muster more men and ships than Lennox had with him, and the attackers had been driven off, to return south.

As well as these invasions there had been troubles on the domestic front. Arising out of Angus's involvement during the Edinburgh attack, there had been a price to pay. For that difficult character had always hated Arran and now, in a position to use his new influence, he was behind a move to unseat the Regent and put the Queen-Mother in his place – as once he had done with the previous Queen-Mother, Margaret Tudor – although this time there was no suggestion as yet as to marrying Marie de Guise. What that lady thought of it all was anybody's guess – but she made no secret of her belief that Arran was too weak for his position. So now there was a faction using her name to undermine the Regent's authority.

Also there had been Church troubles. The Cardinal had paid a semi-pontifical visit to Perth, as Legate, where the Bishops of Dunblane and Dunkeld had been conducting an anti-heresy campaign; and there the trial of four reformers and a woman had been staged. One, named Lamb, was accused of interrupting a friar during his sermon, to deny that prayer to the saints was a necessary means to salvation. Three others were condemned for breaking the Lenten fast and ridiculing an image of St. Francis. And the wife of one of these was charged with failing to pray to the Virgin Mary for aid during her labour with child. All were found guilty, the men hanged and the woman drowned, amidst protests of the Perth citizenry. Davie Beaton, present, could have saved them but did not.

All this, and more, tended to bring the Lord Lyon King of Arms back to Scottish earth with something of a jerk.

Although David would have been well content to stay awhile at Lindifferon with Janet, since he was home rather earlier than had been anticipated, he felt that he was in duty bound to report to Davie Beaton – and it was perhaps significant that it was towards Beaton rather than the Regent or the Queen-Mother that he felt bound. So, after a couple of days, with the Hopes returned to Edinburgh in considerable anxiety to discover what had happened to their families, homes and business during the English attack, David set out for St. Andrews, where Janet understood the Cardinal to be. He took her with him, cherishing each other's company.

But at St. Andrews they found that Beaton was gone, apparently to Melgund in Angus, where it seemed that, of all things, and at such a time, he was building himself a new palace-castle, and was gone to inspect progress. Intrigued, the Lindsays decided to follow him there, since by ferry across Tay it would take them less than four hours.

Melgund lay inland from the coast some eighteen miles, on high ground in Aberlemno parish, Church property. It was a pleasant rural area, with fine views over Strathmore and to the blue buttresses of the Highland Line; but it seemed much off the beaten-track and a strange place for the man who was to all intents ruling Scotland to choose to build.

They learned at least part of the reason before ever they made contact with Beaton, for approaching the site in the slanting mellow sunlight of evening, they saw the walls, already quite high, glowing a most lovely rose-red on a green mound above a curve of a stream, in as fair a scene as was to be come across in many a day's riding. Clearly there had been a small tower-house here before, of the same warm stone, presumably quarried nearby.

They found Davie, and to their great pleasure, Marion Ogilvy with him, occupying very humble quarters in what had been the farmery of the early tower. The meeting was joyful.

The Lindsays had not seen Marion for some time. She was looking well, indeed blooming, carrying her years lightly despite her curious status and situation, a strikingly good-looking woman, clearly still as fond of Davie as ever, although by no means under his thumb. That man was at his best and most likeable, as he always was in Marion's company, and also unfeignedly glad, and surprised, to see the visitors. It was like old times.

"I had not expected you back from foreign parts for a month or six weeks yet, at the least, David," the Cardinal greeted. "Is all well? I hope that this does not signify any hitch or trouble?"

"Not so. The reverse, indeed. We were very fortunate. And you? And Marion? How good to see you both – and together!"

"Aye – we are here to see our new home at its growing. Long planned. Long looked forward to . . ."

"New home? You are not leaving Ethie Castle?"

"Not entirely. It is still Marion's, and will remain so. It is not *mine*. And she has had long years of that windy hold. Secure, yes, and remote, but bleak of a winter . . ."

"I have made no complaint," Marion observed.

"No. But then, you are no complainer, lass. Or you would have rid yourself of me long since! But this Melgund is ours – not mine, nor Marion's but *ours*. We are not so young as once we were, and here is to be our home, in this pleasant, sequestered place on the lip of Strathmore, where Marion comes from. I have built houses for our children at Colliston and Balfour, not far away. Now I build one for *us*. You like its looks, Janet? Is not the rose-coloured stone a joy?"

"Indeed it is. We exclaimed whenever we saw it. I am so glad for you both. This is . . . good. Are you thinking of giving up your direction of affairs, Davie? Your life of rule in Church and state? And becoming just the Laird of Melgund . . .?"

What in someone less discriminating might have been termed a hoot escaped from Marion Ogilvy.

"That may come, in time," David said carefully. "Meanwhile we shall spend as much of our winters here together as we may. But – come. There is still time and sufficient light for you to see what we are doing. The stone comes from a quarry nearby, and Marion fell in love with its colour. The old Carnegie tower was built of it, likewise."

He led them over to the grassy mound above which the masonry, now stained a rich red by the sunset, with violet shadows picking out every feature and aperture, corbels, windows, crowsteps, shot-holes and crenellations, rose almost to the final wallhead save at one corner, the original small tower skilfully incorporated. Conducting them round the outside first, Davie explained his ideas as to what constituted a suitable and comfortable home for such as themselves, stressing that it was for living in, not large entertaining or show any more than for defence, convenient to manage and with not too much climbing of difficult stairs, the normal handicap in tall Scots castles. Although on the outside it approximated in almost all respects to the ancient and traditional aspect with turrets, parapets, machicolations, gunloops and the rest, within it would be much more modern, incorporating all that Marion required and would like.

Walking along the lengthy south front, he pointed up to where, above one of the range of quite large windows, the lintel was carved with a sculptured panel, in relief, bearing four letters, DB and MO. He said nothing.

The significance of that panel was not lost on the visitors. It was what was known as a marriage-stone, and almost every Scots castle had one, representing the initials of the builder and his wife. David had seen scores of them – and never one with the initials of a mistress. He nodded, Janet turning to squeeze Marion's arm.

"Good!" she said.

Within, Beaton indicated the long range of no fewer than seven vaulted basement chambers, kitchen, bake-house, laundry, well-chamber and wine-cellar, but led them straight up the handsome stairway in the tower at the west end. This was much wider than usual and the treads less steep, a turnpike still, but no longer designed to be narrow enough to be defended by one swordsman. Half-way up two more stones were pointed out, inscribed DB and MO, that there be no mistake.

There were two halls, a greater and a lesser, on the first floor, the former a magnificent apartment, well lit by windows larger than usual, again an indication that this was no defensive stronghold but a house designed for gracious living. The great fireplace was splendidly decorative. The lesser hall in the keep was for more private entertainment; and as well there was a withdrawing-room opening off the other, eastern end of the larger hall, this with its own stairway up to bedrooms. These last were not yet finished and the roof not on; but they were to be, the visitors were assured, of a similar standard. Much impressed with all, and with the plans specified for gardens, a plesaunce, orchards, arbours and the like, the Lindsays were escorted back to the farmery.

"Now," Beaton said, "having seen our project and heard of our doings, what of yours? How did your notable journey fare? Let us hear all, David."

"All would take the night to tell. But some, aye some, you *should* hear. I think that you may be . . . interested. First in order, the Netherlands convoy project is agreed, and trade therewith should be much increased and the English pirates foiled. Then the citizenship agreement with France is accepted. Charles, the Cardinal, contrived it with King Francis with no difficulty. But that King does very poorly. He seems to have lost all spirit and fails in body also. I fear that he will not live long."

"You say so? I am sorry to hear that. Francis has been a good friend to Scotland. I knew that he was not well, not himself. Madeleine's death hit him hard. But – the mutual citizenship is good news. It should greatly help us. I scarcely expected it to be fully achieved so swiftly. It *is* now assured?"

"Yes. And the Cardinal sends his warm greetings to you. But in Rome I was less well received. Your Pope is scarcely . . . forthcoming! However, in Italy, with the Duke of Naples, I learned something of some value, I think. Did you know that Henry of England has been selling altars? Taken from English churches and abbeys. Selling them all round the Mediterranean and Adriatic seas."

"Wha-a-at!" It was not often that Davie Beaton reacted like that.

"I thought that you were not likely to know of it. But, yes. He has been doing a trade in these stolen altars, shiploads of them, selling them like any merchant, to whoever will buy them."

"Henry! You are sure, man? This is not just some fable you have been told . . .?"

"No. It is truth. Vouched for by many. I have myself

seen one of the altars. On a Dalmatian island off Dubrovnik – that is, Ragusa." David Lindsay told them the whole story.

He had guessed that Beaton would be more than interested, and he was not disappointed. That the great Protestant reforming monarch, scourge of Holy Church, should be engaged in such a sordid traffic, and with Catholic countries, was something even the realist and down-to-earth Cardinal had never visualised, could scarcely credit. But he was not long in visualising how he could use the information.

"Do you see what this means?" he demanded of them all. "It means that I can inform all the princes of Christendom of the mercenary monster and hypocrite that sits on England's throne and would fain swallow up Scotland. It is proof that Henry is more concerned with money than with faith or belief. How think you his ally the Emperor will view this? Or the reforming German princes? Or the Catholics of England, including Norfolk, his Earl Marshal? To confiscate the Church lands is one thing, but to peddle stolen church furniture is beyond all, for a king."

"So I saw it. But how can it be used to *aid* us against Henry?"

"A king, any king, requires *credit*, as well as armies, fleets and a treasury. Take away his credit in the eyes of other princes and he is at once much diminished. This will help make Henry a laughing-stock, and his credit will suffer. Never fear, I will contrive excellent uses for the information. I bless you for it!"

After that, the account of the Dubrovnik visit and the flint purchase was something of an anti-climax, Beaton's mind being obviously preoccupied elsewhere.

They sought their couches soon afterwards.

In the morning, it was David Lindsay's turn to ask the questions. And inevitably something of the pleasant friendly atmosphere was dissipated, at least between the two men. He indicated that he had not failed to hear of the dire doings at Perth.

"Ah, yes – that was grievous, but necessary," Beaton averred. "St John's Town had become a hotbed of heresy and error. Something had to be done, or it would spread. The forces of anarchy and false doctrine, under the guise of reform, grow ever more bold, more dangerous, encouraged, fomented and paid for by Henry, for his own ill ends."

"I cannot think that Henry of England had much concern with the poor woman in child-birth who omitted to pray to the Virgin Mary!"

"Not directly, perhaps. But it is the general attitude which Henry fosters. Paying leaders of opinion to corrupt others."

"Would he pay those Perth citizens to fail to pray to St. Francis? *I* have never in my life prayed to St. Francis!"

"These were but symbols of more general error. An example had to be made, the rot stopped."

"The rot, aye! I would say that the rot in Holy Church lies in other than failing to pray to saints!"

"But then you, my friend, do not have the responsibility of stopping the rot. It is easy to stand back and criticise. A very small rot in one apple can rot a whole barrel. I seek to purge and counter the corrupt in high places in the Church, and to replace them with better men. I have forced the resignation of many bishops, abbots, priors and priests. But I cannot overlook the smaller folk either, who are nearer to the commonality and therefore affect them more closely."

"Need you have had these slain? You did not slay your corrupt bishops!"

"That was the decision of the diocesan court, the Church's penalty for heresy. These knew it when they sinned. Their bodies destroyed that their souls might be saved. I could not interfere with the court's decision . . ."

"A mercy! You, *you* do not believe that? You, a man of wits and wiles and learning, aye, wiles! That by hanging or burning or drowning a body the soul is saved! That our merciful Saviour demands this? Our God of love?"

"Wiser men than you, or myself, have decided so."

"Weak! Feeble! Is that Davie Beaton I hear speaking? No man's fool. Nor tool. That is but excuse."

The other took a turn away, and back, there in the

yard of the Melgund farmery where they talked while the women were more profitably engaged.

"See you, David – I am fighting a battle, a war. And all but single-handed. I verily believe that if I died this day – as I well might, for my death is plotted – Scotland would fall to England. That is the size of it. Do *you* know any who could, or would, stop Henry, in this realm today? For I do not. The crown is a baby girl, the Regent a weakling, the Privy Council utterly divided, the nobility riddled with disaffection and self-seeking, the parliament leaderless, many of its commissioners Henry's pensioners, the common folk bewildered, helpless. Only the Church can stand fast for Scotland, as it will while I lead it. But I cannot have my hands tied by dissenters, by internal fighting in the Church itself. That is something that we just cannot afford at this present. And Henry knows it, and uses all his powers and wealth to foment it. *You* know that he is no true reformer – you have proved it with this of the altars. He has no religion in him, I think. But he will bring down Scotland through the religious niceties and scruples of its folk, if he can – and we are a nation of hair-splitters. That I will not allow. I must fight Henry with his own weapons, where I have no others. He has burned ten thousand Catholics. If I must burn two or three dissident Scots, to save this realm, then I will do so – and God have mercy on my soul!"

Lindsay stared at this man, his friend and yet so often his opponent, and shook his head, wordless, as again so often.

"There are ten English for every one Scot," Beaton added. "Mighty armies, great fleets and a rich treasury. Aye, and a ruthless monarch who rules them all with an iron fist – and who covets Scotland. Remember that when you rail against me, David Lindsay. If I go, how will you fight?"

The other latched on to that. "What do you mean – if you go? And you said before that your death is plotted. What is this?"

"Henry, I know well, has often sought to have me removed, a thorn in his flesh. But this time I am gaining more evidence. There is a group of the reforming nobles who seek my assassination – Glencairn, Cassillis, Sir George Douglas and the lairds of Brunstane and Ormiston in Lothian. Henry has put them up to it and uses a priest, George Wishart, son to Wishart of Pitarrow, the Lord Justice Clerk, as go-between. He is one of the reformers, and had to flee Scotland six years ago. But he has come back as one more English citizen, in the train of Sadler, over the marriage negotiations with Arran for the child-Queen's hand, a year ago. This Wishart comes and goes between Sadler and these plotters. He is bold and preaches openly, in especial in Dundee and Montrose – Pitarrow is in the Mearns. I could have him taken and tried, at any time. But I prefer to keep him under watch, and to learn of what is plotted. I keep my own folk close to him. I wish to know how my assassination is to be contrived. That way, I may catch not only Wishart but the others."

"This is vile. Should you be here, then? Unguarded?"

"I am perhaps better guarded than I seem, friend! I knew, see you, of your approach here before ever I saw you. But I do not wish to have my life, if it is to be left to me, spoiled by obtrusive guards. Nor Marion's. So they keep their distance."

Inevitably Lindsay had to glance around him, but could see only field-workers some distance away, forking hay.

"Ever you surprise me," he said. He changed the subject. "You have, I hear, been making moves towards Angus. This also surprises."

"Perhaps it surprised the Douglas also! But, yes – Henry has grievously offended Angus and I would be foolish not to seek to profit by it. The Tudor's follies must be my opportunities. I would not trust the Douglas further than I can see him. But he can be useful, if handled with care. As can a hive of bees!"

"And this of his urging that Marie de Guise be Regent instead of Arran? How say you to that?"

"It might be none so ill an exchange."

"Do I detect *your* hand in this?"

"Scarcely that. But the notion has its advantages. And its uses meantime, as both a curb and a spur! It should keep Arran more heedful, prepared to be guided, requiring support. And give me a hold over Angus. Something for which he would seek my aid."

"Aye, I see it. And the Queen-Mother herself? How will *she* like being pawn in your subtle games, man?"

"Oh, Marie and I understand each other. She is a woman of much sense as well as ability. She does not like Angus, but nor does she admire Arran. She would, in fact, make a good Regent – but not for Angus to manipulate. She is still too new to Scotland to be readily accepted by most, and a woman as Regent would not be popular. But with the Queen only one year old, we are going to require regency for long. Marie's time may come. Meanwhile, no harm in letting Angus advocate it. And Henry will not like it."

"Henry might therefore act the more violently and swiftly? This raid of Hertford's and Lisle's, in May – it was grievous indeed. But it was *only* a raid. Not fullest invasion. Lennox's assault in the west, likewise. If Henry were to commit his full strength . . ."

"He will not do that, I think. Not while the de Guise brothers control France. The Duke Francis is moving to besiege Calais – had you heard? Henry dare not commit all against their sister's Scotland and leave south England open to French invasion. The Auld Alliance still serves its turn. Oh, Henry Tudor will attack again, nothing surer. But not outright war, meantime, I think . . ."

Marion and Janet appeared from the house. "You two greybeards have had sufficiently long to set the world to rights!" the former announced. "*We* have been deciding more vital matters – James's wedding. What we shall wear, what we shall eat, and who shall be invited. This concerns you, David. The bride is kin of yours, is she not? A Lindsay, at least."

The men exchanged glances. James Beaton, Davie's eldest son, was to marry Margaret, a daughter of John, fifth Lord Lindsay of the Byres, and so a niece of David's first wife, Kate.

"Far out . . ." he disclaimed. But, of course, that was no valid excuse for them to avoid involvement in the pros and cons of this important matter. Church and state thereafter were relegated to their proper places in the scheme of things.

David Lindsay was not amongst the guests at the Beaton-Lindsay wedding, although Janet did attend. He had intended to be at the Abbey of Arbroath for the ceremony but he was prevented – and it was his projected host thereat who dissuaded him. In mid-August, four days before the event, the Cardinal came hurriedly to Lindifferon in person, from St. Andrews, in some concern.

"Trouble, David," he announced, without preamble. "Trouble in which you can help, I think. We have known for some time that the English are massing again along the border, and have been watching them heedfully. They are in three groups, under Sir Ralph Eure, Sir Brian Layton and Sir Richard Bowes, awaiting Henry's signal to attack. A few days back, my people in Northumberland intercepted an English royal courier and read his letter. It was to Eure from Henry, and was sufficiently explicit. It ordered Eure and the others to invade, in the East and Middle Marches just so soon as they were ready, promising reinforcements and a parallel assault by Wharton on the West March. Also urging the usual terror, savagery and scathe on men, women and children, to throw down and burn every abbey, monastery, town, village, tower, mill and farm. That is his usual style, of course. But there was something new this time. Henry promised Eure in person a specific royal grant of all the lands in the Merse, Teviotdale, Tweeddale, and Lauderdale which he can overrun, under the Great Seal of England, to be held of him, Henry, in perpetuity. Naming in especial Douglas lands amany. Moreover, he ordered Melrose Abbey in particular to be destroyed and the Douglas tombs therein to be defaced. That is Henry Tudor!"

"Save us – the man runs utterly mad! His wits are lost in hatred."

"No doubt. And I must use this madness. Two days ago, I showed Angus that intercepted letter."

"You did? How did that man take it?"

"Need you ask? His fury was daunting. Henry has burned all his bridges with Angus now. But I did more than show him the letter. I persuaded the Regent to appoint him Chief Warden of the Marches."

"What! Angus – Warden? Oh, no!"

"But yes. It is taking a chance, I agree. But in this pass, who better? This time he will not go over to the English, I swear! He is a fighter, an experienced soldier, whatever else. He knows the Borderland – and the border clans will rally to him as they would not to Huntly or Argyll or Atholl. He would not be the man to put over a *national* army, I agree. But a Borders one, yes."

"I would never trust Angus," Lindsay declared flatly.

"Nor I, man. But I can *use* him. See you, I want you to go with him. To accompany him to the Borders. You have campaigned there, many a time – and he knows it. You are Lyon, one of the officers of state, and he cannot object to your presence. So you can watch him, keep an eye on him – aye, and aid him too. For he will need aid. You are the best man for the task, and someone must watch Angus."

"We much mislike each other . . ."

"I know it. But I must work with many that I mislike. It is something which you can do for the realm, which others could not do. You are one of the very few that Angus has got to accept."

Put like that, Lindsay had to agree, if very doubtfully.

"You will miss the wedding. I am sorry. But Angus has already gone to Tantallon and you should join him as soon as you may. I shall be at Arbroath, but not for long. Then to Edinburgh, where you will be able to reach me, at any time, if need be. My information is that these three English forces total some six thousand men. But they are to be reinforced. And Wharton may have more, in the west . . ."

So instead of heading northwards, clad in his best, for Arbroath Abbey, David rode southwards for Tantallon, in half-armour and with a small escort, reluctant both as watch-dog and warrior.

He had not been within the mighty Red Douglas stronghold on the edge of the Norse Sea cliffs since that day all those years ago when, with Patrick, Lord Lindsay, Kate's father, he had bearded Angus in his den, on behalf of the other Chancellor and Archbishop Beaton. He was not now much more warmly received than he had been on that occasion. Angus then had been a hot young man in his early twenties; now he was in his early fifties but still hot, autocratic, and still as full of energy, drive and resentment. His uncles had died, but he still had the support of his brother, Sir George Douglas, and of numerous other Douglas lairds.

"That fox Beaton sent you, no doubt," the Earl accused, when David presented himself at the cliff-edge hoist of the castle courtyard, within the mighty curtain wall and keep which screened off the thrusting headland on which the stronghold was built, where Angus superintended the raising of supplies from boats far below – one of the reasons for Tantallon's invulnerability, since it could be provisioned and reinforced from the sea unhindered.

"The Cardinal-Chancellor believes that I can be of some aid to you in Borders warfare, my lord, since I have had some experience of it," David answered stiffly. To add, "As you know."

The other, who had been the enemy on such occasions, more than once, did know. "I need no guide to hold *my* hand in the Borderland, Lindsay!" he returned.

"No doubt. But even your lordship cannot be in three places at once – and I understand that there are three English groups operating against us at the moment – four, if Wharton on the West March is counted. Moreover, as Lyon, I can speak and act directly in the Queen's royal name, and the Regent's, which others cannot do. An advantage, in these circumstances."

Angus did not admit that directly. "I am Warden and will not be interfered with or hampered by any," he declared. "Mind it." And then, abruptly, "We ride tomorrow."

"To be sure. I did not conceive you able to defend the Border from Tantallon!"

"I have three forces out, watching Eure, Layton and Bowes. I cannot attack in full strength until I know which is chiefest, which will serve best to defeat first. Eure, I think." Eure, David recollected, was the one Henry had sent the letter to and promised all the Douglas lands which he could conquer.

"They are not together, then?"

"Eure harries Teviotdale, Bowes Tweeddale and Lauderdale, Layton the Merse." Most of the Douglas properties were in Teviotdale. "But they could easily switch or link up. I must know who decides."

"How many men have you?"

"Insufficient. For I must keep many on the West March, to watch Wharton. If Beaton had sent me more men, instead of . . ." Angus left the rest unsaid.

"Can Maxwell not hold the west?"

"I do not trust Maxwell. He loves me not."

By that standard Angus would be unable to trust many in Scotland. "So we ride tomorrow. Whither?"

The Earl turned back to the unloading, David in effect dismissed.

With a mere four hundred, but all mounted moss-troopers, the Douglas headed south next morning, David very much cold-shouldered. He understood that they were making for Home Castle in the West Merse. As they passed Dunbar, Dunglass and Pease Dean, memories came flooding back for David, and he marvelled anew at the recurrent changes of fortune, alliance and challenge in the affairs of a nation.

Riding slantwise across the Merse, the devastation, old and new, which met the eye on every hand witnessed anew to the ferocity of the English raiding – and the fact that the Homes no longer held their one-time immunity from assault. The Douglas contingent seemed hardly to notice it all, the blackened ruins, the broken mills, the down-trodden and abandoned fields, the wells choked with bodies, the clouds of flies – it was not Douglas land, of course.

Home Castle on its isolated mound in the great green plain was too strong a place to reduce without heavy cannon and so far it had remained inviolate. It was as good a forward base as any to keep watch on the eastern Borderland, with Lauderdale and Teviot opening off Tweed not far away. Here they found Douglas of Mains already installed, the Lord Home, an inoffensive character, having removed himself to less stressful parts.

Mains, now a grizzled veteran, David knew from of old. He it was who had captured him, and the late Earl of Lennox with him, at the Battle of Linlithgow Bridge when the Bastard of Arran had come up and cold-bloodedly stabbed the wounded Lennox to death before their eyes – to Mains's fury, who thus lost a major ransom. That long-ago encounter on a battlefield scarcely made them friends, but at least it offered them a basis for reminiscence; and David found the older man more tolerant of him than were Angus's closer lieutenants.

Mains reported on the situation in detail, for he had scouts out watching all three areas and sending back information. It seemed that the English were engaged in a curious campaign, different from their usual raiding, an ongoing series of hit-and-run attacks, but co-ordinated and planned to keep the Scots defence confused, extended and unprepared. The three enemy forces, each of about two thousand men, and all horsed, based themselves well behind their own border, Layton behind the defences of Berwick-on-Tweed, Bowes at Wark Castle and Eure in Upper Redesdale, behind Carter Bar and the Redeswire. From these bases they made descents on the Scots districts approximately opposite, which even Eure, the farthest back, could reach in an hour or two's riding, never remaining in the harried parts for more than a couple of grim nights before retiring back to their own sanctuaries. But these raids were clearly not haphazard, planned carefully – for the three units were based not so very far apart, a mere thirty-five miles, and the leaders could keep in close touch. Sometimes all three struck on the same day, sometimes only one, sometimes when the defenders rushed to one savaged area another English assault was mounted behind them. Most evidently the aim was to create maximum havoc but without having to fight pitched battles. And the strategy was proving all too successful. The hard-riding raiders could penetrate twenty or thirty miles in from the borderline in a two-day assault before returning to safety, and Mains conceded that there was now a belt of ravaged territory, two-score miles long by fully a score wide, where there was practically nothing left but smoking ruins and corpses, the survivors fled westwards into the sanctuary of the great Forest of Ettrick. How to attempt to deal with the situation he did not know.

It was clear why Angus was anxious to learn who actually commanded this English terror operation. The three knights, Eure, Layton and Bowes, were all of an equal rank and similar background, captains from Henry's French wars. Any Scots counter-attack should be made on the leader – but which was that? With the limited Scots numbers he could not attempt to assail all three at their bases; and the chances of being able to fall upon a raid in progress, in these circumstances, were not high.

But there was one indication to follow. Berwick-on-Tweed was a mighty walled citadel, and Wark Castle a powerful stronghold, neither to be reduced without prolonged siege and heavy artillery – like this Home Castle. But Upper Redesdale held no such fortress, a few peel-towers, that was all. And Eure was the one who was attacking and menacing the Douglas lands in Teviotdale. Also the one Henry had written to – although he might have sent similar letters to the other two, not intercepted. Angus decided on an attack on Redesdale.

David Lindsay was doubtful – but then, he was apt to be. He was not consulted, anyway. He did express his fears to Mains. Upper Redesdale was wild and empty country, deep in the Cheviot Hills. If Eure did not want a fight – and it looked as though the English did not, at this stage – then nothing would be easier than for him to disperse his people amongst the myriad high valleys and cleuchs of the area and there would be nothing a Scots expedition could do about it save burn a few hill farms and sack a peel-tower or two. And meanwhile Scotland behind them would be wide open to attack.

Douglas of Mains accepted this assessment, but failed to convince Angus that the attack was inadvisable. After all something had to be attempted, inaction already too prolonged.

The call went out for most of the Scots forces watching the enemy concentrations to assemble at Jedburgh, some way up Teviot.

It took a few days to organise this, during which no English raids were reported. On the way to Jedburgh, David was shocked by what he saw; the town of Kelso a ravaged desolation, empty save for the occasional furtive looter and scavenging, snarling dogs, its fine abbey shattered – many of its monks, as well as citizens, had died defending it, they were told; the old royal castle of Roxburgh at the rivers-joining had been ruined for long, blown up by its English captors when they retired, but now its extensive castleton, almost as large as Kelso, was in ruined abandonment; villages, hamlets, miltons and farm-touns, of course, had suffered the same fate, and the fair vale of Teviot was a man-made desert. Jedburgh itself, when they reached it, had not been spared, few buildings left standing, the magnificent abbey roofless, burned out. This dire journey affected Lindsay in a way no amount of reporting could do. They had, of course, heard of all this at Edinburgh, Stirling and St. Andrews and reacted angrily; but the reality appalled.

It certainly upset Angus, for they were now approaching the Douglas lands, and he was breathing threatenings and slaughters. But it greatly added to his problems also, for his host of about five thousand men, here mustered, found little to eat and to feed their horses. Normally, on campaign, they lived off the country, taking – and seldom paying for – cattle, sheep, poultry, oats and forage. But now there was none to take and provisioning even a modestly-sized expedition became ever more difficult. The sooner they were over into unravaged England the better, the Earl declared savagely.

This was mainly Kerr country and the Kerrs supported Douglas. The lairds of Ferniehirst, Cessford, Eckford and others knew of some hidden stocks and stores in secret valleys and deans. But five thousand hungry men take a lot of feeding, and they set off up Jed Water without delay, climbing now into the Cheviots, with largely empty bellies.

Eleven miles up, at the Redeswire Stone, traditional meeting-place of the Scots and English Wardens of the Middle March to settle differences, in happier times, they crossed over into Northumberland, the Borderline unmarked save by this great stone. The views from up here, looking back over the Scots side, were tremendous, the devastation, from this range, not very apparent; but ahead it was all only heather, reeds and deer-hair-grass, on enclosing hills.

Their drove-road followed a well-trodden track, with ample signs of the passage of large numbers of horsemen and cattle, stolen Scots cattle undoubtedly, by what was really just a pass through the Cheviots; until after three miles they emerged into a widening of the valley, wherein was the loch of Catcleuch, with around its mile or so of length two or three unharried hill farms, the first such they had seen for long, with cattle grazing on the slopes. Withstanding the temptation to wreak vengeance here, Angus pressed on. Since Eure was so frequently raiding into Scotland from hereabouts, obviously his base must not be very far ahead, probably at Byrness, a mere two miles on, the nearest actual community to the Borderline, where the River Rede was joined by sundry side-burns. They aimed to surprise him.

They did not, in fact, as David at least had feared. After all, a look-out on the top of one or two of these hills was all that was required to warn Eure of the approach of five thousand men, a column almost a mile long. Presumably such had done so, for when the Scots dropped down from the Catcleuch area towards the hub of lesser valleys which constituted Byrness, it was to find every sign of a great encampment filling the valley-floor, horse-lines, cooking-fires, even abandoned tentage, but no men nor beasts. Clearly there had been a hasty departure. But, gazing as they would up into the radiating glens and cleuchs and hillsides, they could see no sign of decamping horsemen, much less an army. Disappointment and anger was rife.

However, there was some slight compensation. Much food and drink had been left behind, also straying cattle and booty. And, of course, there were the farmeries, cot-houses and mill of Byrness to savage and despoil. So they took over the encampment and settled down. Angus set guards and sent out scouts to try to find the enemy; but they had little fear of actual attack, since Eure was thought to have only two thousand as against their five.

At least they fed well that night, to the light of blazing homesteads.

Next day they scoured Redesdale and the off-branching valleys, but save for seeing the odd horseman in the distance, found no trace of Eure or his force. And now, to be sure, some of the Scots were fretting about what might well be happening behind them, in Scotland, and, David and Mains amongst them, persuaded Angus against continuing on to spread havoc in the North Tyne valley, as he would have liked, but to turn back, the protection of his own Borderland his prime duty. And, sure enough, when they reached the Redeswire heights again, it was to see great new smoke-clouds staining all the sky to the north-east.

Cursing, they rode the faster.

They were much too late, of course, to save the Billie, Bonkyl and Blanerne districts of the Merse, or to catch the raiders, presumably out from Berwick.

Frustrated and out-manoeuvred, they returned to Home Castle, Angus bad company indeed.

In the weeks that followed, that was the pattern of events on the East and Middle Marches; and to a lesser extent on the West too, with Angus having to shuttle to and fro on occasion to assist the Lord Maxwell, the West Warden, to cope with Sir Thomas Wharton. There were no real battles, much as the Scots sought them, only the odd encounter and skirmish. No doubt Angus and his lieutenants managed to save many a district which would otherwise have been devastated; but for all that, the areas of destruction grew and grew as the English were reinforced. The situation seemed all but hopeless, the horror unending, so little that Angus or anyone else seemed to be able to do to counter the strategy of triple assault carefully organised from English strongholds against undefended targets. Oddly enough, a tally of something of the damage done came to them in time, not from their own local informants but from Davie Beaton, whose Northumbrian minions had once again intercepted a courier from Eure to King Henry proudly giving details of achievements to date against the dastardly Scots. This despatch quoted these totals – seven great religious houses burned, sixteen castles and towers brought low, five market towns destroyed, no fewer than two hundred and forty-three villages, hamlets and townships demolished, thirteen mills and three hospices sacked, plus 10,386 cattle, 12,492 sheep and 1,496 horses taken. Even allowing for a little exaggeration, these figures were dire indeed. The Cardinal's unspoken criticism of Angus's defensive strategy was evident.

For himself, David Lindsay hated it all, the bloodshed, the horror, the frustration, his own helplessness. His presence here was useless, for Angus would allow him no command and never directly took his advice – although indirectly, through Mains whom he could influence, he may have achieved a little. And clearly Angus was in no danger of going over to the English again, his hatred and fury at them unbounded. So David's mission was pointless. He sent word, to that effect, to Beaton.

It was not until November, however, that he achieved his recall – although, he recognised, that as Lord Lyon he did not have to wait on the permission of the Chancellor-Primate or any other. Strangely the summons back to Edinburgh came at a period when conditions were rather more tolerable than heretofore at Home Castle, with a lull in the English raiding, however temporary, and Angus absenting himself on unspecified business and leaving his brother, Sir George, in command. Nor did Beaton explain why he urgently required David's presence before St. Machar's Day, 12th November.

So quite thankfully he left Home Castle, his going regretted by none save perhaps Douglas of Mains.

At the capital he found that Beaton had gone to Stirling, and left word for him to follow there. And when he reached that citadel, he discovered it in something of a state of emergency, not to say agitation. He found that Angus himself was there, also Marie de Guise and the young Queen. Beaton took Lindsay to his own quarters, to explain the situation.

Arran had precipitated a crisis. Against Beaton's advice he had called a parliament, as Regent, to condemn Angus's failure to stem the English reign of terror and to remove him from office as Chief Warden – this the week before, in Edinburgh Castle. There were other items put forward, but that was the main reason. Davie had declared this to be folly and worse, dangerous; for if Douglas and Home and Kerr could not hold the Border, who could? But Arran had insisted, and the Cardinal had countered by declaring that he would not attend, as Chancellor. Moreover, he would urge the Spiritual Estate to stay away also. But the Regent had gone ahead without them, holding a very brief and badly attended assembly, declaring it to be a parliament although it was not, in those circumstances. But something had to be done about the situation. So . . .

"Aye – so what?"

Beaton looked just a little uncomfortable. "Marie de Guise is calling another parliament, for 13th November. In the young Queen's name."

"Ah! So that is it. That is why Angus is here. Rival parliaments, now? Scarcely adding to the realm's dignity and repute!"

"Something had to be done," the other repeated. "If Angus is dismissed as Warden, as Arran's assembly has it, who will we get to take his place? We will lose the Douglas power, and possibly that of many of the Borders clans with it. Angus could be thrown back into the English arms. It might well produce civil war in Scotland – which would hand the realm over to Henry, nothing more sure."

"So you have elected to throw in your lot with Angus the renegade, as against Arran – who is still the Regent!"

"Not so. I am acting as go-between. Seeking to preserve some semblance of unity, on the surface at least. Someone must do so. As Chancellor, Primate and Legate, perhaps only I can attempt it. Arran is a fool. He cannot be allowed to remain Regent for much longer."

"You would replace him with Angus?"

"No, no. It will have to be the Queen-Mother, Marie. But that is not yet. See you – this parliament of Marie's. It is difficult. It is necessary, to undo the harm which has been done over Angus. But I do not wish openly to support it, as Chancellor. That would mean taking sides, before all, against the Regent. Better that I seem to remain uncommitted, in the background, meantime. Then it could be said, if necessary, that *neither* was a true parliament, because the Chancellor did not chair either. Yet, this one must have sufficient authority to counter the harm of the Regent's one. You see the problem?"

"I see you caught in coils of your own devising! And you want my help, I take it?"

"Yes, as Lyon. You represent the Queen of Scots, directly. Not the Regent. If you appear with the young Mary at the opening session, as you did many a time with the young James, then that extra authority is given to the proceedings. It still will not be a true parliament, but more so than Arran's was. And so can cancel Angus's dismissal, and other unwise matters passed."

"I see. So you wish me to do what you find it indiscreet to do yourself!"

"That is no way to put it, man! You are a friend of Marie's, and she intends to ask you to do this. Indeed, I do not see how you could refuse, as Lyon, if she asks you in her daughter's name. It commits you to nothing save doing your official duty. And you have been with Angus doing *his* duty, however unsuccessfully. You will much help me. And, I believe, the kingdom."

"So I have no choice?"

"Say that your good sense and goodwill impel you to it."

Three days later, then, in Stirling Castle, David Lindsay

was involved in what seemed to him like a repeat performance of one of his own plays, the ushering in of the Queen-Mother and the infant Scots monarch to the throne, before a bowing assembly in the great hall, announced by trumpeters. Mary, in her mother's arms, was now two years old, a lively and attractive child, reddish-haired like her father, and having outgrown her early frailty. She did not know David so well as James had done, of course, but she made no objection when Marie set her down beside the throne, and Lindsay, in his state tabard, seated her thereon amidst loud acclaim. She sat quite happily in a corner of it, with the man standing at her side and her mother in a chair nearby.

There was quite a large turn-out, much greater apparently than the Regent's gathering of a few days earlier, at Edinburgh, the Spiritual Estate being well represented now, even though neither of the archbishops was present. The Chancellor's place was taken by David Paniter, David's old travelling-companion, still royal secretary but now Bishop-Elect of Ross, he well able to conduct the proceedings. However, he did not have much conducting to do, for the session was the briefest in living memory, basically called only to reverse the dismissal of Angus – it transpired that he had also been accused of high treason by the previous assembly – and in its turn to declare that the Regent was no longer fit to govern, and therefore to discharge all classes of the people from allegiance to him. It did not go so far as to proclaim Marie de Guise Regent, but it was implied that that would follow. That really was all, and took only a few minutes, Angus present but not raising his voice – an unusual situation for that man. So young Mary did not have time to become bored, and in fact seemed to enjoy the stir and colour, even the trumpeting.

So Scotland, ever a dangerously divided realm, to its own continuing hurt, was now a divided land indeed, with two alleged parliaments, a Regent whom many did not recognise, two commanders of the nation's forces and a Church racked with dissension. David Beaton sought to seem to mediate, to fill the gap in some measure, trying to keep a foot in both camps. David Lindsay did the same to a lesser degree, not quite sure where his duty lay.

He was to learn.

14

The wintry weather of 1544–5 tended to inhibit even the enthusiasm of the English raiders, although it did not altogether halt them. But by mid-February the temper of savagery had picked up, and a force under Sir Ralph Eure penetrated as far up Tweed as Melrose, and there, while sacking the lovely red-stone abbey, duly desecrated and defaced the tombs in this, the traditional Douglas family burial-place, as Henry had ordered in the letter. Here the heart of Robert the Bruce was buried.

This, needless to say, sent Angus back to the Borderland hotfoot, in towering rage. He was now calling himself Lieutenant-General of the Realm, and to some degree this title might be justified, for he now had increased forces at his disposal and was supported by others who previously had stood aloof from him, the Earls of Glencairn and Cassillis, the Lords Somerville, Livingstone and Fleming, and even his old enemy, Scott of Buccleuch. But not, on this occasion, by David Lindsay. Beaton, after the tombs desecration, judged that there was little need to fear Angus's desertion to the English.

David was not to escape continuing Border-warfare entanglement, however, for of all things, the unwarlike Arran now decided to take a hand, presumably to prove that he could do better than Angus, and to enhance his flagging authority as Regent. He collected seven thousand men, largely Hamiltons, and requested the Lord Lyon to accompany him.

David was less than eager, but having accompanied Angus previously, to refuse Arran would look very much like taking sides. Beaton urged him to go, in the interests of national unity; besides, he might well be useful, for Arran was no soldier and David knew the Borderland and its warfare.

They rode south-eastwards from Edinburgh, passing

the Byres and Garleton. David learned that they were making for Coldingham where, it seemed, Sir Brian Layton had taken advantage of the winter-time lull to move up from Berwick, and had installed himself in that strongly defensive priory, slaying its Douglas prior. A victory over Layton would have great strategic value and at the same time damage Angus's credit, who had not so far attempted to wipe out this latest Douglas reverse. Arran was going to lay siege to Coldingham.

Past so many places which set memories astir in David's mind, they marched – for this host was not all horsed, indeed with cannon lumbering on behind – Dunbar, Dunglass, Coldbrandspath Tower, and so on to Coldingham Muir, so near to Fast Castle where he had spent that dramatic honeymoon with his Kate.

Their approach to Coldingham could not go unobserved, of course, and being inevitably slow, the English had ample time to take precautions and counter-measures. By the time the Scots arrived in the valley inland from the mighty cliffs of the headland of St. Ebba, who had founded the priory, the enemy were all either safely within its high protecting walls or else departed for Berwick a dozen miles to the south.

But they had come for siege rather than battle and Arran disposed his forces all around to invest the place, ridiculous as it seemed for an army of seven thousand to be assailing one monastery. For himself, David was more than usually unenthusiastic. He had vivid and ominous memories of Coldingham from the time when King James, besieging Tantallon, had heard that Angus had slipped away here and came to apprehend him, with disastrous results. This was a very different situation, but struck Lindsay as unlikely to be much more profitable.

Shot at from the priory walling by hagbuts and crossbows, the besiegers kept their distance, waiting for the arrival of the artillery-train which would enable them to pound the place into submission. The fact that it was a religious establishment of some note seemed to worry no one on either side.

Unfortunately, heavy cannon necessarily travelled even

more slowly than marching men, drawn by teams of ponderous oxen, eight to ten miles a day representing maximum progress. So, with nearly fifty miles to cover, the besiegers would have to wait a day or two; and in February weather, in the open, that was less than comfortable. It all called for great fires, tentage, makeshift shelter, as well as requisitioning the homes of the unfortunate Coldingham villagers. And once all this was organised, an inevitable settled-in atmosphere developed, less than aggressively warlike. David warned of the dangers of this; but secure in their great numbers, the Regent, no soldier anyway, paid little heed. Once the artillery arrived there would be no lack of martial ardour, he asserted.

That might well have been so, save that Sir Brian Layton arrived first. It seemed that he had not shut himself up in the priory but had retired hot-foot to Berwick, and now returned in strength. Even Arran, to be sure, was not such a fool as to fail to have scouts out; but the warning sent by these allowed insufficient time for any adequate reception. Layton, no doubt well informed as to the situation, evidently decided that a night attack would be best, permitting greater surprise, a more screened approach and wider dispersal of the besiegers. All of which in fact proved valid reasoning.

Arran's trumpets sounding the assembly were too late to allow any large proportion of his host to muster effectively from their camp fires, scattered encampments and village billets, before the English, mounted and in disciplined cohorts, descended upon them out of the dusk, swords slashing and lances thrusting; and therefore no coherent defence was practicable. That it should have to be defence, when almost certainly the English attackers did not number half the Scots strength, made it all the sorrier. But that was the way of it. Some Scots groups put up a good fight, and some leaders made brave attempts to rally forces, David Lindsay amongst them. But lacking any strong central command, in the darkness, with Arran in panic, the position was chaotic and all but irremediable. Especially when the English in the priory sallied out to assist their compatriots and many Scots found themselves attacked from behind. No doubt many of Arran's ordinary fighting men had no notion of the overall picture, no idea of the enemy numbers, certainly no clear directives as to tactics, and so conceived self-preservation and escape as the obvious priority. Flight into the blessed obscurity of the night appealed strongly.

As it transpired, this appealed to Arran as much as anyone else, and it was not long before he departed the scene, deciding that the Home castle of Aytoun would serve him better on a night like this. His late brother, the Bastard, would never have acted so – but then, they had always been at odds anyway.

The Regent had retained the loyalty of very few of the great nobles, but the Earl of Bothwell was present and he and David did their utmost to stem the flight, gather men into units, especially the horsed men, and used these to assail enemy formations and to rescue beleaguered groups of their own people. But in the darkness and prevailing confusion, morale inevitably low, they were only moderately successful. Presently it became clear, if anything was clear that night, that there was little more that they could usefully do save try to make a controlled retiral with as many of their folk as they could collect. David, as Lyon, always had his personal trumpeter, and he used this to sound a rallying-call. This did bring in a few stragglers and abandoned men. The risk that it would also bring the enemy leadership down upon them had to be taken; but now the English force was much dispersed also, and the darkness hampering them likewise, away from the fires. At any rate, no major assault on their muster developed, and with a mixture of thankfulness and shame, Lindsay and Bothwell led quite a substantial company out of that fatal valley, westwards, Arran having presumably made for Aytoun. They did not think that they were pursued.

Seldom, surely, had Scotland's military reputation sunk so low.

At Aytoun Castle, four miles away, they found the Regent in nail-biting distress and indecision, humiliated and guilt-ridden. He seemed to find the new arrivals, some twelve-hundred strong, only a further accusation of his own failure.

But Arran had the answer, even so. Angus was not so very far away, with his thousands of men. He must be summoned. Together they would return and teach these English their lesson. Angus was doing nothing, useless. He should be here, with his people. David Lindsay must go for him, forthwith. Fetch him. He had been with Angus earlier, here on the Border. Moreover, he knew the country and could find his way in the darkness.

David suggested that Angus might refuse to come to the aid of the Regent who had dismissed him and accused him of treason, but Arran countered that, if so, it would but prove to all what a dastardly traitor the man was. If he were still calling himself Chief Warden, he could not refuse the Regent's and Lord Lyon's summons.

More doubtful than ever, David set off across the night-bound Merse for Home Castle, about twenty five miles away, with only his personal escort.

As well that he had traversed and criss-crossed this territory so many times, or he would quickly have been hopelessly lost. As it was, there were occasions when he was at a loss and had to back-track, his men, Fifers all, of no use to him here. By trial and error, they rode by Reston and Chirnside and Edrom, all now blackened shells, to the Whitadder. But at Broomhouse, north of Duns, it was not black but red, glowing hot in the night, tower and village both – which meant that the raiders had been here very recently and might still be in the vicinity, Bowes presumably. Making a circumspect wide sweep west-about then, avoiding the marshy area where de la Bastie had been murdered, they headed southwards by Polwarth and Greenlaw, all Home country and all devastated.

It was daylight before they had covered all the weary and depressing miles to Home Castle, gritty-eyed, their nostrils filled with the stink of smoke and death. But at the castle they found Angus gone.

Mains was still there. He told David that they had had word the previous afternoon of this latest raid and that, after the burning of Broomhouse, Bowes had turned westwards for the Melrose area again. The Homes here had been particularly incensed over Broomhouse, for the old Home matriarch there apparently, after yielding the tower against hopeless odds, with her son's family – the son here with Angus – had been driven back inside with the young people, barred in, and then the tower set on fire with them all inside. Angus himself on hearing that the English were again in the Melrose vicinity, had sworn a great oath to catch them this time, and ridden off last night with his fullest force, almost three thousand men.

David, too tired to think clearly what to do next, had to sleep. He would decide thereafter.

By midday, roused, he had made up his mind. He would go on after Angus. Layton was out in the Coldingham area and Bowes here; possibly Eure also was in action – a combined operation. In which case Angus ought to know of it or he could be trapped. Arran's scattered and demoralised host could still be of use, under effective leadership. The two, united, might achieve much. Mains agreed. Leaving only a skeleton garrison to defend Home Castle, with some two hundred Douglas mosstroopers, they set off south-westwards for the Melrose area.

They did not get anywhere near Melrose before, in the late afternoon, on the heights of Muirhouselaw above Ancrum, they were halted abruptly. Ahead of them the wide stretch of Ancrum Muir was alive with men and horses, moving southwards – and not only horses, cattle. So they must be English. No Scots would be driving cattle southwards. There must be thousands of them.

Presumably this was Bowes returning, possibly not having actually been at Melrose. Where then was Angus? This host looked in no sort of hurry, certainly not being pursued or harried; and equally not giving the impression of themselves pursuing anyone. Had Angus not made contact?

It was decided to wait here at Muirhouselaw meantime, as it were hull-down behind the slight ridge, where they could watch without being seen.

It took a considerable time for the English to pass. It

was indeed dusk before the watchers realised that the enemy was not in fact continuing on down into Teviotdale but were settling into camp at the far southern end of this Ancrum Muir, where it rose in folds to the ridge of Peneil Heuch. Many camp fires were beginning to prick the half-light. Then, just before darkness shrouded all, the keen-eyed perceived a great new tide of riders appearing from the south to join the encampment. Coming from that direction, and in such numbers, the probability was that this was Eure, with Jedburgh only four miles to the south. If it were, then there was something especially significant going on, the three English forces all out at the same time.

Where was Angus? Arran also must be informed. Angus had gone to intercept the Melrose raiders, but it looked as though he had not done so. If they had proved too many for him to tackle, it would have been expected either that he would return to Home Castle or that he would be shadowing this force somewhere behind. They themselves had come directly from Home and seen no sign of Angus; therefore the probability was that he was somewhere to north or west. Where or why they could not guess.

Clearly there was nothing that they themselves could do in the darkness – save send messengers back to Arran, telling him that the English were here on Ancrum Muir in great force, and urging him to come on westwards, to help to challenge them, rather than expect Angus to come east to Aytoun. They would stay here and send out scouts at first light in search of Angus, unseen they hoped by the enemy.

Actually their scouts found Angus without much difficulty, camped only three miles away at Bowden, south of Melrose, licking his wounds. It transpired that he had indeed made an attack on Bowes's force, but outnumbered as he was, had been driven off with quite heavy losses. He was now in a state of indecision as to what to do next.

David Lindsay's and Mains' arrival, with their news, scarcely helped, although the Earl was glad to get the extra two hundred horsemen. But the information that the retiring English had been reinforced, presumably by Eure, helped not at all. The fact that Arran was not far away, with at least the remnants of seven thousand, although significant, did not impress Angus, needless to say.

David enlarged on the importance of the fact that seemingly all three English forces were out operating at the same time, this highly unusual. They had halted at Peneil Heuch, which they need not have done, with Jedburgh so near. Why? If Eure had joined Bowes there, it must be for some reason.

Angus had to be interested in this. It occurred to him that, if the English stayed there, a night attack might be possible. But would they wait through this day?

David had been racking his wits to come up with a reason for the English behaviour – and came to a possible conclusion. If Eure had joined Bowes at Peneil Heuch and was waiting there, might they not be waiting for Layton to come from the east? And if so, what was this full strength assembly aimed at? Might it not be the town of Hawick, ten miles or so up Teviot? Hawick, so far, had escaped devastation. It was the largest of the Borderland communities and would demand a large force to reduce it, well guarded as it was, for it was the 'capital' of the great clan of Scott, with Buccleuch's main seat of Branxholm Tower nearby. Might not this be the answer?

Mains, even Angus, agreed that it might well be so. If it were, and the English were indeed waiting for Layton, then they would probably be there overnight again, for it would take considerable time for the other force to cross the entire Merse from Coldingham, some thirty miles.

David well recognised that a night attack such as Angus suggested was a very doubtful proposition. Such, while achieving possible surprise, seldom produced any major victory, since the surprised enemy tended to scatter rather than stand and be defeated – as at Coldingham – and could reassemble, under good leadership and, if in large numbers as here, turn the tables on the less numerous attackers once daylight prevailed. For himself, he proposed a move down into the Teviot valley westwards, unseen, there to wait, hidden, at one of the narrowings of the dale, and so to ambush the enemy as and if they approached Hawick. Possibly at Hornshole, where the Hawick folk had successfully ambushed English raiders the year after Flodden, an epic occasion. An ambush would admittedly not destroy a major army but it could seriously damage the leadership. And if Arran's people, in the process, were to come up behind the enemy, much might be achieved.

Mains was in favour of this plan but Angus still preferred the night attack.

However, the matter was more or less decided for them. A deputation of local folk arrived at Bowden, to urge Angus to attack the hated invaders who had so cruelly ravaged their homes and slaughtered their friends, these from the Melrose and St. Boswells area. They claimed to have assembled a large number of ordinary people, armed after a fashion, determined on vengeance. There were hundreds of them, they said, gathered at Lessudden, near St. Boswells. They needed, demanded, leadership from the Warden. These were still making their appeal when a force of twelve hundred lances under the Master of Rothes arrived from the north, sent by Beaton as reinforcements – to Angus it was to be noted, not to the Regent. This access of strength had barely been absorbed when Scott of Buccleuch himself appeared, from the Hawick area, with another thousand men, having been informed of the new English concentration, guessing, like David, that Hawick might well be the next target, and seeking Angus's aid. Soon after this, who should arrive at Bowden but the Earl of Bothwell, from Aytoun, with another eleven hundred horsemen of the Regent's force and the information that Arran himself was on his way, with the somewhat tattered remains of his army. This major and unexpected enhancement of his power had its due effect on the hot-blooded Angus, who decided there and then on outright attack, not any sort of ambush. Indeed he was not for waiting for darkness, despite the advice of more cautious spirits. It was already mid-afternoon, and even sunny February days were short.

The matter was settled finally when their scouts brought the word that the enemy were in fact breaking camp and on the move, presumably without waiting further for Layton. No doubt their own scouts had seen something of these Scots reinforcements arriving, and they had decided to attack before more appeared – for they were moving north again, down into Ancrum Muir, not south for Teviotdale.

So it was to be battle, large-scale battle, at long last.

At least the Scots had the advantage of better knowing the land. There were a number of ridges and folds between Bowden Muir and Ancrum Muir, which could ensure hidden approach. And, Buccleuch pointed out, the further they moved in a westerly approach, the more the sinking sun would be in the English eyes.

Sending instructions for the local people mustered at St. Boswells to advance, in parallel, due southwards – they would at least serve to confuse the enemy – Angus ordered his enlarged force, an army now, forward. He had over five thousand, mainly horsed.

When they reached, after about four miles, the final main ridge of Williamrig, only the Scots leaders went up to the summit, to peer over. They saw the high moorland filled with the English horsemen, in orderly companies – or the southern half of it, for they had not advanced further yet. This orderly grouping simplified counting, and they reckoned that the enemy were approximately of equal numbers to themselves. If Layton were still to come from the east, then the Scots would be considerably outnumbered.

Buccleuch, who, of course, knew this countryside very well – they were in Scott of Raeburn land here, indeed – pointed out that just below this ridge, but before the level moor, was another and much lower escarpment, with a quite sizeable dip this side of it. If some proportion of their strength were to ride round and into that dip, out of sight, as could be done, and then sent the horses back to mass on this main ridge, in sight of the enemy, then the English almost certainly would believe that this was the main Scots array, afraid to engage. The chances were that they would attack, uphill as it was – and so the hidden

Scots force would be behind them. An assault front and rear, then . . .

Angus did not like seeming to accept lesser men's guidance, especially from an old enemy like Buccleuch; but with everyone agreeing that this sounded an excellent plan, and himself with nothing better to suggest, he conceded it. There was no great enthusiasm amongst the rank-and-file horsemen to fight on foot, but they were not consulted.

So a division of the force was made, some three thousand moving off with Buccleuch in a left-about, circuitous and hidden approach to the dip behind the lesser escarpment, Angus to stay with the remainder on the higher Williamrig, there to mass on the summit and show themselves when the others' horses returned. David elected to go with Buccleuch, as did Bothwell.

Led in round-about ways, to take advantage of every fold and hollow of the land, they reached their long dip, they believed, without being seen. All dismounting, they sent their thousands of horses back whence they had come. Inevitably there would be tracks and droppings to show where such a large cavalcade had passed, but it was to be hoped that the English leadership, advancing mounted uphill in the face of the foe, would not have time to notice or act on this.

Buccleuch's reasoning was that when the invaders saw the massed Scots waiting on Williamrig, and recognised that they were in fact halted there, not coming down to attack, they themselves would resume the initiative. After all, they had been making the running for many months, the Scots always on the defensive, and not very successfully at that. So they would assail the Scots position, but not in any foolish headlong frontal engagement. Probably they would send up flanking attacks, left and right. They might also mount one directly upwards, but with this intermediate low ridge to surmount on the way, they were more likely to avoid the extra climb and dip. So the most likely development would be two main mounted attacks, to north and south of the Scots summit position, pincer-style. Angus would slowly retire westwards downhill before these, in line, and they themselves would swarm up behind the English and cause panic and confusion in the rear, and Angus change to the assault.

It seemed a likely sequence of events.

When, presently, they saw movement up on the main ridge, to the west, it certainly seemed sufficiently authentic. The mass of men and horses up there extended for half a mile, and from below there was no impression that a majority of the horses were riderless, for their owners could be assumed to be dismounted temporarily. Anyway, it was difficult to make out details, for the sinking sun was directly behind Angus's line and dazzling in the eyes of those to the east.

Presently they heard the English trumpets blowing.

Buccleuch, David and Bothwell crept up to the crest of their escarpment, to spy. It was as visualised. The enemy were dividing into three companies, two large and one smaller. One of the larger was already beginning to spur northwards directly below them, obviously the right flanking wing; the other forming to head more or less straight uphill to avoid this escarpment, the left wing. The smaller group remained where it was, meantime, no doubt prepared to reinforce where necessary.

"These we will have to watch," the veteran Buccleuch said.

Timing was now of the essence. It would take some time for the dismounted men to get up on to the main ridge. They wanted the English there first, of course; but not too far in advance or Angus's people could suffer a major mauling. But too early a dash up the hill would spoil the surprise and warn the enemy.

Leaving a scout or two up on the intermediate ridge to watch the third English group, they retired to their hiding men, to ready them for the assault. They were scarcely in position when one of the scouts came running down to announce a new development. A great crowd of people had appeared at the northern lip of the moor, a very few on horses, no doubt the Melrose and St. Boswells folk; and all but a very small knot of the third English group were riding off to meet them.

Buccleuch and the others hailed this news, since it meant that a distinct danger to their backs was removed – although David for one knew a pang of pity for the courageous citizenry who were thus to face a mounted attack by English fighting men; however, they had, after all, chosen to take that risk.

The three thousand waited until they could see the two prongs of the main enemy assault reach the summit of Williamrig, to right and left, with Angus's force and the mass of horses backing away before them, out of sight. Then Buccleuch gave the signal, no blowing of trumpets or horns here, and they set off uphill, rank upon rank. They did not actually attempt a run, armed and part-armoured as they were, for exhausted men would be of little use; but they climbed as fast as was practicable. The hillside was not steep. They had just over half a mile to cover.

Whether any of the enemy spotted their ascent they could not know. Probably not, for mounted men attacking a hilltop host would not be apt to be looking behind them, and the curve of the ridge would help to hide them. At any rate, there was no swinging round of horsemen to face them.

Somewhat breathless, especially the older men, the first ranks reached the summit; and any preoccupation with breathing and leg-weariness was swiftly dispelled by the scene in front. Battle was taking place about three hundred yards ahead on the beginning of the westwards slope. From their position they could see nothing of the Scots, behind the mass of the English cavalry.

Not waiting for the last ranks of their men to come up, Buccleuch launched his people forward, lances discarded, swords, dirks and battle-axes in hand.

It was complete surprise. Running now, without shouting or slogans – and, of course, without hoof-pound to draw attention – the dismounted Scots descended upon the English rear almost before any there were aware of their presence, smiting, stabbing, thrusting. Hamstringing the enemy horses was the favoured strategy, since this could be done from behind, where the rider could not reach back readily, and usually resulted in the said rider toppling back over the collapsing mount's hindquarters, an easy prey to sword or dirk. And the forward ranks of the horsemen, hot in their attack on Angus's front, took a considerable time to become aware of what was going on behind them. The two wings of the English assault had more or less coalesced into a single crescent-shaped front, and now found themselves sandwiched between the two Scots forces.

Where cavalry had freedom of movement they had a considerable superiority over infantry, with height and weight and the power to ride down. But when constricted, hemmed in, they were handicapped, getting in each other's way, less manoeuvrable. So now Buccleuch's men were able to exploit their advantage, cutting off individuals and groups, picking off leaders, preventing break-outs, and always hamstringing and panicking the trapped horses. Angus, to be sure, played his part, changing over from defence to attack, seeking especially to reach and isolate the enemy leaders.

The English fought well enough, but they were taken aback in more ways than one, outwitted, outmanoeuvred, and probably spoiled by too many easy conquests in the past year. Any central command was an early casualty, and the secondary leadership out of its depth. Fairly quickly it became evident that escape rather than regaining the initiative was the general preoccupation.

But escape was not easy, save for fortunate individuals, not with three thousand determined men blocking the way, not to mention hundreds of fallen and flailing hamstrung horses. Buccleuch, commanding all effectively from the rear with his lieutenants, was concerned to plug all possible gaps.

But there was something else concerning him – Sir Brian Layton. If Layton's force were to arrive from the east at this juncture, it could change all. The Scots themselves might become the sandwiched. He sent scouts back up on to the ridge-summit, to keep watch – although it was now dusk, with the sun gone down and the eastern prospect dim.

It would be hard to say just when that strange battle ended, for there was no clear or recognisable finish, no general surrender, with pockets of the English fighting on to the death, others throwing down arms, others achieving escape. Probably the real moment of victory was signalised when somebody stumbled over Sir Ralph Eure's personal banner, its bearer dead, and Eure himself in his fine heraldically painted armour lying nearby. That banner, waved and waved aloft by shouting Scots, spelt the end, for many. And then, shortly afterwards, another resplendent corpse was identified as none other than Sir Brian Layton. As well as considerable bewilderment, there could be no doubt that the day was won and lost, however much individual fighting was still going on. That Layton himself had in fact been with Eure throughout the battle was a major surprise to the Scots; presumably he had left his force at Coldingham and hastened westwards to join his colleagues at Peneil Heuch – which might well account for the delay in arrival on the scene of his people.

It was at this stage that David Lindsay besought Buccleuch to let him take a party, reunited with their horses, to go to the aid of the St. Boswells folk, who might well be in desperate straits. Since there was still no sign of the Coldingham force, and the light failing fast, Scott agreed.

With some two hundred volunteers, then, David spurred northwards along the ridge for a mile or so. Soon the declining noise of the conflict behind was superseded by a similar din ahead – so at least the citizen fighters had not yet been totally overwhelmed.

In the half-dusk this separate battle seemed only an incoherent struggling mass from above. Indeed, as Lindsay's squadron thundered down on it from slightly higher ground, it continued to give that impression, with no line or front apparent, only a confusion of battling men – and women, for the newcomers were astonished to discover females amongst the Scots fighters. The mounted English were the most evident element, slashing and beating down from their superior height; but since a number of fallen horses were to be seen, here too the hamstringing device had seemingly been employed.

The arrival of two hundred fresh-mounted Scots swiftly put an end to this secondary but bloody engagement, with the enemy not slow to perceive that they would be better elsewhere; and no doubt recognising that if the Scots could thus afford a detachment from the main affray, it was unlikely to be a victory for the invaders. Everywhere the mounted English broke off and began instead to cleave their way through the struggling mass southwards, for safety.

David's men, after seeing them on their way, did not attempt any real pursuit, in the now prevailing obscurity. Instead, dismounting, they sought to succour and aid their wounded and dying fellow-countrymen – while not a few of the survivors went about finishing off fallen Englishmen. David was further impressed by the numbers of women they found amongst the combatants – and clearly these were there as combatants themselves, not just helpers, sustainers, camp-followers. Not a few were dead, many wounded and one in especial, apparently called Lilliard, being acclaimed for her effective battling and courage; for even when grievously wounded about the legs, she had fought on, kneeling, and wielding her wood-axe against the enemy horses' hocks. These Borders folk had had a long and large score to settle with the savage invaders, and this day had effected some settlement. Apart from the casualties they had inflicted here, at major cost to themselves, their arrival on the scene had undoubtedly aided the Scots main effort by relieving Buccleuch's force from the threat from behind.

Presently, leaving some of his men and horses to assist in getting the wounded and dead back to their homes, David returned to the Williamrig heights, where he found the Battle of Ancrum Muir over, camp fires being lit and victory celebrated, the first major Scots military success for many a long day. The English losses were clearly enormous, and although Sir Robert Bowes himself appeared to have made his escape, there were a great many knights and landed men, captured, suitable for ransom – always an important matter. And no doubt back at Peneil Heuch there would be booty galore to be acquired, in the morning.

Setting sentries to watch for possible, if unlikely, attack by the Coldingham English, the Scots settled down amongst the dead, dying and wounded, for the night.

Next day, it was not Layton's force but Arran's which arrived at Ancrum Muir – the Regent in extraordinarily fine fettle and pleased with himself, humiliation at Coldingham forgotten. It seemed that he had learned of the English defeat from a group of local folk hastening back to their village of Maxton with the news; and he actually claimed some share in the credit, partly in that he had allowed Bothwell to come to Angus's aid and partly because he claimed that his somewhat discountenanced host had frightened off Layton's force coming to support Eure, and last seen turning tail in the Greenlaw area and heading back for Berwick. Little as David and Bothwell credited this, the fact remained that the enemy from Coldingham had not shown up in mass and seemed unlikely to do so now.

The meeting between Arran and Angus was almost comic, each congratulating himself and denigrating the other – when in fact the victory was more truly Buccleuch's. Not that they suffered much of each other's company, for Angus promptly departed for Tantallon – but via Peneil Heuch, for the booty; and the Regent heading south for Jedburgh, there to proclaim the good news and to issue suitable warnings to King Henry as to the dangers of invading sacred Scottish soil, and threats of retaliation.

Buccleuch and the others were left to deal with the wounded, bury the dead, clean up the battlefield and assist the local folk – after all, it *was* Scott country.

Presently David Lindsay, with Bothwell and much of the army, headed off northwards, thankfully, to inform the Cardinal and Queen-Mother.

15

Strangely, the principal beneficiary of Ancrum Muir did turn out to be Arran, the nation at large, in its relief, thanks to his prompt trumpeting, hailing the Regent as its saviour – much to the fury of Angus, needless to say, and to the amusement of David Lindsay. Davie Beaton was less amused, but typically sought to make use of Arran's sudden and unexpected popularity, for his own, and what he claimed were the nation's, purposes.

For events had not stood still in the rest of Scotland while the Borders campaign was in progress. King Henry was stirring up trouble in the Highland West, granting his pensions to the Island chiefs and sending Lennox with some thousands of men in a fleet of ships to aid them rise against the Scottish crown, in lieu of Angus's lost support. Which was why Argyll, Huntly, Atholl and other loyal lords along the Highland Line had not been represented in the Borders fighting, being concerned with protecting the northern areas and their own lands. As well as this, there was serious trouble in the Church, or at least in religious affairs linked with politics. For the reformer George Wishart, he whom Beaton asserted was concerned in the plot to assassinate himself, was being very active, preaching openly against Rome and its adherents, in places as far apart as Montrose and Dundee, Perth, Ayr and Dumfries. Beaton would have had him apprehended but he was under the strong protection of sundry powerful lords and lairds who were either in Henry's pocket or who professed the reformed faith, including the Earls of Glencairn and Cassillis, Sir George Douglas and the lairds of Brunstane, Ormiston and Calder. Always, at his preachings, Wishart was surrounded by the mail-clad ranks of these nobles' retainers, who also aided in the stirring up of anti-Church feeling and riots amongst the citizenry. At

Dundee, for instance, both the Blackfriars and Greyfriars monasteries had been sacked and burned by the mob.

Surely never, the Cardinal complained, had a nation been plagued with such a treacherous and unruly nobility?

So now he sought to use the tide of Arran's undeserved popularity to strengthen his own position and manoeuvre his enemies into difficulties. He called, not a parliament, which he might not have been able to control, but a convention of the said nobility and senior clergy, in Edinburgh, in theory to congratulate the Regent – and thereby ensuring that Angus would not attend – but in fact to achieve more practical results. He informed the gathering that Lennox and the Isles chiefs were now in Ulster, with a great fleet of galleys, recruiting a major army for the invasion of mainland Scotland – recognising that the introduction of Irishmen on the scene would much inflame Scottish opinion – and succeeded in gaining the Regent's authority to muster the entire strength of the realm forthwith, despite the euphoria generated by the recent victory. He also obtained agreement of the assembly that the Privy Council should be advised to declare Lennox guilty of highest treason, a useful device which made him in theory outlaw. He revealed that King Henry had attacked and captured Boulogne, and in consequence the King of France was prepared to accede to his request, Beaton's, and to send a large French expeditionary force to Scotland, to present the English with the desired war on two fronts. He announced that Holy Church was prepared to pay for most of the costs of the Regent's mustered army, but warned that the Church's position was being grievously undermined by paid agents of Henry Tudor stirring up riot and havoc, in the name of so-called reform, notably the man Wishart, supported by highly placed adherents of England who would have to be shown up and punished for the traitors they were – this last being received in an uncomfortable silence, unlike the rest. He ended by urging all strongly to support the Regent who had so admirably upheld the honour of the realm, even going so far as to suggest that it might well be worth considering a betrothal, in due course, of the infant Queen to the Regent's son and heir, to put an end at least to Henry's excuse for what he called his Rough Wooing. But in a shrewd and final postscript, lest the anti-Arran forces present be too greatly offended, he added that he had recommended the King of France to award the coveted Order of St. Michael to the Earl of Angus in recognition of the part he had played in the Battle of Ancrum Muir.

It was altogether a most skilful solo performance, and achieved most of the desired results, including a promise by the gathering to have a muster of at least twenty-five thousand men at Roslin Muir, in Lothian, by the end of July. Arran beamed, but clearly would have preferred the Order of St. Michael to have come to himself.

David Lindsay marvelled anew at this curious friend of his, and wondered just how Scotland would manage without him.

Henry Tudor was, of course, no less active than was Davie Beaton, however preoccupied with his latest French adventures. His anger against the Scots reached fever-pitch and he sent his trusted Earl of Hertford north again to raise the entire north of England for major invasion, no mere raiding like the Eure-Bowes-Layton campaign but a minimum army of thirty thousand called for – this unless there was immediate agreement by the Scots to wed their infant Queen to his son Edward and to send her to be reared in England.

It looked as though all the Roslin Muir muster was going to be required fairly soon.

David Lindsay, thankfully, was not involved in this new assembling and training of forces in Lothian – he had had enough of matters military for the meantime. He was, however, sent through to the west, to welcome the French contingent which was expected at Dumbarton in the second half of May. It was important that someone directly representing the crown should go, not only for the sake of protocol but because of the position of the Earl of Lennox. Nobody knew just where he was, whether still in Ulster or back in the Hebrides; but he was hereditary keeper of the royal castle of Dumbarton, and that fortress dominated the Clyde estuary and the main west-coast ports, and in hostile hands could gravely embarrass a French landing there. So the Lord Lyon was sent in the Queen's name, to take over the castle from the deputy-keeper, well in advance, with a company of the royal guard. Not really expecting trouble, he took Janet along.

Actually they had no trouble at Dumbarton. The captain, Stirling of Glorat, Lennox's deputy, had already proved co-operative in the past, and now was entirely helpful towards the Queen's representative, installing the Lindsays in the best quarters of the rock-crown fortress and symbolically handing over the keys. He said that he did not know where the Earl of Lennox might be – and clearly wished him far enough away.

So commenced a strange interlude, there on the skirts of the Highland West, perched above the blue, isle-strewn waters of the Firth of Clyde with all the great mountains circling round – for the French delayed, and no problems developed from the north. David, with his wife for company for once, felt almost divorced from the stresses and strains which racked the land, the assembling of armed men everywhere, fears of full-scale invasion, clan feuding and lords' plotting, Church heresy-trials and the like. At Dumbarton the cuckoos called from the braeside hawthorns, the broom glowed golden, the May sun glinted on the sparkling waters, and life could be lived as the Lindsays felt that it ought to be lived, quietly, unhurriedly, appreciatively, even productively – for David did what he had been itching to do for long, started on a new poem, which he would call *Kitty's Confession*, in which he would use the abuse of the confessional by the clergy to give point to a comedy with a message. So they relaxed, rode abroad through the Levenachs, the strath of the Leven from Loch Lomond which gave Lennox his title; they sailed and fished in the firth; they visited the isles of Arran and Bute and penetrated far up the network of sea-lochs and kyles which fretted that lovely coastline, and were thankful to turn their backs, for a while, on the rest of Scotland with its problems, however devoted they might be to their native land and realm.

Then, towards the end of the month, the French squadron arrived, having had to sail round Ireland to avoid the English fleet. Happily they had seen no sign of Lennox and the Islesmen's galleys – although perhaps, since they came in eight well-armed vessels, these last had elected to keep their distance. The French, who were very cautious about putting into the anchorage until they had the assurance that all was well, were under the command of the Sieur Lorges de Montgomerie, a dandified individual who nevertheless quickly proved himself to be nobody's fool and a competent leader. He brought no fewer than three thousand foot soldiers, five hundred horse, a bodyguard of one hundred mounted archers for the Regent, considerable amounts of arms, munitions and supplies, and a large treasure-chest of gold. The Cardinal of Lorraine had not failed his sister. Also, it transpired that he had duly entrusted to his care the insignia of the Order of St. Michael, for Angus.

It took some time to get all this unloaded, the newcomers welcomed and catered for, and all formed up for the march across the waist of Scotland. They would go by the Vales of Leven and Endrick to the great Carse of Forth, so as to call at Stirling and pay due respects to the child-Queen and Marie de Guise, leaving Janet there, before heading for Edinburgh.

Davie Beaton was at the capital, and greatly relieved to have the French contingent and the money. For, despite the superficial success of the Regent's muster at Roslin Muir – there were almost thirty thousand assembled or promised – he was worried.

"These Frenchmen could make all the difference," he told Lindsay.

"With thirty thousand, are they so important?"

"They are, yes. It is the old story, as so often before. The Scots lords are reluctant to cross the border. They will muster to protect our own territory, yes – but not to invade England. They say that is only playing France's game . . ."

"As it is, to be sure. Is not that why King Francis and the de Guises have sent all the men and gold? So that

Henry will have an invasion of Northern England, and so have less power to unleash on France?"

"There is that, to be sure. But an invasion over the Border is much to Scotland's benefit also. It will discourage the northern English from rallying to Hertford, as well as giving Henry pause. It will give our forces the right spirit, of attack not always defence, something they much need. Also provide booty, to compensate for *our* grievous losses, always important."

"And you think that these French will change our lords' minds?"

"Yes – or some of them. For this de Montgomerie has come to invade, not defend. *He* will cross the Borderline whoever else does. If his lead changes sufficient minds – that is the rub. Some he will *not* change."

"Even with the French lead you fear some refusal?"

"I do not fear – I know! I have my sources of information, as you are aware. I have spies planted in sundry camps. I needs must. I would not stay alive otherwise. This assassination plot – I keep ahead of them only thanks to my spies. Their reports. And these reporters have told me, of late, other than plans to do away with me! I have lists of those whom Henry calls his 'assured Scots', lords – aye, and bishops too – who, at the right moment he can rely upon to act in the English interest, his pensioners all. Cassillis is Henry's principal lieutenant now. Cassillis, you will recollect, was one of the Scots earls captured at Solway Moss. Henry gave him his freedom, without ransom, on condition that he served England thereafter. I have a spy in Cassillis's household. It is Cassillis who has the responsibility of getting rid of me! And the priest, or former priest, George Wishart, is his tool in the matter."

"Can you not apprehend Cassillis, then?"

"He is too well-protected, too powerful, an earl of Scotland, with many highly placed friends, even on the Privy Council itself – Glencairn, Somerville, Ruthven and the other so-called reformists. I could not *prove* anything against him. But I will get Wishart, one of these days, and make him confess. But – that is another matter. What I am concerned with now is this of muster and invasion.

Cassillis and Glencairn have conspired to convince a large number of the lords, in especial the south-west lords, who have joined this Regent's muster, not to set one foot over the Borderline. They will go as far as Tweed, and no further. While this is taking place, Wishart will be stirring up riot behind us, in the name of reform, causing men to look back over their shoulders. And at the same time, there is a plot for the English under Wharton, to take over Caerlaverock Castle at Dumfries, the West March Warden's seat, the Master of Maxwell agreeing. His father, the Lord Maxwell, is another of the Solway Moss prisoners and Henry has bought him also. That could cause a panic in the south-west and give the lords thereof excuse to ride for home. Meanwhile, Lennox and the West Highland chiefs are expected to make their long-awaited attack – which will much concern the lords whose lands flank the Highland Line. You see it all? And you see why we need the French?"

"I see a kingdom lost already, without a sword drawn or an arrow shot – and deserving to be lost!"

"Scarcely that. There are still some honest lords. And the folk, the people themselves, are true enough. It is the recurring curse of our nation to have child-monarchs. We need strong kings, to keep the lords in place, since it is the lords who have the manpower – and we get babes! With Henry Tudor to face! Mark you, Henry is having his problems also. He is having to send up more and more foreign mercenaries for Hertford – Irish, Germans, Spaniards, Italians, Greeks even. And why? Because his northern English and Borderers do not like this kind of war, this deliberate savaging of the land, towns and people – people like themselves, fellow-Borderers. They see all too clearly that it could happen to themselves, one day, if the tide of war turns, the English north laid waste. That is why it is so important that we invade now, before Hertford is ready."

Lindsay shook his head. "God help us all!" he sighed. "All caught, caught in a trap. The trap of a man mad for power." And, in a different voice. "And all this, Davie? You tell me all this, for a reason, I think?"

The other nodded. "Yes. You, my modest friend, although you never admit it, are in a very special position in this realm. You are Lyon and can speak with the voice of the monarch, when that monarch has no voice of her own save a babe's cry. You are admired and trusted by the Queen-Mother. But, almost as important in this present situation, you are well known to have, shall we say, reformist leanings! I think that you err in these – but that is another matter. After your *Satire of the Three Estates*, none can doubt your sympathies with Church reform – none. So none is better placed to be trusted by these reformist lords . . ."

"If you desire me to act your master-spy amongst them, then you must forget it! That is not for me."

"No, no – you mistake. It is not another spy that I require, but a guardian. For our little Queen. As you were for her father."

"Does she need another guardian, in Stirling Castle? Other than the Earl Marischal and the keeper, Lord Erskine?"

"I fear that she does. As does her mother. You see, the Earl Marischal too, has become smitten with this reformist disease. Who knows, *you* may well have been responsible, with your play-actings and poems, for he speaks of them often to Marie. Cassillis and Glencairn know this, to be sure, and my spies tell me that there is talk of a plot, instigated of course by Henry, to seize the child, in Stirling, and convey her secretly to England, no doubt by Caerlaverock and Carlisle, with the Earl Marischal's co-operation."

"Lord – he would never do that! Not William Keith. He is a leal man."

"Be not so sure. If others can turn, so may Keith. Religious fervour can change any man – as I know better than most! We dare not take the risk – since if we lose the girl-Queen we have lost all. Nor can we be sure of Erskine. He has always been sound, but he too is interested in this talk of reform . . ."

"If so many good men are become so, Davie, does it not occur to you that *you* ought to be? You, as Cardinal,

Primate and Papal Legate, not to mention Chancellor, could guide and lead all, decently, achieve successful reform, heal the division in the nation, and put Henry Tudor in his place. If you took the lead in this, as you have done in so much else. And you admit that reform is called for."

"Man – I will reform the Church, from within, in my own time. But not with Henry's wolves baying at our gates, Henry's gold flooding the land, Henry plotting my murder. First things first. We must save the house from the robbers before we set its plenishings in new order."

"So what do you want of me? If not to spy."

"I want you to go to Stirling Castle, take Mary and her mother from the Marischal's and Erskine's keeping and convey them to the safety of Dunkeld, inside the Highland Line. Atholl has a house there, with a guard of Highlanders. And the new Bishop, John Hamilton, the Regent's half-brother, is my man. So take the Queen to Dunkeld and keep her there secure, until this ill season is overpast. Will you do that? Marie de Guise agrees."

"But – will the *Marischal* agree? And Erskine?"

"They cannot refuse *you*, the Lyon. With the authority of the Queen-Mother and the Regent – for Arran accepts that it is necessary. And, to be sure, the Chancellor. Only you could do it, David. And be heeded by these reformist lords."

"It is a heavy responsibility to put on me – the Queen's safety."

"Who better? And you carried it for her father, many a time."

Lindsay could not refuse, of course, not with all that authority behind him. And a part of him knew a kind of rejoicing, for it meant that, instead of all the stress and alarms of one more military campaign in the Borderland – which already seemed certain to be anything but trouble-free – he would be in the skirts of the Highlands again, with Janet, in company of Marie de Guise, whom he liked and respected.

Presumably the Queen-Mother was the least surprised at David's so swift return to Stirling, with fifty of the French mounted-archer guard sent for the Regent. Janet was overjoyed, naturally, although the Earl Marischal and the Lord Erskine, friendly as they were towards Lindsay out of long association and co-operation in the royal service, were less so when they learned of the reason for his coming. But, although they questioned the need, and chuntered somewhat about it all being a reflection on their own abilities and trustworthiness as guardians, they were not in a position to contest the matter when confronted with the decision of the Lyon, the Regent and the Chancellor, supported by the Queen-Mother herself. David tactfully sought to soften the blow to their self-esteem by suggesting that it was likely to be only a short absence, and that the child and her mother could well do with a break from fortress-living in this fine summer weather. He was only afraid that the two nobles might propose to come with them; but happily nothing such eventuated.

So, sending ahead a courier to inform the Earl of Atholl that they were on their way, two days later they set out with the French escort and quite a large baggage-train for the north, the Queen, now three years old, riding happily before her mother, Janet or David.

In the circumstances it was a slow progress. It took four days to cover the fifty miles, by the Allan Water and Strathearn, St. John's Town of Perth, the Tay valley and Birnam Wood, stopping overnight at the monkish hospices of St. Mungo's of Gleneglis, the Blackfriars of Perth – where the little Queen's ancestor, James the First had been murdered – and the grange at Auchtergaven. The last day, threading the leafy glades of Birnam Wood, with the steep hillsides now rising sharply on either hand and the Pass of Dunkeld ahead, David told his small liege-lady the story of her two forerunners, MacBeth and Malcolm Canmore, and how Birnam Wood went to Dunsinane, with dire results.

At Dunkeld, the Earl himself had come from Blair-in-Atholl to greet them, with almost an army of Stewart clansmen, wild-looking and bristling with arms. The fiery warrior of Linlithgow Bridge and the open-handed host of the Blair extravaganza of 1534, was growing an old man now, but lacking nothing in spirit. He welcomed Mary in boisterous style, which had her wide-eyed and just a little alarmed, the while he cursed his fellow-Stewart, Matthew Lennox, and the barbarous Island chiefs who were keeping him here guarding the northern approaches when he should have been in the Borderland showing the accursed English how to make war. But at least his young cousin – thus he referred to Mary – would be safe in Atholl, with a thousand men to guard her, a thousand mountains to protect her and a thousand glens to hide her should troublers come. She would not need these Frenchies, who could be sent back to where they were more needed. That was John Stewart of Atholl.

Once Atholl had returned to Blair, less than twenty miles to the north – until which time all was in an uproar inevitably – an extended period of peace enfolded David Lindsay, which made the Dumbarton interlude seem very modest, and the like of which he could scarcely recollect hitherto; and this while so much of the rest of his native land was in such notable stir, tension and a degree of dread. The result, for that man, of course, was guilt, however much he told himself that he was here playing a valuable, perhaps vital, part in the nation's affairs and of much more use than being just one more alleged leader in an army already overburdened with self-appointed leaders; or in aiding the government of one who needed no assistance from him. It is a strange aspect of men's character, particularly of Scots character, that there is something essentially wrong, blameworthy, in being pleasurably engaged, that life must be difficult and taxing to be meaningful, productive.

Not that the days and weeks which followed were inactive or purposeless. There was no lack of things to do north of the Highland Line, and Atholl as good a location as any to do them in. Hunting, hawking and fishing, of course, were the obvious pastimes, with the mountains, moors, glens, lochs and rivers alive with game on a scale and variety unknown in the Lowlands. But as well as this there were places of interest to inspect, many of which David had heard of but never seen, and which had had their own impact on Scotland's story, of major significance to a man of his concerns and temperament; notably, of course, Dunkeld Cathedral itself, a remarkable fane to be found in a Highland valley, wherein was buried, behind the altar of all places, that notorious and excommunicated prince, the Wolf of Badenoch, son of Robert the Second, who had terrorised the north for years and for a whim burned a greater cathedral than this, that of Elgin, the glory of Moray. Dunkeld's bishop, the former Abbot of Paisley, Arran's brother, was seldom there, preferring to be with the Regent – for which David was not ungrateful, Hamilton being a slippery character and notably ambitious, however useful Beaton found him to be.

There were many other shrines and scenes to visit, at no great distance by Highland standards. David was particularly interested in the Pictish remains which dotted the area, being much aware of the neglect of knowledge of and concern with this cultured and talented people, who were after all the ancestors of them all but who, having no written language but communicating by pictures – why the Romans gave them that name – left no written records. Their stone-circles, standing-stones, forts, cairns, souterrains and symbol-stones were much in evidence hereabouts, and provided the Lindsays, and Marie de Guise also, with many a day of exploration and enlightenment.

And then the people themselves were a continuing source of edification, the clansfolk. For, of course, to most Lowlanders the Highlanders were uncouth barbarians and worse, scarcely to be accepted as fellow-countrymen – this through ignorance and a certain fear, and because they spoke an unknown language. David knew better than this, but now learned much that he ought to have known long since, nearly all to the clansmen's advantage, their mannerliness despite often a somewhat wild appearance, their innate hospitality however frugal their means, their pride of race, their loyalty to their chiefs, their knowledge of what might be called the occult but which Lowlanders were apt to term witchcraft. There was no talk of Church reform here. David unfortunately had only a very few words of the Gaelic, and Janet none, but they were learning. The Dean of Dunkeld, who really ran the diocese, a Highlandman himself, was delighted to escort his distinguished visitors around, and to interpret.

But, of course, the best of it all was just to be able to live a normal and undemanding life with his wife; and to get to know and the more appreciate the company of Marie de Guise, who not only improved with the knowing but proved to be a most excellent companion, with no least hint of standing on her dignity nor of superior attitudes. She was shrewd and informed, and very much concerned with matters of state, as well as ambitious for her daughter; but that side of her character was not allowed to obtrude.

As for the child Mary, Queen of Scots, she was a delight, remarkably little trouble, active and intelligent for her age, and won all hearts. If her father had only lived to know her, David, who still grieved for James, felt that he would have been a happier man.

So June passed into July and July to August, with better weather than the usual Scots summer. They were not entirely divorced from what went on elsewhere, for fairly frequent reports came from the secretary, David Paniter, now Bishop of Ross, at Edinburgh; and occasional letters from Davie Beaton himself. The Regent did not see fit to communicate. The muster, apparently, continued to go well at Roslin, with probably the largest army assembling which Scotland had seen since Flodden, although there was the usual friction between Hamiltons and Douglases, reformers and good Catholics, the French forces being useful to act as buffers. Caerlaverock had been handed over, as anticipated, but so far Lennox and his Islesmen had not shown their hands. Beaton wrote that Hertford was still delaying invasion, allegedly waiting until the Scots harvest was cut and gathered, so that he could more readily burn it all and thus add starvation to his other depredations; also that he, Beaton, had not yet caught

Wishart, the man having escaped him narrowly on two occasions, and now was gone back to Dundee, his favourite city, deliberately, where the plague was presently raging and where he had the arrogance to believe that his own ministrations were needed. All of which the more caused David to be thankful that he was where he was, although scarcely assuaging his feelings of guilt.

And then, late in August, with the heather purple on all the mountains, the grouse and blackcock and capercailzie in season and sport at its best, came word that all was in disarray again, the counter-invasion a fiasco, the realm more divided than ever. The Regent's great host had indeed marched for the Border, but at Tweed had staged a major revolt against Arran's leadership and the French influence, using the pretext that the principal commands had been given to Frenchmen and that crossing into England would be wholly in the French interests. In the event Angus had led the confrontation, throwing in his lot with the anti-Regent interests despite his Order of St. Michael. It was all entirely reminiscent of the late Albany's similar effort at invasion which had ended only in the abortive assault on Wark Castle, those years ago; for this followed the same pattern, with only the French crossing Tweed with Arran and his Hamiltons while the vast Scots array watched sullenly. Neither Hertford's nor the English Warden's forces had put in an appearance, and the French, without back-up support, dared not penetrate far into England in case they were cut off. So, after a mere token sweep into the Tillmouth, Wark and Carham area, they had returned frustrated to the Tweed, to find Angus leading off northwards most of the Scots host. It was all complete and shameful folly. The Regent was for arraigning Angus there and then on a charge of treason again, and Angus declaring that if he did so he would raise the land against the Hamiltons.

So it would be civil war, with Hertford still poised to invade.

David Lindsay groaned in spirit. He sent a message to Beaton to ask if there were anything that he could do, to mediate, to aid the lawful authority, to bridge the gap, in the Queen's name or in his own? But the answer came back from St. Andrews to stay where he was, to guard the Queen even more strictly. For if Angus did rise in arms against the Regent, nothing was more likely than that he would seek to grasp young Mary, as he had once grasped young James, to use as his authority. It was not only Lennox now, and Henry's other minions, who must be watched.

So David remained at Dunkeld, and felt no less guilty than heretofore.

They heard of Hertford's invasion in due course, a curious affair in that it was so much more limited in scope than they had feared. It was sufficiently dire for those involved, to be sure; but despite his great numbers, largely mercenaries, Hertford was content to devastate anew the same old area of the Merse, Tweeddale, Teviotdale and Lauderdale, when it had been anticipated that he would be considerably more ambitious, on a par at least with his previous attack on Edinburgh and Lothian. Of course the Merse was a notable grain-growing territory, and he had been said to be deliberately waiting to destroy the harvest; but this seemed an inadequate explanation. Even Beaton was nonplussed – and taken in conjunction with Lennox's delay in attack, it might possibly imply some policy decision on Henry's part.

Whatever the reason, all save the Borderers were supremely thankful when, after three weeks against only limited opposition, Hertford turned back, leaving a smoking wilderness behind him and having spent a major proportion of that time in seeking utterly to demolish, stone by stone, the great abbeys of Kelso, Jedburgh, Melrose and Dryburgh – or what was left of them from earlier raids, as well as lesser shrines. Whether this had been a special remit from his master there was no knowing.

At least civil war in Scotland had not broken out in the interim.

Davie Beaton arrived in person at Dunkeld soon afterwards, not so much to see Lindsay as the Queen-Mother. If he was an anxious man – and he had to be, with all his responsibilities, in the present state of Scotland, not to mention threats of assassination – he did not show it. He could scarcely pretend confidence that all was under control; but he was cheerful, betraying no agitation. Nevertheless it transpired, presently, that what had brought him up into the Highlands was little less than desperation. Somehow the regency had to be strengthened, or the realm was going to fall apart completely, with Angus gaining the mastery in the short term but Henry winning all in the long. Arran was useless. Yet he was still next in line for the throne and would remain so until the child Queen could have offspring of her own. For everyone's sake he should be replaced as Regent – but by whom? If they did not find an alternative swiftly, Angus would take over, one way or another.

There was only one person who had the status to replace Arran and whom Angus and his supporters could scarcely object to lawfully, and that was Marie de Guise herself. There *would* be objections, of course, against a woman, and a foreign woman at that, wielding the supreme authority. But that could be got over by naming her at first as Joint Regent with Arran; and then presently easing him out. Perhaps it would be wise not to use the term Regent at all, at first? Governor, perhaps – Joint Governor.

Marie, who was as anxious over the matter as anyone, saw the need and accepted the challenge, David Lindsay supporting, with reservations.

Beaton declared that although such a development ought to be by decision of parliament, he would prefer not to risk the possibility of major opposition organised by Angus and the Douglases. He did not think that they could rally a majority, or anything like it, against the project, but they could cause unpleasantness and bad feeling. Better to make it by decree of the Privy Council, on which they could be sure to outvote any opposition. If necessary a parliament could confirm this later, once all was established and its benefits perceived.

When David Lindsay, as usual, expressed some dubiety, this time against dispensing with the parliament and the indisputable authority it represented, the Cardinal-Chancellor clapped him on the shoulder.

"Your name should have been Thomas!" he asserted. "Ever the doubter. Trust my wits, man. Trust Davie Beaton."

And that was the trouble, of course. *Could* he trust Davie Beaton? Could anyone?

16

It was extraordinary, in fact, what a difference this device of having Marie de Guise as Joint Regent or Governor made. Arran was unpopular as well as ineffectual, whereas Marie was well thought of and reliable and had never pushed herself forward like her predecessor, Margaret Tudor. And after the first huffs of offence, Arran not only accepted their partnership but more and more came to value it, indeed to rely on Marie's judgement and guidance. The fact was, of course, that he had no leadership in him, no aptitude for making important decisions, out of his depth as a ruler, only really concerned with prestige and status. So long as he had the title of Regent and was acknowledged by all as heir-presumptive to the throne, he was reasonably content to leave the decision-taking to someone as high-born as the Queen-Mother – especially with Beaton ever dangling before him the possibility of young Mary marrying his son, the Master of Arran. So, guided to be sure by Beaton, but nevertheless displaying a will and judgement of her own, Marie quite quickly became the effective Regent and Arran little more than a figurehead. And, by and large, the nation responded to a firm hand at the helm, the nobility prepared to co-operate with the Queen-Mother where they had resented the Hamilton chief; the churchmen had to go along with the Cardinal, at least on the surface; and the people were thankful for a Governor who was above the everlasting feuding, back-stabbing and oppression, even if it was a woman. There was opposition but fortunately it was divided, the reformist faction on the one hand – for Marie was a staunch Catholic and was backing Beaton's policy – and Angus on the other who, whatever else he might be, was no religious reformer. Beaton and Marie between them were skilful in keeping those two factions more or less at loggerheads.

Not that the autumn and winter was an easy time for Scotland; but it was all less dire than it might have been, with Henry deeply involved in France and said to be a sick man, indeed so gross as to be scarcely able to walk – although his spleen remained as virulent as ever, apparently. The Sieur Lorges de Montgomerie was not happy about the inaction of his force, but at least they represented a threat to the English north and so to some extent justified their presence.

The Yuletide festivities were low-key, but not altogether omitted. It was considered safe for David Lindsay and Janet to bring Queen Mary from Dunkeld to Stirling for Christmas.

It was at that festive season of 1545–6 that a fuse was lit which was to explode a charge to alter Scotland's course to a major degree. With the colder weather, the plague had died down at Dundee, and Master George Wishart felt himself free to resume his more general campaign against Rome. It was learned that he was in East Lothian for the Christmas period and had been preaching at Inveresk and Tranent and Haddington, the county-town – where another fiery reformer, a Master John Knox, of that town, had preceded Wishart into the great church of St. Mary actually bearing a huge two-handed sword, with the usual armed guard behind. Now the laird Cockburn of Ormiston was one of Wishart's strongest supporters – also one of Henry's pensioners – and Ormiston was a property in East Lothian only seven miles from Haddington. Davie Beaton put two and two together. That there be no mistake this time, he hastened to Edinburgh, where he collected Arran and Bothwell, who were celebrating Yule in that city, and with the two Earls rode for East Lothian. He sent Bothwell to gather a company of his men-at-arms from his seat of Hailes Castle, the other side of Haddington, while he and the Regent went to wait at Elphinstone Tower, not far from Ormiston, reaching there by night so that their presence would not be known. And in the darkness Bothwell and his men descended upon Cockburn of Ormiston's house and surrounded it. Sure enough, they found George

Wishart lodging within. They arrested him and brought him to the Cardinal at Elphinstone. The preacher was now in Edinburgh Castle awaiting shipment to St. Andrews for trial – by sea, just in case there should be an attempt to rescue him on the part of the reformist lords.

David Lindsay would very much have liked to have been present that night at Elphinstone Tower to witness the meeting of these two churchmen of such opposing views and determined character.

It was in fact February before he saw Beaton again, at Stirling, and by that time the repercussions of Wishart's arrest were stirring the land. The man had become something of a legend, what with his fiery eloquence, his assured prophecies, his outspoken challenges to Holy Church and his self-sacrificing return to plague-stricken Dundee to minister there. Now all who saw the Church as in need of drastic reform were rallying to his cause and demanding his release. And many who had no real interest in matters religious were using his name and case to further their own ends.

"Are you still intending to bring Wishart to trial?" Lindsay demanded of the Cardinal, in a room of the palace at Stirling Castle, which looked out to the blue bastions of the Highland Line. "Despite this uproar in the nation?"

"To be sure, I am. What would you? I have sought to catch this one for sufficiently long. Get rid of Wishart and this kingdom is the safer place."

"Safer? I would not call it that. You are on the way to making a martyr of that man. Will that help Scotland?"

"His removal will. For he has become the standard-bearer for all the troublemakers. I have to take the risk of turning him into a martyr. But that would not last long. For, once the campaigning season starts again, the English will be at our gates once more, nothing surer, and one man's death will be forgotten in the death of thousands."

"Be not so sure. The Scots have long memories. And you say death? That means that you are going to try Wishart for heresy? Before *your* court, the verdict is certain – guilty. Burning! You will burn Wishart?"

"If that is the decision of the court. Wishart has known the penalty, all along."

"That would be utter folly, as well as shame, man. And dangerous. You must see it."

"More dangerous to have him alive, to be the centre for sedition and revolt! And, belike, to achieve my own death! For Wishart is deep in that plot."

"Are you certain? It could be that the others, Glencairn, Cassillis and the rest are but using him."

"I am sure of it." That was short.

"Even if it is so, I say this trial is a mistake. To burn Wishart would be madness, for you, for the Church and for the realm."

"That is your opinion. Mine is otherwise. And the decision is mine."

"Could you not, at least, forbear the burning? Banish him the realm, perhaps . . .?"

"He would just come back, that one. And long imprisonment would merely keep him the martyr longer. No – the trial is fixed for the first day of March, St. David's Day. In St. Andrews Castle."

"Then I do not congratulate you. Indeed, I condemn you, Davie Beaton! You have all but complete power in this realm, and you misuse it. Not only to the hurt of this man Wishart but that of the entire kingdom. For only evil can come of so ill a deed. The Church itself will suffer for it – that I promise you . . ."

"And will that trouble you – *you* who have for so long been an open enemy of the Church which nurtured you?"

"Not an enemy – never that. It is because I have love for Christ's Church that I would see its corruptions washed away, its faults cleansed."

"Wishart says the same! So, watch you! Aye, it could be that you, David Lindsay, are the more dangerous to Holy Church than even Wishart. For your seditious verses and poems are on everyone's lips. All the nation knows that its Lord Lyon is an exponent of heresy. I have long befriended you, protected you, but . . ."

"Ha – but now, no longer? You would unleash the hounds of God on me? Although I think that the good

God, the God of mercy and love, would scarce recognise them as His. Nor you!"

The two Davids stared at each other, almost eye to eye, for moments. Then, without another word, the Cardinal turned and strode from the chamber.

Lindsay remained long, gazing after him, unseeing.

The result of the trial of George Wishart was, of course, never in doubt, a foregone conclusion; although it lasted for days and superficially all was conducted with scrupulous fairness, however inevitable the verdict. The preacher, who conducted himself with dignity throughout, was duly found guilty of the most blatant and repeated heresy, and condemned to be burned at the stake before the castle of St. Andrews on the twenty-eighth day of the said month of March – and might God have mercy on his soul, once purified and redeemed by fire.

Sentence was carried out a few days later, with the Cardinal and Dunbar, Archbishop of Glasgow, with the court of bishops, watching from a castle window.

Scotland seethed.

But that seething, sufficiently basic and pronounced as it might be, was modest indeed compared with that which convulsed the nation on 28th May, so soon after, when the news broke. The Cardinal-Archbishop, Primate and Chancellor was dead, assassinated within his own secure castle of St. Andrews, indeed in the same upper chamber of the Sea Tower from which he had witnessed the burning of George Wishart.

David Beaton had gone to appear before another court, whose jurisdiction he might find less apt for manipulation.

It was some time before David Lindsay, appalled, heard the details. It appeared that, early in the morning, a group of conspirators, led by Norman Leslie, Master of Rothes, and his uncle, with Kirkcaldy of Grange, had managed to gain entrance to the castle dressed as workmen, along with a large party of masons who were carrying out repairs to the walling. Once inside, they had slain the gate-porter and thrown his body in the moat, let in more of their friends, and proceeded to rout out the still sleeping guards, who, along with the genuine masons, were then driven out into the city, and the portcullis dropped and drawbridge raised, all so simple a device. Then most of them had swarmed up the stair of the Sea Tower to the Cardinal's bedchamber at its top – for Leslie knew the castle well, being in theory a friend of the Beaton family. Indeed he had traded on that, for Beaton kept his chamber door locked and when, on the knocking, he had asked who called at such an hour, the other had shouted that it was his friend, Norman Leslie, on urgent business. The Cardinal had risen and opened, and the assassins had streamed in, sixteen of them altogether, daggers already drawn. Naked, Beaton had had no least chance and fell bleeding to the floor. According to the accounts, one of the conspirators, a priest, named James Melville, had at this stage halted the proceedings, holding up his hand and declaring that all was not being done in sufficiently godly fashion and that prayer was called for. So he had had them all kneel down around the fallen Cardinal while he sought to involve the Almighty in the matter. Thereafter they completed their task. When assured that Beaton breathed no more, they hoisted his stabbed and savaged body, and by a cord they had had brought for the purpose, tied round one ankle, hung it out of the window, the same from which their victim had watched the burning of Wishart.

This last refinement was the undoing of them however, for the sight of the body, plainly visible from the street, quickly brought crowds roused by the expelled guards. These massing outside the gatehouse prevented escape, and soon the Provost and town guard arrived. So the attackers were themselves besieged, in as extraordinary a situation as even the Scots could have contrived.

The kingdom reeled under the impact. David Lindsay, in his own consternation and sense of loss, spared a thought for Marion Ogilvy finally left alone in Melgund Castle.

17

As well, indeed, that Marie de Guise had been appointed Joint Regent and Governor previously, and now was able to display her mettle. For, of course, with Beaton holding all the power and offices he had done, in state as well as Church, his abrupt removal left a yawning abyss, a vacuum in the rule and leadership of the realm. Arran was all but useless, in hand-wringing impotence; and Archbishop Dunbar of Glasgow, now elderly and never forceful, was not much better. But the Queen-Mother stepped into the breach, distressed and apprehensive as she was, and coped, with remarkable success. She could not work miracles; but, the mother of the monarch, she supplied the impression of a reasonably firm hand at the helm of the nation, an outwardly calm assurance and a sound judgement. And she had David Lindsay and Bishop Paniter at her right and left hands, to advise.

David felt the responsibility, and his own inadequacy, keenly. It was one thing to question and seek to temper Beaton's subtle but forceful policies; and quite another to provide guidance on most aspects of government, which would probably be acted upon, and even to initiate policy.

Obviously almost the first priority was to call a parliament. But although the forty days' notice could sometimes be dispensed with, not at hay-harvest time, as now, and with a large and representative attendance required. So, a convention of the nobility first, more simple to arrange, to attempt to deal with immediate problems of the emergency.

This was assembled at Stirling on 10th June, less than two weeks after the assassination, a notably speedy achievement, indicative of the recognition by all that Beaton's strong and so capable hand removed meant national crisis indeed. Likewise indicative was the turn-out, practically every interest and faction – save that of the

St. Andrews conspirators themselves – being represented; Angus and the Douglases had some special concern, for Douglas of Longniddry was one of the now besieged party in that castle, and Angus's brother, Sir George of Pittendreich, although not in the castle-assault, was believed to be in the plot; Glencairn and Cassillis and the Lord Gray, of the pro-English party; the Earl Marischal, Ruthven, Livingstone and Somerville, of the reformist but pro-French conviction; Atholl, Argyll and Huntly, assured regency supporters; Erskine, Seton, Ochiltree and Montrose, strong Catholics; Home, Buccleuch and other Borders lords, a law unto themselves; Morton, Crawford, Ogilvy, Caithness and many another, of uncertain allegiance; and, of course, the Hamiltons and their allies; plus the serried ranks of the Lords Spiritual, bishops and mitred abbots. Eying them all, in that great hall of Stirling Castle before the start, the Lord Lyon King of Arms, for one, felt his heart sink. Was it possible that this high-born but hopelessly divided crew could ever come to any sort of agreement to save the kingdom?

There was one item of news, however, which would not be without its effect on all present that day. Word had just reached them that England and France had come to agreement on peace terms, at least for the moment. So Henry would be the less preoccupied abroad. And one of the terms of this new treaty ominously stipulated the return to France forthwith of de Montgomerie's expeditionary force.

To emphasise the importance of the occasion, David led in the child-Queen, before the two Regents, almost as though it had been a true parliament – but without the trumpeting – to the genuflections of all. But at such a council there was no need for Mary to stay. With no Lord Privy Seal nor Chancellor available to conduct the proceedings, old Archbishop Dunbar, a former Chancellor, led off. In a quavering voice he read out a prepared statement detailing the dire situation and listing the identities of the men in St. Andrews Castle, ending with the two Douglas names. This brought forth an immediate and strong denial from Angus that they were there by his will or authority. There were a variety of rumbles from the company.

Dunbar went on to declare that, in view of the offices of state held by the late and esteemed Cardinal, certain positions had to be filled forthwith, at least temporarily, if the essential business of the realm were to be carried on. Of these, that of Chancellor or chief minister was undoubtedly the most vital, at this moment. In the circumstances, it must be held by a man of proven integrity and ability, who had the confidence of the Regents, the people and the Church. The Regents proposed the name of George Gordon, Earl of Huntly.

Thus early, and immediately after the naming of the two Douglas conspirators, the challenge was thrown down, however quivering the voice. And for long moments there was silence, David like many another scarcely daring to breathe. But the pause continued, and it became clear that neither Angus nor any of the other factions considered themselves in a sufficiently strong position at that moment to contest the nomination. With a sigh of relief Dunbar declared the Gordon chief to be interim Chancellor, until such time as a parliament might confirm the appointment or otherwise. The Earl of Huntly to come forward to chair the gathering.

That victory for order, the regency and some semblance of unity, set the tone for the meeting; and although there were inevitable clashes, accusations and taunts thereafter, progress was made, good progress in the circumstances. Huntly managed all firmly, expeditiously, but with some tact, as far as possible avoiding controversy. Arran fortunately said little – although he did announce, plaintively, that his heir, the Master of Arran, had unhappily been captured by the miscreants in St. Andrews and was now being held as hostage in the castle. This produced mixed reactions and only a little sympathy, for the said Master, although second in line for the throne, was little more popular than was his father. But it did in fact help progress just a little, unexpectedly; for when Angus shouted unkindly that at least their young liege-lady was now in no danger of being married off to the Hamilton heir while he was safely in captivity, the Queen-Mother intervened to say that there was no danger of such or any other premature marriage, the Earl of Arran having agreed to leave the matter until, as a previous parliament had decided, the Queen's Grace was at least ten years old. This stumbling-stone for the anti-Hamilton interests removed, helped the proceedings.

An urgent priority was to deal with the St. Andrews situation itself. The conspirators should be tried for the murder of the Cardinal; but until such trial and investigation, individuals could hardly be declared guilty. So they must be summoned, in the Queen's name, to surrender and stand trial. The obvious authority to attend to this formality was the Lord Lyon King of Arms. Sir David Lindsay was ordered by the assembly to proceed to St. Andrews and demand surrender.

National security was debated, and surprise expressed that there had so far this campaigning season been no major English invasion. Why this should be was not known, save perhaps by Glencairn and Cassillis, who remained silent. But this was unlikely to continue and plans were laid for a more effective defence of the Borderlands, with Angus, despite all doubts, confirmed as Chief Warden and Buccleuch his deputy. On this subject there was one improvement. The Lord Maxwell had died in English captivity. He had been hereditary Warden of the West March and owner of Caerlaverock Castle, its strongest fortress; and his son succeeding to both, now that pressure could no longer be brought to bear on him over his sire, resumed allegiance to his own monarch and ejected the English occupants of his castle. So they no longer had that toe-hold in Scotland.

Strangely, the vital matter of the realm's safety did not take nearly so long to decide on as that of the young Queen. With the device of grasping power by taking possession of the infant monarch so long-practised, and by some there present, a majority were concerned to prevent a recurrence. So it was decided that no fewer than a score of lords, temporal and spiritual, be appointed as responsible for the Queen's safety, to act in sets of four, in monthly rotation. The composition of these groups of four was, of course, all-important, in order that no faction should find itself in a position to take over young Mary; so each nominee had to be countered by others of a different complexion. Thus the first quartet consisted of Huntly himself, with the Bishop of Orkney, the reformist Ruthven and a Douglas; the next, Archbishop Dunbar, Angus, the Lord Somerville and the Abbot of Dunfermline. And so on. Working out the permutations was a lengthy and acrimonious process, and tempers were frayed and the atmosphere less co-operative before the meeting closed.

But all in all it had gone a deal better than might have been anticipated, at least by David Lindsay.

He was not very happy about his mission to St. Andrews, with no expectation that it could achieve any success – save the fact that refusal to obey the royal summons to surrender could be construed as treason, which might prove useful. However, going there would give him excuse to proceed on thereafter across Tay, to Melgund in Angus, to see Marion Ogilvy. He could take Janet with him, perhaps . . .

St. Andrews town was as full of stories about the castle as an egg of meat. The Cardinal's body was being preserved in salt in the infamous Bottle-dungeon of the Sea Tower, the Master of Arran confined in the same grim pit. More and more of the reformist sort were coming to join the assassins, or Castilians as they were now being termed, being admitted by night from boats – for part of the castle-walling ran right down to the sea's edge. Amongst the newcomers was the priest John Knox, from Haddington, who was preaching and keeping up the others' spirits, even preaching at the townsfolk in the street, from a castle window. Kirkcaldy of Grange and John Leslie, brother of the Earl of Rothes and Norman's uncle, had been smuggled out and taken passage in a ship for London, to ask King Henry to send up a fleet to deliver them. And so on. None of which encouraged David in his task.

He left Janet in the Blackfriars monastery, and feeling

distinctly foolish, dressed in his Lion Rampant tabard and chain-of-office, attended by the city's Provost and magistrates, rode to the castle on its headland.

The street led right to the high curtain-walling and gatehouse, behind the moat. The drawbridge, of course, was up and the portcullis down. No sign of life was to be seen.

David ordered his trumpeter to blow a rousing summons. It produced a prompt appearance of guards, indicative that their approach had been watched.

"I am the Lord Lyon King of Arms," he shouted. "Sent by the Regents of this realm, in Her Grace the Queen's royal name. I require to speak with whoever is holding this archiepiscopal castle and palace."

There was silence from the gatehouse.

"Fetch him, I say. This is a royal command."

After a wait, a voice spoke. "I am the Master of Rothes, Sir David. We are well acquainted. And of a like mind, I think."

"Not in murder and armed rebellion, sir! I am sent to require the yielding of this castle to the crown."

"It is not the crown's castle but that of the fallen and forsworn Church. The Church *you* have condemned as corrupt, Sir David."

"Archbishop Dunbar wholly supports the crown in this. You must yield."

"No, my Lord Lyon. We shall not."

"No? See you, Leslie – you are no witless loon. *You* know the price of refusal to obey a royal command. Treason! Are you, and yours, prepared to be charged with treason? Forfeiture of your lands and gear? Outlawry? All that follows?"

"We must abide it, if that is the price of doing God's will."

"God's will, man! Murder? Assassination? Is that God's will? Henry Tudor's, rather."

"Aye, God's will," another voice, deeper, sonorous, rang out, the voice of a trained orator. "The man Beaton was a grievous impediment to the work of the Almighty in this kingdom, the cleansing and reform of His body, the Church. You, of all men, Lindsay, should know it."

"I know that those who take the sword shall perish by the sword, sir. Are you the priest, Knox, from Haddington?"

"I am the Lord's humblest servant. My name is no matter . . ."

"Save that it will be necessary for your charge of treason in due course, Master Knox!"

"Only treason to my Creator troubles me, Lindsay."

"You are very bold, Master Knox, behind that wall! It will not save you for ever. I say yield now, in the Queen's name."

"Never."

"Very well. You must all take the consequences . . ."

Having anticipated nothing else, David was not disappointed as he rode away, but he was saddened, for this defiance could only mean further trouble and sorrow for the realm, and prolonged unrest, opportunity for Henry. But there was no more that he could do about it.

Sending the trumpeter and his escort back to Stirling, David and Janet rode on to Ferryport-on-Craig, where they hired the ferry to take them and their horses across Tay to Broughty, in Angus, on their way to Melgund.

They found Marion living alone in the great new, rose-red castle, seemingly her serene and contained self. She welcomed them with a quiet warmth. Any embarrassment in the meeting was on the visitors' part.

She by no means spurned their sympathy, and did not make light of her loss. But nor did she dwell at great length on Davie's death.

"I have known for long that this would be the way of it. Or something of the sort," she said. "Davie warned me sufficiently often. It was only a matter of time, he said. He had wrecked the hopes and schemes of too many unscrupulous men. Oh, Davie himself did not scruple overmuch – but he at least schemed on the realm's behalf, and the Church's. I was almost bound to be left widow, in the end. All the while this house was building, I guessed that it would be only myself who occupied it."

What could they say to that?

"Davie . . . chose well . . . in his woman!" Janet got out.

"I wonder? A different sort of woman, fond of courts and high living, might have served him better, been at his side a deal more. But . . . he has me ever at his side now, at least."

Enquiringly, they looked at her.

"Davie was a believer in the hereafter, whatever else of Church teachings he believed or disbelieved. As am I. Love is eternal and cannot die, he always said. Any more than the soul. Two souls linked by true love will, must, go on into eternity together. Otherwise God is not love – as we know that He is. So Davie and I are possibly nearer to each other now than ever we have been. And will be still nearer hereafter. I am content."

Much moved, they left it at that, the more content in their own hearts.

18

The refusal of the St. Andrews assassins to surrender, plus those who had since joined them, posed a self-evident challenge and problem to the crown which could by no means be ignored. The required parliament was held on 29th July, and after confirming Huntly as Chancellor and making sundry other appointments, its first decision was that the regency should take immediate steps to capture St. Andrews Castle and its occupants and bring them to justice on charges of treason. Since it was scarcely a woman's task to besiege a strong castle, the onus was on Arran, and he was nothing loth, with his son held hostage therein. There was, however, a certain amount of doubt and reluctance expressed, inevitably by the Douglases but also by the Church representatives. After all, St. Andrews Castle was the metropolitan archiepiscopal seat, and a treasure-house of irreplaceable valuables, relics and the like; the last thing they would agree to was that all could risk destruction by cannon-fire. Arran himself was not eager for artillery, with his son endangered. So it would probably be a matter of prolonged siegery and starving-out.

There had still been no major English attack, despite a fine summer, much to the surprise of all; but Henry's sickness reported to be worsening, led to the assumption that without his raging hate there was little impetus for invasion.

One very noticeable aspect of that 1546 parliament was the so-obvious increase in confidence and support of the reformist movement – another reason for moderation towards the St. Andrews conspirators. With the death of the man who had for so long led Holy Church, and the forces against drastic reform, it was clearly felt that the tide was flowing their way. Both the so-called French and English alignments spoke with one voice, in this matter at least. David Lindsay, not unsympathetic, watched and listened. So much would depend on who was appointed, or who rose up, to lead the Church in Scotland, as to whether the movement for reform was more orderly or more violent. Certain it was that it would be a deal stronger spared Davie Beaton.

No great army was required to invest St. Andrews Castle, so Arran set out almost at once on his task. He besought Lyon's assistance, at least at first; and since protection of the Queen was now in theory adequately looked after by the various quartets of lords, there was nothing urgent to detain David at Stirling or Linlithgow. He was fairly certain that there would be no swift surrender to Arran and that therefore the business would develop into a prolonged, time-wasting siege; so the chances were that with the besiegers settled into St. Andrews town, he himself could pass much of the time, with Janet, at Lindifferon, a mere dozen miles away, available if required.

That is how it turned out. Arran was no more heeded than David had been, despite the numbers he deployed. A few shots were fired from arquebuses, on either side, more as gestures than anything else, and all settled down to a waiting game, more comfortable for the investing force than was normal, thanks to the accommodation and facilities of the town. Thankfully David retired to supervise harvesting at the Mount.

It was two weeks before he was sent for, and then in a hurry. It was to find an English squadron of ships lying off in St. Andrews Bay and the Regent highly agitated. He must have more men if he were to resist an enemy landing to relieve the castle. The Lord Lyon was to hasten round Fife raising levies from its lords and lairds.

David pointed out that there were only five ships out there, none of them very large. No major force could disembark therefrom. Arran's people, with the townsmen's help, could surely deal with them? But the Earl was insistent. Men he must have. Lacking enthusiasm, David departed again.

For three days he rode round Fife seeking to persuade

his fellow landowners to provide troops. And when he got back to St. Andrews it was to find the enemy ships gone. Apparently all they had been doing was to send in supplies to the beleaguered garrison. This could be done from small boats, by night, the stores being hauled up to the parapet-walkways by ropes. When Arran had discovered this, he arranged to have local boats patrol the approaches during darkness; and thereafter the English vessels sailed away. But by then the damage had presumably been done, and the Castilians replenished and sustained for further defiance.

The siege went on, in somewhat lack-lustre fashion. David returned to Lindifferon.

Soon the Regent wearied of it, and went back to Stirling, depressed, leaving the Earl of Montrose in charge. Before he went, the Castilians had shouted that if artillery were brought against the castle they would execute the Master of Arran before his father's eyes.

It appeared to be stalemate.

That back-end of the year 1546, at Lindifferon, David Lindsay commenced a poem on the life and death of Davie Beaton, and found it the most difficult that he had ever attempted, in the circumstances. His trouble was how to reconcile his growing belief that Davie's removal was quite possibly to the ultimate benefit of Scotland in the matter of Church reform which was bound to come – and was a deal more likely to come without dire bloodshed and war lacking his presence – with his own admiration for so much that was the man, and his abhorrence of the deed of assassination. Time and again he started it and then tore up the results, dissatisfied. He decided, eventually, that he should wait awhile, until the impact of it all was less racking, and a better perspective attained.

The church bells rang out all over Scotland, that January of 1547, in acclaim and thanksgiving. Henry Tudor, the sorest scourge of the northern kingdom since Edward the First, Hammer of the Scots, was dead. Crazed with hatred, the lust for power and a terrible need for personal domination, he survived his arch-enemy, Davie Beaton, by only a few months. Leaving a nine-year-old and delicate son, as Edward the Sixth, to reign over a war-weary nation. Surely Scotland might now be spared the everlasting threat and fact of invasion, which she had suffered for thirty grievous years?

That Henry's other long-time enemy, and Beaton's friend, King Francis, should have died a month or so later, was rather extraordinary. This proved to be no disadvantage to Scotland either, for his successor on the throne of France, Henry the Second, was still more under the influence of the de Guises than had been his father; and his strong-minded Italian wife, Catherine de Medici, a perfervid Catholic and therefore profoundly anti-English. With Marie's brothers now to all intents ruling France, the Auld Alliance was the stronger. A resident ambassador, one d'Oisell, a de Guise nominee, was sent to the Scots court, along with sundry military advisers, d'Esse and de Thermes being the most prominent. They brought with them the formal proposal that the new Dauphin, Henry's four-year-old son Francis, should be betrothed to the young Queen of Scots.

There were those in Scotland who welcomed all this only doubtfully, the Protestant and reformist elements, who saw their burgeoning cause endangered.

David Lindsay was, as so often, drawn both ways, his desire for the security of the realm clashing with his concern for the cause for true religion and the cleansing of the Church.

At least, this last was somewhat aided, in a quiet and undramatic way, by the ecclesiastical leadership situation. No new Primate and Archbishop of St. Andrews was appointed meantime, this because Beaton's obvious successor would have been Archbishop Dunbar of Glasgow; but he was old and frail and unsuited to the tasks involved. Yet for the Church to nominate someone junior over his head would be unacceptable – especially with John Hamilton, the new Bishop of Dunkeld, Arran's ambitious brother, waiting in the wings and making no secret of his desire to be Primate. Many moderates were alarmed at this possibility; but David was less so. He assessed Hamilton as more concerned with personal advancement than with religious zeal of any sort, and guessed that such a man at the head of the Church might well prove more amenable to reforming pressures than any stern dogmatist.

So Scotland breathed more freely that year than for long – although the news from England presently had a somewhat ominous ring to it in that the Earl of Hertford, Edward Seymour, the Scots-hostile militarist, had been appointed Lord Protector – the equivalent of Regent – for the young Edward the Sixth and created Duke of Somerset. He was, of course, the boy's uncle, brother of the late Queen Jane Seymour.

In August, after fourteen months of siege of a sort, there were developments at St. Andrews Castle at last. The de Guises sent a fleet of no fewer than sixteen armed galleons, well equipped with cannon of every description and calibre, under a picturesque admiral, Leo Strozzi, Prior of Capua – presumably on the principle that a military cleric was the man to take effective measures against an archiepiscopal castle. This fleet anchored in St. Andrews Bay and disgorged some proportion of its artillery, along with expert gunners and some thousands of troops, who took over the entire city in an hour or so, with little or no reference to Montrose or the Scots besiegers. They then somehow positioned their lighter cannon on the highest pinnacles around the castle, including the towers of the cathedral and abbey and steeples of the university colleges, and proceeded to select unprotected targets within the walls, their archers and arquebusiers picking off anyone who showed themselves. After half an hour of this, Admiral Strozzi went to the gatehouse, with heavier cannon, and shouted to the inmates that they had one hour to yield up the castle or he would destroy at leisure every fortification and put a ball through every window. To reinforce his announcement, the galleons out in the bay opened up on the seawards-facing walling with their massive guns, blasting great holes in the masonry.

Well within the stipulated hour the white flag was hoisted from the Sea Tower, and the siege was at an end. It had taken exactly six hours from time of anchoring.

The Frenchmen then entered the castle, marched out the defenders, tied together with ropes in pairs, and then systematically as they had gone about the siege, ransacked the place – allegedly in case another occupation by reformist Scots should endanger the ecclesiastical treasures and relics – and, with these and the prisoners, sailed promptly back to France, leaving a dazed and bewildered St. Andrews, and indeed Scotland generally, behind.

At least the Regent's less effective besiegers could now return home also, likewise the Master of Arran. The Cardinal's body was recovered from its salt-barrel, to be buried decently in his own cathedral.

That was all at the beginning of August. Before the month was out, those January church bells were proved to be premature, to say the least. The new Duke of Somerset was at pains to prove the point.

David and Janet were with the court at Linlithgow Palace when the news reached there. Actually the first tidings were of a fleet of English warships entering the Firth of Forth – and since Linlithgow was only three miles inland from that coast, this was sufficiently alarming. But when, a few hours later, they heard that Somerset had himself crossed Tweed with a major army estimated at between fifteen and twenty thousand, the seriousness of the situation required no emphasising. With that fleet in the Forth, it was obvious that this was no Border raid but full-scale invasion. And the possibility was that the ships, sent in advance, were concerned with the capture of the young Queen.

They would never have been taken by surprise, like this, in Davie Beaton's time his spy-system would not have failed to warn him.

Marie de Guise was anxious to get her daugher out of danger's way. She herself, as Co-Regent now, could not just go and hide away with the child behind the Highland Line; but David and Janet could take Mary somewhere remote and secure while she herself removed to Stirling Castle. If the worst came to the worst, the little Queen might have to be sent to France; so it might be wise to install her somewhere reasonably near to Dumbarton and the Clyde estuary, on the safer side of Scotland from English shipping. D'Oisell strongly recommended this, and declared that Dunkeld, where they had hidden away before, was much too vulnerable, since English vessels might sail far up the Tay towards it. Also it was too far from Dumbarton. It was the Lord Erskine who suggested that one of the islands in the Loch of Menteith was a suitable refuge. Although hereditary keeper of Stirling Castle, his personal house was Cardross Castle in Menteith. There was a priory on Inchmahome, one of the islands in that large loch, where the young monarch could be secret and comfortable, in pleasing surroundings but within half a day's ride of Dumbarton. And the Queen-Mother could ride there from Stirling, if need be, in the same time.

So David Lindsay, with mixed feelings once more, in this emergency acted squire again not only to his five-year-old sovereign-lady but to a clutch of other young girls, for Mary had by now acquired her own small court, youngsters of her own age or little more, in particular four, the daughters of the Lords Seton, Fleming, Livingstone and of Beaton of Creich, a niece of Davie's, all with the name of Mary. With no large train to attract undue attention – the quartet of lords-protector that month saw their duty rather in protecting the kingdom; and besides, the priory on Inchmahome would not accommodate many visitors – they went with the Queen-Mother's cavalcade as far as Falkirk and then struck off westwards into the anonymity of the vast Tor Wood, while Marie continued on to Stirling. The parting of mother and daughter was affecting, with the future uncertain.

The Tor Wood hid their passage for many miles, before they emerged into the central upland valley of the Campsie Fells, wherein they were not likely to be observed, inhabited as it was only by a shepherd's house or two. This brought them eventually to the Fintry area, amongst wooded green braes, where they had to turn northwards, in the dusk now, to head by Arnprior for Cardross Castle, islanded in the intricacies of the huge Flanders Moss, where they were to spend the night. Fortunately Erskine had provided his son and heir, the Master, as guide, otherwise they would never have found their way through the shadowy marshlands and thin rising mists.

The Queen and her young companions, spirited girls every one by careful choice, enjoyed it all, the secrecy an adventure in their normally fairly sheltered lives.

Next day, by devious and hidden ways through the Moss, the vast hundred-square-miles barrier between Lowlands and Highlands, sanctuary of the turbulent MacGregor clan, they came to the south shore of the Loch of Menteith, a lovely sheet of water, island-dotted, lying under the foothills of the Highland Line. There, in a grove of alder trees, the Master of Erskine brought them to a large bell hanging from a bough, which he tolled loud and long. Soon, like a distant echo, they heard an answering ringing from across the water, and presently saw a boat coming to them from the largest island almost a mile away.

The boat, rowed by two muscular young monks, was not large enough to take many of the company; but when the rowers learned that here was the Queen of Scots herself, and her entourage, they ferried over the girls, David and Janet and the Master, to their island, promising to send a larger craft for the others and a barge for the horses. Normally, it appeared, horses were stabled on the mainland nearby, but when secrecy was required, as now, they could be accommodated on the Isle of Dogs.

Inchmahome, their destination, the Isle of St. Colman, a Celtic saint, was less than three hundred yards long but richly wooded and supporting an Augustinian monastery of moderate size, which nevertheless boasted a four-storey bell-tower and a church strangely ambitious for such a site – indeed, their oarsmen told them that Mary's distant predecessor, David the Second, the Bruce's son, had wed Margaret Logie therein. This priory of Inchmahome was to be the Queen's sanctuary meantime. On the next island, Inch Talla, was the old castle of the Earls of Menteith, taking up the entire area; but this, neglected now and bare, would make much less comfortable lodging than would the monastery. The Queen and her young attendants should have the Prior's own quarters.

It was one more strange situation for David Lindsay, hidden away in this delectable spot, while the kingdom faced the terrors of large-scale invasion. He had no notion as to how long he would be required to remain here. But Janet had no qualms, and advised him to make the most of it. He was now a man of fifty years, let him not forget, and should have learned to appreciate the smiles of good fortune when they came. And whether Scotland survived or sank this time would not depend on David Lindsay.

So commenced a blissful interlude in the golden autumn, amidst surroundings and conditions which spoke only of peace, beauty and well-being, while terror and horror must be raging not so far away. Young Mary was no trouble, a pretty child with fetching ways, now in good physical shape and no more difficult to manage than any of her little companions. The island was just large enough for the children not to feel confined, and with its woodland, little beaches and coves, its rocks to clamber over, shallows to paddle in and boats to play in, not to mention monks to involve in their games, was a paradise for youngsters. They could be ferried over to the other islands, and occasionally to the mainland, and be taken on fishing expeditions. The monks helped them to dig and plant a garden of their own, although at that time of year, growth was problematical. All of which left David and Janet with considerable time to themselves – and no excuse for the man not to get to grips with *The Tragedy of the Cardinal*, which more and more he was coming to see as not so much an elegy for Davie Beaton as a vehicle to help advance reform, in a moderate and constructive way, to try to counter the violence which had hitherto beset that cause. Davie, in a better place now, might well defer criticism.

They were not entirely cut off from the rest of the land at Inchmahome, for Marie de Guise sent frequent couriers to them with messages and presents for her daughter. From these they learned that the English fleet, now reinforced to no fewer than thirty-four ships, had attempted a landing at Aberlady Bay, David's old haunt, but had been beaten off by French artillery based, by de Thermes, at Luffness Castle. Balked in this, the enemy had sailed across to Fife, to spread havoc there all along the coast. There was no indication that they had penetrated inland sufficiently far north to reach Lindifferon. But at least they had failed in what had been undoubtedly an attempt to assault Edinburgh in a pincer-movement with the land-based invasion, advancing, it was reported, by the east coast route, with Angus and Buccleuch, vastly outnumbered, managing only minor delaying tactics.

The main Scots army was still assembling on Edinburgh's Burgh Muir.

Other news was that Archbishop Dunbar had died. So there was now no valid reason for delaying the appointment of a new Primate – on whom so much might depend.

Then, on Holy Cross Day, 14th September, Marie de Guise herself arrived at the Loch of Menteith, even that normally calm and assured woman in some agitation, accompanied by the Lord Seton. There had been a great battle, at Pinkie Braes, behind Musselburgh, they reported, a disaster for Scotland. Lothian was now being over-run by the invaders and Edinburgh besieged. Linlithgow was occupied and Stirling itself might well be assailed, for the English fleet was working its way up Forth and had bombarded the royal castle-prison of Blackness in the bygoing.

Seton, having been present at the battle, was able to supply David with details. "It was the usual folly," he declared. "Divided counsels, bad blood between Arran and Angus, overmuch haste, and Highland and Lowlands going their own ways. That, and the English ships . . ."

"Ships? How could ships affect a land battle?"

"They did, to be sure. With their heavy cannon. They sailed into Musselburgh Bay and some way up the mouth of the Esk, and were able to bombard our left flank."

"You were near enough the firth for that?"

"Not at first – that was the folly of it. Somerset advanced into Lothian from the east, by the Merse. He avoided Dunbar and Tantallon castles, crossed Tyne at

East Linton and came on by Longniddry and Tranent. Thereafter he came slowly along the Fawsyde ridge. Fawsyde of that Ilk sought to hold him up, by fire from his castle walls, and sent word to Edinburgh – which was to cost him dear thereafter. Arran marched from the Burgh Muir, now joined by Angus, and came to Edmonstone Edge – you will know it, a strong position facing the Fawsyde ridge distant four miles. They reached it on the evening of the ninth – and there was the first blunder. Home, on the left wing, with fifteen hundred of his Merse mosstroopers, the best cavalry we had, saw the enemy down on the low ground of the Esk. They had captured the old bridge at Musselburgh – as you know, the only bridge across Esk for many a mile. Without consulting Arran or Angus, he charged down the hill. He recaptured the bridge, yes – but then the ships in the river-mouth opened fire. They could see them plainly. Because of the narrow position around the bridge, the mosstroopers could not disperse. They and their horses were scythed down like hay, Home himself sorely wounded. That cavalry was little further use thereafter. Angus was crazy-mad!"

"Angus – was he in command?"

"God knows! There was the rub. He should have been. He calls himself Lieutenant-General and Chief Warden. And, whatever else he is, he is a fighter. But Arran, as Regent and Governor, assumed he had the command. And Huntly, the Chancellor, supported him, Argyll likewise. And Arran's soldiering is as good as my needlework!" Seton glanced apologetically at the Queen-Mother.

"Folly indeed!" David agreed.

"Aye. And next day, Arran threw all away. Somerset remained on the Fawsyde ridge with his main army, his right under Grey de Wilton stretching right down to the coast at Drummore and Salt Preston. The Governor ordered us all to advance. There could be only the one advance from Edmonstone Edge – downhill! So we left our strong position for the low ground, to cross Esk by that devil-damned bridge!"

"Lord – what James the Fourth did at Flodden!"

"The same. Angus refused to move and stayed up on the Edge meantime, with his seasoned Borderers. But the rest of us went – Huntly, Argyll, Atholl, Bothwell, Montrose, myself, fifteen thousand and more . . ."

"Save us, to cross Esk by that narrow bridge, where only two could pass at a time?"

"The foot, yes – which was nine-tenths of us. The horse could ford the river. But we had lost much of our horse the previous day. As we waited to cross, bunched together, those ships' cannon cost us dear again – and nothing that we could do. Then our own cannon came down from Edmonstone, and we could fire back and do some hurt to the ships. Angus came on then, in the rear, and joined Argyll and his four thousand Campbells."

"And Somerset? He was still on the high ground at Fawsyde?"

"Aye, there he bided, curse him! We had one success. Grey de Wilton, with five hundred cavalry, made a flanking attack round by the coast and the east back of Esk, to get behind us. So it was Angus and the rearguard that he reached. Angus's foot had eighteen-foot pikes, and they formed schiltroms, hedgehogs. The English cavalry had only eight-foot lances, and could not win close enough to strike. They lost many men and more horses. And when they were circling round, trying to ride the schiltroms down, Argyll and his Highlanders closed in and surrounded them. Few English escaped, Grey himself down. But that was our only victory."

Marie de Guise sighed. "If only d'Esse or de Thermes had been there, in charge . . ."

"Even Angus himself, Madam. He would never have sent us on into the How Mire."

"The How Mire . . .?"

"The valley between Inveresk and Fawsyde. Shallow, wide, but marshy. A trap of a place. Arran thought to assail Fawsyde ridge from there, the fool! We all protested. Huntly, when he could not prevail on Arran, tried to delay and sent back for Angus. He convinced Arran to let him ride forward, with his banner-bearer, to challenge Somerset up on the high ground. He offered to fight

Somerset himself, hand-to-hand. Or if Somerset felt his years, to name any deputy. Or, if they would not risk that, twenty English against twenty Scots. Or ten against ten. Somerset, to be sure, laughed him to scorn. But Angus was slow in coming. When the English saw him coming, from the Eskside, they charged downhill upon us, in that mire. And it was massacre, total defeat. And shameful flight thereafter . . ."

"The rearguard? Angus and Argyll? Could they not rally some part? Save something . . .?"

"The Highlandmen were over-busy plundering the dead and dying of Grey's force. Angus did form a defensive line with his pikemen, on the firm ground. But when Huntly was unhorsed and captured, and his Gordons lost heart and turned back, others took it for a retreat and turned with them. It became a rout. Angus could not, or did not, stem the flight. He and his retired in fair order. But few others did." Seton shrugged. "A sorry day for Scotland. One more of over many."

"At least we still have some force undefeated," Marie declared, determined to extract what cheer she could from the situation. "Buccleuch was not there. He was holding the Soutra pass out of Lauderdale. Somerset sent a small force there, to mislead. Angus will join him and we shall still have an army. D'Esse and de Thermes will aid."

Seton looked doubtful.

"Huntly is captured, then? So we have no Chancellor again! Arran – did he escape?"

"Aye – he is safe in Edinburgh Castle. I swear we could have spared him better than Huntly!" Again the glance at the Queen-Mother.

"So what now?" David asked.

Marie spread her hands. "We must take all measures that we can. To save the kingdom. Since my lord of Arran is shut up in Edinburgh Castle, *I* must act the Governor. From Stirling, or wherever I may. It may be that I shall have to retire into the Highlands. You, Sir David, must have my royal daughter ready at any moment to go secretly to Dumbarton. D'Esse has a French ship waiting there, to take her to France. I pray God that it may not be necessary, but . . ."

David assured her that he could have Queen Mary in Dumbarton in half a day after receiving word to move her. "But you, Madam – would I not be better with you? Than here, with Her Grace. You will require all the assistance you can gather. Others can guard your daughter on this island."

"Perhaps so, Sir David. It may be that I shall require you at my side. If so, I shall send for you. Meantime, all is uncertain. I shall return to Stirling. Atholl and Argyll are there. If Somerset advances westwards, I may have to retire with them into their Highland fastnesses, there to raise the clans. To drive the English out of this land . . ."

"I greatly admire your spirit, Madam. Would to God others were as sure and true!"

"That good God will uphold the right, never fear. And I shall aid Him, my friend! My brothers will send more help, men and moneys. And I shall write to the Emperor and his aunt, for their assistance. Also the King of Denmark, who is my friend. We shall triumph in the end, never fear."

"Bless you, Madam!" Seton exclaimed. "Would *you* had been at Pinkie!"

David was sent for, to go to Stirling eight days later, but not to flee with the Queen-Mother into the Highlands. The Master of Erskine brought the summons, and with it rather extraordinary news. Somerset had already returned to England, and with his main force, leaving Lord Clinton, the English Lord Admiral, with his ships, in command in Scotland. He had gone, they were informed – and by Huntly of all people, whom Somerset had released on payment of a great ransom and injunctions to use his powers as Chancellor to counter the French influence and to have the young Queen of Scots betrothed to Edward forthwith – because the Lord Protector had learned of a plot in England to unseat him and to grasp the young King. So such behaviour was not confined to Scotland. What made this the more serious for Somerset was that the leader of the conspiracy was alleged to be Dudley, Earl of Warwick, the second most powerful man in England. So Scotland was breathing a mighty sigh of relief – since shipmen, no less savage than soldiers as undoubtedly they could be, seldom went very far from their vessels and therefore most of the land was likely to be spared their attentions.

Even so, Erskine revealed, by no means all had escaped Somerset's ire, in the week before he departed. David's own county of East Lothian, in especial, had suffered. Erskine had no information as to Garleton and The Byres. But nearby Luffness Castle had felt the invader's vengeance, for having driven off Clinton's fleet before Pinkie. Deliberately Somerset had ordered it to be spoiled. His troops had descended upon it, with cannon, battering it into submission, and then systematically demolished it stone by stone, throwing down the extensive curtain walling and angle-towers, gatehouse and drum-towers and all else they could – although the keep itself defeated them, at least its lower storeys where the walling was ten feet thick and the mortar iron-hard. They left the garrison, mainly Lindsays under Bickerton the keeper, hanging from nearby trees.

Nor had Somerset forgotten Fawsyde Castle, which had obstructed him before the battle. That he surrounded, cooped up its laird, family and servants within, and heaping brushwood around it, set fire to all, smoking everyone inside. He had also had time to burn Musselburgh, Dalkeith, Leith and other towns near Edinburgh and to demolish the Abbey of Holyrood, before he left for London – the heavy cannon in Edinburgh Castle, Mons Meg included, heavier than anything he had, kept him from capturing the capital itself.

At Stirling, Marie was holding a council of lords to decide on policy – and a distinctly acrimonious affair it was, with everybody holding others responsible for the defeat at Pinkie, and even accusations of actual collaboration with the English. Fortunately perhaps Arran could not be present, still holed up in Edinburgh Castle, with

Clinton waiting nearby; otherwise matters would have almost certainly been worse, with Angus there.

Marie, presiding, had a difficult and thankless task, but because of her position, birth and innate quiet authority, she achieved what almost anyone else would have found impossible, some degree of harmony however superficial, and sundry agreed decisions as to action.

The most urgent demand, of practically all there, was that Arran should be removed from the regency. This last demonstration of his ineffectiveness had left him with practically no supporters, not even Huntly. The problem was how to eject him, decently and lawfully, or anyhow indeed unless he agreed to resign. He was, whether they liked it or not, next heir to the throne. If young Mary died, and five-year-olds were vulnerable, Arran would be king. He could not be dismissed out-of-hand by anyone there, or anyone anywhere. Marie de Guise, who by no means loved the man, pointed that out.

In all the noisy debate, David Lindsay almost ventured a suggestion, then thought better of it meantime. Perhaps he might mention it privately to the Queen-Mother afterwards.

The question unresolved, they passed on to the matter of the Primacy. It was, to be sure, an issue for the Church; but it was also of major importance to the nation, so integrated were Church and state through the Spiritual Estate of parliament. Indeed the Primate was frequently the Chancellor of the realm. All knew that John Hamilton, Arran's half-brother, wanted the position – and the anti-Hamilton faction was automatically against it. He was presently with Arran at Edinburgh.

This time David did raise his voice. "This could bear on the other matter, that of the regency," he asserted. "Bishop John has much influence with his brother the Earl. If it were hinted to him that the Primacy could be his if he could convince his brother that it would be wise to resign the regency, that might do much. And, see you, Hamilton might serve none so ill as Primate. He is no zealot. But he is ambitious. He would not, I think, risk his position for the sake of one side or the other. He would permit reform in the Church rather than endanger all. Better him than one of the more fanatic priests."

There were murmurs of agreement at that, and Marie nodded.

"Well said, Sir David," she commended. "Your wise counsel is welcome. We shall consider this, indeed. Now, my lords – the matter of France. Is it your will that Her Grace, my daughter, should be declared formally betrothed to the new Dauphin Henry? To end these demands of the English. If it is, then I think that I may promise large French assistance in our present need, of men, ships, cannon and gold."

There were anti-French magnates present but, after Pinkie, none to speak up for an English match. Huntly and Argyll were both fearful of overmuch French influence, as was Angus; but in the circumstances they kept silence, and that vitally important issue was nodded through.

They went on to discuss the young Queen's immediate situation – whether she should remain at Inchmahome meantime, or be brought back to Stirling, now that the major danger was over for the time being, all agreeing that if anything was certain it was that Clinton's ships could not take Stirling Castle, whatever else. David's advice was sought in this. He recommended that, since the child was safe and happy on the island, she should be left there meantime; but when winter set in it would be different, and then she might return to Stirling if conditions still allowed.

This was accepted.

Finally they discussed the military situation. What was required, none could dispute, was a fleet to counter the activities of the English ships. But Scotland had never gone in for warship-building, strangely considering her vast coastline and vulnerability to attack by sea, from Viking times onward. James the Fourth had attempted some rectification of this failure but had been unfortunate with his naval ventures; and this Arran's father, when Lord High Admiral, had actually sold most of what remained of James's fleet to the French. So they were in no position to challenge Clinton at sea. All they could do was to seek to oppose his ship-based troops when they landed. These would not have horses, so they would probably not go far from their vessels; and they would be vulnerable to cavalry. On the other hand, they could sail where they would, unpredictable, and it would be quite impossible to have Scots defending forces within striking distance of most coastal areas in which they might choose to land. All that could be done was to set up a number of very mobile horsed companies, and base these along the seaboards most liable to be attacked – Fife, Gowrie, Angus, the Mearns and to a lesser extent Lothian, the local lords, lairds and burghs co-operating. This was the sort of activity such could almost enjoy, so there was no difficulty in arranging it, although the details took time.

For the rest, Angus not so much accepted as demanded responsibility for the defence of the Borders area, emphasising his claim to be Lieutenant-General of the realm as well as Chief Warden of the Marches. Huntly and Argyll, of course, disputed that; but Marie skilfully deflected argument and passed on to the need for raising a more or less standing army from the clans behind the Highland Line – as distinct from the West Highland and Isles clans who were always inimical, Atholl along with Huntly and Argyll to be in charge of this.

When all was over, and before returning to Menteith, David had a private word with the Queen-Mother.

"This of the Earl of Arran and the regency, Madam," he said. "It is going to take time, I fear, for him to be persuaded to yield it up. He is much concerned with his own standing and position, like many weak men. His brother, the Bishop, will I think much aid us if suitably rewarded. But more is needed, probably. You, Madam, might be able to effect it."

"I, Sir David? I fear not. My lord of Arran does not love me, resents my sharing the regency with him. He would scarcely be persuaded by me."

"Not by your words, no – but perhaps by your deeds. See you, Madam, if you could add to his status and standing in some way, he might be the more prepared to give up as Regent, as all the realm desires. He is, more's the pity, heir presumptive to the throne until your royal daughter may produce a child – which must be near a dozen years hence. If his position as heir could be made more evident to all, more honoured, more pleasing to his vanity, that man would be the happier. He must know that he is not popular and, made the way he is, he cannot *enjoy* the responsibility of rule, I believe. It is only the *title* of Regent that he covets, not the discharge of it, for he is a man of indecision."

"So . . .?"

"A better title. A higher one, yet without the responsibilities of office. You, Madam, can achieve much in France, where your brothers rule. A French dukedom, conferred on Arran, as heir-presumptive to the Scots throne? Make him the only duke in Scotland. Could you effect this? If so, I think that it would greatly please him, hurt none, and much help ease him out of the regency and its problems."

"*Parbleu* – here is a notion, yes! To be sure, that is clever thinking. A duke. My brothers would do that for me, I swear. Make Arran a duke of France."

"Yes." David coughed a little. "And, Madam, while you so consider, think on this also. Huntly and Argyll – you, and the realm, need these two earls greatly, themselves and their many clansmen, Campbells and Gordons. Now, more than ever, with the Highlands to be won over to your cause. These two do not love Angus, especially this of him calling himself Lieutenant-General. We do not want trouble there, in our present state. Yet Angus was given the Order of St. Michael, from France . . ."

"Ha! You think, Sir David, that if these two earls were also made knights of that great Order, they would be the more content?"

"It so occurred to me, Madam."

Marie laughed. "My friend, you much interest me! Always I have recognised your worth and good judgement and kindness to me. But now – now I think, you are taking on the mantle of the good Cardinal Davie! Now that he is gone to God. For this is as good as His Eminence's devising. You step into his shoes, no?"

"God forbid!" David said, fervently.

But, almost guiltily, he pondered that suggestion on his way back to Inchmahome.

19

It could not last, of course. Somerset himself might be preoccupied with plotters, and maintaining his ascendancy with difficulty in the face of Warwick's pressure, but all his minions were not. Sir Thomas, now Lord Wharton, English Warden of the West March, invaded Scotland from Carlisle before the winter was out, in late February 1548, with three thousand men, burned the town of Annan, captured the Jardine stronghold of Castlemilk, with other lesser Annandale and Nithsdale towers, and commenced another siege of Caerlaverock Castle, the Maxwell seat. To support this incursion – or it may have been the other way round, in view of what followed – Clinton's ship-borne force moved at the same time into major action, with the worst of the winter storms past. Hitherto he had contented himself with comparatively small-scale hit-and-run raids on the Fife and Angus coasts, from his base at Leith, all the while posing a threat to Edinburgh. But now he moved most of his fleet north to the Tay estuary, where he set up a new base at Broughty, the quite major ferry-port near to Dundee, guarded by the powerful Broughty Castle. This, shamefully, was handed over freely to the English by its owner, Patrick, fourth Lord Gray – all in the name of religious reform. He was one of the most militant of the Protestant lords, although not otherwise notably pious, and had been one of George Wishart's principal supporters, helping to make the adjacent city of Dundee the most vehement reformist community in the land. From Broughty, no doubt on Gray's advice, Clinton sailed up Tay as far as his ships could go, to St. John's Town of Perth. This walled town his cannon, at point-blank range, soon subdued, and his crews proceeded to sack all, paying particular attention to the many friaries, monasteries and nunneries for which the place was famed, systematically raping the nuns, as the declared whores of Satan, in the cause of reform likewise. While this, no doubt, was a useful demonstration of religious conviction, what Clinton had come to Perth for almost certainly was more subtle. It so happened that the town, comfortably far removed from most danger areas, and so well-endowed with rich religious houses in pleasing situation, was considered a highly suitable place to send the daughters of the nobility for safety and education. The town was full of young females of lofty birth. These Clinton had rounded up, to take back in his ships to Broughty and Dundee, to use as hostages and bargaining-counters in his curious kind of war, since half of the members of the Scots Privy Council had daughters there. Patrick Gray presumably did not.

It was this, rather than Wharton's raid into the south-west – which Angus presently defeated in Nithsdale, with heavy losses on both sides – that set Scotland's aristocracy in a turmoil, and resulted in David Lindsay being given a new task. Young Mary was back to Stirling from Inchmahome, for the winter, and he and Janet with her.

The Queen-Mother explained. Something had to be done about these captured girls: their lordly fathers and brothers were raging mad. An army could march on Dundee and probably take it, but the girls could be removed and embarked on the English ships at Broughty, and no rescue possible. Clinton was demanding repudiation of the French betrothal and the handing over of Queen Mary to him, in exchange for these young hostages. The like had never before been heard of, surely?

David, as concerned and upset as any, did not see what *he* could do about it.

He could go to Denmark, Marie asserted, to King Christian. Denmark and the Netherlands had the only fleets of warships large enough to challenge Clinton's force – and the Netherlands ships were presently engaged in the Emperor's ongoing war with the Grand Turk. David, in a fast vessel from Dysart, could be in Denmark in four days. It was nearer than France; and any French ships, if they could be spared, would take much longer to reach the Tay estuary, having to sail round Ireland and the north of Scotland to avoid battle in the Channel. Christian could send a fleet across the Norse Sea in just a few days, bottle up Clinton in the Tay, and gain the release of these unhappy girls.

David could scarcely believe what he was hearing. Marie de Guise was normally so entirely practical and level-headed; yet she appeared to be wholly serious about this astonishing project.

"But, Madam," he protested, "How can this be? I cannot go and ask the King of Denmark to send a great fleet hundreds of miles to a strange land just to rescue a parcel of girls, however high born. Even in Your Highness's name. He would laugh me to scorn, if not worse . . ."

"Not so, Sir David. Christian is presently in league with France. Against the Hansa Germans, who are supporting Vasa and the Swedes against him in the Baltic Sea. He will see this as a gesture towards France. Moreover, his Danish traders have suffered much at the hands of the English pirates. He will be glad to strike back, I think."

"But – a fleet! Great enough to engage Clinton's. An act of war. For what . . .?"

"For bread, my friend. For grain. The Danes have had two bad harvests. There is near famine. And the Swedes and Hansa Germans will sell them none. Offer Christian Scots grain, at cheap price, and free trade with Scots ports, something he has long sought, and I believe that he will send his ships for it – and challenge Clinton at the same time."

Wonderingly David wagged his head. He could scarcely argue further. Marie needed this gesture to win over many wavering Scots lords to her support; especially reformist lords, and Denmark was a Lutheran Protestant kingdom.

Doubtful still, two days later he slipped out of Dysart harbour in the fastest craft available, on a dark March night of wind and rain, praying that these conditions might ensure that the English ships still based on Leith would remain in ignorance; such precautions were standard procedure for Scots merchant shipmen these days.

The *Kilrenny Maid*, skipper John Durie, might be fast

but she was scarcely comfortable, accustomed to trading in salt-fish to Muscovy, and smelling like it. Skipper Durie, a typically independent Fifer, if he were impressed by the status of his passenger, did not admit it, although he did vacate his own cabin for the Lord Lyon King of Arms, such as it was. He prophesied that if this south-west wind held, as it was apt to do in March, he would have Sir Davie across in Roskilde Fiord in three days and a bittie.

As well that David was a good sailor, for the Norse Sea was wild indeed. He was inclined to compare it, unfavourably, with his last voyaging in the more kindly Mediterranean and Adriatic waters. He scarcely left his cabin throughout, insalubrious as it was – and he had no excuse for failure to work on his poetry. He had still not finished his *Tragedy of the Cardinal*, but, strangely torn emotionally with it, had started something more light-hearted to write, as it were, alongside it, a folly, a play which he was tentatively calling *The History and Testament of Squire Meldrum*. It is to be feared that it was this on which he concentrated during that uncomfortable voyage; that, and the preliminary work for a manual of Scottish arms and heraldry for which, as Lyon, he had long felt the need.

Soon after a grey daybreak on the fourth day out, John Durie summoned his passenger on to the heaving deck to point out proprietorially a long low fang of land on their starboard bow, which he declared to be the Skaw. Unimpressed, David was then informed that this, also known as Skagen, was the most northerly tip of the Danish island of Jutland, which meant that they were now into the Kattegat, the more sheltered sound between Jutland and Sweden, here some forty miles across. If the weather had been clearer they could have seen the Gothenburg coast. So they ought to be in Roskilde Fiord by nightfall, as promised. Expressing due appreciation now, David returned to his cabin. If this were a sheltered waterway, he wondered why the vessel was tossing about as violently as ever, if not more so, to be told scornfully that the shallower the sea the steeper the waves in any sort of wind.

Durie's assertion that they would be in Roskilde Fiord by nightfall was apparently fulfilled. But that did not mean that they were at their destination, Roskilde city. For the fiord proved to be a lengthy and very narrow tideway, fully twenty miles long and not much wider than a broad river, its guardian headlands strongly fortified. This was no place to thread in darkness, indeed a removable boom of chains and timber across the entrance was put down to prevent anything such, for security rather than navigational reasons; and the *Kilrenny Maid*, like sundry other ships, had to lie up in a creek under one of the forts, whose cannon-ports pointed at them menacingly. Apparently this was normal practice however.

In the morning, permitted to be on their way, it was like sailing up a lowland river, in a strung-out convoy, through a seemingly populous and trim countryside of marshland, farms and pasture, oddly normal and peacefulseeming to be the homeland of the warlike Danes and one-time Vikings.

Roskilde, which they reached by midday, was the ancient capital of Zealand, its palace the favourite seat of the Danish kings. But as cities went it was a small place, the Danes never having gone in for town-dwelling in a large way. It was strange indeed to Scots eyes, all being built in timber, not stone, even the palace and a quite large cathedral, built around a pagan mineral-spring sacred to the old Norse gods. Apart from this ancient feature, why Roskilde should be a favoured place for a sea-going race was entirely evident, for here, suddenly, the narrow fiord opened out into a great and sheltered basin, fully two miles across, surrounded by low green hills and fair woodlands, dotted with villages and farmsteads, the waters now filled with shipping, mainly war-vessels it seemed, raising a veritable forest of masts and spars. A safer and more hidden base for a fleet could scarcely have been devised. Abruptly David's mission seemed to become somewhat less improbable. The city, behind its wharves, docks and warehouses, rose fairly steeply towards the cathedral-crowned hill, David noted – but he could see no sign of the palace.

They had difficulty in effecting a disembarkation, so crowded were the jetties and berthing-places, but no hindrance otherwise to their landing. At once David found himself at something of a loss as to how to proceed, for he knew nothing of the language, and those to whom he spoke as evidently did not understand his Scots-English. John Durie knew a few words of Muskovite but no Danish. The skipper did know that the monarch here was termed 'the kong', and by asking for the kong's house they were directed up the hill to what looked like just one more terraced street of houses joined together, but which proved to be in fact one lengthy building right on the street, the Kongsheim Palace, odd-seeming indeed to the Scots, who had been looking for something of a fortress or great castle. It seemed that the Danish monarchs viewed their position in a different light from that of most of the princes of Christendom, and lived much closer to the people.

On application at this modest-seeming royal residence, they found an officer with sufficient English of a sort to inform them that King Christian was in fact not there but had gone to Copenhagen, the present capital, for a meeting of the Rigsdag or parliament. The conversation did not get much beyond that owing to language difficulties involving how they were to get to Copenhagen. Then, abruptly beaming, their informant came out with the odd word "Maccabaeus", or something like that, repeating it, and pointing vaguely eastwards. The only entity David knew approximating to that name was some biblical character; but the other then added Scot man, Scot man, and directed them to the great kirke or church.

Mystified but hopeful they set off for the cathedral.

At that handsome building, much more ambitious than the palace, all of timber but with a tall spire and painted white and blue, they found a sort of small theological college attached; and when they repeated the name Maccabaeus to a black-robed individual there, understanding was forthcoming and they were conducted to something like a classroom where a venerable, grey-bearded man in Lutheran priestly garb was addressing a group of younger men, presumably students. Their guide left them, to listen to a lecture in Danish.

Fortunately it did not go on for long, and when the students trooped out, the elderly individual was left to eye them enquiringly.

"Are you, sir, him they call Maccabaeus?" David asked. "Leastways I think that was the name told us. A Scot, it was said."

"Hech, aye – Maccabaeus is what they cry me here," the other agreed, in a very different and rich Doric voice. "Man – tis good to hear the auld Scots tongue. It is a whilie since I heard it. What brings you here, masters?"

"I am Lindsay of the Mount, Lyon King of Arms, on a mission to King Christian, sir. And this is Skipper John Durie, of Dysart. We cannot speak the language here, and were directed to yourself."

"Lindsay o' the Mount! Och, I've heard tell of you. Aye, and of your bit Satyre o' the Estates, forby. Man, I'm proud to ken you! Och, you struck a right stout blow for true religion with yon play-acting." And the other came forward to grasp and shake David's arms vigorously.

"My poor efforts have sounded as far as Denmark, then? Here is a wonder! How comes that . . .?"

"Och, I hear frae Scotland now and again, mind. And Lindsay o' the Mount and his scrievings are namely wherever honest Christians gather. Against the Whore o' Rome, God be praised."

David coughed. "I am for reform in Holy Church, yes. But not violent upheaval and strife, Master Maccabaeus . . ."

"Man, the name is MacAlpine, Sir Davie. MacBeth MacAlpine. Of the Gregorach, see you. But that was a bittie much for folk at St. Salvators, in St. Andrews, and they cried me MacBee, at the college. And the nearest these Danes can get to that is Maccabaeus – him you'll mind of, Judas Maccabaeus, the hero o' the Jews."

"I see. So you were at St. Andrews also? As was I, long since."

"Mysel' longer, I think! As student. But I was teaching there again, when I was Prior o' the Blackfriars at St.

Johnston. Till yon limb o' Satan, Beaton, made it ower dangerous for those practising reformed doctrine. He'd have had me burned, yon one – so I came here, where the good Martin's teachings are respected. And here I have bided, for a dozen years and mair, well done by."

"You are a teacher in this Lutheran Church, then?"

"That, aye – but a small matter mair, see you. I am Professor of Theology at the University of Copenhagen, where I am translating the Bible into Danish. Forby, I am Chaplain to King Christian."

"Guidsakes! Then you are an important man. And could help me in my mission – if you will." David went on to explain what had brought him to Denmark, a little hesitant about those girls and their plight.

He need not have been, for their new friend expressed himself as sympathetic and entirely willing to assist, so long as it was not to the advantage of the Church of Rome in Scotland. He had, he declared vehemently, no love of the English. Indeed that said, he went on to announce that as there was nothing further to detain him here at Roskilde, he would take Sir Davie with him back to Copenhagen and introduce him to King Christian.

This sounded eminently satisfactory, especially when it transpired that the former Prior could ride to the capital that very day, less than twenty miles by road, whereas the journey by sea, back down the fiord to the Kattegat again and then round by the Elsinore Sound, would be nearer one hundred and fifty miles. So it was agreed that David would ride with MacAlpine while Durie took the *Kilrenny Maid* round the long way.

Travelling through the Zealand countryside, by Taastrup and Glostrup, interested the visitor. He had always thought of the Danes, the descendants of the fierce Vikings who had plagued Scotland so sorely in the past, as a warlike if not savage sea-faring folk; and the great fleet in Roskilde Fiord rather confirmed that notion. But now, riding through a trim, intensively cultivated and notably domesticated land, much more so than Scotland, he gained a totally different impression. His companion and guide assured him that this was a good country to live in, even though he pined whiles for his own land and folk, especially for its mountains, forests and lochs, for he was of Highland extraction. The people here were honest, industrious and more peaceable than the Scots, although much concerned with material things, to a fault. And, to be sure, they had thrown off the yoke of Rome.

They reached Copenhagen, the haven of the merchants as MacAlpine translated, a walled city seemingly as large as Edinburgh, as dusk was falling. There were no hills to break the skyline, here, of roofs and towers and spires. It seemed to be divided by a great waterway, quite wide, up which sea-going ships could sail right into the middle of the town, so that their masts mingled with the gables and steeples. Creeks or canals struck off from this navigable Sound. Clearly it was a great trading centre, as its name implied. The vessels so evident here were not warships, as at Roskilde.

MacAlpine took him directly to the royal palace of Christiansborg, right in the centre of the city, standing on a sort of island formed by the Sound, creeks and canals, where it seemed he had his own quarters, as a royal chaplain. And, as adequate confirmation of his influence with the King, that same evening procured an interview with the monarch. David was much impressed.

Christian the Third of Denmark and Norway was a burly man of forty-five years, with a jovial manner, heavy brows, a down-turning moustache and a square spade-beard. A zealous Lutheran and lusty fighter, he had succeeded his father, Frederic the First, fifteen years earlier, against the wishes of the bishops and Catholic nobility, but also contrary to the desires of much of the merchant burgesses and peasantry, who sought the restoration of Frederic's deposed predecessor, Christian the Second, now a prisoner. Despite these handicaps, he had triumphed over both hostile camps, and in three years was strong enough to abolish the Romish Church in Denmark and introduce a Protestant form of government. Not content with that, he then went to war first with the Hanseatic League and then with that League's protector, the Emperor Charles himself; both of which conflicts ended with the Peace of Spires in 1544, on terms favourable to Denmark. So this was the doughty fighter to whom Marie de Guise looked hopefully, on the basis that the de Guise brothers had caused France to make threatening noises against the Empire at just the right moment, facilitating the said Peace of Spires – even though what they did was as much to France's benefit as Christian's.

The audience developed not so much as an interview and negotiation as a drinking session, the King obviously having a phenomenal capacity for *schnaps* or *akvavit*, a very fiery liquor, seeking to refill his guest's goblet as frequently as his own, to David's growing discomfort. However, that was as far as the discomfort went, for otherwise all proceeded well, almost ridiculously so considering the seriousness and scale of the proposals. Christian spoke no English, so the exchange had to be effected through MacAlpine, who proved both an eloquent and an enthusiastic advocate. Quickly the monarch perceived what was sought of him and began to thump the table and laugh loudly. At first this depressed David, who took it to mean that the suggested naval expedition was being scorned – as indeed did not greatly surprise him. But although the belly-laughter continued, it became evident that MacAlpine was far from put out, and went on with his presentation of the case. David, in his efforts to make the thing seem more reasonable, stressed the grain-export situation and especial trade-terms offered – although he had had doubts about the relevance of this on their ride from Roskilde, for the countryside had looked entirely prosperous and with no hint of want, much less famine, evident. But MacAlpine had admitted that the last two harvests had been very poor, and though the war was over, the Hansa merchants, like the Swedes, were refusing to sell the Danes grain and cattle-feed. It was this last which constituted the major shortage, it seemed, for Denmark was a great cattle-rearing land, and keeping the herds fed over the winter months had grievously lowered the stocks of oats and rye in especial, for human consumption as well as animal. At any rate, the grain offer seemed to go down very well, the suggestion that the warships, after their demonstration, could come back home laden with oats, setting the monarch off into further gales of laughter. While David was still summoning up further inducements in the way of free-trade ports and special import privileges, it dawned on him that Christian, for his part, was summoning fresh supplies of *akvavit* to celebrate their compact. The project was agreed, MacAlpine declared. A fleet would sail from Roskilde just as soon as the ships could be readied, provisioned and the crews rounded up.

It was an hour or so later before David escaped, head spinning, steps unsteady and bladder near to bursting, seeking his couch after an extraordinary day. MacAlpine confided to him, in his handsome lodging, that the King was no doubt glad of an opportunity to provide his seamen with activity, for nothing was worse for ships and sailors than rotting in harbour. The ploy would serve all concerned excellently.

So, mission over almost before it had begun, Scotland's envoy collapsed on the bed provided, bemused if not befuddled. The *Kilrenny Maid* was presumably still somewhere in the Kattegat.

Three days seeing the sights and meeting the prominent of Copenhagen, and evenings spent discussing religious reform and the niceties of Martin Luther's doctrines, and David re-embarked on his ship in the outer harbour for the return voyage, strong in his expressions of gratitude to MacBeth MacAlpine or Maccabaeus. He was assured that the Danish fleet would not be far behind.

He arrived back at Stirling to major developments, even after so brief an absence. Firstly and direly young Queen Mary was ill, stricken down suddenly, without warning. There were the usual whispers of poison, of course. Some of Marie's physicians talked almost equally darkly about smallpox although others diagnosed a sharp attack of measles.

There had also been a letter to the Queen-Mother from Somerset, of all people, in a strangely different tone from previous attitudes, declaring the Lord Protector's entire goodwill towards Scotland and assuring that his, and England's, only desire was a marriage between his young monarch and the child-Queen of Scots, with thereafter the beneficial union of the two kingdoms in perfect equality, and the elimination of the names and identities of both England and Scotland, the joint realm to be called Britain for ever thereafter.

This extraordinary proposal and affirmation met with utter incredulity in the northern realm and was not to be answered. And as a commentary on its sincerity, word had come, at almost the same time, of the activities of two of Somerset's lieutenants. Wharton, on the West March, on his retiral to Carlisle, and mortified by his defeat in Nithsdale, had staged a public trial of sundry prisoners, young Scots nobles, captured before the defeat, on the grounds that he had been assured of the co-operation of what he called his 'assured Scots' and that they had failed him in the event. They were solemnly condemned to death for this peculiar failure, and although six were subsequently reprieved, four were hanged there and then. Not only this, but a number of Scots priests and monks, taken from overrun abbeys and monasteries, were dragged at horses' tails through the streets of Carlisle and then scourged, this in the name of religious correction. And on the East March, Lord Grey was reported to be massing another invading army.

So the Rough Wooing continued.

All this tended to water down somewhat David's good news on the success of his Danish mission, although the need for Christian's gesture was by no means lessened. However, less than a week after David's return, the news reached Stirling that a Danish fleet had already arrived off Leith and was now anchored there, the English ships left there by Clinton having promptly fled. David was sent hot-foot the thirty-five miles down Forth to discover the situation, and to direct the Danes northwards to the Tay estuary, where Clinton's main strength was concentrated.

He arrived at Leith to find the Scandinavians having a high old time in the port and town. The Danish admiral,

Estrup, was relieved to see him, nobody there, he complained, seeming to know just what the situation was, and no information about grain shipments forthcoming. David reassured him on this point and promised that he would immediately arrange for warehousemen and merchants to supply the cargoes, both here in Lothian and over in Fife, and these would be ready for shipment when the Danes returned from Tayside – to be informed that they had already been to the Tay and at sight of their approach Clinton's fleet had hastily up-anchored and departed southwards. They had followed it down to well beyond Berwick-on-Tweed, and then come on here, duty done.

Impressed as he was, David wanted to know what had happened to the girl-hostages. Were they still in Dundee? Or in Broughty Castle? Or had the English taken them with them in the ships? Estrup knew nothing of this, not having landed at Dundee. His task, he said, was to drive off the English. This he had done, with only a token shot or two fired. Now he wanted his oats.

With mixed feelings, David left him, to hurry up to Edinburgh Castle, where Arran was still holed up, and there told the Joint-Regent of the situation, that there was now no danger to him here, but that the position at Dundee and Broughty was obscure and that of the girls likewise. He urged the Earl to send a force up to the Tay forthwith, to reduce Broughty Castle and discover what transpired. No doubt the Danes would transport such force, which need hardly be large, in their ships, while they were waiting for the grain to be brought down to the docks. Arran, probably a little shamefaced over his recent inaction, agreed, and at his brother's urging, said that he would lead the force himself. Meanwhile, Bishop Hamilton would see to the grain collection, for undoubtedly much of it would have to come from Church granaries, abbey-granges and monastic sources, at this time of year, with merchants' stocks beginning to run low.

Although David scarcely trusted Arran to be very effective, he believed that he could rely on his brother to carry out his part. He returned to the Queen-Mother at Stirling.

Young Mary's condition, happily, was improving daily. She was a spirited and lively child, and that helped. All now decided that her affliction was only measles.

Extraordinary news arrived presently from Tayside. Dundee had declared for the English, scarcely believable as this sounded. The Danes had landed Arran and his troops at Broughty Ferry and straight away returned to Leith and Fife ports to load up. Arran was besieging Broughty Castle, but so far without success. Clinton unfortunately had left a garrison therein; but what was more important, a number of heavy ships' cannon with much greater range and power than anything the Regent had available, so that he could not win close enough to storm the place. Moreover, the Dundee citizens were harassing his force's flanks and rear, refusing to supply provisions and otherwise acting in a hostile fashion, declaring themselves to favour the English, and especially the English religion. They had actually sent a letter to Somerset asking for his aid and a replacement of Clinton's fleet, some sound reformed preachers to come, and bring a supply of Bibles in the English tongue and other godly books. But at least Clinton had not taken the girls south with him. Left in Dundee, the city fathers had sent them all back to Perth, where they had come from.

It was all verging on the comic, in its own way, whatever Arran thought of it.

Far from comic was the sequel. Whether as a result of the Dundee appeal, or the lack of reaction to his letter proposing a united kingdom, and no doubt aware that the Danes had now sailed back home, in mid-April Somerset authorised Lord Grey to invade in major force. Marie's pleas to France and the Empire for military aid had not yet produced any such, although the Emperor Charles had promised six thousand German mercenaries and the de Guise brothers were assembling large numbers of men and ships at Boulogne. With Wharton threatening again in the west, Angus had to divide his strength, and was unable seriously to hold up Grey's advance through the Merse and into Lothian. At the Esk, almost on the site of the Pinkie disaster, he managed to hold the ancient bridge and river-crossing, halting Grey at Musselburgh. The English once again burned that long-suffering town and, unable to effect a crossing of Esk, turned away up it, to burn Dalkeith four miles to the south. At this stage, Arran's force, raising the ineffectual siege of Broughty Castle, and joined by Fife levies, came south to join Angus. Grey halted his march on Edinburgh and retired the few miles to Haddington, the East Lothian county-town, behind the strong walls of which he dug in, no doubt to await reinforcements.

So much for unity and equality.

With the English so close and Lennox again threatening trouble in the west Highlands, the object of all the aggression, young Mary Stewart, was deemed to be in real danger of capture. Reluctant as her mother was to give the permission, it was decided by the council that she should be sent to France for safety. Once she was there, especially if she were betrothed to the Dauphin, surely the English would desist from this everlasting pressure to obtain her? David and Janet were once again ordered to take her, not to Inchmahome this time but directly to Dumbarton Castle, there to await arrangements for her transport to France. As before, her four companion Marys went with her. She was now well on the way to recovery.

David was always in two minds about these nursemaid duties with his sovereign-lady. He liked the child, found her no trouble, and was honoured to be so entrusted. But by the very nature of the situation, it was only in times of crisis and national danger that it was necessary for Mary to be hidden away from that danger, which meant that he too kept disappearing into comfortably secure places on such occasions – which must appear less than heroic, to say the least. Not that he had any desire to seem a hero or to be involved in battle and clash. But he was somewhat concerned for his reputation. And there was always the possibility that he might be of more use at the mother's side than the daughter's when vital decisions and steps had to be taken – if that were not rating his advice and wits too highly. After all, as Lyon, he was one of the realm's great officers-of-state. Janet, needless to say, saw it all very differently, and said so.

Dumbarton Castle made a pleasant enough sanctuary, on its enormous rock rearing above the Clyde estuary, although less suitable for little girls than was Inchmahome, in that they could not be left to roam about freely on account of its cliffs and rock-faces. On the other hand, the adjoining town, with its harbour and shipping, was always a source of interest for children; and the accommodation of a royal castle was much superior to that of an island priory. For how long they would have to wait there was anybody's guess.

It was six weeks, in fact, before the French ships came into the Clyde and another three before they left again, with the young Queen aboard, six quiet weeks at Dumbarton but stressful for Scotland, with Grey besieged in Haddington, Clinton bringing back his fleet, with an army aboard, into Aberlady Bay to relieve Grey, being repelled from landing once again by cannon-fire from the ravaged castle of Luffness. There was nowhere else on that coast suitable for large vessels to put in, all shallows and rocks, save at Leith itself which, since Clinton's last occupation, had been hastily fortified and equipped with heavy cannon from Edinburgh Castle. So Clinton, frustrated, had had to transfer his troops and spleen to Fife, where he spread ruin, and then based himself on Dundee and Broughty again, while the siege of Haddington continued.

Then, at last, in June, the long-awaited French and Empire aid arrived at Leith, escorted by a Netherlands fleet which had got all safely past the English blockade in the Norse Sea – six thousand men, artillery, ammunition, money. Also the charter of the French dukedom of Châtelherault for Arran, with the revenues of the town thereof; that, and the Order of St. Michael for Huntly and Argyll. The King of France had actually sent his own royal galley to transport his intended daughter-in-law back to his realm, under de Villegagnon.

The sighs of relief reached Dumbarton – even though it took considerably longer for the French squadron to arrive there, after discharging its troops and supplies at Leith and then sailing right round the north of Scotland.

Marie de Guise appeared well before the ships did, to take farewell of her daughter, and bringing with her news of a parliament held actually just outside Haddington itself, in the Abbey of St. Mary, at which, amongst other decisions, the formal betrothal of Mary to the Dauphin was agreed. The Queen-Mother brought with her the distinguished company which was to escort her daughter to France – for not only the four Marys were going. Lord Erskine was to be in charge, and with him three of the Queen's illegitimate half-brothers, the Lord James, Robert and John Stewart. Also, as Mistress of the Queen's Household, Mary Fleming's mother, Janet, an illegitimate daughter of James the Fourth, whose husband, the Lord Fleming, had fallen at Pinkie – a lively creature, allegedly as generous with her favours as had been her half-brother the late King James.

De Villegagnon arrived, in stormy weather for the time of year, on 28th July, and all embarked next day. It was a sad parting for Marie de Guise, who had had to leave her other child, of her first marriage, the young Duke de Longueville, when she married King James. Janet likewise was in tears, and David himself more moved than he would have admitted, having become quite attached to the little redhead.

In the event, after all the leave-taking and God-speeds, with Marie returned to her regency duties at Stirling, and with the ships still in the estuary, the unseasonable weather blew up again and the squadron was storm-bound for a full week within sight of the Castle-rock of Dumbarton. The pilot, put ashore when eventually they sailed, reported that the little Queen was one of the few passengers not to fall seasick during the heaving interval.

David Lindsay, for one, rode thoughtfully back eastwards. So far as he could ascertain, this was only the second time in Scotland's long story when a reigning monarch had had to flee the country in the interests of safety, unless Bruce's travels after his coronation were counted. Somehow, surely, the Scots people had failed their sovereign. Or was it only the nobility?

20

The bells were ringing all over Scotland – as well they might. For it was peace, at last – not just a truce or a temporary cessation but full peace, negotiated, signed, and vouched for by France and the Empire. How long it would last, of course, none could say; but the signs and probabilities were good.

Two developments were mainly responsible. Firstly, as hoped for, Queen Mary's removal to France and betrothal to the Dauphin had indeed made it clear, even to the English, that any marriage to the young King Edward was no longer possible; so the Rough Wooing was at an end. Secondly, Somerset had fallen, and was now a prisoner in the Tower of London, awaiting sentence. Warwick had triumphed over him and was now supreme in England, not calling himself Lord Protector but more or less holding the King in his power and created Duke of Northumberland. And Warwick, although no lover of peace, was much concerned with consolidating his own position, and saw war with Scotland as something that he could not afford in his circumstances. He had sent up an army, under Shrewsbury, to extricate the besieged English in Haddington; but this done, the joint force had returned to England forthwith. Moreover, Clinton, making one of his raids on Fife, was roundly defeated at St. Monans by the Laird of Wemyss and the young Lord James Stewart, back from France, and himself seriously wounded. He had given up his occupation of Broughty Castle and sailed for home. The small pockets of English occupation remaining in the Borderland found themselves consequently endangered and unsupported, and made haste to depart – not always successfully, with the Scots and French swift to switch to the attack. Indeed the Borderers, after all the years of horror and destruction, and bent on revenge, repaid their debts upon these last English in harshest fashion, slaying without mercy, taking no prisoners, in fact actually buying prisoners taken by the French in order to kill them to their savage satisfaction.

It was the grim harvest of Henry Tudor's sowing.

So now peace was declared and established, the bells rang out, and the Scots could concern themselves with other matters than mustering, invasion, battle and war and the struggle to survive.

But, to be sure, there are other struggles than for mere survival, and the Scots were ever a notably argumentative and cross-grained folk. It did not take long for alternative causes and controversies to loom large and preoccupy, notably in the matter of religion. It was perhaps strange that so awkward a race should be so concerned over the niceties of faith and dogma, but so it was – and now there was less to prevent the tide of reform from advancing. Also there was the situation of the uncomfortable city of Dundee, still vociferous in its anti-Popish zeal and demanding an English-style religious system.

So, this summer day of 1550, David Lindsay was on his way from Linlithgow – where Marie de Guise now held her court in her own fair palace, instead of having to be cooped up in the fortress of Stirling – to attend the Provincial-General Synod of Holy Church, called specifically to try to cope with the developing situation by the new Primate and Archbishop of St. Andrews, John Hamilton. He was going somewhat uneasily, too – it seemed to be that man's lot to occupy uneasy situations – for although he held no office in the Church, he was nevertheless going in an official capacity, not exactly as Lord Lyon but as observer for the Queen-Mother Regent. Marie was, of course, a strong Catholic and anxious that the movement for reform did not get out-of-hand. She confided that she did not trust the new Archbishop Hamilton any more than she trusted the new Duke of Châtelherault, his brother. So she wanted not only a first-hand report on the proceedings but the evident presence thereat of her Lord Lyon King of Arms. Which, considering that David Lindsay had been involved in advising both the appointment of Hamilton to the Primacy and the gaining of the French dukedom for Arran, together with his known predilection for reform in the Church, accounted for his present discomfort.

Marie de Guise undoubtedly had her own brand of cunning.

The Synod was being held, not at St. Andrews, citadel of Holy Church, as was normal, but at Edinburgh, a significant gesture in itself towards reformist interests. The venue was to be the Blackfriars Monastery, the same which had featured so dramatically in the Douglas-Hamilton Cleanse, the Causeway incident of thirty years earlier, since the Abbey of Holyrood was still a blackened ruin after Somerset's burning. Entering, vivid memories crowded in on David Lindsay.

The meeting was to be held in the refectory, and its limited accommodation was already crowded, for this was a very special occasion and most of the ranking clergy of the land were present, unless ill or abroad. Some space had been set aside for spectators, for this was intended to be an exercise in public relations as well as a decision-taking assembly; but this space was limited and only the privileged were able to attend. One of the first persons David noted as he entered was the Duke of Châtelherault, sitting amidst a group of Hamilton notables.

It was rather a strange experience for David, these days, to slip into any public gathering unannounced, since it was normally Lyon's duty to do the announcing. His entry did not pass unnoticed, nevertheless. There were whispers and noddings and nudges, not all welcoming, especially amongst the senior clergy, who no doubt considered him to be an unfortunate influence. He found a less than prominent seat.

Presently, soon after the bells had chimed noonday, a choir of singing boys heralded the Archbishop and select company of prelates, who had been celebrating mass in the adjoining chapel. The Primate preceded by a cross-bearer, led in a procession of six bishops and eight mitred abbots, together with the Provincials of the Black and Grey Friars, plus two very young men, both named James Stewart, the one the Lord James who had accompanied his half-sister to France, aged eighteen and Commendator Prior of St. Andrews; the other, also an illegitimate son of the late King, Commendator Abbot of Melrose.

John Hamilton, despite the magnificence of his canonicals, scarcely made an impressive successor to the debonnaire Davie Beaton, a stringy, gangling figure with a pronounced stoop of the shoulders. He proceeded up on to a dais where he briefly called upon the Almighty to look upon and bless their deliberations; and then took his seat in a throne-like chair. The bishops sat in the stalls on his right, the abbots on his left, the two Provincials standing behind.

The Archbishop's Coadjutor now took over. He happened to be also his half-brother, another illegitimate son of the late Arran, Gavin Hamilton, Abbot of Kilwinning, now raised to the status of bishop. He sat at a table at the edge of the dais, flanked by secretaries, removing his new mitre for the occasion, indicating that he did not speak here as bishop but as chairman. He would conduct the synod more or less as the Chancellor did a parliament.

He read out a preamble and programme, in a flat monotone, giving the distinct impression that the whole affair was unfortunate but probably necessary. They were gathered in full synod to consider and take due action upon certain problems facing Holy Church in this realm. For long there had been unrest and dispute over some aspects of the faith, doctrine and practice, much of it deplorable, even heretical, and as such to be sternly condemned. But there were also certain complaints which were better founded and perhaps legitimate. These could bear examination and amendment. The Primate Archbishop of St. Andrews, whom God preserve, had put his mind to this situation, and with the advice of wise and learned councillors, had set forth a number of possible failures and abuses which the synod could consider, with proposed appropriate action for their rectification and amendment. If the synod saw fit, such amendments could be incorporated forthwith in canons, and so published for guidance and rule in Holy Church hereafter.

Complete silence greeted that unenthusiastic but in fact

quite extraordinary, not to say breath-taking announcement. Was Holy Church actually about to admit error and malpractice? Never before had it done so, not in Scotland at least.

The Coadjutor went on, after his significant pause. "The Archbishop John, for your guidance, lists certain items in which failure might be indicated and betterment made." He coughed. "Item: In the ignorance and lack of learning of much of the clergy, senior and junior. Item: The . . ."

He got no further before his flat voice was drowned in a hubbub of exclamation and shocked protest.

Looking sour and almost as though he agreed with the outrage, the Coadjutor waited. From his chair the Archbishop, his brother, raised a beringed hand. Gradually the noise died away.

"Item: In the corrupt morals of much of the clergy, senior and junior, monastic and parochial."

This time it was not so much outcry as indrawn breaths, gasps, open-mouthed alarm, as everywhere men turned to stare at each other. Monotonously the speaker read on. "Item: Plurality of benefices and offices held by senior clergy."

Even David Lindsay all but choked on that. Plurality! Did not John Hamilton himself still hold on to the abbacy of Paisley and sundry lesser but valuable charges, despite promotion to archbishopric? And this kinsman of his, Gavin Hamilton the Coadjutor, remained Abbot of Kilwinning. Of the bishops sitting smooth-faced there, David knew that Patrick Hepburn, brother of the Earl of Bothwell, was Bishop of Moray and at the same time Abbot of Scone; Andrew, Bishop of Galloway was also Dean of the Chapel-Royal. As to the others, he knew not. Apparently unconcerned, the Lords Spiritual sat there. Presumably all this was being said with their assent, if not advice. Could it be taken seriously?

"So much for complaints as to clergy," Gavin Hamilton proceeded. "Now to failure in worship. Item: In certain cathedrals and in many parish churches the Creed is never rehearsed, the Lord's Prayer never said, the Ten

Commandments never spoken, the Seven Sacraments unknown, and sermons never delivered. This due to the aforesaid ignorance of clergy."

Now the assembly sat tense, synod-members and onlookers alike. The bishops and mitred abbots may have been prepared for this, but clearly the great majority there had not.

"Item: The Holy Bible, when read, is done so only in the Latin, and this is understood by few in this realm, common and noble alike. It is recommended . . ."

This time interruption was not from thunderstruck clergy but from the ranks of the onlookers, reprehensible as this was. However, Coadjutor Hamilton forbore to frown, indeed he actually inclined his tonsured head, for the exclamation came from the Duke of Châtelherault himself. "Good! Good! Excellent!" he cried. James Hamilton had always complained that he could not make head nor tail of Latinity, and had advocated reform in this respect for long.

"Item: The charges levied for baptism, marriage and burial are frequently beyond the ability of the poor to pay, thus denying them the sacramental benefits of Holy Church. These for your consideration and decision." The Coadjutor ended abruptly, without any change of tone or delivery. Folding up his papers, he sat back, as though an unpleasant duty done. Then he recollected, and added, "Master John Winram, Sub-Prior of St. Andrews, to speak to these items, on behalf of my lord Archbishop and his advisers."

Excited talk now broke out all over the refectory. It is safe to say that never had a synod of the Church heard the like in all its five-hundred-year history. There was question, astonishment, offence, even some small satisfaction expressed – but mainly question. What did all this portend?

A small, neat man of middle years rose and came forward to the dais, papers in hand. John Winram had been one of Davie Beaton's trusted lieutenants ever since he had taken over the Primacy. Sub-Prior of St. Andrews did not perhaps sound a particularly lofty or influential position, but none of those who knew the situation looked down their prelatical noses at John Winram. For the Priory of St. Andrews was not like any other priory in Scotland. It was more important than many abbeys in that it was enormously wealthy and was in effect part of the Primacy, responsible for carrying out much that the Primate took in hand, largely acting as the nerve-centre of the archbishopric. But because it was so rich and prestigious, the office of Prior thereof was a much sought-after plum in the clerical polity, always going to the well-born and powerful. In fact, the present Prior of St. Andrews was the eighteen-year-old Lord James Stewart, eldest illegitimate son of the late King and half-brother of Queen Mary, there present. These lofty incumbents seldom took any real interest in the Priory or its affairs, only in its income. So the Sub-Prior was in fact the real master there and consequently the Primate's most useful aide. He had to be effective to reach and retain that position. John Winram was certainly so. In present circumstances, with a new Primate succeeding so forceful a character as Beaton, he was the more influential. David Lindsay sat forward expectantly.

Winram bowed to the Archbishop formally and, without glancing at his papers, launched into a detailed survey, in clear and businesslike fashion with little sign of the ecclesiastical manner.

"On account of the clerical ignorance mentioned, and the lack of learning prevalent, it is recommended that every diocese and cathedral church shall have a doctor or licentiate of theology attached, for the instruction of the clergy great and small throughout each bishopric. Until the clergy thereof are sufficiently learned to themselves instruct in competence, the said doctors shall preach sermons to the people as well as instruct. Such doctors and licentiates shall be supplied from the St. Andrews colleges, under the guidance of Master John Mair, Provost of St. Salvator's College." Winram turned and bowed towards an elderly man, plainly robed, who sat in the front rows of seats in the body of the refectory. There was a stir amongst the delegates. Mair, or Major, had long been a noted exponent of reform, and more than once threatened with removal from his position for near-heresy.

"To aid in this necessary work of education," Winram went on, "a catechism setting forth the true foundations of our Christian faith, in the common Scots tongue, shall be written and published, its study to be binding on all clergy, monastic and parochial, starting with all vicars, parsons and curates. The catechism will include the Apostles' Creed, the Lord's Prayer, the Ten Commandments, the Angelical Salutation and the Seven Sacraments, with instruction thereon. Readings from it will be made to all congregations, on all Sundays and holy days, to the term of one half-hour, where there is no sermon. This book or catechism will not itself be given to the laity, save by the express permission of the bishop."

The murmurs thereat were both doubtful and unhappy, for many there could scarcely read, and only were able to rehearse their abbreviated rituals parrot-fashion in approximate Latin.

"The *Pater Noster* or Lord's Prayer in future not to be said to named saints but only to our Lord Himself. This is an archiepiscopal command, not a recommendation."

There was outcry at that also, anent ancient usage, disrespect of saints, particularly the position of St. Peter, who held the Keys of the Kingdom and was represented on earth by the Pope. Also the heavenly status of the Mother of God, the Blessed Virgin.

Winram waited until the protests died away and then resumed, ignoring them entirely, save in that the Lord's Prayer would be said at the beginning of every service and the *Ave Maria* at the end.

"The holding of a plurality of benefices will cease." The Sub-Prior cleared his throat slightly, for the first time. "In order that there shall be no hardship nor difficulty in filling consequent vacancies, those pluralities presently enjoyed shall remain vested in their beneficiaries, who now hold them, during their lifetime or until voluntary relinquishment."

Oddly, this was accepted without dispute, sighs of relief

coming from many, and hopes for filling the vacancies no doubt interesting others. The bishops thus given remission, sat as expressionless as ever.

"Lastly, a scale of charges or fees to be paid to vicars, parsons and curates will be laid down, for performing the sacraments of baptism, marriage and Christian burial, in maximum. In minimum they may be performed according to the ability to pay, if necessary gratis to the very poor – who may appeal to the diocesan bishop."

This, of course, was a major blow to the lesser parish clergy; but, it being a provincial synod, these were but scantily represented there. Winram had not once looked at his notes. Clearly all this was entirely familiar to him, indeed it almost sounded as though much of it was of his own composition and devising. David Lindsay wondered. John Hamilton had been Primate for far too short a time to have bent his mind to all this. In which case Winram had probably been working towards it for long. On his own initiative – or Davie Beaton's? Could this in fact be Davie's strange swan-song? His final legacy to Holy Church? He had always said that reform must come from within, from the heights down not from the depths up. This seemed to be just that. Lindsay imagined that he could almost see Davie's mocking smile, looking down on them all.

The Sub-Prior laid down his papers. "These recommendations, if approved, will be incorporated in a series of canons covering each severally. And thereafter become binding on all clergy of Holy Church in this land. It is confidently believed that this synod will so agree, decide and authorise." He bowed again briefly to the Archbishop and the Coadjutor, and went to resume his seat. He received no sort of ovation.

Gavin Hamilton said levelly, "This synod is now open for discussion."

There was considerable pause – not to be wondered at, all things considered. Most evidently all this was the decision of the hierarchy, however reluctantly come to, the Primate and College of Bishops – no Archbishop of Glasgow had yet been installed to succeed the late Dunbar,

Huntly's brother's nomination having been appealed against by powerful interests; so there was no alternative archiepiscopal voice. And Holy Church was nothing if not hierarchical. All preferment, appointment and promotion was in the hands of those who were recommending those fairly drastic reforms, so that anyone vehemently opposing them would be a marked man, possibly jeopardising his future, and seen by all to be doing so.

An old and distinctly quavering voice spoke up, quavering with emotion as well as with age, clearly. "I say praise be to God!" Provost John Mair exclaimed. "This indeed is the day that the Lord hath made! Let us rejoice and be glad in it. At last, at last, we set our feet on the road to a better and brighter land. A blessed milestone on the road for Scotland's Church. Praise be, I say! Let none seek to put a stone for stumbling in our way!"

"Amen! Amen to that!" That was John Sinclair, Dean of Restalrig. David had not heard that he was of reformist sympathies.

There were a few murmurs of agreement but the great majority remained silent.

The Coadjutor waited, tapping fingers on his table. Who would be brave enough to lead the opposition which so evidently prevailed?

At length John Paterson, Provincial of the Grey Friars, raised his voice. His position, like that of their host, of the Black Friars, was rather different from that of the others there, being provincial head of an international religious Order, in his case the Franciscans, and his appointment emanating from Rome, not St. Andrews. Not that he would wish to be at public odds with the Primate; but he could not be demoted or expelled save with Vatican agreement.

"My lords and fellow-clergy," he said carefully, "the suggestions and recommendations here made are indeed far-reaching if not severe. Undoubtedly some improvements and reforms are necessary and must be welcomed. But it is perhaps questionable whether all need go quite so far as Master Winram indicated. My Order favours moderation in all things save our commitment to the Lord

Christ. Perhaps some moderation might be advisable here, at this stage."

The first hearty agreement of the session greeted that.

"What specific amendments or deletions does the Provincial suggest?" Dean Sinclair demanded.

"I spoke in general rather than specific terms. Do not mistake me – I agree with much that is proposed. I but suggest some, shall we say, caution, some consideration also of the effect of all this on the realm at large. In especial on those near-heretics agitating for so-called reform. Might not such forcible measures spur them on to still wilder claims and demands? In this regard, all present may not yet have heard that the renegade priest John Knox, along with others, has now been released from being a galley-slave, by the French, and is presently in England, being made much of by the heretical Church there. This man, who gave comfort and blessing to the murderers of our Cardinal-Primate of blessed memory, is threatening to return to Scotland to continue his wicked attack on Holy Church. I ask you, what would be the effect of these measures, if adopted, on John Knox and his like?"

Into the acclaim, old Provost Mair spoke up. "I say that these reforms are no less than what is required, and any reduction in them would be not only folly but sin." Although the eighty-year-old voice itself was weak, the spirit behind it was the reverse. "As to Knox, surely these measures are what is requisite to temper his efforts rather than to inflame them. He may be a man of extremes, but he is honest, I believe. I know him, for I taught him. As I taught *you*, John Paterson, and others amongst the more learned here present! Moderation has its value, but there are higher virtues! It was the sin of the Laodiceans!"

That silenced Master Paterson and left others wary as to crossing swords with the old master.

The Primate took advantage of the pause to make his one and only intervention. "These recommendations are the result of much thought and debate," he observed. "The effects they may have were as deeply considered as any likely to be raised here – and by those who have a fuller knowledge of the prevailing situation in Church and realm. As well as having the authority and responsibility for the Church's guidance. I commend them for acceptance in their entirety."

The silence was profound.

"Is any contrary motion put forward?" the Coadjutor asked.

No voice was raised.

"Then I declare the recommendations carried by this synod, Master Winram to incorporate them in canons, to be endorsed by the Primate and College of Bishops." Patently thankful to have the entire distasteful business over and done with, Gavin Hamilton briefly announced one or two matters of routine and order, and then turning to his half-brother, nodded what might have served as a bow. As an afterthought, he did the same towards his other half-brother, the Duke.

The Primate rose, sketched a benediction, and made for the door, followed in some confusion by the bishops and mitred abbots.

History had been made, however oddly.

As he picked his way out through the suddenly vociferous and noisy company, David Lindsay found his arm gripped by Provost John Mair.

"Bless you, Sir David – bless you!" the old man said. "Much of this day's work is thanks to you, of your doing. You, more than any other, prepared the soil. Without your plays and verse, the seed which we have for so long been seeking to sow would have fallen on stony ground. Bless you, I say!"

Much moved, David pressed the venerable hand and passed on.

He rode back to Linlithgow with a glow in his heart.

Marie de Guise had listened to his account of the synod quietly, without comment, only occasionally seeking elucidation of a point here or there. Now she nodded.

"So it is victory for the reformers," she said. "The Church bows before the storm – and will never be the same again. And you, my friend, I think rejoice?"

"I cannot but do so, Madame. For I conceive it to be a great step forward, for the Church and for the kingdom also. Only good can come of the reform of corruption, venality and ignorance. It had to come. I thank God that it has come thus, by the Church's own decision and not by violence or armed conflict."

"Yet it represents defeat for Holy Church, which will hereafter be the weaker. Having yielded this much, it could be forced to yield more, all will know."

"So long as it was corrupt, it was the weaker, more endangered. Now it is strengthened, rather."

"I wonder. A wall once breached is never so strong again. There are harsh and determined men, Sir David, seeking not *reform* of the Church so much as its downfall, its end. Some honest in their beliefs perhaps, however mistaken. But others, many others, seeking only the Church's wealth, its lands. As in England. This will encourage not a few of your Scots lords to join Glencairn and Cassillis and the others. That they may share, one day, in the rape!"

He could not deny that shrewd observation, but sought to make the point that the common people would henceforth feel much closer to the Church and provide an added strength.

"It is not the people but the nobles who have the power, with their hosts of armed men. Do I not know it!" she returned. "In England, who gained the advantage of their so-called Reformation? The people? Or King Henry and his lords? I much fear that we may see here what happened in England, one day. And what your friend the Cardinal fought so long and so strongly to prevent."

"Madame, it is my belief that he would be none so ill-pleased with what was done at that synod. Who knows, indeed, how much of it was in fact *his* doing? He always accepted that reform must come, but that it must come from the Church's own leaders not be imposed from below. This is what has happened. I cannot think that he will frown, wherever he is!"

"This then, Sir David, is why you urged me to support John Hamilton's claim to the Primacy and to recommend his name to the Pope? That, a self-seeking and ambitious man, he would not stand in the way of these measures? A sorry successor to the Cardinal! You foresaw this, I think?"

David cleared his throat. "Say that I thought it possible. Some of it. And advisable, Madame. I, I do not regret it."

"So be it. The thing is done. And now *I* must seek to deal with the consequences, as Regent. Think you it will ease my task?"

"I think that it well may, yes. There will be more of peace in the realm. Less of tumult and complaint. The problem of Dundee will be over. And now that we have peace with England, this move will give the English churchmen the less excuse to plot against us. Yes, Madame, I think that your task may be the easier."

"We shall see, my friend. And still I name you my friend, Sir David, you see. For I need all the friends I can make, the good God knows!" And she held out her hand to him.

He stooped to kiss it, half-bending one knee. "I am the more honoured," he said simply. "My services, such as they are, like my royal goodwill, are Your Grace's always. As is my admiration . . ."

21

David straightened up slowly after patting the last sheaf of the eight in the stook into place, reflecting, not for the first time, and a trifle ruefully, on the truth of the saying that the years did not come alone. Much as he still enjoyed a day amongst the harvest-field rigs, towards the end of it, as now, his back ached from picking up and stooking, picking up and stooking. It was basic, elementary work – however unsuitable, as his farm-grieve considered, for a laird and great one in the state – which he had always enjoyed and found satisfying, and which moreover, seemed to assist his mind in the process of composing sentences and paragraphs to match the images in his mind's eye. And he could do with such assistance at present, for foolishly perhaps, he was involved in no fewer than three writing projects at once – something he would probably entitle *The History and Testament of Squire Meldrum of Cleish*; the rewriting, he hoped for the last time, of *The Tragedy of the Cardinal*, which he doubted nevertheless would ever satisfy him; and a reappraisal, amendment and indeed extension of his *Satire of the Three Estates* – this at the suggestion of the Queen-Mother herself, who wished it to be performed again and brought up-to-date, with some indication, in the form of a final scene perhaps, showing that reform was in fact in process and that the situation was improved. This for reasons of state.

Back straightened, he shaded his eyes to gaze where the grieve pointed. Yes, five riders were to be seen climbing the track up to his little castle on the Mount of Lindifferon; and even at that range and with not-so-young eyes, he could see that the foremost was clad all in red. For a moment or two it was as though the clock was turned back and Davie Beaton was once again visiting the Mount, as so often, and apt to be dressed in scarlet.

He nodded. "Aye – visitors. A good excuse to stop breaking my back, Wattie!" He patted the grieve's arm, and set off along the slantwise field of stubble for the house.

When he arrived in the courtyard it was to experience a still stronger harking-back impression, for the young man who stood there beside his four escorts, talking to Janet, as well as being so handsomely dressed in red, was extraordinarily like Davie Beaton in feature and build, a little heavier perhaps and lacking the little pointed beard, but sufficiently good-looking and keen-eyed. David, in his shirt-sleeves and oldest clothes, offered a notable contrast, but was past concern with the impression he might make.

"An interesting and welcome visitor, David," Janet introduced. "Here is the Abbot of Arbroath, Master James Beaton. Is this not a, a wonder?"

A wonder indeed. This young man David had, of course, heard of but never met, second son of Davie's eldest brother, John Beaton of Balfour. A protégé of his uncle for long, who had guided his own sons by Marion Ogilvy via lofty marriages and rich endowments to become Angus lairds in fine castles, this youth, older by a few years, he had taken to France with him when he went as envoy there, and had him educated at his expense at the Sorbonne, destining him for the same sort of career as his own. Indeed, at the age of eighteen, in 1542, he had had him appointed Commendator-Abbot of Arbroath in his own stead – although retaining, as his own uncle had done, most of the revenues thereof. The young man had remained in France, and was able to serve as a useful reporter and go-between. Now, here he was back in Scotland, almost a reincarnation of Davie, aged twenty-six years.

"Greetings, Sir David – it is my great privilege to call upon you and your lady," the young Beaton said, bowing. His voice was unusually light and with a basic Scots accent much overlaid by a distinct French intonation. "I bring you the good wishes and regards of the Bishop-Elect of Ross, Master David Paniter, Scots ambassador to France."

"Ah, Paniter, yes – an old colleague. How good to see the nephew of that other colleague and friend, the Cardinal Davie, now with God." David shook hands.

"Abbot James is on his way to St. Andrews," Janet informed. "He says that he will not stay the night."

"I have been delayed," the young man explained. "There were great affairs at Dumbarton, before Queen Marie sailed, and which I could scarcely leave." It was amusing that he mispronounced Dumbarton, putting the accent on the first syllable. "I am to meet the Prior of Arbroath at St. Andrews tonight, to pay my respects to the Archbishop, and to sail for Arbroath Abbey in the morning, there to meet the abbatial council. My first," he added, with a smile, part-rueful, part-mocking and wholly Beaton.

"I see. At least you will take some refreshment before you go. And your men. It is still fifteen miles to St. Andrews." David led the way within, while Janet took the escort to the kitchens.

"The Queen-Mother has sailed, then?" David asked. Marie de Guise, with peace established, at least for the meantime, in state and Church, had decided to visit her homeland, see her daughter, son and brothers, and seek to resolve outstanding issues in the Franco-Scottish alliance. David had bidden her farewell and Godspeed at Linlithgow five days previously, and since Arran, or Châtelherault, was to be acting sole Regent in Marie's absence, and unlikely to require or want his services, he and Janet had thankfully returned to Lindifferon for harvest, a time of the year he always longed to spend on his own land.

"Yes, sir. They sailed two days ago. Prior Strozzi brought six galleys to Dumbarton, including King Henry's own, for her – that is how I gained passage. It was a sight to see – Strozzi had bought one thousand ells of white damask to clothe all aboard, even the galley-slaves and mariners, in the lady's honour! Never have I seen the like!"

"She well deserves all such attentions," David asserted. "She is a great and good princess."

"No doubt, sir. So my uncle always held. Bishop Paniter will meet her at Dieppe, where I left him."

"Ah, yes, the good Bishop. He is well, and does well, in France?"

"To be sure. He labours much for Scotland. And for the young Queen. He sees much of her. He says to tell you that she speaks much of you, sir, of this island in the lake – I have forgot the name. She has indeed made a song of it. She and her four Marys sing it together, with lute and harp. The Queen is very musical. She is of a strong spirit, happy, dances much and rides well. The French court already loves her."

"That is good. For it might have been otherwise. Her father had a different nature; his was not a happy life, and fate was scarcely kind to him. Pray God Mary does better."

"The Bishop also told me to convey to you the greetings of the Cardinal of Lorraine. He thinks highly of you, Sir David." Beaton hesitated just a little. "He, the Cardinal, urges that you become not too close with the reformers, sir. He sees danger there. This man Knox, it seems, has been naming your name. In England. As though you were all but in his camp. There is further trouble ahead, His Eminence fears."

"Ha! So that is why you came to Lindifferon, my lord Abbot! You bring me a warning? From Holy Church!"

"No, sir – no! Not so. I came because Bishop Paniter bade me to. With his good wishes and news of the young Queen. This of the Cardinal of Lorraine is but . . . by the way."

"I understand, my friend. Be not put out. That is the way it goes. However, I think that I can deal with the Master Knox. He is scarcely the Devil's lieutenant, as some seem to fear. I hear that he has been offered an English bishopric. Perhaps he will spare us his further zeal, in Scotland!"

The younger man looked doubtful.

He did not linger after his refreshment, less sure of himself than his uncle had been at that age.

When they had seen him off, at the courtyard gatehouse,

David took Janet's arm and led her to the rustic arbour in the walled orchard which slanted south-facing below the castle, a favourite haunt from which they could survey all the fair vale of Stratheden and the Howe of Fife, spreading east and west below them for a full score of miles.

"There goes one more young venturer on the seas of Scotland's troubles," he said. "Hoping for a haven of profit and power belike. Sakes – he makes me feel old!"

"I am glad that something does, harvester! Or I am like to grow old alone – a sorry fate! Our young friend is extraordinarily like Davie, is he not?"

"Only at first sight, I think. That one will not scale the same heights as his uncle, although he will wish to do so. I sense a flaw in that steel."

"Were there not flaws in Davie's also? In us all, no doubt."

"Not a flaw so much as two tempered steels at war with each other, in Davie. As well, perhaps. Otherwise who knows where he might have led Scotland. As lead Scotland he would. And did, to be sure. He saved us from Henry Tudor – he alone."

"With some little help from others. Yourself for one, my dear."

He shook his head. "I was never near his stature. I did what I could – when I perceived it. Or he pointed it out to me! But he alone was sufficiently strong to counter Henry."

"And yet, and yet David, you say in your *Tragedy of the Cardinal*, that although his assassination was an ill deed, he was well away."

"Aye – the hardest words I ever penned! How often have I scored them through, then written them again! For I am convinced that it was necessary for Scotland, by then, that he went. He had saved the realm from Henry, yes. But he could have wrecked all thereafter. I believe that he aimed to be Pope – Scotland's first! And he could have achieved it, I judge. And, with Davie in the Vatican, what hope of a reformed Church, without bloody war, division and the English seizing their opportunity once more?"

"Perhaps *he* might have made reforms? From Rome?"

"No. The Pope is the Prisoner in the Vatican. Even Davie could not have altered that. The Pontiff must resist change, or his citadel falls. That would have spelled the end of Scotland."

"Scotland!" she murmured. "Always Scotland! This strange land and people. So difficult, so awkward and divided, so unruly. Do other realms demand such devotion, David? Do other nations mean so much to their folk? France? England? The Netherlands? Denmark? You have visited all these, and I have not. Are all the same? Or is it just this Scotland? All your life – aye, and all Davie's too, and so many another no doubt – it has been the same. Tell me, what is it that so binds you, us all, to it?"

He stroked his chin. "A hard question, lass. One that I have scarcely even asked myself, in so many words. As to other realms, I think not. Not quite in the same way. Oh, they can be proud of their own land, to be sure. Seek its good, as well as their own. Fight for it, even die for it, if they must. But, no – I cannot think that it is *part* of the others as Scotland is of the Scots. Or some of the Scots! Angus, now – How would he see it? Or Lennox? Or Glencairn? Others of that kidney. And yet, perhaps I wrong them. Perhaps they too have their own notion of Scotland, love it in their own way. And seek its rule so that *their* wish for it may prevail? As Davie Beaton did. Who knows? Perhaps it is all because we are a small people in numbers, although contrary of will. But so are the Danes. Perhaps because of our past, the oldest kingdom in Christendom, with our kings stretching back beyond recorded time. Or it may be the land itself, so strong, so various, so proud and yet so fair. Aye, the land – it has us all in thrall. Whether we know it or not. The mountains and glens, the fertile vales and rich pastures, the barren rocks and frowning passes, the gold-fringed coasts and thrusting headlands, the far-flung moors and great forests. Can you wonder, woman – can you wonder?"

"There speaks the poet and bard, David . . ."

"Perhaps. But that is only the putting of it into words.

The effect, the force of it, is there for all. Can a land make its folk? Earth and rock, sand and water? Can these mould and shape men and women they support?"

"I think not. Only God can do that."

"True. But God made the land before He made the people on it – long before. And if the people were all to be gone, by war, pestilence and plague or other disaster, the land would still be there, strong, enduring, beautiful, unchanging. So – which moulds which?"

"But that is the same for all lands, is it not? Not just this Scotland."

"All lands may mould their folk, yes. So what makes the Scots so strange a people? So difficult, as you said. So factious, discordant, scarcely governable? A race of leaders, each and all, not to be led? I look at this fair land which we are using and harvesting and dwelling on, and I see the rocks rising, here, there, everywhere, the *rock*. Rich tilth, yes. Lush pastures, yes. Spreading moor and vast forests. The mountains and valleys, the lochs and rivers, the cliffs and shores and strands. But always the rock rising through. The rock always present, close below, where it is not thrusting into view. It is the rock which makes us what we are, I think. Christ said of Simon Peter – on this rock I will found my Church. I think that perhaps His Father said some time before – on this northern rock I will mould the Scots! Why? He must have a purpose. How often I ask myself that question!"

She smiled, shaking her head. "Perhaps just so that you and Davie Beaton and your like *should* ask that question, my dear – and know that you are not gods!"

After a moment he turned to her, wondering almost. "Save us, Janet – you could have it! Guid sakes – it might be even so! Woman, woman – where did you get that?"

"Questions, ever more questions, David! It is the men who are always asking the questions. The women but answer them!"

For long, then, they sat there, hand in hand, watching the day at its dying over the kingdom, a kingdom come but for ever coming.

HISTORICAL NOTE

It took ten more years for the reformers' kingdom fully to come, and the Reformation Parliament of 1560 to turn Scotland into a Protestant state – with a different form of religious intolerance taking over. And fifty-three years before the long warfare between the realms of Scotland and England finally ceased, with the King of Scots mounting the childless Elizabeth's throne and forming a United Kingdom of Great Britain – and oddly, all because of the unlovable Margaret Tudor. Yet still the problems of rule and government remain for both. It was eleven years before Mary Queen of Scots, and Queen-Dowager of France, returned to her own country, a French-reared, Catholic monarch for a now Protestant realm, and trouble inevitable. Her mother, the Regent, had died the year before.

For how long David Lindsay survived David Beaton is uncertain. Some authorities say he died in 1555, some 1558, others declare the date of his death unknown. What is recorded is that a second performance of his great play, *A Pleasant Satire of the Three Estates* was staged at Greenside in Edinburgh, before the Queen-Regent and great ones, in 1552; and Lindsay was certainly alive then for he amended and indeed lengthened the production. Gratified as he must have been, he was not to know that the play would still be featuring in the Edinburgh International Festival in the 1980s, to critical and general acclaim.